Saldur smiled and then struck her hard across the face.

The chains binding Arista's wrists snapped taut as she tried to protect herself. He listened to her crying softly for a moment and then said, "You're a smart girl—too smart for your own good—but you're not *that* smart. Hilfred may have helped you escape arrest. He might even have hidden you for those weeks we searched. But he couldn't have gotten you into the palace or found this prison. Hilfred died wearing the uniform of a fourth-floor guard. You must have had help from some-one on the staff to get that, and I want to know who it was."

"There was no one. It was just me and Hilfred."

Saldur slapped her again. Arista cried out, her body shak-ing, jangling the chains.

"Don't lie to me," he said while raising his hand again.

Arista spoke quickly to stay the blow. "I told you. It was just me. I got a job working in the palace as a chambermaid. I stole the uniform."

"I know all about you posing as Ella the scrub girl. But you couldn't have gotten the uniform without help. It had to be someone in a position of authority. I must know who the trai-tor is. Now tell me. Who was helping you?"

When she said nothing, he struck her twice more.

Arista cringed. "Stop it!"

"Tell me," Saldur growled.

"No, you'll hurt her!" she blurted.

"Her?"

BOOKS BY MICHAEL J. SULLIVAN

THE RIYRIA REVELATIONS

Theft of Swords
Rise of Empire
Heir of Novron

HEIR OF NOVRON

Volume Three of the
Riyria Revelations

MICHAEL J. SULLIVAN

www.orbitbooks.net

Orbit
Hachette Book Group
1290 Avenue of the Americas, New York, NY 10104
www.HachetteBookGroup.com

First Edition: January 2012

Orbit is an imprint of Hachette Book Group, Inc. The Orbit name
and logo are trademarks of Little, Brown Book Group Limited.

The publisher is not responsible for websites (or their content) that
are not owned by the publisher.

The characters and events in this book are fictitious. Any similarity
to real persons, living or dead, is coincidental and not intended by
the author.

Library of Congress Cataloging-in-Publication Data
Sullivan, Michael J.
    Heir of Novron / Michael J. Sullivan. — 1st ed.
      p. cm. — (The Riyria revelations ; 3)
    ISBN 978-0-316-18771-8
    I. Title.
    PS3619.U4437H45 2012
    813'.6 — dc22
                                        2011018070

Printing 17, 2023

Printed in the United States of America

This book is entirely dedicated to my wife, Robin Sullivan.

Some have asked how it is I write such strong women without resorting to putting swords in their hands. It is because of her.

She is Arista
She is Thrace
She is Modina
She is Amilia
And she is my Gwen.

This series has been a tribute to her.

This is your book, Robin.

I hope you don't mind that I put down in words
How wonderful life is while you're in the world.
—ELTON JOHN, BERNIE TAUPIN

CONTENTS

Known Regions of the World of Elan

Estrendor: Northern wastes
Erivan Empire: Elvenlands
Apeladorn: Nations of man
Ba Ran Archipelago: Islands of goblins
Westerlands: Western wastes
Dacca: Isle of south men

Nations of Apeladorn

Avryn: Central wealthy kingdoms
Trent: Northern mountainous kingdoms
Calis: Southeastern tropical region ruled by warlords
Delgos: Southern republic

Kingdoms of Avryn

Ghent: Ecclesiastical holding of the Nyphron Church
Melengar: Small but old and respected kingdom
Warric: Most powerful of the kingdoms of Avryn
Dunmore: Youngest and least sophisticated kingdom
Alburn: Forested kingdom
Rhenydd: Poor kingdom
*Maranon: Producer of food. Once part of Delgos, which was
    lost when Delgos became a republic*
*Galeannon: Lawless kingdom of barren hills, the site of
    several great battles*

The Gods

Erebus: Father of the gods
Ferrol: Eldest son, god of elves
Drome: Second son, god of dwarves
Maribor: Third son, god of men
Muriel: Only daughter, goddess of nature
Uberlin: Son of Muriel and Erebus, god of darkness

Political Parties

Imperialists: Those wishing to unite mankind under a single leader who is the direct descendant of the demigod Novron
Nationalists: Those wishing to be ruled by a leader chosen by the people
Royalists: Those wishing to perpetuate rule by individual, independent monarchs

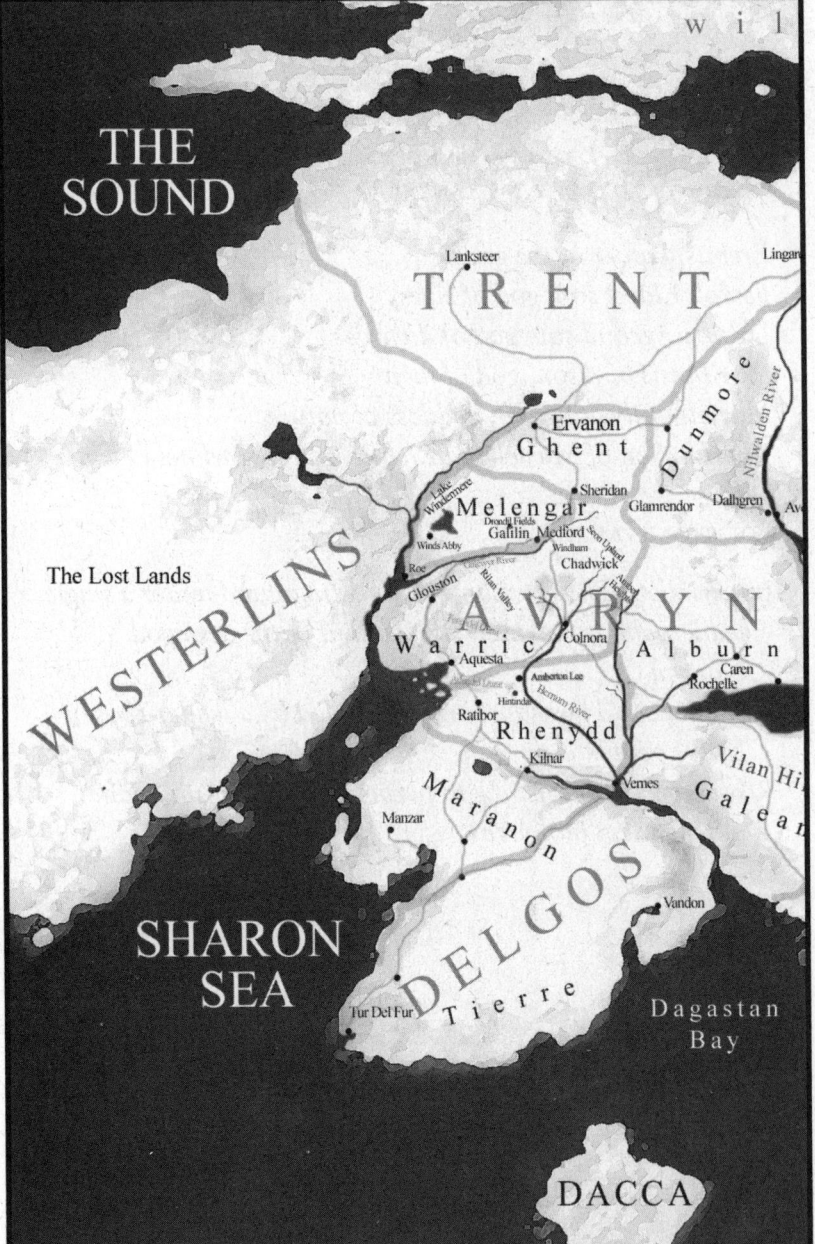

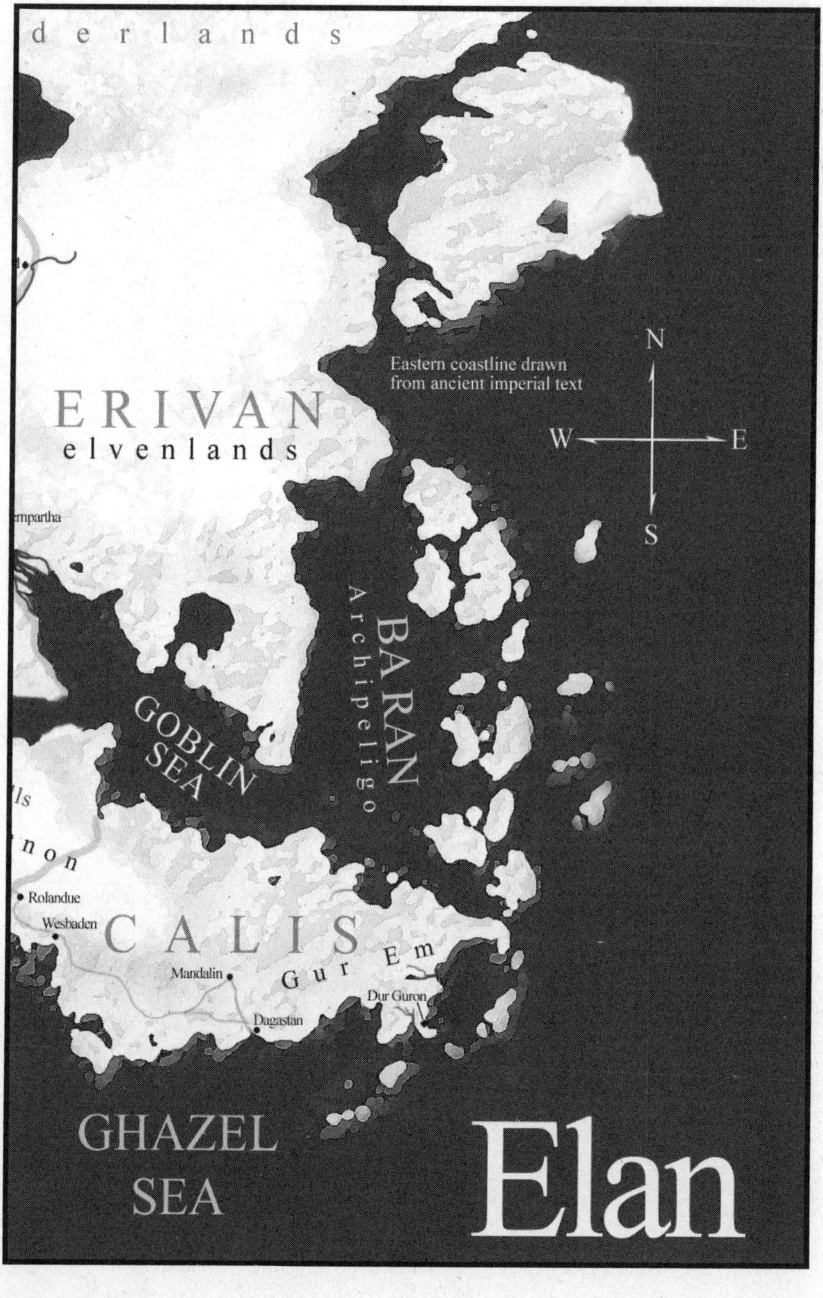

derlands

ERIVAN
elvenlands

Eastern coastline drawn
from ancient imperial text

N

W — E

S

mpartha

BA RAN
Archipeligo

GOBLIN
SEA

ls

non

• Rolandue

Wesbaden

CALIS

Mandalin •

Gur Em

Dur Guron

Dagastan

GHAZEL
SEA

Elan

BOOK V

WINTERTIDE

CHAPTER 1

AQUESTA

Some people are skilled, and some are lucky, but at that moment Mince realized he was neither. Failing to cut the merchant's purse strings, he froze with one hand still cupping the bag. He knew the pickpocket's creed allowed for only a single touch, and he had dutifully slipped into the crowd after two earlier attempts. A third failure meant they would bar him from another meal. Mince was too hungry to let go.

With his hands still under the merchant's cloak, he waited. The man remained oblivious.

Should I try again?

The thought was insane, but his empty stomach won the battle over reason. In a moment of desperation, Mince pushed caution aside. The leather seemed oddly thick. Sawing back and forth, he felt the purse come loose, but something was not right. It took only an instant for Mince to realize his mistake. Instead of purse strings, he had sliced through the merchant's belt. Like a hissing snake, the leather strap slithered off the fat man's belly, dragged to the cobblestones by the weight of his weapons.

Mince did not breathe or move as the entire span of his ten disappointing years flashed by.

Run! the voice inside his head screamed as he realized there was a heartbeat, perhaps two, before his victim—

The merchant turned.

He was a large, soft man with saddlebag cheeks reddened by the cold. His eyes widened when he noticed the purse in Mince's hand. "Hey, you!" The man reached for his dagger, and surprise filled his face when he found it missing. Groping for his other weapon, he spotted them both lying in the street.

Mince heeded the voice of his smarter self and bolted. Common sense told him the best way to escape a rampaging giant was to head for the smallest crack. He plunged beneath an ale cart outside The Blue Swan Inn and slid to the far side. Scrambling to his feet, he raced for the alley, clutching the knife and purse to his chest. The recent snow hampered his flight, and his small feet lost traction rounding a corner.

"Thief! Stop!" The shouts were not nearly as close as he had expected.

Mince continued to run. Finally reaching the stable, he ducked between the rails of the fence framing the manure pile. Exhausted, he crouched with his back against the far wall. The boy shoved the knife into his belt and stuffed the purse down his shirt, leaving a noticeable bulge. Panting amidst the steaming piles, he struggled to hear anything over the pounding in his ears.

"There you are!" Elbright shouted, skidding in the snow and catching himself on the fence. "What an idiot. You just stood there—waiting for the fat oaf to turn around. You're a moron, Mince. That's it—that's all there is to it. I honestly don't know why I bother trying to teach you."

Mince and the other boys referred to thirteen-year-old Elbright as the Old Man. In their small band only he wore an actual cloak, which was dingy gray and secured with a tarnished metal broach. Elbright was the smartest and most accomplished of their crew, and Mince hated to disappoint him.

Laughing, Brand arrived only moments later and joined Elbright at the fence.

"It's not funny," Elbright said.

"But—he—" Brand could not finish as laughter consumed him.

Like the other two, Brand was dirty, thin, and dressed in mismatched clothing of varying sizes. His pants were too long and snow gathered in the folds of the rolled-up bottoms. Only his tunic fit properly. Made from green brocade and trimmed with fine supple leather, it fastened down the front with intricately carved wooden toggles. A year younger than the Old Man, he was a tad taller and a bit broader. In the unspoken hierarchy of their gang, Brand came second—the muscle to Elbright's brains. Kine, the remaining member of their group, ranked third, because he was the best pickpocket. This left Mince unquestionably at the bottom. His size matched his position, as he stood barely four feet tall and weighed little more than a wet cat.

"Stop it, will ya?" the Old Man snapped. "I'm trying to teach the kid a thing or two. He could have gotten himself killed. It was stupid—plain and simple."

"I thought it was brilliant." Brand paused to wipe his eyes. "I mean, sure it was dumb, but spectacular just the same. The way Mince just stood there blinking as the guy goes for his blades. But they ain't there 'cuz the little imbecile done cut the git's whole bloody belt off! Then…" Brand struggled against another bout of laughter. "The best part is that just after Mince runs, the fat bastard goes to chase him, and his breeches fall down. The guy toppled like a ruddy tree. *Wham.* Right into the gutter. By Mar, that was hilarious."

Elbright tried to remain stern, but Brand's recounting soon had them all laughing.

"Okay, okay, quit it." Elbright regained control and went straight to business. "Let's see the take."

Mince fished out the purse and handed it over with a wide grin. "Feels heavy," he proudly stated.

Elbright drew open the top and scowled after examining the contents. "Just coppers."

Brand and Elbright exchanged disappointed frowns and Mince's momentary elation melted. "It felt heavy," he repeated, mainly to himself.

"What now?" Brand asked. "Do we give him another go?"

Elbright shook his head. "No, and all of us will have to avoid Church Square for a while. Too many people saw Mince. We'll move closer to the gates. We can watch for new arrivals and hope to get lucky."

"Do ya want—" Mince started.

"No. Give me back my knife. Brand is up next."

The boys jogged toward the palace walls, following the trail that morning patrols had made in the fresh snow. They circled east and entered Imperial Square. People from all over Avryn were arriving for Wintertide, and the central plaza bustled with likely prospects.

"There," Elbright said, pointing toward the city gate. "Those two. See 'em? One tall, the other shorter."

"They're a sorry-looking pair," Mince said.

"Exhausted," Brand agreed.

"Probably been riding all night in the storm," Elbright said with a hungry smile. "Go on, Brand, do the old helpful stableboy routine. Now, Mince, watch how this is done. It might be your only hope, as you've got no talent for purse cutting."

≫

Royce and Hadrian entered Imperial Square on ice-laden horses. Defending against the cold, the two appeared as ghosts shrouded in snowy blankets. Despite wearing all they had, they were ill-equipped for the winter roads, much less the mountain passes that lay between Ratibor and Aquesta. The all-night snowstorm had only added to their hardship. As the two drew their horses to a stop, Royce noticed Hadrian breathing into his cupped hands. Neither of them had winter gloves. Hadrian had wrapped his fingers in torn strips from his blanket, while Royce opted for pulling his hands into the shelter of his sleeves. The sight of his own handless arms disturbed Royce as they reminded him of the old wizard. The two had learned the details of his murder while passing through Ratibor. Assassinated late one night, Esrahaddon had been silenced forever.

They had meant to get gloves, but as soon as they had arrived in Ratibor, they saw announcements proclaiming the Nationalist leader's upcoming execution. The empire planned to publicly burn Degan Gaunt in the imperial capital of Aquesta as part of the Wintertide celebrations. After Hadrian and Royce had spent months traversing high seas and dark jungles seeking Gaunt, to have found his whereabouts tacked up to every tavern door in the city was as much a blow as a blessing. Fearing some new calamity might arise to stop them from finally reaching him, they left early the next morning, long before the trade shops opened.

Unwrapping his scarf, Royce drew back his hood and looked around. The snow-covered palace took up the entire southern side of the square, while shops and vendors dominated the rest. Furriers displayed trimmed capes and hats. Shoemakers cajoled passers-by, offering to oil their boots.

Bakers tempted travelers with snowflake-shaped cookies and white-powdered pastries. And colorful banners were everywhere announcing the upcoming festival.

Royce had just dismounted when a boy ran up. "Take your horses, sirs? One night in a stable for just a silver each. I'll brush them down myself and see they get good oats too."

Dismounting and pulling back his own hood, Hadrian smiled at the boy. "Will you sing them a lullaby at night?"

"Certainly, sir," the boy replied without losing a beat. "It will cost you two coppers more, but I do have a very fine voice, I does."

"Any stable in the city will quarter a horse for five coppers," Royce challenged.

"Not this month, sir. Wintertide pricing started three days back. Stables and rooms fill up fast. Especially this year. You're lucky you got here early. In another two weeks, they'll be stocking horses in the fields behind hunters' blinds. The only lodgings will be on dirt floors, where people will be stacked like cordwood for five silvers each. I know the best places and the lowest costs in the city. A silver is a good price right now. In a few days it'll cost you twice that."

Royce eyed him closely. "What's your name?"

"Brand the Bold they call me." He straightened up, adjusting the collar of his tunic.

Hadrian chuckled and asked, "Why is that?"

" 'Cuz I don't never back down from a fight, sir."

"Is that where you got your tunic?" Royce asked.

The boy looked down as if noticing the garment for the first time. "This old thing? I got five better ones at home. I'm just wearing this rag so I don't get the good ones wet in the snow."

"Well, Brand, do you think you can take these horses to The Bailey Inn at Hall and Coswall and stable them there?"

"I could indeed, sir. And a fine choice, I might add. It's run by a reputable owner charging fair prices. I was just going to suggest that very place."

Royce gave him a smirk. He turned his attention to two boys who stood at a distance, pretending not to know Brand. Royce waved for them to come over. The boys appeared hesitant, but when he repeated the gesture, they reluctantly obliged.

"What are your names?" he asked.

"Elbright, sir," the taller of the two replied. This boy was older than Brand and had a knife concealed beneath his cloak. Royce guessed he was the real leader of their group and had sent Brand over to make the play.

"Mince, sir," said the other, who looked to be the youngest and whose hair showed evidence of having recently been cut with a dull knife. The boy wore little more than rags of stained, worn wool. His shirt and pants exposed the bright pink skin of his wrists and shins. Of all his clothing, the item that fit best was a torn woven bag draped over his shoulders. The same material wrapped his feet, secured around his ankles by twine.

Hadrian checked through the gear on his horse, removed his spadone blade, and slid it into the sheath, which he wore on his back beneath his cloak.

Royce handed two silver tenents to the first boy, then, addressing all three, said, "Brand here is going to have our horses stabled at the Bailey and reserve us a room. While he's gone, you two will stay here and answer some questions."

"But, ah, sir, we can't—" Elbright started, but Royce ignored him.

"When Brand returns with a receipt from the Bailey, I will pay *each* of you a silver. If he doesn't return, if instead he runs off and sells the horses, I shall slit both of your throats and hang you on the palace gate by your feet. I'll let your blood drip into a pail, then paint a sign with it to notify the city that Brand the Bold is a horse thief. Then I'll track him down, with the help of the imperial guard and *other connections* I have in this city, and see he gets the same treatment." Royce glared at the boy. "Do we understand each other, Brand?"

The three boys stared at him with mouths agape.

"By Mar! Not a very trusting fellow, are ya, sir?" Mince said.

Royce grinned ominously. "Make the reservation under the names of Grim and Baldwin. Run along now, Brand, but do hurry back. You don't want your friends to worry."

Brand led the horses away while the other two boys watched him go. Elbright gave a little shake of his head when Brand looked back.

"Now, boys, why don't you tell us what is planned for this year's festivities?"

"Well…" Elbright started, "I suspect this will be the most memorable Wintertide in a hundred years on account of the empress's marriage and all."

"Marriage?" Hadrian asked.

"Yes, sir. I thought everyone knew about that. Invitations went out months ago, and all the rich folk, even kings and queens, have been coming from all over."

"Who's she marrying?" Royce asked.

"*Lard* Ethelred," Mince said.

Elbright lowered his voice. "Shut it, Mince."

"He's a snake."

Elbright growled and cuffed him on the ear. "Talk like that will get you dead." Turning back to Royce and Hadrian, he said, "Mince has a bit of a crush on the empress. He's not too pleased with the old king, on account of him marrying her and all."

"She's like a goddess, she is," Mince declared, misty-eyed. "I seen her once. I climbed to that roof for a better view when she gave a speech last summer. She shimmered like a star, she did. By Mar, she's beautiful. Ya can tell she's the daughter of Novron. I've never seen anyone so pretty."

"See what I mean? Mince is a bit crazy when it comes to the empress," Elbright apologized. "He's got to get used to Regent Ethelred running things again. Not that he ever really stopped, on account of the empress being sick and all."

"She was hurt by the beast she killed up north," Mince explained. "Empress Modina was dying from the poison, and healers came from all over, but no one could help. Then Regent Saldur prayed for seven days and nights without food or water. Maribor showed him that the pure heart of a servant girl named Amilia from Tarin Vale had the power to heal the empress. And she did. Lady Amilia has been nursing the empress back to health and doing a fine job." He took a breath, his eyes brightened, and a smile grew across his face.

"Mince, enough," Elbright said.

"What's all this about?" Royce asked, pointing at bleachers that were being built in the center of the square. "They aren't holding the wedding out here, are they?"

"No, the wedding will be at the cathedral. Those are for folks to watch the execution. They're gonna kill the rebel leader."

"Yeah, that piece of news we heard about," Hadrian said softly.

"Oh, so you came for the execution?"

"More or less."

"I've got our spots all picked out," Elbright said. "I'm gonna have Mince go up the night before and save us a good seat."

"Hey, why do I have to go?" Mince asked.

"Brand and I have to carry all the stuff. You're too small to help and Kine's still sick, so you need to—"

"But you have the cloak and it's gonna be cold just sitting up there."

The two boys went on arguing, but Royce could tell Hadrian was no longer listening. His friend's eyes scanned the palace gates, walls, and front entrance. Hadrian was counting guards.

❦

Rooms at the Bailey were the same as at every inn—small and drab, with worn wooden floors and musty odors. A small pile of firewood was stacked next to the hearth in each room but never enough for the whole night. Patrons were forced to buy more at exorbitant prices if they wanted to stay warm. Royce made his usual rounds, circling the block, watching for faces that appeared too many times. He returned to their room confident that no one had noticed their arrival—at least, no one who mattered.

"Room eight. Been here almost a week," Royce said.

"A week? Why so early?" Hadrian asked.

"If you were living in a monastery for ten months a year, wouldn't you show up early for Wintertide?"

Hadrian grabbed his swords and the two moved down the hall. Royce picked the lock of a weathered door and slid it open. On the far side of the room, two candles burned on a small table set with plates, glasses, and a bottle of wine. A man, dressed in velvet and silk, stood before a wall mirror, checking the tie that held back his blond hair and adjusting the high collar of his coat.

"Looks like he was expecting us," Hadrian said.

"Looks like he was expecting someone," Royce clarified.

"What the—" Startled, Albert Winslow spun around. "Would it hurt to knock?"

"What can I say?" Royce flopped on the bed. "We're scoundrels and thieves."

"Scoundrels certainly," Albert said, "but thieves? When was the last time you two stole anything?"

"Do I detect dissatisfaction?"

"I'm a viscount. I have a reputation to uphold, which takes a certain amount of income—money that I don't receive when you two are idle."

Hadrian took a seat at the table. "He's not dissatisfied. He's outright scolding us."

"Is that why you're here so early?" Royce asked. "Scouting for work?"

"Partially. I also needed to get away from the Winds Abbey. I'm becoming a laughingstock. When I contacted Lord Daref, he couldn't lay off the Viscount Monk jokes. On the other hand, Lady Mae does find my pious reclusion appealing."

"And is she the one who..." Hadrian swirled a finger at the neatly arranged table.

"Yes. I was about to fetch her. I'm going to have to cancel, aren't I?" He looked from one to the other and sighed.

"Sorry."

"I hope this job pays well. This is a new doublet and I still owe the tailor." Blowing out the candles, he took a seat across from Hadrian.

"How are things up north?" Royce asked.

Albert pursed his lips, thinking. "I'm guessing you know about Medford being taken? Imperial troops hold it and most of the provincial castles except for Drondil Fields."

Royce sat up. "No, we didn't know. How's Gwen?"

"I have no idea. I was here when I heard."

"So Alric and Arista are at Drondil Fields?" Hadrian asked.

"King Alric is but I don't think the princess was in Medford. I believe she's running Ratibor. They appointed her mayor, or so I've heard."

"No," Hadrian said. "We just came through there. She was governing after the battle but left months ago in the middle of the night. No one knows why. I just assumed she went home."

Albert shrugged. "Maybe, but I never heard anything about her going back. Probably better for her if she didn't. The Imps have Drondil Fields surrounded. Nothing is going in or out. It's only a matter of time before Alric will have to surrender."

"What about the abbey? Has the empire come knocking?" Royce asked.

Albert shook his head. "Not that I know of. But like I said, I was already here when the Imperialists crossed the Galewyr."

Royce got up and began to pace.

"Anything else?" Hadrian asked.

"Rumor has it that Tur Del Fur was invaded by goblins. But that's only a rumor, as far as I can tell."

"Not a rumor," Hadrian said.

"Oh?"

"We were there. Actually, we were responsible."

"Sounds...interesting," Albert said.

Royce stopped his pacing. "Don't get him started."

"Okay, so what brings you to Aquesta?" Albert asked. "I'm guessing it's not to celebrate Wintertide."

"We're going to break Degan Gaunt out of the palace dungeon, and we'll need you for the usual inside work," Royce said.

"Really? You do know he's going to be executed on Wintertide, don't you?"

"Yeah, that's why we need to get moving. It would be bad if we were late," Hadrian added.

"Are you crazy? The palace? At Wintertide? You've heard

about this little wedding that's going on? Security might be a tad tighter than usual. Every day I see a line of men in the courtyard, signing up to join the guard."

"Your point?" Hadrian asked.

"We should be able to use the wedding to our advantage," Royce said. "Anyone we know in town yet?"

"Genny and Leo arrived recently, I think."

"Really? That's perfect. Get in touch. They'll have rooms in the palace for sure. See if they can get you in. Then find out all you can, especially about where they're keeping Gaunt."

"I'm going to need money. I was only planning to attend a few local balls and maybe one of the feasts. If you want me inside the palace, I'll have to get better clothes. By Mar, look at my shoes. Just look at them! I can't meet the empress in these."

"Borrow from Genny and Leo for now," Royce said. "I'm going to leave for Medford tonight and return with funds to cover our expenses."

"You're going back? Tonight?" Albert asked. "You just got here, didn't you?"

The thief nodded.

"She's okay," Hadrian assured Royce. "I'm sure she got out."

"We've got nearly a month to Wintertide," Royce said. "I should be back in a week or so. In the meantime, learn what you can, and we'll formulate a plan when I return."

"Well," Albert grumbled, "at least Wintertide won't be boring."

CHAPTER 2

INTO DARKNESS

S omeone was whimpering.
    It was a man's voice this time, one that Arista had heard
before. Everyone cried eventually. Some people even broke
down into fits of hysterics. There used to be a woman who
was prone to screaming, but she had been removed some time
earlier. Arista held no illusions of the woman being set free.
She had heard them drag the body away. The whimpering
man used to cry out but had grown quieter over the past few
days. He never wailed anymore. Although not long before, she
had heard him praying. Arista was surprised that he did not
ask for rescue or even a quick death. All he prayed for was *her*.
He asked Maribor to keep her safe, but in all his ramblings,
the princess never caught the name of the man's lover.

    There was no way to track the passage of time in the dark.
Arista tried counting meals, but her hunger suggested they
came less than once per day. Still, weeks must have passed
since her capture. In all that time, she had never heard Gaunt,
despite having called out to him. The only time she had heard
his voice was the night she and Hilfred had failed to rescue him.

    Since then, she had been confined to her cell, which contained only a pail for waste and a few handfuls of straw. The room was so small that she could touch all four walls at once, making it feel like a cage or a grave. Arista knew that Modina, the girl once known as Thrace, had been kept somewhere just like that. Perhaps even in that very cell. After she had lost everyone and everything that mattered to her, it would have been a nightmare to wake alone in the dark without explanation, cause, or reason. Not knowing where she was or how she had gotten there must have driven the girl mad.

Despite her own tragedies, at least Arista knew she was not alone in the world. Once the news of her disappearance reached him, her brother, Alric, would move the world to save her. The two had grown closer in the years since their father's death. He was no longer the privileged boy, and she was no longer the jealous, reclusive sister. They still had their arguments, but nothing would stop him from finding her. Alric would enlist the help of the Pickerings—her extended family. He might even call on Royce and Hadrian, whom Alric affectionately referred to as the royal protectors. It would not be long now.

Arista pictured Hadrian's lopsided smile. The image stung but her mind refused to let it go. Memories of the sound of his voice, the touch of his hand, and that tiny scar on his chin pulled at her heart. There had been moments of warmth, but only kindness on his part, only sympathy—compassion for a person in pain or need. To him, Arista was just *the princess*, his employer, his job, just one more desperate noble.

How empty an existence I've led that those few I count among my best friends are two people I paid to work for me.

She wanted to believe that Hadrian saw her as something special, that the time they had spent on the road together had endeared her to him—that it meant as much to Hadrian as it did to her. Arista hoped he considered her smarter or more capable than most. But even if he did, men did not want smart or capable. They wanted pretty. Arista was not pretty like Alenda Lanaklin or Lenare Pickering. If only Hadrian saw her the way Emery and Hilfred had.

Then he would be dead too.

The deep rumble of stone against stone echoed through the corridors. Footsteps sounded in the hall. Someone was coming.

Now was not the time for food. While Arista could not count the days in the darkness, she knew food never came until she feared it might never come. They fed her so little that she welcomed the thin, putrid soup, which smelled of rotten eggs.

The approaching footfalls came from two sets of shoes. The first she recognized as a guard who wore metal and made a pronounced *tink-tink*. The other wore hard heels and soles that created a distinct *click-clack*. That was not a guard, nor was it a servant. Servants wore soft shoes that made a *swish-swish* sound or no shoes at all—*slap-slap*. Only someone wealthy could afford shoes that clacked on stone. The steps were slow but not hesitant. There was confidence in the long, measured strides.

A key rattled against the assembly of her lock and then clicked.

A visitor?

The door to her cell opened, and a bright light made Arista wince.

A guard entered, jerked her roughly to one side, and attached a pair of iron bracelets, chaining her wrists to the wall. Leaving her sitting with her arms above her head, the guard exited but left the door open.

A moment later, Regent Saldur entered holding a lantern. "How are you this evening, Princess?" The old man shook his head sadly, making tsking noises. "Look at you, my dear. You are so thin and filthy, and where in Maribor's name did you get that dress? Not that there's much of it left, is there? Those look like new bruises too. Have the guards been raping you? No, I suppose not." Saldur lowered his voice to a whisper. "They had *extremely* strict orders not to touch Modina when she was here. I accused an innocent jailor of improperly touching her and then had him pulled apart by oxen as an example. There were no problems after that. It might seem extreme, but I couldn't have a pregnant empress, now could I? Of course, in your case I really don't care, but the guards don't know that."

"Why are you here?" she asked. Her low raspy voice sounded strange, even to her.

"I thought I would bring you some news, my dear. Kilnar and Vernes have fallen. Rhenydd is now a happy member of the empire. The farmlands of Maranon on the Delgos peninsula had a nice harvest, so we'll have plenty of supplies to feed our troops all winter. We've retaken Ratibor but had to execute quite a few traitors as examples. The peasants must learn the consequences of rebellion. They were cursing your name before we had finished."

Arista knew he was telling the truth. Not because she could read his face, which she barely saw through her matted hair, but because Saldur had no reason to lie. "What do you want?"

"Two things, really. I want you to realize that the New Empire has risen and nothing can stand in its way. Your life, Arista, is over. You will be executed in a matter of weeks. And your dreams are already dead. You need to bury them alongside the sad little graves of Hilfred and Emery."

Arista stiffened.

"Surprised? We learned all about Emery when we retook Ratibor. You really do have such a way with men. First you got him killed and then Hilfred as well. You must make black widows jealous."

"And the second?" She noticed his momentary confusion. "The other reason we're having this little chat?"

"Oh yes. I want to know who you were working with."

"Hilfred—you killed him for it, remember?"

Saldur smiled and then struck her hard across the face. The chains binding Arista's wrists snapped taut as she tried to protect herself. He listened to her crying softly for a moment and then said, "You're a smart girl—too smart for your own good—but you're not *that* smart. Hilfred may have helped you escape arrest. He might even have hidden you for those weeks we searched. But he couldn't have gotten you into the palace or found this prison. Hilfred died wearing the uniform of a fourth-floor guard. You must have had help from someone on the staff to get that, and I want to know who it was."

"There was no one. It was just me and Hilfred."

Saldur slapped her again. Arista cried out, her body shaking, jangling the chains.

"Don't lie to me," he said while raising his hand again.

Arista spoke quickly to stay the blow. "I told you. It was just me. I got a job working in the palace as a chambermaid. I stole the uniform."

"I know all about you posing as Ella the scrub girl. But you couldn't have gotten the uniform without help. It had to be someone in a position of authority. I must know who the traitor is. Now tell me. Who was helping you?"

When she said nothing, he struck her twice more.

Arista cringed. "Stop it!"

"Tell me," Saldur growled.

"No, you'll hurt her!" she blurted.

"*Her?*"

Realizing her mistake, Arista bit her lip.

"So it was a woman. That limits the possibilities considerably, now doesn't it?" Saldur played with a key that dangled from a small chain, spinning it around his index finger. After several minutes, the regent crouched down and placed the lantern on the floor.

"I need a name and you *will* tell me. I know you *think* you can carry her identity to your grave, but whether you hold your tongue out of loyalty to her or to spite me, you should reconsider. You might believe that a few weeks is not long to hold your tongue, but once we start, you'll wish for a quick death."

He brushed her hair aside. "Look at that face. You don't believe me, do you? Still so naive. Still such an optimistic child. As a princess, you've led such a pampered life. Do you think that living among the commoners of Ratibor and scrubbing floors here at the palace has made you strong? Do you think you have nothing else to lose and you've finally hit bottom?"

When he stroked her cheek, Arista recoiled.

"I can see by your expression that you still have some pride and a sense of nobility. You don't yet realize just how far you have to fall. Trust me, Arista, I can strip you of that courage and break your spirit. You don't want to find out just how low I can bring you."

He stroked her hair gently for a moment, then grabbed a handful. Saldur pulled hard, jerking her head back and forcing Arista to look at him. His gaze lingered on her face. "You're still pure, aren't you? Still untouched and locked in your tower in more ways than one. I suspect neither Emery nor Hilfred dared to bed a princess. Perhaps we should begin with that. I will let the guards know that they can—no—I will specifically order them to violate you. It will make both of us very popular. The men will be requesting extra duty so they can desecrate you night and day."

Saldur let go of her hair, allowing her head to drop.

"Once you are thoroughly used and your pride has evaporated, I'll send for the master inquisitor. I'm sure he will relish the opportunity to purge the evil from the infamous Witch of Melengar." Saldur moved closer and spoke softly, intimately. "The inquisitor is very imaginative, and what he can do with chains, a bucket of water, and a searing hot brand is sheer artistry. You'll scream until you lose your voice. You'll black out and wake where the nightmare left off."

Arista tried to turn away, but his wrinkled hands forced her to look at him once again. His expression was not pleased or maniacal. Saldur appeared grim—almost sad.

"You'll experience anguish that you never thought possible. Your remaining courage will evaporate into myth and memory. Your mind will abandon you, leaving behind a drooling lump of scarred flesh. Even the guards won't want you then."

Saldur leaned forward until she could feel his breath and feared he might kiss her. "If, after all that, you've still not given me what I want, I will turn my attention to that pleasant little family who took you in—the Barkers, wasn't it? I will have them arrested and brought here. The father will watch as his wife takes your place with the guards. Then she will witness her husband and sons drawn and quartered one by one. Imagine what it will do to the woman when she sees her youngest, the one you supposedly saved, die. She will blame *you*, Arista. That poor woman will curse your name, and rightly so, for it will be your silence that destroyed her life."

He gently patted Arista's burning cheek. "Don't force me to do it. Tell me the traitor's name. She is guilty of treason, but the poor Barkers are innocent. They have done nothing. Simply tell me the name of this woman and you can prevent all these horrors."

Arista found it difficult to think and fought for breath as

she started losing control. Her face throbbed from his blows, and she was sickened by the salty-metallic taste of blood in her mouth. Guilt conjured images of Emery and Hilfred, both of whom had died because of her. She could not bear to add the Barkers' blood to her hands. To have them suffer for her mistakes.

"I'll tell you," Arista finally said. "But in return I want your assurance nothing will happen to the Barkers."

Saldur looked sympathetic, and she could almost see the grandfatherly face from her youth. How he could make such despicable threats and then return to such a kindly expression was beyond her understanding.

"Of course, my dear. After all, I'm not a monster. Just give me what I want and none of those things will come to pass. Now, tell me...What is her name?"

Arista hesitated. Saldur lost his smile once again—her time was up. She swallowed and said, "There *was* someone who hid me, gave me food, and even helped to find Gaunt. She's been a true friend, so kind and selfless. I can't believe I am betraying her to you now."

"Her *name*?" Saldur pressed.

Tears ran from Arista's eyes as she looked up. "Her name is...is...Edith Mon."

CHAPTER 3

SIR BRECKTON

Archibald Ballentyne, the Earl of Chadwick, stared out the windows of the imperial throne room. Behind him, Saldur shuffled parchments at a table while Ethelred warmed a throne not yet his own. A handful of servants occasionally drifted in and out, as did the imperial chancellor, who briefly spoke with one regent or the other. No one ever spoke to Archibald or asked for his counsel.

In just a few short years, Regent Saldur had risen from Bishop of Medford to the architect of the New Empire. Ethelred was about to trade his king's crown of Warric for the imperial scepter of all Avryn. Even the commoner Merrick Marius had managed to secure a noble fief, wealth, and a title.

What do I have to show for all my contributions? Where is my crown? My wife? My glory?

The answers Archibald knew all too well. He would wear no crown. Ethelred would wed his wife. And as for his glory, the man who had stolen that was just entering the hall. Archibald heard the boots pounding against the polished marble floor. The sound of the man's stride was unmistakable—uncompromising, straightforward, brash.

Turning around, Archibald saw Sir Breckton Belstrad's

floor-length blue cape sweeping behind the knight. Holding his helm in the crook of one arm and wearing a metal breastplate, he looked as if he were just returning from battle. Sir Breckton was tall, his shoulders broad, his chin chiseled. He was a leader of men, victorious in battle, and Archibald hated him.

"Sir Breckton, welcome to Aquesta," Ethelred called as the knight crossed the room.

Breckton ignored him, and Saldur as well, walking directly to Archibald's side, where he stomped dramatically and dropped to one knee. "Your Lordship," he said.

"Yes, yes, get up." The Earl of Chadwick waved a hand at him.

"As always, I am at your service, my lord."

"Sir Breckton?" Ethelred addressed the knight again.

Breckton showed no sign of acknowledgment and continued to speak with his liege. "You called, my lord? What is it you wish of me?"

"Actually, I summoned you on behalf of Regent Ethelred. He wishes to speak with you."

The knight stood. "As you wish, my lord."

Breckton turned and crossed the distance to the throne. His sword slapped against his side, and his boots pounded against the stone. He stopped at the base of the steps and offered only a shallow bow.

Ethelred scowled, but only briefly. "Sir Breckton, at long last. I've sent summons for you six times over the past several weeks. Have the messages not reached you?"

"They have, Your Lordship."

"But you did not respond," Ethelred said.

"No, Your Lordship."

"Why?"

"My lord, the Earl of Chadwick, commanded me to take Melengar. I was following his orders," Breckton replied.

"So the crucial demands of battle prevented you from breaking away until now." Ethelred nodded.

"No, Your Lordship. Only the fall of Drondil Fields remains and the siege is well tended. Victory is assured and does not require my attention."

"Then I don't understand. Why didn't you come when I ordered you to appear before me?"

"I do not serve you, Your Lordship. I serve the Earl of Chadwick."

Archibald's disdain for Breckton did not diminish his delight at seeing Ethelred verbally slapped.

"May I remind you, sir knight, that I will be emperor in just a few weeks?"

"You may, Your Lordship."

Ethelred looked confused. This brought a smile to Archibald's face. He enjoyed seeing someone else trying to deal with Breckton and knew exactly how the regent felt. Was Breckton granting Ethelred permission to remind the knight, or had he just insinuated the regent might not be emperor? Either way, the comment was rude yet spoken so plainly and respectfully that it appeared innocent of any ill intent. Breckton was like that—politely confounding and pointedly confusing. He had a way of making Archibald feel stupid, and that was just one of the many reasons he despised the arrogant man.

"I see this is going to continue to be an issue," Ethelred said. "It demonstrates the point of this meeting. As emperor, I will require good men to help me reign. You have proven yourself a capable leader, and as such, I want you to serve me directly. I am prepared to offer you the office and title of grand marshal of all imperial forces. In addition, I'll grant you the province of Melengar."

Archibald staggered. "Melengar is mine! Or will be when it is taken. It was promised to me."

"Yes, Archie, but times change. I need a strong man in the north, defending my border." Ethelred looked at Breckton. "I will appoint you the Marquis of Melengar. All too fitting, given that you were responsible for taking it."

"This is outrageous!" Archibald shouted, stomping his foot. "We had a deal. You have the imperial crown and Saldur has the imperial miter. What do I get? What is the reward for all my sweat and sacrifice? Without me, you wouldn't have Melengar to bestow to anyone!"

"Don't make a fool of yourself, Archie," Saldur said gently. "You must have known we could never entrust such an important realm to you. You are too young, too inexperienced, too...weak."

There was silence as Archibald fumed.

"Well?" Ethelred turned his attention back to Breckton. "Marquis of Melengar? Grand marshal of the imperial host? What say you?"

Sir Breckton showed no emotion. "I serve the Earl of Chadwick, just as my father and grandfather before me. It does not appear he wishes this. If there is nothing else, I must return to my charge in Melengar." Sir Breckton pivoted sharply and strode back to Archibald, where he knelt once more.

Ethelred stared after him in shock.

"Don't leave Aquesta just yet," Archibald told the knight. "I may have need of you here."

"As you wish, my lord." Breckton stood and briskly departed.

They were silent as they listened to the knight's footfalls echo and fade. Ethelred's face turned scarlet and he clenched his fists. Saldur stared after Breckton with his usual irritated glare.

"It seems you didn't take into account the man's unwavering sense of loyalty when you made your plans," Archibald railed. "But then, how could you, seeing as how you obviously don't understand the meaning of the word yourself? You should have consulted me first. I would have told you what the result would be. But you couldn't do that, could you? No, because it was *me* you were plotting to stab in the back!"

"Calm down, Archie," Saldur said.

"Stop calling me that. My name is Archibald!" Spit flew from his lips. "You're both so smug and arrogant, but I'm no pawn. One word from me and Breckton will turn his army and march on Aquesta." The earl pointed toward the still open door. "They're loyal to him, you know—every last one of the miserable cretins. They will do whatever he says, and as you can see, he worships me."

He clenched his fists and advanced, maddened that his soft heels did not have the same audible impact as Breckton's.

"I could get King Alric to throw his support behind me as well. I could return his precious Melengar in exchange for the rest of Avryn. I could beat you at your own little game. I'd have the Northern Imperial Army in my right hand and what remains of the Royalists in my left. I could crush both of you in less than a month. So don't tell me to calm down, *Sauly*! I've had it with your condescending tone and your holier-than-thou attitude. You're as much a worm as Ethelred. You're both in this together, weaving your webs and plotting against me. You just may have caught your own selves in your sticky trap this time!"

He headed for the door.

"Archi—I mean, Archibald!" Ethelred called after him.

The earl did not pause as he swept past Chancellor Biddings, who was just outside the throne room and gave the earl a concerned look. Servants scattered before Archibald as he marched in a fury through the doorway to the inner ward. Bursting into the brilliant sunshine reflected by the courtyard's snow, he discovered he was unsure where to go from there. After a few moments, Archibald decided that it did not matter. It felt good just to move, to burn off energy, to get away. He considered calling for his horse. A long ride over hard ground seemed like just the thing he needed, but it was cold out. Archibald did not want to end up miles from shelter freezing, tired, and hungry. Instead, he settled for pacing back and forth, creating a shallow trench in the new snow.

Frustration turned to pleasure as he recalled his little speech. He liked the look it had put on both of their faces. They had not expected such a bold response from him. The delight ate up most of the burning anger, and the pacing dissipated the rest. Taking a seat on an upturned bucket, he stomped the snow from his boots.

Would Breckton turn his forces against Aquesta? Could I become the new emperor and have Modina for my own with just a single order?

The answer formed almost as quickly as the question had. The thought was an appealing dream but nothing more. Breckton would never agree and would refuse the order. For all the knight's loyal bravado, everything that man did was subservient to some inscrutable code.

The entire House of Belstrad had been that way. Archibald recalled his father complaining about their ethics. The Ballentynes believed that knights should take orders without question in exchange for wealth and power. The Belstrads believed differently. They clung to an outdated ideal that the ruler — appointed by Maribor — must act within His will to earn a knight's loyalty. Archibald was certain Breckton would not consider civil war to be Maribor's will. Apparently, nothing Archibald ever really wanted fit that category.

Still, he had rocked the regents on their heels, and they

would treat him better. He would finally have respect now
that they realized just how important he was. The regents
would have no clue that he could not deliver on his threats, so
they would try to placate him with a larger prize. In the end,
Archibald would have Melengar and perhaps more.

Chapter 4

Wedding Plans

The Duchess of Rochelle was a large woman in more than just girth. Her husband matched her, as they were both rotund people with thick necks, short pudgy fingers, and cheeks that jiggled when they laughed, which in the case of the lady was often and loud. They were like bookends to each other. A male and female version, cut from the same cloth in every way except temperament. While the duke was quiet, Lady Genevieve was anything but.

Amilia always knew when the duchess was coming, as the lady heralded her own arrival with a trumpetlike voice that echoed through the palace halls. She greeted everyone, regardless of class, with a hearty "Hullo! How *are* you?" in her brassy voice, which boomed off the dull stone. She would hug servants, guards, and even the huntsman's hound if he crossed her path.

Amilia had met the duke and duchess when they first arrived. Saldur was there and had made the mistake of trying to explain why an audience with the empress was not possible. Amilia had been able to excuse herself, but she was certain Saldur had not been so lucky and probably was delayed for hours. Since then, Amilia had been avoiding the duchess, as

the woman was not one to take no for an answer, and she did
not want to repeat Saldur's mistake. After three days Amilia's
luck finally ran out, when she was leaving the chapel.

"Amilia, darling!" the duchess shouted, rushing forward
with her elegant gown billowing behind her. When she reached
Amilia, two huge arms surrounded the imperial secretary in a
crushing embrace. "I've been looking for you everywhere.
Every time I inquire, I'm told you are busy. They must work
you to death!"

The duchess released her grip. "You poor thing. Let me
look at you." She took Amilia's hands and spread her arms
wide. "Oh my, how lovely you are. But, darling, please tell me
this is a washday and your servants are behind. No, don't
bother. I am certain that is the case. Still, I hope you won't
mind if I have Lois, my seamstress, whip you up something. I
do so love giving gifts and it's Wintertide, after all. By the look
of you, it will hardly take any material or time. Lois will be
thrilled."

Lady Genevieve took Amilia's arm and walked her down the
hall. "You really are a treasure, you know, but I can tell they
treat you poorly. What can you expect with men like Ethelred
and Saldur running the show? Everything will be fine, though,
now that I'm here."

They rounded a corner and Amilia was amazed by the
woman's ability to talk so quickly without seeming to take a
breath.

"Oh! I just loved the invitation you sent me, and yes, I
know it was all your doing. It's *all* been your doing, hasn't it?
They have you planning the whole wedding, don't they? No
wonder you are so busy. How insensitive. How cruel! But
don't worry. As I said, I'm here to help you. I've fashioned
many weddings in my day and they've all been wonderful.
What you need is an experienced planner—a wizard of won-

der. We aristocrats expect panache and dazzle at these events and we hate to be disappointed. Being that this is the wedding of the empress, it must be larger, grander, and more amazing than anything that has come before. Nothing less will suffice."

She stopped suddenly and peered at Amilia. "Do you have doves to release? You must have them. You simply must!"

Amilia thought to reply, but the concern fled the duchess's face before she had a chance. Lady Genevieve was walking once more, pulling Amilia along. "Oh, I don't want to frighten you, darling. There is still plenty of time, given the proper help, of course. I am here now, and Modina will be thrilled at what we will achieve together. It will simply astound her."

"I—"

"How many white horses have you arranged for? Not nearly enough, I'm sure. Never mind, it will all come together. You'll see. Speaking of horses, I insist you accompany me on the hawking. I won't stand for you riding with anyone else. You'll love Leopold—he's quiet, just like you are, but a real pumpkin. Do you know what I mean? It doesn't look like you do—but no matter. You two will get on marvelously. Do you have a bird?"

"A bird?" Amilia managed to squeeze in.

"I'll let you use Murderess. She is one of my own goshawks."

"But—"

"No worries, my dear. There's nothing to it. The bird does all the work. All you need to do is just sit on your horse and look pretty—which you will in the new dress Lois will make. Blue would be a good color and will go wonderfully with your eyes. I suppose I will have to arrange a horse as well. We can't have you trudging through the snow and ruining the gown, now can we? I just know Saldur never thinks of such things. He appointed you secretary to the empress, but does he realize the need for clothing? A horse? Jewelry?"

The duchess paused again, still gripping her arm like a cider press. "Oh, my darling, I just realized you aren't wearing any—jewelry, that is. Don't be embarrassed. I understand perfectly. Otto is a fabulous jeweler. He can set a sapphire pendant in the blink of an eye. Won't that look stunning with your new blue gown? Thank Maribor I brought my full retinue. Lord knows the local artisans could never keep up with me. When you think about it, who can?" She laughed, and Amilia wondered just how much longer she could go on.

With another pull, they were off again. "I tend to be a bit much, don't I? It's the way I am. I can't help it. My husband stopped trying to turn me into a proper wife years ago. Of course, now he knows that my exuberance is what he loves most about me. 'Never a dull moment or a moment's peace,' he always says. Speaking of men, have you chosen a champion to carry your favor in the joust?"

"N-no."

"You haven't? But, darling, knights just adore fighting for pretty, young things like you. I'll bet you've driven them mad by waiting so long."

There was a pause, which startled Amilia into speech. "Ah, I didn't know I was supposed to."

"Ha hah!" Lady Genevieve laughed delightedly. "You *are* a marvel, darling. Simply fabulous! Ethelred tells me you're new to the gentry—elevated by Maribor himself. Isn't that delightful? Maribor's Chosen One watching over Maribor's Heir. How amazing!"

They turned the corner into the west wing, where a handful of chambermaids scattered like pigeons before a carriage. "You're a living legend, dear Amilia. Why, every knight in the kingdom will clamor for your favor. There will be none more sought after except the empress herself, but of course, no one would dare insult Ethelred by asking for *her* favor just weeks before his wedding! No one wants to make an enemy of a new emperor. That makes you the darling of the festival. You can have your pick of any eligible bachelor. Dukes, princes, earls, counts, and barons are all hoping for the chance to capture your attention or win the honor of sitting next to you at the feast with a victory on the field of Highcourt."

"I wasn't planning on going to either," Amilia stated.

The mere idea of noblemen chasing her was beyond frightening. While courtly love might be honorable and romantic for princesses and countesses, no noble ever practiced gentleness with a common woman. Serving girls who caught the eye of any noble—whether a knight or a king—could be taken against their will. Amilia had never been attacked, but she had wiped tears and bound wounds for more friends than she cared to count. Although she now possessed the title of *lady* before her name, everyone knew her background, and Amilia feared her flimsy title would be a poor shield against a lust-driven noble.

"Nonsense, you must attend the feasts. Besides, it's your duty. Your absence could very well start a riot! You don't want to be the cause of an insurrection in the weeks leading to your empress's wedding, do you?"

"Ah, no, of course—"

"Good, so it's all settled. Now you just need to pick someone. Do you have a favorite?"

"I don't know any of them."

"None? Good gracious, darling! Do they keep you a prisoner? What about Sir Elgar or Sir Murthas? Prince Rudolf is competing, and he is a fine choice with an excellent future. Of course, there is also Sir Breckton. You couldn't find a better choice than that. I know he *does* have the reputation of being a bit stuffy. It is true, of course. But after his victory in Melengar, he's the hero of the hour—and quite dashing." The duchess wiggled her eyebrows. "Yes, Breckton would be a perfect choice. Why, the ladies of several courts have been fawning over him for years."

A look of concern crossed Lady Genevieve's face. "Hmm... that does bring up a good point. You'll probably need to be careful. While you are certainly the object of every knight's affections, that means you're also the target of every lady's jealousy."

The duchess threw a meaty arm around Amilia's neck and pulled her close, as if she were going to whisper in her ear, but her voice did not drop a bit in volume. "Trust me, these women are dangerous. Courtly love isn't a game to them. You're new to politics, so I am telling you this for your own good. These are daughters of kings, dukes, and earls, and they are used to getting what they want. When they don't, they can be vengeful. They know all about your background. I am certain that many have sent spies to visit your family, trying to dig up any dirt they can. If they can't find any, trust me, they will invent some."

Lady Genevieve tugged her around another corner, this time toward the northern postern and up the steps to the third floor.

"I don't understand what you mean."

"It's quite simple, my dear. On the one hand, they think belittling you should be easy because of your common roots. But, on the other, you've never made any pretense of being otherwise, which negates their effort. It's difficult to demean someone for something they're not embarrassed of, now isn't it? Still, you must turn a deaf ear to any jibes told at your expense. You may hear name-calling, like swine herder and such. Which, of course, you're not. You must remember you're the daughter of a carriage maker and a fine one at that. Why, absolutely everyone who is anyone is beating a path to your father's door. They all want to ride in a coach crafted by the father of the Chosen One of Maribor."

"You know about my father? My family? Are they all right?" Amilia stopped so suddenly that the duchess walked four steps before realizing she had lost her.

Amilia had long feared her family was dead from starvation or illness. They had had so little. She had left home two years earlier to remove an extra mouth from the table, with the intent of sending money home, but she had not counted on Edith Mon.

The head maid had declared Amilia's old clothes unfit and demanded she pay for new ones. This forced Amilia to borrow against her salary. Broken or chipped plates also added to her bill, and in the first few months, there were many. With Edith, there was always something to keep Amilia penniless. Eventually the head maid even began fining her for disobedience or misbehavior, keeping Amilia in constant debt.

How she had hated Edith. The old ogre had been so cruel that there had been nights when Amilia had gone to sleep wishing the woman would die. She fantasized that a carriage would hit her or that she would choke on a bone. Now that Edith was gone, she almost regretted those thoughts. Charged with treason, Edith had been executed less than a week earlier, with all the palace staff required to watch.

In more than two years, Amilia had been unable to save even a single copper to send home and had heard nothing from her family. While the empress had been trapped in her catatonic daze, the regents had sequestered the palace staff to prevent others from learning about her condition. During that time, Amilia had been as much a prisoner as Modina. Writing letters home had been useless. The palace rumor mill maintained that all letters were burned by order of the regents. After Modina recovered, Amilia continued to write, but she never received a single reply. There had been reports of an epidemic near her home, and she feared her family was dead. Amilia had given up all hope of ever seeing them again—until now.

"Of course they're all right, darling. They are more than all right. Your family is the toast of Tarin Vale. From the moment the empress spoke your name during her speech on the balcony, people have flocked to the hamlet to kiss the hand of the woman who bore you and to beg words of wisdom from the man who raised you."

As they reached the third-floor guest chambers, Amilia's eyes began to water. "Tell me about them. Please. I must know."

"Well, let's see. Your father expanded his workshop, and it now takes up an entire block. He's received hundreds of orders from all over Avryn. Artisans from as far away as Ghent beg for the chance to work as his apprentices, and he's hired dozens. The townsfolk have elected him to city council. There is even talk of making him mayor come spring."

"And my mother?" Amilia asked with a quivering lip. "How is she?"

"She's just marvelous, darling. Your father bought the grandest house in town and filled it with servants, leaving her plenty of time for leisure. She started a modest salon for the local artisan women. They mostly eat cake and gossip. Even your brothers are prospering. They supervise your father's workers and have their pick of the women for wives. So you see, my dear, I think it is safe to say your family is doing *very* well indeed."

Tears ran down Amilia's face.

"Oh, darling! What is wrong? Wentworth!" she called out as they reached her quarters. A dozen servants paused in their tasks to look up. "Give me your handkerchief, and get a glass of water immediately!"

The duchess directed Amilia to sit on a settee, and Genevieve dabbed the girl's tears away with surprising delicacy.

"I'm sorry," Amilia said softly. "I just—"

"Nonsense! I'm the one who should apologize. I had no idea such news would upset you." She spoke in a soft motherly voice. Then, turning in the direction the servant had gone, the duchess roared, "Where's that water!"

"I'm all right—really," Amilia assured her. "I just haven't seen my family in so long and I was afraid..."

Lady Genevieve smiled and embraced Amilia. The duchess whispered in her ear, "Dear, I've heard it said that people come from far and wide to ask your family how *you* saved the empress. Their reported response is that they know nothing about that, but what they can say with complete certainty is that you saved them."

Amilia shook with emotion at the words.

Lady Genevieve picked up the handkerchief. "Where's that water!" she bellowed once more. When it arrived, the duchess thrust the cool glass into Amilia's hands. She drank while the big woman brushed back her hair.

"There now, that's better," Lady Genevieve purred.

"Thank you."

"Not at all, darling. Do you feel up to finding out why I brought you here?"

"Yes, I think so."

They were in the duchess's formal reception area, part of the four-room suite that Lady Genevieve had redecorated, transforming the dull stone shell into a warm, rich parlor. Thick woolen drapes of red and gold covered every inch of wall. Facades made the arrow slits appear large and opulent. An intricately carved cherry mantel fronted the previously bare stone fireplace. Layers of carpets covered the entire room, making the floor soft and cozy. Not a stick of the original furniture remained. Everything was new and lovelier than anything Amilia had ever seen before.

A dozen servants, all dressed in reds and golds, returned to work. One individual, however, stood out. He was a tall, well-tailored man in a delightful outfit of silver and gold brocade. On his head he wore a whimsical, yet elegant, hat that displayed a long, billowing plume.

"Viscount," the duchess called, waving the man over. "Amilia, darling, I want you to meet Viscount Albert Winslow."

"Enchanted indeed." He removed his hat and swept it elaborately in a reverent bow.

"Albert is perhaps the foremost expert on organizing grand events. I hired him to mastermind my Summersrule Festival, and it was utterly amazing. I tell you, the man is a genius."

"You are far too kind, my lady," Winslow said softly with a warm smile.

"How you managed to fill the moat with leaping dolphins is beyond me. And the streamers that filled the sky—why, I've never seen such a thing. It was pure magic!"

"I'm pleased to have pleased you, my lady."

"Amilia, you simply must use Albert. Don't worry about the cost. I insist on paying for his services."

"Nonsense, good ladies. I couldn't conceive of taking payment for such a noble and worthwhile endeavor. My time is yours, and I'll do whatever I can out of devotion to you both and, of course, for Her Eminence."

"There now!" Lady Genevieve exclaimed. "The man is as chivalrous as a paladin. You *must* take him up on his offer, darling!"

They both stared at Amilia until she found herself nodding.

"I am delighted to be of service, my lady. When can I meet with your staff?"

"Ah..." Amilia hesitated. "There's only me and Nimbus. *Oh, Nimbus!* I'm sorry but I was on my way to meet with him when you—I mean—when we met. I'm supposed to be selecting entertainment for the feasts and I'm terribly late."

"Well, you should hurry off, then," Lady Genevieve said. "Take Albert with you. He can begin there. Now run along. There is no need to thank me, my dear. Your success will be my reward."

⤚⟡

Amilia noticed that Viscount Winslow was less formal when away from the duchess. He greeted each performer warmly, and those not selected were dismissed with respect and good humor. He knew exactly what was required, and the auditions proceeded quickly under his guidance. All told, they selected twenty acts: one for each of the pre-wedding feasts, three for the Eve's Eve banquet, and five for the wedding reception. The viscount even picked four more, just in case of illness or injury.

Amilia was grateful for the viscount's help. As much as she had grown to rely on Nimbus, he had no experience with event planning. Originally, the courtier had been hired as the empress's tutor, but it had been quite some time since he had educated Modina on poise or protocol. Such skills were not required, as Modina never left her room. Instead, Nimbus became the secretary to the secretary, Amilia's right hand. He knew how to get things done in a royal court, whereas Amilia had no clue.

From his years of service to the nobles in Rhenydd, Nimbus had mastered the subtle language of manipulation. He tried to explain the nuances of this skill to Amilia, but she was a poor student. From time to time he corrected her for doing foolish things, such as bowing to the chamberlain, thanking a steward, or standing in the presence of others, which forced them to remain on their feet. Almost every success she had in the palace was because of Nimbus's coaching. A more ambitious man would resent her taking the credit, but Nimbus always offered his counsel in a kind and helpful manner.

Sometimes when Amilia caught herself doing something particularly stupid, or when she blushed from embarrassment, she noticed Nimbus spilling something on himself or tripping on a carpet. Once he even fell halfway down a flight of stairs. For a long while, Amilia thought he was extremely clumsy, but recently she had begun to suspect Nimbus might be the most agile person she had ever met.

The hour was late and Amilia hurried toward the empress's chamber. Gone were the days when she spent nearly every minute in Modina's company. Her responsibilities kept her busy, but she never retired without checking in on the empress, who was still her closest friend.

Rounding a corner, she bumped headlong into a man.

"I'm sorry!" she exclaimed, feeling more than a little foolish for walking with her head down.

"Oh no, my lady," the man replied. "It is I who must apologize for standing as a roadblock. Please, forgive me."

Amilia did not recognize him, but there were many new faces at the palace these days. He was tall and stood straight with his shoulders squared. His face was closely shaved and his hair neatly trimmed. By his bearing and clothing, she could tell he was a noble. He was dressed well, but unlike those of many of the Wintertide guests, his outfit was subdued.

"It's just that I am a bit confused," he said, looking around.

"Are you lost?" she asked.

He nodded. "I know my way in forests and fields. I can pinpoint my whereabouts by the use of moon and stars, but for the life of me, I am a total imbecile when trapped within walls of stone."

"That's okay, I used to get lost in here all the time. Where are you going?"

"I've been staying in the knights' wing at my lord's request, but I stepped outside for a walk and can't find my way back to my quarters."

"You're a soldier, then?"

"Yes, forgive me. My stupidity is without end." He stepped back and bowed formally. "Sir Breckton of Chadwick, son of Lord Belstrad, at your service, my lady."

"Oh! *You're* Sir Breckton?"

Appearances never impressed Amilia, but Breckton was perfect. He was exactly what she expected a knight should be: handsome, refined, strong, and—just as Lady Genevieve had described—dashing. For the first time since coming to the palace, she wished she were pretty.

"Indeed, I am. You've heard of me, then...For good or ill?"

"Good, most certainly. Why, just—" She stopped herself and felt her face blush.

Concern furrowed his brow. "Have I done something to make you uncomfortable? I am terribly sorry if I—"

"No, no, not at all. I'm just being silly. To be honest, I never heard of you until today, and then..."

"Then?"

"It's embarrassing," she admitted, feeling even more flustered by his attention.

The knight's expression turned serious. "My lady, if someone has dishonored me, or harmed you through the use of my name—"

"Oh no! Nothing as terrible as all that. It was the Duchess of Rochelle, and she said..."

"Yes?"

Amilia cringed. "She said I should ask you to carry my favor in the joust."

"Oh, I see." He looked relieved. "I'm sorry to disappoint you, but I am not—"

"I know. I know," she interrupted, preferring not to hear the words. "I would have told her so myself if she ever stopped talking—the woman is a whirlwind. The idea of a knight— any knight—carrying *my* favor is absurd."

Sir Breckton appeared puzzled. "Why is that?"

"Look at me!" She took a step back so he could get a full view. "I'm not pretty, and as we both now know, I'm the opposite of graceful. I'm not of noble blood, having been born a poor carriage maker's daughter. I don't think I could hope for the huntsman's dog to sit beside me at the feast, much less have a renowned knight such as yourself riding on my behalf."

Breckton's eyebrows rose abruptly. "Carriage maker's daughter? *You* are *her*? Lady Amilia of Tarin Vale?"

"Oh yes, I'm sorry." She placed her hand to her forehead and rolled her eyes. "See? I have all the etiquette of a mule. Yes, I am Amilia."

Breckton studied her for a long moment. At last he spoke. "You're the maid who saved the empress?"

"Disappointing, I know." She waited for him to laugh and insist she could not possibly be the Chosen One of Maribor. While Modina's public declaration had helped protect Amilia, it had also made her uncomfortable. For a girl who had spent her whole life trying to hide from attention, being famous was difficult. Worse yet, she was a fraud. The story about a divine intervention selecting her to save the empress was a lie, a political fabrication—Saldur's way of manipulating the situation to his advantage.

To her surprise, the knight did not laugh. He merely asked,

"And you think no knight will carry your favor because you are of common blood?"

"Well, that and about a dozen other reasons. I hear the whispers sometimes."

Sir Breckton dropped to one knee and bowed his head. "Please, Lady Amilia, I beseech you. Give me the honor of carrying your token into the joust."

She just stood there.

The knight looked up. "I've offended you, haven't I? I am too bold! Forgive my impudence. I had no intention to participate in the joust, as I deem such contests the unnecessary endangerment of good men's lives for vanity and foolish entertainment. Now, however, after meeting you, I realize I must compete, for more is at stake. The honor of any lady should be defended and you are no ordinary lady, but rather the Chosen One of Maribor. For you, I would slay a thousand men to bring justice to those blackguards who would soil your good name! My sword and lance are yours, dear lady, if you will but grant me your favor."

Dumbstruck, Amilia did not realize she had agreed until after walking away. She was numb and could not stop smiling for the rest of her trip up the stairs.

⁓

As Amilia reached Modina's room, her spirits were still soaring. It had been a good day, perhaps the best of her life. She had discovered her family was alive and thriving. The wedding was proceeding under the command of an experienced and gracious man. And a handsome knight had knelt before her and asked for her token. Amilia grasped the latch, excited to share the good news with Modina, but all was forgotten the moment the door swung open.

As usual, Modina sat before the window, dressed in her thin white nightgown, staring out at the brilliance of the snow in the moonlight. Next to her was a full-length intricately carved oval mirror mounted with brass fittings on a beautiful wooden swivel.

"Where did *that* come from?" Amilia asked, shocked.

The empress did not answer.

"How did it get here?"

Modina glanced at the mirror. "It's pretty, isn't it? A pity they brought such a nice one. I suppose they wanted to please me."

Amilia approached the mirror and ran her fingers along the polished edge. "How long have you had it?"

"They brought it in this morning."

"I'm surprised it survived the day." Amilia turned her back on the mirror to face the empress.

"I'm in no hurry, Amilia. I still have some weeks yet."

"So you've decided to wait for your wedding?"

"Yes. At first I didn't think it would matter, but then I realized it could reflect badly on you. If I wait, it will appear to be Ethelred's fault. Everyone will assume I couldn't stand the thought of him touching me."

"Is that the reason?"

"No, I have no feelings about him or anything. Well, except for you. But you'll be all right." Modina turned to look at Amilia. "I can't even cry anymore. I never even wept when they captured Arista... not a single tear. I watched the whole thing from this window. I saw Saldur and the seret go in and knew what that meant. They came back out, but she never has. She's down there right now in that horrible dark place. Just like I once was. When she was here, I had a purpose, but now there is nothing left. It's time for this ghost to fade away. I have served the regents' purpose by helping them build the empire. I've given you a better life, and not even Saldur will harm you now. I tried to help Arista, but I failed. Now it's time for me to leave."

Amilia knelt down next to Modina, gently drew back the hair from her face, and kissed her cheek. "Don't speak that way. You were happy once, weren't you? You can be again."

Modina shook her head. "A girl named Thrace was happy. She lived with the family she loved in a small village near a river. Surrounded by friends, she played in the woods and fields. That girl believed in a better tomorrow. She looked forward to gifts Maribor would bring. Only instead of gifts, he sent darkness and horror."

"Modina, there is always room for hope. Please, you must believe."

"There was one day, when you were getting the clerk to order some cloth, that I saw a man from my past. He was hope. He saved Thrace once. For a moment, one very brief moment, I thought he had come to save me too, only he didn't. When he walked away, I knew he was just a memory from a time when I was alive."

Amilia's hands found Modina's and cradled them as she might hold a dying bird. Amilia was having trouble breathing. As her lower lip began to tremble, she looked back at the mirror. "You're right. It *is* a shame they brought such a pretty one." She put her arms around Modina and began to cry.

CHAPTER 5

FOOTPRINTS IN THE SNOW

S everal miles from Medford, Royce saw the smoke and prepared himself for the worst. Crossing the Galewyr used to
mean entering the bustling streets of the capital, but on that
day, as he raced across the bridge, he found only a charred
expanse of blackened posts and scorched stone. The city he
had known was gone.

Royce never called anywhere *home*. To him the word meant
a mythical place, like paradise or fairyland, but Wayward
Street had been the closest thing he had ever found. A recent
snowfall covered the city like a sheet that nature had drawn
over a corpse. Not a building remained undamaged, and many
were nothing but charcoal and ash. The castle's gates were
shattered, portions of the walls collapsed. Even the trees in
Gentry Square were gone.

Medford House, in the Lower Quarter, was a pile of smoldering beams. Nothing remained across the street except a
gutted foundation and a burned sign displaying the hint of
a rose in blistered paint.

He dismounted and moved to the rubble of the House.
Where Gwen's office used to be, he caught a glimpse of pale
fingers beneath a collapsed wall. His legs turned weak and his

feet foolish as he stumbled over the wreckage. Smoke caught in his throat, and he drew up the scarf to cover his nose and mouth. Reaching the edge of the wall, he bent, trying to lift it. The edge broke away, but it was enough to reveal what was underneath.

An empty cream-colored glove.

Royce stepped back from the smoke. Sitting on the blackened porch, he noticed he was shaking. He was unaccustomed to being scared. Over the years, he had given up caring if he lived or died, figuring that a quick demise spared him the pain of living in a world so miserly that it begrudged an orphan boy a life. He had always been ready for death, gambling with it, waging bets against it. Royce had been satisfied in the knowledge that his risks were sound because he had nothing of value to lose—nothing to fear.

Gwen had changed everything.

He was an idiot and never should have left her alone.

Why did I wait?

They could have been safe in Avempartha, where only he held the key. The New Empire could beat themselves senseless against its walls and never reach him or his family.

A block away, a noisy flock of crows took flight. Royce stood and listened, hearing voices on the wind. Noticing his horse wandering down the street, he cursed himself for not tying her up. By the time he caught the reins, he spotted a patrol of imperial soldiers passing the charred ruins of Mason Grumon's place.

"Halt!" the leader shouted.

Royce leapt on his mare and kicked her just as he heard a dull *thwack*. His horse lurched, then collapsed with a bolt lodged deep in her flank. Royce jumped free before being crushed. He tumbled in the snow and came up on his feet with his dagger, Alverstone, drawn. Six soldiers hurried toward him. Only one had a crossbow, and he was busy ratcheting the string for his next shot.

Royce turned and ran.

He slipped into an alley filled with debris and vaulted over the shattered remains of The Rose and Thorn. Crossing the sewer near the inn's stable, he was surprised to find the plank bridge still there. Shouts rose behind him, but they were distant and muffled by the snow. The old feed store was still standing, and with a leap, he caught the windowsill on the second story. If they tracked him through the alley, the soldiers would be briefly baffled by his disappearance. That was all the head start Royce needed. He pulled himself to the roof, crossed it, and climbed down the far side. He took one last moment to obscure his tracks before heading west.

&

Royce stood at the edge of the forest, trying to decide between the road and the more direct route, through the trees. Snow started to fall again, and the wind swept the flakes at an angle. The white curtain muted colors, turning the world a hazy gray. The thief flexed his hands. He had lost feeling in his fingers again. In his haste to find Gwen, he had once more neglected to purchase winter gloves. He pulled his hood tight and wrapped the scarf around his face. The northwest gale tore at his cloak, cracking the edges like a whip. He hooked it in his belt several times but eventually gave up—the wind insisted.

The distance to the Winds Abbey was a long day's ride in summer, a day and a half in winter, but Royce had no idea how long it would take him on foot through snow. Without proper gear, it was likely he would not make it at all. Almost everything he had was lost with his horse, including his blanket, food, and water. He did not even have the means to start a fire. The prudent choice would be the road. The walking would be easier, and he would at least have the chance of encountering other travelers. Still, it was the longer route. He chose the shortcut through the forest. He hoped Gwen had kept her promise and gone to the monastery, but there was only one way to be certain and his need to see her had grown desperate.

As night fell, the stars shone brightly above a glistening world of white. Struggling to navigate around logs and rocks hidden beneath the snow, Royce halted when he came upon a fresh line of tracks—footprints. He listened but heard only the wind blowing through the snow-burdened trees.

With an agile jump he leapt on a partially fallen tree and nimbly sprinted up its length until he was several feet off the ground. Royce scanned the tracks in the snow below him. They were only as deep as his own, too shallow for a man weighed down by even light armor.

Who can possibly be traveling on foot here tonight besides me?

Given that the footprints were headed the direction he was going, and Royce wanted to keep the owner in front of him, he followed. The going was less difficult and Royce was thankful for the ease in his route.

When he reached the top of a ridge, the tracks veered right, apparently circling back the way he had come.

"Sorry to see you go," Royce muttered. His breath puffed out in a moonlit fog.

As he climbed down the slope, he recalled this ravine from the trip he had taken three years earlier with Hadrian and Prince Alric. Then, as now, finding a clear route had been difficult and he struggled to work his way to the valley below. The snow made travel a challenge, and once he reached level

ground, he found it deep with drifts. He had not made more
than a hundred feet of headway before encountering the footprints once more. Again he followed them, and found the way
easier.

Reaching the far side of the valley, he faced the steep slope
back up. The footprints turned to the right. This time Royce
paused. Slightly to the left he could see an easy route. A
V-shaped ravine, cleared and leveled by runoff, was inviting.
He considered going that way but noticed that directly in front
of him, carved in the bark of a spruce tree, was an arrow-
shaped marker pointing to the right. The trailblazer's footprints were sprinkled with wood chips.

"So you want me to keep following you," Royce whispered
to himself. "That's only marginally more disturbing than you
knowing I'm following you at all."

He glanced around. There was no one he could see. The
only movement was the falling snow. The stillness was both
eerie and peaceful, as if the wood waited for him to decide.

His legs were weak, his feet and hands numb. Royce had
never liked invitations, but he guessed following the prints
would once again be the easier route. He looked up at the
slope and sighed. After following the tracks only a few hundred feet more, he spotted a pair of fur mittens dangling from
the branch of a tree. Royce slipped them on and found they
were still warm.

"Okay, that's creepy," Royce said aloud. He raised his voice
and added, "I'd love a skin of water, a hot steak with onions,
and perhaps some fresh-baked bread with butter."

All around him was the tranquil silence of a dark wood in
falling snow. Royce shrugged and continued onward. The trail
eventually hooked left, but by then the steep bluff was little
more than a mild incline. Royce half expected to find a dinner
waiting for him when he reached the crest, but the hilltop was

bare. In the distance was a light, and the footprints headed straight toward it.

Royce ticked through the possibilities and concluded nothing. There was no chance imperial soldiers were leading him through the forest, and he was too far from Windermere for it to be monks. Dozens of legends spoke of fairies and ghosts inhabiting the woods of western Melengar, but none mentioned denizens that left footprints and warm mittens.

No matter how he ran the scenarios, he could find no way to justify an impending trap. Still, Royce gripped the handle of Alverstone and trudged forward. As he closed the distance, he saw that the light came from a small house built high in the limbs of a large oak tree. Below the tree house, a ring of thick evergreens surrounded a livestock pen, where a dark horse pawed the snow beside a wooden lean-to.

"Hello?" Royce called.

"Climb up," a voice yelled down. "If you're not too tired."

"Who are you?"

"I'm a friend. An old friend—or rather, you're mine."

"What's your name…*friend*?" Royce stared up at the opening on the underside of the tree house.

"Ryn."

"Now see, that's a bit odd, as I have few friends, and none of them is called Ryn."

"I never told you my name before. Now, are you going to come up and have some food or simply steal my horse and ride off? Personally, I suggest a bite to eat first."

Royce looked at the horse for a long moment before grabbing the knotted rope dangling along the side of the tree trunk and pulling himself up. Reaching the floor of the house, he peeked inside. The space was larger than he had expected, was oven warm, and smelled of meat stew. Branches reached out in all directions, each one rubbed smooth as a banister.

Pots and scarves hung from the limbs, and several layers of mats and blankets hid the wooden floor.

In a chair crafted from branches, a slim figure smoked a pipe. "Welcome, Mr. Royce," Ryn said with a smile.

He wore crudely stitched clothes made from rough, treated hides. On his head was a hat that looked like an old flopped sack. Even with his ears hidden, his slanted eyes and high cheekbones betrayed his elven heritage.

On the other side of the room, a woman and a small boy chopped mushrooms and placed them in a battered pot suspended in a small fireplace made of what looked to be river stones. They too were *mir*—a half-breed mix of human and elf—like Royce himself. Neither said a word, but they glanced over at him from time to time while adding vegetables to the pot.

"You know my name?" Royce asked.

"Of course. It isn't a name I could easily forget. Please, come in. My home is yours."

"How do you know me?" Royce pulled up his legs and closed the door.

"Three autumns ago, just after Amrath's murder, you were at The Silver Pitcher."

Royce thought back. *The hat!*

"They were sick." Ryn tilted his head toward his family. "Fever—the both of them. We were out of food and I spent my last coin on some old bread and a turnip from Mr. Hall. I knew it wouldn't be enough, but there was nothing else I could do."

"You were the elf that they accused of thieving. They pulled your hat off."

Ryn nodded. He puffed on his pipe and said, "You and your friend were organizing a group of men to save the Prince of Melengar. You asked me to join. You promised a reward—a fair share."

Royce shrugged. "We needed anyone willing to help."

"I didn't believe you. Who of my kind would? No one ever gave fair shares of anything to an elf, but I was desperate. When it was over, Drake refused to pay me, just as I expected. But you kept your word and forced him to give me an equal share—*and a horse*. You threatened to kill the whole lot of them if they didn't." He allowed himself a little smile. "Drake handed over the gelding with full tack and never even checked it. I think he just wanted to get rid of me. I left before they could change their minds. I was miles away before I finally got a chance to look in the saddlebags. Fruits, nuts, meat, cheese, a pint of whiskey, a skin of cider, those would've been treasure enough. But I also found warm blankets, fine clothes, a hand axe, flint and steel, a knife—and *the purse*. There were gold tenents in that bag—twenty-two of them."

"Gold tenents? You got Baron Trumbul's horse?"

Ryn nodded. "There was more than enough gold to buy medicine, and with the horse I got back in time. I prayed I would be able to thank you before I died, and today I got my chance. I saw you in the city but could do nothing there. I am so glad I persuaded you to visit."

"The mittens were a nice touch."

"Please sit and be my guest for dinner."

Royce hung his scarf alongside his cloak on one of the branches and set his boots to warm near the fire. The four ate together with little conversation.

After she had taken his empty bowl, Ryn's wife spoke for the first time. "You look tired, Mr. Royce. Can we make you a bed for the night?"

"No. Sorry. I can't stay," Royce said while getting up, pleased to feel his feet again.

"You're in a hurry?" Ryn asked.

"You could say that."

"In that case, you will take my horse, Hivenlyn," Ryn said.

An hour earlier, Royce would have stolen a horse from anyone he had happened upon, so he was surprised to hear himself say, "No. I mean, thanks, but no."

"I insist. I named him Hivenlyn because of you. It means *unexpected gift* in Elvish. So you see, you must take him. He knows every path in this wood and will get you safely wherever you need to go." Ryn nodded toward the boy, who nimbly slipped out the trapdoor.

"You need that horse," Royce said.

"I'm not the one trudging through the forest in the middle of the night without a pack. I lived without a horse for many years. Right now, you need him more than I do. Or can you honestly say you have no use for a mount?"

"Okay, I'll *borrow* him. I am riding to the Winds Abbey. I'll let them know he is your animal. You can claim him there." Royce bundled up and descended the rope. At the bottom, Ryn's son stood with the readied horse.

Ryn climbed down as well. "Hivenlyn is yours now. If you have no further need, give him to someone who does."

"You're crazy," Royce said, shaking his head in disbelief. "But I don't have time to argue." He mounted and looked back at Ryn, standing in the snow beneath his little home. "Listen...I'm not...I'm just not used to people...you know..."

"Ride safe and be well, my friend."

Royce nodded and turned Hivenlyn toward the road.

⮜

He traveled all night, following the road and fighting a fresh storm that rose against him. The wind blew bitter, pulling his cloak away and causing him to shiver. He pushed the horse hard, but Hivenlyn was a fine animal and did not falter.

At sunrise they took a short rest in the shelter of fir trees. Royce ate the hard round of mushroom-stuffed bread Ryn's wife had provided and gave Hivenlyn a bit of one end. "Sorry about the pace," he told the horse. "But I'll make sure you get a warm stall and plenty to eat when we arrive." Royce failed to mention that the deal depended on his finding Gwen safe. Anything less, and he would not care about the needs of the horse. He would not care about anything.

The storm continued to rage all through that day. Gale-swept snow blew across the road, forming patterns that resembled ghostly snakes. During the entire trip, Royce did not come across a single traveler, and the day passed by in a blinding haze of white.

As darkness fell, the two finally reached the summit of Monastery Hill. The abbey, silent and still, appeared from behind a veil of falling snow. The quiet of the compound was disturbing, too similar to that visit he had made three years earlier after the Imperialists had burned the church to the ground with dozens of monks locked inside. Panic threatened to overtake Royce as he raced up the stone steps and pulled on the expansive doors. He entered, moving quickly down the length of the east range. He just needed a face, any face, someone he could ask about Gwen. Not a single monk in the abbey could have missed the arrival of a band of prostitutes.

The corridor was dark, as was the hall leading to the cloister. He opened the door to the refectory and found it vacant. The empty dining tables were matched by empty benches. As Royce listened to the hollow echo of his own footsteps, the sense of doom that had driven him through the snow caused him to sprint to the church. Reaching the two-story double doors, he feared that, just as once before, he would find them chained shut. Taking hold of the latches, he pulled hard.

The soft sound of singing washed over him as Royce gazed

down a long nave filled with monks. The massive doors boomed as they slammed against the walls. The singing halted and dozens of heads turned.

"Royce?" a voice said. A woman's voice—her voice.

The forest of brown-clad monks shifted, and he spotted Gwen among them, dressed in an emerald gown. By the time she reached the aisle, he was throwing his arms around her and squeezing until she gasped.

"Master Melborn, please," the abbot said. "We are in the middle of vespers."

CHAPTER 6

THE PALACE

Hadrian drew the drapes and lit a candle on the small table before asking Albert, "What have you discovered?" In the past Royce had always run the meetings, and Hadrian found himself trying to remember all the little things he would do to ensure secrecy.

They were in Hadrian's room at the Bailey, and this was their first meeting since Royce had left. Albert was staying at the palace now, and Hadrian wanted to keep Albert's visits infrequent. A guest of the empress might patronize a seedy inn for entertainment, but too many visits could appear suspicious.

"Genny introduced me to the empress's secretary," Albert said. He was dressed in a heavy cloak, which hid his lavish attire beneath simple wool. "The girl cried tears of joy when Genny told her the news about her family. I think it's safe to say that Lady Amilia loves the duchess and at least trusts me. You should have seen Genny. She was marvelous. And her chambers are exquisite!"

"What about Leo?" Hadrian asked.

"He's quiet as always but playing along. If Genny is all right with it, so is he. Besides, he's always hated Ethelred."

The two sat at the table. The dim, flickering light revealed not much more than their faces. For over a week Hadrian had tried to find out what he could in town, but he was not getting very far. He did not have the head for planning that Royce did.

"And you know how Genny loves intrigue," Albert added. "Anyway, she got me appointed as the official wedding planner."

"That's perfect. Have you learned anything useful?"

"I asked Lady Amilia about places that could be used to temporarily house performers. I told her it's common practice to utilize empty cells, since tavern space is hard to come by."

"Nice."

"Thanks, but it didn't help. According to her, the palace doesn't have a dungeon, just a prison tower."

"Prison tower sounds good."

"It's empty."

"Empty? Are you sure? Have you checked?"

Albert shook his head. "Off-limits."

"Why would it be off-limits if it's empty?"

The viscount shrugged. "No idea, but Lady Amilia assures me it is. Said she was up there herself. Besides, I've watched it the last few nights, and I'm pretty sure she's right. I've never seen a light. Although, I did see a Seret Knight go in once."

"Any other ideas?"

Albert drummed his fingers on the tabletop, thinking for a moment. "The only other restricted area is the fifth floor, which I've determined is where the empress resides."

"Have you seen her?" Hadrian leaned forward. "Have you managed to speak with her?"

"No. As far as I can tell, Modina never leaves her room. She has all her meals brought to her. Amilia insists the empress is busy administrating the empire and is still weak. Apparently, the combination leaves her unable to receive guests. This has been a source of irritation recently. All the visiting dignitaries want an audience with the empress—but all are denied."

"Someone has to see her."

"Lady Amilia certainly does. There is also a chamber-maid…" Albert fished inside his tunic, pulling out a wadded bundle of parchments, which he unfolded on the table. "Yes, here it is. The chambermaid is named Anna, and the door guard is…" He shuffled through his notes. "Gerald. Anna is the daughter of a mercer from Colnora. As for Gerald, his full name is Gerald Baniff. He's from Chadwick. Family friend of the Belstrads." Albert took a moment to flip through a few more pages. "Was once personal aide to Sir Breckton. A commendation for bravery won him the position of honor guard to the empress."

"What about the regents?"

"I assume they *could* see her, but as far as I can tell, they don't. At least, no one I've talked to reports ever having seen them on the fifth floor."

"How can she govern if she never takes a meeting with Ethelred or Saldur?" Hadrian asked.

"I think it's obvious. The regents are running the empire."

Hadrian slumped back in his seat with a scowl. "So she's a puppet."

Albert shrugged. "Maybe. Is this significant?"

"Royce and I knew her—before she became the empress. I thought maybe she might help us."

"Doesn't look like she has any real power."

"Does anyone know this?"

"Some of the nobles may suspect, although most appear colossally unaware."

"They can't all be *that* gullible."

"You have to keep in mind that many of these people are extremely religious and dedicated Imperialists. They accept the story of her being the heir descended from Maribor. From what I've determined, the vast majority of the peasant class feels the same way. The servants and even palace guards view her with a kind of awe. The rarity of her appearances has only reinforced this notion. It's a politician's dream. Since she's hardly seen, no one attaches any mistake to her and instead they blame the regents."

"So no one other than Amilia, the guard, and the chambermaid sees her?"

"Looks that way. Oh, wait." Albert paused. "Nimbus also apparently has access."

"*Nimbus?*" Hadrian asked.

"Yes, he is a courtier from Vernes. I met him several years ago at some gala or ball. No one of account, as I remember, but generally a decent fellow. He's actually the one that introduced Lord Daref and me to Ballentyne, which led to that pair of stolen letter jobs you did for the Earl of Chadwick and Alenda Lanaklin. Nimbus is a thin, funny guy, prone to wearing loud clothes and a powdered wig. Always carries a little leather satchel over his shoulder—rumor is he carries makeup in it. Smarter than he appears certainly. Very alert—he listens to everything. He was hired by Lady Amilia and works as her assistant."

"So what is the likelihood *you* could see the empress?"

"Slim, I suspect. Why? I just told you there's not much chance she can help, or do you think they're keeping Gaunt in Modina's room?"

"No." Hadrian rubbed a hand over the surface of the table amidst the flickering shadows. "I'd just like to—I don't know— to see if she's all right, I guess. I sort of promised her father I'd watch out for her—make sure she was okay, you know?"

"She's the empress," Albert stated. "Or hasn't he heard?"

"He's dead."

"Oh." Albert paused.

"I just would feel better if I could talk to her."

"Are we after Gaunt or the empress?"

Hadrian scowled. "Well, it doesn't look like we're very close to finding where Gaunt is being held."

"I think I've pushed things about as far as I can. I'm a wedding planner, not a guard, and people get suspicious if I start asking about prisoners."

"I really didn't think it would be this hard to find him."

Albert sighed. "I'll try again," he said, standing and pulling the drawstrings on his cloak.

"Hold on a second. When we first arrived, didn't you mention that the palace was recruiting new guards?"

"Yeah, they're expecting huge crowds. Why?"

Hadrian didn't reply right away, staring into the single candle and massaging his callused palms. "I thought I might try my hand at being a man-at-arms again."

Albert smiled. "I think you're a tad overqualified."

"Then I ought to get the job."

⚯

Hadrian waited in line among the weak-shouldered, bent-backed, would-be soldiers. They shifted their weight from foot to foot and blew into cupped hands to warm their fingers. The line of men stretched from the main gate to the barracks' office within the palace courtyard. Being the only man with his own weapons and a decent cloak, Hadrian felt out of place and forced himself to stoop and shuffle when he walked.

Heaps of snow packed the inner walls of the well-shoveled courtyard. Outside the barracks, a fire burned in a pit, where the yard guards would occasionally pause to warm their hands or get a cup of something steaming hot. Servant boys made routine trips back and forth to the well or the woodpile, hauling buckets of water or slings of split logs.

"Name?" a gruff soldier asked as Hadrian entered the dim barracks and stood before a rickety desk.

Three men in thick leather sat behind it. Beside them was a small clerk, whom Hadrian had seen once before in the palace. A disagreeable sort with a balding head and ink-stained fingers, he sat with a roll of parchment, pen, and ink.

"You have a name?" the man in the center asked.

"Baldwin," Hadrian said. The clerk scratched the parchment. The end of his feathered quill whipped about like the tail of an irritated squirrel.

"Baldwin, eh? Where have you fought?"

"All over, really."

"Why aren't you in the imperial army? Ya a deserter?"

Hadrian allowed himself a smile, which the soldier did not return. "You could say that. I left the Nationalists."

This caught the ear of everyone at the table and a few men standing in line. The clerk stopped scribbling and looked up.

"For some reason they stopped paying me," Hadrian added with a shrug.

A slight smile pulled at the edges of the soldier's lips. "Not terribly loyal, are you?"

"I'm as loyal as they come...as long as you pay me."

This brought a chuckle from the soldier, and he looked to the others. The older man to his right nodded. "Put him on the line. It doesn't require much loyalty to work a crowd."

The clerk began writing again and Hadrian was handed a wooden token.

"Take that back outside and give it to Sergeant Millet, near the fire. He'll get you set up. Name?" he called to the next in line as Hadrian headed back out into the blinding white.

Unable to see clearly for a moment, Hadrian blinked. As his eyes adjusted, he saw Sentinel Luis Guy ride through the front gate, leading five Seret Knights. The two men spotted each other at the same instant. Hadrian had not seen Guy since the death of Fanen Pickering in Dahlgren. And while he hoped to one day repay Guy for Fanen's death, this was perhaps the worst possible time to cross paths.

For a heartbeat, neither moved. Then Guy slowly leaned and spoke to the man beside him, his eyes never straying from Hadrian.

"Now!" Guy growled when the knight hesitated.

Hadrian could not think of a worse place to be caught. He had no easy exit—no window to leap through or door to close. Between him and the gate were twenty-six men, still in line, who would jump at the chance to prove their mettle by helping the palace guard. Despite their numbers, Hadrian was the least concerned by the guard hopefuls, as none of them were armed. The bigger problem was the ten palace guards dressed for battle. At the sound of the first clash of swords, the barracks would empty, adding more men. Hadrian conservatively estimated he would need to kill or cripple at least eighteen people just to reach the exit. Guy and his five seret would be at the top of that list. The serets' horses would also need to be dispatched for him to have any chance of escaping through the city streets. The final obstacle would be the crossbowmen on the wall. Among the eight, he guessed at least two would be skilled enough to hit him in the back as he ran out through the gate.

"Just—don't—move," Guy said with his hands spread out in front of him. He looked as if he were trying to catch a wild horse, and did not advance, dismount, or draw his sword.

Just then the portcullis dropped.

"There's no escape," Guy assured him.

From a nearby door, a handful of guards trotted toward Hadrian with their swords drawn.

"Stop!" Guy ordered, raising his hand abruptly. "Don't go near him. Just fan out."

The men waiting in line looked from the soldiers to Hadrian and then backed away.

"I know what you're thinking, Mr. Blackwater," Guy said in an almost friendly tone. "But we *truly* have you outnumbered *this* time."

~

Hadrian stood in an elegantly furnished office on the fourth floor of the palace. Regent Saldur sat behind his desk, fidgeting with a small bejeweled letter opener shaped like a dagger. The ex-bishop looked slightly older and a bit heavier than the last time Hadrian had seen him. Luis Guy stood off to the right, his eyes locked on Hadrian. He was dressed in the traditional black armor and scarlet cape of his position, his sword hanging in its sheath. Guy's stance was straight and attentive, and he kept his hands gripped behind his back. Hadrian did not recognize the last man in the room. The stranger, dressed in an elegant garnache, sat near a chessboard, casually rolling one of the pieces back and forth between his fingers.

"Mr. Blackwater," Saldur addressed Hadrian, "I've heard some pretty incredible things about you. Please, won't you sit?"

"Will I really be staying that long?"

"Yes, I am afraid so. No matter how this turns out, you'll be staying."

Hadrian looked at the chair but chose to remain standing.

The old man leaned back in his seat and placed the tips of his fingers together. "You're probably wondering why you're here instead of locked in the north tower, or at least why we haven't shackled your wrists and ankles. You can thank Sentinel Guy for that. He has told us an incredible story about you. Aside from murdering Seret Knights—"

"The only murder that day was Fanen Pickering," Hadrian said. "The seret attacked us."

"Well, who's to say who did what when? Still, the death of a seret demands a severe penalty. I'm afraid it's customarily an executable offense. However, Sentinel Guy insists that you are a Teshlor—the only Teshlor—and *that* is an unusual extenuating circumstance.

"Now, if I recall my history lessons correctly, there was only one Teshlor to escape the destruction of the Old Empire— Jerish Grelad, who had taken the Heir of Novron into hiding. Legend claims that the Teshlor skills were passed down from generation to generation to protect the bloodline of the emperor.

"The Pickerings and the Killdares are each said to have discovered just a single one of the Teshlor disciplines. These jealously guarded secrets have made those families renowned for their fighting skills. A fully trained Teshlor would be…well… invincible in any one-on-one competition of arms. Am I correct?"

Hadrian said nothing.

"In any case, let's assume for the moment that Guy is not mistaken. If this is so, your presence presents us with an interesting opportunity, which can provide a uniquely mutual benefit. Given this, we felt it might encourage you to listen if we treated you with a degree of respect. By leaving you free—"

The door burst open and Regent Ethelred entered. The stocky, barrel-chested man was dressed in elaborate regal vestments of velvet and silk. He too looked older, and the former king's once-trim physique sported a bulge around the middle. Gray invaded his mustache and beard in patches and left white lines in his black hair. After pulling his cape inside, he slammed the door shut.

"So this is the fellow, I take it?" he said in a booming voice as he appraised Hadrian. "Don't I know you?"

Seeing no reason to lie, Hadrian replied, "I once served in your army."

"That's right!" Ethelred said, throwing up his hands in a large animated gesture. "You were a good fighter too. You held the line at...at..." He snapped his fingers repeatedly.

"At the Gravin River Ford."

"Of course!" He slapped his thigh. "Damn nice piece of work that was. I promoted you, didn't I? Made you a captain or something. What happened?"

"I left."

"Pity. You're a fine soldier." Ethelred clapped Hadrian on the shoulder.

"Of course he is, Lanis. That's the whole point," Saldur reminded him.

Ethelred chuckled, then said, "Too true, too true. So, has he accepted?"

"We haven't asked him yet."

"Asked me what?"

"Hadrian, we have a little problem," Ethelred began. As he spoke, he paced back and forth between Saldur's desk and the door. He kept the fingers of his left hand tucked in his belt behind his back while using his right to assist him in speaking, like a conductor uses a baton. "His name is Archibald Ballentyne. He's a sniveling little weasel. All of the Ballentynes have been worthless, pitiful excuses for men, but he's also the Earl of Chadwick. So, by virtue of his birth, he rules over a province that is worthless in all ways except one. Chadwick is the home to Lord Belstrad, whose eldest son, Sir Breckton, is very likely the best knight in Avryn. When I say *best*, I mean that in every sense of the word. His skill at arms is unmatched, as are his talent for tactics and his aptitude for leadership. Unfortunately, he's also loyal to a fault. He serves Archie Ballentyne and *only* Archie."

Ethelred crossed the room and took a seat by hopping onto Saldur's desk, causing the old man to flinch.

"I wanted Breckton as *my* general, but he refuses to obey the chain of command and won't listen to anyone except Archie. I can't waste time filtering all my orders through that pissant. So we offered Breckton a prime bit of land and a title to abandon Ballentyne, but the fool wasn't interested."

"The war is over, or soon will be," Hadrian pointed out. "You don't need Breckton anymore."

"That is exactly correct," Saldur said.

There was something in the detached way he spoke that chilled Hadrian.

"Even without a war we still need strong men to enforce order," Ethelred explained. Picking up a glass figurine from Saldur's desk, he began passing it from hand to hand.

Saldur's jaw clenched as his eyes tracked each toss.

"When Breckton turned us down, Archie threatened to use his knight and the Royalists against us. Can you believe that? He said he would march on Aquesta! He thinks he can challenge me! The little sod—" Ethelred slammed the figurine down on the desk, shattering it. "Oh—sorry, Sauly."

Saldur sighed but said nothing.

"Anyway," Ethelred went on, dusting off his hands so that bits of glass rained on the desk. "Who could have guessed a knight would turn down an offer to rise to the rank of marquis and command a whole kingdom as his fief? The pissproud pillock! And what's he doing it for? Loyalty to Archie Ballentyne. Who hates him. Always has. It's ridiculous."

"Which brings us to why you're here, Mr. Blackwater," Saldur said. He used a lace handkerchief to gingerly sweep the broken glass off his desk into a wastebasket. "As much as I would like to take credit for it, this is all Guy's idea." Saldur nodded toward the sentinel.

Guy never changed his wooden stance, remaining at attention as if it were his natural state.

"Finding you in our courtyard, Guy realized that you can solve our little problem with Sir Breckton."

"I'm not following," Hadrian said.

Saldur rolled his eyes. "We can't allow Breckton to reach his army at Drondil Fields. We would be forever at the mercy of Archie. He could dictate any terms so long as Breckton controlled the loyalty of the army."

Hadrian's confusion continued. "And...?"

Ethelred chuckled. "Poor Sauly, you deal too much in subtlety. This man is a fighter, not a strategist. He needs it spelled out." Turning to Hadrian, he said, "Breckton is a capable warrior and we had no hope of finding anyone who could defeat him until Guy pointed out that you are the perfect man for the job. To be blunt, we want you to kill Sir Breckton."

"The Wintertide tournament will start in just a few days," Saldur continued. "Breckton is competing in the joust and we want you to battle him and win. His lance will be blunted, while yours will have a war point hidden beneath a porcelain shell. When he dies, our problem will be solved."

"And exactly why would I agree?"

"Like the good regent explained," Guy said, "killing seret is an executable offense."

"Plus," Ethelred put in, "as a token of our appreciation, we will sweeten the deal by paying you one hundred solid gold tenents. What do you say?"

Hadrian knew he could never murder Breckton. While he had never met the man, he was familiar with Breckton's younger brother Wesley, who had served with Royce and Hadrian on the *Emerald Storm*. The young man had died in battle,

fighting beside them at the Palace of the Four Winds. His sacrificial charge had saved their lives. No man had ever proven
himself more worthy of loyalty, and if Breckton was half the
man his younger brother was, Hadrian owed him at least one
life.

"What can he say?" Saldur answered for him. "He has no
choice."

"I wouldn't say that," Hadrian replied. "You're right. I am
a trained Teshlor, and while you've been talking, I've calculated eight different ways to kill everyone in this room. Three
using nothing more than that little letter opener Regent Saldur
has been playing with." He let his arms fall loose and shifted
his stance. This immediately set Ethelred and Guy, the two
fighters, on the defensive.

"Hold on now." Saldur's voice wavered and his face showed
strain. "Before you make any rash decisions, consider that the
window is too small to fit through, and the men in the corridor will not let you leave. If you really are as good as you say,
you might take a great many of them with you, but even you
cannot defeat them all."

"You might be right. We'll soon find out."

"Are you insane? You're choosing death?" Saldur erupted
in frustration. "We are offering you gold and a pardon. What
benefit is there in refusing?"

"Well, he does plan on killing all of you." The man with
the chess piece spoke for the first time. "A good trade, really—
forfeiting one knight to eliminate a knight, a bishop, and a
king. But you offered the man the wrong incentive. Give him
the princess."

"Give—what?" Saldur looked puzzled. "Who? Arista?"

"You have another princess I'm not aware of?"

"Arista?" Hadrian asked. "The Princess of Melengar is
here?"

"Yes, and they plan to execute her on Wintertide," the man answered.

Saldur looked confused. "Why would he care—"

"Because Hadrian Blackwater and his partner, Royce Melborn, better known as Riyria, have been working as the royal protectors of Melengar. They've been instrumental in nearly every success either Alric or his sister has had over the last few years. I suspect they might even be friends with the royal family now. Well—as much as nobles will permit friendship with commoners."

Hadrian tried to keep his face neutral and his breathing balanced.

They have Arista? How did they capture her? Was she hurt? How long have they been holding her? Who is this man?

"You see, Your Grace, Mr. Blackwater is a romantic at heart. He likes his honor upheld and his quests worthy. Killing an innocent knight, particularly one as distinguished as Breckton, would be...well...wrong. Saving a damsel in distress, on the other hand, is an entirely different proposition."

"Would that be a problem?" Ethelred asked Saldur.

The regent thought a moment. "The girl has proven resourceful and given us more than her fair share of trouble but... Medford is destroyed, the Nationalists are disbanded, and Drondil Fields won't last much longer. I can't see any way she could pose a serious threat to the empire."

"Well," Ethelred said, addressing Hadrian, "do we have a deal?"

Hadrian scrutinized the man at the chessboard. While he had never seen his face before, he felt as though he should recognize him.

"No," Hadrian said at length. "I want Degan Gaunt too."

"You see? He is the guardian!" Guy proclaimed. "Or he wishes to be. Obviously Esrahaddon told him Gaunt is the heir."

Ethelred looked concerned. "That's out of the question. We've been after the Heir of Novron for years. We can't let him go."

"Not just years—centuries," Saldur corrected. He stared at Hadrian, his mouth slightly open, the tip of his tongue playing with his front teeth. "Esrahaddon is dead. You confirmed that, Guy?"

The sentinel nodded. "I had his body dug up and then burned."

"And how much does Gaunt know? I've heard you've had several *little chats* with him."

Guy shook his head. "Not much, from what I've been able to determine. He insists Esrahaddon didn't even tell him he's the heir."

"But Hadrian will tell him," Ethelred protested.

"So?" Saldur replied. "What does that matter? The two of them can travel the countryside, proclaiming Gaunt's heritage from the mountaintops. Who will listen? Modina serves us well. The people love and accept her as the unquestionable true Heir of Novron. She slew the Gilarabrywn, after all. If they try to convince people that Gaunt is the heir, they'll get no support from the peasants or nobles. The concern was never Degan, per se, but rather what Esrahaddon could do by using him as a puppet. Right? With the wizard gone, Gaunt is no real threat."

"I'm not certain the Patriarch will approve," Guy said.

"The Patriarch isn't here having a standoff with a Teshlor, is he?"

"And what about Gaunt's children, or grandchildren? Decades from now, they may attempt to regain their birthright. We have to concern ourselves with that."

"Why worry about problems that may never occur? We're at a bit of an impasse, gentlemen. Why don't we deal with our present issues and let the future take care of itself? What do you say, Lanis?"

Ethelred nodded.

Saldur turned to Hadrian. "If you *succeed in killing* Sir Breckton in the joust, we will release Degan Gaunt and Princess Arista into your custody on the condition that you leave Avryn and promise not to return. Do we have a deal?"

"Yes."

"Excellent."

"So I'm free to go?"

"Actually, no," Saldur said. "You must understand our desire to keep this little arrangement between us. I'm afraid we're going to have to insist that you stay in the palace until after your joust with Breckton. While you're here, you will be under constant observation. If you attempt to escape or pass information, we will interpret that as a refusal on your part, and Princess Arista and Degan Gaunt will be burned at the stake.

"Breckton's death has to be seen as a Wintertide accident at best or the actions of an overambitious knight at worst. There can be no suspicions of a conspiracy. Commoners aren't permitted to participate in the tournament, so we'll need to transform you into a knight. You will stay in the knights' quarters, participate in the games, attend feasts, and mingle with the aristocracy, as all knights do this time of year. We will assign a tutor to help you convince everyone that you're noble so there will be no suspicions of wrongdoing. As of this moment, your only way out of this palace is to kill Sir Breckton."

Chapter 7

Deeper into Darkness

Drip, drip, drip.

Arista scratched her wrists, feeling the marks raised by the heavy iron during the regent's interrogation. The itching had only recently started. With what little they fed her, she was surprised her body could heal itself at all. Lying about Edith Mon had been a gamble, and she had worried Saldur would return to her cell with the inquisitor, but three bowls of gruel had arrived since his visit, which led her to conclude he had believed her story.

Whirl . . . splash!

There it was again.

The sound was faint and distant, echoing as if traveling through a long, hollow tube.

Creak, click, creak, click, creak, click.

The noise certainly came from a machine, a torture device of some kind. Perhaps it was a mechanical winch used to tear people to pieces or a turning wheel that submerged victims in putrid waters. Saldur had been wrong about her courage. Arista never had any doubt she would break if subjected to torture.

The stone door to the prison rumbled as it opened.

Footsteps echoed through the corridors. Once more, someone was coming when it was not time for food.

Clip-clap, clip-clap.

The shoes were different and not as rich as Saldur's, but they were not poor either. The gait was decidedly military, but these feet were not shod in metal. They did not come for her. Instead, the footfalls passed by, stopping just past her cell. Keys jangled and a cell door opened.

"Morning, Gaunt," said a voice she found distantly familiar and vaguely unpleasant, like the memory of a bad dream.

"What do you want, Guy?" Gaunt said.

It's him!

"You and I need to have another talk," Guy said.

"I barely survived our last one."

"What did Esrahaddon tell you about the Horn of Gylindora?"

Arista lifted her head and inched nearer the door.

"I don't know how many ways I can say it. He told me nothing."

"See, this is why you suffer in our little meetings. You need to be more cooperative. I can't help you if you won't help us. We need to find that horn and we need it now!"

"Why don't you just ask Esrahaddon?"

"He's dead."

There was a long pause.

"Think. Surely he mentioned it to you. Time is running out. We had a team, but they are long overdue, and I doubt they're coming back. We need that horn. In all your time together, do you really expect me to believe he never mentioned it?"

"No, he never said anything about a damn horn!"

"Either you're becoming better at lying, or you've been telling the truth all along. I just can't imagine he wouldn't tell you *anything* unless...Everyone is so certain, but I've had a nagging suspicion for some time now."

"What's that for?" Gaunt asked, his voice nervous—frightened.

"Let's call it a hunch. Now hold still."

Gaunt grunted, then cried out. "What are you doing?"

"You wouldn't understand even if I told you."

There was another pause.

"I knew it!" Guy exclaimed. "This explains so much. While it doesn't help either of us, at least it makes sense. The regents were fools to kill Esrahaddon."

"I don't understand. What are you talking about?"

"Nothing, Gaunt. I believe you. He didn't tell you anything. Why would he? The Patriarch will not be pleased. You won't be questioned anymore. You can await your execution in peace."

The door closed again and the footfalls left the dungeon.

Esrahaddon's dying words came back to Arista.

Find the Horn of Gylindora—need the heir to find it—buried with Novron in Percepliquis. Hurry—at Wintertide the Uli Vermar *ends. They will come—without the horn everyone dies.*

These words had brought Arista to Aquesta in the first place and were the reason she had risked her and Hilfred's lives trying to save Gaunt. Now she once more tried to understand just what Esrahaddon had meant by them.

❧

Drip, drip, drip.

The protruding bones of Arista's hips, knees, and shoulders ached from bearing her weight on the stone. Her fingernails had become brittle and broken. Too exhausted to stand or sit upright, Arista struggled even to turn over. Despite her weakness, she found it difficult to sleep, and lay awake for hours, glaring into the dark. The stone Arista lay on sucked the warmth from her body. Shivering in a ball, she pushed herself up in the dark and struggled to gather the scattered bits of straw. Running her fingers over the rough-hewn granite, she swept together the old, brittle thatch and mounded it as best she could into a lumpy bed.

Arista lay there imagining food. Not simply eating or touching it, but immersing herself. In her daydreams, she bathed in cream and swam in apple juice. All her senses contributed and she longed for even the smell of bread or the feel of butter on her tongue. Arista was tortured with thoughts of roasted pig dripping with fruit glaze, beef served in a thick, dark gravy, and mountains of chicken, quail, and duck. Envisioning feasts stretching across long tables made her mouth water. Arista ate several meals a day in her mind. Even the vegetables, the common diet of peasants, were welcomed. Carrots, onions, and parsnips hovered in her mind like unappreciated treasures—and what she would give for a turnip.

Drip, drip, drip.

In the dark there was so much to regret and so much time to do so.

What a mess she had made of a life that had started out filled with so much happiness. She recalled the days when her mother had been Queen of Melengar and music filled the halls. There had been the beautiful dress stitched from expensive Calian silk that she had received on her twelfth birthday. How the light had shimmered across its surface as she twirled before her mother's swan mirror. The same year, her father had given her a Maranon-bred pony. Lenare had been so jealous watching as Arista chased Alric and Mauvin over the Galilin hills on horseback. She loved riding and feeling the wind in her hair. Those had been such good days. In her memory, they were always sunny and warm.

Her world had changed forever the night the castle caught on fire. Her father had just appointed her uncle Braga as the Lord Chancellor of Melengar and celebrations ran late. Her mother tucked her into bed that night. Arista did not sleep in the tower then. She had a room across the hall from her parents, but she would never sleep in the royal wing again.

In the middle of that night, she had awoken to a boy pulling her from bed. Frightened and confused, she jerked away, kicking and scratching as he tried to grab hold.

"Please, Your Highness, you must come with me," the boy begged.

Outside her window, the elm tree burned like a torch, and her room flickered with its light. She heard a muffled roar from somewhere deep in the castle, and Arista found herself coughing from smoke.

Fire!

Screaming in terror, she cowered back to the imagined safety of her bed. The boy gripped her hard and dragged her toward him.

"The castle is burning. We have to get out of here," he said.

Where is my mother? Where are Father and Alric? And who is this boy?

While she fought against him, the boy lifted her in his arms and rushed from the room. The corridor was a tunnel of flames formed by the burning tapestries. Carrying her down the stairs and through several doors, he stumbled and finally collapsed in the courtyard. The cool evening air filled Arista's lungs as she gasped for breath.

Her father was not in the castle that night. After settling a dispute between two drunken friends, he had escorted them home. By sheer luck, Alric was also not there. He and Mauvin

Pickering had secretly slipped out to go *night hunting*, what they used to call frog catching. Arista's mother was the only royal who failed to escape.

Hilfred, the boy who had saved Arista, had tried to rescue the queen as well. After seeing the princess to safety, he went back into the flames and nearly died in the attempt. For months following the fire, Hilfred suffered the effects of burns, was beset by nightmares, and had coughing fits so intense that he spat blood. Despite all the agony he endured on her behalf, Arista never thanked him. All she knew was that her mother was dead, and from that day on everything had changed.

In the wake of the fire, Arista moved to the tower, as it was the only part of the castle that did not smell of smoke. Her father ordered her mother's furniture—those few items that had survived the fire—to be moved there. Arista would often cry while sitting before the swan mirror, remembering how her mother used to brush her hair. One day her father saw her and asked what was wrong. She blurted out, "All the brushes are gone." From that day forward, her father brought her a new brush after each trip he took. No two were ever alike. They were all gone now—the brushes, her father, even the dressing table with the swan mirror.

Drip, drip, drip.

Arista wondered if Maribor decreed she should be alone. Why else had she, a princess nearly twenty-eight years old, never had a proper suitor? Even poor, ugly daughters of fishmongers fared better. Perhaps her loneliness was her own fault, the result of her deplorable nature. In the dark, the answer was clearly visible—no one wanted her.

Emery had thought he loved Arista, but he had never really known her. Impressed by her wild ideas of taking Ratibor from the Imperialists, he had been swayed by the romantic notion of a noble fighting alongside a band of commoners. What Emery had fallen in love with was a myth. As for Hilfred, he had worshiped Arista as *his princess*. She was not a person but an icon on a pedestal. That they had died before learning the truth was a mercy to both men.

Only Hadrian had escaped being deceived. Arista was certain he saw her merely as a source of income. He likely hated her for being a privileged aristocrat living in a castle while he scraped by. All commoners were nice to nobility when in their presence—but in private, their true feelings showed. Hadrian probably snickered, proclaiming her too repulsive for even her own kind to love. With or without magic, she was still a witch. She deserved being alone. She deserved to die. She deserved to burn.

Drip, drip, drip.

A pain in her side caused her to turn over slowly. Sometimes she lost feeling in her feet for hours, and her fingers often tingled. After settling onto her back, she heard a skittering sound.

The rat had returned. Arista did not know where it came from or where it went in the darkness, but she always knew when it was near. She could not understand why it came around, as she ate all the food delivered. After consuming every drop of soup, she licked and even chewed on the bowl. Still, the rat visited frequently. Sometimes its nose touched her feet and kicking would send it scurrying away. In the past, she had tried to catch it, but it was smart and fast. Now Arista was too weak even to make an attempt.

Arista heard the rat moving along the wall of the cell. Its nose and whiskers lightly touched her exposed toes. She no longer had the energy to kick, so she let it smell her. After sniffing a few more times, the rat bit her toe.

Arista screamed in pain. She kicked but missed. Still, the

rat scurried off. Lying in the darkness, she shivered and cried in fear and misery.

"A—ris—ta?" Degan asked, sounding horse. "What is it?"

"A rat bit me," she said, once again shocked by her own rasping voice.

"Jasper does that if—" Gaunt coughed and hacked. After a moment, he spoke again. "If he thinks you're dead or too weak to fight."

"Jasper?"

"I call him that, but I've also named the stones in my cell."

"I only counted mine," Arista said.

"Two hundred and thirty-four," Degan replied instantly.

"I have two hundred and twenty-eight."

"Did you count the cracked ones as two?"

"No."

The princess lay there, listening to her own breathing, and felt the weight of her hands on her chest as it rose and fell. She started to drift into and out of sleep when Degan spoke again.

"Arista? Are you really a witch? Can you do magic?"

"Yes," she said. "But not in here."

Arista did not expect him to believe her and had been doubting her own powers after being cut off from them for so long. Runes lined the walls of the prison. They were the same markings that had prevented Esrahaddon from casting spells while incarcerated in Gutaria, but her stay would not last a thousand years as his had. Gutaria's runes halted the passage of time as well as preventing the practice of magic, and the ache in her stomach reminded Arista all too often that time was not suspended here.

Only since the Battle of Ratibor had Arista begun to understand the true nature of magic, or the Art, as Esrahaddon had called it. When touching the strings of reality, she felt no sense of boundaries—only complexity. With time and understanding, anything might be possible and everything achievable. She was certain that were it not for the runes disconnecting her from the natural world, she could break open the ground and rip the palace apart.

"Were you born a witch?"

"I learned magic from Esrahaddon."

"You knew him?"

"Yes."

"Do you know how he died?"

"He was murdered by an assassin."

"Oh. Did he ever talk about me? Did he tell you why he was helping me?" he asked anxiously.

"He never told you?"

"No. I didn't—" He broke into another fit of coughs. "I didn't have much of an army when we met, but then everything changed. He got men to join and follow me. I never had to do much of anything. Esrahaddon did all the planning and told me what to say. It was nice while it lasted. I had plenty to eat, and folks saluted and called me sir. I even had a horse and a tent the size of a house. I should have known all that was too good to last. I should have realized he was setting me up. I'm just curious why. What did I ever do to him?" His voice was weak, coming in gasps by the end of his speech.

"Degan, do you have a necklace? A small silver medallion?"

"Yeah—well, I did." He paused a long while, and when he spoke again, his voice was better. "My mother gave it to me before I left home—my good luck charm. They took it when they put me in here. Why do you ask?"

"Because you are the Heir of Novron. That necklace was created by Esrahaddon nearly nine hundred years ago. There were two of them, one for the heir and one for the guardian trained to defend him. For generations they protected the wearers from magic and hid their identities. Esrahaddon taught me a spell that could find who wore them. I was the one who helped him find you. He's been trying to restore you to the throne."

Degan was quiet for some time. "If I have a guardian, where is he? I could use one right now."

The waves of self-loathing washed over her again. "His name is Hadrian. Oh, Degan, it's all my fault. He doesn't know where you are. Esrahaddon and I were going to find you and tell him, but I messed it all up. After Esrahaddon's death, I thought I could get you out on my own. I failed."

"Yeah, well, it's only my life—nothing important." There was a pause, then, "Arista?"

"Yes?"

"What about that thing Guy mentioned? That *horn*? Did Esrahaddon ever mention it to you? If we can tell them something about it, maybe they won't kill us."

Arista felt the hair on her arms stand up.

Is this a trick? Is he working for them?

Weak and exhausted, she could not think clearly. In the darkness she felt vulnerable and disoriented—exactly what they wanted.

Is it even Gaunt at all? Or did they discover I was coming and plant someone from the start? Or did they switch the real Gaunt while I slept? Is it the same voice?

She tried to remember.

"Arista?" he called out again.

She opened her mouth to reply but paused and thought of something else to say. "It's hard to recall. My head's fuzzy, and I'm trying to piece the conversation together. He talked about the horn the same day I met your sister. I remember he introduced her...and then...Oh, how did it go again? He said, 'Arista, this is...this is...' Oh, it's just beyond my memory. Help me out, Degan. I feel like a fool. Can you remind me what your sister's name is?"

Silence.

Arista waited. She listened and thought she heard movement somewhere beyond her cell, but she was not sure.

"Degan?" she ventured after several minutes had passed. "Don't you know your own sister's name?"

"Why do you want to know her name?" Degan asked. His tone was lower, colder.

"I just forgot it, is all. I thought you could help me remember the conversation."

He was quiet for so long that she thought he might not speak again. Finally, he said, "What did they offer you to find out about her?"

"What do you mean?"

"Maybe you're Arista Essendon, or maybe you're an Imperialist trying to get secrets from me."

"How do I know any different about you?" she asked.

"You supposedly came to free me, and now you doubt who I am?"

"I came to free Degan Gaunt, but who are *you*?"

"I won't tell you the name of my sister."

"In that case, I think I will sleep." She meant it as a bluff, but as the silence continued, she dozed off.

Chapter 8

Sir Hadrian

Hadrian sat on the edge of his bunk, perplexed by the tabard. A single red diagonal stripe decorated each side. Depending on how he wore it, the stripe started from either his right or his left shoulder, and he could not figure out which was correct.

As he finally made a decision and placed it over his head, there was a quiet knock, followed by the timid opening of his door. A man's face, accentuated by a beaklike nose and topped by a foppish powdered wig, peered inside. "Excuse me, I'm looking for Sir Hadrian."

"Congratulations, you found him," Hadrian replied.

The man entered, followed closely by a boy, who remained near the door. Thin and brittle-looking, the man was dressed in bright satin knee breeches and an elaborate ruffled tunic. Even without the outlandish clothing, he would still be comical. Encased in buckled shoes, his feet seemed disproportionally large, and all his limbs were gangly. The teenage lad behind him wore the more conventional attire of a simple brown tunic and hose.

"My name is Nimbus of Vernes, and I am imperial tutor to the empress. Regent Saldur thought you might need some guidance on court protocol and instruction in knightly virtues, so he asked me to assist you."

"Pleased to meet you," Hadrian said. He stood and offered his hand. At first Nimbus appeared confused, but then he reached out and shook.

Motioning toward the tabard Hadrian wore, he nodded. "I can see why I was called upon."

Hadrian glanced down and shrugged. "Well, I figured I had a fifty-fifty chance." Removing the garment, he turned the tunic around. "Is that better?"

Nimbus struggled to suppress a laugh, holding a lace handkerchief to his lips. The boy was not so restrained and snorted, then laughed out loud. This made Nimbus lose his own battle, and finally Hadrian found himself laughing as well.

"I'm sorry. That was most inappropriate of me," Nimbus apologized, getting a hold of himself. "I beg your forgiveness."

"It's no problem. Just tell me what I'm doing wrong."

"Well, to start with, that particular garment is used only for sparring, and no self-respecting knight would wear such a thing at court."

Hadrian shrugged. "Oh, okay, good to know. It was the only thing I saw. Any ideas?"

Nimbus walked to a drape behind the bunk and flung it aside, revealing an open wardrobe filled with tunics, jackets, coats, capes, jerkins, gambesons, vests, doublets, baldrics, belts, breeches, shirts, hose, boots, and shoes.

Hadrian looked at the wardrobe and frowned. "So how was I supposed to know all that was there?"

"Why don't we begin by getting you properly dressed?" Nimbus suggested, and motioned for Hadrian to pick something.

He reached toward a pair of wool pants, but a cough from Nimbus stopped him.

"No?" Hadrian asked.

Nimbus shook his head.

"Okay, what do *you* think I should be wearing?"

Nimbus considered the wardrobe for several minutes, picking out various pieces, comparing them, putting one back, and then choosing another. He finally selected a white shirt, a gold doublet, purple hose, and shiny black shoes with brass buckles. He laid them out on the bunk.

"You're joking," Hadrian said, staring at the array. "That's your best choice? I'm not sure gold and purple are for me. Besides, what's wrong with the wool pants?"

"Those are for hunting and, like the tabard, not appropriate for dress at court. Gold and purple complement each other. They announce you are a man that makes no excuses."

Hadrian held up the clothes with a grimace. "They're loud. *Disturbingly* loud."

"They exude refinement and grace," Nimbus corrected. "Qualities, if you don't mind me saying, from which you could benefit. I know knights in the field dress in order to bully rabble-rousers and brigands, and under such circumstances, it's appropriate to select garments based on certain utilitarian qualities." He took an appraising look at Hadrian's attire. "But you are at the palace now, competing with a higher class of…thug. A strong arm and loud voice will not be enough. You need to sell yourself to the knights you wish to intimidate, to the ladies you wish to bed, to the lords you wish to impress, and to the commoners who will chant your name during the competitions. This last group is particularly important, as it will raise your stature with the others.

"A knight skilled in combat may stay alive, but it is the one skilled in persuasion who wins the king's daughter for his wife and retires to a vast estate. Truly successful knights can obtain multiple fiefs and enter their twilight years as wealthy as any count or earl."

Nimbus lowered his voice. "Regent Saldur mentioned that you might be a bit rough around the edges." He paused briefly. "I think we can both agree I've not been misled. It may take some doing to refine your mannerisms. So, in the meantime, I plan to overcompensate with clothing. We'll blind everyone with dazzle so they won't see the dirt on your face."

Hadrian reached for his cheek.

"That was a metaphor," Nimbus informed him. "Although now that I look at you, a bath is certainly in order."

"Bath? It's freezing outside. You're supposed to groom me, not kill me."

"You may be surprised to discover that in civilized society we bathe indoors in tubs with heated water. You might even find it enjoyable." Turning to the boy, Nimbus ordered, "Renwick, run and fetch the tub and get some others to help carry buckets. We'll also need a bristle brush, soap, oils, and—oh yes—scissors."

The lad ran off and quickly returned with a small army of boys carrying a wooden tub. They left and returned with buckets of hot water. After filling the tub, all the boys left except Renwick. He dutifully stood beside the door, ready for further requests.

Hadrian undressed and tested the water with a hesitant foot.

"Are you versed in the basic concept of bathing? Or do you need me to instruct you?" Nimbus asked.

Hadrian scowled at him. "I think I can handle it," he said, settling into the water. The tub overflowed and created a soapy mess. He grimaced. "Sorry about that."

Nimbus said nothing and turned away to give Hadrian a modicum of privacy.

The hot bath was wonderful. Hadrian had been assigned an interior chamber selected, no doubt, for its lack of windows.

There were a simple bed, two wooden stools, and a modest table, but no fireplace, which left the chamber chilly. If he was desperate, there was a large hearth in the common room at the end of the hall, which also sported carpets and a chess set, but despite the cold, Hadrian preferred to remain in the isolation of his private room. Having not felt comfortably warm in days, Hadrian sank lower to submerge as much of himself as possible.

"Are these yours?" Nimbus asked, noticing Hadrian's weapons resting in the corner of the room.

"Yes, and I know they're worn and dirty *just like me.*"

Nimbus lifted the spadone, still encased in the leather baldric, with a noticeable degree of reverence. Turning it over gingerly, he ran his fingertips along the hilt, grip, and pommel. "This is very old," he said almost to himself. "Wrong sheath, though." He laid the sword across the foot of the bed.

"I thought you were a courtier. What do you know about swords?"

"You'll learn that there are many weapons at court. Survival in the maelstrom of the body politic requires being able to size up another by what little they reveal to you."

Hadrian shrugged. "It's the same in combat."

"Court is combat," Nimbus said. "Only the skills and setting differ."

"So how would you size me up?"

"Regent Saldur told me your background is completely confidential and that divulging anything would result in my — not too painless — demise. The only information he provided was that you were recently knighted. He refrained from any detail about your station or ancestry. The regent merely mentioned you were lacking refinement and instructed me to ensure you fit seamlessly into the Wintertide festivities."

Hadrian kept an unwavering stare on the tutor. "You didn't answer the question."

Nimbus smiled at him. "You really want to know, don't you? You aren't toying with me?"

Hadrian nodded.

The tutor turned to the page. "Renwick?"

"Yes, sir?"

"Fetch Sir Hadrian a cup of wine from the steward in the kitchen."

"There's wine in the common room, sir, and it's closer."

Nimbus gave him a stern look. "I want some privacy, Renwick."

"Oh, I see. Of course, sir."

"Very well, then," Nimbus said after the boy had left. He pursed his lips and tapped them several times with his index finger before continuing. "The truth of the matter is that you are not a knight. You haven't even served as a squire, groom, or page. I doubt you've ever set foot in a proper castle for more than a few minutes at a time. However—and this is the important point—you are indeed *noble*."

Hadrian paused in his scrubbing. "And what makes you think that?"

"You didn't know where the wardrobe was, you've never taken a bath in winter, you shook my hand when we met, and apologized for spilling your bathwater. These are most certainly not the actions of a knight raised from birth to feel and act superior to others."

Hadrian sniffed the scented soap and discarded it.

"Most telling, however, was the handshake itself. You offered it as a simple gesture of greeting. There was no agenda, no flattery, no insincerity. There also was no insecurity or sense that, by virtue of my clothes and mannerisms, I was your better. How odd, considering, as I now know, you were not *raised* a noble." Nimbus looked back at the sword resting on the bed. "It's an heirloom, isn't it?"

Picking up a bottle of oil, Hadrian pulled the cork and deemed it acceptable. He added a bit to the bristles of the brush. "I got it from my father."

The tutor ran his hand along the sheathed blade. "This is a remarkable weapon—a knight's sword—tarnished with time and travel. You don't use it as often as the others. The bastard and short sword are tools to you, but this—ah—this is something else—something revered. It lays concealed in a paltry sheath, covered in clothes not its own. It doesn't belong there. This sword belongs to another time and place. It is part of a grand and glorious world where knights were different, loftier— *virtuous*. It rests in this false scabbard because the proper one has been lost, or perhaps, it waits for a quest yet to be finished. It longs for that single moment when it can shine forth in all its brilliance. When dream and destiny meet on a clear field, then and only then will it find its purpose. When it faces that honorable cause—that one worthy and desperate challenge for which it was forged and on which so much depends—it will find peace in the crucible of struggle. For good or ill, it will ring true or break. But the wandering, the waiting, the hiding will at last be over. This sword waits for the day when it can save the kingdom and win the lady."

Hadrian sat staring, not realizing that he had dropped his brush.

Nimbus appeared to take no notice of Hadrian's reaction and sat on the bunk with a satisfied smile across his face. "Now, while I have your attention, shall we address the task to which I was assigned?"

Hadrian nodded.

"To help me judge where to start, can you tell me what you already know about chivalry?" Nimbus asked.

"It's a code of conduct for knights," Hadrian replied, searching the bottom of the tub for the lost brush.

"Yes—well, you are essentially correct. What do you know of its principles?"

"Be honorable, be brave, that sort of thing."

" 'That sort of thing'? Oh, I'm afraid we'll have to start with the basics. Very well, please pay attention, and don't forget to scrub the bottoms of your feet."

Hadrian frowned but lifted a foot.

"The knightly virtues derive themselves from a standard of ethics passed down from the original empire. There are eight such virtues. The first is proficiency. It is the easiest to achieve, as it merely means skill at arms and can be obtained through practice and observation. Judging from the wear on your weapons, I trust you have a solid understanding of this virtue?"

"I'm able to hold my own."

Nimbus nodded. "Excellent. Next is courage, one of the most important virtues. Courage, however, is not so cheaply bought as by charging against overwhelming odds. It can take many forms. For instance, the bravery to choose life over death, especially if that means living with loss. Or the will to risk all for a cause too noble to let perish. Courage can even be found in surrender—if doing so will mean the survival of something too valuable to lose.

"The third virtue of a knight is honesty. To possess honor, a man must first strive to be honest to men, to women, to children, to great and to small, to the good and to the villainous, but mostly to himself. A knight does not make excuses."

Hadrian made an extra effort to keep his eyes focused on scrubbing his feet.

"Integrity is a virtue that comprises both loyalty and honor. Possessing integrity often means adhering to a pledge or principle. Loyalty to a sovereign is the mark of a goodly knight. However, integrity can also mean defending those in need who cannot help themselves. A knight should always work for the good of the king third, the betterment of the kingdom second, but always place what is right first."

"How does a knight know what is right?" Hadrian interrupted. He put down the brush, letting his foot slip back to the bottom of the tub. "I mean...what if I'm forced to choose between two evils? Someone could get hurt no matter what I do. How do I decide?"

"True nobility lies in the heart. You must do what *you* know to be right."

"How do I know I'm not being selfish?"

"Ah, that brings us to the next virtue—faith. Faith is not simply a belief in the tenets of the church but a belief in virtue itself. A knight does not find fault. A knight believes in the good of all men, including himself. He trusts in this belief. A knight is confident in the word of others, in the merits of his lord, the worth of his commands, and in his own worth."

Hadrian nodded, though the words did not help ease his conscience.

"Generosity is the sixth virtue. A knight should show bounteousness to all, noble and commoner alike. More important than generosity of wares is a generosity of spirit. A knight believes the best of others and always extends the benefit of doubt. A knight does not accuse. He does not assume wrongdoing. Still, a knight grants no benefit to himself and always questions if he is at fault.

"Respect is the virtue concerning the good treatment of others. A knight is not thoughtless. He does not harm through recklessness. He seeks not to injure by lazy words or foolishness. A knight does not mimic the bad behavior of others. Instead, he sees it as an opportunity to demonstrate virtue by contrast."

Nimbus paused. "I don't think you need worry too much about this one either." He offered a smile before continuing.

"The final virtue is sincerity, which is elusive at best. Nobility by birthright is clear, but what is in question here is noblesse of heart and cannot be taught or learned. It must be accepted and allowed to grow. This virtue is demonstrated through bearing, not swagger; confidence, not arrogance; kindness, not pity; belief, not patronage; authenticity, not pretension.

"These are the virtues that comprise the Code of Chivalry," Nimbus concluded, "the path of goodness and truth to which men of high honor aspire. The reality, however, is often quite different."

As if on cue, the door burst open and three men tumbled inside. They were large, stocky brutes dressed in fine doublets with silk trim. The lead man sported a goatee and stood near the door, pointing at Hadrian.

"There he is!" he announced.

"Well, he certainly isn't this little sod," roared a second man, who pushed Nimbus hard in the chest and knocked the tutor back against the bunk. This man was the largest of the three and wore several days of beard growth. The insult, as well as the terrified expression on the courtier's face, brought the new arrivals to laughter.

"What's your name, twig?" the man with the goatee asked.

"I am Nimbus of Vernes," he said while attempting to stand and regain some level of dignity. "I am imperial tutor to—"

"Tutor? He's got a tutor!"

They howled in laughter again.

"Tell us, twig, what are you teaching Sir Bumpkin here? How to wash his arse? Is that your job? Have you taught him to use the chamber pot yet?"

Nimbus did not answer. He clenched his teeth and fixed his eyes on the unkempt man before him.

"I think you're getting under that ruffled collar of his," the last of them observed. He was clean-shaven and sipped wine from a goblet. "Careful, Elgar, he's made fists."

"Is that true?" Elgar looked at the tutor's hands, which were indeed tightly clenched. "Oh dear! Am I impinging on your sacred pedagogical honor? Would you like to throw a punch at me, little twig? Put me in my proper place, as it were?"

"If he takes a big enough swing, it's possible you might actually feel it," the shaved one said.

"I asked you a question, twig," Elgar pressed.

"If you don't mind, we'll continue this another time," Nimbus said to Hadrian. "It would seem you have guests."

Elgar blocked the tutor's path as he tried to leave, and shoved him again. Staggering backward, Nimbus fell onto the bed.

"Leave him alone," Hadrian ordered as he stood and grabbed a towel.

"Ah, Sir Bumpkin, in all his regal glory!" proclaimed the man with the goatee, pointing. "Well, not *that* regal and certainly not *that* glorious!"

"Who are you?" Hadrian demanded, stepping out of the tub and wrapping the towel around himself.

"I am Sir Murthas and the gent with the handsome face beside me here is Sir Gilbert. Over there, that dashing fellow holding the pleasant conversation with the twig is none other than Sir Elgar. We are the three finest knights of the realm, as you will soon discover. We wanted to welcome you to the palace, deliver you a fond tiding, and wish you luck on the field—as luck is all you'll have."

Nimbus snorted. "They're here because they heard a bath was ordered, and wanted to see your scars. Knowing nothing about you, they came to see if you have any fresh bruises or recent wounds they might take advantage of on the field. Also, they are trying to intimidate you, as a man in a tub is at a disadvantage. Intimidation can frequently win a contest before it starts."

Sir Elgar grabbed hold of Nimbus, pulling him up by his tunic. "Talkative little bastard, aren't you?" He raised a fist just as a sopping towel slammed into his face.

"Sorry. Elgar, is it?" Hadrian asked. "Just got done drying my ass and noticed a smudge on your face."

Elgar threw off the towel and drew his sword. In just two steps, the knight cut the distance to Hadrian, who stood naked and unflinching even as Elgar raised the blade's tip toward his throat.

"Brave bugger, I'll give you that much," Elgar said. "But that just means you'll be an easier target along the fence. You might want to save that water. You'll need it after I put you in the mud." Sheathing his sword, he led his friends from the room, nearly colliding with Renwick, who stood outside the door holding a goblet of wine.

"You all right?" Hadrian asked, grabbing a fresh towel.

"Yes, of course," Nimbus replied in an unsteady voice. He smoothed the material of his tunic.

"Your wine, sir," Renwick said to Hadrian.

Without pause, Nimbus took the cup and drained it. "As I was saying, the reality can be quite different."

Chapter 9

Winds Abbey

Royce stood before the window of the bedroom, watching Gwen sleep and thinking about their future. He pushed the thought away and suppressed the urge to smile. Just imagining it would bring disaster. The gods—if they existed— detested happiness. Instead, he turned and looked out over the cloistered courtyard.

The previous night's storm had left everything covered in a new dress of unblemished white. The only exception was a single line of footprints that led from the dormitory to a stone bench, where a familiar figure sat wrapped in a monk's habit. He was alone, yet the movement of his hands and the bob of his head revealed he was speaking with great earnest. Across from the monk was a small tree. Planting it was one of the first things Myron had done when he had returned to the abbey after the fire. It now stood a proud eight feet tall but was so slender it drooped under the snow's weight. Royce knew there was great resiliency in a tree accustomed to bending in the wind, but he wondered if the strain could be endured. There was a breaking point for everything, after all. As if reading his thoughts, Myron rose and gave the tree a light shake. He had to stand close to do so, and much of the snow fell on his head.

The tree sprang back, and without the burden of snow, it appeared more like its former self. Myron returned to his seat and his conversation. Royce knew he was not speaking to the tree but to his boyhood friend who was buried there.

"You're up early," Gwen said from where she lay with her head on a clutched pillow. He could make out the elegant slope of her waist and rise of her hip beneath the covers. "After last night, I would have thought you'd be sleeping late."

"We went to bed early."

"But we didn't sleep," she teased.

"It was better than sleep. Besides, around here, waking after first light *is* sleeping in. Myron is already outside."

"He does that so he can talk privately." She smiled and drew back the covers invitingly. "Isn't it cold next to that window?"

"You're a bad influence," he said, lying down and wrapping his arms around her. He marveled at the softness of her skin. She drew the quilt over both of them and laid her head on his chest.

Their room was one of the bigger guest chambers, which was three times larger than any of the monks' cells. Gwen, who had left Medford a week before Breckton's invasion, had arranged to bring everything with her, even her canopied bed, carpets, and wall hangings. Looking around the room, Royce could easily imagine he was back on Wayward Street. He felt at home, but not because of the decorations. All he needed was Gwen.

"Am I corrupting you?" she asked playfully.

"Yes."

His fingers caressed her bare shoulder and ran along the swirled tattoo. "This last trip Hadrian and I went on, we went to Calis…into the jungles. We stayed in a Tenkin village, where I met an unusual woman."

"Did you? Was she beautiful?"

"Yes, very."

"Tenkin women can be exceptionally attractive."

"Yes, they can. And this one had a tattoo that—"

"Did Hadrian find the heir?"

"No—well, yes, but not how we expected. We stumbled on the news the empire is holding him in Aquesta. They're going to execute him on Wintertide. But this tattoo—"

"Execute him?" Gwen pushed herself up on one elbow, looking surprised—too surprised just to be avoiding questions. "Shouldn't you be helping Hadrian?"

"I will, although I'm not sure why. I was hardly any help on the last trip, and I didn't need to save him. So your little prophecy was wrong."

He thought it would put Gwen at ease to know her prediction of disaster had not come to pass. Instead, she pushed him away—the familiar sadness returned.

"You need to go help him," she said firmly. "I might be wrong about the timing, but I'm not wrong about Hadrian dying unless you are there to save him."

"Hadrian will be fine until I get back."

She hesitated, took a deep breath, and laid her head back down. Hiding her face against his chest, she became quiet.

"What's the matter?" Royce asked.

"I *am* a corrupting influence."

"I wouldn't worry about that," he told her. "Personally, I've always rather liked corruption."

There was a long pause, and he watched her head riding on the swells of his breath. Running his fingers through her hair, he marveled at it—at her. He touched the tattoo again.

"Royce, can we just lie here a little while?" She squeezed him, rubbing her cheek against his chest. "Can we just be still and listen to the wind and make believe it is blowing past us?"

"Isn't it?"

"No," she said, "but I want to pretend."

❧

"There wasn't much of a fight," Magnus said.

Royce always thought the dwarf's voice sounded louder and deeper than it should for someone his size. They sat at a long table in the refectory. Now that Royce knew Gwen was safe, his appetite returned. The monks prepared an excellent meal, accompanied by the first good wine he had tasted in ages.

"Alric just ran," Magnus said while mopping up the last of an egg. For someone so small, he ate a lot and never passed up an opportunity for food. "So Breckton's army took over everything except Drondil Fields, but they'll have that soon."

"Who burned Medford?" Royce asked.

"Medford was burned?"

"When I came through there a couple days ago, it was."

The dwarf shrugged. "If I had to guess, I'd say church-led fanatics out of Chadwick or maybe Dunmore. They've been pillaging homes and hunting elves since the invasion."

Magnus finished eating and leaned back with his feet on an empty stool. Gwen sat beside Royce, clutching his arm as if she owned him. The very idea of belonging to her was so strange that he found it distracting, but he was surprised to discover he enjoyed the sensation.

"So how long are you back for?" the dwarf asked. "Got time to let me see Alver—"

"I'm leaving as soon as Myron gets done." Royce noticed a look from Gwen. "I'm sure it won't take him more than a few days."

"What's he doing?"

"Drawing a map. Myron saw a floor plan of the palace once, so he's off reproducing it. He said it's old...real old... dates back to Glenmorgan, apparently."

"When you leave," Gwen said, "take Mouse. Give Ryn's horse to Myron."

"What does Myron need with a horse?" he asked. Gwen just smiled, and Royce knew better than to question further. "Okay, but I'm warning you now. He'll spoil it rotten."

౼

Myron sat at his desk in the scriptorium carrel, arguably his favorite place in the world. The peaked desk and small stool took up most of the cramped space between the stone columns. To his left, a half-moon window overlooked the courtyard.

Outside, the world appeared frightfully cold. The wind howled past the window, leaving traces of snow in the corners of the leading. The hilltop scrub shook with winter's fury. Peering out, Myron appreciated the coziness of his tiny study. The niche in the room enveloped him like a rodent's burrow. Ofttimes Myron considered how he might like to be a mole or a shrew—not a dusky or a greater white-tooth or even a lesser white-tooth shrew, but just a common shrew, or perhaps a mole. How pleasant an existence it would be to live underground, safe and warm, in small hidden chambers. He could look out at the vast world with a sense of awe and delight in knowing there was no reason to venture forth.

He put the finishing touches on the drawing for Royce and returned to working on the final pages of *Elquin*. This was the masterwork of the fifth-dynastic poet Orintine Fallon. It was a massive tome of personal reflections on how the patterns of nature related to the patterns in life. When completed, it would be the twentieth book in Myron's quest to restore the Winds Abbey library, with a mere three hundred and fifty-two remaining—not including the five hundred and twenty-four scrolls and one thousand two hundred and thirteen individual parchments. For more than two years' work, that accomplishment might not seem impressive, but Myron scribed full-time only in the winter, as the warmer months were devoted to helping put the finishing touches on the monastery.

The new Winds Abbey was nearly completed. To most, it would appear exactly as it once was, but Myron knew better. It had the same types of windows, doors, desks, and beds, but they were not the same ones. The roof was exactly as he remembered, yet it was different—just like the people. He missed Brothers Ginlin, Heslon, and the rest. Not that Myron was unhappy with his new family. He liked the new abbot, Harkon. Brother Bendlton was a very fine cook, and Brother Zephyr was marvelous at drawing and helped Myron with many of his illuminations. They were all wonderful, but like the windows, doors, and beds, they were not the same.

"No, for the last time, no!" Royce shouted as he entered the small scriptorium, pursued by Magnus.

"Just for a day or two," Magnus pleaded. "You can spare the dagger for that long. I only want to look at it—study it. I won't damage it."

"Leave me alone."

The two made their way toward Myron, weaving between the other desks. There were two dozen in the room, but only Myron's was used with any regularity.

"Oh, Royce, I've just finished. But you might want to wait for the ink to dry."

Royce held the map to the light, scanning it critically for several minutes.

Myron became concerned. "Something wrong?"

"I can't believe how things like this are just sitting in your head. It's incredible. And you say this is a map of the palace?"

"The notation reads 'Warric Castle,'" Myron pointed out.

"That's no map," Magnus said with a scowl, looking at the parchment Royce held out of his reach.

"How would you know?" Royce asked.

"Because what you have there are construction plans. You can see the builder's marks."

Royce lowered the scroll and Magnus pointed. "See here, the builder jotted down the amount of stone needed."

Royce looked at the dwarf and then at Myron. "Is that right?"

Myron shrugged. "Could be. I only know what I saw. I have no idea what it means."

Royce turned back to Magnus. "So you understand these markings, these symbols."

"Sure, it's just basic engineering."

"Can you tell me where the dungeon is by looking at this?"

The dwarf took the plans and laid them on the floor, as the desks were too high for him to reach. He motioned for a candle and Royce brought it over. Magnus studied the map for several minutes before declaring, "Nope. No dungeon."

Royce frowned. "That doesn't make sense. I've never heard of a palace or castle that didn't have some kind of dungeon."

"Well, that's not the only strange thing about this place," Magnus said.

"What do you mean?"

"Well, there's nothing, and I mean nothing at all, below ground level. Not so much as a root cellar."

"So?"

"So you can't stack tons of stone on just dirt. It will sink. Rain will erode it. The walls will shift and collapse."

"But it hasn't," Myron said. "The records I reproduced date back hundreds of years."

"Which makes no sense. These plans show no supporting structure. No piles driven down to bedrock, no columns. There's nothing holding this place up. At least nothing drawn here."

"So what does that mean?"

"Not sure, but if I were to guess, it's 'cuz it's built on top of something else. They must have used an existing foundation."

"Knowing that and looking at this...could you give me an idea of where a dungeon is, if you were there?"

"Sure. Just need to see what it's sitting on and give a good listen to the ground around it. I found you that tunnel to Avempartha, after all."

"All right, get packed. You're coming with me to Aquesta."

"What about the dagger?"

"I promise to bequeath it to you when I die."

"I can't wait until then."

"Don't worry. At this rate, it won't be too long." Royce turned back to Myron. "Thanks for the help."

"Royce?" Myron stopped the thief as they started to leave.

"Yeah?"

Myron waited until Magnus left. "Can I ask you something about Miss DeLancy?"

Royce raised an eyebrow. "Is something wrong? Is the abbot upset with her and the girls being here?"

"Oh no, nothing like that. They have been wonderful. It's nice having sisters as well as brothers. And Miss DeLancy has a very nice voice."

"Nice voice?"

"The abbot keeps us segregated from the women, so we don't see them much. They eat at different times and sleep in separate dormitories, but the abbot invites the ladies to join in vespers. A few come, including Miss DeLancy. She always arrives with her head covered and face veiled. She's quiet, but from time to time, I notice her whispering a prayer. Each service begins with a hymn and Miss DeLancy joins in. She sings softly but I can hear her. She has a wonderful voice, haunting, beautiful but also sad like the song of a nightingale."

"Oh." Royce nodded. "Well, good. I'm glad there isn't a problem."

"I wouldn't call it a problem, but…"

"But?"

"I often see her in the mornings when I go to the Squirrel Tree to talk with Renian. Miss DeLancy sometimes takes walks in the cloister, and she always stops by to pay her respects to us when she does." Myron paused.

"And?" Royce prompted.

"Well, it's just that one morning she took my hand and looked at my palm for several minutes."

"Uh-oh," Royce muttered.

"Yes," Myron said with wide eyes.

"What did she say?"

"She told me I would be taking two trips—both sudden and unexpected. She said I would not feel up to it, but I should not be afraid."

"Of what?"

"She didn't say."

"Typical."

"Then she told me something else and was sad like when she sings."

"What was it?" Royce asked.

"She said she wanted to thank me in advance and tell me it wasn't my fault."

"She didn't explain that either, did she?"

Myron shook his head. "But it was very disturbing, the way she said it—so serious and all. Do you know what I mean?"

"All too well."

Myron sat up on his stool and took a breath. "You know her. Should I be concerned?"

"I always am."

⤎

Royce walked the courtyard in the early-morning light. He had a habit of getting up early. To avoid waking Gwen, he had slipped out to wander the abbey's grounds. Scaffolding remained here and there, but the majority of the monastery was finished. Alric had financed the reconstruction as a payment to Riyria for saving Arista when their uncle Braga had tried to kill her. Magnus oversaw its construction and seemed genuinely happy to be restoring the buildings to their former splendor, even though working with Myron frustrated the dwarf. Myron provided detailed, although unorthodox, specifications describing dimensions in the height of several butter churns, the width of a specific book, or the length of a spoon. Despite this, the buildings went up, and Royce had to admit the monk and the dwarf had done an excellent job.

That day, the ground was covered in a thick frost and the sky lightened to a bright, clear blue as Royce made his morning rounds. Myron had finished the map, and he knew he should be leaving soon, but Royce was stalling. He enjoyed lingering in bed with Gwen and taking walks with her in the courtyard. Noticing the sun rising above the buildings, he headed back inside. Gwen would be up, and having breakfast together was always the best part of their day. When he reached their room, Gwen was still in bed, her back to the door.

"Gwen? Are you feeling all right?"

She rolled over to face him and he saw the tears in her eyes.

108 *Michael J. Sullivan*

Royce rushed to her side. "What is it, what's wrong?"

She reached out and hugged him. "Royce, I'm sorry. I wish there was more time. I wish..."

"Gwen? What—"

Someone knocked at the door and the force pushed it open. The portly abbot and a stranger stood awkwardly on the other side.

"What is it?" Royce snapped as he studied the stranger.

He was young and dressed in filthy clothes. His face showed signs of windburn and the tip of his nose looked frostbitten.

"Begging your pardon, Master Melborn," the abbot said. "This man rode in great haste from Aquesta to deliver a message to you."

Royce glanced at Gwen and stood up even as her fingers struggled to hold him. "What's the message?"

"Albert Winslow told me you would pay an extra gold tenent if I arrived quickly. I rode straight through."

"What's the message?" Royce's voice took on a chill.

"Hadrian Blackwater has been captured and is imprisoned in the imperial palace."

Royce ran a hand through his hair, barely hearing Gwen thank the man as she paid him.

⌇

Brilliant sunlight illuminated the interior of the stable as Royce entered. The planks composing the stalls were still pale yellow, not yet having aged to gray. The smell of sawdust mingled pleasantly with the scents of manure, straw, and hay.

"I should have guessed you'd be here," Royce said, startling Myron, who stood inside the stall between the two horses.

"Good morning. I was blessing your horse. Not knowing which you would take, I blessed them both. Besides, someone has to do the petting. Brother James cleans the stalls very well, but he never takes time to scratch their necks or rub their noses. In *The Song of Beringer*, Sir Adwhite wrote: *Everyone deserves a little happiness*. It's true, don't you think?" Myron stroked the dark horse's nose. "I know Mouse, but who is this?"

"His name is Hivenlyn."

Myron tilted his head, working something out while moving his lips. "And was he?" the monk asked.

"Was he what?"

"An unexpected gift."

Royce smiled. "Yes—yes, he was. Oh, and he's yours now."

"Mine?"

"Yes, compliments of Gwen."

Royce saddled Mouse and attached the bags of food the abbot had prepared while Royce had said his goodbyes to Gwen. There had been too many partings over the years, each harder than the one before.

"So you are off to help Hadrian?"

"And when I get back, I'm taking Gwen and we're leaving, going away from everyone and everything. Like you said, 'Everyone deserves a little happiness,' right?"

Myron smiled. "Absolutely. Only..."

"Only what?"

The monk paused before speaking again, rubbing Mouse's neck one last time. "Happiness comes from moving toward something. When you run away, ofttimes you bring your misery with you."

"Who are you quoting now?"

"No one," Myron said. "I learned that one firsthand."

CHAPTER 10

THE FEAST OF NOBLES

The fourteen-day-long Wintertide festival officially began with the Feast of Nobles in the palace's great hall. Twenty-seven colorful banners hung from the ceiling, each with the emblem of a noble house of Avryn. Five were noticeably absent, leaving gaps in the procession: the blue tower on the white field of House Lanaklin of Glouston, the red diamond on the black field of House Hestle of Bernum, the white lily on the green field of House Exeter of Hanlin, the gold sword on the green field of House Pickering of Galilin, and the gold-crowned falcon on the red field of House Essendon of Melengar. In times of peace, the hall welcomed all thirty-two families in celebration. The gaps in the line of banners were a reminder of the costs of war.

The palace shimmered with the decorations of the holiday season. Wreaths and strings of garland festooned the walls and framed the windows. Elaborate chandeliers, draped in red and gold streamers, spilled light across polished marble floors. Four large stone hearths filled the great hall with a warm orange glow. And rows of tall arched windows gowned in snowflake-embroidered curtains let in the last light of the setting sun.

On a dais at the far end of the room, the head table ran along the interior wall. Like rays from the sun, three longer tables extended out from it, trimmed with fanciful centerpieces woven from holly branches and accentuated with pinecones.

As many as fifty nobles, each dressed in his or her finest garments, already filled the hall. Some stood in groups, speaking in lordly voices; others gathered in shadowed corners, whispering in hushed tones; but the majority sat conversing at the tables.

"They look pretty, don't they?" Nimbus whispered to Hadrian. "So do snakes in the right light. Treat them the same way. Keep your distance, watch their eyes, and back away if you rattle them. Do that, and you might survive."

Nimbus looked him over one last time and brushed something off Hadrian's shoulder. He wore the gold and purple outfit—and felt ridiculous.

"I wish I had my swords. Not only do I look silly, but I feel naked."

"You have your pretty jeweled dagger," Nimbus said, smiling. "This is a feast, not a tavern. A knight does not go armed before his liege. It's not only considered rude, it also suggests treason. We don't want that now, do we? Just keep your wits about you and try not to say much. The more you talk, the more ammunition you provide. And remember what I told you about table manners."

"You're not coming?" Hadrian asked.

"I will be seated with Lady Amilia at the head table. If you get in trouble, look for me. I'll do what I can. Now remember, you're at the third table, left side, fourth chair from the end. Good luck."

Nimbus slipped away and Hadrian stepped into the hall. The instant he did, he regretted it, realizing he was not certain which side was left, which table was third, or which end of the table he should count from. Heads turned at his entrance, and the looks on their faces brought back memories of the aftermath of the Battle of RaMar. On that day, carrion birds had feasted on the bodies as Hadrian had walked through the battlefield. Hoping to drive the vultures off, he had shot and killed one of them with an arrow. To his revulsion, the other birds descended on the fresher remains of their fallen comrade. The birds had cocked their heads and looked at him as if to say he had no business being there. Hadrian saw the same look in the eyes of the nobles around him now.

"And who might you be, good sir?" a lady said off to Hadrian's right.

In his single-minded effort to find his seat, and with all the chatter in the room, he paid no attention.

"It is rude to ignore a lady when she speaks to you," a man said. His voice was sharp and impossible to ignore.

Hadrian turned to see a young man and woman glaring at him. They looked to be twins, as each had blond hair and dazzling blue eyes.

"It is also dangerous," the man went on, "when she is a princess of the honorable kingdom of Alburn."

"Um...ah...forgive—" Hadrian started when the man cut him off.

"There you have it. The cause for the slight is that the knight has no tongue! You are a knight, are you not? Please tell me you are. Please tell me you were some bucolic farmer that a drunken lord jokingly dubbed after you chased a squirrel from his manor. I couldn't stand it if you were another illegitimate son of an earl or duke, who crawled from an alehouse, attempting to claim true nobility."

"Let the man try to speak," the lady said. "Surely he suffers from a malady that prevents his mind from forming words properly. It's nothing to make light of, dear brother. It is a true sickness. Perhaps he contracted it from suffering on the battlefield. I am told that placing pebbles in the mouth often helps. Would you care for some, good sir?"

"I don't need any pebbles, thank you," Hadrian replied coolly.

"Well, you certainly need *something*. I mean, you are afflicted, aren't you? Why else would you completely ignore me like that? Or do you delight in insulting a lady, whose only offense is to ask your name?"

"I didn't—I mean, I wasn't—"

"Oh dear, there he goes again," she said with a pitiful look. "Please send a servant to fetch some pebbles at once."

"I daresay," her brother began, "I don't think we have time for the pebbles. Perhaps he can simply suck on one or two of these pinecones. Would that help, do you think?"

"He doesn't have a speech problem," Sir Murthas said as he approached, thumbs hooked in his belt and a wide grin on his face.

"No?" the prince and princess asked together.

"No, indeed, he's merely ignorant. He has his own tutor, you know. When I first met Sir Hadrian—that is the lout's name, by the way—he was in the middle of a bathing lesson. Can you imagine? The poor clod doesn't even know how to wash."

"Oh, now that is troubling." The princess began cooling herself with a collapsible fan.

"Indeed. So at a loss was he at the complexities of bathing that he threw his washcloth at Sir Elgar!"

"Such *rude* behavior is inherent in him, then?" she asked.

"Listen, I—" Hadrian started, only to be cut off again.

"Careful, Beatrice," Murthas said. "You're agitating him. He might spit or drool on you. If he's that uncouth, who knows what degradations he's capable of? I'll lay money that he'll wet himself next."

Hadrian was taking a step toward Murthas when he saw Nimbus rushing toward them.

"Princess Beatrice, Prince Rudolf, and Sir Murthas, a wonderful Wintertide to you all!"

They turned to see the tutor, his arms spread wide, a joyous smile beamed across his face. "I see you've met our distinguished guest Sir Hadrian. I am certain he is far too modest to tell the tale of his recent knighting on the field of battle. A shame, as it is a wonderful and exciting story. Prince Rudolf, I know you'd enjoy hearing it, and in return you can tell of *your own* heroic battles. Oh, I am sorry, I forgot—you've never actually seen a real battle, have you?"

The prince stiffened.

"And you, Sir Murthas, I can't recall—please tell us— where *you* were while the empress's armies fought for their lives. Surely you can relate *your* exploits of the last year and how you fared while other goodly knights died for the cause of Her Eminence's honor?"

Murthas opened his mouth, but Nimbus was quicker. Turning to the woman, he went on, "And, my lady, I want to assure you that you needn't take offense at Sir Hadrian's slight. It is little wonder that he ignored you. For he knows, as we all do, that no honorable lady would *ever* be so bold as to speak first to a strange man in the same manner as a common whore selling her wares on the street."

All three of them stared, speechless, at the tutor.

"If you're still looking for your seat, Sir Hadrian, it's this way," Nimbus said, hauling him along. "Once again, a glorious Wintertide to you all!"

Nimbus directed him to a chair at the end of a table, which so far remained empty.

"Whoa," Hadrian said in awe. "You just called those men cowards and the princess a whore."

"Yes," he said, "but I did so *very* politely." He winked. "Now, please do try to stay out of trouble. Sit here and smile. I have to go." Nimbus slipped back through the crowd, waving to people as he went.

Once more, Hadrian felt adrift amidst a sea of eggshells. He looked back and saw the princess and Murthas pointing in his direction and laughing. Not far away he noted two men watching him. Arms folded, they leaned against a pillar wrapped in red ribbons. The men were conspicuous in that they were the only guests wearing swords. Hadrian recognized the pair, as he had seen them often. They were always standing in the dark, across a room, or just outside a doorway — his own personal shadows.

Hadrian turned away and carefully took his seat. Tugging at his clothes, he tried to remember everything Nimbus had taught him: *sit up straight, do not fidget, always smile, never start a conversation, do not try anything you're unfamiliar with, and avoid eye contact unless cornered into a conversation.* If forced into an introduction, he was supposed to bow rather than shake hands with men. If a lady held out her hand, he should take it and gently kiss its back. Nimbus had advised him to keep several excuses at the ready to escape conversations, and to avoid groups of three or more. The most important thing was to appear relaxed and never draw attention to himself.

Minstrels played lutes somewhere near the front of the room, but he could not see them through the sea of people, who moved in shifting currents. Every so often, insincere laughter burst out. Snide conversations drifted to and fro. The ladies were much better at it than the men. "Oh, my dear, I simply *love* that dress!" A woman's high lilting voice floated from somewhere in the crowd. "I imagine it is insanely comfortable, given that it is so simple. Mine, on the other hand, with all this elaborate embroidery, is nearly impossible to sit in."

"I'm sure you are correct," another lady replied. "But discomfort is such a small sacrifice for a dress that so masterfully masks a lady's physical flaws and imperfections by the sheer complexity of its spacious design."

Trying to follow the feints and parries in the conversations around him gave Hadrian a headache. If he closed his eyes, he could almost hear the clash of steel. He was pleased to see that Princess Beatrice, Prince Rudolf, and Sir Murthas took seats at another table. Across from Hadrian, a man wearing a simple monk's robe took a seat. He looked even more out of place than Hadrian. They nodded silently to each other. Still, the chairs flanking him remained vacant.

At the head table, Ethelred sat beside a massive empty throne. Kings and their queens filled out the rest of the table, and at one end Nimbus was seated next to Lady Amilia. She sat quietly in a stunning blue dress, her head slightly bowed.

The music stopped.

"Your attention, please!" shouted a fat man in a bright yellow robe. He held a brass-tipped staff, which he hammered on the stone floor. The sound penetrated the crowd like cracks of thunder and stifled the drone of conversations. "Please take your seats. The feast is about to begin."

The room filled with the sounds of dragging chairs as the nobility of Avryn settled at their tables. A large man with a gray beard was to the monk's left. To his right sat none other than Sir Breckton, dressed in a pale blue doublet. The resemblance to Wesley was unmistakable. The knight stood and bowed as a large woman with a massive smile sat down on Hadrian's left. The sight of Genevieve Hargrave of Rochelle was a welcome one.

"Forgive me, good sir," she implored as she struggled into her chair. "Clearly they were expecting a dainty princess to sit here rather than a full-grown duchess! No doubt you were hoping for the same." She winked at him.

Hadrian knew a response was expected, and decided to take a safe approach.

"I was hoping not to spill anything on myself. I didn't think beyond that."

"Oh dear, now that *is* a first." She looked across the table at the knight. "I daresay, Sir Breckton, you may have competition this evening."

"How is that, my lady?" he asked.

"This fellow beside me shows all the signs of matching your humble virtue."

"Then I am honored to sit at the same table as he and even more pleased to have you as my view."

"I pity all princesses this evening, for surely I am the luckiest of ladies to be seated with the two of you. What is your name, goodly sir?" she asked Hadrian.

Still seated, Hadrian realized his error. Like Breckton, he should have stood at Genny's approach. Rising awkwardly, he fumbled a bow. "I am...Sir Hadrian," he said, watching for a raised hand. When she lifted it, he felt foolish but placed a light kiss on its back before sitting down. He expected laughter from the others but no one seemed to notice.

"I am Genevieve, the Duchess of Rochelle."

"Pleased to meet you," Hadrian replied.

"Surely you know Sir Breckton?" the duchess asked.

"Not personally."

"He is the general of the Northern Imperial Army and favored champion of this week's tournament."

"Favored by whom, my lady?" Sir Elgar asked, dragging out the seat next to Breckton and sitting with all the elegance of an elephant. "I believe Maribor favors my talents in this year's competition."

"You might like to think that, Sir Elgar, but I suspect your boasting skills are more honed than your riding prowess after so many years of endless practice," the duchess returned, causing the monk to chuckle.

"No disrespect to Her Ladyship," Breckton said in cold seriousness, "but Sir Elgar is correct in that only Maribor will judge the victor of this tournament, and no one yet knows the favor of his choice."

"Do not speak on my behalf," Elgar growled. "I don't need your charity, nor will I be the foundation for your tower of virtue. Spare us your monk's tongue."

"Don't be too quick to shun charity or silence a monk," the robed man across from Hadrian said softly. "Or how else will you know the will of god?"

"Pardon me, good monk. I was not speaking against you but rather rebuking the preaching of this secular would-be priest."

"Wherever the word of Maribor is spoken, I pray thee listen."

A squat, teardrop-shaped man claimed the chair beside the duchess. He kissed her cheek and called her dearest. Hadrian had never met Leopold before, but from all Albert had told him, his identity was obvious. Sir Gilbert took the empty chair next to Elgar.

No one sat to Hadrian's right, and he hoped it would remain that way. With the duchess protecting one flank, if no one took the seat at the other, he had to worry only about a frontal assault. While Hadrian pondered this, another friendly face appeared.

"Good Wintertide, all!" Albert Winslow greeted those at the table with an elegant flourish that made Hadrian envious.

He was certain Albert saw him, but the viscount displayed no indication of recognition.

"Albert!" The duchess beamed. "How wonderful to have you at our table."

"Ah, Lady Genevieve and Duke Leopold. I had no idea I ranked so highly on Her Eminence's list that I should be given the honor of dining with such esteemed personages."

Albert immediately stepped to Genny, bowed, and kissed her hand with effortless grace and style.

"Allow me to introduce Sir Hadrian," the lady said. "He appears to be a wonderful fellow."

"Is he?" Albert mused. "And a knight, you say?"

"That is yet to be determined," Sir Elgar said. "He claims a *Sir* before his name, but I've never heard of him before. Has anyone?"

"Generosity of spirit precludes judging a man ill before cause is given," Sir Breckton said. "As a knight of virtue, I am certain you know this, Sir Elgar."

"Once more, I need no instruction from you. I, for one, would like to know from whence Sir Hadrian hails and how it was he won his spurs."

All eyes turned to Hadrian.

He tried to remember the details drilled into him without looking like he was struggling. "I come from...Barmore. I was knighted by Lord Dermont for my service in the Battle of Ratibor."

"Really?" Sir Gilbert said in a syrupy voice. "I wasn't aware of *that* victory. I was under the impression the battle was lost and Lord Dermont killed. For what were you knighted, and how, pray tell, did His Lordship knight you? Did his spirit fly overhead, dubbing you with an ethereal sword, saying, 'Rise up, good knight. Go forth and lose more battles in the name of the empire, the empress, and the lord god Maribor'?"

Hadrian felt his stomach churn. Albert looked at him with tense eyes, clearly unable to help. Even the duchess remained silent.

"Good evening, gentlemen and lady." From behind him, the voice of Regent Saldur broke the tension, and Hadrian felt the regent's hand on his shoulder.

Accompanying him was Archibald Ballentyne, the Earl of Chadwick, who took the seat to Hadrian's right. Everyone at the table nodded reverently to the regent.

"I was just showing the earl to his seat, but I couldn't help overhearing your discussion concerning Sir Hadrian of Barmore here. You see, it was the empress herself who insisted he attend this festival. I ask him to grant me the guilty pleasure of responding to this honorable inquiry by Sir Gilbert. What do you say, Sir Hadrian?"

"Sure," he replied stiffly.

"Thank you," Saldur said, and after clearing his throat, continued, "Sir Gilbert is correct in that Lord Dermont was lost that day, but reports from his closest aides brought back the tale. Three days of rain made a mounted charge impossible, and the sheer number of the unstoppable Nationalist horde convinced Lord Dermont of the futility of engagement. Overcome with grief, he retreated to his tent in resignation.

"Without Lord Dermont to lead them, the imperial army floundered when the attack came. It was Sir Hadrian—then *Captain* Hadrian of the Fifth Imperial Mounted Guard— who roused the men and set them to ranks. He raised the banner and led them forth. At first, only a handful of soldiers responded. Indeed, only those who served with him answered his call, for they alone knew firsthand his mettle. Ignoring his meager numbers, he trusted in Maribor and called the charge."

Hadrian looked down and fidgeted with an uncooperative toggle on his tunic as the others sat enthralled.

"Although it was suicide, Captain Hadrian rode at the head of the troop into the fen field. His horse threw mud and slop, and a magnificent rainbow burst forth from the spray as he galloped across a stretch of standing water. He drove at the heart of the enemy with no thought of his own safety."

Saldur's voice grew in volume and intensity. His tone and cadence assumed the melodramatic delivery of a church sermon. A few nobles at the other tables turned to listen as he continued.

"His courageous charge unnerved the Nationalist foot soldiers, who fell back in fear. Onward he plunged, splitting their ranks until at last his mount became overwhelmed by the soft earth and fell. Wielding sword and shield, he got to his feet and continued to drive forward. Clashing against steel, he cried out the name of the empress: 'For Modina! Modina! Modina Novronian!' "

Saldur paused and Hadrian looked up to see every eye at the table shifting back and forth between the regent and him.

"Finally, shamed by the bravery of this one lone captain, the rest of the imperial army rallied. They cried to Maribor for forgiveness even as they drew sword and spear and rushed to follow. Before reinforcements could reach him, Hadrian was wounded and driven into the mud. Some of his men bore him from the field and took him to the tent of Lord Dermont. There they told the tale of his bravery and Lord Dermont swore by Maribor to honor Hadrian's sacrifice. He proclaimed his intent to knight the valiant captain.

" 'Nay, lord!' cried Captain Hadrian even as he lay wounded and bleeding. 'Knight me not, for I am unworthy. I have failed.' Lord Dermont clutched his blade and was heard to say 'You are more worthy of the noble title of *knight-valiant* than I am of the title of *man*!' And with that, Lord Dermont dubbed him *Sir* Hadrian."

"Oh my!" the duchess gasped.

With everyone staring at him, Hadrian felt hot, awkward, and more naked than when Elgar had interrupted his bath.

"Lord Dermont called for his own horse and thanked Sir Hadrian for the chance to redeem his honor before Maribor. He led his personal retinue into the fight, where he and all but a few of his men perished on the pikes of the Nationalists.

"Sir Hadrian tried to return to the battle despite his wounds, but fell unconscious before reaching the field. After the Nationalists' victory, they left him for dead and only providence spared his life. He awoke covered in mud. Desperate for food and water, he crawled into the forest, where he came upon a small hovel. There he was fed and tended to by a mysterious man. Sir Hadrian rested there for six days, and on the seventh, the man brought forth a horse and told Sir Hadrian to take it, ride to Aquesta, and present himself to the court. After he handed over the reins, thunder cracked and a single white feather fell from a clear blue sky. The man caught the feather before it reached the ground, a broad smile across his face. And with that, the man disappeared.

"Now, gentlemen and ladies." Saldur paused to look out over the other tables whose attention he had drawn. "I tell you truthfully that two days before Sir Hadrian arrived, the empress came to me and said, 'A knight riding a white horse will come to the palace. Admit him and honor him, for he shall be the greatest knight of the New Empire.' Sir Hadrian has been here, recuperating from his wounds, ever since. Today he is fully recovered and sits before you all. Now, if you'll excuse me, I must take my seat, as the feast is about to begin." Saldur bowed and left them.

No one said a word for some time. Everyone stared at Hadrian in wonder, including Albert, whose mouth hung agape.

It was the duchess who finally found words to sum up their collective thoughts. "Well, aren't you just an astonishment topped with surprises!"

⋙

Dinner was served in a fashion that Hadrian had never seen before. Fifty servants moving in concert delivered steaming plates of exotic victuals in elaborate presentations. Two peacocks were posed on large platters. One peered up as if surprised, while the other's head curled backward as if it were sleeping. Each was surrounded by an array of succulent carved meat. Ducks, geese, quail, turtledoves, and partridges were displayed in similar fashion, and one pure-white trumpeter swan reared up with its wings outstretched as if about to take flight. Rings of nuts, berries, and herbs surrounded glazed slabs of lean venison, dark boar, and marbled beef. Breads of various shades, from snow white to nearly black, lay in heaping piles. Massive wedges of cheese, cakes of butter, seven different types of fish, oysters steamed in almond milk, meat pies, custard tarts, and pastries drizzled with honey covered every inch of the table. Stewards and their many assistants served endless streams of wine, beer, ale, and mead.

Anxiety welled up as he struggled to remember Nimbus's multiple instructions on table etiquette. The list had been massive, but at that moment he could remember just two things: he was not to use the tablecloth to blow his nose and should not pick his teeth with the knife. Following Saldur's prayer to Maribor, Hadrian's fears vanished when all the guests ripped into the bountiful food with abandon. They tore legs off pigs and heads from birds. Bits of meat and grease sprayed the table as nobles groped and pawed to taste a bite of every dish, lest they miss something that might be the talk of the feast.

Hadrian had lived most of his life on black bread, brown ale, hard cheese, salted fish, and vegetable stews. What lay before him was a new experience. He tried the peacock, which, despite its beauty, was dry and not nearly as good as he had expected. The venison had a wonderful hickory-smoked taste. But the best thing by far was the dish of cinnamon baked apples. All conversation stopped when the eating began. The only sounds in the hall were those of a single lute, a lone singer, and scores of chewing mouths.

> *Long is the day in the summertime,*
> *long is the song which I play,*
> *I will keep your memory in my heart,*
> *till you come to me...*

The music was beautiful and strangely haunting. Its melody filled the great hall with a radiance that blended well with the glow of the fireplace and candles. After the setting of the sun, the windows turned to black mirrors and the mood became more intimate. Consoled with food, drink, and music, Hadrian forgot his circumstance and began to enjoy himself—until the Earl of Chadwick nudged him back to reality.

"Are you entered in the joust?" he asked. From his tone and glassy eyes, Hadrian could tell Archibald Ballentyne had started drinking long before the feast.

"Ah, yes—yes I am, sir—I mean, Your Lordship."

"Then you might be riding against my champion Sir Breckton over there." He waved a limp hand across the table. "He's also competing in the joust."

"Then I don't stand much of a chance."

"No, you don't," the earl said. "But you must do your best. There will be a crowd to please." The earl leaned over in a confidential manner. "Now tell me, was what Saldur told us true?"

"I would never dispute the word of a regent," Hadrian replied.

Archibald guffawed. "I think the phrase you were actually looking for is 'never *trust* the word of a regent.' Did you know they promised me Melengar and then just like that..." The earl attempted to snap his fingers. "...like that..." He attempted again. "...like..." He failed yet a third time. "Well, you know what I mean. They took away what they promised me. So you can see why I'm skeptical. That bit about the empress expecting you, was that true?"

"I have no idea, my lord. How could I know?"

"So you haven't met her? The empress, I mean?"

Hadrian paused, remembering a young girl named Thrace. "No, I haven't actually met *the empress*. Shouldn't she be seated up there?"

The earl scowled. "They leave the throne vacant in her honor. She never dines in public. To be honest, I've lived in this palace for half a year and have only seen her on three occasions: once in the throne room, once when she addressed the public, and once when I... Well, what matters is she never seems to leave her room. I often wonder whether the regents are keeping her prisoner up there. I should have her kidnapped— free the poor girl."

Archibald sat up and said, more to himself than to Hadrian, "That's what I should do, and there's just the man I need to talk to." Plucking a walnut from the centerpiece, he threw it down the table at Albert.

"Viscount Winslow," he shouted with more volume than necessary. "I haven't seen you in quite some time."

"No, indeed, Your Lordship. It has been far too long."

"Are you still in contact with those two...phantoms of the night? You know, the magicians that can make letters disappear and who are equally adept at saving doomed princesses from tower prisons?"

"I'm sorry, Your Lordship, but after what they did to you, I terminated my connection with them."

"Yes...what they did..." the earl slurred while looking into his cup. "What they did was put Braga's head in my lap! While I was sleeping, no less! Did you know that? It was a most disagreeable awakening, I tell you." He trailed off, mumbling to himself.

Hadrian bit his lip.

"I had no idea. You have my sincere apology," Albert said with genuine surprise, which was lost on the earl, who had tilted his head back to take another swallow of wine.

New musicians entered and began playing a formal tune as gentlemen, including Gilbert and Elgar, took the hands of ladies and led them to the dance floor. Hadrian had no idea how to dance. Nimbus had not even tried to instruct him. The Duke and Duchess of Rochelle also left to join in. A clear line of sight opened between Hadrian and Albert.

"So, Sir Hadrian, is it?" the viscount asked, shifting down to take Lady Genevieve's vacated chair. "Is this your first time in the banquet hall?"

"Indeed, it is."

"The palace is large and has an impressive history. I'm sure that during your recent recovery you've not had an opportunity to visit much of it. If you aren't planning to dance, I'd be happy to give you a tour. There are some fine paintings and frescoes on the second floor that are exquisite."

Hadrian glanced at the men still watching him.

"I'm sure they are, Viscount, but I think it might be rude to leave the feast so early. Our hosts might look poorly on me for doing so." He motioned toward the head table, where Saldur and Ethelred sat. "I wouldn't want to incur their disfavor so early in the celebrations."

"I understand completely. Have you found your accommodations at the palace to your liking?"

"Yes, indeed. I have my own room in the knights' wing. Regent Saldur has been most generous, and I have nothing to complain about as far as my quarters are concerned."

"So you have reason to complain otherwise?" Albert inquired.

Carefully choosing his words, Hadrian replied, "Not a complaint, really. I am merely concerned about my performance in the coming tournament. I am going to be competing against many renowned knights, such as Sir Breckton here. It is extremely important that I do well in the joust. Some very distinguished people will be watching the outcome quite closely."

"You should not be so concerned," Breckton mentioned. "If you are true to the knight's code, Maribor will guide you. What others may think has no weight on the field. The truth is the truth, and you know whether you live in accord with it or not. From this you will draw your strength or weakness."

"Thank you for your kind words, but I am not merely riding for myself. A success in this tournament will change the fortunes of those I care about as well... my, ah, retinue."

Albert nodded.

Sir Breckton leaned forward. "You are that concerned about the reputation of your squires and grooms?"

"They are as dear to me as family," Hadrian responded.

"That is most admirable. I can't say I have ever met a knight so concerned with the well-being of those who serve him."

"To be honest, sir, it is mainly for their welfare that I ride. I only hope they do nothing to dishonor me, as some of them are prone to poor judgment—rash and risky behavior—usually on my behalf, of course. Still, in this instance, I prefer they would merely enjoy the holiday."

Albert gave another nod and drained the last of his wine.

Ballentyne took another drink as well. He swallowed, burped loudly, and then slouched with his elbow on the table, resting a palm against his cheek. Hadrian surmised that it would not be long before the earl passed out completely.

The monk and the gray-bearded fellow bid the table good night. The two wandered off while debating the Legend of Kile, the significance of Saldur's story, and the true nature of the man Hadrian had allegedly met in the forest.

"Well, it has been a delight to dine with you all," Albert said, rising. "I am not used to such rich living, and this wine has gone to my head. I fear I will make a fool of myself should I remain, so I will retire."

The two knights bid him farewell, and Hadrian watched as Albert left the hall without looking back.

Having no one else left to converse with, Hadrian turned to Breckton. "Did your father not attend, or is he seated somewhere else?"

Breckton, whose attention was focused toward the front of the hall, took a moment to respond. "My father chose not to come. If not for the request of my lord here"—he gestured at the earl, who did not react—"I would not have attended either. Neither of us is in a mood for celebrations. We only recently learned that my younger brother Wesley died in the empress's service."

Hadrian replied in a somber voice, "I'm sorry for your loss. I'm sure he died with honor."

"Thank you, but death in service is not unexpected. It would be a comfort to know the circumstances. He died far from home, serving aboard the *Emerald Storm*, which was lost at sea." Breckton got to his feet. "Please excuse me. I think I'll also take my leave."

"Of course, good evening to you."

He watched Breckton go. The knight had the same stride as his brother, and Hadrian had to remind himself that the two choices he faced were equally unpleasant. Even without his emotional ties, two lives were more valuable than one. Breckton was a soldier, and as he himself had stated, death in service was not unexpected. Hadrian had no choice, but that fact did little to ease his conscience.

Ballentyne's head slipped off his hand, making a solid thud as it hit the table.

Hadrian sighed. Like knighthood, noble feasts were not as illustrious as he had expected.

CHAPTER 11

KNIGHTLY VIRTUE

Albert Winslow walked quickly through Aquesta, holding his heavy cloak tightly around him, its hood raised. He regretted not switching to boots, as his buckled shoes were treacherous on the icy cobblestones. He could have taken a carriage. The palace had a few available for hire, but walking made it easier to determine if he was being followed. Glancing back, Albert found the street empty.

By the time he entered The Bailey Inn, the fire in the common room was burning low. An elderly man slept near the hearth, a cup of brandy nearly spilling in his lap. Albert walked quickly to the stairs and up to his room. He would write out a note, leave it on the table, and then head back to the palace. Formulating the wording in his head, he took out a key and unlocked the door.

How do I begin to explain what I just saw?

Instead of entering a cold, dark room, he found a fire burning, lighted candles on the table, and—lying on his bed with boots still on—a dwarf.

"Magnus?"

The door closed abruptly, and Albert spun to see Royce

behind him. "You should remember to lock your door," the thief said.

Albert smirked. "I won't even dignify that with a comment. When did you get back?"

"Not long enough ago to get any rest," Magnus grumbled. "He drove us like dogs to get here."

"Hey, watch the boots," Albert said, slapping them with the back of his hand.

"What's happened with Hadrian?" Royce spoke sharply, his hood still up.

When Albert first met Royce, the viscount had been a drunk living in a farmer's barn outside Colnora. Reduced to selling his clothes piecemeal to buy rum, he was down to little more than his nightshirt and old rags. Wailing about the misfortune of being the noble son of a spendthrift father, he offered Royce and Hadrian his silk nightshirt for five copper tenents. Royce had made him a better offer. Riyria needed a nobleman to work as a liaison to the wealthy and privileged — a respectable face to sell disreputable services. They cleaned him up, paid for new clothes, and provided all the trappings of success that a viscount required. They gave him back his dignity, and Albert was noble once more. From then on the viscount saw Royce as a friend, but at times like this — when Royce's hood was raised, and his voice harsh — even Albert was scared of him.

"Well?" Royce pressed, stepping closer and causing Albert to back up. "Is he in prison? They didn't..."

"What? No!" Albert shook his head. "You're actually not going to believe this. I just came from the Feast of the Nobles, the big opening party for the Wintertide celebration. Everyone was there, kings, bishops, knights, you name it."

"Get to the point, Albert."

"I am. Hadrian was there too."

Albert saw Royce's hands form fists. "What were they doing to him?"

"Oh no, nothing like that—they were feeding him. He was— They made him a knight, Royce—a knight of the empire. You should have seen the outfit he was wearing."

At this, even the dwarf sat up.

"What? Speak sense, you crazy—"

"I swear. It's the truth! Regent Saldur even came over and told the whole table this nutty story about how Hadrian fought for the Imperialists at the Battle of Ratibor and was knighted because of it. Can you believe that?"

"No, I don't. Have you been drinking again?"

"Just a bit of wine. I'm sober. I swear," Albert said.

"But why would they do such a thing? Were you able to get near him? What did he say?"

"He wasn't able to speak freely and hinted that he was being watched, but I think he's competing in the tournament. It sounded like the regents made him some kind of deal."

"The tournament at Highcourt?"

"Yes. He made it pretty clear that we shouldn't interfere or try to help."

"I don't understand."

"That makes two of us."

❧

"I feel ridiculous," Amilia whispered to Nimbus as she pushed her plate away.

One hundred and twenty-three pairs of eyes stared at her. She knew the exact number. She knew which rulers brought wives and which sat with courtesans. She knew who was sensitive to drafts and who was uncomfortable near the heat of the hearth. She knew which princess refused to sit beside which countess. She knew who held power and which ones were just puppets. She knew every quirk and foible, every bias and fear, every name and title—but not a single face.

They were manageable as slips of parchment, but now they were all here—staring. No, not staring. Their expressions were too malicious and filled with contempt for something as benign as staring. In their eyes she could see the exasperation and she knew what they were thinking: *How is it that she— the poor daughter of a carriage maker—sits at the empress's table?* She felt as though one hundred and twenty-three wolves snarled at her with exposed teeth.

"You look beautiful," Nimbus said. His fingers kept tempo with the pavane. The tutor was apparently oblivious to the waves of hatred crashing over them.

She sighed. There was nothing to do now but struggle through the night as best she could. Sitting up straight, Amilia reminded herself to breathe, which was no easy feat in the tight bodice.

Amilia wore the gown the duchess had presented to her that morning. Far from just an ordinary dress, it was a work of art in blue silk. Ribbons woven into elaborate designs resembling swans adorned the front. The fitted bodice pressed her stomach flat and led to a full, billowing skirt that shimmered like rippling water when she moved. A deep neckline left the tops of her breasts exposed. To Lady Genevieve's dismay, Amilia wore a scarf, covering them and the exquisite jeweled necklace the duchess had lent. Perhaps to avoid a similar concealment with the diamond earrings, the duchess had sent three stylists to put Amilia's hair up. They spent the better part of two hours on the coif and were followed by a pair of cosmetic artists, who painted her lips, eyelids, cheeks, and even her fingernails. Amilia never wore makeup of any kind.

She never styled her hair, and she certainly never exposed her breasts. Out of respect for the duchess, she complied, but she felt like a clown—a buffoonish entertainment on display for those one hundred and twenty-three sets of eyes.

One hundred and twenty-four, she corrected herself. There had been a last-minute addition.

"Which one is he?" she asked Nimbus.

"Who? Sir Hadrian? I squeezed him in over there. He's the one in purple and gold. Saldur is passing him off as a knight, but I've never met a man so unknightly."

"He's cruel?"

"Not at all. He's considerate and respectful, even to servants. He complains less than a monk, and while I am certain he knows the use of a blade, he seems as violent as a mouse. He drinks only moderately, considers a bowl of porridge a feast, and rises at dawn. He is no knight but rather what a knight *should* be."

"He looks familiar," she said, but could not place him. "How is he coming along?"

"Slowly," Nimbus told her. "I just hope he doesn't attempt to dance. I haven't found time to teach him, and I am certain he hasn't a clue."

"*You* know how to dance?" Amilia asked.

"I am exceedingly talented, milady. Would you like me to teach you as well?"

She rolled her eyes. "I hardly think I will need to know *that.*"

"Are you sure? Didn't Sir Breckton seek your favor for the joust?"

"Out of pity."

"Pity? Are you certain? Perhaps you...Oh dear, what have we here?" Nimbus stopped as Sir Murthas navigated the tables, walking straight for them. Wearing a ribbed burgundy doublet that was tight in the waist and sported broad, padded shoulders, he looked quite impressive. An elegant gold chain with a ruby hung around his neck. His dark eyes matched his coal-black hair, and his goatee appeared freshly trimmed.

"Lady Amilia, I am Sir Murthas of Alburn." He held out his hand, covered in thick rings.

Confused, she stared at it until the man awkwardly let it fall. Amilia noticed Nimbus cringing beside her. She had done something inappropriate but did not know what.

"I was hoping, dear lady," Sir Murthas said, pushing on, "that you would honor me with a dance."

Amilia was horrified. She sat rigid and stared at him without saying a word.

Nimbus came to her rescue. "I believe Her Ladyship is not interested in dancing at the moment, Sir Murthas. Another time, perhaps?"

Murthas gave the tutor a loathing look, and then his face softened as he returned his attention to Amilia. "May I ask why? If you are not feeling well, perhaps I could escort you to a balcony for some fresh air? If you don't care for the music, I will have them play a different tune. If it is the color of my doublet, I will gladly change."

Amilia remained unable to speak.

Murthas glanced at Nimbus. "Has *he* been speaking ill of me?"

"I have never mentioned you," the tutor replied, but his words had no effect on the knight.

"Perhaps she's put off by that bit of rat hair on your chin, Murthas," Sir Elgar bellowed as he too approached the table. "Or perhaps she is waiting for a real man to ask her to the floor. What do you say, my lady? Will you do me the honor?" Elgar dwarfed Murthas and brushed the smaller knight to one side as he held out his hand.

"I'm—I'm sorry." Amilia found her tongue. "I choose not to dance."

Elgar's expression darkened to a storm, but he said nothing.

"Gentlemen, gentlemen, 'tis I she is waiting for," Sir Gilbert said, striding forward. "Forgive me, my lady, for taking so long to arrive and leaving you in such company."

Amilia shook her head, stood, and hurried away from the table. She neither knew nor cared where she was going. Frightened and embarrassed, she thought only of getting away. Afraid of catching the eye of another knight, she focused on the floor, and it was in this way that she stumbled once more into Sir Breckton.

"Oh my," she gasped, looking up at him. "I...I..."

"We seem to be making a habit of this," Breckton said with a smile.

Amilia was mortified and felt so foolish that tears welled up and spilled down her cheeks.

When Breckton saw this, his smile vanished; he fell to one knee and bowed his head. "Forgive me, dear lady. I am a fool. I spoke without thought."

"No, no, it's all right," she told him, feeling worse than ever. "Please, I am only trying to get to my chambers. I—I've had my fill of feasting."

"As you wish. Please, take my arm and I will see you safely there."

Amilia was beyond resisting and took hold of the knight as they continued down the hall. Away from the noise and the crowd, Amilia felt more like herself. She wiped her cheeks and let go of his arm.

"Thank you, Sir Breckton, but I do not need you to escort me to my room. I have lived in this palace for a long time and know the way quite well. I can assure you there are no dragons or ogres along my path."

"Of course. Forgive me again for my presumption. I only thought because—"

Amilia nodded. "I know. I was just a little overwhelmed. I'm not used to so much attention. Despite the title, I am still a simple girl, and knights...they still frighten me."

Breckton looked wounded and took a step backward. "I would *never* harm you, my lady!"

"Oh, there I go again. I feel like such a fool." Amilia threw up her hands. "I—I don't know how to be noble. *Everything* I *say* is wrong. Everything I *do* or *don't do* is a mistake."

"I am certain it is not you but I who am at fault," Breckton assured her. "I am not accustomed to the courts. I am a soldier—plain and blunt. I will once more ask your forgiveness and leave you alone, as clearly, I am a terror to you."

"No, no, you are not. You are most kind. It's the others I— You are the only one—" She sighed. "Please, I would be honored if you would escort me."

Breckton snapped smartly to attention, bowed, and offered his arm once more. They walked silently to the stairs and up to the fifth floor. Passing by a set of guards, they proceeded to a chamber door. Breckton nodded and smiled at Gerald, who responded with a salute—something Amilia had never seen the guard do before.

"You are well protected," Breckton remarked.

"Not me; this is the empress's chambers. I always check on her before retiring. To be honest, you shouldn't even be on this floor."

"Then I will take my leave."

He started to turn.

"Wait," she said, reaching out to touch his arm. "Here." She pulled off her scarf and handed it to him.

Breckton smiled broadly. "I will wear it at the tournament proudly and represent you with honor."

Taking her hand, he gently kissed the back of it. Then the knight bowed and left. Amilia's gaze followed him until he reached the stairs and disappeared from sight. When she turned back, she found Gerald grinning. She raised an eyebrow and the guard wiped the expression from his face.

Amilia entered the imperial bedchamber. As always, Modina was at the window. Lying on the stone in her thin white nightgown, the empress looked dead. Amilia found her this way most nights. The mirror was still intact and Modina was merely asleep. Still, Amilia could not help thinking that one day… She pushed the thought away.

"Modina?" She spoke softly as she rocked the empress's shoulder. "Come, it's too cold to lie there."

The girl looked up sadly, then nodded. Amilia put her in bed, covered her with a blanket, and gave her a kiss on the forehead before leaving Modina to sleep.

ᳵ

Hadrian was squeezing melted candle wax between his fingers and listening to the rhythmic snores of the earl. Even his *shadows* looked tired, although they were different men since the shift change. He wondered how long he was expected to remain in the hall.

He saw Sir Breckton return to the feast, but rather than resuming his seat, the knight struck up a conversation with Nimbus. He watched them for a moment and then noticed movement at the head table. To Hadrian's dismay, Regent Saldur picked up his wine goblet and walked directly toward him.

"You've done well," the regent said while taking the seat across from Hadrian. "Or at least it appeared so from over there. Sentinel Guy and Lord Marius speak highly of you."

"Lord Marius? You don't mean *Merrick* Marius?"

"Yes, you remember him, don't you? He was at our little meeting. Oh, how foolish. Perhaps we forgot to introduce him. Marius said he was extremely impressed with a recent assignment that you and your partner performed on his behalf. By the sound of things, it was quite difficult. He even told me that he thought only you two could have accomplished such a feat."

Hadrian clenched his teeth.

"I've been thinking...Perhaps when this business with Breckton is over, you might find working for the empire preferable to exile with Gaunt. I am a pragmatist, Hadrian, and I can see the benefit of having someone like you aiding in what we are trying to accomplish. I'm sure you've heard any number of terrible things about me or what I may have done. But you need to realize I'm trying to rid our world of problems that plague all of us, commoner and noble alike. Roads have gone to ruin. You can hardly travel in spring due to mud. Banditry is rampant, which hampers trade and stifles prosperity. Every city is a cesspool of filth and few have adequate fresh water. There are not enough jobs in the north, not enough workers in the south, and not enough food anywhere."

Hadrian glanced across the hall and saw Breckton and Nimbus leaving the feast together. A little while later, Murthas, Elgar, and Gilbert downed their drinks and left in the same direction.

"The world of men has many enemies," Saldur droned on. "When petty kings war with each other, they weaken the nations with their childish feuds. I have long believed these squabbles leave the doors open for invasion and invite destruction. You might not know this, but the Ghazel and Dacca have been raiding from the south. We don't publicize this information, of course, so few know just how severe it has become, but they have even invaded Tur Del Fur."

Hadrian glared. "If you didn't want the Ghazel as neighbors, you probably shouldn't have invited them."

Saldur looked at him curiously for a moment and then said, "I did what was necessary. Now where was I? Oh yes. Not everyone can keep what they have if things are to change. There must be sacrifices. I have tried to be reasonable, but if a leg is infected and cannot be saved, it must be removed for the good of the body. I hope you can see past these small costs and recognize the larger implications. I am not an evil man, Hadrian. It is the world that forces me to be cruel, but no more so than a father forcing his child to swallow an unpleasant medicine. You can see that, can't you?"

Saldur looked at him expectantly.

"Am I allowed to leave?" Hadrian asked. "The feast, I mean."

Saldur sighed and sat back in his chair. "Yes, you can go. You need to get plenty of sleep. The tournament begins in two days."

⤚

Pinecones and holly garland, the remnants of wayward revelers, littered the hallways along Hadrian's path to the knights' wing. Rounding a corner, he found Nimbus slumped against the corridor wall. The courtier's tunic was torn, and his nose bleeding. Sir Gilbert stood above him, grinning. Through the doorway of the common room, Hadrian spotted Sir Breckton. Armed with only his dress dagger, the knight defended himself against Murthas and Elgar, each of whom wielded a sword as well as a dagger.

"Look who's joined the party," Gilbert said as Hadrian approached.

"Given this situation," Hadrian asked Nimbus while keeping his eyes on Gilbert, "how much *generosity* am I required to extend to these fellow knights?"

In the common room, Murthas swiped at Breckton, who caught the sword with his little blade and cast the stroke aside.

"Given the situation," Nimbus said quickly, "I think the virtue of generosity is not applicable."

"Indeed!" Breckton shouted. "They have forfeited their right to honorable treatment."

Hadrian smiled. "That makes this a lot easier." Drawing his own dagger, he threw it into Gilbert's thigh. The knight cried out and fell to his knees, looking up in astonishment. Hadrian punched him in the face, and his opponent collapsed. Taking both his and Gilbert's daggers, Hadrian advanced.

Elgar sneered as he turned to face Hadrian, leaving Breckton to Murthas.

"I hope you joust better than you wield a sword," Hadrian said, approaching.

"We haven't even fought yet, you fool," Elgar bellowed.

"That's hardly necessary. You hold your sword like a woman. No, that's not true. I've actually known women who can sword fight. The truth is, you're just terrible."

"What I lack in style, I make up for in strength." Elgar charged Hadrian, raising his blade over his head and leaving his entire chest exposed. Hadrian's training made him instinctively want to aim a single thrust at the man's heart, which would kill Elgar instantly. He fought the urge and lowered his weapon. Saldur and Ethelred would not approve. Besides, Elgar was drunk. Instead, he dodged to one side and left a foot behind to trip the knight. Elgar fell, hitting his head on the stone.

"Is he dead?" Nimbus asked, watching Hadrian roll the big man over on his back.

"No, but I think he might have chipped the slate. Now *that's* a hard head."

Hadrian sat down next to Nimbus and inspected the tutor's wounds.

"Shouldn't you help Sir Breckton?"

Hadrian glanced up as Murthas made another lunge.

"I don't think that's necessary, nor would it be proper to step into another man's fight. However..." Picking up Elgar's sword, Hadrian yelled, "Breckton!" before throwing it across the common room. Breckton caught the weapon and Murthas stepped back, looking less confident.

"Damn you!" Murthas shouted, taking one last swing before fleeing.

Hadrian could not suppress the temptation to stick out his foot once more, tripping Murthas as he ran by. Murthas fell, got back to his feet, and ran off.

"Thank you," Breckton said, offering Hadrian a slight nod.

"It's Murthas who should be thanking me," Hadrian replied.

Breckton smiled. "Indeed."

"I don't understand," Nimbus said. "Murthas lost. Why would he thank you?"

"He's still alive," Hadrian explained.

"Oh," was all Nimbus said.

◈

Hadrian managed to stop Nimbus's bleeding. The tutor's nose did not appear broken. Even so, none of them was interested in returning to the banquet hall. Hadrian and Breckton escorted Nimbus to his room, where the slim man thanked the two knights for their assistance.

"You fight well," Breckton said as he and Hadrian walked the palace corridors back toward the knights' wing.

"Why did they attack you?"

"They were drunk."

"Where I come from, drunks sing badly and sleep with ugly women. They don't attack rival knights and courtly gentlemen."

Breckton was quiet for a moment, then asked, "Where *do* you come from, Sir Hadrian?"

"Saldur explained—"

"Some of the men that fought with Lord Dermont and survived the Battle of Ratibor joined my army in the north. Captain Lowell was one of them. His accounting of that day in no way resembles the tale Regent Saldur described. I would not embarrass the regent or you by mentioning it in public, but now that we are alone..."

Hadrian said nothing.

"What Lowell did tell me was the entire imperial army was caught sleeping on that rainy morning. Most never managed to strap on a sword, much less mount a horse."

Hadrian simply replied, "It was a very confusing day."

"So you say, but perhaps you were never there at all. A knight taking credit for another's valor is most dishonorable."

"I can assure you, I *was* there," Hadrian said sincerely. "And that I rode across the muddy field leading men into battle that morning."

Breckton stopped at the entrance of his own room and studied Hadrian's face. "You must forgive me for my rudeness. You have aided me this evening, and I have responded with accusations. It is unseemly for one knight to accuse another without proper evidence. I will not let it happen again. Good night."

He offered Hadrian a curt nod and left him alone in the corridor.

Chapter 12

A Question of Succession

The sun reached its midday peak and Arcadius Vintarus Latimer, the master of lore at Sheridan University, still waited in the grand foyer of the imperial palace. He had been there before, but that was back when it had been called Warric Castle and had been the home of the most powerful king in Avryn. Now it was the seat of the New Empire. The imperial seal etched in the white marble floor was a constant and unavoidable reminder. Arcadius read the inscription that ringed the design, shaking his head in disgust. "They misspelled *honor*," he said aloud, even though he waited alone.

Finally, a steward approached and motioned for him to follow. "The regent Saldur will see you now, sir."

One step closer, Arcadius thought as he headed toward the stairs. The steward was nearly to the fourth floor when he realized Arcadius had reached only the second landing.

"My apologies," the lore master called up to him, leaning on the banister and removing his glasses to wipe his brow. "Are you certain the meeting is all the way up there?"

"The regent asked for you to come to his office."

The old professor nodded. "Very well, I'll be right along."

Another positive development.

While it was unlikely that Saldur would agree to his pro-posal, Arcadius judged his odds of success tripled with each flight he climbed. He did not want to speak in a reception hall filled with gossipy courtiers. Not that he held much hope, no matter where the subject was broached. Still, if this meeting went well, he would be free of his guilt and the burden of responsibility. A private meeting with the regent would be per-fect. Saldur was an intellectual, and Arcadius could appeal to the regent's respect for education. However, when he reached the office, Saldur was not alone.

"Well, of course we need a southern defense," Ethelred was saying when the steward opened the door. "We have a nation of goblins down there now. You haven't seen them, Sauly. You don't know…er…Yes? What is it?"

"May I present Professor Arcadius Latimer, master of lore at Sheridan University," the steward announced.

"Oh yes, the teacher," Ethelred said.

"He's a bit more than that, Lanis," Saldur corrected.

"Not at all, not at all," Arcadius said with a cheerful smile. "Instructing young minds is the noblest act I perform. I am honored."

The lore master bowed to the four people in the room. In addition to the regents, there were two men he did not recog-nize. One, however, was dressed in the distinct vestments of a church sentinel.

"You are a long way from Sheridan, Professor." Saldur addressed him from behind a large desk. "Did you come for the holiday?"

"Why no, Your Grace. At my age it takes a bit more than the allure of jingling bells and sweetmeats to rouse one such as I from warm chambers in the depth of winter. I don't know if you noticed, but there's a great deal of snow outside."

Arcadius took a moment to examine his surroundings.

Hundreds of books sat on shelves, locked behind glass cabinets with little keyholes. A pretty carpet, somewhat muddled in its colors and partially hidden by the regent's desk, portrayed what appeared to be a scene of Novron conquering the world while Maribor guided his sword.

"Your office is so... *clean*," the professor remarked.

Saldur raised an eyebrow and then chuckled. "Oh yes, I seem to recall visiting you once. I don't believe I made it through your door."

"I have a unique filing system."

"Lore master, I don't mean to be short, but we are quite busy," Ethelred said. "Exactly what has brought you so far in the cold?"

"Well," he began, smiling at Saldur, "Your Grace, I was hoping to speak to you—in private." He glanced pointedly at the two men he did not recognize. "I have a sensitive matter to discuss concerning the future of the empire."

"This is Sentinel Luis Guy and over there is Lord Merrick Marius. I assume you already know our soon-to-be emperor, Ethelred. If you wish to discuss the empire's future, these are the men you need to speak with."

Arcadius paused deliberately, took off his spectacles, and cleaned them slowly with his sleeve. "Very well, then." The lore master replaced his glasses and crossed the room to one of the soft chairs. "Do you mind? Standing for too long makes my feet hurt."

"By all means," Ethelred said sarcastically. "Make yourself at home."

Arcadius sat down with a sigh, took a deep breath, and began. "I have been thinking about the New Empire you are establishing, and I must say that I approve."

Ethelred snorted. "Well, Sauly, we can sleep better now that the scholars have weighed in."

Arcadius glared at him across the tops of his glasses. "What I mean is that the idea of a central authority is a sound one and will stop the monarchial squabbles, bringing harmony from chaos."

"But?" Saldur invited.

"But what?"

"I just sensed you were going to find fault," Saldur said.

"I am, but please try not to get ahead of me—it ruins the drama. I've spent several days bouncing over frozen ground, preparing for this meeting, and you deserve to experience the full effect."

Arcadius adjusted his sleeves and waited for what he thought was the precise amount of time to draw their full attention. "I'm curious to know if you've put any thought into the line of succession."

"Succession?" Ethelred blurted from where he sat on the edge of Saldur's desk.

"Yes, you know, the concept of producing an heir to inherit the mantle of leadership. Most thrones are lost because of poor planning on this front."

"I'm not even crowned, and you complain because I haven't fathered an heir yet?"

Arcadius sighed. "It is not *your heir* I am concerned about. This empire is founded on a bedrock of faith—faith that the bloodline of Novron is back on the throne. If the bloodline is not maintained, the cohesion that holds the empire together might dissolve."

"What are you saying?" Ethelred asked.

"Only that should something tragic happen to Modina, and no child of *her blood* be available, you would lose your greatest asset. The line of Novron would end, and without this thin strand of legitimacy, the empire could face dissolution. Glenmorgan's Empire lasted only three generations.

How long will this one endure with only a mere mortal at its head?"

"What makes you think anything will happen to the empress?"

Arcadius smiled. "Let's just say I know the ways of the world, and sacrifices are often required to bring about change. I'm here because I fear you might mistakenly think Modina is expendable once Ethelred wears the crown. I want to urge you not to make a terrible, perhaps fatal, error."

Saldur exchanged looks with Ethelred, confirming that the lore master had guessed correctly.

"But there is nothing to fear, gentlemen, for I've come to offer a solution." Arcadius gave them his most disarming smile, which accentuated the laugh lines around his eyes and showed off his round cheeks, which he guessed were still rosy from his trip. "I am proposing that Modina already bore a child."

"What?" Ethelred asked. He stood and his face showed a mixture of emotions. "Are you accusing my fiancée—the empress—of impropriety?"

"I am saying that if she had a child—a child born a few years ago and no longer dependant on the mother—it could make your lives a great deal easier. It would ensure the continued unification of the empire under the bloodline of Novron."

"Speak plainly, man!" Ethelred erupted. "Are you suggesting such a child exists?"

"I am saying such a child *could* exist." He looked at each of their faces before focusing back on Saldur. "Modina is no more the Heir of Novron than I am, but that is not relevant. The only thing that matters is what her subjects believe. If they accept she has a child, then the pretense of the heir can continue and the masses will be satisfied. After ensuring the line of succession, an unfortunate incident involving the empress would not be such a tragedy. Her people would certainly mourn her, but there would still be hope—hope in the form of a child who would one day take the throne."

"You bring up an interesting point, Professor," Ethelred said. "Modina has…been ill as of late, but I'm sure she could hang on long enough to bear a child, couldn't she, Sauly?"

"I don't see why not. Yes. We could arrange that."

The lore master shook his head as if hearing an incorrect response from one of his students. "But what if she were to die in childbirth? It happens far too often and is too great a risk for something as important as this. Do you really wish to gamble all you are trying to accomplish? A child conceived before the empress even knew Ethelred would not reflect poorly on him. There are ways to present the child that would bolster the new emperor's standing. He can profess that his love for Modina is boundless and agree to raise the child as if it were his own. Such sentiments would endear him to the people."

Arcadius waited a minute before continuing. "Take a healthy child and educate it in philosophy, theology, poetry, history, and mathematics. Fill the vessel with training in civics, economics, and culture. Make the child the most learned leader the world has ever known. Picture the possibilities. Imagine the potential of an empire ruled by an intellectual giant rather than the thug with the biggest stick.

"If you want a better empire, you need to create a better ruler. I can provide this. I can bring you a child that I have already begun to educate and will continue to groom. I can raise the child at Sheridan, away from life at court. We don't want a spoiled brat, pampered from birth, swinging little legs on the imperial throne. What we need is a strong, compassionate leader without ties to the nobility."

"One *you* control," Luis Guy accused.

Arcadius chuckled. "It is true that such a child might be fond of me, and while I know that I cut quite a dashing figure for someone my age, I'm a very old man. I will be dead soon. Most likely, I will pass on long before the child reaches coronation age, so you'll not have to worry about my influence.

"I should point out that I don't intend to be the child's only tutor. Nor could I be in order to ensure success. A task of this magnitude would require historians, doctors, engineers, and even tradesmen. You can send as many of your own instructors as you wish. I would hope you, Regent Saldur, would be one of them. I suspect much of the vision of the New Empire comes from you, after all. Once the wedding is over and things are operating smoothly, you could join us at Sheridan. She will require training that you are uniquely qualified to teach."

"She?" Ethelred said.

"Beg pardon?" Arcadius asked, peering over his glasses again.

"You said *she*. Are you speaking of a girl?"

"Well, yes. The child I am suggesting is a young orphan whom I have been taking care of for some time. She is extremely bright and at the age of five has already mastered letters. She is a delightful girl who shows great promise."

"But—a *girl*?" Ethelred sneered. "What good is a girl?"

"I'm afraid my fellow regent is correct," Saldur said. "The moment she married, her husband would rule, and all your education would be wasted. If it was a boy…"

"Well, there is no shortage of orphan boys," Ethelred declared. "Find a handsome one and we can do the same with him."

"My offer is for *this* girl only."

"Why?" Guy asked.

Arcadius detected a tone in the question he did not like.

"Because I sense in her the makings of a magnificent ruler, the kind who could—"

"But she's a *girl*," Ethelred repeated.

"As is Empress Modina."

"Are you saying you would refuse to tutor another child? One of our choosing?" Saldur asked.

"Yes." Arcadius said the word with the stern conviction of an ultimatum. He hoped the value of knowledge that only he could bestow would be enough to win them over, but he could see the answer before it was spoken.

Saldur was respectful at least and politely thanked him for bringing the subject to their attention. They did not invite him to stay for Wintertide, and Arcadius was uncomfortable about the way Luis Guy watched him as he left.

He had failed.

✦

Royce waited patiently.

He had been in Imperial Square that morning, speaking with vendors who regularly delivered supplies to the palace, when the old battered coach passed by and entered the imperial gates. Recognizing it immediately, Royce wondered what it was doing there.

The palace courtyard had insufficient space for all the visitors' carriages during Wintertide and soon the coach returned and parked along the outer wall. The old buggy, with its paint-chipped wheels, weathered sides, and tattered drapes, looked out of place amidst the line of noble vehicles.

He waited for what must have been hours before he spotted the old man leaving the palace and approaching the carriage.

"What the—" Arcadius began. He was startled by Royce, who sat inside.

The thief placed a finger to his lips.

"What are you doing here?" Arcadius whispered, pulling himself in and closing the door behind him.

"Waiting to ask you that same question," Royce said quietly.

"Where to, Professor?" the driver called as he climbed aboard. The coach bounced with his weight.

"Ah—just circle the city once, will you, Justin?"

"The city, sir?"

"Yes. I'd like to see it before we leave."

"Certainly, sir."

"Well?" Royce pressed as the carriage jerked forward.

"Chancellor Lambert took sick on the day he was to leave for the celebrations here. Because he could not attend, he thought a personal apology was required and asked me—of all people—to deliver his regrets. Now, what about you?"

"We located the heir."

"Did you now?"

"Yeah, and you said finding him would be difficult." Royce drew back his hood and tugged his gloves off one finger at a time. "After Hadrian discovered he was the Guardian of the Heir, he knew exactly what he wanted for a Wintertide present—his very own Heir of Novron."

"And where is this mythical chimera?"

"Right underfoot, as it turns out. We're still pinpointing him, but best guess puts Gaunt in the palace dungeons. He is being held for execution on the 'Tide. We were planning to steal him before that."

"The heir is Degan Gaunt?"

"Ironic, huh? The Nationalist leader trying to overthrow the empire is actually the one man destined to rule it."

"You said *were*...so you're not planning to rescue him anymore?"

"No. Hadrian cut some deal with the regents. They've made him a knight, of all things. If he wins the joust, I think they promised to set Gaunt free. I'm not sure I trust them, though."

The carriage rolled through the streets and up a hill, causing the horse to slow its pace. One of Arcadius's open travel bundles fell to the floor, joining the rest of his clothes, a pile of books, his shoes, and a mound of blankets.

"Have you ever put anything away in your life?" Royce asked.

"Never saw the point. I'd just have to take it back out again. So, Hadrian's in the palace—but what are you doing here? I heard Medford was burned. Shouldn't you be checking on Gwen?"

"Already have. She's fine and staying at the Winds Abbey. That reminds me. You might want to stick around. If all goes well, you can come with us for the wedding."

"Whose?"

"Mine. I finally asked Gwen and she agreed, believe it or not."

"Did she?" Arcadius said, reaching out for one of the blankets to draw over his legs.

"Yeah, and here we both thought she had more sense than that. Can you picture me as a husband and a father?"

"Father? You've discussed children?"

"She wants them and even picked out names."

"Has she now? And how does that sit with you? Whining children and stagnation might be harder for you than all the challenges you've faced before. And this is one you can't walk out on if you decide it's not for you." The old man tilted his head to look over the tops of his glasses, his mouth slightly open. "Are you sure that's what you want?"

"You've been after me to find a good woman for years; now you're second-guessing Gwen? I know I won't find better."

"Oh no, it's not that. I just know your nature. I'm not sure you'll be content with the role of a family man."

"Are you trying to scare me off? I thought you wanted me to settle down. Besides, when you found me, I was a much different person."

"I remember," the wizard said thoughtfully. "You were like a rabid dog, snapping at everything and everyone. Clearly, my genius in matching you up with Hadrian worked wonders. I knew his noble heart would eventually soften yours."

"Yeah, well, travel with a guy long enough and you start picking up his bad habits. You have no idea how many times I almost killed him when we first started. I never bothered, because I expected the jobs would take care of that for me, but somehow he kept surviving."

"Well, I'm glad to see things worked out for you both. Gwen is a fine woman, and you're right—you couldn't do better."

"So you'll wait?"

"I'm afraid not. I was ordered to return immediately."

"But you'll come out to the Winds Abbey afterward, right? If you were not there, it would be like not having my fath—well, an uncle, at least."

Arcadius smiled, but it looked strained. After a moment of silence, the smile disappeared.

"What's wrong?" Royce asked.

"Hmm...oh, nothing."

"No, I've seen that look before. What is it, you old coot?"

"Oh—well, probably nothing," Arcadius said.

"Out with it."

"I was just in with the regents. With them were a sentinel

named Luis Guy and another very quiet fellow. I've never seen him before, but the name was familiar. You used to speak of him often."

"Who?"

"They introduced him as Lord Merrick Marius."

CHAPTER 13

THE HOUSE ON HEATH STREET

Mince was freezing.
The dawn's wind ripped through the coarse woven bag around his shoulders as if it were a fishnet. His nose ran. His ears were frozen. His once-numb fingers—now stuffed in his armpits—burned. He managed to escape most of the heavy gusts by standing in the recessed doorway of a millinery shop, but his feet were lost in a deep snowdrift, protected only by double wraps of cloth stuffed with straw. It would be worth it if he learned who lived in the house across the street, and if that name matched the one the hooded stranger had asked about.

Mr. Grim—or was it Mr. Baldwin?—had promised five silver to the boy who found the man he was looking for. Given the flood of strangers in town, it was a tall order to find a single man, but Mince knew his city well. Mr. Grim—it had to be Mr. Grim—explained the fellow would be a smart guy who visited the palace a lot. That right there told Mince to head to the Hill District. Elbright was checking out the inns, and Brand was watching the palace gate, but Mince was sure Heath Street was the place for someone with palace connections.

Mince looked at the house across the street. Only two stories and quite narrow, it was tucked tight between two others. Not as fancy as the big homes but still a fine place. Built entirely of stone, it had several glass windows, the kind you could actually see through. Most of the houses on Heath Street were that way. The only distinguishing marks on this one were the dagger and oak leaf embossment above the door and the noticeable lack of any Wintertide decoration. While the rest of the homes were bedecked in streamers and ropes of garland, the little house was bare. It used to belong to Lord Dermont, who had died in the Battle of Ratibor the past summer. Mince asked the kids who begged on the street if they knew who owned it now. All they could tell him was that the master of the house rode in a fine carriage with an imperial-uniformed driver and had three servants. Both the master and the servants kept to themselves, and all were new to Aquesta.

"This has to be the right house," Mince muttered, his words forming a little cloud. A lot was riding on him that morning. He had to be the one to win the money—for Kine's sake.

Mince had been on his own since he was six. Handouts were easy to come by at that age, but with each year, things got tougher. There was a lot of competition in the city, especially now, with all the refugees. Elbright, Brand, and Kine were the ones who kept him alive. Elbright had a knife, and Brand had killed another kid in a fight over a tunic—it made others think twice before messing with them—but it was Kine, their master pickpocket, who was his best friend.

Kine had taken sick a few weeks earlier. He began throwing up and sweating like it was summer. They each gave him some of their food, but he was not getting better. For the past three days, he had not even been able to leave The Nest. Each time Mince saw him, Kine looked worse: whiter, thinner, blotchier, and shivering—always shivering. Elbright had seen the sickness before and said not to waste any more food on Kine, as he was as good as dead. Mince still shared a bit of his bread, but his friend rarely ate it. He hardly ate anything anymore.

Mince crossed the street to the front of the house, and to escape the bitter wind, he slipped to the right of the porch stairs. His foot sank deeper than expected and his arms windmilled as he fell down a short flight of steps leading to a root cellar. Mince landed on his back, sending up a cloud of powder that blinded him. He reached around and felt a hinge. His frozen hands continued to search and found a large lock holding the door fast.

He stood and dusted himself off. As he did, he noticed a gap under the stairs, a drain of some kind. His fall had uncovered the opening. Hearing the approach of the butcher's wagon, he quickly slithered inside.

"What will you have today, sir?"

"Goose."

"No beef? No pork?"

"Tomorrow starts Blood Week, so I'll wait."

"I have some right tasty pigeons and a couple of quail."

"I'll take the quail. You can keep the pigeons."

Mince had not eaten since the previous morning, and all their talk about food reminded his stomach.

"Very good, Mr. Jenkins. Are you sure you don't require anything else?"

"Yes, I'm sure that will be all."

Jenkins, Mince thought, *that is probably the servant's name, not the master of the house.*

Footfalls came down the steps and Mince held his breath as the manservant brushed the snow away from the cellar door with a broom. He opened it to allow the butcher entry.

"It's freezing out here," Jenkins muttered, and trotted out of sight.

"That it is, sir. That it is."

The butcher's boy carried the goose, already plucked and beheaded, down into the cellar and then returned to the wagon for the quails. The door was open. It might have been the cold, the hunger, or the thought of five silver—most likely it was all three—that sent Mince scurrying inside quick as a ferret without bothering to consider his decision. He scrambled behind a pile of sacks that smelled of potatoes and crouched low while trying to catch his breath. The butcher's boy returned with the birds, hung by their feet, and stepped out again. The door slammed, and Mince heard the lock snap shut.

After the brilliant world of sun and snow, Mince was blind. He stayed still and listened. The footsteps of the manservant crossed overhead, but they soon faded and everything was quiet. The boy knew there was no way to escape the cellar undetected, but he chose not to worry about that. The next time there was a delivery, he would just make a run for it. He could get through the door on surprise, and no one could catch him once he was in the open.

When Mince looked around again, he noticed that he could see as his eyes adjusted to the light filtering down through gaps in the boards. The cellar was cool, although balmy when compared to the street, and filled with crates, sacks, and jugs. Sides of bacon hung from the ceiling. A small box lined with straw held more eggs than he could count. Mince cracked one of them over his mouth and swallowed. Finding a tin of milk, he took two big mouthfuls and got mostly cream. Thick and sweet, it left him grinning with delight. Looking at all the containers, Mince felt as if he had fallen into a treasure room. He could live there by hiding in the piles, sleeping in the sacks, and eating himself fat. Hunting through the shelves for more treats, Mince found a jar of molasses and was trying to get the lid off when he heard steps overhead.

Muffled voices were coming closer. "I will be at the palace the rest of the day."

"I'll have the carriage brought at once, my lord."

"I want you and Poe to take this medallion to the silversmith. Get him started making a duplicate. Don't leave it, and don't let it out of your sight. Stay with him and watch over it. It's *extremely* valuable."

"Yes, my lord."

"And bring it back at the end of the day. I expect you'll need to take it over several times."

"But your dinner, my lord. Surely Mr. Poe can—"

"I'll get my meals at the palace. I'm not trusting Poe with this. He is going along only as protection."

"But, my lord, he's hardly more than a boy—"

"Never mind that, just do as instructed. Where is Dobbs?"

"Cleaning the bedrooms, I believe."

"Take him too. You'll be gone all day, and I don't want him left here alone."

"Yes, my lord."

My lord, my lord! Mince was ready to scream in frustration. *Why not just use the bugger's name?*

~

Mince listened for a long time before deciding the house was empty. He crossed the cellar, climbed the steps, and tried the door to the house. It opened. Careful and quiet as a mouse, he crept out. A board creaked when he put his weight on it. He froze in terror but nothing happened.

He was alone in the kitchen. Food was everywhere: bread,

pickles, eggs, cheese, smoked meats, and honey. Mince sampled each one as he passed. He had eaten bread before, but this was soft and creamy compared to the three-day-old biscuits he was used to. The pickles were spicy, the cheese was a delight, and the meat, despite being tough from curing, was a delicacy he rarely knew. He also found a small barrel of beer that was the best he had ever had. Mince found himself light-headed and stuffed as he left the kitchen with a slice of pie in one hand, a wedge of cheese in the other, and a stringy strip of meat in his pocket.

The inside of the house was more impressive than the exterior. Sculptured plaster, carved wood, finely woven tapestries, and silk curtains lined the walls. A fire burned in the main room. Logs softly crackled, their warmth spreading throughout the lower floor. Crystal glasses sat inside cherry cabinets, fat candles and statuettes rested on tables, and books filled the shelves. Mince had never held a book before. He finished the pie, stuffed the cheese in his other pocket, and then pulled one down. The book was thick and heavier than he had expected. He tried to open it, but it slipped through his greasy fingers and struck the floor with a heavy thud that echoed through the house. He froze, held his breath, and waited for footsteps or a shout.

Silence.

Picking up the book, he felt the raised leather spine and marveled at the gold letters on the cover. He imagined the words revealed some powerful magic—a secret that could make men rich or grant eternal life. Setting the book back on the shelf with a bit of sadness, Mince moved toward the stairs.

He climbed to the second story, where there were several bedrooms. The largest had an adjoining study with a desk and more books. On the desk were parchments, more mysterious words—more secrets. He picked up one of the pages, turned it sideways and then upside down, as if a different orientation might force the letters to reveal their mysteries. He grew frustrated. Dropping the page back on the desk, he started to leave when a light caught his attention.

A strange glow came from within the wardrobe. He stared at it for a long time before venturing to open the door. Vests, tunics, and cloaks filled the cabinet. Pushed to the rear was a robe — a robe that shimmered with its own light. Mesmerized, Mince risked a hesitant touch. The material was unlike anything he had felt before — smoother than a polished stone and softer than a down feather. The moment he touched the fabric, the garment instantly changed from dark, shimmering silver to an alluring purple and glowed the brightest where his fingers contacted it.

Mince glanced nervously around the room. He was still alone. On an impulse, he pulled the robe out. The hem brushed the floor and he immediately draped it over his arm. Letting the robe touch the ground did not seem right. He started to put it on and had one arm in the sleeve when he stopped. The robe felt cold, and it turned a dark blue, almost black. When he pulled his arm out, the beautiful purple glow returned.

Mince reminded himself he was not there to steal.

On principle, he was not against thieving. He stole all the time. He picked pockets, grabbed-and-ran from markets, and even looted drunks. But he had never robbed a house — certainly not a Heath Street house. Thieving from nobles was dangerous, and the authorities were the least of his worries. If the thieves' guild found out, their punishment would be worse than anything the magistrate would come up with. No one would raise a stink over a starving boy taking food, but the robe was a different matter. With all the books and writing in the house, it was obvious the owner was a wizard or warlock of some sort.

It was too risky.

What would I do with it, anyway?

While it would put old Brand the Bold's tunic to shame, he could never put it on. The robe was too big for him to wear and Mince would not dare cut it. Even if he managed it, the robe would draw every eye in the city. He reached out to put it back in the wardrobe, deciding he could not risk taking it. Once more the robe went dark. Still holding it, he pulled his arm out, and it glowed again. Puzzled but still determined, Mince hung it back up. The moment he let go, the robe fell to the floor. He tried again and it fell once more.

"All right, go ahead and stay there," he said, and started to turn away.

The robe instantly flared to a brilliant white. All shadows in the room vanished and Mince staggered backward, squinting to see.

"Okay, okay. Stop it. Stop it!" he shouted, and the light dimmed to blue again.

Mince did not move. He stood staring at the robe as it lay on the floor. The light was throbbing—growing bright and dim almost as if it were breathing. He watched it for several minutes, trying to figure it out.

Slowly, he stepped closer and picked it up. "Ya want me to take you?"

The robe glowed the pretty purple color.

"Can I wear you?"

Dark blue.

"So . . . ya just want me to steal you?"

Purple.

"Don't ya belong here?"

Blue.

"You're being held against yer will?"

The robe flashed purple so brightly that it made him blink.

"You're not—ya know—*cursed*, are you? Ya aren't going to hurt me—are ya?"

Blue.

"Is it okay if I fold ya up and stuff ya inside my tunic?"

Purple.

As big as it was, the garment compressed easily. Mince stuffed it in the top of his shirt, making him look like a busty girl. Because he was already stealing the robe, he also picked up a handful of parchments and stuffed them in as well. He was not going to find out who lived there while the occupants were out, and Mince did not want to stick around for them to discover that the robe was missing. Mr. Grim looked to be the type to know letters, or know someone who did. Maybe he could tell enough from the parchments for Mince to win the silver.

⚘

Royce sat on the bleachers in Imperial Square, observing the patterns of the city. Wintertide was less than two weeks away and the city swelled with pilgrims. They filled the plaza, bustled by the street vendors and open shops, and shouted holiday greetings and obscenities in equal measure. Wealthy, blanket-wrapped merchants rode in carriages, pointing at the various sights. Visiting tradesmen carried tools over their shoulders, hoping to pick up work, while established vendors scowled at them. Threadbare farmers and peasants visiting Aquesta to see the holy empress huddled in groups, staring in awe at their surroundings.

Betrayal in Medford. Royce read the sign posted in front of a small theater. It indicated nightly performances during the week leading up to Wintertide's Eve. From the barkers on the street, he determined the play was the imperial variation of the popular *The Crown Conspiracy*, which the empire had outlawed. Apparently in this version, the plotting prince and his witch sister decide to murder their father, and only the good archduke stands in the way of their evil plans.

Four patrols of eight men circled the streets. At least one group checked in at each square every hour. They were swift and harsh in their peacekeeping. Dressed in mail and carrying heavy weapons, they brutally beat and dragged away anyone causing a nuisance or being accused of a crime. They did not bother to hear the suspect's side of the story. They did not care who had trespassed on whom, or whether the accusation was truth or fiction. Their goal was order, not justice.

An interesting side effect, which would have been comical if the results had not been so ugly, was that street vendors falsely accused their out-of-town competitors of offenses. Local vendors banded together, forming an alliance to denounce the upstarts. Before long, people learned to gather at the squares just before an imperial patrol was expected to arrive, or follow the men as they patrolled. The spectacle of violence was just one more holiday show.

Two good-sized pigs, attempting to escape their fates of Blood Week, ran through the square, trailed by a parade of children and two mongrel dogs chasing after them. A butcher wearing a bloodstained apron and looking exhausted from running paused to wipe his brow.

Royce spotted the boy deftly dodging his way through the crowd. Pausing briefly to avoid the train chasing the pig, Mince locked eyes with Royce, then casually strolled over to the bleachers. Royce was pleased to see no one watched the boy's progress too closely.

"Looking for me?" Royce asked.

"Yes, sir," Mince replied.

"You found him?"

"Don't know—maybe—never got a name or a look. Got these, though." The boy pulled some parchments from his shirt. "I snatched them from a house on Heath Street. It has a new owner. Can ya read?"

Royce ignored the question as he scanned the parchments. The handwriting was unmistakable. He slipped them into his cloak.

"Where exactly is this house?"

Mince smiled. "I'm right, aren't I? Do I get the coin?"

"Where's the house?"

"Heath Street, south off the top, harbor side, little place right across from Buchan's Hattery. Ya can't miss it. There's a crest of an oak leaf and dagger above the door. Now, what about the money?"

Royce did not respond but focused on the boy's overstuffed tunic, which glowed as if he had a star trapped inside.

Mince saw his look and promptly folded his arms. Tilting his head down, he whispered, "Quit it!"

"Did you take something else from the house?"

Mince shook his head. "It has nothing to do with ya."

"If that's from the same house, you'll want to give it to me."

Mince stuck his lip out defiantly. "It's nothing and it's mine. I'm a thief, see. I took it for myself in case I got the wrong house. I didn't want to risk my neck and get nothing. So it's my bonus. That's how professional thieves work, see? Ya might not like it, but it's how we do things. You and me had a deal and I've done my part. Don't get all high-and-mighty or go on about bad morals, 'cuz I get enough of that from the monks."

The light grew brighter and began flashing on and off.

Royce was disturbed. "What *is* that?"

"Like I said, it's none of yer business," Mince snapped, and pulled away. He looked down once more and whispered, "Stop it, will ya! People can see. I'll get in trouble."

"Listen, I don't have a problem with a little theft," Royce told him. "You can trust me on that. But if you took something of value from *that* house, you'd be wise to give it to me. This might sound like a trick, but I'm only trying to help. You don't understand who you're dealing with. The owner will find you. He's very meticulous."

"What's that mean...*meticulous*?"

"Let's just say he's not a forgiving man. He will kill you, Elbright, and Brand. Not to mention anyone else you have regular contact with, just to be thorough."

"I'm keeping it!" Mince snapped.

Royce rolled his eyes and sighed.

The boy struggled to cover up by doubling over and wrapping his arms around his chest. As he did, the light blinked faster and now alternated different colors. "By Mar, just give me the money, will ya? Before one of the guards sees."

Royce handed him five silver coins and watched as the boy took off. He ran hunched over, emitting a rapidly blinking light that faded and eventually stopped.

⤎

Mince entered the loft by climbing to the roof of the warehouse, pulling back a loose board near the eaves, and scrambling through the hole. The Nest, as they dubbed their home, was the result of poor carpentry. A mistake made when the East Sundries Company had built their warehouse against the common wall of the Bingham Carriage House & Blacksmith Shop. A mismeasurement had left a gap, which was sealed shut with side boards. Over the years, the wood had warped.

While trying to break into the warehouse, Elbright had noticed a gap between the boards that revealed the hidden space. He never found a way into the storehouse, but he had discovered the perfect hideout. The little attic was three feet tall and five feet wide and ran the length of the common wall. Thanks to the long hours of the blacksmiths, who usually kept a fire burning, it was also marginally heated.

A collection of treasures gathered from the city's garbage littered The Nest, including moth-eaten garments, burned bits of lumber, fragments of hides tossed out by the tanner, cracked pots, and chipped cups.

Kine lay huddled in a ball against the chimney. Mince had made him a bed of straw and tucked their best blanket around him, but his friend still shivered. The little bit of his face not covered by the blanket was pale white, and his bluish lips quivered miserably.

"How ya doing?" Mince asked.

"C-c-cold," Kine replied weakly.

Mince put a hand to the brick chimney. "Bastards are trying to save coal again."

"Is there any food?" Kine asked.

Mince pulled the wedge of cheese from his pocket. Kine took a bite and immediately started to vomit. Nothing came up, but he retched just the same. He continued to convulse for several minutes, then collapsed, exhausted.

"I'm like Tibith, ain't I?" Kine managed to say.

"No," Mince lied, sitting down beside him. He hoped to keep Kine warm with his body. "You'll be fine the moment the fire is lit. You'll see."

Mince fished the money out of his other pocket to show Kine. "Hey, look, I got coin—five silver! I could buy ya a hot meal, how would that be?"

"Don't," Kine replied. "Don't waste it."

"What do ya mean? When is hot soup ever a waste?"

"I'm like Tibith. Soup won't help."

"I told ya, yer not like that," Mince insisted, slamming the silver in a cup he decided at that moment to use as a bank.

"I can't feel my feet anymore, Mince, and my hands tingle. I ache all over and my head pounds and…and…I pissed myself today. Did you hear me—I pissed myself! I *am* like Tibith. I'm just like he was and I'm gonna die just like him."

"I said ya ain't. Now quit it!"

"My lips are blue, ain't they?"

"Be quiet, Kine, just—"

"By Mar, Mince, I *don't want to die*!" Kine shook even more as he cried.

Mince felt his stomach churn as tears dripped down his cheeks too. Victims never recovered once their lips went blue.

He looked around for something else to wrap his friend in and then remembered the robe.

"There," he muttered, draping the robe over Kine. "After all the trouble you've been, try to be of some use. Keep him warm or I'll toss ya in the smith's fire."

"W-what?" Kine moaned.

"Nothing, go to sleep."

᠅

Royce heard the key turn. The bolt shifted and the door opened on well-oiled hinges. Four pairs of feet shuffled on the slate of the foyer. He heard the sound of the door closing, the brush of material, and the snap of a cloak. One pair of feet scuffed abruptly as if their owner unexpectedly found himself on the edge of a precipice.

"Mr. Jenkins," Merrick's voice said, "I want you and Dobbs to take the rest of the evening off."

"But, sir, I—"

"This is no time to argue. Please, Mr. Jenkins, just leave. Hopefully I will see you in the morning."

"Hopefully?" This voice was familiar. Royce recognized Poe, the cook's mate on the *Emerald Storm*. It took him a moment, but then Royce understood. "What do you mean you will— Hold on. Is *he* here? How do you know?"

"I want you to go too, Poe."

"Not if he's here. You'll need protection."

"If he wanted me dead, I would already be lying in a bloody puddle. So I think it is fair to surmise that I am safe. You, on the other hand, are a different story. I doubt he knew you would be here. Now that he knows your connection to me, the only thing keeping you alive is that he is more interested in talking to me than slitting your throat, at least for the moment."

"Let him try. I think—"

"Poe, leave the thinking to me. And never tempt him like that. This is not a man to toy with. Trust me, he'd kill you without difficulty. I know. I worked with him. We specialized in assassinations and he's better at it than I am—particularly spur-of-the-moment killings—and right now you're a very tempting spur. Now, get out while you can. Disappear for a while, just to be safe."

"What makes you think he even knows I'm here?" Poe asked.

"He's in the drawing room, listening to us right now. Sitting in the blue chair with its back to the wall, he's waiting for me to join him. I'm sure he has a crystal glass half filled with the Montemorcey wine I bought and left in the pantry for him. He's holding it in his left hand so if, for whatever reason, he has to draw his dagger, he won't need to put the glass down first. He hates to waste Montemorcey. He's swirling it, letting it breathe, and while he's been here for some time, he has yet to taste it. He won't drink until I sit across from him—until I too have a glass."

"He suspects you poisoned it?"

"No, he hasn't tasted the wine because…well, it would just be rude. He'll have a glass of cider waiting for me, as he knows I no longer drink spirits."

"And how do you know all this?"

"Because I know him just as I know you. Right now you're fighting an urge to enter the drawing room to see if I'm right. Don't. You'll never come out again, and I don't want you staining my new carpet. Now leave. I will contact you when I need to."

"Are you sure? Yeah, okay, stupid question."

The door opened, then closed, and footsteps could be heard going down the porch stairs.

There was a pause and then a light flared. Merrick Marius entered the dark room holding a single candle. "I hope you don't mind. I prefer to be able to see you too."

Merrick lit four sconce lights, added some logs to the fire, and stirred the embers to life with a poker. He watched them for a long moment, then placed the tool back on its hook before taking a seat opposite Royce, next to the poured glass of cider.

"To old friends?" Merrick asked, holding up his drink.

"To old friends," Royce agreed, and the two sipped.

Merrick was dressed in a knee-length coat of burgundy velvet, a finely embroidered vest, and a startlingly white ruffled shirt.

"You're doing well for yourself," Royce observed.

"I can't complain. I'm Magistrate of Colnora now. Have you heard?"

"I hadn't. Your father would be proud."

"He said I couldn't do it. Do you remember? He said I was too smart for my own good." Merrick took another sip. "I suppose you're angry about Tur Del Fur."

"You crossed a line."

"I know. I am sorry about that. You were the only one who could do that job. If I could have found someone else..." Merrick crossed his legs and looked over his glass at Royce. "You're not here to kill me, so I'll assume your visit is about Hadrian."

"Is that your doing? This *deal*?"

Merrick shook his head. "Actually, Guy came up with that. They tried to persuade Hadrian to kill Breckton for money and a title. My only contribution was providing the proper incentive."

"They're dangling Gaunt?" Royce asked.

Merrick nodded. "And the Witch of Melengar."

"Arista? When did they get her?"

"A few months ago. She and her bodyguard tried to free Gaunt. He died and she was captured."

Royce took another drink and then set his glass down before asking, "They're going to kill Hadrian, aren't they?"

"Yes. The regents know they can't just let him go. After he kills Breckton, they will arrest him for murder, throw him in prison, and execute him along with Gaunt and Arista on Wintertide."

"Why do they want Breckton dead?"

"They offered him Melengar in order to separate him from Ballentyne. He refused, and now they're afraid the Earl of Chadwick will attempt to use Breckton to overthrow the empire. They're spooked and feel their only chance to eliminate him is by using a Teshlor-trained warrior. Nice skills to have in a partner, by the way—good choice."

Royce sipped his wine and thought awhile. "Can you save him?"

"Hadrian?" Merrick paused and then answered, "Yes."

The word hung there.

"What do you want?" Royce said.

"Interesting that you should ask. As it turns out, I have another job that you would be perfect for."

"What kind?"

"Find-and-recover. I can't give you the details yet, but it's dangerous. Two other groups have already failed. Of course, I wasn't involved in those attempts, and you weren't leading the operation. Agree to take the job and I'll make sure nothing happens to Hadrian."

"I've retired."

"I heard that rumor."

Royce drained his glass and stood. "I'll think about it."

"Don't wait too long, Royce. If you want me to work this, I'll need a couple of days to prepare. Trust me, you'll want my help. A dungeon rescue will fail. The prison is dwarven made."

CHAPTER 14

TOURNAMENT DAY

The morning dawned to the wails and cries of the doomed. The snow ran red as axe and mallet slaughtered livestock whose feed had run out. Blood Week happened every winter, but exactly what day it began depended on the bounty of the fall harvest. For an orphan in Aquesta, the best part of winter was Blood Week.

Nothing went to waste—feet, snouts, and even bones sold—but with so much to cleave, butchers could not keep track of every cut. The city's poor circled the butcher shops like human vultures, searching for an inattentive cutter. Most butchers hired extra help, but they always underestimated the dangers. There were never enough arms carrying the meat to safety or enough eyes keeping lookout. A few daring raids even managed to carry off whole legs of beef. As the day wore on and workers grew exhausted, some desperate butchers resorted to hiring the very thieves they guarded against.

Mince had left The Nest early, looking for what he could scrounge for breakfast. The sun had barely peeked above the city wall when he managed to snatch a fine bit of beef from Gilim's Slaughterhouse. After a particularly sound stroke from Gilim's cleaver, a piece of shank skipped across the slick table, fell in the snow, and slid downhill. Mince happened to be in the right place at the right time. He snatched it and ran with the bloody fist-sized chunk of meat clutched inside his tunic. Anyone noticing the sprinting boy might conclude he was mortally wounded.

He was anxious to devour his prize, but exposing it would risk losing the meat to a bigger kid. Worse yet, a butcher or guard might spot him. Mince wished Brand and Elbright were with him. They had gone to the slaughterhouses down on Coswall, where most of the butchering would be done. The fights there would be fierce. Grown men would struggle for scraps alongside the orphans. Mince was too small to compete. Even if he managed to grab a hunk, someone would likely take it, beating him senseless. The other two boys could hold their own. Elbright was as tall as most men now, and Brand even larger, but Mince had to satisfy himself with the smaller butcher shops.

Arriving on the street in front of the Bingham Carriage House, Mince stopped. He needed to get inside, but the thought of what he might find there frightened him. In his haste to get an early start, he had forgotten about Kine. For the past few days, his friend's loud wheezing had frequently woken Mince, but he could not remember having heard anything that morning.

Mince had seen too much death. He knew eight boys— friends—who had died from cold, sickness, or starvation. They always went in winter, their bodies stiff and frozen. Each lifeless form had once been a person—laughing, joking, running, crying—then was just a thing, like a torn blanket or a broken lantern. After finding remains, Mince would drag them to the pile—there was always a pile in winter. No matter how short a distance he needed to drag the body, the trip felt like miles. He remembered the good times and moments they had spent together. Then he would look down at the stiff, pale thing.

Will I be the thing one day? Will someone drag me to the pile?

He gritted his teeth, entered the alley, climbed to the roof, and pulled back the board. Leaving the brilliant sunlight, Mince crawled blindly into the crevice. The Nest was dark and silent. There was no sound of breathing—wheezing or otherwise. Mince reached forward, imagining Kine's cold, stiff body. The thought caused his hand to shake even as he willed his fingers to spread out, searching. Touching the silken material of the robe, he recoiled as it began to glow.

Kine was not there.

The robe lay on the floor as if Kine had melted during the night. Mince pulled the material toward him. As he did, the glow increased enough to reach every corner of the room. He was alone. Kine was gone. Not even his body remained.

Mince sat for a second, and then a thought surfaced. He dropped the robe in horror and kicked it away. The robe's glow throbbed and grew fainter.

"Ya ate him!" Mince cried. "Ya lied to me. Ya *are* cursed!"

The light went out and Mince backed as far away as possible. He had to get away from the killer robe, but now it was lying between him and the exit.

A silhouette passed in front of the opening, momentarily blocking the sunlight.

"Mince?" Kine's voice said. "Mince, look. I got me lamb chops!"

Kine entered and replaced the board. Mince's eyes adjusted until he could see his friend, holding a pair of bloody bones. His chin was stained red. "I woulda saved you one, but I couldn't find you. By Mar, I was famished!"

"Ya all right, Kine?"

"I'm great. I'm still a little hungry, but other than that, I feel fantastic."

"But last night…" Mince started. "Last night ya—ya—didn't look so good."

Kine nodded. "I had all kinds of queer dreams, that's for sure."

"What kind of dreams?"

"Hmm? Oh, just odd stuff. I was drowning in this dark lake. I couldn't breathe 'cuz water was spilling into my mouth every time I tried to take a breath. I tried to swim, but my arms and legs barely moved—it was a terrible nightmare." Kine noticed the beef shank Mince still held. "Hey! You got some meat too? You wanna cook it up? I'm still hungry."

"Huh? Oh, sure," Mince said as he looked down at the robe while handing the beef to Kine.

"I love Blood Week, don't you?"

◈

Trumpets blared and drums rolled as the pennants of twenty-seven noble houses snapped in the late-morning breeze. People filed into the stands at Highcourt Fields on the opening day of the Grand Avryn Wintertide Tournament. The contest would last ten days, ending with the Feast of Tides. Across the city, shops closed and work stopped. Only the smoking and salting of meat continued, as Blood Week ran parallel to the tournament, and the slaughter could not halt even for such an august event. Many thought the timing was an omen that signaled the games would produce a higher number of accidents, which only added to the excitement. Every year crowds delighted in seeing blood.

Two years before, the baron Linder of Maranon had died when a splintered lance held by Sir Gilbert pierced the visor of his helm. The same year Sir Dulnar of Rhenydd had his right hand severed in the final round of the sword competition. Nothing, however, compared to the showdown five years ago between Sir Jervis and Francis Stanley, the Earl of Harborn. In the final tilt of the tournament, Sir Jervis—who had already borne a grudge against the earl—passed over the traditional Lance of Peace and picked up the Lance of War. Against council, the earl agreed to the deadly challenge. Jervis's lance pierced Stanley's cuirass as if it were parchment and continued on through his opponent's chest. The knight did not escape the encounter unscathed. Stanley's lance pierced Jervis's helm and entered his eye socket. Both fell dead. Officials judged the earl the victor due to the extra point for a head blow.

Centuries earlier, Highcourt Fields had functioned as the supreme noble court of law in Avryn. Civil disputes inevitably escalated until accused and accuser turned to combat to determine who was right. Soon the only dispute became who was the best warrior. As the realms of Avryn expanded, trips to Highcourt became less convenient. Monthly sessions were eventually reduced to biyearly events where all grievances were settled over a two-week session. These were held on the holy days of Summersrule and Wintertide, in the belief Maribor was more attentive at these times.

Over the years, the celebration grew. Instead of merely proving their honor, the combatants also fought for glory and gold. Knights from across the nation came to face each other for the most prestigious honor in Avryn: Champion of the Highcourt Games.

Adorned in the distinct colors of their owners, richly decorated tents of the noble competitors clustered around the fringe of the field. Squires, grooms, and pages polished armor and brushed their lords' horses. Knights entered in the sword competition limbered up with blades and shields, sparring

with their squires. Officials walked the line of the carousel—
a series of posts dangling steel rings no larger than a man's
fist. They measured the height of each post and the angle of
each ring, which men on galloping horses would try to collect
with lances. Archers took practice shots. Spearmen sprinted
and lunged, testing the sand's traction. On the great jousting
field, horses snorted and huffed as unarmored combatants
took practice rides across the course.

Amidst all this activity, Hadrian braced himself against a
post as Wilbur beat on his chest with a large hammer. Nimbus
had arranged for the smith to adjust Hadrian's borrowed
armor. Obtaining a suit was simple, but making it fit properly
was another matter.

"Here, sir," Renwick said, holding out a pile of cloth to
Hadrian.

"What's that for?" Hadrian asked.

Renwick looked at him curiously. "It's your padding, sir."

"Don't hand it to him, lad," Wilbur scolded. "Stuff it in!"

Embarrassment flooded the boy's face as he began wadding
up the cloth and shoving it into the wide gap between the steel
and Hadrian's tunic.

"Pack it tight!" Wilbur snapped. He took a handful of padding and stuffed it against Hadrian's chest, ramming it in
hard.

"That's a bit *too* tight," Hadrian complained.

Wilbur gave him a sidelong glance. "You might not think
that when Sir Murthas's lance hits you. I don't want to be
accused of bad preparation because this boy failed to pack you
properly."

"Sir Hadrian," Renwick began, "I was wondering—I was
thinking—would it be all right if I were to enter the squire
events?"

"Don't see why not. Are you any good?"

"No, but I would like to try just the same. Sir Malness never allowed it. He didn't want me to embarrass him."

"Are you really that bad?"

"I've never been allowed to train. Sir Malness forbade me from using his horse. He was fond of saying, 'A man upon a horse has a certain way of looking at the world, and a lad such as yourself should not get accustomed to the experience, as it will only produce disappointment.'"

"Sounds like Sir Malness was a real pleasant guy," Hadrian said.

Renwick offered an uncomfortable smile and turned away. "I have watched the events many times—studied them, really—and I have ridden but never used a lance."

"Why don't you get my mount and we'll have a look at you?"

Renwick nodded and ran to fetch the horse. Ethelred had provided a brown charger named Malevolent for Hadrian. Bred for stamina and agility, the horse was dressed in a chanfron to protect the animal from poorly aimed lances. Despite the name, he was a fine horse, strong and aggressive, but not vicious. Malevolent did not bite or kick, and upon meeting Hadrian, the horse affectionately rubbed his head up and down against the fighter's chest.

"Get aboard," Hadrian told the boy, who grinned and scrambled into the high-backed saddle. Hadrian handed him a practice lance and the shield with green and white quadrants, which the regents had supplied.

"Lean forward and keep the lance tucked tight against your side. Squeeze it in with your elbow to steady it. Now ride in a circle so I can watch you."

For all his initial enthusiasm, the boy looked less confident as he struggled to hold the long pole and guide the horse at the same time.

"The stirrups need to be tighter," Sir Breckton said as he rode up.

Breckton sat astride a strong white charger adorned with an elegant caparison of gold and blue stripes. A matching pennant flew from the tip of a lance booted in his stirrup. Dressed in brightly polished armor, he had a plumed helm under one arm and a sheer blue scarf tied around the other.

"I wanted to wish you good fortune this day," he said to Hadrian.

"Thanks."

"You ride against Murthas, do you not? He's good with a lance. Don't underestimate him." Breckton studied Hadrian critically. "Your cuirass is light. That's very brave of you."

Hadrian looked down at himself, confused. He had never worn such heavy armor. His experience with a lance remained confined to actual combat, in which targets were rarely knights. As it was, Hadrian felt uncomfortable and restricted.

Breckton motioned to the metal plate on his own side. "Bolted armor adds an extra layer of protection where one is most likely to be hit. And where is your elbow pocket?"

Hadrian was confused for a moment. "Oh, that plate? I had the smith take it off. It made it impossible to hold the lance tight."

Breckton chuckled. "You do realize that *plate* is meant to brace the butt of the lance, right?"

Hadrian shrugged. "I've never jousted in a tournament before."

"I see." Sir Breckton nodded. "Would you be offended should I offer advice?"

"No, go ahead."

"Keep your head up. Lean forward. Use the stirrups to provide leverage to deliver stronger blows. Absorb the blows you receive with the high back of your saddle to avoid being driven from your horse."

"Again, thank you."

"Not at all, I am pleased to be of service. If you have any questions, I will be most happy to answer them."

"Really?" Hadrian responded mischievously. "In that case, is that a token I see on your arm?"

Breckton glanced down at the bit of cloth. "This is the scarf of Lady Amilia of Tarin Vale. I ride for her this day—for her and her honor." He looked out at the field. "It appears the tournament is about to start. I see Murthas taking his position at the alley, and you are up first. May Maribor guide the arm of the worthy." Breckton nodded respectfully and left.

Renwick returned and dismounted.

"You did well," Hadrian told him, taking the squire's place on the charger. "You just need a bit more practice. Assuming I survive this tilt, we'll work on it some more."

The boy carried Hadrian's helm in one hand and, taking the horse's lead in the other, led the mounted knight to the field. They entered the gate, circled the alley, and came to a stop next to a small wooden stage.

Ahead of Hadrian lay the main arena, which an army of workers had spent weeks preparing by clearing snow and laying sand. The field was surrounded by a sea of spectators divided into sections designated by color. Purple housed the ruler and his immediate family; blue was for the ranked gentry, red for the church officials, yellow for the baronage, green for the artisans, and white for the peasantry, which was the largest and only uncovered section.

Hadrian's father used to bring him to the games, but not for entertainment. Observing combat had been part of his studies. Still, Hadrian had been thrilled to see the fights and cheer the victors along with the rest. His father had no use for the winners and cared to discuss only the losers. Danbury questioned Hadrian after each fight, asking what the defeated knight had done wrong and how he could have won.

Hadrian had hardly listened. He was distracted by the spectacle—the knights in shining armor, the women in colorful gowns, the incredible horses. He knew one knight's saddle was worth more than their home and his father's blacksmith shop combined. How magnificent they had all seemed in comparison to his commoner father. It had never occurred to him that Danbury Blackwater could defeat every knight in every contest.

As a youth, Hadrian had dreamed of fighting at Highcourt a million times. Unlike the Palace of the Four Winds, this field was a church to him. Battles were respectful—not to the death. Swords were blunted, archers used targets, and jousts were performed with the Lance of Peace. A combatant lost points if he killed his opponent, and could be expelled from the tournament even for injuring a competitor's horse. Hadrian had found that strange. Even after his father had explained that the horse was innocent, he had not understood. He did now.

A large man with a loud voice stood on a platform in front of the purple section, shouting to those assembled: "...is the chief knight of Alburn and the son of the Earl of Fentin, and he is renowned for his skill in the games and at court. I give to you—Sir Murthas!"

The crowd erupted in applause, drumming their feet on the hollow planks. Ethelred and Saldur sat to either side of a throne that remained as empty as the one in the banquet hall. At the start of the day, officials had announced that the empress felt too ill that morning to attend.

"From Rhenydd he hails," the man on the box shouted as he gestured toward Hadrian, "only recently knighted amidst the carnage of the bloody Battle of Ratibor. He wandered forest and field to reach these games. For his first tournament ever, I present to you—Sir Hadrian!"

Some clapping trickled down from the stands, but it was only polite applause. The contest was already over in the eyes of the crowd.

Hadrian had never held a Lance of Peace. Lighter than a war lance, which had a metal tip, this one was all wood. The broad flared end floated awkwardly but it was still solid oak and not to be underestimated. He checked his feet in the stirrups and gripped the horse with his legs.

Across the sand-strewn alley, Sir Murthas sat on his gray destrier. His horse was a strong, angry-looking steed cloaked in a damask caparison covered in a series of black and white squares and fringed with matching tassels. Murthas himself held a lozenge shield and wore a matching surcoat and cape of black and white diamonds. He snapped his visor shut just as the trumpeters sounded the fanfare and the flagman raised his banner.

Mesmerized by the spectacle, Hadrian let his gaze roam from the stands to the snapping pennants and finally to the percussionists beating on their great drums. The pounding rolled like thunder such that Hadrian could feel it in his chest, yet the roar of the crowd overwhelmed it. Many leapt to their feet in anticipation. Hundreds waited anxiously, with every eye fixed upon the riders. As a boy in the white stands, Hadrian had held his father's fingers, hearing and feeling that same percussive din. He had wished to be one of those knights waiting at their gates—waiting for glory. The wish had been a fantasy that only a young boy who knew so little of the world could imagine—an impossible dream he had forgotten until that moment.

The drums stopped. The flag fell. Across the alley, Murthas spurred his horse and charged.

Caught by surprise, Hadrian was several seconds behind. He spurred Malevolent and lurched forward. The audience sprang to their feet, gasping in astonishment. Some screamed in fear. Hadrian ignored them, intent on his task.

Feeling the rhythm of the horse's stride, he became one with the motion. Hadrian pushed the balls of his feet down, taking up every ounce of slack and pressing his lower back against the saddle. Slowly, carefully, he lowered the lance, pulling it to his side and keeping its movement in sync with the horse's rapid gait. He calculated the drop rate with the approach of his target.

The wind roared past Hadrian's ears and stung his eyes as the charger built up speed. The horse's hooves pounded the soft track, creating explosions of sand. Murthas raced at him, his black and white cape flying. The horses ran full out, nostrils flaring, muscles rippling, harnesses jangling.

Crack!

Hadrian felt his lance jolt, then splinter. Running out of lane, he discarded the broken lance and pulled back on the reins. Hadrian was embarrassed by his slow start and did not want Murthas to get the jump on him again. Intent on getting the next lance first, he wheeled his charger and saw Murthas's horse trotting riderless. Two squires and a groom chased the destrier. Hadrian spotted Murthas lying on his back along the alley. Men ran to the knight's aid as he struggled to sit up. Hadrian looked for Renwick, and as he did, he noticed the crowd. They were alive with excitement. All of them were on their feet, clapping and whistling. A few even cheered his name. Hadrian guessed they had not expected him to survive the first round.

He allowed himself a smile and the crowd cheered even louder.

"Sir!" Renwick shouted over the roar, running to Hadrian's

side. "You didn't put your helm on!" The squire held up the plumed helmet.

"Sorry," Hadrian apologized. "I forgot. I didn't expect them to start the run so quickly."

"Sorry? But—but no one tilts without a helm," Renwick said, an astonished look on his face. "He could have killed you!"

Hadrian glanced over his shoulder at Murthas hobbling off the field with the help of two men and shrugged. "I survived."

"Survived? *Survived?* Murthas didn't even touch you, and you *destroyed* him. That's a whole lot better than just *survived*. Besides, you did it without a *helm*! I've never seen anyone do that. And the way you hit him! You punched him off his horse like he hit a wall. You're amazing!"

"Beginner's luck, I guess. I'm all done here, right?"

Renwick nodded and swallowed several times. "You'll go on to the second round day after tomorrow."

"Good. How about we go see how well you do at the carousel minor and the quintain? Gotta watch that quintain. If you don't hit it clean, the billet will swing around and knock you off."

"I know," Renwick replied, but his expression showed he was still in a state of shock. His eyes kept shifting from Hadrian to Murthas and back to the still-cheering crowd.

❦

Amilia had never been to the tournament before. She had never seen a joust. Sitting in the stands, Amilia realized she had not even been outside the palace in more than a year. Despite the cold, she was enjoying herself. Perched on a thick velvet cushion, she draped a lush blanket over her lap and held a warm cup of cider between her hands. Everything was so pretty. So many bright colors filled the otherwise bleak winter world. All around her the privileged were grouped according to their stations. Across the field, the poor swarmed, trapped behind fence rails. They blended into a single gray mass that almost faded into the background of muddied snow. Without seats, they stood in the slush, shuffling their feet and stuffing hands into sleeves. Still, they were obviously happy to be there, happy to see the spectacle.

"That's three broken lances for Prince Rudolf!" the duchess squealed, clapping enthusiastically. "A fine example of grand imperial entertainment. Not that his performance compares to Sir Hadrian's. Everyone thought the poor man was doomed. I still can't believe he rode without a helm! And what he did to Sir Murthas... Well, it will certainly be an exciting tournament this year, Amilia. Very exciting indeed."

Lady Genevieve tugged on Amilia's sleeve and pointed. "Oh, see there. They are bringing out the blue and gold flag. Those are Sir Breckton's colors. He's up next. Yes, yes, here he comes, and see—see on his arm. He wears your token. How exciting! The other ladies—they're positively drooling. Oh, don't look now, dear, they're all staring at you. If eyes were daggers and glares lethal..." She trailed off, as if Amilia should know the rest. "They all see your conquest, my darling, and hate you. How wonderful."

"Is it?" Amilia asked, noticing how many of the other ladies were staring at her. She bowed her head and kept her eyes focused on her lap. "I don't want to be hated."

"Nonsense. Knights aren't the only ones who tilt at these tournaments. Everyone comes to this field as a competitor, and there can only be one victor. The only difference is that the knights spar in the daylight, and the ladies compete by candlelight. Clearly, you won your first round, but now we must see if your conquest was a wise one, as your victory remains locked with his prowess. Breckton is riding against Gilbert. This should be a close challenge. Gilbert actually killed a man a few years ago. It was an accident, of course, but it still gives him an edge over his opponents. Although, rumor has it that he hurt his leg two nights back, so we shall see."

"Killed?" Amilia felt her stomach tighten as the trumpet blared and the flag flew.

Hooves shook the ground, and her heart raced as panic flooded her. She shut her eyes before the impact.

Crack!

The crowd roared.

Opening her eyes, she saw Gilbert still mounted but reeling. Sir Breckton trotted back to his gate unharmed.

"That's one lance for Breckton," Leo mentioned to no one in particular.

The duke sat on the far side of Genevieve, appearing more animated than Amilia had ever seen him. The duchess ran on for hours, talking about everything and anything, but Leopold almost never spoke. When he did, it was so softly that Amilia thought his words were directed to Maribor alone.

Nimbus sat to Amilia's right, frequently glancing at her. He looked tense and she loved him for it.

"That Gilbert. Look at the way they are propping him up," the duchess prattled on. "He really shouldn't ride again. Oh, but he's taking the lance—how brave of him."

"He needs to get the tip up," Leopold noted.

"Oh yes, Leo. You are right as always. He doesn't have the strength. And look at Breckton waiting patiently. Do you see the way the sun shines off his armor? He doesn't normally clean it. He's a warrior, not a tournament knight, but he went to the metalsmith and ordered it polished so that the wind itself could see its face within the gleam. Now why do you suppose a man who hasn't combed his hair in months does such a thing?"

Amilia felt terrified, embarrassed, and happy beyond what she had believed to be the bounds of emotion.

The trumpet blared, and again the horses charged.

A lance cracked, Gilbert fell, and once again Breckton emerged untouched. The crowd cheered, and to Amilia's surprise, she found herself on her feet along with the rest. She had a smile on her face that she could not wipe away.

Breckton made certain Gilbert was all right, then trotted over to the stands and stopped in front of Amilia's seat in the nobles' box. He tossed aside his broken lance, pulled off his helm, rose in his stirrups, and bowed to her. Without thinking, she walked down the steps toward the railing. As she stepped out from under the canopy into the sun, the cheers grew louder, especially from the commoners' side of the field.

"For you, my lady," Sir Breckton told her.

He made a sound to his horse, which also bowed, and once more the crowd roared. Her heart was light, her mind empty, and her whole life invisible except for that one moment in the sun. Feeling Nimbus's hand on her arm, she turned and saw Saldur scowling from the stands.

"It's not wise to linger in the sun too long, milady," Nimbus warned. "You might get burned."

The expression on Saldur's face dragged Amilia back to reality. She returned to her seat, noticing the venomous glares from the nobles around her.

"My dear," the duchess said in an uncharacteristic whisper, "for someone who doesn't know how to play the game, you are as remarkable as Sir Hadrian today."

Amilia sat quietly through the few remaining tilts, which

she hardly noticed. When the day's competition had ended, they exited the stands. Nimbus led the way and the duchess walked beside her, holding on to Amilia's arm.

"You will be coming with us to the hunt on the Eve's Eve, won't you, Amilia dear?" Lady Genevieve asked as they walked across the field to the waiting carriages. "You simply must. I'll have Lois work all week on a dazzling white gown and matching winter cape so you'll have something new. Where can we find snow-white fur for the hood?" She paused a moment, then waved the thought away. "Oh well, I'll let her work that out. See you then. Ta-ta!" She blew Amilia a kiss as the ducal carriage left.

The boy was just standing there.

He waited on the far side of the street, revealed when the duke and duchess's coach pulled away. A filthy little thing, he stared at Amilia, looking both terrified and determined. In his arms he held a soiled bag. He caught her eye and with a stern resolve slipped through the fence.

"Mi-milady Ami—" was all he got out before a soldier grabbed him roughly and shoved him flat. The boy cowered in the snow, looking desperate. "Lady, please, I—"

The guard kicked him hard in the stomach and the boy crumpled around his foot. His eyes squeezed shut in pain as another soldier kicked him in the back.

"Stop it!" Amilia shouted. "Leave him alone!"

The guards paused, confused.

On the ground, the boy struggled to breathe.

"Help him up!" She took a step toward the child, but Nimbus caught her by the arm.

"Perhaps not here, milady." His eyes indicated the crowd around the line of carriages. Many were straining to see what the commotion was about. "You've already annoyed Regent Saldur once today."

She paused, then glanced at the boy. "Put him in my carriage," she instructed the guards.

They lifted the lad and shoved him forward. He dropped his bundle and pulled free in time to grab it before scurrying into the coach. Amilia glanced at Nimbus, who shrugged. The two followed the youth inside.

A look of horror on his face, the boy cowered on the seat across from Amilia and Nimbus.

The courtier eyed the lad critically. "I'd have to say he's ten, no more than twelve. An orphan, certainly, and nearly feral by the look of him. What do you suppose he has in the bag? A dead rat?"

"Oh, stop it, Nimbus," Amilia rebuked. "Of course it's not. It's probably just his lunch."

"Exactly," the tutor agreed.

Amilia glared. "Hush, you're frightening him."

"Me? He's the one who came at us with the moldy bag of mystery."

"Are you all right?" Amilia asked the boy softly.

He managed a nod, but just barely. His eyes kept darting around the interior of the carriage but always came back to Amilia, as if he were mesmerized.

"I'm sorry about the guards. That was awful, the way they treated you. Nimbus, do you have some coppers? Anything we could give him?"

The courtier looked helpless. "I'm sorry, my lady. I'm not in the habit of carrying coin."

Disappointed, Amilia sighed and then tried to put on a happy face. "What was it you wanted to say to me?" she asked.

The boy wetted his lips. "I—I have something to give to the empress." He looked down at the bag.

"What is it?" Amilia tried not to cringe at the possibilities.

"I heard...well...they said she couldn't be at the tournament today because she was sick and all. That's when I knew I had to get this to her." He patted the bag.

"Get what to her? What's in the bag?"

"Something that can heal her."

"Oh dear. It *is* a dead rat, isn't it?" Nimbus shivered in disgust.

The boy pulled the bag open and drew out a folded shimmering robe unlike anything Amilia had ever seen before. "It saved the life of my best friend—healed him overnight, it did. It's...it's magical, it is!"

"A religious relic?" Nimbus ventured.

Amilia smiled at the boy. "What's your name?"

"They call me Mince, milady. I can't say what my real name is, but Mince works well enough, it does."

"Well, Mince, this is a generous gift. This looks very expensive. Don't you think *you* should keep it? It's certainly better than what you're wearing."

Mince shook his head. "I think it wants me to give it to the empress—to help her."

"*It* wants?" she asked.

"It's kind of hard to explain."

"Such things usually are," the courtier said.

"So can you give this to her?"

"Perhaps you should let *him* give it to her," Nimbus suggested to Amilia.

"Are you serious?" she replied.

"You wanted to atone for the misdeeds of the guards, didn't you? For the likes of him, meeting the empress will more than make up for a few bruises. Besides, he's just a boy. No one will care."

Amilia thought a moment, staring at the wide-eyed child.

"What do you think, Mince? Would you like to give it to the empress yourself?"

The boy looked as if he might faint.

~

Modina had found a mouse in her chamber three months earlier. When she had lit the lamp, it had frozen in panic in the middle of the room. Picking it up, she felt its little chest heave as it panted for breath. Clearly terrified, it looked back at her with its dark, tiny eyes. Modina thought it might die of fright. Even after she set it down, it still did not move. Only after the light had been out for several minutes did she hear it scurry away. The mouse had never returned—until now.

He was not that mouse, but the boy looked just the same. He lacked the fur, tail, and whiskers, but the eyes were unmistakable. He stood fearfully still, the only movement the result of his heaving chest and trembling body.

"Did you say his name was *Mouse*?"

"Mince, I think he said," Amilia corrected. "It is *Mince*, isn't it?"

The boy said nothing, clutching the bag to his chest.

"I found him at the tournament. He wants to give you a gift. Go on, Mince."

Instead of speaking, Mince abruptly thrust the bag out with both hands.

"He wanted to give this to you because Saldur announced that you were too sick to attend the tournament. He says it has healing powers."

Modina took the bag, opened it, and drew forth the robe. Despite having been stuffed in the old, dirty sack, the garment shimmered—not a single wrinkle or stain on it.

"It's beautiful," she said sincerely as she held it up, watching it play with the light. "It reminds me of someone I once knew. I will cherish it."

When the boy heard the words, tears formed in his eyes and streaked his dirty cheeks. Falling to his knees, he placed his face on the floor before her.

Puzzled, Modina glanced at Amilia, but the imperial secretary only offered a shrug. The empress stared at the boy for a moment and then said to Amilia, "He looks starved."

"Do you want me to take him to the kitchen?"

"No, leave him here. Go have some food sent up."

After Amilia left the room, Modina laid the robe on a chair and then sat on the edge of the bed, watching the boy. He had not moved, and remained kneeling with his head still touching the floor. After a few minutes, he looked up but said nothing.

Modina spoke gently. "I'm very good at playing the silent game too. We can sit here for days not saying a word if you want."

The boy's lips trembled. He opened his mouth as if to speak and then stopped.

"Go ahead. It's okay."

Once he started, the words came out in a flood, as if he felt the need to say everything with a single breath. "I just want ya to get better, that's all. Honest. I brought ya the robe because it saved Kine, see. It healed him overnight, I tell ya. He was dying, and he woulda been dead by morning, for sure. But the robe made him better. Then today, when they said you was too sick to see the tournament, I knew I had to bring ya the robe to make ya better. Ya see?"

"I'm sorry, Mince, but I'm afraid a robe can't heal what's wrong with me."

The boy frowned. "But... it healed Kine and his lips were blue."

Modina walked over and sat down on the floor in front of him.

"I know you mean well, and it's a wonderful gift, but some things can never be fixed."

"But—"

"No buts. You need to stop worrying about me. Do you understand?"

"Why?"

"You just have to. Will you do that for me?"

The boy looked up and locked eyes with her. "I would do anything for you."

The sincerity and conviction in his voice staggered her.

"I love you," he added.

Those three words shook her, and even though she was sitting on the floor, the empress put a hand down to steady herself.

"No," she said. "You can't. You just met—"

"Yes, I do."

Modina shook her head. "No, you don't!" she snapped. "No one does!"

The boy flinched as if struck. He looked back down at the floor and, nevertheless, added in a whisper, "But I do. Everyone does."

The empress stared at him.

"What do you mean—'everyone'?"

"Everyone," the boy said, puzzled. He gestured toward the window.

"You mean the people in the city?"

"Well, sure, them, but not just here. Everywhere. Everyone loves you," the boy repeated. "Folks been coming to the city from all over. I hear them talking. They all come to see ya. All of them saying how the world's gonna be better 'cuz you're here. How they would die for you."

Stunned, Modina stood up slowly.

She turned and walked to the window, where she gazed into the distance—above the roofs to the hills and snow-covered mountains beyond.

"Did I say something wrong?" Mince asked.

She turned back. "No. Not at all. It's just that…" Modina paused. She moved to the mirror and ran her fingertips along the glass. "There are still ten days to Wintertide, right?"

"Yes. Why?"

"Well, because you gave me a gift, I'd like to give you something in return, and it looks like I still have time."

She crossed to the door and opened it. Gerald stood waiting outside, as always. "Gerald," she said, "could you please do me a favor?"

CHAPTER 15

THE HUNT

"Merry Eve's Eve, Sir Hadrian," a girl said brightly when he poked his head outside his room. She was just one of the giggling chambermaids who had been extending smiles and curtsies to him since the day of the first joust. After his second tilt, pages bowed and guards nodded in his direction. His third win, although as clean as the others, had been the worst, as it brought the attention of every knight and noble in the palace. After each joust, he had his choice of sitting in his dormitory or going to the great hall. Preferring to be alone, Hadrian usually chose his room.

That morning, like most days, Hadrian found himself wandering the palace hallways. He had seen Albert from a distance on a few occasions, but neither attempted to speak with the other, and there had been no sign of Royce. Crossing through the grand foyer, he paused. The staircase spiraled upward, adorned in fanciful candles and painted wood ornaments. Somewhere four flights up, the girl he had known as Thrace was probably still asleep in her bed. He put his foot on the first step.

"Sir Hadrian?" a man he did not recognize asked. "Great joust yesterday. You really gave Louden a hit he'll not soon forget. I heard the crack even in the high stands. They say Louden will need a new breastplate, and you gave him two broken ribs to boot! What a hit. What a hit, I say. You know, I lost a bundle betting against you the first three jousts, but since then I've won everything back. I'm sticking with you for the final. You've made a believer out of me. Say, where you headed?"

Hadrian quickly drew back his foot. "Nowhere. Just stretching my legs a bit."

"Well, just wanted to tell you to keep up the good work and let you know I'll be rooting for you."

The man exited the palace through the grand entrance, leaving Hadrian at the bottom of the stairs.

What am I going to do, walk into her chambers unannounced? It's been over a year since I spoke with her. Will she hate me for not trying to see her earlier? Will she remember me at all?

He looked up the staircase once more.

It's possible she's all right, isn't it? Just because no one ever sees her doesn't necessarily mean anything, does it?

Modina was the empress. They could not be treating her too badly. When she lived in Dahlgren, she had been happy, and that had been a squalid little village where people were killed nightly by a giant monster.

How much worse can living in a palace be?

He took one last look around and spotted the two shadows leaning casually near the archway to the throne room. With a sigh, Hadrian turned toward the service wing, leaving the stairway behind.

The sun was not fully up, but the kitchen was already bustling. Huge pots billowed clouds of steam so thick that the walls cried tears. Butchers hammered on cutting blocks, shouting orders. Boys ran with buckets, shouting back. Girls scrubbed cutlery, pans, and bowls. The smells were strong and varied. Some, such as that of baked bread, were wonderful, but others were sulfurous and vile. Unlike in the rest of the palace, no holiday decoration adorned the walls or tables. Here, behind the scenes, the signs of Wintertide were reduced to cooling trays of candied apples and snowflake-shaped cookies.

Hadrian stepped into the scullery, fascinated by the activity. As soon as he entered, heads turned, work slowed, and then everything came to a stop. The room grew so quiet that the only sounds came from the bubbling pots, the crackling fires, and water dripping from a wet ladle. All the staff stared at him, as if he had two heads or three arms.

Hadrian took a seat on one of the stools surrounding an open table. The modest area appeared to be the place where the kitchen staff ate their own meals. He tried to look casual and relaxed, but it was impossible with all the attention.

"What's all this now?" boomed a voice belonging to a large, beefy cook with a thick beard and eyes wreathed in cheerful wrinkles. Spotting Hadrian, those eyes narrowed abruptly. He revealed—if only for a moment—that he had another side, the same way a playful dog might suddenly growl at an intruder.

"Can I help you, sir?" he asked, approaching Hadrian with a meat cleaver in one hand.

"I don't mean any harm. I was just hoping to find some food."

The cook looked him over closely. "Are you a knight, sir?"

Hadrian nodded.

"Up early, I see. I'll have whatever you want brought to the great hall."

"Actually, I'd rather eat here. Is that okay?"

"I'm sorry?" the cook said, confused. "If you don't mind me asking, why would a fine nobleman like yourself want to eat in a hot, dirty kitchen surrounded by the clang of pots and the gibbering of maids?"

"I just feel more comfortable here," Hadrian said. "I think a man ought to be at ease when eating. Of course, if it's a problem..." He stood.

"You're Sir Hadrian, aren't you? I haven't found the time to see the jousts, but as you can see, most of my staff has. You're quite the celebrity. I've heard all kinds of stories about you and your recent change in fortune. Are any of them true?"

"Well, I can't say about the stories, but my name is Hadrian."

"Nice to meet you. Name's Ibis Thinly. Have a seat, sir. I'll fix you right up."

He hurried away, scolding his crew to return to work. Many continued to glance over at Hadrian, stealing looks when they felt the head cook could not see. In a short while, Ibis returned with a plate of chicken, fried eggs, and biscuits and a mug of dark beer. The chicken was so hot that it hurt Hadrian's fingers, and the biscuits steamed when he pulled them open.

"I appreciate this," Hadrian told Ibis, taking a bite of biscuit.

Ibis gave him a surprised look and then chuckled. "By Mar! Thanking a cook for food! Them stories *are* true, aren't they?"

Hadrian shrugged. "I guess I have a hard time remembering that I'm noble. When I was a commoner, I always knew what noble meant, but now, not so much."

The cook smiled. "Lady Amilia has the same problem. I gotta say it's nice to see decent folk getting ahead in this world. The news is you've ruled the field at Highcourt. Beat every knight who rode against you. I even heard you opened the tournament by tilting against Sir Murthas without a helm!"

Hadrian nodded with a mouthful of chicken, which he shifted from side to side, trying to avoid a burnt tongue.

"When a man does that," Ibis went on, "and comes from the salt like the rest of us, he wins favor among the lower classes. Yes, indeed. Those of us with dirty faces and sweaty backs get quite a thrill from one such as you, sir."

Hadrian did not know how to respond and contented himself with swallowing his chicken. He had ridden to the sound of roaring crowds every time he had competed, but Hadrian was not there for applause. His task was dark, secret, and not worthy of praise. He had unsaddled five knights and, by the rules of the contest, owned their mounts. Hadrian had declined that privilege. He had no need for the horses, but it was more than just that—he did not deserve them. All he wanted was the lives of Arista and Gaunt. In his mind, the whole affair was tainted. Taking anything else from his victories—even the pleasure of success—would be wrong. Nevertheless, the crowds cheered each time he refused his right to a mount, believing him humble and chivalrous instead of what he was—a murderer in waiting.

"It's just you and Breckton now, isn't it?" Ibis asked.

Hadrian nodded gloomily. "We tilt tomorrow. There's some sort of hunt today."

"Oh yes, the hawking. I'll be roasting plenty of game birds for tonight's feast. Say, aren't you going?"

"Just here for the joust," Hadrian managed to say even though his mouth was full again.

Ibis bent his head to get a better look. "For a new knight on the verge of winning the Wintertide Highcourt Tournament, you don't seem very happy. It's not the food, I hope."

Hadrian shook his head. "Food's great. Kinda hoping you'll let me eat my midday meal here too."

"You're welcome anytime. Ha! Listen to me sounding like an innkeeper or castle lord. I'm just a cook." He hooked a thumb over his shoulder. "Sure, these mongrels quiver at my voice, but you're a knight. You can go wherever you please. Still... if my food has placed you in a charitable mood, I would ask one favor."

"What's that?"

"Lady Amilia holds a special place in my heart. She's like a daughter to me. A sweet, sweet lass, and it seems she's recently taken a liking to Sir Breckton. He's good, mind you, a fine lancer, but from what I've heard, you're likely to beat him. Now, I'm not saying anything against you—someone of my station would be a fool to even insinuate such a thing—but..."

"But?"

"Well, some knights try to inflict as much damage as they can, taking aim at a visor and such. If something were to happen to Breckton... Well, I just don't want Amilia to get hurt. She's never had much, you see. Comes from a poor family and has worked hard all her life. Even now, that bas—I mean, Regent Saldur—keeps her slaving night and day. But even so, she's been happy lately, and I'd like to see that continue."

Hadrian kept his eyes on his plate, concentrating on mopping up yolk with a crust of bread.

"So anyway, if at all possible, it'd be real nice if you went a bit easy on Breckton. So he doesn't get hurt, I mean. I know a'course that you can't always help it. Dear Maribor, I know that. But I can tell by talking with you that you're a decent fellow. Ha! I don't even know why I brought it up. You'll do the right thing. I can tell. Here, let me get you some more beer."

Ibis Thinly walked away, taking Hadrian's mug and appetite with him.

◆

In many ways Amilia felt like a child Saldur had brought into the world that day in the kitchen when he had elevated her to the rank of lady. Now she was little more than a toddler, still trying to master simple tasks and often making mistakes. No one said anything. No one pointed and laughed, but there were knowing looks and partially hidden smiles. She felt out of her element when trying to navigate the numerous traps and hazards of courtly life without a map.

When addressed as *my lady* by a finely dressed noble, Amilia felt uncomfortable. Seeing a guard snap to attention at her passing was strange. Especially since those same soldiers had grinned lewdly at her little more than a year earlier. Amilia was certain the guards still leered and the nobles still laughed, but now they did so behind polite eyes. She believed the only means of banishing the silent snickers was to fit in. If Amilia did not stumble as she walked, spill a glass of wine, speak too loudly, wear the wrong color, laugh when she should remain quiet, or remain quiet when she should laugh, then they might forget she used to scrub their dishes. Any time Amilia interacted with the nobility was an ordeal, but when she did so in an unfamiliar setting, she became ill. For this reason, Amilia avoided eating anything the morning of the hawking.

The whole court embarked on the daylong event. Knights, nobles, ladies, and servants all rode out together to the forest and field for the great hunt. Dogs trotted in their wake. Amilia had never sat on a horse before. She had never ridden a pony, a mule, or even an ox, but that day she found herself precariously balanced atop a massive white charger. She wore the beautiful white gown and matching cape Lady Genevieve had provided her, which, by no accident, perfectly matched her horse's coat. Her right leg was hooked between two horns of the saddle and her left foot rested on a planchette. Sitting this way made staying on the animal's back a demanding enterprise. Each jerk and turn set her heart pounding and her hands grasping for the charger's braided mane. On several occasions,

she nearly toppled backward. Amilia imagined that if she were
to fall, she would wind up hanging by her trapped leg, skirt
over her head, while the horse pranced proudly about. The
thought terrified her so much that she barely breathed and sat
rigid with her eyes fixed on the ground below. For the two-
hour ride into the wilderness, Amilia did not speak a word.
She dared to look up only when the huntsman called for the
party's attention.

They emerged from the shade of a forest into the light of a
field. Tall brown rushes jutted from beneath the snow's cover.
The flicker of morning sunlight was reflected by moving water
where a river cut the landscape. Lacking any wind, the world
was oddly quiet. The huntsman directed them to line up by
spreading out along the edge of the forest and facing the
marsh.

Amilia was pleased to arrive at what she hoped was their
destination and proud of how she had managed to direct her
horse without delay or mishap. Finally at a standstill, she
allowed herself a breath of relief only to see the falconer
approaching.

"What bird will you be using today, my lady?" he asked,
looking up at her from within his red coif. His hands were
encased in thick gloves.

She swallowed. "Ah...what would you suggest?"

The falconer appeared surprised, and Amilia felt as if she
had done something wrong.

"Well, my lady, there are many birds but no set regulation.
Tradition usually reserves the gyrfalcon for a king, a falcon
for a prince or duke, the peregrine for an earl, a bastard
hawk for a baron, a saker for a knight, a goshawk for a noble,
tercel for a poor man, sparrow hawk for a priest, kestrel for a
servant, and a merlin for a lady, but in practice it is more a
matter of—"

"She will be using Murderess," the Duchess of Rochelle announced, trotting up beside them.

"Of course, Your Ladyship." The falconer bowed his head and made a quick motion with his hand. A servant raced up with a huge hooded bird held on his fist. "Your gauntlet, milady," the falconer said, holding out a rough elk-hide glove.

"You'll want to put that on your left hand, darling," the duchess said with a reassuring smile and mischievous glint in her eyes.

Amilia felt her heart flutter as she took the glove and pulled it on.

"Hold your hand up, dear. Out away from your face," Lady Genevieve instructed.

The falconer took the raptor from the servant and carried her over. The hawk was magnificent and blinded by a leather hood with a short decorative plume. While being transferred to Amilia, Murderess spread her massive wings and flapped twice as her powerful talons took hold of the glove. The hawk was lighter than she had expected, and Amilia had no trouble holding her up. Still, Amilia's fear of falling was replaced by her fear of the bird. She watched in terror as the falconer wrapped the jess around her wrist, tethering her to the hawk.

"Beautiful bird," Amilia heard a voice say.

"Yes, it is," she replied. Looking over to see Sir Breckton taking station on her left, Amilia thought she might faint.

"It's the Duchess of Rochelle's. She—" Amilia turned. The duchess had moved off, abandoning her. Panic made her stomach lurch. As friendly as Lady Genevieve was, Amilia was starting to suspect the woman enjoyed tormenting her.

Amilia tried to calm herself as she sat face to face with the one man in the entire world she wanted to impress. With one hand holding the bird and the other locked on to the horse's reins, she realized the cold was causing her nose to run. She could not imagine the day getting any worse. Then, as if the gods had heard her thoughts, they answered using the huntsman's voice.

"Everyone! Ride forward!"

Oh dear Maribor!

Her horse tripped on the rough, frost-heaved ground, throwing her off balance. The sudden jolt also startled Murderess, who threw out her great wings to save herself by flying. Tethered to Amilia's wrist, the hawk pulled on her arm. She might have stayed in the saddle—if not for the bird's insistence on dragging her backward.

Amilia cried out as she fell over the rump of the horse, her nightmare becoming reality. Yet before she cleared the saddle, she stopped. Sir Breckton had caught her around the waist. Though he wore no armor, his arm felt like a band of steel— solid and unmovable. Gently, he drew her upright. The bird flapped twice more, then settled down and gripped Amilia's glove again.

Breckton did not say a word. He held Amilia steady until she reseated herself on the saddle and placed her foot on the planchette. Horrified and flushed with humiliation, she refused to look at him.

Why did that have to happen in front of him!

She did not want to see his face and find the same condescending smirk she had seen on so many others. On the verge of tears, she wanted desperately to be back at the palace, back in the kitchen, back to cleaning pots. At that moment she preferred the thought of facing Edith Mon—or even her vengeful ghost—to that of enduring the humiliation of facing Sir Breckton. Feeling tears gathering, she clenched her jaw and breathed deeply in an effort to hold them back.

"Does it have a name?"

Sir Breckton's words were so unexpected that Amilia replayed them twice before understanding the question.

"Murderess," she replied, thanking Maribor that her voice did not crack.

"That seems…appropriate." There was a pause before he continued. "Beautiful day, isn't it?"

"Yes." She tasked her brain to think of something to add, but it came back with nothing.

Why is he talking like that? Why is he asking about the weather?

The knight sighed heavily.

Looking up at him, she found he was not smirking but appeared pained. His eyes accidentally met hers while she studied his face, and he instantly looked away. His fingers drummed a marching cadence on his saddle horn.

"Cold, though," he said, and quickly added, "Could be warmer, don't you think?"

"Yes," she said again, realizing she must sound like an idiot with all her one-word answers. She wanted to say more. She wanted to be witty and clever, but her brain was as frozen as the ground.

Amilia caught him glancing at her again. This time he shook his head and sighed once more.

"What?" she asked fearfully.

"I don't know how you do it," he said.

The genuine admiration in his eyes only baffled her further.

"You ride a warhorse sidesaddle over rough ground with a huge hawk perched on your arm and are still managing to make me feel like a squire in a fencing match. My lady, you are a marvel beyond reckoning. I am in awe."

Amilia stared at him until she realized she was staring at him. In her mind, she ordered her eyes to look away, but they refused. She had no words to reply, which hardly mattered, as Amilia had no air in her body with which to speak. Breathing seemed unimportant at that moment. Forcing herself to take a breath, Amilia discovered she was smiling. A second later, she knew Sir Breckton noticed as well, as he abruptly stopped drumming and sat straighter.

"Milady," said the falconer's servant, "it's time to release your bird."

Amilia looked at the raptor, wondering just how she was going to do that.

"May I help?" Sir Breckton asked. Reaching over, he removed Murderess's hood and unwound her tether.

With a motion of his own arm, the servant indicated that she should thrust her hand up. Amilia did so, and Murderess spread her great wings, pushed down, and took to the sky. The raptor climbed higher and higher yet remained circling directly overhead. As she watched the goshawk, Amilia noticed Breckton looking at her.

"Don't you have a bird?" she asked.

"No. I did not expect to be hawking. Truth be told, I haven't hunted in years. I'd forgotten the joy of it—until now."

"So you know how?"

"Oh yes. Of course. I used to hunt the fields of Chadwick as a lad. My father, my brother Wesley, and I would spend whole weeks chasing fowl from their nests and rodents from their burrows."

"Would you think ill of me if I told you this was my first time?"

Breckton's face turned serious, which frightened her until he said, "My lady, be assured that should I live so long as to see the day that the sun does not rise, the rivers do not flow, and the winds do not blow, I would *never* think ill of you."

She tried to hide another smile. Once more, she failed, and once more, Sir Breckton noticed.

"Perhaps you can help me, as I am befuddled by all of this," Amilia said, gesturing at their surroundings.

"It is a simple thing. The birds are *waiting on*—that is to say, hovering overhead and waiting for the attack. Much the way soldiers stand in line preparing for battle. The enemies are a crafty bunch. They lay hiding before us in the field between the river and ourselves. With the line made by the horses, the huntsman has ensured that the prey will not come this way, which, of course, they would try to do—to reach the safety of the trees—were we not here."

"But how will we find these hidden enemies?"

"They need to be drawn out, or in this case *flushed* out. See there? The huntsman has gathered the dogs."

Amilia looked ahead as a crowd of eager dogs moved forward, led by a dozen boys from the palace. After they were turned loose, the hounds disappeared into the undergrowth. Only their raised tails appeared, here and there, above the bent rushes as they dashed into the snowy field without a bark or a yelp.

With a blue flag, the huntsman signaled to the falconer, who in turn waved to the riders. He indicated they should move slowly toward the river. With her bird gone, Amilia found it easier to control her horse and advanced along with the rest. Everyone was silent as they crept forward. Amilia felt excited, although she had no idea what was about to happen.

The falconer raised a hand and the riders stopped their horses. Looking up, Amilia saw the birds had matched their movement across the field. The falconer waved a red flag and the huntsman blew a whistle, which sent the dogs bursting forth. Immediately, the field exploded with birds. Loud thumping sounds erupted as quail broke from cover, racing skyward. In their efforts to evade the monstrous dogs, they never saw the death awaiting them in the sky. Hawks swooped down out of the sun, slamming into their targets and bearing them to the ground. One bore its prey all the way to the river, where both hawk and quail hit the water.

"That was Murderess!" Amilia shouted, horrified. Her mind filled with the realization that she had killed Lady Genevieve's prized bird. Without thinking, she kicked her horse, which leapt forward. She galloped across the field and, as she neared the river, spotted a dog swimming out into the icy water. Another quickly followed in its wake. Two birds flapped desperately on the surface, kicking up a white spray.

Just before Amilia charged headlong into the river, Breckton caught her horse by the bit and pulled them both to a halt.

"Wait!"

"But the bird!" was all Amilia could say. Her eyes locked on the splashing.

"It's all right," he assured her. "Watch."

The first dog reached Murderess and, without hesitation, took the hawk in its jaws. Holding the raptor up, the hound circled and swam back. At the same time, the second dog raced out to collect the downed prey. The quail struggled, but Amilia was amazed that the hawk did not fight when the dog set its teeth.

"You see," Breckton said, "dogs and birds are trained to trust and protect one another. Just like soldiers."

The hound climbed out of the water still holding the hawk. Both Amilia and Breckton dismounted as the dog brought the bird to them. Gently, the animal opened its jaws and Murderess hopped onto Amilia's fist once more. She stretched out her wings and snapped them, spraying water.

"She's all right!" Amilia said, amazed.

A boy ran up to her, holding out a dead bird by a string tied around its feet. "Your quail, milady."

⁓

When Hadrian returned later that day, Ibis Thinly was waiting with more than just a plate. The entire table was laden with a variety of meats, cheeses, and breads. The scullery had been cleaned such that extra sacks were removed, shelves dusted, and the floor mopped. The table was set with fresh candles, and a larger, cushioned chair replaced the little stool. He guessed not all of this was strictly Ibis's doing. Apparently, word of his visit had spread. Twice as many servants populated the kitchen as had that morning—most standing idle.

Ibis did not speak to Hadrian this time. The cook was feverishly busy dealing with the flood of game brought in by nobles returning from the hunt. Already maids were plucking away at quail, pheasant, and duck from a long line of beheaded birds that was strung around the room like a garland. With so much to process, even Ibis himself skinned rabbits and squirrels. Despite his obvious urgency, the cook immediately stopped working when Amilia arrived.

"Ibis! Look! I got two!" she shouted, holding the birds above her head. She entered the kitchen dressed in a lovely white gown and matching fur cape.

"Bring them here, lass. Let me see these treasures."

Hadrian had seen Lady Amilia from a distance at each of the feasts, but this was the first time he had seen her up close since he had posed as a courier. She was prettier than he remembered. Her clothes were certainly better. Whether it was the spring in her step or the flush in her cheeks brought on by the cold, she appeared more alive.

"These are clearly the pick of the lot," Ibis said after inspecting her trophies.

"They're scrawny and small, but they're *mine*!" She followed the declaration with a carefree, happy laugh.

"Can I infer from your mood that you did not hunt alone?"

Amilia said nothing and merely smiled. Clasping her hands behind her back, she sashayed about the kitchen, swinging her skirt.

"Come now, girl. Don't toy with me."

She laughed again, spun around, and announced, "He was at my side almost the whole day. A *perfect* gentleman, I might add, and I think..." She hesitated.

"Think what? Out with it, lass."

"I think he may fancy me."

"Bah! Of course he fancies you. But what did the man say? Did he speak plainly? Did he spout verse? Did he kiss you right there on the field?"

"*Kiss me?* He's *far* too proper for such vulgarity, but he was *very* nervous...silly, even. And he couldn't seem to take his eyes off me!"

"Silly? Sir Breckton? Ah, lass, you've got him hooked. You have. A fine catch, I must say, a fine catch indeed."

Amilia could not contain herself and laughed again, this time throwing back her head in elation and twirling her gown. Doing so, she caught sight of Hadrian and halted.

"Sorry, I'm just having a late lunch," he said. "I'll be gone in a minute."

"Oh no. You don't have to leave. It's just that I didn't see you. Other than the staff, I'm the only one who ever comes down here—or so I thought."

"It's more comfortable than the hall," Hadrian said. "I

spend my days tilting with the knights. I don't feel like competing with them at meals too."

She walked over, looking puzzled. "You don't talk like a knight."

"That's Sir Hadrian," Ibis informed Amilia.

"Oh!" she exclaimed. "You helped Sir Breckton and my poor Nimbus when they were attacked. That was very kind. You're also the one who rode in the tournament without a helm. You've—you've unseated every opponent on the first pass and haven't had a single lance broken on your shield. You're...very good, aren't you?"

"And he's riding against Sir Breckton tomorrow for the championship," Ibis reminded her.

"That's right!" She gasped, raising a hand to her lips. "Have you *ever* been unseated?"

Hadrian shrugged self-consciously. "Not since I've been a knight."

"Oh, I wasn't—I didn't mean to—I just wondered if it hurt terribly. I guess it can't feel good. Even with all that armor and padding, being driven from a galloping horse by a pole must not be pleasant." Her eyes grew troubled. "But all the other knights are fine, aren't they? I saw Sir Murthas and Sir Elgar on the hawking just today. They were trotting and laughing, so I'm certain everything will be all right no matter who wins.

"I know tomorrow is the final tilt and winning the tournament is a great honor. I understand firsthand the desire to prove yourself to those who look down on you. But I ask you to consider that Sir Breckton is a good man—a very good man. He would never hurt you if he could help it. I hope you feel the same." She struggled to smile at Hadrian.

He put down the bread he was eating as a sickening

sensation churned his stomach. Hadrian had to stop eating in the kitchen.

⤨

The acrobats rapidly assembled their human pyramid. Vaulting one at a time into the air, they somersaulted before each landed feetfirst on the shoulders of the one below. One after another they flew, continuing to build the formation until the final man reached up and touched the ceiling of the great hall. Despite the danger involved in the exciting performance, Amilia was not watching. She had seen the act before at the audition and rehearsals. Her eyes were on the audience. As Wintertide neared, the entertainment at each feast became grander and more extravagant.

Amilia held her breath until the hall erupted in applause.

They liked it!

Looking for Viscount Winslow, she spotted him clapping, his hands above his head. The two exchanged wide grins.

"I thought I would die from stress toward the end," Nimbus whispered from the seat next to Amilia. The bruises on the tutor's face were mostly gone and the annoying whistling sound had finally left his nose.

"Yes, that was indeed excellent," said King Roswort of Dunmore.

At each feast, Nimbus always sat to Amilia's left and the queen and king sat to her right.

King Roswort was huge. He made the Duke and Duchess of Rochelle appear petite. His squat, portly build was mimicked—in miniature—in his face, which sagged under its own weight. Amilia imagined that even if he were thin, King Roswort would still sag like an old riding horse. His wife, Freda, while no reed herself, was thin by comparison. She was dry and brittle both in looks and manner. The couple were fortunately quiet most of the time, at least until their third glasses of wine. Amilia lost count that evening but assumed number three had arrived and perhaps already gone.

"Are the acrobats friends of yours?" the king asked, leaning around his wife to speak to Amilia.

"Mine? No, I merely hired them," she said.

"Friends of friends, then?"

She shook her head.

"But you know them?" the king pressed further.

"I met them for the first time at the auditions."

"Rossie," Freda said. "She's clearly trying to distance herself from them now that the doors of nobility are open to her. You can't blame her for that. Anyone would abandon the wretches. Leave them in the street. That's where they belong."

"But I—" Amilia began before the king cut her off.

"But, my queen, many are rising in rank. Some street merchants are as wealthy as nobles now."

"Terrible state of affairs," Freda snarled through thin, red-painted lips. "A title isn't what it used to be."

"I agree, my queen. Why, some knights have no lineage at all to speak of. They are no better than peasants with swords. All anyone needs these days is money to buy armor and a horse, and there you have it—presto—a noble. Commoners are even learning to read. Can you read, Lady Amilia?"

"Actually, I can."

"See!" The king threw his hands up. "Of course, you are in the nobility now, but I assume you learned letters before that? It's a travesty. I don't know what the world is coming to."

"At least the situation with the elves has improved," his wife put in. "You have to give Ethelred credit for reducing their numbers. Our efforts to deal with them in Dunmore have met with little success."

"Deal with them?" Amilia asked, but the monarchs continued under their own momentum.

"If they had any intelligence, they would leave on their own. How much plainer can it be that they are not welcome?" the king said. "The guilds prohibit them from membership in any business, they can't obtain citizenship in any city, and the church declared them unclean enemies of Novron ages ago. Even the peasants are free to take measures against them. Still, they don't take the hint. They keep breeding and filling up slums. Hundreds die each year in church-sanctioned Cleansing Days, but they persist. Why not move on? Why not go elsewhere?"

As the king ran out of breath, the queen took over. "They are like rats, festering in every crack. Living among their kind is a curse. It's what brought down the first empire, you know. Even keeping them as slaves was a mistake. And mark my words, if we don't get rid of them all, so that not a single elf walks a civilized street or country lane, this empire will fall to the same ruin."

"True, true, the old emperors were too soft. They thought that they could *fix* them—"

"Fix them!" Freda erupted. "What a ridiculous notion. You can't fix a plague. You can only run from it or wipe it out."

"I know, darling, I agree with you wholeheartedly. We have a second chance now, and Ethelred is off to a good start."

Realizing that the king and queen ran through a conversation as familiar and comfortable to them as a pair of well-worn shoes, Amilia nodded politely without really listening. She had seen elves only once in her life. When she had still been living in Tarin Vale, three of them had come to the village—a family, if they had such notions of kinship. Apparently content to dress in rags, they were dirty and carried small, stained bundles, which Amilia guessed were all they had. They were so thin they looked sick, and walked with their heads bowed and shoulders slumped.

Children had called the elves names and villagers had thrown stones and shouted for them to leave. A rock struck the female's head and she cried out. Amilia did not throw any rocks, but she watched as the family was bruised and bloodied before they fled from town. At the time, she did not understand how they could be a threat. The monk who had been teaching her letters explained elves were responsible for the downfall of the empire. They had seemed helpless, and Amilia could not help feeling sorry for them.

Roswort concluded his tirade by accusing the elves of being responsible for the drought two years before, and Amilia caught Nimbus rolling his eyes.

"You don't share their opinions?" she whispered.

"It's not my place to counter the words of a king, milady," the courtier responded politely.

"True, but I sometimes wonder just what goes on under that wig of yours. Something tells me there's more than courtly etiquette rattling around."

Off to Amilia's right, Roswort and Freda had moved on. "Dwarves aren't much better, but at least they have skills," the king was saying. "Fine stonemasons and jewelers, I'll give them that, but niggardly as an autumn squirrel facing an early snow, the entire lot of them. They can't be trusted. Any one of them would slit your throat to steal two copper tenents. They stick to their own kind and whisper their outlawed language. Living with dwarves is like trying to domesticate a wild animal, can't ever truly be done."

The conversation died down as another performance started. This time a pair of conjurers pulled apples and oddments from their sleeves, then juggled the items. When the act was over, and all the knives and goblets safely caught, Nimbus asked, "Doesn't the empress hail from your kingdom, Your Majesty?"

"Oh yes." Roswort perked up and nearly spilled his drink. "Lived right there in Dahlgren. What a terrible mess that was. Afterward, the deacon ran about babbling his tall tales—and no one believed him. I certainly didn't. Who would have thought that the Heir of Novron would come from that tiny dust speck?"

"How is it that we never see her?" the queen asked Amilia. "She *will* be at the wedding, won't she?"

"Of course, Your Majesty. The empress is saving her strength for just that. She's still quite weak."

"I see," the queen replied coolly. "Surely she is well enough by now to admit guests. Several of the ladies feel it has been most unseemly the way she has been ignoring us. I would very much like a personal audience with her before the ceremony."

"I am afraid that's really not up to me. I only follow her directions."

"How can you follow her directions on something I have just now suggested? Are you a mind reader?"

"Who would have expected Sir Hadrian to be in the finals of the tournament?" Nimbus said loudly. "I certainly didn't think a novice would be challenging for the title tomorrow. And against Sir Breckton! You must admit Lady Amilia certainly backed the right arm-and-shield there. Who are you favoring, Your Majesty?"

Roswort pursed his lips. "I find both of them disagreeable. The whole tournament has been too tame for my taste. I prefer the theatrics of Elgar and Gilbert. They know how to play to a crowd. This year's finalists are as solemn as monks, and neither has done anything other than unseat their opponents. That's bad form, if you ask me. Knights are trained for war.

They should instinctually seek to kill rather than merely bust a pole on a reinforced plate. I think they should be required to use war tips. Do that, and you'll see something worth watching!"

When the last performance finished, the lord chamberlain rapped his brass-tipped staff on the flagstones and Ethelred stood. Conversations trailed off as the banquet hall fell silent.

"My friends," Lanis Ethelred began in his most powerful voice, "I address you as such to assure you that even though you will soon be my loyal subjects, I will always think of you, first and foremost, as my friends. We have weathered a long hard struggle together. Centuries of darkness, hardship, barbarianism, and threats from Nationalists have plagued us. But in just two days' time, the sun will dawn on a new age. This Wintertide we celebrate the rebirth of civilization—the start of a new era. As our lord Maribor has seen fit to bestow onto me the crown of supreme power, I will pledge to be faithful to his design and lead mankind armed with the firm hand of righteousness. I will return to traditional values in order to make the New Empire a beacon to light the world and blind our enemies."

The hall applauded.

"I hope you all enjoyed your game birds, courtesy of the hawking. Tomorrow the finalists of the joust will tilt for the honor of best knight. I hope you will all enjoy the contest between two such capable men. Sir Breckton, Sir Hadrian—where are you?—please stand, both of you." The two knights hesitantly rose to their feet, and the audience applauded. "A toast to the elite of the New Empire!"

Ethelred, along with everyone else in the hall, drank in their honor. The regent sat back down, and Amilia motioned to the musicians to take their places.

As on the previous nights, couples took to the open floor to dance. Amilia spotted Sir Breckton, dressed in a silver tunic, striding her way. When he reached the head table, he bowed before her.

"Excuse me, my lady. Might I enjoy the pleasure of your company for the dance?"

Amilia's heart beat quickly at his invitation, and she could not think clearly. Before remembering that she could not dance, she stood, walked around the table, and offered her hand.

Taking it, the knight gently led her to where pairs of dancers formed into lines. Accompanying him in such an intimate setting felt like a dream. When the first notes of music hit the air, that dream turned to a nightmare. Amilia had no idea what to do. She had watched the dances the past several evenings but not to learn their steps. All she could recall was that the dance started in rows and ended in rows, and at some point in the middle, the dancers touched hands and traded places several times in rapid succession. All other details were a mystery. For a moment, Amilia considered returning to the security of her chair, but to do so now would embarrass her and humiliate Breckton. Light-headed, she hovered on the verge of fainting but managed a curtsy in response to Breckton's bow.

Nothing could save her from the pending disaster. In her mind played a scene, in which she staggered, tripped, and fell. The other nobles would laugh and sneer while tears ran down her cheeks. She imagined them saying, *What possessed you to think you could be one of us?* Not even Breckton's calm gaze was able to reassure Amilia.

She shifted her weight from left to right, knowing some action would be required in a half bar of music. If only she knew which foot to use, she might manage the first step.

Suddenly the music stopped and the entire assemblage halted.

A hush fell as conversations died, replaced by scattered gasps. Everyone stood and all eyes were transfixed as into the great hall strode Her Most Serene and Royal Grand Imperial Eminence, Empress Modina Novronian.

Two fifth-floor guards flanked her as they crossed the hall. The empress was dressed in the formal gown she had worn for the speech on the balcony, the luxurious mantle trailing behind her. Modina's hair was pulled under a mesh cowl, upon which rested the imperial crown. She walked with stunning grace and dignity—chin high, shoulders squared, back straight. As she passed through the silent crowd, she appeared ethereal, like a mythical creature slipping through trees in a forest.

Amilia blinked several times, unsure what she was actually seeing and remained as transfixed as the others. The effect of Modina's appearance was astounding and was reflected by every face in the room. No one moved and few appeared to breathe.

Reaching the front of the room, Modina walked down the length of the main table to the imperial throne left vacant each of the previous nights. The empress paused briefly in front of her seat, raised a delicate hand, and simply said, "Continue."

There was a long pause, and then the musicians began to play once more. Saldur and Ethelred both glared at Amilia, who promptly excused herself from the dance. Her leaving the floor was quite understandable now, though she was sure it no longer mattered. Amilia doubted anyone, except perhaps Sir Breckton, noticed or cared.

She returned to the main table and stood behind Modina.

"Your Eminence, are you certain you are strong enough to be here? Wouldn't you like me to escort you back to your room?" she asked softly.

Modina did not look at Amilia. The empress's eyes scanned the room, taking in the revelry. "Thank you, my dear. You are so kind to inquire, but I am fine." Amilia exchanged glances with Ethelred and Saldur, both of whom looked tense and helpless.

"I think you should not be risking yourself so," Saldur told Modina. "You need to save your strength for your wedding."

"I am certain you are quite correct, Your Grace—as you always are—and I will not stay long. Still, my people deserve to see their empress. Maribor forbid that they come to suspect I don't exist at all. I am certain many couldn't distinguish me from a milkmaid. It would be a sad thing indeed if I arrived at my wedding and no one could tell the bride from the bridesmaids."

Saldur's look of bewilderment was replaced with a glare of anger.

Amilia remained behind the empress's chair, unsure what to do next. Modina tapped her fingers and nodded in rhythm with the music while watching the dance. By contrast, Saldur and Ethelred were as rigid as statues.

At the end of the song, Modina applauded and got to her feet. The moment she rose, all the guests stopped once more, fixing their eyes on her.

"Sir Breckton and Sir Hadrian, please approach," the empress commanded.

Saldur shot another concerned glance at Amilia, who could do nothing but clutch the back of Modina's chair.

The two knights came forward and stood side by side before the empress. Hadrian followed Breckton's lead, bending to one knee and bowing his head.

"Tomorrow you will compete for the glory of the empire, and Maribor will decide your fate. You are clearly both beloved by this court, but I see Sir Breckton wears the token of my secretary, Lady Amilia. This grants him an unfair advantage, but I will not ask him to refuse such a gift. Nor would I ask Lady Amilia to seek its return, as a favor once given is a sacred endorsement of faith. Instead, I will mirror her gesture by granting Sir Hadrian my token. I proclaim my faith in his skill, character, and sacred honor. I know his heart is righteous, and his intentions virtuous." Modina drew out a piece of pure white cloth that Amilia recognized as part of her nightgown, and held it out.

Hadrian took the cloth.

Modina continued, "May you both find honor in the eyes of Maribor and compete *as true and heroic knights*."

The empress clapped her hands and the hall followed her lead, erupting in cheers and shouts. In the midst of the thunder, Modina turned to Amilia and said, "You may escort me back to my room now."

The two walked down the length of the table. As they passed the Queen of Dunmore, Freda looked stricken. "Lady Amilia, what I said earlier—I—I didn't mean anything by that, I just—"

"I'm sure you meant no disrespect. Please sit, Your Majesty. You look pale," Amilia said to the queen, and led Modina out of the room. Saldur watched them go, and Amilia was thankful he did not follow. She knew there would be an interrogation, but she had no idea how to explain Modina's behavior. The empress had never done anything like this before.

Neither woman said anything as they walked arm in arm to the fifth floor. The door to Modina's bedchamber stood unguarded. "Where is Gerald?" Amilia asked.

"Who?" the empress replied with a blank look.

Amilia scowled. "You know very well who. Gerald. Why isn't he guarding your door? Did you send him on an errand to get him out of the way?"

"Yes, I did," the empress replied casually.

Amilia frowned. They entered the bedroom and she closed

the door behind them. "Modina, what were you thinking? Why did you do that?"

"Does it matter?" the empress replied, settling onto her bed with a soft bounce.

"It matters to the regents."

"It's only two days until Ethelred comes to my bedroom and takes me to the cathedral for our marriage. I did no damage. If anything, I reassured the nobles that I exist and am not just a myth created by the regents. They should thank me."

"That still doesn't explain why."

"I have only a few hours left and felt like getting out. Can you begrudge me this?"

The anger melted from Amilia and she shook her head. "No."

Ever since the mirror had appeared in Modina's room, the two had avoided discussing the empress's plans for Wintertide. Amilia considered having it removed, but knew that would not matter. Modina would just find another way. The secretary's only other alternative was to tell Saldur, but the regent would imprison the empress. The ordeal had nearly destroyed Modina once, and Amilia could not be responsible for inflicting that on her again—even to save the empress's life. There seemed to be no solution. Especially considering that if their places were reversed, Amilia would probably do the same thing. She had tried to delude herself into believing that Modina would change her mind, but the empress's words and the reminder of Wintertide's approach brought her back to reality.

Amilia helped Modina out of her gown, tucked the empress into the big bed, and hugged her tightly while trying to hide her tears.

Modina patted Amilia's head. "It will be all right. I am ready now."

✧

Hadrian trudged back to the knights' wing, carrying the white strip of cloth as if it weighed a hundred pounds. Seeing Thrace had removed one burden, but her words had replaced it with an even heavier load. He passed by the common room, where a handful of knights still lingered. They handed around a bottle, taking swigs from it.

"Hadrian!" Elgar shouted. The large man stepped into the hall, blocking his path. Elgar's face was rosy, and his nose red, but his eyes were clear and focused. "Missed you at the hawking today. Come on in and join us."

"Leave me alone, Elgar, I'm in no mood tonight."

"All the more reason to come have a drink with us." The big warrior grinned cheerfully, slapping Hadrian on the back.

"I'm going to sleep." Hadrian turned away.

Elgar gripped him by the arm. "Listen, my chest still hurts from when you drove me off my saddle."

"I'm sorry about that but—"

"Sorry?" Elgar looked at him, clearly confused. "Best clobbering I've taken in years. That's how I know you can take Breckton. I've wagered money on it. I thought you were a joke when you first showed up, but after that flying lesson...Well, if you're a joke, it's not a terribly funny one."

"You're apologizing?"

Elgar laughed. "Not in your lifetime! Summersrule is only six months away, and I'll have another chance to repay in kind. But just between you and me, I'm looking forward to seeing Sir Shiny eat some dirt. Sure you won't have a drink? Send you off to bed right proper?"

Hadrian shook his head.

"All right, go get your beauty rest. I'll keep the boys as

quiet as I can, even if I have to bash a few skulls. Good luck tomorrow, eh?"

Elgar returned to the common room, where at least two of the knights were trying to sing "The Old Duke's Daughter" and doing a terrible job of it. Hadrian continued to his room, opened the door, and froze.

"Good evening, Hadrian," Merrick Marius greeted him. He was dressed in an expensive crimson silk garnache. Around his neck was a golden chain of office. Merrick sat nonchalantly at the chamber's little table, upon which sat the chessboard from the common room. All the pieces were in their proper starting places except for a single white pawn, which was two spaces forward. "I have taken the liberty of making the first move."

The room was too small for anyone to hide in—they were alone. "What do you want?" Hadrian asked.

"I thought that was obvious. I want you to join me. It's your turn."

"I'm not interested in playing games."

"I think it is a bit presumptuous to consider this a mere game." Merrick's voice was paradoxically chilling and friendly, a mannerism Hadrian had witnessed many times before—in Royce.

Merrick's demeanor distressed him. Hadrian had learned to read a man by his tone, his body language, and the look in his eye, but Merrick was impossible to peg. He appeared completely relaxed, yet he should not be. Although larger and heavier than Royce, Merrick was not a big man. He did not look like a fighter, nor did he appear to be wearing any weapons. If Merrick was half as smart as Royce had suggested, he knew Hadrian could kill him. Given how he had manipulated them on the *Emerald Storm*, which had resulted in the death of Wesley Belstrad and the destruction of Tur Del Fur, Merrick should further know it was a real possibility, yet the man showed no sign of concern. It unnerved Hadrian and made him think he was missing something.

Hadrian took the seat across from Merrick and, after glancing at the board for only a moment, slid a pawn forward.

Merrick smiled with the eagerness of a small boy starting his favorite pastime. He moved another pawn, putting it in jeopardy, and Hadrian took it.

"Ah, so you accept the Queen's Gambit," Merrick said.

"Huh?"

"My opening moves. They are referred to as the Queen's Gambit. How you respond indicates acceptance or not. Your move has signaled the former."

"I just took a pawn," Hadrian said.

"You did both. Are you aware chess is known as the King's Game due to its ability to teach war strategy?"

Almost without thought, Merrick brought another pawn forward.

Hadrian did not reply as he looked at the board. His father had taught him the game when he was a boy to strengthen Hadrian's understanding of tactics and planning. Danbury Blackwater had made a board and set of pieces from metal scraps. His father had been the best chess player in the village. It had taken years for Hadrian finally to checkmate him.

"Of course, the game has broader implications," Merrick went on. "I've heard bishops base whole sermons on chess. They draw parallels indicating how the pieces represent the hierarchy of the classes, and the rules of movement depict an individual's duty as ordained by God."

Merrick's third pawn was in jeopardy, and Hadrian took it as well. Merrick moved his bishop, again without pause. The man's playing style disturbed Hadrian, as he expected more contemplation after Hadrian had taken two of his pieces.

"So you see, what you deem a simple, frivolous game is actually a mirror to the world around us and how we move in it. For example, did you know that pawns were not always allowed to move two squares at the start? That advent was the result of progress and a slipping of monarchial power. Furthermore, upon reaching the opposite side of the board, pawns used to only be promoted to the rank of councilor, which is the second-weakest piece, after the pawn itself."

"Speaking of pawns... We didn't appreciate you using us at Tur Del Fur," Hadrian said.

Merrick raised a hand. "Royce has already scolded me on that score."

"Royce—he spoke to you?"

Merrick chuckled. "Surprised I'm still alive? Royce and I have a...an understanding. To him I am like that bishop on the board. I'm right there—an easy target—and yet the cost is too high."

"I don't understand."

"You wouldn't."

"You tricked us into helping you slaughter hundreds of innocent people. Royce has killed for far less."

Merrick looked amused. "True, Royce usually requires a reason *not* to kill. But don't deceive yourself. He's not like you. The deaths of innocents, no matter how many, are meaningless to him. He just doesn't like being used. No, I would venture to say that only one murder has ever caused him to suffer remorse, and that is why I'm still alive. Royce feels the scales are not balanced between us. He feels he still owes me."

Merrick gestured toward himself. "Were you waiting on me? I believe it's your move."

Hadrian decided to be more daring and pulled out his queen to threaten Merrick's king. Merrick moved instantly, sliding his king out of harm's way, almost before Hadrian removed his hand.

"Now where was I?" Merrick continued. "Oh yes, the evolution of chess, which changes just as the world does. Centuries ago there was no such thing as castling, and a stalemate was considered a win for the player causing it. Most telling, I think, is the changing role of the queen in the game."

Hadrian brought forward a pawn to threaten the bishop, and Merrick promptly took it. Hadrian moved his knight out and Merrick did the same.

"Originally there was no queen at all, as all the pieces were male. Instead, a piece called the king's chief minister held that position. It wasn't until much later that the female queen replaced this piece. Back then she was restricted to moving only one square diagonally, which made her quite weak. It wasn't until later that she obtained the ability to move the entire length of the board in any direction, thus becoming the most powerful piece in the game—and the most coveted target to trap or kill."

Hadrian started to move his bishop but stopped when he realized that Merrick's knight was threatening his queen.

"That was an interesting speech the empress delivered at the feast, don't you think?" Merrick asked. "Why do you think she did that?"

"No idea," Hadrian replied, studying the board.

Merrick smiled at him. "I see why Royce likes you. You're not big on conversation. You two are quite the odd pairing, aren't you? Royce and I are far more similar. We each maintain a common pragmatic view of the world and those in it, but you are more an idealist and dreamer. You look like an ale drinker to me, and Royce prefers his Montemorcey."

Another quick succession of moves made Hadrian slow down his play and left him studying the board.

"Did you know I introduced him to that particular wine? That was years ago, when I brought him a case for his birthday. Well, that's not precisely correct. Royce has no idea about the actual date of his birth. Still, it could have been, so we celebrated like it was. I liberated the wine from a Vandon caravan loaded with merchandise, and we spent three whole days drinking and debauching a tiny agrarian village. That town had a surprisingly large proportion of attractive maids. I had never seen Royce drunk before that. He's usually so serious—all dark and brooding—or at least he was back then. For those three days he relaxed and we had arguably the best time of our lives."

Hadrian focused on the board.

"We were quite the team back in our day. I'd plan the jobs and he'd execute them. We had quite a contest going. I tried to see if I could invent a challenge too difficult, but he always surprised me. His skills are legendary. Of course, back then the shackles of morality didn't weigh him down. That's your doing, I suppose. You tamed the demon, or at least think you have."

Hadrian found Merrick's conversation irritating and realized that was the point. He moved his queen to safety. Merrick innocently, almost absentmindedly, slid a pawn forward.

"It's still there, though—the demon within—hiding; you can't change the nature of someone like Royce. In Calis they try to tame lions, did you know that? They take them as cubs and raise them in palaces as pets for princes. They think them safe until one day the family dogs are gone. 'Perhaps the dogs warranted it,' the love-struck prince says. 'Perhaps the hounds attacked the cat or antagonized it,' he says as he strokes his loyal beast. The next day they find the carcass of the prince in a tree. No, my friend, you can't tame a wild animal. Eventually it will return to its true nature."

Hadrian made a series of moves that succeeded in taking the white bishop. He could not determine if Merrick was just toying with him or was not nearly as good at the game as Hadrian had expected.

"Does he ever speak of me?" asked Merrick.

"You sound like an abandoned mistress."

Merrick sat straighter and adjusted the front of his tunic. "You've had a chance to see Breckton joust. Is there any doubt about whether you can defeat him?"

"No."

"That's good. But now comes the important question... will you?"

"I made an agreement, didn't I? You were there."

Merrick leaned forward. "I know you—or at least your type. You're having second thoughts. You don't think it's right to kill an innocent man. You've met Breckton. He's impressive. The kind of man you want to be. You're hating yourself right now, and you hate me because you think I helped arrange it. Only I didn't. I have no part in this—well, beyond suggesting they offer you the princess. Whether you want to thank me or kill me for that, I'd just like to point out that at the time you were threatening to kill everyone in the room."

"So if this is none of your business, then why are you here?"

"I need Royce to do another job for me—an important one—and he'll be far less inclined if you die, which you will if you don't kill Breckton. If, however, you keep your promise, everything should work out nicely. So I've come to affirm what you already know, and what Royce would tell you if he were here. You *must* kill Breckton. Keep in mind you will be trading the life of the most capable enemy of Melengar for its princess and the leader of the Nationalists. Together, they could revitalize the resistance. And let's not forget your legacy. This is your one chance to correct the sin of your father and bring peace to his spirit. If nothing else, don't you think you owe Danbury that much?"

"How do you know about that?"

Merrick merely smiled.

"You're a smug bastard, aren't you?" Hadrian glared at him. "But you don't know everything."

Hadrian reached out to move, but Merrick raised a hand and stopped him.

"You're about to take my rook with your bishop. After that, you will take the other with your queen. How can you not? The poor castle is completely undefended. You'll be feeling quite pleased with yourself at that point. You'll be thinking that I don't play this game anywhere near as well as you expected. What you won't realize is that while you have gained materially, you've systematically given up control of the board. You'll have more troops but discover too late that you can't effectively mount an attack. I will sacrifice my queen. You will have no choice but to kill her. By that time, I will be perfectly positioned to reach your king. In the end, you will have taken a bishop, two rooks, and my queen, but none of this will matter. I will checkmate you on the twenty-second turn by moving my remaining bishop to king's seven." Merrick stood and moved toward the door. "You've already lost, but you lack the foresight to see it. That's your problem. I, on the other hand, do not suffer from that particular malady. I am telling you for your own good, for Royce's sake, for Arista, Gaunt, and even for your father—you must kill Sir Breckton. Good night, Hadrian."

CHAPTER 16

TRIALS BY COMBAT

The sky was overcast, the day a dull gray, and the wind blew a chilled blast across the stands. And yet the crowd at Highcourt was larger and louder than ever. The entire imperial court, and most of the town, had turned out to see the spectacle. Every inch of the bleachers was jammed, and a sea of bodies pushed against the fence. On the staging field only the blue and gold tent of Sir Breckton and the green and white tent of Sir Hadrian remained.

Hadrian arrived early that morning alongside Renwick, who went right to work feeding and brushing Malevolent. Hadrian did not want to be in the palace and risk an encounter with Breckton, Amilia, or Merrick. All he wanted was to be left alone and for this day to be over.

"Hadrian!" a strangely familiar voice called. Along the fence line, he spotted a man amidst the crowd waving at him while a pike-armed guard held him back. "It's me, Russell Bothwick from Dahlgren!"

Leaving Renwick to finish dressing Malevolent, Hadrian walked over to the fence to get a better look. As he did, his shadows from the palace moved closer.

Hadrian shook Russell's hand. His wife, Lena, and his son

Tad stood next to Hadrian's old host. Behind them was Dillon McDern, the town smith, who had once helped Hadrian build bonfires to fend off a monster.

"Let them through," Hadrian told the guard.

"Look at you!" Dillon exclaimed as they passed under the rail to join Hadrian at his tent. "Too bad Theron's not here. He'd be braggin' about how he had taken fencing lessons from the next Wintertide champion."

"I'm not champion yet," Hadrian replied solemnly.

"That's not what Russell here's been saying." Dillon clapped his friend on the back. "He's done his own fair share of bragging at every tavern in town about how the next champion once spent a week living in his home."

"Four people bought me drinks for that," Russell said with a laugh.

"It's very nice to see you again," Lena said, taking Hadrian's hand gently and patting it. "We all wondered what became of you and your friend."

"I'm fine and so is Royce, but what happened to all of you?"

"Vince led us all to Alburn," Dillon explained. "We manage to scratch a living out of the rocky dirt. It's not like it was in Dahlgren. My sons have been taken for the imperial army, and we have to hand over most of what we grow. Still, I guess it could be worse."

"We saved all our coppers to come up here for the holidays," Russell said. "But we had no idea we'd find *you* riding in the tournament. Now that really is something! Rumor is they knighted you on the field of battle. Very impressive."

"Not as much as you might think," Hadrian replied.

"How's Thrace?" Lena asked, still holding his hand.

He hesitated, not sure what to say. "I don't know. I don't get to see her much. But she came to the banquet last night and she looked well enough."

"We just about died when we heard Deacon Tomas was calling for her to be crowned empress."

"Thought the old boy had gone mad, really," Dillon put in. "But then they went and did it! Can you imagine that? Our little Thrace—I mean, Modina—empress! We had no idea she and Theron were descended from Novron. That's probably where the old man got all his stubbornness and she her courage."

"I wonder if she's in love with Regent Ethelred," speculated Verna, Dillon's daughter. "I bet he's handsome. It must be wonderful to be the empress and live in that palace with servants and knights kissing your hand."

"You'd think she woulda remembered some of us *little folk* who cared for her like a daughter," Russell said bitterly.

"Rus!" Lena scolded him. Her eyes drifted to the high walls of the palace visible over Highcourt's tents. "The poor girl has gone through so much. Look up there. Do you think she's happy with all these problems she has to deal with? Wars and such. Do you think she has time to think about old neighbors, much less track us down? Of course not, the poor dear!"

"Excuse me, Sir Hadrian, but it's time," Renwick announced, leading Malevolent.

With the help of a stool, Hadrian mounted the horse, which was decorated in full colors.

"These are friends of mine," Hadrian told the squire. "Take care of them for me."

"Yes, sir."

" 'Yes, *sir*'! Did you hear that?" Dillon slapped his thigh. "Wow, to be knighted and in the final bout of the Wintertide tournament. You must be the happiest man in the world right now."

Hadrian looked at their faces and tried to smile before trotting toward the gate.

The crowd exploded with applause as the two knights rode onto the field. The clouds overhead were heavier than before and appeared to have drained the color from the banners and flags. He felt cold, inside and out, as he took his position at the gate.

Across from him, Breckton waited in the same fashion. His horse's caparison waved in the bitter wind. The squires arrived and took their positions on the podium, beside the lances. The herald, a serious-looking man in a heavy coat, stepped up to the platform. The crowd grew silent when trumpeters blew the fanfare for the procession to begin.

Ethelred and Saldur rode at the head of the line, followed by King Armand and Queen Adeline of Alburn, King Roswort and Queen Freda of Dunmore, King Fredrick and Queen Josephine of Galeannon, King Rupert of Rhenydd — recently crowned and not yet married — and King Vincent and Queen Regina of Maranon. After the monarchs came the princes and princesses, the lord chancellor and lord chamberlain, Lady Amilia and Nimbus, and the archbishop of each kingdom. Lastly, the knights arrived and took their respective seats.

The trumpeters blew once more and the herald addressed the crowd in loud, reverent tones.

"On this hallowed ground, this field of tourney where trials are decided, prowess and virtue revealed, and truth discovered, we assemble to witness this contest of skill and bravery. On this day, Maribor will decide which of these two men shall win the title of Wintertide champion!"

Cheers burst forth from the crowd and the herald paused, waiting for them to quiet.

"To my left, I give you the commander of the victorious Northern Imperial Army, hero of the Battle of Van Banks, son of Lord Belstrad of Chadwick, and favored of our lady Amilia of Tarin Vale — Sir Breckton of Chadwick!"

Again, the crowd cheered. Hadrian caught sight of Amilia in the stands, clapping madly with the rest.

"To my right, I present the newest member to the ranks of knightly order, hero of the Battle of Ratibor, and favored of Her Most Serene and Royal Grand Imperial Eminence, Empress Modina Novronian—Sir Hadrian!"

The crowd roared with such intensity that Hadrian could feel their shouts vibrating his chest plate. Looking at the sea of commoners, he could almost imagine a small boy standing next to his father, waiting in excited anticipation.

"For the title of champion, for the honor of the empire, and for the glory of Maribor these two battle. May Maribor grant the better man victory!"

The herald stepped down to the blasts of trumpets, which were barely noticeable above the cry of the crowd.

"Good luck, sir." A stranger dressed in gray stood at Hadrian's station, holding out his helm.

Hadrian looked around but could not see Renwick anywhere. He took the helm and placed it on his head.

"Now, *the lance*, sir," the man said.

The moment Hadrian lifted it, he could tell the difference. The weapon looked the same, but the tip was heavy. Holding it actually felt better to him, more familiar. There was no doubt he could kill Breckton with it. His opponent was a good lancer, but Hadrian was better.

Hadrian glanced once more at the stands. Amilia stood with her hands pressed to her face. He tried to think of Arista and Gaunt. Then his eyes found the empty space between Ethelred and Saldur—the throne of the empress—Modina's empty seat.

I proclaim my faith in his skill, character, and sacred honor. I know his heart is righteous, and his intentions virtuous. May you both find honor in the eyes of Maribor and compete as true and heroic knights.

The flags rose and he took a deep breath, lowering his visor. The trumpets sounded, the flags dropped, and Hadrian spurred his horse. Breckton responded at the same instant and the two raced toward each other.

Hadrian crossed only a quarter of the field before pulling back on the reins. Malevolent slowed to a stop. The lance remained in its boot, pointing skyward.

Breckton rode toward him. A bolt of gold and blue thundering across the frozen ground.

Excellent form.

The thought came to Hadrian as if he were a spectator, safe in the stands, like that boy so long ago holding his father's hand along the white rail, feeling the pounding of the hooves. He closed his eyes and braced for the impact. "I'm sorry, Da. I'm sorry, Arista," he muttered within the shell of his helm. With luck, Breckton's blow might kill him.

The hoofbeats drummed closer.

Nothing happened. Hadrian felt only the breeze of the passing horse.

Did he miss? Is that possible?

Hadrian opened his eyes and turned to see Breckton riding down the alley.

The crowd died down, shuffling as a low murmur drifted on the air. Hadrian removed his helm just as Breckton pulled his horse to a stop. The other knight also removed his helm and trotted back to meet Hadrian at the rail.

"Why didn't you tilt?" Breckton asked.

"You're a good man. You don't deserve to die by treachery." Hadrian let the tip of his lance fall to the ground. Upon impact, the broad ceramic head shattered to reveal the war point.

"Nor do you," Breckton said. He slammed his own pole and revealed that it too had a metal tip. "I felt its weight when

I charged. It would seem we are both the intended victims of deceit."

The sergeant of the guard led a contingent of twenty soldiers onto the field and said, "The two of you are ordered to dismount! By the authority of the regents, I place you under arrest."

"Arrest?" Breckton asked, looking confused. "On what charge?"

"Treason."

"Treason?" Breckton's face revealed shock at the accusation.

"Sir, dismount now or we will use force. Try to run and you *will* be cut down."

On the far side of the field, a contingent of seret entered in formation, and mounted troops blocked the exits.

"Run? Why would I run?" Breckton sounded bewildered. "I demand to hear the details of this charge against me."

No answer was provided. Outnumbered and out-armed, Breckton and Hadrian dismounted. Seret surrounded them and rushed the two knights off the field. As they did, Hadrian spotted Luis Guy in the stands near Ethelred and Saldur.

The crowd erupted. They booed and shouted. Fists shook and Highcourt Fields was pelted with whatever they could find to throw. More than once Hadrian heard the question "What's going on?"

The seret shoved them out of the arena through a narrow corridor of soldiers that created a path leading them out of the crowd's sight and into a covered wagon, which hauled them away.

"I don't understand," Breckton said, sitting among the company of five seret. "Someone conspires to kill us and we are accused of treason? It doesn't make sense."

Hadrian glanced at the hard faces of the seret and then down at the wagon floor. "The regents were trying to kill you…and I was supposed to do it. You were right. I'm not a knight. Lord Dermont never dubbed me. I wasn't even a soldier in the imperial army. I led the Nationalists *against* Dermont."

"Nationalists? But Regent Saldur vouched for you. They confirmed your tale. They—"

"Like I said, they wanted you dead and hired me to do it."

"But why?"

"You refused their offer to serve Ethelred. As commander of the Northern Imperial Army, that makes you a threat. So they offered me a deal."

"What *kind* of deal?" Breckton asked, his voice cold.

"I was to kill you in exchange for the lives of Princess Arista and Degan Gaunt."

"The Princess of Melengar and the leader of the Nationalists?" Breckton fell into thought once more. "Are you in her service? His?"

"Neither. I never met Gaunt, but the princess is a friend." Hadrian paused. "I agreed in order to save their lives. Because if I failed to kill you, they will die tomorrow."

The two traveled in silence for some time, rocking back and forth as the wooden wheels of the wagon rolled along the snow-patched cobblestone. Breckton finally turned to Hadrian and asked, "Why didn't you do it? Why didn't you tilt?"

Hadrian shook his head and sighed. "It wasn't right."

⤜

"There are over a hundred rioters just in Imperial Square," Nimbus reported. "And more arriving every minute. Ethelred has pulled the guards back and closed the palace gates."

"I heard some guards were killed. Is that true?" Amilia asked from her desk.

"Only one, I think. But several others were badly beaten. The rioters are calling for the empress."

"I've heard them. They've been chanting for the last hour."

"Since the tournament, they don't trust Ethelred or Saldur. The crowd wants an explanation and they'll accept it only from the empress."

"Saldur will be coming here, won't he? He'll want me to have Modina say something. He'll order me to have the empress make a statement about Breckton and Hadrian plotting to take the throne."

Nimbus sighed and nodded. "I would suspect so."

"I won't do it," Amilia said defiantly. She rose and slapped her desk. "Sir Breckton isn't a traitor and neither is Sir Hadrian. I won't be a party to their execution!"

"If you don't, it's likely you will share their fate," Nimbus warned. "After tomorrow, Ethelred will be the emperor. He will officially rule and there will be precious little need for Modina's nursemaid."

"I love him, Nimbus." This was the first time she had said the words—the first time she had admitted it, even to herself. "I can't help them kill him. I don't care what they do to me."

Nimbus gave her a sad smile and sat down in the chair near her desk. This was the first time that Amilia could remember him sitting in her presence without first asking permission. "I suppose they will have even less need for a tutor. Hadrian obviously did *something* wrong and I will likely be blamed."

Someone walked by outside the office and both shot nervous glances at the closed door.

"It's like the whole world is ending." Tears ran down Amilia's cheeks. "This morning I was so happy. I think I woke up happier than I'd ever been."

They paused anxiously as they heard several more people running past the door.

"Do you think I should check on Modina?" Amilia asked.

"It might be wise." Nimbus nodded. "The empress always sits by that window. She's bound to hear the protests. She'll be wondering what's going on."

"I should talk to her. After the way she acted at the feast, who knows what she's thinking?" Amilia stood.

Just as the two moved toward the door, it burst open and Saldur stormed in. The regent was red-faced, his jaw clenched. He slammed the door behind him.

"Here!" Saldur shoved a parchment in Amilia's face. A few lines of uneven text were scrawled across it. "Make Modina learn this and have her reciting it on the balcony in one hour — *exactly* as written!"

Wheeling to leave, he opened the door.

"No," Amilia said softly.

Saldur froze. Slowly, he closed the door and turned around. He glared at her. "What did you say?"

"I won't ask Modina to lie about Sir Breckton. That's what this is, isn't it?" She looked at the parchment and read aloud, "'My loyal subjects…'" She skipped down. "'…found evidence…Sir Breckton and Sir Hadrian…guilty of treason against the empire…committed the vilest crime both to man and god and must pay for their evil.'" Amilia looked up. "I won't ask her to read this."

"How dare you." Saldur rose to his full height and glowered down at her.

"How dare *you*?" she retorted defiantly. "Sir Breckton is a great man. He is loyal, considerate, kind, honora —"

Saldur struck Amilia hard across the face, sending her to the floor. Nimbus started to move to her but stopped short. Saldur ignored him.

"You were a scullery girl! Or have you forgotten? I *made* you! Have you enjoyed pretending to be a lady? Did you like

wearing fine dresses and riding off to the hunt, where knights
fawned all over you? I'm sure you did, but don't let your feelings for Breckton go to your head. This is no game and you
should know better. I understand you're upset. I understand
you like the man. But none of this matters. I am building an
empire here! The fate of future generations is in our hands.
You can't toss that aside because you have a crush on someone
you think looks dashing in a suit of armor. You want a knight?
I'll arrange for you to have any knight in the kingdom. I promise. I can even arrange a marriage with a crown prince, if that
is what you wish. How's that? Is that *grand* enough for you,
Amilia? Would you like to be a queen? Done. What matters
right now is that we keep the empire from crumbling. I've
given you power because I admire your cunning. But *this* is
not negotiable. Not this time.

  "There might only be a few hundred rioters out there now,"
Saldur said, pointing to her window, "but word will spread
and in a day or two we could be facing a civil war! Do you
want that? Do you want to force me to send the army out to
slaughter hundreds of citizens? Do you want to see the city set
on fire? I will not have it. Do you hear me?"

  Saldur grew angrier and more animated as his tirade continued. "I like you, Amilia. You've served me well. You're
smarter than any ten nobles, and I honestly plan to see you
rewarded handsomely for your service. I'm serious about making you a queen. I will need loyal, intelligent monarchs governing the imperial provinces. You've proved I can count on
you and that you can think for yourself. I value such qualities.
I admire your spirit, but not *this* time. You will obey me,
Amilia, or by Maribor's name, I'll have you executed with the
rest!"

  Amilia shook. Her lower lip trembled even as she clenched
her jaw. Still clutching the paper, she balled her hands into

tight fists and breathed deeply as she tried to control herself.
"Then you'd better order another stake for the bonfire," she
said, tearing the parchment in two.

He glared at her for a moment longer and then threw open
the door and two seret entered. "Take her!"

Chapter 17

The Final Darkness

J asper was back.

Arista lay on her side, face flat against the stone. She heard the rat skittering somewhere in the dark. The sound sent chills through her.

Everything hurt from lying on the floor. Worst of all, her feet and hands were numb nearly all the time now. Occasionally, Arista woke to the feel of her leg moving—the only indication that Jasper was eating her foot. Horrified, she would try to kick only to find her effort barely shifted her leg. She was too weak.

No food had arrived for a very long time, and Arista wondered how many days ago they had stopped feeding her. She was so feeble that even breathing took concentrated effort. The coming flames were now a welcome thought. That fate would be better than this slow death, being eaten alive by a rat she called by name.

Terrible ideas assailed her exhausted, unguarded mind.

How long will it take for a single rat to eat me? How long will I stay conscious? Will he remain content to gnaw off my foot, or once he realizes I can no longer resist, will he go for softer meat? Will I be alive when he eats my eyes?

Shocked to realize there were worse things than burning alive, Arista hoped Saldur had not forgotten her. She found herself straining, listening for the sounds of the guards and praying to Maribor that they would arrive soon. If she had the strength, Arista would gladly light the pyre herself.

She heard pattering, scratching on the floor, tiny nails clicking. Her heart fluttered at the sounds. Jasper was moving toward her head. She waited.

Patter, patter, patter—he came closer.

She tried to raise a hand, but it did not respond. She tried to raise her head, but it was too heavy.

Patter, patter, patter—closer still.

Arista could hear Jasper sniffing, smelling. He had never come this close to her face before. She waited—helpless. Nothing happened for several minutes. Starting to fall asleep, she stopped herself from drifting off. She did not want to be unconscious with Jasper so close. There was nothing she could do to keep him from feeding, but being awake was somehow better than not knowing.

When a minute had passed with no further noise, Arista thought the rat might have moved away. The sound of sharp teeth clicking told her Jasper was right next to her ear. He sniffed again and she felt him touch her hair. As the rat tugged, Arista began to cry, but she had no tears to weep.

Rumble.

Arista had not heard the sound in quite some time. The stone-on-stone grinding told her the door to the prison was opening.

There were sounds of gruff voices and several sets of footsteps.

Tink-tink!

Guards, but others were with them, others with softer shoes—boots perhaps? One walked; the other staggered.

"Put 'em in numbers four and five," a guard ordered.

More steps. A cell door opened. There was a scuffle and then the door slammed. More steps and the sound of a burden dragged across the stone. They came closer and closer but stopped just short of her door.

Another cell opened. The burden dropped—a painful grunt. *Tink-tink.*

The guards went back out and sealed them in. It was only a deposit. There would be no food, no water, no help, not even the salvation of an execution.

Arista continued to lie there. The noise had not scared Jasper away. She could hear him breathing near her head. In a moment or two, the rat would resume his meal. She began to sob again.

"Arista?"

She heard the voice but quickly concluded she had only imagined it. For the briefest moment she thought it was—

"Arista, it's Hadrian. Are you there?"

She blinked and rocked her head side to side on the stone floor.

What is this? A trick? A demon of my own making? Has my mind consumed itself at last?

"Arista, can you hear me?"

The voice sounded so real.

"Ha—Hadrian?" she whispered in a voice so faint she feared he would not hear.

"Yes!"

"What are you doing here?" Her words came out as little more than puffs of air.

"I came to save you. Only I'm not doing very well."

There was the sound of tearing cloth.

Nothing made sense. Like all dreams, this one was both silly and wonderful.

"I messed up. I failed. I'm sorry."

"Don't be..." she said to the dream, her voice cracking. "It means a lot...that you...that anyone tried."

"Don't cry," he said.

"How long until...my execution?"

There was a long pause.

"Please..." she begged. "I don't think I can stand this much longer. I want to die."

"*Don't say that!*" The dungeon boomed with his voice. The sudden outburst sent Jasper skittering away. "Don't you *ever* say that."

There was another long pause. The prison grew silent once more, but Jasper did not return.

The tower was swaying. She looked under the bed, but still she couldn't find the brush. How was that possible? They were all there except the first one. It was the most important. She had to have it.

Standing up, she accidently caught sight of her reflection in the swan mirror. She was thin, very thin. Her eyes had sunk into their sockets like marbles in pie dough. Her cheeks were hollow, and her lips stretched tight over bone, revealing rotted teeth. Her hair was brittle and falling out, leaving large bald areas on her pale white skull. Her mother stood behind her with a sad face, shaking her head.

"Mother, I can't find the brush!" she cried.

"It won't matter soon," her mother replied gently. "It's almost over."

"But the tower is falling. Everything is breaking and I have to find it. It was just here. I know it was. Esrahaddon told me I needed to get it. He said it was under the bed, but it's not here. I've looked everywhere and time is running out. Oh, Mother, I'm not going to find it in time, am I? It's too late. It's too late!"

Arista woke. She opened her eyes, but there was no light to indicate a difference. She still lay on the stone. There was no tower. There were no brushes, and her mother was long dead. It was all just a dream.

"Hadrian...I'm so scared," she said to the darkness. There was no answer. He had been part of the dream too. Her heart sank in the silence.

"Arista, it will be all right." She heard his voice again.

"You're a dream."

"No. I'm here."

His voice sounded strained.

"What's wrong?" she asked.

"Nothing."

"Something's wrong."

"Just tired. I was up late and—" He grunted painfully.

"Wrap the wounds tight," another man said. Arista did not recognize him. This voice was strong, deep, and commanding. "Use your foot as leverage."

"Wounds?" she asked.

"It's nothing. The guards just got a bit playful," Hadrian told her.

"Are you bleeding badly?" the other voice asked.

"I'm getting it under control...I think...Hard to tell in the dark. I'm...feeling a bit dizzy."

The dungeon's entrance opened again and once more there was the sound of feet.

"Put her in eight," a guard said.

The door to Arista's cell opened and the light of the guard's torch blinded her. She could barely make out Lady Amilia's face.

"Eight's taken," the guard shouted down the corridor.

"Oh yeah, number eight gets emptied tomorrow. Don't worry about it, for one night they can share."

The guard shoved the secretary inside and slammed the door, casting them into darkness.

"Oh dear Novron!" Amilia cried.

Arista could feel her kneeling beside her, stroking her hair. "Dear Maribor, Ella! What have they done to you?"

"Amilia?" the deep voice called out.

"Sir Breckton! Yes, it's me!"

"But—why?" the knight asked.

"They wanted me to make Modina denounce you. I refused."

"Then the empress knew nothing? This is not her will?"

"Of course not. Modina would never agree to such a thing. It was all Saldur's and Ethelred's doing. Oh, poor Ella, you're so thin and hurt. I'm so sorry."

Arista felt fingers brushing her cheek gently and realized she had not heard Hadrian in a long time. "Hadrian?"

She waited. There was no response.

"Hadrian?" she called again, fearful this time.

"Ella—er—Arista, calm down," Amilia said.

Arista felt her stomach tighten as she realized just how important it was to hear his voice, to know he was still alive. She was terrified he would not speak again. "Had—"

"I'm…here," he said. His voice was weak and labored.

"Are you all right?" Arista asked.

"Mostly, but drifting in and out."

"Has the bleeding stopped?" Breckton asked.

"Yeah…I think."

෴

As the night wore on, Modina could still hear them—voices shouting in anger and crying out in rage. There must be hundreds, perhaps thousands, by then. Merchants, farmers, sailors, butchers, and road menders all shouted with one voice.

They beat on the gate. She could hear the pounding. Earlier, Modina had seen smoke rising just outside the walls. In the darkness she could see the flicker of torches and bonfires.

What is burning? An effigy of the regents? The gate itself? Maybe it is just cook fires to feed all of them while they camp.

Modina sat at the window and listened to the wails the cold wind brought her.

The door to her bedroom burst open. She knew who was there before turning around.

"Get up, you little idiot! You're going to make a speech to calm the people."

Regent Saldur crossed the dim chamber with Nimbus in tow. He held out a parchment toward Nimbus.

"Take this and have her read it."

Nimbus slowly approached the regent and bowed. "Your Grace, I—"

"We don't have time for foolishness!" Saldur exploded. "Just make her read it."

The regent paced with intensity while Nimbus hurriedly lit a candle.

"Why is there no guard at this door?" Saldur asked. "Do you have any idea what could happen if someone else had waltzed up here? Have soldiers stationed as soon as we leave or I'll find someone *else* to replace Amilia."

"Yes, Your Grace."

Nimbus brought over the candle and said, "His Grace respectfully requests that—"

"Damn you." Saldur took the parchment from Nimbus. He brought it over and held it so close to Modina's face that she could not have read it even if she had known how. "*Read it!*"

Modina did not respond.

"You spoke well enough for Amilia. You always speak for *her.* You even opened your mouth when I threatened her for letting you play with that damn dog. Well, how's this, my little empress? You get out there and read this—clearly and accurately—or I will have your sweet little Amilia executed tomorrow along with the rest. Don't think I won't. I've already sent her to the dungeon."

Modina remained as unmoving as a statue.

Saldur struck her across the face. She rocked back but made no sound. Not a hand rose in defense. She did not flinch or blink. A tear of blood dripped from her lip.

"You insane little bitch!" He hit her again.

Once more, she showed no notice, no fear, no pain.

"I'm not certain she can even hear you, Your Grace," Nimbus offered. "Her Eminence has been known to go into a kind of trance when overwhelmed."

Saldur stared at the girl and sighed. "Very well, then. If the crowd doesn't disperse by morning, we'll send out the army to cut us a path to the cathedral. But the wedding *will* go on as scheduled and then we can finally be rid of her."

Saldur turned and left.

Nimbus paused to set the candle on Modina's table. "I'm so very sorry," he whispered before following the regent from the room.

The door closed.

Cool air on her face soothed the heat left by Saldur's hand.

"You can come out now," Modina said.

Mince crawled out from under the bed. He was pale in the light of the single flame.

"I'm sorry you had to hide, but I didn't want you to get into trouble. I knew he would be coming."

"It's okay. Are you cold? Do you want the robe?" he asked.

"Yes, that would be nice."

Mince crawled back under the bed and pulled out the shimmering cloth. He shook it a few times before gently draping it over her shoulders.

"Why do you sit next to this window? It's awfully chilly and the stone is hard."

"You can sit on the bed if you like," she said.

"I know, but why do *you* sit here?"

"It's what I do. It's what I've done for so very long now."

There was a pause.

"He hit you," Mince said.

"Yes."

"Why did you let him?"

"It doesn't matter. Nothing matters anymore. Soon it will all be over. Tomorrow is Wintertide."

They sat in silence for several minutes. She kept her eyes on the city, reflected by the flickering fires beyond her window. Behind her, Mince shifted and fidgeted occasionally, but he did not speak.

Eventually Modina said, "I want you to do something for me."

"You know I will."

"I want you to go back to the city again. This time I want you to stay there. You need to be careful and find somewhere safe until the rioting is over. But—and this is the important thing—I don't want you to come back here again. Will you promise me that?"

"Yes, if that is what you want," Mince told her.

"I don't want you to see what I must do. Or be hurt afterward because of it. I want you to remember me the way I've been over these last few days with you."

She got up, crossed to the boy, and kissed him on the forehead. "Remember what I said, and keep your promise to me."

Mince nodded.

Modina waited until he left the room and his footsteps faded down the hall. She blew out the candle, took the water pitcher from the dresser, and shattered the mirror.

❦

From under the tarpaulin draped over a potato cart, Royce peered around the courtyard. He took special care to study the darkened corners and the gap behind the woodpile. A yellow glow rose from beyond the front gate as if the city was ablaze. Shouts were still coming from the far side, growing louder and demanding the release of Hadrian and Breckton. The unseen mob called for the empress to show herself. It was a perfect diversion but also put every guard in the palace on alert.

"Are we going in or not?" Magnus grumbled, half buried in tubers. Royce answered by slipping out. The dwarf followed, and as they made their way to the well, Royce was impressed by how quietly Magnus moved. Royce kept a constant check on the guards facing the gate. No one was paying attention to the courtyard.

"You want to crank me down, or do you want to go first?" Magnus whispered.

"There's no power in existence that could cause me to let you do the lowering."

Magnus muttered something about a lack of trust and sat on the bucket, holding the rope tight between his legs. Royce waited for the dwarf to get settled, then lowered him until Magnus signaled him to stop. When the weight left the bucket, Royce lowered the pail to the bottom, braced the windlass, and climbed down the rope.

Albert had gained the dwarf access to the inner ward as a member of the wedding event crew. It had taken Magnus just five minutes to determine the dungeon's location. A few stomps told him where to find empty spaces below. A nighttime lowering into the well by Royce had revealed the rest. Magnus deduced that the well, peppered with small air ducts, ran along the outer wall of the prison, granting the dwarf access to the face of the ancient stone. For eleven nights, Magnus had worked, cutting an entry. Merrick had been right—the prison was dwarven made—but he had never expected Royce to bring his own dwarf, especially one with experience in burrowing through stone.

As Royce descended, he spotted a faint glow from an opening in the side of the shaft. The hole itself was really more like a tunnel, due to the thickness of the ancient stone. He removed the bundle he carried, containing a sword and lantern, and passed it through the hole to the dwarf. Even with all Magnus's skill, the stone must have been difficult to dig through, as the passage was narrow. While sufficient for a dwarf, it was a tight squeeze for Royce, and he hoped Hadrian would fit.

Emerging from the tunnel, Royce found himself peering around a small cell, where a dead body was lying on the floor. Dressed in a priest's habit and curled into a tight ball, the dead man gave off a terrible stench. The room was tiny, barely large enough to accommodate the corpse. Magnus stood awkwardly against the wall, holding a crystal that glowed with a faint green radiance.

Royce pointed at the rock. "Where'd you get the stone?"

"Beats the heck out of flint and steel, eh?" Magnus grinned and winked. "I dug it up. I'm a dwarf, remember?"

"Really trying to forget that," Royce said. He crossed to the door, picked the lock, and peered down the hallway outside. The walls had the same kind of markings he had seen in Gutaria Prison—small spidery patterns. He examined the seam where the walls met the floor.

"What are you waiting for? Let's get on with it," Magnus said.

"You in a hurry?" Royce whispered.

"It's cold. Besides, I can think of a lot better places to be than here. Heck, the stench is reason enough. I'd like to be done with this."

"I'm heading in. You wait here and watch for anyone coming behind us — and be careful."

"Royce?" Magnus asked. "I did good, right? With the stonework, I mean."

"Sure. You did fine."

"After this is over...you think you could let me study Alverstone for a while? You know, as kind of a reward — to show your appreciation and all."

"You'll be paid in gold, just like Albert. You've got to get over this obsession of yours."

Royce entered the hallway. The darkness was nearly absolute, the only illumination coming from Magnus's green stone.

He made a quick sweep of the corridors — no guards. Most of the cells were empty but he could hear faint movement and breathing from behind four doors. The only other sound was the *drip, drip, drip* of the well echoing off the stone walls. After he was sure it was safe, Royce lit the lantern but kept the flame low. He picked the lock on one of the cells and found a man lying motionless on the floor. His blond hair was a little longer than Royce remembered, but Royce was certain this was the man he had seen in the tower of Avempartha — Degan Gaunt. He was dangerously thin but still breathing. Royce shook him, but he did not wake. Royce left the door open and moved on.

He unlocked the next cell, and a man sitting on the floor looked up. The resemblance was unmistakable and Royce recognized him immediately.

"Who's there?" Breckton Belstrad asked, holding up a hand to block the glare of the lantern.

"No time to chat. Just wait here for a minute. We'll be leaving soon."

Royce moved to the next cell. Inside, two women slept. One he did not know, and the other he almost did not recognize. Princess Arista was ghastly thin, dressed in a rag, and covered with what looked to be bite marks. He left them and moved to the last cell.

"Fourth time's the charm," he whispered under his breath as he opened the final door.

Hadrian sat leaning against the wall. He was shirtless. His tunic had been torn into strips and tied around his leg, arm, and midsection. His shirt was fashioned into a pad pressed tight to his side. Each piece of material was soaked dark, but Royce's partner was still breathing.

"Wake up, buddy," Royce whispered, nudging him. Hadrian was damp with sweat.

"About time you got here. I was starting to think you ran off and left me."

"I considered it, but the thought of Magnus as my best man kinda forced the issue. Nice haircut, by the way. It looks good on you—very knightly."

Hadrian started a laugh that turned to grunts of pain.

"They skewered you good, didn't they?" Royce asked, adjusting the cloth strips. He pulled the midsection one tighter.

Hadrian winced. "The prison guards don't like me much. They lost money betting against me five jousts in a row."

"Oh, well, that's understandable. I would have stuck you too."

"You got Arista, right? And Gaunt? Is he alive?"

"Yeah, she's sleeping next door. As for Gaunt, he's in pretty bad shape. I'll have to drag him out. Can you walk?"

"I don't know."

Royce gripped Hadrian around the waist and slowly helped him up. Together they struggled down the corridor to the end cell with the well breach. Royce pushed on the door but it did not budge. He put more effort into it but nothing happened.

"Magnus, open the door," Royce whispered.

There was no answer.

"Magnus, come on. Hadrian is hurt and I'm gonna need your help. Open up."

Silence.

CHAPTER 18

WINTERTIDE

In the darkness of the prison, Amilia lay cradled in Breckton's arms, pondering the incomprehensible—how it was possible to drown simultaneously in bliss and fear.

"Look," Sir Breckton whispered.

Amilia raised her head and saw a weak light leaking around the last cell's door. In the pale glow, the figures in the prison appeared ghostly faint, devoid of all color. Princess Arista, Sir Hadrian, and Degan Gaunt lay in the corridor, on a communal bed built from straw gathered from all the cells. The three looked like corpses awaiting graves. Sir Hadrian's torso was wrapped in makeshift bandages stained frighteningly red. The princess was so thin that she no longer looked like herself, but Degan Gaunt was the worst of all. He appeared to be little more than skin stretched over bone. If not for his shallow breathing, he could have been a cadaver, several days dead.

During the night, a man had broken into the prison in an attempt to free them. He had opened the doors to the cells, but the plan to escape had failed. Now the man prowled around the prison.

"It's morning," Sir Breckton said. "It's Wintertide."

Realizing the light indicated a new day, Amilia began to cry. Breckton did not ask why. He simply pulled her close. From time to time the knight patted her arm and stroked her hair in a manner she could hardly have thought possible less than a day before.

"You'll be all right," he reassured her with surprising conviction. "As soon as the empress discovers the treachery of the regents, I am certain nothing will stop her from saving you."

Amilia pressed her quivering lips tightly together. She gripped the knight's arm and squeezed it.

"Modina is also a prisoner," Arista stated.

Amilia had thought the princess was sleeping. Looking over, she saw Arista's eyes were open and her head was tilted just enough to see them.

"They use her as a puppet. Saldur and Ethelred run everything."

"So she's a complete fabrication? It was *all* just a ruse? Even that story about slaying Rufus's Bane?" Breckton asked her.

"That was real," Arista replied. "I was there."

"You were there?" Amilia asked.

Arista started to speak, then coughed. She took a moment, then drew in a wavering breath. "Yes. She was different then—strong, unwavering. Just a girl, but one determined to save her father and daunted by nothing. I watched her pick up a bit of broken glass to use as a weapon against an invincible monster the size of a house."

"There now, my lady," Breckton said. "If the empress can do that, I am certain—"

"She can't save us!" Amilia sobbed. "She's dead!"

Breckton looked at her, stunned.

She pointed at the light under the door. "It's Wintertide. Modina killed herself at sunrise." She wiped her face. "The

empress died in her room, in front of her window, watching
the sun rise."

"But...why?" he asked.

"She didn't want to marry Ethelred. She didn't want to live.
She didn't have a reason to go on. She...she..." Overcome
with emotion, Amilia rose and moved down the corridor.
Breckton followed.

ଵ

Hadrian woke to the sound of Arista coughing. He struggled
to sit up, surprised at his weakness and wincing at the pain.
He inched close enough to lift the princess's head and rest it
on his thigh.

"How are you?" he asked.

"Scared. How about you?"

"I'm great. Care to dance?"

"Maybe later," Arista said. Her body was bruised and covered with ugly red marks. "This sounds terrible," she said,
"but I'm glad you're here."

"This sounds stupid," he replied, "but I'm glad I am."

"That is stupid."

"Yeah, well, I've had a run of stupidity as of late."

"I think we all have."

Hadrian shook his head. "Not like mine. I actually trusted
Saldur. I made a deal with him—and Luis Guy, of all people.
You and Royce wouldn't have made that mistake. Royce
would have used the time between jousts to break you out.
And you—you would've probably figured some way to take
over the whole empire. No, you two are the smart ones."

"You think I'm smart?" she asked softly.

"You? Of course. How many women could have taken a

city in armed conflict with no military training? Or saved their brother and kingdom from a plot to overthrow the monarchy? And how many would have tried to single-handedly break into the imperial palace?"

"You could have stopped before that last one. If you didn't notice, that was a colossal failure."

"Well, two out of three isn't so bad." He grinned.

"I wonder what is happening up there," Arista said after a time. "It's probably midday. They should have come and taken us to the stakes by now."

"Well, maybe Ethelred had a change of heart," Hadrian said.

"Or maybe they've decided to just leave us down here to starve."

Hadrian said nothing and Arista stared at him for a long time.

"What is it?" he asked.

"I want to ask you to do me a favor."

"What is it?"

"It's not an easy favor to ask," she said.

He narrowed his eyes. "Name it."

She still hesitated and then took a deep breath. Looking away at first, she said, "Will you kill me?"

Hadrian felt the air go out of him.

"What?"

She looked back at him but said nothing.

"Don't talk like that."

"You could strangle me." Reaching out, she took his hand and placed it to her neck. "Just squeeze. I'm certain it won't take long. I don't think it will hurt much. Please, I'm so weak already, and Royce didn't bring any food or water. I—I want it to be over. I just want this nightmare to end..." She started to cry.

Hadrian stared at her, feeling the warmth of her neck against his hand. His lips trembled.

"There's this rat, and he's going to…" She hesitated. "Please, Hadrian. Oh, please. Please?"

"No one is going to be eaten alive." Hadrian looked again at the marks on her skin. "Royce is working on a way out. This is what he does, remember? This is what we always do. We're miracle workers, right? Isn't that what Alric calls us? You just need to hang on."

Hadrian took his hand from her throat and pulled her close with his good arm. He felt dead inside, and only the stab wounds reminded him he was otherwise. He stroked Arista's hair while her body jerked with the sobs. Gradually, she calmed down and drifted back to sleep. Hadrian faded in and out as well.

"You awake?" Royce asked, sitting down next to Hadrian.

"Am now. What's up?"

"How you feeling?"

"I've had better days. What have you come up with? And it better be good, because I already told Arista how brilliant you are."

"How's she doing?" Royce asked.

Hadrian looked at the princess, who remained asleep, her head still resting against him.

"She asked me to kill her."

"I'll take that as *not well*."

"So? What have you found out?" Hadrian asked.

"It's not good. I've been over every inch of this dungeon three times now. The walls are solid and thick. There are no cracks or worn areas. Even with Magnus doing the digging with his special chisels, it took over a week to dig in. No telling how long it would take to tunnel out. I found some stairs leading up to what I assume is the entrance, but there's no lock. Heck, there isn't even a door. The stairway just ends at the stone ceiling. I still don't know what to make of that."

"It's a gemlock. Like Gutaria. A seret in the north tower has a sword with an emerald in the hilt."

"That would explain it. The door I came through won't budge. It's not locked, so it must be jammed somehow. It's probably our best chance at getting out. It's made of wood, so feasibly we could try to burn it down. It's pretty thick, though, so I'm not sure I can get it to catch even by using the straw and oil from the lantern. And the smoke—if it doesn't kill us first—could signal our escape and guards would be waiting at the top."

"Arista and Gaunt can't climb out through a well," Hadrian pointed out.

"Yeah, but that's just one of the problems. I'm positive the rope isn't there anymore. I'm not sure if they grabbed Magnus or if he's responsible. Either way, anyone bothering to spike the door would take the rope too."

"So where does that leave us?"

Royce shrugged. "The best I can come up with is to wait for dark and then try to burn down the door. Maybe no one will see the smoke. Maybe we won't suffocate before we can break it down. Maybe I can slip out unnoticed. Maybe I can kill the guards. Maybe I can rig a way to pull you out of the well."

"That's a lot of maybes."

"No kidding. But you asked." Royce sighed. "You got anything?"

"What about Arista?" Hadrian looked down at her sleeping face again, which he held cradled with his good arm. "She's weak but maybe—"

Royce shook his head. "There are runes all over the walls. Just like the ones in the prison Esrahaddon was in. If she could do anything, I'm pretty sure she would have by now."

"Albert?"

"If he has half a brain, he'll lie low. At this point he can't do anything but draw attention to himself."

"What about the deal Merrick offered?"

"How do you know about that?" Royce asked, surprised.

"He told me."

"You two talked?"

"We played chess."

Royce shrugged. "There's no deal. He'd already told me what I wanted to know."

They sat side by side in silence awhile. Finally Hadrian said, "I doubt this is any consolation, but I do appreciate you coming. I know you wouldn't be here if it weren't for me."

"Don't you ever get tired of saying that?"

"Yeah, but I'm pretty sure this will be the last time. At least I finally got to Gaunt. Some bodyguard I turned out to be. He's nearly dead."

Royce glanced over. "So that's the Heir of Novron, eh? I sort of expected more, you know? Scars, maybe, or an eye patch—something interesting, distinctive."

"Yeah, a peg leg, maybe."

"Exactly."

They sat together in the dim light. Royce was conserving the lantern oil. Eventually Breckton and Amilia returned and sat beside Arista. Lady Amilia's eyes were red and puffy. She placed her head on Breckton's shoulder, and he nodded a greeting to Hadrian and Royce.

"Royce, this is Sir Breckton," Hadrian said, introducing them.

"Yeah, I recognized him when I opened the door. For a moment, I thought it was Wesley looking back at me."

"Wesley? You've met my brother?"

Hadrian said, "We both have. I'm sorry I couldn't say

anything at the feast. Royce and I served with him on the *Emerald Storm*. Your brother had taken command after the captain was killed. I've followed many officers over the years, but I can truthfully say I never served under a more worthy and honorable man. If it wasn't for Wesley's bravery in battle, Royce and I both would have died in Calis. He made a sacrificial charge so others would live."

Royce nodded in agreement.

"You never cease to amaze me, Sir Hadrian. If that is indeed true, then I thank you. Between the two of us, Wesley was always the better man. I only hope I shall meet my end half as well as he did."

⁓

Saldur fumed as he started up the stairs to the fifth floor. It was past midday and they should have left for the cathedral hours earlier. The Patriarch himself was waiting to perform the ceremony.

As far back as Saldur could recall, which was a good many years, the Patriarch had never left his chambers in Ervanon. Those wishing to see him, to seek his council or blessing, had to travel to the Crown Tower. Even then, he accepted audiences only on rare occasions. The Patriarch had a reputation for refusing great nobles and even kings. Even the highest-ranking members of the church never saw him. Saldur had been bishop of Medford for nearly ten years without ever meeting the man. As far as the regent knew, even Galien, the former Archbishop of Ghent, who lived with the Patriarch in the Crown Tower, had never had a face-to-face meeting. That the sentinels made frequent visits to the tower was common knowledge, but Saldur doubted if any actually stood in the presence of the Patriarch.

That the Patriarch had left the Crown Tower for this auspicious occasion was a personal triumph for Saldur. He genuinely looked forward to meeting the great leader of the Nyphron Church—his spiritual father. The wedding was supposed to be a wondrous and moving event, a lavish production complete with a full orchestra and the release of hundreds of white doves. This day was the accumulation of years of careful planning, dating back to that fateful night in Dahlgren when the plan to elevate Lord Rufus to emperor had failed.

At that time, Deacon Tomas had been raving like a lunatic. He claimed to have witnessed the miracle of a young girl named Thrace killing the Gilarabrywn. Seeing as how Saldur himself had proclaimed that only the *true* Heir of Novron could slay that beast, the deacon's claim was perceived as a problem. Sentinel Luis Guy planned to erase the incident by killing both the deacon and the girl, but Saldur saw other possibilities.

The Patriarch had wanted to name Saldur as the next Archbishop of Ghent, to take the place of Galien, who had died in the Gilarabrywn's attack. The position was the highest in the church hierarchy, just below the Patriarch himself. The offer was tempting, but Saldur knew the time had arrived for him to take the reins of shaping a New Empire. He abandoned his holy vestments and donned the mantle of politics—something no officer of the church had done since the days of Patriarch Venlin.

Saldur weathered the condemnation of kings and bishops in his battle against ignorance and tradition. He pressured, cajoled, and murdered to reach his goal of a strong, unified empire that could change the world for the better. With his guidance, the glory of the Old Empire would rise once more. To the feeble minds of Ethelred and his ilk, that just meant one man on one throne. To Saldur it meant *civilization*. All that once was would be again. Wintertide marked the culmination of all his efforts and years of struggle. This was the last uphill battle and it was proving to be a challenge.

Saldur had expected the peasants to tire themselves out overnight, but their fury seemed to have increased. He was irked that the city, which had been quiet and orderly for years, chose this moment to rampage. In the past, people had been taxed penniless and starved to provide banquets for kings. Despite all this, they had never revolted. That they did so now was strange, but moreover, it was embarrassing.

Even Merrick had been surprised by the reprisal, which had appeared to come out of nowhere and everywhere at once. Saldur had expected some disappointment at the outcome of the joust and anticipated a few troublemakers. He knew there was a chance that one of the knights would live and supporters of the fallen champion might lash out. What he had not counted on was both competitors surviving. With no obvious crime, their arrests appeared unwarranted. Still, the response was curiously impassioned.

At first he thought it would be an easy matter to contend with, and ordered a dozen heavily armed soldiers to silence the agitators. The men returned bloodied and thinned in ranks. What they had met was not a handful of dissidents but a citywide uprising. The whole matter was frustrating, but of no actual concern. He had sent for the Southern Army, and it was on its way to restore order. That would take a day or so. In the meantime, Saldur proceeded with the wedding.

The ceremony had been delayed a few hours, as Saldur had needed the morning to arrange armed escorts for the carriage's trip to the cathedral. That had gone well and now he just needed to transport the bride and groom. He was anxious to get the final procession under way, but Ethelred had not returned with Modina. If he had not known better, Saldur might have thought Lanis was exercising his husbandly rights a bit early. Whatever the delay, he was tired of waiting.

Saldur reached the empress's bedroom and found two guards posted outside the door. At least Nimbus was following orders. Without a word to either guard, Saldur threw the door open, entered, and halted just past the threshold. The regent stood, shocked, as he took in the grisly scene.

The first thing he saw was the blood. A large pool spread across the white marble floor of the chamber. The second was the broken mirror. Its shards were scattered like brilliant islands in a red sea.

"What have you done!" he exclaimed before he could catch himself.

Modina casually turned away from the window to face him, the hem of her white nightgown soaked red to the knee. She looked at the regent without qualm or concern.

"He dared to place a hand on the empress's person," she said simply. "This cannot be allowed."

Ethelred's body lay like a twisted doll, an eight-inch shard of glass still protruding from his neck.

"But—"

Modina cocked her head slightly to one side like a bird and looked curiously at Saldur.

She held another long, sharp shard. Despite its being wrapped in material, her grip was so tight blood dripped down her wrist.

"I wonder how a feeble old man such as yourself would fare against a healthy, young farm girl armed with a jagged piece of glass."

"Guards!" he shouted.

The two soldiers entered the room but showed little reaction at the scene before them.

"Restrain her," Saldur commanded.

Neither of them moved toward the empress. They simply stood inside the doorway, unheeding.

"I said restrain her!"

"There's no need to shout," Modina said. Her voice was soft, serene. Modina moved toward Saldur, walking through the puddle. Her feet left macabre tracks of blood.

Panic welled in Saldur's chest. He looked at the guards, then back at the empress, who approached with the knifelike glass in her hand.

"What are you doing?" he demanded of the soldiers. "Can't you see she's crazy? She *killed* Regent Ethelred!"

"Your forgiveness, Your Grace," one guard said, "but she *is* the empress. The descendant of Novron. The child of god."

"She's *insane!*"

"No," Modina said, cold and confident. "I'm not."

Saldur's fear mingled with a burning rage. "You might have these guards fooled, but you won't succeed. Men loyal to me— the whole Southern Imperial Army—are already on their way."

"I know," she told him in her disturbingly dispassionate voice. "I know everything." She nodded at the guard and added, "As is fitting for the daughter of Novron.

"I know, for example, that you killed Edith Mon for aiding Arista, which incidentally she didn't—I did. The princess lived for weeks in this very room. I know you arranged to have Gaunt captured and imprisoned. I know you hired Merrick Marius to kill Esrahaddon. I know you made a deal with him that handed the port city of Tur Del Fur over to the Ba Ran Ghazel. I know how you bargained with a dwarf named Magnus to betray Royce Melborn in exchange for a dagger. I know you convinced Hadrian to kill Sir Breckton in the tournament. I know you slipped Breckton a war tip. Only neither knight killed the other. I like to think I had a hand in that.

"You thought you had anticipated everything, but you hadn't expected a riot. You didn't know about the rumors circulating through the throngs of the city to expect treachery at the joust as proof of your treason. Yesterday's crowd wasn't watching for entertainment—but for confirmation of that rumor.

"I also know that you were planning to kill me." She glanced down at Ethelred's body. "That was actually his idea. He doesn't care for women. You, on the other hand, just wanted to lock me up again in that hole. That hole that nearly drove me mad."

"How do you know all this?" Saldur felt real fear. This girl, this child, this peasant's daughter *had* slain the Gilarabrywn. She had butchered Ethelred, and now she knew— She knew everything. It was as if...as if she really were...

She smiled.

"Voices came to me. They told me everything." She paused, seeing the shock on his face. "No, the words were not Novron's. The truth is worse than that. Your mistake was appointing Amilia, who loved and cared for me. She freed me from my cell and brought me to this room. After so many months in the dark and cold, I was starved for sunlight. I spent hours sitting beside the window." She turned and looked at the opening in the wall behind her. "I had nothing to live for and had decided to kill myself. The opening was too small, but when I tried to fit through it, I heard the voices. Your office window is right below mine. It's easier to hear you in the summer, but even with your window closed, I can still make out the words.

"When I first came here, I was only a stupid farm girl, and I didn't care what was being said. After my family died, I didn't care about anything. As time went on, I listened and learned. Still there was nothing to care about—no one to live for. Then one day a little mouse whispered a secret in my ear that changed everything. I learned I have a new family, a family that loves me, and no monster will ever take them from me again."

"You won't get away with this! You're just a—a—"

"The word you are searching for is *empress*."

∽

That morning Archibald woke feeling miserable, and his spirits only fell as the day progressed. He did not bother going to the cathedral. He could not bear to see Ethelred taking *her* hand. Instead, he wandered the palace, listening to the sounds of the peasants shouting outside. There was the blast of an army trumpet coming from somewhere in the city. The Southern Army must be arriving.

A pity, he thought.

Even though he would fare poorly at the hands of the mob, should the rioters breach the gate or walls, he still reveled in the knowledge that the regents would suffer more.

He entered the great hall, which was empty except for the servants readying it for the wedding feast. They scurried about like ants, feverishly carrying plates, wiping chairs, and placing candles. A few of the ants bowed and offered the obligatory *my lord* as he passed. Archibald ignored them.

Reaching another corridor, he found himself walking toward the main stair. Archibald was halfway up the first flight before he realized where he was headed. The empress would not be there, but he was drawn to her room just the same. Modina would be at the altar by now, her room empty. A vacant space never to be filled again now that she was...He refused to think about it.

Out of the corner of his eye, he caught the movement of figures. Turning, he spotted Merrick Marius standing at the end of the corridor, speaking to someone Archibald did not recognize—an old man wrapped in a cloak. When they spotted him, the pair abruptly slipped around a corner. Archibald wondered whom Merrick was speaking with, as he was always up to no good. Just then, a commotion overhead interrupted his thoughts. Hearing a man cry out, he ran for the stairs.

When he reached the fourth floor, he found a guard lying dead. Blood dripped down the marble steps in tiny rivers. Archibald drew his sword and continued to climb. On the fifth floor he discovered two more slain guards.

In the corridor ahead, Luis Guy was fighting another palace guard. Archibald had almost reached them when the sentinel delivered a quick thrust and the guard fell as dead as the others.

"Thank Maribor you've arrived!" Saldur's voice echoed from Modina's room as Guy entered the chamber. The regent sounded shaken. "We have to kill her. She's been faking all this time and eavesdropping. She knows everything!"

"But the wedding?" Guy protested.

"*Forget the wedding!* Ethelred is dead. Kill her and we'll tell everyone she is still sick. I will rule until we can find a replacement for Ethelred. We will announce that the new emperor married her in a private ceremony."

"No one will believe that."

"We don't have a choice. Now kill her!"

Archibald peered in. Guy stood, sword in hand, with Saldur. Beyond them, near the window, was Modina in her red-stained nightdress. Presumably the blood belonged to Ethelred, who lay dead on the floor. Sunlight glinted off a shard of glass gripped tightly in the empress's hands.

"How do I know you're not going to just saddle *me* with both their murders?"

"Do *you* see another way out of this? If we let her live, we are all dead men. Look around you. Look at the guards you just killed. Everyone believes she really *is* the empress. You *have* to kill her!"

Guy nodded and advanced on her.

Modina took a step back, still holding the shard out.

"Good afternoon, gentlemen," the Earl of Chadwick announced as he entered. "I hope this isn't a private party. You see, I was growing bored. Waiting for this wedding is very dull."

"Get out of here, Archie," Saldur snapped. "We don't have *time* for you. *Get out!*"

"Yes, I can see you're very busy, aren't you? You have to hurry up and kill the empress, but before you do…perhaps I can be of assistance. I would like to propose an alternative."

"Such as?" Saldur asked.

"I've wanted to marry Modina for some time—and still do. Now that the old bugger's dead"—he looked down at Ethelred's body and offered a wry smile—"why not choose me? I'll marry her and things can go on as planned, only with me on the throne instead of Ethelred. Nothing has to change. You could say I dueled him for the right of her hand. I won and she swooned for me."

"We can't let her leave the room. She'll talk," Saldur said.

Archibald considered this as he strolled around Saldur. He eyed the empress, who stood defiantly even though Guy's sword was only a few feet away.

"Consider this. I'll hold the point of a dagger hidden by my cloak at her ribs during the ceremony. She either does as we want or dies on the altar. If I kill her in front of all the crowned heads, neither of you will be held responsible. You can claim innocence of the whole affair. Her death will fall on me—that crazy lunatic *Archie* Ballentyne."

Saldur thought for a moment, then shook his head. "No,

we can't risk letting her out of this room. If she gets to people, she can take control. Too many are devoted to her. It has to end here. We'll pick up the pieces afterward. Kill her, Guy."

"Wait!" Archibald said quickly. "If she's going to die—let me do it. I know it sounds strange, but if I can't have her, I will take some satisfaction from denying her to anyone else."

"You are a twisted little git, aren't you, Ballentyne?" Guy said with a disgusted look.

Archibald moved closer. For each step he took forward, Modina took a step back, until she had no more room to retreat.

Archibald raised his sword, and while keeping his eyes focused on Modina, he plunged the blade toward Luis Guy. The sentinel did not see the attack coming, but Archibald's ruse prevented an accurate strike. His thrust landed poorly. Instead of piercing Guy's heart, the blade glanced off a rib and merely sliced through his side. Archibald quickly withdrew his blade, turned, and tried to strike again. Guy was faster.

The earl felt Guy's blade enter his chest. The last thing Archibald Ballentyne saw before he died was Modina Novronian running past Saldur, slicing his arm as he unsuccessfully tried to stop her.

❧

Royce's head turned abruptly.

"What—" Hadrian began, but stopped when Royce held up a hand.

Getting to his feet in one fluid motion, Royce paused midstride on a single foot, listening. He waited a moment and then moved swiftly to the cell door, which admitted the light. He lay down and placed his ear to the crack at the bottom.

"What is it?" Hadrian asked.

"Fighting," he replied at last.

"Fighting? Who?" Hadrian asked.

"I can't hear the color of their uniforms." Royce smirked. "Soldiers, though. I hear swords on armor."

They all looked at the door. Soon Hadrian heard it too. Very faint at first, like the rustle of leaves in autumn, but then he picked out the sounds of steel on steel and the unmistakable cries of men in pain. Within the prison, new sounds rose—the main entrance opened, shouts rang out, and footsteps echoed down the hall.

Royce picked up the sword he had brought and held it out toward Hadrian.

He shook his head. "Give it to Breckton. I doubt I can even hold it."

Royce nodded, handed the weapon to the knight, and raced down the hall with Alverstone drawn.

Breckton left Amilia's side and moved to stand in front of them all. Hadrian knew whoever was coming would have to kill the knight to get by.

Hard heels and soles echoed off the stone. A man cried out in terror.

"By Mar!" Hadrian heard Royce say. "What are *you* doing here?"

"Where is she?" responded a young man's voice. Hadrian recognized him but could not understand how he could possibly be there.

Torchlight filled the hall, growing brighter as footsteps hurried near. The group appeared first as dark silhouettes, the prisoners wincing at the brilliance. Hadrian raised an arm to shield his eyes.

"Alric? Mauvin?" Hadrian asked, stunned, then quickly added, "Breckton, *stop*! Don't fight!"

The King of Melengar and his best friend were leading a

party of men into the dungeon. Renwick, Ibis Thinly, and several others Hadrian did not know crowded the stone corridor. When Alric Essendon saw the prisoners, he wavered and a sickened expression crossed his face.

"You two—go back." Alric barked orders to his retinue. "Fetch stretchers." He raced to his sister's side. "Arista! Good Maribor, what have they done to you?" Over his shoulder he shouted, "Bring water! Bring bandages and more light!"

"You're not looking too good, my friend," Mauvin Pickering said, kneeling beside Hadrian. Mauvin was dressed in shimmering mail, his blood-spattered tabard bearing the crest of the Essendon falcon.

"They have indeed treated you poorly, sir," Renwick agreed, looking distraught. He was also dressed in bloodstained mail, and his face and hair were thick with sweat.

"I don't understand," Royce said. "Last we heard, Drondil Fields was under siege and about to fall."

"It was," Mauvin replied. "Then the damndest thing happened. The flag of truce went up from the vanguard of the Northern Imperial Army. A rider advanced and asked permission to speak at the gates. He explained that new orders had arrived along with a personal message to King Alric. If that wasn't strange enough, the personal guard of Empress Modina had delivered them."

He nodded toward a palace guard who was providing water to Amilia. "His name is Gerald. Anyway, the message said that Regents Ethelred and Saldur were traitors, and they were keeping the empress a prisoner in her own palace. It also said the war against Melengar was their personal quest for power, and that their commander, Sir Breckton, was either dead by treachery or falsely imprisoned and awaiting execution."

Hadrian started to speak, but Mauvin stopped him. "Wait... wait... it gets better. The orders commanded the acting leader of the Northern Army to cease all aggression against Melengar, extend the empress's sincerest apologies to King Alric, and return to Aquesta with all haste. The messenger went on to explain that Arista was scheduled for execution on Wintertide, and Empress Modina requested Alric to send whatever assistance he could spare."

"What did Alric say?" Hadrian asked Mauvin, as the king was consumed with aiding his sister.

"Are you kidding? He figured it was a ploy. Some trick to get us to come out. We all thought so. Then Alric yells down, more as a joke than anything, 'To prove you are telling the truth, lay down your weapons!' We laughed real hard until the commander, a guy named Sir Tibin—who's a decent enough fellow once you get to know him—did just that. We all stood on the parapet watching in disbelief as the Imperialists made this huge pile of spears, swords, and shields.

"That convinced Alric. He told them that not only would he send help, but he would personally lead the detachment. We rode day and night and expected to have a rough time breaching the city walls, but when we arrived, the gates were open. The people were rioting in the empress's name and shouting for Ethelred's and Saldur's heads. We stormed the palace and found only token resistance—just some foot soldiers and a few seret."

"Your sword has blood on it," Hadrian noted, pointing to Mauvin's blade.

"Yeah, funny that. I was determined never to draw it again, but when the fighting started, it just kind of came out by itself."

"What about Modina?" Amilia asked. "Is she...is she..."

Gerald's face was grave.

"What?" Amilia begged.

"There was an unfortunate incident in her bedroom this morning," the guard said.

Tears rose in Amilia's eyes. "Did she..."

"She killed Regent Ethelred."

"She what?"

"She stabbed him with a piece of broken glass from her mirror. She escaped an attempt on her life and ran to the courtyard. She rallied the soldiers who were loyal to her. When we arrived, she was ordering her men about like a seasoned general. Her troops managed to open the palace gates for us. Along with the Melengarians and the Northern Army, we suppressed the remaining seret and the palace guards loyal to the regents."

"Where is she now?" Amilia asked.

"She's on her throne, accepting vows of allegiance from the monarchs, nobles, and knights—everyone that had come for the wedding."

Men with stretchers appeared in the hall. Amilia turned to Sir Breckton. With tears in her eyes, she let out an awkward laugh and said, "You were right. She did save us."

CHAPTER 19

NEW BEGINNINGS

Modina stood alone on the little hill just beyond the city. This was the first time she had been outside the palace gates in more than a year. Four men with pickaxes had worked the better part of three days, cutting through the frozen ground to make a hole deep enough for the grave. What had taken days to dig was filled in just minutes, leaving a dark mound on a field of white.

Her reunion with the world was bittersweet, because her first act was to bury a friend. The gravediggers tried to explain it was customary to wait until spring, but Modina insisted. She had to see him put to rest.

Seventeen soldiers waited at the base of the hill. Some trotted a perimeter on horseback, while others kept a watchful eye on her or the surrounding area. As she stood quietly in that bleak landscape, her robe shimmered and flapped in the wind like gossamer.

"You did this to me," she accused the dirt mound before her.

Modina had not seen him since Dahlgren. She knew *of* him the way she knew about everything.

Saldur enjoyed the sound of his own voice, which made him an excellent tutor. The regent even talked to himself when no one else was around. When he did not know something, he always summoned experts to the sanctity of his office, the one place he felt safe from prying ears. Most of the names and places had been meaningless at first, but with repetition, everything became clear. Modina learned of Androus Billet from Rhenydd, who had murdered King Urith, Queen Amiter, and their children. Androus succeeded where Percy Braga had failed when trying to seize control of Melengar. She learned how Monsignor Merton, though loyal to the church, was becoming a liability because he was a true believer. She heard that the regents could not decide if King Roswort of Dunmore's biggest asset was his cowardice or his greed. She learned the names of Cornelius and Cosmos DeLur, men the regents saw as genuine threats unless properly controlled. Their influence on trade was crucial to maintaining imperial stability.

In the beginning Modina heard without listening as the words just flowed past. Over time, their constant presence filtered through the fog, settling like silt upon her mind. The day *his* name floated by was the first time she actually paid attention to what was being said.

The regents were toasting him for their success. Initially, Modina thought he was in Saldur's study, sharing a glass of spirits with them, but eventually it became apparent they were mocking him. His efforts were instrumental to their rise, but he would not share in the rewards. They spoke of him as a mad lunatic who had served his purpose. Instead of executing him, he had been locked in the secret prison—that oubliette for refuse they wanted to forget.

He died alone in the darkness. The doctors said it was due to starvation, but Modina knew better. She was intimately familiar with the demons that visited prisoners trapped in that darkness: regret, hopelessness, and most of all, fear. She knew how the fiends worked—entering in silence, filling a void, and growing until the soul was pushed out, until nothing remained. Like an old tree, the trunk could continue to stand while the core rotted away, but when all strength was gone, the first breeze would snap the spirit.

She knelt down and felt the gritty texture of a cold clump of dirt in her hand. Her father had loved the soil. He would break it up with his huge leathery fingers and smell it. He even tasted it. Field and farm had been his whole world, but they would not be hers.

"I know you meant well," she said. "I know you believed. You thought you were standing up for me, protecting me, saving me. In some ways, you succeeded. You might have saved my life, but you did not save *me*. What fate might we have had if you hadn't championed my cause? If you hadn't become a martyr? If we stayed in Dahlgren, you could have found us a new home. The Bothwicks would have raised me as their own daughter. I would have carried wounds, but perhaps I would have known happiness again. Eventually. I could have been the wife of a farmer. I would have spun wool, pulled weeds, cooked turnips, raised children. I would have been strong for my family. I would have fought against wolves and thieves. Neighbors would say, *She got that strength from the hardships of her youth.* I could have lived a small, quiet life. But you changed all that. I'm not an innocent maid anymore. You hardened and hammered me into a new thing. I know too much. I've seen too much. And now I've killed."

Modina paused and glanced up at the sky. There were only a few clouds on the field of blue, the kind of clear blue seen only on a crisp winter day.

"Perhaps the two paths really aren't so different. Ethelred was just a wolf who walked like a man, and the empire is my family now."

Placing a hand on the grave, she softly said, "I forgive you." Then Modina stood and walked away, leaving behind the mound with the marker bearing the name Deacon Tomas.

❧

The candles had burned down to nubs and still they were not through the list. Amilia's eyes drooped and she fought the urge to lay her head down on the desk. She sat wrapped in a blanket with part of it made into a hood.

"Should we stop here and come back to it tomorrow?" she asked hopefully.

The empress shook her head. She was wearing the robe Mince had given her. Amilia had not seen her wear anything else since Modina had taken control of the empire. Other than on the night of the hawking feast, the empress had never donned the crown or mantle of her office. "I want to get through this last set tonight. I can't afford to have these positions left vacant. Isn't that right, Nimbus?"

"It would be best to settle on the remaining prefects, at least. If I may speak plainly, Your Eminence, you relieved over one-third of all office holders. If new ones are not appointed soon, the resulting void might give warlords an opportunity to exert authority and fracture the empire."

"How many do we still have to go?" Modina asked.

Nimbus shuffled through parchments. "Ah, there are still forty-two vacant positions."

"Too many. We have to finish this."

"If only you hadn't removed *so* many," Amilia said in a tired voice.

Since taking power, Modina had worked tirelessly and demanded the same of her aides. The change in her was amazing. The once quiet, shy waif, who had sat before a window each day, had transformed into an empress, commanding and strong. She organized meetings of state, judged the accused, appointed new officials, and even demanded that Nimbus teach her letters and history.

Amilia admired her but regretted Modina's dedication. With so much required of her, Amilia had only a few moments each day to spend with Sir Breckton. The secretary found herself strangely nostalgic for the hours they had spent imprisoned together.

Each day the empress, Nimbus, and Amilia met in Saldur's old office. Modina insisted on working there because it contained numerous charts, maps, and scrolls. These imperial records were meticulously organized and provided details on all aspects of the kingdom. Not being able to read, Modina had to rely on Nimbus and Amilia to sift through the documents and find answers to her questions. Nimbus was a greater help than Amilia, but still Modina insisted on her presence.

"I just wish I could remove some of the nobles as well," Modina said. "There are several kings and dukes that are as bad as Saldur. Saldur got King Armand of Alburn his throne through the assassination of King Reinhold, and I hate that he is rewarded for such treachery. Are you certain I can't remove him?"

Nimbus cringed. "*Technically* you can. As empress and the descendant of Novron, you are semidivine and your authority is absolute to all those who call Maribor god. However, such notions are fine in *theory*, but you must function based on *reality*. A ruler's power comes from the support and loyalty of her nobles. Offend enough of them and not only will they not obey you, they will almost certainly raise armies against you. Unless you are prepared to govern by the strength of Maribor's will alone, I suggest we keep the ruling nobles, if not happy, at least content."

Nimbus shifted in his seat. "A number of Ethelred and Saldur supporters are most likely preparing for a coup. Given the current situation, however, I am certain they are puzzled how best to proceed. For over a year the regents actively promoted you as empress and a goddess—supreme and infallible. Now that you actually wield power, it will take some creative manipulation to convince others to act against you. Finding allies won't be easy, but they have some advantages. For instance, you are inexperienced and they expect you to make mistakes, which they will hope to exploit. The key is to avoid making any."

Modina thought for a moment and then asked, "So although I am all powerful, I have to obey the nobles?"

"No, you merely have to keep them from wanting to get rid of you. You can do this in two ways. Keep them placated by providing things they want, such as wealth, power, and prestige. Or make the idea of opposing you more distasteful than bowing to you. Personally, I suggest doing both. Feed their egos and coffers, but build your base around loyal leaders. Men like Alric of Melengar would be a good start. He's proven himself to be trustworthy, and you've already won his gratitude by saving his kingdom. Bolster his position by providing income through preferential trade agreements. Grow that seed of an alienated monarchy into an economic, political, and military ally. With powerful supporters, the nobles will not be so quick to attack you."

"But Melengar isn't even in the empire."

"All the better. Those inside the empire will compete for power amongst themselves. Everyone on the ladder wants to be on a higher rung. Because Alric isn't part of that ladder, no one will feel slighted when he receives preferential status. If you were to act similarly with a noble within the empire, you will generate resentment of that favoritism. You can proclaim aid to Melengar as *prudent foreign affairs*. By endorsing Alric, you'll be building a supporter who won't be easily assailable. And one who will be more grateful than those who consider it their due."

"But won't this be expensive? Where will I get the funds? The people are already suffering under a heavy tax," the empress said.

"I would suggest meeting with the DeLurs. They generally operate outside *official* channels, but offering them legitimacy can provide mutual benefit. Given recent events with the Ba Ran Ghazel in Delgos, Cornelius DeLur in particular should be most receptive to a proposal of imperial protection."

"I've been thinking about Cornelius DeLur quite a bit lately. Do you think I should appoint him as trade secretary?"

Nimbus smiled, started to speak, paused, and then eventually said, "I think that might be a little too much like placing a drunk in charge of a tavern, but you're thinking along the proper lines. Perhaps a better choice might be to appoint Cornelius DeLur Prefect of Colnora. Until recently, Colnora was a merchant-run city, so recognizing this officially would go a long way toward good relations with merchants in general and the DeLurs in particular. Best of all, it won't cost you anything."

"I like the idea of Cornelius as prefect," Modina said, and turned to Amilia. "Please summon him for an audience. We can present the idea and see what he says." The empress returned her attention to Nimbus. "Is there anything else I need to be looking into at present?"

"I suggest creating sanctioned imperial representatives, trained here in Aquesta, to travel and relay instructions. They can be your eyes and ears to check up on local administrators. You might consider drawing these representatives from the monasteries. Monks are usually educated, used to living in poverty, and will be especially devoted because of your Novronian lineage. Religious fervor can often be more powerful than wealth, which will keep your agents bribe-resistant. Oh, one other thing, be certain to avoid appointing anyone to a province who is from that area, and be sure to rotate them often. This will prevent them from becoming too familiar with those they administer."

"As if I didn't have enough to do." Modina sighed. "The best approach is to divide and conquer. Do you have a short list for the remainder of the prefects, Nimbus?"

"Yes." He reached into his piles and pulled out a stack of parchments. "I've compiled what I think are the best candidates. Shall we go through them?"

"No, I trust your judgment."

Nimbus looked disappointed.

"To save time, call in your top choices and interview them yourself. If you're satisfied, I want you to go ahead and appoint them. What's next?"

"What about Saldur?" Nimbus asked.

Modina sighed once more and slouched in her chair.

"Many of the others can be tried for treason, but he's different," Nimbus explained. "He wasn't just the regent. He was also once a very powerful officer in the Nyphron Church. An execution would be...well...*awkward*. Saldur is too dangerous to let go and too dangerous to execute. I suppose we could keep him imprisoned indefinitely."

"No!" Modina suddenly said. "I can't do that. You're right in that his situation is unique, but we must settle the matter one way or another. Even though he's in the tower and not the dungeon, I won't let anyone stay locked up forever. Even with adequate food, water, and light, the knowledge that you'll never be free has a way of destroying you from the inside. I'll not do that to anyone, not even *him*."

"Well, the Patriarch hasn't left for Ervanon yet. He's taken up residence in the cathedral. If we could convince him to denounce Saldur, that would make it possible to execute the ex-regent without fear of reprisal. Shall I set up a meeting?"

Modina nodded.

"Is that it?" Amilia asked. "Can we go to bed?"

"Yes, I think that will do for now," Modina told them. "Thank you both for all of your assistance. I couldn't hope to do any of this without you."

"You're most welcome, Your Eminence," Nimbus replied.

"You know, Nimbus, you don't have to be so formal. We are alone, after all. You can call me Modina."

"Don't bother," Amilia said. "You can't stop him. Trust me. I've tried. I've badgered him for nearly a year, yet he still calls me milady."

"My respect for you both prevents me from doing otherwise."

"Honestly, Nimbus," Modina told him, "you should be chancellor permanently. You are already doing the job behind the scenes. I don't know why you won't officially take the position."

"I am happy to serve now, in your time of need, but who is to say what the future might bring?"

Modina frowned.

"Oh, one more thing," Nimbus said. "There have been some strange rumors from the north. The information is sketchy, but there appears to be some kind of trouble."

"Like what?"

"I don't know exactly. All I've heard is that the roads from Dunmore are choked with refugees fleeing south."

"You might want to send someone to find out what's happening," Modina told him.

"I already did. I asked Supreme General Breckton to investigate, and he has sent three separate patrols. Quite some time ago, in fact."

"And?" the empress inquired.

"None of them have returned," Nimbus replied.

"What do you make of it?"

Nimbus shrugged. "Perhaps they are delayed by bad weather or flooding. Although, to be honest, the most likely answer would point toward pestilence. If the patrols visited a plague-ridden city, they would remain rather than risk bringing the disease back with them. Even so, illnesses have a way of traveling on their own. It might be best to brace for an epidemic."

Modina sighed. "Will it never end?"

"Wishing you were back at your window now, aren't you?" Amilia asked.

৵

Hadrian had found himself in the infirmary along with Arista Essendon and Degan Gaunt. For the first three days, he did little more than sleep and was only marginally aware that his wounds had been stitched and wrapped. Whenever he woke, Royce was beside the bed, enveloped in a cloak with the hood covering his face. With his feet propped up on a chair, the thief appeared to be sleeping, but Hadrian knew better.

As Hadrian regained enough strength to focus, Royce entertained him with current events. The good news was that Modina seemed to have matters concerning the empire well in hand. The bad news was that Merrick Marius and Luis Guy had managed to escape and had not been seen since Wintertide.

By the seventh day, Hadrian felt strong enough to try walking, and he had been moved out of the infirmary and into a bedroom on the third floor. Each day he walked down the corridor, holding on to Royce, Albert, or Renwick. The squire and viscount were frequent visitors, but Hadrian did not have the opportunity to thank the Duke and Duchess of Rochelle for their help before they returned home. Like the other nobles gathered for the wedding, they swore fealty to Modina before departing. Albert continued to stay in Genny and Leo's suite, as the viscount was in no hurry to trade the luxurious palatial accommodations for his austere cell at the monastery. From time to time, Mauvin and Alric stopped by, usually on their way to visit Arista. Even Nimbus peeked in once or twice, but Royce and Renwick, who took turns as his steadfast sentries, tended to Hadrian day and night.

The princess rested two doors down. Though still thin and weak, Arista was recovering faster than Hadrian, judging by the pace of her strides past his door. At first Alric or Mauvin escorted her, but recently she had started passing by unaided. Hadrian was disappointed that she never came to his room, and he, in turn, never visited hers.

Degan Gaunt had been at death's door when first pulled from the dungeon, and few had expected him to survive. At Hadrian's insistence, Royce checked in on him and relayed updates on his condition. Even when given thin chicken broth, Gaunt had choked and vomited. One night the doctors had called in a priest of Nyphron, but somehow Gaunt pulled through. The latest reports indicated Degan was now eating solid foods and starting to regain weight.

"Ready for another walk?" Royce asked, handing Hadrian a cloak.

Recently woken, Hadrian was still rubbing his eyes. "Wow, you're in a hurry. Mind if I relieve myself first? Is somebody getting a bit anxious to get back to Gwen?"

"Yes, and you're milking all the attention. Now get up."

Royce helped Hadrian to his feet. Feeling the tug on his stitches, Hadrian grimaced as he slowly stood.

"How's the head today?" Royce asked.

"Much better. Not dizzy at all. I think I can walk on my own."

"Maybe so, but lean on me anyway. I don't want you falling down the stairs and ripping your side open. If you do, I'll be stuck here playing nursemaid another week."

"Your compassion is overwhelming," Hadrian said, wincing as he slipped a tunic over his head.

"Let's just start by getting you down to the courtyard. If you're still feeling okay after that, then you can try going on your own."

"Oh, may I?" Hadrian replied.

Using Royce as a crutch, Hadrian limped out to the hallway.

He let his friend lead him toward the main landing. He expected pain but felt only a modest twinge.

"You know, I meant what I said in the dungeon. I appreciate you coming for me," Hadrian said.

Royce laughed. "You do realize that I really didn't *do* anything? Everything would have turned out exactly the same if I had stayed at Windermere with Gwen. She keeps insisting I'm needed to save you, but you seem pretty self-sufficient these days. Well, not right now, but you know what I mean."

They reached the courtyard and Royce helped Hadrian down the stairs. A warm spell had moved in and the weather was unusually pleasant. Hadrian heard the sound of dripping water everywhere as the snow melted.

"Early spring?" Hadrian asked.

"Only temporary, I'm sure," Royce replied. "Nothing this nice stays long. Okay, now that you're on level ground, try walking to the gate. I'll wait here."

Even after two weeks, the courtyard still bore signs of combat. Dark smears and sooty smudges on the walls, a broken cart, a missing door, and several shattered windows all told the story of what had happened while he had been in the prison.

Hadrian spotted another patient out for her daily exercise. Arista wore a simple blue dress and had gained enough weight to start looking like herself again. She swung her arms and took deep breaths of fresh air while circling the ward. Her hair was down and blowing in the breeze.

"Hadrian!" Arista cried out after seeing him.

He tried to straighten up and winced.

"Here, let me help you." She rushed forward.

"No, no, I'm trying to go solo today. Royce is releasing some of his tyrannical control." He hooked a thumb toward his friend, waiting at the palace doors. "I'm surprised Alric lets you wander around alone."

She laughed and pointed at two well-armed guards whose eyes never wavered from her as they stood a short distance away. "He has turned into a mother hen. It's kind of embarrassing, but I'm not going to complain. Did you know he cried the night they carried us out? Alric has always been more like our mother than I am. How can I be mad at someone for caring?"

They walked together to a bench. It was clear of snow; the warm sun had dried it clean. The two of them sat down and Hadrian was grateful for the rest.

"Alric did well," he said. "I'm sure it was difficult for him to leave Medford and go to Drondil Fields. Royce tells me he took quite a few of the citizenry with him."

She nodded. "Yes, and doing so made the siege difficult. Hundreds of people were jammed into the corridors, halls, and all around the courtyard. Food was scarce after only a month because there were so many mouths to feed. Alric's advisors told him he had to deny food to the sick to save others, but he refused to listen. Some of the weak actually died. Count Pickering said Alric needed to surrender in order to save those he could. I heard from Mauvin that Alric was planning to do just that. He was just waiting until after Wintertide. I'm proud of my brother. He knew they would kill him, but he was willing to sacrifice himself for his people."

"How are things now at Drondil Fields?"

"Oh, fine. Supplies are flowing again and Count Pickering is administrating from there. I'm not sure if you know, but Medford was destroyed. Drondil Fields will need to function as the capital until Alric can rebuild. That's funny, as it served just such a purpose in the beginning."

Hadrian nodded and the pair continued to sit while quietly looking around the courtyard. Arista unexpectedly took his hand and squeezed. Glancing down, he saw her looking at him with a warm smile.

"I want to thank you for trying to rescue me," Arista said. "You have no idea how much it meant. When I was in the..." She paused and looked away, staring at some distant, unseen point. A shadow crossed her face and lingered long enough to make her lip quiver. When she spoke again, her voice was softer and less confident. "I felt very alone. More so than I imagined a person could be."

Arista chuckled softly. "I was so naive. When I was first captured, I believed I could face death bravely—like Alric was going to." Arista paused again, studying the fallow garden and wetting her lips. "I'm ashamed to say that I'd completely given up by the end. I didn't care about anything. I just wanted the fear to stop. I was terrified, so terrified that... And then... then I heard your voice." She gave another sad little smile. "I couldn't believe what I heard at first. You sounded like a bird-song in the dead of winter... so warm, so friendly, so very out of place. I was falling into an abyss, and at the very last moment, you reached out and caught me. Just your voice. Just your words. I don't think I can ever express how much they meant."

He nodded and squeezed her hand back. "I'm pleased to have been of service, my lady." Hadrian gave a reverent little bow of his head.

They sat quietly again for some time. When the silence was nearly uncomfortable, Hadrian asked, "What are you going to do now? Go with Alric to Drondil Fields?"

"Actually, that's something I need to talk to you about—but not today. We both have healing yet to do. It will wait until we are stronger. Did you know Esrahaddon is dead?"

"Yeah, we found that out."

"He came to me the night he was killed and told me something. Something involving Degan Gaunt..." Her voice faded as she glanced toward the main gate, a look of curiosity crossing her face. "Who is that?" She pointed.

Hadrian followed her gaze and saw a lone figure entering on horseback. The rider was thin, small, and wearing a monk's frock. The man rode slumped over the horse's neck. Once inside the palace's gate, he fell face-first into the slush. Royce was the farthest away, but he was still able to reach the man first. Several servants were right behind him. Hadrian and Arista approached, and by the time they arrived, Royce had already rolled the man over and pulled back his hood.

"Myron?" Hadrian said in disbelief. He stared down at the familiar face of their friend from the Winds Abbey. The monk was unconscious, but there was no sign of a wound.

"Myron?" Arista asked, puzzled. "Myron Lanaklin of Windermere? I thought he never left the abbey."

Hadrian shook his head. "He doesn't."

◌

The little monk lay on a cot in the infirmary. Two chamber-maids and the palace physician busied themselves tending to him. They brought water and cleaned the mud from his face, arms, and legs, looking for wounds. Myron woke with a star-tled expression, looked around in a panic, and collapsed again. A miserable moan escaped his lips, followed by, "Royce?"

"What's wrong with him?" Hadrian asked.

"Just exhausted, as far as I can tell," the doctor replied. "He needs food and drink." Just as he said this, a maid entered with a steaming bowl.

"I'm so sorry," Myron said, opening his eyes again and focusing on Royce. "I'm so sorry. I'm sure it was my fault. I should have done *something*...I don't know what to say."

"Slow down," Royce snapped. "Start at the beginning and tell me everything."

"*Everything?*" Hadrian asked. "Remember who you're talking to."

"It was four days ago and me and Miss DeLancy were out talking with Renian. I was telling him about a book I had just finished. It was early and no one was in the garden but us. Everything was so quiet. I didn't hear anything. Maybe if I had heard..."

"Get to the point, Myron." Royce's irritation increased.

"He just appeared out of nowhere. I was talking with Renian when I heard her gasp. When I turned, he was behind her with a knife to her throat. I was so scared. I didn't want to do anything that might get Miss DeLancy hurt."

"What did he look like? *Who* put a knife to her throat?" Royce asked intently.

"I don't know. He didn't say his name. He looked a little

like you, only larger. Pale skin, like new vellum—and dark eyes—very dark. He told me, 'Listen carefully. I've been told you can remember exactly what you hear or read. I hope that is true for *her* sake. You will travel to the palace in Aquesta, find Royce Melborn, and deliver him a message. Any delay or mistake may cost her life, so pay attention.'"

"What's the message?" Royce asked.

"It was very strange, but this is what he told me: 'Black queen takes king. White rooks retreat. Black queen captures bishop. White rook to bishop's four, threatening. Check. White's pawn takes queen and bishop. Jade's tomb, full face.'"

Royce looked devastated. He stepped back and actually stumbled. Breathing hard, he sat on a vacant bed.

"What is it?" Hadrian asked anxiously. "Royce?"

His friend did not answer. He did not look at him or at anyone. He merely stared. Hadrian had seen the look before. Royce was calculating, and from his intense expression, Hadrian could tell he was doing so in earnest.

"Royce, talk to me. What did that mean? I know it's a code but for what?"

Royce got up. "Gwen's in danger. I have to go."

"Let me get my swords."

"No," he said bluntly. "I want you to stay out of this."

"Stay out of it? Stay out of what? Royce, since when do—"

Royce's face turned to a mask of calm. "Look at you—you're hobbling around. I can handle this. You get some rest. It's not that bad."

"Don't do that. Don't try to manage me. Something terrible is happening. It's Merrick, isn't it? He likes chess. What did that message mean? I was the one who got you to help me find Gaunt, and if there is a price to be paid, I want to help. What's Merrick up to?"

Royce's face changed again. The calm faded, and what lay

behind it was an emotion Hadrian had never seen on his partner's face before—terror. When he spoke, his voice quavered. "I have to go, and I *need* you to stay out of it."

Hadrian noticed Royce's hands were shaking. When Royce saw them too, he pulled them under his cloak.

"Don't follow me. Get well and take your own path. We won't be seeing each other again. Goodbye."

Royce bolted from the room.

"Wait!" Hadrian called. He struggled to stand and follow, but it was useless. Royce was already gone.

Chapter 20

The Queen's Gambit Accepted

It was late as Arista walked the balcony of her room. The storm from the night before had left the handrails mounded with snow, and icicles dangled from the eaves. In the light of the nearly full moon everything was so pretty, like a fairy tale. Pulling her cloak tight, Arista lifted the hood such that she looked out through a fur-lined tunnel. Still the cold reached her. She considered going back inside, but she needed to be out. She needed to see the sky.

Arista could not sleep. She felt uneasy—restless.

Despite her exhaustion, sleeping was nearly impossible. The nightmares were not a surprise, given what she had gone through. She often woke in the dark, covered in sweat, certain she was still in the dungeon—certain that the sounds of snow blowing against the window were the scratches of a rat named Jasper. Afterward, lying awake brought thoughts of Hadrian. The hours of darkness trapped in that hole had stripped her bare and forced her to face the truth. In Arista's most desperate moment, her thoughts had turned to him. The mere sound of his voice had saved her, and the thoughts of her own death were extinguished when she feared he was hurt.

She was in love with Hadrian.

The revelation was bitter, as it was clear he did not feel the same. In those last hours, the only words that passed his lips were ones of common comfort, the same encouragement anyone would give. He might care about her, but he did not love her. In one way, she found that a blessing, as every man who ever had loved her had died. She could not bear to see Hadrian die as well. She concluded they would remain friends. Close friends, she hoped, but she would not endanger that friendship by admitting anything more. She wondered if somewhere Hilfred was watching her and laughing at the irony or crying in sympathy.

Still, it was not thoughts of Jasper or Hadrian that kept Arista walking the balcony that night. Another ghost stalked her troubled mind, whispering memories. Something was happening. She had felt it building ever since they had pulled her from the prison. At first she assumed it was the lingering effect of starvation, a form of light-headedness affecting her senses. Now she realized it was more than that.

...at Wintertide the Uli Vermar *ends. They will come— without the horn everyone dies. Only you know now—only you can save...*

The words of Esrahaddon echoed in her head, but she could not understand what they meant.

What is the Uli Vermar? *And who is coming?*

Something had clearly happened. Somehow the world had changed on Wintertide. She could feel it. She could taste it. The air sizzled with the sensation. While she had known how to tap the natural power of the world, Arista was shocked to discover that the world could talk back, speaking to her in a language she did not fully understand. It came in subtle impressions, vague feelings she might have previously dismissed as imagination. All the signals spoke of a great shift. She, like all living things in tune with the natural world, was aware of the change just as if it were the coming dawn. Something about *this* Wintertide had been different. Something rare, something old, something great had transpired. She looked to the northeast. It was there, hurtling toward them.

They are coming.

A voice startled her. "Anna said you were out here."

Arista spun to see Modina standing behind her. She wore a simple kirtle dress. Her arms folded across her chest, fending off the cold. She looked more like the girl Arista had first met in Dahlgren than an empress.

"Sorry, didn't mean to scare you," Modina said.

Arista gathered herself and curtsied as best she could. "Not at all, Your Eminence."

Modina sighed. "Please don't. I have enough people kissing the floor. I refuse to take it from you. And I'm sorry for taking so long to visit."

"You are the empress—the *real* empress. I'm sure your time is limited. And because I am still the Ambassador of Melengar, I really should greet and address you properly."

Modina frowned. "Perhaps, but can't we skip the formalities when in private?"

"If that is your wish."

"I wanted to let you know that we are officially allies now. I signed a preferred trade agreement and defense pact this morning with Alric."

"That's wonderful." Arista smiled. "Although you're putting me out of a job by going over my head like that."

"Can we go inside? It's freezing out here." Modina led the way back into Arista's room.

In the dim light, Arista noticed something lying folded neatly on the bed.

"I was so worried about you," Modina whispered as she unexpectedly hugged the princess, squeezing her tight. "And just so you know, I did visit you—nearly every night. You've just been asleep."

"You saved my life, my brother, and my kingdom," Arista replied, returning the embrace. "Do you really think I can feel slighted by you?"

Modina let go. "I'm sorry it took so long. I'm sorry that you had to stay in that…that…place. I didn't save Deacon Tomas, and I didn't save Hilfred. Perhaps if I had acted sooner…"

"Don't," Arista said, seeing the empress's eyes watering. "You have nothing to apologize for."

Modina wiped the tears and nodded. "I wanted to give you something…something special." She walked to the bed and held up a familiar robe, which unfolded in shimmering cascades.

"Do you recognize it?"

Arista nodded.

"I can't imagine there are two such robes in all the world. I think he would want you to have it, and so do I."

✧

Modina had just left Arista's room and was passing Degan's half-open door when he called out, "Hang on there!"

She pushed the door open and stood on the threshold, looking at him.

Tall and still very thin, he sat propped against a bank of pillows in bed. "My chamber pot needs emptying, and the room is starting to stink. Wanna get in here and take care of it?"

"I'm not the chambermaid," Modina replied.

"Oh? Are you a nurse? 'Cause I'm still not feeling well. I could use some more food. Some beef would be nice—steak, perhaps?"

"I'm not a nurse or scullery maid either."

Degan looked irritated. "What good are you, then? Listen, I just got out of the dungeon, and they literally starved me. I deserve some sympathy. I need more food."

"If you want, I can walk you down to the kitchen and we can find something there."

"You're joking, right? Didn't you just hear what I said? I'm sick. I'm weak. I'm not about to go rummaging around like a rodent."

"You won't regain your strength by sitting in bed."

"I thought you said you weren't the nurse. Listen, if you won't bring it to me, find someone who will. Don't you realize who I am?"

"You're Degan Gaunt."

"Yes, but do you know *who* I am?"

She looked at him, puzzled. "I'm sorry...I don't kn—"

"Can you keep a secret?" he asked, leaning forward and speaking in a conspiratorial tone.

Modina nodded.

"As it turns out, I'm the Heir of Novron." Modina feigned surprise and Gaunt grinned in reply. "I know—I was shocked too. I only recently learned myself."

"But I thought Empress Modina was the heir."

"From what I heard, that's just what the old regents wanted everyone to believe."

"So do you plan to overthrow the empress?"

"Don't need to," he said with a wink. "I heard she's young and beautiful, so I figure I'll just marry her. I also hear she's popular too, so I can benefit from the goodwill she already has. See how smart that is?"

"What if she won't marry you?"

"Hah! Why wouldn't she? I'm the Heir of Novron. You can't do no better than that."

Modina noticed Gaunt looking her over more intently. His tongue licked his upper lip, sliding back and forth. "Say, you're kinda pretty, you know that?" He glanced past her, into the hallway. "What do ya say you shut the door and slip on over here?" He patted the covers.

"I thought you were sick and feeble."

"I said I was weak, not feeble, and I'm not *that* weak. If you won't get me something to eat, the least you can do is help warm my bed."

"I don't think that is the least I can do. Yes, I can definitely think of less."

He furrowed his brow at her. "You know, I'm gonna be the emperor just as soon as I get well enough. You might want to be nicer to me. We can keep this thing going, even after the wedding. I expect I'll have several *ladies-in-waiting*, if you know what I mean. I'll be taking good care of them too. This is your chance to get in early and be the first."

"And what exactly does that mean?"

"Oh, you know. I take care of you. Give you a room here at the palace. See that you get some fine dresses. That kind of stuff."

"I already have those things."

"Sure, but you might not after I take over. This way you can make sure that your future is protected. So, what do you say?"

"Remarkably, I think I will pass."

"Suit yourself." Gaunt waved her away. "But hey, if you do see a maid, tell her to get her ass in here and get rid of this pot, okay?"

When Modina reached the stair, she met a gate soldier climbing up.

"Your Eminence." He approached, bowed, and waited.

"Yes?" she asked.

"A man at the palace gates is requesting an audience."

"What? Now?"

"Yes, Your Eminence. I told him it wasn't possible."

"It's getting kind of late. Ask him to see the palace clerk in the morning."

"I already told him that, but he says he and his family must leave at first light. They came for Wintertide, and he wanted to make one last attempt to see you before departing. He said you would know him."

"Did he give you his name?"

"Yes, Russell Bothwick of Dahlgren."

Modina lit up. "Where is he now?"

"I had him wait at the gate."

When she had lived in Dahlgren, the Bothwicks had been as close as family. They had taken her in after the death of her mother, and the excitement of seeing her old friends overtook Modina. She trotted down the stairs to the main entry, causing the guards to rush to open the huge double doors for her. Modina hurried into the snowy courtyard and regretted not having brought a cloak the moment she stepped outside. The night was dark, and as she crossed the courtyard toward the front gate, she realized she could have used a lantern as well. Seeing Russell and Lena was too good to be true. She would give them the finest suite in the palace and stay up all night reminiscing about old times... better times.

As she passed the stable, a voice close by said, "Thrace?"

She spun around and was surprised to find Royce there. "What are you doing out here? Come with me to the gate. The Bothwicks are here."

"I want you to know I am very sorry about this," Royce told her.

"About what?"

He had a sad expression in his eyes as one hand clamped

over her mouth. She struggled for a moment, but it was over quickly. The last thing she heard was his voice whispering in her ear, "*I'm sorry.*"

∽

The palace bell rang before dawn. Hadrian and the other residents of the third floor stepped into the hallway. Arista wore Esrahaddon's glimmering robe, and Degan Gaunt yawned while clutching a blanket around his shoulders.

Amilia and Breckton led a troop of guards into the corridor.

"Have any of you seen the empress?"

"Not since last night," Arista said.

"What's going on?" Gaunt grumbled irritably. This was the first time Hadrian had seen him since the dungeon.

"The empress is missing," Breckton announced. He motioned to the soldiers, who opened doors and swept into the rooms.

"So what's all the fuss? Check the quarters of the best-looking servant," Gaunt said. "She probably just fell asleep afterward."

"Bishop Saldur is also missing," Breckton said. "And the guard at the tower and two gate sentries are dead."

The soldiers finished searching the rooms and returned to the hallway.

"How could Saldur have gotten out?" Arista asked. "And why would he take Modina?"

Hadrian glanced at her and then at the floor. "It wasn't Saldur."

"But who could have—" Arista started.

Hadrian interrupted her. "Royce took her. He has taken them both. 'White's pawn takes queen and bishop.' It's the Queen's Gambit and Royce has accepted."

CHAPTER 21

LANGDON BRIDGE

Directly overhead the full moon peered through a break in the clouds, making the Bernum River glisten like a dark, oily snake as it wound through the heart of Colnora. Numerous warehouses perched on the high banks, sleeping like behemoths on the cold winter night. Far from the residential neighborhoods, the mercantile district was desolate at this hour. Frost-covered lampposts fashioned in the shapes of swans dotted the length of the Langdon Bridge, illuminating icicles hanging from every ledge and ornament. Snow started to fall once more, and fluffy flakes caught in the lamplight twirled and drifted on air currents rising from the river gorge. The sound of the Bernum roared up from the depths as if the river were some monstrous, insatiable beast.

Royce stood in the shadows on the north side of the bridge. Despite the cold, he was drenched in sweat. Behind him, Saldur and Modina stood silently with their wrists tied behind their backs. Royce did not use gags—they were not required. He had given his prisoners several reasons to remain silent.

Extracting Saldur from the prison tower had been easy enough. The ex-regent offered no resistance and obeyed every whispered command promptly and quietly. Royce had been disappointed, as he was eager for any excuse to correct that particular captive's behavior. Modina was another matter. He honestly regretted taking her. He simply had no choice. Royce had squeezed her neck with the least amount of pressure and for the shortest interval necessary to drop her painlessly into unconsciousness. He was certain she woke with a terrible headache but suffered no other harm.

Royce studied the warehouses on the far side of the bridge. One had a four-leaf clover painted on its side. That was the place where he had mistakenly killed Merrick's lover. It had happened back when all three of them had been assassins in the Black Diamond thieves guild. *Jade's tomb.* He worried about the message Merrick was sending with his choice of location.

After glancing up again and checking the location of the moon, Royce lit a lantern and stepped into the street. Two nerve-wracking moments later, another light appeared in reply from the far end of the bridge. Merrick was there. And Gwen was with him.

She's alive!

Royce's heart leapt. Relief mixed with anxiety. She was so close, yet not close enough. No one else was visible—the Black Diamond were conspicuously absent. Royce had expected members of the thieves' guild to descend the instant he entered the city. Either Merrick had arranged for safe passage, or they had decided they did not want any part of *this* transaction.

"Show them." Merrick's voice carried on the cool, crisp air.

Royce motioned and Modina and Saldur stepped from the shadows next to him.

"I'll double your reward for this, Marius," Saldur shouted. "You'll be Marquis of Melengar. I'll—" He cried out in pain as Royce dragged Alverstone along his shoulder blade. The gleaming knife sliced through the regent's robes and into his skin.

"Did we forget our agreement?" Royce snapped.

Royce looked at Modina, who stood quiet and still. The empress displayed no fear, anger, or malice. She did not struggle. She merely waited.

"Send them across," Merrick ordered.

"Don't run, Saldur," Royce said. "You need to match Gwen's pace. I'm good at throwing a dagger, and you won't be out of my range until you reach the bridge's midpoint. If you pass it before she does, it will be the last step you ever take."

The captives stepped forward at the same time as Gwen. She wore a heavy wool cloak and boots that were not her own. Tears streamed down her cheeks. With her arms tied behind her back, she could not push away her tangled hair or free her mouth from the gag. They walked toward each other at an agonizingly slow pace.

For Royce, nothing on the face of the world stirred except for the three hostages on the bridge. The prisoners passed at the bridge's center, exchanging only brief glances. The wind blew harder, throwing the snow and Gwen's hair askew. Royce's heart thundered in his chest as she broke into a run. He no longer cared about the others. Saldur could rule all of Elan, so long as he could have Gwen. They would go to Avempartha—leave that very night. The wagon was already filled with supplies and hitched to a strong team. He would take her beyond everyone's reach. Royce would finally have a place to call home and have a life worth living. Every night he would sleep with Gwen in his arms, knowing he would never need to leave her again. Together they would walk through open fields without Royce having to look over his shoulder. They would have children, and he would delight in watching them grow. Royce would be content to grow old with Gwen at his side.

He was sprinting to her. He did not recall telling his feet to move, yet they raced toward her. As the distance between them closed, Royce threw out his arms to embrace Gwen. Suddenly her eyes widened with shock, then shut tight with anguish. She stiffened and arched her back as the crossbow bolt exited the front of her body. Royce felt a spray of blood.

She fell.

"*Gwen!*" he screamed.

He slid to his knees and turned her over so they could see each other. Dark blood pooled around her, staining the snow. He cradled Gwen in his arms, pulled her to him, and brushed the hair from her face. Royce's hands shook as he cut her restraints. He pulled away the gag, which was soaked in blood.

She coughed. "Roy-Roy-ce." She struggled to speak. "Roy-ce...my love..."

"Shh," he told her. "It will be all right. I'll find a doctor. I'll take care of you. We're going to get married right away. No more waiting. I swear it!"

"No." She shook her head in his hands. "I don't...need a doctor."

Royce wiped the blood from her mouth and supported her head as her eyes fought for focus.

Her hand twitched as she tried to lift it toward his face. "Don't cry," she said.

Royce had not been aware that he was until that moment. Tears ran down his cheeks and fell to her face, mixing with the thin line of blood that trickled from the side of her mouth.

This cannot be happening, his mind screamed. *We are going away together. The wagon is ready!*

He shook and shuddered as if he might break in two.

"Don't leave me, Gwen. I love you. Please don't leave me."

"It's okay, R-Royce...Don't you see?"

"No, no—it's not. It's not okay! It's—" His voice broke. He swallowed. "How can this be okay? How can you leaving me alone be all right?"

She jerked in his arms. Her eyes closed and she coughed once more. When her eyes opened again, her chest heaved for breath. A thick gurgling sound came from her throat.

"It's the fork in your lifeline," she managed to say, her voice weaker now—only a coarse whisper. "You reached it...The death of the one you love most. Only I was wrong...I was wrong. It wasn't Hadrian...It was me...It was me all along."

"Yes," he cried, kissing her forehead.

"And what did I tell you about that? What did I say? Do you remember?"

"You said...You said that you could die a happy woman if only that were true."

She looked up at him tenderly, but her eyes lost focus and began to wander. "I can't see you, Royce. It's dark. I can't see in the dark like you can. I'm scared."

He clenched her hand. "I'm here, Gwen. I'm right beside you."

"Royce, listen to me. You have to hang on," she said, her voice suddenly urgent. "Don't let go. Don't you dare let go. Do you hear me? Are you listening to me, Royce Melborn? You have to hang on, Royce. Please...give me your hand. Give me your hand!"

He squeezed her hand tighter. "I'm here, Gwen. I have you. I'm not letting go. I'll never let go."

"Promise me. You must promise. Please, Royce."

"I promise," he told her.

"I love you, Royce. Don't forget...Don't let go..."

"I love you."

"Don't...let..."

Her body hitched again. She struggled to breathe, stiffened

in his arms, and then slowly…gradually…fell limp. Her head tilted backward. Clutching her tightly to his chest, he kissed her face. Gwen was gone and Royce was alone.

∽

Amilia, Breckton, Hadrian, and Arista led thirty horsemen to the gates of Colnora. The cavalry detachment was selected from the Northern Imperial Army and included Breckton's best soldiers. Most of them had been at the siege of Drondil Fields only weeks before. These were not the sons of counts and dukes. They did not wear elaborately decorated armor of full plate. They were grim, battle-hardened men who honed their skills on bloody fields.

In the wake of Modina's abduction, Amilia found herself in the surreal position of imperial steward. The former scullery maid now ruled the empire. She tried not to think about it. Unlike Modina, she was not descended from Novron and held no pedigree to protect her station. And she had no idea how long she had before her power, her station, and perhaps her very life ended.

She had no idea what to do, but to her great relief, Sir Breckton mobilized his men and vowed to find the empress. When Sir Hadrian and Arista volunteered to join them, Amilia decided to ride as well. She could not sit in the palace. She did not know how to administrate, so she left Nimbus in charge until her return. If she could not find Modina, there might be no point in returning at all. They had to find her.

"Open the gate!" Sir Breckton shouted toward the watch-tower that sat atop the wall in Colnora.

"City gate opens at dawn," someone replied from above.

"I am Sir Breckton, commander of the imperial hosts, on a

mission of grave importance to Her Eminence. I demand that you open at once!"

"And I am the gatekeeper with strict orders to keep this gate sealed between dusk and dawn. Come back at first light."

"What are we going to do?" Amilia asked as panic threatened to consume her. The absurdity of the situation was overwhelming. The empress's life was at stake, and they were at the mercy of a foolish man and a wooden gate.

Breckton dismounted. "We can lash tree branches together to make ladders and go over the walls. Or we can build a ram—"

"We don't have time for that," Hadrian interrupted. "The full moon's high. Royce is doing the exchange at the Langdon Bridge. We have to get inside and down to that bridge—now!"

"This is all your fault!" Amilia burst out, and shook with fury. "You and your *friend*. First you attempt to kill Sir Breckton, and now *he's* taken Modina."

Breckton reached up and took her hand. "Although he had the power to do so, Sir Hadrian did not kill me. He is not responsible for the actions of his associate. He is trying to help."

Amilia wiped tears from her eyes and nodded. She did not know what to do. She was no general. She was just a stupid peasant girl whom the nobility would soon execute. Everything was so hopeless. The only one who did not seem upset was Arista.

The princess was humming.

Already off her horse, she stood with her eyes closed and her hands outstretched. Her fingers moved delicately through the air and a low vibration echoed from deep in her throat. The sound was not a tune or a song of any kind. There was no discernible melody, and as Arista's voice grew louder, the air seemed to grow thick and heavy. Then there was another hum. An echo resonated from the gate. The wooden beams moved like a man quivering in the cold. They cracked and buckled. The great hinges rattled, and bits of stone fractured where they met the walls. Arista stopped humming. The gate ceased its trembling. Then, in one burst of voice, she uttered an unrecognizable word, and the gate exploded in flying bits of splintered wood and scattered snow.

❧

Modina tested the ropes on her wrists, but the movement only caused them to bite deeper. Merrick Marius and two men she did not know had dragged her off the bridge and into a nearby warehouse. Saldur was allowed to walk freely. The building was cavernous, abandoned, and in need of repair. Broken windows let in snow, which drifted across the bare floorboards. Torn sacks and broken glass littered the floor.

"Excellent, my boy. Excellent." Saldur addressed Merrick Marius as another man cut his hands free. "I will honor my offer to reward you handsomely. You will—"

"Shut up!" Merrick ordered harshly. "Get them both upstairs."

One of the men threw Modina over his shoulder like a sack of flour and carried her up the steps.

"I don't understand," Saldur said, even as the other stranger steered him upstairs too.

"This isn't over," Merrick replied. "DeLancy is dead. You have no idea what that means. The scales are balanced. The demon is unleashed."

He said more, but his voice faded as Modina was carried up several flights. The man carrying her dropped her in an empty room on the third floor. He pulled a wad of twine from his pocket and bound her ankles tight. When he was done, he moved to the broken window and peered out.

Moonlight fell across his face. He was a short, husky brute with a rough beard and flat nose. He wore a dark cowl over a coarse woolen garnache, but Modina's eyes were focused on the leather girdle from which two long daggers hung. He crouched on one knee, looking at the street below.

"Be very quiet, miss," he murmured, "or I'll have to slit your throat."

✒

With trembling hands, Royce laid Gwen's lifeless body near the side of the bridge. He closed her eyes and kissed her lips one last time. Folding her arms gently across her chest, he covered her as best he could with the rough, oversized cloak as if putting her to bed. He could not bring himself to cover her face and stared at it for a long while, noting the smile she wore even in death.

Turning from her, he got up and, without conscious thought, found himself crossing the bridge.

"Stop right there, Royce!" Merrick shouted when he had reached the far side.

From the sound and angle of his voice, Royce knew Merrick was on the second floor of the warehouse.

"All of the lower doors and windows are sealed. I have a man with a dagger to the empress's throat."

Royce ignored him. He deftly climbed up the closest lamppost, shattered the lantern, and snuffed out the flame. He repeated this twice more, darkening the area.

"I mean it, Royce," Merrick shouted again. The tinge of panic in his voice betrayed that his old partner could no longer see him. "Don't make the mistake of killing another innocent woman tonight."

Royce tore the bottom of his cloak and soaked the scrap in the lamppost reservoir. Then he walked to the warehouse.

"You can't get to me without killing her!" Merrick shouted again. "Get back where I can see you."

Royce began coating the base of the walls with oil.

"Damn it, Royce. I didn't do it. I didn't kill her. It wasn't me."

Royce struck a light, catching the oiled cloth on fire, and pushed it under the door. The wood was old and dry, and the flames hungrily took hold. The brisk winter wind did its part, spreading flames to the clapboard sides.

"What are you doing?" asked Saldur's voice, rising in terror. "Marius, do something. Threaten to cut Modina's throat if he doesn't—"

"I did, you idiot! He doesn't care about the empress. He's going to kill us all!" Marius shouted.

The flames spread quickly. Royce went back for more oil to lure the fire across the timbers. The exterior of the storehouse blazed, and sheets of flame raced upward. Royce stepped back and watched the building burn. He felt the heat on his face as the flaming building lit up the street.

Shouts came from inside, fighting to be heard over the crackling of the fire. Royce waited, watching the cloverleaf insignia burn away.

It was not long before the first man jumped from a second-story window. He managed to land well enough, but Royce was on him in an instant. Alverstone flickered in the firelight. The man screamed, but Royce was in no hurry and took his time. He cut the tendons of the man's legs, making it impossible for him to run. Then, sitting on his chest, he severed the man's fingers. It had been a long time since Royce had used Alverstone to dismember someone. He marveled at how well the white dagger cut through the toughest cartilage and even through bone. Royce left the first man to bleed when he noticed another one jump. This one came from a third-story window. He landed awkwardly, and Royce heard a bone break.

"No!" the man cried, struggling to crawl away as Royce's dark form flew toward him. The man scraped desperately at the snow. Once more, Royce was slow and methodical. The man howled with each cut. When he stopped moving, Royce removed his heart. He stood up, drenched in blood, his right arm soaked to the elbow, and threw the organ through the window the man had leapt from.

"You're next, Saldur," he taunted. "I can't wait to see if you actually have one or not."

There was no response.

Out of the corner of his eye, Royce saw a dark figure moving from the back of the building. Merrick was barely noticeable as he slipped through the dancing shadows. Royce guessed he was planning to hide on the lip under the Langdon Bridge, which the Black Diamond used to ambush targets. Royce left Saldur to burn. The fire completely engulfed the second floor. It would be just a matter of time. The only way out was for the regent to jump, and a man his age would fare poorly in a three-story drop to frozen ground.

Royce chased after Merrick, who abandoned stealth to make an open run for it. Royce caught up quickly, and Merrick gave up near the middle of the bridge. He turned, his dagger drawn, his face covered in sweat and soot.

"I didn't kill her," he shouted.

Royce did not respond. He rapidly closed the remaining distance and attacked. The white dagger lashed out like a snake. Merrick dodged. He avoided the first swipe but Royce caught him on the return stroke, slicing across his chest.

"Listen to me," Merrick said, still trying to back away.

"Why would I kill her? You *know* me! Don't you think I knew she was my protection? Have you *ever* seen me do anything as stupid as that? Just ask yourself—why would I do such a thing? What would I gain? Think, Royce, think. What reason would I have to kill her?"

"The same reason that I'm going to kill you—revenge."

Royce lunged. Merrick tried to move, but he was too slow. He would have died instantly if Royce had aimed for his heart or throat. Instead, Alverstone caught Merrick in the right shoulder.

It plunged deep and Merrick dropped his weapon.

"*It doesn't make sense!*" Merrick screamed at him. "This has nothing to do with Jade. If I wanted revenge, I could have killed you years ago. I only wanted Saldur and the empress. I was never going to hurt her. We've made our peace with each other, Royce. I was serious about that offer to work together again. We are not enemies. Don't make the same mistake I did. You were set up when Jade died, but I couldn't see that—I didn't want to. Now someone is doing the same thing to me. I've been set up, don't you see? Just like you were. Use your brain! If I had a bow, would I have let you burn the warehouse? It wasn't me. It was someone else!"

Royce made a show of looking around. "Funny, I don't see anyone else here."

He pounced again. Merrick retreated and his heel hit the short curb of the bridge.

"You're running out of room."

"Damn it, Royce, you have to believe me. I would never kill Gwen. I swear to you—I didn't do it!"

"I believe you," Royce said. "I just don't care."

With one final thrust, he stabbed Alverstone into Merrick's chest.

Merrick toppled backward. He reached out for the only

thing he could grab, and together he and Royce fell over the edge.

⬿

When the gate had burst open, Hadrian did not wait for the others. Instead, he spurred his horse and raced toward the river. Malevolent slipped on the snow and nearly fell as he rounded the corner to Langdon Bridge. On the far side, the warehouse burned like a giant pyre. The streetlamps on that side of the bridge were dark. On his side, the iron swans, dusted with snow, flickered with an eerie orange light. The tall lampposts cast wavering shadows—thin, dark, dancing spears that fluttered and jabbed.

Hadrian saw her lying near the side of the bridge.

"Oh dear Maribor, no!" He ran to Gwen's side. Flakes of snow gathered on her closed eyes and clung to her dark lashes. He put his head to her chest. There was no heartbeat—she was dead.

"*It doesn't make sense!*" Hadrian heard someone cry out. Looking down the bridge, he saw them at the very apex of the span. Royce had Merrick backed up along the edge. Merrick was hurt, unarmed, and screaming. Jumping to his feet, Hadrian sprinted forward, his boots slipping on the slick snow. From only a few strides away, Hadrian saw Royce stab Merrick and watched as both of them tumbled over the side.

He slid, caught himself against the lip, and looked over. His heart pounded in his chest. Far below, the churning water of the Bernum River revealed itself as a dark line broken by moonlit explosions where water crashed against rocks. He saw something dark still falling. A moment later, it hit the surface with a brief flash of white.

❧

Arista flexed her fingers and climbed back on her horse. Breck-ton remounted as well and rode forward to speak with the shouting gate guards. Hadrian had already disappeared into the twisting streets.

No one mentioned anything about the exploding gate.

Without Hadrian to guide them, Sir Breckton led the detachment through Colnora. They crossed the Bernum using the Warpole Bridge and were midway across when they saw the warehouse ablaze near a bridge farther down the river, sig-naling their destination. Rather than backtrack, Breckton continued across the Warpole and arrived at the Langdon Bridge on the warehouse side, causing them to pass in front of the monstrous blaze.

The building was an inferno. The burning hulk mesmer-ized Arista. Huge spirals of flames reached to the sky. All four stories were on fire. The north wall blistered and snapped. The east wall curled and partially collapsed, releasing a burst of sparks and a rain of burning debris that hissed when it struck snow. White smoke billowed out from shattered win-dows and a nearby oak tree blazed, its naked limbs turned into a giant torch.

Arista heard a woman cry out.

"That's Modina!" Amilia shrieked, pulling back so hard on her horse's reins that the beast shook its head and backed up a step. *"She's inside!"*

Sir Breckton and several of his men dismounted and rushed to the doorway. They broke down the bolted door, but the heat forced them back. Breckton pulled his cloak over his head and started to enter.

"Stop!" Arista shouted as she slid from her horse.

The knight hesitated.

"You'll die before you reach her. I'll go."

"But—" Breckton said, then stopped. Rubbing his jaw, he looked at the fire and then back at Arista. "Can you save her?"

Arista shook her head. "I don't know. I've never done this before, but I stand a better chance than you do. Just keep everyone else back."

She pulled the sleeves of Esrahaddon's robe over her hands and the hood up around her head and face as she approached the crumbling warehouse. Realizing she could sense the fire's movements was exhilarating. The blaze moved and acted like a living thing. It withered, snapped, and fed on the old wood like a ravenous beast. It was hungry, starved for nourishment, a never-ending want, boundless greed. Approaching the blaze, she sensed it noticing her, and the fire regarded Arista with desire.

No, she told it. *Eat the wood. Ignore me.*

The fire hissed.

Leave me alone or I will snuff you out.

Arista knew she could conjure a rainstorm, or even a whirlwind, but rain would take too long, and wind would collapse the fragile building. Perhaps there was a way to eliminate the fire altogether, but she was not certain how to go about it and Modina could not wait for her to figure it out.

The fire snapped. She felt its elemental eye turn away and Arista entered the blackened doorway. She walked into an inferno of smoke and fire. Everything around her was burning. Hot currents of air whipped and gusted, blasting through the building's interior. She moved through a raging river of smoky air that parted around her.

After finding the scorched wooden stairs, she carefully began to climb. Beneath her feet the planks fractured, splintered, and popped. With the protection of Esrahaddon's robe, she felt warmth but nothing more. Breathing through the material, Arista found fresh, cool air.

"Thanks, Esra," she muttered, pushing forward into the thick, surging smoke.

She heard a muffled cry from above and climbed. On the third floor, she found Modina. The empress was in the center of a small room, hands and feet bound. The fire was busy enjoying the older, drier timber of the main brace on the far side of the room and ignored the greener floorboards where Modina lay. Running along the rafters, it ate into the supporting beams with wolfish delight.

"Not much time," the princess said, glancing up. "Can you walk?"

"Yes," Modina answered.

Arista cursed herself for not wearing a dagger as her fingers struggled to untie the empress's hands. Once loose, they worked to free her feet.

Modina coughed and gagged. Arista removed the robe. Instantly the intense heat slammed into her. She wrapped the garment over their shoulders like a blanket and held one of the sleeves to her mouth.

"Breathe through the robe," she told Modina over the roaring blaze.

The two women moved down the stairs together. Arista kept her focus on the fire's intentions and warned it away when it came too close. A timber cracked overhead and crashed with the sound of thunder. The building shuddered with the blow. A step snapped under Arista, and Modina pulled her forward in time to save the princess from a two-story fall.

"We can thank the dungeon for you not weighing much," Modina said through the sleeve pressed against her mouth.

They reached the ground floor and raced out together. The moment Modina emerged, Amilia threw her arms around her.

"There's someone else up there," Sir Breckton announced. "In that upper window near the end."

"Help!" Saldur cried. "Someone help me!"

A few looked to Arista, but she made no move to reenter the building.

"*Help me!*" he screamed.

Arista stepped back to get a better view. The old man was in tears. His face was transfigured with horror.

"Arista!" he pleaded, spotting her. "In the name of Novron...help me, child."

"It's a shame," she shouted back, her voice rising above the roar of the fire, "that *Hilfred* isn't here to save you."

There was another loud *crack* and Saldur's eyes filled with panic. He grabbed the windowsill and clung to it as the floor gave way beneath him. With a final scream, his fingers slipped and Maurice Saldur, former bishop of the Nyphron Church, co-regent and architect of the New Empire, vanished from view into the flames.

⁂

Hadrian was bent over the bridge's edge, looking over the side. His eyes fixated on the spot far below where the body had hit the river. A gust of wind revealed a familiar cloak that flapped out from below the skirt of the bridge.

His heart beat faster as he spotted four fingers clinging to a hidden lip that ran beneath the span. He hurriedly wrapped his feet around a lamppost and lowered himself farther. Royce was there, just out of reach. His left hand held the underside of the Langdon, his feet dangling free.

"Royce!" Hadrian called.

His partner did not look up.

"Royce—damn you, look at me!"

Royce continued to stare down into the foaming waters as the wind whipped his black cape like the broken wings of a bird.

"Royce, I can't reach you," Hadrian shouted, extending his arm toward his friend. "You have to help me. You need to reach with your other hand so I can pull you up."

There was a pause.

"Merrick is dead," Royce said softly.

"I know."

"Gwen is dead."

Hadrian paused. "Yes."

"I—I burned Modina alive."

"Royce, goddamn it! That doesn't matter. Please, look at me."

Slowly, Royce tilted his head up. His hood fell away and tears streaked his cheeks. He refused to meet Hadrian's eyes.

"*Don't do it!*" Hadrian yelled.

"I—I don't have anything left," Royce muttered, his words almost stolen by the wind. "I don't—"

"Royce, listen to me. You have to hang on. Don't let go. Don't you dare let go. Do you hear me? Are you listening to me, Royce Melborn? You have to hang on, Royce. Please... give me your hand. Give me your hand!"

Royce's head snapped up. He focused on Hadrian and there was a curious look in his eyes. "What—what did you say?"

"I said I can't reach you. I need your help."

Hadrian extended his arm farther.

Royce sheathed Alverstone and swung his body. The momentum thrust his right hand upward. Hadrian grabbed it and lifted.

BOOK VI

PERCEPLIQUIS

Chapter 1

The Child

Miranda had been certain that the end of the world would begin like this—without warning, but with fire. Behind them, the sky glowed red as flames and plumes of sparks rose into the night sky. The university at Sheridan was burning.

Holding Mercy's little hand, Miranda was terrified she might lose the girl in the dark. They had been running for hours, dashing blindly through the pine forest, pushing their way past unseen branches. Beneath the laden boughs, the snow was deep. Miranda fought through drifts higher than her knees, breaking a path for the little girl and the old professor.

Struggling somewhere behind, Arcadius called out, "Go on, go on, don't wait for me."

Hauling the heavy pack and dragging the little girl, Miranda was moving as fast as she could. Every time she heard a sound or thought a shadow moved, Miranda fought back a scream. Panic hovered just below the surface, threatening to break free. Death was on their heels and her feet were anchors.

Miranda felt sorry for the child and worried that hauling her forward was hurting her arm. Once, Miranda had pulled too hard and dragged Mercy across the surface of the snow. The girl had cried when her face skimmed the powder, but her whimpering was short-lived. Mercy had stopped asking questions, stopped complaining about being tired. She had given up talking altogether and trudged behind Miranda as best she could. She was a brave girl.

They reached the road and Miranda knelt down to inspect the child. Her nose ran. Snowflakes clung to her eyelashes. Her cheeks were red, and her black hair lay matted with sweat to her forehead. Miranda took a moment to brush several loose strands behind her ears while Mr. Rings kept a close eye on her. As if he were a fur stole, the raccoon curled around the girl's neck. Mercy had insisted on freeing the animals from their cages before leaving. Once released, the raccoon had run up Mercy's arm and held tight. Apparently, Mr. Rings also sensed something bad was coming.

"How are you doing?" Miranda asked, pulling the girl's hood up and tightening the broach holding her cloak.

"My feet are cold," she said. The child's voice was little more than a whisper as she stared down at the snow.

"So are mine," Miranda replied in the brightest tone she could muster.

"Ah, well, that was fun, wasn't it?" the old professor said while climbing the slope to join them. He puffed large clouds and shifted the satchel over his shoulder, his beard and eyebrows thick with snow and ice.

"And how are *you* doing?" Miranda asked.

"Oh, I'm fine, fine. An old man needs a bit of exercise now and again, but we need to keep moving."

"Where are we going?" Mercy asked.

"Aquesta," Arcadius replied. "You know what Aquesta is, don't you, dear? That's where the empress rules from a big palace. You'd like to meet her, wouldn't you?"

"Will she be able to stop them?"

Miranda noticed the little girl's gaze had shifted over the old man's shoulder to the burning university. Miranda looked as well, watching the brilliant glow rising above the treetops. They were many miles away now, and yet the light still filled the horizon. Dark shadows flew above the fire's light. They swooped and circled over the burning university, and from their mouths spewed torrents of flame.

"We can hope, my dear. We can hope," Arcadius said. "Now let's keep moving. I know you're tired. I know you're cold. So am I, but we have to go as fast as we can. We have to get farther away."

Mercy nodded or shivered. It was difficult to discern which.

Miranda dusted the snow from the child's back and legs in an attempt to keep her from getting wetter than she already was. This drew a cautious glare from Mr. Rings.

"Do you think the other animals got away?" Mercy asked.

"I'm certain they did," Arcadius assured her. "They are smart, aren't they? Maybe not as smart as Mr. Rings here— after all, he managed to get a ride."

Mercy nodded again and added in a hopeful voice, "I'm sure Teacup got away. She can fly."

Miranda checked the girl's pack and then her own to ensure they were still closed and cinched tight. She looked down the dark road before them.

"This will take us through Colnora and right into Aquesta," the old wizard explained.

"How long will it take to get there?" Mercy asked.

"Several days—a week, perhaps. Longer if the weather stays bad."

Miranda saw the disappointment in Mercy's eyes. "Don't worry, once we are farther away, we will stop, rest, and eat. I'll make something hot and then we'll sleep for a bit. But for now, we have to keep going. Now that we are on the road, it will be easier."

Miranda took the little girl's hand and they set off again. She was pleased to discover that what she had told the child turned out to be true. Trenches left by wagons made for easy going, even more so due to the downhill slope. They kept a brisk pace, and soon the forest rose to blot out the fiery glow behind them. The world became dark and quiet, with only the sound of the cold wind to keep them company.

Miranda glanced at the old professor as he trudged along, holding his cloak tight to his neck. The skin of his face was red and blotchy, and he labored to breathe. "Are you sure you are all right?"

Arcadius did not respond at first. He drew near, forced a smile, and whispered softly in Miranda's ear, "I fear you may need to finish this journey without me."

"What?" Miranda said too loudly, and glanced down at the little girl. Mercy did not look up. "We'll stop soon. We'll rest and take our time tomorrow. We've gone a good distance today. Here, let me take your satchel." She reached out.

"No. I'll hang on to it. It's very fragile, as you know—and dangerous. If anyone dies carrying it, I want it to be me. As for resting, I don't think it will make a difference. I'm not strong enough for this sort of travel. We both know that."

"You can't give up."

"I'm not. I'm handing off the charge to you. You'll manage."

"But I don't know what to do. You've never told me the plan."

Arcadius chuckled. "That's because it changes frequently. I had hoped the regents would have accepted Mercy as Modina's heir, but they refused."

"So now what?"

"Modina is on the throne now, so we have a second chance.

The best you can do is get to Aquesta and seek an audience with her."

"But I don't know how—"

"You'll figure it out. Introduce Mercy to the empress. That will be a start in the right direction. Soon you will be the only one who knows the truth. I hate placing this burden on you, but I have no choice."

Miranda shook her head. "No, it was my mother who placed the burden on me. Not you."

"A deathbed confession is a weighty thing." The old man nodded. "But doing so allowed her to die in peace."

"Do you think so? Or is her spirit still lingering? Sometimes I feel as if she is watching—haunting me. I'm paying the price for her weakness, her cowardice."

"Your mother was young, poor, and ignorant. She witnessed the death of dozens of men, the butchery of a mother and child, and narrowly escaped. She lived in constant fear that someday, someone would discover there were twins and she rescued one of them."

"But," Miranda said bitterly, "what she did was wrong and unconscionable. And the worst part is she couldn't let the sin die with her. She had to tell me. Make it my responsibility to correct her mistakes. She should—"

Mercy came to an abrupt halt, tugging on Miranda's arm.

"Honey, we need to…." She stopped upon seeing the girl's face. The faint light of an early dawn revealed fear as Mercy stared ahead to where the road dipped toward a large stone bridge.

"There's a light up ahead," Arcadius said.

"Is it…?" Miranda asked.

The old teacher shook his head. "It's a campfire—several, it looks like. More refugees, I suspect. We can join with them and the going will be easier. If I'm not mistaken, they are camped on the far bank of the Galewyr. I had no idea we'd come so far. No wonder I'm puffing."

"There now," Miranda said to the girl as they once more started forward. "See? Our troubles are already over. Maybe they will even have a wagon that an old man can ride in."

Arcadius gave her a smirk but allowed himself a smile. "Things may be looking up at that."

"We'll be—"

The girl squeezed Miranda's hand and stopped once more. Up the road, figures on horseback trotted toward them. The animals snorted white fog as their hooves drove through the iced tracks. The riders sat enveloped in dark cloaks. With hoods drawn up and scarves wrapped, it was difficult to determine much, but one thing was certain—they were just men. Miranda counted three. They came from the south but not from the direction of the campfires. These were not refugees.

"Who do you think?" Miranda asked. "Highwaymen?"

The professor shook his head.

"What do we do?"

"Hopefully nothing. With luck they are just good men coming to our aid. If not…" He patted his satchel grimly. "Get to those campfires and ask for shelter and protection. Then see to it that Mercy reaches Aquesta. Avoid the regents and try to tell the empress Mercy's story. Tell her the truth."

"But what if—"

The horses approached and slowed.

"What do we have here?" one rider asked.

Miranda could not tell who spoke, but guessed it was the foremost. He studied them while they stood still, listening to the deep throaty pant of the horses.

"Isn't this convenient?" he said, and dismounted. "Of all the people in the world—I was just coming to see you, old man."

The leader was tall and held his side gingerly, moving stiffly. His piercing eyes glared out from under his hood, his nose and mouth shrouded by a crimson scarf.

"Out for an early stroll in a snowstorm?" he asked, closing the distance between them.

"Hardly," Arcadius replied. "We're in flight."

"I'm sure you are. Clearly if I had waited even a day, I would have missed you, and you might have slipped away. Coming to the palace was a foolish mistake. You exposed too much. And for what? You should have known better. But age must bring with it a degree of desperation." He looked at Mercy. "Is this the girl?"

"Guy," Arcadius said, "Sheridan is burning. The elves have crossed the Nidwalden. The elves have attacked!"

Guy! Miranda knew him, or at least his reputation. Arcadius had taught her the names of all the church sentinels. From the professor's viewpoint, Luis Guy was the most dangerous. All sentinels were obsessed, all chosen for their rabid orthodoxy, but Guy had a legacy. His mother's maiden name was Evone. She had been a pious girl who had married Lord Jarred Seret, a direct descendant of the original Lord Darius Seret, who had been charged by Patriarch Venlin to find the heir of the Old Empire. In the realm of heir hunters, Luis Guy was a fanatic among fanatics.

"Don't play me for a fool. This is the girl-child you spoke to Saldur and Ethelred about, isn't it? The one you wanted to groom as the next empress. Why would you do that, old man? Why pick *this* girl? Is this another ruse? Or were you actually trying to slip her past us? To atone for your mistake." Guy crouched down to get a better look at Mercy's face. "Come here, child."

"No!" Miranda snapped, pulling Mercy close.

Guy stood up slowly. "Let go of the child," he ordered.

"No."

"Sentinel Guy!" Arcadius shouted. "She's just a peasant girl. An orphan I took in."

"Is she?" He drew his sword.

"Be reasonable. You have no idea what you're doing."

"Oh, I think I do. Everyone was so focused on Esrahaddon that you went by unnoticed. Who could have imagined that you would point the way to the heir not just once, but twice?"

"The heir? The Heir of Novron? Are you insane? Is that why you think I spoke to the regents?"

"Isn't it?"

"No." He shook his head, an amused smile on his face. "I came because I suspected they hadn't thought about the question of succession, and I wanted to help educate the next imperial leader."

"But you insisted on this girl—only *this* girl. Why would you do that unless she really is the heir?"

"That makes no sense. How could I know who the heir is? Or even if an heir still lives?"

"How indeed. That was the missing piece. You are actually the only one who could know. Tell me, Arcadius Latimer, what did your father do for a living?"

"He was a weaver, but I fail to see—"

"Yes, so how did the poor son of a weaver from a small village become the master of lore at Sheridan University? I doubt your father even knew how to read, and yet his son is one of the most renowned scholars in the world? How does that happen?"

"Really, Guy, I would not think I would need to explain the merits of ambition and hard work to someone such as you."

Guy sneered back. "You disappeared for ten years, and when you came back, you knew a lot more than when you left."

"You're just making things up."

Guy smirked. "The church doesn't let just anyone teach at their university. Did you think they didn't keep records?"

"Of course not. I just didn't think you'd see them." The old man smiled.

"I'm a sentinel, you idiot! I have access to every archive in the church."

"Yes, but I didn't think my scholastic examination would be of any interest. I was a rebel in my youth—handsome too. Did the records indicate that?"

"It said you found the tomb of Yolric. Who was Yolric?"

"And here I thought you knew everything."

"I didn't have time to linger in libraries. I was in a hurry to catch you."

"But why? Why are you after me? Why is your sword out?"

"Because the Heir of Novron must die."

"She's not the heir. Why do you think she is? How could I even know who the heir was?"

"Because that is one of the secrets you brought back. You discovered how to locate the heir."

"Bah! Really, Guy, you have quite an imagination."

"There were other records. The church called you in for questioning. They thought you might have gone to Percepliquis like that Edmund Hall fellow. And then, only days after that meeting, there was a fight in the city of Ratibor. A pregnant mother and her husband were killed. Identified as Linitha and Naron Brown, they and their child were executed by Seret Knights. After centuries of looking, I find it interesting that my predecessor managed to locate the Heir of Novron just days after the church interrogated you." Guy glared at the professor. "Did you make a deal with the church? Did you trade information in exchange for freedom? I'm sure they told you they wanted to find the heir so they could make him king again. When you discovered what they really did, I imagine you felt used—the guilt must be awful."

Guy paused for Arcadius to respond but the professor said nothing.

"After that everyone thought the bloodline had ended, didn't they? Even the Patriarch had no idea another heir still lived. Then Esrahaddon escapes and he goes straight to Degan Gaunt. Only Degan isn't the heir. I was fooled for a long time too, but imagine my shock when he failed the blood test that he previously passed. No doubt the result of the same potion Esrahaddon used on King Amrath and Arista that made Braga suspect the Essendons. I suppose, looking back on it, we should have guessed a wizard of the Old Empire wasn't a fool and would never lead us to the real heir.

"But there was another, wasn't there? And you performed whatever trick you did the first time to find her." Guy peered at Mercy. "What is she? A bastard child? A niece?" He advanced toward Miranda. "Hand her over."

"No!" the old professor shouted.

One of the soldiers grabbed Miranda, and the other pulled the girl from her.

"But let's be certain, shall we? I will not make the same mistake twice." With a deft sweep of his wrist, Guy slashed Mercy across her hand. She screamed and Mr. Rings hissed.

"That's uncalled for!" Arcadius said.

"Watch them," Guy ordered his men while he moved to his horse.

"Hush now, be a brave girl for me," Miranda told Mercy.

Guy carefully laid his sword on the ground, then withdrew a small leather case from his saddlebag. From it, he pulled forth a set of three vials. He uncorked the first, tilted it slightly, and tapped on it with his finger until a bit of powder sprinkled onto the bloodstained end of his sword.

"I want to leave now," Mercy whimpered as the guard held her fast. "Please can we go?"

"Interesting," Guy muttered to himself, then applied the contents of the next vial. This one held a liquid that hissed and fizzled when it landed on the blade.

"Guy!" Arcadius shouted at him as he stepped forward.

"*Very* interesting," Guy continued. He uncorked the last vial.

"Guy, don't!" the old man yelled.

He poured a single drop on the tip of the sword.

Pop!

The sound was like a wine bottle cork coming free and the flash was as brilliant as lightning.

The sentinel stood up, staring at the end of his sword, and began to laugh. It was a strange and eerie sound, like the song of a madman. "At last. At long last, I have found the Heir of Novron. The quest of my ancestors will be achieved through me."

"Miranda," Arcadius whispered, "you can do nothing more by yourself." The old man's eyes glanced toward the refugee camp.

As the morning light rose, Miranda could see several columns of smoke. Possible help was tantalizingly close. Only a few hundred yards at most.

"I've devoted my life to correcting my mistake. But now it is up to you to do what must be done," Arcadius said.

Luis Guy took the girl and hoisted her onto his horse. "We'll take her to the Patriarch."

"What about these two, sir?" one of the hooded men asked.

"Take the old man. Kill the woman."

Miranda's heart skipped as the soldier reached for his sword.

"Wait!" Arcadius said. "What about the horn?" The old

professor was backing away, clutching his satchel. "The Patriarch will want the horn too, won't he?"

Guy's eyes flashed at the bag Arcadius held.

"You have it?" the sentinel asked.

Arcadius shot a desperate look toward Miranda, then
turned and fled back down the road.

"Watch the child," Guy ordered one of his men. Turning to
the other, he waved, and together they chased after Arcadius,
who ran faster than Miranda would have ever imagined
possible.

She watched him—her closest friend—racing back the
way they had come, his cloak flying behind him. She might
have thought the sight comical except she knew what Arcadius actually had in his satchel. She knew why he was running
away, what that meant, and what he wanted her to do.

Miranda reached for the dagger under her cloak. She had
never killed anyone before, but what choice did she have? The
man standing between her and Mercy was a soldier, and likely
a Seret Knight. He turned his back on her to get a better grip
on Guy's horse, focusing his attention on Mercy and the hissing raccoon that snapped at him.

Miranda had only seconds before Guy and the other man
caught up to Arcadius. Knowing what would happen made
her want to cry. They had come so far together, sacrificed so
much, and just when it seemed like they were finally close to
their goal...to be stopped like this...to be murdered on a
roadside...*Tragic* was too weak a word to frame the injustice.
There would be time for tears later. The professor was counting on her and she would not let him down. That one look had
told her everything. This was the final gamble. If they could
get Mercy to Modina, everything might be made right again.

She drew the dagger and rushed forward. With all her
strength, Miranda stabbed the soldier in the back. He was not

wearing mail or leather and the sharp blade bit deep, passing through clothes, skin, and muscle.

He spun and swatted her away. The back of his fist connected with her cheek and left her reeling from the blow. She fell to the snow, still holding the dagger, the handle slick with blood.

On the horse, Mercy held tight to the saddle and screamed. The raccoon chattered, its fur up.

Miranda got back to her feet as the soldier drew his sword. He was badly hurt. Blood soaked his pant leg and he staggered toward her. She tried to get away, reaching for Mercy and the horse, but the seret was faster. His sword pierced her side somewhere near her waist. She felt it go in. The pain burned, but then she suddenly felt cold. Her knees buckled. She managed to hold fast to the saddle as the horse, frightened by the violence and Mercy's screaming, moved away, dragging her with it.

Behind them, the soldier fell to his knees, blood bubbling from his lips.

Miranda tried to pull herself up, but her legs were useless. They hung limp and she felt the strength draining from her arms. "Take the reins, Mercy, and hang on tight."

Down the road, Guy and the other man had caught up to Arcadius. Guy, who had stopped at the sound of the girl's screams, lagged behind, but the other soldier tackled the old professor to the snow.

"Mercy," Miranda said, "you need to ride. Ride over there—ride to the campfires. Beg for help. Go."

With her last bit of strength, she struck the horse's flank. The animal bolted forward. The saddle ripped from Miranda's hands and she fell once more into the snow. Lying on her back, she listened to the sound of the horse as it raced away.

"Get on your—" she heard Guy shout, but it was too late. Arcadius had opened the satchel.

Even from hundreds of feet away Miranda felt the earth shake from the explosion. An instant later, a gust of wind threw stinging snow against her face as a cloud billowed into the morning sky. Arcadius, and the man who wrestled with him, died instantly. Guy was blown off his feet. The remaining horses scattered.

As the snowy cloud settled, Miranda stared up at the brightening sky, at the rising dawn. She was not cold anymore. The pain in her side was going away, growing numb along with her legs and hands. She felt a breeze cross her cheek and noticed her legs and waist were wet, her dress soaked through. She could taste iron on her tongue. Breathing became difficult— as if she were drowning.

Guy was still alive. She heard him cursing the old man and calling to the horses as if they were disobedient dogs. The crunch of snow, the rub of leather, then the sound of hooves galloping away.

She was alone in the silence of the cold winter's dawn.

It was quiet. Peaceful.

"Dear Maribor, hear me," she prayed aloud to the brightening sky. "Oh Father of Novron, creator of men." She took her last breath and with it said, "Take care of your only daughter."

✧

Alenda Lanaklin crept out of her tent into the brisk morning air. She wore her thickest wool dress and two layers of fur, but still she shivered. The sun was just rising—a cold milky haze in the soup of a heavy winter sky. The clouds had lingered for more than a week and she wondered if she would ever see the sun's bright face again.

Alenda stood on the packed snow, looking around at the

dozens of tents pitched among the pine forest's eaves. Camp-fires burned in blackened snow pits, creating gray tails of smoke that wagged with the wind. Among them wandered figures, hooded and bundled such that it should have been difficult to identify male from female. Yet there was no such dilemma— they were all women. The camp was filled with them as well as children and the elderly. People walked with bowed heads, picking their way carefully through the trampled snow.

Everything appeared so different in the light, so quiet, so still. The previous night had been a terror of fire, screams, and a flight along the Westfield road. They had paused only briefly to take a head count before pushing on. Alenda had been so exhausted that she barely recalled the camp being set.

"Good morning, my lady," Emily greeted her from beneath a blanket, which was wrapped over her cloak. Her words lacked their normal cheerfulness. Alenda's maid had always been bright and playful in the morning. Now she stood with somber diligence, her reddened hands quivering, her jaw shak-ing with the chill.

"Is it, Emmy?" Alenda cast another look around. "How can you tell?"

"Let's find you some breakfast. Something warm will make you feel better."

"My father and brothers are dead," Alenda replied. "The world is ending. How can breakfast possibly help?"

"I don't know, my lady, but we must try. It's what your father wanted—for you to survive, I mean. It's why he stayed behind, isn't it?"

A loud boom, like a crack of thunder, echoed from the north. Every head turned to look out across the snowy fields. Every face terrified that the end had arrived at last.

Reaching the center of the camp, Alenda found Belinda Pickering; her daughter, Lenare; old Julian, Melengar's lord high chamberlain; and Lord Valin, the party's sole protector. The elderly knight had led them through the chaos the night before. Among them, they composed the last vestiges of the royal court, at least those still in Melengar. King Alric was in Aquesta lending a hand in the brief civil war and saving his sister, Arista, from execution. It was to him they now fled.

"We have no idea, but it is foolish to stay any longer," Lord Valin was saying.

"Yes, I agree," Belinda replied.

Lord Valin turned to a young boy. "Send word to rouse everyone. We will break camp immediately."

"Emmy," Alenda said, turning to her maid. "Run back and pack our things."

"Of course, my lady." Emily curtsied and headed toward their tent.

"What was that sound?" Alenda asked Lenare, who only shrugged, her face frightened.

Lenare Pickering was lovely, as always. Despite the horrors, the flight, and the primitive condition of the camp, she was radiant. Even disheveled in a hastily grabbed cloak, with her blonde hair spilling out of her hood, she remained stunning, just as a sleeping baby is always precious. She had gotten this blessing from her mother. Just as the Pickering men were renowned for their swordsmanship, so too were the Pickering women celebrated for their beauty. Lenare's mother, Belinda, was famous for it.

All that was over now. What had been constants only the day before were now lost beyond a gulf too wide to clearly see across, although at times it appeared that Lenare tried. Alenda often had seen her staring north at the horizon with a look somewhere between desperation and remorse, searching for ghosts.

In her arms, Lenare still held her father's legendary sword.

The count had handed it to her, begging that she deliver it safely to her brother Mauvin. Then he had kissed each member of his family before returning to the line where Alenda's own father and brothers waited with the rest of the army. Since then, Lenare had never set the burden down. She had wrapped it in a dark wool blanket and bound it with a silk ribbon. Throughout the harrowing escape, she had hugged the long bundle to her breast, at times using it to wipe away tears.

"If we push hard today, we might make Colnora by sunset," Lord Valin told them. "Assuming the weather improves." The old knight glared up at the sky as if it alone were their adversary.

"Lord Julian," Belinda said. "The relics...the scepter and seal—"

"They are all safe, my lady," the ancient chamberlain replied. "Loaded in the wagons. The kingdom is intact, save for the land itself." The old man looked back in the direction of the strange sound, toward the banks of the Galewyr River and the bridge they had crossed the night before.

"Will they help us in Colnora?" Belinda asked. "We haven't much food."

"If news has reached them of King Alric's part in freeing the empress, they should be willing," Lord Valin said. "Even if it has not, Colnora is a merchant city, and merchants thrive on profit, not chivalry."

"I have some jewelry," Belinda informed him. "If needs be, you can sell what I have for..." The countess paused as she noticed Julian still staring back at the bridge.

Others soon lifted their gazes, and finally Alenda looked up to see the approach of a rider.

"Is it...?" Lenare began.

"It's a child," Belinda said.

Alenda quickly realized she was right. A little girl raced at them, clutching to the back of the sweat-soaked horse. Her hood had blown back, revealing long dark hair and rosy cheeks. She was about six years old, and just as she clutched the horse, a raccoon held fast to her. They were an odd pair to be alone on the road, but Alenda reminded herself that "normal" no longer existed. If she should see a bear in a feather cap riding a chicken, that too might be normal now.

The horse entered the camp and Lord Valin grabbed the bit, forcing the animal and rider to a stop.

"Are you all right, honey?" Belinda asked.

"There's blood on the saddle," Lord Valin noted.

"Are you hurt?" the countess asked the child. "Where are your parents?"

The girl shivered and blinked but said nothing. Her little fists still clutched the horse's reins.

"She's cold as ice," Belinda said, touching the child's cheek. "Help me get her down."

"What's your name?" Alenda asked.

The girl remained mute. Deprived of her horse, she turned to hugging the raccoon.

"Another rider," Lord Valin announced.

Alenda looked up to see a man crossing the bridge and wheeling toward them.

The rider charged into the camp and threw back his hood, revealing long black hair, pale skin, and intense eyes. He bore a narrow mustache and a short beard trimmed to a fine point. He glared at them until he spotted the girl.

"There!" he said, pointing. "Give her to me at once."

The child cried out in fear, shaking her head.

"No!" Belinda shouted, and pressed the girl into Alenda's hands.

"My lady," Lord Valin said. "If the child is his—"

"This child does not belong to him," the countess declared, her tone hateful.

"I am a Sentinel of Nyphron," the man shouted so all could hear. "This child is claimed for the church. You will hand her over now. Any who oppose me will die."

"I know very well who you are, Luis Guy," Belinda said, seething. "I will not provide you with any more children to murder."

The sentinel peered at her. "Countess Pickering?" He studied the camp with renewed interest. "Where is your husband? Where is your fugitive son?"

"I am no fugitive," Denek said as he came forward. Belinda's youngest had recently turned thirteen and was growing tall and lanky. He was well on his way to imitating his older brothers.

"He means Mauvin," Belinda explained. "This is the man who murdered Fanen."

"Again I ask you," Guy pressed. "Where is your husband?"

"He is dead and Mauvin is well beyond your reach."

The sentinel looked out over the crowd and then down at Lord Valin. "And he has left you poor protection. Now, hand over the child."

"I will not," Belinda said.

Guy dismounted and stepped forward to face Lord Valin. "Hand over the child or I will be forced to take her."

The old knight looked to Belinda, whose face remained hateful. "My lady does not wish it, and I shall defend her decision." The old man drew his sword. "You will leave now."

Alenda jumped at the sound of steel as Guy drew his own sword and lunged. In less than an instant, Lord Valin was clutching his bleeding side, his sword arm wavering. With a shake of his head, the sentinel slapped the old man's blade away and stabbed him through the neck.

Guy advanced toward the girl with a terrifying fire in his eyes. Before he could cross the distance, Belinda stepped between them.

"I do not make a habit of killing women," Guy told her. "But nothing will keep me from this prize."

"What do you want her for?"

"As you said, to kill her. I will take the child to the Patriarch and then she must die, by my hands."

"Never."

"You cannot stop me. Look around. You have only women and children. You have no one to fight for you. Give me the child!"

"Mother?" Lenare said softly. "He is right. There is no one else. Please."

"Mother, let me," Denek pleaded.

"No. You are still too young. Your sister is right. There is no one else." The countess nodded toward her daughter.

"I am pleased to see someone who—" Guy stopped as Lenare stepped forward. She slipped off her cloak and untied the bundle, revealing the sword of her father, which she drew forth and held before her. The blade caught the hazy winter light, pulling it in and casting it back in a sharp brilliance.

Puzzled, Guy looked at her for a moment. "What is this?"

"You killed my brother," Lenare said.

Guy looked to Belinda. "You're not serious."

"Just this once, Lenare," Belinda told her daughter.

"You would have your daughter die for this child? If I must kill all your children, I will."

Alenda watched, terrified, as everyone backed away, leaving a circle around Sentinel Guy and Lenare. A ripping wind shuddered the canvas of the tents and threw Lenare's golden hair back. Standing alone in the snow, dressed in her white traveling clothes and holding the rapier, she appeared as a mythical creature, a fairy queen or goddess—beautiful in her elegance.

With a scowl, Luis Guy lunged, and with surprising speed and grace, Lenare slapped the attack away. Her father's sword sang with the contact.

"You've handled a blade before," Guy said, surprised.

"I am a Pickering."

He swung at her. She blocked. He swiped. She parried. Then Lenare slashed and cut Guy across the cheek.

"*Lenare*," her mother said with a stern tone. "Don't play games."

Guy paused, holding a hand to his bleeding face.

"He killed Fanen, Mother," Lenare said coldly. "He should be made to suffer. He should be made an example."

"No," Belinda said. "It's not our way. Your father wouldn't approve. You know that. Just finish it."

"What is this?" Guy demanded, but there was a hesitation in his voice. "You're a woman."

"I told you—I am a Pickering and you killed my brother."

Guy began to raise his sword.

Lenare stepped and lunged. The thin rapier pierced the man's heart and was withdrawn before he finished his stroke.

Luis Guy fell dead, facedown in the blood-soaked snow.

CHAPTER 2

NIGHTMARES

Arista woke up screaming. Her body trembled; her stomach suffered from a sinking sensation—the remaining residue of a dream she could not remember. She sat up, her left hand crawling to her chest, where she felt the thundering of her heart. It was pounding so hard, so fast, beating against her ribs as if needing to escape. She tried to remember. She could only recall brief snippets, tiny bits that appeared to be disjointed and unrelated. The one constant was Esrahaddon, his voice so distant and weak she could never hear what he said.

Her thin linen nightgown clung to her skin, soaked with sweat. Her bedsheets, stripped from the mattress, spilled to the floor. The quilt, embroidered with designs of spring flowers, lay waded up nearly on the other side of the room. Esrahaddon's robe, however, rested neatly next to her, giving off a faint blue radiance. The garment appeared as if a maid had prepared it for her morning dressing. Arista's hand was touching it.

How is it on the bed? Arista looked at the wardrobe. The door she remembered closing hung open, and a chill ran through her. She was alone.

A soft knock at the door startled her.

"Arista?" Alric's voice came from the other side.

She threw the robe around her shoulders and immediately felt warmer, safer. "Come in," she called.

Her brother opened the door and peered in, holding a candle a bit above his head. Dressed in a burgundy robe, he had a thick baldric buckled around his waist, the Sword of Essendon hanging at his side. The weapon was huge, and as he entered, Alric used one hand to tilt it up to keep the tip from dragging on the floor. The sight reminded her of the night their father was murdered—the night Alric became king.

"I heard you cry out. Are you all right?" he asked, his eyes searching the room and settling on the glowing robe.

"I'm fine—just a nightmare."

"Another one?" He sighed. "You know, it might help if you didn't sleep in that *thing*." He gestured toward the robe. "Sleeping in a dead man's clothes...it's creepy—sort of sick, really. Don't forget he was a wizard. That thing could be— well, I'll just say it—it *is* enchanted. I'm sure it is responsible. Do you want to talk about your dream?"

"I don't remember much. Like all the others, I just...I don't know. It's hard to describe. There's this sense of urgency that's overwhelming. I feel this need to find something—that if I don't, I'll die. I always wake up terrified, like I am walking off a cliff and don't see it."

"Can I get you something?" he asked. "Water? Tea? Soup?"

"Soup? Where will you get soup in the middle of the night?"

He shrugged. "I just thought I'd ask. You don't have to beat me up for it. I hear you scream, I jump out of bed and rush to your door, I offer to play servant for you, and this is the thanks I get?"

"I'm sorry." She frowned playfully but meant what she

said. Having him there did chase the shadows away and took her mind off the wardrobe. She patted her bed. "Sit down."

Alric hesitated, then set the candle on her nightstand and took a seat beside her. "What happened to the sheets and quilt? Looks like you were wrestling."

"Maybe I was. I can't remember."

"You look terrible," he said.

"Thanks."

He sighed.

"I'm sorry. I'm sorry. But you're still my little brother and this new protective side of yours is hard to get used to. Remember when I fell off Tamarisk and broke my ankle? It hurt so bad that I couldn't see straight. When I asked you to get help, you just stood there laughing and pointing."

"I was twelve."

"You were a brat."

He frowned at her.

"But you're not anymore." She took his hand and cupped it in both of hers. "Thank you for checking on me. You even wore your sword."

Alric looked down. "I didn't know what beast or scoundrel might be attacking the princess. I had to come prepared to do battle."

"Can you even draw that thing?"

He frowned at her again. "Oh, quit it, will you? They say I fought masterfully in the Battle of Medford."

"Masterfully?"

He struggled to stop himself from smiling. "Yes, some might even say heroically. In fact, I believe some did say heroically."

"You've watched that silly play too many times."

"It's good theater, and I like to support the arts."

"*The arts.*" She rolled her eyes. "You just like it because it makes all the girls swoon and you love all the attention."

"Well…" He shrugged guiltily.

"Don't deny it! I've seen you with a crowd of them circling like vultures and you grinning and strutting around like the prize bull at the fair. Do you make a list? Does Julian send them to your chambers by hair color, height, or merely in alphabetical order?"

"It's not like that."

"You know, you do have to get married, and the sooner, the better. You have a lineage to protect. Kings who don't produce heirs cause civil wars."

"You sound like Father. Maribor forbid I should have any enjoyment in my life. I have to be king—don't make me have to be a husband and father too. You might as well just lock me up and get it over with. Besides, there's plenty of time. I'm still young. You make it sound like I am teetering on the edge of my grave. And what about you? You're pushing old-maid status now. Shouldn't we be searching for suitable nobles? Do you remember when you thought I arranged a marriage for you with Prince Rudolf, and—Arista? Are you all right?"

She turned away, wiping the moisture from her eyes. "I'm fine."

"I'm sorry." She felt his hand on her shoulder.

"It's okay," she replied, and coughed to clear her throat.

"You know I would never—"

"I know. It's all right, really." She sniffled and wiped her nose. They sat in silence for a few minutes; then Arista said, "I would have married Hilfred, you know. I don't care what you or the council would have said."

A look of surprise came over him. "Since when have you ever cared…Hilfred, huh?" He smirked and shook his head.

She glared back.

"It's not what you think," he said.

"What is it, then?" she asked with an accusing tone, thinking that the boy who had laughed at her falling from her horse had reappeared.

"No slight to Hilfred. I liked him. He was a good man and loved you very much."

"But he wasn't noble," she interrupted. "Well, listen—"

"Wait." Her brother held up a hand. "Let me finish. I don't care if he was noble or not. Truth is he was nobler than just about anyone I can think of, except maybe that Breckton fellow. How Hilfred managed to stand by you every day, while not saying anything—that was real chivalry. He wasn't a knight, but he's the only one I ever saw who acted like one. No, it's not because he wasn't noble-born, and it's not because he wasn't a great guy. I would have loved to have him as a brother."

"What, then?" she asked, this time confused.

Alric looked at her, and in his eyes was the same expression she had seen when he had found her in the dark of the imperial prison.

"You didn't love him," he said simply.

The words shocked her. She did not say anything. She could not say anything.

"I don't think there was anyone in Essendon Castle who didn't know how Hilfred felt. Why didn't you?" he asked.

She could not help it. She started crying.

"Arista, I'm sorry. I just..."

She shook her head, trying to get enough air into her lungs to speak. "No—you're right—you're right." She could not keep her lips from quivering. "But I would have married him just the same. I would have made him happy."

Alric reached out and pulled her close. She buried her head into the thick folds of his robe and squeezed. They did not say anything for a long while and then Arista sat up and wiped her face.

She took a breath. "So when did you get so romantic, anyway? Since when does love have anything to do with marriage? You don't love any of the girls you spend your time with."

"And that's why I'm not married."

"Really?"

"Surprised? I guess I just remember Mom and Dad, you know?"

Arista narrowed her eyes at him. "He married Mother because she was Ethelred's niece and he needed the leverage with Warric to combat the trade war with Chadwick and Glouston."

"Maybe at the start, but they grew to love each other. Father used to tell me that wherever he was, if Mom was there, it was home. I always remembered that. I've never found anyone who made me feel that way. Have you?"

She hesitated. For a moment she considered telling him the truth, then just shook her head.

They sat again in silence; then finally Alric rose. "Are you sure I can't get you anything?"

"No, but thank you. It means a lot to know that you care."

He started to leave, and as he reached the door, she said, "Alric?"

"Hmm?"

"Remember when you and Mauvin were planning on going to Percepliquis?"

"Oh yeah, believe me, I think about that a lot these days. What I wouldn't give to be able to—"

"Do you know where it is?"

"Percepliquis? No. No one does. Mauvin and I were just hoping we'd be the ones to stumble on it. Typical kid stuff, like slaying a dragon or winning the Wintertide games. It sure would have been fun to look, though. Instead, I guess I have to go home and look for a bride. She'll make me wear shoes at dinner—I know she will."

Alric left, closing the door softly behind him and leaving her in the blue glow of the robe. She lay back down with her eyes open, studying the stone and mortar above her bed. She saw where the artisan had scraped his trowel, leaving an impression frozen in time. The light of the robe shifted with her breaths, creating the illusion of movement and giving her the sensation of being underwater, as if the ceiling were the lighted surface of a winter pond. It felt like she was drowning, trapped beneath a thick slab of solid blue ice.

She closed her eyes. It did not help.

Soup, she thought—warm, tasty, comforting soup. Perhaps it was not such a bad idea after all. Maybe someone would be in the kitchen. She had no idea what time it was. It was dark, but it was also winter. Still, it had to be early, since there had been no scuttling of castle servants past her door. It did not matter. She would not fall back to sleep now, so she might as well get up. If no one was awake, she might manage on her own.

The idea of doing something for herself, of being useful, got her going. She was actually excited as her feet hit the cold stone and she looked around for her slippers. The robe glowed brighter, as if sensing her need. When she entered the dark hall, it remained bright until she descended the stairs. As she entered into torchlight, the robe dimmed until it only reflected the firelight.

She was disappointed to find several people already at work in the kitchen. Cora, the stocky dairymaid with the bushy eyebrows and rosy cheeks, was at work churning butter near the door, pumping the plunger in a steady rhythm, trading one hand for another. The young boy Nipper, with his shoulders powdered in snow, stomped his feet as he entered from the dark courtyard, carrying an armload of wood, pausing to shake his head like a dog. He threw a spray that garnered a curse from Cora. Leif and Ibis stoked the stoves, grumbling to each other about damp tinder. Lila stood on a ladder like a circus performer, pulling down the teetering bowls stacked on the top shelf. Edith Mon had always insisted on having them dusted at the start of each month. While the ogre herself was gone, her tyranny lived on.

Arista had looked forward to rustling around in the darkened scullery, searching for a meal like a mouse. Now her adventure was ruined and she considered returning upstairs to avoid an awkward encounter. Arista knew all the scullery servants from her days posing as Ella the chambermaid. She might be a princess, but she was also a liar, a spy, and, of course, a witch.

Do they hate me? Fear me?

There was a time when the thought of servants had not bothered her, a time when she had hardly noticed them at all. Standing at the bottom of the steps, watching them scurry around the chilly kitchen, she could not determine if she had gained wisdom or lost innocence.

Arista pivoted, hoping to escape unnoticed back up the stairs to the sheltered sanctuary of her chamber, when she spotted the monk. He sat on the floor near the washbasins, where the stone was wet from a leaky plug. His back rested against the lye barrel. He was small, thin, and dressed in the traditional russet frock of the order of the Monks of Maribor. Delighted by rubbing the shaggy sides of Red, the big elkhound who sat before him, he had a great smile on his face. The dog was a fixture in the kitchen, where he routinely cleared scraps. The dog's eyes were closed, his long tongue hung dripping, and his body rocked as the monk scratched him.

Arista had not seen much of Myron since the day he had

arrived at the castle. So much had happened since then that she forgot he was still there.

Walking forward, she adjusted her robe, straightening it and fixing the collar. Heads looked up. Cora was the first to see her. The pace of her plunging slowed. Her eyes tracked Arista's movements with interest. Nipper, having dropped his load, stood up and was in the process of brushing the snow off when he stopped in mid-stroke.

"Ella—ah, forgive me, Your Highness." Ibis Thinly was the first to speak.

"Actually, I'd prefer Arista," she replied. "I couldn't sleep. I was hoping to maybe get a little soup?"

Ibis grinned knowingly. "It can get cold up in them towers, can't it? As it happens, I saved a pot of last night's venison stew, froze it out in the snow. If that's all right, I'll have Nipper fetch it. I can heat it up in two shakes. It'll warm you nicely, and how about some hot cider and cinnamon to go with it? Still got some that ain't quite turned yet. It will have a bit of a bite, but it's still good."

"Yes, thank you. That would be wonderful."

"I'll have someone run it up to your chambers. You're on the third floor, right?"

"Ah, no. Actually, I was thinking of eating down here—if that's okay?"

Ibis chuckled. "Of course it is. Folks been doing that a good deal these days, and I'm sure you can eat anywhere that pleases you, 'cepting maybe the empress's bedroom—course rumor has it you did that already." He chuckled.

"It's just that"—she looked at the others, all of whom were watching and listening—"I thought I might not be welcome after...after lying to all of you."

The cook made a dismissive *pfft* sound. "You forget, we worked for Saldur and Ethelred. All they ever did was lie and they sure never scrubbed floors or emptied no chamber pots along with us. You take a seat at the table, Your Highness. I'll get you that stew. Nipper, fetch the pot and get me the jug of cider too!"

She took a seat as instructed and whether they agreed with Ibis's sentiments or not, none of them said a word. They returned to work and only occasionally glanced at her. Lila even ventured a tiny smile and a modest wave before returning to her struggle with the bowls.

"You're Myron Lanaklin, aren't you?" Arista asked, turning on her stool to face the monk and the dog.

He looked up, surprised. "Yes, yes, I am."

"Pleased to meet you. I'm Arista. I believe you know my brother, Alric?"

"Of course! How is he?"

"He's fine. Haven't you seen him? He's just upstairs."

The monk shook his head.

No longer being scratched, Red opened his eyes and looked at Myron with a decidedly disappointed expression.

"Isn't he wonderful?" Myron declared. "I've never seen a dog this big. I didn't know what he was at first. I thought he might be a shaggy breed of deer that they housed in the kitchen, much like we used to keep pigs and chickens at the abbey. I was so happy to discover he was not a future meal. His name is Red. He's an elkhound. Although, I think his days of hunting wolves and boar are over. Did you know that in times of war, they can take knights down off horses? They kill their prey by biting the neck and crushing the spine, but really he's not vicious at all. I come down here every day to see him."

"Do you always get up this early?"

"Oh, this isn't early. At the abbey this would be lazy."

"You must go to sleep early, then."

"Actually, I don't sleep much," he said as he resumed petting the dog.

"Me neither," she admitted. "Bad dreams."

Myron looked surprised. Again, he stopped stroking Red, who nosed his hand in protest. She thought he was about to say something, but then he returned his attention to the dog.

"Myron, I'm wondering if you can help me?" she asked.

"Of course. What are the nightmares about?"

"Oh no. I wasn't speaking of that. It's just that my brother mentioned you read quite a bit."

He shrugged. "I found a little library on the third floor, but there are only about twenty books there. I'm on my third time through."

"You've read all the books in the library three times?"

"Almost. I always have trouble with Hartenford's *Genealogy of Warric Monarchs*. It's almost all names and I have to sound most of them out. What do you need to know?"

"I was actually thinking about information you might have read about while at the Winds Abbey. Have you ever heard of the city of Percepliquis?"

He nodded. "It's the capital city of the original empire of Novron."

"Yes," she said eagerly. "Do you know where it is?"

He thought a moment and smiled to himself. "In every text, they always refer to everything else by way of it. Hashton was twenty-five leagues southeast of Percepliquis. Fairington, a hundred leagues due north. No one ever mentioned where Percepliquis was, I presume because everyone already knew."

"If I got you a map, would it be possible to find it based on the references to other places?"

"Maybe. I'm pretty sure that's how Edmund Hall found it. Although, all you really need is his journal. I've always wanted to read that one."

"I thought reading his journal is considered heresy. Isn't that why they locked Hall and his journal in the top of the Crown Tower?"

"Yes."

"And yet you would still read it? Alric never mentioned what a rebel you are."

Myron looked puzzled, then smiled. "It is heresy for a member of the Nyphron Church to read it."

"Oh, that's right. You're a Monk of Maribor."

"And blessedly, we have no such restrictions on our reading material."

"It makes you wonder, doesn't it?" Arista said. "All the things that might be hidden at the top of the Crown Tower."

"Makes you wish you could get inside, doesn't it?"

"Yes—yes, it does."

⁓

They arrived late that evening, the whole castle buzzing with the news. Trumpets blared, servants rushed, and before she could get dressed, two servants, as well as Alric and Mauvin, had stopped by to tell Arista of the caravan that had just arrived from the north bearing the falcon crest and the banners of gold and green.

She hoisted the hem of the robe and raced down the steps with the rest. A crowd formed on the front steps. Servants, artisans, bureaucrats, and nobles mingled and pushed to see the sight. Guards formed an aisle allowing her to pass to the front, where she stood next to Mauvin and Alric. To her left, she spotted Nimbus draping Amilia's shoulders with his cloak, leaving the skinny man looking like a twig in the wind. She did not see the empress.

Wind-whipped torches and a milky moon illuminated the

courtyard as the caravan entered. There were no soldiers, just elderly men who walked behind carriages. Toward the rear of the procession came wagons bearing a shivering cargo. Women and children, crammed tightly together, huddled for warmth beneath communal blankets. The first carriage reached the bottom of the steps and Belinda and Lenare Pickering stepped out, followed by Alenda Lanaklin. The three women looked up at the crowd before them hesitantly.

Mauvin ran forward to embrace his mother.

"What are you all doing here?" he exclaimed excitedly. "Where's Father, or didn't he—" Arista saw Mauvin stiffen and pull back.

There was no joy at this meeting. The women's faces were sorrowful. They were pale, drawn, and gray, and only their eyes and noses held color—red and sore from crying and the bitter wind. Belinda held her son, wringing his clothes with her fists.

"Your father is dead," she cried, and buried her face in his chest.

Moving slower than the rest, Julian Tempest, the elderly lord chamberlain of Melengar, climbed carefully down out of the carriage. When Arista saw him, her stomach tightened. She could think of very few things that might cause Julian to leave Melengar, and none of them good.

"The elves have crossed the Nidwalden River," Julian announced to the crowd. His voice fought against the wind that viciously fluttered the flags and banners. He walked gingerly, placing his feet upon the frozen ground as if it might be pulled out from beneath him. The old man's stately robes snapped about him like living things, his cap threatening to fly off. "They've invaded and taken all of Dunmore and Ghent." He paused, looked at King Alric, took a breath, and said, "And Melengar."

"The north has fallen? To elves?" Alric sounded incredulous. "But how?"

"These are not the *mir*, Your Majesty. They are not the half-breeds we are familiar with. Those that attacked are pure-blooded elves of the Erivan Empire. Terrible, fierce, and merciless, they came out of the east and crushed all in their path." The wind gained a grip on the old man's cap, throwing it across the yard and revealing his balding head, wreathed in thin white hair. His hands flew up in a futile effort and remained at face level, quivering and forgotten. "Woe to the House of Essendon, the kingdom is lost!"

Alric's gaze lifted to the caravan. He stood staring at the long line of wagons, studying its length, the number of faces crawling from them, and Arista knew what he was thinking.

Is this all?

Julian and the ladies were ushered inside. Arista watched them enter but remained on the steps. She recognized a face or two. One had been a barmaid at The Rose and Thorn. Another, a seamstress at the castle. Arista had often seen her daughter playing near the moat with a doll her mother had made from scraps. She did not have the doll now and Arista wondered, *What became of it? What became of everything?*

"There's not that many," Amilia was saying to Sebastian. He was a ranking castle guard, but she could not recall his specific position. "Find room for them in the gallery for now."

He snapped a salute.

"And have someone run and tell Ibis to get some food prepared; they look hungry."

Amilia turned back toward the castle doors when she made eye contact with Arista. She bit her lip in a sad expression. "I'm sorry," she managed to say, and then walked away.

Arista remained on the steps as the stable hands broke

down the harnesses and the wagons emptied. A line of refugees filed past her, heading inside.

"Melissa!" Arista called.

"Your Highness." Melissa curtsied.

"Oh, forget that." She ran down the remaining steps and gave the girl a hug. "I'm so happy you are all right."

"Are you the empress?" a little girl asked, holding on to Melissa's hand.

Arista had been away from Melengar for some time—only a few months short of a year—but this child could not have been Melissa's. The girl had to be six or seven. She stood on the step beside Arista's maid, bouncing on anxious feet and clutching a bundle to her chest with her free hand.

"This is Mercy," Melissa said, introducing her. "We found her on the way here." She lowered her voice and whispered, "She's an orphan."

There was something familiar about the little girl. Arista was certain she had seen her before. "No, I'm sorry. I'm not the empress. My name is Arista."

"Can I see the empress?"

"I'm afraid not. The empress is very busy."

The child's eager expression collapsed to one of disappointment, and her head drooped to look at her feet. "Arcadius said I would meet the empress when we got to Aquesta."

Arista studied her face a moment. "Arcadius? Oh yes, I remember you. We met last summer, wasn't it?" Arista looked around the few remaining refugees but did not see her old teacher among them. Just then, she noticed the bundle move. "What have you got in there?"

Before the girl could answer, the head of a raccoon poked out. "His name is Mr. Rings."

Arista bent down, and as she did, the robe brightened slightly—a soft pink glow. The girl's eyes widened excitedly.

"Magic!" she exclaimed. She reached out, then paused and looked up.

"You can touch it," Arista told her.

"It's slippery," she said, rubbing the material between her fingers. "Arcadius could do magic too."

"Where is Arcadius?" The little girl did not answer as she shivered in the cold. "Oh, I'm sorry, you both must be freezing. Let's get inside."

They stepped from the pale blue winter into the dark fire-lit hall. The howl of the wind silenced at the closing of the doors, which boomed, echoing in the vaulted chamber. The little girl looked up in awe at the flight of steps, the stone columns and arches. A number of refugees, wrapped in blankets, shivered as they waited for directions.

"Your Highness," Melissa whispered. "We found Mercy alone on a horse."

"Alone? But where is..." She hesitated, seeing Melissa's downcast eyes.

"Mercy hasn't said much, but...well, I'm sorry."

The light of her robe dimmed and the color turned blue. "He's dead?" *First Esrahaddon, now Arcadius.*

"The elves burned Ghent," Melissa said. "Sheridan and Ervanon are gone."

"Gone?"

"Burned."

"But the tower of Glenmorgan, the Crown Tower..."

Melissa shook her head. "We joined with some people fleeing south. Several saw it fall. One said it looked like a child's toy being toppled. Everything is gone." Melissa's eyes glistened. "They're...unstoppable."

Arista expected tears, but all she felt was a numbness—too much loss all at once. She gently touched Mercy's cheek.

"Can I let Mr. Rings play in here?" Mercy asked.

"What? Oh, I suppose, as long as you keep a sharp eye on him," Arista said. "There's an elkhound that might gobble him up if he goes too far."

She set the raccoon down. It sniffed the floor and cautiously skittered to the wall near the steps, where it began a systematic smelling along all the baseboards. Mercy followed and took a seat on the lowest step.

"I can't believe Arcadius is dead."

...at Wintertide the Uli Vermar *ends. They will come— without the horn everyone dies.* The words of Esrahaddon echoed in Arista's head. Words of warning mingled with words she still did not fully understand.

Mercy yawned and rested her chin on her hands as Mr. Rings inched along the length of the step, exploring the world.

"She's tired," Arista said. "I think they are handing out soup in the great hall. Would you like some soup, Mercy?"

The girl looked up, smiled, and nodded. "Mr. Rings is hungry too, aren't you, Mr. Rings?"

The city was more beautiful than anything Arista had ever seen. White buildings, taller than the highest tree, taller than any building she had ever seen, rose up like slender fingers reaching for the sky. Sweeping pennants of greens and blues trailed from their pinnacles snapping in the breeze and shimmering like crystal. A road, broad enough for four carriages, straight as a maypole, and paved with smooth stone, led into the city. Upon it moved a multitude of wagons, carts, wains, coaches, and buggies. No wall or gate hindered the flow of traffic. No guardhouse gave them pause. The city lacked towers, barbican, and moat. It stood naked and beautiful— fearless and proud with only a pair of sculptured lions to

intimidate visitors. The breadth of the city was hard to accept, hard for her to believe. It dominated three full hills and filled the vast valley where a gentle river flowed. It was a lovely place—and it was so familiar.

Arista, you must remember.

She felt the urgency, a tightness in her stomach, a chill across her back. Arista had to think; she needed to solve the puzzle. So little time remained, but such a sight as this would be impossible to forget. She could not have seen it before.

You were here.

She was not. Such a place as this could not even exist. This was a dream, an illusion.

You must trust me. You were here. Look closely.

Arista was shaking her head. It was ridiculous...and yet...something about the river, the way it curved near the base of the northern hill. Yes, the hill. The hill did look familiar. And the road—not so wide. It had been overgrown and hidden. She remembered finding it in the dark; she remembered wondering how it had come to be there.

Yes, you were here. On the hill, look at the Aguanon.

Arista did not understand.

The northern hill, look at the temple on the crest.

She spotted it. Yes, it was familiar, but it did not look the same in her memory. It was broken, fallen, mostly buried, but it was the same. Arista had been there and it frightened her to remember. Something bad had happened to her here. She had nearly died on this hill before the broken stones, amidst the splintered remains of shattered columns and breaching slabs. But she had not died. She did something on that hill, something awful, something that made her rip the dewy grass with her fists and beg Maribor for forgiveness.

At last, Arista understood where she was, what she was seeing.

This is it. This was my home. Go there, dig down, find the tomb, bring forth the horn. Do it, Arista! You must! There is no time left! Everyone will die! Everyone will die! EVERY-ONE WILL—

Arista woke up screaming.

CHAPTER 3

PRISONS

"Get out of the way!" Hadrian shouted, his voice booming through the corridor. He stood just a few feet from the guard glaring at him, breathing on him. The two guards who watched from the end of the hall ran forward. He heard their chain mail jingling, their empty scabbards slapping their thighs. Both stopped short of sword's length.

"It's the Teshlor," one warned in a whisper.

The soldier who blocked the door stood his ground. Hadrian sensed the tension, the fear, the lack of confidence, but he also felt the courage and loyalty that refused to let him waver. He usually respected such qualities in a man, but not this time. This man was merely in his way.

Behind him, a latch lifted and a door creaked. "What's going on?" a befuddled woman's voice asked.

Hadrian glanced. It was Amilia. She shuffled forward, wiping her eyes and fumbling with the tie of her robe.

"I need to speak to the empress," he growled. "Tell them to stand down."

"It's the middle of the night!" she exclaimed in a whisper. "You can't see her. If you want, I'll try to arrange an appointment in the morning, but I must tell you, Her Eminence is very busy. The news —"

Hadrian's hands rose and he took hold of his sword grips. The three soldiers tensed and all but the door guard took a step back. The man before him let his own hand settle slowly on his weapon but he did not pull it.

This guard is a cool one, Hadrian thought, and took another half step closer, until their noses nearly touched. "Get out of my way."

"Hadrian? What are you doing?" This time it was Arista's voice echoing down the hallway.

"I'm seeking an audience with the empress," he said through gritted teeth. He broke his stare to turn and see the princess trotting up the fifth-floor corridor. As always these days, she was dressed in Esrahaddon's robe, which was a dull blue and, at the moment, only reflected the fire of the torches hanging in the wall sconces.

"They have him locked up. They won't even let me see him," Hadrian told her.

"Royce?"

"He didn't want to kidnap the empress, but he would have done anything to get Gwen back. They should give him a medal for killing Saldur and Merrick." Hadrian sighed. "Gwen died in his arms and he wasn't thinking straight. He never meant to harm Modina. I found out he's being held in the north tower. I don't think Modina even knows. So I'm going to tell her. Don't try and stop me."

"I'm not," she said. "I have to see her as well."

"What for?"

The princess looked uncomfortable. "I had a bad dream."

"*What?*"

"No one is seeing the empress tonight!" Amilia declared.

Six more guards arrived, trotting toward them. "I'll turn out the whole castle regiment if I have to!"

Hadrian glanced at the imperial secretary. "Do you think they'll stop me?"

"The door has a bolt on the inside," the door guard said. "Even if you got past us, there's half a foot of solid oak in your way."

"That won't be a problem," Arista assured them. "But I should warn you, I can't be responsible for wounds from flying splinters." Her robe began to glow. It gave off a hazy gray light that slowly brightened, bleaching their faces and weakening the torch-fed shadows. Hadrian noticed a faint breeze in the corridor. A warm wind was rising, swirling around Arista like a tiny cyclone, fluttering the hem of her robe and the ends of her hair.

Amilia stared, horrified.

"Open the door, Amilia, or I'll remove it."

Amilia looked as if she might scream.

"Let them in, Gerald." The voice emanated from the other side of the door.

"Your Eminence?"

"Yes, Gerald. It isn't locked. Let them in."

The door guard lifted the latch and gave a push. The door swung inward, revealing the darkness of the imperial bedroom. Amilia said nothing. She was breathing faster than normal, her fists clenched at her sides. Hadrian entered first, with Arista behind, both followed by Amilia and Gerald.

It was cold in the bedroom. The fireplace was dark and the only light came in through the open window in the far wall. To either side, sheer white curtains billowed inward, dancing in the faint moonlight like a pair of ghosts. Dressed in only her nightgown, Empress Modina rested on the floor, looking out at the stars. She sat on her knees, hands in her lap, her shoulders drawn up against the cold. Bare toes poked out from within the pool of white linen that gathered around her. Blonde hair fell down her back in tangles. She appeared much like the girl Hadrian had seen under the Tradesmen's Arch in Colnora so long ago.

"They arrested Royce," Hadrian told her. "They've locked him in a cell in the tower."

"I know."

"You know?" he said incredulously. "How long have —"

"I ordered it."

Hadrian stared at her, stunned. "Thrace — I mean, Modina," he said softly. "You don't understand. He never meant to harm you. He only did what he had to. He was trying to save the person he loved most in the world. How could you do this to him?"

At last she turned. "Have you ever lost the one person in the world that meant everything to you? Did you watch them die, knowing it was your fault?"

Hadrian said nothing.

"When my father was killed," she continued, looking back out the window, "I remember I found it almost too painful to breathe. I had not just lost my father; it was as if the whole world had died, but somehow I was left behind — alone. I just wanted it to end. I was tired. I wanted the pain to stop. If I had the chance — if they hadn't taken me away, if they hadn't locked me up, I would have thrown myself into the falls." She turned and looked at Hadrian once more. "Believe me. He is well cared for — at least, as much as he will allow. Ibis makes him good meals that he doesn't eat. Can you think of a better place for Royce right now?"

Hadrian's shoulders slumped; his arms fell loose at his sides. "Can I at least see him?"

Modina thought a moment. "Yes, but only you. In his present state, he is a danger to anyone else. Still, I'm not sure he will hear you. You can visit him in the morning." She leaned over so she could see Amilia. "Can you see to it that he has access?"

"Yes, Your Eminence."

"Good," the empress said, then looked at Arista. "Now what is it that you have that can't wait until morning?"

The Princess of Melengar stood shifting her feet, folding and refolding her hands before her, the robe a tranquil dark blue. She looked at the empress, then at Hadrian, Amilia, and even Gerald, who stood stiffly just inside the door. When her eyes once more returned to Modina, she said, "I think I know how to stop the elves."

❧

Hadrian had just descended to the third floor, where several people were returning to their rooms now that all the shouting had died down. He caught a glimpse of Degan Gaunt. The ex-leader of the Nationalists stood in his nightshirt, peering up the steps, both curious and irritated. This was the first time Hadrian had seen the man since the two of them had been released from the dungeon. His neck and nose were narrow, and his lips were so thin they were almost nonexistent. There were creases across his brow and lines about his eyes that spoke of a hard life. Hadrian could tell by the way he carried his weight, and the motions of his body, that he felt awkward, lost in his own skin. He had a faraway look in his eyes, two days' growth of beard, and a plume of hair that hung out of place. If he had to guess, Hadrian might have pegged him as a poor poet. He seemed nothing like the descendant of emperors.

"What's going on up there?" Gaunt asked a passing servant.

"Someone looking to see the empress, sir. It's over now."

Gaunt appeared dubious.

This was not how Hadrian had planned on meeting Gaunt. Hadrian had waited, giving them both time to fully heal. After that, he hesitated out of nerves. He wanted their meeting to go well, to be perfect. This was not perfect, but now that they stood face to face he could hardly walk away.

"Hello, Mr. Gaunt, I am Hadrian Blackwater," he said, introducing himself with a bow.

Degan Gaunt greeted him with his nose crinkled up as if he smelled something bad. He critically observed Hadrian, then frowned. "I thought you'd be taller."

"I'm sorry," Hadrian apologized.

"You're supposed to be my servant, right?" Gaunt asked. He began walking around Hadrian, orbiting him in slow, lazy circles, carrying a frown around with him.

"Actually, I'm your bodyguard."

"How much am I expected to pay for this privilege?"

"I'm not asking for money."

"No? What is it, then? You want me to make you a duke or something? Is that why you're here? Boy, people come out of the woodwork when you've got money and power, I guess. I mean, I don't even know you and here you come begging for privileges before I'm even crowned emperor."

"It's not like that. You're the Heir of Novron; I am the defender of the heir, just like my father before me. It's a...tradition."

"Uh-huh." Gaunt stood slouching, sucking on his teeth for a moment before jamming his pinky finger into his mouth to struggle with something caught between them. After a few minutes, he gave up.

"Okay, here's what I don't get. I'm the heir. That makes me head of the empire, and head of the church. I'm even part god, if I get that right—great-great-grandson of Maribor or some kind of which or whether. So if I'm gonna be emperor and have a whole castle of guards and an army to protect me, what do I need you for?"

Hadrian didn't say anything. He didn't know what he could say. Gaunt was right. His role as bodyguard was only important so long as the heir was in hiding.

"Well, guarding you is sort of a family tradition that I would hate to break," he finally told Gaunt. The words sounded silly even to him.

"You any good with a sword?"

"Pretty good."

Gaunt scratched his stubbly chin. "Well, since you aren't charging anything, I guess I'd be stupid not to take you on. Okay, you can be my servant."

"Bodyguard."

"Whatever." Gaunt waved at him as if shooing away a pesky fly. "I'm going back to bed. You can wait outside my door and do your guard thing if you like."

Gaunt returned to his room and Hadrian waited outside, feeling decidedly foolish. That had not gone as well as he had hoped. He failed to impress Gaunt, and he had to admit, Gaunt did nothing to impress him. He did not know what exactly he had expected. Maybe he thought Gaunt would be the embodiment of the noble poor. A man of staggering integrity, a beacon of enlightenment, who had grown out of the earth's salt and struggled to the pinnacle. Sure, his standards were high, but after all, Degan was supposed to be part god. Instead, just being near him made Hadrian want to go bathe.

He leaned against the wall outside the door, looking up and down the quiet hallway.

This is ridiculous. What am I doing?

The answer was obvious—nothing. But there was nothing to do. He had missed his opportunity and was now useless.

From somewhere inside, he heard Gaunt begin to snore.

∽

The next morning Hadrian found Royce sitting on the floor of the cell, his back resting against the wall, one knee up, cocked like a tent pole. His right arm rested on it, his hand hanging limp. He wore only his black tunic and pants. His belt and boots were missing, his feet bare, the soles blackened with dirt. He hung his head back, tilted upward resting against the wall and revealing a week's worth of dark stubble that covered his chin, cheeks, and neck. Lengths of straw littered his hair and clothing, but on his lap lay a neatly folded, meticulously clean scarf.

He did not look up when Hadrian entered the cell. He was not sleeping—no one could get this close to Royce without his waking, but more obviously, his eyes were open. He stared at the ceiling, not seeing it.

"Hey, buddy," Hadrian said, entering the cell.

The guard closed the door behind him. He heard the lock slide in place. "Call me when you want out," he told Hadrian.

The cell had a small window near the ceiling, which cast a square of light where the wall and floor met. Through its shaft, he could see straw dust lingering in the air. A cup of water, a glass of wine, and a plate of potato and carrot stew sat beside the door. All untouched, the stew having dried into a solid brick.

"Am I interrupting breakfast?"

"That was dinner," Royce said.

"That bad, huh?" Hadrian sat across from him on the bed. It had a thick mattress, a half dozen warm blankets, three soft pillows, and fine linen sheets. It had not been slept in. "Not too bad in here," he said, making a show of looking around. "We've been in much worse, but you know, this was pretty much the last place I was thinking you'd be. I sort of thought the idea was for you to disappear and give me time to explain why you kidnapped the empress. What happened?"

"I turned myself in."

Hadrian smirked. "Obviously."

"Why are you here?" Royce replied, his eyes dull and empty.

"Well, now that I know you're here, I thought you could use some company. You know, someone to talk to, someone who can smuggle you fig pudding and the occasional drumstick. I could bring up a deck of cards. You know how much you love beating me at... Well, you just like beating me."

Royce made an expression that was almost like a smile. He reached out with his left hand and grabbed up a handful of straw. He crushed it in his fist letting the bits fall through his fingers and watching them in the shaft of light. When the last of it fell, he opened his hand palm-up, stared at it, turning it over and back as if he had never really seen it before.

"I want to thank you, Hadrian," he said, still looking at his hand, his voice soft, lingering, disconnected.

"Awfully formal, aren't you? It's just a card game," Hadrian said, and smiled.

Royce lowered his hand, laying it on the floor like a forgotten toy. His attention turned vaguely toward the ceiling again. "I hated you when we first met, did you know that? I thought Arcadius was crazy making me take you along on that heist."

"So why did you?"

"Honestly? I expected you'd be killed; then I could go to the nutty wizard, laugh, and say, *See? What did I tell you? The clumsy fool died*. Only you didn't. You made it all the way to the top of the Crown Tower, no complaining, no whining."

"Did you respect me then?"

"No. I figured you suffered from beginner's luck. I expected you'd die on the return trip that next night when he made us put it back."

"Only, again I lived."

"Kinda made me mad, actually. I'm not usually wrong, you know, about people? And man, you could fight. I thought Arcadius was feeding me a load of crap the way he went on about you. 'The best warrior alive,' he said. 'In a fair fight Hadrian can best anyone,' he said. That was the telling part— a fair fight. He knew not all your battles would be fair. He wanted me to educate you in the world of backstabbing, deceit, and treachery. I guess he figured I knew something about that."

"And I was supposed to teach honor, decency, and kindness to a man raised by wolves."

Royce rolled his head to the side and looked at him. "He told you about me?"

"Not everything, just some of the ugly parts."

"Manzant?"

"Just that you were there, that it almost killed you, and that he got you out."

Royce nodded. His face drooped, his eyes stared again, his hand absently scooped up another handful of straw to crush.

Hadrian's eyes drifted around the cell. Centuries of captives had left a dark smoothness to all the stones a bit higher than halfway up, like a flood line. On the far wall, a year's worth of old hatch marks scratched a pattern that looked like a series of bound bales of wheat. Up in the window, a bird had built a nest, tucked on the outside corner of the sill. It was empty, frosted in snow. Occasionally, he heard a cart, a horse, or the sound of people in the courtyard below them, but mostly it was quiet, a heavy, dull-gray silence.

"Hadrian," Royce began. He'd stopped playing with the straw, his hands flat, his stare focused on the wall, his voice weak and hesitant. "You and Arcadius...you're the only family I've ever known. The only two people in this whole world—" He swallowed and bit his lower lip, pausing.

Hadrian waited.

Finally he went on. "I want you to know—It's important that..." He turned away from Hadrian, facing the wall. "I wanted to say thank you for being there for me, for being here. For being the closest thing to a brother I'll ever know. I just— I just want you to know that."

Hadrian did not say anything. He waited for Royce to turn back, to look at him. It took several minutes, but the silence drew the look. When he did, Hadrian glared at him. "Why? Why do you want me to know that?"

"What do you mean?"

"Tell me—no, don't look at the wall; look at me. Why is it so important that I know this?"

"It just is, okay?" Royce said.

"No, it's not *okay*. Don't give me this crap, Royce. We've been together for twelve years. We've faced death dozens of times. Why is it you're telling me this now?"

"I'm upset. I'm distraught. What do you want from me?"

Hadrian continued to stare but slowly began to nod. "You've been waiting, haven't you? Just sitting here, leaning against that wall, waiting—waiting for me to show up."

"In case you forgot, they arrested me. I'm in a locked cell. There's not much else I can do."

Hadrian snorted.

"What?"

Hadrian stood. He needed to move. There wasn't much

space but he still paced back and forth between the wall and, the door. Three steps each way. "So when are you going to do it? As soon as I leave? Tonight? How about a nice morning suicide? Huh, Royce? You could be poetic and time it with the rising of the sun, or just the drama of midnight, how would that be?"

Royce scowled.

"How are you gonna do it? Your wrists? Throat? Gonna challenge the guard to fight when he brings dinner? Call him names? Or are you gonna make an even bigger splash? Head for Modina's room and threaten the empress's life again. You'll find some young idiot, a big one, someone with an ego. You'll draw a blade, something little, something not too scary. He'll draw his sword. You'll pretend to attack, but he won't know you're faking."

"Don't be this way."

"*This way?*" Hadrian stopped and whirled on him. He had to take a breath to calm down. "How do you expect me to be? You think I should be—what? Happy, maybe? Did you think I'd just be okay with this? I thought you were stronger. If anyone could survive—"

"That's just it—I don't want to! I've always survived. Life is like a bully that gets laughs by seeing how much humiliation you'll put up with. It threatens to kill you if you don't eat mud. It takes everything you care about—not because it wants what you have, or needs it. It does it just to see if you'll take it. I let it push me around ever since I was a kid. I did everything it demanded just to survive. But as I've gotten older, I realize there are limits. You showed me that. There's only so far I can go, only so much I can put up with. I'm not going to take it anymore. I won't eat mud just to survive."

"So it's my fault?" Hadrian slumped down on the mattress once more. He sat there running his hand through his hair for a moment, then said, "Just so you know, you're not the only one who misses her. I loved her too."

Royce looked up.

"Not like that. You know what I mean. The worst part is..." His voice cracked. "It really is my fault, and that's what I will be left with. Did you think of that? You were right and I was wrong. You said not to take the job from DeWitt, but I talked you into it. 'Let's leave Dahlgren; this isn't our fight,' you said, but I got you to stay. 'You can't win against Merrick,' you said, so you went to protect me. You told me Degan Gaunt would be an ass, and you were right about that too. You didn't do what you knew was right because of me. I pulled you along while trying to redeem myself to the memory of a dead father. Gwen is gone because of me. I destroyed what little good there was in your life trying to accomplish something that in the end means nothing.

"I'm not the hero who saves the kingdom and wins the girl. Life isn't like that." Hadrian laughed bitterly. "You finally taught me that one, pal. Yep. Life isn't a fairy tale. Heroes don't ride white horses, and the good don't always win. I just—I guess I just *wanted* it to be that way. I didn't think there was any harm in believing it. I never knew it would be you and Gwen that would pay."

"It's not your fault," Royce told him.

"You tell me that a few million more times and I might actually start believing it. Only that's not going to happen, now is it? You're not going to be around to remind me, are you? You're going to give up. You're going to walk out on me and that will be my fault too. Damn it, Royce! You *have* a choice. I know it doesn't seem like it, and I know I'm a fool that believes in a fantasy world where good things can happen to good people, but I do know this. You can either head into darkness and despair or into virtue and light. It's up to you."

Royce jerked his head up and looked at Hadrian, a shocked expression on his face. Shock turned quickly to suspicion.

"What?" Hadrian asked, concerned.

"How are you doing that?" Royce demanded, and for the first time since Hadrian had entered the cell, he saw the old Royce—cold, dark, and angry.

"How am I doing what?"

"That's the second time you've quoted Gwen, once on the bridge and now—this. She said that same thing to me once, those exact words."

"Huh?"

"She read my palm and told me there was a fork—a point of decision. I had to choose to head into darkness and despair or into virtue and light. She told me this would be precipitated by a traumatic event—the death of the one I loved the most."

"Gwen?"

He nodded. "But you weren't there. You couldn't have heard her say that. We were alone in her office at the House. It was *a year* ago. I only remember because it was the night Arista came to The Rose and Thorn, and you were getting drunk and ranting about being a parasite. So how did you know?"

Hadrian shrugged. "I didn't, but…" He felt a chill run up his spine. "What if *she* did? What if I'm not quoting her— what if she was quoting me?"

"*What?*"

"Gwen was a seer," Hadrian said. "What if she saw your future, bits and pieces like Fan Irlanu did in that Tenkin village?" Now he was staring at the wall, his eyes wandering aimlessly as he thought. "She could have seen us on the bridge, and here in this cell. She knew what I would say, and she also knew you wouldn't listen to me. She must have known you wouldn't listen to me at the bridge either. That's why she said those things." He was speaking quickly now, seeing it all before him. "She knew you would ignore me, but you can't ignore her. Royce, Gwen doesn't want you to die. She agrees with me. I may have been wrong in the past, but not this time. This time I'm right, and I know I'm right because Gwen saw the future and she's backing me up." He sat against the wall, folding his hands behind his head in victory. "You can't kill yourself," he said jubilantly, as if he had just won some unspoken bet. "You can't do it without betraying her wishes!"

Royce looked confused. "But if she knew, why didn't she stop it? Why did she let me go with you? Why didn't she tell me?"

"It's obvious, isn't it? She wanted us to go, and either she couldn't avoid her death, or—"

"Or what? She wanted to die?" he said sarcastically.

"No, I was going to say, she knew she *had* to die."

"Why?"

"I don't know—something else she saw, maybe, something that hasn't happened yet. Something so important it was worth dying on the bridge for, but whatever it is, it doesn't include you killing yourself. She made that pretty clear, I think."

Royce threw his head back against the stone wall hard enough to make an audible thud and clenched his eyes shut. "Damn it."

⋙

Mauvin Pickering stood on the fourth-floor balcony, looking out at the palace courtyard. It was snowing again, thick wet flakes. They fell on the muddy earth, slowly filling in where carts had left deep ruts. One after another, the flakes hit the ground and melted, but somehow, they managed to overcome.

The puddles receded; the dirt disappeared; the world turned white and pure once more.

Beyond the wall he could see the roofs of the city. Aquesta stretched out below him, hundreds of snow-covered thatched peaks clustered together, huddling against the winter storm. The buildings ran to the sea and up the hill north. His gaze rose to the gap he knew was Imperial Square, and farther out to Bingham Square, where he could see the top of the Tradesmen's Tower marking the artisan district. He continued to look up, his gaze reaching out beyond the open patches of farm fields to the forested hills—a hazy gray line in the distance, and the suggestion of higher hills beyond—masked by the snowy curtain. He imagined he could see Glouston, and beyond it, across the river, Melengar, the kingdom of the falcon-crested kings, the land of his birth, his home. Drondil Fields would be blanketed in snow, the orchard frosted, the moat frozen. Vern would be out breaking the ice on the well, dropping his heavy hammer tied to the end of a rope. He would be fearful the knot would come loose like it had five years earlier, leaving his favorite tool at the bottom of the well. It was still there, Mauvin thought, still lying in the water, waiting for Vern to claim it, but now he never would.

"You'll catch your death out there," his mother said.

He turned to see her standing in the doorway in her dark blue gown—the closest thing she had to black. Around her shoulders was the burgundy shawl Fanen had given her for Wintertide three years before—the year he died. It became a permanent part of her attire that she wore year-round, explaining how it kept the chill away in the winter and the sun off her shoulders in the summer. That morning he noticed she was also wearing the necklace. The awkward thick chain weighed down by the huge pendant was hard to miss. It was supposed to look like the sun. A big emerald pressed into the gold setting, and lines of rubies forming the rays of light. It was an ugly, gaudy thing. He had seen it only a few times before in the bottom of her jewelry box. It had been a gift from his father.

Even after bearing four children, Belinda Pickering still turned heads. Too many for his father's comfort, if the stories were true. Rumors had circulated for decades of the numerous duels fought over her honor. Legend asserted there were as many as twenty, all sparked by some man looking at her too long. They all ended the same, with the death of the offender via Count Pickering's *magic* sword. That was the legend, but Mauvin knew of only two actual incidents.

The first had occurred before he was born. His father had told him the story on his thirteenth birthday, the day he had mastered the first tier of the Tek'chin. His father explained that he and Mauvin's mother had been traveling home alone and were waylaid by highwaymen. There had been four bandits and his father was willing to give up their horses, his purse, and even Belinda's jewelry to escape without incident. But his father had seen the way the thieves looked at Belinda. As they whispered back and forth, he saw the hunger in their eyes. His father killed two, wounded one, and sent the last one running. They had given his father a scar nearly a foot long.

The second had happened when Mauvin was just ten. They had come to Aquesta for Wintertide and the Earl of Tremore became angry when Count Pickering refused to enter the sword competition. The earl knew that even if he had won the tournament, he would still be considered second best, so he challenged Pickering to a duel. Mauvin's father refused. The Earl of Tremore had grabbed Belinda and kissed her before the entire court. She slapped him and pulled away. When he made a grab for her, he tore free the neckline of her gown, exposing her. She fell to the floor, crying, struggling to cover herself. Mauvin remembered with perfect clarity his father drawing his sword and telling him to help his mother back to their room. He did not kill the Earl of Tremore, but the man lost a hand in the battle.

Still, it was easy to see how the stories spread. Even he could see how lovely his mother was. Only now, for the first time, did he notice the gray in her hair and the lines on her face. She had always stood so straight and tall, but now she leaned forward, bowed as if by an invisible weight.

"I haven't seen you much," she said. "Where have you been?"

"Nowhere."

He waited for her to press, to demand more information. He expected it—but she just nodded. His mother had been acting this way since arriving and it unnerved him.

"Chancellor Nimbus was by earlier. He wanted to let you know that the empress is calling a meeting this evening and you are requested to attend."

"I know. Alric already told me."

"Did he say what it was to be about?"

"It'll be about the invasion, I'm sure. She will want to mount a full-scale retaliation. Alric expects she will use this crisis to demand Melengar join the empire."

"What will Alric do?"

"What can he do? Alric isn't a king without a kingdom. I should warn you that I intend to join him. I will gather what men Alric still has, form a troop, and volunteer to fight."

Once more the quiet, submissive nod.

"Why do you do that? Why must you give in to me without even a protest? If I had said I was going off to war a month ago, I would have never heard the end of it."

"A month ago you were my son; today you are Count Pickering."

He watched her clutch the shawl with a white-knuckled fist, her mouth set, her other hand holding the doorframe.

"Maybe he survived," Mauvin said. "He's gotten through tough situations before. There's a chance he could have fought his way out. With his sword no one could ever beat him—not even Braga."

Her lips trembled; her eyes grew glassy. "Come," she said, and disappeared back into the castle. He followed as she led the way to her chambers. There were three beds in the room. With all the refugees, space was tight in the palace these days. The chamberlain did his best to accommodate them according to rank, but there was only so much he could do. Mauvin bunked with Alric and now his brother Denek as well. Mauvin knew his mother shared her room with his sister, Lenare, and the lady Alenda Lanaklin of Glouston, neither of whom was there at that moment.

The room was a fraction of the size of her bedchamber back home. The beds themselves were small single bunks. The plain headboards were dressed with quilts adorned with patterns of roses. Leaded glass windows let the light in, but sheer white curtains turned the brilliance into a muted fog, which felt heavy and oppressive. The room had the air of a funeral. On the dresser he spotted the familiar statuette of Novron that used to be in their chapel. The demigod sat upon his throne, one hand upraised in a gesture of authority. Beside it was a single salifan candle, still burning. On the floor before it lay her bed pillow, two dents side by side where she had knelt.

His mother walked to the wardrobe and withdrew a long blanket-wrapped bundle. She turned and held it out. There was a formality in her movement, a solemnness in her eyes. He looked at the bundle—long and thin, tied with a green silk ribbon, the kind she and Lenare used to bind their hair. The blanket it held was like a shroud over a dead body. Mauvin did not want to touch it.

"No," he said without meaning to, and took a step backward.

"Take it," she told him.

The door opened abruptly.

"I don't want to go alone," Alenda Lanaklin said as she and his sister, Lenare, entered. The two women were also dressed in dark conservative gowns. Lenare carried a plate of food, and Alenda a cup. "It's awkward. I don't even know him. Oh—" They both stopped.

Mauvin hastily took the bundle from his mother. He did not look at it and quickly moved toward the door.

"I'm sorry," Alenda said. She was staring at him, her face troubled.

"Excuse me, ladies," Mauvin muttered, and walked past them. He kept his eyes focused on the floor as he went.

"Mauvin?" Alenda called down the hallway.

He heard her steps behind him and stopped, but he did not turn.

He felt her touch his hand. "I'm sorry."

"You said that."

"That was for interrupting."

He felt her press against him, and she kissed his cheek.

"Thank you." He watched as she worked hard to force a smile even as a tear slipped down her cheek.

"Your mother hasn't eaten. She hardly even leaves the room. Lenare and I went to get her something."

"That's very kind."

"Are *you* all right?"

"I should be asking you that. I lost a father, but you lost a father and two brothers as well."

She nodded and sniffled. "I've been trying not to think

about it. There's so much—too much. Everyone has lost someone. You can't have a conversation anymore without people crying their eyes out." She half laughed, half cried. "See?"

He reached up and wiped her tears. Her cheeks were amazingly soft; the wetness made them shine.

"What were you and Lenare talking about?" he asked.

"Oh, that?" she said, sounding embarrassed. "It will sound foolish."

"Perhaps foolishness is needed right now." He made a face and winked at her.

She smiled, this time more easily.

"Com'on," he said, taking her hand and pulling her with him down the hall. "Tell me this terrible secret."

"It's not a secret. I just wanted Lenare to come with me when I meet my brother."

"Myron?"

She nodded. "I'm a little nervous about it—frightened, actually. How do I explain why I never bothered to see him?"

"Why didn't you?"

She shrugged self-consciously. "I should have. I just— He was a stranger. If only my father had taken me, but he didn't. He seemed like he wanted to forget Myron existed. I think he was ashamed of him and some of that rubbed off on me, I guess."

"And now?"

"Now I'm scared."

"Scared of what?"

"Of him."

"You're scared of *Myron*?" He started to chuckle, but he stopped abruptly when he saw the seriousness in her eyes.

"I knew you'd think me foolish!"

"It's just that we're talking about Myron and—"

"He's the marquis now!" she exclaimed. "He's the head of my house. By law, I have to do as he says, go where he orders, marry whom he chooses. What if he hates me? What if he decides to punish me for the hardships he has had to endure? I've lived in a castle with servants who dressed, fed, and bathed me. I've attended feasts and tournaments, galas and picnics. I've worn silk, lace, finely embroidered gowns, and jewelry. While he—" She stopped. "Since the age of four, Myron has been sequestered at the Winds Abbey. He has been forced to work with his hands in the dirt, worn coarse wool, and never gone anywhere or seen anyone—not even his family. Now they are all dead, except for me. Of course he hates me. Why wouldn't he? He'll curse me and I'll be the target of all his pain and frustration. He'll deny me, just as we denied him. He'll send me away, strip me of my title, and leave me penniless. And...and...I can't even blame him."

She looked up at Mauvin's face, confused. "What? What?"

CHAPTER 4

FALL THE WALL

"How is Royce?" Arista asked Hadrian as they took seats next to each other near the end of the table. There were no place cards, and Hadrian had no clue where they might want him to sit. He looked to the princess for guidance, but all she offered was a shrug.

"Not great, but who is these days?" He glanced at Alric, who was taking a seat across from Arista, then at Mauvin, who sat next to his king. "I was sorry to hear about your father," he offered.

Mauvin replied with an almost imperceptible nod. Arista stood, reached across the table, and took Mauvin's hand. She did not say a word but merely looked into his eyes, offering a weak smile.

"See, that's the difference," Mauvin said. "I suffer a loss and people console me. Royce suffers a loss and whole towns evacuate." He offered a sad smile. "I'm fine, really. My father led a good life, married the most beautiful woman in the realm, raised four children, outlived one, and died in battle defending his home. I should hope to do half as well."

"It's hard to imagine that anyone could break through Royce's shell," King Alric said.

Only a few years had passed since Hadrian had first met Alric. He, Royce, and later Myron spent three days roaming the hills of Melengar with the prince just after King Amrath's death. It seemed like only yesterday, but Alric appeared decades older. His eyes showed a maturity and his boyish face was gone—hidden behind a full beard. He looked more like his father now, brooding and withered. The small white scar on his forehead was still there—a ghostly reminder of that day he nearly died, when his face was pushed into the dirt.

"She was a remarkable woman," Hadrian explained.

"I wish I had met her," Arista said, sitting back down.

"You would have liked Gwen, and I know she thought highly of you. She was"—Hadrian paused—"unique."

They gathered in the great hall, the largest chamber in the palace. Four stone hearths filled the room with warmth and a ruddy-orange glow. Above each massive fireplace, arrays of steel shields and glimmering swords were displayed as a sign of power. Thirty-two banners displaying the emblems of all the noble houses of Avryn hung from the ceiling in two rows along the length of the room. Five had been added since the last time Hadrian had sat there. The banners of the House of Lanaklin of Glouston, the House of Hestle of Bernum, the House of Exeter, the House of Pickering of Galilin, and the gold crowned falcon on a red field of the House of Essendon of Melengar— all restored to their rightful places.

The table where they waited was the only one in the room. Placed in the center of the hall, it was longer than the bar at The Rose and Thorn, and nine chairs lined each side, along with one at the end. This was the same room where Hadrian spent his first feast masquerading as a noble. He felt as out of place now as he had then as the room filled with the other invited guests—each noble.

He knew most of the faces that entered. Armand, King of

Alburn, claimed a seat near the head of the table, his son, Prince Rudolf, at his right hand. Not to be outdone, Fredrick, King of Galeannon, sat across from him. King Vincent of Maranon chose to sit two chairs down from Fredrick, making Hadrian wonder if there was an issue between the two bordering kingdoms. Not everyone was a royal. Sir Elgar, Sir Murthas, and Sir Gilbert, as well as Sir Breckton, who wore the gold sash of his new office as imperial high marshal, entered together.

Stewards began pouring wine while seven seats remained open, including the one at the head of the table, where no one dared sit. Hadrian took a sip from the goblet before him and grimaced.

"That's right," Arista mentioned. "You aren't a wine drinker, are you?"

Hadrian set the goblet back down and continued to sneer at it. "It's probably very good," he said. "It just tastes like spoiled grape juice to me, but you have to remember I was raised on Armigil's beer."

Hadrian's old tutor, the awkwardly thin imperial chancellor, Nimbus, entered along with Amilia, the imperial secretary, and they took their seats to the immediate left and right of the table's head. Degan Gaunt wandered in, looking lost. He was dressed in an expensive doublet and breeches with buckle shoes, none of which suited him. Looking at the heir, Hadrian could not help comparing him to the Duchess of Rochelle's pet poodle, which she dressed in tailored vests. Gaunt circled the table three times before choosing a lonely seat in the vacant space two up from Mauvin and one down from Sir Elgar, both of whom he eyed suspiciously.

Two more men entered. The first he did not know, a heavy-set elderly man with a bald head and sagging cheeks. He was dressed in a long, handsomely brocaded coat with large silver buttons, accompanied by a ruffled silk shirt. Following him was a younger but fatter duplicate of the first. Hadrian recognized him as Cosmos DeLur, the wealthiest man in Avryn and infamous head of the Black Diamond thieves guild. He guessed the other man must be his father, Cornelius DeLur, formerly the unofficial leader of the Republic of Delgos.

Two chairs left.

Several conversations occurred simultaneously. Hadrian tried to make sense of them. Tilted heads, knowing smiles, sidelong glances, murmurs, whispers. He could catch only a handful of words here and there. Most often, what he caught were discussions about the empress. Many of those at the table had seen her only that one night before the final Wintertide joust, when she made her brief, but dramatic, appearance, and once more when they swore fealty after the uprising. This would be the first opportunity for them to have an audience with her.

Trumpets blared.

All conversations halted, each head turned, and everyone stood as the empress entered the hall. Her Eminence Modina Novronian passed through the arched doorway, looking every inch the daughter of a god. She wore a black gown gorgeously hand embroidered with a rainbow of colored thread and adorned with diamonds, rubies, and sapphires. Around her neck, a starched ruff rose in the shape of a Calian lily. She wore long sleeves with wrist ruffs that scalloped her hands. On her ears dangled sparkling earrings, and on her breast lay a necklace of pearl. As she walked, a long black velvet mantle embroidered with the imperial crest trailed behind her. The days of begging a clerk for dress material were long gone.

The woman Hadrian saw before him had the face of Thrace Wood, but she was not the little girl he had once pulled from the gutter on Capital Street in Colnora. She walked tall, her shoulders back, her gaze elevated. She did not look at anyone, nor turn her head prematurely, her sight fixed by the direction she faced. She took her time, walking elegantly, in an arc that allowed her train to straighten before she reached the head of the table.

Hadrian smiled to himself as he remembered how a madam had once suggested that, to save her from starvation, she should join the roster at the Bawdy Bottom Brothel. He had responded with the prophetic words "Something tells me she's not a prostitute."

A steward removed the mantle from her shoulders and placed the chair behind her, but the empress did not sit. Hadrian noted a slight stiffening of her posture as she surveyed her guests. He followed her line of sight, noting the last empty chair.

She addressed Nimbus. "Did you notify the Patriarch of my summons?"

"I did, Your Eminence."

She sighed, then looked upon her subjects.

"Lords and ladies, forgive me. I will forgo customary traditions. My chancellor tells me there are many formalities I am expected to follow; however, such things take time and time is a luxury we can't afford."

It was eerie, Hadrian thought, seeing her addressing heads of state, as calmly as if she were holding a tea party for children.

"As most of you already know, Avryn has been invaded. We believe the attack began more than a month ago, but we were uncertain until very recently. The information comes from the refugees fleeing south and twelve teams of scouts I had sent north, many of whom never returned. Sir Breckton, if you will please explain the situation as it now stands..."

Sir Breckton rose and stood before the assembly, wearing a

long black cape over his dress tunic. All eyes turned to him, not just because he was about to speak, but because Sir Breckton was one of those men who commanded attention. There was something in the way he held himself. He managed to appear taller, straighter, and stouter than other men. Breckton made a formal bow to the empress, then faced the table.

"While none of the scouts managed to pierce the advance troops to report on the main body of the elven army, what we have learned is unsettling enough. We now believe that at midnight on Wintertide, elements of the Erivan Empire crossed the Nidwalden River with a force estimated at over a hundred thousand. They conquered the kingdom of Dunmore in less than a week and Glamrendor is gone. King Roswort, Queen Freda, and their entire court—lost, presumably on their return trip from the Wintertide celebration."

Heads turned left and right and Hadrian heard the words *hundred thousand* and *less than a week* repeated between them. Breckton paused for only a moment before speaking again.

"The elven host continued west, entering unopposed into Ghent. Estimates suggest they conquered it in eight days. Whether Ghent put up a fight, we don't know. It has been confirmed, however, that the university at Sheridan was burned and Ervanon destroyed."

The men at the table shifted with more anxiety but less was said.

"They entered Melengar next," he told them, and a few heads turned toward Alric. "Drondil Fields made a last stand, heroically providing time for as many as possible to escape south. The fortress managed to hold out for one day."

"A day?" King Vincent exclaimed. He looked at Alric, who nodded solemnly. "How can this be?"

"King Fredrick." The empress addressed the monarch seated to her left. "Please repeat what you told us."

King Fredrick stood up, brushing the folds from his clothes. He was a squat, balding man with a round belly that pressed the limits of the front of his tunic.

"Not long after the Wintertide holiday—perhaps a few days at most—travelers brought news of trouble in Calis. They told stories of Ghazel hitting the coast in droves. They called it The Flood. Hundreds of thousands of the mongrels stormed the cliffs at Gur Em Dal."

"Are you saying the elves are in league with the Ghazel?" Cornelius DeLur asked.

The king shook his head. "No, they weren't warriors. Well, some may have been, but the impression I got was that they too were refugees. They were fleeing and running where they could. The Calian warlords slaughtered many on the eastern coast, but the deluge was so great they could not entirely stem the wave. Within a week, bands of Ghazel were on the border of Galeannon and slipping into the Vilan Hills. We lost all communication with Calis—no more travelers have come out."

Fredrick took his seat.

"As of this very afternoon," Sir Breckton said, "we received word that a ship by the name of the *Silver Fin* was five days out of its port in Kilnar when it saw Wesbaden burning. Beyond it, the captain said he saw another column of smoke rising in the distance, which he guessed to be Dagastan."

"Why would the elves launch an attack on both the Ghazel and us? Why open two fronts?" Sir Elgar asked.

"It's likely they don't consider either the Ghazel or ourselves to be a serious threat," Breckton told them. "Sources report the elven host is accompanied by scores of dragons who burn everything in their path. Other reports speak of equally disturbing capabilities, such as the ability to control the weather and call down lightning. There are stories of huge monsters that shake the earth, burrowing beasts, lights that blind, and a mist that...devours people."

"Are these fairy stories you would have us believe, Breckton?" Murthas asked. "Giants, monsters, mists, and elves? Who were these scouts? Old wives?"

This brought chuckles from both Elgar and Gilbert and a smile from Rudolf.

"They were good men, Sir Murthas, and it does not befit you to speak ill of the courageous dead."

"I grieve for the lives of the men who died," King Armand said. "But seriously, Breckton, a mist that kills people? You make them out to be the sum of all nightmares, as if every tale of boogeyman, ghost, or wraith spills out of the wood across the Nidwalden. These are only elves, after all. You make them sound like invincible gods that—"

> *They came with hardly a warning,*
> *thousands both beautiful and terrible;*
> *They came on brilliant white horses*
> *wearing shining gold and shimmering blue;*
> *They came with dragons and whirlwinds,*
> *and giants made of stone and earth;*
> *They came and nothing could stop them.*
> *They are coming still.*

The voice issued from the doorway and all heads turned as into the great hall entered an old man. It was hard to say what caught Hadrian's eyes first, as so much was startling. The man's hair, which did not begin until well behind his balding forehead, was long enough to reach the back of his knees and was beyond gray, beyond white, appearing almost purple, like the edges of a rotting potato. His mouth lacked lips, his eyes were without brows, and his cheeks were shriveled. He wore a cascade of glittering purple, gold, and red—robes displayed with relish—flaunting it with dramatic sweeps of his arms as he walked using a tall staff. Brilliant blue eyes shifted restlessly around the room, never pausing for too long on any one person. His jaw, held taut in an openmouthed grin, showed a surprising full complement of teeth, his expression a silent laugh.

Behind him entered two equally shocking guards. They wore shimmering gold breastplates over top shirts of vertical red, purple, and yellow stripes with long cuffs and billowing sleeves. Matching pants plumed out, gathering just below the knee into long striped stockings. Across their chests, stretching from their shoulders, hung silver braids and tassels of honor. They wore gold helms with messenger wings that hid their faces. Each held unusual weapons, long halberds with ornately curved blades at both ends, which they held tight to their sides with one arm straight down and the other high across their chests.

The guards halted in perfect unison, snapping their heels in one audible *clack*. The old man continued forward, approaching Modina. He stopped before her, slamming the metal tip of his staff down on the stone floor.

"Forgive me, Your Eminence," the old man announced in a loud voice, and followed with an elaborate bow, which allowed him the opportunity to further display the grandeur of his robes. "My apologies cannot begin to elevate the depth of my sadness at having failed to arrive at the appointed time, but alas, I was irrevocably detained. I do hope you can forgive a feeble old man."

Modina stared at him, her expression blank. She said nothing.

The old man waited, shifting his weight, tilting his head from side to side.

Modina glanced at Nimbus.

"Patriarch Nilnev," the chancellor addressed the old man. "If you will please take your seat."

The Patriarch looked at Nimbus, then back to Modina. With a curious expression, he nodded, walked to the empty chair, clacking his staff with each step, and sat down.

"Patriarch Nilnev," Breckton said. "Can you explain your interruption of King Armand's comments?"

"I was quoting an ancient text: '*And lo the sylvan gods prey on Man. They that death does not visit and time does not mar. Firstborn fairy kings, undisputed lords, mankind cowers before thee.*'" He recited the words with reverence and paused before continuing, "The ancient writings speak clearly of the power of the elves. So much time has passed, so much dust covers the years, that man has forgotten the world as it was before the coming of our lord Novron. Before his sacred birth, the elves ruled all the land. Every fair place, every sunlit hill and green valley, lay under their dominion. They were firstborn, greatest of the inhabitants of Elan. We forgot because the miracle of Novron made such amnesia possible. Before his coming, the elves *were* invincible."

"Forgive me, Your Holiness." Sir Elgar spoke up, his voice like the growl of a bear. "But that's a load of bull. Elves are as weak as women and dumber than cattle."

"Have you crossed the Nidwalden, Sir Elgar? Have you seen a true member of the Erivan Empire? Or are you speaking of the *mir*?"

"What's a *mir*?"

"A *mir*—or *kaz* in Calian—is one of those wretched, vile creatures that so often used to defile the streets of cities throughout Apeladorn. Those emaciated, loathsome perversions with pointed ears and slanted eyes who carry a muddied mix of human and elven blood are abominations. *Mirs* are remnants of a conquered people that have less in common with elves than you do with a goldfish. Elf and human cannot coexist. They are mortal enemies by divine providence. The mixing of their blood in a single body has produced a contemptible walking insult to both Maribor and Ferrol, and the gods' wrath has fallen upon them. You should not presume to look at a *mir* and guess at the nature of an elf."

"Okay, I get the point. Still, I've never come across any creature that draws breath who is immune from the sharpened tip of a sword," Elgar said.

This produced pounding of fists on the table and grunts of agreement from the other knights — all except Breckton.

"The ancient text tells us that prior to the coming of Novron, no elf was ever killed by a man. Moreover, due to their long life, no human ever saw an elven corpse. This gave rise to the belief that they were immortal gods. '*Soft of foot, loud as thunder, terrible as lightning, greater than the stars, they come, they come, they come to conquer.*'"

"So if they were so great, how did Novron stop them?" Elgar challenged.

"He was the son of a god," the Patriarch replied simply. "And" — he paused briefly, his grin widening to display even more teeth — "he had help in the form of the Rhelacan."

"The divine sword?" Sir Breckton asked skeptically.

The Patriarch shook his head. "It was created by the gods, but the Rhelacan is not a sword; it is the Trumpet of Ferrol, the Call of Nations, the *Syord duah Gylindora* that Novron used to defeat the Erivan Nation. Many make the same mistake. In the Old Speech the word *syord* means *horn*, but that bit of information was lost when some sloppy translator thought it meant *sword*. The name Rhelacan is merely Old Speech for *relic* or *artifact*. So the *Syord duah Gylindora*, or Horn of Gylindora, became the *sword that is a great relic*, or the Rhelacan — the weapon that Novron used against the elves."

"How can this...*horn*...defeat an army?" Sir Breckton asked.

"It was made by the hand of their god, Ferrol, and holds dominion over them. It gave Novron the power to defeat the elves."

"And where might this marvelous trumpet be?" Cornelius DeLur spoke up. "I only ask because in our present circumstances, such a delightful treasure could prove to be quite useful."

"Herein lies the great question. The Rhelacan has been lost for centuries. No one knows what became of the Horn of Gylindora. The best accounts place it in the ancient capital of Percepliquis, just before the city vanished."

"Vanished?" Cornelius asked, leaning forward as far as his immense girth would allow.

"Yes," the Patriarch said. "All accounts from that time report that the city was there one day and gone the next. Percepliquis was consumed, lost, it is said, in a single day." The Patriarch closed his eyes and spoke in a musical tone:

> *Novron's home, seat of power*
> *White roads, walls, roofs, and towers*
> *Upon three hills, fair and tall*
> *Gone forever, fall the wall.*

> *Birthplace of our wondrous queen*
> *Mounted flags of blue and green*
> *Exquisite mansions, wondrous halls*
> *Goodbye forever, fall the wall.*

> *City of Percepliquis*
> *Ever sought, forever missed*

Pick and shovel, dig and haul
Search forever, fall the wall.

Gala halted, city's doom
Spring warmth chilled with dust and gloom
Darkness sealed, blankets all
Death upon them, fall the wall.

Ancient stones upon the Lee
Dusts of memories gone we see
Once the center, once the all
Lost forever, fall the wall.

"I know that," Hadrian blurted out, and regretted it the moment he did, as all eyes looked his way. "It's just that I remember hearing that as a kid. Not the whole thing, just the last part. We used to sing it when we played a game called Fall-the-Wall. We didn't know what it meant. We didn't think it meant anything. Although some of the kids thought it had something to do with the ruins of Amberton Lee."

"It does!" Arista broke in. "Amberton Lee is all that remains of the ancient capital of Percepliquis."

Hadrian heard the reactions of disbelief around the table.

"How do *you* know this?" Sir Murthas asked inquisitorially. "Scholars and adventurers have searched for centuries and a wit—" He caught himself. "A *princess* just happens to know where it is? What proof do you have?"

"I had—" Arista began when the empress cut her off.

"Princess Arista has provided to me irrefutable proof that what she says is indeed true." Modina glared at the knight.

Sir Murthas looked as if he might protest, but he closed his mouth in defeat.

"I believe the city is buried," Arista went on. "I think Edmund Hall found a way in. If only we had his journal ... but the Crown Tower is gone, along with everything in it."

"Wait a minute," Hadrian said. "Was it a beat-up brown leather notebook? About this big?" He gestured with his hands.

"Yes," the Patriarch said.

Arista looked back and forth between them. "How do you know that?"

"I know it because I have lived in the Crown Tower," the Patriarch said.

"And you?" Arista looked at Hadrian, who hesitated.

"Ha-ha! Of course, of course. I knew it!" Cosmos DeLur chuckled and clapped his hands together in single applause while smiling at Hadrian. "Such a wonderfully delightful rumor as that had to be true. That is an exquisite accomplishment."

"You stole it?" Arista asked.

"Yes, he did," the Patriarch declared.

"Actually," Hadrian said, "Royce and I did, but we put it back the next night."

"Riyria's reputation is well founded," Cosmos said.

"I did not wish to lose such an important treasure again, so since then, I've kept it with me at all times." The Patriarch pulled out a small ruddy-brown leather book and lay it on the table. "This is the journal of Edmund Hall, the daily account of his descent into the ancient city of Percepliquis and what lies within."

Everyone stared at the book for a moment in silence.

"The princess is correct," the Patriarch continued. "The city lies beneath Amberton Lee and Hall did find a means in. He also found a great deal more than that. The journal speaks of a terrible shaft of darkness, an underground sea that must be crossed, insidiously complex tunnels and tight crevices, bloodthirsty tribes of Ba Ran Ghazel, and a monster so terrible Hall could not fully describe it."

"You're saying the ancient capital is only three miles from Hintindar?" Hadrian asked.

"Yes," Modina said, "and I plan on sending in a party to retrieve this horn."

"Having read Hall's journal," the Patriarch said, "I believe you will need several skilled warriors, someone with historical knowledge of the city, someone with spelunking skills, and someone with sailing experience. I have already sent three teams on this very mission. Perhaps I—"

"I know," the empress said. "They all failed. Princess Arista will organize my team."

"If we could borrow Hall's journal," Arista said, "that would be of great assistance. I promise you'll have it returned before the party sets out."

The Patriarch's smile seemed to waver, but he nodded. "Of course. It is the least I can do."

Modina gestured toward Arista. "Your Highness, if you will..."

The princess stood up and faced the table. Before she could talk, however, Sir Elgar got to his feet. "Hold on," he said. "Are you saying we aren't even going to try and fight them? We're just going to sit here and wait for some fairy-tale horn that might not even exist anymore? I say we form ranks, march north, and hit them before they hit us!"

"Your courage is commendable," Sir Breckton said, "but in this instance foolish. We have no idea where our enemy is, the size or strength of their force, or their path of movement. Without even the faintest hint about our enemy we would be as a blind man fumbling around for a bear in the forest. And all attempts to discover anything about our foe have met with failure. I have sent dozens of scouts and few have returned."

"It seems wrong to just wait."

"We won't just be waiting," the empress said. "You can be assured that Sir Breckton has drawn up excellent plans for the defense of Aquesta, which I expect each of you to support. We have already begun overstocking the city with supplies and reinforcing the walls. We should not deceive ourselves: this war—this storm—is coming and we must be prepared for it. I assure you, we will stand, we will fight, and we will pray. As I find myself faced with annihilation, I am not above throwing support to even the thinnest promise. If there is a chance that finding this horn can save my people—my family—we must try. I will do whatever it takes to protect us. I would even make a deal with Uberlin himself if that is what is needed."

When she was done, no one said a word until she once more gestured toward Arista.

The princess took a breath. "I have already discussed this with the empress. The team will be small, no more than twelve, I think. Two people must go. For the rest, I will ask for volunteers, starting from a list we have already prepared. I will speak with those on the list individually, in order to allow for the privacy of each person's decision."

"And who are these two?" Murthas asked. "The ones that must go. Can we know their names?"

"Yes," Arista said. "They are Degan Gaunt and myself."

Several people spoke at once. Sir Elgar and the other knights laughed, and Alric started to protest, but by far the loudest voice in the room came from Degan Gaunt.

"Are you insane?" he shouted, jumping to his feet. "I'm not going anywhere! Why do I have to go? This is just another plot of the aristocracy to silence me. Can't you see what this really is? This elven threat is a hoax, an excuse to oppress the common man once more!"

"Sit down, Mr. Gaunt," Modina said. "We'll discuss this in private as soon as the meeting is over."

Gaunt dubiously sat down and slumped in his chair.

The empress rose and the room went silent. "This concludes this meeting. Sir Breckton will begin by convening a war council here in one hour to specify in detail the reorganization of troops and the requisition of supplies and arms necessary to develop a proper defense for the city. Those not asked to join the Percepliquis party should meet back here at that time. In the future, Chancellor Nimbus and Secretary Amilia will be on hand in their offices to answer any additional questions. May Maribor protect us all."

The room filled with the sounds of scraping chairs and low conversations. Hadrian rose to his feet but stopped when he felt Arista's hand on his arm.

"We stay here," she told him.

He glanced up the length of the table as the kings and knights began filing out of the room. The empress made no indication of leaving, nor did Amilia or Nimbus. He even caught the spindling chancellor subtly patting the table with his hand, as further indication that Hadrian should sit back down. Alric and Mauvin stood but did not advance toward the exit.

The Patriarch, flanked by his bodyguards, exited the hall. He looked back, nodding and smiling, his staff clicking on the stone. He was the last one out of the hall, and with a nod from Nimbus, guards closed the doors. A dull but—Hadrian felt— ominous thud echoed with their closing.

"I'm going," Alric told his sister.

"But—" she started.

"No buts," he said firmly. "You went to meet with Gaunt against my wishes. You tried to free him from these dungeons instead of coming home. You even managed to be on hand when Modina slew the Gilarabrywn. I'm tired of being the one sitting home worrying. I may no longer have a kingdom, but I am still the king! If you go, I go."

"Me too," Mauvin put in. "As Count of Galilin, it falls to me to keep both of you safe. My father would have insisted."

"I was just going to say, before you interrupted," Arista began, "that you're both already on the list. I'll just check you both off as agreeing."

"Good." Alric smiled triumphantly, folding his arms across his chest, then grinned at Mauvin. "Looks like we'll make it to Percepliquis after all."

"And you can take me off your bloody list!" Degan Gaunt shouted. He was on his feet. "I'm not going!"

"Please sit down, Degan," Arista told him. "I need to explain."

Degan remained furious, his eyes wide, his hands tugging at his doublet and his tight collar. "You!" He pointed at Hadrian. "Are you just going to sit there? Aren't you supposed to protect me?"

"From what?" he asked. "They only want to talk."

"From the brutish manhandling of the common man by the rich aristocracy!"

"That's actually what we need to speak about," Modina explained. "You are the true Heir of Novron, not I. That is why Ethelred and Saldur locked you up."

"Then why haven't I been acknowledged? I've seen precious little benefit from that wondrous title. I should be the emperor—I should be on the throne. Why hasn't my pedigree been announced? Why do you feel it is necessary to speak about my lineage in private? If I really am this heir, I should be sitting for my coronation right now, not going on some suicide mission. How stupid do you think I am? If I really were this descendant of a god, I would be too valuable to risk. Oh no, you want me out of the way so you can rule! I am an inconvenience that you have found a convenient way to dispose of!"

"Your lineage hasn't been announced for your own safety. If—"

Gaunt cut Modina off. "My own safety? You people are the only ones that threaten me!"

"Will you let her finish?" Amilia told him.

Modina patted her hand and then continued. "The heir has the ability to unite the four nations of Apeladorn under one banner, but I have already accomplished that, or rather the late regents, Saldur and Ethelred, have. Through their diligent, misguided efforts, the world already believes the heir sits on the imperial throne. At this moment, we are in a war with an adversary we have little chance of defeating. This is no time to shake the people's belief. They must remain strong and confident that the heir already rules. We must remain united in the face of our enemy. If we revealed the truth now, that confidence would be shaken and our strength destroyed. If we manage to survive, if we live to see the snow melt and the flowers bloom again, then you and I can talk about who sits on the throne."

Degan stood with less conviction now. He leaned on the table, pulling on his collar. "I still don't see why I need to go on this loony trip into a buried city."

"The ability to unite the kingdoms was thought to be the sum of the heir's value, but we now believe it is trivial compared to your true importance."

"And that is?"

"Your ability to both find and use the Horn of Gylindora."

"But I don't know anything about this—this horn thingy. What is it I'm supposed to do, exactly?"

"I don't know."

"What will happen if I use it?"

"I don't know."

"Then I don't know that I am going. You said that if everything works out, we'll talk about who sits on the imperial throne, but I say we have that discussion now. I will go on this quest of yours, but in return I demand the throne. I want it in writing, signed with your hand, that I will be Emperor of Apeladorn upon my return, regardless of success. And I want two copies, one which I will take with me in case the other is *somehow* lost."

"That's outrageous!" Alric declared.

"Perhaps, but I won't go otherwise."

"Oh, you'll go," Mauvin assured him with a smirk.

"Sure, you can tie me up and drag me, but I'll hang limp— a dead weight that will slow you down. And at some point you'll need me to do something, which I assure you I will not. So if you want my cooperation, you will give me the throne."

Modina stared at him. "All right," she said. "If that is your price, I will pay it."

"You're not serious!" Alric exclaimed. "You can't agree to put this—this—"

"Careful," Gaunt said. "You are speaking of your next emperor, and I remember slights against me."

"What will happen to Modina?" Amilia asked.

Gaunt pursed his lips, considering. "She was a farmer once, wasn't she? She can go back to that."

"Empress," Alric began, "think about what you are doing."

"I am." She turned to Nimbus. "Take Gaunt. Have the scribe write up whatever he wants. I will sign it."

Gaunt smiled broadly and followed the chancellor out of

the hall. A silence followed. Alric started to speak several times but stopped himself and finally slumped in his seat.

Arista looked at Hadrian and took his hand. "I want you to go."

Hadrian glanced at the door. "Being his bodyguard, I don't suppose I have a choice."

She smiled, then added, "I also want Royce to come."

Hadrian ran a hand through his hair. "That might be a bit of a problem." He looked toward Modina.

"I have no objection," she said.

"We need the best team I can put together," Arista added.

"That's right," Alric said. "If ever there was a need for my miracle team, this is it. Tell him I'll make it worth his time. I still have *some* fortune left."

Hadrian shook his head. "This time it won't be about money."

"But you will talk to him?" Arista asked.

"I'll try."

"Hey," Alric said to Arista, "why is it that *you* feel compelled to go? I never remember you having any interest in Percepliquis before."

"To be honest, I would rather not go, but it's my responsibility now."

"Responsibility?"

"Perhaps *penance* is a better word. You could say I am haunted." Her brother did not appear to understand, but she did not elaborate. "We still need a historian. If only Arcadius had...but now..."

"I know someone," Hadrian said, picking up Hall's journal. "A friend with an appetite for books and an uncanny memory."

Arista noded. "What about someone with sailing experience?"

"Royce and I spent a month on the *Emerald Storm*. We know a little about ships. It's a shame I don't know where Wyatt Deminthal is, though. He was the helmsman on the *Storm* and a fantastic seaman."

"I'm familiar with Mr. Deminthal," Modina said, drawing a curious look from Hadrian. "I'll see if I can convince him to sign on."

"That just leaves the dwarf," Arista said.

"The what?" Hadrian stared at her.

"Magnus."

"You've found him?" Alric asked.

"Modina did."

"That's wonderful!" Alric exclaimed. "Can we execute him before our departure?"

"He's going with you," Modina told him.

"He killed my father!" Alric shouted. "He stabbed him in the back while he was at prayer!"

"While I can see your point, Your Majesty," Hadrian said to Alric, "there is a more pressing issue. He nearly killed Royce twice. If he sees Magnus, the dwarf is dead."

"Then perhaps you should be the one to hang on to this." Modina produced the white dagger and slid it down the table, where it came to rest, spinning slightly before Hadrian. "I know all about Magnus's crimes. His obsession with Royce's dagger caused him to make poor decisions, including the one that got him arrested when he tried to steal it from the storehouse. You are going underground, perhaps deep underground. There will be no maps or road signs and I can't afford for you to get lost."

"Alric, Modina and I agree on this," Arista said. "Remember he was my father as well. We are setting out on a journey that may decide the fate of our race! The elves don't want to push us from our lands and lock us in slums. They plan to eradicate us. They won't ever let us have a second chance to hurt them. If we don't succeed, it's over—all of it. No more Melengar, no more Warric, no more Avryn. We will cease to exist. If I must tolerate—even forgive—a murderer as payment for the safety of everyone and everything I've ever known...Why, I'd marry the little cretin if that was the modest price Maribor put on *this* prize."

There was a silence after the princess stopped speaking.

"All right," Alric said grudgingly. "I guess I can put up with him."

Hadrian reached out and picked up Alverstone. "I will definitely need to hold on to this."

"Wow," Mauvin said, looking at Arista. "You'd marry him? That's really sick."

"Supplies are being prepared," Modina explained. "Food kits designed by Ibis Thinly will be packed along with lanterns, ropes, harnesses, axes, cloth, pitch, blankets, and everything else we can think of that you might need."

"Then we will leave as soon as the supplies are ready," Arista declared.

"So it's settled." Modina stood and all the others followed suit. "May Maribor guide your steps."

THE MARQUIS OF GLOUSTON

Myron sat curled up on his bunk, bundled deep in several layers of blankets. He had his hood up and a candle in his hand, which hovered over a giant book spread across his knees. He shared Hadrian's room in the knights' dormitories. The room lacked a window and fireplace, leaving it dark as well as cold. Only a plain green drape covering one wall interrupted the drab space. Myron did not mind; he liked the room.

He took his meals in the kitchen. Breakfast was early and supper late, working on abbey time. He visited Red, the elkhound, daily and said his prayers alone. In many ways, it reminded him of the abbey. He had expected he would be homesick by now, but the feeling never came. This surprised him at first, but *home*, he realized, was not so much a place as an idea that, like everything else, grew and blossomed along with the person. Being away gave him a new insight that the abbey was no longer his home — he carried his home with him now, and his family was not just a handful of monks.

He forced his eyes to focus on the book before him. Lord Amberlin of Gaston Loo had just discovered that he was descended from the Earl of Gast, who had defeated the invading Lumbertons at the Battle of Primiton Tor. He had no idea who Lord Amberlin was nor who the Lumbertons might be, but it was fascinating just the same. Everything he read still fascinated him.

A knock at the door caused him nearly to spill the candle. He put the book away and, opening up, was greeted by a familiar page.

"My lord."

Myron smiled. The boy always called him that, and Myron found each instance funny. "The lady Alenda requests an audience with you in the small east parlor. She is there now. Will you see her or shall I respond with a message?"

Myron stood puzzled for a moment. "Lady who?"

"The lady Alenda of Glouston."

"Oh," he said. "Ah, I'll go, but…ah, could you show me the way? I don't know where the east parlor is."

"Certainly, my lord."

The page turned and began walking, leaving Myron to quickly close the door and trot after him. "What is Lady Alenda like?" Myron asked.

The page glanced at him, surprised. "She's your sister, my lord. At least, that is what she said."

"Yes, she is, but…Do you know what she wants?"

"No, my lord. The lady Alenda did not say."

"Did she sound angry?"

"No, my lord."

They reached the small parlor, with its hearty fire's warm glow. The room was filled with many soft upholstered chairs and couches, lending the chamber a friendly feel. Rich tapestries depicting a hunt, a battle, and a spring festival covered the walls.

Two women jumped to their feet the moment he entered. The foremost was dressed in a beautiful black gown of brocade with a high collar and tight bodice composed of many buttons, lace, and trimming. The second wore a much simpler, but nonetheless rich, black gown of kersey.

Having spent almost his entire life in a monastery on top of a remote hill, Myron had met few people, and even fewer women—and none like these two. They were both as beautiful as a pair of deer.

They promptly curtsied and Myron was not sure what that meant.

Am I supposed to curtsy as well?

Before he could decide, one of them spoke. "My lord," the nearest woman said while still bent down. "I am your sister, Alenda, and with me is my maid Emily."

"Hello," he said awkwardly. "I'm Myron."

He held out his hand. Alenda, still in full curtsy, looked up, confused. She spotted his outstretched arm and gave an odd glance to the other woman before taking it. She kissed the back of his hand.

Myron hauled his hand back, shocked. A long uncomfortable silence followed.

"I really wish I had some cookies to offer you," he said at length.

Again, silence.

"We always had cookies at the abbey for guests."

"I want to ask your forgiveness, Your Lordship," Alenda burst out in a quavering voice, "for failing to meet you before this. I know it was wrong of me and that you have every reason to be angry. I have come now to beg you to be merciful."

Myron looked at the woman before him, baffled. He blinked several times.

"You are begging mercy—from *me*?"

Alenda looked at him, horrified. "Oh please, my lord, have pity. I didn't even know you lived until I was fourteen, and then I heard about you only in passing during a dinner conversation. It really wasn't until I was nineteen that I fully realized I had another brother and that Father had sentenced you to that awful place. I know I am not blameless. I realize my misdeeds and fully admit to you my foul nature. When I heard you lived, I should have come at once and embraced you, but I did not. Still, you must understand I am not accustomed to traveling abroad and visiting strange men, even if they are my long-lost brother. If only our father had brought me to you— but he refused and sadly I did not press."

Myron stood frozen in place.

Looking at him, Alenda wailed, "Sentence me as you must, but please do not torture me any longer. My heart cannot stand it."

Myron's mouth opened, but nothing came out. He stepped back, stunned.

Alenda stood wavering on her feet. In the silence between them, she looked at the frayed, coarse woolen frock he wore and her eyes filled with tears. She stepped toward him, her hands shaking. She reached out, touching his garment, letting it play between her fingers, and whispered with a closing throat, "I am sorry for how Father treated you. I am sorry for how I treated you. I am sorry for all that you have been forced to endure by our selfishness, but please don't turn me out into the cold. I'll do whatever you ask, but please have pity." Alenda fell to her knees before him weeping into her hands.

Myron fell to his own knees and, reaching out, put his arms around his sister and hugged her. "Please stop crying. I don't know what I did to hurt you, but I'm very sorry." He looked up at Emily and mouthed, "Help me."

The maid just stared at him in shock.

Alenda looked up, dabbing the tears from her eyes with a lace handkerchief. "You aren't going to strip me of my title? Drive me off our land and force me to fend for myself?"

"Oh dear Maribor, no!" Myron exclaimed. "I could never do that! But—"

"You won't?"

"Of course not! But—"

"Will you—could you also grant me my dowry of the Rilan Valley?" she said, and then very quickly added, "I only ask because no decent man would ever marry a woman without an adequate dowry. Without this I would continue to be a burden to you and the estate. Of course, the Rilan is very good land and I understand that you may not want to part with it, but Father promised it to me. Still I would be happy with anything you are willing to grant."

"But I can't give you anything. I'm only a monk of the Winds Abbey." He pulled the cloth of his frock out from his chest. "This is all I own. This is all I've ever owned. And technically I think this belongs to the abbey."

"But—" Alenda looked at him, stunned. "Don't you know?" Myron waited, blinking again.

"Our father and brothers are all gone, fallen in the battle against the elves. They died at Drondil Fields—"

"I'm so sorry to hear that," Myron said. He patted her hand. "I mourn for your loss. You must feel awful."

"They were your family as well."

"Yes, of course, but I was not as close to them as you were. Actually, I only met Father, and just once. But that does not diminish my sympathy for you. I am so sorry for you. Is there anything I can do?"

A questioning furrow across her brow, Alenda exchanged looks with Emily.

"I'm not sure you understand. With their passing, our family's fortune and title passes to you. They left you your inheritance. You are the Marquis of Glouston. You own thousands of acres of land, a castle, villages—barons and knights are all yours to command. You control the lives of hundreds of men and women who live or die at your decree."

Myron shivered and grimaced. "No, no. I'm sorry, you must be mistaken. I want none of that. I don't suppose I could trouble you to take care of those things?"

"So I can have the Rilan Valley?"

"Oh no—well, I mean, yes—I mean, everything. I don't want it. You can have it all—well, are there any books?"

"A few, I think," Alenda said, dazed.

"Then can I have those?" he asked. "You can have them back if you want after I read them, but if you don't, I'd like to make them part of the library at Windermere. Would that be all right?"

"Are you saying you want me to assume ownership of all of Glouston? Everything—except the books?"

Myron nodded and glanced at Emily. "If that is too much trouble, perhaps your friend could help. Maybe she could have some of those castles and knights—you know, many hands make light work."

Alenda nodded with her mouth still open.

Myron smiled. "Was there anything else?"

Alenda shook her head slowly.

"Okay, well, it was very nice meeting you." He reached out and shook Alenda's hand. "Both of you." He shook Emily's as well. Neither said a word.

He exited through the door and leaned with his back against the wall, feeling as if he had just escaped death itself.

"There you are," Hadrian called to him as he approached up the corridor, clutching a small notebook. "The page told me you were here."

"The strangest thing just happened," Myron told him, pointing back at the parlor door.

"Save it." He held out the book. "You need to read this tonight. The whole thing. Can you do that?"

"Just the one?"

Hadrian smiled. "I knew I could count on you."

"What is it?"

"Edmund Hall's journal."

"Oh my!"

"Exactly. And tomorrow you can tell me all about it on the road. It will help to pass the time."

"Road—tomorrow?" Myron asked. "Am I going back to the abbey?"

"Better—you're going to be a hero."

CHAPTER 6

VOLUNTEERS

As far as prison cells went, Wyatt Deminthal had seen far worse. Despite the stone, it was surprisingly warm and remarkably similar to the solitary cell he had been occupying for the past several weeks. The small bed he sat on was nicer than most of the rooms he had rented and much better than the ship hammocks he was used to. A small window, high up, allowed light to splash the far wall. Wyatt had to admit it was a fine room. He might have even found it comfortable if not for the locked door and the dwarf staring at him.

The dwarf had already been in the cell when they had brought Wyatt in, and the guards had not bothered with introductions. He had a brown braided beard and a broad flat nose, and he was dressed in a blue leather vest, with large black boots. Despite having been roommates for several hours, neither had said a word. The dwarf grumbled occasionally, shuffled his boots as he shifted position, but said nothing. Instead, he had a nasty habit of staring. Little round eyes peered out from beneath bushy eaves—eyebrows that matched his beard in color if not in neatness. Wyatt had known few dwarves, but they always sported carefully groomed beards.

"So you're a sailor," the dwarf muttered.

Wyatt, who had been passing the time by playing with the feather in his hat, raised his head and nodded. "And you're a dwarf."

"What was your first clue?" The little fellow smirked. "What'd you do?"

Wyatt did not see any point in avoiding the question. Lies were told to protect one's future, and Wyatt had no illusions of his. "I'm responsible for destroying Tur Del Fur."

The dwarf sat up, interested. "Really? What part?"

"The whole city—well, technically all of Delgos, if you think about it. I mean, without the protection of Drumindor, the port is lost and the rest is helpless."

"You destroyed an entire country?"

"Pretty much." Wyatt nodded miserably, then sighed.

The dwarf continued to stare at him, now in fascination.

"How about you?" Wyatt asked. "What did you do?"

"I tried to steal a dagger."

Now it was Wyatt's turn to stare. "Really?"

"Sure, but you have to remember—I'm a dwarf. You'll probably get a slap on the wrist. After all, you only destroyed a country. I'll likely be ripped apart by wild dogs."

The door to the chamber opened, and while Wyatt had never actually seen her before, there was no mistaking Empress Modina Novronian. She entered flanked by guards and a spindly man in a foppish wig.

"Both of you are guilty of crimes," she said. "Punishable by execution."

Wyatt was surprised at the sound of her voice. He had expected an icier tone, a shrill superiority common to high nobility. She sounded—oddly enough—like a young girl.

"Wyatt Deminthal," the spindly man in the wig said formally. "For wanton acts that precipitated and enabled the invasion of Delgos and the destruction of Tur Del Fur by the

Ba Ran Ghazel, you are hereby found guilty of high treason against mankind and this empire. Punishment will be execution by beheading, to be carried out immediately."

The empress then turned to the dwarf and once more the thin man spoke. "Magnus the dwarf, for the murder of King Amrath, you are hereby found guilty and sentenced to death by beheading, also to be carried out at once."

"Seems you left something out," Wyatt said to the dwarf, who only grumbled in response.

"Both of your lives are over," Modina said. Then: "When I leave this room, the headsman will escort you to the block in the courtyard, where your punishment will be administered. Is there anything you would like to say before I leave?"

"My daughter…" Wyatt began, "she's innocent. So is Elden— the big guy with her. I beg you, please don't punish them."

"They are safe and free to go. But where do you think they will go once you're dead? You've been caring for them both for many years, haven't you? While Elden may make a fine babysitter, he's not much of a provider, is he?"

"Why are you saying this?" It mystified Wyatt that such a young girl could be so cruel.

"Because I would like to make you an offer, Mr. Deminthal. I would like to make both of you an offer. Given your positions, I think it is a very good one. I want the two of you to do a task for me. It will involve a difficult journey that I suspect will be very dangerous. If you agree, then upon your return, I shall absolve you both of your crimes."

"And if I don't come back? What happens to Elden and Allie?"

"Elden will go with you. I need experienced sailors and strength. I think he'll be useful."

"What about Allie? I won't have her going to some prison or orphanage. Can she come as well?"

422 *Michael J. Sullivan*

"No, as I mentioned, the trip will be dangerous, so she will remain with me. I will be her guardian while you are away."

"What if I don't come back? What if neither Elden or I…"

"If that happens, I promise that I will personally adopt her."

"You will?"

"Yes, Mr. Deminthal. If you succeed, you will be forgiven of all crimes you have committed. If you fail, I will make your daughter my daughter. Of course, you can refuse my offer, in which case I have to ask if you would prefer a blindfold or not. It's your choice."

"And me?" Magnus asked.

"I offer you the same thing. Do as I ask, and you'll live. I'll consider your service as fulfillment of your sentence. In your case, however, there is one additional stipulation. Mr. Deminthal has proved that his ties to his daughter are strong enough to hold him to his commitments. You, on the other hand, have no such attachments and have a talent for disappearing. I can't afford to let you out of this cell without some insurance. I know a sorceress who can find anyone, anywhere, using only a strand of hair, and your beard is ever so long."

Magnus's eyes widened in alarm.

"It's your choice, master dwarf, your beard or your neck."

"Do we at least get to know where we are going, and what we will be doing?" Wyatt asked.

"Does it matter?"

Wyatt thought a moment, then shook his head.

"You'll be accompanying a team to the ancient city of Percepliquis to find a very important relic that might just save mankind. If you succeed at that, I think you deserve to be forgiven for any crime.

"There is just one more thing. You'll be accompanied by Royce Melborn and Hadrian Blackwater. As for you, Wyatt, they know nothing of your involvement with Merrick. I suggest you keep it that way. Merrick is dead, and nothing good can come from revealing your involvement in Tur Del Fur."

Wyatt nodded toward the dwarf. "I already told him."

"That's all right. I doubt Master Magnus will be speaking to them much. Magnus has had, shall we say, his own misunderstandings with Riyria, not to mention the children of King Amrath, who will also be along for the trip. I suspect he'll be on his best behavior, won't you, Magnus?"

The dwarf's face showed concern but he nodded.

"So, gentlemen, the choice is yours. Risk your lives for me and have a chance to become heroes of the empire, or refuse and die now as criminals."

"That's not much of a choice," the dwarf growled.

"No—no, it isn't. But it is all you have."

❧

Hadrian slowly climbed the steps. It felt like there were more of them this time. Aside from speaking to Myron, Hadrian had spent all night, and a good part of the next day, walking the corridors and courtyard, trying to formulate an argument— a reason that would convince Royce to go.

The guard heard him coming and was on his feet, key in hand. He looked bored. "You've come to take him?" he asked without interest. "I was told you'd be by—expected you earlier."

Hadrian only nodded in reply.

"So much fuss about this little guy? From hearing the talk around the palace, you'd think he was Uberlin himself," the guard continued as he placed the key in the lock. "He's been quieter than a mouse. A few nights ago, I heard him crying— muffled sobs, you know? Not exactly the demon I was warned about."

Royce had not moved. Nothing in the cell had changed since Hadrian's last visit.

"You wanna give me a minute?" Hadrian asked the guard, who stood behind him.

"Huh? Oh—sure. Take your time."

Hadrian stood silently at the open door. Royce did not move. He continued to sit with his head bowed.

Hadrian sighed. After all his searching, his thinking, his wandering, his solution seemed feeble at best. He had held dozens of mental debates in which he had played both sides of the arguments, but when he sat across from Royce, he had only one thing he could say. "I need your help."

Royce looked up as if his head weighed a hundred pounds, his eyes red, his face ashen. He waited.

"One last job," Hadrian told him, then added, "I promise."

"Is it dangerous?"

"Very."

"Is there a good chance I'll get killed?"

"Odds are definitely in favor of that."

Royce nodded, looked down at the scarf in his lap, and replied, "Okay."

CHAPTER 7

THE LAUGHING GNOME

Arista lugged her pack out into the cold. Three stewards and one soldier, an older man with a dark beard who held the door open, offered to carry it for her. She shook her head and smiled. The pack was light. Gone were the days of bringing six silk dresses, hoopskirts, corsets, girdles, and a headdress—just in case. She planned to sleep in the clothes she traveled in and learn to do without almost everything else. All she really needed was the robe. The wind blew snow in her face, freezing her nose. Her feet felt the cold, but the rest of her was immune, protected by the shimmering garment.

As she crossed the courtyard, the only light came from within the stable, and the loudest noise from her boots as they crushed the snow.

"Your Highness!" A boy chased after her, gingerly holding a steaming cup in both hands. "Ibis Thinly sent this to you." He shivered, dressed only in light wool.

She took the cup. "Tell him thank you."

The boy made a feeble bow and turned so fast to run back that his foot slipped and he fell to one knee.

The cup contained tea, and it felt wonderfully hot in her chilled fingers. The steam warmed her face as she sipped. Ibis had prepared a wonderful meal for everyone, laying it out across two tables. Arista had only glanced at the plates. It was too early to eat. She rarely ate breakfast. Her stomach needed time to wake up before going to work. That morning the thought of food was abhorrent. Her stomach was knotted and riding high. She knew she would pay later for skipping the meal. Somewhere along the road she would regret not having eaten something.

The stable smelled of wet straw and horse manure. Both doors stood open, leaving a path for the wind, which jingled the harnesses. Gusts harassed the lanterns and ripped through gaps in the walls, producing a loud fluttering howl as if a massive flock of sparrows were taking flight every few seconds.

"I'll take that, Your Highness," a groom offered. He was a short, stocky older man with a bristling beard and a knit hat that slumped to one side. He had two bridles draped around his neck and a bale hook hanging from his belt. He grabbed her pack and walked to the wagon. "You'll be riding back here," he told her. "I've made a right comfortable spot for you. I got a soft pillow from a chambermaid and three thick blankets. You'll ride in style, you will."

"Thank you, but I'll be needing a horse and a sidesaddle."

The groom looked at her with a blank stare, his mouth open, his lips thick and cracked. "But—Your Highness, where you're going—it's quite a ways from here, ain't it? Right awful weather too. You won't want to be atop no horse."

She smiled at him, then turned and walked up the aisle between the stalls. The aisle was brick, the stalls were dirt, and everything lay covered in bits of straw. The rear ends of a dozen horses faced her, swishing tails and shifting weight from one hoof to the other. Cobwebs gathered in corners, catching hay and forming snarled nests even in the rafters. The walls all bore a stain a full foot from the bottom—the high manure mark, she guessed. She stopped without thinking before a stall. This was where she had spent a night with Hilfred, where he had held her, where he had stroked her hair—kissed her. A pleasant-looking gray mare was there now. The horse turned her head and Arista saw a white nose and dark eyes. "What do you call this one?"

The groom slapped the horse's rump fondly. "This here girl is called Princess."

Arista smiled. "Saddle her for me."

Arista led Princess out into the courtyard. The groom followed close behind with the wagon. The team of horses puffed great clouds into the morning air. A crowd of people came out to the steps of the palace wrapped in dark cloaks, heads draped in hoods. They spoke in soft voices and whispers, clustering in small groups; some cried. The gathering reminded Arista of a funeral.

She knew many of the faces, even if she did not know all the names.

Alenda Lanaklin stood beside Denek, Lenare, and Belinda Pickering as they said goodbye to Mauvin and Alric. Mauvin threw his head back, laughing at something. It sounded wrong—too loud, too much effort. With her left hand, Belinda dabbed at her eyes with a cloth; her right hand gripped Mauvin's sleeve with white fingers. Alenda looked over the crowd, managing to catch Myron's attention. She waved to him. The monk paused in his efforts to pet the noses of the team of brown geldings harnessed to the wagon. He smiled and hesitantly waved back.

Not far away, two men Arista did not know spoke with the empress. One wore a plumed cavalier hat, a red and black doublet, high leather boots, and a heavy sailor's wrap. The other man towered over everyone present. His head reminded Arista of a barrel, wide and flat on top and bottom, with vertical creases like wooden slats. He was mostly bald and missing one ear and sporting several ugly scars, one that split his lower lip. A thick, untailored cape draped him like a tent. Arista speculated he had merely cut a hole in a thick blanket and pulled his head through. At his side was a huge, crude axe, hanging naked from a rough bit of raw leather.

"Do what the empress tells you," Arista heard the sailor say. "She'll take care of you until I come back."

A few feet away, Hadrian stood speaking with a man, a refugee from Melengar. He was a viscount, but she did not know his name. An attractive young woman rushed up, went up on her toes, and kissed Hadrian. The viscount called her Emerald.

What kind of name is that?

Hadrian hugged her, pulling Emerald off the ground. She giggled. Her left leg bent at the knee. She was very cute — smaller than Arista, thinner, younger. The princess wondered if he had dozens of women like this all over Avryn, or if this Emerald was special. Watching them together, seeing his arms around her, watching them kiss, she felt an emptiness, as if there were a hole inside her. She felt an ache, a pain like a weight pressing on her chest, and told herself to look away. After another minute, she actually did.

Twelve riding horses and two hitched to the wagon, fourteen animals in all, stood waiting in the snow. On four of the horses sat five young boys — squires, Hadrian called them — who he had recruited to act as servants and watch after the animals. All Arista knew about them were their names: Renwick, Elbright, Brand, Kine, and Mince. The last boy was so small that he rode double with Kine. They waited sitting straight and trying to look serious and grown up.

The buckboard, filled with their provisions and covered with a heavy canvas tarp, had its wheels removed and was fitted with snow runners. Huddled on the forward bench, glancing only occasionally at the crowd and adjusting his hood with a disgusted, angry expression, was the dwarf. Beneath his heavy brows, beneath his large nose and frowning mouth, his long braided beard had recently been cut short. The dwarf's fingers absently played with it the way a tongue might play with the space left by a missing tooth. He grumbled and sneered, but she could not find any sympathy for him. It was the first time she had seen Magnus since the day he had slammed the door in her face—less than a week after his hand had murdered her father.

Royce Melborn stood alone in the snow. He waited silently across the courtyard near the gate, his dark cloak fluttering lightly with the breeze—a small shadow near the wall. No one appeared to notice him except Hadrian, who kept a watchful eye, and Magnus, who repeatedly glanced over nervously. Royce never looked at any of them. His head faced the gate, the city, and the road beyond.

Amilia exited the palace, wrapped in heavy wool. She pushed through the crowd and crossed the yard to Arista. Trapped under her arm was a parchment, wrinkled and creased. In her hands was what looked to be a short whip.

"This is for you," she said, holding out what Arista now recognized as the severed half of the dwarf's beard, still neatly braided. "Being aware of Magnus's tendency to disappear, Modina took the precaution of snipping some hair for you."

She nodded. "Give her my thanks. Do you know where Gaunt is?"

"He's coming."

The castle doors opened once more and Degan Gaunt stepped out. He was clad in a belted fur-lined houppelande and a chaperon hat with a full bourrelet wrapped around his head and a long cornette that streamed nearly to the ground.

The elaborate houppelande was worn complete with huge bell sleeves and a long train, which dragged across the ground, softly grading the snow behind him.

"The future emperor has arrived," Amilia whispered, and then added, "He thought his clothes needed to reflect his future status and he didn't want to be cold."

"Can he ride in that?"

Before the secretary could answer, a page ran out before Gaunt carrying two large silk pillows and a blanket. He proceeded to lay them out on the wagon's bench. The dwarf forgot his beard as he looked at the pillows beside him with another sneer.

"I'm not riding beside a dwarf. Get that runt off of there," Gaunt said. "Hadrian will drive the wagon." When no one made a move, he added, "Do you hear me?"

Arista pulled herself onto Princess's back, swung her leg over the sidesaddle horn, and trotted rapidly to Gaunt. She reined the animal only a few feet short of Gaunt, causing him to step back. She glared down at him. "Magnus rides on the wagon because he's too short for the horses, and he is perfectly capable of driving it, true?"

The dwarf nodded.

"Good."

"But I do not wish to travel with him."

"Then you may ride on a horse."

Gaunt sighed. "I've been told this will be a long journey and I do not wish to spend it on the back of a horse."

"Then you can sit beside Magnus. Either way—it doesn't matter."

"I just told you I don't want to sit beside a dwarf." Gaunt glared at Magnus with a grimace. "And I don't appreciate your tone."

"And I don't appreciate your obstinacy. You can ride beside

Magnus, ride on a horse, or walk, for all I care. But regard-less, we are leaving." She raised her head and her voice. "Mount up!"

At her command, they all found their rides and climbed aboard. Looking livid, Gaunt stood staring at the princess.

Arista pulled on the reins and turned her mare to face Modina, who was holding Allie's hand. This left Gaunt facing the rear of her mare.

"I swear I will do all I can to find the horn and return with it as soon as possible."

"I know," Modina replied. "May Maribor guide your path."

&

Alric and Mauvin rode at the head of the party, although the king did not know where they were going. He had studied many maps but only set foot out of Melengar on three occa-sions. Alric had never traveled that far south and he had never heard of Amberton Lee before the meeting. He trusted some-one would tell him when to turn—Arista, most likely.

They traveled the Old Southern Road, which Alric knew from maps ran all the way to Tur Del Fur, at the southern tip of Delgos. As they passed through the Adendal Durat, the road was little more than a cleft in the ridge that sliced through the rocky mountains as it dropped down from the plateau of Warric to the plain of Rhenydd. Snow drifted in the pass such that on occasion, they needed to dismount and pull the horses through, but the road remained passable. Months of sun fol-lowed by bitter nights had left a crust on the surface that crunched under the horses' hooves and left icicles, hanging thick like frozen waterfalls, across the face of the rocky cliffs. The height of winter was over, days grew longer, and while the world lay buried, it was not as deep as it once had been.

No one talked much during the course of the morning. Gaunt and Magnus were particularly quiet, neither saying a word nor looking at each other. Degan sat bundled, his long train wrapping his body and head so only his nose remained exposed. Magnus appeared oblivious to the cold as he drove the wagon with bare ruddy hands. His breath iced his mustache and what remained of his beard, leaving him with a frozen grimace of irritated misery. Alric felt better seeing his discomfort.

Royce and Hadrian rode at the rear of the party, and Alric never noticed either speak. Royce rode absently, his hood up, his head down, bobbing as if he were asleep. The five boys were with them. They whispered among themselves occasionally, as servants were prone to do. The sailor they called Wyatt rode beside his giant friend. Alric had never seen a man that size before. They had provided him a draft horse and still his feet hung nearly to the ground, the stirrups left dangling. Wyatt had whispered a few words to the giant at the start, but Elden never spoke.

The only conversation, the only break from the droning crunch of snow and panting breath of the animals, was that of Myron and Arista. A quarter hour did not pass without the monk pointing out some curiosity to her. Alric had forgotten Myron's fascination with everything—no matter how trivial. Myron found the twenty-foot icicles hanging from the cliff-side nothing short of a miracle. He also pointed out designs he found in the rock formations—one he swore looked like the face of a bearded man. Arista smiled politely and even offered a laugh on occasion. It was a girl's laugh, high and light, natural and unburdened. Alric would feel self-conscious to laugh so openly. His sister did not seem to care what those around her thought.

Alric hated how she had taken charge when setting out. As

much as he had enjoyed the look on Gaunt's face when she had barked at him in the courtyard, he disliked the bold way his sister acted. If only she had given him the time to act. He was the king, after all. The empress might have given Arista authority to *organize* the expedition, but that did not extend to leading it. She had never satisfactorily explained why she was along, anyway. He had assumed she would ride quietly in the wagon and leave commanding the venture to him but he should have known better. Given her theatrics in the courtyard, it was surprising that she still rode sidesaddle and had not taken to wearing breeches. They escaped the tight pass before noon as morning clouds finally gave up their tight grip on the world. Ahead the land dropped away, leaving a magnificent view to the south. Alric spotted Ratibor in the distant valley. The whole city appeared no larger than his thumb and from that distance it looked beautiful, a clustered glen in a sea of forest and field.

"There," Hadrian announced from the rear, pointing toward a shining river to the east. "You can see Amberton Lee—sort of. Down near the Bernum River, where it bends. See there, how the land rises up into three hills."

"Yes, that's it," Arista agreed. "I remember." She looked up at the sky. "We won't make it today."

"We could spend the night in Ratibor," Hadrian offered. "It's only a few miles. We could reach it by nightfall."

"Well, I don't—" Arista began.

"We will head to Ratibor," Alric declared quickly, causing Arista to look at him in surprise.

"I was just going to say," she went on, "if we veer east now, we'll be that much closer in the morning."

"But there is no road," Alric told her. "We can't be wandering through the snowy fields."

"Why not?"

"Who knows how deep that snow is and what lies beneath?"

"Royce can find us a route through; he's good at that," Hadrian said.

"That's what I was thinking," Arista agreed.

"No, Ratibor is a much better choice," Alric said loudly. "We'll get a good night's rest, then push on at first light and be there by noon."

"But, Alric—"

"You heard my decision!" He kicked his horse and trotted down the road, feeling their eyes on his back.

Hooves trotted up behind him. He expected it to be his sister and dreaded the argument, but he would not back down. Alric turned hotly only to see Mauvin with his hair flying. The rest of the group followed twenty feet behind them, but they were moving in his direction. He let his horse slow to a walk.

"What was that all about?" Mauvin asked, moving alongside, where the two horses naturally fell into the same pace.

"Oh, nothing." He sighed. "Just trying to remind her who's king. She forgets, you know."

"So many years, so few changes," Mauvin said softly, brushing the hair out of his eyes.

"What's that supposed to mean?"

Mauvin only smiled. "Personally, I prefer your idea. Who wants to sleep in the snow if you can have a bed? Besides, I'd like to see Ratibor. It was on our list, remember?"

Alric nodded. "We were also supposed to go to Tur Del Fur."

"Yeah, but let's save that for another time, since it's under new management and all," Mauvin mentioned. "I still can't believe we are on our way to Percepliquis. That was always the big prize—the dream."

"Still hoping to find the Teshlor Codes?"

Mauvin chuckled. "That's right. I was going to discover the secret techniques of the Teshlor Knights. You remember that, do you? I was supposed to be the first one in a thousand years to possess that knowledge. I would have guarded it jealously and been the greatest warrior alive." Mauvin glanced behind them. "Not much chance of that now. Even if I did find them, I could never match Hadrian. He grew up with it and was taught by a master. That was a stupid dream, anyway. A boy's fantasy. The kind of thing a kid thinks before actually seeing blood on a blade. When you are young, you think you can do anything, you know? And then..." He sighed and turned away. Alric noticed his hand go up to his face briefly before settling on the pommel of his sword, only it was not Mauvin's sword.

"I didn't notice before," Alric told him, nodding toward Mauvin's side.

"This is the first time I've worn it." He pulled his hand away self-consciously. "I've wanted it for so long. I used to see my father wield it—so beautiful, so elegant. I dreamed of it sometimes. All I ever wanted to do was hold it, swing it, and hear it sing in the air for me."

Alric nodded.

"What about you?" Mauvin asked. "Are you still interested in finding Novron's crown?"

The king huffed and might have laughed if the statement had not seemed so ironic. "I already have a crown."

"Yeah," Mauvin said sadly.

Alric spoke in a voice just loud enough for Mauvin to hear. "Sometimes the price of dreams is achieving them."

※

They were just closing the city gate for the night when the party arrived in Ratibor. Arista did not recognize the guard. He was a burly, balding man in a rough stitched rawhide coat who waved at them impatiently to get inside.

"Where is a good place to find lodgings for the night, my good man?" Alric asked, circling his mount on the guard as he went about locking down the city.

"Aquesta. Ha!" The man laughed.

"I meant here."

"I knows what ya meant," he said gruffly. "The Gnome has open rooms, I think."

"The Gnome?"

"It's a tavern," Arista explained. "The Laughing Gnome—King's Street and Lore."

The guard eyed her curiously.

"Thank you," she said, quickly kicking her horse. "This way."

The heavy scent of manure and urine that Arista had remembered as the prominent smell of Ratibor was replaced by the thick smell of wood smoke. Other than that, the city had changed little from the last time she had been there. Streets ran in awkward lines, forcing adjoining buildings to conform to the resulting spaces often with strange results, such as shops in the shapes of wedges of cheese. The wooden planks that used to bridge the rivers of muck lay buried beneath a thick layer of snow. The winter had stolen the leaves from the trees and the wind ripped along empty streets. Nothing but the snow moved. Arista had expected winter would brighten the place and bury the filth, but instead she found it bleak and barren.

She rode in the lead now. Behind her, she could hear Alric grumbling. He spoke too low for her to catch the words, but his tone was clear. He was unhappy with her—again. Any other time, she might have fallen back, apologized for whatever it was she had done wrong, and tried to make him feel better. But she was cold, hungry, and tired. She wanted to get to the tavern. His feelings could hurt at least until they were settled.

As they approached Central Square, she tried to keep her eyes down and focus on the snow where Princess walked, but she could not resist. When they were in the exact middle of the square, her eyes ignored her will and looked up. The post was still there, but the ropes were gone. Dark and slender, nearly blending into the background, it was a physical reminder of what might have been.

There is blood under the snow, she thought.

Her breath shortened and her lip began to quiver. Then she noticed someone riding beside her. Arista was not aware if she had heard his approach, or merely sensed his presence, but suddenly Hadrian was an arm's length away. He did not look at her or speak. He merely rode quietly alongside. This was the first time he had left Royce's side since they had started out, and she wondered what had brought him forward. Arista wanted to believe he joined her because he knew how she felt. It was silly, but it made her feel better to think it.

The signboard above the door at the public house was crowned in snow and yet remained as gruesome as ever. The obscenely large open mouth, hairy pointed ears, and squinting eyes of the namesake gnome glared down at them.

Arista halted, slid off her mount, and stepped onto the boardwalk. "Perhaps the rest of you should wait here while Hadrian and I make arrangements."

Alric coughed and she caught him glaring at her.

"Hadrian and I know this city. It will just be faster if we go," she told him. "*You* were the one that wanted to come here."

He frowned and she sighed. Waving for Hadrian to follow, she passed under the sign of The Laughing Gnome. A flickering yellow light and warm air that smelled of grease and smoke greeted them. A shaggy spotted dog scampered over, trying to lick their hands. Hadrian caught him just as he jumped up toward her. He let the dog's forepaws rest on his thighs as he scrubbed behind its ears, causing the animal to hang its tongue.

The common room was empty except for two people huddled near the hearth—so different from the first time she had been there. She stared off at a spot near the center where a fiery-haired young man had once held the room spellbound.

This was the place. It was here I saw Emery for the very first time.

She had never thought about it before, but this revelation made the room sacred to her. She felt a hand on her shoulder. Hadrian gave her a gentle squeeze.

She spotted Ayers behind the bar, wiping out mugs. He was wearing the same apron, which appeared to have the same stains. The innkeeper had not shaved in a day or two, and his hair was mussed, and his face moist.

"What can I do ya for?" he asked as they approached, the dog trailing behind, pawing at Hadrian for more attention.

"We'd like rooms." Arista counted on her fingers. "There are fifteen in our party, so maybe four rooms? Do your rooms sleep four?"

"They can, but I usually charge by the pair."

"Oh, okay, so then seven rooms if you have them, I guess— the boys can all sleep in one room. Do you have vacancy?"

"Oh, I've got 'em. No one here but the mice. All the folk heading down from Wintertide passed through weeks ago. No one travels this time a' year. No need to…" He trailed off as he looked intently at Arista. His narrow eyes began widening. "Why, ain't you—I mean, yer her—ain't you? Where have you been?"

Embarrassed, she glanced at Hadrian. She had been hoping to avoid this. "We'd just like the rooms."

"By Mar! It is you!" he said, loud enough to catch the

attention of the two near the fire. "Everyone said you was dead."

"Almost. But really, we have people waiting in the cold. Can we get rooms? And we have horses too that—"

"Jimmy! Jimmy! Get your arse in here, boy!"

A freckle-faced kid, as thin as a Black Diamond member, rushed out of the kitchen, bursting through the doors with a startled look on his face.

"Horses outside need stabling. Get on it."

The boy nodded, and as he stepped by Ayers, the proprietor whispered something in his ear. The lad looked at Arista and his mouth opened as if it had just gained weight. A moment later he was running.

"You understand we're tired," Arista told the innkeeper. "It has been a long day of riding and we need to leave early in the morning. We are just looking for a quiet night."

"Oh, absolutely! But you'll be wantin' supper, right?"

Arista glanced at Hadrian, who nodded. "Yes, of course."

"Wonderful. I'll get something special for you."

"That's not necessary. We don't want to cause any—"

"Nonsense," Ayers told her. "Rusty!" he shouted over her head toward the two at the hearth, who were now on their feet, hesitantly inching closer. "Run and tell Engles I want his cut of pork."

"Pork?" the man replied. "You can't serve her no smoked pork! Benjamin Braddock got a prize lamb he's kept alive all winter, feeds it like a baby, he does."

"Yeah, real sweet animal," the other man said.

"Okay, okay, tell him to get it to Engles and have it butchered."

"How much you willing ta pay?"

"Just tell him who it's for, and if he wants to come ask *her* for money, let him."

"Oh please, this isn't necessary," Arista said.

"He's been saving that lamb for a special occasion," Rusty told her, and smiled. "I can't see how he can expect a better one."

The door opened and the rest of the party entered, dusting snow off their heads and shoulders and stomping their feet. Once inside, Gaunt let go his train and threw back his hood, shivering. He walked directly toward the fire with his hands outstretched and brought to Arista's mind the image of a giant peacock.

Rusty nudged his buddy. "That's Degan Gaunt."

"By Mar," Ayers said, shaking his head. "If'n you get a drop, it's a flood. And look at him all dressed up like a king. He's one of your group?"

Arista nodded.

"Blimey," Rusty said, staring now at Hadrian. "I seen this fella afore too—just a few weeks ago. He's the tourney champion. He unhorsed everyone 'cept Breckton, and he only missed 'cuz he didn't want ta kill him." He looked at Hadrian with admiration. "You woulda dropped him if'n you'd had the chance. I know it."

"Who else you got with you?" Ayers asked, looking overwhelmed. "The Heir of Novron?"

Arista and Hadrian exchanged glances.

"Our rooms—where are they?" Alric asked, joining them as he shook the wet out of his hood.

"I—ah—let me show you." Ayers grabbed a box of keys and led the way up the stairs.

As she climbed, Arista looked down at the empty space below and remembered how they had spent forty-five silver to sleep there. "How much for the rooms?"

Ayers paused, turned, and chuckled.

When they reached the top of the stairs, he threw his arms out. "Here you are."

"Which rooms?"

Ayers grinned. "Take the whole floor."

"How much?" Alric asked.

Ayers laughed. "I'm not charging you—I can't charge you. I'd be strung up. You get settled in and I'll call you when dinner is ready."

Alric grinned. "See? I told you it was worth coming. They are very friendly here."

"For her," Ayers said, nodding in Arista's direction, "nothing in this city has a price."

Alric frowned.

"That is very kind," she told him. "But given our situation, I think five rooms will still be best."

"What? Why?" Alric said.

"I don't think we want to leave Magnus or Gaunt unsupervised, do you?"

Hadrian, Royce, Myron, and Gaunt took one room. Wyatt, Elden, Magnus, and Mauvin took the second, and the boys took the third. Alric insisted on his own room, which left Arista alone as well.

"Relax as long as you like," Ayers told them. "Feel free to come down and enjoy the hearth. I'll roll out my best keg and uncork my finest bottles. If you choose to sleep, I'll send Jimmy to knock on your doors as soon as the meal is ready. And I just want to say, it's a great honor to have you here." He said the last part while staring at Arista.

She heard Alric sigh.

∽

Wyatt lay on one of the beds, stretching out his sore muscles. Elden sat across from him on the other bed, his huge head in his hands, his elbows on his knees. The bed bent under the pressure. Wyatt could see the ropes drooping down below the frame. Elden caught Wyatt's look and stared back with sad, innocent eyes. Like Allie, Elden trusted him. He gave the big man a reassuring smile.

"Stop! Don't touch that!" Mauvin shouted, and every head in the room turned. The count was hanging his cloak on a string with the other wet clothes. He glared at Magnus, who had a hand outreached toward the pommel of Pickering's sword, which was sheathed and hanging by a belt slung over the bedpost.

Magnus raised a bushy eyebrow and frowned. "What is it with you humans? And you call us misers! Do you think I'll stuff it under my shirt and walk off with it? It's as tall as I am!"

"I don't care. Leave it be."

"It's a fine weapon," the dwarf said, his hand retreating, but his eyes drinking it in. "Where did you get it?"

"It was my father's." Mauvin advanced to the end of the bed and grabbed his sword.

"Where did he get it?"

"It's a family heirloom, passed down for generations." Mauvin held the sword in his hand gingerly, as if it were an injured sparrow needing reassuring after its narrow escape from the dwarf. Wyatt had not noticed the weapon before, but now that his attention was drawn, he saw that it was an uncommonly attractive sword. It was elegant in its simplicity; the lines were perfect and the metal of the hilt shone bright. Almost imperceptible were fine decorative lines.

"I meant, how did yer family come to have it? It is a rare man who owns such a blade as this."

"I suppose one of my ancestors made it, or paid for it to be made."

The dwarf made a disgusting noise in his throat. "This was

not made by some corner blacksmith with a brat pumping a bellows. That there, lad, was forged in natural fires in the dark of a new moon. Your kind didn't touch it for centuries."

"My kind? Are you saying this is dwarven?"

Again the noise of reproach. "Bah! Not by my kin—that blade is elvish and a fine one at that, or I've never worn a beard."

Mauvin looked at him skeptically.

"Does she sing when she travels the air? Catch the light around her and trap it in her blade? Never grow dull even if used as a shovel or an axe? Cut through steel? Cut through other blades?"

Mauvin's face answered the dwarf. The count slowly drew it out. The blade shimmered in the lamplight like glass.

"Oh yes, she's an elven blade, boy, drawn from stone and metal, formed in the heat of the world, and tempered in pure water by the First Ones, the Children of Ferrol. No finer blade have I laid my eyes on save one."

Mauvin slipped it back and frowned. "Just don't touch it, okay?"

Wyatt heard the dwarf grumble something about having his beard cut off; then Magnus moved to the bed on the other side of the room, where he was too far for Wyatt to hear. Mauvin still held the blade, rubbing his fingers over the pommel; his eyes had a faraway look.

They were strangers to Wyatt. Mauvin, he knew, was a count of Melengar and close friend of King Alric. He had also heard that he was a good sword fighter. His younger brother had been killed in a sword fight some years back. His father had died recently—killed by the elves. He seemed a decent sort. A bit moody, perhaps, but all right. Still, he was noble and Wyatt had never had many dealings with them, so he decided to be cautious and quiet.

He kept a closer eye on the dwarf and wondered about the "misunderstandings" the empress had spoken of.

How do I keep getting myself into these situations?

Poor Elden. Wyatt had no idea what he made of all this.

"How you feeling?" Wyatt asked.

Elden shrugged.

"Want to go down for the meal, or have me bring you back a plate?"

Again a shrug.

"Does he talk?" Mauvin asked.

"When he wants to," Wyatt replied.

"You're the sailors, right?"

Wyatt nodded.

"I'm Mauvin Pickering," he said, putting out his hand.

Wyatt took it. "Wyatt Deminthal, and this is Elden."

The count looked Elden over. "What does he do on a ship?"

"Whatever he wants, I should think," Magnus muttered. This brought a reluctant smile to everyone's lips, including those of the dwarf, who clearly had not meant it as a joke but gave in just the same.

"Where are you from—Magnus, is it?" Wyatt asked. "Is there a land of dwarves?"

The dwarf's smile faded. "Not anymore." He clearly meant that to be the end of it, but Wyatt continued to stare and now Mauvin and Elden were doing likewise. "From up north—the mountains of Trent."

"Is it nice there?"

"It's a ghetto—dirty, cramped, and hopeless, like every place they let dwarves live. Satisfied?"

Wyatt regretted saying anything. An awkward silence followed until the tension was broken by a pounding at the door and a cheerful shout: "Meal is ready!"

❧

The knock came to their door announcing supper and Hadrian and Myron were first on their feet. Royce, who sat on a stiff wooden chair in the corner by the window, did not stir. His back was to them as he stared out at the dark. Perhaps his elven eyes could see more than the blackness of the glassy pane, perhaps he was watching people moving below, or the windows of the shops across the street, but Hadrian doubted he was even aware of the window itself.

Royce had not said a word since they had left Aquesta. When he bothered, he communicated in nods. Royce was always quiet, but this was unusual even for him. More disturbing than his silence were his eyes. Royce always watched the road, the eaves of the forest, the horizon, always looking, scanning for trouble, but not that day. The thief rode for over nine hours without once looking up. Hadrian could not tell if he stared at the saddle or the ground. Royce might have been asleep except that his hands continually played with the ends of the reins, twisting them with such force that Hadrian could hear the leather cry.

"Hadrian, fetch me a plate of whatever they are handing out down there," Degan told him as he lay on his bed, staring up at the ceiling.

Upon first entering the room, Gaunt had immediately claimed the bed nearest the fireplace. He had cast off his houppelande and chaperon, throwing them on the floor. Then he had flung himself on the mattress, where he sprawled, moaning about his aches.

"And make sure it's lean," Gaunt went on. "I don't want a bunch of fat. I want the good stuff. And I'll take dark bread if they have it, the darker the better. And a glass of wine—no, make that a bottle, and be sure it's good stuff, not—"

"Maybe you should come down and pick out what you want. That way there won't be any mistakes."

"Just bring it up. I'm comfortable—can't you see I'm comfortable here? I don't want to mingle with all the local baboons. An emperor needs his privacy. And for Novron's sake, pick up my clothes! You need to hang those up so they can dry properly." He looked quizzical. "Hmm…I suppose that should be *for my ancestor's sake*, now wouldn't it? Perhaps even for *my* sake." He smiled at the thought.

Hadrian rolled his eyes. "Let me rephrase. Get your own food or go hungry."

Gaunt glowered and slapped his mattress so that even Royce looked over. "What bloody good is it having a personal servant if you never do anything for me?"

"I'm not your servant; I'm your…bodyguard," he said with reluctance, the word tasting stale. "How about you, Royce? Can I bring you something?"

Royce didn't bother even to shake his head. Hadrian sighed and headed for the door.

When he descended the stairs, Hadrian found The Laughing Gnome filled to the walls. People packed the common room. Considering their numbers, the crowd was keeping remarkably quiet. Rather than being filled with a roar of conversation and laughter, the room barely buzzed with a low hum of whispers. All heads turned expectantly when he and Myron emerged from the steps. That was followed quickly by signs of disappointment.

"Right this way, gentlemen," Ayers called, pushing forward. "Clear a path! Clear a path!"

Hadrian caught a few muttered *false knight* and *joust champion* comments as Ayers escorted them from the bottom of the stairs around to a large table set up in a private room.

"I'm keeping them out so you can eat in peace," Ayers told

them. "But I can't kick them out of the inn altogether. I have to live in this town, and I'd never hear the end of it."

Wyatt, Mauvin, Magnus, and Alric already sat at the table with empty plates before them. Jimmy, dressed now in a stained apron, rushed about filling cups. He held a pitcher in each hand and danced around the table like a carnival juggler. The room was a small space adjacent to the kitchen. Fieldstone made up half of the wall, along with the corner fireplace. Thick milled timbers and plaster formed the upper portion. The room's three windows remained shuttered and latched.

"Are they all here to see *us*?" Myron asked. He paused at the doorway, looking back at the crowd, mirroring their expressions of awe.

Hadrian had just taken a seat when a cheer exploded beyond the closed door in the common room. Alric drained his glass and held it up to Jimmy, shaking it.

"Are you all right? Where have you been?" voices, muffled by the wooden door, called out in the common room. "Were you kidnapped? Will you resume your office? We missed you. Will you drive out the empire again?"

"Forgive me, dear people, but I have traveled long today," Arista said from the other room. "I am very tired and cannot hope to answer all your questions. Just know this: the tyrants that once controlled the empire are gone. The empress now— and for the first time—rules, and she is good and wise."

"You met her?"

"I have. I lived with her for a time and have just come from Aquesta. Evil men held her prisoner in her own palace and ruled in her name. But...she rose up against her captors. She saved my life. She saved the world from a false imperium. Now she is in the process of building the true successor to the Empire of Novron. Show her the trust you have given me, and

I promise you will not be disappointed. Now, if you will allow me, I am very hungry."

Cheering. Applause.

The door opened and Arista stepped inside, then closed it behind her and leaned on it as if she were barricading it with her body. "Where'd they all come from?"

"Word spread," Ayers replied, looking self-conscious. "I need to get back to the bar. I can't leave the mob too long without refreshment."

As Ayers exited, Hadrian spotted Mince standing with the other boys just outside the doorway. Hadrian waved them in. All five entered the dining room in single file and stood just inside—afraid to move farther.

"They came to our room and told us there was food down here, sir," Renwick said to Hadrian. "But we don't know where to go."

"Take a seat at the table," Hadrian replied.

All the boys reacted with the same shocked expression, a mixture of fear and wonder.

"Oh, we aren't going to have the servants eat with us," Alric said, causing the boys to halt.

"There are enough chairs," Arista pointed out.

"But honestly, stableboys? Look at them. They're not just servants; they're children. There must be somewhere else they can eat."

"Actually, if I may…" Hadrian spoke loudly, stood up, and grabbed a hold of Mince, who was attempting to worm his way out of the room. "These young men here," Hadrian said, pointing to Elbright, Kine, and Brand, "assisted in rousing the people of Aquesta to open the gates for you and your army. And Renwick"—Hadrian pointed at the oldest—"was a tremendous help to me as my squire during the time I pretended to be a knight."

"Still am, sir. I don't care what they say."

Hadrian smiled at him. "He also fought in the palace court-yard and was one of the first into the dungeon, if you recall. And this young man here," he said, holding the squirming boy with both hands, "is Mince. This *child*, as you call him, has been singled out by the empress herself as being instrumental in the overthrow of Ethelred and Saldur. Without them, it is very likely that your sister, Royce, I, and even the empress would all be dead. Oh, and of course, so would you and Mauvin. Not bad for a stableboy. So for all that they have done, don't you think they deserve a place at our table?"

"Yes, yes, of course, of course," Alric said quickly, looking a bit ashamed.

"Sit down," Hadrian told them, and they each took a seat, smiles across their faces.

A rotund woman with short, ratty hair and saddlebag cheeks backed into the room from the kitchen, carrying a deep tray of spit-roasted lamb. She wore a gray wool dress and yet another grease-stained apron.

She approached the table and stopped abruptly, looking at the diners with a disappointed—even irritated—expression. "Missing three," she said, her high voice reminding Hadrian of a squeaking door.

"I'll bring a plate up for Royce. He's…he's not feeling well," Hadrian explained.

Arista glanced at him. "Is it okay to leave him alone?"

Hadrian nodded. "I think so. Besides, if he wanted to do something, who's going to stop him?"

"Elden will also be staying in his room," Wyatt mentioned. "He has a thing about crowds."

The cook nodded. Her large breasts, outlined by the apron, hung over the edge of the pan, threatening to nudge the steam-ing lamb. No one else spoke. Finally she asked, "And where's that scoundrel Degan Gaunt? I can't imagine him turning down a free meal."

"Scoundrel?" Hadrian said, surprised. "I thought he was a hero here in Ratibor."

"Hero?"

He nodded. "Yeah, you know. Local boy who went off to seek his fortune, became a pirate, and returned to lead the liberation movement."

The cook laughed, though it was more like a cackle that juggled its way out of her round throat. She put down the tray and began cutting the meat.

Everyone at the table exchanged glances.

Wyatt shrugged. "I don't know his background, but Gaunt was no pirate. That I do know."

Again, the cook cackled and this time put a hand to her lips, which turned the laughter inward and caused her shoulders and chest to bounce.

"Are you going to let us in on the joke?" Alric asked.

"Oh, well, it's not my place to be spreading rumors, now is it?" she said, and followed the statement by making a show of biting her lower lip. Her hands slowed in their work and then stopped. She looked up and a huge grin pushed the saddlebags apart.

"Okay, so it's this way," she said, lowering her voice. "I grew up only a few doors down from Gaunt—right there on Degan Street. Did you know that his mother named him Degan because it was the only word she knew how to spell, having seen the street sign for so many years?"

Now that her mouth was going, so were her hands, and she sliced portions and delivered them to their plates, heedless of the little trails of grease she left. "Anywho, his mother and mine were close and I used to be best friends with his sister, Miranda. She was a joy, but Degan—well, even as a boy he was a demon.

We stayed clear of him when we could. He was a pitiful little wretch. He got caught stealing dozens of times, and not because of need. I mean, I don't agree with theft, but pinching a loaf of bread from Briklin's Bakery when the old man has his back turned to surprise your mother with on Wintertide is one thing. I ain't saying it is right, but I overlook something like that.

"Well, as for Degan, he goes in for stuff like smashing the window on the curio shop so he can have a porcelain rabbit he had his eye on. Thing is, everyone knows he's a no-good. You can see it in the way shopkeepers watch him or shoo him out the door. They can spot the likes of him a mile away."

Just then, Ayers barged in. "Jimmy, get to the cellar and roll out another keg. They've already drained the one we pulled up earlier." The boy put down his pitchers and ran toward the kitchen. Ayers stared at the cook. "You're not bothering these folks, are you, Bella? Is she bothering any of you?"

"Not at all," Arista replied, and all the heads at the table nodded in agreement.

"Well, keep it that way. She has a way of yammering, she does."

Bella blinked her eyes innocently.

Jimmy appeared, rolling a barrel from the kitchen.

"How many we got left?" the innkeeper asked.

"Four."

Ayers frowned. "I shoulda ordered more, but who knew…" He pointed at the diners and shrugged. Ayers took control of the barrel and returned to the tavern. Bella waited a moment, staring at the door. Then a grin filled her face and she went on.

"Now, just ta give you an idea about how bad things got for ole Degan, he even received a visit from the BD telling him to cut it out. Course he don't and yet somehow managed to avoid punishment. Miranda and I used to talk about how that boy was charmed. But after his mother's death, he got into

some *real* trouble. Now, I wasn't there to see it, but rumor is—
and it sure seemed like the kinda thing that idiot would do—
he got drunk and raped Clara, the candle maker's daughter.
Well, her old man had connections. Not only was he a favorite
merchant to the royal chamberlain, but his nephew was in
the BD."

"BD?" Myron asked. "I don't understand."

"BD—Black Diamond," Mauvin told him.

Myron still looked confused.

"Not a lot of literature on them," Hadrian said. "The Black
Diamond is a very powerful thieves' guild. They control all
the illegal activity in a city, just like a potters' guild controls
the pottery market."

The monk nodded. The cook was standing still again,
holding a lamb chop between two greasy, stubby fingers, waiting, as if her body could not move unless her mouth was.

"I'm sorry, please continue," Myron said. "This is a wonderful story."

"Well now," she went on, dumping the chop onto Myron's
plate so roughly and off center that it nearly flipped over. "I
remember there were patrols combing the streets for him.
They was angry too, shouting that they was gonna hang him,
only they never found ole Degan. Turns out that a press-gang
near the docks caught him that very night. They didn't know
who he was. They just needed hands for a ship and hauled him
off to sea. Like I said, the man is charmed.

"Okay, so this next part I know from reliable folk. Some
years later, the ship he was on was attacked by pirates. They
done killed the whole crew but somehow ole Degan survived.
Who knows how he done it? He probably convinced them
pirates he knew where a treasure was buried er sumptin. Anywho, he gets away. Some folks say a storm wrecked the pirate
ship, and again he's the lone survivor. That seems a mite bit

lucky for anyone, but for Degan it doesn't seem so strange. So he ends up in Delgos and gets into trouble again. He's back to his old tricks, this time stealing from the merchant families at the border villages. He's going to be executed for sure this time, but then he spins his greatest tale.

"He says he was only taking the money to finance his dream of freeing the common man from the boot of the aristocracy. Can you believe it? Degan Gaunt, a man of the people? Well, that kinda talk plays real well down that way. Those folks on the peninsula hate the monarchies. They swallow it and, what do you know, not only do they let him go—they give him money for his cause! Well, this just tickles Degan, as you could imagine, and he decides to keep the thing going. He travels all over, giving speeches and getting donations. I heard him once when he was preaching his spiel in Colnora. He was actually pretty good at it—all shouts for liberty and freedom, banging his fist on a podium and working up a sweat. Then a'course he passes the hat. But then—" She stopped talking as she struggled to free a troublesome lamb chop from the rest.

"But then?" Alric asked.

"Oh, sorry," she said. "Somehow he goes from being this traveling sideshow to actually running an army—and a successful one at that! That's just strange. It's one thing to be—"

The crowd outside the door began clapping, and a moment later the door to the dining room opened and Degan stepped inside. He had a disapproving sneer on his face.

"You started serving without me?"

No one answered and the cook puckered her lips, continuing to dish out the meal in silence. Degan took a seat and waited impatiently for his plate. Everyone stared at him until he glared back, irritated. "What?"

"This is very good." Wyatt spoke up, pointing to the lamb on his plate.

"Thank you," the cook replied.

"If it is, it will be the first time this place has served anything eatable," Gaunt muttered. "Hurry up, woman!"

The cook, who stood behind him, made a *see what I mean?* face and dropped a chop on his plate.

"What time will you folks be getting up?" the cook asked. "You'll be wanting breakfast, won't you?"

"We'll be leaving early," Arista said. She caught a look from her brother. "Isn't that right, Alric?" she added.

"Yes, yes, ah—dawn, I should think," he said. "Breakfast should be before that. Something hot, I hope."

"Seeing the business you're bringing him, old Ayers would pay to poach venison if you wanted it. Course he ain't gonna be too pleased you're leaving tomorrow. I'm sure he's hoping you'll be here a week at least."

"We're in a hurry," Arista explained.

Bella looked as if she might say more when the common room door opened again. "Bella, quit bugging them. I don't pay you to chatter. I have orders for food. I need five stews and a plowman's meal."

"All right, all right!" she bellowed back. She turned to the diners and, with an awkward curtsy, rushed off to the kitchen.

◁৯

The room was dark except for the moonlight that entered through the window and the glow of hot coals in the fireplace. Outside, the wind blew snow against the building. Royce could hear the muffled sounds of voices rising through the floorboards as everyone ate dinner. The shift of furniture, the clink of glasses—he had heard it all before.

Royce's eyes focused on the street corner outside. He could see the start of the alley between Ingersol's Leather Shop and a silversmith. It was right there—on that very corner, that exact spot.

"That's where I came from." Royce spoke to the empty room, his words condensing on the window's glass, making a tiny fog.

He remembered nights like this—cold, windy nights when it was hard to get to sleep. Most nights he had slept in a barrel packed with straw, but when it was really cold—the kind of cold that killed—he had climbed into barns and squeezed between sheep and cattle. Doing so was dangerous. Farmers listened to their animals, and if they found intruders, they assumed they were stealing.

Royce had been only eight, maybe ten years old. He had been freezing, his feet and hands numb, his cheeks burning. It was late and he had crawled into the stable on Legends Avenue. The rear stall was blocked off into a makeshift manger for four sheep. They lay curled up as one big wooly bed, their sides rising and falling like breathing pillows. Royce carefully crawled into the middle, feeling their body heat and the soft wool. They bleated at his intrusion, but given the size of the stall, they suffered his presence. In just a few minutes he fell asleep.

He woke to a farmer with a pitchfork. The farmer jabbed and nearly got Royce in the stomach. Royce rolled, taking the tongs in his shoulder. He screamed and scattered the sheep, which bounced off the walls. In the confusion, Royce escaped into the snow. The hour was late. It was still dark, and blood ran down his arm. He had not yet discovered the sewers and had no place to go. He returned to the barrel on the corner and climbed in, pulling as much straw over him as he could.

Royce remembered hearing "Ladies of Engenall" played on a fiddle from inside the Gnome. He listened to them all night: people singing, laughing, clinking glasses—all warm, safe, and happy while outside he shivered and cried. His shoulder screamed in pain. The rags he wore hardened as the blood froze. Then it started to snow. He felt the flakes on his face and thought he would die that night. He was so certain that he prayed, and that was the first and last time he had ever asked the gods for help. The memory was so vivid he could almost smell the straw. He recalled lying there shivering, his eyes shut tight as he had whispered aloud to Novron, asking to be saved. He pleaded, reminding the god that he was only a child—a boy—only he knew that was a lie. He was not a boy—boys were human.

Royce was not human—not entirely. He was a *mir*, a half-breed, a mongrel.

He knew Novron would not help him. Novron and his father, Maribor, were the gods of men. Why would they listen to the words of an elf, a hated cur whose own parents had thrown him away as trash? Still, he begged for his life anyway. Because he did not look like an elf, the young Royce reasoned that maybe Novron would not notice.

Right down there, on that corner, Royce had begged to live.

He traced a circle on the window with his finger.

He always remembered it as the worst night of his life—he had been alone, terrified, dying. And he had been so happy the next morning when he was still alive. Starved, shaking from the cold, stiff from sleeping in a ball, shoulder throbbing, but as happy as a person could be.

Here I am, warm and comfortable in The Laughing Gnome, and I'd give anything to be in that barrel again.

A board creaked and Myron entered quietly. He hesitated at the door, then slowly crossed the room toward Royce and sat down on the bed near him.

"I used to sit for hours too," the monk said, his voice soft, just a tad above a whisper. "I used to remember things… times and places, both good and bad. I would see something that reminded me of my past and wish I could go back. I wished I could be the way I used to be, even if that meant pain. Only I could never find my way around the wall. Do you know what I mean by *the wall*?"

Royce refused to answer. Myron did not seem to mind.

"After the burning of the abbey, I never felt whole again. Half of me was missing—gone—more than half. What was left was lost, like I didn't know where I was or how to get back."

Royce stared. He was breathing faster without knowing why.

"I tried to find a way to go on. I could see familiar traces of the path that was my life, but there was always the wall behind me. Do you know what I mean? First you try and climb, pretending it never happened, but it's too tall. Then you try to go around, thinking you can fix it, but it is too far. Then, in frustration, you beat on it with your hands, but it does nothing, so you tire and sit down and just stare at it. You stare because you can't bring yourself to walk away. Walking away means that you're giving up, abandoning them.

"There is no way back. There is only forward. It's impossible to imagine there's any reason to move ahead, but that isn't the real reason you give up. The real fear—the terror that keeps you rooted—is that you might be wrong."

Royce reeled. It was as if Myron were rifling through his heart, opening sealed closets and exploring locked drawers. Royce gave Myron a withering look. If he were a dog, Royce would be growling, yet Myron seemed not to notice.

The little monk went on.

"Instead of passion, you have regret. In place of effort, you are mired in memory. You sink in nothingness and your heart drowns in despair. At times—usually at night—it's a physical pain, both sharp and dull. The anguish is unbearable."

Royce reached out and grabbed Myron by the wrist. He wanted him to stop—needed him to stop.

"You feel you have no choices. Your love for those who have gone makes you hold tight to their memory and the pain of their loss. You feel to do anything else would be disloyal to them," Myron went on, placing his free hand on top of Royce's and patting it gently.

"While the idea of leaving is at first impossible to contemplate, the question you need to ask is, how would they feel knowing that you are torturing yourself because of them? Is this what they would want? Is that what you would want them to do if the situation was reversed? If you love them, you need to let go of your pain and live your life. To do otherwise is a selfish cruelty."

Hadrian opened the door and nearly dropped the plate of lamb. He stepped in hesitantly. "Everything all right here?" he asked.

"Get him away from me, before I kill him," Royce growled between gritted teeth, his voice unsteady, his eyes hard.

"You can't kill Myron, Royce," Hadrian said, rapidly pulling the monk away as if he had found a child playing with a wild bear. "It would be like killing a puppy."

Royce did not want to kill Myron. He honestly did not know what he wanted, except for him to stop. Everything the monk had said hurt, because it was all true. The monk's words were not close. They were not worrisomely accurate. What he said was dead-on, as if he were reading Royce's mind and speaking his innermost thoughts aloud—holding his terrors to the light and exposing them.

"Are you all right, Royce?" Hadrian asked, still holding Myron close. His tone was cautious, nervous.

"He'll be fine," Myron replied for him.

∽

The five boys and Myron had left the dinner table, followed shortly by Hadrian and Wyatt, who took plates up to Royce and Elden respectively. Alric, who had eaten his fill, loosened his belt but made no move to leave. He sat back, smiling, as Ayers brought out another bottle of wine and set it on the table before them. For the first time since they had started this trip, Alric was feeling good. This was more like it. He could see the same expression in Mauvin's eyes. This was the dream of their youth: riding hard, exploring, seeing strange new sights, and in the evening settling in at a local inn for a fine meal and a night of drinking, laughing, and singing. At last, the carefree days of his boyhood—once stolen—now returned. This was an adventure at last. This was a man's aspiration, a chance to live life to the fullest.

"My finest stock," Ayers told them with pride.

"That's awfully kind of you," Arista said. "But we need to be getting up early tomorrow."

"It's not polite to insult a host like that, Arista," Alric said, feeling her hands trying to strangle his dream.

"I didn't—Alric, you can't stay up all night drinking and expect to get an early start in the morning."

He frowned at her. This was why she had never been included in his and Mauvin's plans. "The man wants to honor us, all right? If you're tired, go to bed and leave us be."

Arista huffed loudly and threw her napkin on the table before walking out.

"Your sister isn't pleased with you," Gaunt observed.

"Are you just discovering that now?" Alric replied.

"Shall I open it?" Ayers asked.

"I don't know," Alric muttered.

"It would be best to do as she tells you," Gaunt said.

"What's that?"

"I only meant her being in charge and all. You don't want to become the nail sticking out. I can see why you're afraid of her and I sympathize, believe me. You saw the way she treated me when we left—but what can we do? She holds all the power."

"She's not in charge," Alric growled. "I am." He looked at Ayers. "Open that bottle, my good man, and pour liberally."

Gaunt smiled. "I guess I misjudged you, Your Majesty. I've actually been doing too much of that. Take Magnus here, for example."

Alric preferred not to. The idea that he had just finished a meal with—and was about to drink at the same table with—his father's killer sickened him.

"I was offended that I had to ride with a dwarf, but it turns out he's not a bad companion. True, he's not exactly a big talker, but he's interesting just the same. Did you know he's held here by the hairs of his beard—literally? He's another member of our exclusive club who your sister controls and forces to do her bidding."

"My sister doesn't control me," Alric snapped.

"And you had best watch your tongue, my friend," Mauvin advised Gaunt. "You are treading on dangerous ground."

"My apologies. Perhaps I am mistaken. Please forgive me. It's just that I've never seen a woman lead a mission like this before. It's shocking to me, but then again, you come from the north, and I come from the south, where women are expected to stay behind while their men go off to fight. Allow me to toast her." He raised his glass. "To the princess Arista, our lovely leader."

"I told you, she's not in charge. I am," Alric said with more force.

Gaunt smiled and raised his other hand defensively. "I meant no offense." He raised his glass again. "To you, then, to King Alric, the true leader of this mission."

"Hear! Hear!" Alric joined him and drank.

Chapter 8

Amberton Lee

*P*eople were singing in the streets. They danced and it did not seem to matter with whom. Streamers flew through the air and explosions of light illuminated the sky like magic. Bands played and every face reflected their joy. The doors to all the shops were open, their wares free to the people on the street—free bread, free cakes, free meats, free drinks. People took whatever they liked and the owners smiled and waved.

"Good Founding!" they shouted to each other. "Good Founding to you! May Novron bless his home and people!"

She felt disturbed at this, although she did not know why. Something was wrong. She looked at the faces. They did not know.

Know what? she wondered. She had to hurry. Time was running out. Running out? What is going to happen?

She had to move, but not too quickly. It was important not to give them cause for suspicion. She must get to the rendezvous. She squeezed the necklaces in her hand. Working the spell had taken all night. There was not even time to say goodbye to Elinya and that broke her heart.

As she hurried along, she knew she would never see Elinya again. Turning onto the Grand Mar, she saw the imperial

*guards waiting in the eaves. Each group was led by a Teshlor
knight. The three swords the knights carried marked them as
surely as their imperial armor did. Heroes of the realm, the
protectors of the emperor—assassins all.*

She had to find Nevrik and Jerish.

*Pausing at the Column of Destone, she turned. The palace
was straight ahead, not more than another half mile. She
could see the great golden dome. Emperor Nareion and his
family were there. Her heart pounded, and her breath came in
short gasps. She could go. She could face them. She could
fight. They would not expect that and she could get the first
incantation. She would blow the whole miserable palace
apart and let the glass and stone rip through the bleeding bastards. But she knew it would not be enough. This would not
stop them, but she would kill a few and hurt many others.
Not Venlin, though, and not Yolric. They would kill her—
maybe not Yolric, but Venlin certainly. Venlin would not hesitate. She would be dead, the imperial family would follow,
and Nevrik and Jerish would be lost.*

*No, she needed to sacrifice the father for the son. It was the
emperor's wish, his order. The line must endure at all costs.
The line must survive.*

*She turned and ran down Ebonydale, weaving her fingers,
masking her movement. She had to get the necklaces to them.
Then they could hide. The empire would be safe—at least
one small piece. Once the amulets were safely around their
necks and they were on their way, she would turn back. And
Maribor help the traitors then, for she was done hiding. They
would see the power of a Cenzar unleashed, unrestrained by
edict. She would destroy the entire city if she needed to. Lay it
all to waste. Bury it deep beneath the earth and let them
spend eternity picking through the rubble.*

For now, though, she had to hurry. It was time to go.

Time to go.

Time to—

Arista woke up.

It was dark, but as always, the robe was glowing faintly, revealing the small, sparse room. She felt as if she had fallen from one world to another. She was in a hurry to do something, but that was only a dream. Out the window, she could just make out the first hints of morning light. Slowly she remembered she was in The Laughing Gnome in Ratibor. She kicked off the blankets and reached out with her toes, looking for her boots. The fire was out and the room was cold. Touching the floorboards was like standing on ice.

In just a few moments, she was moving up the corridor, knocking on doors, hearing people groan from behind them. Downstairs, the crowd from the night before was gone; the common room looked like a storm had passed through. Bella was up and Arista smelled leftover lamb and onions. The rest staggered down groggily, wavering as they wiped their eyes. Mauvin's hair was worse than ever, as several locks stood up on one side. Magnus could not stop yawning, and Alric kept dragging his hands over his face as if trying to remove a veil. Only Myron appeared alert, as if he had been up for some time.

While they ate, Ayers ordered Jimmy into the cold to saddle the animals. Hadrian and Mauvin took pity on the boy, and along with the other boys, they all went out to help him. By the time the sun breached the horizon, they were ready to leave.

"Arista?" Alric stopped her as she headed for the door. They were alone in the common room, standing beside the bar, where a dozen mugs reeked of stale beer. "I would appreciate it if you were a little less quick to give orders in my presence. I am king, after all."

"What did I... Are you mad that I woke everyone up?"

"Well, yes—to be honest—I am. That and everything else you've done. You are constantly undermining my authority. You make me…well, you make me look weak and I want you to stop."

"All I did was get people out of bed so we could get an early start. If you were up pounding on doors, I wouldn't have to. I told you that staying up late wasn't a good idea, but you didn't listen. Or would you rather we had waited until noon?"

"Of course not, and I'm glad you got everyone up, but…"

"But what?"

"It's just that you are always doing that, always taking command."

"Seems to me I wanted to ride on to Amberton Lee yesterday, but you ordered us here. Did I argue?"

"You started to. If I hadn't ridden off, we'd still be debating it."

Arista rolled her eyes. "What do you want me to do, Alric, not talk anymore? You want me to crawl in with the rest of the supplies in the sled and pretend I'm not here?"

"That's just it. You—you insert yourself into everything. You shouldn't be here at all. This is no place for a woman."

"You may be king, but this is *my* mission. Modina didn't assign this task to me. I went to her to explain where I was going. This was my idea—my responsibility. I would have gone even if no one else did, even if Modina forbade me. And let me remind you that unless we succeed, you won't be king of anything."

Alric's face was red, his cheeks full, his eyes angry.

"Lovers' quarrel?" Mauvin asked, walking in with a smile. When neither replied, he dropped the expression. "Okay— never mind. I just forgot my gloves—but, ah…the horses are ready." He picked the gloves up off a table and quickly slipped back out.

"Listen," Arista said in a quieter tone. "I'm sorry, okay? I'll try to be more of a *lady* if you want, and I'll let you lead." She gestured outside. "They would probably prefer taking orders from a man, anyway."

There was a long pause and she said, "Still hate me?"

Alric wore a nasty look on his face, but the storm had passed. "Let's go. People are waiting."

He walked past her and Arista sighed and followed him.

⚜

By midmorning, they found the ancient road. Royce seemed better and rode with Hadrian at the head of the column, guiding them along narrow trails, paths, and even frozen rivers. Alric took his position right behind them. Arista stayed back. She rode with Myron once more, this time just behind the wagon. They left the farmlands and entered an unclaimed wilderness of fields and thickets. Not long after reaching the woods, they came upon a broad avenue. It did not look the same as when Arista had ridden on it with Etcher. The snow hid the paving stones and weeds. Arista stopped Princess broadside in the avenue and looked up and down its length. "Straight as a maypole," she muttered.

The monk looked at her.

"This is it," she told him. "The road to Percepliquis. Under this snow are stones laid thousands of years ago by order of Novron."

Myron looked down. "It's nice," he replied politely.

They followed the tracks left by the sled ahead of them. There was silence as they rode through the trees. Here the snow was a soft powder and muffled everything, the sound of the horses and sled smothered to a whisper.

Once more, they traveled without much comment. Not

long after they had started up the road, Magnus brought up the subject of lunch, and she was pleased to hear Alric say they would eat when they reached the Lee. The sun had passed overhead and shadows were forming on the other side of the trees when they began climbing a steep hill. As they cleared the gray fingers of the forest, Arista saw the snow-crowned summit ahead. On it were broken shapes of cut stone, ruins of a great city poking up through the surface. Ancient walls buried now in earth and snow caught the pale light of a late-winter afternoon.

It is a grave, she thought, and wondered how she could have missed this before. A sense of sadness and loss radiated from the mounds now that she understood what she was seeing. Pillars lay half buried in the hillside, mammoth headstones of a giant's graveyard; broken steps of marble and walls of stone lay crumbled. Only one tree stood upon the hill—it appeared dead but, like the rest of the ruins, still stood long after its time. The strange shapes rose from the earth, casting blue shadows. The scene was beautiful—beautiful but sad, in the way a lake can still be beautiful even when frozen.

Royce raised a hand for them to stop when they reached the base of the open hillside. He dismounted and went ahead on foot. They all waited, listening to the jangle of the bridles as the horses shook their heads, unhappy with the interruption.

When he returned, he spoke briefly with Hadrian and Alric. Arista's brother glanced back at her as if he might say something or call her up to ask advice. He looked away and the party moved on once more. Arista fought the urge to trot ahead and inquire about what was happening. It was frustrating to sit in the dark, sentenced to the corner like a naughty child, but it was important for Alric to hold the reins. She squeezed her hands into fists. She loved her brother, but she did not trust him to make the right decisions.

Hadrian is up there with him, she thought. *He won't let him do anything stupid.* Thank Maribor she had Hadrian with her. He was the only one in the party she felt she could rely on, the only one she could lean on without fear of breaking or offending. Just looking at the back of him as he bounced on his horse was comforting.

They climbed to the summit and dismounted.

"We'll have lunch," Alric announced. "Myron, come up here, will you?"

Royce, Alric, and Myron spoke together for several minutes while Arista sat on some stone, absently eating strips of smoked beef and exhausting her jaws in the attempt. Ibis had sent full meals, but she was in no mood. The chewing gave her something to do besides walking over there.

She turned away to see Elden staring at her. He looked away bashfully, pretending to search in his pack for something.

"Don't mind him, my lady," Wyatt said. "Or should I address you as Your Highness?"

"You can call me Arista," she said, and watched his eyes widen.

"Seriously?"

She nodded. "Of course."

He shrugged. "Okay, then, *Arista*." He spoke the word gingerly. "Elden here, he doesn't get out much, and when he has, it's been on board ships where there aren't any women. I suspect you're the first lady he's seen up close in—well, as long as I've known him. And I'm sure you're the only noblewoman he's ever seen."

She touched her matted hair and the robe that hung on her like a smock. "Not a very good example, I'm afraid. I'm not exactly Lady Lenare Pickering, am I? I'm not even the best-looking princess here. My horse takes that title. Her name is Princess." She smiled.

Wyatt looked at her, puzzled. "You sure don't speak like a noblewoman. I mean, you do—but you don't."

"That's very coherent, Mr. Deminthal."

"There, you see? Those are the words of a princess—putting me in my place with eloquence and grace."

"As well she should," Hadrian said, appearing beside her. "Do I need to keep an eye on you?" he asked Wyatt.

"I thought you were *his* bodyguard." He pointed at Gaunt, who remained on the wagon with the dwarf, their lunches resting on the bench between them.

"You'd think that, wouldn't you?"

"What did Royce find?" Arista asked.

"Tracks, but they're old."

"What kind of tracks?"

"Ghazel—probably a scouting party. Looks like King Fredrick was right about *the flood*. But we are still a ways from Vilan Hills. I'm surprised they are scouting out this far."

She nodded thoughtfully. "And Alric has Myron and Royce trying to find the entrance?"

"Yep, they're looking for a river. Hall's book tells of a river flowing into a hole."

"What about the tracks?"

"What about them?"

"Have you followed them?"

"They're too old to be a threat. Royce guesses they were made more than a week ago."

"Maybe they aren't from Vilan Hills. The Patriarch said Ghazel were in Percepliquis. Follow the tracks...They might lead to the entrance. And get Magnus off the wagon. Isn't he supposed to be an expert at finding underground passages?"

Hadrian stared at her stupidly. "You're absolutely right." He started to return to the others.

"Hadrian?" She stopped him.

"Yeah?"

"Don't tell Alric I said anything. Say it was your idea."

He looked confused for a second, then said, "Oh—right." He nodded with sympathy. Hadrian started to climb the hill, then waved at Wyatt. "Com'on, sailor, you can help look too."

"But I'm still—"

Hadrian gave him a smirk.

"Okay, okay. Excuse me, my lady—ah—Arista."

The two climbed to the top of the hill and disappeared over the rise. Elden came over and sat beside her. He reached into his pocket and withdrew a small bit of wood, holding it out in his huge palm. It was a figurine, deftly carved in the shape of a woman. She took it and, upon closer inspection, realized it was her. The detail was perfect, right down to her messy hair and Esrahaddon's robe.

"For you," she heard him whisper.

"It's beautiful, thank you."

Elden nodded; then, standing up slowly, he moved off to sit by himself.

Arista held the statuette in her fingers, wondering when he had found time to make it. She tried to determine whether he had whittled in the saddle or carved it the night before while the rest of them were eating dinner.

Myron left the top of the hill and Arista waved him over.

"So what does Mr. Hall have to say about how he got in?"

Myron smiled comically. "Not a lot that is of much help. Although, he did have some nice diagrams that showed the ruins, so we are in the right place. As for getting in, all he said was that he went into a hole. From his accounts, it was really deep. He started climbing down and fell. A nasty fall by the sound of it too. His handwriting afterwards was shaky and he only bothered to write short sentences: *Fell in a hole. No way out. The pile! They eat everything! Cyclone of darkness. River running. Stars. Millions. Crawling, crawling, crawling. They eat everything.*"

Arista sneered. "Doesn't sound all that pleasant, does it?"

"It gets worse," he said. "Down near the underground sea, just before he reached the city, he encountered the Ba Ran Ghazel, but that wasn't the worst of it. He actually made it to the great library when—"

A whistle sounded.

"Found it!" Alric shouted.

⁊

The hole was not on the summit of the hill.

Hadrian had watched as Magnus and Royce had located the passage, each coming at it from a different direction. Royce traced Ghazel tracks and Magnus followed what he called the sound of an underground hollow. They came together down the back side of the slope, where the angle grew steep and danger-ous. A patch of trees and thick thorny brambles wreathed what appeared to be a minor depression. The only clue that some-thing more lurked there was the faint echo of falling water.

"Looks slippery," Mauvin said as they all gathered on the icy ridge above. "Who's going first?"

Before anyone could answer, Royce appeared carrying a heavy coil of rope, wearing his climbing harness and slipping on his hand-claws—brass wraps with sharpened hooks that jutted out of his palms. Hadrian helped him get situated; then Royce lay on his stomach and inched along, leaving a trough in the soft snow as he eased off the ridge.

As he started down the slope, Royce began to slide. He tried to get a grip, but his hands and claws found only snow. He picked up speed like a sled and Hadrian worked at taking up the slack in the rope. Then Royce crashed through the thickets and disappeared from view. Mauvin joined Hadrian on the rope, which was now as taut as a bowstring.

"Get the end," Hadrian ordered. "Tie it to that tree."

Magnus moved to grab the line.

"No, not you!" Hadrian shouted, and the dwarf scowled. Hadrian looked to the next-closest person. "Wyatt, could you tie the end off?"

The sailor grabbed the end of the rope and dragged it around the base of the little birch.

"How ya doing, Royce?" Hadrian called.

"Dangling," Royce replied. "Pretty slick up there. Give me some slack."

They stood in a circle, each keeping a safe distance, all of them standing on their toes, trying to see down. Overhead, the winter clouds made it hard to tell the time. There was no sun, just a vague gray light that filled the sky, leaving everything murky and drained of color. Hadrian guessed they had only four hours of light left.

Mauvin and Hadrian let out the rope until it hung from the tree, although Hadrian continued to hold on to it just the same. He could not see Royce and stared instead at the thin rope. It too was mostly lost, buried in the snow, leaving only a telltale mark.

"Can you reach the bottom?"

"How much rope do we have?" Royce's voice returned like an echo from the bottom of a well.

Hadrian looked at Arista.

"Ten coils of fifty feet each," she replied. "All told, there should be five hundred feet's worth," she shouted, tilting her head up a bit as if throwing her voice into the hole.

"Not half good enough," Royce replied.

"That's a deep hole," Hadrian said.

The rope shifted and twisted at the edge.

"What're you doing, buddy?"

"Trying something."

"Something stupid?"

"Maybe." He sounded winded.

The rope stopped moving and went slack.

"Royce?" Hadrian called.

No answer.

"Royce?"

"Relax," came his reply. "This might work. I'm on a ledge, big enough for all of us, I think. Icy, but doable. We can tie on here too. Looks like we'll have to work our way a leg at a time. Might as well start sending down the gear."

They brought up the wagon and began lowering supplies, each package disappearing through the opening in the brush.

"I'll go first," Alric announced when the wagon was empty.

Hadrian and Mauvin tied the safety rope around his waist and legs. Once tethered, the king took hold of the guide rope and, sitting down on the snow, scooted forward. Mauvin and Hadrian were careful this time to let out the rope slowly, and soon Alric reached the thickets and peered through.

"Oh dear Maribor!" Alric exclaimed. "You have me, right?" he shouted back at them.

"You're not going anywhere until you want to," Mauvin replied.

"Oh lord," he repeated several times.

Royce was offering suggestions, but too faintly for Hadrian to hear exactly what they were.

"Okay, okay, here I go," Alric said. He turned himself over and, lying flat on his stomach, started backing into the hole, clutching tightly to the guide rope. "Slowly now," he warned as Mauvin and Hadrian let out the tether, and inch by inch he slipped over the edge and out of view.

"Oh sweet Maribor!" they heard him exclaim.

"You okay?" Hadrian called.

"Are you crazy? Of course I'm not! This is insane."

"Lower him," Royce shouted.

They let out the line until Hadrian felt a tug that he guessed was Royce pulling Alric to the ledge. The rope went slack, Royce shouted the all clear, and they reeled up the empty harness. Feeling it best to send him early so they still had enough people to man the rope, they sent Elden next. He went over the side quietly, although his eyes told a story similar to Alric's.

"Degan, you're next," Hadrian informed him.

"You are joking," Gaunt replied. "You don't expect me to go down there?"

"Kinda why you're here."

"That's insane. What if the rope breaks? What if we can't reach the bottom? What if we can't get back up? I'm not doing this. It's—it's ridiculous!"

Hadrian just stared at him, holding the harness.

"I won't."

"You have to," Arista told him. "I don't know why, but I know the Heir of Novron must accompany us for this trip to be successful. Without you there's no need for any of us to go."

"Then fine, none of us go!"

"If we don't, the elves will kill everyone."

He looked at her and then at the others with a desperate, pleading face. "How do you know this? I mean, how do you know I have to come?"

"Esrahaddon told me."

"That loon?"

"He was a wizard."

"He's dead. If he was so all-knowing, how come he's dead? Huh?"

"Waiting down here," Alric shouted up.

"You have to go," Arista told him.

"And if I refuse?"

"You won't be emperor."

"What good is being emperor if I'm dead?"

No one spoke; they all just looked at him.

Degan slumped his shoulders and grimaced. "How do you put this damn thing on?"

"Put your feet through the loops and buckle it around your waist," Hadrian explained.

After Gaunt and Arista were down, Wyatt took over Hadrian's position on the rope, freeing him to speak with Renwick. "You have supplies to last a week, perhaps more if you conserve," he told him and the other boys as they gathered around. "Take care of the horses and stay off the hilltop. Make camp in that hollow. For your own safety, I'd avoid a fire in the daylight. The smoke will be visible at a distance. It would be best not to attract any uninvited guests."

"We can handle ourselves," Brand declared.

"I'm sure you can, but still it would be best not to wander, and try to keep unnoticed."

"I want to go with you," Renwick said.

"Me too," Mince added.

Hadrian smiled. "You're all very brave."

"Not me," Elbright said. "A man would have to be a royal fool to go into something like that."

"So you're the sensible one," Hadrian told him. "Still, we need all of you to do your job here. Keep the camp, and take care of the horses for us. If we aren't back in a week, I suspect we won't be coming back and it will probably be too late if we do. If you see fire in the north or west, that will likely mean the elves have overrun Aquesta or Ratibor. Your best bet would be to go south. Perhaps try to catch a ship to the Westerlins. Although I have no idea what you'll find there."

"You'll be back," Renwick said confidently.

Hadrian gave the boy a hug, then turned to look at the monk, who was, as usual, with the horses. "Com'on, Myron, it's nearly your turn."

Myron nodded, petting his animal one last time, whispering to it. Hadrian put an arm around him as they walked toward the ridge, where Wyatt and Mauvin were in the process of lowering Magnus.

"What did you say to Royce last night?" Hadrian asked the monk.

"I just spoke with him briefly about loss and coping with it."

"Something you read?"

"Sadly, no."

Hadrian waited for more, but the monk was silent. "Well, whatever it was, it worked. He's—I don't know—alive again. Not singing songs and dancing, of course. If he did that, I suppose I'd worry. But you know, kinda normal, in a Royce sort of way."

"He's not," Myron replied. "And he'll never be the way he was again. There's always a scar."

"Well, I'm just saying the difference is like summer and winter. You should be thanked, even if Royce will never say it. There aren't many who would face him like that. It's like pulling a thorn from a lion's paw. I love Royce, but he *is* dangerous. The life he's lived denied him a proper understanding of right and wrong. He wasn't kidding when he said he might have killed you."

"I know."

"Really?"

Myron nodded. "Of course."

"You didn't even seem worried. What happened to my little naive shut-in who walked in awe of the world? Where did all the wisdom come from?"

Myron looked at him, puzzled. "I'm a monk."

ॐ

Hadrian was the last to enter the hole, lowering himself hand over hand, sliding on his stomach to the edge, where at last he looked over and saw what Alric and the rest already had. An abyss opened below him. From the rim of the bowl, the opening looked small, but it was an illusion. The aperture was huge, an almost perfect circle of irregular rock, like the burrow of some enormous rabbit, and it went straight down. As in the pass, long icicles decorated the upper walls, stretching down from stony cliffs, and snow dusted the crevices.

He could not see the bottom. The setting sun cast an oblique light across the opening and against the far wall, leaving the depths lost to darkness. Far below, so far he would not have ventured an arrow shot, swallows flew, their tiny bodies appearing as insects, highlighted by the sunlight and brilliant against the black maw as they swirled and circled.

A bit light-headed, Hadrian stared down into the space below his feet. His stomach lightened and it took conscious effort to breathe. He got a firm hold of the rope, slipped over the side, and dangled in midair. The sensation was disturbing. Only the thin line separated him from eternity.

"You're doing great," Arista called to him as if she were an old pro now, her voice hollow as it echoed across the mouth of the shaft. He felt Royce pulling him in toward the side. Looking down, he saw all of them crouched on a narrow ledge that was glassy with ice, their gear stacked at one end.

He touched down, feeling hands on his waist pulling him to the safety of the wall.

"That was fun," he joked, only then realizing how fast his heart was racing.

"Yeah, we should do this all the time," Mauvin said, and followed it with a nervous laugh.

"Want us to leave the rope or untie it?" Renwick called down.

"Have him leave it," Royce said. "That lip will be a problem otherwise. From this point on, I'll come last and bring the rope with me. Wyatt, you have the most climbing experience. Why don't you find the next ledge?"

Hadrian could see tension on the sailor's face as they tied on the harness.

The interior of the hole was a wall of stone with many handholds. Hadrian guessed that even he could climb it with little fear if not for the ice and the knowledge that he was hundreds of feet from the ground.

Wyatt found a landing point, a new ledge some ways down, and they began the moving process again. The next ledge was narrower and shorter. There was not enough room for everyone, and Wyatt was forced to move on before all of them were down. Royce brought up the rear, untying the rope, coiling it around his body, and climbing down untethered, using just his claws.

The next two levels Hadrian did not consider ledges at all. They were merely a series of hand- and footholds where only three could pause. As they were forced to cling to the rock without ropes, their gear was left to dangle.

The next ledge was the widest yet, being the width of a country lane, and upon reaching it, several of them collapsed, lying down on their backs, their chests heaving, sweat dripping. Hadrian joined them, yawning to relieve the growing pressure in his ears. When he opened his eyes, he saw a circle of white light above them that was no larger than his thumb held at arm's length. A seemingly solid shaft of light, like a pale gray pillar, beamed down into the hole. Through its luminescent column, the swallows swooped at eye level, rising and falling, dancing through the shaft. The far wall was still so distant it appeared hazy in the ethereal light.

"It's like being bloody spiders," Alric remarked.

"I'm not sure even being ruler of the world is worth all this," Degan moaned.

"I can see how Edmund Hall fell now, but he must have gotten down a long way to have survived," Arista said. "Could you imagine doing this alone?"

"He wasn't alone," Myron said. "He had two friends and several servants."

"What happened to them? Were they locked up as well?"

"No," Myron replied.

"They didn't survive, did they?"

"I'm afraid not."

Hadrian sat up. His clothes were wet. Around him droplets fell, cascading down the walls. Looking across the shaft, he could see a clear division between a bright level of ice and snow and a much darker level of damp stone. "It's warmer," he said.

"We need to keep going," Royce told them. "The light is fading. Anyone want to do this holding a torch?"

"Try and find thicker ledges," Alric told Wyatt.

"I find what I find."

The lower they went, the darker it became, regardless of the daylight, which, to Hadrian's dismay, was fading quickly. They dropped down four more ledges. Their efficiency grew with repetition, but their progress was being hampered by the failing light. The walls were black, while overhead the opening had changed from a brilliant gray to a sickly yellow, with one side dipping into a rosy purple as the sun began to set.

Arista was on the rope, climbing down, when he heard her scream. Hadrian's heart skipped. He was holding the rope—had it wrapped around his waist—when he felt her weight jerk him.

"Arista!" he shouted.

"I'm all right," she called up.

"Did you slip?" Alric yelled from farther below.

"I—I put my hand on a bat," she said.

"Everyone quiet," Royce ordered.

Hadrian could hear it too, a faint squeaking, but on a massive droning scale. That was followed by a hum, a vibration that bounced within the shaft until it grew to a thunder. The air moved with a mysterious wind, swirling and gusting.

"What's going on?" Arista called out, her voice hard to hear behind the growing roar.

"Hang on!" Hadrian shouted back.

They felt a rushing movement, like an eruption that issued from below, as the world filled with the fluttering of endless wings and high-pitched squeals. Hadrian braced himself, holding tight to the rope, as Arista screamed once more and the shaft filled with a cloud of bats that swirled with the force of a cyclone.

With his head down, Hadrian clutched the rope, wrapping it tight around his forearm. Mauvin and Royce grabbed hold of him. Arista was not going anywhere.

In less than a minute the hurricane of bats passed by.

"Lower me down!" Arista called. "Before something else happens."

He felt her touch down, and as he reeled up the harness, Hadrian looked up. The small patch of mauve sky was filled with a dark swirling line. A cloud of bats snaked like the tail of a serpent, twisting, looping, circling. Like a magic plume of smoke, they were mesmerizing to watch. Hadrian guessed there had to be millions.

Looking back down, he noticed there was a light below, a bright light that filled the shaft, revealing the glistening walls.

"What's going on down there?" he called.

"I'm tired of not being able to see," Arista yelled back.

"She's got her robe glowing," Alric said uncomfortably.

When Hadrian got down, he saw the princess perched on an outcropping of rock. Her legs dangled over the edge, scissoring in the air, her robe glowing white. Whenever she moved, the shadows shifted. Everyone stole repeated glances, as if it might be impolite to stare. Gaunt had no such reservation as he gaped, openly horrified.

On they went, following the same order, all of them doing their job with a rhythm. They traveled in silence except for the necessary calls of "down" and "clear." It took five more descents before he heard Wyatt call up, "Stop! I'm at the bottom!"

"You're still on the rope," Hadrian shouted back, confused. "You haven't touched down yet? You need more slack?"

"*No!* No slack! I would prefer not to touch down."

"River?" Arista asked.

"Nope, but it's moving."

"What is?"

"Can't really tell. It's too dark down here. Give me a minute to find a place to land."

In time, they all descended to an island of rock that jutted up from the floor of the cavern. Even with Arista beside him, it was too dark for Hadrian to see clearly what lay around them. All he knew was that they stood on an island within a sea of dark movement. He smelled a foul odor and heard a soft chattering coming from the floor. The smell was very much like an old chicken coop. "What is it, Royce?"

"I really think you need to see this for yourself," Royce replied. "Arista, can you turn that thing up?"

Before he finished his sentence, Esrahaddon's robe increased in brilliance, a phosphorous light illuminating the entire base of the shaft. What they saw left them speechless. They were not actually at the bottom. They stood on the tip of an up-thrusted rock, tall enough to breach the surface of a monolithic pile of bat droppings. The cone-shaped mound of guano stood easily three hundred feet high. Every inch of it moved, as across its surface scurried hundreds of thousands of cockroaches.

"By Mar!" Mauvin exclaimed.

"That's disgusting," Alric said.

There was more there than cockroaches. Hadrian spotted something white and spidery darting across the surface—a crab, and there was not just one, but hundreds all scuttling along. There was a faint squeal lower down and he saw a rat. The rodent was scrambling to escape the pile as a horde of beetles swarmed it. The rat toppled and was pulled onto its back, where it floundered, struggling in the soft guano. It squealed again. Its feet, tail, and head quivered and thrashed above the surface as an endless mob of beetles pulled it down, until only the trembling, hairless tail was visible, and then it too vanished.

" 'Crawling, crawling, crawling. They eat everything,' " Myron quoted.

"Anyone want to try walking across that?" Royce asked.

Wyatt replied with an uncomfortable laugh, then said, "No, seriously, how do we get down?"

"What if we jump and run real fast?" Mauvin offered.

This idea garnered several grimaces.

"What if it's not solid? Can you imagine it being so soft that you went under, like water?" Magnus muttered.

"You're thinking something," Hadrian said to Royce. "You saw this from above. You wouldn't have come down if you didn't have some kind of plan."

He shook his head. "Not me, but I was hoping she would." He gestured at Arista.

All eyes turned to the princess and she returned the looks with an expression of surprise and self-doubt.

"You need to provide us with a path or something," Royce told her. "Some means of getting down the slope of this pile. There's an opening over there, a crack in the wall—see it?" He pointed. "It will be tight, but I think we can get through. Of course, we'll have to crawl, possibly even dig our way out. So really, anything you can do to distract the meat-eating beetles would be nice."

She nodded and sighed. "I really don't have a lot of experience at this."

"You do what you can," Hadrian told her.

"The only other alternative is Mauvin's idea—we run for it and hope to get out before we're completely eaten."

Arista made a face and nodded again. "Everyone should stand behind me. I don't know exactly what will happen."

"What's she gonna do?" Gaunt asked. "What's going on?"

"Just do as she says," Royce told him.

The princess took a position on the edge of the rock and faced the mound. The rest gathered behind her, shifting their feet so as not to fall. Arista stood with her arms at her sides, rotating her palms out toward the mound, and slowly, softly, she began to hum. Then the light of her robe went out.

Darkness swallowed them.

Their only reference point was the tiny circle of starlit sky that lingered overhead, and in the absence of sight, the chattering sounds of a million roaches echoed. They all stood close to each other, huddled against the black, when tiny lights began appearing. Pinpricks flashed and died in the air before them. While the sparks lived, they swirled and drifted, riding currents of spinning air. More appeared, until Hadrian felt he was seeing the top of a giant campfire. There was no flame, only the swarm of sparks that rose high into the air, carried up as if the shaft were an enormous chimney.

In addition to the sparks, there was heat. It felt as if Hadrian stood before his father's forge. He could feel it baking his clothes and flushing his skin. With the heat came a new smell; far worse than the musty ammonia scent, this was thick and overpowering—the gagging stench of burning hair. As they watched, the pile before them began to radiate light, a faint red glow, like embers in a neglected fireplace. Then spontaneously flames caught, flaring here and there, throwing tall demonic shadows dancing on the walls.

"All right! All right!" Alric shouted. "That's enough! That's enough! You're burning my face off!"

The flames subsided, the red glow faded, and the soaring sparks died. Arista's robe once more glowed, but fainter and with a bluish tint. Her shoulders slumped and her legs wavered. Hadrian grabbed hold of her by the elbow and waist.

"Are you all right?"

"Did it work? Is anyone hurt?" she asked, turning to look.

"A little seared, perhaps," he said.

Royce ventured a foot out onto the pile. There was an audible crunch, as if he were stepping on eggshells. The surface of the mound looked dark and glassy. Nothing moved anymore.

Royce took two steps, then returned promptly to the island. "Still a tad warm. We might want to wait a bit."

"How did you do that?" Degan asked, astonished, while at the same time shifting away from her as far as the tiny perch allowed.

"She's a witch," Magnus said.

"She's not a witch!" In the otherwise silent cave, the volume of his own voice embarrassed Hadrian. It echoed twice. He noticed Alric looking at him, surprised, and he felt suddenly crowded. He stepped off and started walking.

He felt the surface of the pile crackle beneath his weight, the heat under his boots as if he were striding across sunbaked sand. He shuffled down the side of the pile, kicking the roasted remains of crabs aside. Light bobbed behind him and he knew at least Arista followed. They reached the crack. It was larger than it had seemed at a distance, and he was able to pass through without so much as ducking.

CHAPTER 9

WAR NEWS

The two girls sprinted along the parapet, their dark winter cloaks waving in their wake. Mercy jerked to a halt and Allie nearly ran her down. They bumped and both giggled into the cold wind. The sky was as gray as the castle walls they stood on, their cheeks a brilliant red from the cold, but they were oblivious to such things.

Mercy got to her hands and knees, and crawling between the merlons, she peered down. Huge blocks of unevenly colored stone formed a twenty-foot-high wall, the squares seeming to diminish in size the farther away they were. At the bottom lay a street, where dozens of people walked, rode, or pushed carts. The sight made Mercy's stomach rise, and her hands felt so weak that squeezing anything caused a tickling sensation. Still, it was wonderful to see the world from so high, to see the roofs of houses and the patterns formed by streets. With the snow, almost everything was white, but there were splashes of color: the side of a red barn on a distant hill, the three-story building painted sky blue, the bronze patches of road where snow retreated before the heat of traffic. Mercy had never seen a city before, much less one from this height. Being on the battlements of the palace made her feel as if she were the empress of the world, or at least a flying bird—both of equal delight in her mind.

"He's not down there!" Allie shouted, her voice buffeted by the wind so that her words came to Mercy as if from miles away. "He doesn't have wings!"

Mercy crawled back out of the blocks of stone and, bracing her back against the battlement, paused to catch her breath.

Allie was standing before her—grinning madly, her hood off, dark hair flying in the wind. Mercy hardly noticed Allie's ears, or the odd way her eyes narrowed, anymore. Mercy had been fascinated by her that first day, when they had met in the dining hall. She had wandered away from the Pickerings' table to get a closer look at the strange elven girl. Allie had been just as interested in Mr. Rings, and from then on the two were inseparable. Allie was her best friend—even better than Mr. Rings, for although Mercy confided all her secrets to each, Allie could understand.

Allie sympathized when Mercy told her how Arcadius had refused to let her roam the forests near the university. She had suffered equally from similar hardships, such as when her father refused to let her roam their home city of Colnora. Both girls spent long nights by candlelight sharing horror stories of their adventure-impoverished childhoods, rendered such by overprotective guardians who refused to see the necessity of finding tadpoles or obtaining the twisted metal the tinsmith threw away.

They tried on each other's clothes. Allie's wardrobe consisted of boyish outfits, mostly tunics and trousers, all faded and worn, with holes in the knees and elbows, but Mercy found them marvelous. They were much easier to wear than dresses when climbing trees. Allie had very few clothes compared to the many dresses, gowns, and cloaks Mercy used to have at the university, but of course, now Mercy had only the one outfit Miranda had dressed her in the day they had fled Sheridan. In the end, all they managed to do was trade cloaks. Mercy's was thicker and warmer, but she liked how Allie's old tattered wrap made her look dashing, like some wild hero.

Allie let Mercy play with the spare sextant her father had given her, showing her how to determine their position by the stars. In return, Mercy let Allie play with Mr. Rings, but began regretting the decision now that he climbed on Allie's shoulder more often than her own. Late at night she would scold the raccoon for his disloyalty, but he only chattered back. She was not at all certain he understood the gravity of the problem.

"There!" Allie shouted, pointing farther up the parapet, where Mercy spotted the raccoon's tiny face peering at them from around the corner. The two bolted after him. The face vanished, a ringed tail flashed and was gone.

The two slid on the snow as they rounded the corner. They were at the front of the palace now, above the great gates. On the outside was a large square, where vendors sold merchandise from carts and barkers shouted about the best leather, the slowest-burning candles, and the bargain price of honey. On the inside lay the castle courtyard and, beyond it, the tall imposing keep, rising as a portly tower with numerous windows.

The raccoon was nowhere to be seen.

"More tracks!" Mercy cried dramatically. "The fool leaves a trail!"

Off they ran once more, following the tiny hand-shaped imprints in the snow.

"He went down the tower stairs, lasses," the turret guard informed them as they raced by. Mercy only glanced at him. He was huge, as all the guards were, wearing his silver helm and layers of dark wool, and holding a spear. He smiled at her and she smiled back.

"There!" Allie shouted, pointing across the courtyard at a dark shadow darting under a delivery cart.

They scrambled down the steps, bounded to the bottom, and raced across the ward. They caught up to him when he neared the old garden. The two split up like hunters driving their quarry. Allie blocked Mr. Rings's path, forcing him toward Mercy, who was closing in. At the last minute, Mr. Rings fled toward the woodpile outside the kitchen. He easily scaled the stacked logs and scampered through a window, left open a crack to vent smoke.

"Crafty villain!" Allie cursed.

"You can't escape!" Mercy shouted.

Mercy and Allie entered the yard door to the kitchen and raced through the scullery, startling the servants, one of whom dropped a large pan, which rang like a gong. Shouts and curses echoed behind them as they sped up the stairs, past the linen storeroom, and into the great hall, where Mercy finally made a spectacular diving grab and caught Mr. Rings by the back foot. His tiny claws skittered over the polished floor, but to no avail. She got a better grip and pulled him to her.

"Gotcha!" she proclaimed, lying on her back, hugging the raccoon and panting for breath. "It's the gallows for you!"

"A-hem."

Mercy heard the sound and instantly knew she was in trouble.

She rolled over and, looking up, saw a woman glaring down, her arms folded and a stern look across her face. She wore a brilliant black gown decorated with precious stones that twinkled like stars. At the nearby table, another woman and eight men with grim faces stared at them.

"I don't recall inviting you to this meeting," the woman told Mercy. "Or you," she said to Allie, who had tumbled in behind Mercy. She then focused on Mr. Rings. "And I know I didn't invite you."

"Forgive us, Your Eminence," the two door guards said in near unison as they rushed forward, the foremost taking a rough hold of Allie. The second guard grabbed for Mercy, who scrambled to her feet, frightened.

The lady raised a delicate hand, bending it slightly at the wrist, and instantly the guard halted.

"You are forgiven," she told him. "Let her go."

The guard holding Allie obeyed and the little girl took a step away, looking at him warily.

"You're the empress?" Mercy asked.

"Yes," she replied. "My name is Modina."

"I'm Mercy."

"I know. Allie has told me all about you. And this is Mr. Rings, correct?" the empress asked, reaching out a hand and stroking the raccoon's head. Mr. Rings tilted his snout down in a shy gesture as he was awkwardly held to Mercy's chest, his belly exposed. "Is he the one causing all the trouble?"

"It's not his fault," Mercy blurted out. "We were just playing a game. Mr. Rings was the despicable thief who stole the crown jewels and me and Allie were on the hunt tracking him down to face the axman's justice. Mr. Rings just happens to be a really good thief."

"I see, but alas, we are in the middle of a very important meeting that does not include thieves, axmen, or little girls." She focused on Mr. Rings, as if she were speaking only to him. "And raccoons, no matter how cute, are not allowed. If you two would be so kind as to take him back to the kitchen and ask Mr. Thinly to make him a plate of something, perhaps that will keep him out of mischief. See if he can also find some sweetmeats for the two of you—toffee, perhaps? And while he is being so kind, you might return the favor by asking if there are any chores you can do for him."

Mercy was nodding even before she finished.

"Away with you, then," she said, and the two sprinted back
the way they had come, exchanging wide-eyed looks of relief.

᠅

Modina watched them race out, then turned back to the council. She did not resume her seat but preferred to walk, taking
slow steps, circling the long table where her ministers and
knights waited. The only sounds in the room were the crackle
of the fire and the click of her shoes. She walked more for
effect than from need. As empress, she had discovered the
power and necessity of appearances.

The dress was an outward expression of this. Stiff, tight,
restraining, noisy, and generally uncomfortable, it was nonetheless impressive. She noticed the expressions of awe in the
eyes of all who beheld her. Awe begot respect; respect begot
confidence; confidence begot courage, and she needed her
people to be brave. She needed them to cast aside their doubts
even in the face of a terrible growing shadow. She needed them
to believe in the wisdom of a young woman even when faced
with annihilation.

The men at the table were not fools. They would not be
there if she thought them so. They were practical, clear-
thinking, war-hardened leaders. Such romantic notions as the
infallibility of a daughter of Novron did not impress them.
The count of spears and a calculated plan were more to their
liking. Still, even such efforts she knew to be futile. Warriors
on a battlefield and the belief in a demigod empress would
stand equal chance of saving them now. They had but one
hope and — as a goddess, or as a thoughtful ruler — she needed
their blind acceptance to raise the payment needed to buy
time. So she walked with her head bowed, her fingers tapping
her lower lip in apparent contemplation, giving the impression

that she calculated the number of swords and shields, their positions at the choke points, the river dams set to be broken, the bridges set to be destroyed, the units of cavalry, the state of preparedness of the reserve battalions. More than anything she did not wish to appear to these old men as a flighty girl who held no understanding of the weight she bore.

She paused, looking at the fire, leaving her back to the table. "You are certain, then?" she asked.

"Yes, Your Eminence," Sir Breckton replied. "A beacon is burning."

"But only one?"

"We know that the elves are capable of swiftness and stealth. It's why we had so many signal patrols."

"Still, only one?"

"It's no accident."

"No, of course not," she said, pivoting on a heel so that her mantle swept gracefully around. "And I do not doubt it now, but it shows something of their ability. Out of twenty-four, only one man had enough time to lay a torch to a pile of oiled wood." She sighed. "They have crossed the Galewyr, then. Trent has fallen. Very well, send orders to clear the countryside, evacuate the towns and villages, and break the dams and bridges. Seal us off from the rest of the world—except for the southern pass. That we leave open for the princess. Thank you, gentlemen."

The meeting was over and the council stood. Breckton turned to Modina. "I will leave immediately to personally take charge of destroying the bridges in Colnora."

She nodded and noticed Amilia wince at his words. "Sir Breckton, I hope you do not take offense, but I would like to have my secretary accompany you so that she can report to me. I don't want to take you away from your duties just to keep me informed."

Both of them looked shocked. "But, Your Eminence, I will be riding north—there is risk—"

"I will leave it to her, then. Amilia? Will you go?"

She nodded. "As my empress wishes," she said solemnly, as if this were a terrible hardship that she would endure only for the sake of the empire. Amilia, however, was not a very good actress.

"As you will be passing by Tarin Vale, see that you check on Amilia's family, and ensure they are sent here to the palace." This time Amilia lit up with genuine surprise.

"As you wish," Sir Breckton said with a bow.

Amilia said nothing but reached out and squeezed Modina's hand as she passed her.

"One more thing," Modina said. "See to it that the man—the one that lit the fire—see that he receives a commendation of some kind. He should be rewarded."

"I will indeed, Your Eminence."

Servants entered the hall carrying plates but pulled up short with guilty looks.

"No, no, come in." She waved them forward. "Chancellor, you and I will continue in my office to allow these people to set up for the evening meal."

Outside the great hall, the corridors and public rooms buzzed with dozens of people walking, working, or just gathering to talk. She liked it this way; the castle felt alive. For so long she had lived within a cold hollow shell—a ghost within a mausoleum. But now, packed tightly with guests, all fighting for access to washbasins and seats at tables, and arguing over snoring and blanket stealing, it felt like a home. At times, she could almost imagine they were all relatives arriving as guests for a grand party or, perhaps, given the lingering mood, a funeral. She had never met most of those she saw, but they were family now. They were all family now.

Guards escorted them through the corridor and up the central stairs. Since the Royce Incident, as Breckton called it, he insisted she have bodyguards at all times. They ordered people in gruff tones to step back. "Empress!" they would call out, and crowds would gasp, look around nervously, dividing and bowing. She liked to smile and wave as she passed, but on the stairs she had to hold the hem of her dress. The dress, for all its expense, was no end of problems and she looked forward to the end of the day, when she could retire to her room and slip into her linen nightgown.

She half considered going there now. Nimbus would not mind. He had seen her in it hundreds of times, and while he was a shining example of protocol himself, he was silent to the foibles she made. As Modina climbed the stairs, it occurred to her she would have no more reservation about changing her clothes in front of him than she would about doing so in front of Red or Amilia, as if he were a doctor or priest.

They entered what had once been Saldur's office. She had had most of the church paraphernalia and personal items removed. The chambermaids might even have scrubbed it— as the room did smell better.

The sun was setting outside the window, the last of the light quickly fading.

"How long has it been?" she asked Nimbus as he closed the office door.

"Only two days, Your Eminence," Nimbus replied.

"It seems so much longer. They must have reached Amberton Lee by now, right?"

"Yes, I should think so."

"I should have sent riders with them to report back. I don't like this waiting. Waiting to hear from them, waiting to hear the trumpet blare of invasion." She looked out at the dying light. "When they seal the northern pass and destroy the bridges in Colnora, the only way in or out of this city will be by sea or the southern gate. Do you think I should put more ships out to guard against a water invasion? We are vulnerable to that."

"It's possible, yet unlikely. I've never heard of elves being ones for sea going. I don't believe they brought ships with them across Dunmore. Breckton destroyed the Melengar fleet and—"

"What about Trent? They might have gone there for the ships."

The slender man nodded his powdered-wig-covered head. "Except that there was no need at that time. There will be no need until your men close the roads. Usually one doesn't go to great lengths unless one has to, and so far—"

"They have had an easy time of killing us. Will it be any harder for them here?"

"I think so," Nimbus said. "Unlike the others, we have had time to prepare."

"But will it be enough?"

"Against any human army we would be impregnable, but..."

Modina sat on the edge of her desk, her gown puffing out as she did. "The reports said swarms of Gilarabrywn. You've never seen one, Nimbus, but I have. They're giant, brutal, terrifying flying monsters. Just one of them destroyed my home—burned it to ash. They are unstoppable."

"And yet you stopped it."

"I killed one—the man said swarms! They will burn the city from the sky."

"The shelters are almost complete. The buildings will be lost, but the populace will be safe. They will not be able to take the city by Gilarabrywn. You have seen to that."

"What about food?"

"We've been lucky there. It was a good year. We have more

in store than is usual for late winter. Fishermen are working around the clock harvesting, salting, and smoking. All meats and grain are rationed and underground. Even here at the castle the bulk of the stores are already in the old dungeon."

"It should slow them down, shouldn't it?"

"I think so," he said.

She looked back out the window at the snow-covered roofs. "What if Arista and the others had trouble? What if they were attacked by thieves? They might have died even before reaching the city."

"Thieves?" Nimbus asked, stifling a laugh. "I daresay I should pity any band of *thieves* that had the misfortune of assaulting that party. I am certain they have entered Amberton Lee safely."

She turned to face him. His tone was so confident, so certain that it set her at ease. "Yes, I suppose you're right. We just have to hope they are successful. What obstacles they will face beneath the Lee will certainly be more formidable than a band of thieves."

Chapter 10

Beneath the Lee

Arista had no idea what time it was or how long they had walked since reaching the bottom of the shaft. Her feet, sore and heavy, slipped and stumbled over rocks. She yawned incessantly and her stomach growled, but there was no stopping—not yet.

They followed a series of narrow crevices so small and tight it often required crawling and, in the case of Elden, a sucked-in stomach and the occasional tug-of-war. It was frighteningly claustrophobic at times. She moved sideways through narrow slits where her nose passed within inches of the opposite side. During this period, Arista's robe was the only source of light. At times, she noticed it dim or flicker briefly, which gave her concern. She would stiffen and instantly the light grew steady, often brighter, but as the night dragged on, the light drifted steadily from white to darker shades of blue.

The passage widened and constricted, but Royce usually found a way to move ahead. On a few occasions, he was wrong and they needed to backtrack and find another way. At such times, Arista heard Magnus mumble. Royce must have heard him too, but the thief never spoke or looked in his direction. The dwarf, who moved through the tunnels like a fish in water, did not elaborate on his grumblings. He remained generally quiet and traveled in the rear or middle of the group, yet occasionally when Royce entered a crevice, Magnus might cough with a disapproving tone. Royce ignored him and invariably returned with a scowl. After a few missteps, Royce started turning away from an appealing path the moment Magnus made a sound, as if a new thought had just occurred to him. Silently worked out and agreed upon, the system functioned well enough for both of them.

The rest of the party followed mindlessly, focused only on their own feet. After the first hour, Alric, who had begun the march giving the occasional obvious direction or asking questions, then nodding his head as if approving some sort of action, gave up the pretense altogether. Soon he dragged himself along like the rest, blindly following wherever Magnus and Royce led.

"Mmm," Arista heard Magnus intoning somewhere ahead, as if he had just tasted something wonderful.

The princess was fumbling forward, ducking and twisting to get by as they struggled through another long narrow fissure. The blue light of her robe made the rock appear to glow.

"Wonderful," the dwarf muttered.

"What is?"

"You'll see."

They inched onward through the crevice, which became tighter. She felt forward with her feet, kicking away loose stones to find footing.

"Whoa." She heard Royce's voice from somewhere up ahead, speaking the word slowly with uncharacteristic awe. She attempted to look forward, but Mauvin and Alric, standing ahead of her in the narrow pass, blocked her view.

Alric soon exclaimed, "By Mar! How is that possible?"

"What's happening?" Degan said behind her.

"No clue—not there yet," she replied. "Mauvin's big head is blocking me."

"Hey!" he retorted. "It's not my fault. It gets really narrow in—Oh my god!"

Arista pushed forward.

Mauvin was right—the path did grow very tight—and she had to bend, squeeze, and step through. Her shoulders brushed the stone, her hair caught on jagged rocks, and her foot was almost stuck as she shifted her weight. She held her breath and pulled her body through the narrowest gap.

Once on the far side, the first thing she noticed was that she was standing in a large cavern, which, after the hours of crawling like a worm, was wonderful. The action of some forgotten river had cut the walls out in scoops and brushed them to a smooth wavy finish. Elongated pools of water that littered the floor shone as mirrors divided from each other by smooth ridges of rock.

The second thing she noticed was the *stars*.

"Oh my," she found herself saying as she looked up. The roof of the cavern appeared just like the night sky. Thousands of tiny points of light glowed bright. Captured in the enclosed space, they illuminated the entire chamber. "Stars."

"Glowworms," Magnus corrected as he walked out ahead of her. "They leech on to the ceiling stone."

"They're beautiful," she said.

"Drome didn't put all his grandeur on the outside of Elan. Your castles, your towers, they are sad little toys. Here are the real treasures we hoard. They call us misers on the surface— they have no idea. They scrape for gold, silver, and diamonds, never finding the real gems beneath their feet. Welcome to the house of Drome; you stand on his porch."

"There's a flat table of rock up there," Royce told them, pointing ahead at a massive plate of stone that lay at a slight angle. "We'll camp, get some food, and sleep."

"Yes, yes, that sounds wonderful," Alric agreed, bobbing his head eagerly.

They walked around the pools filled with the reflected starlight. Myron and Elden, both with their eyes locked on the distant ceiling, missed their footing several times, soaking their feet—neither seemed to care. They climbed to the surface of the table rock, which was as large as the floor of the palace's great hall. It was a vague triangle, and the long point rose at the center of the cavern like the prow of a ship breaching a wave.

With no wood and no need for tents, making camp consisted entirely of dropping their packs and sitting down. Arista had the lightest pack, carrying only her own supplies of food, bedding, and water, but still, her shoulders ached and did so even more noticeably once she set her burden down. She planted herself on the prow, her legs dangling over the edge, and leaned back on her hands, rolling her head. She felt the aches in her neck and looked up at the false night sky. Elden was the first to join her; he settled in and mimicked her actions exactly. He smiled bashfully when he caught her looking. The big man's forehead and his left cheek had ugly scrapes and his tunic was torn across the chest and along his right shoulder. It was a wonder he had made it through at all.

From her pack she pulled one of the meals, in a neatly sewn bag. She tore it open and found salted fish, a preserved egg with a green look to it, a bit of hard bread, walnuts, and a pickle. Just as she had once devoured the pork stew Hadrian and Royce had given her the first night she had traveled with them, she consumed this meal, and when finished, she searched the bag for any remaining crumbs. Sadly, she found only two more walnuts at the bottom. She considered opening another bag, but reason fought against the idea. Partially sated, her hunger lost its edge and gave up.

Most of the group found seats along the edge of the shelf and lined up like birds on a fence, their legs dangling at various rates of swing. Royce was the last to settle. As in the past, he spent some time exploring ahead and checking behind. Degan and Magnus sat together some distance from the rest, speaking together softly.

"Blessed Maribor, am I starved!" Mauvin declared as he tore open a bag of his own. His expression showed his disappointment, but he was not discouraged. After he tasted the contents, a smile returned. "That Ibis is a genius. This fish is wonderful!"

"I—have—the pork," Alric managed to get out around the food in his mouth. "Good."

"I feel as if I am back on a ship," Wyatt mentioned, but did not pause to explain why as he tore his bread with his teeth.

Myron negotiated a trade with Elden over walnuts—a discussion held without words. The little monk looked exhausted but managed to smile warmly at the giant as they debated with hand gestures and nods. Elden grinned back, delighted by the game.

After eating, Arista looked around for a place to sleep. It was not like bedding down in a forest, where you looked for a flat area clear of roots and stones. Here everything was rock. One place was as good as another, and all appeared to offer little in the way of comfort. With her pack in hand, she wandered toward the center of the shelf, thinking that at the very least she did not want to roll off. She spotted Hadrian far down at the low end of the rock. He was lying on his back, his knees up, his head on his blanket, which he had rolled into a pillow.

"Something wrong?" she asked, approaching cautiously.

He turned on his side and looked up. "Hmm? No."

"No?" She got down on her knees beside him. "Why are you all the way over here?"

He shrugged. "Just looking for some privacy."

"Oh, then I'm probably bothering you." She got up.

"No—you're not." He stopped her. "I mean…" He sighed. "Never mind."

He sounded upset, frustrated, maybe even angry. She stood hovering over him, unsure of what to do. She hoped he would say something, or at least smile at her. Instead, he refused to look her way. His eyes focused on the darkness across the cavern. The miserable, bitter sound of the words *never mind* echoed in her head.

"I'm going to sleep," she said at last.

"That's a good idea," he replied, still not bothering to look at her.

She walked slowly back to the center of the table, glancing at him over her shoulder. He continued to lie staring at nothing. It bothered her. If it were Royce, she would not give it a second thought, but this was not like him. She spread out her blankets and lay down, feeling suddenly awful, as if she had lost something valuable. She just was not sure what.

Her robe was dark. She had not noticed until that moment and could not recall when it had faded. They were all tired, even the robe. She looked up at the glowworms. They did look like stars. There must be hundreds of thousands.

⋖⋗

The boy was pale, ghostly, his eyes sallow. His mouth hung slightly agape as if perpetually on the verge of asking a ques-

tion, only he could no longer form words. She guessed it took all his mental capacity to keep from screaming. Jerish stood next to him. The fighter towered over the lad with a look that reminded her of a cornered mother bear. They were both dressed in common clothes, his armor and emblems left at the palace. He appeared to be a poor merchant or tradesman, perhaps, except for the long sword slung to his back, the pommel rising over his left shoulder as if keeping watch.

"Grinder," the boy said as she entered the station.

"Nary," she greeted him, and it took effort not to bow. He looked so much like his father—the same lines, the same clarity in his eyes, the cut of his mouth—the lineage of the emperor so obvious.

"Were you followed?" Jerish asked.

She smirked.

"A Cenzar cannot be followed?"

"No," she said bluntly. "Everyone still thinks I am loyal to the cause. Now we have to be quick. Here." She held out the necklaces. "This one is for you, Nary, and this is Jerish's. Put them on and never take them off. Do you understand me? Never take them off. They will hide you from magical eyes, protect you from enchantments, allow me to find you when the time is safe, and even provide you with a bit of luck."

"You intend to fight them?"

"I will do what I can." She looked at the boy. Her efforts had to be for him now, for his safety and his return.

"You cannot save Nareion," Jerish told her bluntly. She looked at the boy and saw his lips tremble.

"I will save what is dearer to him, his son and his empire. It may take time—a long time, perhaps—but I swear I will see the empire restored even if it costs me my life." She watched as they slipped the necklaces on. "Be sure to hide *him well. Take him into the country, assume the life of a commoner. Do nothing to draw attention, and await my call."*

"Will these really protect us from your associates?"

"I will have no associates after today."

"Even old Yolric?"

She hesitated. "Yolric is very powerful, but wise."

"If he is so wise, why is he with them? Is it not wisdom to preserve the empire and show loyalty to the emperor?"

"I am not certain Yolric is with them. He has always remained an island. Even the emperors do not influence him. Yolric does as he wishes. I cannot say what he will do. I hope he will join with me, but should he side with Venlin..." She shook her head sadly. "We must hope."

Jerish nodded. "I trust you to watch our backs. I never thought I would ever say that—not to a Cenzar...not to you."

"And I entrust you with the future of the empire and ultimately the fate of mankind—I certainly did not expect to be saying that to you."

Jerish tore off his glove and held out his hand. "Goodbye, Brother."

She took his hand in hers. This was the last time she would ever shake anyone's hand.

How do I know that?

"Goodbye, Nary," she told the boy. At the sound of her voice, Nevrik rushed forward and threw his arms about her. She hugged him back.

"I'm scared," he said.

"You must be brave. Remember, you are the son of Nareion, the emperor of Apeladorn, the descendant of Novron, the savior of our race. Know that the time will come when the blood descendant of Novron must protect us again—your descendant, Nary. It may take many years for me to defeat

the evil that has risen today, so you must not wait. If you find a girl who makes your heart smile, make her your wife. Remember, Persephone was a mere farmer's daughter and she mothered a line of emperors. You must find a girl like that and have a family. Give your child your necklace and stay safe. Do what Jerish says. After this day, there will be no warrior greater than he. I will see to that as well." She noticed a dark look come over Jerish. *"It is necessary,"* she told him, surprised at the ice in her own voice.

Jerish nodded miserably.

"What exactly do you intend to do?"

"Just make certain you are not in the city when I do it."

Tink! Tink! Tink!

Arista woke up cold and confused. The sense of urgency, the fear and concern, lingered. Her back hurt. The hard, damp stone tortured her strained muscles, leaving her feeling crippled. She rolled to her side with a miserable groan.

Tink! Tink! Tink! The sound of stone striking stone echoed.

She looked up but saw nothing. It was all black now. The worms were gone or no longer giving off light.

Tink!

There was a spark of white light and in that brief flash she spotted Magnus, hunched over a pile of rocks, only a few feet from her.

Tink!

"*Ba, durim hiben!*" he growled. She heard him shift position.

"How long have I been asleep?" she asked.

"Six hours," the dwarf replied.

Tink! Another flash, another incomprehensible grumble.

"What is it you are doing?"

"Frustrating and embarrassing myself."

"What?"

"It's just been so long, although that's really no excuse. I can hardly call myself a Brundenlin if—"

Tink! Another flash—this time it did not go out. The spark appeared to linger, amazingly bright. Instantly Magnus bent down and she could hear him blowing. The spark grew brighter with each puff. Soon she could clearly see the face of the dwarf—the ridges of his cheeks, the tip of his nose, the beard trimmed short, all highlighted by the flickering glow. His dark eyes glistened, eagerly watching the flame he breathed life into.

"We have no wood," she said, puzzled, as she sat up.

"Don't need wood."

She watched him pile fist-sized stones on top of the little flame. He blew again and the fire grew. The stone was burning.

"Magic?"

"Skill," he replied. "Do you think they only have fire on the outside? Drome taught the dwarves first. In the deep, the blood of Elan bubbles up. There are rivers of burning stone, red and yellow, flowing thick and hot. We taught the secret of fire to the elves, much to our regret."

"How old are you?" she asked. It was common knowledge that elves lived longer—much longer—than humans, but she had no idea about dwarves.

Magnus looked at her through squinting eyes and pursed his lips as if he had tasted something bitter. "That's not a polite question, so I will be just as rude and ignore it. Since you feel you still need me, I trust you won't burn me to a cinder for it."

Arista rocked back. "I would never do such a thing. Perhaps you've forgotten I am not the one who randomly commits murder."

"No? My mistake. Apparently you're only content with enslavement." He tugged at his cropped beard.

"Would you have come if the empress had merely asked?"

"No. What care is it of mine if the elves erase you? It would restore the world. Humans have always been a blight, like the Ba Ran Ghazel, only with the Ghazel you know where you stand. They don't pretend to accept you when they want something, then shove you out in the cold when they're done with you. No, the Ghazels' hatred is up front and honest, not like the lies of the humans."

"I'd listen to him, Princess. He is an expert on betrayals."

The voice, low and threatening, came out of the darkness and Magnus jumped up, scrambling toward her, as if for protection. A moment later Royce appeared at the edge of the fire's light.

"I just wanted the dagger," Magnus replied, a hint of desperation in his voice, which rose an octave higher than normal.

"I understand, and I promise that the moment this business is done, I will make a present of it to you," Royce told him with a hungry look in his eyes that gave even Arista's heart pause. "Be sure to keep me informed of his usefulness, won't you, Your Highness?"

"He's actually being very helpful—so far," she replied.

"Too bad," Royce said. "Still, I have every confidence that will change. Won't it, Magnus?" He glared at the dwarf for several minutes as if expecting an answer; then the thief looked at her. "Better get everyone up. It's time we got moving."

Royce turned and disappeared silently into the cave's gloom. When she looked back at the dwarf, Magnus was staring at her with a surprised, almost shocked, expression, as if something about her suddenly mystified him. He turned away and grumbled something she did not catch before returning to his pile of burning rocks.

Magnus's campfire made the process of getting up and having breakfast almost cheerful and lent a sense of normality to their queer surroundings. The bright yellow flicker reminded Arista of her days traveling with Royce and Hadrian, and of her trip to Aquesta. It was shocking to think of those days as better times. Her life since the death of her father had been one long cascading fall that had left her tripping over ever greater troubles.

She could hardly imagine a more desperate state than the one she faced now. There wasn't much that could top the extinction of mankind. She was certain, however, that it would never come to that. Even should the elves prevail, even if they sought to eradicate humans, she suspected there would be pockets that survived. It would be like trying to kill all the mice in the world. A few would always survive. She looked around the cave as she sat tying up her hair for the day's journey. Hundreds, perhaps thousands, could live down there alone. Like her father, she was not an overly religious person, and yet she could not believe that Maribor would let his people vanish from the face of Elan. He had saved them before. He had sent Novron to snatch them from the brink, and she suspected he would do so again.

Myron ate breakfast with Elden much as he had dinner. The two communicated in silence while Wyatt rolled up blankets. She had no idea what to make of Wyatt. He and Elden kept mostly to themselves, rarely speaking, and usually only to each other. They did not seem a bad sort, not like Gaunt. Degan bothered her like a splinter in her skin. How he could be the descendant of Novron was bewildering, and not for the first time she wondered if perhaps Esrahaddon had gotten it wrong.

They lit lanterns from the dying flames of the campfire,

and after packing up, Royce roamed about the cavern, disappearing from view occasionally. Only the glow of his lantern showed his position.

"Wrong way," she heard Magnus mutter, his arms folded, his foot tapping the stone. "Better…better…now up… up—yes!"

From across the cavern they could see Royce swinging his light and they marched forward. They climbed a sheer cliff to a crack in the rock and sliced through to another chamber. Then they climbed down into another long passage into yet another cavity. Each looked the same as the ones before, smooth walls and wet, pool-scattered floors.

"I thought caverns were supposed to have long cone-shaped stones hanging down from the ceiling," Alric mentioned as they entered yet another chamber.

"Not old enough," Magnus said.

"What's that?" the king asked.

"These caves, they're not old enough for dripstones to form. It takes tens of thousands of years. These…" He looked around, pursing his pudgy lips. "These tunnels are young. I doubt they have existed for more than a few thousand years and most of that time this was underwater from a powerful river. That's what carved the walls and rounded the rocks. You also need limestone and this isn't that kind of cave. Actually…" He paused, then stopped to pick up a rock. As he weighed it in his hand, a puzzled look came over his face.

"What is it?" Mauvin asked.

"The rocks here are from the surface." He shrugged. "Perhaps the river carried them." He continued to stare, licking his teeth, for several seconds before dropping it and moving on.

They entered another narrow space but not nearly so tight as before. This was an irregular passage about the size of a

typical second-story castle corridor. Low ceilings caused them
to duck and rough ridges made them step around, but the way
was considerably easier and more comfortable than those previously encountered. The passage was in a constant descent,
growing more pronounced with each step. They followed the
glow of Royce's lantern and kept track of the back of their
procession by the bob of Hadrian's. As on the previous day,
Arista walked in the middle, her robe glowing softly.

They heard a rush, as if someone far away was beating a
drum. The sound echoed, making it hard to determine what
direction it was coming from. They all paused, looking around
nervously. Arista felt a slight breeze forming and realized what
was coming. At the same instant, she knew that outside, the
sun had just risen.

"Here they come," Hadrian called out.

Arista crouched down, pulling the hood of her robe up over
her head as through the corridor swept the same multitude of
bats that had frightened her in the shaft the evening before.
The world around her filled with squeaks and flutters; then
the wind passed and the sound moved away. She stood up and
peeked out and saw the others lowering their arms as well. A
few slow strays continued to fly by when one not far from
Myron was snatched from the air. The monk staggered backward with a gasp and fell in front of Elden, who picked the
monk up as if he were a doll.

"Snake," Wyatt announced. "A big black one."

"There's dozens of them," Royce explained.

"Where?" Alric asked.

"Mostly behind you on the walls."

"What?" the king said, aghast. "Why didn't you say
something?"

"Knowing would only make traveling slower."

"Are they poisonous?" Mauvin asked.

They could all see the silhouetted shoulders of Royce's shadow on the far wall shrug.

"I demand you inform me of such things in future!" Alric declared.

"Do you want to know about the giant millipedes, then too?"

"Are you joking?"

"Royce doesn't make jokes," Arista told him as she looked around, anxiously hugging herself. Immediately her robe brightened and she spotted two snakes on the walls, but they were a safe distance away.

"He must be joking," Alric muttered quietly. "I don't see any."

"You aren't looking up," the thief said.

Arista did not want to. Some instinct, a tiny voice, warned her to fight the impulse, but in the end she just could not help herself. On the low ceiling, illuminated brightly by the robe, slithered a mass of wormlike bugs with an uncountable number of hairlike feet. Each was nearly five inches in length and close to the width of a man's finger. There were so many that they swarmed over each other until it was hard to tell if the ceiling was rock at all. Arista felt a chill run down her back. She clenched her teeth, forced her eyes to the floor, and focused on walking forward as quickly as possible.

She promptly passed Alric and Mauvin, both moving quicker than normal. She reached Royce, who stood outside the corridor on a boulder at the entrance to a larger passage.

"I guess I was wrong. Looks like I should have told you earlier," Royce said, watching them race forward.

"Are there...?" she asked, pointing upward without looking.

Royce glanced up and shook his head.

"Good," she replied. "And please, if Alric wants to know these things, fine, but don't tell me. I could have gone the rest of my life not knowing they were there." She shivered.

Everyone scurried out of the corridor except Myron, who lingered, staring up at the ceiling and smiling in fascination. "There are millions."

They entered another chamber, a smaller cavern of dramatic boulders that thrust up and out. Arista thought they appeared how the timbers of a house might look if a giant stepped on it. As soon as they entered, they faced a mystery on the far wall, where three darkened passages awaited, one large, one small, and one narrow. The party waited as Royce disappeared briefly into each one. When he returned, he did not look pleased.

"Dwarf!" he snapped. "Which one?"

Magnus stepped forward and poked his head into each. He placed his hands on the stone, groping over the surface as if he were a blind man. He pressed his ear to the rock, sniffed the air in each opening, and stepped back with a perplexed look. "They all go deep, but in separate directions."

Royce continued to stare at him.

"The stone doesn't know where we want to go, so it can't tell me."

"We can't afford to pick the wrong path," Arista said.

"I say we choose the largest," Alric stated confidently. "Wouldn't that be the most sensible?"

"Why is that sensible?" Arista asked.

"Well—because it is the biggest, so it ought to go the farthest and, you know—get us there."

"The largest might not remain that way," Magnus replied. "Cracks in rock aren't like rivers. They don't taper evenly."

Alric looked irritated. "Okay, what about you?" he asked Arista. "Can you do anything to—well—you know—find which is the right one?"

"Like what?"

"Do I need to spell it out? Like..." He waved his hands in the air in a mysterious fashion that she thought made him look silly. "Magic."

"I knew what you meant, but what exactly do you expect me to do? Summon Novron's ghost to point us in the right direction?"

"Can you do that?" the king asked, sounding both impressed and apprehensive.

"No!"

Alric frowned and slapped his thighs with his hands as if to indicate how horribly she had let him down. It irritated her how everyone seemed so disgusted by her talent and yet was even more upset when they found her ability lacking.

"Myron?" Hadrian said softly to the monk, who stood silently, staring at the passages.

"*Three openings. What to do?*" Myron said eerily.

"Myron, yes!" Alric smiled. "Tell us, which way did Hall go?"

"That's what I am reciting to you," he replied, trying to hide a little smile. " 'Three openings. What to do? I sat for an hour before I gave up trying to reason it out and just picked. I chose the closest.' "

Myron stopped, and when he failed to say more, Alric spoke. "The closest? What does that mean? Closest to what?"

"Is that all Hall wrote?" Arista asked. "What came next?"

Everyone crowded around the little man as he cleared his throat.

" 'Down, down, down, always down, never up. Slept in the corridor again. Miserable night. Food running low. Big-eyed fish looking better all the time. This is hopeless. I will die in here. I miss Sadie. I miss Ebot and Dram. I should never have come. This was a mistake. I have placed myself in my own grave. Feet are always wet. Want to sleep, but don't want to lie in water.

" 'A pounding. Pounding up ahead. A way out maybe!

" 'Pounding stopped. I don't think it was from the outside. I think someone else is down here—something else. I hear them—not human.

" 'Ba Ran Ghazel. Sea goblins. A whole patrol. Nearly found me. Lost my shoe.

" 'Bread moldy, salted ham nearly gone. At least there is water. Tastes bad, brackish. Slept poorly again. Bad dreams.

" 'I found it.' "

"The shoe?" Wyatt asked.

"No," Myron replied, smiling, "the city."

"Interesting," Gaunt said. "But that doesn't help us with the passages, does it? By the sound of things he traveled for days and never listed any landmark. It's pointless."

"We could split up," Alric said, considering. "Two groups of three and one of four. One group is bound to reach Percepliquis."

Arista shook her head. "That only works if we can divide up Mr. Gaunt in three parts. He is the one who has to reach the city."

"So you keep reminding me," Gaunt said. "But you refuse to tell me exactly what you expect me to do. I am not a man of many talents. There is nothing I can do that someone else in this party can't. I hope to Maribor you don't expect me to slay one of those Gilly-bran things. I'm not much of a fighter."

"I suppose you have to—I don't know—blow the horn."

"Couldn't I have done that after you returned with it?"

Arista sighed. "There's something else. I don't know what. I just know you have to be here."

"And yet we have no idea where _here_ is," he said indignantly.

Arista sighed and sat down on a rock, staring at the entrances. As she did, Alric stared at her.

"What?" she asked.

Alric smiled and glanced back at the passages. "I was wrong. Hall went in the narrow passage on the right."

He sounded so certain that everyone looked at him.

"Care to tell us how you know that?" Arista asked.

He grinned, obviously very pleased with himself. "Sure, but first you have to tell me why you sat there," he said to her.

"I don't know. I was tired of standing and this might take a while."

"Exactly," Alric said. "What did you say, Myron? It took an hour for Hall to decide which passage?"

"Close. 'I sat for an hour before I gave up trying to reason it out and just picked,' " the monk corrected.

"He sat for an hour trying to decide," Alric replied. "He sat right where you are."

"How do you know?" Gaunt asked. "How do you know it was on *that* rock and not someplace else?"

"Ask Arista," the king replied. "Why did you sit there and not someplace else?"

She shrugged and looked around. "I didn't really think about it. I just sat. I guess because it looked like the most comfortable place."

"Of course it is. Look around. That rock is perfect for sitting. All the others are sharp on the top or at steep angles or too big or small. That is the perfect sitting rock for looking at those passages! And that's the same reason Hall chose that spot, and the closest passage is the narrow one. Hall went in there. I'm positive."

Arista looked at Royce, who looked at Hadrian, who shrugged. "I think he might be right."

"Sounds good to me," Royce said.

Arista nodded. "I think so too."

Everyone seemed pleased except for Gaunt, who frowned but said nothing.

Alric adjusted his pack and, taking the lantern from Royce, promptly led the way.

"That lad might amount to something yet," Mauvin said, chuckling, as he followed his king.

CHAPTER 11

THE PATRIARCH

Monsignor Merton shuffled along the dark snowy road, his black hood up, his freezing fingers gripping the neck of his frock. He shuffled for fear of falling on the ice he could not feel. The tip of his nose and the tops of his cheeks had gone from feeling cold to burning unpleasantly.

Maybe I have frostbite, he thought. *What a sight I will be without a nose.* The thought did not bother him much; he could get along fine without one.

The hour was late. The shop windows were all black, dull sightless eyes reflecting his image. He had passed fewer than a dozen people since leaving the palace and all of them were soldiers. He felt sorry for the men who guarded the streets. The shopkeepers complained when they collected taxes, the vagrants wailed when they drove them off, and the criminals cursed them. They were half-shaven, blunt-nosed, loud, and always seen as bullies, but no one saw them on nights like this. The shopkeepers were all asleep in their beds, the vagrants and thieves tucked in their holes, but the soldiers of the empress remained. They felt the cold, suffered the wind, and endured exhaustion, but they bore their burdens quietly. As he shuffled on, Merton said a quiet prayer to Novron to give them strength and make their night rounds easier. He felt foolish doing so. *Surely Novron knows the plight of his own. He does not need me reminding him. What an utter annoyance I must be, what a bother. It's little wonder that I should lose my nose. Perhaps both feet should be taken as well.*

"Without feet, Lord, how will I serve?" He spoke softly. His voice came out in clouds that drifted by as he walked. "For I am not fit for much else these days beyond carrying messages."

He stopped. He listened. There was no answer.

Then he nodded. "I see, I see. Stop being a fool and walk faster and I will keep my feet. Very wise, my lord."

On he trudged, and reaching the top of the hill, he turned off Majestic Avenue and entered Church Square. At the center of the dark void glowed the clerestory lights of the great cathedral, the Imperial Basilica of Aquesta. Now that Ervanon was no more—crushed and defiled by the elven horde—this was the seat of power of the Nyphron Church. Here emperors would be crowned, married, and laid to rest. Here Wintertide services would be performed. Here the Patriarch and his bishops would administer to the children of Maribor. While it had nowhere close to the majesty of the Basilica of Ervanon, it had something Ervanon had never had—the Heir of Novron, their earthly god returned. And not a moment too soon, was how Merton saw it, but gods had a flair for dramatic timing. He considered himself blessed to be granted life in such a wondrous time. He would be a living witness to the fulfillment of the promise and the return of Novron's Empire, and in some small way he might even be allowed to contribute.

He climbed the steps to the massive doors and tugged on the ring. Locked. It always mystified Merton why the house of Novron should be sealed. He beat against the oak with his frozen fist.

The wind howled; the cold ripped mercilessly through his thin wool. He looked up, disappointed not to see stars overhead. He liked the stars, especially how they looked on cold nights, as if he could reach up and pluck one. As a boy, he had imagined that he might scoop them up and slip them into his pocket. He never imagined doing anything with the stars; he would just run his fingertips through them like grains of sand.

The door remained closed.

He hammered again. His hand made a feeble fleshy sound against the heavy wood.

"Is it your will that I freeze to death here on your steps?" he asked Novron. "I certainly should not think it would look good to have the body of your servant found here. People might get the wrong idea."

He heard a latch slide.

"Thank you, my lord, forgive my impatience. I am but a man."

"Monsignor Merton!" Bishop DeLunden exclaimed as he held up a lantern and peered out. "What are you doing out so late on a night like this?"

"God's will."

"Of course, but certainly our lord could wait until morning. That's why he makes new ones every day." DeLunden was more the curator of the church than its bishop these days, now that the Patriarch had taken up residence. He was like the captain of a ship that ferried an admiral.

Bishop DeLunden had unusually dark skin even for a Calian, which made his wreath of short white hair stand out against his balding head, the top of which looked like a dark olive set in cream. The bishop had a habit of wandering the halls at night like a ghost. Exactly what he did on his walks about the cathedral Merton had no idea, but tonight he was more than thankful for his nocturnal habits. "And it wasn't

Novron who sent you out on such a night; it was Patriarch Nilnev." He pulled the great door closed and slid the bolt. "Back from the palace again, are you?"

"These are troubled times and he needs to keep informed. Besides, if not for my wanderings, who would praise the beauty of our lord's nights?"

"Those farther south, I imagine," DeLunden retorted gruffly. "Put your hands on the lantern. Warm them lest they fall off."

"Such compassion," Merton said. "And for the likes of an Ervanonite like me."

"Not all Ervanonites are bad."

"There's only four of us."

"Yes, and of the four I can say that you are a good, devout, and gentle man."

"And the others?"

"I don't speak of them at all. I still find it altogether strange that only he and his guards managed to escape the desolation of Ervanon while all others perished."

"I am here."

"Novron loves you. Our lord pointed you out on the day of your birth and told his father to watch over you."

"You are too kind, and surely Novron loves everyone, and the leader of his church most of all."

"But the Patriarch is not—not anymore." The bishop peered from the vestibule toward the interior. "I don't like how he treats you."

Since the Patriarch had arrived, Bishop DeLunden had been very vocal about how the Patriarch treated everyone and, more importantly, *his* cathedral. It was a matter of jealousy, but Merton would never say anything. If Novron wished the bishop to learn this lesson, he would find a worthier vessel than him to explain.

"I also don't like how he holds court in the holy chancel, as

if he were Novron himself. The altar deserves more respect.
Only the empress should occupy that space, only the blood of
Novron, but he sits there as if *he* is the emperor."

"Is he there now?"

"Of course he is—him and his guards. Why does he need
guards, anyway? I don't have guards and I meet dozens of
people every day. He meets no one but is never separated from
them—and what strange men. They speak only to him, and
always in whispers. Why is that? He unnerves me. I am glad I
never met the man when I was a deacon, or I should never
have devoted my life to Novron."

"And that would have been a terrible loss to us all," Merton assured him. "Now if you do not mind, I must speak with
the Patriarch."

"Patriarch! That's another thing. The man has a name—he
was born with a name, just like the rest of us—but no one ever
uses it. We refer to our lords as Novron and Maribor, but
Nilnev of Ervanon must be referred to as *the Patriarch*, out of
respect for his office as head of the church, but as I said, he's
not the head anymore. Novron's child has returned to us, but
still he sits there. Still he rules. I don't like it—I don't like it one
bit, and I don't think the empress approves either. If she doesn't,
we can be assured our lord Novron isn't too pleased."

"Would you like me to speak to him about your concerns?"

DeLunden scowled. "Oh, he knows. Believe me, he knows."

Merton left the bishop in the narthex and entered the nave.
He stopped briefly, looking down the long cavernous room
with its magnificent arched ceiling, shaped like a great ship's
keel—the word *nave*, Merton had learned, was derived from
the ancient term *navis*, meaning *ship*. Towering rows of ribbed
pillars, like bunches of reeds bound together, rose hundreds of
feet, spilling out at the tops, which spread to form the vaulted
ceiling. To either side, lower aisles flanked the nave, encased in

the arcades—the series of repeating archways and columns. Above them, the clerestory, or second story, was pierced by tall quatrefoil windows, which normally flooded the floor with light. Tonight they remained black and oily as they reflected the fire of the candles. The same was true of the great rose window at the far end of the cathedral, which appeared as one giant eye. Merton often thought of it as the eye of god watching them, but just as the clerestory lights were dark, so too the great eye remained shut.

Reaching the altar, Merton found alabaster statues of Maribor and Novron. Novron, depicted as a strong handsome man in the prime of his youth, was kneeling, sword in hand. The god Maribor, sculpted as a powerful, larger-than-life figure with a long beard and flowing robes, loomed over Novron, placing a crown on the young man's head. The statues were the same in every church and chapel; only the materials differed, depending on the means of the parishioners.

"Come forward, Monsignor," he heard the Patriarch say. His voice carried in echoes from the altar. The cathedral was so large that from where he stood, those in the chancel appeared tiny, dwarfed by distance and made small by the height of the ceiling and the breadth of the walls.

Merton walked the long pathway, listening to the sounds of his shoes against the stone floor.

Just as DeLunden had described, the Patriarch sat at the altar on a chair, his gold and purple robes draped to the floor. Rumors circulated it was the same chair he had used in Ervanon, which he had ordered brought with him at great effort. Merton had never interviewed with His Holiness while in Ervanon, so he could not say if that rumor was true. Few could— His Holiness had rarely seen anyone in his days sequestered in the Crown Tower.

He might have been sleeping, the way the old did, regardless of where they happened to be. To either side of him stood the guards, matching their charge perfectly in color and fashion. DeLunden was right, at least about the guards: they were a peculiar pair. They stood like statues, without expressions, and for a moment he considered how their eyes reminded him of the windows.

Upon reaching the Patriarch, Merton knelt and kissed his ring, then stood once more. The Patriarch nodded. The guards did not move—not even to blink.

"You have news," Nilnev prompted.

"I do, Your Holiness. I have just come from a meeting with Her Eminence and her staff."

"So tell me, what is the empress doing to protect us?"

"She has done a great deal. Supplies have been stored to last the city an estimated two years with proper rationing, which she has already instituted. In addition, the grounds of Highcourt Fields will be opened to farmers come spring. This and other areas of the city will produce grain and vegetables from stored seed. Already manure is being delivered as fertilizer. Fish are being netted around the clock and salt houses are preserving the cod in bulk. A saltworks has been built near the docks to provide pans for raking. These measures could very well provide the city and its people with food for years— indefinitely, perhaps, should the fishing fleet be free to farm the sea.

"All stores are being kept underground in bunkers being dug by the populace in the event of attacks from the sky similar to what was seen at Dahlgren. In most instances, this is merely an expansion or adaptation of an existing dungeon. A series of tunnels have already been built that allow access to freshwater. The wastes from latrines are being channeled through newly built sewers. Given the frozen ground, progress is slow, but it is believed that adequate space is already available to save the population—although it will be most uncomfortable. Plans to continue the expansion underground could take two or three more months. The empress actually feels that having it uncompleted is beneficial, as it gives the people something to do."

"So she plans to become a city of moles, hiding in the dirt?"

"Well, yes and no, Your Holiness. She has also strengthened the defenses of the city. A series of catapults are in various states of construction around the outer walls, and soldiers are being drilled by officers appointed by Marshal Breckton. He has devised a number of redundant procedures for every contingency, allowing a means of giving commands in the form of horns, drums, and flags to be flown from the high towers. Archers have stockpiled thousands of arrows and any able-bodied citizen not already employed is working to gather wood for more. Even children are scouring the forest floors. Oil and tar vats are prepared and in ample supply at all gates.

"Signal fires were placed to burn the moment the elves were spotted. One was lit and the empress has ordered all of the roads leading to the city to be destroyed, save the southern gate. All bridges and dams are to be broken in order to prevent—"

"Destroyed?" the Patriarch interrupted. "When did she give this order?"

"Just last night."

"Last night?" The Patriarch looked concerned. "Is there anything else?"

"The empress asked me to inquire what precautions you will be taking."

"That is none of her business," he replied.

Merton was shocked. "Begging your pardon, Your Holiness, but she is the empress as well as the head of the church.

How is it not her business to know what efforts you have taken to secure her flock?"

The Patriarch glared at him for a moment, then softened his expression. "You are a good and devout member of the church, Merton of Ghent, and as our lord has seen fit to make you my liaison to the empress, I think perhaps it is time you were made aware of certain truths."

"Your Holiness?"

"Empress Modina is not the head of this church," the Patriarch declared simply.

"But she's the Heir of Novron—"

"That's exactly the problem—she is not." The Patriarch licked his nonexistent lips and continued. "Bishop Saldur and Archbishop Galien overstepped their mandate while in Dahlgren. They took it upon themselves to declare the girl the anointed heir. It was a well-intentioned mistake. They were too impatient to wait for Novron to show the way, so they sought to artificially create a new empire. They picked this girl at random, using the unexpected incidents on the Nidwalden to serve as proof. What happened there, however, was proof of nothing. It's a fabrication that a Gilarabrywn can only be slain by the blood of Novron. They used the ignorance of the masses to build this false empire."

"Why didn't you stop it?"

"What could I do? Did you think I *chose* to live my life in seclusion?"

Merton looked at the Patriarch for a moment, confused; then the revelation dawned on him. "You were a prisoner?"

"Why else would I be locked away at the top of the Crown Tower all these years, never seeing anyone?"

"These guards?"

"The only two souls I know to be truly loyal to me. They tried to free me once. They spoke out and Galien had their tongues sliced off. Only now, with Saldur and the others dead, and Ervanon destroyed, am I able to speak freely."

"I can hardly believe it," the monsignor said. "The archbishop, and Saldur as well? But they both seemed so kindly."

"You have no idea of their ruthlessness. Now, as a result of their actions, a false god sits on the throne of our lord and our fate is in peril."

"But you can do something about it now, can't you?"

"What can I do? You've heard the mutterings of even old Bishop DeLunden. Imagine what the world would think if I tried to tell the truth. I would be labeled a jealous old man, clinging to lost power. No one would believe me. The empress would see me murdered, just as she eliminated Ethelred and Saldur when they stood in her way. No, I cannot act openly — not yet."

"What do you intend to do, then?"

"There is a greater issue at stake. We do not face just the extinction of the empire, but of mankind. Modina and her actions will doom all of us."

"Her preparations to defend the city certainly appear to —"

"Her efforts are useless, but that is not of which I speak."

"You're referring to the mission to Percepliquis?"

"Yes! It's by this that she imperils all."

"But you were at the meeting. Why didn't you say anything?"

"Because that mission *is* necessary. It's imperative that the horn be found. The danger lies in *who* finds it. That horn is a weapon of incredible power. What Modina does not know — what even Saldur and Ethelred did not know — is that they have been fooled into searching for it. The enemy needs to lay hands on it as much as we do. Whoever wields it controls all. It's *he* who they obey. They have always been his pawn. For centuries, he has planned this, his hand guiding every move, hidden in the shadows, manipulating forces unseen. They think he is gone, that he is dead, but he is not. He is clever and crafty, his magic is beyond imagining, and he seeks revenge. A millennium of preparation comes down to this moment and it is he who desires the horn and with it will make all of mankind bow to him. Even the elves will pay for crimes committed a thousand years ago. They will hand the horn to him, for they do not see the danger traveling with them.

"Right now, in the depths of this world, ten individuals are delving into the past and discovering what never should be known, and with that knowledge the world will be undone, unless..."

Merton waited, and when the Patriarch said nothing more, he asked, "Unless what?"

The old man, with his barren brows and bluish hair, looked back as if pulled from a terrible nightmare. "I did what I could. I managed to strike a deal with a member of the empress's team. At the right moment, my agent will betray them."

"Who?"

"I will not say. You are a good servant of Novron, but I cannot take a chance of revealing his identity even to you — not with so much at stake."

"Can you at least tell me who this evil one is? Who can span the course of a thousand years to bring this about?"

"Think hard, Monsignor, and you will know, but for now pray — pray to Novron that my agent will succeed in his charge."

"I will, Your Holiness. I will."

"Good, and pack your bags lightly."

"Am I going somewhere?"

"We both are."

CHAPTER 12

THIEVES END

R oyce heard whispering.
He estimated it was an hour before dawn. Although he
wasn't certain, it would surprise him if he was very far off. Royce
had experience keeping track of time underground. He had
developed a surprisingly accurate method during his incarceration in Manzant. During those days, tracking minutes had
focused his mind, keeping it off other, more painful thoughts.
This was the first time in many years he had allowed himself to
remember those days. He had carefully locked them away, packaged them into a back corner of his mind with a dark blanket
laid over top, just in case he accidentally looked that way. Only
now did he welcome the memories. The pain they caused worked
much the same way as keeping track of time had in Manzant,
much the same as biting a finger, or squeezing his fist until the
fingernails dug half-moons into his palm. They distracted him
from thoughts of loss far more fresh—far more crippling.

More than a decade had passed since the First Officer of
the Black Diamond had betrayed him, since he had tragically
killed Jade and as a result was sent to Manzant Prison by his
best friend. Manzant was a dwarven-constructed prison and
salt mine. He could still remember the dark rock with streaks

of white and fossils of shellfish. The walls were shored up with timber. Dwarves never used wood. Men added that years later as they carved deeper, hauling the chunks of rock salt out to the elevator in baskets. It was easy to tell the man-made sections from the dwarven by the height of the ceiling. Those being punished worked in the dwarven tunnels, and Royce often found himself there.

He recalled the constant clink of pick on stone and the heat of the fires boiling the brine out of underwater lakes. Huge pans, bubbling and hissing, filled the stale air with steam. If he closed his eyes, he could see the line of bucket men and the walkers chained by their necks to the huge wheel powering the pump. He could also see men driven to exhaustion until they collapsed into the furnace pit.

Water was plentiful, so it was available to those who worked, but Ambrose Moor, the owner of the prison mine, did not waste his profits on food. They were lucky to receive a single small meal a day, usually the spoiled remnants of what a crew of indentured sailors refused to eat. This was just one of many deals Ambrose arranged to minimize operation costs. Royce would fall asleep to dreams of killing Ambrose and the thoughts lingered throughout the day. In the two and a half years he spent in Manzant, he killed Ambrose five hundred and thirty-seven times—no two alike. He killed many people in Manzant and not all of them were imaginary. He never thought of them as people. They were all animals, monsters. Whatever humanity a man had possessed going in was leached out by the salt, pain, and despair. They all fought for rotten food, a place to sleep, a cup of water. He learned how to sleep light and how to appear like he was sleeping when he was not.

Never seeing daylight, never breathing fresh air, and being worked to exhaustion each day, and beaten for mere recreation, had killed many and driven others insane. For Royce, Manzant was only part of his prison, the latest incarnation. The real walls he had been building up brick by brick for years. Escaping Manzant was impossible, but it was ultimately easier than escaping the prison of his own making.

Nim had started him on the path, and later Arcadius and Hadrian had guided his way, but it was Gwen who had finally unlocked the cell door. She shoved it open and stood just outside calling, assuring him it was safe. He could smell the fresh air and see the brilliance of the sun. He was almost through, almost out—almost.

The whispering came from near the pool.

He thought everyone was asleep. They had traveled a long distance that day over hard terrain. No one had called for him to stop, but he had seen them stumbling—all except the dwarf. The little rat never seemed to tire but continued to scurry, and more than once, Royce had spotted a little smile behind the mustache and remains of his beard.

He had almost killed Magnus that first night they had spent at The Laughing Gnome. The thought had danced teasingly on his mind. That was before Myron came back from dinner and got all chatty. Royce would not admit it to anyone, but the dwarf was useful, and on surprisingly good behavior—which showed even more good sense. More than that, he discovered he no longer had the desire. Like everything else, the dwarf's crime had been made trivial by Gwen's death. Both love and hate were banished from him. He was a desert, dry of all passion. Mostly he was tired. He had one last job to do and he would do it, not for the empire, not even for Hadrian—this was for Gwen.

He got to his feet silently, out of curiosity more than concern. The whispering was definitely coming from the party— not some intruder. He spotted the princess lying on her side, wrapped in twisted blankets. She was jerking and thrashing again, that creepy robe glowing different colors, fading out and lighting up. He had no idea if the robe was causing her to dream so violently or if her dreams sparked the robe's response. He did not see how it was any of his business and moved on.

At first, he thought it might be Magnus and Gaunt whispering. He frequently spied them traveling together and talking when the rest were too far to hear. Drawing closer, he discovered the source—it was Elden. He could see the huge reclined form up on one elbow under the blanket. His conspirator was on the far side and blocked from view. Wyatt lay a short distance away. He too was awake and watching.

"What's going on?" Royce whispered to the sailor. "Who's Elden talking to?"

"The monk."

"Myron?"

Wyatt nodded.

"Is it normal for him to talk to strangers like that?"

Wyatt looked at him. "He's talked more to that little monk in the last three days than he has to me in the last decade. They were doing this last night too, and I swear I heard Elden crying. I once watched while a ship's surgeon put a red-hot poker to a wound on his thigh. Elden didn't make a sound, but last night that little monk had him weeping so bad his eyes were red the next morning."

Royce said nothing.

"Funny thing, though, he was smiling. All day long, I saw Elden grinning from ear to ear. That's just not like him."

"Best get back to sleep," Royce told him. "I'll be waking everyone in another hour."

༄

Royce stopped again.

Hadrian could see him over the heads of the others from

his position at the rear. This time, Royce knelt down, placed the lantern on the ground beside him, and scraped the dirt. Alric approached and stood slightly to one side.

The party spent most of that day, like the one before, traveling in a single column in the narrow corridor. Overhead, water dripped, soaking their heads and shoulders; likewise, their feet felt pickled from wading through ankle-deep pools.

"What is it this time?" he heard Degan mutter with disdain. "He's stopping every twenty feet now. This is the problem with monarchies and the whole feudal system, for that matter. Alric is in charge by no other virtue than his birth, and the man is clearly incompetent. He lost his own kingdom twice over in a single year, and now he is in charge of us? We should have a leader who is elected on merit, not lineage. Someone who is the most talented, the most gifted, but no—we have Alric. And the king in all his minuscule wisdom has chosen Royce to guide us. If I were in charge, I would put Magnus out front. He's obviously far more gifted. He's constantly correcting Royce's mistakes. We would be making twice the time we are now. I've observed that people respect you."

Hadrian noticed Gaunt was looking at him. Up until that moment, he had not known who Gaunt was speaking to.

"No one says it, no one bows or anything, but you are highly regarded, I can tell—more than Alric, that's for certain. If you were to support me, I think we could persuade the others to accept my command of this group. I know Magnus would."

"Why you?" Hadrian asked.

"Huh?"

"Why should you be in charge?"

"Oh—well, for one thing I am the descendant of Novron and will be emperor. And second, I am smarter than that oaf Alric, by far."

"I thought you said you wanted a system based on merit, not lineage."

"I did, but like I said, I am far better suited to the task than he is. Besides, why else am I here if not to lead?"

"Alric has led men into battle, and when I say *led*, I mean it. He personally charged the gates of Medford under a hail of arrows ahead of everyone, even his bodyguards."

"Exactly, the man is a fool."

"All right, it might not have been the smartest choice, but it did show courage and an unwillingness to sit back in safety while sending others into peril. That right there gives him credit in my book. But okay, I see your point. He might not be the smartest leader. So if you want someone with brains and merit, then Princess Arista is your clear choice."

Degan chuckled, apparently taking his comments as a joke. When he saw Hadrian's scowl, he stopped. "You're not serious? She's a woman—an irritating, manipulative, bossy woman. She shouldn't even be on this trip. She's got Alric wrapped around her finger and it will get us all killed. Did you know she tried to free me from that dungeon all by herself? She failed miserably, got herself captured and her bodyguard killed. That's what she does, you know. She gets people killed. She's a menace. And on top of that she's also a wit—"

Degan struck the wall with the back of his head, bounced off, and fell to his knees. Hadrian felt the pain in his knuckles and only then realized he had hit him.

Gaunt glared up, his eyes watering, his hands cupping his face. "Crazy fool! Are you mad?"

"What's going on?" Arista called back down the line.

"This idiot just punched me in the face! My nose is bleeding!"

"*Hadrian* did?" the princess said, stunned.

"It was...an accident," Hadrian replied, knowing it sounded

feeble, but not knowing how else to describe his actions. He had not meant to hit Gaunt; it had just happened.

"You *accidentally* punched him?" Wyatt asked, suppressing a chuckle. "I'm not sure you have a full understanding of the whole bodyguard thing."

"Hadrian!" Royce called.

"What?" he shouted back, irritated that even Royce was going to join in this embarrassing moment.

"Come up here. I need you to look at something."

Degan was still on his knees in a pool of water. "Um—sorry 'bout that."

"Get away from me!"

Hadrian moved up the line as Wyatt, Elden, and Myron pressed themselves against the walls to let him pass, each one looking at him curiously.

"What did he do?" Arista whispered as he reached her.

"Nothing, really."

Her eyebrows rose. "You punched him for no reason?"

"Well, no, but—it's complicated. I'm not even sure I understand it. It was sort of like a reflex, I guess."

"A...reflex?" she said.

"I told him I was sorry."

"Anytime today would be nice," Royce said.

Arista stepped aside, looking at him suspiciously as he passed.

"What was all that about?" Alric asked as he approached.

"I, ah—I punched Gaunt in the face."

"Good for you," Alric told him.

"About time someone did," Mauvin said. "I'm just sorry you beat me to it."

"What do you make of this?" Royce asked, still on his knees and pointing to something on the ground beside his lantern.

Hadrian bent down. It was a leather string with a series of stone beads, feathers, and what looked like chicken bones threaded through it.

"It's a Trajan ankle bracelet," he told them. "Worn for luck by warriors of the Ankor tribe of the Ghazel."

"The ends aren't torn," Royce said. "But look how they are bent and twisted. I think it just came untied. And it is partially buried under the dirt, so I am thinking it's been here awhile. Regardless, we are in their neighborhood, so we'd better start moving a bit more cautiously. See if you can keep the chatter down to a minimum."

Hadrian looked at the bracelet and caught Royce by the arm as he was about to move forward again.

"Here," he said, keeping his body positioned to block the view of the rest of the party. He placed Alverstone into Royce's hand.

"I was wondering where that went."

"Time to re-claw the cat, I think," Hadrian said. "Just be a good boy, okay?"

"Look who's talking."

The party moved forward again. Hadrian did not return to the rear. He thought it was more likely they would encounter Ghazel from the front, and he also did not relish the idea of returning to Gaunt.

The corridor widened until they could walk three abreast. Then abruptly the passageway ended. It stopped in a small room where the far side narrowed to no more than a crack. In the center was nothing more than a sizable pile of rocks.

Gaunt shook his head in disgust. "I told you he was incompetent," he said, pointing at Alric. "He was so sure this was the right passage, and here we are days later standing at a dead end."

"You said *I* was incompetent?" the king asked, then looked to Hadrian. "No wonder you hit him. Thanks."

"What about us?" Gaunt asked. "How many days of food do we have? How much time have we wasted? We've been down here—what? Three days now? And it took us two days from Aquesta. That's five days. Add five days to get back and even if we were to leave right now, we will have been gone ten days! How long do you think we have until the elves reach Aquesta? Two weeks? We'll blow most of that time just retracing our steps."

"I did not hear you suggesting a different choice," Arista said. "Alric picked as best he could and I don't think anyone here could have chosen any better."

"How surprising—*his sister* is defending him."

Mauvin stepped toward Gaunt and drew his blade. The sword picked up the light from the lanterns on its mirrored surface and flashed as Mauvin raised the point to Gaunt's neck. "I warned you before. Do not speak of my king without respect in my presence."

"Mauvin, stop!" Arista ordered.

"I'm not going to kill him," he assured her. "I'll just carve my initials in his face."

"Alric." She turned to her brother. "Tell him to stop."

"I'm not certain I should."

"See! This is the oppression I spoke of!" Gaunt shouted. "The evils of a hereditary authority."

"Somebody shut him up," Royce snapped.

"Mauvin," Hadrian said.

"What?" Mauvin looked at him, confused. "You punched him!"

"Yeah, well—that was then."

"Lower your blade, Mauvin," Alric said, relenting. "My honor can wait until we are through with this."

Mauvin sheathed his weapon and Gaunt pushed himself

away from the wall, breathing heavily. "Threatening me doesn't change the situation. We are still at a dead end and it is—"

"It's not a dead end," Magnus stated. He stomped his boot twice, got to his knees, and placed his ear to the ground. Then he looked up and glared at the pile of rocks. He got back to his feet and began throwing the rocks aside. Beneath were several pieces of wooden planking and, below them, a hole.

"That was hidden on purpose," Wyatt said.

"This doesn't mean we are in the right passage," Gaunt argued. "I don't remember the monk ever saying anything about going in a hole. There's no way to tell this is the right way."

"It is," Myron replied.

Gaunt turned on the little monk. "Oh, so you're keeping information from us, is that it? Or are you merely incompetent and just forgot to tell us about this part of the journal?"

"No," he said meekly. "There's nothing in the journal about this."

"Then surely you are more pious than I thought, for Maribor himself must be giving you information he keeps from the rest of us."

"Maybe," Myron replied. "All I know is that's Edmund Hall's mark." He pointed. "See there, carved into the stone."

Royce was first to it and, holding his light above the floor, revealed the etched inscription:

$$E\!\!/\!\!H$$

"E.H.," Gaunt read. "How do we know that stands for Edmund Hall?"

"You think there's a parade of people coming through here with those initials, do you?" Royce asked.

"That's the exact way he wrote his initials in the journal," Myron explained.

"What about these, Myron?" Royce asked as he pushed more rocks away to reveal more etchings. These were much brighter—fresher than the *EH*.

Myron glanced at them for only a moment before saying, "I don't know anything about those."

Hadrian stepped up, blew the dirt away. Then he turned to Arista and Alric. "Didn't the Patriarch say he sent other teams?"

"Yes, he did," Alric agreed. "Three of them, I think."

"According to the empress, they all failed," Arista added.

Hadrian glanced at Royce. "I think we know about the third group he sent, but they didn't come this way. Still, I'm guessing these are the initials of either the first or the second team." He looked at Royce again. "If you were going to hand-pick a group to come down here, and you could choose anyone, who would you pick to lead such a group?"

"Breckton, maybe," Royce replied. "Or possibly Gravin Dent of Delgos."

"Well, we know they didn't pick Breckton, and look at the first initials, GD. Now when was the last time anyone saw Gravin? He wasn't at the Wintertide games this year."

"Not last year either," Alric said.

"He was at Dahlgren," Mauvin said.

"Yes, he was!" Arista confirmed. "I remember Fanen pointing him out and saying what a great adventurer he was and how he worked mainly for the Church of Nyphron. He called him something...a—a—"

"Quester?" Mauvin asked.

"Yes, that's it!"

"Now let's think about that," Hadrian said. "They would need a scholar, a historian. Dent was at Dahlgren. Wasn't there someone else too? That funny guy with the catapult, what was his name?"

"Tobis Rentinual?" Mauvin asked. "He was a real nut."

"Yeah, but do you remember him saying something about how he named the catapult after Novron's wife, because of all the research he did into ancient imperial history?"

"Yes. He said something about having to learn a language or something, didn't he? He was all boastful about it, remember?"

"That's right." Hadrian was nodding. "Look at that second set of initials, TR."

"Tobis Rentinual," Mauvin said. "It even looks like how he would draw his letters."

"What about the others?" Alric asked.

Hadrian shrugged. "I'm really only guessing at the first two. I have no idea about the others."

"I do," Magnus said. "Well, one of them, at least. HM, that's Herclor Math."

"Who?" Hadrian asked, and looked around, but everyone shrugged.

"Of course none of you would know him. He's a mason— a *dwarf* mason—and a good one. I would recognize his inscription anywhere. The Maths are an old family. A Math even worked on the design team of Drumindor. His clan goes back a long way."

"Why did they initial the stone?" Wyatt asked.

"Maybe to let anyone who might follow know they got this far," Magnus replied.

"Why didn't they mark the bloody three-choice passage?" Mauvin asked.

"Maybe they planned to," Arista said. "Maybe—like us— they didn't know if they picked the right one, but planned to mark it on the way out, only—only they never came out."

"Maybe we should carve our initials too," Mauvin suggested. "So others will know we were here."

"No," Arista said. "If we don't come back out, there will be no others to follow us."

Each of them looked toward the hole with apprehension.

"At any rate," Royce said, "this looks like the place. Who's carrying the rope?"

They tied three lengths of rope together, and with Hadrian on the line, Royce climbed in. They fed out two-thirds of it before Hadrian felt the line stop and Royce's weight come off.

He waited.

They all waited. Some sat down on whatever flat spots they could find. Elden remained standing. He had an unpleasant look on his face as he eyed the hole. Despite Arista's comments, the dwarf busied himself carving each of their initials into the stone.

"You want to call down to him?" Alric asked. "He's been in there a while."

"It's better to be patient," he replied. "Royce will either call up or yank on the line when he wants us to come down."

"What if he fell?" Mauvin asked.

"He didn't. On the other hand, what is more likely is that there's a patrol of Ghazel and he's waiting for them to pass. If you get nervous and start yelling down, you'll get him killed, or angry. Either way it's not a good idea."

Mauvin and Alric both nodded gravely. Hadrian had learned his lesson the hard way on that first trip the two made to Ervanon. Learning to trust Royce when it was dark, you were alone, and the world was so quiet you could hear your own breathing was not something you did overnight.

Hadrian remembered the wind whipping them as they climbed the Crown Tower. *That* was a *big* tower. He must have climbed a hundred of them with Royce since, but aside from Drumindor, that was the tallest—and the first. He had marveled at how the little thief could scale the sheer wall like a fly with nothing but those hand-claws. He gave Hadrian a pair and sat smirking as he tried to use them.

"Hopeless," was all he said, taking the claws back. "Can you at least climb a rope?"

Hadrian had just returned from his days in the arenas of Calis, where he had been respected and cheered by roaring crowds as the Tiger of Mandalin. He was less than pleased with this little twig of a man treating him as if he were the village idiot. So infuriated had he been by Royce's smug tone that Hadrian had wanted to beat him unconscious, only Arcadius had warned him to be patient. "He's like the pup of a renowned hunting dog who's been beaten badly by every master he's had," the old wizard had told him. "He's a gem worthy of a little work, but he'll test you—he'll test you a lot. Royce doesn't make friends easily and he doesn't make it easy to be his friend. Don't get angry. That's what he's looking for. That's what he expects. He'll try to drive you away, but you'll fool him. Listen to him. Trust him. That's what he won't expect. It won't be easy. You'll have to be very patient. But if you do, you'll make a friend for life, the kind that will walk unarmed into the jaws of a dragon if you ask him to."

Hadrian felt a light tug on the rope.

"Everything okay, pal?" he called down softly.

"Found it," Royce replied. "Come on down."

It was like a mine shaft, tight and deep. Hadrian had descended only a short distance when his eyes detected a faint light below. The pale blue-green light appeared to leak into the base of the shaft, which, he could now estimate, was no more than a hundred feet deep. As he reached the bottom, he felt a strong breeze and heard a sound. A very out-of-place sound—the crash of waves.

He stood in an enormous cavern so vast he could not see the far wall. At his feet were shells and black sand, and before him lay a great body of water with waves that rolled in white and frothy. Along the beach, he spotted clumps of seaweed and algae that glowed bright green and the ocean gave off an emerald light, which the ceiling reflected in such a way as to make it seem like they were not underground at all. He felt like he was standing on the beach at night under a cloudy, albeit green, sky. His nose filled with the pungent scent of salt, fish, and seaweed. To the right lay nothing but endless water, but straight out, just visible at the horizon, were structures—the outlines of buildings, pillars, towers, and walls.

Across the sea lay the city of Percepliquis.

Royce stood on the shore, staring across the water, and glanced over his shoulder when Hadrian touched down. "Not something you see every day, is it?"

"Wow," he replied.

It did not take long before all of them stood on the black sand, gazing out at the sea and the city beyond. Myron looked as if he were in shock. Hadrian realized the monk had never seen an ocean, much less one that glowed bright green.

"Edmund Hall mentioned an underground sea," Myron said at length. "But Mr. Hall is not terribly good at descriptions. This—*this* is truly amazing. I've never thought of myself as big in any sense, but standing here, I feel as small as a pebble."

"Anyone lose an ocean? 'Cause I think we just found it," Mauvin announced.

"It's beautiful," Arista said.

"Whoa," Wyatt muttered.

"How are we going to get across it?" Gaunt asked.

They all looked to Myron. "Oh, right—sorry. Edmund Hall made a raft from stuff he found washed up on the beach.

He said there was a lot of it. He lashed planking with a rope he had with him and formed a rudder out of one side of an old crate. His sail was a patchwork of sewn bags, his mast a tall log of driftwood."

"How long did it take him?" Gaunt asked.

"Three weeks."

"By Mar!" he exclaimed.

Alric scowled at him. "There's ten of us and we have an expert sailor and better gear. Let's get looking for our raw material."

They all spread out like a group of beachcombers looking for shells and starfish on a lovely summer's day.

There was a good deal of debris on the shore. Old bottles and broken crates, poles and nets, all amazingly well preserved after having been down there for a thousand years. Hadrian picked up a jug with writing on one side. He carefully turned it over, realizing he was holding an artifact that by its mere age was profoundly valuable. He did not expect to be able to read it. Everything from the ancient time of Percepliquis would be in Old Speech. He looked at the markings and was stunned to find he could understand them: BRIG'S RUM DISTILLERY. DAGASTAN, CALIS.

He blinked.

"Where's Myron?" It was not so much the question as the voice that pulled Hadrian's attention away from the jug.

Elden had spoken. The big man stood like a wave break on the sand, his head twisting around, searching. "I don't see him."

Hadrian glanced up and down the beach. Elden was right—the monk was gone.

"I'll find him," Royce said, annoyed, and trotted off.

"Elden?" Wyatt called. "Can you give me a hand here?" he said, trying to pull up a large weathered plank mostly buried in the sand. "We can use this as the keel, I think."

Alric and Mauvin were dragging over what looked like the side of a wooden crate. "There's another side to this back there among those rocks," the king informed Wyatt.

"That's great, but right now can the two of you help us dig this beam out?"

Gaunt wandered the beach halfheartedly, kicking over rocks, as if he might find a mast hiding under one. Magnus noticeably avoided the water, sticking to the high beach area and glancing over his shoulder at the waves as if they were barking dogs he needed to constantly assure himself were chained.

Arista came running down to where the four dug the beam out of the sand. "I found a huge piece of canvas!" she said, and did a little dance.

Hadrian noticed her feet were bare. She held her shoes in her hands, swinging them by the heels, her robe swaying. As he looked at her just then, she could have been any number of girls he had known from taverns or small towns—not a princess at all.

"Don't you like my celebratory dance?" she asked him.

"Is that what that is?"

She rolled her eyes. "Com'on and help me get the canvas. It will make the perfect sail."

She ran back down the beach and Hadrian followed. She stopped and, bending down, pulled on the corner of a buried piece of canvas. "We'll have to dig it out, but I bet it is big. I think—" She stopped when she spotted Royce and Myron walking toward them.

"There you are," Hadrian said in a reprimanding tone. "You had Elden worried, young man."

"I saw a crab," Myron said, embarrassed. "They have these huge claws and run sideways—they scurry very fast—like big spiders. I chased him down the beach, but he disappeared into a hole before I could get a good look. Have you ever seen a crab?"

"Yes, Myron. I've seen crabs before."

"Oh, so you know how fascinating they are! I was literally carried away—well, not literally. I mean, I wasn't actually *carried* by the crab; *lured* is more accurate."

"Royce, look at the canvas I found!" Arista said, repeating her little dance for him.

"Very nice," the thief replied.

"You don't seem suitably impressed. It's going to be our sail," she told him proudly. "Maybe we should have a contest for the person who finds the best part of the raft." She followed this with a greedy grin.

"We could do that." Royce nodded. "But I don't think you'll win."

"No? Did you find something better?"

"Myron did."

"Better than the crab?" Hadrian asked.

"You could say that." Royce motioned for them to follow.

They walked around an arm of the cliff wall that jutted into the sea, causing them all to wade up to their ankles for a short bit. On the far side, resting on the sand about a half mile down the beach, was a small single-mast boat that listed off the keel. Its pair of black sails dangled from the yards, feebly flapping in the sea breeze.

"By Mar!" Hadrian and Arista said together.

❧

A loose board on the boat's deck creaked under Hadrian's weight and Royce glared at him. Twelve years they had worked together, and still Royce did not seem capable of understand-

ing that Hadrian could not float. The problem was that Royce
apparently could. He made it look so easy. Hadrian walked
like the caricature of a thief—on his toes, his arms out for
balance, wavering up and down as if he were on a tightrope.
Royce walked as casually as if he were sauntering down a city
street. They communicated as they always did on the job, with
facial expressions and hand gestures. Royce had learned sign
language as part of his guild training but had never bothered
teaching Hadrian more than a few signals. Royce was always
able to communicate what he needed by pointing, counting
with his fingers, or making simple obvious signs like scissoring his fingers across his level palm, imitating legs walking on
a floor. He expressed most of his silent dialogue the way he was
now: through rolled eyes, glares, and the pitiable shaking of
his head. Given how irritated he so often looked, it was a mystery why he put up with Hadrian. After the first trip to the
Crown Tower, both were convinced Arcadius was insane in
pairing them. Royce hated him and the feeling was mutual.
Just as Royce recently confirmed, the only reason they had
gone back together was out of spite—their shared dislike
compelled them. Royce wanted to see Hadrian give up, or die,
and Hadrian refused to give him the satisfaction of either. Of
course, what ended up happening was something neither of
them expected—they were caught.

Royce held a hand out palm up, and Hadrian stopped moving, freezing in place as if he were playing a kid's game. He
could see Royce tilting his head like a dog trying to listen. He
shook his head and motioned for him to follow again.

The two had left the rest of the party on the beach, safely
back near where Arista had found the canvas, as they scouted
the ship. It looked abandoned, but Royce refused to take
chances. What they found on deck only further suggested it
was deserted. The wood was rough and weathering badly,

paint was peeling, and crabs scurried about as if they had lived there for some time. The bow plaque indicated the name: *Harbinger*. Still, one last mystery needed investigation. The little ship was tiny compared to the *Emerald Storm*, just large enough to support a below-deck cabin, and they needed to see what was inside.

The door lay closed and Royce inched up on it as if it were a viper ready to strike. When he reached the cabin, he glanced back at Hadrian, who drew his swords. Royce carefully twisted the latch. The corroded metal stuck and he struggled to free it. Then the door fell inward with a creek and banged against the inner wall. Hadrian rushed forward just in case. He fully expected the cabin to be empty, but to his surprise, the faint light falling through the doorway revealed a man.

He lay on a small bed within the small cabin. He was dead, his face rotted, the eyes and lips gone and most of the flesh eaten, perhaps by the crabs. Hadrian guessed the man had died not too long ago, less than a year certainly, perhaps only six months. He wore sailors' clothes and around his neck was a white kerchief.

Hadrian whispered, "My god, is that…"

Royce nodded. "It's Bernie."

Hadrian remembered Bernie as the wiry topman from the *Emerald Storm*. He along with Staul—whom Royce had killed—Dr. Levy, and the historian Antun Bulard had worked for Sentinel Thranic. They were the third and final team the Patriarch had sent in to obtain the horn. The last Hadrian had seen of them was in the dungeons beneath the Palace of the Four Winds.

"This looks like blood on the bed and floor," Royce said.

"I'll take your word for it—I just see a shadow—but what's that around his belly?"

"Linen—bloodstained. Looks like he died from a stab

wound to the stomach, but it was slow." Royce climbed out of the cabin and looked around the ship, bending down to study the decking and the lines.

"What are you looking for?"

"Blood," he replied. "There's blood all over the place, spots on the deck, handprints on the ropes, and on the wheel. I think he set sail wounded."

"He could have been attacked on board."

"Maybe, but I doubt it. He looks to have initially survived whatever fight gave him the wound, that means the other guy must have been hurt worse, only there's no other body."

"Might have dumped it in the sea."

"Mighta, but there would still be signs of a fight and blood—a lot of blood—somewhere. All I see are dribbles and drips. No, I think he was wounded, got the boat rigged, and set sail..." Royce ran to the wheel, then the stern. "Yep, rudder is tied. He set the ship, tied the rudder; then, feeling weak, he lay down below, where he slowly bled to death."

"So who knifed him?"

Royce shrugged. "Ghazel?"

Hadrian shook his head. "It's been—what? Three, four months? You saw that bracelet back there. The Ghazel have passed by here. They've seen this ship but haven't touched it. If they killed him, they would have taken it. No, Thranic had a deal with the Ghazel, remember? He said something about a guide and safe passage."

"So Merrick or the Patriarch managed to cut a deal with the Ghazel, letting them come in here?"

"Seems to be the case."

Hadrian waved to the others and dropped a rope ladder over the side.

"All safe and sound, I trust?" Alric asked, coming aboard.

"Safe," Hadrian said. "As for sound, I defer to our resident expert in the ways of seafaring."

Wyatt stood in the middle of the ship and slammed his feet down on the wood of the deck. He then grabbed a rope and climbed up to the masthead, inspecting the lines and the canvas. Lastly, he went below. When he returned, he said, "A little worn and neglected, but she's a fine ship as far as Tenkin doggers go."

"Tenkin?" Mauvin asked.

Wyatt nodded. "And that's Bernie in the cabin, right?"

"Pretty sure," Hadrian replied.

"Then that means this isn't just some underground salt lake."

"What do you mean?"

"This boat sailed here from the Palace of the Four Winds. This must open out to the Goblin Sea—some cove the Ba Ran Ghazel discovered that goes underground and is navigable all the way under Alburn to here."

"That's how the Ghazel have been getting in and managing to send scouting parties around Amberton Lee," Hadrian said.

"As nice as all that is," Alric began, "how are we going to get this ship into the water?"

"We aren't," Wyatt told him. "It will do that all by itself, in about six hours."

"Huh?"

"This ship is just going to jump in the water in six hours?" Mauvin asked incredulously.

"He's talking about the tide," Arista said.

"It's low tide right now, or near it. I'm guessing at high tide the watermark will be up to the cliff's edge. There won't even be a beach here. Of course, the ship may still be touching bottom. We'll set sail and hope the wind can pull us. If not, we'll have to kedge off."

"Kedge off?" Mauvin asked, and glanced at Arista, who this time shrugged.

"You take the ship's anchor, put it on a launch, paddle it out, drop it in the water, and then with the capstan you crank and pull the ship toward the anchor. It's not a fun drill. Sometimes the anchor doesn't catch, and sometimes it catches too well. Either way, turning the capstan is never pleasant. All I can say is thank Maribor we have Elden.

"Of course, a ship this size doesn't have a launch, so we'll need to make something to float the anchor out with. Since we have six hours to kill, we might as well do that. I'll need Royce, Hadrian, and Elden to help me set the ship in order, so could His Majesty grab a few of the remaining people and make a raft?"

"Consider it done, Captain," Alric told him.

"We should also dispose of old Bernie, I'm afraid," Wyatt said. "While it is tempting to just dump him in the sea, we probably should bury him."

"Don't look at me," Gaunt said. "I didn't even know the man."

"I'll do it," Myron told them. "Can someone help me get him to the beach?"

"Good, then we're all squared away," Wyatt said. "We'll set sail in six hours—hopefully."

CHAPTER 13

THE VOYAGE OF THE HARBINGER

The tide had come in and Arista noticed most of the shore was gone. Waves slammed against the cliff edge, hammering the wall. Seawater sluiced in and out of the shaft they had come down, making a vague sucking sound with each roll out. The ship sat upright, the deck flat, and the whole thing rocked with each new set of waves, which lifted the stern.

Myron stood on the deck of the *Harbinger*, casting his eyes upward at the sails as Royce flew about on ropes, tying off the braces. Soaked to the bone, the monk created a puddle where he stood. His frock stuck to his skin, a bit of glowing seaweed was on his shoulder, and he had black sand in his hair and on his cheeks.

"All done, then?" Hadrian asked, tying the end of one of the lines Royce had dropped to him.

Myron nodded. "Well, mostly, but I thought..." He looked up once more. "I thought Royce might be willing to say a few words, since he knew him best."

"Royce is a bit busy," Hadrian replied.

Myron's shoulders slumped.

"How about if I come? I knew him too."

"Can I come?" Arista asked. She had been on deck coiling ropes and generally clearing the clutter. No one had asked her to. No one had asked her to do anything. Women were unexpected on board a ship and she did not think Wyatt knew what to do with her. She had tried helping Alric with building the raft for the anchor, but that had gone badly. Her brother noticeably winced each time she suggested something to Mauvin, Degan, or Magnus. After only an hour, she excused herself, saying she was not feeling well, and returned to the ship. She hoped Wyatt would have some use for her, but he only smiled and nodded politely as he passed.

"Of course," Myron said eagerly, a smile brightening his face.

Arista jumped to her feet, feeling oddly relieved. Somehow she had expected Myron would exclude her as well. She regretted volunteering, as getting off the ship required wading in chest-deep water. It was very cold and took her breath away. Her robe billowed around her as she struggled to find traction in the ground below.

A strong wave struck her from behind and she started to fall face forward. Hadrian caught her by the elbow and held her up.

"Thank you. I thought I was going for a swim there," she told him.

"Bad form on the wave's part, sneaking up and attacking you from the back like that."

"Not very chivalrous, was it?"

"Not at all—I'd complain."

Myron moved ahead of them, splashing his way to a high point where the water was only a few inches deep. "He's under here—at least, he used to be." Myron looked about, concerned.

"I'm sure he still is," Hadrian said.

"We'd best get started before he slips away," Arista said as a wave's retreat sucked her feet into the sand. "You start us off, Myron."

"Dear Maribor, our eternal father, we are gathered here to say farewell to our brother Bernie. That's his name, right?" Myron whispered.

Hadrian nodded.

"We ask that you remember him and see that he crosses the river to the land of the dawn." He looked to Hadrian, motioning with his hand for him to speak.

"Ah..." Hadrian thought a moment. "Bernie wasn't a good man, exactly. He was a thief, and a grave robber, and he tried to knife Royce once—"

Seeing Myron's expression, Arista nudged Hadrian.

"But, um...he didn't actually ever try to kill any of us. He was just doing his job, I guess. I suppose he was pretty good at it." Hadrian stopped there, looking awkward.

"Would *you* like to say something?" Myron asked Arista.

"I didn't know him."

"At this point I don't think he'd mind," Myron said.

"Okay. I suppose." She thought a second, then said, "Although none of us knew him well, I am certain Mr. Bernie had virtues as well as shortcomings, like any of us. He likely helped people, or showed courage in the face of adversity when others might not. He must have had some good in him; otherwise Maribor would not have sent one of his most compassionate and thoughtful servants here to ensure he had a proper passing."

"Wow, that was much better than mine," Hadrian whispered.

"Shh," Arista said.

"And so, Lord," Myron concluded with a bowed head, "we say farewell to Bernie. May the light of a new dawn rise upon his soul." Then in a light voice Myron sang:

> *Unto Maribor, I beseech thee*
> *Into the hands of god, I send thee*
> *Grant him peace, I beg thee*
> *Give him rest, I ask thee*
> *May the god of men watch over your journey.*

"Is that it?" Hadrian asked.

"That's it," Myron replied. "Thank you both for coming and standing in the cold water."

"Let's get back. My feet are going numb," Arista said, hopping through the surf.

"Your Highness?" Myron asked, chasing her. "I can't help but ask. Who is the servant of Maribor you were speaking of?"

She looked at him, surprised. "You, of course."

"Oh."

When they got back, Alric and the rest were tying up their makeshift raft to the side of the *Harbinger*. Arista was impressed. The raft was eight feet square, lashed tight and caulked with pitch.

On board, Wyatt and Elden were pushing everything that could be moved from the bow to the stern. The back of the ship began to rock in earnest, making it hard to stand.

Once everyone was on board, Wyatt looked up as if to the heavens and shouted, "Loose the tops'l!"

She gasped as Royce pulled a line, then without hesitation ran across the yard to the far side and pulled another. The topsail fell open and Royce dropped to the masthead and, running along the top of the mainsail yard, tied off the sheets.

"Loose the mains'l!" Wyatt shouted, and Royce released the big sail. "Hands to the sheets!"

Hadrian and Elden, on opposite sides of the ship, pulled ropes connected to the lower corners of the sail, stretching it out taut.

"Hands to the braces! Back all sails!"

Elden and Hadrian grabbed hold of ropes attached to the ends of the yards and pulled, twisting them around so that they caught the wind on an angle, pushing the ship backward toward the sea. They looked to Wyatt, who waved them over until they had the right angle; then they tied off the braces.

"Everyone to the stern!" Wyatt called, and each of them moved to the back of the ship. The wind and the waves rocked them, and at times it seemed they were lifting, but the ship failed to move.

"The keel's dug in," Wyatt said, then sighed. "We'll need to kedge off. Elden and Hadrian, hoist the anchor to the raft and lash it tight. Alric—forgive me, Your Majesty, but I need to use you like a deckhand and will be dispensing with formalities. I hope you understand. Please take Mauvin and launch the raft as soon as the anchor is on it. Now this is what you must remember: paddle out *directly* behind the ship. Any angle will reduce our traction. We want to pull the ship in perfect line with the keel. When you are out so far that the chain is fully extended, drop the anchor, then return to the ship as fast as you can."

Alric nodded, and with Mauvin following, they climbed over the side of the ship. Using the pulleys attached to the main yard, Hadrian and Elden hoisted the anchor out over the raft, which bobbed and bucked in the surf. Alric and Mauvin straddled it, tying the anchor fast to the deck; both were sprayed and soaked by crashing waves. Hadrian handed paddles down, and with one on each side, the two worked to push the weighted craft out over the swells.

The chain played out through Wyatt's own hands as he stood at the stern, carefully watching their progress. Alric and Mauvin appeared like two rats on a barrel lid when the chain went taut. Arista saw the flash of Mauvin's blade, and the anchor went into the water, nearly flipping the raft.

"Hands to the capstan!" Wyatt called. "That's everyone—except, of course, you, Your Highness."

Arista sighed but was just as happy to stand at the stern rail and watch Alric and Mauvin, who were paddling back. They were moving much faster now that they had the swells pushing them.

In the center of the ship, poles were passed through the holes in the big wheel and everyone put their weight into pushing the capstan around. Arista could hear the rapid *clank, clank, clank* of the pawls as they took up the slack. Then the sound grew slower, the time between the clanks longer.

Everyone aside from her, including Wyatt, heaved on the capstan. Each pole had two people on it except for Elden's. The giant commanded his own pole and his face was turning red from the strain. Arista heard a fearful creaking as the anchor and the ship fought each other.

"Show us the waves, Arista!" Wyatt called to her. "Put your arms up and drop them just before a wave is about to hit the ship!"

She nodded and looked out to sea. Alric and Mauvin were already coming alongside. She looked at the swells. They were in a lull, but she could see three humps in the distance rolling toward them like the slithering backs of serpents.

"It will be a minute," she shouted back.

"Everyone rest," Wyatt told them. "When you see her drop her arms, really put your back into it."

Mauvin and Alric scrambled over the side, soaked and exhausted. They flung themselves down on the deck.

"No time to rest!" Wyatt shouted at them. "Find a spot on the poles."

The swells were nearing and Arista raised her arms. "Get ready!"

They all braced themselves and took deep breaths.

The first swell rushed in and Arista dropped her arms, but she did so too late.

They heaved. There was a grinding sensation; then it stopped and the men fell, exhausted, hanging from the poles.

"I timed it wrong," Arista shouted. "I was too late. Here comes another." She raised her arms and they all braced again, with Mauvin and Alric finding places at the poles.

Arista watched the swell rushing at her. This time she lowered her arms while the wave was still a few feet away. By the time the men heaved, the rear of the ship was rising. There were a noticeable lurch and more grinding. This time she heard the sound of wood scraping and felt movement.

"One more!" she shouted, raising her arms and then dropping them almost as soon as they were up.

Once more the men pushed, the chain tightened, and the boat rose. This time a gust of wind managed to catch the topsail and the ship lurched dramatically. The bottom scraped and broke out of the sludge. They rocked smooth and free, drifting backward.

A cheer rose and everyone was grinning. Wyatt ran back to the stern beside Arista and grabbed hold of the wheel. "That was lucky," he said, sweat dripping from his forehead. "Great job, by the way."

"Thanks."

"Keep cranking! Let's see if we can save the anchor."

The men pushed the capstan around easily now. They quickly covered the distance Alric and Mauvin had paddled and passed it. Arista watched the cable swing down beneath them. There was a sudden lurch that staggered her; then she heard the rapid clanking of the pawls as the anchor came in.

"Man the braces!" Wyatt shouted. "Stand by to come about!"

Wyatt looked out at the swells and gave the wheel a hard

spin. The ship turned. "Swing round the yards—starboard tack!"

Everyone else cleared out of the way as Hadrian, Elden, and Royce went to work twisting the yards and tying off. The ship turned its nose out to sea and the wind filled the sails, pushing it over to one side. "Tacks and sheets, catch that wind!"

Arista grabbed hold of the rail, frightened at the sudden speed the ship acquired and the disturbing tilt of the deck. Concerned that they were about to capsize, she watched apprehensively as the mast leaned and the ship rode on its side.

"There she goes!" Wyatt exclaimed with a great smile on his lips. "Fly, *Harbinger*, fly!" As if the ship heard him, the bow broke through a crest, dove forward, and hurdled the surface until it splashed down with a burst of spray. "Atta girl!"

⁓

Arista carried the hot cup with difficulty. She held it with both hands, but the deck refused to stay in one place for long and caused her to stagger. She approached Myron, who sat shivering with his back against the base of the mast.

"Here," she said, kneeling down and holding out the steaming cup.

"For me?" he asked, and she nodded. He took the cup and sniffed. "It's tea?" he said as if the drink were some kind of miracle. "It's hot tea."

"You seemed like you could use something warm to drink."

Myron looked at her with an expression of such gratefulness she thought for a moment that he might cry. "I—I don't know what to say."

"It's just tea, Myron. It wasn't much work."

"You had to get the stove going, and that must have been difficult. I wouldn't know how to do that on board a ship."

"I—ah, I didn't use the stove."

"But you had to boil the water...Oh," he said, lowering his voice.

"Yeah, I used a little trick." She wiggled her fingers.

He looked back down at the cup.

"If you don't want it, that's okay. I just thought—"

He lifted the cup and took a noisy sip. "It's wonderful. Created by magic and made for me by a royal princess. This is the best tea I've ever had. Thank you."

She laughed a bit and sat down before the lurching of the ship knocked her over. "Lately, I sometimes forget I am a princess. I haven't thought of myself that way for a really long time."

"Still, it is astoundingly thoughtful."

"It's what I can do," she said. "I feel useless lately. The least I can do is cook. Problem is, I really don't know how. But I can boil water like nobody's business. I'd like to make a cup for Royce. Hadrian says he gets seasick and I always thought tea soothed the stomach, but he's up in the rigging. Still, at the rate we're traveling I don't think it will be much longer before we land."

Myron tilted the cup to his lips and sipped. "It tastes wonderful. You did an excellent job."

She smirked at him. "You'd say that even if it was awful. I get the impression I could serve you dishwater and you'd act perfectly happy."

He nodded. "That is true, only I wouldn't be acting."

She opened her mouth to protest, then stopped. "You really mean that, don't you?"

He nodded and took another sip.

"It doesn't take much to please you, does it, Myron?"

"Antun Bulard once wrote 'When you expect nothing from the world—not the light of the sun, the wet of water, nor the air to breathe—everything is a wonder and every moment a gift.'"

"And you expect nothing from the world?"

He looked at her, puzzled. "I'm a monk."

She smiled and nodded. "You need to teach me to be a monk. I expect too much. I want too much...things I can't have."

"Desire can be painful, but so can regret."

"*That* is the one thing I have too much of."

"Sail!" Royce shouted from somewhere above them.

"Where?" Wyatt called from the wheel.

"Off the starboard bow, you'll be able to see it in another minute."

Arista and Myron got to their feet and moved to the rail. The dark prow of the *Harbinger* cut a white slice through the luminous green waves. Ahead, the city was much closer. Arista could see some detail in the buildings—windows, doorways, stairs, and domes.

"Which side is the starboard side?" she asked.

"The right side," Myron told her. "*Starboard* is derived from what they used to call the rudder—the sterobord—which was always on the right side of a ship, because most people are right handed. As a result, when docking, the one steering a ship always pulled up placing the opposite side of the ship next to the pier so it didn't interfere with his paddling, or the rudder. And of course that side, the left side, was the *port* side. Or so Hill McDavin explained in *Chronicles of Maritime Commerce and Trade Practices of the Kilnar Union*."

"Hadrian said you could do stuff like that—but until you see it, it's hard to believe. It's amazing that you can remember so many things."

"Everyone has talents. It's like magic, I guess."

"Yes," she said, nodding slowly. "I suppose it is."

"Look," Myron told her, pointing.

She spotted dark sails coming out of the dim light. They were far larger than their own—big sweeping triangles of black canvas with a white mark emblazoned on them. The design was a symbol of slashes that looked vaguely like a skull.

"Everyone get down!" Wyatt shouted. "Royce, tell me if they change course toward us!"

Arista and Myron lay down on the deck but continued to peer out at the approaching vessel. The hull came into view as if out of a green fog. It too was black and glistened with the ocean's spray, looking like smoked glass. With the underside reflecting the unholy glow of the sea, the ship appeared ominous. It looked as if it were something not of their world at all.

A light flashed from the top of the masts.

"They are signaling us," Royce called down.

"Damn," Wyatt said. "That's going to be a problem."

"She's changing course toward us."

"Hands to the braces!" Wyatt shouted as he spun the wheel and the *Harbinger* turned away from the oncoming ship. "They're onto us now."

Arista heard a faint shout across the water and she could see movement; small dark figures loped across the deck. As she saw them, a chill ran through her. Like anyone, she had heard tales of the Ba Ran Ghazel—the sea goblins. They were the stuff of legends. Nora, Arista's nursemaid, had told her fairy stories at bedtime. Most often the tales were about greedy dwarves that kidnapped spoiled princesses, who were always saved by a dashing prince in the end. But sometimes, she spoke about the Ghazel. No prince ever saved a princess from them, no matter how dashing. The Ghazel were vile creatures of the dark, inhuman monsters, the children of a malevolent god. Nora's tales of the Ghazel always included villages burned, warriors killed, and children taken—not to be ransomed but to be feasted on. The Ghazel always ate their victims.

When Arista was sitting in her bed, wrapped in blankets, surrounded by pillows, and safe in the warmth and light of a crackling fireplace, Nora's tales were fun. She always imagined dwarves as nasty little men and fairies as tiny winged girls, but the Ghazel she could never conjure entirely—even in the vast imaginings of her childish mind. They were always as they appeared now: distant threatening shadows exhibiting fast jerky movements that no human could make. Nora had always begun her stories the same way: "Not all of this story is true, but enough is..." Looking out at the ship, and the dark figures on the deck, Arista wondered if Nora had realized just how true they were.

The *Harbinger* pivoted under Wyatt's deft hand, sheering away to the left. Arista and Myron lost sight of the Ghazel ship. They ran back to the stern, where Wyatt stood holding the wheel with one hand while looking back over his shoulder. The Ghazel ship had matched their tack and was coming up on their stern.

"Everyone to the lee side!"

"Oh, now which side is that?" Arista asked Myron.

"Opposite of windward, ah—right now it is the starboard side."

"What in Maribor's name is wrong with *left* and *right*?"

As soon as they reached the starboard rail, she knew why Wyatt had ordered them there. As he cranked the wheel, the wind pressed the *Harbinger's* sails and bent the ship over on its beam, forcing it dangerously close to capsizing. The starboard side rose higher and higher.

Arista wrapped her arms around the rail to keep from sliding and Myron did the same. Farther up the deck, Magnus looked terrified as he clutched the side, his feet skidding and slipping on the wet boards. If the ship had flown before, it was doing something unheard of now. They no longer dipped and rose, but like a bar of soap running across a washboard, they hammered the crests as they went. The ship felt like a stone being skipped across a lake.

"Ha-ha!" Wyatt jeered, the wind ripping the words from his mouth so that she barely heard him. "Match that with your overweight trow!"

She watched Wyatt, with his feet in place against the stock, his arms holding the wheel, hugging it to his chest like a lover, his hair blowing, the spray bathing him. He wore a grin and she was not certain whether she should be happy or concerned. The rest of them hung on in desperation as the race sent them across the luminous sea.

Arista noticed the pain in her arm lessening, the ship righting itself, their speed dropping. She glanced at Wyatt and saw a look of concern.

"They're stealing our wind," he grumbled.

"How are they doing that?" Alric asked.

"They are putting us in their wind shadow, moving their ship in line with ours, blocking it—depriving us. Hands to the braces! Starboard tack!"

The ship was nearly flat now, allowing Hadrian and Elden to run. They cast off ropes and pulled the yard around again, the big sail flapping as Wyatt turned the ship to catch the wind from the other side. Overhead, Royce moved among the top lines, working the upper sail.

"Haul those sheets in!" They caught the wind once more and the ship set off again. "All hands to port!"

Arista was ahead of him, already running across the deck to renew her grip on the rail. She knew what was coming this time and got her feet planted securely before the side of the ship rose. Beyond the stern, she could see the following ship already turning to mimic their action, the great black sails with the skull-like symbols flapping loose as they came around. They were much closer now. She could clearly see the creatures crawling across the deck, climbing ropes. Dozens of them had gathered near the bow. It frightened her to see them move. They skidded along on all fours like spiders—a shipload of huge black tarantulas—so tightly packed they climbed over each other just to move about.

The *Harbinger* skipped the waves again, racing directly at the city, but it was no use. The following ship, with its larger bank of sails, was still eating up the distance between them and moved to cut their wind again.

"Elden, Hadrian!" Wyatt called. "I will be going about, but when I do, I will then change my mind and go back to my previous tack, do you understand? The moment you get my signal, run the jib up to port."

Hadrian looked at Elden, who was nodding. "Show him, Elden. This has to go perfectly or we're dead in the water. Also, get Alric and Mauvin on the lines. More hands will make this easier. The moment we are back on tack and under way, drop the jib. Let's see how good their crew is. They have the advantage of more canvas, so let's turn that against them. With all that sail, it will take them longer to recover, and if they don't pull back in time, they will stall."

"Your Highness," he said, addressing Arista, "I will need to be facing forward to time this just right, so you need to be my eyes astern. I need you to watch the Ghazel ship and tell me the moment you see them starting to come around, got that?"

"Yes," she replied, nodding in case her feeble voice was lost in the wind.

"Then get forward and hang on."

She nodded again and began crawling to the front of the ship, moving hand over hand along the rail.

"Stand by to come about!" Wyatt shouted.

He waited. She watched as the Ghazel ship once more glided over, aligning itself, eclipsing their wind. Wyatt flexed his fingers on the wheel and took a deep breath. He even closed his eyes for a moment, perhaps saying a silent prayer; then he stiffened his back and turned the wheel hard over.

The ship sheered back to port. "Tacks and sheets!"

Elden and Hadrian went to work once more, and Mauvin and Alric followed their directions, pulling the yards round. Arista focused her gaze on the Ghazel ship behind them. She could feel the *Harbinger* shifting, sensed it slowing underneath her as it started to lose the wind.

"They're turning!" she shouted as she saw the Ghazel coming about. The tiny spiders scattered across their deck in sudden fury. They were not just trying to match their turn; they were trying to beat them to it.

Wyatt did nothing.

"They're turning," she yelled again.

"I heard you," he said. "We need to wait for them to be fully committed."

Arista gripped the rail with nervous hands, feeling the ship moving slower and slower.

"Avast!" he finally shouted. "Back all braces! Raise the jib!"

The ship still had some wind, still some forward motion to it, and when Wyatt turned the wheel, it responded. The jib out front had the angle and caught what was left of the wind, turning the bow. A wave caught them dead on and broke, washing the deck, but the ship held true. The sails caught the wind and filled. Elden hauled down the jib as once more the *Harbinger* flew.

Behind them, the Ghazel realized their mistake but were

too late. They tried to mimic the turn and she watched as their sails went slack.

Wyatt looked behind them. "They're lost, stalled in the eye of the wind," he declared, grinning, his chest heaving with excitement. "It will take them several minutes to catch it again. By then we will—"

"Sail!" Royce shouted. "Starboard bow!"

Wyatt's grin melted as his head turned. Ahead of them appeared a ship that looked nearly identical to the one behind. It flashed a light and behind them the other Ghazel ship replied.

Wyatt looked fore and aft and she could see the story written clearly in lines of fear on his face. Through great skill, and a bit of luck, they had barely managed to avoid one ship. They would not fare well against two.

"Sail! Port bow!" Royce shouted, and she could see Wyatt visibly slump against the wheel as if struck from behind.

Wyatt lay off the wheel and let the ship slow and level off. There was no need to hasten their approach. Everyone on board looked to him.

"What now?" Alric asked, coming aft.

Wyatt did not reply. He just turned his head, looking back and forth at the ships. His forehead glistened. He bit his lip, and Arista noticed his left hand starting to shake.

"We're out of options, aren't we?" Alric asked.

"This ship doesn't even have nets to impede boarders," Wyatt replied.

"How will they attack?" Hadrian asked. "Will they board?"

"Eventually, yes, but first they will clear the deck with arrows."

"Fire?"

"No," Wyatt replied. "They have us. We're boxed in, overwhelmed. They will want the ship."

"Do we have to surrender?" Alric asked.

"Ghazel don't take prisoners," Hadrian told him. "They don't even have a word in their language for *surrender*."

"What do we do, then?" the king asked.

"We don't really have a lot of options, Your Majesty," Wyatt told him. "Those ships hold sixty, maybe as many as a hundred Ghazel each, and we don't even have a means of shooting back. Their archers will drive us into the cabin; then they will grapple on and come aboard uncontested. At that point they could lock us in and sail us to their port."

"Which they will do," Hadrian added. "Then they will drag us into a ring and…and, well, you get the idea. No sense in spoiling the surprise."

"I hate ships!" Magnus growled. "Infernal things. There's nowhere to go. Nowhere to hide."

"We're going to…die?" Gaunt asked, stunned. "I—I can't die. I'm going to be emperor."

"Yeah, well, we all had plans, didn't we?" Hadrian said.

"I didn't," Royce said, climbing down from the rigging. Arista noted a modest smile on his lips. "I don't think I'll be joining you in the cabin. I don't mind a game of arrow dodging."

"Actually only Arista and Myron should go in the cabin," Hadrian said. "The rest of us will remain on deck. We'll need shields—anything of wood about an inch thick will do, or metal even thinner. Trilons don't have much penetration power. We can also use the mast as cover."

Arista looked out at the approaching ships, coming at angles to intercept them. The Ba Ran Ghazel were coming and there would be no rescue by a dashing prince—*the Ghazel always ate their victims*.

"Not this time," she told herself, and letting go of the rail, she walked forward. She stepped around Wyatt at the wheel and passed through the group of men in the waist.

"Arista?" Hadrian called. "You should get in the cabin."

She looked out at the water.

"Mr. Deminthal," she shouted, "take hold of that wheel. Everyone else...hang on to something."

Taking a breath, Arista calmed herself and reached out into the dark—into the energy that lay around them, above and below. She could feel the depths of the ocean, the weight of the water, the floor of the sea, the fish, the seaweed, the glowing algae. She felt the breeze and grabbed it tight.

The wind, which had been a constant presence since they had climbed out of the shaft to the beach, abruptly died. The sails drooped; the incessant quiver and clank of pulleys and ropes halted. Not a breath remained and the world became silent. Even the waves perished. The ships stopped as the sea became as tranquil as a bathtub. The silence was deafening.

Then across the water the hush was broken by Ghazel voices. She could hear them, like the barks and howls of dogs. She felt them too. She felt everything and held it all in her grip.

She raised her hand, holding her fingertips lightly.

Fire? she thought. She had played that note before. She knew just how to do it. But as enticing as the thought of three flaming pyres against the water was, the light would alert the shore.

Wind? She could sense that chord. It was powerful. She could shatter the ships. *No.* Too unwieldy, like trying to pick up a coin with mittens.

Water? Yes! It was everywhere. She twisted three fingers in the air and the world responded with movement.

The sea swirled.

Currents formed, churning, building, rotating, and spinning. The three Ghazel ships began to rotate, revolving as if they were toy boats in a tub she had flicked with a finger.

Whirlpools formed.

Beneath the goblin ships, circles appeared—large swirling funnels of spinning water. Faster and faster they moved, the centers giving way, dropping lower as the speed of the rotation increased. They widened, spreading out, and grew in strength. Even the *Harbinger* began to rock noticeably as the maelstroms reached out to pull on the strength of the whole sea.

The barks of the Ghazel became cries and screams as the ships continued to spin. A *crack* issued across the water as a mast snapped. Then another, and another, poles the size of tree trunks popped like twigs. The Ghazel shrieked and wailed, their voices blurring into one note, which Arista also held.

The sheer enormity of the power she worked was incredible. It was so easy and all at her command. Everything— every droplet, every breath, every heartbeat—it was all hers. She felt them, touched them, played with them. It was irresistible, like scratching a terrible itch. She let the power run. It was so big, so potent. She did not just control the power; she *was* the power, and it was her. She whirled, she frothed, and she wanted to run, to spin and grow. Like a ball sent off a hill, she felt the building momentum. It excited her and she loved the motion—the *freedom*! She felt herself letting go, giving herself to it, spreading out and becoming a part of the symphony she played—so grand—so beautiful. All she wanted was to blend with the whole, to become—

Stop it!

The idea was a discord. An off note. A broken thread.

Stop it! Pull back!

A distant voice called to her, struggling to be heard over the crescendo of the music she played.

Regain control!

She didn't want to listen; she didn't like the sound. It clashed with the melody.

You're killing them!
Of course I'm killing them. That is the whole point.
The Ghazel are gone. That is not who you are killing! Stop!
No. I can't.
You can!
I won't. I don't want to. It's too wonderful to stop, too in-
credible. I have to keep going. I love it so—

⛬

Arista woke with a wrenching headache. It was so painful her
eyes hurt just from opening. She was in the cabin, lying on the
bed where they had found Bernie. A lantern hanging from a
hook on the ceiling swayed back and forth, casting shadows
that sloshed from one wall to the next.

She turned her head and pain swelled behind her eyes.
"Ow," she whispered.

Arista raised a hand and found a bandage wrapped around
her head. There was stiffness at the back of her head where
the bandage pulled at her hair. Drawing her hand away, she
found blood on her fingertips.

"Are you all right?" Myron asked. He sat beside her on a
little stool and took her hand in his.

"What happened?" she asked. "My head is killing me."

"Excuse me a moment," the monk said, and opened the
door to the deck. "She's awake," he called.

Immediately, Hadrian and Alric entered, ducking inside
and dodging the lantern. "Are you all right?"

"Why does everyone keep asking me that? And yes, I'm
fine...mostly. But my head hurts." She sat up slowly.

Hadrian looked pained. "I'm sorry about that."

She narrowed her eyes at him, which made her head hurt
even more. "You hit me?"

He nodded.

"Why?"

"He had to," Alric put in, his expression grave. "You—you lost control, or something."

"What do you mean?"

Arista saw him glance toward the doorway. "What is it? What happened?"

She stood up, weaving a bit, her head still not right, and she felt tired to the point of being groggy. Hadrian extended a hand and steadied her. She ducked her head, careful to avoid banging it against the doorframe, and stepped out onto the deck.

"Oh dear Maribor!" she gasped.

The *Harbinger* was in shambles. The mast was gone; all that remained was a splintered stump. The beams of the deck were warped. One board was cracked to the point of splintering, and on the starboard side near the bow there was a gaping hole that revealed the hull below. The topsail was gone, along with the topsail yard, but the mainsail lay across the bow, torn and tattered. The railing on the port side was missing as well, sheared away.

"*I* did this?" she asked, shocked. "Oh my—is anyone..." She looked around, searching for faces—Gaunt, Magnus, Mauvin, Alric, Hadrian... "Where's Royce, Wyatt, and Elden?"

"They're okay. They're working on the ship. Everyone's okay," Alric told her. "Thanks to Hadrian. We tried talking to you, shaking you. Wyatt even poured water over your head. You just stood there mumbling and fiddling with your fingers while the ship came apart."

Mauvin was smiling at her and nodding. On his forehead a deep cut stood out, and his cheek was red and blotchy.

"Did I do that?"

"Actually a flying pulley did that. I was just too stupid to duck." He was still smiling at her, but there was something behind it—something terrible—something she had never seen on Mauvin's face before: fear—fear of her.

She sat down where she was, feeling the strength melt out of her legs. "I'm so sorry," she whispered.

"It's all right," her brother told her, again with apprehension in his voice. They made a circle around her, but no one came near.

"I'm sorry," she repeated. Her eyes filled with tears and she let them run down her cheeks. "I just wanted…" Her voice gave up on her and she began to weep.

"There's nothing to be sorry for," Hadrian said. He came forward and knelt beside her. "You saved us. The Ghazel are gone."

"Yeah," Mauvin said. "Scariest thing I've ever seen. It was like—like what they said Esrahaddon could do, only *he* never did. It was—"

"It was what we needed," Hadrian broke in over him. "If she hadn't, we'd all be dead now, and trust me, it would have been a very unpleasant death. Thank you, Your Highness."

She looked up at Hadrian. He appeared blurry through her watering eyes. He was smiling. She wiped her face and peered at him again carefully. She studied his eyes.

"What?" he asked.

"Nothing," she said.

His hand reached out and brushed her cheeks dry. "What?" he asked again.

"I—I don't want—" She hesitated and took a breath. "I just don't want people to be afraid of me."

"That arrow's already flown," Degan Gaunt said.

"Shut it, Gaunt," Alric snapped.

"Look at me," Hadrian told her, and putting his hand under her chin, he gently lifted it. He took her hands in his. "Do I look frightened?"

"No," she said. "But...maybe you should be."

"You're tired."

"I am—I'm really very tired."

"We're going to be drifting here for a bit, so why don't you lie down and get some rest? I'm sure things will look better when you wake up."

She nodded and her head felt like a boulder rocking on her shoulders.

"Com'on," he said, pulling her to her feet. She wavered and he slipped an arm around her waist and escorted her back into the cabin, where Myron had the bed ready.

"Myron will watch over you," Hadrian assured Arista as he tucked the blankets tightly around her. "Get some sleep."

"Thank you."

He brushed her wet hair from her eyes. "It's the least I can do for my hero," he said.

◆

She walked swiftly up the Grand Mar, the broad avenue beautifully lined with flowering trees. The rose-colored petals flew and swirled, carpeting the ground, scenting the air, and creating a blizzard in spring.

It was festival day, and blue and green flags were everywhere. They flew over houses and waved in the hands of passersby. People clogged the streets. Wandering minstrels filled the air with music and song. Drums announced another parade, this one a procession of elephants followed by chariots, prancing horses, dancing women, and proud soldiers. Stall keepers called to the crowd, handing out cakes, nuts, confections, and fermented drinks called Trembles, made from the sweet blossoms of the trees. Young girls rushed from door to door, delivering small bouquets of flowers in the imperial colors.

Noblemen on their chariots wore their bright-colored tunics; gold bracelets flashed in the afternoon sun. Older women stood on balconies, waving colored scarves and shouting words impossible to hear. Boys who dodged and slipped through the crowd carried baskets and sold trinkets. You could get three copper pins for three piths, or five for a keng. There was always a contest to collect the largest variety of pins before the day was out.

It was a beautiful day.

She hurried past the rivers of people into Imperial Square. To her right stood the stone rotunda of the Cenzarium and to the left the more brutish columned facade of the blocked Hall of Teshlor. Before her, at the terminus of the boulevard, rose the great golden-domed imperial palace—the seat of the emperor of the world. She walked past the Ulurium Fountain, across the Memorial Green, to the very steps of the palace—not a single guard was on duty. No one noticed. Everyone was too busy celebrating. That was part of the plan that Venlin had laid well.

She entered the marbled hall, so cool, so elegant, and scented with incense that made her think of tropical trees and mountaintops. The palace was a marvel, large, beautiful, and so sturdy it was hard to imagine what she knew was happening.

She reached the long gallery, the arcade of storied columns, each topped with three lions looking down from their noble perch at all who passed that way.

Yolric was waiting for her.

The old man leaned heavily on his staff. His long white beard was a matted mess. "So you have come," he greeted her. "But I knew you would. I knew someone would. I could have guessed it would be you."

"This is wrong. You of all people should see that!"

Yolric shook his head. "Wrong, right—these words have no meanings except in the minds of men. They are but illusions. There is only what is and what isn't, what has been and what will be."

"I am here to define that value for you."

"I know you are. I could have predicted it. My suspicions, it would seem, have weight. This is the second time now. It has taken a long time to find, but there is a pattern to the world. Wobble it and it corrects, which should be impossible; chaos should beget chaos. Order should be only one possibility and drowned by all the other permutations. But if it corrects again, if order prevails, then there can be only one answer. There is another force at work—an invisible hand— and I think I know what that force is."

"I don't have time to discuss this theory of yours again."

"Nor do I have need of you. As I said, I have finally worked it out. You see, the legends are true."

She was irritated with him; he barred her path but did not attack. He merely babbled on about unimportant theories. This was no time for metaphysical debates about the nature of existence, chaos versus order, or the values of good and evil. She needed to get by him, but Yolric was the one person she could not hope to defeat. She could not take the chance of instigating a battle if it could be avoided. "Do you side with Venlin or not?"

"Side with the Bishop? No."

She felt a massive sense of relief.

"Will you help me? Together we could stop him. Together we can save the emperor. Save the empire."

"I wouldn't need your help to do that."

"So you will let it happen?"

"Of course."

"*Why?*"

"*I need the wobble. One does not a pattern make. I need to see if it will correct again and, perhaps, how. I must find the fingerprint, the tracks that I can trace to the source. The legends are true — I know that now, but I still want to see his face.*"

"*I don't know what you are talking about!*"

"*I know you don't. You couldn't.*"

"*Are you going to try and stop me or not?*"

"*The wobble, my boy. I never touch it once I have it going. You go, do what you must. I am only here now to watch. To see if I can catch a glimpse at the face behind the invisible hand.*"

She was confused, baffled by Yolric's unconcerned attitude, but it did not matter; what did was that he would not interfere. Her greatest obstacle was gone. Now it was just between her and Venlin.

"*Goodbye, then, old master, for I fear I shall never see you again.*"

"*No, you won't. I would wish you luck, but I do not believe it exists. Still, I suspect you have better than mere luck on your side — you have the invisible hand.*"

CHAPTER 14

THE COLD

The ceiling of the grand imperial throne room was a dome painted to mimic the sky on a gentle summer's day, and Modina still thought it beautiful. Dressed once more in her formal gown, she sat on the gaudy bird-of-prey throne with the wings, spread into a vast half circle, forming the back of the chair. The throne was mounted on a dais that had twelve steps to climb. She could not help remembering the days they had forced her to practice before it.

"Do you remember the board you ordered sewn into my dress?" she asked Nimbus, who looked suddenly uncomfortable.

"It worked," he replied.

"Who's next?"

Nimbus studied the parchment in his hands. "Bernard Green, a candlemaker from Alburn."

"Send him in, and get another log on the fire. It's freezing in here."

Unlike the great hall, the throne room was rarely used, or at least that had been the case until now. When the empress had been a mythical creature, the room had been sealed. Now that she existed in the flesh, the room was opened once more, but it always felt cold, as if it would take time to recover the warmth after those years of neglect.

Nimbus waved to the clerk, and a moment later, a short, soft-looking man entered. His eyes were small, his nose narrow and sharp. Modina immediately thought of a squirrel and recalled how she used to remember the court of Ethelred by similar associations before she learned their names.

"Your Grand Imperial Eminence," he said with a shaky voice, and bowed so low his forehead touched the floor.

They all waited. He did not move.

"Ah—please stand up," she told him. The man popped up like a child's toy, but he refused to look at her. They all did that. She found it irritating but understood it was a tradition and it would be even more unnerving for them to try to change. "Speak."

"Ah—Grand Imperial Eminence—I, ah—that is—ah—I am from Alburn, and I—am a candlemaker."

"Yes, I know that, but what is your problem?"

"Well, Your Grand Imperial Eminence, since the edict, I have moved my family here, but—you see—I have little means and no skills other than making candles, but the merchant guild refuses to grant me a license of business. I am told that I cannot have one as I am not a citizen."

"Of course," Nimbus said. "Citizenship is a prerequisite for applying to a guild and only guild members are allowed to conduct a trade within the city."

"How does one obtain citizenship?" Modina asked.

"Usually by inheritance, although it can be granted to individuals or families as recognition for some extraordinary service. Regardless, one must be a member of a guild to gain citizenship."

"But if you need to be a guild member to apply for citizenship and you need to be a citizen to be a guild member, doesn't that make it extraordinarily difficult to become a citizen?"

"I believe that is the point, Your Eminence. Cities guard against invasions from outside tradesmen that might disrupt the order of established merchants and reduce the profitability of existing businesses."

"How many citizens are there?"

"At present, I believe about ten to fifteen percent of the city's population are citizens."

"That's ridiculous."

"Yes, Your Eminence. It's also a drain on the treasury, because only citizens are required to pay taxes. Also, only citizens have the right of a trial in a court, or are required to serve to protect the city walls in the event of attack."

Modina stared at him.

"Shall I summon the city's merchant council and organize a meeting in order to review the guild policy, say, tomorrow?" Nimbus asked.

"Please do." She looked back down at Bernard Green. "Rest assured I will address this matter immediately, and thank you for bringing it to my attention."

"Bless you, Your Grand Imperial Eminence, bless you." He bowed once more with his head to the floor.

Modina waved her hand and the master-at-arms escorted him out. "I don't so much mind the bowing—that's actually nice. It's the scraping I can't stand."

"You are not just the empress," Nimbus told her. "You are a demigod. You must expect a little scraping."

"Who's next?"

"A fellow by the name of Tope Entwistle, a scout from the north," he replied.

"A scout? A scout follows the candlemaker?"

"He just has a status report—nothing urgent," Nimbus

told her. "And the candlemaker had been waiting for three days."

A stocky man entered wearing a heavy wool tunic with a little copper pin in the shape of a torch on his breast. He also sported wool pants wrapped in leather strips. His face was blotchy, his skin a ruddy leather. The tip of his nose was more than red; it was a disturbing shade of purple. His knuckles and the tips of his fingers were a similar color. He walked with an unusual gait, a hobbled limp, as if his feet were sore.

"Your Imperial Eminence." The man bowed and sniffled. "Sir Marshal Breckton sends word. He reports that there has been no confirmed movement by the elves since the initial crossing. In addition, he sends word that all bridges and roads have been closed. As for the lack of movement on the part of the elven force, it is his estimated opinion that the elves may have gone into winter quarters. He has also sent several quarter-master lists and a detailed report, which I have here in this satchel."

"You can give those to the clerk," Nimbus told him.

He slipped the satchel off and sneezed as he held out the bag.

"And how are things in Colnora?"

"Excuse me, Your Highness." He stuck a finger in his ear and wiggled it. "I've been fighting a cold for a month and my head is so clogged I can barely hear."

"I asked, how are things in Colnora?" she said louder.

"They are fine in Colnora. It's the road between that gets a tad chilly. Course I can't complain. I've been up on the line in the wilderness and there it is colder than anything. Not even a proper fire allowed, on account of not wanting to give away our positions to the elves."

"Is there anything you need?"

"Me? Oh, I don't need much. I already had me a good hot

meal and a sit near a hearth. That's all I need. Course a soft, warm place to sleep awhile before I head back would certainly be appreciated."

Modina looked at Nimbus.

"I will inform the chamberlain," he told her.

"Thank you, Your Eminence," the scout said, and bowed again before leaving.

"I never really thought about how it must be out there for them, waiting," Modina said.

"Next is Abner Gallsworth, the city administrator," Nimbus said, and a tall, thin man entered. He was the best dressed of the lot that morning, wearing long heavy robes of green and gold draped nearly to the floor. On his head was a tall hat with flaps that drooped down the sides of his head like a hound's ears. His face was long and narrow, qualities made more noticeable by the sagging of age.

"Your Imperial Eminence." He bowed, but more shallowly than anyone else so far, and there was no scraping to be seen. "While I am pleased to report that all the provisioning you have commanded has been achieved, and that the city is functioning at high efficiency, I nevertheless regret to tell you that there is a problem. We are becoming overcrowded. Refugees are still arriving from the surrounding towns and villages — even more so since the news of troops sealing the roads and passes has leaked into the countryside.

"We now have several hundred people living on the streets, and with the winter's cold, I have daily reports coming across my desk of frozen corpses in need of disposal. At present we are carting the bodies outside the walls and piling them in a fallow field to await a spring burial. This solution, however, has attracted wild animals. Packs of wolves have been reported and those still outside the city walls are complaining. I would like to request permission to dispose of the bodies at sea. To do this, I will require access to a barge. As all ships are presently under imperial edict, my request has been repeatedly denied. Hence I am here, appealing to you."

"I see," Modina said. "And what provisions have you made to prevent the future deaths of more refugees?"

"Provisions?" he asked.

"Yes, what have you done to stop the peasants from freezing to death?"

"Why...nothing. The peasants are dying because they have no shelter. They have no shelter because they cannot afford any or none can be found. I can neither create money nor construct housing. Therefore, I do not understand your question."

"You cannot commandeer ships to dispose of bodies either and yet you stand before me requesting that."

"True, but a barge is an achievable goal. Preventing future peasants from dying is not. The city has been overcrowded for weeks and yet just this morning another large group has arrived from Alburn. There are perhaps fifty families. If a viable solution is what you desire, I suggest preventing any more displaced people from entering the city. Seal it off and be done with it. Let those that come here looking for charity learn that they must provide for themselves. Allowing them entry will only cause a higher rate of mortality."

"I suspect you are right," Modina told him. "I also suspect you would feel quite differently if it was you and your family standing on the other side of our locked gate. I am the empress of all the people. It is my responsibility to keep them safe, not the other way around."

"Then please tell me what you would like me to do, for I can see no solution to this problem. There is simply no place for all these people."

Modina looked around her, at the painted dome and the great stone hearth burning the new log she had ordered.

"Chancellor?" she said.

"Yes, Your Eminence?" Nimbus replied.

"How many people could we fit in this hall?"

He raised his eyebrows in surprise, then pursed his lips. "Perhaps a hundred if they do not mind squeezing together."

"I think if faced with freezing to death, they will not mind."

"You will open the throne room to the public?" Gallsworth asked, stunned. "How will you conduct the business of the empire?"

"This *is* the business of the empire, and no, I am not going to open the throne room to the public." She looked at Nimbus. "I am opening the entire palace. I want the gates opened at once. Line the halls, corridors, even the chapel. I want every square inch used. There will not be a single man, woman, or child left in the cold as long as there is any room to spare. Is that understood?"

"Absolutely, Your Eminence."

"Furthermore," she said, turning to Gallsworth, "I want a study done of the city to locate any other sources of shelter that could be utilized. I don't care how hallowed or privileged. This is an emergency and all space is to be used."

"You're serious?" he said, amazed.

"I will not have my people dying on my doorstep!" she declared in a raised voice that left no room for question.

Guards looked up, concerned by her unusual outburst. Servants appeared nervous and several noticeably cringed. The city administrator did not. He remained straight, his eyes focused on her own. He said nothing for a moment; then his lips began to move about as if he were sucking on something, and finally he began to nod.

"Very well," he said. "I will begin to look into the matter, but I can tell you right now where there is a large unused space. The Imperial Basilica of Aquesta has the capacity to house perhaps a thousand and at present is home to no more than eight individuals."

"If you knew this, why did you not say something before?"

"I would never presume to fill the house of god with poor, filthy peasants."

"Then what in Maribor's name is it for?"

"The Patriarch will not be pleased."

"Damn the Patriarch!" Modina barked. "Nimbus—"

"At once, Your Eminence."

❧

"Why are the two of you not asleep?" Modina asked, entering her bedroom to find Mercy and Allie wide-awake.

Modina insisted that Allie stay in her room as part of her initiative to free up as much space as possible. When Allie asked for Mercy to join them, Modina could not refuse. Now both girls were in their nightgowns, wrapped in blankets, facing the darkened, frost-covered window. At her question, the girls looked at her and then quickly wiped their cheeks.

"Too cold," Mercy replied unconvincingly, and sniffled.

"It's freezing," Allie agreed. "We couldn't even play outside today."

"Even Mr. Rings won't set foot out there." Mercy glanced to where the raccoon was curled up near the fire.

"It is very cold, isn't it?" Modina said, looking out the window at the starry sky. The night was always clear when the temperature was frigid.

"It freezes the water in your eyes!"

"It makes my ears hurt."

Modina put her hand to the frosted glass—the same window she had spent so many hours kneeling before. It was like ice to her touch. "Yes, the cold is troublesome, but it might just be the miracle we need."

"We need it to be cold?" Allie questioned.

"Well, if Mr. Rings won't go outside, I don't suspect anyone else will want to be out there either."

"You mean the elves?" Mercy asked.

"Yes," she replied. She didn't see the point in lying.

"Why do they want to kill us? Allie is an elf, but she doesn't want to kill us, do you?"

Allie shook her head.

"I don't know why," Modina said. "I'm not certain anyone knows. The reason is likely very old, too old for anyone to remember."

"Will they—will they kill us when it gets warmer?" Allie asked.

"I'm not going to let them. Your father isn't going to let them either. Is that why you were crying? You miss him, don't you?"

The girl nodded.

"And you?" Modina looked at Mercy.

"I miss Arcadius and Miranda. She used to put me to bed at night, and he would tell me stories when I couldn't sleep."

"Well, I think I can help with that. I know a story—a story that a dear friend once told me when I was feeling very bad. So bad, in fact, that I couldn't even eat. How about we get more wood for the fire, curl up in my big bed, and I will tell it to you?"

She watched the two padding about in their bare feet, collecting armloads of split logs.

The empress smiled.

Everyone commented on how gracious she was for taking them in and sharing her personal chambers. Although, there were some who thought that it was a political ploy—that her generosity was extended to make it impossible for any duke to suggest such indignities were beneath him. This was not the reason, only a convenient secondary benefit. Modina did it because she had promised Wyatt she would look after Allie, and she meant to fulfill that oath. As there was no separating the two girls, Modina inherited twins. Having done so, she realized that even if Wyatt returned that night, and the winter melted to summer and all the problems with her kingdom were swept away by some miracle, she would still want the children to live with her. Carefree laughter was something Modina had not heard in a great while. She had stared out her window at a free blue sky to avoid the gray world of grim-faced men. Now a bit of that sky bounced within her chambers. They reminded her of Maria and Jessie Caswell, childhood friends who had died too soon.

She tucked the girls in and lay beside Allie, stroking her hair.

"This is called *Kile and the White Feather*. The father of the gods, Erebus, had three sons: Ferrol, Drome, and Maribor. They were the gods of elves, dwarves, and men. He also had a daughter, Muriel, who was the loveliest being ever created. She held dominion over all the plants and animals. Well, one night Erebus became drunk and...well, he hurt his own daughter. In anger, her brothers attacked their father and tried to kill him, but of course, gods can't die.

"Filled with guilt and grief, Erebus returned to Muriel and begged her forgiveness. She was moved by her father's remorse but still could not bear to look at him. He begged, pleading for her to name a punishment. He would do anything to win her forgiveness. Muriel needed time to let the fear and pain pass, so she told him, 'Go to Elan to live. Not as a god, but as a man to learn humility.' To repent for his misdeeds, she charged him with doing good works. Erebus did as she requested and took the name of Kile. It is said that to this day, he walks the world of men, working miracles. For each act that pleases her, Muriel bestows upon him a white feather from her magnificent robe, which he keeps in a pouch forever by his side. Muriel decreed that when the day came when all the feathers were bestowed, she would call her father home and forgive him. It is said when all the gods are reunited, all will be made right and the world will transform into a paradise."

"Empress?" Mercy said.

"Yes?"

"When you die, do you meet others who have died?"

"I don't know. Who is it you want to meet?"

"I miss my mother."

"Oh, that's different," she told her. "I am quite certain daughters and mothers are *always* reunited."

"Really?"

"Of course."

"She was very pretty, my mother. She used to say I was pretty too."

"And you are."

"She told me I would grow up to be a fairy princess one day, but I don't think I will now. I don't think I will grow up at all."

"Don't talk like that. If your mother said you would be a fairy princess, you trust her—mothers know these things." She hugged the girl and kissed her cheek. Mercy felt so small, so delicate. "Now it is late and time for you to go to sleep."

A bright moon was rising.

Modina thought of the fifty-eight men outside, pitched on a snowy hillside, ordered by her to remain in the cold. Some would lose fingers, others toes, noses, or ears, and some might be dying right then, like her father almost had the night of the blizzard. They might be huddled in a shallow frozen hole they had chipped out of the snow, trying in vain to keep warm with only a thin wool blanket and a few layers of clothes separating them from the bitter winds. They would shiver uncontrollably, their teeth chattering, their muscles tight as they pulled into balls, snow and ice forming on their beards and eyelashes. The unlucky ones would fall into a deep warm sleep, never to wake up.

She thought of the men, imagined their pain and fear, and felt guilt. They were dying on her command, but she needed them to be there. As much as she wished it could be better for them, as much as she wished she could pray for warmer weather, she looked out at the sparkling stars and whispered, "Please, Maribor, I know I am not your daughter. I am but a poor peasant girl who shouldn't even be here, but please, please make it stay cold."

She fell asleep and woke a few hours later. The room was dark, the new logs having burned low, and everything outside the covers felt chilled.

It was Mercy who had woken her. She was kicking and twisting in the covers, her eyes still closed. She wrestled, her arms twitching, her eyes darting fretfully under her lids. From her mouth came fearful utterances like the cries of terror from one gagged.

"What's wrong with her?" Allie asked with a sleepy face and matted hair.

"Bad dream, I suspect." Modina took hold of Mercy's shoulder and gave it a gentle squeeze. "Mercy?" she said. "Mercy, wake up."

The little girl kicked once more, then lay still. Her eyes fluttered open and then shifted left and right nervously.

"It's okay. It was just a bad dream." Mercy clutched at Modina, shaking. "It's all right, everything is okay now."

"No," the little girl replied with a hitching voice. "It's not.

I saw them. I saw the elves coming into the city. Nothing stopped them."

Modina patted her head. "It was just a dream, a nightmare brought on because of what we were saying just before you fell asleep. I told you I won't let them hurt us."

"But you couldn't stop them—no one could. The walls fell down and flying monsters burned the houses. I heard the men screaming in the fog. There was lightning, the ground broke, and the walls fell. They poured in riding white horses all dressed in gold and blue."

"Gold and blue?" Modina asked.

She nodded.

Modina's heart felt as if it skipped a beat. "Did you see the elves when you escaped the university?"

"No, just the flying monsters. They were really scary."

"How did you know they dressed in gold and blue?"

"I saw them in my dream."

"What else did you see? Which way did they come?"

"I don't know."

"You said they were on horses. Did they arrive here on horses or did they come by boat?"

"I don't know. I just saw them on horses coming into the city."

"Do you know which gate?"

She shook her head, looking more frightened as Modina quizzed her. The empress tried to calm down, tried to smile, but she could not. Instead, she stood up. The floor was cold, but she barely noticed. She paced, thinking.

It's not possible for a child to see the future in a dream—is it? But that's what the Patriarch said when he was quoting at the meeting. "They came on brilliant white horses, wearing shining gold and shimmering blue." Still, that ancient account might not apply to these elves.

"Can you remember where you were when you saw them enter the gate?"

Mercy thought a moment. "We were on the wall out front of the courtyard, where Allie and I play with Mr. Rings."

"Was it day or night?"

"Morning."

"Could you see the sun?"

She shook her head and Modina sighed. If only she—

"It was cloudy," Mercy told her.

"Could you tell which side the sea was on while looking at the gate?"

"Ah—this side, I think," she said, taking her right hand out of the covers and shaking it for her.

"Are you sure?"

The girl nodded.

"You were looking at the *southern* gate," Modina said.

"You two get back to sleep," she told the girls, and left them staring as she rushed out of the bedroom, pulling on a robe. The guard outside spun around, startled.

"Wake up the chancellor and tell him I want to see that scout Entwistle right now. I will meet them in the chancellor's office. Go."

She closed the door and ran down the steps to the fourth floor without bothering to get dressed.

"You there!" She caught a guard yawning. He snapped to attention. "Get a light on in the chancellor's office."

By the time Nimbus and the scout arrived, she had the map of the kingdom of Warric off the shelf and spread out over the desk.

"What's going on?" the chancellor asked.

"You are from the south, aren't you, Nimbus?"

"I am from Vernes, Your Eminence."

"That's down here at the mouth of the Bernum?"

"Yes."

"Do you know of any place south of Colnora to cross the Bernum River?"

"No, Your Eminence."

She looked back at the map for a moment and the two men waited patiently. "So the elves can't get at us from the west unless they have seaworthy ships, and they can't approach us from the north because of the mountains?"

She looked up, this time at the scout.

"Yes, Your Eminence, we started an avalanche on the Glouston road and it won't be clear until late spring. The bridges in Colnora were destroyed as well."

"And they can't come at us from the east or the south because of the Bernum. What about the Rilan Valley? Can't they get through there?"

"No, the snow is too deep in the fields. An elf might be able to walk over it with proper shoes, but he won't be able to bring horses or wagons. And even if they did, they would still have to cross the Farendel Durat, and those passes are closed."

She looked again at the map, studying the little lines on it.

"If the elven army was to attack us from our southern gate, how best would they get here?"

"They can't," the scout said. "The only bridges across the Bernum River gorge were in Colnora and they have been destroyed."

"What if they went *around* Colnora? What if they crossed the Bernum south of there?"

"The river south of Colnora is wide and deep. There's no ford or bridge except those in Colnora, which aren't there anymore."

Modina drummed her fingers on the desk, staring at the map.

"What is it, Your Eminence?" Nimbus asked.

"I don't know," she said. "But we're missing something.

592 Michael J. Sullivan

It's not the cold slowing down their advance. Maybe they want us to think it is, but I'm certain they're circling around us. I think they will attack from the southeast."

"But that's not possible," the scout said.

"These are elves. Do we really know what is possible for them? If they were able to get across, what would that do?"

"That would depend on where they crossed. It could wind up dividing us from Breckton's forces in the east, or they could walk in unopposed from the south."

"Your Eminence, I know every inch of the Bernum. I used to float goods down it from Colnora to Vernes with my brother as boys. We worked it year-round. There is no place to cross. It is as wide and deep as a lake and has a deadly current. Even in summer, without a boat, a man can't get across. In winter it would be suicide."

The decision was too important to base on the nightmare of a child even though her heart told her she was right. Her eyes fell on the little copper pin in the shape of a torch on Tope Entwistle's chest. "Tell me," she said. "What is that you are wearing on your breast?"

He glanced down and smiled self-consciously. "Sir Breckton awarded that to me for successfully lighting the fire signaling the elves' move across the Galewyr."

"So you actually saw the elven army?"

"Yes, Your Eminence."

"Tell me, then, what color are the uniforms of the elves?"

He looked surprised at the question and then replied, "Blue and gold."

"Thank you, you can leave. Go back to sleep. Get some rest."

The scout nodded, bowed, and left the office.

"What are you thinking, Your Eminence?" the chancellor asked.

"I want word sent to Colnora to recall Breckton and his troops," she said. "We aren't going to survive, Nimbus. Even after everything we've done. They are going to break through our defenses, throw down our walls, and burst into this palace."

Nimbus said nothing. He remained straight and calm.

"You knew that already, didn't you?"

"I harbor few illusions, Your Eminence."

"I won't let my family be slaughtered—not again."

"There is still hope," he told her. "You have seen to that. All we can do is wait."

"And pray."

"If you feel that will help."

"You don't believe in the gods, Nimbus?"

He smiled wryly. "Oh, I most certainly believe in them, Your Eminence. I just don't think they believe in me."

CHAPTER 15

PERCEPLIQUIS

The *Harbinger* limped to shore without much dignity. Wyatt managed to create a small sail from what remained, and hoisted it to a pole he lashed to the stump of the old mast. They no longer flew across the waves; they barely drifted, but it was enough to make the far shore. Farther down the shore Royce spotted what looked to be a dock, which they avoided, and instead they anchored in at a sheltered cove. Here the beach was only a small spit of land surrounded by large blocks of broken stone, each one half the height of a man. They lay tumbled and scattered like the toys of some giant toddler after a tantrum. The stones glistened from the sea spray, and those closest to the water wore glowing beards of what looked like long stringy moss.

"What bothers me is the lack of gulls," Wyatt said, tying off the bowline to a rock that rose out of the sand like a colossal finger. "Only a godforsaken beach is without seagulls."

"Really?" Hadrian asked. "The gulls? I would have figured the glowing green water would have you more concerned."

"There's that too."

Magnus was one of the first off the boat. He hit the sand and ran up the slope to the stone blocks, touching them with

his hands as if to assure himself they were real. Royce was off
next. His face had started to take on a green all its own. His
elven heritage made him subject to seasickness and Hadrian
recalled the days of misery his friend had spent aboard the
Emerald Storm. Royce climbed to the top of a large sturdy
rock and lay down. Alric and Mauvin arrived on the beach
wide-eyed, looking up at the ruined stone with awe. Arista
was the last off, accompanied by Myron, who held her hand.
She had slept for more than two hours and still had deep shadows beneath her eyes. After reaching the beach, she turned
around to view the *Harbinger* and a look of remorse crossed
her brow.

"She's not in much shape for a return trip," Wyatt stated,
looking at the princess. "I was thinking that maybe Elden and
I ought to stay here and work on her while the rest of you fetch
that horn. I could rig a few pulleys in these rocks, and with
Elden's help, I might be able to set a new mast if we manage to
find something we can use for one. At the very least, I could
run a jib line and reinforce the pole we have. I also think the
rudder needs some work and I need to stop the leaks that
opened up or she'll sink on the way back. I have the pitch for
that; I just need to make a fire and get the hull out of the water,
which the tide should help with."

"And if the Ghazel spot you?" Arista asked.

"Well, I will do my best to avoid that, but if they come
around, I suppose we'll hide among the rocks. I'm hoping that
after today, we won't be seeing any more of them for a while.
Perhaps we have at least a few days before another ship arrives.

"Thing is, I'm on this trip for my sailing skills, right? I can't
handle a sword as well as a Pickering or Hadrian, and I wasn't
brought along for that, anyway. Neither was Elden. Besides,
you can leave the excess gear here, and travel lighter."

Arista nodded. She did not look strong enough to argue.

"I really didn't mean to hit you so hard," Hadrian told her as Arista sat down on the sand.

"What?" she asked sluggishly. "Oh no, it's not my head. It's just that I feel exhausted, even after sleeping. I feel like I've walked for miles and been up for weeks. You know better than I do—do you get that from being whacked in the head?"

"No, not really," he replied. "It just usually throbs awhile and aches after that."

"I feel sort of like you do when coming down with a cold—weak, tired. My mind just wanders and I can't stay focused. It doesn't help that anytime I sleep, I have dreams."

"What kind of dreams?"

"You'll think I'm crazy," she said, embarrassed.

"I thought that from the first time we met."

She smirked at him. "In my dreams I'm not me—I actually think I'm Esrahaddon, only it's years ago, before this city was destroyed, before the emperor was killed, before he was locked up."

"That's what you get from wearing that robe."

She looked down. "It's a really nice robe—very warm, and have you ever seen one that lights up for you?"

"It's a little creepy."

"Maybe."

They sat in silence for a minute. Elden and Wyatt walked around the ship, looking at the hull. They were wasting no time assessing the damage. Alric and Mauvin climbed up in the rocks, exploring like children. Myron sat only a few feet away and appeared to be watching them.

Hadrian stared at the waves as they rolled ashore, splashing just beyond their feet. They would head off soon, but for now, it was good to sit on solid ground. He would nudge Royce in a bit, but he wanted to give him a few minutes. He expected dangers would be greater from that point on, and preferred Royce to be in top form.

"I should thank you," Arista said with downcast eyes and a quiet voice, as if it were a confession.

He looked at her curiously. "For what?"

"For the crack on the head," she replied, raising a hand to rub the spot. She took the bandage off. "Alric was right. I'd lost control." Her hair fell across her face—an auburn curtain hiding everything but the tip of her nose. "It's hard to explain the feeling of it—the power—it's as if I can do anything. Can you imagine knowing you can do *anything*? It's exciting, alluring—it draws you in and you want it like a hunger. You feel yourself becoming part of something bigger, joining with it, working with it. You sense every drop of water, every blade of grass, and you become them—everything—the air and the stars. You want to see how far you can go, where the edges are, only some part of you knows—there are no edges.

"I never did anything that big before. I spread out too far. I joined with it too much. I was losing myself, I think. It was just so amazing, feeling the world respond to me like it was a part of me, or I was a part of it. I don't know—I wasn't thinking anymore. I was just feeling and I don't know what might have happened if you hadn't..."

"Whacked you?"

"Yeah."

"I'm just glad you aren't mad," he said, and meant it. "Most people I hit wake up with a slightly different attitude."

"I suppose they do." She pulled the curtain of hair back and tilted her head up at him. She had a self-conscious smile on her face. "I'd also like to thank you for something else."

He looked at her once more—confused and a little worried.

"I want to thank you for not being afraid of me."

Her hair was tangled, her face drawn and weary. She had
drooping eyes and thin pale pink lips. There was a pinch of
sand on the tip of her nose. Creases marked her forehead, thin
lines of worry.

Is there anyone quite like her?

He fought an urge to brush the sand from her nose.

"Who says I'm not afraid of you?" he asked her.

He saw her turning that comment over in her mind and felt
it was best to end the conversation before he said something
stupid. He got up, dusted the sand off himself, and went looking for his pack. He had just reached the ship, where Wyatt
was coiling a length of rope, when the two scouts returned.

"There's a passage up that way," Mauvin announced,
grinning.

They came to the side of the ship, where they found their
packs and, pulling out their water sacks, threw their heads
back and guzzled to quench their thirst.

"It's amazing," Alric said, wiping the water from his beard.
"There are these huge statues of lions—their paws are taller
than I am! This really is Percepliquis. I want to go in. We
should get going."

"Wyatt and Elden are planning to stay here," Hadrian
told him.

"Why?" he asked, concerned and perhaps a bit annoyed.

"They plan to fix the ship while we're gone and have it
ready for us by the time we get back."

"Oh, okay, that makes sense—good sense. That's great.
Now let's get our stuff and get going. I've waited all my life to
see this." Alric and Mauvin trotted back aboard the *Harbinger* to find the rest of their gear.

"Kings," Hadrian said to Wyatt with a shrug.

"Be careful," Wyatt told him. "And keep an eye on Gaunt."

"Gaunt?"

"You're too trusting," Wyatt said. He nodded to where Gaunt sat near the dwarf on a large stone slab. "He spends a lot of time with Magnus and he was unusually friendly with me and Elden, like he was buddying up with the drafted members of the party, trying to form a group of dissenters. Remember what I told you on the *Emerald Storm*? There's always one member of any crew who's looking for a mutiny."

"And he's our only hope," Hadrian replied with a lilt of irony in his voice. "You'd better be careful too. As you know, the Ghazel are no joke. Keep an eye out. Don't sleep on the ship. Don't light any fires."

"Trust me, I remember the arena at the Palace of the Four Winds. I have no desire to cross swords with them a second time."

"That's good, because this isn't an arena and there are no rules. Out here they'll swarm over you like an army of ants."

"Good luck."

"Same to you and make sure this ship is ready to sail when we get back. I've been on enough jobs with Royce to know that while the going in may be slow, the coming out is usually a race."

The ruins of the city began at the water's edge, although this was not entirely evident until they left the sand and moved inland, where they had a wider perspective. The large stone blocks were part of the broken foundation of white marble columns that had once stood a hundred feet tall. They knew this by discovering three remaining columns still upright, yet how they had managed to remain this way was bewildering, as the blocks had shifted precariously.

They found the passage Alric and Mauvin had discovered, which began at the feet of two huge lions carved from stone. Each was easily two hundred feet tall, although one was missing its head, which had fallen away. The remaining lion

showed a fierce face with teeth bared and a full and flowing
mane.

"The Imperial Lions," Myron muttered as they passed
under their shadow and Royce paused to light his lantern.

"I've seen these before," Arista whispered, her head back,
looking up at the sculptures. "In my dreams."

"What do you know of this place, Myron?" Royce asked,
lifting his light and peering forward into a vast labyrinth of
crumbled stone and silhouetted ruins.

"Which author would you like to hear from? Antun Bulard
did a wonderful study of the ancient texts as well as—"

"Summarize, please."

"Right, okay, well, legend has it that this was once a small
agrarian village, the home of a farmer's daughter named Persephone. They lived in fear of the elves, who had reportedly
burned nearby villages and slaughtered the inhabitants right
down to every man, woman, and child. Persephone's village
was next but a man called Novron appeared in the village. He
fell in love with Persephone and vowed to save her. He begged
her to leave the village but she refused, so he decided to stay
and swore to protect her.

"He took charge and rallied the men. When the attack
came, he defeated the forces of the elves, saving the village. He
revealed himself to be Novron, the son of Maribor, sent to
protect his children from the greed of the Children of Ferrol.

"Many battles later, Novron defeated the elves at the Battle
of Avempartha and a time of peace with the elves began. Novron wished to build a capital for his great empire and a home
for his wife. Although he ruled vast tracks of land, Persephone
refused to live anywhere other than her village. So it was here
that Novron built his capital, naming it Percepliquis—*the city
of Persephone.*

"Over the years it became the largest and most sophisticated city in the world. It is chronicled as being five miles across and the seat of a famous university and library. Scholars came from across the empire to study. The Grand Imperial Palace was built here and it was a place of temples, gardens, and parks. Records report that the city had clean water fountains open to the public and baths where citizens lounged in heated pools.

"Percepliquis was also the home of the imperial bureaucracy, a vast system of offices that administered the empire, controlling its economy and social and political institutions. There were agents responsible for rooting out potential dissidents, suspected criminals, and corrupt officials. And of course, it was home to the Teshlor Guild and the Cenzar Council—the imperial knights and the college of wizards that advised and protected the emperor.

"Through his bureaucracy the emperor controlled everything, from the forests to mines, farms, granaries, shipyards, and cloth mills. Corruption was held in check by appointing more than one head of each department and by rotating them out frequently. They never appointed local men who might have ties to those they administered to. Even prostitution was regulated by the empire.

"Percepliquis was a place of great wealth. The center of the empire's trade that spanned all of Apeladorn and reached even into the exotic Westerlins and north into Estrendor, it bustled with richly dressed merchants and the roads were legendary. They were huge, wide thoroughfares of well-laid stone, perfectly straight, that ran for miles in all directions. Trees were planted on either side of them to provide shade, and they were well maintained and marked with milestones. Wells and shelters were placed at regular intervals for the comfort of travelers.

"There was no famine, no crime, no disease or plague. No

droughts were ever recorded, nor floods, nor even harsh frosts. Food was always plentiful, and no one was poor."

"I can see why the Imperialists want to recapture that ideal," Alric observed.

"Which just goes to show how foolish people can be," Gaunt said. "No famine, no drought, no disease, no poor? There's about as much chance of that happening as—"

"As you becoming emperor?" Royce asked.

Gaunt scowled.

"So what should we be looking for?" Royce asked.

Myron shook his head. "I don't know," he replied, and glanced at Arista.

"The tomb of Novron," the princess told them.

"Oh." Myron brightened. "That would be under the palace in the center of the city."

"Any way to identify it?"

"It's a huge white building with a solid-gold dome," Arista answered for him, gaining several surprised looks. She shrugged. "I'm guessing."

Myron nodded. "Good guess."

They moved on as before, with Royce in the lead, fleet of foot as always, investigating shadows and crevices, his light bobbing. Alric and Mauvin followed at a distance in a manner that reminded Hadrian of a fox hunt. Arista and Myron walked together, both staring up at their surroundings with great interest. Gaunt and Magnus followed them, occasionally speaking in whispers. Hadrian brought up the rear once more, glancing over his shoulder repeatedly. He already missed Wyatt and Elden.

They followed a passage that wove between collapsed rockfalls until they reached a street of neatly paved stones, each cut in a hexagon and fitted with stunning precision.

Here, at last, the mounds of rubble gave way, allowing them to view the shattered remains of the once-magnificent city that rose around them.

Great buildings of rose or white stone, tarnished by age and curtained in debris, had lost none of their beauty. What immediately captured Hadrian's attention was how tall they were. Pillars and arches soared hundreds of feet in the air, supporting marvelously decorated entablatures and pediments. Great domes of burnished bronze and stone-crowned buildings with diameters in excess of a hundred feet were far larger than anything he had ever seen before. Colonnades supporting a row of arches ran for hundreds of yards as mere decoration, standing out before load-bearing walls. Statues of unknown men were exquisitely sculpted such that they might move at any minute. They adorned silent fountains, pedestals, and building facades.

The grandeur of the city was stunning, as was its rattled state. Each building, each pillar, each stone appeared to have dropped from some great height. Blocks of stone lay askew and shifted out of place. Some teetered beyond imagination, loose, twisted, and misaligned so that it looked as if the weight of a sparrow would topple a structure of a thousand tons. The devastation was not even or predictable. Some buildings missed whole walls. Most no longer had roofs, while others revealed the shift of only a few stones. Despite the disarray, other aspects of the city were astonishingly preserved. A seller's market stood untouched; brooms remained standing, stacked on display. A pot stall exhibited several perfect clay urns, their brilliant ceramic glazes of red and yellow dimmed only by a coat of fine dust. On the left side of the street, in front of a disheveled four-story residence, lay three skeletons, their clothes still on them but rotted nearly to dust.

"What happened to this place?" Gaunt asked.

"No one knows exactly," Myron replied, "although there have been many theories. Theodor Brindle asserted that it was the wrath of Maribor for the murder of his blood. Deco Amos the Stout found evidence that it was destroyed by the Cenzar, in particular the wizard Esrahaddon. Professor Edmund Hall, whose trail we are on, believed it was a natural catastrophe. After crossing the salty sea and seeing the state of the city, he concluded in his journal that the ancient city sat upon a cavern of salt, which was dissolved with a sudden influx of water, thus causing the city above to collapse. There are several other more dubious explanations, such as demons, and even one rumor concerning the bitterness of dwarves and how they pulled it down out of spite."

"Bah!" Magnus scoffed. "Humans always blame dwarves. A baby goes missing and it was a dwarf that stole it. A princess runs off with a second son of a king and it was a dwarf who lured her to a deep prison. And when they find her with the prince—lo, she was rescued!"

"A king is stabbed in the back in his own chapel, and a princess's tower is turned into a death trap," Royce called back to them. "Friends are betrayed and trapped in a prison— yes, I can see your surprise. Where do they get such ideas?"

"Damn his elven ears," Magnus said.

"What?" Gaunt asked, shocked. "Royce is an elf?"

"No, he's not," Alric said. He looked back over his shoulder. "Is he?"

"Why don't you ask him?" Arista replied.

"Royce?"

The bobbing light halted. "I don't see how this is the time or place for discussing my lineage."

"Gaunt brought it up. I was just asking. You don't look elven."

"That's because I am a *mir*. I'm only part elven, and since I never met my parents, I can't tell you any more than that."

"You're part elven?" Myron said. "How wonderful for you. I don't think I've ever met an elf. Although I have met you, so perhaps I have met others and don't know it. Still, it is quite exciting, isn't it?"

"Is this going to be an issue?" Royce asked the king. "Are you planning on questioning my allegiance?"

"No, no, I wasn't," Alric said. "You've always been a loyal servant—"

Hadrian started walking forward, wondering if he had returned Royce's dagger too soon.

"Servant? Loyal?" Royce asked, his voice growing lower and softer.

Never a good sign, Hadrian thought. "Royce, we need to keep moving, right?"

"Absolutely," he said, staring directly at Alric.

"What did I say?" the king asked after Royce resumed his advance. "I was merely—"

"Stop," Hadrian told him. "Forgive me, Your Majesty, but just stop. He can still hear you and you'll only make matters worse."

Alric appeared as if he would speak again, but then scowled and moved on. Arista offered her brother a sympathetic look as she passed him.

They continued in silence, following the light. On occasion Royce whispered for them to wait, and they sat in silence, tense and worried. Hadrian kept his hands on the pommels of his swords, watching and listening. Then Royce would return and off they would go once more.

They moved to a much wider boulevard. The buildings became more elaborate, taller, often with facades of chiseled columns. Pillars lined the avenue, tall monoliths covered in detailed engravings, epigraphs and images of men, women, and animal figures. One very large building was totally shattered, forcing them to climb over a mountain of rubble. The going was treacherous, with slabs of broken rock the size of houses that were loose enough to shift with their weight. Driven to inch along ledges and crawl through dark holes, they all welcomed a rest on the far side.

They sat on what had once been a great flight of marble steps, which now went nowhere and looked down the city's main road. Each building was tall and made from finely carved stone, usually a white marble or rose-colored granite. Fountains appeared intermittently along the wide thoroughfare, and as he stared, Hadrian could imagine a time when children ran in the streets, splashing in the pools and swinging from the spear arm a statue held out. He could almost see the colorful awnings, the markets, the crowds. Music and the smells of exotic food would fill the air, much like in Dagastan, only here the streets were clean, the air cool. What a wonderful place it must have been, what a wonderful time to have lived.

"A library," Myron whispered as they sat, his eyes fixed on a tall circular building with a small dome and a colonnade surrounding it.

"How do you know?" Arista asked.

"It says so," he replied. "On top there: IMPERIAL REPOSITORY OF TOMES AND KNOWLEDGE, roughly translated, at least. I don't suppose I could..." He trailed off, his eyes hopeful.

"If you go in there, we might never get you out," Hadrian said.

"We need to camp and we still don't know anything about the horn," Arista said. "If Myron could find something..."

"I'll take a look," Royce said. "Hadrian, come with me. Everyone else wait here."

Just as if he were on a job, Royce circled the library twice, making a careful study of the entrances and exits before moving to the two great bronze doors, each decorated in ornate sculptured relief depicting a bisected scene of a man handing a scroll and a laurel to a younger man amidst the aftermath of a great battle. Hadrian noticed a river and a familiar-looking tower at the edge of a waterfall in the upper right. The doors were marred badly, dented and bent, bearing marks from a large blunt hammer.

Hadrian slowly, quietly drew one sword. Royce set down and hooded the lantern, then pulled the doors open and slipped inside. One of the many rules Hadrian had learned from the start was never to follow Royce into a room.

That was how it all had gone so bad in Ervanon.

Royce had slipped into the Crown Tower as delicately as a moth through a window. Yet unlike on the previous night, the room was not empty. A priest sat in the small outer chamber. It did not matter, as he had not seen or heard Royce, but then Hadrian blundered in. The man screamed. They ran — Royce one way, Hadrian the other. It was a coin flip that Hadrian won. The guards came around the tower on Royce's side. While they were busy chasing and wrestling Royce down, Hadrian made it back to the rope. He was safe. All he had to do was climb back down, retrieve his horse from the thickets, and ride away. That was exactly what Royce expected him to do, what Royce would have done in his place, but back then Royce did not know him.

Hadrian heard the three taps from inside the library and, grabbing the lantern, crept inside. It was black and he was met with a terrible confluence of smells. The dominant odor was a thick burnt-wood scent, but a more pungent rotted-meat stink managed to cut through. From the darkness, he heard Royce say, "We're clear, light it up."

Hadrian lifted the lantern's hood to reveal a scorched hall. Burned black and filled with piles of ash, the room was still beautiful beyond anything else Hadrian had ever seen. Four stories tall, the walls circling him were marvelously crafted tiers of marble arcades. Towering pillars ringed the coffered dome and supported the great arches joining the arcades to each other. Around the rim, a colonnade of white marble was interspersed with lifelike bronze statues of twelve men, each of which had to be at least twenty feet tall. From the floor they appeared life-sized. Great chandeliers of gold hung around the perimeter. The black cracked remains of tables formed a circular pattern of desks with a great office in the center. A fresco painting of wonderful scenes of various landscapes formed the lower part of the dome, while the greater portion, made of glass, now lay in shards scattered across the beautiful mosaic floor.

In the center of the room, near the office bench, was its only inhabitant. Surrounded by a few singed books, papers, quills, three lanterns, and an oilcan lay what remained of an old man. He was on his back, his head resting on a knapsack, his legs wrapped in a blanket. Like Bernie, this man was dead, and as he had Bernie, Hadrian recognized him.

"Antun Bulard," he said, and knelt beside the body of the elderly man he had befriended in Calis. He was not as ravaged by death as Bernie—no sea crabs here. Bulard, who had always been pale in life, was now a bluish gray, his complexion waxy. His white hair was brittle and spectacles still rested on the end of his nose.

"Bernie was right," Hadrian told Bulard. "You didn't survive the trip, but then again, neither did he."

Hadrian used the old man's blanket to wrap him up and together they carried his body out and set it off to the side under a pile of rocks. The smell lingered, but it was not nearly as pungent.

When the others arrived, they stared with disappointment, Myron most of all. Exhaustion won out and they threw their packs down while Royce relocked the door.

Myron looked up, his eyes scanning the tiers and countless aisles where books must have once lay, but now they housed only piles of ash, and Hadrian noticed the monk's hands tremble.

"We'll rest here for a few hours," Royce said.

"Here?" Gaunt asked. "The smell is awful, charcoal and something else...What is that disgusting—" Gaunt asked.

"We found a body," Hadrian told them. "Another member of the last team the Patriarch sent in, from the same group as Bernie, from the *Harbinger*...and a friend. We took his remains out."

"Was he burned?" Myron asked fearfully.

"No." Hadrian placed a hand on his shoulder. "I don't think anyone was here when it caught fire."

"But it was burned recently," the monk said. "It wouldn't still smell like this after a thousand years."

"Perhaps our resident sorceress can do something about the stench?" Gaunt asked.

This brought stern looks from Hadrian, Alric, and Mauvin.

"What?" Degan asked. "Are we to continue to tiptoe around it? She is a magician, a mage, a wizardess, a sorceress, a witch—pick whatever term you prefer. Beat me senseless if you like, but after our little boat ride, there is no debating the reality of that fact."

Alric strode toward Gaunt with a threatening look and a hand on his sword.

"No." Arista stopped him. "He's right. There's no sense hiding it or pretending. I suppose I am a— Did you say *wizardess*? That one's not too bad." As she said this, her robe glowed once more and a mystical white light filled the chamber with a wonderful brilliance, as if the moon had risen in their midst. "That's fine—best that it is out in the open, best that we can all say it. Royce is an elf, Hadrian a Teshlor, Mauvin a count and a Tek'chin swordsman, Alric a king, Myron a monk with an indelible mind, Magnus a dwarven trap smith, Degan the Heir of Novron, and I—I am a wizardess. But if you call me a witch again, I promise you'll finish this journey as a frog in my pocket. Are we clear?"

Gaunt nodded.

"Good. Now, I am exhausted, so you will have to live with the smell."

With that, Arista threw herself down, wrapped up in her blankets, and closed her eyes. As she did, the robe dimmed and faded until at last it was dark. The rest of them followed her lead. Some swallowed a handful of food or a mouthful of water before collapsing but no one spoke. Hadrian tore open another packaged meal, surprised at how few he had left. They had better find the horn soon or they might all end up like Bulard.

What happened to him?

It was the question he drifted to sleep on.

∽

Hadrian felt a nudge and opened his eyes to Mauvin's face and wild hair hanging over him.

"Royce told me to wake you. It's your watch."

Hadrian sat up groggily. "How long and who do I wake?"

"You're last."

"Last? But I just fell asleep."

"You've been snoring for hours. Give me the chance to get a little sleep."

Hadrian wiped his eyes, wondering how he could best estimate the length of an hour, and shivered. He always felt chilled when he woke up, before his blood got running properly. The cool subterranean air did nothing to help. He wrapped his blanket around his shoulders and stood up.

The party all lay together like blanket-shrouded corpses, bundles of dark lumps on the floor. Each had swept the broken glass back and it clustered in a ring marking the border of their camp. The lantern was still burning, and off to one side, near where he had found Bulard's body, huddled in a ball and wrapped in his hooded frock and blanket, sat Myron.

"Tell me you did not stay up reading," he whispered, sitting down next to him among the piles of papers and books, which Myron had neatly stacked.

"Oh no," he replied. "I was beside Mauvin when Alric woke him for his watch. I just couldn't get back to sleep, not in here. These papers," he said, picking up a handful. "They were written by Antun Bulard, a famous historian. I found them scattered. He was here. I think he is the one who died."

"He used to say he couldn't remember anything unless he wrote it down."

"Antun Bulard?" Myron looked astonished. "You've met him!"

"I traveled briefly with him in Calis. A nice old man and a lot like you in many ways."

"He wrote the *The History of Apeladorn*, an incredible work. It was the book I was scribing the night you found me at the Winds Abbey." Myron lifted the parchments, holding them up to Hadrian. "His legs were broken. They left him here with some food and water and the lantern for light. His notes are sloppy, lines running over one another. I think he wrote them in the dark to save oil for reading, but I can read most of it. He was with three others, a Dr. Levy, Bernie—who we laid to rest—and Sentinel Thranic, who I gather was their leader. Antun wasn't very pleased with him. There was also a man named Staul, but he died before they set sail."

"Yes, we knew them too. What happened?"

"Apparently, they acquired the *Harbinger* from a warlord of some sort called Er An Dabon. He also arranged for a Ghazel guide to take them into the city. All went well, if not a bit tense, until they arrived at this library. Here they found evidence that this had been the last stand for a previous team and he mentioned the names Sir Gravin Dent, Rentinual, Math, and Bowls."

"So it *was* them."

"They apparently barricaded themselves inside, but the doors were forced open. Bulard's group found their gear, bloodstains, and lots of Ghazel arrows—but no bodies."

"No, they wouldn't."

"Antun suggested they leave him to sit and read while they went on to explore for the horn."

"So the library—"

"It was fine—*perfect*, to use the words of Antun Bulard— filled with thousands and thousands of books. Bulard wrote, 'There is perhaps a hundred tomes on birds—just birds—and above those, another hundred on the imperial seafaring mercantile industries. I followed an aisle back to a swirling brass stair that corkscrewed up to yet another floor, like an attic, and it was filled to the ceiling with records of the city—births, deaths, land titles, and transfers—amazing!' "

"What happened?"

"Thranic burned it," Myron said. "They had to hold Antun down. After that, he refused to go any farther. Thranic broke both his legs to prevent him from escaping the city and left him here, just in case they had a question he needed to answer.

"Antun salvaged these from the ash." He pointed to the small stack of five books. "He lived for nearly three months. In the end, with the oil gone, he was trying to feel the words on the page with his fingertips."

"Nothing about what happened to the others?"

"No, but he appeared to realize something of tremendous importance. He began writing about it in earnest, but it must have been after the oil ran out and I suspect starvation was taking its toll. His quill work was abysmal. He wrote something about a betrayal, a murder, and something he referred to as the Great Lie, but the only thing he wrote clearly was the phrase *Mawyndulë of the Miralyith*, which was underlined twice. The rest is indecipherable, although it goes on for ten more pages and there are many exclamation points. Only the last line is fully readable. It says, 'Such a fool was I, such fools are we all.' "

"Any idea what this Maw-drool-eh of the Mirrorleaf *is*?"

"Maw-in-due-lay and Meer-ah-leeth," he corrected. "The Miralyith is, or was, one of the seven tribes of elves."

"Seven tribes?"

"Yes, actually Bulard wrote of them in his first book years ago. There were seven tribes of elves named from the ancestors that founded them. The Asendwayr, known as the hunters; the Gwydry, the farmers; the Eilywin, the builders; the Miralyith, the mages; the Instarya, the warriors; the Nilyndd, the crafters; and the Umalyn, the priests of Ferrol. Everyone knows that Ferrol created the elves first and for thousands of years only they and the creations of Muriel existed on the face of Elan. Bulard discovered that there was friction from the beginning. Elves once fought elves, clan against clan. A feud existed between the Instarya and the Miralyith to where—"

Arista quivered in her sleep and let out a muffled cry.

"She's been like that all night," Myron told him.

Hadrian nodded. "She told me she's been suffering from

nightmares, but I think they are more than dreams." Hadrian watched her. As he did, he felt Myron's hand on his. Looking up, he saw the monk offer him a sad smile.

Hadrian drew his hand away. "I think I'd better start waking people."

Myron nodded as if he understood more than Hadrian had meant to say.

CHAPTER 16

THE WHITE RIVER

Mince was convinced that the vast majority of his ten long years—soon to be eleven—had been spent with frozen feet. Even the empress's gifts of thick wool cloaks, hats, mittens, boots, and scarves were incapable of withstanding the biting winds. His fingers kept going numb, and he had to make fists to keep the blood flowing.

This must be the coldest winter the world has ever seen. If the water in my eyes freezes, will I be unable to blink?

Mince stood with a bucket in hand and stomped on the river with his frozen feet—solid as stone. He heard no cracking, nor the gurgle of liquid lapping beneath the surface. There would be no water again, which meant another miserable day warming cups of snow under their tunics. Hadrian had ordered them not to build a fire and Renwick was adamant about obeying. The task was unpleasant, but they could make do. Mince was not sure how much longer the horses could go without.

Lack of water was not the horses' only problem. Even though the boys had tethered them in a tight pack, and built a windbreak from pine boughs and thickets, the animals were still suffering from the cold. Ice formed on their backs, icicles hung from their noses, and that morning Mince had seen two of them lying down. One was producing a small puff of white mist at frighteningly long intervals. The other did not appear to breathe at all. The ones lying down were the horses on the outside of the pack—the ones exposed to the most wind.

The Big Freeze, as Kine had named it, had occurred three days earlier and come upon them overnight. The previous day they had run around in warm sunshine, playing tag without scarves or hats; then the sky had turned gray and a frigid air blew in. That morning Elbright had returned from fetching the water reporting that only a narrow stream ran down the center of the river. The day after, the river was gone completely—replaced by a smooth expanse of white. That afternoon when the snow started to fall, the flakes were no larger than grains of sand.

The five boys had been living in a snow cave beneath the eaves of a holly tree, and when the freeze came, they dug their shelter deeper and built a windbreak by covering the opening with lashed pine boughs.

Time passed slowly after the Big Freeze. With the temperature so bitter, they no longer went out except to relieve themselves. The only fun they had had was when Brand discovered the *trick*. He got up miserable, shivering, and cursing, and in a fit of frustration, he spit. It was so cold that the liquid cracked in the air. They spent the next few hours trying to see who could get the loudest snap. Kine was the best, but he had always been the best spitter. As fun as cracking spit was, it pushed away the boredom only temporarily and they tired of the game. As the cold wind blew, and the temperature continued to drop, Mince could not help wondering how long they would have to stay.

He should have headed back to the Hovel, what they began calling their snow cave, but instead scanned the length of the broad white trail that ran north and south like a shining crystal road. Mince was trying to see if some portion was clear. Perhaps there was a place where the current prevented the ice from forming. He looked for a change in color, but there was nothing but a never-ending expanse of white. Still, something caught his eye. Far to the north he saw movement.

A long gray line crossed the river. There were people, tall and slender, wearing identical cloaks. He stared, amazed at the sight, and wondered if perhaps they were ghosts, for in the stillness of the winter's morning he heard no sound of their passing. Mince stood staring but it was not until he saw a glint of armor that it occurred to him what he was actually seeing. The revelation froze him as instantly as if he were spit turning solid in the morning air.

Elves!

As he watched the spectral cavalcade, they marched three abreast in the muted light, passing like phantoms on the ridge. They rode on steeds that even at a distance Mince could tell surpassed any breed raised by men. With broad chests, tall ears, proud arched necks, and hooves that pranced rather than walked, these animals were ethereal. Their bridles and equestrian gowns were adorned in gold and silk, as if the animals were statelier than the noblest human king. Upon them, each rider wore a golden helm and carried a spear with a streaming silver banner licking the air.

The sound of music reached his ears—a wild, capricious but beautiful euphony that haunted his spirit and caused him to unwillingly take a step forward. Joining the sound was the wonderful lilt of voices. They were light and airy and reminded Mince of flutes and harps speaking to one another. They sang in a language Mince could not understand, but he did not need to. The melody and plaintive beauty of the sound carried him with it. He felt warm and content and took another step forward. Before long, the music faded, as did the sight of them as they finished crossing the river and disappeared into the foothills.

"Mince!" He heard Elbright and felt hands shaking him. "He's over here! The little idiot fell asleep on the ice. Wake up, you fool!"

"What's he doing way up here? I found the bucket a half mile back." Kine's voice was more distant and out of breath.

"It's almost dark. We need to get him back. I'll carry him. You run ahead and tell Renwick to get a fire started."

"You know what he'll say."

"I don't care! If we don't get him warm, he'll die."

There were the sounds of feet on snow, sounds of urgency and fear, but Mince did not care. He was warm and safe and still remembered the music lingering in his head, calling to him.

❧

When Kine returned to camp, only Brand was there — Brand the Bold, as he liked to call himself. It was a bold boast for a kid of thirteen, but no one questioned it. Brand had survived a knife fight, and that was more than any of them could claim.

"We need to get a fire started," Kine said, returning to the Hovel. "We found Mince and he's near dead with cold."

"I'll get kindling," Brand replied, and ran out into the snow.

Kine got the tinderbox from the supplies they had not touched and cleared a space near the front of the shelter. Brand was back in minutes with a sheet of birch bark, a handful of brown grass, tiny dry twigs, and even a bit of rabbit fur. He dropped the treasures off and set back out. As he did, Kine spotted Elbright carrying Mince on his back. The boy's head rolled with each step. It reminded him of how deer looked when hunters brought them in.

Elbright said, "Make a bed, put down lots of needle branches—pile them up—we want to keep him off the snow."

Kine nodded and ran out of the shelter past the horses—two more were lying down. He entered a grove of spruce trees, where he tore the branches from the trunks, getting his mittens sticky from the sap. He made four trips, and when he finished, Mince had a thick bed to lie on.

Elbright had a small, delicate flame alive on the birch sheet. His mittens were on the snow beside him. His bare fingers were red, and he frequently breathed on them or slapped his thigh as he squatted in the snow. "Fingers go numb in seconds."

"What are you doing?" Renwick said, coming up the slope from the south.

When Mince had not returned after going for water, they all went searching in different directions. Renwick took the southern riverbank and returned only now that the sky was darkening and the temperature plummeted.

Although he was also an orphan, Renwick was not one of their gang. He lived at the palace, where his father used to be a servant. While really no more than a page, the boy had served as squire to Sir Hadrian during Wintertide. All the boys were impressed by Hadrian's spectacular success during the games and this admiration spilled over to Renwick. The boy was also older—perhaps a year or two Elbright's senior. Unlike those of the rest, Renwick's clothes fit him properly and even matched in color.

"We have to get a fire going," Elbright told him even as he fed the tongues of flame little sticks. "We found Mince on the ice. He's freezing to death."

"We can't build a fire. Hadrian—"

"Do you want him to die?"

Renwick looked at the growing fire and the tendrils of white smoke snaking from it, then at Mince lying on the spruce bed. Kine could see the debate going on inside him.

"He's my best friend," Kine told him. "Please."

Renwick nodded. "It's getting dark. The smoke won't be visible, but we need to contain the light as much as we can. Let's bank the snow walls higher. Damn, it *is* cold."

Brand returned with more wood, larger branches and even a few broken logs. His cheeks and nose were red and ice crystals formed around his nose and mouth.

"You need to keep him awake," Elbright told him as he tended the fire as if it were a living thing. "If he stays asleep, he'll die."

Kine shook Mince and even slapped him across the face, but the boy did not seem to notice. Meanwhile, Renwick and Brand boosted the windbreak wall, which not only contained the light, but also reflected the heat. Elbright coaxed the fire, cooing to it like it was a child he had brought into the world. "Com'on, baby, eat that branch. Eat it, that's right, there you go. Tastes good, doesn't it? Eat all of it. It will make you strong."

Elbright's baby became a full-grown fire and soon the frigid cold fell back. It was the first time in days any of them had known real warmth. Kine's feet and fingers began to ache and his cheeks and the tip of his nose burned as he thawed out.

Beyond the mouth of their snow cave, darkness fell, made deeper by the bright light of the fire. Renwick grabbed a pot from the supplies, filled it with snow, and set it near the fire to melt. Elbright refused to let him put it on his fire. They sat in silence, listening to the friendly sound of the flames.

Soon the shelter was warm enough that Elbright took off his hat and even his cloak. The rest of them followed his lead, with Kine laying his over Mince.

"Can we eat now?" Brand asked.

Renwick had established a firm rule that they ration their food and they all ate together to make certain no one had more than his share. Like the cups of water, they kept their meals inside their shirts, up against their skin, since it was the only way to keep the food from freezing solid.

"I suppose," Renwick said passively, but looked just as hungry as any of them.

Brand pulled out his stick of salt pork and set it near the fire. "I'm having a hot meal tonight."

The rest of them mimicked him, and before long, the smell of hot meat filled the cave. They all waited to see how long Brand could hold out. It was not long and soon everyone was ripping into the pork and making exaggerated smacks of ecstasy.

In the midst of their revelry, Mince sat up.

"Supper?"

"You're alive!" Kine exclaimed.

"You're not eating my share, are you?"

"We should!" Elbright yelled at him. "You little idiot. Why did you decide to take a nap on the ice?"

"I fell asleep?" Mince asked, surprised.

"You don't remember?" Kine asked. "We found you curled up on the river, snoring."

"You should thank Maribor for your life," Elbright added. "And what were you doing so far north?"

"I was watching the elves."

"Elves?" Renwick asked. "What elves?"

"I saw the elven army crossing the river, a whole line of them."

"There were no elves," Elbright declared. "You dreamed it."

"No, I saw them on horseback, and they played this beautiful music. I started listening and—"

"And what?"

"I don't know."

"Well, you fell asleep is what," Elbright told him. "And if I hadn't heard you snoring, you'd be dead by now."

"He would, wouldn't he?" Renwick muttered, looking out at the dark. "The elves—you said they were all on horseback? None on foot? How about wagons?"

"No, no wagons, just elves on horses, beautiful horses."

"What is it?" Elbright asked.

"He didn't see the elven army."

"I know that," Elbright replied with a chuckle. "It was a dream."

"No—no, it wasn't," Renwick corrected. "He saw elves, but it wasn't the army. It was only the vanguard—the advance patrol. I heard the knights talking—the elven army travels at night, but hardly anyone has ever seen them and no one knows why, but I think I do—I do now."

They all looked at Mince.

"He'd be dead," Elbright said, nodding. "But that means the army is—It's night!"

They all looked at the fire, which had melted down a half foot into the snow so that it burned in its own little well. Elbright was the one who kicked it out. It made a dying hiss as the snow swallowed the flames. They all worked to bury the embers until it was a small mound of dirty brown with sticks and grass sticking out.

No one said a word as they felt around in the faint light for their cloaks and mittens. Silence hung in the air. Since it was winter, they did not expect the sounds of birds or frogs, but now not even the wind breathed. The constant rustle of naked branches was absent, as were the random cracks and snaps.

They poked their heads out of the cave, lifting them attentively above the blind and around the bundle of pine boughs. They could not see anything.

"They're out there," Renwick whispered. "They are crossing the frozen river and sneaking up on Aquesta from the south. We have to warn them."

"You want us to go out *there*?" Elbright asked incredulously. "Where *they* are?"

"We have to try."

"I thought we had to stay here and watch the horses."

"We do, but we also have to warn the city. I'll go. The rest of you stay here. Elbright, you'll be in charge. You can explain to Hadrian why I left." As he spoke, he moved to the gear and began picking supplies. "Keep the fire out. Stay inside and…" He paused a moment, then said, "Cover your ears if you hear any music."

No one said a word as he slipped out. They all watched as he inched nervously to the horses. He picked the one closest to the middle of the bunch and saddled it. When he was gone, all that remained was the deep silence of a cold winter's night.

CHAPTER 17

THE GRAND MAR

The party had stopped again. Since they'd left the library, their progress through the ancient city had been tedious, as Royce was pausing frequently. Sometimes he forced them to wait for what felt like hours as he scouted ahead—the rest of them sitting among the rubble. This time, he had left them in the middle of what appeared to be an alley with tall buildings towering on either side. Arista sighed and leaned against one wall. Someone ahead of her had stepped on a piece of fabric, the boot print revealing the faded colors of blue and green. She bent down and picked a small flag from under a thick coating of dust and dirt. This one was a handheld version, the sort people waved at celebrations. Looking up, she spotted a window, and hanging from that was an old and faded banner that read FESTIVIOUS FOUNDEREIONUS!

"What does that say?" she asked Myron, but she was certain she already knew.

" 'Happy Founder's Day,' " the monk replied.

Next to where she found the flag, she noticed a small object. Reaching out, she found a copper pin in the shape of the letter *P.* Now more than ever she wished she could remember the dream from the night before, but the more she tried to recall, the more it slipped away.

Royce returned, waving them forward, and then he led them in a circle back to the boulevard. Here they began to see skeletons. They were in groups of twos and threes, lying crumpled to the ground as if they had died right where they stood. The only way to tell how many there were was by the number of skulls in the piles. As they progressed, the bone count increased. Skeletons lined either side of the road with skull counts of ten deep.

They entered a small square, a portion of which was flooded where the ground was cracked and sank away at a dramatic angle. The same green light that illuminated the sea lit the square and revealed a raised platform on which was a great statue of a man. He stood twenty feet tall, with a strong, youthful physique. A sword was in his right hand and a staff in the other. Arista had seen similar statues several times throughout the city and in each case the head was missing, broken at the neck and shattered.

Royce stopped again.

"Any idea if we are getting close to the palace?" he asked, looking at Myron.

"I only know that it is near the center," the monk replied.

"The palace is at the end of the Grand Mar," Arista told them. "That's what they used to call the boulevard we're on now. So it is just up ahead."

"The Grand Mar?" Myron said, more to himself than to her, and then nodded. "The Marchway."

"What are you babbling about?" Alric asked.

"There was said to be a great avenue in Percepliquis called the Grand Imperial Marchway, so called as it was often the site of parades. Ancient descriptions declared it to have been wide enough for twelve soldiers to walk abreast and that it was made up of two lanes divided by a row of trees. Imperial troops would march down the right side to the palace, where the emperor would review them from his balcony, and then they would return down the other side."

"They were fruit trees," Arista said. "The trees that grew in the center of the Grand Mar—fruit trees that blossomed in spring. They used to make a fermented drink from the blossoms called...Trembles."

"How do you know that?" Myron asked.

She looked at him and pretended to be surprised. "I'm a wizardess."

They paused to have a short meal on the steps of an impressive building off the main boulevard. Stone lions, similar to those that guarded the entrance to the city, sat on either side. A fountain stood in the street at the center of an intersection. The water no longer sprayed and the pool was filled with a black liquid.

"What books have you got there?" Alric asked, seeing Myron sift through his pack and pull out one of the five that Bulard had saved.

"This one is called *The Forgotten Race* by Dubrion Ash. It deals mostly with the history of the dwarves."

"What's that now?" Magnus asked, leaning over to look closer at the pages.

"According to this, mankind is actually native to Calis— isn't that interesting? And dwarves started in what we know as Delgos. The elves of course are from Erivan, but they quickly occupied Avryn."

"What about the Ghazel?" Hadrian asked.

"Funny you should ask," he said, flipping back several pages. "I was just reading about that too. You see, men appeared in Calis during the *Urintanyth un Dorin* and would have—"

"Huh?" Mauvin asked.

"It means *the Great Struggle with the Children of Drome.* You see, the dwarves warred with the elves for centuries, nearly six hundred years, in fact, until the fall of Drumindor in 1705—that's pre-imperial reckoning, of course—about two thousand years before Novron built this city. The dwarves went underground after that. As it turns out, the early human tribes would have failed—perished—if not for the contact they had with the exiled dwarves who traded with them."

"Aha!" the dwarf said. "And how do they treat us for our kindness now? Ghettos, refusals of citizenship, bans on dwarven guilds, special taxes, persecution—it's a sad reward."

"Quiet!" Royce suddenly told everyone, and stood up. He looked left and then right. "Get ready to move," he said, and leaving the lantern, he climbed down the steps, heading back the way they had come.

"You heard him," Hadrian said.

"But we just sat down," Alric complained.

"If Royce says get ready to move, and he has that look on his face, you do what he says if you want to live."

They gathered their belongings back into their bags. Arista took one more mouthful of salt pork and a swallow of water before stashing the rest in her pack. She was just pulling the straps over her shoulders when Royce reappeared.

"We're being tracked," he told them in a whisper.

"How many?" Hadrian asked.

"Five."

"A hunting party." Hadrian drew his swords. "Everyone get moving. Royce and I will catch up."

"But they're just five," Arista protested. "Can't we avoid them?"

"It's not the five I am worried about," Hadrian told her. "Now go. Just keep moving up the avenue."

He and Royce moved back down the road at a trot. She watched them go as a sinking feeling pulled at her stomach. Alric led them forward at a run, past the fountain and on up the Grand Mar.

This part of the city was familiar to her. This road, these buildings—she had seen them before. Gone were the brilliant white alabaster walls and brightly painted doors. Now they were dingy and brown, cracked, fractured, chipped, and like everything else, covered in a layer of dirt. As in the rest of the city, the columned halls stood on misaligned stones.

Alric led them around a massive fallen statue whose head had severed at its neck and lay on its side, its features bashed and broken. They then leapt a fallen column, and as soon as she cleared it, Arista stopped. She knew this pillar; it was the Column of Destone. She turned left and saw the narrow road Ebonydale. That was the way Esrahaddon had gone to meet Jerish and Nevrik. She looked forward down the Mar. She should be able to see the dome, but it was not there. Ahead was only rubble.

"Arista!" She heard Alric calling to her and she ran once more.

᠊ꝥ᠊

Royce and Hadrian paused near the headless statue, where the algae in the water cast an eerie green radiance to the underside of all things. Royce motioned with two spread fingers that a pair were coming up one side of the street and two on the other. While the two pairs were mere shadows to Hadrian, the fifth was quite visible as he loped up the center of the boulevard like an ape hunched over and traveling on three limbs. His massive claws clicked intentionally on the stone as signals to the others. Every few feet he would pause, raise his head, and sniff the air with his hooked, ring-pierced nose. He wore a headdress made from the blackened fin of a tiger shark, a mark of his station—a token he would have obtained alone in the sea with no more than his claws. He was the chief warrior of the hunting party—the largest and meanest—and the others looked to him for direction. They all carried the traditional sachel blades—curved scimitars, narrow at the hilt and wider at the tip, where a half-moon scoop formed a double-edged point. Like all Ghazel, he also carried a small trilon bow with a quiver slung over one shoulder.

Royce drew out Alverstone and nodded to Hadrian as he slipped into the darkness. Hadrian gave him a minute; then, taking a breath, he also moved forward. He closed the distance, keeping the statue between him and the Ghazel. To his surprise, he was able to reach the platform before the warrior noticed him and let out the expected howl. Immediately arrows whistled and glinted off the stone.

The warrior rushed him, his sachel slicing the air. Fighting a Ghazel was always different from fighting men, but the moment the two swords connected, Hadrian no longer needed to think. His body moved on its own, a step, a lunge. The fin-endowed warrior responded exactly as Hadrian wanted. Hadrian caught the warrior's next stroke with his short sword and saw the momentary shock in the Ghazel's eyes when his bastard sword came around, removing his arm at the elbow. A short spin and Hadrian took the warrior's head, fin and all.

A high-pitched shriek announced the charge of two more Ghazel. Hadrian always appreciated how they announced their attacks. He was able to step out from his shelter now—the rain of arrows having ended.

The two bared their pointed teeth and black gums, cackling.

Hadrian shoved the length of his short sword into the stomach of the closest. Dark blood bubbled up from the wound. Without looking to see the reaction of the remaining Ghazel, he swung his other blade behind him and felt it sink into flesh.

Hadrian heard fast-moving footsteps and looked up. Across the open square Royce ran at him, carrying a Ghazel bow and quiver of arrows. The thief was making no attempt at stealth, his cloak flying behind him.

"What's up? Did you get the others?"

"Yep," he said. As he ran by, he tossed the bow and quiver to Hadrian and added, "You might need these."

Hadrian chased after him as he ran back up the Grand Mar. "What's the hurry?"

"They weren't alone."

Hadrian glanced back over his shoulder but saw nothing. "How many?"

"A lot."

"How many are a lot?"

"Too many to stand around and count."

∽

The party reached the end of the boulevard, which looked nothing like what Arista remembered from her dream. The Ulurium Fountain—with its four horses bursting out of the frothing waters—was gone, crushed by giant stones. To the right, the rotunda of the Cenzarium still stood, but it was a faded, broken version of its former self, the dome gone, the walls blackened. To the left, the columned facade of the Hall of Teshlor remained intact. While it had weathered the years better, the building was just as grime-covered as the rest. Most importantly, the great golden dome of the magnificent palace— in fact, the whole palace—was missing. Before her, only a hopeless mountain of rubble remained. All around the perimeter, every inch of space was carpeted with bones of the dead.

Reaching the end of the road, Alric spun around and held the lantern high. "Arista! Which way?"

She shook her head and shrugged. "The palace—it should be just ahead of us. I think—I think it's destroyed."

"That's just great!" Gaunt bellowed. "Now what do we do?"

"Shut up!" Mauvin barked at him.

"Is this as far as Hall got?" Alric asked Myron.

"No," the monk replied. "He wrote that he entered the palace."

"How?"

"He found a crevice."

"Crevice? Where?"

"He wrote 'Fearful of the drums in the darkness, and afraid to sleep in the open, I sought refuge in a pile of rocks. I found a crevice just large enough for me to slip through. Expecting nothing more than a mere pocket to sleep in, I was elated to discover a buried corridor. On my way out I was careful to mark it so that I might find it should I return this way again.' "

They began searching, crawling among the boulders and broken stones. The collapse of the building covered the entire breadth of the broad boulevard with a mass of fallen stones containing hundreds of crevices, each of which might hide an entrance. They had only begun looking when Royce and Hadrian returned, their weapons still drawn and slick with dark blood.

"That's not good," she heard Hadrian say the moment he saw the pile.

"There's a crevice somewhere that leads inside," Arista said.

"There's a horde of Ghazel right behind us," Royce told her.

"Everyone inside that building on the left," Hadrian shouted.

They ran across the square, struggling over the piles of bones and rocks that blanketed the walk and steps to the Hall of Teshlor. Yelps and cries erupted behind them. Looking back, Arista spotted goblins skidding across the stone, scratching their claws like dogs on a hunt. Their eyes flashed in the darkness with a light from within, a sickly yellow glow rising behind an oval pupil. Muscles rippled along hunched backs and down arms as thick as a man's thigh. Mouths filled with rows and rows of needle-like teeth spilled out the sides as if there was not enough room in their mouths to contain them.

"Don't watch, run!" Hadrian shouted, grabbing hold of her arm and pulling her across the loose mounds of bones.

Alric and Mauvin sped up the steps, heaving themselves simultaneously against the great doors.

Hadrian threw Arista to the ground, where she fell, scraping her knee and bruising her cheek.

"Wha—" Her protest was silenced as a hail of arrows peppered around them, sparking off the stones. He hauled her to her feet once more and shoved her forward.

"Go!" Hadrian ordered.

She ran as fast as she could, charging up the steps. Myron and Magnus, who had just slipped inside the big double doors, waved at her to hurry. She glanced behind her. Gaunt was just reaching the base of the steps.

Arrows flew again.

Arista heard the hiss and Hadrian pulled her behind the pillars, but Gaunt had no such protection. An arrow caught him in the leg and he fell, sliding to a stop.

He rolled over to his back and cried out as the first goblin reached him.

"Degan!" Arista screamed.

A white dagger slit the Ghazel's throat, and the princess

spotted Royce straddling the fallen Gaunt. Three more Ghazel rushed forward. Two fell dead almost instantly as Hadrian joined Royce, taking one with each of his swords. Distracted, the third turned toward the new threat just as Royce stepped behind him and the goblin fell.

"Get up, you fool!" Royce shouted at Gaunt, grabbing him by his cloak and pulling him to his feet. "Now run!"

"Arrow in my leg!" was all Gaunt managed to say through gritted teeth.

"Look out!" Arista shouted as nearly a dozen more Ghazel charged.

Hadrian's swords flashed as he threw himself into the fight. Royce vanished only to reappear and vanish again, his white dagger flashing like a sparkling star in the night.

"Back into your holes, you beasts!" Alric shouted as he suddenly ran out with a lantern in one hand and his sword in the other. Mauvin chased after his king as Alric leapt into the fray fearlessly, cleaving into the nearest goblin. Her brother took an arm off his opponent and then ran him through. Arista's heart stopped as Alric failed to see the blade of another Ghazel swinging from the side at his head. Mauvin saw it. A lightning-quick flash of his sword blocked the attack, sliced through the blade, and killed the goblin in one stroke.

Gaunt was up and hobbling forward.

Arista hiked up her robe and ran back down the stairs to him. "Put your arm around me!" she shouted, moving to his wounded side.

Gaunt put his weight on her. From behind them more goblins entered the square. Twenty—perhaps as many as thirty—ran forward shrieking and yelping, their claws clicking the stone, and a drone came from them like the sound of a swarm of locusts.

"Time to go!" Hadrian declared. Reaching Alric, he pulled

634 Michael J. Sullivan

the lantern from the king's hand and smashed it on the stone before the attacking Ghazel. A burst of flame rose along with more cries and squeals.

"I've got him!" Hadrian told her. "Run!"

They all bolted for the doors that Magnus and Myron held open. As soon as they entered, the monk and the dwarf pulled them shut. Royce slid the latch.

"Get that stone bench in front of the door!" Royce shouted.

"What bench?" Mauvin asked. "It's pitch-black in here!"

Arista barely thought about it and her robe glowed with a cold blue light that revealed the entrance hall. Musty and stale, it was much like the library, covered in cobwebs and dust. The white-and-black-checkered floor was cracked and uneven. A chandelier that had hung from the ceiling rested in the center of the floor. Braziers lay toppled, stone molding was scattered, and plaster chips littered the ground. Great tapestries still clung to either wall. Faded and dirty, they were otherwise unmarred, as were long curtains that draped the walls. Stairs led up from either side of the front doors and past two tall, narrow windows that looked out onto the square. It was then that Arista realized how much like a small castle-fortress the Teshlor Guild was.

Boom! Boom! The goblins hammered against the door, shaking the dust off the walls.

Having laid Gaunt down near the center of the room, Hadrian pulled the goblin bow from his shoulder and ran up the steps. He made use of the arrow slits to fire on the goblins outside. She heard a cry for every twang of the tiny bow and soon the hammering stopped.

"They've moved off," Hadrian said, leaning heavily against the wall. "Out of bow range, at least, but now that they know they have guests, they won't leave us alone."

Royce looked around, scanning the stairs, the ceiling, and the walls. "Question is...is there another way in here? And perhaps more importantly, another way out?" He pulled the remaining lanterns from Myron's pack and began lighting them.

Arista moved to Gaunt's side. The short, foul-looking arrow had penetrated through his calf with both ends sticking out. "I can see why you were having such trouble running," she told him as she pulled her dagger and started to cut his trouser leg.

"At least someone gives me credit," he growled.

"You're lucky, Mr. Gaunt," Hadrian said, coming down the stairs and approaching them. He grabbed the first lit lantern and knelt down beside him. "If the tip was still inside your leg, this next process would hurt a lot more."

"Next process?"

Hadrian bent down, and before Arista or Gaunt knew what was happening, he snapped off the arrow's tip. Gaunt howled in pain.

"Get some bandages ready," he told Arista. Myron was already there holding two rolls out to her. "Now this will hurt some."

"*This* will?" Gaunt asked incredulously. "What you did befo—"

Hadrian pulled the shaft from his leg. Gaunt screamed.

Blood flowed from the wounds on either side of the leg and Hadrian quickly began wrapping and pulling the cloth.

"Put your hands on the other side and squeeze tight—real tight," he told Arista. Blood soaked through the white linen, turning it red.

"Squeeze harder!" he told her as he unrolled a second length of cloth.

As she did, Gaunt cried out again, throwing his head back. His eyes went wide for a moment and then squeezed shut.

"I'm sorry," she told him.

Gaunt groaned through gritted teeth.

Blood seeped through her fingers. It was warm—and slicker than she had expected, almost oily. This was not the first time she had found her hands covered in blood. In the square of Ratibor, with Emery in her arms, there was much more, but she did not notice it then.

"Okay, let go," Hadrian told her, and he redressed the wound. Once again he had her squeeze as soon as he was finished. More blood soaked the bandages, but it was spotty this time and did not consume the whole linen.

Hadrian wrapped another length and tied it off. "There," he said, wiping his hands. "Now you just have to hope there was nothing nasty on that shaft."

Royce handed him a lantern. "We should look for other entrances."

"Mauvin, Alric? Keep watch out the windows, shout if they return."

"I need water," Gaunt said, his face dripping with sweat. Arista slipped a pack under his head and grabbed his water pouch. It appeared more of it dribbled down his chin than went in his mouth.

"Rest," she said, and brushed the hair from his brow.

He gave her a suspicious look.

"Don't worry, I'm not going to enchant you," she said.

ж

When she entered, her robe illuminated the grand hall with a cold azure light. A great stone table stood in the center with dozens of tall chairs surrounding it. A few had fallen to their sides, as had a half dozen metal goblets that rested on the table. The chamber was four stories tall, with great windows lining the high gallery and skylights in the ceiling. She imagined that they had once filled this room with a wonderful radiance of sunlight. Painted on the upper walls and parts of the ceiling were astounding scenes of battle. Knights rode on horseback with streamers flying from long poles, vast valleys were filled with thousands of soldiers, and castle gates, defended by archers, were assailed by machines of war. In one scene, three men battled on a hilltop against three Gilarabrywn. Those same men were seen in other images, and in one, they were pictured in a hall with a throne where one sat with a crown and to either side stood the other two. Below the paintings, a varied array of weapons lined the room: swords, spears, shields, bows, lances, and maces. The one thing they all had in common: even after a thousand years, they still gleamed.

Words were engraved in a band encircling the room and could also be found on recessed plaques, yet Arista's training in the Old Speech was verbal, not written. Unable to decipher the meanings, she did spot the words *Techylor* and *Cenzlyor*.

A majestic stair gave access to the gallery above and she climbed it. At the top were a series of doors. Some rooms lay open and she spied small chambers, living quarters with beds, shelves, and closets. Lantern light spilled from one.

She found Hadrian standing near the bed, staring up at the opposite wall as if entranced. He was looking at a suit of armor, a shield, and a set of weapons. The armor was not at all like the traditional heavy breastplates, pauldrons, vambraces, and tassets of typical knight attire. This was one piece and appeared as a long formal coat, but made from leaves of gold-colored metal. It hung from a display with a great plumed helm like the head of an eagle resting on top.

"Planning on moving in?" she asked. "I got a little worried when you didn't come back."

"Sorry," he said, embarrassed. "I didn't hear any shouts. Is everything all right?"

"Gaunt is sleeping, Myron reading, Magnus is arguing with Alric, Royce still hasn't returned, and Mauvin wandered off. And what are you doing?"

She sat down on the bed, which promptly collapsed under her weight, issuing a cloud of dust.

"You all right?" he asked, helping her up.

"Yes," she said, coughing and waving her hand before her face. "I guess the wood rotted over the years."

"This is it," he said.

"What?" She brushed the dust from her robe.

"This is Jerish's room, Jerish Grelad, the Teshlor Knight who went with the emperor's son into hiding."

"How do you know?"

"The shield," he said, and pointed across the room at the heater shield hanging on the wall. On it was an emblem of twisted and knotted vines around a star supported by a crescent moon. Hadrian reached back and drew forth the long spadone sword. He held it up so that she could see the small engraving at the center of the pommel that matched the one on the shield. Then he stood up and crossed the room. As he did, she noticed for the first time that the suit of armor had no sword, but there was a sheath of gold and silver. Hadrian fitted the tip into the opening and let the great sword slide home. "You've been parted a long time."

"Doesn't quite match anymore," Arista said, noticing how the sword was marred to a dull finish.

"It has seen a thousand years of use," Hadrian said, defending it. He looked back at the armor. "The sword was the only thing he took. I suppose he couldn't expect to hide very well dressed in shiny gold armor." His fingers played over the gleaming surface of the metal.

"Looks like it would fit," she said.

He smirked. "What would I do with it?"

She shrugged. "Still, it seems like you should have it. Goes with the sword, anyway."

"It does, doesn't it?"

He lifted the coat. "So light," he said, stunned.

Arista looked back down at the bed and, as she did, noticed a small object—a figurine carved from a bit of smoky quartz. She picked it up and rubbed it clean. It was a statuette of three people, a boy flanked by two men, one in leaf armor and the other in a robe. The likeness of Esrahaddon was remarkable, except that this figure had hands. Whoever the artist was had a rare gift.

"Interested in what he looked like?" she said, and held out the figurine.

"He was young," Hadrian replied, taking the statuette and turning it over in his hands. "A good face, though." Then his eyes shifted and he smiled and she knew he was looking at Esrahaddon. "So this must be Nevrik, the heir. Doesn't look like Gaunt, does it?"

"How many generations are there in a thousand years?" she asked. "Funny that he left this. It's so beautiful you would have thought he'd taken it with him, or at least..." She paused and glanced around the room. Except for the expected silt of a thousand years, the room was neat and ordered, the bed made, drawers and cabinets closed, a pair of boots standing side by side at the foot of the bed.

"Did you...straighten up in here at all?" she asked.

He looked at her curiously and appeared as if he might laugh. "No," he told her.

"It's just that it's so tidy."

"What, because he was a knight you think— Okay, so there is Elgar, but he's more of an exception. No one is as messy as he is, but—"

"That's not what I meant. It's just that after Jerish left— after he took Nevrik and ran—I would have thought they would have searched this room, tore it apart looking for clues, but nothing looks out of place. And this figurine—don't you think they would have taken it? Why didn't they ransack the room? It's been a thousand years. You'd think they would have gotten around to it by now, unless...maybe they never got the chance."

"What do you—"

The blare of a horn blowing from somewhere outside the guildhall reached them, followed by the distant beat of drums.

⤚

"What's happening?" Hadrian asked, returning with Arista to the front of the hall, where Alric was once again at the windows. He carried the armor in a bundle and the shield over his back.

Alric shrugged. "I don't know. I can't see a thing out there. Did you find an exit?"

"No, everything is sealed by rubble. So on the one hand, we're safe, but on the other, trapped."

"I think more are arriving out there," Alric mentioned.

"Get your head back from the window before you catch an arrow," Royce told him, returning from a side hall Arista had not taken.

She knelt down beside Gaunt and looked over his wound. The bleeding had finally stopped, but his face was still moist despite the chill in the air.

"Anything?" Hadrian asked.

Royce shook his head; then he looked around, concerned. "Where's Myron and Mauvin?"

"This is the Teshlor Guild," Alric said. "Mauvin has wanted to explore this since he was ten."

"And Myron?"

Alric glanced at Gaunt, who looked up painfully, blinking. Then all of them turned to Magnus.

"Don't look at me like that. I don't know where he went. He wandered off."

"I'll look for him," Royce said.

"Wait." Alric stopped him. "How are we going to get out of here?"

"Don't know," Royce replied.

Alric slumped against the front wall with a miserable look on his face. "He's not serious, is he?"

"You're the king," Gaunt said. "You tell us. You wanted to be in charge. What does your family heritage and blue-blood breeding say now? What insight has it provided you that we commoners can't see?"

"Shut it, Gaunt," Mauvin ordered, trotting down the stairs.

"There you are," Royce said.

"I'm just saying that he's the king," Gaunt went on. "He's in charge. So far all that he's managed is to get me bleeding to death and all of us trapped. This is a perfect chance for him to shine and prove his worth. All the other teams that came in here didn't have a noble king to lead them. Surely he will not leave us to the same fate as they. Isn't that right, Your Majesty?"

"I said, shut it," Mauvin repeated in a lower, more threatening voice. "Have you forgotten he just risked his life to help save yours?"

Alric looked at each of them as they sat around the entrance hall in the flickering light of four lanterns, each casting four separate shadows of everything.

"I don't know," he said. He peeked back out the window. "You heard the horn and the drums. There could be dozens of goblins out there by now."

"I doubt that," Hadrian replied, and Alric looked hopefully at him. "I would say there were hundreds by now. Ghazel prefer uneven battles, the more one-sided, the better, as long as it is in their favor. Those horns and drums are calling all goblins within earshot. Yeah, I would say a couple hundred at least are gathering."

Alric stared at him, shocked. "But...how are we going to get out, then?"

No one replied.

Even Gaunt gave up his taunting and lay back down. "And I was going to be emperor."

"The imperial hunts were massive." They heard Myron's voice echo as Royce led him back. "You can see by that tapestry. Hundreds participated—thousands of animals must have been killed, and did you see the chariots?"

"He was looking at the art," Royce told them.

"They were master bronze craftsmen, did you see?" the monk asked. "And this building, this is the guildhall, the knights' guildhall. This is the very place mentioned in hundreds of books of lore, often thought to be a myth—the Hall of Techylor—and isn't that amazing—not Teshlor at all.

"It's astounding, really, in all the years of reading about the Old Empire I never found anything about it, but clearly it was true. Techylor is not a combat discipline or martial art any more than Cenzlyor is a discipline of mystical arts. They're names. Names! Techylor and Cenzlyor were the names of people who were with Novron at the first battle of the Great

Elven War. The Teshlor Knights were literally the knights trained by Teshlor, or actually Techylor."

"This is hardly the time for studying history!" Alric snapped. "We need to find a way out, before they find a way in!"

"I see a light," Mauvin announced. "There's a fire, or a torch, or some— Uh-oh."

"What?" Gaunt asked.

"Well, two things, really," the young count Pickering began. "Hadrian was right. I can only see silhouettes but—oh yeah—there's a lot out there now—a whole lot."

"Second?" Hadrian asked.

"Second, it looks like they're setting up for flaming arrows."

"What good is that?" Alric asked. "This place is stone. There's nothing to burn."

"Smoke," Hadrian replied. "They'll smoke us out."

"That doesn't sound good," Gaunt said.

"Another locked room," Hadrian said to Royce. "How many is this? I've lost track."

"Too many, really."

"Ideas?"

"Only one," the thief said, and then looked directly at Arista.

She watched Hadrian nod.

"No," she said instantly. She stood up and backed away from them. "I can't."

"You have to," Royce told her.

She was shaking her head so that her hair whipped her face, her breath short and rapid and her stomach tightening, starting to churn. "I can't," she insisted.

Hadrian moved toward her slowly, as if he were trying to catch a spooked horse.

Her hands were starting to shake. "You saw—you know what happened last time. I can't control it."

"Maybe," Hadrian told her, "but outside that door are anywhere from, I'm guessing, fifty to a few hundred Ba Ran Ghazel. All the bedtime stories, legends, and fables are true. I know firsthand, and actually, they don't tell even half the story—no one would dare tell the real stories to children.

"I served as a mercenary for several years in Calis. I fought for warlords in the Gur Em Dal—the jungle on the eastern end of the peninsula that the goblins took back. I've never spoken about what happened there, and I won't now—honestly, I work very hard not to think about it. Those days that I lived under the jungle canopy were a nightmare.

"The Ghazel are stronger than men, faster too, and they can see in the dark. They have sharp teeth and, if they get the chance, will hold you down and rip into the flesh of your throat or stomach. The Ghazel want nothing better than a meal of human meat. Not only are we a delicacy to them, but they also use their victims as part of their religious ceremonies. They will make a ritual out of killing us, take us alive if they can—eat us while we still breathe. They'll drink their black cups of gurlin bog and smoke tulan leaves while we scream.

"That door is the only way out of here. We can't sneak out, we can't create a diversion and hope to catch them off guard, we can't hope for a rescue. Either you do something or we all die. It's as simple as that."

"You don't know what you're asking me to do. You don't know what it's like. I can't control it. I—I don't know what will happen. The power is—it's—I don't know how to describe it, but I could kill everyone. It just gets out of control, it just runs away."

"You can handle it."

"I can't. I can't."

"You can. It caught you off guard before. You know what to expect now."

"Hadrian, if I go too far—" She tried to imagine and realized she did not want to. There was an excitement in the thought of the power, a thrill like standing on the edge of a cliff, or playing with a sharp knife; the exhilaration came from the risk, the very real fear that she could step too far. It lured her like the still beauty of a deep lake. Even as she spoke about it, she remembered how it felt, the desire, the hunger. It called to her. "If I reach beyond—if I go too far—I might not come back." She looked at Hadrian. "I'm scared what would happen. I don't think I would be human anymore. I'd be lost forever."

He took her hands. Until he touched her, she had not realized she was shaking. His hands felt warm, strong. "You can do it," he told her firmly. He stared into her eyes and she could not help looking back. There was peace there, a gentle understanding familiar to her now, comforting, reassuring.

How does he do it?

Her hands stopped shaking.

An arrow whizzed through Mauvin's window, just missing him. It streaked a thick dark smoke that stank of sulfur. It flew to the far wall and bounced off the stone, continuing to smolder and burn. Two more managed to find their way into the narrow slits while outside it sounded as if it were raining. Then a line of smoke began to leak in through the cracks of the door.

"You have to try," Hadrian told her.

She nodded. "But I want you with me. Don't leave me...no matter what happens."

"I swear I will not leave you." His voice and the look in his eyes were so sincere, so resolute.

Degan began to cough, and Mauvin and Alric climbed down from the stairs.

"Everyone gather," she told them in a soft voice, trying to keep her eyes on Hadrian. "I don't know exactly what's going to happen. Just try and stay as close as you can, and don't you let go of me, Hadrian."

CHAPTER 18

DUST AND STONE

The smoke was growing thick and it was becoming hard to breathe as Arista remained standing still, muttering, her eyes closed, her hands twitching.

"Is she going to do something?" Gaunt asked, and followed this with a series of coughs.

"Give her a second," Hadrian told him.

As if in response, a light breeze moved within the room. Where it came from Hadrian could not tell, but it moved around the chamber, swirling and stealing away the smoke. The wind grew stronger and soon it ruffled the edges of their cloaks, slapping their hoods and spinning the dust into little whirlwinds that twirled, dancing about. All at once, the flames in the lanterns went out and the wind stopped. Everything was deathly still for a heartbeat.

Then the front wall of the guildhall exploded.

Arista's robe flared brilliantly as from beyond the missing wall, Hadrian heard the cries of goblins, like a million squealing rats. The square cast in darkness for a thousand years lay revealed, illuminated as if the sun had returned to the Grand Mar. They could finally see the beauty that once had been, the city of Novron, the city of Percepliquis, the city of light.

"Gather your things," Arista shouted, opening her eyes, but Hadrian could tell she was not fully with them. She was breathing deep and slow, her eyes never focusing, as if blind to what was around her. She was not seeing with her eyes anymore.

Mauvin and Alric hoisted Gaunt between them. He grunted but said nothing as he hopped on his good leg.

"Come," she told them, and began to walk toward the collapsed pile that had once been a palace.

"You're doing great," Hadrian told her. She showed no sign of hearing him.

The goblins stayed back. Whether they retreated from the explosion of stone, the harsh light, or some invisible sorcery that Arista was manifesting, all Hadrian could tell was that they refused to approach.

The party walked as a group clustered around Arista.

"This is crazy," Gaunt said, his voice quavering. "They'll kill us."

"Don't leave the group," Hadrian told them.

"They're fitting arrows," Mauvin announced.

"Stay together."

Struggling to shield their eyes as they bent their bows, the Ghazel launched a barrage. All of the party flinched except Arista. A hundred dark shafts flew into the air, burst into flame, and vanished into streaks of smoke. More howls arose from the Ghazels' ranks, but no more arrows flew, and now more than ever, the goblins showed no willingness to advance.

"Find the opening!" she shouted, sounding out of breath, her tone impatient, like someone holding up heavy furniture.

"Magnus, try and find the hollow corridor," Hadrian barked.

"To the left, up there, a gap. No over farther—there!"

Royce was on it, throwing rocks back. "He's right—there's an opening here."

"Of course I'm right!" Magnus shouted.

"Something…" Arista said dreamily.

"What was that, Arista?" Hadrian asked. She mumbled and he did not catch the last few words. He kept his hands on her shoulders, squeezing slightly, although he was not certain if by doing so he was reassuring her or himself.

"Something…I feel something—something fighting me."

Hadrian looked up and stared out over the Grand Mar at the colony of goblins, a writhing mass of insidiously twisted bodies, with dripping teeth and brilliant claws clacking along the length of spears and swords. He spotted what he looked for beyond them, moving in a ring around the Ulurium Fountain. The small, slim figure of the oberdaza, dressed in a skirt and headdress of feathers, shaking a tulan staff and dancing his methodic steps. He spotted two more joining the first.

"We need to get in now!" Hadrian shouted.

Royce threw Myron and a lantern inside the dark hole and then shoved Magnus after him before following them inside. Gaunt, Mauvin, and Alric followed.

"We need to go," Hadrian told Arista.

Across the span of the square, he could hear chanting as two more witch doctors joined in the dance.

"Something," Arista muttered again. "Something taking shape, something growing."

"That's why we need to get moving."

A light appeared in the center of the square. No more than a candle flame, it wavered, hovering in midair; then it began to grow. The light swirled, flared, popped, and grew to the size of an apple. The host of the Ghazel army joined in the chant of the three oberdaza as the hovering ball of fire continued to grow and take shape. Hadrian began to see what looked like limbs and a head emerging from the withering fire.

"Okay, we *really* have to go," Hadrian said, and grabbed

hold of the princess. The moment he did, she staggered back, looking shocked and frightened. The glow of her robe went out.

"What's happening?" Arista asked.

He did not answer but merely grabbed her tightly by the wrist and drew her up the rubble to the opening, where he shoved her headfirst into the hole. Behind him he heard the thrum of a hundred arrows taking to the air and dove into the hole after her.

"Go! Crawl!" he shouted to Arista as he did his best to shove rocks up against the opening. She obeyed and somewhere in the darkness he heard her scream.

"Arista!" He turned and scrambled forward, only to fall.

Dropping ten feet, he landed next to her, and the two found themselves lying in a corridor illuminated by a lantern in Myron's hand.

"You two all right?" Royce asked. "That drop is a bit of a surprise."

"I'm sorry," Arista was saying, rubbing her back. "I couldn't hold them. There was something fighting me, something I've never felt before, another power."

"It's okay," Hadrian told her. "You did great. We're in."

"We are?" the princess asked, looking around, surprised.

"What about getting back out?" Gaunt asked.

"I'd be more concerned about them following us right now," Hadrian told him. "The narrow passage will slow their progress, but they'll be coming."

"Talk as you walk," Royce said. "Or run if you're up to it. Give me the lantern, Myron. I don't want to fall into any more holes."

"Maybe we should stay behind and kill them as they come down," Mauvin said to Hadrian.

"You'll run out of strength before they run out of goblins,"

Hadrian told him. "And then there's that—that thing the oberdaza were making."

"*Thing?*" Arista asked.

They jogged down the corridor with Royce out front holding the lantern high. To either side were white marble walls, and beneath them, a dark polished floor of beautiful mosaic design.

"I don't suppose you saw a map of this place," Royce said to Myron.

"Actually, yes, but it was very old, and parts were missing."

"Better than nothing. Any idea where we are?"

"Not yet."

At first Hadrian thought they stumbled into a room—a great hall, by the size of it—but soon it became clear that it was a corridor, but far larger than any Hadrian had ever before seen. Suits of armor, each similar to the one he had found in Jerish's room, stood on either side. The walls were sculptured relief images of men, scenes of battles, scenes of remembrance; they flashed, frame by frame, as the party raced past.

Hadrian saw a long succession of men being crowned, with the cityscape in the background; in each one the city was smaller, the crowning ceremony less lavish. Two things caught his notice as they ran. The first was that in every instance, the head of the man being crowned was scratched out, deliberately chipped away. The second was that in each depiction, although the crowd always appeared different, Hadrian could swear the artist used the same model for one figure—a tall, slender man—who appeared in the forefront in each scene. And while in the dim fluttering lantern light it was difficult to tell, Hadrian was certain he had seen the man before.

They came to a four-way intersection. To the left was an

incredible door, five stories tall, made completely of gold and inlaid with stunning geometric designs of such artistry each of them expelled a sound of awe.

"The imperial throne room," Myron said. "In there once sat the ruler of the world."

"You know where we are, then?" Royce asked.

Myron nodded, looking at the walls. "Yes...I think so."

"Which way to the crypts?"

The monk hesitated, closing his eyes for a second. "This way." He pointed forward. "Down two doors, then we take a stair down on the left."

They quickly reached the stair and Royce led them down. Gaunt grunted, limping along with one arm around Myron's shoulders, his fist holding on to the monk's rope belt.

"Oberdaza?" Arista said to Hadrian as they chased the end of the line. "You mentioned them before, when we were in Hintindar, didn't you? You said they were witch doctors who used Ghazel magic."

"Scary little buggers."

"What was that *thing* they were making?"

"No idea, but it was on fire and growing."

"I could sense something, something disrupting the rhythm, breaking my pattern, my connection. I've never encountered anything like that before. I didn't know what to do."

"I think you did great," he told her. "You controlled it real well too—didn't even get close to losing you this time."

In the dim light he managed to catch a little smile on her face. "I did control it better, didn't I? You helped. I could sense you near me, this warm light I could cling to, an anchor to keep me grounded."

"You were probably just afraid I'd hit you again." Behind them, down the corridor, echoed a tremendous *boom!* The ground shook under them and dust blew off the walls. "Uh-oh."

They reached another stair.

"We keep going down, right?" he heard Royce ask. "This tomb-thing is at the bottom?"

"Yes," Myron replied. "The imperial crypt is on the lowest level. The palace was actually built over the tomb of Novron as a shrine to glorify his memory. It became a ruling palace long after."

They came to still another stair and raced down it, Magnus grunting with each drop. At the bottom lay corridors smaller and narrower, with shorter ceilings. They moved single file now, Gaunt struggling, hopping. A three-way intersection stopped them. Three statues of long-bearded men holding shields stood before them, staring back.

"Well?" Royce asked the monk.

"This is where the map was torn," he replied apologetically. "The rest is just white space."

"Great," Royce said.

"But we should be close. There wasn't much room left, so it has to be—Look!" The monk pointed at the wall on the right corridor, where an *EH* was scratched.

"Let's hope the Ghazel can't read," Royce said, pushing on.

"They don't need to; they can smell," Hadrian explained.

They ran as best they could, chasing the bobbing lantern. Behind them, the sounds of pursuit grew as the Ghazel gained on them. They passed doors on either side of the corridor, which Royce ignored as he rushed forward. Some were partially open. Hadrian tried to look inside, yet the interior of each was too dark to see anything.

Drums echoed, and the blast of a horn rang down the stone corridors. Gaunt was bleeding again. Hadrian could see dark drops on the floor behind them. If the Ghazel had had any trouble tracking them before, they would have none now.

Again they stopped, this time at a T-intersection at the

center of which stood a large stone door beside a stone table. They all saw letters above it, carved deep into the arch.

"Myron, translate," Royce ordered.

"This is it," he said excitedly. " *'Tread lightly, with fear and reverence, all ye who enter these halls, for this is the eternal resting place of the emperors of Elan, rulers of the world.'* "

Before Myron finished reading, Hadrian heard the chilling sound of claws on stone. "They're coming!"

Royce pulled on the door and struggled with it. Hadrian and Mauvin pushed forward. Together they grabbed hold of the edge and pulled to the sound of heavy stone grinding.

The sharp clacking of hundreds of three-inch nails grew louder as behind them a fiery red light appeared and grew. They all passed through the opening and together pulled the door shut. As they did, as the door closed, Hadrian peered out the closing crack and glimpsed the sight of a giant, stooping figure made of flame striding down the corridor at them.

"There's no way to lock it!" Alric shouted.

"Outta my way!" The dwarf fell to his knees and, drawing his hammer, pounded on the hinges. There was an immediate crack. "That will slow them."

Ahead was another, very narrow downward stair. Here the stone was different. It cast a bluish hue and was carved in fluid curving lines.

Boom!

The Ghazel reached the door and struck it hard.

"Run!" Hadrian called forward, and Royce reached the bottom of the stairs in seconds, waiting for the rest to join him.

Boom!

Hadrian glanced over his shoulder, watching Myron help Gaunt down. There was a loathsome clicking on the far side of the door, and he imagined all those claws scratching. Magnus remained on his knees, picking up wedges of broken stone and hammering them into cracks to hold the door tight.

Boom!

A red glow was visible, seeping in around the edges. Licks of flame curled through like long fingers reaching, searching.

"The door won't stop them," Arista said. She too remained on the landing, standing before the door, and Hadrian could see tension in her face. "And we can't keep running. They will eventually catch us. I have to stop them. Go on ahead."

"You tried that," Hadrian told her sternly.

"I didn't understand then. I'll do better this time." Her little body was breathing fast as she stared unblinking at the door, her hands clenching and unclenching.

"There's three of them and only one of you, and there's this fire thing. You—"

"Go!" she shouted. "It's the only way!"

Boom!

Cracks appeared across the face of the door. Bits of stone chipped off and fell on the dwarf's head.

"Go on, all of you!" She closed her eyes and began to mutter. Myron and Gaunt were finally at the bottom. Magnus followed quickly, vaulting down the steps. Mauvin and Alric hesitated partway down, but Hadrian remained—reluctant to leave her.

Boom!

The door fractured, the hands of flames bending around, gripping tight, ripping at the stone.

Arista's robe burst forth a brilliant white light, the stairs illuminated so harshly everyone shielded their eyes.

Boom!

The door buckled.

"No, you don't!" Arista shouted above the thunder of the stone.

White light rushed to the door, circling it and forcing back the red fire, filling the gaps. The flaming fingers recoiled and fought. Writhing and twisting, sparks erupted where the two met. From the far side they all heard an unnatural howl of pain that shook the bowels of the stone. A loud crack shuddered through the walls and, like a candle she blew on, the fiery light went out with a snap.

Arista remained on the landing, her face slick with sweat, her arms up, her fingers weaving in the air as if she were playing an invisible harp. The stone of the doors glowed with a blue light, brightening and ebbing like a luminous heartbeat. Her movements became faster, her hands jerking. She grunted and cried out as if in alarm.

"No!" she shouted.

A wind filled the space around her; Arista's hair whirled and snapped, her robe blowing, billowing out, shimmering like the surface of a moonstruck lake.

"Arista?" he called to her.

"They're—they're—" She was clearly struggling, fighting something. The pulsing light on the door sped up, growing faster and faster. She screamed and this time her head dodged to one side. She took a step backward and with another grunt struggled to throw her weight forward. "They're fighting me!"

She cried out again and Hadrian felt a powerful gust of wind burst through the door. It staggered both of them. Hadrian placed a hand on the wall to keep from falling.

"More than three!" she said. "Oh dear Maribor! I can't—"

Her face was straining, her jaw clenched; her eyes watered and tears fell down her cheeks. "I can't hold them. Run! *Run!*"

The door exploded. Bits of stone flew cracking across the walls, splitting and whizzing. Dust blossomed in a cloud. Arista flew back, crumpling to the floor—her light all but out. The robe managed only a quivering purple glow.

"No!" Hadrian shouted. He grabbed hold of her and lifted just as through the door the goblin horde charged.

They broke through the fog of dust with snarling teeth and glowing eyes. They attacked with sachels held high, fanged mouths spitting curses and dripping with anticipation.

Alric drew forth the sword of Tolin Essendon. "In the name of Novron and Maribor!" he shouted fiercely as he charged up the steps with Mauvin close behind. The shimmering blade of Count Pickering slid free of its sheath. "Back!" the king cried. "Back to Oberlin, you mangy beasts!"

Hadrian ran down the steps, clutching the princess to his chest. Behind him, he could still hear Alric's cursing the goblins, the blades' ringing, and the Ghazels' screams.

As Hadrian reached the bottom, Arista was stirring, her eyes fluttering open. He handed her to Myron. "Keep her safe!"

He turned, drew his swords, and ran back up the steps with Royce right behind. Above him, Mauvin and Alric fought as dark blood splattered the walls and spilled down the steps. Already a mound of bodies lay on the landing. He was still three steps away when Alric cried out and fell.

"*Alric!*" Mauvin shouted. He turned to his fallen king just as a sachel blade stabbed out.

Mauvin cried out in pain but managed to cleave the head from the goblin's shoulders.

"Fall back, Mauvin!" Hadrian shouted, stepping over Alric.

Standing shoulder to shoulder, the two filled the width of the corridor and fought like a single man with four arms. The whirl of their blades was daunting, and after three attempts the goblins hesitated. The goblins paused their assault and stood beyond the broken door, staring at them across a pile of Ghazel bodies.

"Mauvin, take Alric and go!" Hadrian ordered, breathing hard.

"You can't hold them yourself," Mauvin replied.

"You're bleeding, and I can hold them long enough. Get your king away."

Mauvin glared at the grinning teeth across from him.

Hadrian could see at least two of the oberdaza lying face-down on the stone table and thought, *She gave as good as she got.*

"Take him, Mauvin. Your duty is to him. Alric may yet live. Take him to Arista."

Mauvin sheathed his sword, and stooping, he lifted Alric and retreated down the steps. The goblins moved a step forward, then hesitated once more as Royce appeared beside Hadrian.

"Ugly little buggers." He appraised the faces across the threshold.

Pressure from the back was pushing the goblins reluctantly forward.

"How long before they remember they have bows?" Royce whispered.

"They aren't the brightest, particularly when scared," Hadrian explained. "In many respects they are like a pack of herd animals. If one panics, they all follow suit, but yeah, they'll figure it out. I'm guessing we got maybe a minute or two. Looks like we should have been winemakers after all, huh?"

"Oh, now you think of it," Royce chided.

"We'd be in our cottage around a warm fire right now. You'd be sampling our wares and complaining it wasn't good enough. I'd be making lists for the spring."

"No," Royce said. "It's five in the morning. I'd still be in bed with Gwen. She'd be curled up in a ball, and I'd be watching her sleep and marveling at how her hair lay upon her cheek as if Maribor himself had placed it there in just that way for me. And in the crib my son, Elias, and my daughter, Mercedes, would be just waking up." Hadrian saw him smile then for the first time since Gwen's death.

"Why don't you go down with the others and leave me here?" Royce said. "You might be able to get a little farther — a little closer to the tomb. Maybe there's another door — a door with a lock. You've spent enough time with me already."

"I'm not going to leave you here," Hadrian told him.

"Why not?"

"There are better ways to die."

"Maybe this is my fate, my reward for the life I lived. I wish these bastards had been at the bridge that night, or at least that Merrick had fought better. I regret it now — killing him, I mean. He was telling the truth. He didn't kill Gwen. I guess I'll just tack that on to all the other regrets of my life. Go on. Leave me."

"Royce! Hadrian!" Myron called to them from the bottom. "Run!"

"We can't —" Hadrian said when he noticed a white light growing below them and felt a rising wind. "Oh son of —!"

The stairs trembled and rock cracked. Bits of stone shattered and flew in all directions, hitting them like stinging bees. Hadrian grabbed hold of Royce and leapt headlong down the steps. A loud roar issued from above them as goblins screamed and the ceiling collapsed.

⁊

"Hadrian!" Arista cried out. Her robe brightened, and Myron held his lantern high, but she could not see through the cloud of dust. She staggered on her feet, light-headed and dizzy. Her legs were weak and her thoughts muddy. Swaying with her arms reaching out for balance, she stared into the gloom of swirling dirt, her heart pounding. "Oh god, don't let them be dead!"

"Cut that a little close, didn't you?" She heard Hadrian's voice emerging out of the murk.

The fighter and the thief crawled out of the haze covered in what looked to be a fine coating of gray chalk. They waved their hands before their faces and coughed repeatedly as they climbed over the rubble to join the others in the narrow corridor. Behind them, the way was sealed.

Royce looked back. "Well, that's one way to lock them out. Not a good way—but a way."

"I didn't know what else to do. I didn't know what else to do!" she said while her hands opened and closed nervously. Arista felt on the edge of losing control; she was exhausted and terrified.

"You did great," Hadrian told her, taking her hands and holding them gently. Then, looking past her, he asked Mauvin, "How is he?"

"Not good," the count replied with a quavering voice. "Still alive, though."

The new Count Pickering was on his knees, holding Alric and brushing the king's hair from his face. Alric was unconscious. A large amount of dark blood pooled on the ground around him.

"The fool," Mauvin said. "He put his arm up to block, like he had a shield—'cause he always practiced with a shield. The blade cut his arm open from the shoulder to the elbow. When he tried to turn, they sliced open his stomach." Mauvin wiped tears from his eyes. "He fought well, though—really well. Better than I've ever seen—better than I thought he could. It was almost like...like I was fighting beside Fanen again." The tears continued to run down Mauvin's cheeks, faster than he could brush them away.

Alric's chest was moving, struggling up and down. A terrible gurgle bubbled up his throat with each raspy breath.

"Give me the lantern." Hadrian rapidly bent down over the king. He tore open his shirt, revealing the wound. The moment Hadrian saw it, he stopped. "Oh dear Novron," he said.

"Do something," Arista told him.

"There's nothing I can do," he told her. "The sword—it went through. I've seen this before—there's just nothing— The bleeding won't stop, not the way he's—I can't— Damn, I'm so sorry."

His lips sealed together and his eyes closed.

"No," Arista said, shaking her head. "No!" She fell and crawled to Alric's side. Placing her hand on his head, she felt he was hot and drenched in sweat. "No," she repeated. "I won't allow it."

"Arista?" She heard Hadrian, but she had already closed her eyes and began to hum. She sensed the dull solid forms of the old walls, the dirt and the stone, the air between them, their bodies, and the flow of Alric's blood as it spilled on the ground. She could see it in her mind as a glowing river of silver and the glow was fading.

"Arista?" The sound of Hadrian's voice echoed, but it was faint, as if coming from a distance.

She saw a sliver of darkness that appeared as a tear, a dark rip in the fabric of the world. She reached out and felt the edges, pulling them wider until she was able to pass through.

Inside it was dark—darker than night, darker than a room after blowing out a candle—it was the darkness of nothing. She peered deep into the void, searching. Alric was there, ahead of her, and drifting away, pulled by a current, like some dark river. She chased after him.

"Alric!" she called.

"Arista?" she heard him say. "Arista, help me!"

Ahead she saw a light, a single point that glimmered white.
"I'm trying. Stop and wait for me."

"I can't."

"Then I'll come and get you," she said, and pushed forward.

"I don't want to die," Alric told her.

"I won't let you. I can save you."

Arista struggled forward, but progress was hard. The river
that pulled Alric away pushed her backward and confounded
her legs. She fought, driving against the wash even as Alric
glided across the surface.

Despite the difficulty, she was getting closer. Her brother
looked back at her, his face frightened. "I'm sorry," he said.
"I'm sorry I wasn't a better brother, a better king. Arista, you
should have ruled instead of me. You were always smarter,
stronger, more courageous. I was jealous. I'm sorry. Please
forgive me."

She reached out and almost caught hold of him, their fingertips touched briefly, then he slipped away. She watched as he
picked up speed. The current grew stronger, pulling him away,
rushing him forward, stealing him from her.

Ahead the light was closer, brighter, and in it, she thought
she saw figures moving. "Alric, you have to try and slow
down, you're moving too fast, I can't get—I can't grab you.
Alric, you're speeding up! Alric, reach out to me! Alric! *Alric!*"

She dove forward but her brother rushed away, washing
toward the light at a speed she could not match. She watched
as he grew smaller and smaller until he was lost in the brilliance of the light.

"No! *No!*" she cried, staring forward, blinded by the
whiteness.

"*Arista.*" She heard a voice call—not Alric's, but familiar.
"Arista. Your brother is here with us now. It's okay."

"Daddy?"

"*Yes, dear, it's me. I'm sorry I have no hairbrush to give you at this meeting, but there is so much more, so much more than a hairbrush waiting. Come join us.*"

"I—I shouldn't," she told him, although she was not certain why.

The light did not hurt to look at, but it made it impossible to see more than vague shapes, all blurred and hazy, as if they moved on the far side of a frosted glass.

"*It's all right, honey,*" her father said. "*And it's not just us waiting. You have other friends here, others who love you.*"

"*My burns are gone,*" Hilfred told her. "*Come see.*"

She saw their wispy outlines before her; they were growing clearer and more defined. The current was no longer fighting against her and she was starting to pick up speed. She needed to stop, she needed to go back, there was something that—

"*Arista my love.*" This was a voice she had not heard for a long, long time and her heart leapt at the sound.

"Mother?"

"*Come to me, honey, come home. I'm waiting for you.*"

There was music playing, soft and gentle. The light was growing all around her such that the dark of the void was fading. She let herself go, let herself drift on the current that carried her forward faster and faster.

"Arista," another voice called. This one was faint and distant, coming from somewhere behind her.

She could almost make out the faces in the light. There were so many and they were smiling with outstretched arms.

"Arista, come back." The voice was not in the light; it was calling to her from the darkness. "Arista, don't leave!"

It came as a cry, a desperate plea, and she knew the voice.

"Arista, please, please don't leave. Please come back. Let him go and come back!"

It was Hadrian.

"*Arista*," her mother called, "*come home.*"

"Home," Arista said, and as she said it, she stopped. "Home," she repeated, and felt a pulling in her stomach as the light diminished.

"*I'll be waiting for you always.*" She heard her mother's voice as it drifted away.

"*Good luck,*" Alric called, his voice almost too faint to hear.

She felt herself flying backward, then—

Her eyes snapped open.

Arista lay on the stone, gasping and struggling to breathe. She inhaled long and hard but still could not manage to get enough air. The world was whirling above her, dark except for a faint purple glow. In this dim haze, she saw Hadrian crouched over her and felt him squeezing her hands. His own were shaking. Suddenly his strained look was replaced with a burst of joy.

"She's okay! See! She's looking around!" Mauvin shouted.

"Can you hear me?" Hadrian asked.

She tried but could not speak. All she could manage was a slight nod and her eye caught sight of Alric.

"He's gone," Hadrian told her sadly.

Again she managed a shallow nod.

"Are you sure you're all right?" Hadrian asked.

"Very...tired," she whispered as her eyes closed, and she fell asleep.

◢

As both Arista and Gaunt slept, Hadrian worked on Mauvin. The count's side was drenched in blood. A stab wound cut through the meat of his arm behind the upper bone. He had been holding it shut with his hand without complaint such that Hadrian had not noticed until Mauvin staggered.

Together, Hadrian and Magnus, with Myron holding the lantern, sewed Mauvin's wound. Hadrian was forced to push muscle back in as he stitched, yet Mauvin made no cry and soon passed out. When they finished, Hadrian wrapped his arm. It was a good, clean job and they had stopped the bleeding. Mauvin would be fine even if his left arm would never be as strong as it once had been. Hadrian checked Gaunt's leg and changed that bandage as well. Then, in the utter silence of the tombs, in the dim light of the lantern, they all slept.

When he woke, Hadrian felt every bruise, cut, scratch, and strained muscle. A lantern burned beside him, and with its light, he found his water skin. They all lay together in the narrow corridor, flopped haphazardly in dirt and blood like a pile of dead after a battle. He took a small sip to clear his mouth and noticed Royce was not with them.

He lifted the lantern and glanced at the pile of rubble where the stairs had once been. The way was blocked by several tons of stone.

"Well, I'm guessing you didn't go that way," he whispered to himself.

Turning, he noticed the corridor bent sharply to the left. Along the walls, he discerned faint, ghostly images etched in the polished stone like burnished details on glass. The images told a story. At the start of the hall was a strange scene: a group of men traveling to a great gathering in a forest where a ruler sat upon a throne that appeared to be part of a tree, yet none of the men had heads. In each instance, they were scraped away. In the next scene, the king of the tree throne fought one of the men in single combat—again no heads.

Hadrian raised the lantern and wiped the dust with his hands, looking closer at the images of the men fighting. He let his fingertips trace the weapons in their hands, strange twisted poles with multiple blades. He had never seen their

666 Michael J. Sullivan

like before and yet he knew them. He could imagine their weight, how his hands would grasp, and how to scoop the lower blade in order to make the upper two slice the air. His father had taught him to use this weapon, the polearm for which he had no name.

In the next scene, the king was victorious and all bowed to him save one. He stood aside with the rest of the men who had traveled together in the first scene, and in his arms, he held the body of the fallen combatant. Still no heads—each one carefully scratched out. On the ground lay bits of chipped stone and white dust.

Hadrian found Royce at the end of the hall before a closed and formidable-looking stone door.

"Locked?" Hadrian asked.

Royce nodded as his hands played over the door's surface.

"How long you been here?"

The thief shrugged. "A few hours."

"No keyhole?"

"Locked from the inside."

"Inside? That's creepy. Since when do dead men lock themselves into their own graves?"

"Something is alive in there," Royce said. "I can hear it."

Hadrian felt a chill run down his back as his mind ran through all the possibilities of what might lie beyond the door. Who knew what the ancients could have placed in their tombs to protect their kings: ghosts, wraiths, zombie guards, stone golems?

"And you can't open the door?"

"Haven't found a way yet."

"Tried knocking?"

Royce looked over his shoulder incredulously.

"What would it hurt?"

Royce's expression eased. He thought a moment and

shrugged. He stepped back and waved toward the door. "Be my guest."

Hadrian drew his short sword and, using the butt, tapped three times on the stone. They waited. Nothing happened. He tapped three more times.

"It was worth a—"

Stone scraped as a bolt moved. Silence. A snap, then another bolt was drawn. The stone slab shuddered and shook.

Royce and Hadrian glanced nervously at each other. Hadrian handed the lantern to Royce and drew his bastard sword. Royce pushed on the door and it swung inward.

Inside, it was dark and Hadrian held up the lantern with his left hand, probing forward with his sword. The light revealed a small square room with a vaulted ceiling. At the center was a great headless statue. The walls were filled with holes filled with piles of rolled scrolls, several of which lay ripped to pieces, their remains scattered across the floor. On the far side was another stone door, closed tight. Hadrian could see large bolts holding it fast. The ground also contained clay pots, clothes, blankets, and the melted remains of burned candles. Not far away the room's only occupant was in the process of sitting back down on his blanket. When the man turned, Hadrian recognized him immediately.

"Thranic?" Hadrian said, stunned.

Sentinel Dovin Thranic moved slowly, painfully. He was very thin. His normally pale face was drawn and ghostly white. His dark hair, which had always been so neatly combed back, hung loose in his face. His once-narrow mustache and short goatee were now a full ragged beard. He still wore his black and red silks, which were now mere shades of their former glory, torn and filthy.

The sentinel managed a strained smile as he recognized them through squinting eyes. "How loathsome that it is *you* that finds me." He focused on Royce. "Come for your revenge at last, elf?"

Royce stepped forward. He looked down at Thranic and then around the room. "How could I possibly top this? Sealed alive in a tomb of rock. My only regret is that I had nothing to do with it."

"What happened?" Hadrian asked.

Thranic coughed; it was a bad sound, as if the sentinel's chest was ripping apart from the inside. He reclined, trying to breathe, for a moment. "Bulard went lame—the old man was a nuisance and we left him at the library. Levy—Levy was killed. Bernie ran out on me—deserted." Thranic shifted uneasily; as he did, Hadrian noticed a bloodstained cloth wrapped his left thigh.

"How long have you been here?"

"Months," he replied. He glanced across the room at a pile of small humanoid bones and grimaced. "I did what I must to survive."

"Until the wound," Hadrian added.

The sentinel nodded. "I couldn't sneak up on them well enough anymore."

Royce continued to stare.

"Go ahead," Thranic told Royce. "Kill me. It doesn't matter anymore. It's over and you'll fare no better. No one can get the horn. It's what you came for, isn't it? The Horn of Novron? The Horn of Gylindora? It lies through there." He pointed at the far door. "On the other side is a large hall, the Vault of Days, which leads to the tomb of Novron itself, but you will never reach it. No one has...and no one will. Look there." He pointed to the wall across from him, where words lay scratched. "See the *EH*? This is as far as Edmund Hall ever got. He turned back and escaped this vile pit, because he was smart. I stayed, thinking I could somehow solve the riddle, somehow find a way to cross the Vault of Days, but it can't be done. We tried. Levy was the slowest—not even his body remains. Bernie wouldn't go back in after that."

"You stabbed him," Royce stated.

"He refused orders. He refused to make another attempt. You found him?"

"Dead."

Thranic showed no sign of pleasure or remorse; he merely nodded.

"What is it about this Vault of Days?" Hadrian asked. "Why can't you cross it?"

"Look for yourself."

Hadrian started across the room and Thranic stopped him. "Let the elf do it. What can you hope to see in there with your human eyes?"

Royce stared at the sentinel. "So what kind of trick is this?"

"I don't like it," Hadrian said.

Royce stepped to the door and studied it. "Looks okay."

"It is. What's on the other side, however, is not."

Royce touched the door and closely inspected the sides.

"So distrusting," Thranic said. "It won't bite if you open the door, only if you enter the room."

Slowly he drew the bolts away.

"Careful, Royce," Hadrian said.

Very slowly Royce pushed the door inward, peering through the gap. He looked left and right, then closed it once more and replaced the bolts.

"What is it?" Hadrian asked.

"He's right," Royce said dismally. "No one is getting through."

Thranic smiled and nodded until he was beset by another series of coughs that bent him over in pain.

"What is it?" Hadrian repeated.

"You're not going to believe it."

"What?"

"There's a—a thingy."

"A what?"

"You know, a thingy thing."

Hadrian looked at him, puzzled.

"A Gilarabrywn," Thranic said.

CHAPTER 19

SEALING OF THE GATE

Renwick stood on the fourth floor of the imperial palace. In front of him the registrar shuffled and rolled parchments, occasionally muttering to himself and scratching his neck with long slender fingers dyed black at the tips. A little rabbit-faced man with precise eyes and a large gap between his front teeth, he sat behind his formidable desk, scribbling. The sound of his quill on parchment reminded Renwick of a mouse gnawing at wood.

Members of the palace staff hurried by, entering the many doors around him. Some faces turned his way, but only briefly. At least the administration wing of the fourth floor was free of refugees. Every other inch of the castle seemed to be full of them. People lined the hallways, sitting with knees up to allow people passage, or sleeping on their sides with bundles under their heads, their arms wrapped tight around their bodies. Renwick guessed the bundles contained what little was left of their lives. Dirty, frightened faces looked up whenever anyone entered the corridors. Families mostly—farmers with sets of children who all looked alike—had come from the countryside, where homes lay abandoned.

He tapped his toes together, noticing that the numbness

was finally leaving. The sound caused the scribe to look up in irritation. Renwick smiled, but the scribe scowled and returned to his work. The squire's face still felt hot, burned from the cold wind. He had ridden nonstop from Amberton Lee to Aquesta and delivered his message directly to Captain Everton, commander of the southern gate. Afterward, starved and cold, he went to the kitchen, where Ibis was kind enough to let him have some leftover soup. Returning to the dormitories, he found a family of three from Fallon Mire sleeping in his bed — a mother and two boys, whose father had drowned in the Galewyr a year earlier trying to cross the Wicend Ford during the spring runoff.

Renwick had just curled up in a vacant corner of the hallway to sleep when Bennington, one of the main hall guards, grabbed him. All he said was that Renwick was to report to the chancellor's office immediately, and he berated the boy about how half the castle had been looking for him for hours. Bennington gave him the impression that he was in trouble, and when Renwick realized that he had left Amberton Lee without orders, his heart sank. Of course the empress and the imperial staff already knew about the elven advance. An army of scouts watched every road and passage. It had been arrogant and shortsighted.

They would punish him. At the very least, Renwick was certain to remain no more than a page, forced back to mucking out the stable and splitting the firewood. Dreams of being a real squire vanished. At the age of seventeen, he had already peaked with his one week of serving Hadrian — the false squire and the false knight. His sad and miserable life was over, and he could hope for no better fortune to befall him now.

No doubt he would also get a whipping, but that would be the worst of it. If Saldur and Ethelred were still in charge, the punishment would be more severe. Chancellor Nimbus and the imperial secretary were good, kind people, which only made his failure that much harder to bear. His palms began to sweat as he imagined—

The door to the chancellor's office opened. Lord Nimbus poked his head out. "Has no one found—" His eyes landed on Renwick. "Oh dash it all, man! Why didn't you let us know he was out here?"

The scribe blinked innocently. "I—I—"

"Never mind. Come in here, Renwick."

Inside the office, Renwick was shocked to see Empress Modina herself. She sat on the window ledge, her knees bent, her body curled up so that her gown sprayed out. Her hair was down, lying on her shoulders, and she appeared so oddly human—so strangely girlish. Captain Everton stood to one side, straight as an elm, his helm under one arm, water droplets from melted snow still visible on the steel of his armor. Another man in lighter, rougher dress stood in the opposite corner. He was tall, slender, and unkempt. This man wore leather, wool, and a thick ratty beard.

Lord Nimbus took a seat at the desk and motioned to Renwick. "You are a hard man to find," he said. "Please, tell us exactly what happened?"

"Well, like I told Captain Everton here, Mince—that's one of the boys with me—he saw a troop of elves crossing the Bernum."

"Yes, Captain Everton told us that, but—"

"Tell us everything," the empress said. Her voice was beautiful and Renwick was astounded that she had actually spoken to him. He felt flustered, his tongue stiff. He could not think, much less talk. He opened his mouth and words fell out. "I—ah—every—um…"

"Start at the beginning, from the moment you left here," she said. "Tell us everything that has happened."

674 Michael J. Sullivan

"We must know the progress of the mission," Nimbus clarified.

"Oh—ah—okay, well, we rode south to Ratibor," he began, trying to think of as much detail as he could, but it was difficult to concentrate under her gaze. Somehow, he managed to recount the trip to Amberton Lee, the descent of the party into the shaft, and the days he and the boys had spent in the snow. He told them of Mince and the sighting, and of his long, hard trip north, racing to stay ahead of the elven vanguard. "I'm sorry I didn't stay at my post. I have no excuse for abandoning it and willingly accept whatever punishment you see fit to deliver."

"Punishment?" the empress said with a tone of humor in her voice as she climbed down from her perch. "You will be rewarded. The news your daring ride has brought is the hope I've looked for."

"Indeed, my boy," Nimbus added. "This news of the mission's progress is very reassuring."

"*Very* reassuring," the empress repeated, then let out a sigh of relief, as if it allowed her to take one more breath. "At least we know they made it in safely."

She crossed the room to him. He stood locked in place, every muscle frozen, as she reached out. She took his face in her hands and kissed him, first on one cheek, and then the other. "Thank you," she whispered, and he thought he saw her eyes glisten.

He could not breathe or look away and thought he might die. The very idea that he would collapse right there at her feet and pass away did not trouble him in the least.

"The lad is going to fall," Everton said.

"I—I just—I haven't—"

"He hasn't had a chance to rest," Nimbus said, saving him. Renwick shut his mouth and nodded.

"Then see to his needs," she said. "For today he is my hero."

✧

Modina left the office feeling better than she had in days. *They found the way in!* Nimbus was right—there was still hope. It was a mere sliver, a tiny drop, but that was the way with hope. She had lived without it for so long that she was unaccustomed to the feeling, which made her giddy. It was the first time in what felt a century that she looked to the future without dread. Yes, the elves were coming. Yes, they were not in winter quarters. Yes, they would attack the city within the week—but the party was safe and she knew where the enemy would strike. There was hope.

She reached the stair and sighed. People filled the entire length of the steps. Families clustered together along the sides, gathering like twigs on a riverbank until they created a dam. They had to stop doing that.

"Sergeant," she called down to a castle guard on the main floor who was having a dispute with a man holding a goat. Apparently the man insisted on keeping it in the palace.

"Your Eminence?" he replied, looking up.

Upon hearing this, the crowd went silent and heads turned. There were whispers, gasps, and fingers pointed toward her. Modina did not roam the castle. Since her edict to grant shelter to the refugees—to quarter them anywhere possible—she had returned to her old habit of being a recluse. She lived in her chambers, visiting the fourth-floor offices and the throne room only once a day, and even then by back stairways. Her appearance in the halls was an uncommon sight.

"Keep these stairs clear," she told him, her voice sounding loud in the open chamber. "I don't want people falling down them. Find these good people room somewhere else. Surely there are more suitable quarters than here."

"Yes, Your Eminence. I'm trying, but they—well, they are afraid of getting lost in the palace, so they gather within sight of the doors."

"And why is that goat in here? All livestock was to be turned over to the quartermaster and recorded by the minister of city defense. We can't afford to have families keeping pigs and cows in the palace courtyard."

"Yes, Your Eminence, but this fellow, he says this goat is part of his family."

The man looked up at her, terrified, clutching the goat around its neck. "She's all the family I 'ave, Yer Greatness. Please don't take 'er."

"Of course not, but you and...your family...will have to stay in the stable. Find him room there."

"Right away, Your Eminence."

"And get these steps clear."

"Thrace?" The word rose out of the sea of faces. The faint voice was nearly swallowed by the din.

"Who said that?" she asked sharply.

The room went silent.

Someone coughed, another sneezed, someone shuffled his feet, and the goat clicked its hooves, but no one spoke for a full minute. Then she saw a hand rising above the crowd and waving slightly side to side.

"Who are you? Come forward," she commanded.

A woman stepped through the throng of bodies, moving across the floor of the entry hall below. Modina could not tell anything from looking down at the top of her head. A handful of others followed her, pushing through the pack, stepping around the blankets and bundles.

"Come up here," she ordered.

As the woman reached the stairs, those squatting on the steps rose and moved aside, granting her passage. She was thin, with light brown hair, cut straight across the bottom at the level of her earlobes, giving her a boyish look. She wore a pathetic rag of a dress made of poor rough wool. It was stained, hanging shapelessly from her shoulders, and tied at the waist with a bit of twine.

She was familiar.

Something in her walk, in the way she hung her head, in the weak sag of her shoulders, and the way she dragged her feet. She knew this woman.

"Lena?" Modina muttered.

The woman stopped and raised her head at the sound. She had the same sharp pointed nose speckled with freckles and brown eyes with no visible brows. The woman looked across at Modina with a mixture of hope and fear.

"Lena Bothwick?" the empress shouted.

Lena nodded and took a step back as Modina rushed toward her.

"Lena!" Modina threw her arms around the woman and hugged her tight. Lena was shaking as tears ran down her cheeks.

"What's wrong?"

"Nothing," Lena said. "It's just I—I didn't know if you'd remember us."

Behind her were Russell and Tad. "Where are the twins?"

Lena frowned. "They died last winter."

"I'm so sorry."

She nodded and they hugged once more.

Russell stood beside his wife. Like Lena, he was thin, dressed in a frayed and flimsy shirt that hung to his knees and was tied about the waist with a length of rope. His face was older, cut with more lines, and his hair was grayer than she remembered. Tad was taller and broader. No longer the boy she remembered, he was a man, but just as haggard and gaunt as the rest.

"Empress!" Russell stated. "Oh, you're your father's daughter, all right. Stubborn as a mule and strong as an ox! The elves are foolish to even think about crossing paths with one of the Woods of Dahlgren."

"Welcome to *my* house," she said, and hugged him.

◆

"Dillon McDern had come here with us during Wintertide just a few months ago. We watched Hadrian joust," Russell told her.

She had brought them back to her bedroom, where she sat on the bed with Lena while Russell—who was never one to sit while telling a story—stood before her. Tad was at the window, admiring the view.

"It was a great day," he went on, but there was regret in his voice. "We tried to see you, but they turned us away at the gate, a'course. Who's gonna let the likes of us in to see the empress? So we went back to Alburn.

"After Dahlgren, Vince found us all plots on Lord Kimble's land. We was grateful to get it at the time but it turned out not to be such a good idea. Kimble took most of the yield and charged us for seed and tools. He took Dillon's sons for his army and they was both killed. When he came to take Tad here, well, I didn't see no reason to stay for that.

"Dillon and I were drinking one night and he told me, he says, 'Rus, if I had it to do over again, I'd a run.' I knew what he was getting at, and we said goodbye to each other like tomorrow would never come. We packed that night and we ran out. Thing is we was only running 'cause we didn't want

Tad to be pressed into Kimble's army. We got as far as Stockton Bridge when we heard the elves had invaded Alburn. We heard they torched the place. Dillon, Vince, even Lord Kimble are all dead now, I suppose. We come here 'cause we didn't know where else to go. We hoped, but we never expected to see you."

The door to the bedroom burst open and the girls and Mr. Rings came bounding in, all three halting short when they saw the Bothwicks. They stood still and silent. Modina held out an inviting arm and the girls shifted uneasily toward her, the raccoon climbing to the safety of Mercy's shoulder.

"This is Mercy and Allie," Modina told them.

Lena smiled at the two curiously, then stared at Allie's pointed ears. "Is she—"

Modina cut her off. "They're as dear to me as daughters. Allie's father is on a very important mission and I promised I would watch over her until his return. Mercy is—" She hesitated briefly. She had never said it in the girl's presence before. "She is an orphan, from the north, and one of the first to see the elves attack."

"Speaking of elves…" Russell continued where his wife had left off.

"Yes, Allie is of elvish descent. Her father saved her from a slave ship bound for Calis."

"And you've got no problem with that?" Russell asked.

"Why would I? Allie is a sweet little girl. We've grown quite fond of each other. Haven't we?" Modina brushed a loose strand of hair behind a pointed ear.

The girl nodded and smiled.

"Her father may have to fight me for her when he gets back." Modina smiled at them both. "And where have you two mischief-makers been?"

"In the kitchen, playing with Red."

Modina raised an eyebrow. "With Mr. Rings?"

"They get along fine," Mercy said. "Although..."

"What?"

Mercy hesitated to speak, so Allie stepped forward. "Mercy is trying to get Red to let Mr. Rings ride on his back. It's not going so well. Mr. Thinly chased us out after Red knocked over a stack of pans."

Modina rolled her eyes. "You are a pair of monsters, aren't you?"

Lena began to cry and put her arms around Russell, who held her.

"What?" Modina asked, going to Lena.

"Oh, it's nothing." Russell spoke for her. "The girls—you know—she misses the twins. We almost lost Tad too, didn't we, boy?"

Tad, who was still looking out the window, turned and nodded. He had not said a word, and the Thaddeus Bothwick Modina remembered had never been quiet.

"We survived all those terrible nights in Dahlgren," Lena said, sobbing. "But living in Alburn killed my little girls and now—and now..."

"You're going to be all right," Modina told her. "I'll see to that."

Russell looked at her, nodding appraisingly. "Damned if you ain't your father's daughter. Theron would be real proud of you, Thrace. Real proud."

⚓

Renwick had no idea what to do. For the third day in a row, he was confused and uncomfortable. He wanted to return to Amberton Lee, but the empress forbade him. The elven army would be between them now. He tried to resume his castle page duties only to discover he was not wanted, once more due to an edict from the empress. Apparently he had no assigned duties.

He wore a new tunic, far nicer than any he had ever had before. He ate wonderful meals and slept right under Sir Elgar and across from Sir Gilbert of Lyle, in a berth in the knights' dormitories.

"You'll get work plenty soon enough, lad," Elgar told him. He and Sir Gilbert were at the table, engaged in a game of chess that Gilbert was winning easily. "When those elves arrive, you'll be earning your keep."

"Hauling buckets of water to the gate for the soldiers," Renwick said dismally.

"Hauling water?" Elgar questioned. "That's page work."

"I am a page."

"Hah! Is that a page's bed you sleep in? Is that a page's tunic? Are you eating page meals? Slopping out the stables? You *were* a page, but the empress has her eye on you now."

"What does that mean?"

"It means you are in her favor, and you won't be hauling no water."

"But what—"

"Can you handle a blade, boy?" Gilbert asked while sliding a pawn forward and making Elgar shift uneasily in his seat.

"I think so."

"You *think* so?"

"Sir Malness never let me—"

"Malness? Malness was an idiot," Elgar growled.

"Probably why he broke his neck falling off his horse," Gilbert said.

"He was drinking," Renwick pointed out.

"He was an idiot," Elgar repeated.

"It doesn't matter," Gilbert said. "When the fight begins, we'll need every man who can hold a blade. You might have been a page yesterday, but tomorrow you will be a soldier. And with the eye of the empress on you—fight well, and you may find yourself a knight."

"Don't fill his head with too much nonsense," Elgar said. "He's not even a squire."

"I squired for Sir Hadrian."

"Hadrian isn't a knight."

A horn sounded and all three scrambled out of the dormitory and raced past the droves of refugees to the front hall. They pushed out into the courtyard, looking to the guards at the towers.

"What is it?" Elgar called to Benton.

The tower guard heard his voice and turned. "Sir Breckton and the army have returned. The empress has gone to welcome them home."

"Breckton," Gilbert said miserably. "Com'on, Elgar, we have a game to finish."

The two turned their backs on the courtyard and returned inside, but Renwick ran out past the courtyard and through the city toward the southern gate. The portcullis was already up by the time he arrived, and the legion bearing Breckton's blue-and-gold-checkered standard entered.

Drums sounded, keeping beat with the footfalls of men. As the knight-marshal rode at the head of his army, the sun shone off his brilliant armor. At his side rode the lady Amilia, wrapped in a heavy fur cloak, which draped across the side and back of her mount. Renwick recognized other faces: King Armand, Queen Adeline, Prince Rudolf and his younger brother Hector, along with Leo, Duke of Rochelle, and his wife,

Genevieve, who composed the last of the Alburn nobility. With their arrival it was official—the eastern provinces were lost. Sir Murthas, Sir Brent, Sir Andiers, and several others he knew from the rosters formed ranks in the armored cavalry. Behind them, neat rows of foot soldiers marched. These were followed by wagons of supplies and people—more refugees.

Modina ran to embrace Amilia the moment she climbed off her horse. "You made it!" she said, squeezing her. "And your family?"

"They are on the wagons," Amilia told her.

"Bring them to the great hall. Are you hungry?"

She nodded, smiling.

"Then I will meet them and we will eat. I have people for you to meet as well. Nimbus!" Modina called.

"Your Eminence." The chancellor trotted to her side and Amilia hugged the beanpole of a man.

Renwick could not see anymore as the army filled the street. He moved to the wall and climbed steps to the top of the gate, where Captain Everton was once more on duty, watching the progress of the army's return below him.

"Impressive, isn't he?" Everton said to him as they watched the column from the battlements. "I for one will sleep easier tonight knowing Sir Breckton is here, and none too soon, I suspect."

"How do you mean?"

"I don't like the sky."

Renwick looked up. Overhead a dark haze swirled a strange mix of brown and yellow, a sickly soup of dense clouds that churned and folded like the contents of some witch's brew.

"That doesn't look natural to me."

"It's warmer too," Renwick said, having just realized that

he was outside without a cloak and not shivering. He breathed out and could not see his breath.

He rushed to the edge of the battlement and looked southeast. In the distance, the clouds were darker still and he noticed an eerie green hue to the sky. "They are coming."

"Blow the horn," Everton ordered as the last of the troops and wagons passed through. "Seal the gate."

CHAPTER 20

THE VAULT OF DAYS

*R*unning *through the corridors, she heard the clash of steel and the cries of men. She had done her duty, her obligations complete. Descending to the tombs, she entered the Vault of Days. The emperor lay on the floor as the last of his knights died on the swords of those loyal to Venlin. A rage boiled in her as she spoke. The room shuddered at the sound of her words and the would-be killers of her emperor—ten Teshlor Knights—screamed as their bodies ripped apart.*

She fell to her knees.

"Emperor!" she cried. "I am here!"

Nareion wept as in his arms he clutched the dead bodies of his wife, Amethes, and Fanquila, their daughter.

"We must go," she urged.

The emperor shook his head. "The horn?"

"I placed it in the tomb."

"My son?"

"He is with Jerish. They have left the city."

"Then we will end this here." Nareion drew his sword. "Enchant it with the weaving-letters."

She knew what he meant to do. She wanted to tell him not to. She wanted to assure him there was another way, but even

*as she shook her head, she placed her hand on the blade and
spoke the words, making the blade shimmer and causing letters to appear. They moved and shifted as if uncertain where
they should settle.*

*"Now go, meet him. I will see to it that he never enters the
tomb." The emperor looked down at his dead family and the
shimmering sword. "I will make certain no one else will."*

*She nodded and stood. Looking back just once at the sad
scene of the emperor crying over the loss of his family, she left
the Vault of Days. She no longer rushed. Time was unimportant now. The emperor was dead, but Venlin had not killed
him. He had missed his chance. Venlin would win the battle
but lose the war.*

*"He is dead, then." She heard the voice—so familiar. "And
you are here to kill me?"*

"Yes," she replied.

*She was in the corridor just outside the throne room. He
was inside, his voice seeping out.*

*"And you think you can? Such is the folly of youth. Even
old Yolric is not so foolish as to challenge me. And you—you
are the youngest of the council, a pup—you dare bring your
inexperience and meager knowledge of the Art against me? I
am the Art—my family invented it. My brother taught Cenzlyor. The entire council flows from the skills and knowledge
of the Miralyith. You have ruined much. I did not suspect you.
Jerish was obvious, but you! You wanted power, you always
wanted power; all of you did. You hated the Teshlor more than
anyone. Above all, I thought I could count on your support."*

*"That was before Avempartha, before I discovered who
you are—murderer. You will not succeed."*

*"I already have. The emperor is dead; I know this. I have
just one loose end to tie up. Tell me, where is Nevrik?"*

"I will die before telling you that."

"There are worse things than dying."

"I know," she told him. "That's why I choose death. Death for me, death for you..." She looked down the corridor to where the sunlight was streaming in. She could still hear the parade marching past the cheering crowds. *"Death for everyone. It ends here, and Nevrik will return to his throne. It is time to bury the dead at last."*

She looked out at the sun one more time and thought of Elinya. *"Maribor take us both,"* she said, and closing her eyes, began the weave.

❧

"He did it."

Arista woke up sweating, her heart pounding.

She lay in a small dark room lit by a single lantern. A thin blanket separated her from the cold floor, another was placed over her, and a bag supported her head. The room was not much bigger than her old bedroom in the tower. It was a perfect square with a vaulted ceiling, the arches forming a star shape as they joined overhead. On either side of the room, two doors faced each other. One opened to the corridor; the other was shut tight and locked from their side. Nooks with brass lattice doors covered the walls, each alcove filled with piles of neatly placed scrolls, round tubes of yellowed parchment. Many of the little grates were open; several scrolls lay spilled on the floor, some of them torn to pieces. In the center of the room was a statue. She recognized it as a version of those she had seen in churches and chapels throughout her life. It was a depiction of Novron, only this one was missing the head. Its remains lay shattered and beaten to powder on the floor.

Hadrian's was the first face she saw, as he sat beside her. "You're awake at last," he said. "I was getting worried."

Myron was just to her left. He was the closest to the light, sitting in a mound of scrolls. The monk looked up, smiled, and waved.

"You're all right?" Hadrian asked with concern in his voice.

"Just exhausted." She wiped her eyes and sighed. "How long have I been asleep?"

"Five hours," Royce said. She only heard his voice, as he was somewhere just outside the ring of light.

"Five? Really? I feel like I could sleep another ten," she said, yawning.

Arista noticed in the corner an unpleasant-looking man—pale and withered—like a sickly molting crow. He sat hunched over, watching them, his dark marble eyes glaring.

"Who's he?"

"Sentinel Thranic," Hadrian told her. "The last living member of the previous team. I'd introduce you, but we sort of hate each other, seeing as how he shot Royce with a crossbow last fall—nearly killed him."

"And he's still alive?" Arista asked.

"Don't look at me. I haven't stopped him," Hadrian told her. "Hungry?"

"I hate to say it, given the circumstances, but I'm famished."

"We thought you died," Mauvin told her. "You stopped moving and even stopped breathing for such a long time. Hadrian slapped you a few times, but it did nothing."

"You hit me again?" She rubbed her cheek, feeling the soreness.

He looked guilty. "I was scared. And it worked last time."

She noticed the bandage on Mauvin's arm. "You're wounded?"

"More embarrassed than anything. But that's bound to

happen when you're a Pickering fighting beside Hadrian. Doesn't really hurt that much, honest."

"Hmm, let's see." She heard Hadrian rummaging around in a pack. "Would you like salt pork...or perhaps...let's see now...how about salt pork?" he asked with a smile, handing a ration to her. She tore it open with shaking hands.

"You sure you're all right?" he asked, and she was surprised at the concern in his voice.

"Just weak—like a fever broke, you know?" Hadrian did not indicate whether he knew, but sat watching her as if she might drop over dead any minute. "I'm fine—really."

Arista took a bite of the meat. The heavily salted and miserably dry pork was a joy to swallow, which she did almost without chewing.

"Alric?" she asked.

"He's in the corridor," Hadrian told her.

"You haven't buried him yet, have you?"

"No, not yet."

"Good, I would like to take him back to Melengar to be laid in the tomb of his fathers."

The others looked away, each noticeably silent, and she saw a disturbing grin stretch across Thranic's face. The sentinel appeared ghoulish in the lantern light; his malevolence chilled her.

"What is it?" she asked.

"It doesn't look like we will be getting back to Melengar," Hadrian told her.

"The horn isn't here?"

"Apparently it's through that door, but we haven't—"

"Through that door is death," Thranic told her. He spoke for the first time, his voice a hissing rasp. "Death for all the children of Maribor. The last emperor's guardian watches the Vault of Days and will not suffer anyone's passage."

"Guardian?" she asked.

"A Gilarabrywn," Hadrian told her. "A big one."

"Well, of course it's big, if it's a Gilarabrywn."

Hadrian smiled. "You don't understand. This one is *really* big."

"Is there a sword? There has to be a sword to slay it, right?"

Hadrian sighed. "Royce says there's another door on the far side. Maybe it's over there. We don't know. Besides, you realize there's no reason for the sword to be down here at all."

"We have to look. We have to…"

The sword.

"What is it?" Hadrian asked.

"Is the Gilarabrywn bigger than the one in Avempartha?"

"A lot bigger."

"It would be," she said, remembering her dream. "And the sword is there, on the far side of the room."

"How do you know?"

"I saw it…or at least, Esrahaddon did. Emperor Nareion created the Gilarabrywn himself. Esrahaddon enchanted the blade of the king's sword with the name and Nareion conjured the beast. Only he did it with his own blood. He sacrificed himself in the making, adding power to the Gilarabrywn and assigning it the task of guarding the tombs where Esrahaddon hid the horn."

The sentinel eyed her curiously. "The Patriarch was not aware of its existence, nor did *we* realize it was there until we opened that door. No spell, no stealth, no army, no wishful thinking will grant anyone access to the room beyond. The quest for the horn ends here."

"And *someone* sealed the way out," Gaunt reminded her. He reclined on his pack. His fur-lined houppelande, pulled tight to his chin, was torn and stained. His chaperon hat was a rumpled mess, the folds ripped and pulled down over his ears.

The liripipe was missing altogether and Arista only then real-ized the same black cloth of Gaunt's headdress wrapped Mauvin's arm. "Which means we're trapped in this room until we die of thirst or starvation. At least this bugger was able to live off goblins. What are we going to do, carve up each other?"

"Don't be so optimistic, Mr. Sunshine," Mauvin told him. "You might just get our hopes too high, and then we'll be dis-appointed in the end."

"We have to try something," she said.

"We will," Hadrian assured her. "Royce and I don't give up that easily—you know that—but you should rest more before we do anything. We might need you. By the way, what did you mean by 'he did it'?"

"What?"

"When you woke up, you said, 'He did it.' It sounded important. Another one of your dreams?"

"Oh, that, yeah," she said, confused for a moment, trying to remember. Already the memory was fogged and blowing away. "It was Esrahaddon, he did this."

"Did what?"

"All this," she said, pointing up and whirling her hand around. "He destroyed the city—just like they said he did. You remember what I did at the stairs? Well, he was a bit more powerful. He collapsed the entire city, sunk and buried it."

"So he wasn't kidding when he said he was better with hands," Royce observed.

"And the people?" Mauvin asked.

"They were having a Founder's Day celebration. The city was packed with people, all the dignitaries, all the knights and Cenzars, and…yes, he killed everyone."

"Of course he did!" Thranic shouted as best he could. "Did you think the church lied? Esrahaddon destroyed the empire!"

"No," she said. "He tried to save it. It was Patriarch Venlin who betrayed the emperor. He was behind it all. Somehow, he convinced the Teshlor and the Cenzar to join him. He wanted to overthrow the emperor, kill him and wipe out his entire family. I think it was his intention to become the new ruler. But Esrahaddon stopped him. He got the emperor's son, Nevrik, out, then destroyed the city. I think he was trying to kill everyone associated with the rebellion, literally crushing all the enemies of Nevrik in one stroke. He expected to die along with them."

"But Esrahaddon survived," Hadrian said.

"So did Venlin," she added. "I don't know how. Maybe Yolric, or no—Venlin may have done something—cast some spell."

"The Patriarch was a wizard?" Hadrian asked.

She nodded. "A very powerful one, I think. More powerful than Esrahaddon."

"That's blasphemy!" Thranic said accusingly, and then fell into a coughing fit that left him exhausted.

"He was so powerful that Esrahaddon never even considered fighting him. He knew he'd lose and Esra was capable of destroying this entire city and nearly everyone in it."

Arista paused and turned her head back the way they had come. "They were all out there, lining the streets. I think they were having a parade. Each of them singing, cheering, eating sweets, dancing, drinking Trembles, enjoying the spring weather—then it all ended.

"I can still feel the chords Esrahaddon used. The deep chords, like the ones I touched on the ship just before you hit me. I barely touched those strings, but Esrahaddon played them loudly. His heart broke as he did it. A woman he loved lived in the city, a woman he planned to marry. He didn't have time to get her out."

"This is larger than your loss! It is larger than the loss of a hundred kings and a thousand fathers. Do you think I enjoyed it? Any of it? You forget—I lost my life as well. I had parents of my own, friends, and—"

Arista finally knew the unspoken words from their last meeting in the Ratibor mayoral office. Her hand touched the material of the robe as she remembered the way she had treated him. She had had no idea.

As a wizard, you must understand personal vengeance and gain are barred to you. We are obligated to seek no recognition, fame, nor fortune. A wizard must work for the betterment of all—and sacrifices are always necessary.

She stared at the floor, recalling the memory of the dream and the memories of the past, feeling sadness and loss. Beside her, Hadrian began humming a simple tune and then sang softly the words to the old song:

Gala halted, city's doom
Spring warmth chilled with dust and gloom
Darkness sealed, blankets all
Death upon them, fall the wall.

Ancient stones upon the Lee
Dusts of memories gone we see
Once the center, once the all
Lost forever, fall the wall.

"I grew up believing it was all just nonsense, something kids made up. We used to join hands, forming lines, and sing that while someone tried to pull the others down or break the line. If they did, they could take their place. We had no idea what any of it meant."

"Lies! All of it, lies!" Thranic shouted at them, straining to his knees. He was shaking, but Arista couldn't tell if it was from weakness or rage—perhaps both.

"I don't think so," Myron said from within a pile of scrolls.

"You shouldn't be reading those," the sentinel snapped. "The church placed a ban on all literature found here. It is forbidden!"

"I can see why," Myron replied.

"You are defying the Church of Nyphron by even touching them!"

"Luckily, I am not a member of the Church of Nyphron. The Monks of Maribor have no such canon."

"You're the one who ripped up these other scrolls," Hadrian said accusingly.

"They are evil."

"What was on them? What was so terrible? You were the one that burned the library. What are you trying to hide?" Hadrian thought a moment, then gestured toward the statue. "And what's with the heads? You did that too. Not just this one, but all throughout the city. Why?"

When Thranic remained silent, Hadrian turned to Myron. "What did you find out?"

"Many things. The most significant is that elves were never enslaved by the empire."

"What?" Royce asked.

"According to everything I've read since we've entered, elves were never enslaved. There's overwhelming evidence that the elves were equal citizens—even revered."

"I demand that you stop!" Thranic shouted. "You will bring down the judgment of Novron upon us all!"

"Careful, Myron," Mauvin said. "We wouldn't want matters to take a bad turn."

"Blasphemers! Wretched fools! This is why it was wrong to allow those outside the church to learn the Old Speech. This is why the Patriarch locked up Edmund Hall and sealed off the entrance, because he knew what could happen. This is why the heir had to die, because one day you would come down here. I failed to reach the horn, but I can still serve my faith!"

Thranic moved with a speed unexpected from his withered appearance; he reached out and grabbed the lantern. Before even Royce could react, he threw it at Myron, smashing it. The glass burst with a popping sound. Oil splashed across the parchments, across the floor, across Myron. Flames rushed forth, low blue tongues licking along the glistening oil pool. Fire blazed over the scrolls and raced up Myron's legs, chest, and face.

Then vanished.

With an audible crack, the room went black.

"That wasn't very nice," Arista said in the dark. Her robe began to glow, revealing the room in a cold bluish radiance. She was glaring at Thranic. The pulsating light shining up from underneath lent her a fearful image. "Are you all right, Myron?"

The monk nodded as he sat wiping the oil from his face. "Just a little warm," he replied. "And I think my eyebrows are gone."

"You bastard!" Mauvin shouted at Thranic, getting to his feet and reaching for his sword. "You could have killed him! You could have killed all of us!"

Even Gaunt was on his feet, but Thranic took no notice. The sentinel did not move. He slouched backward, resting against the wall in an odd twisted position. Thranic's eyes were open, staring at the ceiling, but he was not breathing.

"What's wrong with him?" Gaunt asked.

Mauvin reached out. "He's...dead."

Heads turned.

"I only extinguished the flames," Arista told them.

Heads turned again.

Royce was sitting in a different place than he had been before the fire. Arista looked back at Thranic's body. Blood dripped from a thin red line at the neck.

Mauvin let go of his sword and sat back down. "You sure you're all right, Myron?"

"I'm fine, thank you." Myron stood up. He walked to the sentinel's side and knelt down. He took a moment to close Thranic's eyes, and taking the sentinel's hand, he bowed his head and softly sang:

> *Unto Maribor, I beseech thee*
> *Into the hands of god, I send thee*
> *Grant him peace, I beg thee*
> *Give him rest, I ask thee*
> *May the god of men watch over your journey.*

"How can you do that?" Gaunt asked. "He tried to kill you. He tried to burn you alive. Are you so ignorant that you don't see that?"

Myron ignored Gaunt and remained beside Thranic, his head bowed, his eyes closed. A silence passed; then Myron folded Thranic's hands over his chest and stood up. He paused before Gaunt. " 'More valuable than gold, more precious than life, is mercy bestowed upon he who hast not known its soft kiss' — Girard Hily, *Proverbs of the Soul*."

The monk took another lantern out of Mauvin's pack. "Starting to run low on these," he said, opening it and reaching for the tinder kit.

"Better let me," Hadrian said. "A stray spark could light you up instead."

The monk handed the lantern over and looked at the rest of them. "Will anyone help me bury him?"

Degan made a sound like a laugh and limped away.

"I will." Magnus spoke up from where he still sat on the far side of the room. "We can use the stones from the cave-in."

Without a word, Hadrian got up and lifted Thranic's body, which folded in the middle like a thick blanket. His arms splayed out to either side, white and limp. Arista watched as he left a trail of dark droplets on the dusty stone. She looked back at the space behind, at the clutter in the corner where Thranic had lain. Pots, cups, torn cloth, soiled blankets, trash—it reminded her of a mouse's den. *How long was he here? How long did he lie in this room alone waiting to die? How long will we?*

Arista stood up and, turning away from the trash and the puddle of blood, moved to the sealed door. She touched the stone and the metal rods that held it closed. The door was cold. She pressed her palms flat against the surface and laid her head close. She heard nothing. She reminded herself that it was *not a living creature* and did not grow restless. She could feel it, a power radiating, pushing against her like the opposite pole of a magnet. Her encounter with the oberdaza made her sensitive to magic. The new smell that had confused her before the palace was no longer a mystery. Beyond the door lay magic, but not the vague, shifting sort that defined the oberdaza. The Ghazel witch doctors appeared in her mind as shadows that darted and whirled, pulsating irregularly, but this...this was greater. The power on the other side was clear, intense, and amazing. In it, she could detect elements of the weave. She could see it with her feelings, for there was more than magic that formed the pattern. An underlying sadness dominated and endowed the spell with incredible strength. An incomprehensible grief and the strength of self-sacrifice were bound together by a single strand of hope. It frightened her, yet at the same time, she found it beautiful.

Outside in the hallway, she could hear the clack of stones being stacked. Hadrian returned, wiping his hands against his clothes as if trying to wipe off a disease. He sat beside Royce in the shadows, away from the others.

She crossed the room, knelt down before them, and sat on her legs with the robe pooling out around her.

"Any ideas?" she asked, nodding toward the sealed door.

Royce and Hadrian exchanged glances.

"A few," Royce said.

"I knew I could count on you." She brightened. "You've always been there for us, Alric's miracle workers."

Hadrian grimaced. "Don't get your hopes up."

"You stole the treasure from the Crown Tower and put it back the next night. You broke into Avempartha, Gutaria Prison, and Drumindor—*twice*. How much harder can this be?"

"You only know about the successes," Royce said.

"There've been failures?"

They looked at each other and smiled painfully. Then they both nodded.

"But you're still alive. I should have thought a failure—"

"Not all failures end in death. Take our mission to steal DeWitt's sword from Essendon Castle. You can hardly call that a success."

"But there was no sword. It was a trap. And in the end it all worked out. I hardly call that a failure."

"Alburn was," Royce said, and Hadrian nodded dramatically.

"Alburn?"

"We spent more than a year in King Armand's dungeon," Hadrian told her. "What was that, about six years ago? Seven? Right after that bad winter. You might remember it, real cold spell. The Galewyr froze for the first time in memory."

"I remember that. My father wanted to hold a big party for my twentieth birthday, only no one could come."

"We stayed the whole season in Medford," Royce said. "Safe and comfortable—it was nice, actually, but we got soft and out of practice. We were just plain sloppy."

"We'd still be in that dungeon right now if it wasn't for Leo and Genny," Hadrian said.

"Leo and Genny?" Arista asked. "Not the Duke and Duchess of Rochelle?"

"Yep."

"They're friends of yours?"

"They are now," Royce said.

"We got the job through Albert, who took the assignment from another middleman. A typical double-blind operation, where we don't know the client and they don't know us. Turns out it was the duke and duchess. Albert broke the rules in telling them who we were and they convinced Armand to let us out. I'm still not certain how."

"They were scared we'd talk," Royce added.

Hadrian scowled at him, then rolled his eyes. "About what? We didn't know who hired us at the time."

Royce shrugged and Hadrian looked back at Arista.

"Anyway, we were just lucky Armand never bothered to execute us. But yeah, we don't always win. Even that Crown Tower job was a disaster."

"You were an idiot for coming back," Royce told him.

"What happened?" Arista asked.

"Two of the Patriarch's personal guards caught Royce when we were putting the treasure back."

"Like the two at the meeting?"

"Exactly—maybe the same two."

"He could have gotten away," Royce explained. "He had a clear exit, but instead the idiot came back for me. It was the first time I'd ever seen him fight, and I have to say it was impressive—and the two guards were good."

"Very good," Hadrian added gravely. "They nearly killed us. Royce had been beaten pretty badly and took a blade to the shoulder, while I was stabbed in the thigh and cut across the chest—still have the scar."

"Really?" Arista asked, astounded. She could not imagine anyone getting the better of Hadrian in a fight.

"We just barely got away, but by that time the alarm was up. We managed to hide in a tinker's cart heading south. The whole countryside was looking for us and we were bleeding badly. We ended up in Medford. Neither of us had been there before.

"It was the middle of the night in this pouring rain when we crawled out, nearly dead. We just staggered down the street into the Lower Quarter looking for help—a place to hide. News hit the city about the Crown Tower thieves and soldiers found the cart. They knew we were there. Your father turned out the city guard to search for us. We didn't know anyone. Soldiers were everywhere. We were so desperate that we banged on doors at random, hoping someone would let us in—that was the night we met Gwen DeLancy."

"I still can't understand why you came back," Royce said. "We weren't even friends. We were practically enemies. You knew I hated you."

"Same reason why I took the DeWitt job," Hadrian replied. "Same reason I went looking for Gaunt." He looked across the room at Degan and shook his head. "I've always had that dream of doing what's right, of saving the kingdom, winning the girl, and being the hero of the realm. Then I'd ride back home to Hintindar, where my father would be proud of me and Lord Baldwin would ask me to dine with him at his table, but…"

"But what?" Arista asked.

"It's just a boy's dream," he said sadly. "I became a champion in Calis. I fought in arenas where hundreds of people would come to cheer me. They chanted my name—or at least the one they gave me—but I never felt like a hero. I felt dirty, evil. I guess since then I just wanted to wipe that blood off me, clean myself of the dirt, and I was tired of running. That's what it came down to that day in the tower. I ran from my father, from Avryn, even from Calis. I was tired of running—I still am."

They sat in silence for a minute; then Arista asked, "So what *is* the plan?"

"We send Gaunt in," Royce replied.

"What?" She looked over at Degan, who was lying down on his blankets, curled up in a ball.

"You yourself said that he needed to be here, but why?" Hadrian asked. "He's been nothing but a pain. Everyone on this trip has had a purpose except him. You said he was absolutely necessary to the success of this mission. Why?"

"Because he's the heir."

"Exactly, but how does that help?"

"I think because he needs to use this horn thing."

"That's obvious, but that doesn't explain why we need him *here*. We could just have brought it to him. Why does he have to come with us?"

"We think that, being the heir, he can cross that room," Hadrian told her.

"What if you're wrong?" she asked. "We also need him to blow the horn. If he dies—"

"He can't blow it if he doesn't have it," Royce interjected.

"But that's where you come in," Hadrian said. "You need to shield him, just in case. Can you do that?"

"Maybe," she said without the slightest hint of confidence.

702 Michael J. Sullivan

"Everything with me is try-and-see. What are your other ideas?"

"Only have one other," Royce said. "Someone walks in and diverts its attention while the rest make a mad dash for the far side in the hopes that at least one of us makes it. Hopefully blowing the horn can somehow stop the beast."

"Seriously?"

They nodded.

She glanced over her shoulder. "I guess I'll break the bad news to him."

◈

"Absolutely not!" Degan Gaunt declared, rising to his feet, his hat tilted askew and flat on one side from his lying on it.

When Myron and Magnus had returned, Arista had gathered the group in a circle around the lantern. While they ate sparingly from their remaining provisions, she explained the plan.

"You have to," Arista told him.

"Even if I do, even if I succeed, what good is that? We're still trapped!"

"We don't know that. No one has ever crossed this room. There could be a means to escape on the far side, another exit, or the power of the horn could be such that we could escape with it. We don't know, but an unknown is far better than a certainty of death."

"It's stupid! That's what it is—stupid!"

"Think of it this way," Hadrian told him. "If you fail and that thing eats you, it will be over like that." He snapped his fingers. "Don't do it, and you linger here starving to death for days."

"Or smother," Royce put in. Everyone looked at him. He

rolled his eyes. "The air is getting stale. We have a limited amount."

"If you're going to die, why not die doing something noble?" Hadrian told him.

Gaunt just shook his head miserably.

"That's just it," Mauvin said, disgusted. He held his wound, a pained look on his face. "Hadrian, you've got it right there. Gaunt is not noble. He doesn't even know what it means. You want to know the real difference between you and Alric? You made fun and lurid speeches about nobility, about blue blood and incompetence, but while you might have the blood of the emperor in you, it must be diluted until it is practically non-existent. Your lineage has long forgotten its greatness—your base side is firmly in control. Your wanton desire is unchecked by purpose or honor.

"Alric might not have been the best king, but he was courageous and honorable. The idea of walking through that door, of facing death, must terrify you. How terrible it must be to give up your life when you've never taken the chance to live it. How cheated you must feel, like losing a coin before spending it. To what can you hang on to and feel pride? Nothing! Alric could have walked through that door, not because he was king, not even because he was noble-born, but because of who he was. He wasn't perfect. He made mistakes, but never on purpose, never with an intent to do harm. He lived his life the best way he knew how. He always did what he felt was right. Can you say that?"

Gaunt remained silent.

"We can't force you to do this," Arista told him. "But if you don't, Hadrian is right—we will all die, because there is no going back, and there is no going forward without you."

"Can I at least finish my meal before I answer?"

"Of course," she told him.

She ran a hand through her hair and took a deep breath. She was still so tired—so exhausted—and everything was so hard now. She knew it would be difficult to convince Gaunt, but worse than that, she had no idea what to do if he tried and failed.

Gaunt raised a bite to his lips, then stopped and frowned. "I've lost my appetite." He looked up at the ceiling, his eyes drooping, his lip quivering, his breathing coming loudly through his nose. "I knew this would happen." His hand rose absently to his neck as if searching for something. "Ever since I lost it, ever since they took it, nothing's been the same."

"Took what?" she asked.

"The good luck charm my mother gave me when I was a boy, a beautiful silver medallion. It warded off evil and brought me the most marvelous luck. It was wonderful. When I had it, I could get away with anything. My sister always said I lived a charmed life, and I did, but he took it."

"Who did—Guy?" Arista asked.

"No, another man. Lord Marius, he called himself. I knew nothing would be the same after that. I never had to worry— now it's all falling on me." He looked at the door to the Vault of Days. "If I go in there, I'll die. I know it."

Hadrian reached into his shirt and pulled a chain over his head. Gaunt's eyes widened as the fighter held it up. "Esrahaddon made the medallion you wore, just as he made this one. Just as you received yours from your mother, my father left me this. I am certain they are the same. If you agree to go in—to try and cross the room—I will give it to you."

"Let me see it!"

Hadrian handed the necklace to him. Gaunt fell to his knees next to the lantern and studied the amulet's face. "It *is* the same."

"Well?" Hadrian asked.

"Okay," Gaunt replied. "With this I'll do it...but I'll keep it afterward, right? It's mine for good now, yes? I won't do it otherwise."

"I will let you keep it, but on one more condition. Modina keeps the crown."

Gaunt glared at him.

"Tear up the contract you had with her. If you agree to let her remain empress, then you can keep it."

Gaunt felt the medallion between his fingers. He rubbed it, his eyes shifting in thought. He looked back at the door to the vault and sighed. "Okay," he said, and slipped the chain over his head, smiling.

"The agreement?"

Gaunt scowled, then pulled the parchment from his clothes and gave it to Hadrian, who tore it up, adding the scraps to the pile on the floor.

"How about you?" Hadrian asked Arista.

"Still a bit tired, but I won't get any sleep now."

Hadrian stood up and walked to the door. "Myron, you might want to start praying."

The monk nodded.

"Degan?" Arista called. "Degan?"

Gaunt looked up from his new necklace with an annoyed expression.

"When you get across," Arista told him, "look for the horn in the tomb. I don't know where it will be. I don't even know what it will look like, but it *is* there."

"If you can't find it," Hadrian said, "look for a sword with writing on the blade. You can kill the Gilarabrywn with it. You just have to stab it. It doesn't matter where. Just drive the word written on the blade into its body."

"If something goes wrong, run back and I will try to protect you," Arista said.

Hadrian handed Gaunt the lantern. "Good luck."

Gaunt stood before them, clutching his new medallion and the light. His long cloak was discarded in tatters on the floor, his hat disheveled, his face sick. Hadrian and Royce slid the latches and drew back the bolts. The metal made a disturbing squeal; then the door came free. Hadrian raised his foot and kicked the door open. It swung back with a groan, a large hollow sound that suggested the vast volume of the chamber beyond.

Gaunt took a step, raised the lantern, and peered in. "I can't see anything."

"It's there," Royce whispered to him. The thief stood behind Gaunt. "Right in the middle of the room. It looks like it's sleeping."

"Go on, Degan," Arista said. "Maybe you can sneak by."

"Yeah—sneak," he said, and stepped forward, leaving Arista and Royce standing side by side in the doorway with Hadrian looking over their shoulders.

"Stop breathing so hard," Royce snapped. "Breathe through your mouth, at least."

"Right," he said, and took another step. "Is it moving?"

"No," Royce told him.

Gaunt took three more steps. The lantern in his hand began to jingle a bit as his arm shook.

"Why doesn't he just scream, 'Come eat me!'?" Royce hissed in frustration.

Arista watched as the lantern bobbed. The light revealed nothing of the walls or ceiling and illuminated only one side of Gaunt as he appeared to walk into a void of nothingness.

"How big *is* this room?" she asked.

"Huge," Royce told her.

She tried to remember the dream. She vaguely recalled the emperor on the floor of a large chamber with painted walls and a series of statues—statues that represented all the past emperors—a memorial hall.

"He seems to be doing pretty good," Hadrian observed.

"He's halfway to it," Royce reported. "Walking real slow."

"I think I can see it," Arista said. Something ahead of Gaunt was finally illuminated by his light. It was big. "Is that it? Is that— Oh my god, that's just its foot?"

"I said it was big," Royce told her.

As Gaunt approached, his lantern revealed a mammoth creature. A clawed foot lay no more than ten feet away, yet its tail stretched too far into the darkness to see. Its two great leathery wings were folded at its sides as towering tents of skin stretched out on talon-endowed poles. Its huge head, with a long snout, raised ears, and fanged teeth, lay between its forefeet, making it seem as innocent as a sleeping dog—only it was not sleeping. Two eyes, each one larger than a wagon wheel, watched him, unblinking.

The moment it raised its head, Degan stopped moving. Even across the distance, they heard his labored, rapid breath.

"Don't run," Arista called, stepping forward into the room. "Tell it who you are. Tell it you are the heir. Order it to let you pass."

The Gilarabrywn rose to its feet. As it did, its massive wings expanded. They sounded like distant thunder rolling and Arista felt a gust of air.

"Gaunt, tell it!"

"I—I—I am—I am Degan Ga—Gaunt, the Heir of Novron, and I—"

"Damn it!" Royce rushed forward.

Arista saw it too—the beast lifted its head and opened its mouth. Closing her eyes, she pushed out with her senses. There it was—the beast. In her mind's eye, she could see its massive size, its overwhelming power, and it was pure magic.

She could see it as such, hear its music, feel its vibration, and everything she sensed told her it was about to kill Degan.

"Run!" Hadrian shouted.

In that same instant, panic gripped her. The creature was not a force she could act upon; it was like smoke. She could not grasp, push, burn, or harm it. It *was* magic and acting upon it with magic would have no more effect than blowing at the wind or spitting in a lake.

She opened her eyes. "I can't stop it!"

The beast arched its back to strike.

In one tremendous burst, Arista's robe exploded with the brilliance of a star. Light filled the room, flooding every corner of the great vault. Gold and silver reflected the light, creating dazzling effects that blinded and bewildered. Even Arista could not see, but she heard the beast groan and sensed it recoil. The light went out as quickly as it had appeared, but still she could not see.

She heard footfalls running toward her. They brushed by and she was pulled through the doorway. Still blinking, her eyes still adjusting, she could barely make out Hadrian throwing back the bolts, sealing it out and them in. From the other side they heard a roar that shook the walls, then silence.

Royce and Gaunt lay on the floor panting. Hadrian collapsed near the door, and Arista found herself sliding down a wall to her knees. Tears filled her eyes.

It was over. Thranic had been right. No one was going to cross that room...ever.

CHAPTER 21

THE SACRIFICE

Hadrian raised the lantern and looked up at the collapse. Shattered rock and broken stone crushed into a solid wall blocked the corridor and obliterated the stair. He looked at Magnus at his side. "Well?"

The dwarf shook his head with a scowl. "If I had a month, perhaps two, I could tunnel it."

"We have six, maybe seven, days' worth of food and perhaps three days of water," Hadrian told him. "And who knows how much air? I'm also guessing Wyatt and Elden won't wait much beyond five days before setting sail home."

"And don't forget the Ghazel," Magnus reminded him. "By now, how many do you think there might be? Five hundred? A thousand? Two thousand? How many more oberdaza have they brought up to deal with the princess? They will be watching the other end of this for some time, I think."

Hadrian sighed. "It's not looking good, is it?"

"No," Magnus replied sadly. "I'm sorry."

When they returned to the room, Arista was still sitting in the corner by herself. Since the attempt to cross the Vault of Days, she slept a lot and he wondered if she was looking for answers in her dreams. Mauvin lay on the floor, not bothering to use a blanket to cover the stone. He stared up at the ceiling blankly. Gaunt lay curled in the opposite corner from Arista, holding the amulet with both hands, his eyes closed.

By contrast, Royce and Myron sat chatting next to the last remaining lantern. To Hadrian the two appeared surreal. Myron spoke excitedly, sitting cross-legged on the floor, sifting through the piles of parchments he gathered around him. Each one had been carefully wiped clean of oil. Royce leaned comfortably against the wall, his feet up on Gaunt's pack, his boots off as he flexed his toes. They could have been in the Dark Room at The Rose and Thorn or any cozy pub.

"The Ghazel conquered Calis," Myron was saying. "They came out of the east on ships and attacked. Neither the men nor dwarves had ever seen them before. The men called them the spawn of Uberlin, but it was the dwarves that named them the Ba Ran Ghazel—sea goblins. They overran Calis and drove the clans of men west into Avryn while the dwarves returned underground. The elves warned men not to cross the Bernum River and when they did, the elves declared war."

Myron stopped speaking as Hadrian and Magnus approached, both of them looking up expectantly. "No luck, then?" Royce asked, reading his face, which Hadrian was certain was no great feat.

"No," he replied with a sigh. He was aware his shoulders were slumped, his head hanging. He felt beaten, defeated by stone, dust, and dirt. Exhausted, he lay down and, like Mauvin, stared at the ceiling. "There's no way out of here."

Magnus nodded. "The stone they used is solid and the princess did an excellent job as well. The collapse is hundreds of feet deep. I think she took out the entire stair and a good deal of the corridor beyond. Perhaps with a crew of twenty dwarves and a month to work with, I could clear the wreckage, build supports and reinforcements, and form a new stair, but as it is, we'll be dead before I could tunnel a foot-wide hole."

The dwarf sat down amidst the scrolls and, picking one up, glanced at it.

"Can you read Old Speech?" Myron asked.

"Not likely," Magnus replied. "Dwarves aren't even scholars in our own language. Are you finishing that story? The one about how the dwarves saved mankind?"

"Ah—well, yes, I suppose."

"Well, go on. I liked that one."

"Um, I was just saying that when the goblins arrived, it drove men west. They had little choice, and those who crossed the river were mostly women and children, refugees of the goblin push. According to what I read, the elves knew this and some argued to allow the humans to stay, but there was more to consider.

"Elves had already entered into agreements with men that had proved disastrous. The problem was that humans only live for a few decades. A treaty made with one chieftain would be forgotten in just a few hundred years. More than this, though, was the rate of reproduction. Elves had only one child over the course of their long lives, spanning hundreds, sometimes thousands of years. But humans reproduced like rabbits and the king, a chieftain of the Miralyith at that time, thought that men would choke the world with their number and be more plentiful than ants. It was decided to wipe mankind out to the last woman and child before they grew too numerous to be stopped. At that time the Ghazel were attacking the eastern coast of Avryn and the southern coast of Erivan, taking control of what we know as the Goblin Sea."

"Were did you get all this?" Hadrian asked.

Myron pulled out a red leather-bound book. "It's called *Migration of Peoples* by Princess Farilane, daughter, incidentally, to Emperor Nyrian, who reigned from 1912 to 1989 of imperial reckoning. It has wonderful charts and maps showing how the various clans of man shifted out of Calis and into Avryn. There were originally three main clans. Bulard theorized that these distinct groups, both in tradition and linguistic foundations— temporarily homogenized by the empire—created the ethnic divisions and the basis for the three kingdoms after the fall of the empire."

"Nothing in those books about the horn, then?"

Myron shook his head. "But I'm still reading."

"Speaking of linguistics..." Royce began. "The names you found in the Teshlor guildhall, Techylor and, ah—What was it?"

"Cenzlyor?"

"Yeah, him. I knew a man once—a very smart man—who told me words like that and others, like Avryn, and Galewyr, were elven in origin."

"Oh absolutely," Myron replied. "*Techylor* is actually *swift of hand* in elvish, and *Cenzlyor* is *swift of mind*."

"Is it possible that Techylor and Cenzlyor were actually elves?" Royce asked.

"Hmm." The monk thought for a bit. "I don't know. Until we got here, I never even knew they were people." Myron looked at Magnus. "Is there really no way of digging out? I would so much like to get back to that library again. If Mr. Bulard found these, there may be other books that survived the fire."

"*That's* why you want to get out?" Gaunt exclaimed, sitting up and casting his blanket back. "We're dying here! You know that, right? Your little bookish brain isn't so dense as to not realize that, is it? We will be dead bodies lying on this stone floor soon, and all you can think of are books? You're crazy!"

"This is going to sound really strange," Mauvin began,

"but I have to agree with His Heir-ness on this one. How can you just sit there yapping about ancient history at a time like this?"

"Like what?" Myron asked.

Even Arista was taken aback. "Myron, we are going to die here — you understand that, don't you?"

The monk considered it a moment, then shrugged. "Perhaps."

"You don't find that disturbing?"

Myron looked around. "Why? Should I?"

"Why?" Gaunt laughed. "He is nuts!"

"I just mean — well, how is this different from any other day?" They all looked at him incredulously. Myron sighed. "The morning before the Imperialists arrived and burned the abbey was a lovely fall day. The sky was blue and the weather surprisingly warm. On the other hand, it was a horribly cold and wet night when I met the King of Melengar, Royce, and Hadrian, who opened my eyes to untold wonders. When I traveled south through the snow with the awful news about Miss DeLancy, I had no idea that journey would save my life from the elven invasion. So you see, it is impossible to tell what Maribor has in store for us. A beautiful day might bring disaster, while a day that begins trapped inside an ancient tomb might be the best one of your life. If you don't abandon hope on pleasant days, why do so on those that begin poorly?"

"The odds of death are a bit better than usual, Myron," Magnus pointed out.

The monk nodded. "We may indeed die here, that's true. But we will all die anyway — is there any denying that? When you think of all the possible ways you might go, this is as fine a place as any, isn't it? I mean, to end one's life surrounded by friends, in a comfortable, dry room with plenty to read... that doesn't sound too awful, does it?

"What is the advantage of fear, or the benefit of regret, or the bonus of granting misery a foothold even if death is embracing you? My old abbot used to say, 'Life is only precious if you wish it to be.' I look at it like the last bite of a wonderful meal—do you enjoy it, or does the knowledge that there is no more to follow make it so bitter that you would ruin the experience?" The monk looked around, but no one answered him. "If Maribor wishes for me to die, who am I to argue? After all, it is he who gave me life to begin with. Until he decides I am done, each day is a gift granted me, and it would be wasted if spent poorly. Besides, for me, I've learned that the last bite is often the sweetest."

"That's very beautiful," Arista said. "I've never had much use for religion, but perhaps if I had you as a teacher rather than Saldur—"

"I should never have come," Gaunt complained. "How did I ever get involved in this? I can't believe this is happening. Is anyone else finding it hard to breathe?" He lay back down, pulled his blanket over his head, and moaned.

In the silence that followed, Myron got up and looked around for more unopened scrolls still resting in the many holes.

"Who was he?" Magnus asked Royce. "The one who taught you elvish?"

"What's that?"

"A bit ago you mentioned a man taught you about elvish words. Who was he?"

"Oh," Royce said, wriggling his toes again. "I met him in prison. He was perhaps the first real friend I ever had."

This caught Hadrian's attention. Royce had never spoken of his time in Manzant before, and because he knew everyone Royce had ever called a friend, except one, he took a guess. "He was the one who gave you Alverstone."

"Yes," Royce said.

"Who was he?" the dwarf asked. "How did he come by it? Was he a guard?"

"No, an inmate like me."

"How did he smuggle a dagger in?"

"I asked him the same thing," Royce said. "He told me he didn't."

"What? He found it? Digging in the salt mine? He uncovered that treasure down there?"

"Maybe, but that's not what he told me, and he wasn't the type to lie. He said he made it himself—made it for me. He told me I would need it." Royce looked off thoughtfully. "When I was locked away, I swore to myself never to trust anyone again. Then I met him. I would have died in my first month if I hadn't. He kept me alive. He had absolutely no reason—no reason at all—but he did. He taught me things: how to survive in the mine, where to dig and where not to, when to sleep and when to pretend to. He taught me some mathematics, reading, history, and even a bit of elvish. He never once asked for anything in return.

"One day I was hauled out before Ambrose Moor, to meet an old man named Arcadius who called himself a wizard. He offered to buy my freedom if I did a special job for him—the Crown Tower robbery, as it turned out." Royce looked at Hadrian. "I said I would do it if he also paid for the release of my friend. Arcadius refused. So I pretended to go along just to get out. I told my friend that when I got clear of the prison, I would slit the old man's throat, steal his money, and return to buy his freedom."

"What changed your mind?" Hadrian asked.

"He did. He made me promise not to kill Arcadius or Ambrose Moor—it was the only thing he ever asked of me. It was then that he gave me Alverstone and said goodbye."

"You never went back?"

"I did. A year later I had plenty of coin and planned to buy him, but Ambrose told me he died. They threw his body in the sea like all the others." Royce flexed his hands. "I never had the chance to thank him."

⤜

Hours went by. Like the others, Hadrian lay on the floor drifting into and out of sleep. He dreamed he fought beside his father against shadowy creatures who were trying to kill the emperor—who looked vaguely like Alric. In another dream, he sat in the burned-out shell of The Rose and Thorn with Gwen and Albert, waiting for Royce, but Royce was late— very late. Gwen was frightened something awful had happened, and he assured her Royce could take care of himself. "Nothing," he told her, "absolutely nothing, can keep Royce from your side, not even death."

He woke up groggy and tired, as if he had not slept at all. The cold floor punished his muscles, leaving him stiff and sore. The air grew thin, or at least Hadrian thought so. It was not hard to breathe, but it did feel as if he were sleeping with his head under a blanket.

How much is real and how much imagination? Is the flame in the lantern dwindling?

Everyone was sleeping, Gaunt in his corner, Magnus against the wall—even Myron was asleep, surrounded by scrolls. The princess lay curled up on her side, near the center of the room. She too was asleep, her eyes closed, head on hands, her face revealed by the lantern light. She was not as young as she once had been and no longer looked like a girl. Her face was longer, her cheeks less round, and there were small lines around her mouth and eyes. Smudges of dirt streaked her face. Her lips were chapped and dark circles formed under her eyes. Her hair was a mess. The lack of a brush left her with snarls and mats. She was beautiful, he thought, not despite these things, but because of them. Looking at her made him feel terrible. She believed in him—counted on him—and he had failed her. He had also failed Thrace and even her father. Hadrian had promised Theron that he would watch after his daughter and keep her safe. He had even failed his own father, who had left him this one last chance to bring meaning to his life.

He sighed, and as he did, he noticed Royce was not among the sleeping. The thief was not even in the room. Getting up, Hadrian stepped into the hallway and found him sitting in the dark a few feet from the mound of stones piled over Thranic's body. He could barely see Royce, as so little of the lantern light spilled into the corridor.

Hadrian let his back slap against the corridor wall and slid down to the floor to sit beside his friend.

"I've finally figured it out," Royce said.

"What, the perfect career for us? Not spelunking, I hope?"

Royce looked at him and smirked. Hadrian could see his friend only by the single shaft of light that crossed the bridge of his nose and splashed his left cheek.

"No. I realized that the key is *you*—you can't die."

"I'm liking this so far—I have no idea what you're talking about, but it's starting out good."

"Well, think about it. This can't be the end because you can't die. That's the whole thing right there."

"Are you planning on making sense anytime soon?"

"It's Gwen, remember? She said I had to save your life, right? She was adamant about it. Only I haven't. Ever since she sent us out to search for Merrick, I've never once saved your life. So either she was wrong or we're missing something. And as you know, Gwen has never been wrong. We must be missing something and now I know what it is. *This* is it. This is where I save your life."

"That's wonderful, only how are you going to do that, pray tell?"

"Our second plan—I'm the diversion."

"What?" Hadrian said, feeling like Royce had just hit him.

"I'll draw the beast's attention just like Millie did in Dahlgren and you run, get the sword, and slay it. I don't know why I didn't think of it sooner. It makes perfect sense."

"You do remember what happened to Millie, right?"

"Yes," he said simply. The single word issuing out of the darkness sounded like a verdict. "But don't you see? This is what I'm supposed to do. I've even considered if this was why she died. Maybe Gwen knew *everything.* She knew we could not go off and make a life together because I needed to be here to sacrifice myself. Maybe that's why she was on the bridge that night, maybe she went to her death for me—or rather for you and everyone else, but at least so that I could have the strength to die for you."

"That's a whole lot of ifs and maybes, Royce."

"Maybe," he said.

There was a pause.

"But it has to be," Royce went on. "We know she had the sight. We know she knew the future. We know she planned for it, and that she said I would save your life. She knew that without me you would die, and from your death a horrible thing would occur. So if I save you now, we still have a chance to get the horn."

"But what if the future changed? What if we did something in the meantime to alter it?"

"I don't think it works that way. I don't think you can alter the future. If you could, she would have seen that."

"I don't know," Hadrian replied, finding it hard to discuss rationally the virtues of Royce's killing himself.

"Okay, let me put it this way," Royce said. "Can you think of any other way out of here?"

Hadrian was starting to feel a little sick, the air harder to breathe than before.

"So your plan is to draw it away and keep it occupied while I run for the sword?"

"Yep, you get the sword and kill it. I think I can buy you at least two minutes, but I'm hoping for as much as five. More than that I think is dreaming. After five minutes of dodging it, I will get tired and it will get frustrated to the point of using fire. I can't dodge that. Still, even two minutes should be plenty of time to cross that room and find the sword."

"What if it's locked?"

"It's not. I saw it when I was in there getting Gaunt. It's standing open. Hadrian, you know I'm right. Besides, it's not just you I'm thinking about. There are five other people who will die unless I do this—granted their lives don't mean as much to me, but I know it matters to you."

"And you're sure you want to do this?"

"I want to do it for Gwen. Hadrian, what else do I have to live for? The only thing I have is to fulfill her last request. That's all. After I do that..."

Hadrian closed his eyes and rapped his skull against the wall behind him, creating a dull thud. There was a pressure behind his eyes, a throbbing in his head.

"You know I'm right," Royce said.

"What do you want? You want me to say, 'Hooray, thanks, pal, for saving us'?"

"I don't want anything, except for you to live—you and the rest of them—even Magnus and Gaunt. It's what I can give you and the only thing I can give her. If I manage to save you, and you do get this stupid horn and it saves everyone, it will make her death mean something—mine too, I suppose. That's more than either of us could have hoped for. A prostitute and a no-good thief saving the world—it's not a bad epitaph. You can see I'm right, can't you?"

Hadrian let his head rest and stared out at the black. "Don't you get tired of always being right?"

"We made a good team, didn't we?" Royce replied. "Arcadius wasn't such a fool putting us together after all."

"Speak for yourself."

"Watch it. I'm about to die to save your ass, so be nice."

"Thanks for that, by the way."

"Yeah, well, you'll be happy to be rid of me. You can go back to blacksmithing in Hintindar and live a quiet happy life. Do me a favor and marry some pretty farm girl and train your son to beat the crap out of imperial knights."

"Sure," Hadrian told him. "And with any luck he'll make friends with a cynical burglar who'll do nothing but torment him."

"With any luck."

"Yeah," Hadrian said. "With any luck."

The two sat in silence for a moment. In the room, Hadrian could hear Gaunt snoring.

"We should do this sooner than later," Royce told him. "Just in case the air is running out and while you still have plenty of water and food to escape with, right?"

"I suppose."

"You know, when I'm dead, and it's dead—assuming there's anything left of me, it wouldn't be such a bad thing if you laid me to rest in the tomb of Novron. Can't ask for better accommodations, really, and tell Myron to say something nice, something poetic, something about Gwen and me."

❧

"What? No!" Arista shouted.

She was standing against the wall, a blanket pulled around her shoulders, her fingers white where they clutched the dark wool. Her head was shaking from side to side in a slow constant motion, like the ticking of a pendulum clock.

Magnus and Mauvin flanked her. Neither said a word as Royce explained the plan. In their eyes, Hadrian could see concern, but also resignation. Gaunt was up and looking hopeful, his eyes bright for the first time since they had entered the room.

"It's the only way," Royce assured her as he sat down on his pack, where he had left his boots. "And it will work. I know it will."

"You'll die!" she shouted. "You'll die and I won't be able to save you."

Royce pulled his boots on. "Of course I will, and I don't want you to," he said, and paused a moment before adding, "It will all be over—finally."

"No, you'll both die, I know it." Arista looked up at Hadrian with the same expression of terror on her face. "Don't do this. Please."

Hadrian turned away and unbuckled his belt, dropping his swords. He would be able to run faster without them. "Which way you gonna go, Royce?"

"Right, I think," he said, throwing off his cloak. "That will put me on its left; maybe it's right-handed. I'll try to keep it busy as long as possible, but we'll see how fast it is. I'm going to try to sneak to the right corner and get as far in as possible before I draw its attention, so wait for me to yell. With luck, you'll have an open field to run across."

"You're doing it now?" The princess's head was shaking even faster.

Hadrian leaned against the wall and stretched his legs, then jogged in place for a few seconds. "No sense putting it off."

"Please," Arista begged in little more than a whisper. Taking a step toward Hadrian, she reached out and then stopped.

Royce approached Magnus, who took a step back. The thief reached into his cloak and pulled out Alverstone, still in its sheath. He held it out to the dwarf. "I was wondering if you could watch after this for me."

"Are you serious?" the dwarf asked.

Royce nodded.

Slowly, warily, Magnus touched the weapon gingerly with both hands, cradling it like a newborn.

"You're really going to do this?" the dwarf asked, nodding at the Vault of Days.

"It's all that's left to try."

"I—I could go," Magnus said, still looking at the dagger. "I could take a lantern—"

"With your little legs?" Royce laughed. "You'd just get Hadrian killed."

Magnus looked up, his brows running together, his lips shifting as if he were chewing something. "I should be the last person..." The dwarf stopped.

"Let's just say recent events have made me realize I've done a number of things I shouldn't have. Bad things. Worse, I suppose, than what you've done. Right now, hating you seems... stupid." Royce smiled.

The dwarf nodded. "I'll—I'll hold on to it for you, take good care of it, but just until you need it again."

Royce nodded and moved to the door. He reached up and drew back the seals. "Shall we, partner?"

"See you on the other side, pal."

Hadrian threw his arms around the thief and, surprisingly, felt Royce hug him back. With one final smile, Royce pushed open the door and disappeared into the darkness of the Vault of Days.

Hadrian waited at the doorway. He could not see anything, nor could he hear a sound, but he did not expect to.

"Do you want the lantern?" Myron whispered.

"No," Hadrian replied. "I'll run faster without it, but maybe the princess could stand here and make her robe bright when I start to run." He said this without turning, without looking at her.

"Of...course," he heard her say, her voice strained, stalling in her throat.

They all waited, staring into the black room, listening carefully. Hadrian peered into the dark, trying to guess where it was, where either of them was.

"Hadrian, I—" Arista began in a whisper and he felt a light hand on the small of his back.

"Over here, monster!" Royce shouted, his voice booming across the great darkened expanse, echoing off the distant walls. "Come get me before I find the sword with your name on it and drive it through your foul excuse for a heart!"

∽

Royce watched as Arista's robe lit up, throwing white light in the room, at the sound of his voice. It was not nearly as bright as before, but enough to reveal the far wall, the open door, and the great beast in the middle of the room.

The Gilarabrywn was looking right at him. Royce braced himself, trying to decide whether it would strike with its mouth or a taloned foot.

724 Michael J. Sullivan

How fast is it? How quickly can it cover the distance between us? Royce was far enough away that even as big as it was, the beast would have to take at least ten steps to reach him. He wondered if it would lumber due to its size. He reminded himself it was not a real creature; it was magic and perhaps the same rules might not apply. It was possible that it could sprint like a tiny lizard or lash out like a snake. He stayed on the balls of his feet, shifting his weight back and forth, waiting for the lunge.

"Come on," he shouted. "I'm in your lousy room. You know you want me."

The beast took a slow step toward him, then another.

"Go!" Royce shouted.

Hadrian ran out the door. He had cleared only five strides when the monster whirled on him. Hadrian dug in his heels and slid to the ground as the giant head snapped around with amazing speed.

"Get back!" Arista screamed.

Royce ran forward. "Over here! You stupid thing," he shouted, waving his hands over his head.

The Gilarabrywn ignored Royce and charged Hadrian, who scrambled back toward the light of Arista's robe, which once more brightened.

"Gilarabrywn!" Royce called. The beast stopped its pursuit. "Over here, you stupid thing! What? Don't you like me? Am I too thin?" The beast looked toward Royce but did not move away from the door.

"By Mar!" Royce exclaimed in frustration.

"*Minith Dar,*" the Gilarabrywn said, and its voice rumbled the chamber like thunder.

"It spoke," Royce said, stunned.

"That's right. They talk in Old Speech." He heard Arista.

"What did it say?"

"I'm not sure. I don't know the language well. I think he said, '*Comprehension is missing*,' but I don't know," she shouted.

"I do." It was Myron's voice coming into the darkness. "It said, '*I don't understand*.'"

"It doesn't understand what?"

"Royce can't hear a shrug, Myron," Hadrian said.

"I don't know," the monk replied.

"Ask it," Arista suggested.

There was a pause; then Myron spoke again. "*Binith mon erie, minith dar?*"

The creature ignored Myron and continued to stare at Royce.

"Maybe he didn't hear you."

Myron shouted louder. Still the beast ignored him, his eyes fixed on Royce.

"By Mar," Royce said again.

"*Minith Dar*," the Gilarabrywn replied.

"That's it!" Myron shouted. "*Bimar! Bimar* means *hungry* in Old Speech."

"Yeah, that's right," Arista confirmed. "But it only seems to hear Royce."

"He's elvish," Hadrian said. "Maybe—"

"Of course!" the princess shouted. "It's just like Avempartha! Say something to it in Old Speech, ask it a question. Say, '*Ere en kir abeniteeh?*'"

"*Ere en kir abeniteeh?*" Royce repeated.

"*Mon bir istanirth por bon de havin er main*," the Gilarabrywn replied.

"What'd I say—and what did it say?"

"You asked its name, and it said..." Arista hesitated.

"It said," Myron started, taking over, "'My name is written upon the sword of my making.'"

"You can talk to it, Royce!" Arista told him.

"Wonderful, but why isn't it eating me?"

"Good question," the princess replied. "But let's not ask that. No sense giving it any ideas."

Royce stepped forward. The Gilarabrywn did not move. He took another step, then another, staying on the balls of his feet. He knew the beast was clever and this was just the sort of ploy it might use to get him off his guard. Another step and then another. He was within striking distance; still the Gilarabrywn did not move.

"Careful, Royce," Hadrian told him.

Another step, then another and the Gilarabrywn's tail was just inches away.

"I wonder how it feels about having its tail pulled." Royce reached out and touched it. Still the Gilarabrywn did not move. "What's wrong with it? Myron, how do you say *move away?*"

"*Vanith donel.*"

Royce stood before the giant creature and in a strong voice ordered, "*Vanith donel!*"

The Gilarabrywn backed up.

"Interesting," Royce said. He closed the distance between them. "*Vanith donel!*"

Again the Gilarabrywn retreated.

"Try coming out," Royce said.

The moment Hadrian set foot outside the door, the Gilarabrywn advanced once again. Hadrian retreated into the room.

"How do you say *stop?*"

"*Ibith!*"

Royce ordered it to halt and it froze.

"Myron, how do you say *do not harm anyone?*"

Myron told him and Royce repeated the phrase.

"And how do you say *allow their passage through this room?*"

"*Melentanaria, en venau brenith dar vensinti.*"

"Really?" Royce said, surprised.

"Yes, why?"

"I know that one." Esrahaddon had taught him *Melentanaria, en venau* in Avempartha. Once more Royce repeated Myron's words, and for a third time Hadrian stepped out of the room into the Vault of Days. This time, the Gilarabrywn did not move.

"*Vanith donel!*" Royce shouted, and the Gilarabrywn stepped back, granting them passage.

"This is amazing," Arista said, entering the room with Hadrian. "It's obeying you."

"I wish I had known I could do this back in Avempartha," Royce said. "It would have been real handy."

Royce herded the Gilarabrywn back against the far wall, the great beast stepping backward before the tiny figure of the thief, its head glaring down at him, but showing no signs of violence.

"*Alminule* means *stay,*" Myron said.

"*Alminule,*" Royce said, and backed up. The Gilarabrywn remained where it was. "Everybody cross. Just stay spread out a bit—just in case."

One by one, they ran the expanse. Arista waited in the open beside Royce to provide light until Gaunt—the last to leave—made the crossing.

CHAPTER 22

NOVRON THE GREAT

The stone door on the far side of the Vault of Days was partially open, and taking the lantern from Myron, Hadrian was the first to enter. Inside, tall columns held up a high ceiling. The room was musty and stale. Large painted pots, urns, chests, and bowls lined the walls, as did life-sized statues, braziers, and figures of various animals, some easily identified, others he had never seen before. A colonnade lined both sides with arches framing openings, chambers within which lay stone sarcophagi. Above the arches words were carved and above them paintings of people.

Hadrian heard Arista gasp behind him as the lantern revealed the floor at the center of the room, where three skeletons lay—two adults and a child. Beside them rested two crowns and a sword.

"Nareion," she whispered, "and his wife and daughter. He must have pulled them in here after Esrahaddon went to meet Venlin."

Hadrian wiped the blade with his thumb, revealing a fine script. "This is the sword, isn't it?"

Arista nodded.

"Which one is Novron's coffin?" Mauvin asked.

"The largest," Gaunt guessed. "And it would be on the end, wouldn't it?"

Arista shrugged.

Myron had his head back reading the inscriptions on the walls above the arches, his lips moving slightly as he did.

"Can you tell which it is?" Gaunt asked.

Myron shook his head. "Up there." He pointed at text on the ceiling. "It says this is the tomb of all the emperors."

"We know that, but which is Novron?"

"The tomb of all the emperors, but…" Myron looked at the coffins, counting them with his index finger. "There're only twelve coffins here. The empire lasted for two thousand one hundred and twenty-four years. There should be hundreds."

Hadrian moved around the room, looking at the sarcophagi. They were made of limestone and beautifully carved, each one different. A few had details of hunting and battle scenes, but one depicted nothing but a beautiful lake surrounded by trees and mountains. Another showed a cityscape and buildings being raised. Several of the archways were empty.

"Could they have been moved?" Hadrian asked Myron.

"Perhaps. Still, there are only twenty alcoves allotted here. Why so few?"

"The rest are probably behind this door," Magnus suggested. He was at the far end of the crypt, appearing even smaller than normal against the backdrop of the great pillars and statues. "There's an inscription."

The rest of them moved to the rear of the tomb to a plain wall with a single door and, over it, a single line of words.

"What does it say, Myron?" Royce asked.

" 'HERE LIES NYPHRON THE GREAT, FIRST EMPEROR OF ELAN, SAVIOR OF THE WORLD OF MAN.' "

"There you are," Magnus said. "The first emperor is inside."

Royce moved forward. The door was cut from rock. A set of stone pins held it fast and a lever hung recessed in the wall beside it. Royce took hold of the arm and rotated it, drawing out the pins, which ground loudly, until at last they came clear.

With a gentle push, Royce opened the tomb of Novron.

Hadrian held the lantern high as everyone stood behind Royce, who was the first to enter. Hadrian followed directly behind, along with Arista, whose robe helped illuminate the chamber. The first thing Hadrian saw was a pair of giant elephant tusks standing to either side of the door. They were arranged such that the points arched toward each other. Black marble pillars supported the four corners of the crypt, and within the space between them, treasure filled the tomb.

There were golden chairs and tables, great chests, and cabinets. To one side stood a chariot made entirely of gold, to the other an elaborately carved boat. Spears lined one wall, and a group of shields another. Statues of men and animals cast of gold and silver, draped with jewelry, stood like silent guards. In the center of the room, raised high on a dais, rested a great alabaster sarcophagus. On the sides were divided frames similar to those etched on the walls—the story of a council, a battle, and a war. Nowhere was there the scene of Maribor bestowing the crown, which Hadrian thought odd, as it was the quintessential image found in every church.

"This is it," Mauvin muttered in awe. "We've found it, the crypt of Novron himself." The count touched the chariot, grinning. "Do you think this was his? Was this what he rode into battle?"

"Doubt it," Hadrian said. "Gold is a bit heavy for horses to pull."

Arista moved around the room, her eyes searching.

"What is the horn supposed to look like?" Royce asked.

"I don't know exactly," she said. "But I think it is in the coffin. In fact, I know it is. Esrahaddon placed it there for Nevrik. We need to open it."

Magnus wedged his chisel under the stone lid and Hadrian, Gaunt, and Mauvin took up positions around the lid. Myron held the lantern high as the dwarf struck his hammer to the spike. The men heaved the lid off.

Inside lay the coffin. Wrought of solid gold, it was body-shaped and sculpted to depict a face, hands, and clothing. They all stared at the image of a small slender man with angled eyes and prominent cheekbones wearing an elaborate helm.

"I don't understand," Gaunt said. "What—what are we seeing?"

"It's only a case," Mauvin said. "Just decoration. We need to open this one too."

The nimble fingers of the dwarf found latches and popped them, and everyone helped lift the lid. Once more, they all peered in. Before them lay the remains of Novron the Great.

Hadrian had expected a pile of brittle decaying bones, perhaps even dust, but instead they found a body complete with skin, hair, and clothes. The cloth was gray and rotted such that their breath caused it to flake. The skin was still intact but dry and dark like smoked beef. The eyes were gone, only cavities remaining, but the corpse was remarkably preserved.

"How is this possible?" Gaunt asked.

"Amazing," Myron said.

"Indeed," Magnus put in.

"It can't be," Mauvin declared.

Hadrian looked at the face in fascination. Like the outer lid, it was sharp and delicate in feature, with angled eyes and unmistakably pointed ears. The hands were elegant, with long thin fingers still graced with three rings, one of gold, another silver, and one of black stone. They were neatly folded over a metal box on which were scraped the words

To Nevrik
From Esrahaddon

"Careful," Royce said, studying the hands.

"There's something there," Arista told him. "I sense magic."

"You should if it's the horn, right?" Hadrian asked.

"It's not the horn. It's something on the box—a charm of some kind."

"It will likely strike dead anyone but the heir," Magnus guessed.

They all looked to Gaunt.

"Can't I just poke it with a stick or something?" he asked.

"Esrahaddon wouldn't have done anything that could hurt you," Arista told him. "Go on, take it. He left it for you, more or less."

Gaunt took hold of his medallion and rubbed, then reached out and grabbed hold of the box, pulling it free of Novron's hands.

Sconces around the walls burst into blue flame. A cold breeze coursed around the tomb and Gaunt dropped the box.

"Welcome, Nevrik, mine old friend," a voice said, and they all spun to see the image of Esrahaddon standing before them. He was dressed in the same robe Arista wore, except it was perfectly white. He looked the same as when Hadrian had last seen him in Ratibor.

"If thine ears to these words attest, then terror's shadow hast fled and thou art emperor. Wish I but knew if Jerish stood at thy side. On chance that dreams abide in mortal

spheres, I offer to him that which I withheld in life—my gratitude, my admiration, and my love.

"Stained upon my hands, the blood of innocents brands
my soul with such a crime forgiveness gapes appalled. 'Tis my
sin that shattered stone and rent flesh. 'Twas I who laid waste
to our beloved home. Though to speak of it now feels like
folly, for yet hath spark been struck. Still, committed am I.
For not a breath nor heartbeat flutter can be granted onto a
single Cenzar or Teshlor when the morrow comes. Their evil
with me shall I take, the threat resolved, the night consumed,
that thou may walk beneath the sun of a better day.

"Convinced stand I, here within these hallowed halls of thy
father's reckoning and their solemn rest, certain that Mawyndulë yet lives. Their whispers become a wail as mine eyes focus
upon a murder left two thousand years unavenged. Foul is the
spirit that haunts these walls, for beyond imaginings are the
depths to which his depravity strains. We knew but half!
Banned by horn and god alike, 'tis my belief the fiend aims
with intent to outlast the law. A crevice hath he found and
stretched to slip, for no restriction blocks his way should after
a trio of a thousand years he survive. I go now to ensure he
does not. While master beyond my art, my art will end him.
To slay a fiend, a fiend I must become. Murderer of thousands,
I will be stained and accept this as price paid for extinguishing
this flame that seeks consumption of all.

"The horn be thine. Render it safe. Deliver it unto thine
children with warning against the day of challenge to present
same at Avempartha. Look to Jerish as champion—the secrets
of the Instarya remain the thread upon which all hope
dangles.

"Fare thee well, emperor's son, mine emperor, my student,
my friend. Know that I go now to face Mawyndulë honored
to die that you might live. Make me proud—be a good ruler."

Esrahaddon's image vanished as quickly as it had appeared and the fires in the sconces died, leaving them once more with only the light of the lantern between them and the darkness.

"Did everyone catch that? I wish I had something to write it down with," Hadrian said. Then, noticing Myron, he smiled. "Even better."

Royce knelt down and examined the box. There was no lock and he carefully lifted the lid. Inside was a ram's horn. It was plain, without gold, silver, gems, or velvet. The only adornment it possessed were numerous markings that ringed the surface, letters in a language he could not read but that he recognized.

"Not much to look at, is it?" Magnus observed.

Royce placed the horn back in the box.

"What does this all mean?" Mauvin asked. Looking doleful, he sat down on a gold chair in the pile of treasure. His eyes moved from one to another, searching.

"Novron was an elf," Royce said. "A pure-blooded elf."

"The first true emperor, the savior of mankind, wasn't even a man?" Magnus muttered.

"How can that be?" Mauvin asked. "He led the war *against* the elves. Novron *defeated* the elves!"

"Legends tell of Novron falling in love with Persephone. Perhaps he did it out of love," Myron offered as he wandered around the room, looking at the objects.

"Techylor and Cenzlyor were elves, then?" Hadrian said. "They may even have been Novron's actual brothers."

"That explains the small number of sarcophagi," Myron pointed out. "The generations were longer. Oh! And Old Speech isn't old speech at all—it's elvish. The native language of the first emperor. Imagine that. The language of the church is not similar to elvish...it *is* elvish."

"That's why Thranic was lopping heads off statues," Royce

said. "They were accurate depictions of the emperors, and perhaps Cenzlyor and Techylor."

"But how could it have happened?" Mauvin asked. "How could an elf be the emperor? This has to be a mistake! Novron is the son of Maribor, sent to save us from the elves—the elves are—"

"Yes?" Royce asked.

"Oh, I don't know," Mauvin said, shaking his head. "But this isn't how it's supposed to be."

"It isn't what the church wanted to be known," Royce said. "That's why they locked up Edmund Hall. They knew. Saldur knew, Ethelred knew, Braga knew—"

"Braga!" Arista exclaimed. "That's what he meant! Before he died, he said something about Alric and me not being human—about letting filth rule. He thought we were elves! Or that we had retained at least some elven blood. If the Essendons were heirs to Novron, then we would have. That's the secret—that's why they have hunted the heir. The church has been trying to wipe out the line of Novron so that elves would no longer rule mankind. That's what Venlin was trying to do. That's how he persuaded the Teshlor Guild and the Cenzar Council to unite against the emperor—for the greater good of mankind—to rid them of *elven* rule."

"Instarya," Myron muttered from the corner, where he looked at a worn and battered shield that hung in a place of prominence.

"What's that?" Hadrian asked.

"The markings on the shield here," he said. "They are of the elven tribe Instarya, the warriors. Novron was from the Instarya clan."

Arista asked, "Why was it that Novron fought his own people?"

"None of this matters," Gaunt told them. "We're still

trapped. Unless one of you spotted a door I didn't see. This treasure-filled tomb is a dead end unless, of course, blowing on this does something." Gaunt looked down at the horn.

"No, wait!" Arista shouted, but it was too late.

Everyone cringed as Gaunt lifted the horn to his lips and blew.

✍

Nothing happened.

Not even a sound emanated from the instrument. Gaunt merely turned red-faced, his cheeks puffed out silently as if he were performing a pantomime of a trumpeter. He looked down at it, frustrated. He put his eye to the mouthpiece and peered inside. He stuck his pinky finger in and wiggled it around, then tried to blow it again. Nothing. He blew again and again and then finally threw it to the floor, disgusted. Without a word, he walked to the chariot and sat down, putting his back against a golden spoked wheel.

Arista picked up the instrument and turned it over in her hands. It was just a simple horn, a bit over a foot in length, with a pleasant arc. It was dark, almost black, near the point and faded rapidly to near white at the wide end. Several rings of finely etched markings circled it. There was nothing special about it. The horn just looked old.

"Myron?" she called, and the monk looked up from the treasures. "Can you read any of this?"

Myron took the horn near the lantern and peered at it. "It's Old Speech—or elvish, I suppose, now isn't it?" He looked at the horn and squinted, his mouth and nose crinkled up as his eyes worked and his fingers rotated the horn. "Ah!"

"What?"

"It says '*Sound me, 'O son of Ferrol, spake argument with thine lord, by mine voice wilt thee challenge, no longer by the sword.*'"

"What does that mean?" Mauvin asked.

Myron shrugged.

"Is that all?" Arista asked.

"No there's more. It also says:

> *Gift am I, of Ferrol's hand*
> *these laws to halt the chaos be,*
> *No king shall die, no tyrant cleaved*
> *save by the perilous sound of me.*
>
> *Cursed the silent hand that strikes*
> *forever to his brethren lost,*
> *Doomed of darkness and of light*
> *so be the tally and the cost.*
>
> *Breath upon my lips announce*
> *the gauntlet loud so all may hear,*
> *Thine challenge for the kingly seat*
> *so all may gather none need fear.*
>
> *But once upon a thousand three*
> *unless by death I shall cry,*
> *No challenge, no dispute proceed*
> *a generation left to die.*
>
> *Upon the sound, the sun shall pass*
> *and with the rising of the new,*
> *Combat will begin and last*
> *until there be but one of two.*

*A bond formed betwixt opponents
protected by Ferrol's hand,
From all save the blade, the bone,
and skill of the other's hand.*

*Should champion be called to fight
evoked is the Hand of Ferrol,
Which protects the championed from all
and champion from all—save one—from peril.*

*Battle is the end for one
for the other all shall sing.
For when the struggle at last is done
the victor shall be king.*

"It's not a weapon at all," Hadrian said. "It's just a horn. It's used to announce a ceremonial challenge for the right of leadership, like throwing down a gauntlet or slapping someone's face. Myron, remember you told us that the elves had troubles in the old days with infighting between the clans? This must have been the solution. How the elves decide who rules them. It said that they are only allowed to challenge once—What did you say? A thousand and three years?"

"I actually think that means once every three thousand years."

"Right, well, Novron must have used it to challenge the king of the elves to combat and won, ending the war and making himself king of both the elves and men."

"I don't see how this helps us," Gaunt said. "Why did we bother coming down here? How is this supposed to stop the elven army?"

"By blowing it, Gaunt just announced his challenge for the right to rule them," Arista said. " '*So all may gather none need fear.*' My guess is they have to stop fighting now and await the outcome of the one-on-one combat between Gaunt and their king."

"What?" Gaunt looked up, concerned.

"Only Gaunt didn't blow it," Hadrian said. "It's like it's busted or something."

So the horn isn't getting us out of here?" Gaunt asked.

"No," Arista said sadly. "No, it's not."

"Well, let's see what a dwarf can do, then," Magnus said, and taking out his hammer, began examining the walls, tapping here and there, placing his ear to them, even licking the stone. He circled Novron's tomb and then moved out into the larger crypt of kings. The rest of them wandered around, looking at the contents of the tomb, while Hadrian looked through the packs.

"There's probably thousands of pounds of gold here," Gaunt said, picking up a vase and staring at it miserably, as if it were mocking him by its mere existence. "What good is it?"

"I'd trade it all for a nice plate of Ella's apple pie right now," Mauvin said. "I wouldn't even mind her stew—and I never really liked her stew."

"I never had her stew, but I remember her pie," Myron said. He was crouched against the wall, still studying the horn. "It was very nice."

They all listened quietly for a time to the tapping of the dwarf's hammer in the other room. Its faint *tink!* jarred Arista's nerves.

"I pretended to *be* Ella when I worked at the palace," Arista said. "But I just scrubbed floors. I didn't cook. She did make great apple pie. Did she—"

Mauvin shook his head. "She was killed during the flight."

"Oh." Arista nodded.

"What do you think this is?" Gaunt asked, holding up a statuette that looked to be a cross between a bull and a raven.

Arista shrugged. "Pretty, though."

"How much?" Mauvin asked as Hadrian sat down on the wheel of the chariot.

"Three days," he said, "if we conserve."

The sound of the dwarf's hammer stopped and Magnus returned. His long face said everything. He entered and sat on a pile of gold coins, which jingled gaily. "There are worse places to be buried, I suppose."

"Alric," Arista said suddenly. "I suppose we should put him to rest properly, then."

"He'll be well buried," Myron told her. "And in a king's tomb."

She nodded, trying to appear comforted.

"Royce and I will get him," Hadrian said.

"I think I should be one of his pallbearers as well," Mauvin said, and followed them out.

They returned with his body and gently laid it on a golden table. Arista draped a blanket over him, and they gathered around it in a circle.

"Dear Maribor, our eternal father," Myron began, "we are gathered here to say farewell to our brother Alric Essendon. We ask that you remember him and see him across the river to the land of the dawn." He looked to Arista, whose eyes were already tearing again.

"Alric was my broth—" She stopped short as tears overtook her. Hadrian put his arm around her shoulders.

"Alric was my best friend," Mauvin continued. "My third brother, I always said. He was my rival for women, my fellow conspirator in plans of adventure, my prince, and my king. He was crowned before his time, but we did not know then how little time he had left. He ruled in an era of terror and he ruled well. He showed valor and courage befitting a king right to the end." He paused and looked down at the blanketed form and laid a hand on Alric's chest. "The crown is off now, Alric. You are free of it at last." Mauvin wiped the tears from his face.

"Does anyone else—" Myron began when Gaunt stepped forward, and all eyes turned cautiously toward him.

"I just wanted to say"—he paused a moment—"I was wrong about you." He hesitated for several seconds, as if he might say more, and then glanced awkwardly at the others before stepping back. "That's all."

Myron looked to Arista again.

"He's fine," she said simply while nodding. "At least I know that."

"And so, Lord," Myron continued with a bowed head, "we say farewell to our king, our brother, and our good friend. May the light of a new dawn rise upon his soul."

Myron then began the song of final blessing, and all of them, even Magnus, joined in.

Unto Maribor, I beseech thee
Into the hands of god, I send thee
Grant him peace, I beg thee
Give him rest, I ask thee
May the god of men watch over your journey.

Mauvin stepped out of the tomb into the crypt and returned with a dusty crown, which he lay upon Alric's chest. "Sometimes the price of dreams is achieving them."

Arista could not stay any longer. She felt like she was suffocating and walked out into the crypt. Entering one of the alcoves, she crouched down and hid behind one of the sarcophagi. She sat with her back in the crux of the corner. Her knees were up, and once settled, she let herself cry. She shook so hard that her back bounced against the wall. Tears ran down her face. She let them run unabated, dripping onto the robe, which dimmed until it went out.

She wanted to believe that when Gaunt blew the horn it had stopped the elves, that perhaps they had heard and were coming to dig them out, but it felt like a lie. She was deluding herself because there was nothing else to hope for, nothing to expect beyond despair. In the darkness, she laid her head down on her arms and cried until she fell asleep.

CHAPTER 23

THE SKY SWIRLS

The booming thunder continued shaking the walls and the floors beneath their feet as the metalsmith hammered the last rivet into the helm. The old man's face was etched with deep lines partially hidden behind a mass of gray bristles, a beard he had no time to shave away. "There you are, lad. As fine a helm as you'll find. It will take care of you. Protect that noggin of yours right well. War is upon us, my boy, but don't worry—that's only thunder yer hearing."

"It's *their* thunder," Renwick replied.

The metalsmith looked at him curiously for a moment; then Renwick saw fear cross the man's face as he put the pieces together.

"Yer the boy, aren't you? The one who warned us? The one who rode up ahead of the elven army. You've seen 'em, haven't you?"

Renwick shook his head. "Not me, but yes, my friend did."

"Did he tell you what the devils look like? Rumor has it anyone seeing an elf turns to stone."

"No, but I wouldn't turn an ear to their music."

"You're Breckton's squire now, eh? Aide-de-camp to the marshal-at-arms?"

Renwick shrugged. "I don't even know what an aide-de-camp is."

The old smith chuckled, wiping the sweat from his face with a filthy cloth as overhead an especially loud roll of thunder boomed. Renwick felt it in his chest.

"An adjutant," the smith told him. Renwick shrugged again. "You're like his butler, messenger, and squire all rolled into one, except you're more like an assistant than a servant, which means you'll get some respect."

"But what am I supposed to do?"

"Whatever he says, lad—whatever he says."

Renwick placed the helm on his head. It fit snug around the forehead and the thick batten felt soft and cushioning. He banged his head with the heel of his fist. The helm absorbed the blow. He felt almost nothing.

"It's good."

"You'll be all right. Now get back to Breckton. I have more work to do, as I suspect you do too."

Outside, the streets were wet; warmer air had melted some of the snow. Icicles dripped, sounding like rain, as overhead the sky swirled and thunder crashed.

He jumped a large puddle but did not account for the added weight of the armor. He had never worn any before. It was only a breastplate and helm, but with the shield and sword added, it was enough to throw off his balance. He came up short and splashed in the middle, soaking his foot with ice-cold water. He felt foolish holding the shield as if he expected to be attacked at any moment. The other soldiers wore shields slung on their backs. He paused in the street, examining the straps and trying to determine how to do that, when a flash of lightning arced across the sky and he heard a terrible crack. People on the street ducked into doorways, their eyes skyward. This got him moving again and he jogged the rest of the way to Imperial Square.

Men filled the open area. Soldiers and knights sat on the dry sections of cobblestone or stood in puddles. He worked his way in, trying not to hit anyone with either his shield or his sword. Renwick felt conspicuous. Men with missing teeth and scarred faces glared at him as he picked his way through the crowd. He felt a heat building on his skin, his face flushing with embarrassment as he realized how ridiculous he must look. Renwick knew he did not belong there and so did they.

"Renwick! Over here, lad!" He heard a familiar voice and saw Sir Elgar waving from the center of the square. Never before had he been happy to see him.

"Make room!" Elgar bellowed, and kicked Sir Gilbert and Sir Murthas until they shifted over. Renwick quickly sat down, trying to become invisible.

"Here, lad." Elgar took the shield from him. "Carry it like this." He pulled his arm out roughly and slipped the long strap over his shoulder. "A lot easier that way."

"Thanks," he said, making sure his sword lay flat behind him and was not in anyone's way. Suddenly he felt a jolt as Elgar struck him hard in the chest with his fist like a hammer. Renwick rocked back and looked up, stunned.

"Good armor!" The knight grinned at him and nodded.

A moment later Murthas drew his dagger and hit him hard with the pommel. The sound rang and again Renwick rocked back, shocked, but unharmed. "Excellent."

"Stop!" Renwick shouted, looking at them fearfully.

The two laughed.

"Tradition, boy," Elgar told him. "It is good luck to have new armor tested by friends before enemies. Just praise Novron we're sitting down!"

"Aye!" Sir Gilbert said. "When I got my first helm, Sir Biffard rang it so hard I passed out, but I woke up in the care of Lady Bethany, so I can attest to the good luck of a sound beating on new armor!"

The knights all laughed again.

"Who is this pup?" the man seated across from Renwick asked. His blond hair came nearly to his shoulders, his blue eyes as bright as sapphires. He wore ornate armor inlaid with gold designs of ivy and roses. Over his shoulders he wore a purple velvet cape, held by a solid-gold broach.

"This is Renwick, Your Highness," Murthas replied. "I don't know if he has any other name. He was a page in the palace until recently. Now he is aide-de-camp to Sir Breckton."

"Ah!" the man said. "The fearless rider!"

"Indeed, Your Highness—the same."

"You've done a great service for us, Renwick. I shall be pleased to fight beside you."

"Ah—thank you—ah—"

"You have no idea who I am, do you?" he chuckled, and the rest followed him.

"This is Prince Rudolf of Alburn, son of King Armand," Murthas told him.

"Oh!" Renwick said. "I am honored, Your Highness."

"And well you should be," Murthas said. "There are precious few princes willing to fight beside their knights these days, much less sit with us before the battle."

"Ha!" Rudolf laughed. "Don't flatter me, Murthas. I'm here only to get away from the smothering chatter of women and children. There's a stuffiness to the castle these days. She has them filling the corridors, packed like sausage. You can't piss without a child or woman passing by. And they don't appreciate fine liquor!"

The prince drew forth a crystal decanter of amber liquid,

which he sloshed about merrily. He took the first swallow, smacked his lips loudly, then passed it to Sir Elgar on his right. "From the empress's private stash," the prince told them in an exaggerated whisper. "But I hear she doesn't drink and I'm certain she will not begrudge her knights a bit of warmth on *this* day."

Elgar took a mouthful and handed Renwick the bottle, which he held but did not drink from.

"Ha-ha!" Elgar said, looking at him. "The lad is afraid of getting drunk before his first fight! Drink up, lad, I guarantee that won't be a problem. You could down two such bottles and the fire in your belly would burn up that liquor before it ever reached your head."

Renwick tipped the bottle, swallowed, and felt the liquor burn its way down his throat.

"That-a-boy!" Elgar cheered. "We'll make a man of you today, that's for sure!"

He passed the bottle on to Murthas as overhead huge black clouds swirled and the sky grew dark until it appeared as if dusk had fallen at midday. What light remained cast an eerie green radiance. Lightning continued to flash and thunder cracked. Yet sitting shoulder to shoulder among the stable of men, smelling their sweat, listening to their carefree laughter and the sounds of their belches, curses, and dirty jokes, Renwick felt safe. The liquor warmed him, relaxed him. He placed his hand on the grip of his new sword and squeezed. He thought they could win this battle. He felt that they *would* win, and he would stand among the victors.

"Hide the bottle!" the prince shouted, and Sir Gilbert guiltily stowed it under his shield with a comical look on his face just as Sir Breckton arrived and walked into the center of the circle.

"So there you are!" he said, spotting Renwick. "Got your

armor and sword, I see. Good." He raised his hands to quiet
the crowd. "Men! I have called you together here on behalf of
the empress. Everyone take a knee!"

The soldiers made a loud shuffling of feet and swords. Renwick saw the small, slender figure of the empress Modina
dressed all in white enter the mass of men like a flake of snow
amidst a mound of mud and ash. She stepped up on a box
placed at the center and looked around her, smiling. Several of
the men bowed their heads, but Renwick could not; it was
impossible to take his eyes off her. She was the most beautiful
thing he had ever beheld and he still felt the kiss she had left
on his cheeks. Before that day, he had seen her only once,
when she had addressed the city from the balcony. That day
he had stood in awe like the rest, marveling at her—so
impressive, so powerful. Now, like in the fourth-floor office,
what he saw before him was a woman. The picture of innocence wrapped in a pristine white dress that hung from her as
if she were bathed in light. Modina wore no coat or cloak. Her
unbound hair, glimmering like gold, fell to her shoulders. She
appeared so young, not much older than him, and yet in her
eyes was the aging from years of pain and hard-won wisdom.

"The elves are coming," she began, her voice soft and faint
against the wind. "Reports tell of a host moving up the road
from the south. No one has yet provided an accurate number
or assessment of troops." She looked to the sky and took a
breath. "We are the last stronghold of mankind. You are the
last army, the last warriors, the last defenders of our race. If
they should take this city…" She hesitated and a few bowed
heads looked up.

She looked back as if taking in each face.

"None of you know me," she said, her voice changing, losing its formal tone. "Some have seen me on a balcony or in a
corridor. Some have heard stories about me, of me being a

goddess and the daughter of Novron—your savior. But you don't know me." She raised her arms out at her sides and slowly turned around. "I am Thrace Wood of Dahlgren Village, daughter of Theron and Addie. I was but a poor peasant from a family of farmers. My brother Thaddeus—Thad— was going to be a cooper until one night I left the door to my home open when I went to find my father. The light..." She hesitated and the pause gripped Renwick's heart. "The light through the open door attracted an elven monster. It ripped my home apart and killed my family. It killed the boy I hoped that I might one day marry. It killed my best friends, their parents, even the livestock. Then it killed my father—the last reason I had to live. But it did not kill me. I survived. I did not want to. My family—my life—was gone."

She looked out at them and he watched as her soft chin hardened as she gritted her teeth.

"But then I found a new family—a new life." She held her hands out to them and tears glistened in her eyes even as her voice grew stronger, louder. "You are my family now, my fathers, my brothers, my sons, and I will never leave the door open again. I will *not* let the beast in. I will never let it win again! It has taken too much from me, from you, from all of us! It has destroyed Dunmore, Ghent, Melengar, Trent, and Alburn. Many of you have lost your homes, your land, your families and now it comes here, but it shall go no farther! Here we stop it! Here we fight! Here we face our enemy without running, without flinching, without bending. Here we stand our ground and here we kill it!"

The knights cheered; the soldiers rose to their feet and beat their swords on their shields.

"The enemy comes, Sir Breckton," she shouted over the clamor. "Sound the alarm."

Breckton waved a hand and men on the roofs of shops

stood up and blared fanfares of long brass horns. The sound was repeated throughout the city as other horns echoed the call. Soon Renwick could hear the bells of the churches ringing. People in the streets quickly heeded the signal and headed for the shelters.

"To the walls, men!" Breckton ordered, and they all rose.

Lightning cracked again; this time Renwick saw the crooked finger of light strike the grain silo on Coswall Avenue. There were a flash and then flame as the roof exploded in fire.

≼

"Everyone into the dungeon!" Amilia shouted, standing on top of the wagon in the center of the courtyard as, overhead, lightning flashed and tower roofs exploded.

Only minutes before, a strike had hit something not too far behind her in the city. She felt a strange tingle on her skin and her hair rose as if lifted by dozens of invisible fingers. There was the taste of metal in her mouth; then a blinding light was followed instantly by a deafening crack. Something exploded and nearly threw her from the cart. Shaking, like a bird on a rock in the middle of a surging river, she remained on the wagon, shouting to the throng of people exiting the castle. She pointed them toward the north tower and the entrance to the old dungeon. They all had the same expression, terror imprinted over bewilderment. Poor and rich, peasant and noble, they filed out pushing and crowding, heads tilted toward the sky, cringing with each flash, screaming with each boom of thunder.

"Inside the tower! Move to your left! Don't push!" She swept her arms to the side in frustration, as if this would somehow move the crowd where she wanted them to go.

The attack came all too suddenly. They had expected horns. They had expected drums. They had expected to see an army coming up the road. They had expected plenty of time to move the population of the city underground—they had never expected this.

At least Amilia's family was already in the dungeon. They had all been lingering in the courtyard, having just seen Modina off to her troop address, when the storm began and the alarm sounded. But now she worried about Modina and Breckton. The empress would be gone only a short time, she knew, but Breckton would be going to the fight. She ached the moment he had left her side, and she worried for his safety all the time. Even while they were together, even when he had stood before her father asking for her hand in marriage, there was a shadow, a fear. It hovered and spoke to her of dangers that awaited him—dangers she would not be allowed to share. Fate had a way of making men like him into heroes, and heroes did not die quietly in bed while holding their wife's hand after a long and happy life.

Crack!

She cringed as a flash blinded her. The silver necklace—an engagement gift from Sir Breckton—buzzed around her throat like a living thing and then the roof of the south tower exploded. Chips of slate rained on the ward, the tower became a flaming torch. A sea of screams surrounded her as people scattered or fell to their knees, throwing hands over their heads and wailing at the sky. Amilia watched a young boy collapse under the push of the crowd. A woman, struck in the face with a slate shingle, fell in a burst of blood.

All around the city, lightning struck as if the gods themselves made war upon them. Smoke rose and flames terrified people who struggled to reach the safety of the shelters.

"Amilia! It's no good!" Nimbus called to her as he forced his way with a pair of soldiers against the human current, pushing out of the tower toward her. "The dungeon is filled!"

"How can that be? Are you sure?"

"Yes, yes, all those refugees, we didn't account for them. The cells and corridors are packed solid. We have to send the rest back inside."

"Oh dear Novron," she said, and began waving her arms over her head. "Listen to me! Listen to me. Stop and listen. You need to go back inside!"

No one responded. Maybe they could not hear her, or maybe it did not matter as they continued to be swept forward by the current. Another loud boom of thunder sounded and the people pushed all that much harder. A thick forest of bodies pressed up against the tower and the stables. She could see women and old men being crushed against the stone.

"Stop! *Stop!*" she cried, but the mob was deaf. Like a herd of mindless sheep, they pushed and shoved. A man tried to climb over the woman in front of him in an attempt to get past the mass of people. He was thrown down and did not come up again.

Bodies pressed against the sides of the cart and shook it. Amilia staggered and gripped the side in fear. A hand grabbed her wrist. "Help me!" an elderly woman with bloody scratch marks down the side of her face screamed at her.

A trumpet blared and a drum rolled. Amilia spun to look back at the courtyard's gate. There she saw a white horse and on it was Modina in her equally white dress. She was a vision, riding straight and tall. Her hair and dress billowed behind her. Arms reached out of the swarm of bodies with fingers pointing and Amilia heard shouts of "The empress! The empress!"

"There is no more room in the dungeon," Amilia shouted

to her, and saw Modina nod calmly as she urged her mount forward, parting the crowd.

She raised a hand. "Those of you who can hear my voice, do not fear, do not despair," she shouted. "Return quietly to the castle. Go to the great hall and await me there."

Amilia watched in amazement at the magical effect her words had on the mob. She could feel a collective sigh, a relief pass across the courtyard. The tide changed and the herd reversed direction, moving back into the palace, moving slower, some pausing to help others.

"You should come inside too," Modina told Amilia, and soldiers helped the empress dismount and Amilia climb down from the wagon.

"Breckton? Is he..."

"He's doing his job," she said, handing her reins over to a young boy. "And we need to do ours."

"And what is our job?"

"Right now it is to get everyone inside and keep them as calm as possible. After that, we'll see."

"How do you do it?" Amilia slapped her sides in frustration. "How?"

"What?" Modina asked.

"How can you remain so calm, so unaffected, when the world is coming to an end?"

Modina smirked. "I've already seen the world end once. Nothing is ever as impressive the second time around."

"Do you really think it is coming to an end?" Nimbus asked as the three of them moved—far too slowly for Amilia—toward the palace doors, where the last of the crowd disappeared.

"For us, perhaps," Amilia replied. "And just look at that sky! Have you ever seen clouds swirl like that? If they can control the weather, call down lightning, and freeze rivers, how can we hope to survive?"

"We can always hope," Nimbus told her. "I never give up hope, and I've seen that spark perform miracles."

❧

The lightning storm that ripped through the city stopped. Even the wind paused, as if holding its breath. Renwick stood on the battlement of the southern gate between Captain Everton and Sir Breckton at the center of a line of men with armor glinting in shafts of light that moved across the wall. They stood bravely with grim faces, holding shields and swords, waiting.

"Look at them, lad," Sir Breckton told him, nodding down the length of the wall. "They are all here because of you. Every man on this wall is prepared because of your warning." His hand came down on Renwick's shoulder. "No matter what else you do today, remember that—remember you are already a hero who has given us a fighting chance."

Renwick looked beyond the battlements to the hills and fields. In his left hand, he held on to a bit of wax he picked off a candle at breakfast, which at that moment felt like a month earlier. He played with it between his fingers, squeezing it, molding it. He could still taste the liquor on his tongue, still smell it, but the warmth was gone.

Outside the city the world was melting. The road was dark brown even though the hills remained white. In the stillness, he could hear the drizzle of water. Streaks of wetness teared down the face of the stone and soaked into the earth. Water streamed in the low places, gurgling in a friendly, playful manner. On the trees, buds grew large on the tips of branches. Spring was coming, warmer days, grass, flowers, rain. In another month or so, they would welcome the first caravans to visit the city bringing fresh faces and new stories. A few weeks after that, vendors would open their street stands in the squares and farmers would plow the fields. The smell of manure would blow in, pungent and earthy. Girls would cast aside their heavy cloaks and walk the streets once more in bright-colored dresses. People would speak of coming fairs, the new fashions, and the need for more workers to clear the remains of winter's debris. Renwick found it strange that he had not realized until that moment just how much he loved spring.

He did not want to die that day, not while the promise of so much lay before him. He looked at the line of men again.

Are we all thinking the same thing?

He felt comfort in their numbers, a consolation in knowing he was not alone. If they failed, farmers would not plow their fields, girls would not sing in the streets, and there would be no more fairs. Spring might still come but only for the flowers and trees. Everything else, all that he loved, would be gone.

He thought of Elbright, Brand, Mince, and Kine back under the holly tree in the Hovel.

Do they wonder what happened to me? What will they do once Aquesta is gone? When I'm gone with it? Will they remember me?

Movement to the south broke his thoughts and Renwick looked out along the road. A column of riders approached slowly like a parade—no, a funeral procession. He spotted only glimpses of them through the shutter of dark trees and gray stones, blue and gold on white horses. Accompanying them was the sound of music.

"Wax your ears!" Breckton shouted.

The command relayed down the line and everyone, including Renwick, stuffed the soft substance in his ears. Breckton turned to him, nodded, and smiled, sharing their secret.

Renwick smiled back.

The troop of elves came into full view and fanned out in the field before the southern wall. Mince had been right about them. The elves were dazzling. Each rider wore a golden helm in the shape of a wolf's head and carried a golden spear. The foremost riders bore streaming silver banners. They wore strange armor—shirts of leafed metal that looked light and flexible and greaves that seemed no more than soft satin, all of which shone brilliantly beneath a column of sunlight that followed them.

They sat on animals that Renwick called horses because he had no other word, but they were unlike any he had seen before. These noble creatures pranced rather than walked. They moved in unison with such grace as to mesmerize and bewitch. They wore bridles and caparisons of gold and silk that glistened as if made of water and ice. They formed up and waited with only their banners moving in the breeze and Renwick wondered if they made the wind for just that purpose.

Renwick counted a hundred, no more. A hundred in light armor could be defeated.

Perhaps they won all their other battles by putting their enemies to sleep.

Renwick's heart leapt at the possibility, but as he watched, trying to look into their eyes, he saw more movement on the road. Another column was coming, foot soldiers with heavier banded mail, large curved shields as bright as mirrors, and long spears with strange hooked blades. Their helms were the faces of bears. These troops moved in perfect unison. Like a school of fish or a flock of birds, they banked and turned. Their movements were graceful beyond anything Renwick had ever seen of men. They formed up in rows, and once in position, not one shifted or so much as adjusted a helm or coughed. Three deep they stood in a line that ran the length of the wall, and still more came. These new troops, in light armor like the cavalry's, wore bows with tips that swirled like the tendrils of ivy, and strings that glimmered blue when the sunlight touched them. Their helms were in the shape of hawks' faces.

Still more issued into sight, and even with waxed ears, Renwick could feel the march of these new elements drum against his chest. Great beasts the likes of which he had never seen approached. Powerful animals twice the size of any bull or ox, with horns on their heads. They hauled great devices two and three stories tall, built of poles and levers of white, silver, and green. Ten such devices emerged from the brown bristle tops of barren trees to take position at the rear.

When the last troop was in place, there were at least two thousand elves waiting before the wall. Then more riders appeared. There were no more than twenty and yet to Renwick they were the most frightening yet. They rode black horses, wore no armor, and were dressed only in shimmering robes that appeared to change color. On their heads were masks of spiders. Behind them came twenty more riders. These wore chest plates of gold and long sweeping capes of rich purple. Their helms were the heads of lions.

As Renwick watched, those on the black horses raised their arms in unison and all made identical motions of a complicated pattern that seemed like a dance of arms and hands. He stood fascinated by the fluid gestures. The dance abruptly ended as the twenty clapped their hands, and even through the wax Renwick heard the *boom*.

The ground quaked, and a tremor shook the wall. He felt it sway and saw the men beside him stagger. Cracks formed, fissures opened, chips of stone splintered and fell. Beyond the wall, trees shook as if alive and the earth broke apart. Hills separated from each other, one rising, the other lowering. Great gulfs appeared, ravines forming, jagged cracks that sundered the land and raced at them.

Another jolt struck the wall. Renwick felt the stone snap, the shudder shooting up his legs, making his teeth click. More cracking, more tremors, and then, between the fourth and fifth towers, the curtain wall collapsed. Men screamed as they fell along with thousand-pound blocks of stone into a cloud of exploding dust. The tower to the left of the southern gate slipped its footing, wavered, and toppled, raining stone on a dozen men. The tremor, having passed through the wall, continued through the city like a wave. Buildings collapsed. Streets broke apart and trees fell. Imperial Square divided itself in two — the platform the empress had recently stood on was swallowed by a jagged crevasse. In the distance, the imperial cathedral's tower cracked and fell.

The shaking of the earth stopped but the elves did not move. They did not advance.

"We need reinforcements on that shattered wall now!" Sir Breckton shouted down the line as he reached for his horn, his voice muffled, sounding like Renwick was hearing it underwater. "Wave the red flag!"

Renwick turned to see Captain Everton lying dead, crushed by a block of stone. He did not think. He took up the flag dropped on the stone and waved it above his head. Beside him, Breckton blew on his trumpet until another flag responded.

The mist of dust had only just begun to settle when Renwick heard a cry that no amount of wax could block out. The screech came from overhead and he felt a burst of air as a great shadow flashed across the ground. Looking up, he caught sight of a horror that seized him with fear. A great serpent beast with a long tail and leathery wings flew above him. Clearing the wall, the creature dove with claws that cleaved roofs and walls; then, like a barn swallow, the monster swooped upward, hovered for just a moment, and as Renwick watched, let loose a torrent of flame that bathed the homes and shops below. The creature was not alone. Renwick spotted others; dozens of winged serpents swept out of the swirling clouds and descended on the city. Like a swarm of bats, they swooped, banked, and dove, crushing, clawing, and burning. Within minutes, the whole city was ablaze.

Renwick felt tears on his cheeks. Smoke filled his nostrils, and even through the wax, he could hear the screams. Breckton's hand grabbed him roughly and shoved him back hard. He cried out, but it was too late. Renwick lost his balance and fell off the battlement, plummeting and crashing through the thatch roof of the guardhouse stable. He hit the soft, manure-warmed ground on his back, and every bit of air was driven from him. He could not move or breathe. The wax was out of his ears and sounds flooded his head. The hammering of hooves and the cries of horses were the loudest. Farther away—screaming, snapping, splintering wood, cracking fire, and always the screeching shrieks from the flying beasts.

Renwick managed short shallow breaths as he worked to fill his lungs again. His arms and legs moved once more, and he rolled carefully to his side. It hurt. His head throbbed, his neck ached, and his back was sore. Just as he got to his knees, the stable's roof was ripped away and three horses were stolen from their stalls. They were pulled into the air by two great talons.

He ran, his feet struggling to stay out ahead of him. Fire was everywhere. He was looking toward the gate, searching for Sir Breckton and his post, but everything was gone—the entire southern gate was missing. Only rubble and a shattered bit of slivered wood remained. Under the pile, he saw hands and feet.

The massive stone wall that had ringed the city was gone. Renwick stood on the street, looking out at the elven forces, feeling naked. Then the front row of hawk-helmed archers bent their bows and the sky darkened with a flight of arrows.

It felt like someone else controlled his body as his hands reached behind him and pulled his shield free of his shoulder. He slid one arm through the straps and raised it over his head. The sound was like hail as the arrows peppered the ground, glinting off the cobblestone around him and lodging in the wood of buildings. Three punched through his shield, safely caught, but one went through the back of his hand. He saw it before feeling the pain. Blood sprayed his face. He stared at the shaft protruding through his palm as if it were another person's hand.

"You're alive!" Sir Elgar shouted, his hulking frame casting a shadow over him. "That-a-boy! But get your ass up. This is no time to rest."

"My hand!" Renwick screamed.

Sir Elgar looked under the shield and grinned. Without a word he snapped off the arrow's point and pulled the shaft out. The pain made Renwick's legs weak and his breath shudder. He fell to his knees.

"Up, boy!" Elgar shouted at him. "It's only a scratch."

As absurd as it seemed, Renwick nodded, knowing Elgar was right, and marveled at how little it hurt. Pushing off the ground with the edge of his shield, still ornamented with the four white-feathered shafts, he got to his feet.

Elgar's own shield held two similar decorations. Another arrow was embedded in the knight's shoulder and Renwick grimaced when he saw it.

"Ha-ha! A bee sting is all." The knight laughed. His right cheek bled from a deep gash along the bone. "Murthas, Rudolf, Gilbert—all dead. The wall is gone. There's nothing for it. It's back to the palace for us. We have but one task remaining, one defense left to make."

"Breckton?"

"Alive."

"Where? I must go—"

"His orders are to defend the empress." Elgar grinned and drew his blade. "Break that stick off me, will ya?"

⋘

Everyone in the great hall sat looking up, watching the progress of the crack that formed along the ceiling of the room. It started at the eastern side and rapidly traced a jagged path to the west. Bits of plaster fell, flakes and chips; then whole clumps dropped and people dove aside as the pieces shattered on the marble floor, scattering white chalk in all directions. The robin's egg–blue sky was falling.

Modina ignored the ceiling. She moved slowly through the crowd, taking note of each person, each face, making eye contact and offering a reassuring smile. Mostly women and children were there. A few peasant families, like the Bothwicks, sat on the floor in small packed groups. They rocked and prayed, whispered and wept. All those who did not find room in the dungeon gathered around the great chamber, where only a few months earlier knights and ladies had dined on their Wintertide meals. Tables that had once served venison and duck for kings now provided protection from falling debris for cobblers, midwives, and charwomen. Even the man and his goat found a space under one of the oak tables. The castle guards, servants, and kitchen staff also came when the tremors began.

Knights and soldiers entered the hall torn and bloody, blackened from fire, telling tales of destruction and flight. Duke Leo of Rochelle was carried in on a stretcher by the viscount Albert Winslow and a man called Brice the Barker. They set him down before the duchess, who took her husband's hand and kissed his bald forehead, saying, "You've had your fun, now stay with me. Do you hear me, old man? It's not over. Not yet."

Brice pushed through the crowd to his family, huddled near the statue of Novron, and joined them with tears filling his eyes. His wife looked up, searching the crowd. Her eyes met Modina's but she was not who the woman looked for.

The Pickerings, Belinda, Lenare, and Denek, sat with Alenda and her maid Emily as well as Julian, the chamberlain of Melengar. Not far away, Cosmos DeLur and his father, Cornelius, sat against the east wall under the tapestry of ships returning from a voyage. The two fat men sprawled in their fine clothes and jeweled rings. A group of thin gangly men circled them, crouching like nervous dogs at the foot of their master's feet during a thunderstorm.

Modina walked by a cluster of women in low-cut gowns. Their tears left dark trails through heavy makeup. One looked up with curious eyes and nudged another, who scowled and shook her head. It was not until Modina was several steps past the group that she recalled the faces of Clarisse and Maggie from Colnora's Bawdy Bottom Brothel.

She returned to Allie and Mercy, who sat with Amilia, Nimbus, Ibis, Cora, Gerald, and Anna. They formed a ring within which the two girls sat. Mr. Rings was taking shelter on Mercy's shoulder, while Red, the elkhound, sat beside Ibis, the big cook holding him close.

"Will they kill me too?" Allie asked.

"I don't know," Anna told her.

"I don't want to be left," the little girl said, burying her head in Anna's lap. Sir Elgar and Renwick entered, both bleeding. Amilia spotted them and stood up, looking beyond them toward the door.

"Sir Breckton?" Amilia asked as they approached. "Is he..."

"Alive the last I saw him, milady," Elgar replied. "The wall is gone, the line broken, Your Eminence," he said to Modina. "A whirlwind ripped apart the flanking cavalry Breckton had hidden to the north. I watched it throw a two-ton stone around like a feather. Then the elves came. They moved like deer and struck like snakes, blades swinging faster than the eye could follow. The encounter lasted just minutes. They even killed the horses.

"Then the flying beasts came, and the arrows. Our troops are mostly dead. Those that live are scattered, wounded, blinded by smoke, and blocked by fire. The elves already have the city. They will be coming here next."

Modina did not respond. She wanted to sit—to fall down—but she remained standing. She had to stand. Around her, everyone was watching, checking to see if she was still with them, still unafraid.

She was afraid.

Not for herself—not a thought of her own welfare crossed her mind. She could not recall the last time she worried for her own safety. She worried for them. The scene was all too familiar. She had been here before, with a family to protect and no means to do so. A weight in her chest made it difficult to breathe.

A loud boom thundered outside, followed by screams. Heads turned toward the windows in fear. Then, from across the room, near the glowing hearth, an elderly woman with gray hair and a torn dress began to sing. The song was soft—a lilting lullaby—and Modina recognized the tune immediately, although she had not heard it in many years. It was a common tune among the poor, a mother's lament often sung to children. She remembered every word, and like the others in the hall, she found herself joining in as a hundred whispered voices offered up the prayer.

In the dark, when night's chill cuts
Cold as death they climb the hill
Breaking door and windowpane
They come to burn, slash, and kill.

Shadows pounding on the door
They beat the drums of fear
Place your faith in Maribor
And loudly, so he hears.

Waves they crash upon the bow
Of withered ship at sea
Wind and weather rip the sails
There's little hope for thee.

Shadows pounding on the hull
They beat the drums of fear
Place your faith in Maribor
And loudly, so he hears.

Within darkling wood you walk
So foolish after all
Footsteps follow, catching up
You run until you fall.

Shadows pounding on the path
They beat the drums of fear
Place your faith in Maribor
And loudly, so he hears.

When man stood upon the brink
Novron saved us all

Sent by god above he was
In answer to our call.

Shadows pounding on the gate
They beat the drums so near
If your faith's in Maribor
He's with you, never fear.

Another tremor shook the room. The marble floor snapped like a thin cracker splitting as one side rose sharply and the other fell. The room exploded with screams. The maid, Emily of Glouston, fell over the side of the forming chasm and was caught at the last moment by Lenare Pickering and Alenda Lanaklin, who each managed to grasp a wrist. Another shudder rocked the hall and all three slid toward the edge. Tad and Russell Bothwick lunged out, grabbing ankles and pulling back, hauling the ladies to higher ground.

"Hang on to each other, for Novron's sake!" the Duchess of Rochelle shouted. Cold air was blowing. Modina could feel it against her cheek. A great fissure had ripped apart the windowed side of the hall. The wall wavered like a drunken man.

"Get away!" Modina ordered, motioning with her hands.

Bodies scurried as the partition collapsed amidst cries and screams cut horribly short. Stone and ceiling came down, exploding in bursts that cracked the floor. Modina staggered as she watched thirty people die, crushed to death.

Those nearby pulled the wounded from the debris. Modina saw a hand and moved forward, digging into the rubble, scraping at the stone, hurling rocks aside. She recognized him by his ink-stained fingers. She lifted the scribe's limp head to her chest, wondering painfully why it was by his hand and not by his face she knew him. He was not breathing and blood dripped from his nose and eyes.

"Your Eminence." Nimbus spoke to her.

"Modina?" Amilia called, her voice shaking.

Modina turned and saw everyone watching her, the room silent. Every face frightened, every pair of eyes pleading. She stood up slowly, as she might within a flock of birds. Panic was a moment away. She could hear the frantic breathing all around her, the cry of children, the tears of mothers, the hum of men who rocked back and forth.

She took a deep breath and wiped the scribe's blood on her gown, leaving a streaked handprint. She faced the open air of the missing wall and walked the way Nimbus and Amilia had once taught her to, her head up and shoulders back. Modina waded through the room of stares, like a pond of murky water. Only the sight of her checked their fear. She was the last remaining pillar that held up the sky, the last hope in a place that hope no longer called home.

When she reached the courtyard, she stopped. Half the great hall was gone, but the courtyard was in ruins. The towers and front gate lay on the ground like so many scattered children's blocks. The bake house and chapel collapsed along with one side of the granary—barley spilling across the dirt. Oddly, the woodpile near the kitchen was still stacked.

Without the outer wall enclosing the ward, she could see the city. Columns of fire rose from every quarter. Black smoke and ash billowed like ghosts across the rendered landscape. Men lay dead or dying. She could see bodies of soldiers, knights, merchants, and laborers lying in the streets. Missing buildings formed gaps across a vista she knew so well, old friends once framed by her window—gone. Others stood askew, tilted, missing pieces. In the dark air, familiar shapes flew, circling. She saw them turn, wheeling in arcs, banking like hawks, coming around toward her. A thunderous shriek screamed from above the courtyard and a great winged Gilarabrywn landed where once there had been a vegetable garden.

She looked behind her.

"Do you believe in me?" she asked simply. "Do you believe I can save you?"

Silence, but a few heads nodded, Amilia's and Nimbus's among them.

"I am the daughter of the last emperor," she said with a loud clear voice. "I am the daughter of Novron, the Daughter of Maribor. I am Empress Modina Novronian! This is my city, my land, and you are my people. The elves will not have you!"

At the sound of her voice, the Gilarabrywn turned and focused on her.

Modina looked back at those in the great hall. Russell Bothwick had his arms around Lena and Tad, and Nimbus had his arms around Amilia, who looked back at her and began to cry.

CHAPTER 24

THE GIFT

It is as silent as a tomb, Hadrian thought as he sat in the darkness. The last lantern had died some time ago, as had the last conversation. Royce had been quizzing Myron on linguistics, but even that stopped.

He was in the tomb of Novron, the resting place of the savior of mankind. This place was thought to be mythical, a fable, a legend, yet here he was. Hadrian was one of the first to reach it in a thousand years. Truly a feat—an astounding achievement.

Hadrian rested against a wall, his right arm on what was most likely an urn worth ten thousand gold tenents. His feet were up on a solid-gold statue of a ram. He would die a very rich man, at least.

Look what you have come to. He heard his father's voice ringing in his head, deep and powerful, the way he always remembered it being when he was a boy. He could almost see his old man towering above him covered in sweat, wearing his leather apron, and holding his tongs.

You took all that I taught you and squandered it for money and fame. What has it bought you? You have more riches at your feet than any king and they still chant Galenti *in the east, but was your life worth living now that it has come to its end? Is this what you sought when you left Hintindar? Is this the greatness you desired?*

Hadrian took his hand off the urn and pulled his feet off the ram.

You told me you were going to be a great hero. Show me, then. Show me one thing worth the life you spent. One thing wrought. One thing won. One thing earned. One thing learned. Does such a thing exist? Is there anything to show?

Hadrian tilted his head and looked out toward the crypt. There, in the distance, he saw the dim blue glow.

He stared at it for some time. In the darkness he could not tell how long. The light grew and fell slightly—with her breathing, he guessed. He had no real idea how it worked, whether the shift was of her making or the robe's.

Is there anything to show? he asked himself.

Hadrian stood up and, reaching out with his hands, moved along the wall to the opening into the crypt. There was no one out here but her. She was in one of the alcoves, sitting behind a sarcophagus, the one with the scenes of natural landscapes carved on the sides. Her head was resting on her knees, her arms wrapped around her legs.

He sat beside her, and as he did, the light from her robe brightened slightly and her head lifted. Her cheeks were streaked from tears. She blinked at him and wiped her eyes.

"Hi," she said.

"Hello," he replied. "Dream?"

Arista paused, then shook her head sadly. "No—no, I didn't. What does that mean, I wonder."

"I think it means we're done."

Arista nodded. "I suppose so."

"Everyone is in the tomb. Why did you come over here?"

"I dunno," she said. "I wanted to be alone, I guess. I was

reviewing my life—all the things I regret. What I never did. What I should have. What I did that I wished I hadn't. You know, fun, entertaining stuff like that. That kind of thinking is best done alone, you know? What about you? What were you thinking?"

"Same sort of thing."

"Oh yeah? What did you come up with?"

"Well," he said, clearing his throat. "Funny you should ask. There's a whole lot of things I wished I hadn't done, but... as turns out, there's really only one thing I wished I had done but didn't."

She raised her eyebrows. "Really? You're a fortunate man—almost as good as Myron."

"Heh, yeah," he said uncomfortably.

"What is it, this thing you haven't done?"

"Well, it's like this. I'm—I'm actually envious of Royce right now. I never thought I'd say that, but it's true. Royce had the kind of life that mothers warn their children they will have if they don't behave. It was like the gods had it out for him the day he was born. It's little wonder he turned out as he did. When I first met him, he was quite scary."

"Was?"

"Oh yeah, not like he is now—*real* scary—the never-turn-your-back brand of scary. But Arcadius saw something in him that no one else did. I suppose that's something wizards can do, see into men's souls. Notice what the rest of the world can't about a person."

Hadrian shifted uneasily, feeling the cold stone of the floor through a thick layer of fine dust. He crossed his legs and leaned slightly forward.

"It took Royce a long time to trust anyone. To be honest, I'm not even sure he fully trusts me yet, but he did trust her. Gwen changed Royce. She did the impossible by making him happy. Even now, the idea of Royce smiling—in a good way—is—I dunno, like snow falling in summer, or sheep curling up with wolves. You don't get that kind of thing from just liking a girl. There was something special there, something profound. He only had her briefly, but at least he knows what that feels like. You know what I mean?"

"Yes," she said. "I do."

"That's what I regret."

"You can't regret that," she said, nearly laughing. "How can you regret never having found true love? That's like saying you regret not being born a genius. People don't have control over such things. It either happens or it doesn't. It's a gift—a present that most never get. It's more like a miracle, really, when you think of it. I mean, first you have to find that person, and then you have to get to know them to realize just what they mean to you—that right there is ridiculously difficult. Then..." She paused a moment, looking far away. "Then that person has to feel the same way about you. It's like searching for a specific snowflake, and even if you manage to find it, that's not good enough. You still have to find its matching pair. What are the odds? Hilfred found it, I think. He loved me."

"Did you love him?"

"Yes, but not the way he wanted me to. Not the way he loved me. I wish I had. I feel I should have. It was the same with Emery. I actually feel guilty that I didn't. Maybe with time I could have loved Emery, but I hardly knew him."

"And Hilfred?"

"I don't know. He was more like a brother to me, I suppose. I wanted to make him happy, the way I wanted to see Alric happy. But you see, that's just what I'm talking about. Most people never come near their true love, or if they do, it's one sided. That is perhaps more tragic than never finding love at all. To know joy lies forever just beyond your reach—in a way, it's a kind of torture. So you see, if you don't have control, if it's not a choice, then not finding the one you love is really nothing to regret, is it?"

"Well, that's just the thing. I did find her and I never told her how I feel."

"Oh—that *is* awful," she said, then caught herself and raised a hand to cover her mouth. "I'm so sorry. That was terrible of me. No wonder I was such a lousy ambassador. I'm just the embodiment of tact, aren't I? Here your— Oh!" she suddenly exclaimed as a look of revelation came over her face. "I know who she is."

Hadrian suddenly felt very warm; his skin prickled uncomfortably under his shirt.

"She's very pretty, by the way."

"Ah—" Hadrian stared at her, confused.

"Her name isn't actually Emerald, is it? I heard someone call her that."

"Emerald? You think I'm talking about—"

"Aren't you?" She appeared embarrassed and cautiously said, "I saw her kissing you when we left."

Hadrian chuckled. "Her real name is Falina and she is a nice girl, but no, I'm not speaking of her. No, the woman I'm talking about is *nothing* like her."

"Oh," the princess said softly. "So why have you never told her how you feel?"

"I have a list somewhere." He patted his shirt with his hands, trying to be funny, but he just felt stupid.

She smiled at him. He liked seeing her smile.

"No really—why?"

"I'm not kidding. I really do have a list. It's just not written down. I keep adding items to it. There's so many reasons on it now."

"Give me a few."

"Well, the big one is that she's noble."

"Oh, I see," she said gravely, "but that's not impossible. It depends on the girl, of course, but noble ladies have married common men before. It's not unheard of."

"Rich merchants, perhaps, but how many ladies do you know of that ran off with a common thief?"

"You're hardly a common thief," she chided him sternly. "But I suppose I can see your point. You're right that there aren't many noblewomen who could see past both a common background and a disreputable career. Lenare Lanaklin, for one—it's not her, is it?" She cringed slightly.

"No, it's not Lenare."

"Oh, good." She sighed, pretending to wipe sweat from her brow. "Don't get me wrong, I love Lenare like a sister, but she's not right for you."

"I know."

"Still, some women, even noblewomen, can be attracted to outlaws. They hear tales of daring and they can get swept away by the intrigue—I've seen it."

"But what about obligations? Even if she wanted to, she couldn't turn her back on her responsibilities. There are titles and land holdings at stake."

"Another good point."

"Is that what kept *you* from getting married?" he asked.

"Me? Oh dear Maribor, no." She smiled bitterly. "I'm sure Alric wanted to marry me off to a number of prominent allies for that very reason. If my father hadn't been killed, I'm sure I would be married to Prince Rudolf of Alburn right now." She shivered dramatically for effect. "Thankfully, Alric was a kind man—I never would have expected it from him when we were younger, but he never would force me. I don't know of too many others who would have done the same."

"So why didn't you?"

"Marry, you mean?" She laughed a little uneasily. "You might find this hard to believe, Hadrian—given my immense beauty and all—but Emery was the first man to show an interest. At least, he was the first to actually say anything to me. I'm not like Lenare or Alenda. Men aren't attracted to me and the whole witch thing doesn't help. No, Emery was the first, and I honestly believe that if he'd gotten to know me better, he would have changed his mind. He didn't live long enough to figure out it was just infatuation. It was the same with Hilfred." She paused and looked away from him, a sadness overtaking her. "I suppose I should be happy that so few have ever showed an interest in me, or I might have more blood on my hands."

"I don't follow."

"Only Emery and Hilfred expressed feelings for me." She hesitated a moment. "And each time, within something less than a week, they died."

"It wasn't your fault."

"It was my idea to stage the revolt that killed Emery, and it was my plan to save Gaunt that killed Hilfred. My plans— always my plans."

"Emery would have died in the square if it wasn't for you."

"And Hilfred?" she taunted.

"Hilfred made his own choice, just as you did. I'm sure he knew the risks. It wasn't your fault."

"I still feel cursed, like I'm not supposed to be happy— that way."

He thought she might speak again and waited. They sat in silence for several minutes. He watched her close her eyes and he took another breath. This was harder than he had expected.

"The real reason I never told her," Hadrian went on, his

own voice sounding awkward to him, odd and off key, "if I am honest with myself, is that I'm scared."

She rolled her head to look at him with a sidelong glance. "Scared? You? Really?"

"I guess I was afraid she'd laugh at me. Or worse, become angry and hate me. That's the worst thing I can think of—that she would hate me. I'm not sure I could live with that. You see, I'm very much in love with her, and I'd rather be drawn and quartered than have her hate me."

He watched as Arista's shoulders sank. Her eyes drifted from his face, and her mouth tightened. "Sounds like a lucky woman. It's a shame she's not here now. There's not much to lose at this point. It could give you the courage to tell her, knowing that if she hates you, you'll not have to endure the pain for long."

Hadrian smiled and nodded.

Arista took a breath and sat up. "Do I know her?" She cringed again, as if expecting to be struck.

Hadrian sighed heavily.

"What?" she asked. "I do know her, don't I? You would have told me her name by now if I didn't. Oh come on. It hardly seems worth keeping the secret at this point."

"That's it exactly," he said. "The reason I was thinking all this is because..." He paused, looking into her eyes. They were like pools he was preparing to jump into without knowing the temperature of the water. He braced himself for the shock. "The one thing I regret the most in my life is the one thing I can still change before it's too late."

Arista narrowed her eyes at him. She tilted her head slightly the way a dog might when it heard an odd sound. "But how are you going to—" She stopped.

Her mouth closed and she stared at him without speaking,

without moving. Hadrian was not certain she was still
breathing.

Slowly her lower lip began to tremble. It started there and
he watched as the tremor worked its way down her neck to her
shoulders, shaking her body so that her hair quivered. Without warning tears spilled down her cheeks. Still she did not
speak, she did not move, but the robe changed from blue to
bright purple, surrounding both of them with light.

What does that mean?

"Arista?" he whispered fearfully. The look on her face was
unfathomable.

Fear? Shock? Remorse? What is it?

He desperately needed to know. He had just thrown himself off a cliff and could not see the bottom.

"Are you upset?" he asked. "Please don't be mad—don't
hate me. I don't want to die with you hating me. This is exactly
why I never said anything. I was afraid that—"

Her fingers came up to his lips and gently pressed them
shut.

"Shh," she managed to utter as she continued to cry, her
eyes never leaving his face.

She took his hands in hers and squeezed. "I don't hate
you," she whispered. "I just—I—" She bit her lip.

"What!" Hadrian said in desperation, his eyes wide, trying
to see everything, searching for any clue. She was torturing
him on purpose—he knew it.

"This is going to sound really stupid," she told him, shaking her head slowly.

"I don't care—say it. Whatever it is, just say it!"

"I—" She laughed a little. "I don't think I've ever been
happier in my entire life than I am right now."

It was his turn to stare. His mouth opened but his mind

could not supply words. He was lost in her eyes and realized he could breathe once more.

"If you knew that I—how much I hoped—" She tilted her head down so that her hair hid her face. "I never thought that you saw me as anything more than a—a job." She raised her head and sniffled. "And the way you and Royce talked about nobles..."

Hadrian noticed his heart was beating again. It pounded in his chest, and despite the chill in the crypt, his shirt was soaked with sweat, his hands trembling.

"We're gonna die here," she told him, and abruptly started laughing. "But suddenly I don't care anymore. I never thought I could be so happy."

This got him laughing too. Somewhere inside him, relief and joy were mixing together to create an intoxicant more powerful than any liquor. He felt drunk, dizzy, and—more than ever before—alive.

"I feel—I feel so..." She laughed once and looked embarrassed.

"What?" he asked, reaching up and wiping the tears from her cheeks.

"It's like I'm not buried alive in a crypt anymore. It's like—like I just came home."

"For the first time," he added.

"Yes," she said, and tears began anew.

He reached out. She fell into him, and he closed his arms around her. She felt so small. She had always been such a force that he had never imagined she could feel so delicate—so fragile. He could die now. He laid his head back on the stone, taking in a breath and feeling the wonderful sensation of her head riding up and down on his chest.

Then they heard the rock begin to shatter.

❦

No one could see anything and they gathered around the light of Arista's robe as she and Hadrian came out of the alcove. The bright purple light shifted to white, revealing everyone's faces, making them look pale and ghostly.

"What's going on?" Hadrian asked as another round of thunderous ripping occurred. The noise came from the direction of the Vault of Days, the sound bouncing around the stone walls.

"I don't know. Maybe the Ghazel are tunneling in," Mauvin replied; then he narrowed his eyes at Arista. "Are you all right?"

"Me?" Arista said, smiling. "Yeah, I'm great."

Mauvin looked confused but shrugged. "Should we barricade?"

"What's the point?" Hadrian replied. "If they can cut through that rubble, a few golden chairs aren't going to stop them."

"So what are we going to do?" Gaunt asked.

Hadrian looked around, mentally tallying the faces. "Where's Royce?"

Around the circle of light of Arista's robe were Myron, Magnus, Gaunt, Mauvin, Arista, and Hadrian. Royce was nowhere to be seen. Hadrian turned toward the sound and began walking. Behind him, the others followed. When he reached the Vault of Days, he paused, and together with Arista he carefully entered the room.

"Where is it?" Hadrian asked no one in particular.

"Where's what?" Mauvin said.

"The creature, it's not in the corner anymore."

"It's not?" Gaunt said fearfully. "It ate him!"

"I don't think so," Hadrian said, and taking Arista by the

hand, he led them all across the open room. Partway there the air grew foul with dust. A cloud obscured the door ahead like a fog; the grinding and breaking sounds grew louder.

When they reached the far side, they found the door to the scroll room was missing—along with a good portion of the wall separating the two. The scroll room itself had also been destroyed. The far wall was down and stones lay scattered across the floor. Ahead, where there had once been a corridor leading to the collapsed stairs, was a giant tunnel from which came the thunderous noise and the clouds of dust.

They found Royce sitting on his pack, his feet outstretched, his back against the wall.

"I was wondering how long it would take," he greeted them.

Hadrian looked at him for a moment, then started to move past him toward the tunnel.

"Don't go in there," Royce warned. "The thing isn't careful about where he tosses the stones."

"Maribor's beard!" Hadrian exclaimed, and started to laugh.

"By Drome!" Magnus muttered.

"We thought the Ghazel were coming through," Mauvin said, waving a hand before his face, trying to clear the air.

"I'm sure they will be," Royce replied.

"That's right!" Mauvin said. "There's armor in the tomb— shields. We should—"

"I wouldn't worry about it," Royce told him. "I told Gilly to deal with them too."

Hadrian started to laugh, which brought a smile to Royce's lips.

"Aren't they going to be surprised to see what comes out?" the thief chuckled.

"We're going to get out of here?" Arista said, shocked.

"It's a distinct possibility." Royce nodded. "It took a while to master the right phrases, but once I got him going, old Gilly—boy—he took to it like a knife to a soft back."

"Gilly?" Hadrian asked, laughing.

"A pet has to have a name, doesn't it? Later I'm planning to teach it *fetch* and *roll over*, but for now, *dig* and *sic 'em* will do."

Another loud collision of stone rattled the floor and shook dirt from the ceiling, causing all of them to flinch. A thick cloud billowed out of the tunnel.

"Loosens the teeth when he really gets going like that," Royce said. "Wait here while I check on his progress."

The thief stood, wrapped his scarf around his face, and walked into the dark cloud. The ground continued to shudder and the sound was frightening, as if gods were holding a war in the next room.

"How is it fitting through the corridor?" Myron asked.

"I'm pretty sure it's making a whole new one," Magnus replied.

"Better pack up," Royce told them when he emerged. "Gilly has got a rhythm going, so it won't be long."

They gathered their things and returned to the tomb, where Arista placed the horn in her pack. They replaced the lids on Novron's coffin and Gaunt, Mauvin, and Magnus picked up a few small treasures, which they called souvenirs. Royce, much to Hadrian's surprise, did not touch a thing, not even a handful of gold coins. He merely waited for the rest of them. They all bid one last farewell to Alric before heading back to the tunnel.

Hadrian was the last out of the tomb, and as he was leaving, he caught sight of something small lying on the floor just before Arista's light faded. Picking it up, he stuffed it into his pack before trotting out to join the others.

The dust had settled by the time Royce led them through the tunnel. It was no longer a corridor, but a gaping passage like something a monstrous rabbit might burrow. It was round and at least fifty feet in width. The walls were compact rock and stone held together by weight and pressure. The passage ran level for several feet, then angled upward. There was no sign of the Gilarabrywn, but ahead they heard the familiar beat of drums.

"Ghazel—how nice," Hadrian said miserably. "They waited."

The tunnel ended at the great wide hallway with suits of armor and sculptured walls that they had passed through on the way in. While large enough for the Gilarabrywn to walk through, there was no sign of it.

"Where's your pet, Royce?"

He shrugged. "Perhaps I need to get him a leash."

"What did you tell him to do?" Mauvin asked.

"Well, that's the thing...I don't know exactly. I hope I told it to clear the way of all debris and danger up to the square outside the palace, but who knows what I really said? I might have told it to clear the world of all decency and rangers up to the lair outside the ballast."

Magnus and Mauvin both chuckled; even Hadrian smiled. Then Myron spoke up. "He's not joking. That's actually what he said the first time he repeated the phrase back to me. And of course we're assuming I got it right to begin with."

The sounds of yelps and cries cut through the empty hallway. Hadrian and Mauvin drew their swords. They waited a moment but there was only silence.

Royce shrugged and led them onward, always several dozen feet in front. His head turned from side to side. Royce always reminded Hadrian of a squirrel when he had his ears up. He had the same twitchy behavior.

They passed by the doorway to the throne room, the ornate entrance still closed. Royce halted, raising a hand and tilting his head. The rest of them heard it too. A horn, drums, shouts, cries, it all came from ahead of them—faint and muffled.

"Blood," Royce mentioned, pointing up ahead.

As Arista approached, they could see a disturbing splatter that sprayed across the far wall, creating a ghastly painting that still dripped. A dozen arrows lay widely scattered like fallen branches after a storm.

They proceeded until they reached the end of the corridor, where another Gilarabrywn-sized tunnel ran upward. Through it, they felt fresh salt air and began climbing. They reached the end and Royce poked his head out first before waving for the rest to follow. They stood in the square between the Cenzarium and what Arista had left of the Teshlor guildhall. In the center, where the fountain used to be, the Gilarabrywn lay on a shallow lake of blood, its tail shifting lazily from side to side, hitting the ground with moist slaps. Bodies of Ghazel littered the square, forming mounds like shadowy snowdrifts running out beyond the range of Arista's light. Swords, bows, headdresses, arms, clawed hands, and heads speckled the stone in a macabre collage of death.

"There must be hundreds of bodies," Mauvin whispered.

"And those are the ones it didn't eat," Magnus added.

"Is it safe?" Hadrian asked Royce, looking at the Gilarabrywn.

"Should be."

"Should be?"

Royce gave him a sinister grin.

"If it wasn't, we'd already be dead," Arista pointed out.

"What she said," Royce told him.

They stepped out onto the square, their shoes making wet noises as they walked across the bloody puddle. They made a slow circle around the beast, which remained quiet and still except for the ever-slapping tail.

"I think it got all of them," Hadrian announced. "Ghazel always take their dead if they can."

"I wish I had a sugar cube or something to give him," Royce said, looking at the Gilarabrywn with a sympathetic expression. "He's been such a good boy."

&

They reached the sea quicker than Hadrian would have expected. They followed a more direct route, not needing to dodge the Ghazel, and of course, return trips always seemed shorter. No one stopped to stare at the city. No one had any desire to explore. Their feet were no longer weighted by the dread of the unknown. A sense of urgency filled the party and drove them forward without pause.

Despite a lengthy series of language lessons with Myron, Royce was unable to persuade Gilly to leave the city. It refused to pass the lions and Royce had no choice but to abandon his newfound pet. He sent it back to resume its old duties in the Vault of Days but did not mention why.

"Look at that!" Hadrian exclaimed when they came in sight of the *Harbinger* once again. The ship was where they had left it in the sheltered cove, but not how they had left it. A new mast was set and a beautiful sail furled across a new yard. New boards and caulking were visible along the hull near the glowing green waterline, and parts of the cabin were touched up with new boards as well. "Wyatt and Elden have been busy."

"Amazing!" Magnus said, clearly impressed. "And just the two of them."

"With Elden it is more like three and a half," Hadrian corrected.

"And look," the dwarf said, trotting forward to where a series of planks were supported by floating barrels and linked by rope. "They built a gangway. Excellent craftsmanship, especially for the time given."

Magnus was the first on board, followed by Mauvin, with Hadrian and Arista coming up behind. Royce lingered on the rocks, eyeing the rocking ship with a sour look.

"Wyatt, Elden?" Hadrian called.

The ship was in fine shape. The mast, rail, and wheel block had a new whitewash and the deck was nicely scoured.

"Where did they get the paint?" Arista asked.

Hadrian was looking up. "I'm still impressed by this mast. Even with Elden, how did they set it?"

Not finding them on deck, they headed for the cabin. In the timeless world of the underground, it was possible they were both sleeping. Magnus was the first one through the door and the dwarf abruptly stopped, making an odd sound like a belch.

"Magnus?" Mauvin asked.

The dwarf did not answer. He collapsed as more than a half dozen goblins burst out of the hold, shrieking and skittering like crabs. Mauvin retreated, pulling his sword, and in the same motion cut the head off a charging Ghazel. Hadrian pushed Arista behind him and stood next to Mauvin, who had moved beside him.

Five Ghazel advanced across the deck holding their curved blades and small round shields adorned with finger-painted triangle symbols and tassels of seabird feathers and bone. They hissed as they approached in a line. Four more emerged from behind the cabin; three had bows and one, far smaller than the rest, was decorated in dozens of multicolored feathers. This one danced and hummed. There was one missing. Hadrian was sure he had seen another exit the cabin, not a warrior, not an oberdaza.

"Gaunt, Myron, Arista, get off the ship," he told them as he and Mauvin spread out to block the Ghazels' advance. Mauvin stroked his blade through the air, warming up, and

Hadrian could see he was off tempo. His wounded arm would not allow him to move as he needed to.

Myron backed up but Arista and Gaunt refused.

"No," Gaunt said. "Give me that big sword of yours."

"Do you know how to fight?"

"Ha! I was the leader of the Nationalist Army, remember?"

Hadrian lunged forward, but it was a feint and he dodged left, spinning in a full circle. One of the goblins took the bait, rushed forward, and was in just the right spot when Hadrian came around with his swords. The goblin died with two blades in his body. Hadrian drew them out dramatically and shouted a roar at the others, causing them all to hesitate. While they did, he stepped on the dead goblin's fallen sachel and slid it behind him to Gaunt. He roared again and kicked the shield back as well.

"*Galenti!*" he heard one of the Ghazel say, and the others immediately began to chatter.

"*Yes!*" he said in Tenkin. "*Get off my ship, or you will all die!*"

Arista and Mauvin looked at him, surprised. No one moved on either side except Gaunt, who picked up the shield and sword.

"*Known are you, but leave not. Our ship, borrowed for a time—but ours again. Leave it. Fight no more, you and we. I—Drash of the Klune—I too fight in arena. We all fight.*" He pointed at the ground at the dead. "*Not them. Those young fish, not sharks.*" He pointed at Gaunt, Myron, and Arista. "*Young fish and breeder. Like ones we find here— young fish too—good eating. You not want to fight. You leave.*"

Hadrian brought his swords together and let them clash loudly. He held them high above his head in an X and glared at the goblin chieftain, which caused them all to step back.

"*You saw me in the arena,*" Hadrian said. "*You know these swords. I come from old city, where no Ghazel drum beats—no horn blows—all dead. I did this.*" He gestured behind him. "*We do this. You leave my ship now.*"

The chieftain hesitated and Hadrian realized the ploy too late. The focus of his opponent's eyes shifted to something behind Hadrian. At that moment, he realized his mistake. He had given the finisher enough time to move into position. The missing Ghazel, the assassin, was behind him. *No*, he thought, not behind him. The finisher would not kill the chief of a clan; he would seek the oberdaza, the witch doctor—Arista!

From behind him she screamed.

Hadrian spun, knowing before he did that he was too late. The poisoned blade would already be through her back. Like Esrahaddon, Arista was helpless to a blow she had never seen coming. As soon as he turned, the chief launched his attack. It was a sound plan and Hadrian knew it.

All three ranges had targeted him and let loose the moment they heard Arista scream. Three arrows struck Hadrian in the back and he felt the missiles—soft muffled hits. Two landed between his shoulders and one near the kidneys, but there was no pain. Turning back, he saw the arrows lying on the deck, the tips blunted.

The chieftain stared at him, shocked, and for a moment, Hadrian was equally bewildered, until he felt the weight as he moved. Slung on his back was Jerish's shield, which was so light Hadrian had forgotten about it. The thin metal had stopped the arrows like a block of stone.

They had killed Arista. They had killed Wyatt and Elden. Hadrian felt the blood pound in his ears and his swords moved on their own. Three Ghazel died in seconds, including the chieftain. Somewhere beside him Mauvin was fighting, but he hardly noticed as he cast caution aside and fought forward, dashing madly, wildly through the ranks, killing as he went. Another round of arrows flew at Hadrian as he charged. Without a shield to protect him, with no time to turn, he was dead. He expected to feel the shafts pierce his chest and throat. They never reached him. Instead the arrows exploded in flame and burst into ash an instant after leaving their bows.

Hadrian cleaved the archers aside.

Only the oberdaza remained.

A wall of fire erupted between the two of them and flared up whenever Hadrian tried to move toward him. The song and dance of the Ghazel witch doctor changed to a scream of terror as his own wall rushed back at him. The flames attacked their master like dogs too often beaten and the oberdaza was consumed in a pillar of fire that left no more than a charred black spot in the deck and a foul smell in the air.

Arista?

Hadrian turned and saw her standing unharmed in her glowing robe. The finisher lay dead on the deck with a length of rope around his neck. Royce stood beside her. Mauvin and even Gaunt waited with blood-covered blades. There were smears on Degan's face and a dark stain on his chest, and his arms and hands were dripping.

"Are you all right?" Hadrian asked.

Gaunt nodded with a surprised expression. "They still fight with one arm," he replied, sounding a little dazed.

"Magnus!" Arista shouted as she rushed forward.

The dwarf lay facedown in a pool of dark blood.

They carefully rolled him over. The wound was in his stomach and spewed rich, dark blood. Magnus was still awake, still alert, his eyes rolling around as he looked at each of their faces.

His hand shook as the dwarf fumbled at his belt. He managed to knock Alverstone loose and it fell to the deck. "Give to — Royce — won — der — ful blade."

His eyes closed.

"No!" Arista shouted at him. She sat down, laid a hand on his chest, and started humming.

"Arista, what are you doing?" Hadrian asked.

"I'm pulling him back," she replied.

"No! You can't! Last time you —"

She grabbed his hand. "Just hold on to me and don't let go."

"No! Arista!" he shouted, but it was too late. He could tell she was already gone. "Arista!"

She knelt with her eyes closed, her breathing quick. A soft, gentle humming came from her, as if she were a mother cat. Hadrian cradled her small hand in both of his, trying not to squeeze too hard but making certain to keep a tight hold. He had no idea what good it did, but because she had told him not to let go, he swore that only death would break his grip.

"Nothing else around," Hadrian heard Royce say. "There's a Ghazel ship down the coast, but it's about a mile away and I didn't see any activity. Is he dead?"

"I think so," Mauvin replied. "Arista is trying to save him."

"Not again," Royce said dismally. "Didn't that almost kill her last —"

"Shut up, okay?" Hadrian snapped. "Both of you, just shut up!"

Hadrian stared at her face, watching her head droop lower and lower, as if she were falling asleep.

What does that mean? Is she losing? Slipping away? Dying?

Frustration gripped him. His stomach twisted and every muscle tensed.

Her shoulders slumped and she tilted. He caught her with

his free hand and pulled her to him, pressing her limp head to his chest.

Still humming—is that a good sign?

He thought it was. He cradled her with his left hand while still holding tight with his right, his palm growing slick with sweat.

Arista jerked her head as if she were having a dream. She did it again and her humming stopped and she mumbled something.

"What is it?" he asked. "I didn't hear you. What did you say?"

Another mumble, too soft, too slurred.

She jerked again and appeared to cry out. He held tight as her body went limp against him, her head hanging.

"Arista?" he said.

She stopped breathing.

"Arista!"

He shook her. "*Arista!*"

Her head flopped, her hair whipping back and forth.

"Arista, come back! Come back to me! Goddamn it! Come back!"

Nothing.

She lay like a dead weight against him, as loose as a doll.

He pulled her tight. "Please," he whispered. "Please come back to me. Please. I can't lose you—not now."

He lifted her head. She appeared to be sleeping, the way he had seen her dozens of times. There was a beauty about her face when she slept that he could never explain, a calm softness—only she was not sleeping now. There was no reassuring rise of her chest, no breath on his face. He pressed his lips against hers. He kissed her, but her lips did not move. They remained slack, lifeless, and when he pulled back, she still hung in his arms. He hoped that maybe some power from within him could awaken her, like in a fairy tale. That the kiss—their first—could somehow call her back, awaken her.

But nothing happened. Their first kiss—their last—and she never felt it.

"Please," he muttered as tears began running down his cheeks. "Oh dear Maribor, please, don't do this."

His own breath shortened, his chest too tight. It felt as if a blade had sliced through his stomach and he was falling to his own death. He held tight to her, pressing her body against his, her cheek against his face, as if holding her could keep him—

Her hand jerked.

Hadrian held his breath.

He felt a squeeze.

He squeezed back, harder than he had planned.

Her body stiffened. Her head flew back. Her eyes and mouth opened wide and she inhaled. Arista sucked in a loud breath, as if she just surfaced from a deep dive.

She could not speak and drew in breath after breath, her body rocking with the effort. Slowly she turned to look at him and her expression filled with sadness. "You're crying," she said as her hand came up and wiped his cheek.

"Am I?" he replied, blinking several times. "Must be the sea air."

"Are you all right?"

Hadrian laughed. "Me? How are you?"

"I'm fine—tired as usual." She grinned. "But fine."

"He's alive!" Mauvin shouted, stunned.

They simultaneously turned their heads just in time to see the dwarf rising groggily. Magnus looked at Arista and immediately began to weep.

"The wound," Mauvin said, shaking his head in disbelief. "It's healed."

"Told you I could do it," she whispered.

❧

Arista woke to the gentle motion and creaking of the ship at sea. She felt physically drained again, her body weighted. Both arms shook when she lifted them, her hands quivering. She found her pack left beside the bed and reached in, feeling around for food. She pulled out a travel meal and silently thanked Ibis Thinly as if he were the god of food. Just as before, she devoured the salt pork, hard bread, and pickle. She swallowed three mouthfuls of water and leaned back against the wall for a moment. Eating exhausted her.

In the dark, she listened to the ship. It creaked and groaned—verse and chorus—riding up and down. She let the movement rock her head, feeling the food work its magic.

She thought of Alric and in the darkness saw his face. Young and yet strangely lined, with that silly beard that had never looked right on him—his kingly beard—meant to make him appear older. It had never fully filled in. She thought of her father and the hairbrushes he had brought her—his way of saying he loved her. She remembered her mother's swan mirror, lost when the tower collapsed. It was *all* gone now, certainly all of Medford, perhaps all of Melengar as well. She could still hear the sound of her mother's voice and remembered how it had come to her from out of the light.

What is that place?

She had come close to it twice now. It had been easier with Magnus; she had not seen her loved ones, only his. They spoke to him in dwarvish. She did not know the words, but the meaning was clear—kindness, forgiveness, love.

What is that place? What is it like inside?

She sensed peace and comfort and knew it would be a good place to rest. Arista needed rest, but not there, not yet. Taking the remaining walnuts from her meal, she climbed out to the deck. The length of the ship lay before her, illuminated by the green sea. Royce was in the rigging with an unpleasant, sickly look on his face. Hadrian was at the stern, both hands on the wheel, his teeth clenched as he focused intently on the rising and falling waves. Myron and Degan worked together near the bow, tying off a loose rope that was allowing the jib to flap. Gaunt pulled and Myron tied. Magnus sat at the waist coiling a length of rope, looking like a bearded child left to play on the floor.

"The sleeping princess awakes!" It was Mauvin calling down from the yard above. She smiled at him and he waved back.

"Forget her," the thief barked. "Get to the end of that yard!"

Arista walked across the deck, pausing once reaching the dwarf. She popped another walnut into her mouth. "Feeling all right?" she asked.

The dwarf nodded without looking at her.

"Oh good." She sat down beside him. A warm wind came off the sea and blew through her hair, clearing her face. She looked up and spotted Hadrian taking a precious moment away from steering to look at her and wave with a smile. She waved back, but by then his eyes had turned back to the problems of the sea.

She looked around the deck again; then her head tilted up and she scanned the rigging. Everything was illuminated eerily from below by the glowing sea, which gave the whole ship a ghostly appearance.

"Where're Wyatt and Elden?" she asked Magnus.

"Dead," the dwarf said coldly.

"Oh," she replied, unsettled by the blunt response. She leaned back on her hands, forgetting to chew the walnut as she remembered the two sailors. She had liked them both and regretted now that she had never spoken to either very much, but then, she guessed no one but Myron had spoken much to Elden. She slipped her hand in her pocket and withdrew the little figurine Elden had carved of her and rubbed it with her thumb.

"Poor Allie," she said, shaking her head sadly. Then a thought came to her. "Are you sure they're dead? Or did the goblins just take them? Did anyone actually see—"

"Found them partially eaten," Magnus growled. "Wyatt's legs and arms were gone, his chest torn open—gnawed out like a turkey ready for stuffing. Only half of Elden's face was there, the skin hung off one side and bite marks on his—"

"That's enough!" She stopped him, raising her hands up before her face. "I understand! You don't have to be so—so graphic!"

"You asked," he said tartly.

She stared at him.

He ignored her.

Magnus huffed, stood up, and began to walk away.

"Magnus," she said, stopping him. "What's wrong?"

"Whatcha mean?" he said, but did not turn. He looked out over the side of the ship, watching the luminous waves roll.

"You act as if you're angry with me."

He grumbled to himself, something in dwarvish, still refusing to face her.

Overhead the wind was still ruffling the jib. Myron and Gaunt had paused in their work, both staring at them. Royce was yelling at Mauvin about mainstays and yards.

"Magnus?" she asked.

"Why did you do it?" the dwarf blurted out.

"Do what?"

He whirled at last to face her. His eyes were harsh and accusing. "Why did you save my life?"

She did not know what to say.

"What do you care if I die!" he snapped at her, his eyes fiery. "What difference does it make—you're a princess, I'm just a dwarf! You forced me on this trip. I never wanted to come. You took half my beard. Do you know what a beard means to a dwarf? Of course you don't, I can see it in your eyes. You don't know anything about dwarves!" He flicked the bottom of his severed whiskers at her. "You got what you wanted out of me— you have the blasted horn! And you can find your own way back out. You don't need me anymore. So why, then? Why'd ya do it? Why did you—why did you—" He clenched his teeth, squeezed his eyes shut, and turned his head away.

She sat back, shocked.

"Why did you risk your life to save mine?" he said, his voice now little more than a whisper. "Hadrian said you almost *died*—you stopped breathing like you did with Alric. He said he thought for sure you were dead this time. *He* was your brother!" Magnus shouted. "But me...I murdered your father! Have you forgotten that? I was the one who locked you in the tower. I closed the door on you and Royce and sealed you all in the dungeon under Aquesta, leaving you to starve to death. Did all that just slip your mind? Now Alric is dead. Your family is gone. Your kingdom is gone—you have nothing, and Royce..."

He pulled out the glistening dagger. "Why did he give me this? I wanted to see it, yes! I would have been his slave for the chance to study it for a week. And then he just gave it to me. He hasn't taken it back or even said a word. This—this—this is the most beautiful thing I have ever seen—worth more than a mountain of gold, more than all that back in the tomb. He just gave it to me. After what I did...he should have killed me with it! He should still kill me. So should you. Both of you should have laughed and sang when I..." A hand went to his stomach and he bit his lower lip, making the remains of his beard stand up. "So why did you do it? *Why?*"

He stared at her now with a desperate look on his face — a pained expression, as if somehow she were torturing him.

"I didn't want you to die," she said simply. "I didn't really think beyond that. You were dying and I could save you, so I did."

"But you could have died — couldn't you?"

She shrugged.

Magnus continued to glare at her as if he might either attack her or burst into tears.

"Why is this such a problem for you? Aren't you happy to be alive?"

"*No!*" he shouted.

Over his shoulder, she saw Myron and Gaunt still staring, but now with concerned faces.

"You should have let me die — you should have let me die. Everything would have been fine if you had just let me die."

"Why?" she asked. "Why would it have been better?"

"I don't deserve to live, that's why. I don't and now..." A dark expression came over him and he looked back out at the sea.

"What? What happens now?"

"That's just it, I don't know. I don't know what to do anymore. I've hated you for so long."

"Me?" she asked, shocked. "What did I —"

"All of you — humans. The water flooded the caverns, so we came to you for help — not a handout, but a fair trade, work for payment. You agreed and to a fair price. Then you herded us into the Barak Ghetto in Trent. We mined the Dithmar Range and you paid us all right, then came the taxes. Taxes for living in your filthy shacks, taxes on what we bought and sold, taxes on crops we raised, taxes for not being members of the Nyphron Church—taxes for being dwarves. Taxes so high a number of us turned their backs on Drome to worship your god, but still you did not accept us. You denied us the privilege to carry weapons, to ride horses. We worked night and day and still did not make enough to feed ourselves. We fell into your debt and you made slaves of us. Your kind whipped my kin to make us work, and killed us when we tried to leave. They called us thieves, just for trying to be free." He shook his head miserably. "My whole family—Clan Derin— slaves to humans." He spat the words. "The elves never treated us that badly. And it wasn't just my family, it was all the dwarves."

He hooked a thumb at Myron. "He knows. He told you how centuries ago the dwarves helped you, saved you when you were desperate. And how did you repay us? Tell me, Princess, can a dwarf be a citizen in Melengar?" He did not wait for her answer. "Dwarves are never granted citizenship anywhere. Without it you can't practice a trade. You can't join a guild or open a business. You can't legally work at all. And even in Melengar you put us in the most vile corners, the downhill alleys where all the sewage runs, where the shacks are rotting, and where on a warm day you can't breathe. That's what you've done to us—to dwarves. My great grandfather worked on Drumindor!" He straightened up as he spoke the name of the ancient dwarven fortress. "Now humans defile it."

"Not anymore," she reminded him.

"Good for them, you deserve what you got."

He placed his hands on the rail and stared down the side of the ship.

Myron left Gaunt alone with the rope to listen.

"I'm the last of Clan Derin—the only one to escape—a fugitive, an outlaw because I chose to be free. They hunted me for years. I got good at disappearing. You found that out too, didn't you?

"Your people disgraced and killed mine. Your kind never did anything unless it was for profit—and you call us greedy! I've heard your tales of evil dwarves kidnapping, killing, imprisoning—but that was all your doing. Why would a dwarf kidnap a princess or anyone? That was you using us as an excuse for your own sins.

"Every few years, knights would come into the ghettos and burn them. Those so-called defenders of the law and decency would come in the middle of the night and set fire to our miserable shacks in the dark—and always in winter."

He turned and faced her once more. "But you..." He sighed, his eyes losing their fire, fogging instead with bewilderment and weariness. "You risked yourself and saved my life. It doesn't make sense."

He sat down, looking exhausted. "I've hated you for so long and you go and do this." He put his face in his hands and began to rock forward and back.

"Maybe," Myron said, coming behind the dwarf and placing a hand on his back. "Maybe Magnus did die."

The dwarf looked up and scowled.

"Maybe you should let him die," the monk added. "Let the hate, fear, and anger die with him. This is a chance to start over. The princess has given you a new life. You can choose to live it any way you want starting right now."

The dwarf lost his scowl.

"It's scary, isn't it?" Myron said. "Imagining a different life? I was scared too, but you can do it."

"He's right," Arista said. "This could be a new start."

"That all depends," Magnus replied, "and we'll find out soon enough."

The dwarf stood up.

"Royce!" he shouted. "Come down a second."

The thief looked irritated but grabbed a line and slid down, touching the deck lightly.

"What is it? I can't leave Mauvin up there alone, and I'm not feeling very well as it is."

Magnus held out Alverstone. "Take it back."

Royce narrowed his eyes. "I thought you wanted it."

"Take it. You might need it—sooner than you think."

Royce took the dagger suspiciously. "What's going on?"

Magnus glanced at Arista, and Myron, and lastly at Gaunt, who had finally secured the jib and walked over.

"Before we left Aquesta, I made a bargain with the Patriarch."

"What *kind* of bargain?" Royce asked.

"I was supposed to kill Degan after we found the horn, but before we left the caves. I was hired to kill him and return the horn to His Grace."

"You planned to betray us—again?" Royce asked.

"Yes."

"You were going to kill me?" Gaunt asked.

Royce stared at Magnus and looked down at the dagger.

Myron and Arista watched him closely, tense, waiting.

"Why are you telling me this?"

The dwarf hesitated briefly. "Because…Magnus died before he could go through with it."

Royce stared at the dwarf, turning Alverstone over and over in his hands and pursing his lips. He glanced at Arista and at Myron, then nodded. "You know, I never did like that short son of a bitch." He held out the dagger. "Here, I don't think I'll be needing it."

Magnus did nothing for several minutes but stare at the dagger. He seemed to have trouble breathing. He finally stood up straight. "No." The dwarf shook his head. "Magnus thought—when you gave him that dagger—it was the most valuable gift he could ever receive. He was wrong."

Royce nodded and slipped Alverstone back into the folds of his cloak. He gripped the rope and began to climb.

Magnus stood looking lost for a moment.

"Are you all right?" Myron asked.

"I don't know." He looked down at the deck. "If Magnus died, then who am I?"

"Whoever you want to be," the monk said. "It's a pretty wonderful gift."

᪥

"How far are we?" Arista asked Hadrian, sitting down on the wheel box beside him. The fighter was still grappling with the ship, still struggling to keep its sails balanced.

"Not sure, but judging from the last crossing, we should see land in the next hour, unless Royce and I messed up really bad on the course or I wreck us. Too far this way and the sails collapse and we lose headway, which means we can't steer. Too far the other way and the wind will flip us. Wyatt made this look so easy."

"Is it true what Magnus told me? Did you really find them?"

Hadrian nodded sadly. "He was a good man—they both were. I keep thinking of Allie. They were the only family she had. Now what's going to happen to her?"

She nodded. So much death, so much sadness there were times she felt she might drown. Overhead the canvas fluttered, like the sheet of a maid making up a bed. The rings rattled against the poles and the waves crashed into the hull.

She watched Hadrian standing at the wheel, his chin up, his back straight, and his eyes watching the water. The breeze blew back his hair, showing a worn face, but not hard or broken. He had his sleeves rolled up to his elbows and the muscles of his forearms stood out. She noted several scars on his arms. Two looked new—red and raised. His hands were broad and large, and his skin so tanned that his fingernails stood out lighter. He was a handsome man, but this was the first time she had really noticed. His looks were not what attracted her. It was his warmth, his kindness, his humor, and how safe it felt to sit beside him on a cold, dark night. Still, she had to admit that he was a handsome man in his tattered, coarse cloth and raw leather. She wondered how many women had noticed, and how many he had known. She glanced back across the sea behind them; the crypt of emperors seemed very far away.

"You know, we really haven't had a chance to talk since getting out." She looked at the waves breaking at the bow. "I mean—you said some things in there that—well, maybe they were only meant for in there. We both thought we were dying and people can—"

"I meant every word," he told her firmly. "How about you, do you regret it?"

She smiled and shook her head. "When I woke up, I thought it might have been a beautiful dream. I never really considered myself the kind of woman men wanted. I'm pushy, controlling, I butt into places I shouldn't, and I have far too many opinions on far too many subjects—subjects women aren't supposed to be interested in. I never even bothered to try to make myself more appealing. I avoided dances and never presented myself with my hair up and neckline down. I don't have a clue about flirting." She sighed and ran a hand over her matted hair. "I never cared how I looked before, but now... for the first time I'd like to be pretty... for you."

"I think you're beautiful."

"It's dark."

"Oh, wait." Hadrian reached over to his backpack. "Close your eyes."

"Why?"

"Just do it and hold out your hands."

She did as instructed, feeling a bit silly as she heard him rummaging through his pack, then silence. A moment later she felt something in her hands. Her fingers closed and she knew what it was before she opened her eyes. She began to cry.

"What's wrong?" Hadrian asked in a sudden panic.

"Nothing," she said, wiping the tears away and feeling foolish. She had to stop this. He was going to think she cried all the time.

"Then why are you crying?"

"It's okay. I'm happy."

"You are?" Hadrian asked skeptically.

She nodded, smiling at him as tears continued to run down her cheeks.

"It's not worth getting all that excited over, you know. Everything else in that place was gold and encrusted in jewels. I'm not even sure this is real silver. I was actually so disappointed that I considered not giving it to you, but after what you said—"

"It's the most wonderful gift you could have given me."

Hadrian shrugged. "It's just a hairbrush."

"Yes, it is," she said. "It really is."

CHAPTER 25

THE ARRIVAL

Modina faced the Gilarabrywn. She waited for it to attack, to kill her and the rest of her family. But the beast did none of those things. The monster stared at her for a moment, then spread its wings and lifted off, flying away.

They all waited, staring out through the missing wall.

"Horses," someone said, and soon Modina also heard the sound of trotting hooves.

Twelve elves rode on white mounts. They wore lion helms and long purple capes that draped over the back of their mounts. Drawing off their helms in unison, they revealed long white hair, sharp pointed ears, angled brows, and luminous eyes of green, as if a magical fire burned within.

The lead rider looked about the shattered ruins of the castle; the mere turning of his head revealed a startling, unworldly grace and it was easy to understand how they were once thought to be gods. His eyes settled on Modina, and Amilia wondered how she could manage to stand beneath his stare.

"*Er un don Irawondona fey Asendwayr. Susyen vie eyurian Novron fey Instayria?*" he said. His voice sounded like the ringing of fine crystal.

Modina continued to stare back at the elf.

Nimbus rose and, moving to Modina's side, replied, "*Er un don Modina vie eyurian Novron fey Instayria.*"

The elf stared at Modina for a long moment, then dismounted, his movements as fluid as silk blowing in the wind. Amilia thought his expression was filled with contempt, but she knew nothing about elves.

"What did you two say?" Modina asked.

"He introduced himself as Lord Irawondona of the Asendwayr tribe. He said the Gilarabrywn heard your claim and came to ask if you were in fact the daughter of Novron. I told him yes."

"*Vie eyurian Novron un Persephone, cy mor guyernian fi hyliclor Gylindora dur Avempartha sen youri? Uli Vermar fie veriden ves uyeria! Ves Ferrol boryeten.*"

"He asks, if you are the daughter of Novron and Persephone, why have you not presented the horn for challenge at Avempartha? He says that the *Uli Vermar* ended some time ago and by failing to present the horn you stand in violation before Ferrol."

"*Vie hillin jes lineia hes filhari fi ish tylor baliyan. Sein lori es runyor ahit eston.*"

"He says that by not producing the horn, your violation releases them from all treaties, agreements, and requirements to abide your commands."

"Tell him I'm in the process of retrieving the horn."

Nimbus spoke in the musical language and the elven lord replied.

"He insists that you must present it at once."

Nimbus spoke again, and the elf turned and consulted with one of the mounted riders.

"I explained that it was in the ancient city of Percepliquis and would be brought here soon. I hope that I did not overstep my—"

Modina took Nimbus's face in her hands and kissed him on the mouth. "I love you, Nimbus."

The chancellor looked befuddled and, stepping back, checked to see if his wig was on straight.

"He is coming back," Amilia told them.

Once more Nimbus did the talking. There appeared to be some kind of minor dispute and once the elven lord looked over Nimbus's shoulder at the girls sitting on the floor, then nodded. With the tone of general agreement, the elf remounted his horse and rode back out of the courtyard with the others.

"What?" Modina asked.

"They have decided not to wait and will go to Percepliquis to meet the horn. Should you be telling the truth, they will hold the challenge ceremony there. If you are lying, Irawondona will claim his right to rule through default. I presume that will mean they will continue in their march to rid the world of mankind. Either way you must go with them."

"When?"

"You have just enough time to grab a change of clothes, I think. I tried to arrange a small retinue, but they refused. I did manage to gain agreement for the girls to go. Allie deserves to be with her father when he returns and Mercy will comfort her if he does not. I told him they were your daughters."

"Thank you, Nimbus, you may very well have saved all our lives."

"I fear it may only be a stay of execution."

"Not if Arista succeeds, and every day granted to us is another day to hope."

∽

Mince climbed out of the Hovel, pulling his hood up and yawning. The others had kicked him awake, as it was his turn to check the horses. The rule in their group had always been that those who worked ate. It was a simple rule, with little room for interpretation, but early on a cold winter's morning, when he was bundled in blankets and half-asleep, the thought of going outside in the wind and snow made forgetting even simple rules easy. Finally he had relented, knowing they would just kick him harder.

He stood up and stretched his back as he did every morning, thinking about how old he was getting. It was still early, and the sun was only now breaching the tree line, casting sharp angles of golden light in slants, making the snow crystals glimmer. It was warmer, but the night's chill still lingered. He decided it was the wetness that made it feel worse; at least when it was cold, the air and even snow were dry.

Mince walked to the line of horses waiting for him. He knew them all by name and they knew him. Each of their heads turned, their ears rotating his way. They were lucky. The bitter cold had ended abruptly and none of the horses had died. Even the one Mince was certain had stopped breathing survived.

"Morning, ladies and gents," he greeted them as he did each day, with a nod of his head and a wave of his hand. "How are we this miserable excuse of a day, huh? What's that, Simpleton? You don't agree? You think it is a fine day, you say? Much warmer than yesterday morn? Well, I don't know if I can agree with you, sir. What's that, Mouse? You agree with Simpleton? Hmm, I don't know. It just seems . . . too quiet—far too quiet."

It did. Mince stood still with his feet in the slush and listened. There were no wind or sound. It was a strange sort of stillness, as if the world were dead.

Perhaps it is.

Who knew what had happened up north, or to the south, for that matter.

*What if they are all dead now? What if the four of us are all
that are left?*

A crow cawed in a nearby tree; the stark call made the
silence desolate. A sense of emptiness and loss hung in the air.
Mince felt the line tethering the horses, making sure it was
still secure, then pulled open the feed bags. Normally they jostled each other, trying to stick their noses in, but this morning
something drew their attention. The horse's heads turned,
their ears twitching to the left, their big eyes peering.

"Someone's coming?" Mince whispered to Princess. Her
head bounced up and down, which shocked him, but then she
quickly followed that with a shaking as well.

A few moments later, he heard hooves and he ran to the
Hovel to wake the others.

"Who is it?" Brand whispered.

"How should I know?" Mince replied, pulling himself fully
inside.

"It's certainly not Hadrian and the rest," Elbright pointed
out. "They left their horses with us."

"Maybe it's Renwick coming back?" Kine suggested hopefully, and this returned several positive looks and nods.

"One of us should look," Elbright said commandingly, getting to his knees and pulling on his cloak.

"Not me," Mince said. "Let Brand do it. He's the bold one."

"Hush," Elbright snapped, "I'm going."

He pulled a bit of the tarp aside and looked out.

"Do you see 'em?" Kine asked.

"No."

"Maybe they—"

"Shh!" Elbright held up his hand. "Listen."

Faint voices carried across the stillness of the winter
morning.

"*They went down here,*" a voice said.

"Oh my! That does look rather unpleasant. Is Your Grace certain?"

"Absolutely."

"They don't sound like elves," Kine whispered.

"Like you know how elves talk," Mince said.

"It doesn't sound like Renwick either," Brand added.

"Will you all shut up!" Elbright hissed, slapping Kine on the head.

"It's so deep you can't see the bottom." The faint voice spoke again.

"It's very deep indeed."

"There are no tracks near it."

"They are still inside, still down there, still dredging up secrets and stirring old memories, but they are coming. Already they are quite near and they have the horn."

"How do you know that?"

"Call it...an old man's intuition."

"That's good, isn't it? That they have the horn?"

"Oh yes, that is very good."

The sound of crunching snow could be heard, growing louder.

"They're coming this way," Elbright said.

"Can you see them yet?" Kine asked.

"There are four of them. One looks like a priest in a black frock, two are soldiers, and there's an old man in bright-colored robes with long white hair. The soldiers are kind of strange-looking."

"What are they doing here?" Brand asked.

"Their horses," a voice outside said. They were much closer now. The boys could hear the squishing of the slushy ground. *"You can come out, young men."*

They looked at each other nervously.

"Renwick, Elbright, Brand, Kine, Mince, come, we are going to have breakfast."

Elbright was the first one out, emerging from the tarp carefully. His head turned from side to side. They each followed him slowly, squinting in the sunlight, and just as Elbright had described, four men stood before them in the small clearing. They looked terribly out of place. The man with the long white hair was wearing purple, red, and gold robes and he leaned on a staff. To either side stood the soldiers, in gold breastplates, helms, and sleeves. They also wore colorful pants of red, purple, and yellow. Each held a spear and wore a sword. The priest was the only normal-looking fellow, standing with his weight on one leg in the traditionally drab black habit of a Nyphron priest.

"Who are you?" Elbright asked.

"This is His Grace the Patriarch of the Nyphron Church," the priest told him.

"Oh," Elbright said, nodding. Mince could tell he was trying to sound like he knew who that was, but his friend knew better. Elbright was always doing that, making out like he was more worldly than he was.

"These are his bodyguards and I am Monsignor Merton of Ghent."

"Guess you already know us," Elbright said. "What are you doing here?"

"Just waiting," the Patriarch replied. "Like you—waiting for them to climb back out of that hole and change the nature of the world forever. Certainly you can't begrudge us the desire of a front-row seat."

The old man looked at his guards and they trudged off.

"How's Renwick?" Mince asked. "Did he make it to Aquesta?"

"I'm sorry," Monsignor Merton replied kindly. "We traveled by sea around the horn to Vernes and then by coach. We left quite some time ago, so it is entirely possible that he arrived after we left. Was he a friend?"

Mince nodded.

"He rode to Aquesta with news that the elves were attacking from the southeast," Brand said. "They came right by here, they did."

"I'm sorry I can't tell you more," the priest said.

"Pleasant little place you have here," the old man mentioned, looking around. "It's nice that you put your camp under the holly tree. I like the splash of green on such a day as this, when it seems as if all the color has been stolen. It has been a long, cold winter, but it will soon be over. A new world is about to bloom."

Mince heard the distant sound of music and instantly he threw his hands to his ears.

"Is that...?" Elbright asked, alarmed, raising his own hands as Mince bobbed his head.

"Relax, boys," the Patriarch said. "That melody is not enchanted. It is the "Ibyn Ryn," the Ervian anthem."

"But it's the elves!" Elbright said. "They're coming!"

"Yes." The Patriarch glanced up the hill and then down at the hole. "It's a race now."

CHAPTER 26

THE RETURN

I love this chamber," Arista said as they spread out blankets on the same flat rock. Overhead the glowworms glimmered and winked, and she noticed for the first time how much she missed seeing the sky.

Magnus gathered his rocks in the center once more. "This is nothing compared to the wonders that I have seen in the deep. My grandfather once took me into the mountains of the Dithmar Range of Trent to a place only he knew. He told me that I needed to know where I came from. He took me deep into a crevasse to where a river went underground. We disappeared inside for weeks. My mother and father were furious when we finally returned. They didn't want me to *get ideas*. They had already given up, but my grandfather—he knew."

Magnus sparked a stone against another. "The things he showed me were amazing. Chambers hundreds of times the size of this one made of shimmering crystal so that a single glow stone could make it bright as day. Stone cathedrals with pillars and teeth, and waterfalls that dropped so far you could not hear the roar. Everything down there was so vast, so wide, so big—we felt immeasurably small. It is sometimes hard to believe in Drome, seeing what has become of his people, but in places like this, and certainly in halls like the ones my grandfather showed me, it's like seeing the face of god firsthand."

Arista spread her blanket next to Hadrian.

"What are you trying to do there, Magnus?" Hadrian asked.

"Provide a little light. There are lots of this kind of stone here. My grandfather showed me how to make them burn—smolder, really."

"Let me help." Arista made a modest motion and the trio of rocks ignited and burned as a perfect campfire.

The dwarf frowned. "No, no. Stop it. I can get it."

Arista clapped and the fire vanished. "I just wanted to help."

"Yeah, well, that's not natural."

"And making rocks glow by slamming them together is?" Hadrian asked.

"Yes—if you're a dwarf."

Magnus got his rocks glowing and the rest gathered around them to eat. They were each down to their last meals and hoped to emerge aboveground the following day, or the last leg of the trip would be a hungry one.

"Aha!" Myron said. He had laid his books out near the rocks, giddy that there was enough light to read by.

"Discover the proper pronunciation to another name?" Hadrian asked. "Is Degan's real name Gwyant?"

"Hum? Oh, no, I found Mawyndulë—the one Antun Bulard and Esrahaddon spoke of."

"You *found* him?"

"Yes, in this book. Ever since I read Mr. Bulard's last scribbled words, I've been trying to find information on him. I reasoned that he must have read something shortly before he died. As these were the only books he had with him in the library, it stood to reason that Mawyndulë was mentioned somewhere in one of them. Wouldn't you know it would be in the last book I read? *Migration of Peoples* by Princess Farilane.

It is really a very biased accounting of how the Instarya clan took control of the elven empire. But it mentions Nyphron, the horn, and Mawyndulë."

"What does it say?" Arista asked.

"It says the elves were constantly warring between the various tribes, and quite a bloody and violent people until they obtained the horn."

"I mean, what does it say about Mawyndulë?"

"Oh." Myron looked embarrassed. "I don't know. I haven't read that yet. I just saw his name."

"Then let's be quiet and let the man read."

Everyone remained silent, staring at the monk as he scanned the pages. Arista wondered if all the glaring distracted Myron, but as he rapidly turned page after page of dense script, she realized that the monk was unflappable with a book before him.

"Oh," Myron finally said.

" 'Oh' what?" Arista asked.

"I know why the horn didn't make a sound when Degan blew it."

"Well?" Hadrian asked.

The monk looked up. "You were right. Like you said in the tomb, it's a horn of challenge."

"And?"

"Degan's already king. He can't challenge himself, so it made no sound."

"What does all this have to do with Mawyndulë?" Arista asked.

Myron shrugged. "Still reading."

The monk returned his attention to the book.

"We should be out tomorrow, right?" Arista asked Hadrian, who nodded. "How long have we been down here?"

Hadrian shrugged and looked to Royce.

The thief, having completed his survey of the perimeter, took a seat around the glow of the rocks with the rest of them and fished in his pack for his meal. "At least a week."

"What will we find up there?" she asked herself as much as anyone else. "What if we're too late?"

"So the *Uli Vermar* is the reign of a king," Myron said. "Usually three thousand years—the average life span of an elf, apparently."

"Really?" Mauvin asked, and glanced at Royce. "How old are you?"

"Not that old."

"Remember the emperors in the tomb?" Arista said. "Mixing elven blood with human reduces the life span."

"Yeah, but he'll still outlive everyone here, except maybe Gaunt, right?"

"Why me?" Gaunt, who had been miserably picking at the remains of his meal, looked up.

"You're an elf too."

Gaunt grimaced. "I'm an elf?"

"You're related to Novron, right?"

"But...I don't want to be an elf."

"You'll get used to it." Royce smirked.

"Ah, here it is," Myron said. "Mawyndulë was a member of the Miralyith, and during the time before Novron, they were the ruling tribe." He paused and, looking up, added, "Unlike us, elves don't have consistent nobility. Whichever tribe the king is from becomes the ruling one and holds power over the rest, but only for one generation, or the length of the *Uli Vermar*. Then they face the challenge and if a new king wins the throne, his tribe becomes the new ruling elite."

"But not anyone in the tribe can challenge for the chance to be king, I'll bet," Gaunt said. "There is still a hereditary nobility in the tribes, right? There always is."

"For once I have to side with him," Royce said. "People might like to give the appearance of giving up power, but actually giving it up—that doesn't happen."

"Technically, I think anyone can challenge," Myron explained. "But true, traditionally it is the leader of a given tribe. However, he is elected by the clan leaders."

"Interesting," Mauvin said. "A society without nobility, where leaders are elected. See, Gaunt? You really are an elf."

"So someone blows the horn, fights, wins the challenge, and becomes king," Arista stated. "He's expected to rule for three thousand years, but what if he doesn't? If he dies in an accident, then the crown goes to his next of kin. That part I get. But what happens if the king dies and doesn't have any blood relatives? Then what?"

"That would also end the *Uli Vermar*," Myron said. "And the first person to blow the horn then becomes the new king, and he then presents it to anyone else to challenge him. And that's exactly what appears to have happened." Myron tapped the page in the book. "After the battle of Avempartha, as Nyphron was poised to invade his homeland—"

"Wait a second," Mauvin said. "Are Nyphron and Novron the same person?"

"Yes," Myron, Arista, and Hadrian all said together.

"Just as *Teshlor* is the bastardized pronunciation of the elf warrior Techylor, *Novron* is the bastardized form of Nyphron. So as I was saying, Nyphron was poised to invade his homeland when the *Uli Vermar* ended, and the elven high council presented the horn to Novron, making him king and ending the war."

"The *Uli Vermar* ended just then? That sounds awfully convenient," Royce said. "I'm guessing the elven king didn't die of natural causes."

Myron looked back down and read aloud. " 'And so it came to pass that in the night of the day of the third turn, thus was sent Mawyndulë of the tribe Miralyith. And by the council he was thus charged with the…' " Myron stopped speaking, but his eyes raced across the page.

"What is it?" Arista asked, but Myron raised a finger to stall her.

They all watched as Myron reached up and turned another page, his eyes widening, his eyebrows rising.

"By Mar, monk!" Magnus erupted. "Stop reading and tell us."

Myron looked up with a startled expression. "Mawyndulë murdered the elven king."

"And if he had any children, they were also murdered, weren't they?"

"No," Myron said, surprising Royce. "His only son survived."

"But that doesn't make sense," Arista said. "If his son was alive, why didn't he become king? Why did the *Uli Vermar* end?"

"Because," Myron replied, "Mawyndulë was his son."

It took a moment for this to register. The timing was different for each of them as around the circle of flickering light, they each made a sound of understanding.

"So Mawyndulë couldn't become king because he had committed murder?" Hadrian asked.

"Regicide," Myron corrected. "Significantly more deplorable in elvish society, for it places at risk the very foundation of their civilization and the peace that Ferrol granted them with the gift of the horn. As a result Mawyndulë was banished—stricken from elvish society and cursed by Ferrol, thereby barred from Alysin, the elvish afterlife."

"So why did he do it?" Arista asked.

"Princess Farilane doesn't actually say. Perhaps no one knows."

"So Novron blew the horn and became king and that ended the war." Hadrian finished the last of his meal and folded up his pack.

"That was certainly the plan," Myron said. "No one was supposed to blow the horn after Novron did. No one was supposed to challenge his rule. According to the laws of the horn, if it is presented but no challenger blows the horn within the course of a day, then the king retains his crown."

"But someone challenged?"

"Mawyndulë," Myron said. "As it happens there are no restrictions on who can blow the horn other than they must be of elven blood. Even an outcast, even one cursed by Ferrol, can still challenge. And if he wins—"

"If he wins, he's back in," Royce finished.

"Yes."

"But he lost, right?" Mauvin asked.

"Novron was a battle-hardened veteran of a lengthy war," Hadrian concluded. "And Myron said Mawyndulë was just a kid?"

"Yes." The monk nodded. "It was a quick and humiliating defeat."

"But this doesn't make sense," Arista said. "Esrahaddon told us he was convinced that Mawyndulë was still alive."

"Nyphron did not kill Mawyndulë. While the challenge is usually a fight to the death, Nyphron let him live. Perhaps because he was so young, or maybe because as an outcast he was no threat. What is known is that Mawyndulë was exiled, never allowed in Erivan again."

"So how did Novron die?" Mauvin asked.

"He was murdered."

"By who?"

"No one knows."

"I would wager on Mawyndulë," Royce said.

"Hmm..." Arista pulled on her lower lip, deep in thought.

"What?" Royce asked.

"I was just thinking about what Esrahaddon said when he was dying. He warned that the *Uli Vermar* was ending and that I had to take the heir to Percepliquis to get the horn. But his very last words were 'Patriarch...is the same...' I always assumed that he was never able to finish the sentence before he died, but what if he said all he meant to? Myron, how many patriarchs have there been?"

"Twenty-two including Patriarch Nilnev."

"Yes, and how old is he?"

"I don't recall reading about his birth, but he's been patriarch for sixty years."

"Myron, what are some of the other patriarchs' names?"

"Before Patriarch Nilnev was Patriarch Evlinn. Before him was Patriarch Lenvin. Before that—"

Arista's eyes widened. "Is it possible?"

"Is what possible?" Royce asked.

Arista got to her knees. "Does anyone have anything to write with?"

"I have a bit of chalk." Myron produced a white nib from a pouch.

"Nilnev, Evlin, Lenvin, Venlin..." Arista scrawled the words on the flat rock.

"There are two *n*'s on *Evlinn*," the monk corrected.

She looked up and smiled. "Of course there are. There would have to be. Don't you see? Esrahaddon was right. He changed his name, his appearance. He must have found a position in the Cenzar Council of Emperor Nareion, which would have been easy given his mastery of the Art. Esrahaddon knew that Venlin and Nilnev were the same. In fact, every patriarch since the first has been the same person—Mawyndulë."

"It would explain why the church was so intent on finding the heir," Hadrian said. "If they killed the bloodline of Novron, the *Uli Vermar* would end early."

"Which would be fine, if Mawyndulë had the horn. The fact that he didn't was probably the only thing keeping Gaunt alive when they had him locked up. This explains why the Patriarch has sent so many teams down here. What he didn't realize, though, is you actually needed the heir to succeed. Esrahaddon took precautions. That's why he told me that the heir had to come. I'm not sure exactly what he did, but I venture to say that anyone other than Gaunt touching the horn's box would have been killed."

"That also explains why the Patriarch hired Magnus to kill Gaunt. With the heir dead, a single toot of the horn would make Nilnev king by default, just as it was supposed to do with Novron," Hadrian said.

"Yes, but if the Patriarch blows the horn and Gaunt is still alive, then he's not claiming an empty throne but rather announcing his right to challenge, right?" Arista looked to Myron, who nodded. "So if Gaunt wins, he becomes king of the elves and they have to do whatever he says. And if he tells them to go back across the Nidwalden and leave us alone, they will."

"Theoretically," Myron said.

"So all we have to do is make the Patriarch think he succeeded. We'll tell him Gaunt is dead and keep him hidden until the horn is blown. Then we'll spring the trap."

"Are you forgetting about this fight-to-the-death thing?" Gaunt asked.

"That won't be a problem," Arista reassured him. "He's old, even for an elf. A breath of wind could kill him. He doesn't want to fight you. He's terrified of a fight. That's why he wants you dead."

Gaunt sat silent, his eyes working.

"So what do you say, Degan?" Arista asked. "You wanted to be emperor. How does king of the elves sound to you?"

❧

Arista reached the surface and lay on the wet ground, exhausted. The dazzling morning light shone in her eyes and played across her skin. She had so missed the sun that she lay with arms outstretched, bathing in its warmth. The fresh air was so wonderful that she drank it in as if it were cool water discovered after crossing an arid desert.

For a time she had thought she might not make it out of the hole and back to Amberton Lee. Even with the rope around her, she clung to rocks, shaking from both exhaustion and fear. Hadrian was always there offering encouragement, calling to her, pushing her to try harder. There were a few places where Royce and Hadrian had to pull her up a particularly difficult section and her progress was often slow. Even with his wounded arm Mauvin climbed faster. Still, now that it was over, she was proud of her accomplishment and the sun on her face was the reward.

She was awakened from her reverie when she heard Magnus quietly say, "He's here."

Getting up, she saw four men walking swiftly toward them. The Patriarch was flanked by two guards and behind them was Monsignor Merton, whom Arista had met once in Ervanon. They appeared out of place, descending the ragged slope with the bottoms of their robes wet from being dragged across the melting snow.

Accompanied by Hadrian, Mauvin, Magnus, and Myron,

Arista moved away from the open maw of the shaft and pushed through a large copse of forsythia, threatening to bloom. Hadrian took her hand and pulled her close.

"Give me the horn, quickly," the Patriarch said, extending his hand. Glancing over his shoulder toward the hilltop, he added, "The elves have arrived."

Arista pulled off her pack and took out the box. "Gaunt died before he could blow it."

The Patriarch smirked at her as he took the box. His eyes were transfixed as he drew out the horn and held it up.

"At last," the old man said, and placed it to his lips. He blew into the horn and a long clear note of ominous tone cut through the air. It lacked any musical quality, sounding instead like a cry—a scream of hate and loathing. Each of them instinctively took a few steps backward until Arista felt the little branches of the forsythia jabbing her. The old man lowered his arms, a smile on his face. "You did very well."

Horses thundered over the top of the hill. Arista was amazed by the elegance and grace of the elven lords, dressed in gold and blue with lion helms. With them was Modina, accompanied by Mercy and Allie, who looked exhausted.

One of the riders dismounted, removed his helm, and approached the group. He pointed to the horn and spoke quickly in elvish. Arista could not decipher every word but caught the gist of his introduction as Irawondona of the Asendwayr, who had been the acting Steward of Erivan. He inquired who had blown the horn.

The Patriarch stood before the elven lord and raised his arms. As he did, his features changed. His face grew longer, his nose narrowed, his brows slanted, his ears sharpened, and his eyes sparkled with a luminous green. His frame became slighter, his fingers longer, thinner. The only thing that remained unchanged was the white, near-purple hair. *"Behold*

Mawyndulë of the Miralyith, soon to be King of Erivan, Emperor of Elan, Lord of the World." The words were spoken slowly, deliberately, such that even Arista understood each one.

He threw his head back, cast his arms straight out to his sides, and slowly rotated, giving them all a fair view. Everyone, including the elves, stared, stunned by the transformation.

Mawyndulë and the elven lord spoke quickly to each other. Irawondona pointed toward Modina during the exchange. Arista was catching only bits and pieces but her heart sank when she heard Myron mutter, "Uh-oh."

He added, "Mawyndulë knows about Gaunt."

"What?" Arista asked.

"He just told Irawondona that he blew the horn, and the elven lord said he has brought his opponent. But Mawyndulë said Modina is not the heir, that Degan is, and that Degan is hiding in the hole behind us."

Mawyndulë turned to face them. "I know all about your plan. Your guardian should have paid more attention to Esrahaddon's warnings. Or did you merely forget what he told you the last time you met?"

Arista looked at Hadrian quizzically.

"He said a lot of things."

"He explained," Mawyndulë said, "that he couldn't tell you anything because all his conversations were being overheard."

"You've been listening?" Arista asked.

"I paid close attention to Esrahaddon until he died, but he rarely said anything of importance. Listening to him was easy, as I knew him so well. While you were on your little trip, I monitored the dwarf. The Art did not work as well with him, but it was enough." He looked at Magnus. "I'll deal with you after I'm crowned. In the meantime, you might as well signal to Royce to bring Gaunt up. He's quite safe. No one can harm him or me now that the blessing of Ferrol is upon us. We are

822 Michael J. Sullivan

protected from everyone. It's only during the competition that we can be harmed and only by each other. So the last of Novron's line is safe until dawn tomorrow. There are rules to this ritual and we must observe them."

A rustle in the thickets announced the approach of two figures from the mouth of the hole. Degan shuffled forward with Royce behind him. Gaunt looked sick, pale and sweaty such that his bangs stuck to his forehead.

Mawyndulë turned to Lord Irawondona and announced in elvish, "*This is the heir of Nyphron.*" He then motioned toward Gaunt.

The elven lords and an old owl-helmed elf looked skeptically at Gaunt. They appraised him for several minutes, then spoke at length with Mawyndulë. When they were finished, the elves, along with Mawyndulë, returned up the hillside, leaving the party in the snow.

"What happened?" Hadrian asked.

"The challenge will begin at sunrise tomorrow," Myron explained.

⁓

The elves made camp on the crest of the hill. The rest of them gathered outside the Hovel, which hid in the shelter of holly trees partway up the slope. Hadrian built a fire and asked the boys to gather more wood, which they did, restricting their search toward the bottom of the hill. The process was slow, as the boys continued to look over their shoulders toward the top of the hill.

Modina and the girls were permitted to *join their own kind* and she found a place for the girls near the fire before approaching Arista. She was dressed in a dark lavish gown and raised the hem to pick her way around the others.

"What's going on?" the empress asked.

Arista reached out and took her hand the moment she was near. "It will be fine. Degan, as Novron's last descendant, will fight tomorrow. If he wins, he'll become ruler of the elves and they must obey him."

Modina's face was creased with worry. She looked at those circled around the fire. "If Degan loses, we have no hope. You have no idea what the elves are capable of. Aquesta was destroyed in just a few minutes. The walls fell and every building not made of stone has been burned. I'm afraid to even consider the number of dead. I tried, I tried everything, but... they walked through us with so little effort. If Degan fails..."

"He won't fail," Hadrian said. "Arista has a plan."

"I can't take the credit," she said. "It was Esrahaddon's idea. I think this was his intent from the moment he escaped Gutaria."

"What is it?" the empress asked.

Arista and Hadrian exchanged looks before Arista said, "I can't tell you."

Modina raised her eyebrows.

"The Patriarch is really an elf and a very powerful wizard. He's the one who challenged Degan. Apparently he has the ability to eavesdrop on conversations like this one."

Modina nodded. "Then don't say a word. I trust you. You haven't let me down yet."

"How are the girls?" Arista asked.

"Frightened. Allie has been asking about her father and Elden. I assume they are..."

"Yes, they were killed. As was my brother."

Modina nodded. "I'm sorry. If there is anything I..." The empress choked up and paused. She wiped her eyes. "Dear, sweet Maribor, I swear Gaunt can have the throne and I will go back to farming for the rest of my life and be content with an empty stomach if only he can win. I want you to know

that we are all in your debt for what you have done, for the
sacrifices of Alric, Wyatt, and Elden. Whatever happens
tomorrow, you are all heroes today."

Hadrian, Royce, and Mauvin took Gaunt aside for some
last-minute sparring tips. Arista focused her attention on the
hilltop, where multicolored tents rose to the sounds of alien
voices singing ancient songs. The tension around the fire was
palpable. Out of everyone, except perhaps Gaunt, Monsignor
Merton showed the greatest anxiety. He sat on an upturned
bucket, staring into the fire. Before long Myron sat beside him
and the two had a lengthy talk.

Myron was the only one who showed no signs of concern.
After speaking to Merton, he spent his time with the boys,
discovering how they had built the Hovel and asking numerous questions about how the horses had fared while they were
gone. They told him how the cold cracked their spit and the
monk marveled at their tales. He helped them cook a fine dinner and generally kept the boys busy with chores both in preparation and cleanup.

The sun set and darkness enveloped them save for the light
of the campfire. It was not unlike the one Arista had sat beside
less than a year earlier and very close to the same spot. A little
farther up the slope, perhaps. So much had happened, so much
had changed since the night she had ridden with Etcher.
Amberton Lee was a different place now. With him she had felt
lost in the wilderness. Now she was at the center of the world.

Ancient stones upon the Lee
Dusts of memories gone we see
Once the center, once the all
Lost forever, fall the wall.

She too was different. Perhaps they all were.

"Why don't you and the girls bed down in the shelter there?" Hadrian said to Modina, seeing the girls yawning. "You don't mind, do you, boys?"

They all shook their heads, staring, as they had been for some time, at the empress.

"Where will Degan sleep?" Modina asked, looking across the fire to where Degan was repeating the girls' yawns.

"Near the fire with the rest of us, I suppose," Hadrian responded.

The empress lifted her voice and said, "Degan, you will sleep with me in the shelter tonight."

Degan rolled his eyes. "I appreciate the offer—I do—but really this isn't the night for—"

"I need you rested. The fate of our race depends on your victory tomorrow. The shelter is the most comfortable place. You will *sleep* there, do you understand?"

He nodded with an expression that showed no will to argue.

Modina stood, looked at Arista, and then embraced and kissed her. "Again, thank you."

She went around the fire, thanking, embracing, and kissing each. Then, wiping her face, Modina returned to the shelter of the Hovel.

"Do you think it will work?" Arista asked Hadrian, who smirked. "Sorry. I'm just nervous. This was my idea, after all."

"And a damn fine one at that. Have I mentioned how smart you are?"

She scowled at him. "I'm not that smart—you're just blinded by love."

"Is that a bad thing?"

Her expression softened. "No."

He sat propped against one of the trees and she lay down in his arms. When he squeezed her, she felt a weight lifted and she reveled in the warmth and safety of his embrace. Her eyes drifted to the stars. She wanted to tell them not to leave, to order the sun never to rise, because for this one moment everything was perfect. She could stay as she was, stay in Hadrian's arms, and forget about what was to come.

"One of the great disappointments about living so long is that when the moment of triumph comes, there is no one to share it with," Mawyndulë said as he stepped into the ring of firelight, looking at them with a pleasant smile. His guards followed and placed his chair for him. Mawyndulë sat, showing no disappointment with their glares.

Arista closed her eyes and reached out delicately. She sensed Mawyndulë's power. In her mind, magic appeared as a light in darkness. The oberdaza flickered like torches but Mawyndulë burned like the sun. She avoided him and focused on his guards. They were not men or even elves. They were the same as the Gilarabrywn—pure magic.

"It's a bit chilly, isn't it?" the old elf said. "And what a pitiful excuse for a fire."

Mawyndulë clapped his hands and the flames grew tall and bright. The boys jerked back in fear. Monsignor Merton got up and took several steps back, his eyes wide.

The old man held his hands out to the licking flames and rubbed them together. "Ah, much better. My old bones can't take the cold like they used to."

"Magic," Merton whispered, "is forbidden by the church."

"Of course it is. I don't want mongrels practicing my Art; it's insulting. Would you like it if I wore your clothes? Took them out, got them all dirty, and made fun of them in public? Of course not, and I won't allow humans to defile what is mine."

"How is magic…yours?" Royce asked.

"Inheritance. My family invented the Art, so it is mine.

Wretched thieves stole it, so I took it back. Esrahaddon was the last of the thieves. He used my Art to destroy Percepli-quis." The old man's eyes drifted off, looking at something unseen. "He killed all of them—did it to stop me, but he failed. Not only did I survive, but I was able to keep him alive as well. I needed to know where the boy was, you see. I thought in time he would relent and eventually he did, although unknowingly." The old man smirked and looked back at them. "Is anyone else hungry?"

Mawyndulë spoke words unknown to Arista and made a gesture with his fingers, and before them a banquet of food appeared. A tableful of hams, ducks, and quails were roasted to bronze perfection and wreathed in vegetables, candied wal-nuts, and berries.

"What's wrong, Merton?" Mawyndulë asked without bothering to look at the priest, who had an expression of hor-ror across his face. "Are you shocked? Of course you are, and with good reason, but please eat. The food is delicious and I do so hate to dine alone. Go ahead, everyone, dig in."

Mawyndulë did not wait for them and began tearing off chucks of ham. Glass goblets appeared on the table and filled themselves with a deep-red liquid. The Patriarch picked up one and drained it to wash down the ham. The goblet was full again before he set it back onto the table.

No one else touched the food.

"Where is he?" Mawyndulë asked. "Where is my worthy adversary? Hasn't run off, has he? The rules clearly state that if he fails to show, I win by default."

"He's sleeping," Hadrian said.

"Ah, getting a good night's rest. Very wise. Personally I can never sleep before these things. Gaunt takes after his ancestor. Nyphron slept the night before too. I knew him, you know, your beloved Novron. Ah, but yes, you already discovered that little fact. Here's something the books won't tell you. He was an ass. All those tales about him saving humanity for the love of a farmer's daughter are absolute rubbish. He was no different than anyone else, and like everyone, he sought power. His tribe was small and weak, so he harnessed all of you as fodder for his battles. The Instarya are the best warriors, of course. I will grant them that. There's no point in denying it. That is *their* art, and he taught it to your knights. Still, humans would not have won if not for Cenzlyor, who taught them my Art as well.

"Novron was so arrogant, so sure of himself. He played the wise, forgiving conqueror at Avempartha and those in power were more than willing to bow before him. They were all frightened children at his feet—the boy from the inferior clan. Your great god was just a vindictive brat bent on revenge."

The old man bit into a leg of duck and sat back with a glass of wine in his other hand. He leaned on one arm of the chair and looked up toward the stars. He followed the duck with a fresh strawberry and swooned. "Oh, you've *got* to try one of these. They're perfect. That's the problem with the real thing—you can never find them at their peak. Or they're too big or too small, too tart or sweet. No, I must admit, I pride myself on creating a good strawberry."

He licked his fingers and looked at them. No one moved.

"It was *you*," Merton said at last. "The one you spoke of at the cathedral, the ancient enemy controlling everything."

"Of course," the old man said. "I told you that if you thought hard enough, you'd figure it out, didn't I?" He picked a grape this time but grimaced as he chewed. "See, I'm not nearly as good at these. Far too sour."

"You *are* evil."

"What do you know of evil?" Mawyndulë's tone turned harsh. "You know nothing about it."

"I do," Royce said.

Mawyndulë peered at the thief and nodded. "Then you know that evil is not born, but created. I was turned into what I have become. The council did that to me. They made me believe what they said. They put the dagger in my hand and sent me out with words of blessing. Elders who I revered, who I respected and trusted as the wisest of my people, told me what needed to be done. I believed them when they said the fate of our race was upon me. Back then, we were as you are now, a flickering flame in a growing wind. Nyphron had taken Avempartha. The council convinced me that I was our nation's last hope. They told me my father was too stubborn to make peace and that he would see us all die. As long as he breathed, as long as he was king, we were doomed. No one dared move against him, as the murderer would pay first in this life and then in the next."

Mawyndulë plucked another strawberry but hesitated to eat. He held it between his fingers, rolling it.

"Ten priests of Ferrol swore I would be absolved. Because the existence of the elven race was at stake, they convinced me that Ferrol would see me as a savior, not a murderer. The council agreed to support me, to waive the law. They were so sincere and I was...so young. As my father died, I saw him cry, not for himself but for me, because he knew what they had done, and what my fate would be."

"Why are you here?" Arista asked.

Mawyndulë seemed to have just become aware of them around him. "What?"

"I asked why you were here. Won't they allow you in the elven camp? Are you still an outcast?"

Mawyndulë glanced over his shoulder. "After I am king, they will accept me. They will do whatever I say."

He shifted in his seat and stroked one of the long arms of

the chair. It was of unusual design but strangely familiar in shape. It was not until he moved that Arista realized she had seen similar ones in Avempartha. The Patriarch had brought his own chair with him—not from Aquesta, not from Ervanon, but from home.

He hasn't touched anything but that chair.

She imagined Mawyndulë sealed in the Crown Tower, living in isolation, surrounded by elven furnishing, doing what he could to separate himself.

Mawyndulë looked over to where Magnus sat. "I would have honored our agreement, dwarf. Your people could have had Delgos once more. I have no use for that rock. Of course, now I will have to kill you. As for the rest, you've done me a great service by retrieving the horn and for that I am tempted to let you all live. I could make you court slaves. You will be wonderful novelties—the last humans! A shame you die so quickly, but I suppose I could breed you. The princess looks healthy enough. I could raise a small domestic herd. You could perform at feasts. Oh, don't look so distraught. It's better than dying."

Mauvin's expression hardened and Arista noticed the muscles on his sword arm tighten. She threw him a stern look. He glared back but relaxed.

"Why bother to create the New Empire," Arista asked quickly, "just to destroy it?"

"I broke Esrahaddon's spell and released the Gilarabrywn from Avempartha to show my brothers how weak the human world is, to encourage them to march the moment the *Uli Vermar* ended. Others took it upon themselves to use the occasion to their advantage. Still, I took advantage of Saldur, Galien, and Ethelred's blundering to press for the eradication of the half-breeds. While my word will be undisputed as king, killing any who bear even a small amount of elven blood might not be popular with my kin once I assume the throne. And I cannot abide having their abomination survive. I was the one who started the idea that elves were slaves in the Old Empire. It made it easier, you see—it is so simple to hate those you feel are inferior."

"You're so sure of yourself," Mauvin said. "This protection of Ferrol is some sort of religious blessing. Placed on you by your god. It's supposed to prevent anyone—other than Gaunt—from harming you, right? Thing is, a week ago Novron was a god too. Turns out that was just a lie. A story invented to control us. So what if this is too? What if Ferrol, Drome, and Maribor are all just stories? If it is, I could draw my sword and cut through that miserable throat of yours and save everyone here a lot of trouble."

"Mauvin, don't," Arista said.

Mawyndulë chuckled. "Ever the Pickering, aren't you? Go on, dear count. Swing away."

"Don't," Arista told him firmly.

Mauvin's eyes showed that he was considering it, but the count did not move.

"You are wise to listen to your princess." He paused. "Oh, but I forget, you're his queen, aren't you? King Alric is dead. You left him down there, didn't you? Abandoned him to rot. What poor help you turned out to be."

"Mauvin, please. Let it go. He'll be dead tomorrow."

"Do you really think so?" Mawyndulë snapped his fingers and a huge block of stone making up a portion of the ruins exploded, throwing up a cloud of dust. Everyone jumped.

The old man laughed and said, "I don't agree with your assessment. I think the odds are decidedly in my favor. It's a shame, though, that there will be so few of you left." He paused to look them over. "Is this all that survived? A queen, a count, a thief, the Teshlor, and…" He looked at Myron. "Who exactly would you be?"

"Myron," he said with his characteristic smile. "I'm a Monk of Maribor."

"A Monk of Maribor, indeed—the heretical cult. How dare you worship something other than an elf?" He smirked. "Didn't you just hear your friend? Maribor is a myth, a fairy tale to make you think that life is fair or to provide the illusion of hope. Man created him out of fear, and ambitious men took advantage of that fear—I know of what I speak. I created an entire church—I created the god Novron out of the traitor Nyphron and a religion out of ignorance and intolerance."

Myron did not look concerned. He listened carefully, thoughtfully, then recited: " '*Erebus, father unto all that be, creator of Elan, divider of the seas and sky, brought forth the four: Ferrol, the eldest, the wise and clever; Drome, the stalwart and crafty; Maribor, the bold and adventurous; Muriel, the serene and beautiful—gods unto the world.*' "

"Do not quote me text from your cultish scriptures," Mawyndulë said.

"I'm not," Myron said. "It's yours—section one, paragraph eight of the Book of Ferrol. I found it in the tomb of Nyphron. I apologize if I did not get all the words correct. I am not entirely fluent in elvish."

Mawyndulë's grin faded. "Oh yes, I recall your name now. You are Myron Lanaklin from the Winds Abbey. You were the one left as a witness while the other monks were burned alive, is that right? That incident was Saldur's doing—he had a fetish for burning things—but you are as much to blame, aren't you? You forced him by refusing to reveal what you knew. How do you live with all that guilt?"

"Seemingly better than you live with your hatred," Myron replied.

"You think so?" Mawyndulë asked, and leaned forward.

"You're about to become a slave while I am about to be crowned king of the world."

His attempt at intimidation had no effect on the monk, who, to Arista's astonishment, leaned forward and asked, "But for how long? You are ancient, even by elven standards. How short-lived will your victory be? And at what cost will you have achieved that which you *think* is so great? What have you had to endure to reach this moment? You wasted your long life to obtain a goal you can't possibly live to appreciate. If you hadn't allowed hatred to rule you, you might have spent all those years in contentment and love. You could have—"

"I'm already enjoying it!" Mawyndulë shouted.

"You have forgotten so much." Myron sighed with obvious pity. " '*Revenge is a bittersweet fruit that leaves the foul aftertaste of regret.*'—Patriarch Venlin, The Perdith Address to the Dolimins, circa twenty-one thirty-one."

"You are clever, aren't you?" Mawyndulë said.

" '*Clever are the Children of Ferrol, quick, certain, and dark their fate.*'—Nyphron of the Instarya."

"Shut up, Myron," Hadrian growled.

Arista also saw the flare in the elf's eyes but Myron appeared oblivious. To her relief, Mawyndulë did not strike out. Instead he stood and walked away. His two guards followed with the chair. The banquet vanished and the fire's flames dwindled to mere embers.

"Are you insane?" Hadrian asked Myron.

"I'm sorry," the monk said.

"I'm not." Mauvin clapped the monk on the back, grinning. "You're my new hero."

CHAPTER 27

THE CHALLENGE

Trumpets announced the gray light of the predawn.

The elves had transformed the top of Amberton Lee overnight. Where once only the desolate remains of ancient walls and half-buried pillars stood, the crest of the hill now displayed seven great tents marked by shimmering banners. In the misty haze of melting snow, a low wall of intertwined brambles created an arena marked by torches that burned blue flames. Drums followed a loud fanfare and beat to an ominous rhythm—the heartbeat of an ancient people.

Degan shivered in the cold, looking even worse than the night before. Hadrian, Royce, and Mauvin fed him coffee that steamed like some magical draft. Gaunt clutched the mug with both hands and still the liquid threatened to spill from his shaking. Arista stood with her feet in the cold dew, every muscle in her body tense as she waited. Everyone waited. Aside from the three whispering last-minute instructions into Gaunt's ear, no one else spoke. They all stood like stones on the Lee, unwilling witnesses.

Modina waited with the girls, prepared to face what could be their last sunrise. The boys stood only a few feet from her with Magnus and Myron. The lot of them formed a straight line, uniformly standing with their arms folded across their chests—all eyes on Degan.

Mawyndulë appeared relaxed as he sat in his chair, his legs outstretched and crossed, his eyes closed as if sleeping. The rest of the elves milled about in small groups, speaking in hushed, reverent tones. Arista guessed this was a sacred religious event for them. For those in her party, it was just terrifying.

She turned when she heard Monsignor Merton say, "I know you have a good reason." At first, she thought he was speaking to her, but when she saw him, his eyes were looking up. "But you have to understand I'm but the ignorant fool you made. I don't mean that as an insult, of course. Perish the thought. Who am I to pass judgment on your creation? Still, I hope you have enjoyed our talks. I am entertaining at least, aren't I, Lord? You wouldn't want to lose that, would you? Many of us are entertaining and it would be a shame if we disappeared altogether. Have you considered how you might miss us?" He paused as if listening, then nodded.

"What did he say?" Arista asked.

Merton looked up, startled. "Oh? What he always says."

She waited, but the monsignor never explained further.

The drums grew louder, the rhythm faster. The sky began to lighten and birds, newly returned to the north, began to sing. The faces of the men and elves grew more serious as the priest of Ferrol entered the ring with a thurible burning Agarwood incense. He began singing softly in elvish.

Gaunt placed a hand to his chest, rubbed his shirt, and whispered to himself. Arista cringed and Hadrian said something sharply but quietly and Gaunt pulled his hand away. Arista glanced at Mawyndulë and suspected the damage was done. The old elf narrowed his gaze at his opponent.

Mawyndulë rose from his seat and walked toward Gaunt.

He glanced to the eastern horizon. "Not long now," he said. "I just wanted to wish you good luck."

The once Patriarch held out his hand. Gaunt looked at it hesitantly but reached out to shake. Mawyndulë was quick and nimble and he tore Gaunt's collar wide, revealing the medallion hanging there. He staggered backward as Hadrian and Royce quickly pulled Gaunt away. Mawyndulë sneered and glanced at Arista, then Hadrian, and lastly Myron. He looked about quickly, nervously.

"Not long now," Royce reminded him. "And how will you fare when your magic is useless?"

Mawyndulë smiled and with clenched teeth he began to laugh.

"*Muer wir ahran dulwyer!*" Mawyndulë shouted suddenly. All the elves turned to face him. Everyone else looked at Myron.

"He evokes the Right of Champion," Myron said.

"What does that mean?" Royce asked.

"It means he asks for someone else to fight in his stead."

"Can he do that?" Arista asked.

"Yes," Myron replied. "Remember the inscription on the horn:

> *Should champion be called to fight*
> *evoked is the Hand of Ferrol,*
> *Which protects the championed from all,*
> *and champion from all—save one—from peril.*

"If the champion wins, Mawyndulë will be king."

"*Byrinith con duylar ben lar Irawondona!*" Mawyndulë shouted and there was a loud murmur among the elves as they all turned to face the elven lord.

"Oh damn," Hadrian said. "He had to pick the big guy. I'm pretty sure he knows how to fight."

Lord Irawondona stepped forward in his shimmering armor. He said something that none of them could hear. Mawyndulë replied by nodding and Lord Irawondona raised his hands and shouted, "*Duylar e finis dan iskabareth ben Mawyndulë!*"

"He just accepted," Myron reported.

Gaunt, who had been shaking his head, erupted, "I'm not fighting him. I'm supposed to fight the old guy, not this guy."

"Myron." Arista spun the monk to face her. "Can Gaunt do the same? Can he pick a champion?"

"Ah—yes. I believe so. It would only make sense, as the entire competition is designed for a fair contest between the opponents."

She watched Lord Irawondona remove his cloak. The elf looked imposing even from across the field. "Hadrian is the only one who has any chance of winning. Name him your champion. Myron, tell Gaunt the words he needs to say."

"They weren't on the horn."

"You just heard him," Royce reminded him. "Just repeat what you heard Mawyndulë say, and quickly."

"Oh, right. *Muer wir ahran dulwyer,*" Myron said.

"Degan, say it! Say it loud!"

"*Muer wir*—ah—*ahran*—ah—" Gaunt stumbled and hesitated.

"*Dulwyer,*" Myron whispered.

"*Dulwyer!*" Gaunt shouted.

The heads of the elves turned.

"Now the next line and substitute my name for Irawondona," Hadrian said.

Myron fed him the words and Gaunt recited them. The

elves looked confused for a moment, until Gaunt pointed at Hadrian. Myron gave Hadrian the next line and Arista stood shaking as she heard him recite it aloud, accepting the role of Gaunt's champion.

"Degan," she said, "give Hadrian the medallion back."

"But he said—"

"I know what he said, and he'll let you have it after the fight, but right now he needs all the help he can get. Give it to him now!" Degan tore the chain off his neck and handed it to her.

"Boys!" Hadrian shouted. "Fetch me that bundle near my blanket and the shield!"

The four boys sprinted down the slope to the camp.

"You *can* beat him, can't you?" Arista asked while slipping the chain over his head. She was trembling. "You will beat him for me, won't you? You can't leave me like Emery and Hilfred. You know I couldn't take that, right? You know that—you *have* to win."

"For you? Anything," he said, and kissed her hard, pulling her to him.

The boys returned and threw open the bundle, revealing the brilliant armor of Jerish Grelad. "Help me on with this," Hadrian said, and everyone, including Degan and Myron, looked for ways to assist.

An elf appeared before them, holding one of the strange halberd weapons they had seen images of in Percepliquis. He held it out to Hadrian.

"You know how to use this?" Arista asked.

"Never touched one before."

"Something tells me *he* has," she said as across the field Lord Irawondona lifted his own halberd with both hands spread apart, holding it like a double-bladed quarterstaff. He spun it with remarkable speed such that the blades hummed.

"Yeah, I think you're right."

Hadrian took a breath and turned to her. Their eyes met just at the moment the sun broke over the trees and shone on their faces. Hadrian looked beautiful, glimmering in his golden armor. He appeared like an ancient god reborn onto the world of man.

The priest of Ferrol shouted something and neither needed Myron to translate.

It was time.

Arista found it hard to breathe and her legs grew weak as she watched Hadrian enter the ring of torches. He stepped to the center and waited, planting his feet in the packed snow and shifting his grip on the strange weapon.

She looked at Mawyndulë and saw he was no longer smiling; his face showed concern as Irawondona entered the ring. The blue torches flared with his passing and the elven lord strode about the space casually, confidently.

"Hadrian's the best in the world, Arista," Mauvin whispered to her. "Better than any Pickering, better than Braga, better than—"

"Better than an *elven lord*?" she asked sharply. "He's probably played with that weapon since he was a child—some fifteen hundred years ago!"

The drums rolled and the horns blared once more in a sharply definitive sound that hurt her ears. She tried to swallow but found her throat tight. In her chest, her heart hammered, and her hands rose to her breast in an attempt to contain it.

Hadrian waited awkwardly as if uncertain whether the fight had begun. Irawondona walked around the circle of blue burning torches, spinning his spear, rolling it across his shoulders, down his arm, and around his wrist, grinning at the crowd. He threw the weapon up, where it rotated above his head, and whirled it such that it made the sound of birds in flight. He caught it again and laughed.

"How good is he?" Arista asked Mauvin. "Can you tell by the way he moves?"

"Oh, he's good."

"How good? You've fought Hadrian. Can he beat him?"

"He's real good."

"Stop saying that and answer the damn question!"

"I don't know, okay?" Mauvin admitted. "I can only say that he's really fast, faster than Hadrian, I think."

"What about all the whirling? What can you tell from that?"

"That's nothing, he's just trying to intimidate."

"Well, it's working on me."

Hadrian stood still, waiting.

Irawondona continued to spin the spear with his hands. "I must commend you on at least knowing how to hold the *ule-da-var*," Irawondona told him.

"Yeah, but I don't know how to do all that fancy spinning stuff," Hadrian replied. "Does that help? Or is it just needlessly tiring your muscles?"

Irawondona closed the distance between them with brilliant speed and slashed at Hadrian. One stroke aimed down and across with the top blade and another up with the bottom blade. Hadrian dodged the first strike and parried the second with a last-minute swing.

"That was good," Mauvin whispered. "I'd be dead right now."

"In the first exchange?" Arista asked.

"Yeah, contrary to popular belief, sword fights don't last long, a few minutes at best. I watched his feet and they fooled me—he's *very* good."

Irawondona jabbed—Hadrian slapped the blade aside. He jabbed again, and again; each time Hadrian caught the stroke.

"Very nice," Irawondona said. "Now let's see how good you really are."

The elf slapped the shaft of his spear, causing it to hum and the blade to quiver. He jabbed again, this time too fast for Arista to see. Hadrian blocked, caught, and slapped but then Irawondona swung.

"Duck!" Mauvin shouted. "Oh no!"

Hadrian did duck, stabbing his lower blade into the snow. Irawondona's first stroke passed over Hadrian's head, but then the second came down. Before it landed, Hadrian pulled on his planted pole and slid himself across the snow on his knees, leaving Irawondona to strike nothing but the bare ground.

Both combatants paused, breathing hard.

"Whoa!" Mauvin said. "That was really good."

"You don't move like a human," Irawondona said.

"And you fight surprisingly well for a talking *brideeth*."

The reaction on Irawondona's face was immediate. His happy grin vanished.

Arista looked to Myron.

"I don't know that word," the monk replied.

"I wouldn't think you would," Royce said. "I taught him that one."

Irawondona lashed out again. He moved with blinding speed, spinning forward so that the dual blades flashed in the growing sunlight, their movement visible only by the streaks of light they left. She could hear the sound of the humming knives vibrating the air.

Hadrian leapt back, looking uncertain how to deal with the oncoming whirlwind of metal. He dodged and dodged again as the blades swept close to his head and legs equally. The elf lord drove him back to the edge of the thicket wall. Once there, he flicked the bottom blade, slashing out at Hadrian's

chest. With an agile spin, Hadrian traded places and slammed
the elf lord with his elbow while tripping him with the pole.
Lord Irawondona quickly somersaulted to his feet with a look
of shock on his face.

"You fight like…" Lord Irawondona stopped. He was
breathing hard and eyeing Hadrian with concern.

Hadrian now advanced.

This time the blades collided. Staccato strikes sounded
across the hilltop. Poles spun up against each other, striking,
crossing, clipping. Again there were the hum of bees and then
more strikes. Irawondona pushed Hadrian back, jamming
him, driving him off balance, his whirling pole streaking in
the golden light. Hadrian stumbled and staggered off balance,
and the elf lord flashed a grin. He pressed his attack but then
Hadrian made an unexpected twist and raked Irawondona
across the side with his long blade. A clean stroke—Hadrian's
blade sliced from neck to leg.

The elven lord fell back, shocked. He felt along his side
with fear on his face, at the same time Hadrian looked at his
weapon—neither found blood. They looked bewildered for a
moment; then Irawondona shook it off and regained his
stance. He no longer made an effort at exhibitionism.

They circled each other, more hesitant than before, each
feinting and falling back, reaching, searching for a weakness
in the other. Irawondona charged again; once more the blades
clamored, ringing with a sound horrible to hear. One blow
after another the metal collided edge to edge, razors striking
razors. Just listening to the noise made Arista weak.

Once more Hadrian fell and again Irawondona stabbed,
this time faster, forcing Hadrian to log roll away. Irawondona
chased but was not fast enough and Hadrian was able to get
back on his feet and caught the elf in mid-stride. The elf lord

was too late to pull back and Hadrian's short blade sliced down the back of Irawondona's exposed calf.

"Ha-ha!" Hadrian laughed. "Not fast enough! Now you're—"

No blood.

Once more the two looked at the clean blade and the unscarred flesh and slowly Irawondona began to smile.

"Oh dear Maribor!" Arista cried. "Not again, oh please god, not again."

"What is it?" Mauvin asked. "What's wrong?"

"Hadrian can't harm him. I don't understand. Did we make a mistake when naming him as champion?"

The elf lord, grinning with confidence, attacked again, this time more openly. Hadrian dodged and counterattacked and his strike found Irawondona's neck. The long blade came slicing across from under the exposed throat from the bottom up. Irawondona's head jerked up, but once more, the blade did not bite.

The elf lord laughed. "I am a god," he said, and began to strike out at Hadrian without fear.

"No!" Arista screamed. She looked to the others desperately, tears filling her eyes. "Oh god, Royce, do something. Save him! Please, you have to save him!"

✧

Royce looked at Hadrian as he retreated under the constant bombardment from Irawondona. The elven lord was not letting him rest. It was all Hadrian could do to dodge or glance aside the blows. It would not be long now.

He pulled Alverstone from its sheath. He had never found anything that the blade could not cut. Hadrian had even used it to blind the Gilarabrywn and that was supposed to be impervious to all weapons except the one bearing its name.

In the ring, Irawondona struck wildly from high over his head. Hadrian lifted his pole to block and the long blade struck it. The crack was tremendous as the pole broke in two. The blade struck Hadrian in the chest. The armor prevented the blade from penetrating, but Royce heard something snap and Hadrian cried out. Still, he managed to trip Irawondona to the ground. Hadrian was breathing hard, his face clenched in pain. He spat blood and staggered. "I'm sorry, Arista—I'm so sorry."

"Say goodbye to your champion, Gaunt," Mawyndulë declared. "I will be king now, as it was meant to be."

Royce sprinted for the old elf.

Mawyndulë looked amused for a moment, then shocked. His guard stepped out but at the last minute Royce sidestepped and dove for Mawyndulë. He drove the dagger at the old man's chest. The chair toppled, with both of them falling over and sprawling across the snow.

They got to their feet simultaneously.

Mawyndulë remained unharmed.

"The blessing of Ferrol is upon me, fool! You can't harm me—but no such protection defends you!"

With a wave of his hand, a column of flame formed around Royce. Fire coursed up his body and engulfed him.

"*Royce!*" Arista shouted. She raised her hands to counter the spell, but before she could, the thief stepped out of the flames.

Everyone stopped.

Even Irawondona paused.

When the flames abated and died away, Royce remained unharmed.

"That can't be," Mawyndulë said.

Then the old elf's eyes widened. "Irawondona!" he shouted. "Forget that one! Kill this one. Kill Royce Melborn!"

The elf lord looked puzzled, glancing back at Hadrian, who had collapsed to his knees and was struggling to breathe, his arm and legs drenched in blood.

"Gaunt isn't the heir; Hadrian is worthless," Mawyndulë shouted. "It's this one. Royce Melborn is the Heir of Novron. Kill him. Kill him now!"

⤙

Royce looked as stunned as anyone.

Irawondona left Hadrian and walked toward Royce and Mawyndulë.

"Myron! Mauvin!" Arista shouted. "Water—bandages—now!"

She entered the ring and threw her arms around Hadrian, lying him down. "Royce?" Hadrian asked. "*Royce* is the heir?"

"Yes!" Arista told him as she poured water over his wounds and began binding them tightly with linen. "Why didn't I see it? Arcadius didn't just happen to bring you two together. Somehow he knew. He was reuniting the heir and the guardian. Esrahaddon must have known too. Gaunt was just a diversion. When he begged me to help find the heir, he never said *Degan Gaunt*, he just said *the heir*! He's why we were able to reach the horn. Esrahaddon knew that only the *true* heir could get past the Gilarabrywn. All this time the heir and the guardian *were* together."

"But why didn't Esrahaddon tell us?"

"To keep him safe. That's why he led everyone to Gaunt. Can Royce defeat Irawondona?"

Hadrian shook his head. "Not a chance."

"Then we have to hurry. You still have a fight to win."

"But I can't hurt him."

"Only because the true heir never named you as champion. Once Royce does, you'll be able to hurt him. You'll have to fight and this time you *must* win."

She stood up and shouted, "Royce! Don't fight. Just give me some time and then name Hadrian as your champion." She knelt back down to tend to his wounds.

"Arista, I can't." Hadrian lay on his back, his chest heaving for air, blood smeared on his cheek and pooling around him.

"You *can* beat him," Myron said as he tore more bandages.

"No, I can't—"

"You don't understand," the monk interrupted. "I speak not from faith in you, but from fact. You are a Teshlor Knight. Techylor was the best warrior in the world and the leader of the Instarya warrior tribe. Irawondona is from the hunters' tribe, he doesn't know how to fight."

"Believe me, he does."

"Not like you do."

"Okay, fine, but you fail to take into account that I can't move. My ribs are broken. I can't even stand up."

"Leave that to me," Arista told him, and began to hum.

⊷

Irawondona spoke briefly to Mawyndulë in elvish as Royce slowly retreated from them, backing away between the tents and down the snowy hill.

"*Just kill him!*" Mawyndulë demanded as his guards helped right his chair.

Royce stopped his retreat and crouched, digging his feet in the snow and feeling the weight of Alverstone in his hand. He had heard what Arista had shouted and he looked over to where Hadrian lay. His friend was in bad shape, but Arista was going into one of her trances.

"Come here, little prince," Irawondona jeered, walking toward him. Royce was surprised that the elf could speak Apelanese. "It is our turn to dance." He waved the halberd, spinning it like he had when fighting Hadrian.

Royce looked at Arista once more, then tossed Alverstone away.

Irawondona smiled. "So you're going to make this easy for me, are you?"

"Not really," Royce replied. "I just don't want to accidentally hurt you."

"I don't think you understand how this works, little prince."

"On the contrary, I think it's you who is confused."

"Just kill him and get it over with, you idiot!" Mawyndulë ordered.

Irawondona advanced, racing down the slope, and lunged. Royce dodged, backing farther away.

"You're quick," Irawondona told him. "But then, you are the descendant of one of us."

The elf lord spun his pole once more and advanced. Irawondona attacked and with each swipe Royce dodged and withdrew farther down the slope on the east side of the Lee, nearing the place where Arista had killed two Seret Knights.

"Stop running, little prince, accept your fate. We are done with human rule. I would prefer to wear the crown, of course, but even a Miralyith is better than a mixed blood. It is time that mankind left Elan for good."

"And then you'll live happily ever after?"

"Indeed we will. We will roam the world as we once did. We will destroy the goblins and then it will be just the dwarves and us again, and eventually...just us. Then Erivan will rule Elan again. When that day comes, Ferrol will walk among us once more."

"Do you really think Mawyndulë will honor any agreement he made with you? He hates you more than he does us. It was *your* people that betrayed him. They convinced him to kill his own father. He wants to be your king so he can enact his revenge on those who hurt him the most."

"You're lying."

"Am I? For three thousand years he's sought his revenge. Kill me and you will place a tyrant on your throne and his first order will be your death."

"He is still an elf. Better that he rule than a half-breed like you."

"Whatever bonds of kinship he had, he lost long ago."

"Even so, even if he kills me, if my death and the death of every clan leader is the cost, so be it. We will be rid of your kind—of your blood."

He struck out and once more Royce dodged. But this time he realized too late his own mistake. Irawondona had anticipated the move; he saw the feint and compensated, swinging around with the long blade. Royce was caught. The metal entered him with a surprisingly quiet hiss. Looking down, he saw the blood-coated tip as Irawondona pulled the blade free.

Royce collapsed.

"Royce!" he heard Hadrian cry. "Do it, do it now!"

The elf lord raised his blade once more. "Farewell, Son of Nyphron."

Royce took a breath. *"Byrinith con—duylar ben—Hadrian Blackwater,"* he said as loud as he could manage.

"Duylar e finis dan iskabareth ben Royce Melborn!" Hadrian replied quickly even as Irawondona's stroke came down.

The tip of the long blade slammed against Royce's chest but

he barely felt it. A bright spark flashed and a loud crack echoed as the blade shattered and sent bits of metal skipping down the hillside.

Irawondona stood above him, stunned.

Royce muttered and coughed. "My friend is going to kill you."

Irawondona looked down at him, confused, but Royce took little notice now. He lay staring up at the blue sky. "You *were* right, Gwen. You were right."

◆

The elven lord looked over his shoulder and saw Hadrian, bandaged and standing in the ringed arena. With what sounded like an elvish curse, Irawondona spat on Royce, glared at Mawyndulë, and walked back toward the ring.

Irawondona entered. "Your weapon is destroyed," the elf said in a pitying voice as he gestured at the halberd, lying in two pieces.

"No, it's not." Hadrian reached behind him and drew out the great spadone blade.

Irawondona hesitated but then threw aside his broken pole and drew his own sword, which gleamed much the same way as Mauvin's. The two moved to the center of the ring.

Irawondona attacked first, spinning and swinging. Hadrian took hold of the advance guard of his sword with his off hand, gripping his blade up to the flanges, and caught the attack with two hands much the same as if he had still wielded the pole. He pivoted and spun the sword around but the elf slipped away. He riposted instantly, but Hadrian was there with the hilt guard again. There was a spark and the two separated once more; this time they both panted for breath.

Irawondona attacked again and feinted. Hadrian saw the

ruse and moved to cut—but then the elf leapt in the air and
spun. Irawondona flew from the ground so nimbly that he
appeared to fly, leaving Hadrian's sword nothing but air. Irawondona flipped, and as he touched down, he struck Hadrian
across the back with a hammer punch from his sword's pommel. The blow drove Hadrian to the dirt once more.

Hadrian was down as Irawondona attacked. Once more,
reflex saved him. Hadrian rolled aside and kicked Irawondona
in the knee, causing the elf to stagger back long enough for
Hadrian to gain his footing.

⤝

Arista, Mauvin, Magnus, and Myron rushed to Royce where
he lay on the hillside, struggling to breathe. Arista was not a
doctor, but Royce looked bad. Already the earth around him
was dark with blood. His chest and sides were slick and shiny,
violently thrusting to breathe; both eyes were rolled up, exposing only whites.

"Stay alive, Royce," Arista told him. "Do you hear me?
You need to stay alive!"

Royce muttered something and drew in air with a horrid
gurgle. "I saved—I saved him."

"Not yet you haven't. It's not over! Royce, listen to me."
Arista took his hands. "You can't die, do you understand? Do
you hear me?"

He jerked, his head twitching.

"Damn it!" she said, and placing her hands on his chest,
she closed her eyes and began the chant. Immediately she felt
the resistance, a solid separation, as if a wall stood between
them. The Hand of Ferrol left no cracks or seams. The shield
was perfect and impervious.

She opened her eyes. "I can't help him," she told the others. "Hadrian! Hurry! He's dying!"

⁓

At the sound of her voice Irawondona smiled. "I don't even have to fight to win. I'm faster than you are. I can avoid you until he dies. Then Mawyndulë will be king. But rest assured I will kill you then. You will be the first; then I will kill your woman, and that empress of yours, then every last man, woman, and child on the face of Elan."

Hadrian nodded. "You could do that. And when your son and grandson ask about this day, you can tell them how in the fight that decided everything, you did nothing. You chose to run until time ran out, because you were afraid of being killed in a fair fight by a human—a fight ordained by your god, Ferrol. Then they will know that your race gained their dominance through cowardice and that mankind was truly the greater race."

Irawondona glared.

"Go on, you can admit it. You're afraid of me." Hadrian raised his voice. "You're afraid of me, and I'm only a human. I'm not even a noble or a knight. Do you know what I am? I'm a thief. Both of us are, Royce and I." Hadrian pointed down the hill. "We're nothing but a pair of common thieves. My father was a lowly blacksmith. He worked in a pathetic village not far from here." Hadrian let himself laugh. "An orphan and a blacksmith's son—two human thieves who terrify the invincible elven lords. It's so pathetic."

"I'm afraid of no human."

"Then prove it. Don't wait for him to die. Don't be a coward. Have at me."

Irawondona did not move.

"I thought as much," Hadrian said, and turned his back on the elf.

There was no sound. Hadrian knew there would not be. Years with Royce had taught him so. It was the look on the faces of those who watched that let him know Irawondona had moved.

Hadrian had already shifted his grip on the two-handed pommel of the spadone. His fingers spread in the fashion his father had taught him. His knees bent as his back bowed and his arm moved. One minute he was on the hill at Amberton Lee and the next he was in Hintindar behind the forge as his father shouted instructions.

Don't look! Danbury ordered, tying on the blindfold. *Trust your instincts. Don't guess; know what he is doing. Believe it. Act on it!*

Hadrian swung outward to his right. The great sword of Jerish Grelad caught the morning sun on its worn blade and glinted, shining for one brief moment.

It's more than fighting, Haddy, Danbury said. *It's what you are. It's what you will be—what you must be. Trust in it.*

Hadrian's knees hit the snow, sending up a burst of ice crystals. He could see the shadow now, the rushing darkness of Irawondona running at him from behind. Pulling against the weight of the spadone, he started the pivot, the collapsing rotation.

It was a blind attack.

You don't have to see your opponent to kill him, his father had explained. *You just have to know where he will be. That's the key to everything. And if you know, what good are eyes? What good is seeing? Trust in what I've taught you and you'll hit him.*

Hadrian continued the spin, one knee coming up, his shoulder twisting his waist as he put his full weight into the arc. He did not look. He did not need to. He knew. He knew exactly where Irawondona was and where he would be.

He felt metal kiss metal as Irawondona tried to parry. The force of the spadone, the weight behind it, was too much to deflect. The metal sang, but there was hardly a quiver to the stroke as it carried through the weak defense, driving the sword from Irawondona's grip. The spadone continued in its stroke and Hadrian hardly felt the impact as it cut into the elf's side. Irawondona's body offered even less resistance than his blade, and Hadrian completed the swing as if he were performing it alone behind the blacksmith's shop. The only difference was the splash of blood.

The blue torches flared brilliantly white, then went out with a loud snap.

"*Ir a wondon*," the priest of Ferrol announced, and then, looking at Hadrian, added, "It is done."

"*No!*" Mawyndulë cried, raising his arms. He looked as if he was trying to speak when he coughed and blood sprayed the front of his robes. To either side, his guards started to draw their weapons but disappeared with a loud *pop*.

Mawyndulë collapsed face-first. Behind him, Monsignor Merton stood holding the bloodstained Alverstone in both hands.

The elves did not move or react. Instead they stood silently, their faces solemn, their eyes downcast. No one looked at Irawondona and none bothered with Mawyndulë; instead they started down the hill toward Royce.

"*Hadrian!*" Arista screamed.

He pushed his way through the elves, then finally past Modina, the girls, and the boys to find Arista kneeling on the ground clutching Royce. The ground was soaked and his friend's eyes were closed.

"Help him!" Hadrian told her.

"I can't! I tried!" she cried, her eyes frightened.

"But I won," he said, and looked to Myron. "The blessing is gone now, right?"

The monk nodded.

"There—see? Do it, do it now! Pull him back!"

"I tried!" she shouted at him. "Don't you think I tried! I was waiting, and the second the wall was gone, I went in. But I still can't reach him. Hadrian...he doesn't want to be saved. I think he wants to die."

Hadrian felt the strength at last go out of his legs and he collapsed to his knees.

"He sees her, Hadrian," Arista cried, cradling Royce's head on her lap. "He sees her in the light. He doesn't even hear me. All he sees is her and he keeps saying he did it, he saved you."

Hadrian nodded. Tears filled his eyes and he reached out and brushed the hair away from Royce's face. "Damn it, Royce! Don't leave me, pal. Com'on, buddy, you have to come back. I finally did it. I killed the bad guy, saved the kingdom, won the girl, and you're ruining it all for me. You don't want to do that, do you? Please, we still need you."

"What happens if he dies?" Gaunt asked from above him.

"The elves will be without a king," Myron said in a shaking voice. "The next elf to blow the horn will be king, unless there is another challenger and a fight. But either way, an elf will be crowned."

"Do you hear that, Royce? It isn't over. You have to live or we all die. You won't have saved me after all. Com'on, pal." He lifted him, cradling Royce in his arms. "You can't leave now."

Hadrian studied his face—no change.

"There's just nothing keeping you here anymore, is there?" Tears ran down Hadrian's cheeks. "I love you, buddy," he said, and laid him back down.

Those watching fell silent as they listened to Royce's breathing. It grew shallower and slower, fainter with each rasping in and out. Somewhere a bird sang, and the wind blew across the hilltop.

"Who is he?"

Hadrian heard a small voice disturb the silence.

"Mercy, shush," the empress Modina said. "His name is Royce, now be quiet."

Hadrian looked up suddenly.

"What?" Arista asked.

"Gwen," he said.

"Huh?"

"Gwen told me how to save him."

"She did?"

"Yes, something about... It was the last time I saw her— one of the last things she ever told me. I—I didn't realize..."

"Realize what?" Arista asked.

"She knew."

"Knew what?"

"She knew everything," Hadrian replied. "I remember she told me what to do to save him but at the time I didn't understand. Damn, I wish I had Myron's brain!"

Hadrian took a breath and tried to calm down. "I was with her in The Rose and Thorn, at the table. Royce was there— no—no, he wasn't—he was in the kitchen doing something. He was happy—happy about... about... *the wedding!* Yes, we were talking about the wedding and about how Royce had changed over the years. I felt bad taking him away from her and she said that he had to go or I would die." He looked back toward the arena, where Irawondona's body still lay. "She meant this. She saw this! But then she said something else. She said... Oh, what did she say?"

He struggled to remember her voice, her words: *He's seen*

too much cruelty and betrayal. He's never known mercy.
That was what she had said but then there was something else,
something she wanted him to do. *You have to do this,*
Hadrian. You have to be the one to show him mercy. If you
can do that, I know it will save him.

"No," he said, stunned. "Not show him mercy—oh god!
She wanted me to show him Mercy!"

He leapt to his feet and grabbed the little girl standing
beside Modina. She pulled back, frightened.

"Relax, honey. Don't be afraid," he said softly. "Just tell
me your name."

The girl looked at Modina, who nodded.

"Mercy."

"No—no, what's your *full* name?"

"Mercedes, but no one calls me that except my mother—at
least, she used to."

"What's your mother's name, honey?" Hadrian asked, his
hands trembling as he held her.

"My mother is dead."

"Yes, dear, but what was her name?"

The little girl smiled. "Gwendolyn DeLancy."

"Did you hear that, Royce!" Hadrian shouted. "Her name
is Mercedes."

He kept shouting at him. "Elias or Sterling if a boy, right?
But there was only one name for the girl, *Mercedes*. There was
only one name because Gwen had already named her! This is
your daughter, Royce! This is your and Gwen's daughter!
How old are you, sweetie? Five? Six?"

"Six," she said proudly.

"She's six, Royce. That would have been the year we spent
locked up in Alburn, remember? Gwen took her baby to Arcadius. She probably didn't want you to feel trapped, or maybe
she didn't want her growing up in a whorehouse. In any case,

she knew she would die before introducing you to your daughter. That's why she told me to. Royce, you have a daughter, you old bastard!" He reached out and took hold of Royce's face. "Part of Gwen is still here! Do you hear me?"

"Is he my father?" Mercy asked, drawing closer. "My mother told me that one day I would meet my father and that he would take me to live in a beautiful place and I would become a fairy princess and a queen of the forest."

Royce's eyelids twitched.

"Now!" Hadrian told Arista, but it was not necessary. She was already chanting. The chanting quieted to a hum and then Arista went silent. She jerked abruptly and violently. Hadrian took hold of her. He had one hand on each of them as he prayed to Maribor. Every muscle in Arista's body was taut and her head hitched as if she were being slapped. Then suddenly she shook and her breath shortened to gasps. The time between gasps grew until she stopped breathing entirely.

All around them the crowd stopped breathing as well.

"Royce!" Hadrian screamed at him. "She's your daughter, and if you die, she'll be an orphan, just like you! Are you going to abandon her and leave her alone like your parents did? *Royce!*"

Both bodies lurched in unison and they gasped for air. Arista, damp with sweat, laid her head against Hadrian. Royce breathed deeply, and slowly his eyes fluttered open. He did not speak, but his eyes focused on the little girl.

CHAPTER 28

FULL CIRCLE

The rear wheel of the wagon fell into another hole and bounced so hard that Arista woke. She pulled back the blanket and squinted at the sky. The sun was low on the horizon and the movement of the wagon made the forest on a hill to their right look as if it were marching in the opposite direction. Her neck and back were sore, her muscles stiff, and she was still groggy. She realized that despite the bouncing buckboard, she had slept the day away. Now her stomach ached from hunger. Her teeth felt fuzzy, almost sandy, and her left hand was numb from her lying on it. She rode in the back of the wagon that Magnus and Degan drove. Hadrian had made her the best bed he could, laying down all their blankets as padding in the space left by the consumed supplies.

Modina and the girls rode with her. Allie and Mercy were asleep between her and the empress. The two curled up in tight balls, their knees pulled to their chests. Modina sat with a blanket around her shoulders, staring off at the landscape. The sled runners had been replaced by wheels and they traveled on a rutted, muddy road that formed a dark line between two fields of snow that occasionally showed a patch of matted, tangled weeds. Seeing them got her thinking. She wiped her face with the blanket and, digging her brush out of a nearby pack, began the arduous process of clearing the snarls from her hair.

She pulled, grunted, and then sighed. Modina looked over with a questioning expression, and Arista explained by letting go of the brush and leaving it to hang.

Modina smiled and crawled over to her. "Turn around," she said, and taking the brush, the empress began working the back of Arista's head. "You have quite the rat's nest here."

"Be careful one doesn't bite you," Arista replied. "Do you know where we are?"

"I have no idea. I'm not really much of a world traveler, you know."

"This doesn't look like the road to Aquesta."

"No," Modina said as she worked on a particularly tough snarl. "It's too late to travel that far today, and neither you, Royce, nor Hadrian were up for a long trip. After all, you three had a pretty big day."

"But the people in —"

Modina patted her shoulder. "It's all right. I sent Merton back with instructions for Nimbus and Amilia, and Royce sent the elves with him — well, most of them. A few insisted on staying with their new king. There's nothing left in Aquesta to go back to. The city was destroyed. I ordered the remaining stores to be divided between those who survived. The people will be sent to Colnora, Ratibor, Kilnar, and Vernes, but organized into equal groups so no one city is too overwhelmed."

Arista laughed and shook her head, making it hard for Modina to work. "Are you sure you're the same Thrace Wood I once knew?"

"No, I don't suppose I am," Modina replied. "Thrace was a wonderful girl, naive, starry-eyed, bursting with life. For a long time I thought she was dead and gone, but I think—no, I know—some part of her still exists, but I'm Modina now."

"Well, whoever you are, you're amazing. You truly are the empress worthy of ruling all of mankind."

Modina lowered her voice and said, "I'll tell you a secret— it's not me at all, really. Sure, on occasion, I come up with something intelligent—and I am usually surprised by it myself—but the real genius behind my throne is Nimbus. Amilia deserves everything this empire can give her for hiring him. The man is a wonder: quiet, unassuming, but utterly brilliant. If he had a mind to, he could replace me in a heartbeat. I am convinced he could organize a perfectly lovely coup, but he has no aspirations for power at all. I haven't been in politics long, but even I can see that a man as capable as he and yet so absent of greed is a rare thing. Do you know he still sleeps in his cubicle? Or at least he did until the castle was destroyed. Even though he was chancellor of the empire, he lived in a tiny stone cell. He, Amilia, and Breckton are my jewels, my treasures. I don't know how I could have survived without them."

"Don't forget Hadrian," Arista reminded her.

"Hadrian? No, he's not a treasure of *mine* and neither are you." She paused in her brushing and Arista felt Modina kiss her head. "There's not a word that can describe how I feel about the two of you, except perhaps…miracle workers."

❧

The center of the village clustered along the main road. Wood, stone, and wattle-and-daub buildings with grass-thatched roofs lined either side, beginning at the little wooden bridge and ending before the slope that climbed a hill to the manor house. They consisted of a ramshackle assortment of shops, homes, and hovels, casting long shadows. Beyond them,

Hadrian could see people in the fields working in the strips closest to the village. Down in the valley, near the river, the fields were nearly clear of snow and villeins worked to spread manure from large carts. Hooded in wool cowls, the workers labored. Long curved rakes rose and fell in the faltering light. In the village, smoke rose from a few of the buildings and shops, but none came from the smithy.

As they approached, their horses announced their arrival with a loud hollow *clop clip clop* as they crossed the bridge. A pair of dogs lifted their heads, the sign above the shoemaker's shop squeaked as it swayed, and farther down the road a stable door clapped absently against its frame. The intermittent warbling wail of lambs called out from hidden pens.

Hadrian and Royce led the procession through the village. Behind them rode three elves—Royce's new shadows. Now that Royce was their king, and given what happened to Novron, and his predecessor, they were adamant about his protection.

The change in the elves' demeanor had been dramatic. The moment Royce got to his feet, they all knelt. The sneering looks of contempt were replaced instantly with reverence. If they were acting, Hadrian thought they were all remarkable performers. Perhaps it was seeing Royce come back from the dead, or some magic of the horn, but the elven lords could not appear to be more devoted to him.

Royce did not protest his new protectors. He said little on the subject and rode as if they were not there. Hadrian guessed he was humoring them—for now. Everyone, especially Royce, was too exhausted to think, much less argue, and Hadrian had just a single thought—to find shelter before dark. With that in mind, he headed south, following the little tributary of the Bernum River he knew simply as the South Fork, which brought them to his boyhood home of Hintindar.

A man sitting in front of the stable was filing the edges of

the coulter on a moul board plow when he caught sight of
them. He had a bristling black beard and a dirty, pockmarked
face. He was dressed in the usual hooded cowl and knee-
length tunic of a villein. The man stared, shocked, for a handful of seconds, then emitted a brief utterance that might have
been a squeak. He ran to the bell mounted on the pole in the
middle of the street and rang it five times, then bolted up the
main street toward the manor house.

"Peculiar man," Hadrian remarked, stopping his horse at
the well and, in turn, halting the whole party.

"I think you scared him," Royce said.

Hadrian glanced back at the elves sitting in a perfect line
on their great white stallions in their gleaming gold armor, the
center one holding aloft a ten-foot pole with a long blue and
gold streamer flapping from it. "Yeah, it was probably me."

The two continued to watch the man run. He appeared
only as tall as an outstretched thumb, but Hadrian could still
hear his feet slapping the dirt.

"Know him?" Royce asked.

Hadrian shook his head.

"What's the bell for?" Royce asked.

"Emergencies, fires, the hue and cry—that sort of thing."

"I'm guessing he didn't see a fire."

"Are we stopping here?" Myron asked. He and Mauvin sat
on their mounts just behind the elves and just before the
wagon. "The ladies want to know."

"Might as well. I sort of planned to ride up to the manor to
announce ourselves but...I think that's being taken care of."

He dismounted, letting his horse drink from the trough.
The others got down as well, including Arista and Modina—
the empress still wrapped in her blanket. They left the sleeping
girls wrapped up in their covers.

Hadrian was just about to rap on the bakery's door when a crowd of people began filing into the village, following the cow path from the fields. They carried rakes over their heads and trotted into the street, stopping the moment they saw them. Hadrian recognized most of the faces: Osgar the reeve, Harbert the tailor, Algar the woodworker, and Wilfred the carter.

"Haddy!" Armigil shouted. The old brew mistress pushed her way through. Her broad hips cut a swath through the crowd. "How did ya—What aire ya doin' 'ere, lad? And what 'ave you brought with ya?"

"I—" was all he got out before she went on.

"Never ya mind answering. Ya needs to be gone. Take the lot of ya and go!"

"You need to work on your manners, dear," Hadrian told her. "The last time I came to town, you hit me, and now—"

"Ya don't understand, lad. Things have changed. There's no time to explain. You need to get out of here. His lairdship caught the storm after you left last time."

"Haddy?" Dunstan the baker and his wife approached, staring at him in disbelief. They were both dressed in worn wool, covered in speckles of mud, and their bare feet and legs were caked with drying earth.

"How are you, Dun?" Hadrian asked. "What are you doing in the field?"

"Plowing," he replied dully as he stared at the strangers on his street. "Well, trying to. Things have warmed up a lot, but the ground's still not quite soft enough."

"Plowing? You're a baker."

"We bake at night."

"When do you sleep, then?"

"Quit yer yammering and go, shoo! Away with ya!" Armigil shouted, waving at him as if he were a cow in her vegetable garden. "Haddy, you don't understand. If they find you here—"

"That's right!" Dunstan agreed, as if he suddenly woke from a dream. "You need to go. If Luret sees you—"

"Luret? The envoy? He's still here?"

"He never left," Osgar said.

"He charged Lord Baldwin with disloyalty," Wilfred the carter put in.

"Siward died in the fightin'," Armigil said sadly. "Luret locked up poor old Baldwin in his own dungeon, and that's why you and yer friends need to get!"

"Too late," Royce said, looking down the road toward the manor house. "A line of men are marching down the hill."

"Who are they? Imperial troops?" Hadrian asked.

"Looks like it. They're wearing uniforms," Royce said.

"What's going on?" Arista asked, coming forward. She beamed a smile at Dunstan and Arbor.

"Oh, Emma!" Arbor spoke to her with a fearful tone but said nothing more. Arista appeared puzzled for a moment and then laughed.

"Oh dear," Armigil went on when she noticed the wagon, where Allie and Mercedes were stretching and yawning. A sorrowful expression came over the brew mistress. "Ye got wee ones with ya too?"

"Is it too late to hide them?" Arbor asked.

"They can see us from there," Osgar answered.

Mauvin stepped up near Royce, peering up the road at the small figures coming down the hill. "How many do you count?"

"Twelve," Royce replied, "including Luret."

"Twelve?" Mauvin said, surprised. "Seriously?"

Royce shrugged. "Maybe the fella that ran up there mentioned we had women and children."

"But twelve?"

"Eleven, really."

Mauvin rolled his eyes and folded his arms across his chest in disgust as he watched them approach.

"So Luret has you all working in the fields?" Hadrian asked as he dismounted and tied up his horse.

"Are you daft man?" Armigil shouted. "What ere you makin' conversation fer? They're coming to arrest ya—if you're lucky, that is! They'll haul you to the dungeon, beat you, starve you, and likely torture you. That Luret is not right in the head."

Mince and the boys took it upon themselves to gather the horses and tie them to the wagon, taking time to pause and nod politely to the townspeople.

They soon heard the stomp of feet as the soldiers from the manor house marched at them in an even rhythm. They moved in a two-line formation of six men in back and five in front. They wore chain mail and flat helms. Those in front carried spears, those in the rear, crossbows. Luret rode behind them on a pale speckled mare with a black face and one white-circled eye. Luret looked much the same as he had the last time Hadrian had seen him. The man still had hawkish features and brutal eyes. His attire, however, had improved. He wore a thick brocade tunic along with a velvet cape and handsome long gloves neatly embroidered with chevrons that ran up his wrists. His legs were covered in opaque hose, and his feet covered by leather shoes with brass buckles, which caught what remained of the setting sun.

"Aha! The blacksmith's son!" Luret exclaimed the moment he saw Hadrian's face clearly. "Back to claim your inheritance? Or have you run out of places to hide? And who is this rabble?" He smirked, and waved his hand in the air. "Outlaws the lot of you, I'm sure." He paused a moment as he took notice of the elves, but his sight fell back to Hadrian again. "You've brought them here to roost, eh? Think you can hide out amongst your old friends?" He pointed at Royce. "Oh yes, I remember you, and you too." He looked at Arista. "I don't think they will be quite so quick to take you in this time, not after the beating I gave them." He looked at Dunstan, who stared down at his own feet. "They learned their lesson about harboring fugitives. Now it's time for you to learn a lesson too. Arrest the lot of them. I want chains on these two." He pointed at Hadrian and Royce.

The soldiers managed only one step forward before Hadrian drew his swords. The rest followed his lead. To his left, Degan stepped up, and beside him Magnus held his hammer. To his right the elves advanced to stand in front of Royce, causing him to sigh. Even the boys drew daggers, except for Kine and Mince, who did not have any, but they put up their fists, nonetheless.

The soldiers hesitated. Luret drummed his fingers on his saddle horn. "I said arrest them!"

One of the soldiers near Royce jabbed forward with his spear. The nearest elf severed the metal tip from the shaft. The guard backed up, holding the wooden staff.

None of the others moved.

Luret's face reddened. "You are defying arrest! You are challenging an imperial envoy and duly appointed magistrate and executor of this estate. I demand you surrender at once! Surrender or by the power invested in me by the empress herself I will have you shot where you stand!"

No one moved.

"I don't recall investing anything in you, much less the power to kill members of my personal entourage," Modina said as she walked forward from the rear of the party.

Luret put a hand to shield his eyes from the setting sun and squinted in her direction. "Who is this now?"

"You don't recognize me?" Modina asked in a light and lilting voice. "And yet you are so quick to evoke my name. Allow me to introduce myself. Perhaps it will jog your memory. I am the slayer of Rufus's Bane, the high priestess of the Church of Nyphron, Her Most Serene and Royal Grand Imperial Majesty, Empress Modina Novronian."

She cast off the blanket.

Several people in the crowd gasped. Arbor staggered backward, causing Dunstan to catch hold of her, and Hadrian was certain he heard Armigil mutter, "I'll be buggered."

The empress stood in her lavish gown. She was also adorned in the long black velvet mantle embroidered with the imperial crest, which she'd put on before presenting herself.

"This— No, it's not possible!" Luret muttered. "It's a trick. A trick, I say! I won't be hoodwinked. Look at this child. She is an impostor. A fake. All of you lay down your arms and come peacefully and I will only execute the blacksmith's son and his companion. Defy me and all of you will die!"

At that moment, the six soldiers with the crossbows began to sniffle. They blinked hard, their eyes watered, and they crinkled their noses. One by one, they began to sneeze, and then the thick sinewy skein of the crossbows snapped in loud pops, the metal bolts dropping helplessly to the dirt.

Hadrian glanced at Arista, who smiled mischievously at him.

"Before you get yourself into any more trouble," Modina said, addressing Luret, who was now clearly concerned, "allow me to introduce the rest of my contingent. This is the princess—or rather now Queen Arista of Melengar, conqueror of Ratibor, and sorceress extraordinaire."

"I think she prefers *wizardess*," Myron whispered.

"Pardon me, *wizardess*. This is Royce Melborn, newly crowned king of the ancient realm of Erivan. With him, as you may have noticed, are three of his elven lords. This short gentleman is Magnus of the Children of Drome, a master of stone and earth. Beside him is Degan Gaunt, leader and hero of the Nationalists. Over here is the legendary sword master Count Pickering of Galilin. This is the Marquis of Glouston, the famed and learned monk of Maribor. And while he shouldn't require any introduction, before you stands Hadrian Blackwater, Teshlor Knight, Guardian of the Heir of Novron, champion of the empire, and hero of the realm.

"These defenders of the empire have passed through the underworld, fought armies of goblins, crossed treacherous seas, entered and returned from the lost city of Percepliquis, and this very day halted the advance of an unstoppable army and defeated the being who long ago murdered our savior Novron the Great. They saved not only the empire but all of you as well. You owe them your lives, your respect, and your eternal gratitude."

She paused to stare at the wide-eyed Luret. "Well, envoy, magistrate, and executor, what say you?"

Luret looked at the faces around him. He saw his men laying down their weapons. He glanced at the faces of the villagers, then kicked his horse and bolted. He did not head back up the road to the manor but rather fled out to the open fields.

"I could make him fall off the horse," Arista mentioned, but Modina shook her head.

"Let him go." She looked at the soldiers. "The rest of you can go as well."

"Wait," Hadrian said. "Lord Baldwin is imprisoned at the manor, is that right?"

The soldiers slowly nodded, their faces coated in concern.

"Go free him at once," Modina said. "Tell him what you have seen and that I will be visiting him and his household tomorrow. In fact, tell him he will have the honor of hosting me and my court until such time as I arrange more permanent accommodations."

They nodded, bowed, and walked backward for a dozen steps before giving up, turning, and running up the street.

"I think you made an impression," Hadrian told her, then looked at the villagers.

They all stood like posts, staring at Modina, their mouths agape.

"Armigil, you do still brew beer, right?" Hadrian asked.

"What, Haddy?" she said, dazed, still staring at the empress.

"Beer, you know…barley, hops…It's a drink. We could really do with a barrel about now, don't you think?" He waved a hand in front of Dunstan. "Maybe a warm place to rest. Perhaps a bite of food?" He snapped his fingers three times. "Hello?"

"Is that really *the* empress?" Armigil asked.

"Yeah, so she's gonna be able to pay you if that's what you're worried about."

This snapped her out of her daze. The old woman scowled at him and shook a finger. "Ya know better than that, ya overgrown skunk! 'Ow dare ya be callin' me inhospitable! Whether she's the empress or a tart dragged from the gutter, ya know they both would be equally welcome to a pint and a plate in Hintindar—at least now that Uberlin 'imself is gone." She looked at Dunstan and Arbor. "And what are ya doing standing there and gawking fer? Throw some dough in the oven. Osgar, Harbert, get over 'ere and lend a 'and with a barrel. Algar, see if'n yer wife has any more of that mince pie and tell Clipper to cut a side of salt pork from—"

"No!" Hadrian, Arista, Mauvin, and Degan shouted all at once, startling everyone. They all began to laugh.

"Please, anything but salt pork," Hadrian added.

"Is—is mutton okay?" Abelard asked, concerned. Abelard the shearer and his wife, Gerty, had lived across the street from the Blackwaters for years. He was a thin, toothless, balding man who reminded Hadrian of a turtle, the way his head poked out of his cowl.

They all nodded enthusiastically.

"Mutton would be wonderful."

Abelard smiled and started off.

"And bring your fiddle and tell Danny to bring his pipe!" Dunstan shouted after him. "Looks like spring came a bit early this year, eh?"

❧

Arista was being careful, having learned her lesson before. This time she limited herself to just one mug of Armigil's brew; even then, she felt a tad light-headed. She sat next to Hadrian on top of flour sacks piled on the wide pine of the bakery floor. The floor itself was slippery from the thin coating of flour that the girls loved playing on. Allie and Mercy slid across the floor as if it were a frozen pond, at least until enough people arrived to make a good slide impossible. Arista thought about offering to help Arbor, but she already had half a dozen women working in her cramped kitchen, and after everything, it felt too good just sitting there leaning against him, feeling Hadrian's arm curled around her back. She smelled the sweet aroma of baking bread and roasting lamb. She listened to the gentle chatter of friendly conversations all around her and drank in the warmth and comfort. It made her wonder if this was what Alric had found within the light. She

wondered if it smelled of baking bread, and remembering, she
was almost certain it had.

"What are you thinking?" Hadrian asked.

"Hmm? Oh, I was hoping Alric was happy."

"I'm sure he is."

She nodded and Hadrian raised his mug. "To Alric," he
said.

"To Alric," Mauvin agreed.

Everyone in the room with a glass, mug, or cup—even
those who had never heard of Alric—raised drinks. Her eyes
landed on Allie, who now sat between Modina and Mercy
nibbling like a bird on a hunk of brown bread.

"To Wyatt and Elden," she whispered, too quietly even for
Hadrian to hear, and downed the last of her cup.

"I wanted to say how sorry I am, Dun," Hadrian told his
friend as he handed out another helping of food. "Was it bad,
what happened after we left?"

Dunstan glanced up to see where his wife was. "It was hard
on Arbor," he said. "I think I looked worse than I was. She
had to do most of the work around here for close to six weeks,
but all that is over. I'm used to getting my head cracked now
and again." Dunstan grinned, then stared curiously at
Hadrian and Arista, sitting arm in arm. Royce had just entered
and Dunstan glanced nervously over at him. "You better
watch yourself. He doesn't look the type to be understanding
about such things."

Dunstan moved away, leaving Arista and Hadrian looking
at each other, puzzled.

Royce hesitated at the door, his eyes on the girls as they sat
at Modina's feet. The empress was one of the few in the room
to sit on a chair. It was not her idea, but the Bakers insisted.
He walked over and sat beside Hadrian.

"Where are your shadows?" Hadrian asked.

"You look concerned."

"Just that if you've started another war, I'd like a heads-up is all."

"The level of confidence you have in my diplomatic skills is overwhelming."

"What diplomatic skills?"

Royce frowned. "They're outside. I talked with them about space," Royce said.

"You did?"

"They speak Apelanese. And I do know some elvish, remember."

Royce sat back against the table leg, his eyes on Mercy as she giggled at something Allie whispered in her ear.

"Why don't you go talk to her?" Hadrian asked.

Royce shrugged, his brow creased with worry.

"What is it?"

"Nothing." Royce stood up. "It's a little warm in here for me."

They watched him gingerly step around those on the floor and slip back out. Hadrian looked at Arista.

"Go ahead," she told him.

"You sure?"

"Of course I am. Go."

He smiled, gave her a kiss, and then stood to chase after Royce.

Arista sat for a moment looking around her at all the friendly, rosy faces, talking, laughing, smiling. The bowls of steaming pottage were coming off the open hearth and making their rounds. Abelard, seated on an overturned bucket, was rosining his bow and plucking strings on his fiddle while he waited for Danny, who sat beside him finishing up a plate of lamb. The place was filling up and sitting room was getting scarce. Despite the crowd, a wide berth was maintained around Modina, who planted herself in the corner across from the door, smiling more brightly than Arista had ever seen her. Only the girls dared come within an arm's length, but every eye in the room repeatedly glanced her way.

Arista stood up and found Arbor throwing a round loaf in the oven. She leaned against the counter and wiped her head with the back of her flour-covered hands. "That's the last of it," she said, and smiled at her. "I was worried about you," she told Arista. "We both were."

"Really?"

"Oh yes! The way you left that night, and then when the soldiers came—we were afraid for you. The village was in turmoil that whole week. Men came through here four times spilling the flour and searching. I didn't know what they wanted you for—I still don't."

"It doesn't matter anymore," Arista said. "That's all over and everything is going to be different from now on."

Arbor's expression showed she did not know what to make of that.

"Say, do you still have that dress I gave you?"

"Oh yes!" She looked down at Arista's robe. "You'll be wanting it back, of course." She started to leave and Arista took her hand.

"No, that's not why I was asking."

"But it's okay. I took real fine care with it—never wore it once. I just looked at it a few times, you know."

"I was just thinking you should try it on, because I think you're going to be needing it."

"Oh no, I'll never need a dress that fine. Like I told you before, there's no chance of me going to a fancy ball or anything like that."

"That's just it," Arista told her. "I think you will—that is, if you accept."

"Accept what?"

"I'd like you to be the maid of honor at my wedding."

Arbor looked back at her, confused. "But, Erma, you're already married to Vince."

It was Arista's turn to look puzzled and then she laughed aloud.

᪥

Hadrian caught up with Royce at the footbridge. It was dark, but the moon was bright and he spotted his friend's dark figure leaning over the rail, staring into the dark waters trickling below.

"Crowd getting to you?" Hadrian asked. Royce did not reply. He did not even look up. "So what will you do now?"

"I don't know," Royce said softly.

"You realize that being the real descendant of Novron makes you not only the King of Erivan but Emperor of Apeladorn as well. Have you spoken with Modina?"

"She already told me she would step down."

"Emperor Royce?" Hadrian said.

"Doesn't really sound right, does it?"

Hadrian shrugged and leaned against the same rail. "It could in time."

Except for the bakery, the street was dark, although there were some lights on at the manor house. They were tiny dots from where they stood, like bright yellow stars at the top of the hill.

"I hear you're going to marry Arista."

"Where'd you hear that?"

"Myron mentioned something about doing the honors."

"Ah—right. Well, I thought he'd do a good job, and nei-

ther of us are real thrilled with the idea of a Church of Nyphron ceremony."

"I think it's a good idea." Royce looked back at the water
below. "And don't wait. Marry her right away and start being
happy."

The breeze rustled the bare limbs of the nearby trees and
blew a faint hiss as it passed under the bridge. Hadrian pulled
his collar tight and looked over the edge. He stared down at
the dark waters below.

"So are you going to look for who killed her?" Hadrian
asked. "You know, don't you? Do you want me to come?"

"No," Royce replied. "He's already dead."

"Really? How do you feel about that?"

Royce shrugged.

"I knew it wasn't Merrick," Royce said, tearing a leaf and
throwing it over the edge of the bridge. "I still remember his
face, looking up at me. Telling me it wasn't him. Explaining
how it couldn't have been him. He was confounded by it. Merrick confounded—that was my first clue. Today I got the final
clue."

"What clue?"

"Emperor Royce—he was terrified of that possibility. Royce
Melborn on the throne—could there be a more frightening
thing? That's why he never told us. He brought us together hoping you would change me, but he couldn't fix me. I'd spent too
many years learning to hate. I'd lost the value of life. Then he
learned about Mercedes. I'd lost my humanity, but she was
clean. He could educate her, make her into the perfect ruler."

"Arcadius? But why would he kill Gwen?"

"That's my fault as well. I told him that she had agreed
to marry me. He knew we would come for Mercedes and all
that he invested in her would be lost. He never thought in his

wildest dreams that I would ever take that step with Gwen, and when he found out, he had to kill her before she had the chance to tell me about my daughter."

He looked up at the stars and ran a hand across his face. When he spoke, his voice quavered. "I told Arcadius she was at the Winds Abbey. He hired Merrick to take her and bring her to Colnora. He was there before the meeting, hiding with a crossbow."

Royce turned to Hadrian and his eyes were moist. "But what I can't understand is that he loved her too. So how could he pull that trigger? How could he watch her scream and fall? How frightened must he have been to do that? How much of a horror am I?"

"Royce." Hadrian placed a hand on his shoulder. "You're not like that anymore. You've changed. I've seen it. Arista and Myron, they've mentioned it as well."

Royce laughed at him. "I killed Merrick, didn't I? I never even gave him a chance. And if it wasn't for Arista, Modina would have died in the fire I set. I can't be a father, Hadrian. I can't raise...I'm evil."

"You didn't kill Magnus. Even after he told you his plans to double-cross you again, you let him go—you *forgave* him. The old Royce didn't know what forgiveness was. You aren't him anymore. It's as if—I don't know—it's like some part of Gwen came to you when she died. She's still alive in there somewhere, still literally your better half."

Royce wiped his eyes. "I loved her so much—I miss her so much. I can't help feeling it's my fault, my punishment for the life I've led."

"And Mercedes?"

"What about her?"

"Is she a punishment? She's your daughter. A part of Gwen that still lives. She has her eyes, you know...and that smile.

The gods don't give a gift that precious to someone so undeserving."

"Are you my priest now?"

Hadrian stared at him.

Royce looked back down at the stream below. "She doesn't even know me. What if she doesn't like me? Few people do."

"She might not at first. Maribor knows I didn't. But you have a way of growing on a person." He smiled. "You know, like lichen or mold."

Royce looked up and scowled. "Okay, forget what I said. Definitely steer clear of the priesthood." He paused, then said, "She does look like Gwen, though, doesn't she? And her laugh—have you heard it?"

"She told me that her mother said her father would make her a fairy princess and that they would live in a beautiful place where she would be a queen of the forest."

"Did she?"

Hadrian nodded. "Seems a shame to disappoint her, and if Gwen told her that, it must be true."

Royce sighed.

"So will you take the throne from Modina?"

"Emperor Royce? I don't think so. But I'm stuck with the job of elven king, aren't I?"

"How's that going, by the way?"

"Funny as it sounds, I think they're terrified of me."

"A lot of people are terrified of you, Royce."

He laughed. "I feel like one of those guys in the circus that train bears with just a chair and a whip. They destroyed half of Apeladorn without a single loss of life on their side and the only thing stopping them from finishing the job is me and their crazy religion. They really hate humans but are convinced I was chosen by Ferrol to be their ruler. To disobey me is to disobey their god. To kill me is unthinkable. So here they are, ruled by a human who they must obey and can't kill. You know they've got to be panicking."

"Only you aren't human."

"No—I'm neither."

"Maybe that will help."

"Perhaps."

"So you still haven't told me. What do you plan to do?"

Royce shrugged. "I don't know yet. How could I? I don't know anything about them, really. I do know that I've seen cruelty from both sides. After seeing how Saldur's empire treated people like me, I can understand the elves' hatred. The old me certainly remembers that feeling, the certitude of justice, the purity of unquestioned purpose."

"And the new you?"

Royce shook his head. "I forgave Magnus, for Maribor's sake."

"Why did you?"

"Tired, I guess. Tired of killing—no, that's not really it. The real reason, I think, is that part of me wondered what Gwen would think. I can't imagine her wanting me to kill Magnus any more than she would want me to punish the elves for what they did. She was such a better person than I am, and now that she's gone, I..."

Hadrian squeezed his shoulder. "Trust me—she's proud of you, pal." He gave him a second, then in a bright tone said, "How is it we never had *king* and *emperor* on our list of potential careers? When you think about it, it beats the heck out of winemakers, actors, and fishermen."

"You always think everything is so easy," Royce replied, wiping his eyes.

"I'm just a glass-half-full kinda guy. How's your glass looking these days?"

"I have no idea. I'm still trying to get over the sheer size of it."

Hadrian nodded. "Speaking of glasses…" He lifted his head when he heard the sound of a fiddle and pipe. He put his arm around Royce's shoulder and led him off the bridge. "How about a nice pint of Armigil's brew?"

"You know I hate beer."

"Well, I'm not sure you can really call what she brews beer. Think of it more as… an experience."

FROM OUT OF A CLEAR BLUE SKY

A surprising number of people survived the attack on Aquesta and came out of their underground bunkers to find a different world. The elves were gone and so was the city. All that remained were the bodies of the dead and the shattered rubble of the once-strong walls. In the weeks that followed, the weather grew warm, the snow melted, and people took to the roads. Many dispersed south or east to Colnora, which had managed to survive unscathed. Some, those originally from there, ventured north to find a ravaged land, which they vowed to rebuild. A few remained in Aquesta, picking up the stones and brushing away the dirt.

The empress took up residence at the unlikely estate of Lord Baldwin. It took several weeks before the full contingent of the imperial government was reestablished, but soon messengers in imperial uniforms were racing across the roads bearing news and orders from the empress.

Much to the dismay of the Aquestians, the empress decided not to return. She announced plans to build a new city at Amberton Lee, which would be named New Percepliquis, after the ancient imperial capital. She called on all artisans, engineers, mapmakers, stone workers, wood carvers, road layers, and a host of others to come. With many out of work and, in many cases, homeless, they came in droves. Among this assortment of workers came a surprisingly large number of dwarves, the largest assembly of little folk seen in centuries. No one knew from where they came, but once they arrived, the work began in earnest and those passing near the Lee remarked at the sounds of hammers in the dark of night.

Rumors spread along with the people. One story maintained that it was not the elves who had destroyed Aquesta, but Nationalists who invented the lies about them to strike fear across the countryside. These stories told that Degan Gaunt fought in single combat against the empress's champion, Sir Hadrian, to decide the fate of the empire. Another bit of gossip held that Rufus's Bane had risen from the dead and laid waste to the countryside, hunting the empress. When it found her in Aquesta, she led it away to save her people and single-handedly slew it once again on a hilltop. They said it remained there in a secret place guarded by priests, who watched over it to make certain that it did not rise again.

The most outlandishly incredible—and therefore most popular—tale was one replete with amazing adventures, monsters, heroes, and villains. It was a story about how the elves invaded, and nothing could stand against them. In this version the empress in her wisdom sent ten heroes into the bowels of Elan to seek the Rhelacan from the tomb of Novron. Among them were the Teshlor Sir Hadrian, a dwarven prince who they befriended in the depths, a pious monk, the last giant to walk the world, and the good wizardess Arista— whose evil twin sister was the Witch of Melengar. The story told of how this courageous band fought through caves, sailed across underground seas of glowing water, battled hordes of goblins, and slew a Gilarabrywn. It told how three of them fell in battle, but the remainder emerged victorious.

According to this story, Sir Hadrian, armed with the Rhelacan, defeated the king of the elves and saved the empire. The tale grew with each passing tinker and new characters were added, including a thief, a sailor, and a master swordsman. All that really mattered was that the empress was alive and well and that Amilia the Beloved was with her. Not all the news was welcome, however, as edicts declared dwarves and half-elves were to be recognized as full citizens of the empire. This touched off the Spring Riots in Colnora and Vernes, which Sir Breckton squelched with a contingent of imperial troops.

In the north, the realm of Melengar all but vanished. What the imperial invasion had not destroyed, the elves had. The young king Alric, who never married and had no heirs, did not return, nor did his sister. After more than seven hundred years, the line of Essendon ended, and it was Count Mauvin Pickering, now Imperial Governor Pickering, who returned to administrate the province of Melengar. By all accounts, he was a good and just man, and before long rumors of his marriage to Lady Alenda Lanaklin circulated.

The death of Archibald Ballentyne left the province of Chadwick vacant of a lord. The seat was replaced when the empress appointed Degan Gaunt earl. In her announcement speech, she said that the appointment was not only deserved but appropriate.

By Summersrule, heralds were crossing the empire shouting in every village about the news from New Percepliquis. The first buildings were standing on the mount at Amberton Lee, just enough to allow the empress to move her court, and she was using the holiday to celebrate the move and commemorate those who had given their lives to save the empire.

The games where held in the newborn city, which was little more than chalk and string outlines. Thousands came hoping to glimpse Sir Hadrian or Sir Breckton on the field, but neither entered the competition. Sir Renwick won top honors, un-horsing Sir Elgar in the final tilt.

The highlight of the celebration, however, was the marriage of Sir Breckton to Lady Amilia in a moonlight ceremony performed by Patriarch Merton. On the last day of the celebrations, Empress Modina made the startling announcement that she had adopted, as daughter and heir, the half-elf child Allie, henceforth to be known as the imperial crown princess Alliena Novronian.

The celebration lasted a full two weeks, and when it was over, the roads were filled with carts and wagons of soon-to-be-footsore travelers on their long journeys home. The hilltop at Amberton Lee, now officially renamed New Percepliquis, was once more filled with the sounds of hammers, chisels, and saws. Sheep grazed on the southern slope, and milk cows on the north.

As the sun began to set, lights appeared in the windows of the "palace"—a simple thirty-room blockhouse. It was the first of the dwarven constructions and designed to be servants' quarters for stable hands and groundskeepers. For now it housed the whole of the imperial government.

On the front steps, which were broad and afforded a fine view from the hilltop, a small group gathered to watch the sunset and the approach of the imperial carriage.

"It really is coming along nicely," Hadrian told the dwarf as he sat with his arm around Arista. He was dressed in a soft tunic and she in a comfortable blue linen dress. "It's hard to imagine this is where I fought only four months ago."

The now leveled land revealed tiers where buildings would be constructed partially into the sides of the hill. Huge blocks of stone marked corners that anchored string lines held in place with stakes that designated future walls, roads, and pathways. Most were rectangular, but some were octagonal or completely circular. Still others defied any description, looking haphazard and bewildering from their footprints in string.

"It's beautiful," Arista said.

"Bah! You can't tell a thing yet!" Magnus scoffed. He tapped his temple. "If you could see what's in here, then you could really appreciate it. This city will make the old one below us an embarrassment." He looked out across the hill. "But it will take time—years—decades, really—but yes, it *will be* beautiful."

The laughter of children blew in with the evening summer breeze as down the slope Allie and Mercy chased fireflies, where a holly tree stood and five boys once spent days in a tent they called the Hovel.

The carriage pulled to a stop, and when the door opened, the white-wigged chancellor Nimbus stepped out. He was dressed in his usual outlandish colors, and on his chest was the massive gold chain of his office. He smiled at Modina and Amilia and greeted them all with a sweep of his hand and a lavish bow.

"It's about time you arrived," Modina said, rising to meet him.

"Forgive me, Your Eminence," he said, dusting himself off. "But there was a great deal to be done before blowing out the last candle in Aquesta."

"How long will you be staying?" Amilia asked.

"I'm afraid not long. I've really only come to see what you've started here and to say goodbye."

"I can't believe you won't stay. I don't know how I will get along without you."

"Alas, as I told Your Eminence in our correspondence, it really is time for me to move on. You have matters well in hand. New Percepliquis is coming along nicely. When I accepted this chain of office, we both knew it was temporary. I will be leaving in the morning."

"Really?" Amilia asked. "So soon? I thought we'd have a few days at least."

"I am afraid so, my lady. I've had many farewells and found that they are best kept short."

"You've been wonderful," Modina told him, squeezing his hand. "This empire wouldn't have survived without you. Every citizen owes you a debt of gratitude."

Nimbus addressed Amilia while gesturing toward the empress. "We did all right with her, didn't we? I think that board really helped."

"Yes," Amilia agreed, and raced down the steps and hugged him tight. She kissed his cheek, startling the chancellor. "Thank you—thank you for everything."

Modina motioned for Nimbus to come closer and briefly whispered in his ear.

"Oh yes, the new couple," Nimbus said, looking at Hadrian and Arista. "Congratulations on your wedding. What will you do now?"

"Yes," Modina said. "Now that the honeymoon is over and you've been duly knighted, Sir Hadrian, what are your plans?"

"Don't look at me. Arista is running this show. I thought we'd be back in Medford by now."

"Oh right." She rolled her eyes. "I could just see you as king in the royal court, listening to the earls and barons griping about who has the right to water cattle on the north bank of the Galewyr, or settling a dispute with the clergy over their refusal to pay a tax on the vast tracks of church-owned land. No, I know how it would turn out. I would be the one left alone in the throne room sorting through the tangled string of a dozen petitions while you're off hunting or jousting. I'm sorry but I've had more than my share of ruling and it would only make us both miserable. That's why I gave Melengar to Mauvin. It also made it easier to admit Melengar to the empire, as he didn't have any problem with accepting a governorship as opposed to a crown.

"Do you know what our good knight here has actually been doing with his time? During our honeymoon?" Arista bumped Hadrian with her shoulder. "Why he was too busy to take part in the joust?"

Everyone looked slightly uneasy, wondering what she might say next.

Arista paused a suitable moment to let their minds wander, then said, "He's been working as the smithy in Hintindar."

Magnus chuckled, Modina modestly smiled, but Russell Bothwick roared. He slapped his thigh until his wife, Lena, laid a calming hand on his leg. "You're a romantic, you are," he said through laughter-invoked tears. "Stoking a forge instead of—"

"*Russell!*" Lena burst out.

"What?" he asked, looking at his wife, bewildered. "I'm just saying that the man has got his priorities all wrong."

"Well, it's not like I'm there *all* day and night," Hadrian said, defending himself. "The fact is they don't have one. Grimbald left over a year ago and they have all this work. They're desperate. I hate seeing my father's forge lying cold. It was taking twice as long to till the fields with dull hoes and spades."

"But it hardly seems the best use of time for the last living Teshlor Knight," Nimbus remarked. "And you." He looked at Arista. "The last master of the Art…what have *you* been doing?"

"I learned to bake bread really well." She too received many surprised looks, not the least of which came from Modina, Amilia, and Lena. "No, seriously, I've gotten good. Arbor says I'm ready to marble rye and wheat together."

Nimbus glanced at Modina, who nodded.

The empress leaned forward. "I would like to ask you both something. The lord chancellor and I have been corresponding on this matter and I think he is right. There is so much that needs to be done. There will be warlords, more uprisings like the riots this spring. With the elves back across the river, goblins have begun raiding again. And of course something must be done about Tur Del Fur."

"I'll second that," Magnus grumbled. "It was bad enough when humans controlled Drumindor; now there's Ghazel wandering its halls."

"The empire needs people of good character to guide and protect the people, good arms, strong arms, wise arms. I can only do so much." She gestured at those in her court. "We can only do so much. The realm is vast and we can't be everywhere. Plus, there is the matter of stability. While I am alive, the empire will be strong, but even small kingdoms have fractured at the passing of a monarch. The larger the empire, the greater the threat. With no structure in place, no solid tradition to hold us together, the empire could break into civil wars."

"Two of the things that made the Old Empire so strong—so cohesive," Nimbus told them, "were the Cenzarium and Teshlor Guild. The Grand Council was created from the best and brightest of both. They maintained order and could govern in the absence of a ruler. Until these institutions are restored—until wizards and knights of the old order patrol the roads and visit the courts of distant governors to ensure they are upholding the law—until they guard the borders of Calis and Estrendor, the empire will not be safe or whole."

"Imagine what a hundred Hadrians and a hundred Aristas could do," Modina told them. "And you." She glanced at Myron. "We need a new university. Sheridan is gone. We can think of no one better to lead such a project."

"But I—" the monk began.

"Think of it as a bigger monastery," Nimbus interrupted. "Administering to a larger flock. You will teach them of lore, philosophy, engineering, languages—including elvish—and of course about Maribor. Teams can be sent into the old city to retrieve any volumes that still remain there. They can be the seeds that can help you spread knowledge to all who are willing to learn."

"We will collect all the works and place them under a huge dome of the greatest library ever constructed," Modina added.

"That does sound nice, but my brother monks…"

"There will be plenty of work for all."

"I've already started laying the foundation for the scriptorium," Magnus told him. "It's five times the size of what we had at the Winds Abbey."

"And the Cenzarium?" Arista looked at the dwarf.

Magnus smiled sheepishly. "The walls are already going up. If you look out there, to the left, you can see them."

"So this has already been settled on?" she asked, pretending to sound indignant.

"While certainly no one," Nimbus replied deftly, "least of all those present here—would ever ask any more of you two, and while you have earned a long and well-deserved rest, I was confident you would not abandon your empress, or the empire you fought so hard to establish."

"Where's the guildhall to be?" Hadrian asked.

Magnus pointed. "Across the square from the Cenzarium, of course. Just like in the old city."

"At least we will be close neighbors," Hadrian said.

"We can have lunches together." Arista grinned at him.

"And in between them will be a fountain and statue of Alric, Wyatt, and Elden," Modina explained.

"Well?" Hadrian asked her.

Arista narrowed her eyes and pursed her lips. "You're replacing yourself with us, aren't you?" she asked Nimbus.

"Yes, you are to be the seeds of a new grand council."

"At least you're honest. All right," she said, and then glared at Magnus. "But *I* will be the one to decorate the interior of the Cenzarium. I've seen dwarven tastes and it isn't conducive to the Art."

Magnus scoffed and grumbled something under his breath.

The door to the palace opened and Royce stepped out. "Hadrian, do you know where—" Royce stopped the instant he saw Nimbus, a look of shock on his face.

"Royce?" Hadrian asked.

Royce said nothing but continued to stare at the wigged chancellor.

"Oh, that's right," Modina said. "You've never met Nimbus, have you?"

"Yes—yes, I have," Royce said. He stepped forward, approaching the chancellor. "I thought you were dead."

"No," Nimbus replied. "I'm still alive, my dear friend."

Everyone looked at them, confused.

"But how?"

"Does it matter?"

"I came back," Royce told him. "I tried to free you. I tried to save you, but Ambrose told me..."

"I know, but I wasn't the one who needed to be freed, and I wasn't the one you needed to save."

❦

The morning arrived bright and clear. Golden sunlight slanted across Amberton Lee, casting shadows marking the growing city that spread out like a newly planted field of hope. In the valley, a low mist, like a white cloud, shrouded the twisting Bernum River and the air was still and quiet even on the hilltop.

Modina was already up. She wrapped a cape over her shoulders and headed out to the porch. She found Royce sitting there, his feet dangling from the side, watching the girls as they raced down the dewy hillside, chasing after Mr. Rings.

"You realize you're taking one of my favorite girls from me," she said.

He nodded. "I made Lord Wymarlin of the Eilywin tribe steward and gave him orders to set Erivan on a peaceful footing. I've left them alone too long and need to check on his progress." Royce looked out at the girls. "Besides, I don't want her growing up only knowing half the story. I need to learn it too. I have to cross the Nidwalden where no man has ever set foot, see Estramnadon and the First Tree. Three thousand years seems impossibly long now, but one day... It will be better if both sides became friendlier neighbors, I think. They aren't ready to embrace men, and men aren't prepared to welcome them yet, but in time... maybe.

"I've asked a number of those with mixed blood to pack their belongings and meet me at Avempartha. There aren't many of us left now—a shame, as they could make perfect ambassadors—a foot in each world, as it were. They can be bridges for the future. We'll start there, and then I'll send them back here. Perhaps one day we'll see an actual bridge across the Nidwalden with carts going both ways." He pointed at the two girls. "That is the start of it, the heir of one throne and the heir of the other chasing an overgrown rodent together."

Hadrian and Arista came out to the porch. They took up seats beside Royce and nodded good-morning greetings.

"Just make sure you take good care of her," Modina said.

"Believe me—no harm will come to that little girl so long as I live."

Hadrian laughed suddenly and Modina and Arista turned to him.

"What?" Arista asked.

"Sorry, but I just got a vision in my mind of Mercedes's poor would-be suitors. Can you imagine the courage of the lad capable of asking *him* for her hand?"

They all laughed except Royce, whose face darkened as he muttered, "Suitors? I never really thought—"

Hadrian slapped Royce on his shoulder. "Come on, I'll help you with your gear."

⮞

Royce finished loading the last saddlebag onto a packhorse the grooms had brought out. He once again checked the cinches of the pony Mercedes would ride. He was not about to trust the security of her saddle to anyone.

Myron was there, petting the horses' noses and saying a blessing over them. When he caught Royce watching, he smiled and said one over the new king as well. "Goodbye, Royce. I'm so pleased to have met you. Do you remember what we talked about at the Winds Abbey the last time we were there?"

A smile tugged at the corners of Royce's mouth. "Everyone deserves a little happiness."

"Yes, never forget that. Oh, and if you find any books across the Nidwalden, bring them the next time you visit. I'd love to learn more about the elves."

"So this is goodbye," Hadrian said as he and Arista came down the palace steps hand in hand.

"You'll finally be rid of me," Royce told him.

"You'll be visiting again soon, won't you?" Arista asked.

He nodded and smiled. "I doubt they have Montemorcey on the other side of the river. I only have room to bring a few bottles."

"Then I will be sure to always have it on hand," Arista told him. In her hands, she held out the Horn of Gylindora. "It's supposed to go with the ruler of the elves."

"Thanks."

"No escort for the king?" Hadrian asked, looking around.

"They are meeting us at the crossroads at the bottom of the hill beyond the forest. I didn't want them staring at me while we said goodbye."

He took Arista's hand and placed Hadrian's on top of it. "I am officially turning him over to you. He's your problem now. You'll have to watch out for him and that won't be easy. He's naive, gullible, immature, horribly unsophisticated, ignorant about anything worth knowing, and idealistic to a fault." He paused to make a show of thinking harder. "He's also indecisive, pathetically honest, a horrible liar, and too virtuous for words. He gets up twice each night to relieve himself, wads his clothes rather than folds them, chews with his mouth open, and talks with his mouth full. He has a nasty habit of cracking his knuckles every morning at breakfast, and, of course, he snores. To remedy that, just put a rock under his blanket."

"That was you? All those nights when we camped?" Hadrian looked shocked.

Arista put her arms around the thief and hugged him tight. Royce squeezed her back, then looked into her eyes for a long moment. "He's a very lucky man."

She smiled and kissed him goodbye.

Hadrian grabbed him next, hugging him and clapping him on the back. "Be careful out there, pal."

"I'm always careful. Oh, and do me a favor. See that Magnus gets this." Royce handed him Alverstone. "Wait until I'm gone, and tell him—tell him the maker said he should have it."

Modina, Amilia, and Nimbus came out of the palace with the two girls and Mr. Rings, who Amilia held awkwardly in her arms. The empress was wiping tears from her cheeks and struggling to keep her lips from shaking. When she got to the steps, she bent down and hugged Mercedes, holding her for several minutes before letting her go. When she did, the little girl ran down the steps and pointed. "Is that my pony?"

Royce nodded and Hadrian threw her up onto it.

"Bye-bye, Allie!" she shouted, petting the pony's mane. "I am off to become a fairy princess." Amilia handed up the raccoon.

Nimbus was dressed in traveling clothes, a small pack on his back and his familiar leather satchel at his side.

"You're leaving now as well?" Amilia hugged Nimbus.

"I regret to say I must be off, Your Ladyship. It is time to go."

"I am sure your family in Vernes will be happy to see you return."

He smiled and, dipping his head, removed his chain of office and placed it in her hands.

"Where's your horse?" Hadrian asked.

"I don't need one," Nimbus replied.

"I think the empire can spare at least that much," Modina told him.

"I am certain it can, Your Eminence, but I honestly prefer walking."

It took another round of hugs, kisses, waves, and wishes of safe travels before Royce, Mercedes, and Nimbus actually started down the slope. Allie ran alongside all the way to the trees and then waved madly before turning and running back to Modina.

Nimbus walked with them and Royce was careful to keep a slow, even pace.

They entered the forest and soon lost all sight of the palace, the city, and the hill. They traveled in silence, listening to the morning symphony of birdsongs and honeybees. Mercedes was mesmerized by her new pet.

"What's my pony's name?" she asked.

"I don't think it has one yet. Would you like to name it?"

"Oh yes ... Let me see ... What's yours called, Daddy?"

"Mine is Mouse. The empress gave her that name."

Mercedes crinkled her nose. "I don't like that. Is mine a boy or a girl?"

"Boy," Royce told her.

"Boy ... okay, hmm." She tapped her lips with a perplexed expression, then furrowed her brow in serious thought.

"How about Elias?" Nimbus suggested. "Or perhaps Sterling."

Royce stared at the ex-chancellor, who smiled pleasantly in return.

"Sterling is nice," Mercedes said.

The forest thinned and they reached the open field where the old road crossed the new ones, freshly pressed by holiday travelers, leading west to Ratibor and north to Colnora. A short distance away a group of riders in gold and blue on white mounts waited.

"This is where we part," Nimbus told them.

Royce stared at the thin man in the wig. "Who are you really?"

Nimbus smiled. "You already know that."

"If it hadn't been for you ..." Royce paused. "I've always regretted that I never said thank you."

"And I wish to thank you as well, Royce."

He was puzzled. "For what?"

"For reminding me that anyone, no matter what they've done, can find redemption if they seek it."

The thin man turned and walked down the road toward Ratibor. Royce watched him go, then turned to his daughter. "Let's go visit the elves, shall we?" he asked. Just then, thunder cracked from overhead, shaking the ground and rustling the leaves on the trees.

Royce looked up at the clear blue sky, confused.

"Look!" Mercedes said, pointing down the road.

Royce turned to see Nimbus standing still, his head bent back, his eyes looking up.

A white feather drifted downward. It swirled, blowing on a gentle breeze until it was close enough that the tall spindly man in the white powdered wig reached up and caught it between his fingers. He kissed it gently, then slipped it into his leather pouch. He pulled the bag closed and continued on his way, whistling a merry tune, until he passed behind a hill and was gone.

GLOSSARY OF TERMS AND NAMES

ABNER GALLSWORTH: Aquesta city administrator

ADAM: Wheeler from Ratibor

ADDIE WOOD: Mother of Thrace/Modina, wife of Theron, killed in Dahlgren

ADELINE: Queen of Alburn, married to Armand, sons: Rudolf and Hector, daughter: Beatrice

ADWHITE, SIR: Knight and poet, wrote *The Song of Beringer*

ALBERT WINSLOW: Landless viscount used by Riyria to arrange assignments from the gentry

ALBURN: Kingdom of Avryn ruled by King Armand and Queen Adeline, member of the New Empire

ALENDA LANAKLIN: Daughter of the marquis Victor Lanaklin and sister of Myron the monk

ALGAR: Woodworker in Hintindar

ALLIE: Daughter of Wyatt Deminthal, half-elf, once held hostage by Merrick Marius

ALRIC ESSENDON, KING: Ruler of Melengar, brother of Arista, son of Amrath

ALVERSTONE: \al-ver-stone\ Dagger used by Royce

ALYSIN: Elven afterlife

AMBERTON LEE: Hill with old ruins not far from Hintindar, site where Arista killed two seret

AMBROSE MOOR: Administrator of the Manzant Prison and Salt Mine

AMILIA: Secretary to the empress, carriage maker's daughter, born in Tarin Vale

AMITER, QUEEN: Second wife of King Urith, sister of Androus, killed by Imperialists

AMRATH ESSENDON, KING: \am-wrath\ Former ruler of Melengar, father of Alric and Arista, killed by the Nyphron Church

AMRIL: \am-rill\ Countess that Arista cursed with boils

ANDROUS BILLET: Viceroy of Ratibor, murdered King Urith, Queen Amiter, and their children

ANKOR: Tribe of Ghazel

ANNA: Chambermaid of Empress Modina

ANTUN BULARD: Historian and author of *The History of Apeladorn*, passenger on the *Emerald Storm*, hired to find the Horn of Gylindora

APELADORN: \ah-pell-ah-dorn\ The four nations of man, consisting of Trent, Avryn, Delgos, and Calis

APELANESE: Language spoken by the four kingdoms of men

AQUESTA: \ah-quest-ah\ Capital city of the kingdom of Warric, seat of power for the New Empire

ARBOR: Baker in Hintindar, married to Dunstan, shoemaker's daughter, first love of Hadrian

ARCADIUS VINTARUS LATIMER: Professor of lore at Sheridan University, caretaker of Allie

ARCHIBALD BALLENTYNE: Earl of Chadwick, commander of Sir Breckton, promised providence of Melengar for service to the New Empire, infatuated with Empress Modina, nickname: Archie

ARISTA ESSENDON, PRINCESS: Sister of Alric, daughter of Amrath, Princess of Melengar, leader of rebel victory in Ratibor, former mayor pro tem of Ratibor, former regent of Rhenydd, Witch of Melengar, imprisoned in Aquesta after trying to free Degan Gaunt

ARMAND, KING: Ruler of Alburn, married to Adeline, sons: Rudolf and Hector, daughter: Beatrice

ARMIGIL: Brew mistress of Hintindar, family friend of the Blackwaters

ART, THE: Magic, generally feared due to superstition

ARVID MCDERN: Son of Dillon McDern of Dahlgren

ASENDWAYR: Tribe of elves, hunters

AVEMPARTHA: Ancient elven tower, home of Gilarabrywn that attacked Dahlgren

AVRYN: \ave-rin\ The central and most powerful of the four nations of Apeladorn, located between Trent and Delgos

AYERS: Proprietor of The Laughing Gnome in Ratibor

BA RAN ARCHIPELAGO: Island of the goblins

BA RAN GHAZEL: Goblins of the sea

BACKING: Rigging a sail such that it catches the wind from its forward side, having both backed and regular rigged sails can render a ship motionless

BAILEY INN, THE: Boardinghouse routinely used by Riyria when in Aquesta

BAILIFF: Officer who is employed to make arrests and administer punishments

BALDWIN: Lord whose landholdings include Hintindar

BALLENTYNE: \bal-in-tine\ The ruling family of the earldom of Chadwick

BANNER: Crew member of the *Emerald Storm*, one of the few survivors

BARAK: Ghetto in Trent inhabited by dwarves

BARKERS: Refugee family living in Brisbane Alley of Aquesta, father Brice, mother Lynnette, sons Finis, Hingus, and Wery

BARTHOLOMEW: Carriage maker of Tarin Vale, father of Amilia

BARTHOLOMEW: Priest in Ratibor

BASIL: Officers' cook on the *Emerald Storm*, died at sea

BASTION: Servant in the imperial palace

BATTLE OF MEDFORD: Skirmish that occurred during Arista's witch trial

BATTLE OF RAMAR: Bloody fight that Hadrian once fought in

BATTLE OF RATIBOR: Rebellion against Imperialists, led by Emery Dorn and Arista

BEATRICE, PRINCESS: Daughter of King Armand, Princess of Alburn, sister to Rudolf and Hector

BELINDA PICKERING: Extremely attractive wife of Count Pickering, mother of Lenare, Mauvin, Fanen, and Denek

BELLA: Cook at The Laughing Gnome in Ratibor

BELSTRADS: \bell-straads\ Noble family from Chadwick, including Sir Breckton and Wesley

BENDLTON, BROTHER: Cook at the rebuilt Winds Abbey

BENNINGTON: Guard in Aquesta

BENTLY: Sergeant in the Nationalist army, promoted by Hadrian to adjunct general

BERNARD: Lord Chamberlain of the imperial palace

BERNARD GREEN: Candlemaker from Alburn, living in Aquesta

BERNICE: Former handmaid of Arista, killed in Dahlgren

BERNIE DEFOE: Topsail crew member of the *Emerald Storm*, former member of the Black Diamond thieves' guild, hired to find the Horn of Gylindora

BERNUM HEIGHTS: Wealthiest residential district in Colnora

BERNUM RIVER: Waterway that bisects the city of Colnora

BERYL: Senior midshipman on the *Emerald Storm*, died at sea

BETHAMY, KING: Ruler reputed to have had his horse buried with him

BETRAYAL IN MEDFORD: Imperialist version of the play *The Crown Conspiracy*

BIDDINGS: Chancellor of the imperial palace

BISHOP: Lieutenant aboard the *Emerald Storm*, died at sea

BLACK DIAMOND: International thieves' guild centered in Colnora

BLACKWATER: Last name of Hadrian and his father, Danbury

BLINDEN: Quartermaster's mate on the *Emerald Storm*, died at sea

BLOOD WEEK: Time of the year when stock that won't be able to be fed during the winter is butchered

BLYTHIN CASTLE: Castle in Alburn

BOATSWAIN: Petty officer on a ship who controls the work of other seamen

BOCANT: Family who built a lucrative industry from pork, second-wealthiest merchants in Colnora

BOTHWICKS: Family of peasant farmers of Dahlgren, father: Russell, mother: Lena

BRAGA, PERCY: Former Archduke and Lord Chancellor of Melengar, expert swordsman, uncle-in-law to Alric and Arista, killed by Count Pickering, commissioned the murder of Amrath

BRAND: Street urchin, reputed to have killed a kid in a fight to win a tunic, nickname: Brand the Bold

BRECKTON: Sir Breckton Belstrad, son of Lord Belstrad, brother of Wesley, commander of the Northern Imperial Army, knight of Chadwick, considered by many to be the best knight of Avryn

BRIDEETH: Elven swear word, highest insult

BRIGHT STAR: Ship sunk by Dacca

BRISTOL BENNET: Boatswain on the *Emerald Storm*, died at sea

BRODRIC ESSENDON: Founder of the Essendon dynasty

BUCKET MAN: Term for assassin in the Black Diamond thieves' guild

BULARD, ANTUN: See Antun Bulard

BURANDU: \bur-and-dew\ Lord of the Tenkin village of Oudorro

BYRNIE: Long (usually sleeveless) tunic of chain mail formerly worn as defensive armor

CALIAN: \cal-lay-in\ Pertaining to the nation of Calis

CALIANS: Residents of the nation of Calis, with dark skin tone and almond-shaped eyes

"CALIDE PORTMORE": Folk song often sung while drinking

CALIS: \cal-lay\ Southern- and easternmost of the four nations of Apeladorn, considered exotic, in constant conflict with the Ba Ran Ghazel

CAPSTAN: Spoked wheel on a ship that turns to raise the anchor

CARAT: Young member of Black Diamond thieves' guild

CARREL: Small individual study area in a library

CASWELL: Family of peasant farmers from Dahlgren

CENZAR: \sen-zhar\ Wizards of the Old Novronian Empire

CENZARIUM: Home of the Cenzar Council in Percepliquis

CHAMBERLAIN: Someone who manages the household of a king or nobleman

CHANFRON: A piece of plate armor used to protect a horse's head

CODE OF CHIVALRY: Eight virtues each knight should aspire to

COLNORA: \call-nor-ah\ Largest, wealthiest city in Avryn, merchant-based city, grew from a rest stop at a central crossroads of various major trade routes

CONSTANCE, LADY: Noblewoman, fifth imperial secretary to Empress Modina

CORA: Dairymaid at the imperial palace

CORNELIUS DELUR: Rich businessman, rumored to finance Nationalists and involved in illegal trade good markets, father of Cosmos

COSMOS SEBASTIAN DELUR: Son of Cornelius, also known as the Jewel, head of the Black Diamond thieves' guild

COXSWAIN: Helmsman of a racing ship

CRANSTON: Professor at Sheridan University, tried and burned for heresy

CRIMSON HAND: Thieves' guild operating out of Melengar

THE CROWN CONSPIRACY: Play reputed to be based on the murder of King Amrath, follows the exploits of two thieves and the Prince of Melengar

CROWN TOWER: Home of the Patriarch and center of the Nyphron Church

CUTTER: Moniker used by Merrick Marius when a member of the Black Diamond thieves' guild

DACCA: A fierce seafaring people who live on the island of Dacca, south of Delgos

DAGASTAN: Major and easternmost trade port of Calis

DAHLGREN: \dall-grin\ Remote village on the bank of the Nidwalden River, site of Gilarabrywn attack

DANBURY BLACKWATER: Father of Hadrian

DANTHEN: Woodsman from Dahlgren

DAREF, LORD: Noble of Warric, associate of Albert Winslow

DARIUS SERET: Founder of the Seret Knights

DAVENS: Squire who Arista had a youthful crush on

DAVIS: Crew member of the *Emerald Storm*, died at sea

DEACON TOMAS: Priest of Dahlgren, witnessed destruction of Gilarabrywn, proclaimed Thrace Wood as the Heir of Novron

DEFOE, BERNIE: See Bernie Defoe

DEGAN GAUNT: Leader of the Nationalists, sister of Miranda, Heir of Novron, imprisoned in Aquesta by Imperialists

DELANCY, GWEN: Calian prostitute and proprietor of Medford House and The Rose and Thorn Tavern in Medford, girlfriend of Royce Melborn

DELANO DEWITT: Alias used by Wyatt Deminthal when he framed Hadrian and Royce for King Amrath's death

DELGOS: One of the four nations of Apeladorn. The only republic in a world of monarchies, Delgos revolted against the Steward's Empire after Glenmorgan III was murdered and after surviving an attack by the Ba Ran Ghazel with no aid from the empire

DELORKAN, DUKE: Nobleman from Calis

DELUNDEN, BISHOP: Head of the Nyphron Church in Aquesta

DELUR: Family of wealthy merchants, father: Cornelius, son: Cosmos

DEMINTHAL, WYATT: Quartermaster and helmsman of the *Emerald Storm*, father of Allie, blackmailed by Merrick Marius to ensure Riyria disabled defenses of Drumindor

DENEK PICKERING: Youngest son of Count Pickering

DENNY: Worker at The Rose and Thorn

DERIN: Clan of dwarves

DERMONT, LORD: General of the Southern Imperial Army, killed in the Battle of Ratibor

DERNING, JACOB: Maintop captain on the *Emerald Storm*, member of Black Diamond, rescued Royce and Hadrian from Tur Del Fur jail

DESTRIER: Unusually large warhorse used by knights

DEVON: Monk of Tarin Vale, taught Amilia to read and write

DEWITT, DELANO: See Delano DeWitt

DIGBY: Guard at Essendon Castle

DILLADRUM: Erbonese guide, hired to take crew of the *Emerald Storm* to the Palace of the Four Winds, killed during escape

DIME: Crew member of the *Emerald Storm*, died at sea

DIOYLION: \die-e-leon\ *The Accumulated Letters of Dioylion*, a very rare scroll

DIXON TAFT: Bartender and manager of The Rose and Thorn Tavern, lost an arm in the Battle of Medford

DOBBS: Servant in the employ of Merrick Marius

DOGGER: Type of small ship, often used by Tenkin

DOVIN THRANIC: Sentinel of the Nyphron Church, half-elf, hired to find the Horn of Gylindora

DR. GERAND: Physician in Ratibor

DR. LEVY: Physician, hired to find the Horn of Gylindora

DRASH: Ghazel chieftain, arena fighter, known as Drash of the Klune

DREW, EDGAR: Old seaman

DROME: God of the dwarves

DRONDIL FIELDS: Count Pickering's castle, once the fortress of Brodric Essendon, the original seat of power in Melengar

DRUMINDOR: Dwarven-built fortress located at the entrance to Terlando Bay in Tur Del Fur, can utilize lava from the nearby volcano for its defense, overrun by goblins after the defenses were disabled by Royce and Hadrian

DRUNDEL: Peasant family from Dahlgren consisting of Mae, Went, Davie, and Firth

DUBRION ASH: Author of *The Forgotten Race*, a history of the dwarves

DULNAR, SIR: Knight who lost a hand in the Wintertide games

DUNLAP, PAUL: Former carriage driver of King Urith, dead

DUNMORE: Youngest and least sophisticated kingdom of Avryn, ruled by King Roswort, member of the New Empire

DUNSTAN: Baker in Hintindar, childhood friend of Hadrian, married to Arbor

DUR GURON: Easternmost portion of Calis

DURBO: Tenkin dwelling

DUSTER: Moniker used by Royce while a member of the Black Diamond

ECTON, SIR: Chief knight of Count Pickering, military general of Melengar

EDGAR DREW: See Drew, Edgar

EDITH MON: Head maid in charge of the scullery and chamber servants in the imperial palace

EDMUND HALL: Professor of geometry at Sheridan University, found Percepliquis, declared a heretic by the Nyphron Church, imprisoned in the Crown Tower, husband of Sadie, father of Ebot and Dram

EDMUND HALL'S JOURNAL: Heretical document of journey into Percepliquis, one of the treasures kept in the Crown Tower

EILYWIN: Tribe of elves, builders

ELAN: The world

ELBRIGHT: Street urchin, leader of a small band consisting of Mince, Brand, and Kine, nickname: the Old Man

ELDEN: Large man, friend of Wyatt Deminthal

ELGAR, SIR: Knight of Galeannon, friend of Gilbert and Murthas

ELINYA: Esrahaddon's lover

ELLA: Cook at Drondil Fields

ELLA: Alias used by Arista while masquerading as a maid in the imperial palace

ELLIS FAR: Melengarian ship used to send envoy to Nationalists, captured by Imperialists

ELQUIN: Masterwork of Orintine Fallon, poet

ELVEN: Pertaining to elves

EMERALD STORM: Ship of the New Empire, captained by Seward

EMERY DORN: Young revolutionary from Ratibor, in love with Arista, killed in the Battle of Ratibor

EMPRESS MODINA: Previously Thrace Wood of Dahlgren, locked in a near catatonic state after loss of family and village, appointed empress of the New Empire

ENDEN, SIR: Knight of Chadwick, considered second best to Breckton, killed in Dahlgren

ENILD, BARON: \in-illed\ Nobleman of Galien of Melengar

ERANDABON GILE: Panther of Dur Guron, Tenkin warlord, madman

ERBON: Region of Calis northwest from Mandalin

EREBUS: Father of the gods, also known as Kile when in human form

ERIVAN: \ear-ah-van\ Elven empire

ERLIC, SIR : A knight who survived the destruction of Dahlgren

ERMA EVERTON: Alias used by Arista while in Hintindar

ERVANON: \err-vah-non\ City in northern Ghent, seat of the Nyphron Church, once the capital of the Steward's Empire as established by Glenmorgan I

ESRAHADDON: \ez-rah-hod-in\ Wizard, former member of the Cenzar, convicted of destroying the Old Empire, sentenced to imprisonment, held in Gutaria, killed by Merrick

ESSENDON: \ez-in-don\ Royal family of Melengar

ESSENDON CASTLE: Home of the ruling monarchs of Melengar

ESTRAMNADON: \es-tram-nah-don\ Believed to be the capital or at least a very sacred place in the Erivan Empire

ESTRENDOR: \es-tren-door\ The northern wastes

ETCHER: Member of the Black Diamond thieves' guild, traitor who turns Arista over to seret

ETHELRED, LANIS: \eth-el-red\ Former King of Warric, co-regent of the New Empire, Imperialist

EVERTON: Alias used by Arista, Hadrian, and later Royce

EVERTON, CAPTAIN: Commander of Aquesta's southern gate

EVLIN: City along the banks of the Bernum River

EXETER: Family name of the rulers of Hanlin

FALINA BROCKTON: Real name of Emerald, waitress at The Rose and Thorn

FALLON MIRE: City where Merton prevented the spread of a terrible disease

FALLON, ORINTINE: Poet who wrote about how patterns in nature relate to patterns in life

FALL-THE-WALL: Children's game

FALQUIN: Professor at Sheridan University

FAN IRLANU: Visionary of Oudorro, seer, fortune-teller, predicted Royce's future, including the death of someone near to him

FANEN PICKERING: \fan-in\ Middle son of Count Pickering, killed by Luis Guy

FAQUIN: Inept magician who uses alchemy rather than channeling the Art

FARILANE, PRINCESS: Wrote *Migration of Peoples*

FAULD, THE ORDER OF: \fall-ed\ A post-imperial order of knights dedicated to preserving the skill and discipline of the Teshlor Knights

FENITILIAN: Monk of Maribor, made warm shoes

FERROL: God of the elves

FESTIVIOUS FOUNDEREIONUS: Celebration to commemorate the founding of Percepliquis

FINILESS: Noted author

FINISHER: Stealthy Ghazel fighter

FINLIN, ETHAN: Member of the Black Diamond, stores smuggled goods, owns a windmill

FLETCHER: Maker of arrows

FORECASTLE: Raised portion in the bow of a ship containing living quarters of senior crew members

FORREST: Ratibor citizen with fighting experience, son of a silversmith

FREDA, QUEEN: Queen of Dunmore, wife of Roswort

FREDRICK, KING: Ruler of Galeannon, husband of Josephine

GAFTON: Imperial admiral

GALEANNON: \gale-e-an-on\ A kingdom of Avryn, ruled by Fredrick and Josephine, member of the New Empire

GALENTI: \ga-lehn'-tay\ Calian nickname attributed to Hadrian, Calian word for *killer*

GALEWYR RIVER: \gale-wahar\ Marks the southern border of Melengar and the northern border of Warric and reaches the sea near the fishing village of Roe

GALIEN: \gal-e-in\ Former archbishop of the Nyphron Church

GALILIN: \gal-ah-lin\ Province of Melengar ruled by Count Pickering

GARNACHE: Loose outer garment

GAUNT, DEGAN: See Degan Gaunt

GEMKEY: Gem that opens a gemlock

GEMLOCK: Dwarven invention that seals a container, can be opened only with a precious gem of the right type and cut

GENEVIEVE HARGRAVE: Duchess of Rochelle, wife of Leopold, patron of Riyria, nickname: Genny

GENTRY SQUARE: Affluent district of Melengar

GERALD BANIFF: Primary bodyguard of Empress Modina, family friend of the Belstrads

GERTY: Midwife in Hintindar who delivered Hadrian, married to Abelard

GHAZEL: \gehz-ell\ Ba Ran Ghazel, the dwarven name for goblins, literally: sea goblins

GHAZEL SEA: Southern body of water east of the Sharon Sea

GHENT: Ecclesiastical holding of the Nyphron Church, member of the New Empire

GILARABRYWN: \gill-lar-ah-bren\ Elven beast of war; once escaped Avempartha, destroyed the village of Dahlgren, and was killed by Thrace

GILBERT, SIR: Knight of Maranon, friend of Murthas and Elgar

GILL: Sentry in the Nationalist Army

GINLIN: \gin-lin\ A Monk of Maribor, winemaker, refused to touch a knife

GLAMRENDOR: \glam-ren-door\ Capital of Dunmore

GLENMORGAN: 326 years after the fall of the Novronian Empire, this native of Ghent reunited the four nations of Apeladorn; founder of Sheridan University; creator of the great north-south road; builder of the Ervanon palace (of which only the Crown Tower remains)

GLENMORGAN II: Son of Glenmorgan. When his father died young, the new and inexperienced emperor relied on church officials to assist him in managing his empire. They in turn took the opportunity to manipulate the emperor into granting sweeping powers to the church and nobles loyal to the church. These leaders opposed defending Delgos against the invading Ba Ran Ghazel in Calis and the Dacca in Delgos, arguing the threat would increase dependency on the empire.

GLENMORGAN III: Grandson of Glenmorgan. Shortly after assuming the stewardship, he attempted to reassert control over the realm his grandfather had created by leading an army against the invading Ghazel that had reached southeastern Avryn. He defeated the Ghazel at the First Battle of Vilan Hills and announced plans to ride to the aid of Tur Del Fur. Fearing his rise in power, in the sixth year of his reign, his nobles betrayed and imprisoned him in Blythin Castle. Jealous of his popularity and growing strength, and resentful of his policy of stripping the nobles and clergy of their power, the church charged him with heresy. He was found guilty and executed. This began the rapid collapse of what many called the Steward's Empire. The church later claimed the nobles had tricked them, and condemned many, most of whom reputedly ended their lives badly.

GLOUSTON: Province of northern Warric bordering on the Galewyr River, ruled by the marquis Lanaklin, invaded and taken over by the New Empire

GNOME, THE: Nickname of The Laughing Gnome Tavern

GRADY: Seaman on the *Emerald Storm*, died in the arena fight in the Palace of the Four Winds

GRAND MAR: Main avenue of Percepliquis, leads to the imperial palace

GRAVIN DENT, SIR: Well-respected knight from Delgos

GRAVIS: Dwarf who sabotaged Drumindor

GREAT SWORD: Long sword designed to be held with both hands

GREEN: Lieutenant on the *Emerald Storm*, died at sea

GREIG: Carpenter aboard the *Emerald Storm*, one of the few survivors

GRELAD, JERISH: Teshlor Knight, first Guardian of the Heir, protector of Nevrik

GRIBBON: The flag of Mandalin, Calis

GRIGOLES: \gry-holes\ Author of *Grigoles Treatise on Imperial Common Law*

GRIMBALD: Blacksmith in Hintindar, had taken over the shop from Danbury Blackwater

GRONBACH: Dwarf, fairy tale villain

GRUMON, MASON: \grum-on\ Blacksmith in Medford, worked for Riyria, died in the Battle of Medford

GUARDIAN OF THE HEIR: Teshlor, protector of the Heir of Novron

GUNGUAN: Vintu pack ponies

GUR EM: Thickest part of the jungle in Calis, as it butts up against the eastern tip of Calis

GUTARIA: \goo-tar-ah\ Secret Nyphron prison, designed to hold Esrahaddon

GUY, LUIS: Sentinel of the Nyphron Church, killed Fanen Pickering, son of Evone and Jarred

GWEN DELANCY: See DeLancy, Gwen

GWYDRY: Tribe of elves, farmers

HADDY: Childhood nickname of Hadrian

HADRIAN BLACKWATER: Mercenary, one-half of Riyria, Guardian of the Heir, known throughout Calis as Galenti, renowned arena fighter

HALBERD: Two-handed pole used as a weapon

HANDEL: Master at Sheridan University, originally from Roe, proponent to have Delgos's republic officially recognized

HARBERT: Tailor in Hintindar, husband of Hester

HARBINGER: Ship used by Dovin Thranic, Antun Bulard, Bernie Defoe, and Dr. Levy

HARKON, ABBOT: Abbot of the rebuilt Winds Abbey

HARTENFORD: Author of *Genealogy of Warric Monarchs*

HARVEST MOON: The full moon nearest the fall equinox

HEIR OF NOVRON: Direct descendant of demigod Novron, destined to rule all of Avryn

HELDABERRY: Wild-growing fruit often used to make wine

HERCLOR MATH: Dwarven mason

HESLON: A Monk of Maribor, great cook

HESTLE: Family name of rulers of Bernum

HIGHCOURT FIELDS: Once the site of the supreme noble judicial court of law in Avryn, location of the Wintertide games

HILFRED, REUBEN: Bodyguard and lover of Arista, severely burned in Dahlgren, killed in Aquesta while trying to free Degan Gaunt

HILL DISTRICT: Affluent neighborhood in Colnora

HILL MCDAVIN: Author of books on maritime commerce

HIMBOLT, BARON: Nobleman of Melengar

HINGARA: Calian guide, died in the jungles of Gur Em

HINKLE, BROTHER: Monk who cleans the stable in the new Winds Abbey

HINTINDAR: Small manorial village in Rhenydd, home of Hadrian Blackwater

HIVENLYN: Ryn's horse, name means *unexpected gift* in elvish

HOBBIE: Stableboy in Hintindar

HORN OF DELGOS: Landmark used by sailors to determine the southernmost tip of Delgos

HORN OF GYLINDORA: Item Esrahaddon indicates is buried in Percepliquis; Dovin Thranic, Dr. Levy, Bernie Defoe, and Antun Bulard were hired to retrieve it

HOUSE, THE: Nickname used for Medford House

HOVEL, THE: Nickname of snow fort used by Renwick, Mince, Elbright, Brand, and Kine

HOYTE: Onetime First Officer of the Black Diamond, set up Royce to kill Jade, sent Royce to Manzant Prison, killed by Royce

IBIS THINLY: Head cook at the imperial palace

IMP: Slang for *Imperialist*

IMPERIAL PALACE: Seat of power of the New Empire, originally named Warric Castle

IMPERIAL SECRETARY: Caretaker of Empress Modina

IMPERIALISTS: Political party that desires to unite all the kingdoms of men under a single leader who is the direct descendant of the demigod Novron

INSTARYA: Tribe of elves, warriors

IRAWONDONA, LORD: Elf, member of the hunter tribe

JACOB DERNING: See Derning, Jacob

JADE: Assassin in the Black Diamond, girlfriend of Merrick, mistakenly killed by Royce

JASPER: Rat in the imperial palace dungeons

JENKINS: Merrick Marius's head servant

JENKINS TALBERT: Squire in Tarin Vale

JEREMY: Guard at Essendon Castle

JERISH GRELAD: See Grelad, Jerish

JERL, LORD: Nobleman, neighbor of the Pickerings, known for his prizewinning hunting dogs

JERVIS, SIR: Killed during a Wintertide joust with the Earl of Harborn

JEWEL, THE: Head of the international Black Diamond thieves' guild, also known as Cosmos DeLur

JIMMY: Tavern worker at The Laughing Gnome

JOQDAN: \jok-dan\ Warlord of the Tenkin village of Oudorro

JOSEPHINE, QUEEN: Queen of Galeannon, married to Fredrick

JULIAN TEMPEST: Elderly chamberlain of the kingdom of Melengar

Kaz: Calian term for anyone with mixed elven and human blood

KENDELL, EARL: Nobleman of Melengar, loyal to Alric Essendon

KENG: Form of currency used by the Old Empire

KHAROLL: Long dagger

KILE: Name used by Erebus when sent to Elan, performs good deeds in the form of a man

KILNAR: City in the south of Rhenydd

KINE: Youngest of Elbright's street urchins, best friend of Mince

KNOB: Baker at the imperial palace

KRINDEL: Prelate of the Nyphron Church and historian

KRIS DAGGER: Weapon with a wavy blade, sometimes used in magic rituals

"LADIES OF ENGENALL": Lively popular tune played on a fiddle

LAMBERT, IGNATIUS: Chancellor of Sheridan University

LANAKLIN: Once ruling family of Glouston, in exile in Melengar, opposes the New Empire

LANDONER: Professor at Sheridan University, tried and burned for heresy

LANGDON BRIDGE: Swan-decorated bridge in the warehouse district of Colnora that spans the Bernum River

LANKSTEER: Capital city of the Lordium kingdom of Trent

LAUGHING GNOME, THE: Inn in Ratibor, run by Ayers

LAVEN: Citizen of Ratibor, turned rebel Emery Dorn in to the Imperialists

LEIF: Butcher and assistant cook at the imperial palace

LENA BOTHWICK: Wife of Russell, mother of Tad, from a poor family in Dahlgren

LENARE PICKERING: Daughter of Count Pickering and Belinda, sister of Mauvin, Fanen, and Denek

LEOPOLD HARGRAVE, DUKE: Duke of Rochelle, husband of Genevieve, patron of Riyria, nickname: Leo

LINDER, BARON: Nobleman killed by Gilbert in a Wintertide joust

LINGARD: Capital city of Relison, kingdom of Trent

LINROY, DILLNARD: Royal financier of Melengar

LIVET GLIM: Port controller at Tur Del Fur

LONGWOOD: Forest in Melengar

LOTHOMAD THE BALD, KING: Ruler of Lordium, Trent, expanded territory following the collapse of the Steward's Reign, pushing south through Ghent into Melengar, where Brodric Essendon defeated him in the Battle of Drondil Fields in 2545

LOUDEN, SIR: One of several knights defeated by Sir Hadrian in the Wintertide joust

LOWER QUARTER: Impoverished section of the city of Melengar

LOZENGE SHIELD: Shield decorated with alternating colors of diamonds

LUGGER: Small fishing boat rigged with one or more lugsails

LUIS GUY: See Guy, Luis

LURET: Imperial envoy to Hintindar, arrested Royce and Hadrian

MAE, LADY: Love interest of Albert Winslow

MAGNUS: Dwarf, killed King Amrath, sabotaged Arista's tower, discovered entry into Avempartha, rebuilding the Winds Abbey, obsessed with Royce's dagger

MALEVOLENT: Sir Hadrian's horse

MALNESS, SIR: Former knight to squire Renwick

MANDALIN: \man-dah-lynn\ Capital of Calis

MANZANT: \man-zahnt\ Infamous prison and salt mine, located in Manzar, Maranon, Royce Melborn is only prisoner to have been released from it

MARANON: \mar-ah-non\ Kingdom in Avryn, ruled by Vincent and Regina, member of the New Empire, rich in farmland

MARES CATHEDRAL: Center of the Nyphron Church in Melengar, formerly run by Bishop Saldur

MARIBOR: \mar-eh-bore\ God of men

MARIUS, MERRICK: Former member of the Black Diamond, alias: Cutter, master thief and assassin, former best friend of Royce, known for his strategic thinking, boyfriend of Jade, murderer of Esrahaddon, planned destruction of Tur Del Fur, blackmailed Wyatt to betray Royce and Hadrian

MAUVIN PICKERING: \maw-vin\ Eldest of Count Pickering's sons, friends since childhood with Essendon royal family, bodyguard to King Alric

MAWYNDULË: A powerful wizard

McDERN, DILLON: Blacksmith of Dahlgren

MEDFORD: Capital of Melengar

MEDFORD HOUSE: Brothel run by Gwen DeLancy and attached to The Rose and Thorn

MELENGAR: \mel-in-gar\ Kingdom in Avryn ruled by the Essendon royal family, the only Avryn kingdom independent of the New Empire

MELENGARIANS: Residents of Melengar

MELISSA: Head servant of Arista, nickname Missy

MERCS: Mercenaries

MERCY: Young girl under the care of Arcadius Latimer and Miranda Gaunt

MERLON: Solid section between two crenels in a crenellated battlement

MERRICK MARIUS: See Marius, Merrick

MERTON: Monsignor of Ghent, savior of Fallon Mire, speaks aloud to Novron

MESSKID: Container used to transport meals aboard a ship, resembles a bucket

MILBOROUGH: Melengarian Baron, died in battle

MILFORD: Sergeant in the Nationalist army

MILLIE: Formerly Hadrian's horse, died in Dahlgren

MINCE: Orphan living on the streets of Aquesta, best friend to Kine

MIR: Person with both elven and human blood

MIRALYITH: Tribe of elves, mages

MIRANDA GAUNT: Sister of Degan Gaunt, helping Arcadias raise Mercy

MIZZENMAST: Third mast from the bow in a vessel having three or more masts

MODINA: See Empress Modina

MON, EDITH: See Edith Mon

MONTEMORCEY: \mont-eh-more-ah-sea\ Excellent wine imported through the Vandon Spice Company

MOTTE: A man-made hill

MOUSE: Royce's horse, named by Thrace, gray mare

MR. RINGS: Baby raccoon, pet of Mercy

MURDERESS: Lady Genevieve's prize hunting bird

MURIEL: Goddess of nature, daughter of Erebus, mother of Uberlin

MURTHAS, SIR: Knight of Alburn, son of the Earl of Fentin, friend of Gilbert and Elgar

MYRON LANAKLIN: Sheltered Monk of Maribor, indelible memory, son of Victor, brother of Alenda

MYSTIC: Name of Arista's horse when traveling to Ratibor

NAREION: \nare-e-on\ Last emperor of the Novronian Empire, father of Nevrik

NARON: Heir of Novron who died in Ratibor in 2992

NATIONALISTS: Political party led by Degan Gaunt that desires rule by the will of the people

NATS: Nickname of the Nationalists

NEST, THE: Nickname of both the Rat's Nest, home to the Ratibor Black Diamond thieves, and the adopted home of four street orphans in Aquesta

NEVRIK: \nehv-rick\ Son of Nareion, the heir who went into hiding, protected by Jerish Grelad, nickname Nary

NEW EMPIRE: Second empire uniting most of the kingdoms of man, ruled by Empress Modina, administered by co-regents Ethelred and Saldur

NIDWALDEN RIVER: Marks the eastern border of Avryn and the start of the Erivan realm

NILYNDD: Tribe of elves, crafters

NIMBUS: Tutor to the empress, assistant to the imperial secretary, originally from Vernes

NIPPER: Young servant assigned primarily to the kitchen of the imperial palace

NOVRON: Savior of mankind, demigod, son of Maribor, defeated the elven army in the Great Elven Wars, founder of the Novronian Empire, builder of Percepliquis, husband of Persephone

NOVRONIAN: \nov-ron-e-on\ Pertaining to Novron

NYPHRON CHURCH: The worshipers of Novron and Maribor

NYPHRONS: \nef-rons\ Devout members of the Nyphron Church

OBERDAZA: \oh-ber-daz-ah\ Tenkin or Ghazel witch doctor

OLD EMPIRE: Original united kingdoms of man, destroyed one thousand years in the past after the murder of Emperor Nareion

ORRIN FLATLY: Ratibor city scribe, assistant of Arista

OSGAR: Reeve of Hintindar

OSTRIUM: Tenkin communal hall where meals are served

OUDORRO: Friendly Tenkin Village in Calis

PALACE OF THE FOUR WINDS: Home of Erandabon Gile in Dur Guron

PARKER: Quartermaster and later commander of Nationalist army, killed in Battle of Ratibor

PARTHALOREN FALLS: \path-ah-lore-e-on\ The great cataracts on the Nidwalden near Avempartha

PATRIARCH: Head of the Nyphron Church, lives in the Crown Tower of Ervanon

PAULDRON: Piece of armor covering the shoulder

PERCEPLIQUIS: \per-sep-lah-kwiss\ Ancient city and capital of the Novronian Empire, named for the wife of Novron, destroyed and lost during the collapse of the Old Empire

PERCY BRAGA: See Braga, Percy

PERIN: Grocer from Ratibor

PERSEPHONE: Wife of Novron, Percepliquis was named after her

PICKERING: Noble family of Melengar and rulers of Galilin, Count Pickering is known to be the best swordsman in Avryn and believed to use a magic sword

PICKILERINON: Seadric, who shortened the family name to Pickering

PITH: Small-value coin of the Old Empire

PLANCHETTE: Footrest for a woman's sidesaddle

PLESIEANTIC INCANTATION: \plass-e-an-tic\ A method used in the Art to draw power from nature

POE: Cook's assistant aboard the *Emerald Storm*, Merrick's assistant

POLISH: Head of the Black Diamond thieves' guild in Ratibor

PRALEON GUARDS: \pray-lee-on\ Bodyguards to the king in Ratibor

PRICE: First Officer of the Black Diamond thieves' guild

PRINCESS: Name of Arista's horse on the ride to Percepliquis

QUARTZ: Member of the Ratibor thieves' guild

QUEEN'S GAMBIT: Series of moves used to open a chess game

QUINTAIN: Used in training for the joust; when hit, it will spin and can knock the rider off his saddle

RATIBOR: Capital of the kingdom of Rhenydd, home of Royce Melborn

RAT'S NEST, THE: Hideout of the Black Diamond thieves' guild in Ratibor

RED: Old elkhound, large dog frequently found in the kitchen of the imperial palace

REEVE: Official who supervises serfs and oversees the lands for a lord

REGAL FOX INN, THE: Least expensive tavern in the affluent Hill District in Colnora

REGENT: Someone who administers a kingdom during the absence or incapacity of the ruler

REGINA, QUEEN: Wife of Vincent, Queen of Maranon

RENDON, BARON: Nobleman of Melengar

RENIAN: \rhen-e-ahn\ Childhood friend of Myron the monk, died at a young age

RENKIN POOL: Citizen of Ratibor with fighting experience

RENQUIST: Commander of the Nationalist army, promoted to the position by Hadrian

RENTINUAL, TOBIS: History professor at Sheridan University, built a catapult to fight the Gilarabrywn

RENWICK: Imperial page, assigned to act as Sir Hadrian's squire

RHELACAN: \rell-ah-khan\ Great sword given to Novron by Maribor, forged by Drome, enchanted by Ferrol, used to defeat and subdue the elves

RHENYDD: \ren-yaed\ Poor kingdom of Avryn, ruled by King Urith, now part of the New Empire

RILAN VALLEY: Fertile land that separates Glouston and Chadwick

RIONILLION: \ri-on-ill-lon\ Name of the city that first stood on the site of Aquesta, destroyed during the civil wars that occurred after the fall of the Novronian Empire

RIYRIA: \rye-ear-ah\ Elvish for *two*, a team or a bond, name used to refer collectively to Royce Melborn and Hadrian Blackwater

RONDEL: Common type of stiff-bladed dagger with a round handgrip

ROSE AND THORN, THE: Tavern in Medford run by Gwen DeLancy, used as a base by Riyria

ROSWORT, KING: Ruler of Dunmore, husband of Freda

ROYALISTS: Political party that favors rule by independent monarchs

ROYCE MELBORN: Thief, one-half of Riyria, half-elf

RUDOLF, PRINCE: Son of King Armand, Prince of Alburn, brother to Beatrice and Hector

RUFUS, LORD: Ruthless northern warlord, intended emperor for the New Empire, killed by a Gilarabrywn in Dahlgren

RUFUS'S BANE: Name given to the Gilarabrywn slain by Thrace/Modina

RUPERT, KING: Unmarried king of Rhenydd

RUSSELL BOTHWICK: Farmer in Dahlgren, married to Lena, father of Tad

RYN: Half-elf who helped save Alric from Baron Trumbul

SALDUR, MAURICE: Former bishop of Medford, former friend and advisor to the Essendon family, co-regent of the New Empire, nickname: Sauly

SALIFAN: \sal-eh-fan\ Fragrant wild plant used in incense

SALTY MACKEREL, THE: Tavern in the shipping district of Aquesta

SARAP: Meeting place or talking place in the Tenkin language

SAULY: Nickname of Maurice Saldur, used by those closest to him

SENON UPLAND: Highland plateau overlooking Chadwick

SENTINEL: Inquisitor generals of the Nyphron Church, charged with rooting out heresy and finding the lost Heir of Novron

SERET: \sir-ett\ The Knights of Nyphron. The military arm of the church, first formed by Lord Darius Seret, commanded by sentinels

SET: Ratibor member of the Black Diamond thieves' guild

SEWARD: Captain of the *Emerald Storm*, died at sea

SHARON SEA: Southern body of water west of the Ghazel Sea

SHERIDAN UNIVERSITY: Prestigious institution of learning, located in Ghent, Arista studied there

SHIP'S MASTER: Highest non-officer, in charge of running the daily workings of the ship

SHIRLUM-KATH: Small parasitic worm found in Calis, can infect untreated wounds

SIWARD: Bailiff of Hintindar

SKILLYGALEE: \skil`li-ga-lee\ Oatmeal porridge served to sailors for breakfast

SPADONE: Long two-handed sword with a tapering blade and an extended flange ahead of the hilt allowing for an extended variety of fighting maneuvers. Due to the length of the handgrip and the flange, which provides its own barbed hilt, the sword provides a number of additional hand placements, permitting the sword to be used similarly to a quarterstaff and as a powerful cleaving weapon. The spadone is the traditional weapon of a skilled knight.

STANLEY, EARL FRANCIS: Nobleman of Harborn, killed in a Wintertide joust with Sir Jervis

STAUL: Tenkin warrior aboard the *Emerald Storm*, hired to find the Horn of Gylindora, killed by Royce in jungles of Calis

SUMMERSRULE: Popular midsummer holiday, celebrated with picnics, dances, feasts, and jousting tournaments

TABARD: Tunic worn over armor, usually emblazoned with a coat of arms

TAD BOTHWICK: Son of Lena and Russell, from a poor farming family of Dahlgren

TALBERT, BISHOP: Head of the Nyphron Church in Ratibor

TARIN VALE: Hometown of Amilia

TARTANE: Small ship used for fishing and coastal trading; single mast, large sail

TEK'CHIN: One of the fighting disciplines of the Teshlor Knights, preserved by the Knights of the Fauld, handed down to the Pickerings

TEMPLE: Ship's master of the *Emerald Storm*, second in command

TENENT: The most common form of semi-standard international currency. Coins of gold, silver, and copper stamped with the likeness of the king of the realm where the coin was minted

TENKIN: Community of humans living in the manner of Ghazel and suspected of having Ghazel blood

TERLANDO BAY: Harbor of Tur Del Fur

TESHLOR: Legendary knights of the Novronian Empire, greatest warriors ever to have lived

HALL OF TESHLOR: Building in Percepliquis were Teshlors trained and lived

THEOREM ELDERSHIP: Secret society formed to protect the heir

THERON WOOD: Father of Thrace, farmer of Dahlgren, killed by the Gilarabrywn

THRACE WOOD: Daughter of Theron and Addie, name changed to Modina by the regents, crowned Empress of the New Empire, killed the Gilarabrywn in Dahlgren

THRANIC, DOVIN: See Dovin Thranic

TIBITH: Friend of Mince and Kine who died

TIGER OF MANDALIN: Moniker given to Hadrian while in Calis

TILINER: Superior side sword, used frequently by mercenaries in Avryn

TOLIN ESSENDON: Son of Brodric, moved the Melengar capital to Medford, built Essendon Castle, also known as Tolin the Great

TOPE ENTWISTLE: Northern scout, signaled the elven advance

TOPMEN: Members of a ship's crew who work high up in the rigging and sails

TORSONIC: Torque-producing, as in the cable used in crossbows

TRAMUS DAN: Guardian of Naron, later changed his name to Danbury Blackwater

TREMBLES: Fermented sweet drink made from flowers

TRENCHON: City bailiff of Ratibor

TRENT: Northern mountainous kingdoms not yet controlled by the New Empire

TRILON: Small, fast bow used by Ghazel

TRUMBUL, BARON: Mercenary, hired by Percy Braga to kill Prince Alric

TULAN: Tropical plant, found in southeastern Calis, used in religious ceremonies, leaves are dried and burned as offerings to the god Uberlin, smoke of the leaves produces visions when inhaled

TUR: Legendary village believed to have once been in Delgos, site of the first recorded visit of Kile, mythical source of great weapons

TUR DEL FUR: Coastal city in Delgos, on Terlando Bay, originally built by dwarves, was overrun by goblins when the city's volcanic defenses were disabled by Royce and Hadrian

UBERLIN: God of the Dacca and the Ghazel, son of Erebus and his daughter, Muriel

ULI VERMAR: Obscure reference used by Esrahaddon

ULURIUM FOUNTAIN: Great sculptured fountain at the end of the Grand Mar, before the palace in Percepliquis

UMALYN: Tribe of elves, priests of Ferrol

URITH, KING: Former ruler of Ratibor, died in a fire

URLINEUS: Last of the Novronian Empire cities to fall, located in eastern Calis, constantly attacked by Ghazel. After its collapse, it became the gateway for the Ghazel into Calis

UZLA BAR: Ghazel chieftain, challenging Erandabon Gile for control of Ghazel

VALIN, LORD: Elderly knight of Melengar, known for his valor and courage, no strategic skills

VANDON: Port city of Delgos, home to the Vandon Spice Company, pirate haven, grew into a legitimate business center when Delgos became a republic

VAULT OF DAYS: Large hall outside Novron's tomb

VELLA: Kitchen servant in the imperial palace

VENDEN POX: Poison, impervious to magic remedies

VENLIN: Patriarch of the Nyphron Church during the fall of the Novronian Empire

VERNES: Port city at the mouth of the Bernum River

VIGAN: Sheriff of Ratibor

VILLEIN: Person who is bound to the land and owned by the feudal lord

VINCE EVERTON: Alias used by Royce Melborn while in Hintindar

VINCE GRIFFIN: Founder of Dahlgren Village

VINCENT, KING: Ruler of Maranon, married to Queen Regina

VINTU: Native tribe of Calis

WANDERING DEACON OF DAHLGREN: Name that refers to Deacon Tomas

WARRIC: A kingdom of Avryn, once ruled by Ethelred, now part of the New Empire

WATCH OFFICER: Officer of the watch, in charge during a particular shift, responsible for everything that transpires during this time

WESBADEN: Major trade port city of Calis

WESLEY: Son of Lord Belstrad, brother of Sir Breckton, junior midshipman on the *Emerald Storm*, killed in the arena fight in the Palace of the Four Winds

WESTBANK: Newly formed province of Dunmore

WESTERLINS: Unknown frontier to the west

WHERRY: Light rowboat, used for racing or transporting goods and passengers on inland waters and harbors

WICEND: \why-send\ Farmer in Melengar, name of the ford that crosses the Galewyr into Glouston

WIDLEY: Professor at Sheridan University, tried and burned for heresy

WILBUR: Armor smith in Aquesta

WILFRED: Carter in Hintindar

WINDS ABBEY: Monastery of the Monks of Maribor, rebuilt by Myron Lanaklin with the help of Magnus the dwarf after being burned

WINSLOW, ALBERT: See Albert Winslow

WINTERTIDE: Chief holiday, held in midwinter, celebrated with feasts and games of skill

WITCH OF MELENGAR: Derogatory title attributed to Arista

WYATT DEMINTHAL: See Deminthal, Wyatt

WYLIN: \why-lynn\ Master-at-arms at Essendon Castle

WYMAR, MARQUIS: Nobleman of Melengar, member of Alric's council

YOLRIC: Teacher of Esrahaddon

ZEPHYR, BROTHER: Monk at rebuilt Winds Abbey, illustrator

ZULRON: Deformed *oberdaza* of Oudorro

extras

orbit

meet the author

Michael J. Sullivan

After finding a manual typewriter in the basement of a friend's house, MICHAEL J. SULLIVAN inserted a blank piece of paper and typed: "It was a dark and stormy night, and a shot rang out." He was just eight. Still, the desire to fill the blank page and see where the keys would take him next wouldn't let go. For ten years Michael developed his craft for writing by reading and studying authors such as Stephen King, Ayn Rand, and John Steinbeck, to name a few. He wrote more than ten novels, and after finding no traction in publishing, he quit, vowing to never write creatively again.

His hiatus from writing lasted nearly ten years. The itch returned when he decided to write books for his then thirteen-year-old daughter, who was struggling in school because of dyslexia. Intrigued by the idea of a series with an overarching story line told through individual, self-contained episodes, he created the Riyria Revelations. While he wrote the series with no intention of publishing it, he was surprised that after presenting his book in manuscript form to his daughter, she declared that it had to be a "real" book, bound and formatted, in order for her to be able to read it.

So began his second adventure on the road to publication, which included drafting his wife to be his business manager, signing with a small independent press, and creating his own publishing company. He sold more than sixty thousand books as a self-published author and leveraged this success to achieve mainstream publication through Orbit (the fantasy imprint of Hachette Book Group) as well as foreign translation rights for France, Spain, Russia, and the Czech Republic.

Born in Detroit, Michigan, Michael presently lives in Fairfax, Virginia, with his wife and three children and continues to fill the blank pages with three projects under development: a modern fantasy novel, a literary fiction piece, and a prequel to his best-selling Riyria Revelations.

Find out more about the author at www.michaelsullivan-author.com.

introducing

If you enjoyed
HEIR OF NOVRON,
look out for

THE DRAGON'S PATH

Book 1 of The Dagger and the Coin

by Daniel Abraham

*Marcus's hero days are behind him. He knows too well
that even the smallest war still means somebody's death.
When his men are impressed into a doomed army,
staying out of a battle he wants no part of requires
some unorthodox steps.*

*Cithrin is an orphan, ward of a banking house. Her job
is to smuggle a nation's wealth across a war zone, hiding
the gold from both sides. She knows the secret life of
commerce like a second language, but the strategies of
trade will not defend her from swords.*

*Geder, sole scion of a noble house, has more interest in
philosophy than in swordplay. A poor excuse for a soldier, he is a
pawn in these games. No one can predict what he will become.*

*Falling pebbles can start a landslide. A spat between
the Free Cities and the Severed Throne is spiraling
out of control. A new player rises from the depths of history,
fanning the flames that will sweep the entire region
onto the Dragon's Path — the path to war.*

The Apostate

The apostate pressed himself into the shadows of the rock
and prayed to nothing in particular that the things riding
mules in the pass below him would not look up. His
hands ached, the muscles of his legs and back shuddered with
exhaustion. The thin cloth of his ceremonial robes fluttered
against him in the cold, dust-scented wind. He took the risk
of looking down toward the trail.

The five mules had stopped, but the priests hadn't dismounted. Their robes were heavier, warmer. The ancient
swords strapped across their backs caught the morning light
and glittered a venomous green. Dragon-forged, those blades.
They meant death to anyone whose skin they broke. In time,
the poison would kill even the men who wielded them. All the
more reason, the apostate thought, that his former brothers
would kill him quickly and go home. No one wanted to carry

those blades for long; they came out only in dire emergency or deadly anger.

Well. At least it was flattering to be taken seriously.

The priest leading the hunting party rose up in his saddle, squinting into the light. The apostate recognized the voice.

"Come out, my son," the high priest shouted. "There is no escape."

The apostate's belly sank. He shifted his weight, preparing to walk down. He stopped himself.

Probably, he told himself. *There is* probably *no escape. But perhaps there is.*

On the trail, the dark-robed figures shifted, turned, consulted among themselves. He couldn't hear their words. He waited, his body growing stiffer and colder. Like a corpse that hadn't had the grace to die. Half a day seemed to pass while the hunters below him conferred, though the sun barely changed its angle in the bare blue sky. And then, between one breath and the next, the mules moved forward again.

He didn't dare move for fear of setting a pebble rolling down the steep cliffs. He tried not to grin. Slowly, the things that had once been men rode their mules down the trail to the end of the valley, and then followed the wide bend to the south. When the last of them slipped out of sight, he stood, hands on his hips, and marveled. He still lived. They had not known where to find him after all.

Despite everything he'd been taught, everything he had until recently believed, the gifts of the spider goddess did not show the truth. It gave her servants something, yes, but not *truth.* More and more, it seemed his whole life had sprung from a webwork of plausible lies. He should have felt lost. Devastated. Instead, it was like he'd walked from a tomb into the free air. He found himself grinning.

The climb up the remaining western slope bruised him.

His sandals slipped. He struggled for finger- and toeholds. But as the sun reached its height, he reached the ridge. To the west, mountain followed mountain, and great billowing clouds towered above them, thunderstorms a soft veil of grey. But in the farthest passes, he saw the land level. Flatten. Distance made the plains grey-blue, and the wind on the mountain's peak cut at his skin like claws. Lightning flashed on the horizon. As if in answer, a hawk shrieked.

It would take weeks alone and on foot. He had no food, and worse, no water. He'd slept the last five nights in caves and under bushes. His former brothers and friends—the men he had known and loved his whole life—were combing the trails and villages, intent on his death. Mountain lions and dire wolves hunted in the heights.

He ran a hand through his thick, wiry hair, sighed, and began the downward climb. He would probably die before he reached the Keshet and a city large enough to lose himself in.

But only *probably*.

In the last light of the falling sun, he found a stony overhang near a thin, muddy stream. He sacrificed a length of the strap from his right sandal to fashion a crude fire bow, and as the cruel chill came down from the sky, he squatted next to the high ring of stones that hid his small fire. The dry scrub burned hot and with little smoke, but quickly. He fell into a rhythm of feeding small twig after small twig into the flame, never letting it grow large enough to illuminate his shelter to those hunting and never letting it die. The warmth didn't seem to reach past his elbows.

Far off, something shrieked. He tried to ignore it. His body ached with exhaustion and spent effort, but his mind, freed now from the constant distraction of his journey, gained a dangerous speed. In the darkness, his memory sharpened. The sense of freedom and possibility gave way to loss, loneliness, and dislocation. Those, he believed, were more likely to kill him than a hunting cat.

He had been born in hills much like these. Passed his youth playing games of sword and whip using branches and woven bark. Had he ever felt the ambition to join the ranks of the monks in their great hidden temple? He must have, though from the biting cold of his poor stone shelter, it was hard to imagine it. He could remember looking up with awe at the high wall of stone. At the rock-carved sentries from all the thirteen races of humanity worn by wind and rain until all of them—Cinnae and Tralgu, Southling and Firstblood, Timzinae and Yemmu and Drowned—wore the same blank faces and clubbed fists. Indistinguishable. Only the wide wings and dagger teeth of the dragon arching above them all were still clear. And worked into the huge iron gate, black letters spelled out words in a language no one in the village knew.

When he became a novice, he learned what it said. BOUND IS NOT BROKEN. He had believed once that he knew what it meant.

The breeze shifted, raising the embers like fireflies. A bit of ash stung his eye, and he rubbed at it with the back of his hand. His blood shifted, currents in his body responding to something that was not him. The goddess, he'd thought. He had gone to the great gate with the other boys of his village. He had offered himself up—life and body—and in return...

In return the mysteries had been revealed. First, it had only been knowledge: letters enough to read the holy books, numbers enough to keep the temple's records. He had read the stories of the Dragon Empire and its fall. Of the spider goddess coming to bring justice to the world.

Deception, they said, had no power over her.

He'd tested it, of course. He believed them, and still he had tested. He would lie to the priests, just to see whether it could be done. He'd chosen things that only he could know: his father's clan name, his sister's favorite meals, his own dreams. The priests had whipped him when he spoke false, they had spared him when he was truthful, and they were never, *never* wrong. His certainty had grown. His faith. When the high priest had chosen him to rise to novice, he'd been certain that great things awaited him, because the priests had told him that they did.

After the nightmare of his initiation was over, he'd felt the power of the spider goddess in his own blood. The first time he'd felt someone lie, it had been like discovering a new sense. The first time he had spoken with the voice of the goddess, he'd felt his words commanding belief as if they had been made from fire.

And now he had fallen from grace, and none of it might be true. There might be no such place as the Keshet. He believed there was, so much so that he had risked his life on flight to it. But he had never been there. The marks on the maps could be lies. For that matter, there might have been no dragons, no empire, no great war. He had never seen the ocean; there might be no such thing. He knew only what he himself had seen and heard and felt.

He knew *nothing*.

On violent impulse, he sank his teeth into the flesh of his palm. His blood welled up, and he cupped it. In the faint firelight, it looked nearly black. Black, with small, darker knots. One of the knots unfurled tiny legs. The spider crawled mindlessly around the cup of his hand. Another one joined it. He watched them: the agents of the goddess in whom he no longer believed. Carefully, slowly, he tipped his hand over the small flame. One of the spiders fell into it, hair-thin legs shriveling instantly.

"Well," he said. "You can die. I know *that*."

The mountains seemed to go on forever, each crest a new threat, each valley thick with danger. He skirted the small villages, venturing close only to steal a drink from the stone cisterns. He ate lizards and the tiny flesh-colored nuts of scrub pine. He avoided the places where wide, clawed paws marked paths in the dirt. One night, he found a circle of standing pillars with a small chamber beneath them that seemed to offer shelter and a place to recover his strength, but his sleep there had been troubled by dreams so violent and alien that he pushed on instead.

He lost weight, the woven leather of his belt hanging low around his waist. His sandals' soles thinned, and his fire bow wore out quickly. Time lost its meaning. Day followed day followed day. Every morning he thought, *This will probably be the last day of my life. Only probably.*

The *probably* was always enough. And then, late one morning, he pulled himself to the top of a boulder-strewn hill, and there wasn't another to follow it. The wide western plains spread out before him, a river shining in its cloak of green grass and trees. The view was deceptive. He guessed it would still be two days on foot before he reached it. Still, he sat on a wide, rough stone, looked out over the world, and let himself weep until almost midday.

As he came nearer to the river, he felt a new anxiety start to gnaw at his belly. On the day, weeks ago, when he had slipped over the temple's wall and fled, the idea of disappearing into a city had been a distant concern. Now he saw the smoke of a hundred cookfires rising from the trees. The marks of wild animals were scarce. Twice, he saw men riding huge horses in the distance. The dusty rags of his robe, the ruins of his sandals, and the reek of his own unwashed skin reminded him that this was as difficult and as dangerous as anything he'd done to now. How would the men and women of the Keshet greet a wild man from the mountains? Would they cut him down out of hand?

He circled the city by the river, astounded at the sheer size of the place. He had never seen anything so large. The long wooden buildings with their thatched roofs could have held a thousand people. The roads were paved in stone. He kept to the underbrush like a thief, watching.

It was the sight of a Yemmu woman that gave him courage. That and his hunger. At the fringe of the city, where the last of the houses sat between road and river, she labored in her garden. She was half again as tall as he was, and broad as a bull across the shoulders. Her tusks rose from her jaw until she seemed in danger of piercing her own cheeks if she laughed. Her breasts hung high above a peasant girdle not so different from the ones his own mother and sister had worn, only with three times the cloth and leather.

She was the first person he had ever seen who wasn't a Firstblood. The first real evidence that the thirteen races of humanity truly existed. Hiding behind the bushes, peeking at her as she leaned in the soft earth and plucked weeds between gigantic fingers, he felt something like wonder.

He stepped forward before he could talk himself back into cowardice. Her wide head rose sharply, her nostrils flaring. He raised a hand, almost in apology.

"Forgive me," he said. "I'm…I'm in trouble. And I was hoping you might help me."

The woman's eyes narrowed to slits. She lowered her stance like a hunting cat preparing for battle. It occurred to him that it might have been wiser to discover if she spoke his language before he'd approached her.

"I've come from the mountains," he said, hearing the desperation in his own voice. And hearing something else besides. The inaudible thrumming of his blood. The gift of the spider goddess commanding the woman to believe him.

"We don't trade with Firstbloods," the Yemmu woman growled. "Not from those twice-shat mountains anyway. Get away from here, and take your men with you."

"I don't have any men," he said. The things in his blood roused themselves, excited to be used. The woman shifted her head as his stolen magic convinced her. "I'm alone. And unarmed. I've been walking for...weeks. I can work if you'd like. For a little food and a warm place to sleep. Just for the night."

"Alone and unarmed. Through the mountains?"

"Yes."

She snorted, and he had the sense he was being evaluated. Judged.

"You're an idiot," she said.

"Yes," he said. "I am. Friendly, though. Harmless."

It was a very long moment before she laughed.

She set him to hauling river water to her cistern while she finished her gardening. The bucket was fashioned for Yemmu hands, and he could only fill it half full before it became too heavy to lift. But he struggled manfully from the little house to the rough wooden platform and then back again. He was careful not to scrape himself, or at least not so badly as to draw blood. His welcome was uncertain enough without the spiders to explain.

At sunset, she made a place for him at her table. The fire in the pit seemed extravagant, and he had to remind himself that the things that had been his brothers weren't here, scanning for signs of him. She scooped a bowl of stew from the pot above the fire. It had the rich, deep, complex flavor of a

941

constant pot; the stewpot never leaving the fire, and new hanks of meat and vegetables thrown in as they came to hand. Some of the bits of dark flesh swimming in the greasy broth might have been cooking since before he'd left the temple. It was the best meal he'd ever had.

"My man's at the caravanserai," she said. "One of the princes s'posed to be coming in, and they'll be hungry. Took all the pigs with. Sell 'em all if we're lucky. Get enough silver to see us through storm season."

He listened to her voice and also the stirring in his blood. The last part had been a lie. She *didn't* believe that the silver would last. He wondered if it worried her, and if there was some way he could see she had what she needed. He would try, at least. Before he left.

"What about you, you poor shit?" she asked, her voice soft and warm. "Whose sheep did you fuck that you're begging work from me?"

The apostate chuckled. The warm food in his belly, the fire at his side, and the knowledge that a pallet of straw and a thin wool blanket were waiting for him outside conspired to relax his shoulders and his belly. The Yemmu woman's huge gold-flecked eyes stayed on him. He shrugged.

"I discovered that believing something doesn't make it true," he said carefully. "There were things I'd accepted, that I believed to my bones, and I was...wrong."

"Misled?" she asked.

"Misled," he agreed, and then paused. "Or perhaps not. Not intentionally. No matter how wrong you are, it's not a lie if you believe it."

The Yemmu woman whistled—an impressive feat, considering her tusks—and flapped her hands in mock admiration.

"High philosophy from the water grunt," she said. "Next you'll be preaching and asking tithes."

"Not me," he said, laughing with her.

She took a long slurp from her own bowl. The fire crackled. Something—rats, perhaps, or insects—rattled in the thatch overhead.

"Fell out with a woman, did you?" she asked.

"A goddess," he said.

"Yeah. Always seems like that, dunit?" she said, staring into the fire. "Some new love comes on like there's something different about 'em. Like God himself talks whenever their lips flap. And then..."

She snorted again, part amusement, part bitterness.

"And what all went wrong with your goddess?" she asked.

The apostate lifted a scrap of something that might have been a potato to his mouth, chewed the soft flesh, the gritty skin. He struggled to put words to thoughts that had never been spoken aloud. His voice trembled.

"She is going to eat the world."

Royce watched the courier ride out of sight before taking off his imperial uniform.

Turning to face Hadrian, he said, "Well, that wasn't so hard."

"Will?" Hadrian asked as the two slipped into the forest.

Royce nodded. "Remember yesterday you complained that you'd rather be an actor? I was giving you a part: Will, the Imperial Checkpoint Sentry. I thought you did rather well with the role."

"You know, you don't need to mock *all* my ideas." Hadrian frowned as he pulled his own tabard over his head. "Besides, I still think we should consider it. We could travel from town to town performing in dramatic plays, even a few comedies." Hadrian gave his smaller partner an appraising look. "Though maybe you should stick to drama—perhaps tragedies."

Royce glared back.

"What? I think I would make a superb actor. I see myself as a dashing leading man. We could definitely land parts in *The Crown Conspiracy*. I'll play the handsome swordsman that fights the villain, and you—well, you can be the other one."

RISE OF EMPIRE

Volume Two of the
Riyria Revelations

MICHAEL J. SULLIVAN

www.orbitbooks.net

Orbit
Hachette Book Group
1290 Avenue of the Americas, New York, NY 10104
www.HachetteBookGroup.com

First Edition: December 2011

Orbit is an imprint of Hachette Book Group, Inc. The Orbit name
and logo are trademarks of Little, Brown Book Group Limited.

The publisher is not responsible for websites (or their content) that
are not owned by the publisher.

Library of Congress Cataloging-in-Publication Data
Sullivan, Michael J.
    Rise of empire / Michael J. Sullivan.—1st ed.
        p. cm.—(The Riyria revelations ; v. 2)
    Summary: "The birth of the Nyphron Empire has brought war
to Melengar. To save her kingdom, Princess Arista runs a desperate
gamble when she defies her brother and hires Royce and Hadrian
to perform a dangerous mission behind enemy lines"—Provided by
publisher.
    ISBN 978-0-316-18770-1
    I. Title.
    PS3619.U4437R57 2011
    813'.6—dc22

                                                    2011015271

Printing 19, 2023

Printed in the United States of America

To Robin, for breathing life into Amilia,
giving comfort to Modina, and saving
two others from death

To the members of goodreads.com and
the book blogging community, both of which
have supported the series and invited
others to join the adventure

And to the members of the Arlington
Writers Group, for their generous support,
assistance, and feedback

CONTENTS

BOOK III

Nyphron Rising

BOOK IV

The Emerald Storm

Known Regions of the World of Elan

Estrendor: Northern wastes
Erivan Empire: Elvenlands
Apeladorn: Nations of man
Ba Ran Archipelago: Islands of goblins
Westerlands: Western wastes
Dacca: Isle of south men

Nations of Apeladorn

Avryn: Central wealthy kingdoms
Trent: Northern mountainous kingdoms
Calis: Southeastern tropical region ruled by warlords
Delgos: Southern republic

Kingdoms of Avryn

Ghent: Ecclesiastical holding of the Nyphron Church
Melengar: Small but old and respected kingdom
Warric: Most powerful of the kingdoms of Avryn
Dunmore: Youngest and least sophisticated kingdom
Alburn: Forested kingdom
Rhenydd: Poor kingdom
Maranon: Producer of food. Once part of Delgos, which was
   lost when Delgos became a republic
Galeannon: Lawless kingdom of barren hills, the site of
   several great battles

The Gods

Erebus: Father of the gods
Ferrol: Eldest son, god of elves
Drome: Second son, god of dwarves
Maribor: Third son, god of men
Muriel: Only daughter, goddess of nature
Uberlin: Son of Muriel and Erebus, god of darkness

Political Parties

*Imperialists: Those wishing to unite mankind under a
    single leader who is the direct descendant of the
    demigod Novron*
*Nationalists: Those wishing to be ruled by a leader chosen
    by the people*
*Royalists: Those wishing to continue rule by individual,
    independent monarchs*

THE
SOUND

w i l

Lanksteer

Lingar

T R E N T

Ervanon

Dunmore

G h e n t

Nilwalden River

Lake
Windermere

Sheridan

Dahlgren

Melengar

Glamrendor

Droudf Fields

The Lost Lands

Gatilin   Medford

Winds Abby

Windham

Sten Upland

Roc

Chadwick

WESTERLINS

Glouston

Rilan Valley

A V R Y N

A l b u r n

Warric

Colnora

Caren

Aquesta

Rochelle

Amberton Lee

Bernum River

Ratibor

Hintindar

Kilnar

R h e n y d d

Vilan Hil

Vernes

G a l e a

Manzar

M a r a n o n

SHARON
SEA

Vandon

D E L G O S

Fur Del Fur

T i e r r e

Dagastan
Bay

DACCA

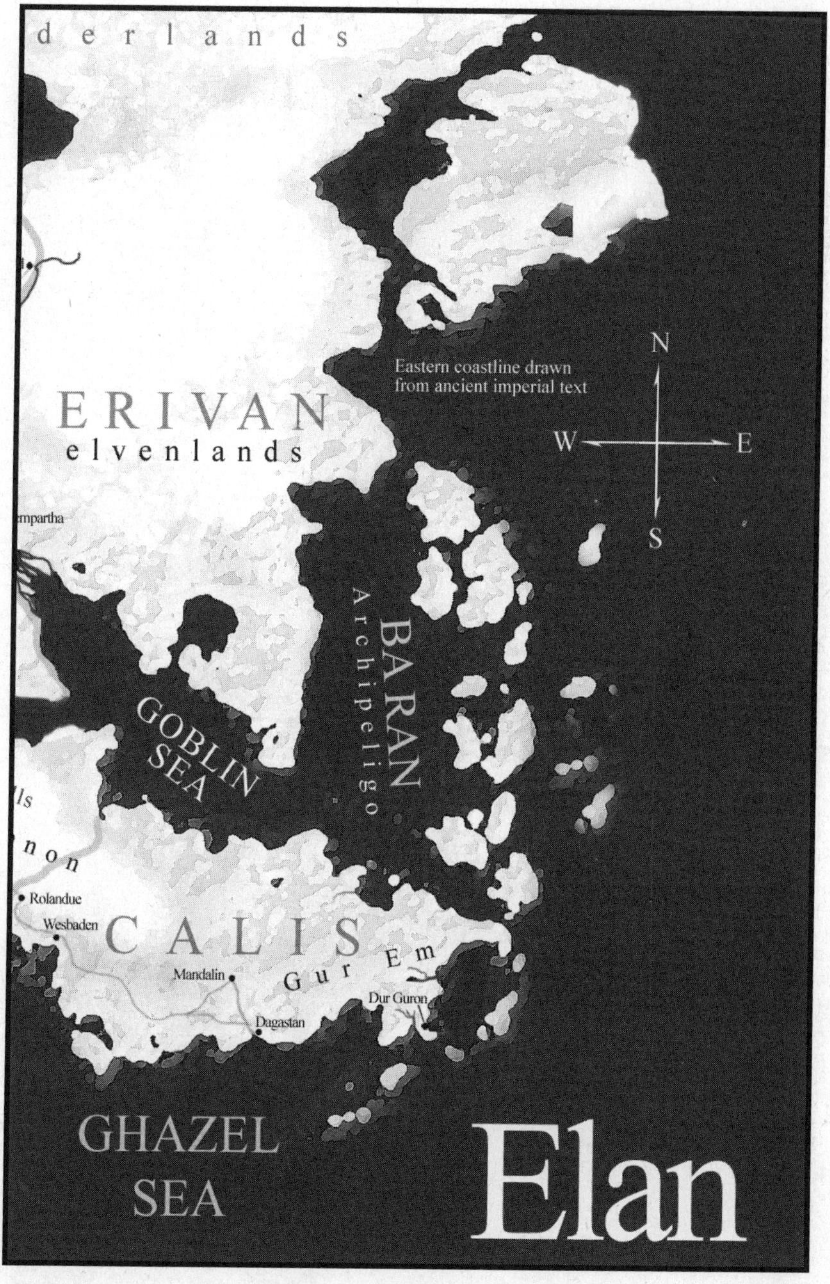

derlands

ERIVAN
elvenlands

Eastern coastline drawn
from ancient imperial text

N

W   E

S

mpartha

BARAN
Archipeligo

GOBLIN
SEA

ls

non

• Rolandue

• Wesbaden

CALIS

Mandalin   Gur Em

Dagastan   Dur Guron

GHAZEL
SEA

Elan

BOOK III

NYPHRON RISING

CHAPTER 1

THE EMPRESS

Amilia made the mistake of looking back into Edith Mon's eyes. She had never meant to—she had never planned on raising her stare from the floor—but Edith startled her and she looked up without thinking. The head maid would consider her action defiance, a sign of rebellion in the ranks of the scullery. Amilia had never looked into Edith's eyes before, and doing so now, she wondered if a soul lurked behind them. If so, it must be cowering or dead, rotting like a late-autumn apple; that would explain her smell. Edith had a sour scent, vaguely rancid, as if something had gone bad.

"This will be another tenent withheld from yer pay," the rotund woman said. "Yer digging quite a hole, ain't you?"

Edith was big and broad and missing any sign of a neck. Her huge anvil of a head sat squarely on her shoulders. By contrast, Amilia barely existed. Small and pear-shaped, with a plain face and long, lifeless hair, she was part of the crowd, one of the faces no one paused to consider—neither pretty nor grotesque enough to warrant a second glance. Unfortunately, her invisibility failed when it came to the palace's head maid, Edith Mon.

"I didn't break it." *Mistake number two*, Amilia thought.

A meaty hand slapped Amilia's face, ringing ears and

watering eyes. "Go on," Edith enticed her with a sweet tone, and then whispered, "lie to me again."

Gripping the washbasin to steady herself, Amilia felt heat blossom on her cheek. Her gaze now followed Edith's hand, and when it rose again, Amilia flinched. With a snicker, Edith ran her plump fingers through Amilia's hair.

"No tangles," Edith observed. "I can see how ya spend yer time, instead of doing yer work. Ya hoping to catch the eye of the butcher? Maybe that saucy little man who delivers the wood? I saw ya talking to him. Know what they sees when they looks at ya? They sees an ugly scullery maid is what. A wretched filthy guttersnipe who smells of lye and grease. They would rather pay for a whore than get ya for nothing. You'd be better off spending more time on yer tasks. If ya did, I wouldn't have to beat ya so often."

Amilia felt Edith winding her hair, twisting and tightening it around her fist. "It's not like I enjoy hurting ya." She pulled until Amilia winced. "But ya have to learn." Edith continued pulling Amilia's hair, forcing her head back until only the ceiling was visible. "Yer slow, stupid, and ugly. That's why yer still in the scullery. I can't make ya a laundry maid, much less a parlor or chambermaid. You'd embarrass me, understand?"

Amilia remained quiet.

"I said, do ya understand?"

"Yes."

"Say yer sorry for chipping the plate."

"I'm sorry for chipping the plate."

"And yer sorry for lying about it?"

"Yes."

Edith roughly patted Amilia's burning cheek. "That's a good girl. I'll add the cost to yer tally. Now as for punishment..." She let go of Amilia's hair and tore the scrub brush from her hand, measuring its weight. She usually used a belt;

the brush would hurt more. Edith would drag her to the laundry, where the big cook could not see. The head cook had taken a liking to Amilia, and while Edith had every right to discipline her girls, Ibis would not stand for it in his kitchen. Amilia waited for a fat hand to grab her wrist, but instead Edith stroked her head. "Such long hair," she said at length. "It's yer hair that's getting in the way, isn't it? It's making ya think too much of yerself. Well, I know just how to fix both problems. Yer gonna look real pretty when I—"

The kitchen fell silent. Cora, who had been incessantly plunging her butter churn, paused in mid-stroke. The cooks stopped chopping and even Nipper, who was stacking wood near the stoves, froze. Amilia followed their gaze to the stairs.

A noblewoman adorned in white velvet and satin glided down the steps and entered the steamy stench of the scullery. Piercing eyes and razor-thin lips stood out against a powdered face. The woman was tall and—unlike Amilia, who had a hunched posture—stood straight and proud. She moved immediately to the small table along the wall, where the baker was preparing bread.

"Clear this," she ordered with a wave of her hand, speaking to no one in particular. The baker immediately scooped his utensils and dough into his apron and hurried away. "Scrub it clean," the lady insisted.

Amilia felt the brush thrust back into her hand, and a push sent her stumbling forward. She did not look up and went right to work making large swirls of flour-soaked film. Nipper was beside her in an instant with a bucket, and Vella arrived with a towel. Together they cleared the mess while the woman watched with disdain.

"Two chairs," the lady barked, and Nipper ran off to fetch them.

Uncertain what to do next, Amilia stood in place watching

the lady, holding the dripping brush at her side. When the noblewoman caught her staring, Amilia quickly looked down and movement caught her eye. A small gray mouse froze beneath the baker's table, trying to conceal itself in the shadows. Taking a chance, it snatched a morsel of bread and disappeared through a small crack.

"What a miserable creature," she heard the lady say. Amilia thought she was referring to the mouse until she added, "You're making a filthy puddle on the floor. Go away."

Before retreating to her washbasin, Amilia attempted a pathetic curtsy. A flurry of orders erupted from the woman, each announced with perfect diction. Vella, Cora, and even Edith went about setting the table as if for a royal banquet. Vella draped a white tablecloth, and Edith started setting out silverware only to be shooed away as the woman carefully placed each piece herself. Soon the table was elegantly set for two, complete with multiple goblets and linen napkins.

Amilia could not imagine who could be dining there. No one would set a table for the servants, and why would a noble come to the kitchen to eat?

"Here now, what's all this about?" Amilia heard the deep familiar voice of Ibis Thinly. The old sea cook was a large barrel-chested man with bright blue eyes and a thin beard that wreathed the line of his chin. He had spent the morning meeting with farmers, yet he still wore his ever-present apron. The grease-stained wrap was his uniform, his mark of office. He barged into the kitchen like a bear returning to his cave to find mischief afoot. When he spotted the lady, he stopped.

"I am Lady Constance," the noblewoman informed him. "In a moment I will be bringing Empress Modina here. If you are the cook, then prepare food." The lady paused a moment to study the table critically. She adjusted the positions of a few items, then turned and left.

"Leif, get a knife on that roasted lamb," Ibis shouted. "Cora, fetch cheese. Vella, get bread. Nipper, straighten that woodpile!"

"The empress!" Cora exclaimed as she raced for the pantry.

"What's she doing coming here?" Leif asked. There was anger in his voice, as if an unwelcome, no-account relative was dropping by and he was the inconvenienced lord of the manor.

Amilia had heard of the empress but had never seen her—not even from a distance. Few had. She had been coronated in a private ceremony over half a year earlier on Wintertide, and her arrival in Aquesta had changed everything.

King Ethelred no longer wore his crown, and was addressed as "Regent" instead of "Your Majesty." He still ruled over the castle, only now it was referred to as the imperial palace. The other one, Regent Saldur, had made all the changes. Originally from Melengar, the former bishop had taken up residence and set builders working day and night on the great hall and throne room. Saldur had also declared new rules that all the servants had to follow.

The palace staff could no longer leave the grounds unless escorted by one of the new guards, and all outgoing letters were read and needed to be approved. The latter edict was hardly an issue, as few servants could write. The restriction on going outside the palace, however, was a hardship to almost everyone. Many with families in the city or surrounding farms chose to resign, because they could no longer return home each night. Those remaining at the castle never heard from them again. Regent Saldur had successfully isolated the palace from the outside world, but inside, rumors and gossip ran wild. Speculations flourished in out-of-the-way corridors that giving notice was as unhealthy as attempting to sneak away.

The fact that no one ever saw the empress ignited its own

set of speculations. Everyone knew she was the heir of the original, legendary emperor, Novron, and therefore a child of the god Maribor. This had been proven when she had been the only one capable of slaying the beast that had slaughtered dozens of Elan's greatest knights. That she had previously been a farm girl from a small village confirmed that in the eyes of Maribor, all were equal. Rumors concluded that she had ascended to the state of a spiritual being, and only the regents and her personal secretary ever stood in her divine presence.

That must be who the noblewoman is, Amilia thought. The lady with the sour face and perfect speech was the imperial secretary to the empress.

They soon had an array of the best food they could muster in a short time laid out on the table. Knob, the baker, and Leif, the butcher, disputed the placement of dishes, each wanting his wares in the center. "Cora," Ibis said, "put your pretty cake of cheese in the middle." This brought a smile and blush to the dairymaid's face and scowls from Leif and Knob.

Being a scullion, Amilia had no more part to play and returned to her dishes. Edith was chatting excitedly in the corner near the stack of oak kegs with the tapster and the cupbearer, and all the servants were straightening their outfits and running fingers through their hair. Nipper was still sweeping when the lady returned. Once more everyone stopped and watched as she led a thin young girl by the wrist.

"Sit down," Lady Constance ordered in her brisk tone.

Everyone peered past the two women, trying to catch the first glimpse of the god-queen. Two well-armored guards emerged and took up positions on either side of the table. But no one else appeared.

Where is the empress?

"Modina, I said sit down," Lady Constance repeated.

Shock rippled through Amilia.

Modina? This waif of a child is the empress?

The girl did not appear to hear Lady Constance and stood limp with a blank expression. She looked to be a teenager, delicate and deathly thin. Once she might have been pretty, but what remained was an appalling sight. The girl's face was white as bone, her skin thin and stretched, revealing the detailed outline of her skull beneath. Her ragged blonde hair fell across her face. She wore only a thin white smock, which added to the girl's ghostly appearance.

Lady Constance sighed and forced the girl into one of the chairs at the baker's table. Like a doll, the girl allowed herself to be moved. She said nothing and her eyes stared blankly.

"Place the napkin in your lap this way." Lady Constance carefully opened and laid the linen with deliberate movements. She waited, glaring at the empress, who sat, oblivious. "As empress, you will never serve yourself," Lady Constance went on. "You will wait as your servants fill your plate." She was looking around with irritation when her eyes found Amilia. "You—come here," she ordered. "Serve Her Eminence."

Amilia dropped the brush in the basin and, wiping her hands on her smock, rushed forward. She lacked experience with serving but said nothing. Instead, she focused on recalling the times she had watched Leif cutting meat. Taking up the tongs and a knife, she tried her best to imitate him. Leif always made it look effortless, but Amilia's fingers betrayed her and she fumbled miserably, managing to place only a few shredded bits of lamb on the girl's plate.

"Bread." Lady Constance snapped the word like a whip and Amilia sliced into the long twisted loaf, nearly cutting herself in the process.

"Now eat."

For a brief moment, Amilia thought this was another order

for her and reached out in response. She caught herself and stood motionless, uncertain if she was free to return to her dishes.

"Eat, I said." The imperial secretary glared at the girl, who continued to stare blankly at the far wall.

"*Eat, damn you!*" Lady Constance bellowed, and everyone in the kitchen, including Edith Mon and Ibis Thinly, jumped. She pounded the baker's table with her fist, knocking over the stemware and bouncing the knives against the plates. "*Eat!*" Lady Constance repeated, and slapped the girl across the face. Her skin-wrapped skull rocked with the blow and came to rest on its own. The girl did not wince. She merely continued her stare, this time at a new wall.

In a fit of rage, the imperial secretary rose, knocking over her chair. She took one of the pieces of meat and tried to force it into the girl's mouth.

"What's going on?"

Lady Constance froze at the sound of the voice. An old white-haired man descended the steps into the scullery. His elegant purple robe and black cape looked out of place in the hot, messy kitchen. Amilia recognized Regent Saldur immediately.

"What in the world…" Saldur began as he approached the table. He looked at the girl, then at the kitchen staff, and finally at Lady Constance, who at some point had dropped the meat. "What were you thinking…bringing her down here?"

"I—I thought if—"

Saldur held up his hand, silencing her, then slowly squeezed it into a fist. He clenched his jaw and drew a deep breath through his sharp nose. Once more he focused on the girl. "Look at her. You were supposed to educate and train her. She's worse than ever!"

"I—I tried, but—"

"Shut up!" the regent snapped, still holding up his fist. No one in the kitchen moved. The only sounds were the faint crackle of the fire in the ovens and the bubbling of broth in a pot. "If this is the result of a professional, we may as well try an amateur. They couldn't possibly do worse." The regent pointed at Amilia. "You! Congratulations, you are now the imperial secretary to the empress." Turning his attention back to Lady Constance, he said, "And as for you—your services are no longer required. Guards, remove her."

Amilia saw Lady Constance falter. Her perfect posture evaporated as she cowered and stepped backward, nearly falling over the upended chair. "No! Please, no," she cried as a palace guard gripped her arm and pulled her toward the back door. Another guard took her other arm. She grew frantic, pleading and struggling as they dragged her out.

Amilia stood frozen in place, holding the meat tongs and carving knife, trying to remember how to breathe. Once the pleas of Lady Constance faded, Regent Saldur turned to her, his face flushed red, his teeth revealed behind taunt lips. "Don't fail me," he told her, and returned up the stairs, his cape whirling behind him.

Amilia looked back at the girl, who continued to stare at the wall.

⮜

The mystery of why no one saw the empress was solved when a soldier escorted the girls to Modina's room. Amilia expected to travel to the eastern keep, home of the regents' offices and the royal residence. To her surprise, the guard remained on the service side and headed for a curved stair across from the laundry. Chambermaids used this stairwell to service rooms on the upper floors. But here, the soldier went down.

Amilia did not question the guard, her thoughts preoccupied with the sword that hung at his side. His dark eyes were embedded in a stone face, and the top of her head reached the bottom of his chin. Each of his hands was the size of two of hers. He was not one of the guards who had taken Lady Constance away, but Amilia knew he would not hesitate when her time came.

The air turned cool and damp as they descended into darkness cut only by three mounted lanterns. The last dripped wax from an unhinged faceplate. At the bottom of the stairs a wooden door stood open, which led to a tiny corridor with more doors on either side. In one room Amilia spotted several casks and a rack of bottles dressed in packs of straw. Large locks sealed two other doors, and a third door stood open, revealing a small stone room, empty except for a pile of straw and a wooden bucket. When they reached it, the soldier stood to one side, his back to the wall.

"I'm sorry..." Amilia began, confused. "I don't understand. I thought we were going to the empress's bedchamber."

The guard nodded.

"Are you saying this is where Her Eminence sleeps?"

Again the soldier nodded.

As Amilia stared in shock, Modina wandered forward into the room and curled up on the pile of straw. The guard closed the heavy door and began fitting a large lock through the latch.

"Wait," Amilia said, "you can't leave her here. Can't you see she's sick?"

The guard snapped the lock in place.

Amilia stared at the oak door.

How is this possible? She's the empress. She's the daughter of a god and the high priestess of the church.

"You keep the empress in an old cellar?"

"It's better than where she was," the soldier told her. He had not spoken until then, and his voice was not what she expected. Soft, sympathetic, and not much louder than a whisper, his tone disarmed her.

"Where was she?"

"I've said too much already."

"I can't just leave her in there. She doesn't even have a candle."

"My orders are to keep her here."

Amilia stared at him. She could not see his eyes. The visor of his helm and the way the shadows fell cast darkness on everything above his nose. "Fine," she said at last, and walked out of the cellar.

She returned a moment later carrying the wax-laden lantern from the stairwell. "May I at least keep her company?"

"Are you sure?" He sounded surprised.

Amilia was not but nodded anyway. The guard opened the door.

The empress was lying huddled on the bed of straw, her eyes open, staring but not seeing. Amilia spotted a blanket wadded up in the corner. She set the lantern on the floor, shook out the wool covering, and draped it over the girl.

"They don't treat you very well, do they?" she said, carefully brushing back the mass of hair that lay across Modina's face. The strands felt as stiff and brittle as the straw that littered them. "How old are you?"

The empress did not answer, nor did she stir at Amilia's touch. Lying on her side, the girl clutched her knees to her chest and pressed her cheek against the straw. She blinked occasionally and her chest rose and fell with each breath but nothing more.

"Something bad happened, didn't it?" Amilia ran her fingers lightly over Modina's bare arm. She could circle the girl's wrist with her thumb and index finger with room to spare. "Look, I don't know how long I'm going to be here. I don't expect it'll be too long. See, I'm not a noble lady. I'm just a girl who washes dishes. The regent says I'm supposed to educate and train you, but he made a mistake. I don't know how to do any of that." She petted Modina's head and let her fingers run lightly over her hollow cheek, still blotchy where Lady Constance had struck her. "But I promise I won't ever hurt you."

Amilia sat for several minutes searching her mind for some way to reach the girl. "Can I tell you a secret? Now don't laugh...but...I'm really quite afraid of the dark. I know it's silly but I can't help myself. I've always been that way. My brothers tease me about it all the time. If you could chat with me a bit, maybe it would help me. What do you say?"

There was still no reaction.

Amilia sighed. "Well, tomorrow I'll bring some candles from my room. I've a whole bunch saved up. That will make things a bit nicer. You just try to rest now."

Amilia had not been lying about her fear of the dark. But that night it had to stand in line behind a host of new fears as she struggled to find sleep huddled beside the empress.

※

The soldiers did not come for Amilia that night and she woke when breakfast was brought in — or rather was skipped across the floor on a wooden plate that spun to a stop in the middle of the room. On it were a fist-sized chunk of meat, a wedge of cheese, and thick-crusted bread. It looked wonderful and was similar to Amilia's standard meals, courtesy of Ibis. Before coming to the palace, she had never eaten beef or venison, but now it was commonplace. Being friends with the head cook had other advantages as well. People didn't want to offend the man who controlled their diet, so Amilia was generally well treated, except by Edith Mon. Amilia took a few bites and loudly voiced her appreciation. "This is sooooo good. Would you like some?"

The empress did not respond.

Amilia sighed. "No, I don't suppose you would. What would you like? I can get you whatever you want."

Amilia got to her feet, grabbed up the tray, and waited. Nothing. After a few minutes, she rapped on the door and the same guard opened it.

"Excuse me, but I have to see about getting a proper meal for Her Eminence." The guard looked at the plate, confused, but stepped aside, leaving her to trot up the stairs.

The kitchen was still buzzing over the events of the previous night, but it stopped the moment Amilia entered the kitchen. "Sent ya back, did they?" Edith grinned. "Don't worry, I done saved yer pile of pots. And I haven't forgotten about that hair."

"Hush up, Edith," Ibis reprimanded with a scowl. Returning his attention to Amilia, he said, "Are you all right? Did they send you back?"

"I'm fine, thank you, Ibis, and no, I think I'm still the empress's secretary—whatever that means."

"Good for you, lassie," Ibis told her. He turned to Edith and added, "And I'd watch what you say now. Looks like you'll be washing that stack yourself." Edith turned and stalked off with a *humph*.

"So, my dear, what does bring you here?"

"I came about this food you sent to the empress."

Ibis looked wounded. "What's wrong with it?"

"Nothing, it's wonderful. I had some myself."

"Then I don't see—"

"Her Eminence is sick. She can't eat this. When I didn't feel well, my mother used to make me soup, a thin yellow broth that was easy to swallow. I was wondering, could you make something like that?"

"Sure," Ibis told her. "Soup is easy. Someone shoulda told me she was feeling poorly. I know exactly what to make. I call it Seasick Soup. It's the only thing the new lads kept down their first few days out. Leif, fetch me the big kettle."

Amilia spent the rest of the morning making trips back and forth to Modina's small cell. She removed all her possessions from the dormitory: a spare dress, some underclothing, a nightgown, a brush, and her treasured stash of nearly a dozen candles. From the linen supply, she brought pillows, sheets, and blankets. She even snuck a pitcher, some mild soap, and a basin from an unoccupied guest room. Each time she passed, the guard gave her a small smile and shook his head in amusement.

After removing the old straw and bringing in fresh bundles from the stable, she went to Ibis to check on the soup. "Well, the next batch will be better, when I have more time, but this should put some wind in her sails," he said.

Amilia returned to the cell and, setting down the steaming pot of soup, helped the empress to sit up. She took the first sip to check the temperature, then lifted the spoon to Modina's lips. Most of the broth dribbled down her chin and dripped onto the front of her smock.

"Okay, that was my fault. Next time I'll remember to bring one of those napkins that lady was all excited about." With her second spoonful, Amilia cupped her hand and caught most of the excess. "Aha!" she exclaimed. "I got some in. It's good, isn't it?" She tipped another spoonful and this time saw Modina swallow.

When the bowl was empty, Amilia guessed most of the soup was on the floor or soaked into Modina's clothes, but she was certain at least some got in. "There now, that must be a little better, don't you think? But I see I've made a terrible mess of you. How about we clean you up a bit, eh?" Amilia washed Modina and changed her into her own spare smock. The two girls were similar in height; however, Modina swam in the dress until Amilia fashioned a belt from a bit of twine.

Amilia continued to chatter while she made two makeshift beds with the straw and purloined blankets, pillows, and sheets. "I would have liked to bring us some mattresses but they were heavy. Besides, I didn't want to risk too much attention. People were already giving me strange looks. I think these will do nicely, don't you?" Modina continued her blank stare. When everything was in order, Amilia sat Modina on her newly sheeted bed in the glow of a handful of cheery candles and began gently brushing her hair.

"So, how does one get to be empress, anyway?" she asked. "They say you slew a monster that killed hundreds of knights. You know, you really don't look like the monster-slaying type—no offense." Amilia paused and tilted her head. "Still not interested in talking? That's okay. You want to keep your past a secret. I understand. After all, we've only just met.

"So, let's see…What can I tell you about myself? Well, I come from Tarin Vale. Do you know where that is? Probably not. It's a tiny village between here and Colnora. Just a little town people sometimes pass through on their way to more exciting places. Nothing much happens in Tarin. My father makes carriages and he's really good at it. Still, he doesn't make much money." She paused and studied the girl's face to try to determine if she heard any of what Amilia was saying.

"What does your father do? I think I heard he was a farmer; is that right?"

Nothing.

"My da doesn't make much money. My mother says it's

because he does *too good* of a job. He's pretty proud of his work, so he takes a long time. It can take him a whole year to make a carriage. That makes it hard, because he only gets paid when it's done. What with buying the supplies and all, we sometimes run out of money.

"My mother does spinning and my brother cuts wood, but it never seems like enough. That's why I'm here, you see. I'm not a very good spinner but I can read and write." One side of the girl's head was now free of tangles and Amilia switched to the other.

"I can see you're impressed. It hasn't done me much good, though. Well, except I guess it did get me a foot in the door, as it were.

"Hmm, what's that? You want to know where I learned to read and write? Oh well, thank you for asking. Devon taught me. He's a monk that came to Tarin Vale a few years ago." Her voice lowered conspiratorially. "I liked him a lot and he was cute and smart—*very smart*. He read books and told me about faraway places and things that happened long ago. Devon thought either my dad or the head of his order would try to split us up, so he taught me so we could write each other. Devon was right, of course. When my da found out, he said, 'There's no future with a monk.' Devon was sent away and I cried for days."

Amilia paused to clear a particularly nasty snarl. She tried her best to be gentle, but was sure it caused the girl pain, even if she did not show it. "That was a rough one," she said. "For a minute I thought you might have a sparrow hiding in there.

"Anyway, when Da found out I could read and write, he was so proud. He bragged about me to everyone who came to the shop. One of his customers, Squire Jenkins Talbert, was impressed and said he could put in a good word for me here in Aquesta.

"Everyone was so excited when I was accepted. When I found out the job was just to wash dishes, I didn't have the heart to tell my family, so I've not been home since. Now, of course, they won't let me go." Amilia sighed but then put on a bright smile. "But that's okay, because now I'm here with you."

There was a quiet knock and the guard stepped in. He took a minute to survey the changes in the cell and nodded his approval. His gaze shifted to Amilia and there was a distinct sadness in his eyes. "I'm sorry, miss, but Regent Saldur has ordered me to bring you to him."

Amilia froze, then slowly put the brush down and with a trembling hand draped a blanket around the young girl's shoulders. She rose, kissed Modina on the cheek, and in a quivering voice managed to whisper, "Goodbye."

CHAPTER 2

THE MESSENGER

He always feared he would die this way, alone on a remote stretch of road far from home. The forest pressed close from both sides, and his trained eyes recognized that the debris barring his path was not the innocent result of a weakened tree. He pulled on the reins, forcing his horse's head down. She snorted in frustration, fighting the bit—like him, she sensed danger.

He glanced behind him and to either side, scanning the trees standing in summer gowns of deep green. Nothing moved in the early-morning stillness. Nothing betrayed the tranquil facade except the pile before him. The deadfall was unnatural. Even from this distance, he saw the brightly colored pulp of fresh-cut wood—a barricade.

Thieves?

A band of highwaymen no doubt crouched under the cover of the forest, watching, waiting for him to draw near. He tried to focus his thoughts as his horse panted beneath him. This was the shortest route north to the Galewyr River, and he was running out of time. Breckton was preparing to invade the kingdom of Melengar, and he must deliver the dispatch before the knight launched the attack. Before he had embarked, his commander, as well as the regents, had personally expressed

the importance of this mission. They were counting on him—
she was counting on him. Like thousands of others, he had
stood in the freezing square on Coronation Day just to catch a
glimpse of Empress Modina. To the crowd's immense disappointment, she never appeared. An announcement came after
many hours, explaining she was occupied with the affairs of
the New Empire. Recently ascended from the peasant class,
the new ruler obviously had no time for frivolity.

He removed his cloak and tied it behind the saddle, revealing the gold crown on his tabard. They might let him pass.
Surely they knew the imperial army was nearby, and Sir Breckton would not stand for the waylaying of an imperial messenger. Highwaymen might not fear that fool Earl Ballentyne, but
even desperate men would think twice before offending Ballentyne's knight. Other commanders might ignore a bloodied
or murdered dispatch rider, but Sir Breckton would take it as a
personal assault on his honor, and insulting Breckton's honor
was tantamount to suicide.

He refused to fail.

Brushing the hair from his eyes, he took a fresh grip on the
reins and advanced cautiously. As he neared the barricade, he
saw movement. Leaves quivered. A twig snapped. He pivoted
his mount and prepared to bolt. He was a good rider—fast
and agile. His horse was a well-bred three-year-old, and once
she was spurred, no one would catch them. He tensed in the
saddle and leaned forward, preparing for the lurch, but the
sight of imperial uniforms stopped him.

A pair of soldiers trudged to the road from the trees and
grudgingly peered at him with the dull expression common to
foot soldiers. They were dressed in red tabards emblazoned
with the crest of Sir Breckton's command. As they approached,
the larger one chewed a stalk of rye while the smaller man
licked his fingers and wiped them on his uniform.

"You had me worried," the rider said with a mix of relief and irritation. "I thought you were highwaymen."

The smaller one smiled. He took little care with his uniform. Two shoulder straps were unfastened, causing the leather tongues to stand up like tiny wings on his shoulders. "Did ya hear that, Will? He thoughts we was thieves. Not a bad idea, eh? We should cut us some purses—charge a toll, as it were. At least we'd make a bit o' coin standin' out here all day. Course Breckton would skin us alive if'n he heard."

The taller soldier, most likely a half-wit mute, nodded in silent agreement. At least he wore his uniform smartly. It fit him better and he took the time to fasten everything properly. Both uniforms were rumpled and stained from sleeping outdoors, but such was the life of an infantryman—one of the many reasons he preferred being a courier.

"Clear this mess. I have an urgent dispatch. I need to get through to the imperial army command at once."

"Here now, we've orders too, ya know? We're not to let anyone pass," the smaller said.

"I'm an imperial courier, you fool!"

"Oh," the sentry responded with all the acumen of a wooden post. He glanced briefly at his partner, who maintained his dim expression. "Well, that's a different set of apples, now ain't it?" He petted the horse's neck. "That would explain the lather you've put on this here girl, eh? She looks like she could use a drink. We got a bucket and there's a little stream just over—"

"I've no time for that. Just get that pile out of the road and be quick about it."

"Certainly, certainly. You don't have to be so rough. Just tell us the watchword, and Will and me, we'll haul it outta yer way right fast," he said as he dug for something caught in his teeth.

"Watchword?"

The soldier nodded. He pulled his finger out and sniffed at something with a sour look before giving it a flick. "You know, the password. We can't be lettin' no spies through here. There's a war on, after all."

"I've never heard of such a thing. I wasn't informed of any password."

"No?" The smaller soldier raised an eyebrow as he took hold of the horse's bridle.

"I spoke to the regents themselves, and I—"

The larger of the two pulled him from his horse. He landed on his back, hitting the ground hard and banging his head. A jolt of pain momentarily blinded him. When he opened his eyes, he found the soldier straddling him with a blade to his throat.

"Who do you work for?" the large sentry growled.

"Whatcha doin', Will?" the smaller one asked, still holding his horse.

"Tryin' to get this spy to talk, that's what."

"I—I'm not a spy. I'm an imperial courier. Let me go!"

"Will, our orders says nothin' about interrogatin' them. If'n they don't know the watchword, we cuts they's throats and tosses them in the river. Sir Breckton don't have time to deal with every fool we get on this here road. Besides, who ya think he works for? The only ones fightin' us is Melengar, so he works for Melengar. Now slit his throat and I'll help you drag him to the river as soon as I ties up this here horse."

"But I *am* a courier!" he shouted.

"Sure ya is."

"I can prove it. I have dispatches for Sir Breckton in the saddlebag."

The two soldiers exchanged dubious looks. The smaller one shrugged. He reached into the horse's bags and proceeded to search. He pulled out a leather satchel containing a wax-sealed parchment, and breaking the seal, he examined it.

"Well, if'n that don't beat all. Looks like he's tellin' the truth, Will. This here looks like a real genuine dispatch for His Lordship."

"Oh?" the other asked as worry crossed his face.

"Sure looks that way. Better let him up."

His face downcast, the soldier sheathed his weapon and extended a hand to help the courier to his feet. "Ah—sorry about that. We were just followin' orders, ya know?"

"When Sir Breckton sees this broken seal, he'll have your heads!" the courier said, shoving past the large sentry and snatching the document from the other.

"Us?" The smaller one laughed. "Like Will here said, we was just followin' his orders. You were the one who failed to get the watchword afore ridin' here. Sir Breckton, he's a stickler for rules. He don't like it when his orders ain't followed. Course ya'll most likely only lose a hand or maybe an ear fer yer mistake. If'n I was you, I'd see if'n I could heat the wax up enough to reseal it."

"That would ruin the impression."

"Ya could say it was hot and, what with the sun on the pouch all day, the wax melted in the saddlebag. Better than losin' a hand or an ear, I says. Besides, busy nobles like Breckton ain't gonna study the seal afore openin' an urgent dispatch, but he will notice if'n the seal is broken. That's fer sure."

The courier looked at the document flapping in the breeze and felt his stomach churn. He had no choice, but he would not do it here with these idiots watching. He remounted his horse.

"Clear the road!" he barked.

The two soldiers dragged the branches aside. He kicked his horse and raced her up the road.

ᕤ

Royce watched the courier ride out of sight before taking off his imperial uniform. Turning to face Hadrian, he said, "Well, that wasn't so hard."

"Will?" Hadrian asked as the two slipped into the forest.

Royce nodded. "Remember yesterday you complained that you'd rather be an actor? I was giving you a part: Will, the Imperial Checkpoint Sentry. I thought you did rather well with the role."

"You know, you don't need to mock *all* my ideas." Hadrian frowned as he pulled his own tabard over his head. "Besides, I still think we should consider it. We could travel from town to town performing in dramatic plays, even a few comedies." Hadrian gave his smaller partner an appraising look. "Though maybe you should stick to drama—perhaps tragedies."

Royce glared back.

"What? I think I would make a superb actor. I see myself as a dashing leading man. We could definitely land parts in *The Crown Conspiracy*. I'll play the handsome swordsman that fights the villain, and you—well, you can be the other one."

They dodged branches while pulling off their coifs and gloves, rolling them in their tabards. Walking downhill, they reached one of the many small rivers that fed the great Galewyr. Here they found their horses still tied and enjoying the river grass. The animals lazily swished their tails, keeping the flies at bay. "You worry me sometimes, Hadrian. You really do."

"Why not actors? It's safe. Might even be fun."

"It would be neither safe nor fun. Besides, actors have to travel and I'm content with the way things are. I get to stay near Gwen," Royce added.

"See, that's another reason. Why not find another line of

work? Honestly, if I had what you do, I would never take another job."

Royce removed a pair of boots from a saddlebag. "We do it because it's what we're good at, and with the war, Alric is willing to pay top fees for information."

Hadrian released a sarcastic snort. "Sure, top fees for us, but what about the other costs? Breckton might work for that idiot Ballentyne, but he's no fool himself. He'll certainly look at the seal and won't buy the story about it softening in the saddlebag."

"I know," Royce began as he sat on a log, exchanging the imperial boots for his own, "but after telling one lie, his second tale about sentries breaking the seal will sound even more outlandish, so they won't believe anything he says."

Hadrian paused in his own efforts to switch boots and scowled at his partner. "You realize they'll probably execute him for treason?"

Royce nodded. "Which will neatly eliminate the only witness."

"You see, that's exactly what I'm talking about." Hadrian sighed and shook his head.

Royce could see the familiar melancholy wash over his partner. It appeared too often lately. He could not fathom his friend's moodiness. These strange bouts of depression usually followed successes and frequently led to a night of heavy drinking.

He wondered if Hadrian even cared about the money anymore. He took only what was needed for drinks and food and stored the rest. Royce could have understood his friend's reaction if they had been making a living by picking pockets or robbing homes, but they worked for the king now. Their jobs were almost too clean for Royce's taste. Hadrian had no real concept of filth. Unlike Royce, he had not grown up in the muddy streets of Ratibor.

Royce decided to try to reason with Hadrian. "Would you rather they find out and send a detachment to hunt us down?"

"No, I just hate being the cause of an innocent man's death."

"No one is innocent, my friend. And you aren't the cause... You're more like"—he searched for words—"the grease beneath the skids."

"Thanks. I feel *so* much better."

Royce folded the uniform and placed it, along with the boots, neatly into his saddlebag. Hadrian still struggled to rid himself of his black boots, which were too small. With a mighty tug, he jerked the last one off and threw it down in frustration. He gathered it up and wrestled his uniform into the satchel. Cramming everything as deep as possible, he strapped the flap down and buckled it as tight as he could. He glared at the pack and sighed once more.

"You know, if you organized your pack a little better, it wouldn't be so hard to fit all your gear," Royce said.

Hadrian looked at him with a puzzled expression. "What? Oh—no, I'm...It's not the gear."

"Then what is it?" Royce pulled on his black cloak and adjusted the collar.

Hadrian stroked his horse's neck. "I don't know," he replied mournfully. "It's just that...I thought by now I'd have done something more—with my life, I mean."

"Are you crazy? Most men work themselves to death on a small bit of land that isn't even theirs. You're free to do as you choose and go wherever you want."

"I know, but when I was young, I used to think I was... well...special. I imagined that I would triumph in some great purpose, win the girl, and save the kingdom, but I suppose every boy feels that way."

"I didn't."

Hadrian scowled at him. "I just had this idea of who I would become, and being a worthless spy wasn't part of that plan."

"We're hardly worthless," Royce said, correcting him. "We've been making a good profit, especially lately."

"That's not the point. I was successful as a mercenary too. It's not about money. It's the fact that I survive like a leech."

"Why is this suddenly coming up now? For the first time in years, we're making good money with a steady stream of *respectable* jobs. We're in the employ of a king, for Maribor's sake. We can actually sleep in the same bed two nights in a row and not worry about being arrested. Just last week I passed the captain of the city watch and he gave me a nod."

"It's not the amount of work. It's the *kind* of work. It's the fact that we're always lying. If that courier dies, it'll be our fault. Besides, it's not sudden. I've felt this way for years. Why do you think I'm always suggesting we do something else? Do you know why I broke the rules and took that job to steal Pickering's sword? The one that nearly got us executed?"

"For the unusual sum of money offered," Royce replied.

"No, that's why *you* took it. I wanted to go because it seemed like the right thing to do. For once I had the chance to help someone who really deserved to be helped, or so I thought at the time."

"And becoming an actor is the answer?"

Hadrian untied his horse. "No, but as an actor, I could at least *pretend* to be virtuous. I suppose I should just be happy to be alive, right?"

He did not answer. The nagging sensation was surfacing again. Royce hated keeping secrets from Hadrian, and it weighed heavily on his conscience, which was amazing, because he had never known he had one. Royce defined right and wrong by the moment. Right was what was best for him—wrong was everything else. He stole, lied, and even killed when necessary. This was his craft and he was good at it. There was no reason to apologize, no need to pause or reflect. The world was at war with him and nothing was sacred.

Telling Hadrian what he had learned ran too great a risk. Royce preferred his world constant, with each variable accounted for. Lines on maps were shifting daily and power slipped from one set of hands to another. Time flowed too fast and events were too unexpected. He felt like he was crossing a frozen lake in late spring. He tried to pick a safe path, but the surface cracked beneath his feet. Even so, there were some changes he could still control. He reminded himself that the secret he kept from Hadrian was for his friend's own good.

Climbing onto his short gray mare, Mouse, Royce thought a moment. "We've been working pretty hard lately. Maybe we should take a break."

"I don't see how we can," Hadrian replied. "With the imperial army preparing to invade Melengar, Alric is going to need us now more than ever."

"You'd think that, wouldn't you? But you didn't read the dispatch."

CHAPTER 3

THE MIRACLE

Princess Arista Essendon slouched on the carriage seat, buffeted by every rut and hole in the road. Her neck was stiff from sleeping against the armrest and her head throbbed from the constant jostling. Rising with a yawn, she wiped her eyes and rubbed her face. An attempt to straighten her hair trapped her fingers in a mass of auburn knots.

The ambassadorial coach was showing as much wear as its passenger, having traveled too many miles over the past year. The roof leaked, the springs were worn, and the bench was becoming threadbare in places. The driver had orders to push hard to return to Medford by midday. He was making good time, but at the expense of hitting every rut and rock along the way. As Arista drew back the curtain, the morning sun flashed through gaps in the leafy wall of trees lining the road.

She was almost home.

The flickering light revealed the interior of the coach; dust entering the windows coated everything. A discarded cheesecloth and several apple cores covered a pile of parchments spilling from a stack on the opposite bench. Soiled footprints patterned the floor where a blanket, a corset, and two dresses nested along with three shoes. She had no idea where the fourth was, and only hoped it was in the carriage and not left in Lanksteer. Over the past six months, she had felt as if she had left bits of herself all over Avryn.

Hilfred would have known where her shoe was.

She picked up her pearl-handled hairbrush and turned it over in her hands. Hilfred must have searched the wreckage for days. This one came from Tur Del Fur. Her father had given her a brush from every city he had traveled to. He had been a private man and saying *I love you* had not come easy, even when speaking to his own daughter. The brushes were his unspoken confessions. Once, she had owned dozens— now this was the last. When her bedroom tower had collapsed, she had lost them and it had felt as if she had lost her father all over again. Three weeks later this single brush appeared. It must have been Hilfred, but he never said a word or admitted a thing.

Hilfred had been her bodyguard for years, and now that he was gone, she realized just how much she had taken him for granted.

She had a new bodyguard now. Alric had personally picked him from his own castle guards. His name began with a T— Tom, Tim, Travis—something like that. He stood on the wrong side of her, talked too much, laughed at his own jokes, and was always eating something. He was likely a brave and skilled soldier, but he was no Hilfred.

The last time she had seen Hilfred had been over a year ago in Dahlgren, when he had nearly died from the Gilarabrywn attack. That had been the second time he had suffered burns trying to save her. The first had been when she was only twelve—the night the castle caught fire. Her mother and several others had died, but a boy of fifteen, the son of a sergeant-at-arms, had braved the inferno to pull her from her bed. At Arista's insistence, he went back for her mother. He

never reached her, but nearly died trying. He suffered for
months afterward, and Arista's father rewarded the boy by
appointing him her bodyguard.

His wounds back then had been nothing like what he had
suffered in Dahlgren. Healers had wrapped him from head to
toe and he had lain unconscious for days. To her shock he had
refused to see her upon awaking and left in the back of a
wagon without saying goodbye. At Hilfred's request, no one
would tell her where he had gone. She could have pressed. She
could have ordered the healers to talk. For months, she looked
over her shoulder expecting to see him, waiting to hear the
familiar clap of his sword against his thigh. She often wondered if she had done the right thing in letting him go. She
sighed at yet another regret added to a pile that had been
building over the past year.

Taking stock of the mess around her increased her melancholy. This is what came from refusing to have a handmaid
along, but she could not imagine being cooped up in the carriage with anyone for so long. She picked up her dresses and
laid them across the far seat. When she spied a document
crushed into a ball and hanging in the folds of the far window
curtain, her stomach churned with guilt. With a frown, she
plucked the crumpled parchment and smoothed it out by
pressing it in her lap.

It contained a list of kingdoms and provinces with a line
slashed through each and the notation *IMP* scrawled beside
them. That the Earl of Chadwick and King Ethelred were the
first in line to kiss the empress's ring was no surprise. But she
shook her head in disbelief at the long list. The shift in power
had occurred virtually overnight. One day nothing, the
next—*bang!* There was a New Empire and the Avryn kingdoms of Warric, Ghent, Alburn, Maranon, Galeannon, and
Rhenydd had all joined. They pressured the small holdouts,

like Glouston, then invaded and swallowed them. She ran her finger over the line indicating Dunmore. His Highness King Roswort had graciously decided it was in his kingdom's best interest to accept the imperial offer of extended landholdings in return for becoming part of the New Empire. Arista would not be surprised if Roswort had been promised Melengar as part of his payment. Of all the kingdoms of Avryn, only Melengar refused to join.

It all happened so fast.

A year ago, the New Empire was merely an idea. She had spent months as ambassador trying to strike alliances. Without support, without allies, Melengar could not hope to stand against the growing colossus.

How long do we have before the empire marches north, before—

The carriage came to a sudden halt, throwing her forward, jerking the curtains, and creaking the tired springs. She looked out the window, puzzled. They were still on the old Steward's Road. The wall of trees had given way to an open field of flowers, which she knew placed them on the high meadow just a few miles outside Medford.

"What's going on?" she called out.

No response.

Where in Elan is Tim, or Ted, or whatever the blazes his name is?

She pulled the latch and, hiking up her skirt, pushed out the door. Warm sunlight met her, making her squint. Her legs were stiff and her back ached. At only twenty-six, she already felt ancient. She slammed the carriage door and, holding a hand to protect her eyes, glared as best she could up at the silhouettes of the driver and groom. They glanced at her, but only briefly, then looked back down the slope of the road ahead.

"Daniel! Why—" she started, but stopped after seeing what they were looking at.

The high meadowlands just north of Medford provided an extensive view for several miles south. The land sloped gently down, revealing Melengar's capital city, Medford. She saw the spires of Essendon Castle and Mares Cathedral and, farther out, the Galewyr River, marking the southern border of the kingdom. In the days when her mother and father had been alive, the royal family had come here in the summer to have picnics and enjoy the cool breeze and the view. Only that day the sight was quite different.

On the far bank, in the clear morning light, Arista saw rows and rows of canvas tents, hundreds of them, each flying the red-and-white flags of the Nyphron Imperial Empire.

"There's an army, Highness." Daniel found his voice. "An army is a stone's throw from Medford."

"Get me home, Daniel. Beat the horses if you must, but get me home!"

⁓

The carriage had barely stopped when Arista punched open the door, nearly hitting Tommy—or Terence, or whoever he was—in the face when he foolishly attempted to open it for her. The servants in the courtyard immediately stopped their early-morning chores to bow reverently. Melissa spotted the coach and rushed over. Unlike Tucker—or Tillman—the small redheaded maid had served Arista for years and knew to expect a storm.

"How long has that army been there?" Arista barked at her even as she trotted up the stone steps.

"Nearly a week," Melissa replied, chasing after the princess and catching the traveling cloak as Arista discarded it.

"A week? Has there been fighting?"

"Yes, His Majesty launched an attack across the river just a few days ago."

"Alric attacked them? Across the river?"

"It didn't go well," Melissa replied in a lowered voice.

"I should think not! Was he drunk?"

Castle guards hastily pulled back the big oak doors, barely getting them open before the princess barreled through, her gown whipping behind her.

"Where are they?"

"In the war room."

She stopped.

They stood in the northern foyer. A wide gallery of polished stone pillars displayed suits of armor and hallways led to sweeping staircases.

"Missy, fetch my blue audience gown and shoes to go with it and prepare a basin of water—oh, and send someone to bring me something to eat. I don't care what."

"Yes, Your Highness." Melissa made a curt bow and raced up the stairs.

"Your Highness," her bodyguard called, chasing after her. "You almost lost me there."

"Imagine that. I'll just have to try harder next time."

✺

Arista watched as her brother, King Alric, stood up from the great table. Normally this would require everyone else to rise as well, but Alric had suspended that tradition inside the council chamber, as he had a habit of rising frequently and pacing during meetings.

"I don't understand it," he said, turning his back on all of them to begin his slow, familiar walk between the table and the window. As he moved, he stroked his short beard the way another man might wring his hands. Alric had started the beard just before Arista left on her trip. It still had not filled in. She guessed he grew it to look more like their father. King Amrath had worn a dark, full beard, but Alric's light brown wisps only underscored his youth. He made matters worse by drawing attention to it with his constant stroking. Arista recalled how their father used to drum his fingers during state meetings. Under the weight of the crown, pressures must build up until action sought its own means of escape.

Her brother was two years her junior, and she knew he had never expected to wear the crown so soon. For years she had heard Alric's plans to roam the wilds with his friend Mauvin Pickering. The two wanted to see the world and have grand adventures that would involve nameless women, too much wine, and too little sleep. They had even hoped to find and explore the ancient ruins of Percepliquis. She had suspected that when he tired of the road, he would be happy to return home and marry a girl half his age and father several strong sons. Only then, as his temples grayed and when all of life's other ambitions were accomplished, would he expect the crown to pass to him. All that changed the night their uncle Percy arranged the assassination of their father and left Alric king.

"It could be a trick, Your Majesty," Lord Valin suggested. "A plan to catch you off your guard."

Lord Valin, an elderly knight with a bushy white beard, was known for his courage, but not for his strategic skills.

"Lord Valin," Sir Ecton addressed the noble respectfully, "after our failure on the banks of the Galewyr, the imperial army can overrun Medford with ease, whether we are on or off our guard. We know it and they know it. Medford is their prize for the taking whenever they decide to get their feet wet."

Alric walked to the tall balcony window, where the afternoon light spilled into the royal banquet hall of Essendon Castle. The hall served as the royal war room out of the need for a large space to conduct the defense of the kingdom. Where once festive tapestries hung, great maps now covered the walls, each slashed with red lines illustrating the tragic retreat of Melengar's armies.

"I just don't understand it," Alric repeated. "It's so peculiar. The imperial army outnumbers us ten to one. They have scores of heavy cavalry, siege weapons, and archers— everything they need. So why are they sitting across the river? Why stop now?"

"It makes no sense from a military standpoint, Sire," Sir Ecton said. A large powerful man with a fiery disposition, he was Alric's chief general and field commander. Ecton was also Count Pickering's most accomplished vassal and regarded by many as the best knight in Melengar. "I would venture it's political," he continued. "It's been my experience that the most foolish decisions in combat are the result of political choices made by those with little to no field experience."

Earl Kendell, a potbellied fussy man who always dressed in a bright green tunic, glared at Ecton. "Careful with your tongue and consider your company!"

Ecton rose to his feet. "I held my tongue, and what was the result?"

"Sir Ecton!" Alric shouted. "I'm well aware of your opinion of my decision to attack the imperial encampment."

"It was insanity to attempt an assault across a river without even the possibility to flank," Ecton shot back.

"Nevertheless, it was my decision." Alric squeezed his hands into fists. "I felt it was...necessary."

"Necessary? Necessary!" Ecton spat the word as if it were a vile thing in his mouth. He looked like he was about to speak again but Count Pickering rose to his feet and Sir Ecton sat down.

Arista had seen this before. Too often Ecton looked to Count Pickering before acting on an order Alric had given. He was not the only one, and it was clear that although her brother was king, Alric had failed to earn the respect of his nobles, his army, or his people.

"Perhaps Ecton is right." Young Marquis Wymar spoke up. "About it being political, I mean." He then hastily added, "We all know what a pompous fool the Earl of Chadwick is. Isn't it possible that Ballentyne ordered Breckton to hold the final attack until Archibald could arrive? It would certainly raise his standing in the imperial court to claim he personally led the assault that conquered Melengar for the New Empire."

"That would explain the delay in the attack," Pickering replied in his fatherly tone, which she knew Alric despised. "But our scouts are reporting that large numbers of men are pulling out and by all accounts are heading south."

"A feint, perhaps?" Alric asked.

Pickering shook his head. "As Sir Ecton pointed out, there would be no need."

Several of the other advisors nodded thoughtfully.

"Something must be going on for the empress to recall her troops like this," Pickering said.

"But what?" Alric asked no one in particular. "I wish I knew what kind of person she was. It's impossible to guess the actions of a total stranger." He turned to his sister. "Arista, you met Modina, spent time with her in Dahlgren. What's she like? Do you have any idea what would cause her to pull the army back?"

A memory flashed in Arista's mind of her and a young girl trapped at the top of a tower. Arista had been frozen in fear, but Thrace had rummaged through a pile of debris and human limbs, looking for a weapon to fight an invincible beast. Had it been bravery or had she been too naive to understand the futility? "The girl I knew as Thrace was a sweet, innocent child who wanted only the love of her father. The church may have changed her name to Modina, but I can't imagine they changed her. She didn't order this invasion. She wouldn't want to rule her tiny village, much less conquer the world." Arista shook her head. "She's not our enemy."

"A crown can change a person," Sir Ecton said while glaring at Alric.

Arista rose. "It's more likely we are dealing with the church and a council of conservative Imperialists. I highly doubt a child from rural Dunmore could influence the archaic attitudes and inflexible opinions of so many stubborn minds who would strive to resist, rather than work with, a new ruler," she said while glaring at Ecton. Over the knight's shoulder, she noticed Alric cringe.

The door to the hall opened and Julian, the elderly lord chamberlain, entered. With a sweeping bow, he tapped his staff of office twice on the tiled floor. "The royal protector Royce Melborn, Your Majesty."

"Show him in immediately."

"Don't get your hopes too high," Pickering said to his king. "They're spies, not miracle workers."

"I pay them enough for miracles. I don't think it unreasonable to get what I pay for."

Alric employed numerous informants and scouts, but none were as effective as Riyria. Arista had originally hired Royce and Hadrian to kidnap her brother the night their father had been assassinated. Since then, their services had proved invaluable.

Royce entered the banquet hall alone. The small man with dark hair and dark eyes always dressed in layers of black. He wore a knee-length tunic and a long flowing cloak and, as always, carried no visible weapons. Carrying a blade in the presence of the king was unlawful, but given he and Hadrian had twice saved Alric's life, Arista surmised the royal guards did not thoroughly search him. She was certain Royce carried his white-bladed dagger and regarded the law as merely a suggestion.

Royce bowed before the assembly.

"Well?" her brother asked a bit too loudly, too desperately. "Did you discover anything?"

"Yes, Your Majesty," Royce replied, but his face remained so neutral that nothing more could be determined for good or ill.

"Well, out with it. What did you find? Are they really leaving?"

"Sir Breckton has been ordered to withdraw all but a small containment force and march south immediately with the bulk of his army."

"So it really is true?" Marquis Wymar said. "But why?"

"Yes, why?" Alric added.

"Because Rhenydd has been invaded by the Nationalists out of Delgos."

A look of surprise circulated the room.

"Degan Gaunt's rabble is invading Rhenydd?" Earl Kendell said in bewilderment.

"And doing quite well from the dispatch I read," Royce informed them. "Gaunt has led them up the coast, taking every village and town. He's managed to sack Kilnar and Vernes."

"He sacked Vernes?" Ecton asked, shocked.

"That's a good-sized city," Wymar mentioned.

"It's also only a few miles from Ratibor," Pickering observed. "From there it's what—maybe a hard day's march to the imperial capital itself?"

"No wonder the empire is recalling Breckton." Alric looked at the count. "What were you saying about miracles?"

෯

"I can't believe you couldn't find anyone to ally with." Alric berated Arista as he collapsed on his throne. The two were alone in the reception hall, the most ornate room in the castle. This room, the grand ballroom, the banquet hall, and the foyer were all that most people generally ever saw. Tolin the Great had built the chamber to be intimidating. The three-story ceiling was an impressive sight and the observation balcony that circled the walls provided a magnificent view of the parquet floor, inlaid with the royal falcon coat of arms. Double rows of twelve marble pillars formed a long gallery similar to that of a church, yet instead of an altar there was the dais. On seven pyramid-shaped steps sat the throne of Melengar—the only seat in the vast chamber. When they had been children, the throne had always appeared so impressive, but now, with Alric slouched in it, Arista realized it was just a gaudy chair.

"I tried," she offered, sitting on the steps before the throne as she had once done with her father. "Everyone had already sworn allegiance to the New Empire." Arista gave her brother the demoralizing report on her past six months of failure.

"We're quite a pair, you and I. You've done little as ambassador and I nearly destroyed us with that attack across the river. Many of the nobles are being more vocal. Soon Pickering won't be able to control the likes of Ecton."

"I must admit I was shocked when I heard about your attack. What possessed you to do such a thing?" she asked.

"Royce and Hadrian had intercepted plans drafted by Breckton himself. He was about to launch a three-pronged assault. I had to make a preemptive strike. I was hoping to catch the Imperialists by surprise."

"Well, it looks like it worked out after all. It delayed their attack just long enough."

"True, but what good will that do if we can't find more help? What about Trent?"

"Well, they haven't said no, but they haven't said yes either. The church's influence has never been strong that far north, but they also don't have any ties to us. All they want is to be on the winning side. They're at least willing to wait and watch. They won't join us because they don't think we have a chance. But if we can show them some success, they could be persuaded to side with us."

"Don't they realize the empire will be after them next?"

"I said that, but…"

"But what?"

"They really weren't very amenable to what I had to say. The men of Lanksteer are brutish and backward. They respect only strength. I would have fared better if I'd beaten their king senseless." She hesitated. "I don't think they quite knew what to make of me."

"I should never have sent you," Alric said, running a hand over his face. "What was I thinking, making a woman an ambassador?"

His words felt like a slap. "I agree that I was at a disadvantage in Trent, but in the rest of the kingdoms I don't think the fact that I am a woman—"

"A witch, then," Alric said, lashing out. "Even worse. All those Warric and Alburn nobles are so devoted, and what do I do? I send them someone the church tried for witchcraft."

"I'm not a witch!" she snapped. "I wasn't convicted of anything, and everyone with a brain between their ears knows that trial was a fabrication of Braga and Saldur to get their hands on our throne."

"The truth doesn't matter. Everyone believes what the church tells them. They said you're a witch, so that makes it so. Look at Modina. The Patriarch proclaims that she's the Heir of Novron, so everyone believes. I should have never made an enemy of the church. But between Saldur's betrayal and their sentinel killing Fanen, I just couldn't bring myself to bend my knee.

"When I evicted the priests and forbade Deacon Tomas from preaching about what happened in Dahlgren, the people revolted. They set shops in Gentry Square on fire. I could see the flames from my window, for Maribor's sake. The whole city could have burned. They were calling for my head— people right in front of the castle burning stuffed images of me and shouting, 'Death to the godless king!' Can you imagine that? Just a few years ago they were calling me a hero. People toasted to my health in every tavern, but now…well, it's amazing how fast they can turn on you. I had to use the army to restore order." Alric reached up and pulled his crown off, turning the golden circlet over in his hands.

"I was in Alburn at the court of King Armand when I heard about that," Arista said, shaking her head.

Alric laid the crown on the arm of the throne, closed his eyes, and softly banged his head against the back of the chair. "What are we going to do, Arista? The Imperialists will return. As soon as they deal with Gaunt's rabble, the army will come back." His eyes opened and his hand drifted absently toward his throat. "I suppose they'll hang me, won't they? Or do they use the axe on kings?" His tone was one of quiet acceptance, which surprised her.

The carefree boy she had once known was vanishing before

her eyes. Even if the New Empire failed and Melengar stood strong, Alric would never be the same. In many ways, their uncle had managed to kill him after all.

Alric looked at the crown sitting on the chair's arm. "I wonder what Father would do."

"He never had anything like this to deal with. Not since Tolin defeated Lothomad at Drondil Fields has any monarch of Melengar faced invasion."

"Lucky me."

"Lucky us."

Alric nodded. "At least we've got some time now. That's something. What do you think of Pickering's idea to send the *Ellis Far* down the coast to Tur Del Fur and contact the Nationalist leader—this Gaunt fellow?"

"Honestly, I think establishing an alliance with Gaunt is our only hope. Isolated, we don't stand a chance against the empire," Arista agreed.

"But the Nationalists? Are they any better than the Imps? They're as opposed to monarchies as much as the empire. They don't want to be ruled at all."

"Alone and surrounded by enemies is not the time to be choosy about your friends."

"We aren't completely alone," Alric said, correcting her. "Marquis Lanaklin joined us."

"A lot of good that does. The empire took his holdings. He's nothing more than a refugee now. He only came here because he has no place else to go. If we get more help like that, we'll go broke just feeding them. Our only chance is to contact Degan Gaunt and form an alliance. If Delgos joins with us, that may be enough to persuade Trent to side in our favor. If that happens, we could deal a mortal blow to this new Nyphron Empire."

"Do you think Gaunt will agree?"

"Don't know why not," Arista said. "It's to our mutual benefit. I'm certain I can talk him into it, and I must say I'm looking forward to the trip. A rolling ocean is a welcome change from that carriage. While I'm away, have someone work on it, or better yet order a new one. And put extra padding—"

"You aren't going," Alric told her as he put his crown back on.

"What's that?"

"I'm sending Linroy to meet with Gaunt."

"But I'm the ambassador and a member of the royal family. He can't negotiate a treaty or an alliance with—"

"Of course he can. Linroy is an experienced negotiator and statesman."

"He's the royal financier. That doesn't qualify him as a statesman."

"He's handled dozens of trade agreements," Alric interjected.

"The man's a bookkeeper!" she shouted, rising to her feet.

"It may come as a surprise to you, but other people are capable of doing things too."

"But why?"

"Like you said, you're a member of the royal family." Alric looked away and his fingers reached up to stroke his beard. "Do you have any idea what kind of position it would put me in if you were captured? We're at war. I can't risk you being held for ransom."

She stared at him. "You're lying. This isn't about ransom. You think I can't handle the responsibility."

"Arista, it's my fault. I shouldn't have—"

"Shouldn't have what? Made your witch-sister ambassador?"

"Don't be that way."

"I'm sorry, Your Majesty, what way would you like me to

be? How should I react to being told I'm worthless and an embarrassment and that I should go sit in my room and—"

"I didn't say any of that. Stop putting words in my mouth!"

"It's what you're thinking—it's what all of you think."

"Have you become clairvoyant now too?"

"Do you deny it?"

"Damn it, Arista, you were gone six months!" He struck the arm of the throne with his fist. The dull thud sounded loudly off the walls like a bass drum. "Six months, and not a single alliance. You barely got a maybe. That's a pretty poor showing. This meeting with Gaunt is too important. It could be our last chance."

She stood up. "Forgive me, Your Majesty. I apologize for being such an utter failure. May I please have your royal permission to be excused?"

"Arista, don't."

"Please, Your Majesty, my frail feminine constitution can't handle such a heated debate. I feel faint. Perhaps if I retire to my room, I could brew a potion to make myself feel better. While I'm at it, perhaps I should enchant a broom to fly around the castle for fresh air."

She pivoted on her heel and marched out, slamming the great door behind her with a resounding *boom!*

She stood with her back against the door, waiting, wondering if Alric would chase after her.

Will he apologize and take back what he said and agree to let me go?

She listened for the sound of his heels on the parquet.

Silence.

She wished she did know magic, because then no one could stop her from meeting with Gaunt. Alric was right: this was their last chance. And she was not about to leave the fate of Melengar to Dillnard Linroy, statesman extraordinaire.

Besides, she had failed and that made it her responsibility to correct the situation.

She looked up to see Tim—or Tommy—leaning against the near wall, biting his fingernails. He glanced up at her and smiled. "I hope you're planning on heading to the kitchens. I'm starved—practically eating my fingers here." He chuckled.

She pushed away from the door and quickly strode down the corridor. She almost did not see Mauvin Pickering sitting on the broad sill of the courtyard-facing window. Feet up, arms folded, back against the frame, he crouched in a shaft of sunlight like a cat. He still wore the black clothes of mourning.

"Troubles with His Majesty?" he asked.

"He's being an ass."

"What did he do this time?"

"Replaced me with that sniveling little wretch Linroy. He's sending him on the *Ellis Far* in my place to contact Gaunt."

"Dillnard Linroy isn't a bad guy. He's—"

"Listen, I really don't want to hear how wonderful Linroy is at the moment. I'm right in the middle of hating him."

"Sorry."

She glanced at his side and he immediately turned his attention back to the window.

"Still not wearing it?" she asked.

"It doesn't go with my ensemble. The silver hilt clashes with black."

"It's been over a year since Fanen died."

He turned back sharply. "Since he was killed by Luis Guy, you mean."

Arista took a breath. She was not used to the new Mauvin. "Aren't you supposed to be Alric's bodyguard now? Isn't that hard to do without a sword?"

"Hasn't been a problem so far. You see, I have this plan. I sit here and watch the ducks in the courtyard. Well, I suppose it's not really so much a plan as a strategy, or maybe it's more of a scheme. Anyway, this is the one place my father never thinks to look, so I can sit here all day and watch those ducks walking back and forth. There were six of them last year. Did you know that? Only five now. I can't figure out what happened to the other one. I keep looking for him, but I don't think he's coming back."

"It wasn't your fault," she told him gently.

Mauvin reached up and traced the lead edges of the window with his fingertips. "Yeah, it was."

She put her hand on his shoulder and gave a soft squeeze. She did not know what else to do. First her mother, then her father and Fanen, and finally Hilfred—they were all gone. Mauvin was slipping away as well. The boy who loved his sword more than Wintertide presents, sweet chocolate cake, or swimming on a hot day refused to touch it anymore. The eldest son of Count Pickering, who had once challenged the sun to a duel because it had rained on the day of a hunt, spent his days watching ducks.

"Doesn't matter," Mauvin remarked. "The world is coming to an end, anyway." He looked up at her. "You just said Alric is sending that bastard Linroy on the *Ellis Far*—he'll kill us all."

As hard as she tried, she could not help laughing. She punched his shoulder, then gave him a peck on the cheek. "That's the spirit, Mauvin. Keep looking on the bright side."

She left him and continued down the hall. As she passed the office of the lord chamberlain, the old man hurried out. "Your Highness?" he called, looking relieved. "The royal protector Royce Melborn is still waiting to see if there is something else needed of him. Apparently he and his partner are thinking of taking some time off, unless there is something pressing the king requires. Can I tell him he's excused?"

"Yes, of course you— No, wait." She cast a look at her bodyguard. "Tommy, you're right. I'm hungry. Be a dear and fetch us both a plate of chicken or whatever you can find that's good in the kitchen, will you? I'll wait here."

"Sure, but my name is—"

"Hurry before I change my mind."

She waited until he was down the corridor, then turned back to the chamberlain. "Where did you say Royce was waiting?"

Chapter 4

The Nature of Right

The Rose and Thorn Tavern was mostly empty. Many of its patrons had left Medford, fearful of the coming invasion. Those who remained were the indentured or those simply too poor, feeble, or stubborn to leave. Royce found Hadrian sitting alone in the Diamond Room—his feet up on a spare chair, a pint of ale before him. Two empty mugs sat on the table, one lying on its side while Hadrian stared at it with a melancholy expression.

"Why didn't you come to the castle?" Royce asked.

"I knew you could handle it." Hadrian continued to stare at the mug, tilting his head slightly as he did.

"Looks like our break will have to be postponed," Royce told him while pulling over a chair and sitting down. "Alric has another job. He wants us to make contact with Gaunt and the Nationalists. They're still working out the details. The princess is going to send a messenger here."

"Her Highness is back?"

"Got in this morning."

Royce reached into his vest, pulled out a bag, and set it in front of Hadrian. "Here's your half. Have you ordered dinner yet?"

"I'm not going," Hadrian said, rocking the fallen mug with his thumb.

"Not going?"

"I can't keep doing this."

Royce rolled his eyes. "Now don't start that again. If you haven't noticed, there's a war going on. This is the best time to be in our business. Everyone needs information. Do you know how much money—"

"That's just it, Royce. There's a war on and what am I doing? I'm making a profit off it rather than fighting in it." Hadrian took another swallow of ale and set the mug back on the table a little too heavily, rattling its brothers. "I'm tired of collecting money for being dishonorable. It's not how I'm built."

Royce glanced around. Three men eating a meal looked over briefly and then lost interest.

"They haven't all been just for money," Royce pointed out. "Thrace, for example."

Hadrian displayed a bitter smile. "And look how that turned out. She hired us to save her father. Seen him lately, have you?"

"We were hired to obtain a sword to slay a beast. She got the sword. The beast was slain. We did our job."

"The man is dead."

"And Thrace, who was nothing but a poor farm girl, is now empress. If only all our jobs ended so well for our clients."

"You think so, Royce? You really think Thrace is happy? See, I'm thinking she'd rather have her father than the imperial throne, but maybe that's just me." Hadrian took another swallow and wiped his mouth with his sleeve.

They sat in silence for a moment. Royce watched his friend staring at a distant point beyond focus.

"So you want to fight in this war, is that it?"

"It would be better than sitting on the sidelines like scavengers feeding off the wounded."

"Okay, so tell me, for which side will you be fighting?"

"Alric's a good king."

"Alric? Alric's a boy still fighting with the ghost of his father. After his defeat at the Galewyr, his nobles look to Count Pickering instead of him. Pickering has his hands full dealing with Alric's mistakes, like the riots here in Medford. How long before the count tires of Alric's incompetence and decides Mauvin would be better suited to the throne?"

"Pickering would never turn on Alric," Hadrian said.

"No? You've seen it happen plenty of times before."

Hadrian remained silent.

"Oh hell, forget about Pickering and Alric. Melengar is already at war with the empire. Have you forgotten who the empress is? If you fought with Alric and he prevailed, how will you feel the day poor Thrace is hanged in the Royal Square in Aquesta? Would that satisfy your need for an honorable cause?"

Hadrian's face had turned hard, his jaw clenched stiffly.

"There are no honorable causes. There is no good or evil. Evil is only what we call those who oppose us."

Royce took out his dagger and drove it into the table, where it stood upright. "Look at the blade. Is it bright or dark?"

Hadrian narrowed his eyes suspiciously. The brilliant surface of Alverstone was dazzling as it reflected the candlelight. "Bright."

Royce nodded.

"Now move your head over here and look from my perspective."

Hadrian leaned over, putting his head on the opposite side of the blade, where the shadow made it black as chimney soot.

"It's the same dagger," Royce explained, "but from where you sat it was light while I saw it as dark. So who is right?"

"Neither of us," Hadrian said.

"No," Royce said. "That's the mistake people always make, and they make it because they can't grasp the truth."

"Which is?"

"That we're both right. One truth doesn't refute another. Truth doesn't lie in the object, but in how we see it."

Hadrian looked at the dagger, then back at Royce.

"There are times when you are brilliant, Royce, and then there are times when I haven't a clue as to what you're babbling about."

Royce's expression turned to one of frustration as he pulled his dagger from the table and sat back down. "In the twelve years we've been together, I've never once asked you to do anything I wouldn't do, or didn't do with you. I've never lied or misled you. I've never abandoned or betrayed you. Name a single noble you even suspect you could say the same about twelve years from now."

"Can I get another round here?" Hadrian shouted.

Royce sighed. "So you're just going to sit here and drink?"

"That's my plan at present. I'm making it up as I go."

Royce stared at his friend a moment longer, then finally stood up. "I'm going to Gwen's."

"Listen." Hadrian stopped him. "I'm sorry about this. I guess I can't explain it. I don't have any metaphors with daggers I can use to express how I feel. I just know I can't keep doing what I've been doing anymore. I've tried to find meaning in it. I've tried to pretend we achieved some greater good, but in the end, I have to be honest with myself. I'm not a thief, and I'm not a spy. So I know what I'm not. I just wish I knew what I am. That probably doesn't make much sense to you, does it?"

"Do me a favor at least." Royce purposely ignored the question, noticing how the little silver chain Hadrian wore peeked out from under his collar. "Since you're going to be here anyway, keep an eye out for the messenger from the castle while I'm at Gwen's. I'll be back in an hour or so."

Hadrian nodded.

"Give Gwen my love, will ya?"

"Sure," Royce said, heading for the door and feeling that miserable sensation creeping in, the dull weight. He paused and looked back.

It won't help to tell him. It will just make matters worse.

⁓

It had been only a day and a half but Royce found himself desperate to see Gwen. While Medford House was always open, it did not do much business until after dark. During the day, Gwen encouraged the girls to use their free time learning how to sew or spin, skills they could use to make a bit of coin in their old age.

All the girls at the brothel, better known as the House, knew and liked Royce. When he came in, they smiled or waved, but no one said a word. They knew he enjoyed surprising Gwen. That night they pointed toward the parlor, where she was concentrating on a pile of parchments, a quill pen in hand and her register open. She immediately abandoned it all when he walked through the door. She sprang from her chair and ran to him with a smile so broad her face could hardly contain it and an embrace so tight he could barely breathe.

"What's wrong?" she whispered, pulling back and looking into his eyes.

Royce marveled at Gwen's ability to read him. He refused to answer, preferring instead to look at her, drinking her in.

She had a lovely face, her dark skin and emerald eyes so familiar, yet mysterious. Throughout his entire life and in all his travels he had never met anyone else like her.

Gwen provided use of a private room at The Rose and Thorn, where he and Hadrian conducted business, and she never blinked at the risks. They no longer used it. Royce was too concerned that Sentinel Luis Guy might track them there. Still, Gwen continued banking their money and watching out for them, just as she had done from the start.

They had met twelve years ago, the night soldiers had filled the streets and two strangers had staggered into the Lower Quarter covered in their own blood. Royce still remembered how Gwen had appeared as a hazy figure to his clouding eyes. "I've got you. You'll be all right now," she told him before he passed out. He never understood what had motivated her to take them in when everyone else had shown the good sense in closing their doors. When he had woken, she had been giving orders to her girls like a general marshaling troops. She sheltered Royce and Hadrian from the mystified authorities and nursed them back to health. She pulled strings and made deals to ensure no one talked. As soon as they were able, they left, but he always found himself returning.

He had been crushed the day she refused to see him. It did not take long for him to discover why. Clients often abused prostitutes, and the women of Medford House were not exempt. In Gwen's case the attacker had been a powerful noble. He had beaten her so badly she did not want anyone to see. Regardless of whether the client was a gentleman or a thug, the town sheriff never wasted his time on complaints by whores.

Two days later the noble had been found dead. His body hung in the center of Gentry Square. City authorities had closed Medford House and arrested the prostitutes. They had been told to identify the killer or face execution themselves. To everyone's surprise, the women spent only one night in jail. The next day Medford House had reopened and the sheriff of Medford personally delivered a public apology for their arrest, adding that swift punishment would follow any future abuse of the women, regardless of rank. From then on, Medford House prospered under unprecedented protection. Royce had never spoken of the incident, and Gwen never asked, but he was certain she knew—just as she had known about his heritage before he had told her.

When he had returned from Avempartha the previous summer, he had decided to reveal his secret to her, to be completely open and honest. Royce had never told anyone about being an elf, not even Hadrian. He expected that she would hate him, either for being a miserable *mir* or for deceiving her. He had taken Gwen for a walk down the bank of the Galewyr, away from people to lessen the embarrassment of her outrage. He had braced himself, said the words, and waited for her to hit him. He had decided to let her. She could scratch his eyes out if she wanted. He owed her at least that much.

"Of course you're elven," she had said while touching his hand kindly. "Was that supposed to be a secret?"

How she had known, she never explained. He had been so overwhelmed with joy to bother asking. Gwen just had a way of always knowing his heart.

"What is it?" she asked again now.

"Why haven't you packed?"

Gwen paused and smiled. That was her way of letting him know he would not get away with it. "Because there is no need. The imperial army isn't attacking us."

Royce raised an eyebrow. "The king himself has his things packed and his horse at the ready to evacuate the city on a moment's notice, but you know better?"

She nodded.

"And how is that?"

"If there was the slightest chance that Medford was in danger, you wouldn't be here asking me why I haven't packed. I'd be on Mouse's back holding on for dear life as you spurred her into a run."

"Still," he said, "I'd feel better if you moved to the monastery."

"I can't leave my girls."

"Take them with you. Myron has plenty of room."

"You want me to take whores to live in a monastery with monks?"

"I want you to be safe. Besides, Magnus and Albert are there too, and I can guarantee you *they're* not monks."

"I'll consider it." She smiled at him. "But you're leaving on another mission, so it can wait until you get back."

"How do you know these things?" he asked, amazed. "Alric ought to hire you instead of us."

"I'm from Calis. It's in our blood," she told him with a wink. "When do you leave?"

"Soon…tonight, perhaps. I left Hadrian at The Rose and Thorn to watch for a messenger."

"Have you decided to tell Hadrian yet?"

He looked away.

"Oh, so that's it. Don't you think you should?"

"No, just because a lunatic wizard—" He paused. "Listen, if I tell him what I saw, his reason will disappear. If Hadrian were a moth, he'd fly into every flame he could find. He'll sacrifice himself if necessary, and for what? Even if it's true, all that stuff with the heir happened centuries ago and has nothing to do with him. There's no reason to think that Esrahaddon wasn't just— Wizards toy with people, okay? It's what they do. He tells me to keep quiet, makes a big stink about how I have to take this secret to my grave. But you know damn well he expects me to tell Hadrian. I don't like being used, and I won't let Hadrian get himself killed at the whim of some wizard's agenda."

Gwen said nothing but looked at him with a knowing smile.

"What?"

"Sounds like you're trying to convince yourself and you're not doing very well. I think it might help if you consider you're one kind of person and Hadrian is another. You are trying to look out for him, but you're using *cat's eyes*."

"I'm doing what?"

Puzzled for a moment, Gwen looked at Royce, then chuckled quietly. "Oh, I suppose that must be a common saying only in Calis. Okay, let's say you're a cat and Hadrian's a dog and you want to make him happy. You give him a dead mouse and are surprised when he isn't thrilled. The problem is that you need to see the world through the eyes of a dog to understand what's best for him. If you did, you would see that a nice juicy bone would be a better choice, even though to a cat it's not very appealing."

"So you think I should let Hadrian go off and get himself killed?"

"I'm saying that for Hadrian, maybe fighting—even dying—for something or someone is the same as a bone is to a dog. Besides, you have to ask yourself, is keeping quiet really for his sake—or yours?"

"First daggers, now dogs and cats," Royce muttered.

"What?"

"Nothing." He let his hands run through her hair. "How did you get so wise?"

"Wise?" She looked at him and laughed. "I'm a thirty-four-year-old prostitute in love with a professional criminal. How wise can I possibly be?"

"If you don't know, perhaps you should try seeing with my eyes."

He kissed her warmly, pulling her tight. He recalled what Hadrian had said and wondered if he was being stupid for not settling down with Gwen. He had noticed for some time a growing pain whenever he said goodbye and a misery that dogged him whenever he left. Royce had never meant for it to happen. He always tried to keep her at a distance, for her own good as well as his. His life was dangerous and only possible so long as he had no ties, nothing others could use against him.

Winters had caused him to crack. Deep snows and brutal cold kept Riyria idle in Medford for months. Huddled before the warmth of hearth fires through the long dark nights, they had grown close. Casual chats had turned into long intimate conversations, and conversations had changed to embraces and confessions. Royce found it impossible to resist her open kindness and generosity. She was so unlike anyone, an enigma that flew in the face of all he had come to expect from the world. She made no demands and asked for nothing but his happiness.

His feelings for Gwen had led to Royce and Hadrian's longest imprisonment, six years earlier. They had taken a job in the spring, sending them all the way to Alburn. The thought of leaving her dragged on him like a weight, especially because she was not feeling well. Gwen had contracted the flu and looked miserable. She claimed it was nothing, but she looked pale and barely ate. He almost did not go but she insisted. He could still remember her face with that brave little smile that had quivered oh so slightly at the edges as he had left her.

The job had gone badly. Royce's concentration had suffered, mistakes had been made, and they had been left rotting in the dungeons of Blythin Castle. All he could do was sit and think about Gwen and wonder whether she was all right. As

the months stretched out, he had begun to realize that if he
survived, he would need to end their relationship. He resolved
never to see her again, for both of their sakes. But the moment
he had returned, the moment he had seen her again, felt her
hands and smelled her hair, he knew leaving her would never
be possible. Since that time, his feelings had only increased.
Even now, the thought of leaving her, even for a week, was
agony.

Hadrian was right. He should quit and take her away
somewhere, perhaps get a small bit of land where they could
raise a family. Somewhere quiet where no one knew Gwen as
a prostitute or him as a thief. They could even go to Avempartha, that ancient citadel of his people. The tower stood vacant,
far beyond the reaches of anyone who did not know its secrets,
and would likely remain that way indefinitely. The thought
was appealing, but he pushed it back, telling himself he would
revisit it soon. For now, he had people waiting, which brought
his mind back to Hadrian.

"I suppose I could look into Esrahaddon's story. Hadrian
would be a fool for dedicating his life to someone else's dream,
but at least I'd know it was genuine and not some kind of wizard's trick."

"How can you find out?"

"Hadrian grew up in Hintindar. If his father was a Teshlor
Knight, maybe he left behind some indication. At least then I
would have someone else's word instead of just Esrahaddon's.
Our job is taking us south. I could make a stop in Hintindar
and see if I can find something out. By the way," he told her
gently, "I'll be gone a good deal longer than I have been. I
want you to know so you don't worry needlessly."

"I never worry about you," she told him.

Royce's face reflected his pain.

Gwen smiled. "I *know* you'll return safely."

"And how do you know this?"

"I've seen your hands."

Royce looked at her, confused.

"I've read your palms, Royce," she told him without a trace of humor. "Or have you forgotten I also make a living as a fortune-teller?"

Royce had not forgotten, but had assumed it was just a way of swindling the superstitious. Not until that moment did he realize how inconsistent it would be for Gwen to deceive people.

"You have a long life ahead of you," she went on. "Too long— that was one of the clues that you weren't completely human."

"So I have nothing to worry about in my future?"

Gwen's smile faded abruptly.

"What is it?"

"Nothing."

"Tell me," he persisted, gently lifting her chin until she met his eyes.

"It's just that...you need to watch out for Hadrian."

"Did you look at his palms too?"

"No," she said, "but your lifeline shows a fork, a point of decision. You'll head either into darkness and despair or vir-tue and light. This decision will be precipitated by a traumatic event."

"What kind of event?"

"The death of the one you love the most."

"Then shouldn't you be worried about yourself?"

Gwen smiled warmly at him. "If only that were so, I'd die a happy woman. Royce, I'm serious about Hadrian. Please watch out for him. I think he needs you now more than ever. And I'm frightened for you if something were to happen to him."

❦

When Royce returned to The Rose and Thorn, he found Hadrian still seated at the same table, only he was no longer alone. Beside him sat a small figure hooded in a dark cloak. Hadrian sat comfortably. Either the person sitting next to him was safe, or he was too drunk to care.

"Take it up with Royce when he gets here," Hadrian was saying and looking up, added, "Ah! Perfect timing."

"Are you from—" Royce stopped as he sat down and saw the face beneath the hood.

"I do believe that is the first time I've ever surprised you, Royce," Princess Arista said.

"Oh no, that's not true," Hadrian said, chuckling. "You caught him way off guard when we were hanging in your dungeon and you asked us to kidnap your brother. That was *much* more unpredictable, trust me."

Royce was not pleased with meeting the princess in the open tavern room, and Hadrian was speaking far too loudly for his liking. Luckily, the room was empty. Most of the limited clientele preferred to cluster around the bar, where the door hung open to admit the cool summer breeze.

"That seems a lifetime ago," Arista replied thoughtfully.

"She has a job for you, Royce," Hadrian told him.

"For *us*, you mean."

"I told you." Hadrian looked at him but allowed a glance at the princess as well. "I'm retired."

Royce ignored him. "What's been decided?"

"Alric wants to make contact with Gaunt and his Nationalists," Arista began. "He feels, as the rest of us do, that if we can coordinate our efforts, we can create a formidable assault. Also, an alliance with the Nationalists could very well be the advantage we need to persuade Trent to enter the war on our side."

"That's fine," Royce replied. "I expected as much, but did you have to deliver this information yourself? Don't you trust your messengers?"

"One can never be too careful. Besides, I'm coming with you."

"What?" Royce asked, stunned.

Hadrian burst into laughter. "I knew you'd love that part," he said, grinning with the delight of a man blessed with immunity.

"I am the Ambassador of Melengar, and this is a diplomatic mission. Events are transpiring rapidly and negotiations may need to be altered to suit the situation. I've got to go because neither of you can speak for the kingdom. I can't trust anyone, not even you two, with such an important mission. This meeting will likely determine whether or not Melengar survives another year. I hope you understand the necessity of having me along."

Royce considered the proposal for a few minutes. "You and your brother understand that I cannot guarantee your safety?"

She nodded.

"You also understand that between now and the time we reach Gaunt, you'll be required to obey Hadrian and myself and you won't be provided any special treatment because of your station?"

"I expect none. However, it must also be understood that I'm Alric's representative and, as such, speak with his voice. So where safety and methods are concerned, you're granted authority, and I'll follow your direction, but as far as overall mission goals are concerned, I reserve the right to redirect or extend the mission if necessary."

"And do you also possess the power to guarantee additional payment for additional services?"

"I do."

"I now pronounce you client and escort," Hadrian said with a grin.

"As for you," Royce told him, "you'd better have some coffee."

"I'm not going, Royce."

"What's this all about?" Arista asked.

Royce scowled and shook his head at her.

"Don't shut her up," Hadrian said. He turned to the princess and added, "I've officially resigned from Riyria. We're divorced. Royce is single now."

"Really?" Arista said. "What will you do?"

"He's going to sober up and get his gear."

"Royce, listen to me. I mean it. I'm not going. There is nothing you can say to change my mind."

"Yes, there is."

"What, have you come up with another fancy philosophical argument? It's not going to work. I told you I'm done. It's over. I'm not kidding. I've had it." Hadrian watched his partner suspiciously.

Royce simply looked back with a smug expression. At last, Hadrian asked, "Okay, what is it? I'm curious now. What do you think you could possibly say to change my mind?"

Royce hesitated a moment, glancing uncomfortably at Arista, then sighed. "Because I'm asking you to—as a favor. After this mission, if you still feel the same way, I won't fight you and we can part as friends. But I'm asking you now—as my friend—to please come with me just one last time."

Just then, the barmaid arrived at the table.

"Another round?"

Hadrian did not look at her. He continued to stare at Royce, then sighed.

"Apparently not. I guess I'll take a cup of coffee, strong and black."

CHAPTER 5

SHERIDAN

Trapped in her long dress and riding cloak, Arista baked as the heat of summer arrived early in the day. Making matters worse, Royce insisted she travel with her hood up. She wondered at its value, as she guessed she was just as conspicuous riding so heavily bundled as she would be if riding naked. Her clothes stuck to her skin and it was difficult to breathe, but she said nothing.

Royce rode slightly ahead on his gray mare, which, to Arista's surprise, they called Mouse. A cute name — not at all what she had expected. As always, Royce was dressed in black and grays, seemingly oblivious to the heat. His eyes scanned the horizon and forest eaves. Perhaps his elven blood made him less susceptible to the hardships of weather. Even after finding out a year ago, she still marveled at his mixed race.

Why had I never noticed?

Hadrian followed half a length behind on her right — exactly where Hilfred used to position himself. It gave her a familiar feeling of safety and security. She glanced back at him and smiled under her hood. He was not immune to the heat. His brow was covered in sweat and his shirt clung to his chest. His collar lay open. His sleeves were rolled up, revealing strong arms.

A noticeable silence marked their travel. Perhaps it was the heat or a desire to avoid prying ears, but the lack of conversation denied her a natural venue to question their direction. After slipping out of Medford before sunrise, they had traveled north across fields and deer paths into the highlands before swinging east and catching the road. Arista understood the need for secrecy, and a roundabout course would help confuse any would-be spies, but instead of heading south, Royce led them north, which made no sense at all. She had held her tongue as hours had passed and they continued to ride out of Melengar and into Ghent. Arista was certain Royce took this route for a reason, and after she agreed to follow their leadership, it would be imprudent to question his judgment so early in their trip.

Arista was back in the high meadowlands where only the day before she had caught her first sight of the imperial troops gathered against Melengar. A flurry of activity was now under way on the far side of the Galewyr as the army packed up. Tents collapsed, wagons lined up, and masses of men started forming columns. She was fascinated by the sheer number and guessed there could be more imperial soldiers than citizens remaining in the city of Medford.

The meadowlands gave way to forest and the view disappeared behind the crest. The shade brought little relief from the heat.

If only it would rain.

The sky was overcast but rain was not certain. Arista knew, however, that it was possible to *make* it rain.

She recalled at least two ways. One involved an elaborate brewing of compounds and burning the mixture out of doors. This method should result in precipitation within a day but was not entirely reliable and failed more often than it succeeded. The other approach was more advanced and instantaneous, requiring great skill and knowledge. It could be accomplished with only hand movements, a focused mind, and words. The first technique she had learned as part of her studies at Sheridan University, where the entire class had attempted it without producing a single drop. The latter Esrahaddon had tried to teach her, but because the church had amputated his hands, he could not demonstrate the complex finger movements. This had always been the major obstacle in studying with him. Arista had nearly given up trying when one day, almost by accident, she made a guard sneeze.

Feeling the power of the Art for the first time had been an odd sensation, like flipping a tiny lever and sliding a gear into place. She had succeeded, not due to Esrahaddon's instructions, but rather because she had been fed up with him. To alleviate her boredom during a state dinner, Arista had been running Esrahaddon's instructions through her head. She purposely ignored his directions and instead tried something on her own. Doing so had felt easier, simpler. Discovering the right combination of movements and sounds had been like plucking the perfect note of music at exactly the right time.

That sneeze, and a short-lived curse placed on Countess Amril, had been her only magical successes during her apprenticeship with Esrahaddon. Arista had failed the rain spell hundreds of times. After her father had been murdered, she stopped attempting magic altogether. She had become too busy helping Alric with their kingdom to waste time on such childish games.

Arista glanced skyward and thought, *What else do I have to do?*

She recalled the instructions, and letting the reins hang limp on her horse's neck, she practiced the delicate weaving patterns in the air. The incantation she recalled easily enough, but the motions were all wrong. She could feel the awkwardness in the movements. There needed to be a pattern to the motion—a rhythm, a pace. She tried different variations and discovered she could tell which motions felt right and which felt wrong. The process was like fitting puzzle pieces together while blindfolded, or working out the notes of a melody by ear. She would simply guess at each note until, by sheer chance, she hit upon the right one. Then after adding it to the whole, she moved on to the next. Doing it this way was tedious, but it kept her mind occupied. She caught a curious glance from Hadrian, but she did not explain, nor did he ask.

Arista continued to work at the motions as the miles passed, until, mercifully, it began to rain on its own. She looked up so that the cool droplets hit her face and wondered if boredom had prompted her recollection of her magical studies, or if it was because they had steered off the Steward's Highway and were now on the road to Sheridan University.

Sheridan existed for the sons of merchants and scribes who needed to know mathematics and writing. Nobility rarely attended, and certainly not future rulers. Kings had no need for mathematics or philosophy. For that, he employed advisors. All he needed to know was the correct way to swing a sword, the proper tactics of military maneuvers, and the hearts of men. School could not teach these things. While it had been rare for a prince or a duke's son to attend the university, the thought of a princess going there was unheard of.

Arista had spent some of her happiest years within the sheltered valley of Sheridan. Here the world had opened up to her, and she had escaped the suffocating vacuum of courtly life. In Melengar her only purpose had been the same as the statues', an adornment for the castle halls. At Sheridan she could forget that she would eventually be a commodity—married for the benefit of the kingdom.

Arista's father had not been pleased with her abnormal interest in books, but he had never forbidden her from reading them. She had kept her habit discreet, which had caused her to spend more and more time alone. She had taken books from the scribe's collection and scrolls from the clergy. Most often she *borrowed* tomes from Bishop Saldur, who had left behind stacks of them after visits with her father. She had spent hours reading in the sanctuary of her tower, whisked away to far-off lands, where for a time she was happy. Books filled her head with ideas, thoughts of a larger world, of adventures beyond the halls, and the dream of a life lived bravely, heroically. Through these treasures she learned about Sheridan and later about Gutaria Prison.

Arista remembered the day she had asked her father for permission to attend the university. At first, he had adamantly refused and laughed, patting her head. She had cried herself to sleep, feeling trapped. All her ideas and ambitions sealed forever in a permanent prison. When her father had changed his mind the next day, it had never occurred to her to ask him why.

What are we doing here?

It irked her not knowing—patience was a virtue she still wrestled with. As they descended into the university's vale, she felt a modest inquiry would not hurt. She opened her mouth but Hadrian beat her to it.

"Why are we going to Sheridan?" he asked, trotting up closer to Royce.

"Information," Royce replied in his normal curt manner, which betrayed nothing else.

"It's your party. I'm just along for the ride."

No, no, no, she thought, *ask more*. Arista waited. Hadrian let his horse drift back. This was her opening. She had to say something. "Did you know I attended school there? You should speak to the master of lore, Arcadius. The chancellor is a pawn of the church, but Arcadius can be trusted. He's a wizard and used to be my professor. He'll know or be able to find out whatever it is you're interested in."

That was perfect. She straightened up in her saddle, pleased with herself. Common politeness would demand Royce reveal his intentions now that she had shown an interest, demonstrated some knowledge on the subject, and offered to help. She waited. Nothing. The silence returned.

I should have asked a question. Something to force him to respond. Damn.

Gritting her teeth, she slumped forward in frustration. Arista considered pressing further, but the moment had passed and now it would be difficult to say anything more without sounding critical. Being an ambassador had taught her the value of timing and of being conscious of other people's dignity and authority. Since she had been born a princess, it was a lesson not easily learned. She opted for silence, listening to the rain drum on her hood and the horses plod through the mud as they descended into the valley.

The stone statue of Glenmorgan, holding a book in one hand and a sword in the other, stood in the center of the university. Walkways, benches, trees, and flowers surrounded the statue on all sides, as did numerous school buildings. A growing enrollment had required the addition of several lecture halls and dormitories, each reflecting the architectural style of its time. In the gray sheets of rain, the university looked like a mirage, a whimsical, romantic dream conceived in the mind of a man who spent his entire life at war. That an institution of pure learning existed in a world of brutish ignorance was more than a dream; it was a miracle, a testament to the wisdom of Glenmorgan.

Glenmorgan had intended the school to educate laymen at a time when hardly anyone but ecclesiastics could read. Its success was unprecedented. Sheridan achieved eminence above every other seat of learning, winning the praises of patriarchs, kings, and sages. Early on, Sheridan also established itself as a center for lively controversy, with scholars involved in religious and political disputes. Handel of Roe, a master of Sheridan, had campaigned for Ghent's recognition of the newly established republic of Delgos against the wishes of the Nyphron Church. Also, the school had been decidedly pro-Royalist in the civil wars following the Steward's Reign. That had come to be an embarrassment to the church, which had retained control of Ghent. The humiliation led to the heresy trials of the three masters Cranston, Landoner, and Widley, all burned at the stake on the Sheridan commons. This quieted the school's political voice for more than a century, until Edmund Hall, professor of geometry and lore at Sheridan, claimed to use clues gleaned from ancient texts to locate the ruins of Percepliquis. He disappeared for a year and returned with books and tablets revealing arts and sciences long lost, spurring an interest in all things imperial. At this time, a greater orthodoxy had emerged within the church and it outlawed owning or obtaining holy relics, as all artifacts from the Old Empire had been deemed. They arrested Hall and locked him in Ervanon's Crown Tower along with his notes and maps. The church later declared that Hall had never found the city and that the books were clever fakes, but no one ever heard from Edmund Hall again.

The traditions of Cranston, Landoner, Widley, and Hall were embodied in the present master of lore—Arcadius

Vintarus Latimer. Arista's old magic teacher had never appeared to notice the boundaries of good taste, much less those of political or religious significance. Chancellor Lambert was the school's head, because the church found his political leanings satisfactory to the task, but Arcadius was Sheridan's undisputed heart and soul.

"Should I take you to Master Arcadius?" Arista asked as they left their horses in the charge of the stable warden. "He really is very smart and trustworthy."

Royce nodded and she promptly led them through the now driving rain into Glen Hall, as most students referred to the original Grand Imperial College building in deference to Glenmorgan. An elaborate cathedral-like edifice, it embodied much of the grandeur of the Steward's Reign that was sadly missing from the other university buildings. Neither Royce nor Hadrian said a word as they followed her up the stairs to the second floor, shaking the water from their travel cloaks and their hair. Inside it was quiet, the air stuffy and hot. Because several people could easily recognize her, Arista remained in the confines of her hood.

"So as you can see, it would be possible to turn lead into gold, but it would require more than the gold's resulting worth to make the transformation permanent, thus causing the process to be entirely futile, at least using this method."

Arista heard Arcadius's familiar voice booming as they approached the lecture hall.

"There are some, of course, who take advantage of the temporary transformation to dupe the unwary, creating a very realistic fool's gold that hours later reveals itself to be lead."

The lecture room was lined with tiers of seats, all filled with identically gowned students. At the podium stood the lore master, a thin elderly man with a blue robe, a white beard, and spectacles perched on the end of his nose.

"The danger here is that once the ruse has been discovered, the victim is often more than mildly unhappy about it." This comment drew laughter from the students. "Before you put too much thought into the idea of amassing a fortune based on illusionary gold, you should know that it's been tried. This crime—and it *is* a crime—usually results in the victim taking out his anger on the perpetrator of the hoax in the form of a rather unceremonious execution. This is why you don't see your master of lore, dressed in the finest silks from Vandon, traveling about in an eight-horse carriage with an entourage of retainers."

More laughter.

Arista was unclear whether the lecture was at an end or if Arcadius spotted the party on the rise and cut the class short. In any case, the lore master closed his instruction for the day with reminders about homework and dates of exams. As most of the students filed out, a few gathered around their professor with questions, which he patiently addressed.

"Give me a chance to introduce you," Arista said as they descended the tiers. "I know Arcadius looks a little...odd, but he's really very intelligent."

"And the frog exploded, didn't it?" the wizard was saying to a young man wearing a sober expression.

"Made quite a mess too, sir," his companion offered.

"Yes, they usually do," Arcadius said in a sympathetic tone.

The lad sighed. "I don't understand. I mixed the nitric acid, sulfuric acid, and the glycerin and fed it to him. He seemed fine. Just as you said in class, the blackmuck frog's stomach held the mixture, but then when he hopped..." The boy's shoulders slumped while his friend mimicked an explosion with his hands.

The lore master chuckled. "Next time, dissect the frog first and remove the stomach. There's a lot less chance of it jumping then. Now run along and clean up the library before Master Falquin gets back."

The two boys scampered off. Royce closed the door to the lecture hall after them, at which point the princess felt it was safe to remove her cloak.

"Princess Arista!" Arcadius exclaimed in delight, walking toward her with his arms wide. The two exchanged a fond embrace. "Your Highness, what a wonderful surprise! Let me look at you." He stepped back, still holding her hands. "A bit disheveled, soaking wet, and tracking mud into my classroom. How nice. It's as if you're a student here again."

"Master Arcadius," the princess began formally, "allow me to introduce Royce Melborn and Hadrian Blackwater. They have some questions for you."

"Oh?" he said, eyeing the two curiously. "This sounds serious."

"It is," Hadrian replied. He took a moment to search the room for any remaining students while Royce locked the doors.

Arista saw the puzzled expression on her instructor's face and explained, "You have to understand they're cautious people by trade."

"I can see that. So I'm to be interrogated, is that it?" Arcadius asked accusingly.

"No," she said. "I think they just want to ask a few questions."

"And if I don't answer? Will they beat me until I talk?"

"Of course not!"

"Are you so sure? You said that you *think* they're here to ask questions. But I think they're here to kill me, isn't that right?"

"The fact is you know too much," Royce told the wizard,

his tone abruptly turning vicious. He reached into his cloak and drew out his dagger as he advanced on the old man. "It's time we silenced you permanently."

"Royce!" Arista shouted in shock. She turned to Hadrian, who sat relaxed in the front row of the lecture hall, casually eating an apple plucked from the lore master's table. "Hadrian, do something," she pleaded.

The old man shuffled backward, trying to put more distance between him and Royce. Hadrian did not respond, eating the apple like a man without a worry in the world.

"Royce! Hadrian!" Arista screamed at them. She could not believe what she was seeing.

"Sorry, Princess," Hadrian finally said, "but this old man has caused us a great deal of trouble in the past, and Royce is not one to forgive debts easily. You might want to close your eyes."

"She should leave," Royce said. "Even if she doesn't see, she'll hear the screams."

"So you're not going to be quick?" the old man whispered.

Hadrian sighed. "I'm not cleaning the mess up this time."

"But you can't! I—I—" Arista stood frozen in terror.

Royce closed the distance between him and Arcadius in a sudden rush.

"Wait." The wizard's voice quavered as he held up a hand to ward him off. "I think I'm entitled to ask at least one question before I'm butchered."

"What is it?" Royce asked menacingly, his dagger raised and gleaming.

"How is your lovely Gwen doing?"

"She's fine," Royce replied, lowering his blade. "She told me to be certain to tell you she sends her love."

Arista glared at each of them. "But what—I—you know each other?"

Arcadius chuckled as Hadrian and Royce snickered sheepishly. "I'm sorry, my dear." The professor held up his hands and cringed slightly. "I just couldn't resist. An old man has so few opportunities to be whimsical. Yes, I've known these two surly characters for years. I knew Hadrian's father before Hadrian was born, and I met Royce when he was..." The lore master paused briefly. "Well, younger than he is today."

Hadrian took another bite of the apple and looked up at her. "Arcadius introduced me to Royce and gave us our first few jobs together."

"And you've been inseparable ever since." The wizard smiled. "It was a sound pairing. You have been a good influence on each other. Left on your own, the two of you would have fallen into ruin."

There was a noticeable exchange of glances between Royce and Hadrian. "You only say that because you don't know what we've been up to," Hadrian mentioned.

"Don't assume too much." Arcadius shook a menacing finger at him. "I keep tabs on you. So what brings you here?"

"Just a few questions I thought you would be able to shed some light on," Royce told him. "Why don't we talk in your study while Hadrian and Arista settle in and get out of their wet things? Is it all right if we spend the night here?"

"Certainly. I'll have dinner brought up, although you picked a bad day; the kitchen is serving meat pies." He made a grimace.

Arista stood stiffly, feeling her heart still racing. She narrowed her eyes and glared. "I hate all of you."

❧

Barrels, bottles, flasks, exotic instruments, jars containing bits of animals swimming in foul-smelling liquids, and a vast array of other oddities cluttered the small office and spilled out into the hallway. Shelves of web-covered books lined the walls. Aquariums displayed living reptiles and fish. Cages stacked to the ceiling housed pigeons, mice, moles, raccoons, and rabbits, filling the cramped office with the sounds of chirps, chatters, and squeaks, which accompanied the musky scent of books, beeswax, spices, and animal dung.

"You cleaned up," Royce said with feigned surprise as he carefully entered and stepped around the books and boxes scattered on the floor.

"Quiet, you," the wizard scolded, looking over the top of his glasses, which rested at the end of his nose. "You hardly ever visit anymore, and you don't need to be impertinent when you do."

Royce closed the door and slid the bolt, which drew another look from the wizard. Then from his cloak he pulled out a silver amulet hanging from a thin chain. "What can you tell me about this?"

Arcadius took the jewelry from him and moved to his desk, where he held it near the flame of a candle. He looked at it only briefly, then lifted his spectacles. "This is Hadrian's medallion. The one his father gave him when he turned thirteen. Are you trying to test me for senility?"

"Did you know Esrahaddon made it?"

"Did he?"

"Remember when I spoke with him in Dahlgren last summer? I didn't mention it before, but according to him, the church instigated a coup against the emperor nine hundred years ago. He insists that he remained loyal and made two amulets. One he gave to the emperor's son and the other to the boy's bodyguard. He claimed to have sent them into hiding while he stayed behind. These amulets are supposed to be enchanted so only Esrahaddon could find them. When Arista and I were with him in Avempartha, he conjured images of the people wearing his necklaces.

"And you saw Hadrian?"

Royce nodded.

"As the guardian or the heir?"

"Guardian."

"And the heir?"

"Blond hair, blue eyes, no one I recognized."

"I see," Arcadius said. "But you haven't told Hadrian what you saw."

"What makes you say that?"

The wizard let the amulet and the chain fall into his palm. "You're here alone."

Royce nodded. "Hadrian's been moody lately. If I tell him, he'll want to fulfill his destiny—go find this long-lost heir and be his whipping boy. He won't even question it, because he'll want it to be true, but I don't think it is. I think Esrahaddon is up to something. I don't want either of us to be pawns in his effort to bring his choice for emperor to the throne."

"You think Esrahaddon is lying? That he conjured false images to manipulate you?"

"That's what I came here to find out. Is it even possible to make enchanted amulets? If so, is it possible to locate the wearers by magic? And you knew Hadrian's father. Did he ever say anything to you about being the guardian to the Heir of Novron?"

Arcadius turned the amulet over in his hand. "*I* don't have the Art to enchant objects to resist magic, nor can I use magic to seek people, but a lot was lost when the Old Empire crumbled. Preserving him in that prison for nearly a thousand years makes Esrahaddon unique in his knowledge, so I can't intelligently say what he is or isn't capable of. As for Danbury Blackwater, I don't recall him ever telling me he was the

Guardian of the Heir. That isn't the kind of thing I would likely forget."

"So I'm right. This is all a lie."

"It may not be a lie, per se. You realize it's possible—even likely—that Danbury could have the amulet and not be anyone special. Nine hundred years is a long time to expect an heirloom to stay in the possession of one family. The odds are weighed heavily against it. Personal effects are lost every day. This is made of silver, and a poor man, in a moment of desperation and convinced any story he was told is just a myth, could be tempted to sell it for food. Moreover, what should happen if the owner died—killed in an accident—and this medallion was taken from the dead body and sold? This has likely passed through hundreds of hands before ever reaching Danbury. If what you say is true, Esrahaddon's incantation merely revealed the wearer of the amulet and not the identity of the original owner's descendants. So it's possible Esrahaddon may be sincere and still be wrong.

"Even if Danbury was the descendant of the last Teshlor, he might not have known any more than Hadrian does. His father, or his father before him, could have failed to mention it because it didn't matter anymore. The line of the heir may have died out, or the two became separated centuries ago."

"Is that what you think?"

Arcadius took off his glasses and wiped them.

"For centuries people have searched for the descendants of Emperor Nareion and no one has ever found them. The empire itself searched for Nareion's son, Nevrik, with all the power of great wizards and questing knights at a time when they could identify him by sight. They failed—unless you accept the recent declaration that they found the heir in the form of this farm girl from Dahlgren."

"Thrace is not the heir," Royce said simply. "The church

orchestrated that whole incident as theatrics to anoint their choice for ruler. They botched the job and she accidently caught the prize."

The wizard nodded. "So I think common sense decrees that an heir no longer exists...if he ever existed to begin with. Unless..." He trailed off.

"Unless what?"

"Nothing." Arcadius shook his head.

Royce intensified his stare until the wizard relented.

"Just supposition, really, but, well...it just seems too romantic that the heir and a bodyguard could have lived all alone on the run for so long, managing to hide while the entire world hunted them."

"What are you suggesting?" Royce asked.

"After the emperor's death, when Nevrik fled with his bodyguard, the Teshlor Jerish, wouldn't they have had friends? Wouldn't there have been hundreds of people loyal to the emperor's son willing to help conceal him? Support him? Organize an attempt to put him back on the throne? Of course this organization would have to act in secrecy, given that the bulk of the dying empire was in control of the church."

"Are you saying such a group exists?" Royce asked.

Arcadius shrugged. "I'm only speculating here."

"You're doing more than just speculating. What do you know?"

"Well, I've come across some odd references in various texts to a group known only as the Theorem Eldership. I first discovered them in a bit of historical text from 2465, about the time of the Steward's Reign of Glenmorgan the Second. Some priest made a brief notation about a sect by that name. Of course, at that time, anyone who opposed the church was considered heretical, so I didn't give it much thought. Then I spotted another reference to the same group in a very old letter sent from Lord Darius Seret to Patriarch Venlin dating back to within the first twenty years after the death of Emperor Nareion."

"Lord Seret?" Royce asked. "As in, Seret Knights?"

"Indeed," Arcadius said. "The duke was commanded by the Patriarch to locate the whereabouts of Nevrik, Emperor Nareion's missing son. He formed an elite band of knights who swore an oath to find the heir. A hundred years after the death of Darius the knights adopted their official name, the Order of Seret Knights, which was later shortened out of convenience. Quite ironic, actually, as their responsibilities and influence broadened dramatically. You would hardly know it, as the seret work mostly in secret—hidden so they can perform their duties invisibly. They still report directly to the Patriarch. It's really just a matter of perceptive logic. Given that there is a pseudo-invisible order of knights seeking to hunt down the heir, doesn't it seem sensible to conclude that there is another unseen group to protect him?"

Arcadius stood up and, with no trouble navigating his way through the room's debris, reached the far wall. There a slate hung and with a bit of chalk he wrote:

Theorem Eldership

Then he crossed out each letter and underneath wrote:

Shield the Emperor

He returned to his desk and sat back down.

"If you decide to search for the heir," Arcadius told Royce in a grave tone, "be very careful. This is not some bit of jewelry you seek and he may be protected and hunted by men who will sacrifice their lives and use any means against you. If any of this is true, then I fear you'll be entering into a world of shadows and lies where a silent, secret war has been waging for nearly a thousand years. There will be no honor and no quarter given. It's a place where people disappear without a trace and martyrs thrive. No price will be too great, no sacrifice too awful. What's at stake in this struggle—at least in their eyes—is the very future of Elan."

❧

The number of students at Sheridan always diminished in summer, so Arcadius arranged for them to sleep in the vacated top floor, known as Glen's Attic. The fourth-floor dormitory in Glen Hall lacked even a single window and was oven hot in summer. Home to the sons of affluent farmers, the upper dorm was deserted this time of year, as students returned home to tend crops. This left the entire loft to them, a single long room with a slanted ceiling so low even Arista had to watch her head or risk hitting a rafter. Cots jutted out from the wall where the ceiling met the floor, each nothing more than a straw mattress on simple wooden frames. Personal belongings were absent, but every inch of wood was etched with a mosaic of names, phrases, or drawings—seven centuries of student memoirs.

Arista and Hadrian worked at drying their wet gear. They laid everything made of cloth across the floor, and damp stains spread across the ancient timbers. Everything was soaked, and smelled of horse.

"I'll get a drying line up," Hadrian told her. "We can use the blankets to create a bit of privacy for you at the same time." He gave her a quizzical look.

"What?"

He shook his head. "I've just never seen a soaking-wet

princess before. You sure you want to do this? It's not too late. We can still head back to Medford and—"

"I'll be fine." She headed for the stairs.

"Where are you going?"

"To bring up the rest of the bags."

"It's probably still raining and I can get those just as soon—"

Arista interrupted him. "You have ropes to tie and, as you pointed out, I'm already soaked." She descended the steps. Her shoes squished and her wet dress hung with added weight.

No one thinks I can handle this.

Arista knew she had led a pampered life. She was no fool, but neither was she made of porcelain.

How much fortitude does it take to live like a peasant?

She was the Princess of Melengar and daughter of King Amrath Essendon—she could rise to any occasion. They all had her so well defined, but she was not like Lenare Pickering. She did not sit all day considering which dress went best with her golden locks. Arista stroked her still dripping head and felt her flat tangled hair. Lenare would have fainted by now.

Outside, the rain had stopped, which left the air filled with the earthy smell of grass, mud, and worms. Everything glistened, and breezes touched off showers beneath trees. Arista had forgotten her cloak. It lay four flights up. She was going only a short distance and would be quick, but by the time she reached the carriage house, she regretted her decision. Three gown-draped students stood in the shadows, talking about the new horses.

"They're from Melengar," the tallest said with the confident, superior tone of a young noble speaking to lesser men. "You can tell by the Medford brand on that one."

"So, Lane, you think Melengar has fallen already?" the shortest of them asked.

"Of course. I'll wager Breckton took it last night or maybe early this morning. That's why the owners of these horses are here. They're probably refugees, cowards fleeing like rats from a sinking ship."

"Deserters?"

"Maybe," Lane replied.

"If Melengar really did fall last night, it might have been the king himself who fled," the short one speculated.

"Don't be a rube!" the second tallest told him. "A king would never ride on nags like these."

"Don't be too sure about that." Lane came to the little one's defense. "Alric isn't much of a *real* king. They say he and his witch sister killed their father and stole the throne just as he was about to name Percy Braga his successor. I even heard that Alric has taken his sister as his mistress, and there's talk of her becoming queen."

"That's disgusting!"

"The church would never allow that," said the other.

"Alric kicked the church out of Melengar months ago because he knew it would try to stop him," Lane explained. "You have to understand that the Melengarians aren't civilized people. They're still mostly barbarians and slip further back into their tribal roots every year. Without the church to watch over them, they'll be drinking the blood of virgins and praying to Uberlin before the year is out. They allow elves to run free in their cities, for Maribor's sake. Did you know that?"

Arista could not see their faces as she stood beyond the doorway, carefully keeping herself hidden.

"So perhaps this *is* the nag the king of Melengar escaped on. He could be staying in one of the dorm rooms right now, plotting his next move."

"Do you think Chancellor Lambert knows?"

"I doubt it," Lane replied. "I don't think a good man like Lambert would allow a menace like Alric to stay here."

"Should we tell him?"

"Why don't you tell him, Hinkle?" Lane said to the short fellow.

"Why me? You should do it. After all, you're the one that noticed them."

"Me? I don't have time. Lady Chastelin sent me another letter today and I need to work on my reply lest she drives a dagger into her chest for fear I've forgotten her."

"Don't look at me," said the remaining one. "I'll admit it — Lambert scares me."

The others laughed.

"No, I'm serious. He scares the wax out of me. I was sent to his office last semester because of that rabid rat stunt Jason pulled. I'd rather he'd just cane me."

Together they walked off, continuing their chatter, which drifted to Lady Chastelin and doubts of her devotion to Lane.

Arista waited a moment until she was certain they were gone, then found the bags near the saddles and stuffed one under her arm. She grabbed the other two and quickly, but carefully, returned across the commons and slipped back up the stairs of Glen Hall.

Hadrian was not in the loft when she returned, but he had the lines up and blankets hanging from them to divide the room. She slipped through the makeshift curtain and began the miserable task of stringing out her wet things. She changed into her nightgown and robe. They had been near the center of her bag and only slightly damp. Then she began throwing the rest of her clothes over the lines. Hadrian returned with a bucket of water and paused when he spotted Arista brazenly hanging her petticoats and corset. She felt her face flush as she imagined what he was thinking. Not only did she travel unescorted with two men, but she was bedding down in the same room—albeit a large and segmented hall—and now she hung her undergarments for them to see. She was surprised they had not questioned her more intently. She knew the unusual circumstances she traveled under would eventually come up. Royce was not the type to miss something as suspicious as a maiden princess traveling alone in the company of two rogues, no matter how highly esteemed by the crown. As for her clothes, there was no other way or place to dry them safely, so it was this or wear them wet in the morning. There was no sense being prissy about it.

Royce entered the dorm as she finished her work. He was wearing his cloak with the hood up. It dripped a puddle on the floor.

"We'll be leaving well before dawn," he pronounced.

"Is something wrong?" Hadrian asked.

"I found a few students snooping around the carriage house when I made my rounds."

"He does that," Hadrian explained to Arista. "Sort of an obsession he has. Can't sleep otherwise."

"You were there?" she asked.

Royce nodded. "They won't be troubling us anymore."

Arista felt the blood drain from her face. "You...you killed them?" she asked in a whisper. As she said it, she felt sick. A few minutes earlier, listening to their horrible discussion, she had found herself wishing them harm, but she had not meant it. They were little more than children. She knew, however, that Royce might not see it that way. She had come to realize that for him, a threat was a threat no matter the package.

"I considered it." No tone of sarcasm tempered his words. "If they had turned left toward the chancellor's residence, instead of right toward the dormitories...But they didn't. They went straight to their rooms. Nevertheless, we'll not be waiting until morning. We'll be leaving in a few hours. That way even if they do start a rumor about horses from Melengar, we'll be long gone by the time it reaches the right ears. The empire's spies will assume we're heading to Trent to beg their aid. We'll need to get you a new mount, though, before heading to Colnora."

"If we're leaving as soon as that, I should go see Arcadius about that meal he promised," Hadrian said.

"No!" Arista told him hastily. They looked at her, surprised. She smiled, embarrassed by her outburst. "I'll go. It will give you two a chance to change out of your wet things without me here." Before they could say anything, she slipped out and down the hallway to the stairs.

It had been nearly a year since that morning on the bank of the Nidwalden River when Esrahaddon had put a question in her head. The wizard had admitted using her to orchestrate the murder of her father to facilitate his escape, but he had also suggested there was more to the story. This could be her only chance to speak with Arcadius. She took a right at the bottom of the stairs and hurried to his study.

Arcadius sat on a stool at a small wooden desk on the far side of the room, studying a page of a massive tome. Beside him was a brazier of hot coals and an odd contraption she had never seen before—a brown liquid hung suspended above the heat of the brazier in a glass vial as a steady stream of bubbles rose from a small stone immersed in the liquid. The steamy vapors rose through a series of glass tubes and passed through another glass container, filled with salt crystals. From the end of that tube, a clear fluid slowly dripped into a small flask. A yellow liquid also hung suspended above the flask, and through a valve one yellow drop fell for each clear one. As these two liquids mixed, white smoke silently rose into the air. Occasionally he adjusted a valve, added salt, or pumped bellows, causing the charcoal to glow red hot. At her entrance, Arcadius looked up.

He removed his glasses, wiped them with a rag from the desk, and put them back on. He peered at her through squinting eyes.

"Ah, my dear, come in." Then, as if remembering something important, he hastily twisted one of the valves. A large puff of smoke billowed up, causing several of the animals in the room to chatter. The stone fell to the bottom of the vial, where it lay quietly. The animals calmed down, and the elderly master of lore turned and smiled at Arista, motioning for her to join him.

This was no easy feat. Arista searched for open floor to step on and, finding little, grabbed the hem of her robe and opted to step on the sturdiest-looking objects in the shortest path to the desk.

The wizard waited patiently with a cheery smile, his high rosy cheeks causing the edges of his eyes to wrinkle like a bedsheet held in a fist.

"You know," he began as she made the perilous crossing, "I always find it interesting what paths my students take to reach me. Some are direct, while others take more of a roundabout approach. Some end up getting lost in the clutter and others find the journey too much trouble and give up altogether without even reaching me."

Arista was certain he implied more than he said, but she had neither the time nor the inclination to explore it further. Instead, she replied, "Perhaps if you straightened up a bit, you wouldn't lose so many students."

The wizard tilted his head. "I suppose you're right, but where would be the fun in that?"

Arista stepped over the rabbit cage, around the large pestle and mortar, and stood before the desk on a closed cover of a book no less than three feet in height and two in width.

The lore master looked down at her feet, pursed his lips, and nodded his approval. "That's Glenmorgan the Second's biography, easily seven hundred years old."

Arista looked alarmed.

"Not to worry, not to worry," he told her, chuckling to himself. "It's a terrible book written by church propagandists. The perfect platform for you to stand on, don't you think?"

Arista opened her mouth, thought about what she was going to say, and then closed it again.

The wizard chuckled once more. "Ah yes, they've gone and made an ambassador out of you, haven't they? You've learned to think before you speak. I suppose that's good. Now tell me, what brings you to my office at this hour? If it's about dinner, I apologize for the delay, but the stoves were out and I needed to fetch a boy to get them fired again. I also had to drag the cook away from a card game, which he wasn't at all pleased about. But a meal is being prepared as we speak and I'll have it brought up the moment it is finished."

"It's not that, Master—"

He put up a hand to stop her. "You are no longer a student here. You are a princess and Ambassador of Melengar. If you call me Arcadius, I won't call you Your Highness, agreed?" The grin of his was just too infectious to fight. She nodded and smiled in return.

"Arcadius," she began again, "I've had something on my mind and I've been meaning to visit you for some time, but so much has been happening. First there was Fanen's funeral. Then, of course, Tomas arrived in Melengar."

"Oh yes, the Wandering Deacon of Dahlgren. He came here as well, preaching that a young girl named Thrace is the

Heir of Novron. He sounded very sincere. Even I was inclined to believe him."

"A lot of people did and that's part of the reason Melengar's fate is so precarious now."

Arista stopped. There was someone at the door—a pretty girl, perhaps six years old. Long dark hair spilled over her shoulders, and her hands were clasped together, holding a length of thin rope that she played with, spinning it in circles.

"Ah, there you are. Good," the wizard told the girl, who stared apprehensively at Arista. "I was hoping you'd turn up soon. He's starting to cause a fuss. It's as if he can tell time." Arcadius glanced at Arista. "Oh, forgive me. I neglected to introduce you. Arista, this is Mercy."

"How do you do?" Arista asked.

The little girl said nothing.

"You must forgive her. She's a bit shy with strangers."

"A bit young for Sheridan, isn't she?"

Arcadius smiled. "Mercy is my ward. Her mother asked me to watch over her for a while until her situation improved. Until then I try my best to educate her, but as I learned with you, young ladies can be most willful." He turned to the girl. "Go right ahead, dear. Take Mr. Rings outside with you before he rips up his cage again."

The girl moved across the room's debris as nimbly as a cat and removed a thin raccoon from his cage. He was a baby by the look of it, and she carried him out the door, giggling as Mr. Rings sniffed her ear.

"She's cute," Arista said.

"Indeed she is. Now, you said you had something on your mind?"

Arista nodded and considered her words. The question Esrahaddon had planted she now presented to her old teacher. "Arcadius, who approved my entrance into Sheridan?"

The lore master raised a bristled eyebrow. "Ah," he said. "You know, I always wondered why you never asked before. You are perhaps the only female to attend Sheridan University in its seven-hundred-year history, and certainly the only one to study the arcane arts at all, but you never questioned it once."

Arista's posture tightened. "I'm questioning it now."

"Indeed...indeed," the wizard replied. He sat back, removed his glasses, and rubbed his nose briefly. "I was visited by Chancellor Ignatius Lambert, and asked if I would be willing to accept a gifted young lady into my instructions on arcane theory. This surprised me. You see, I didn't teach a class on arcane theory. I had wanted to, and I requested to have it added to the curriculum on many occasions, but I was always turned down by the school's patrons. It seemed they didn't feel that teaching magic was a respectable pursuit. Magic uses power not connected to a spiritual devotion to Maribor and Novron. At best, it was subversive and possibly outright evil in their minds. The fact that I practiced the arcane arts at all has always been an embarrassment."

"Why haven't they replaced you?"

"It could be that my reputation as the most learned wizard in Avryn lends such prestige to this school that they allow me my hobbies. Or it may be that anyone who has tried to force my resignation has been turned into the various toads, squirrels, and rabbits you see about you."

He appeared so serious that Arista looked around the room at the various cages and aquariums, at which point the wizard began to chuckle.

She scowled at him—which only made him laugh harder.

"As I was saying," Arcadius went on once he regained control of himself, "Ignatius was in one sentence offering me my desire to teach magic if I was willing to accept you as a student.

Perhaps he thought I would refuse. Little did he know that unlike the rest of them, I harbor no prejudices concerning women. Knowledge is knowledge, and the chance to instruct and enlighten a princess—a potential leader—with the power to help shape the world around us was not a deterrent at all. On the contrary, I saw it as a bonus."

"So you're saying I was allowed entrance because of a plan of the school's headmaster that backfired?"

"Not at all. That is merely how it happened, not why. *Why* is a much more important question. You see, School Chancellor Ignatius Lambert was not alone in my office that morning. With him was another man. He remained silent and stood over there, just behind and to the left of you, where the birdcage is now. The cage wasn't there then, of course. Instead, he chose to stand on a discarded old coat and a dagger. As I mentioned, it's always interesting to see the paths people take when they enter this office, and where they choose to stand."

"Who was he?"

"Percy Braga, the Archduke of Melengar."

"So it *was* Uncle Percy."

"He certainly was involved, but even an archduke of Melengar wasn't likely to have influence over those running Sheridan University, especially on a matter as volatile as teaching magic to young noble ladies. Sheridan is in the ecclesiastical realm of Ghent, where secular lords have no sway. There was, however, another man with them. He never entered my office but stood in the doorway, in the shadows."

"Could you tell who it was?"

"Oh yes." Arcadius smiled. "These are reading glasses, my dear. I can see long distances just fine, but then, I can see that is a common mistake people make."

"Who was it, then?"

"A close friend of your family, I believe. Bishop Maurice Saldur of Medford's Mares Cathedral, but you probably already knew that, didn't you?"

∽

Good to his word, Arcadius sent steaming meat pies and red wine. Arista recalled the pies from her days as a student. They were never very good, even when fresh. Usually they were made from the worst cuts of pork, because the school saved lamb for the holidays. The pies were heavy on onions and carrots and thin on gravy and meat. Students actually gambled on how many paltry shreds of pork they would find in their pies—a mere five stood as the record. Despite their complaints, the other students wolfed down their meals, but she never had. Most of the other students' indignation she guessed was only bluster—they likely ate no better at home. Arista, however, was accustomed to three or four different meats roasted on the bone, several varieties of cheese, freshly baked breads, and whatever fruits were in season. To get her through the week, she had servants bring deliveries from home, which she had kept in her room.

"You could have mentioned that you knew Arcadius," Arista told them as they sat down together at the common table, an old bit of furniture defaced like everything else. It wobbled enough to make her glad the wine was in a jug with cups instead of a bottle and stemmed glasses.

"And ruin the fun?" Hadrian replied with a handsome grin. "So Arcadius was your professor?"

"One of them. The curriculum requires you to take several classes, learning different subjects from the various teachers. Master Arcadius was my favorite. He was the only one to teach magic."

"So you learned magic from Arcadius as well as Esrahaddon?" Royce asked, digging into his pie.

Arista nodded, poking her pie with a knife and letting the steam out.

"That must have been interesting. I'm guessing their teaching styles were a bit different."

"Like night and day." She took a sip of wine. "Arcadius was formal in his lessons. He followed a structured course, using books and lecturing very professorially, like you saw this evening. His style made the lessons seem right and proper, despite the stigma associated with them. Esrahaddon was haphazard, and he seemed to teach whatever came to his mind. Oftentimes he had trouble explaining things. Arcadius is clearly the better teacher, but..." She paused.

"But?" Royce asked.

"Well, don't tell Arcadius," she said conspiratorially, "but Esrahaddon seems to be the more skilled and knowledgeable. Arcadius is the expert on the history of magic, but Esrahaddon *is* the history, if you follow me."

She took a bite of pie and got a mouthful of onions and burnt crust.

"Having learned from both, doesn't that make you the third most skilled mage in Avryn?"

Arista smirked bitterly and washed the mouthful down with more wine. While she suspected Royce was correct, she had cast only two spells since leaving their tutelage.

"Arcadius taught me many important lessons. Yet his classes concerned themselves with using knowledge as a means to broaden his students' understanding of their world. It's his way of getting us to think in new directions, to perceive what is around us in terms that are more sensible. Of course, this didn't make his students happy. We all wanted the secrets to power, the tools to reshape the world to our liking. Arcadius doesn't really give answers, but rather forces his students to ask questions.

"For instance, he once asked us what makes noble blood different from a commoner's blood. We pricked our fingers and ran tests, and as it turns out, there is no detectable difference. This led to a fight on the commons between a wealthy merchant's son and the son of a low-ranking baron. Master Arcadius was reprimanded and the merchant's son was whipped."

Hadrian finished eating, and Royce was more than halfway through his pie, but he had left his wine untouched after grimacing with the first sip. Arista chanced another bite and caught a mushy carrot, still more onions, and a soggy bit of crust. She swallowed with a sour look.

"Not a fan of meat pie?" Hadrian asked.

She shook her head. "You can have it if you like." She slid it over.

"So how was studying with Esrahaddon?"

"He was a completely different story," she went on after another mouthful of wine. "When I couldn't get what I wanted from Arcadius, I went to him. You see, all of Arcadius's teachings involved elaborate preparations, alchemic recipes that are used to trigger the release of nature's powers and incantations to focus it. He also stressed observation and experimentation to tap the power of the natural world. Arcadius relied on manual techniques to derive power from the elements, but Esrahaddon explained how the same energy could be summoned through more subtle enticement, using only motion, harmonic sound, and the power of the mind.

"The problem was Esrahaddon's technique relied on hand movements, which explains why the church cut his off. He tried to talk me through the motions, but without the ability to demonstrate, it was very frustrating. Subtle differences can separate success from failure, so learning from him was hopeless. All I ever managed to do was make a man sneeze. Oh, and once I cursed Countess Amril with boils." Hadrian poured the last of the wine into his and Arista's cups after Royce waved him off. "Arcadius was angry when he found out about the curse and lectured me for hours. He was always against using magic for personal gain or for the betterment of just a few. He often said, 'Don't waste energy to treat a single plague victim; instead, search to eliminate the illness and save thousands.'

"So yes, you're right. I'm likely the most tutored mage in all of Avryn, but that's really not saying much. I would be hard-pressed to do much more than tickle someone's nose."

"And you can do that just with hand movements?" Royce asked skeptically.

"Would you like a demonstration?"

"Sure, try it on Hadrian."

"Ah no, let's not," Hadrian protested. "I don't want to be accidently turned into a toad or rabbit or something. Didn't you learn anything else?"

"Well, he tried to teach me how to boil water, but I never got it to work. I would get close, but there was always something missing. He used to..." She trailed off.

"What?" Hadrian asked.

She shrugged. "I don't know. It's just that I was practicing gestures on the ride here and I—" She squinted in concentration as she ran through the sequence in her mind. They should be similar. Both the rain and the boiling spell used the same element—water. The same motion should be found in each. Just thinking about it made her heart quicken.

That is it, isn't it? That is the missing piece. If I have the rest of the spell correct, then all I need to do is...

Looking around for the bucket that Hadrian had brought up, she closed her eyes and took several deep breaths. Boiling water, while harder than making a person sneeze, took a short, simple incantation, one she had attempted without success hundreds of times. She cleared her mind, relaxed, then reached out, sensing the room—the light and heat emanating from the candles, the force of the wind blowing above the roof, the dripping of water from their wet clothes. She opened her eyes and focused on the bucket and the water inside. Lukewarm, it lay quiet, sleeping. She felt its place in the world, part of the whole, waiting for a change, wanting to please.

Arista began to hum, letting the sounds follow the rhythm that spoke to the water. She sensed its attention. Her voice rose, speaking the few short words in a melody of a song. She raised a single hand and made the motions, only this time she added a simple sweep of her thumb. It felt perfect—the hole that evaded her in the past. She closed her hand into a fist and squeezed. The moment she did, she could feel the heat, and across the room steam rose.

Hadrian stood up, took two steps, and then stopped. "It's bubbling," he said, his voice expressing his amazement.

"Yeah, and so are our clothes." Royce pointed to the pieces of wet clothing hanging on the line, which were beginning to hiss as steam rose from them.

"Oops." Arista opened her hand abruptly. The wash water stopped boiling and the clothes quieted.

"By Mar, that's unbelievable." Hadrian stood grinning. "You really did it."

Royce remained silent, staring at the steaming clothes.

"I know. Can you believe it?" she said.

"What else can you do?"

"Let's not find out," Royce interrupted. "It's getting late and we'll be leaving in a few hours, so we should get to sleep."

"Killjoy," Hadrian replied. "But he's probably right. Let's turn in."

Arista nodded, walked behind the wall of blankets, and only then allowed herself a smile.

It worked! It really worked.

Lying on the little cot without bothering with a blanket, she stared at the ceiling and listened to the thieves moving about.

"You have to admit that was impressive," she heard Hadrian say.

If Royce made a reply, she did not hear it. She had frightened him. The expression on his face had said more than words ever could. Lying there, looking up at the rafters, she realized she had seen that look before—the day Arcadius had reprimanded her. She had been leaving his office when he had stopped her. "I never taught curses in this class, boils or otherwise. Did you cause them by mixing a draft that she drank?"

"No," she recalled saying. "It was a verbal curse."

His eyes widened and his mouth gaped, but he said nothing more. At the time, she had thought his look was one of amazement and pride in a student exceeding expectations. Looking back, Arista realized she had seen only what she had wanted to see.

Chapter 6

The Word

As Amilia watched, the playful flicker of candlelight caught the attention of the empress, which briefly replaced her blank stare.

Is that a sign?

Amilia often played this game with herself, looking for any improvement. A month had passed since Saldur had summoned her to his office to explain her duties. She knew she could never do half of what he wanted, but his main concern was the empress's health, and Amilia was doing well in that regard. Even in this faint light, she could see the change. Modina's cheeks were no longer hollow, her skin no longer stretched. The empress was now eating some vegetables and even bits of meat hidden in the soup. Still, Amilia feared the progress would not be good enough.

Modina still had not said a word—at least, not while awake. Often when the empress slept, she mumbled, moaned, and tossed about restlessly. Upon awakening, the girl cried, tears running down her cheeks. Amilia held her, stroked her hair, and tried to keep her warm, but the empress did not seem to notice her presence.

To pass the time, Amilia continued to tell Modina stories,

hoping it might prompt her into speaking, perhaps to ask a question. After telling her everything she could think of about her family, she moved on to fairy tales from her childhood. There was Gronbach, the evil dwarf who kidnapped a milk-maid and imprisoned her in his subterranean lair. The maiden solved the riddle of the three boxes, snipped off his beard, and escaped.

She even recounted scary stories told by her brothers in the dark of the carriage workshop. She knew they had been pur-posefully trying to frighten her, and even now the tales gave Amilia chills. But anything was worth a try to snap Modina back to the land of the living. The most disturbing of these were about elves, who put their victims to sleep with music before eating them.

When she ran out of fairy tales, she turned to stories she remembered from church, like the epic tale of how, in their hour of greatest need, Maribor sent the divine Novron to save mankind. Wielding the wondrous Rhelacan, he defeated the elves.

Thinking Modina would like the similarities to her own life, Amilia told the romantic account of the farmer's daughter Persephone, whom Novron took to be his queen. When she refused to leave her simple village, he built the great imperial capital right there and named the city Percepliquis after her.

"So what story shall we have this evening?" Amilia asked as the two girls lay across from each other, bathed in the light of the candles. "How about *Kile and the White Feather*? Our monsignor used it from time to time when he wanted to make a point about penance and redemption. Have you heard that one? Do you like it? I do.

"Well, you see, the father of the gods, Erebus, had three sons: Ferrol, Drome, and Maribor; the gods of elves, dwarves, and men. He also had a daughter, Muriel, who was the loveliest being ever created, and she held dominion over all the plants and animals. Well, one night Erebus became drunk and raped his own daughter. In anger, her brothers attacked their father and tried to kill him, but of course, gods can't die."

Amilia saw the candles flicker from a draft. It was always colder at night, and she got up and brought them each another blanket.

"So, where was I?"

Modina merely blinked.

"Oh, I remember, racked with guilt and grief, Erebus returned to Muriel and begged for her forgiveness. She was moved by her father's remorse but still could not look at him. He pleaded for her to name a punishment. Muriel needed time to let the fear and pain pass, so she told him, 'Go to Elan to live. Not as a god, but as a man, to learn humility.' To repent for his misdeeds, she charged him to do good works. Erebus did as she requested and took the name of Kile. It's said that he walks the world of men to this day, working miracles. For each act that pleases her, she bestows a white feather to him from her magnificent robe, which he places in a pouch kept forever by his side. On the day when all the feathers have been awarded, Muriel promised to call her father home and forgive him. The legend says that when the gods are reunited, all will be made right, and the world will transform into a paradise."

This really was one of Amilia's favorite stories and she told it hoping for miraculous results. Perhaps the father of the gods would hear her and come to their aid. Amilia waited. Nothing happened. The walls were the same cold stone, the flickering flames the only light. She sighed. "Well, maybe we'll just have to make our own miracles," she told Modina as she blew out all but a single candle, then closed her eyes to sleep.

៚

Amilia woke with a newfound purpose. She resolved to free Modina from her room, if only for a short while. The cell reeked of the scent of urine and mildew, which lingered even after scrubbing and fresh straw. She wanted to take Modina outside but knew that would be asking too much. Amilia tried to convince herself that Lady Constance had been dragged away because of Modina's failing health, and not because she had taken her to the kitchen. But even so, no matter the consequences, Amilia had to try.

Amilia changed both herself and Modina into their day clothing and, taking her gently by the hand, led her to the door and knocked. When it opened, she faced the guard straight and tall and announced, "I'm taking the empress to the kitchen for her meal. I was appointed the imperial secretary by Regent Saldur himself, and I'm responsible for her care. She can't remain in this filthy cell. It's killing her."

She waited.

He would refuse and she would argue. She tried to organize her rebuttals: noxious vapors, the healing power of fresh air, the fact that they would kill her if the empress did not show improvement. Why that last one would persuade him she had not worked out, but it was one of the thoughts pressing on her mind.

The guard looked from Amilia to Modina and back to Amilia again. She was shocked when he nodded and stepped aside. Amilia hesitated; she had not considered the possibility he would relent. She led the empress up the steps while the soldier followed.

She made no announcement like Lady Constance. She simply walked in with the empress in tow, bringing the kitchen once more to a halt. Everyone stared. No one said a word.

"The empress would like her meal," Amilia told Ibis, who

nodded. "Could you please put some extra bread at the bottom of the bowl, and could she get some fruit today?"

"Aye, aye," the big man acknowledged. "Leif, get on it. Nipper, go to the storage and bring up some of those berries. The rest of you, back to work. Nothing to see here."

Nipper bolted outside, leaving the door open. Red, one of the huntsman's old dogs, wandered in. Modina dropped Amilia's hand.

"Leif, get that animal out of here," Ibis ordered.

"Wait," Amilia said. Everyone watched as the empress knelt down next to the elkhound. The dog, in turn, nuzzled her.

Red was old, and his muzzle had gone gray, and his eyes clouded with blindness. Why the huntsman kept him was a mystery, as all he did was sleep in the courtyard and beg for handouts from the kitchen. Few took notice of his familiar presence, but he commanded the empress's attention. She scratched behind his ears and stroked his fur.

"I guess Red gets to stay." Ibis chuckled. "Dog's got important friends."

Edith Mon entered the kitchen, halting abruptly at the sight of Amilia and the empress. She pursed her lips, narrowed her eyes, and without a word pivoted and exited the way she had come.

⟡

Amidst the sound of pounding hammers, Regent Maurice Saldur strode through the palace reception hall, where artisans were busy at work. A year ago this had been King Ethelred's castle, the stark stone fortress of Avryn's most powerful monarch. Since the coronation of the empress, it had become the imperial palace of the Nyphron Empire and the home of the Daughter of Maribor. Saldur had insisted on the renovations: a grand new foyer, complete with the crown seal etched in white marble on the floor; several massive chandeliers to lighten the dark interior; a wider ornate balcony from which Her Eminence could wave to her adoring people; and of course, a complete rework of the throne room.

Ethelred and the chancellor had balked at the expense. The new throne cost almost as much as a warship, but they did not understand the importance of impressions the way Saldur did. He had an illiterate, nearly comatose child for an empress, and the only thing preventing disaster was that no one knew. Saldur's edict restricting servants from leaving the castle had been issued to contain most of the gossip. Brute-force opulence would further the misdirection.

How much silk, gold, and marble does it take to blind the world?

More than he had access to, he was certain, but he would do what he could.

These past few weeks, Saldur had felt as if he had been balancing teacups on his head while standing on a stool, strapped to the back of a runaway horse. The New Empire had manifested itself in just a matter of weeks. Centuries of planning had finally coalesced, but as with everything, there were mistakes and circumstances for which they could not possibly account.

The whole fiasco in Dahlgren had been only the start. The moment they had declared the establishment of the New Empire, Glouston had gone into open revolt. Alburn had decided to haggle over terms, and of course, there was Melengar. The humiliation was beyond words. Every other Avryn kingdom had fallen in step as planned, all except his. He had been the bishop of Melengar and close personal advisor to the king, as well as the king's son, and yet Melengar remained independent. Saldur's clever solution to the Dahlgren problem had kept him from fading into obscurity. He had drawn victory from ashes, and for that the Patriarch had appointed him the church's representative, making him co-regent alongside Ethelred.

The old king of Warric maintained the existing systems, but Saldur was the architect of the new world order. His vision would define the lives of thousands for centuries to come. Although it was a tremendous opportunity, Saldur felt as if he were rolling a massive boulder up a hill. If he should trip or stumble, the rock would roll back and crush him and everything else with it.

When Saldur reached his office, he found Luis Guy waiting. The church sentinel had just arrived, hopefully with good news. The Knight of Nyphron waited near the window, as straight and impeccable as ever. He stood looking out at some distant point with his hands clasped behind his back. As usual, he wore the black and scarlet of his order, each line clean, his beard neatly trimmed.

"I assume you've heard," Saldur said, closing the door behind him and ignoring any greeting. Guy was not the type to bother with pleasantries—something Saldur appreciated about the man. Over the past several months, he had seen little of Guy, whom the Patriarch kept occupied searching for the real Heir of Novron and the wizard Esrahaddon. This was also to his liking, as Guy, who was one of only two men in the world with direct access to the Patriarch, could be a formidable rival. Strangely, Guy appeared to have little interest in carving out a place for himself in the New Empire—something else to be grateful for.

"About the Nationalists? Of course," Guy responded, turning away from the window.

"And?"

"And what?"

"And I would like to know what—" Saldur halted when he noticed another man in the room.

The office was comfortable in size, large enough to accommodate a desk, bookshelves, and a table with a chessboard between two soft chairs, where the stranger sat.

"Oh yes." Guy motioned to the man. "This is Merrick Marius. Merrick, meet Bishop—forgive me—*Regent* Saldur."

"So this is him," Saldur muttered, annoyed that the man did not rise.

He remained sitting comfortably, leaning back with casual indifference, staring in a manner too direct, too brazen. Merrick wore a thigh-length coat of dark red suede—an awful shade, Saldur thought—the color of dried blood. His hair was short, his face pale, and aside from his coat, his attire was simple and unadorned.

"Not very impressive, are you?" Saldur observed.

The man smiled at this. "Do you play chess, Your Grace?"

Saldur's eyebrows rose and he glanced at Guy. This was his man, after all. Guy had been the one who dug him up, unearthing him from the fetid streets, and praised his talents. The sentinel said nothing and showed no outward sign of outrage or discontent with his pet.

"I'm running an empire, young man," Saldur replied dismissively. "I don't have time for games."

"How strange," Merrick said. "I've never thought of chess as a game. To me it's really more of a religion. Every aspect of life, distilled into sixteen pieces within sixty-four black and white squares, which from a distance actually appear gray. Of course, there are more than a mere sixty-four squares. The smaller squares taken in even numbers form larger ones, creating a total of two hundred and four. Most people miss that. They see only the obvious. Few have the intelligence to look deeper to see the patterns hidden within patterns. That's part of the beauty of chess—it is much more than it first appears, more complicated, more complex. The world at your finger-

RISE OF EMPIRE   *107*

tips, so manageable, so defined. It has such simple rules, a near infinite number of possible paths, but only three outcomes.

"I've heard some clergy base sermons on the game, explaining the hierarchy of pieces and how they represent the classes of society. They correlate the rules of movement to the duties that each man performs in his service to Maribor. Have you ever done that, Your Grace?" Merrick asked, but he did not wait for an answer. "Amazing idea, isn't it?" He leaned over the board, his eyes searching the field of black and white.

"The bishop is an interesting piece." He plucked one off the board and held it in his hand, rolling the polished stone figure back and forth across his open palm. "It's not a very well-designed piece, not as pretty perhaps as, say, the knight. It's often overlooked, hiding in the corners, appearing so innocent, so disarming. But it's able to sweep the length of the board at sharp, unexpected angles, often with devastating results. I've always thought that bishops were underutilized through a lack of appreciation for their talents. I suppose I'm unusual in this respect, but then, I'm not the type of person to judge the value of a piece based on how it looks."

"You think you're a very clever fellow, don't you?" Saldur challenged.

"No, Your Grace," Merrick replied. "Clever is the man who makes a fortune selling dried-up cows, explaining how it saves the farmers the trouble of getting up every morning to milk them. I'm not clever—I'm a genius."

At this, Guy interjected, "Regent, at our last meeting I mentioned a solution to the Nationalist problem. He sits before you. Mr. Marius has everything worked out. He merely needs approval from the regents."

"And certain assurances of payment," Merrick added.

"You can't be serious." Saldur whirled on Guy. "The Nationalists are sweeping north on a rampage. They've taken

Kilnar. They're only miles from Ratibor. They will be marching on this palace by Wintertide. What I need are ideas, alternatives, solutions—not some irreverent popinjay!"

"You have some interesting ideas, Your Grace," Merrick
told Saldur, his voice calm and casual, as if he had not heard a
word. "I like your views on a central government. The benefits of standardizations in trade, laws, farming, even the
widths of roads are excellent. It shows clarity of thought that I
would not expect from an elderly church bishop."

"How do you know anything of my—"

Merrick raised his hand to halt the regent. "I should explain
right away that how I obtain information is confidential and
not open for discussion. The fact is, I know it. What's more—I
like it. I can see the potential in this New Empire you're
struggling to erect. It may well be exactly what the world needs
to get beyond the petty warfare that weakens our nations and
mires the common man in hopeless poverty. At present, however, this is still a dream. That is where I come in. I only wish
you came to me earlier. I could have saved you that embarrassing and now burdensome problem of Her Eminence."

"That was the result of an unfortunate error on the part of
my predecessor, the archbishop. Something he paid for with
his life. I was the one who salvaged the situation."

"Yes, I know. Some idiot named Rufus was supposed to
slay the mythical beast and thereby prove he was the fabled
Heir of Novron, the descendant of the god Maribor himself.
Only instead, Rufus was devoured and the beast laid waste to
everything in the vicinity. Everything except a young girl, who
somehow managed to slay it, and in front of a church deacon,
no less—oops. But you're right. That wasn't your fault. You
were the smart one with the brilliant idea to use her as a
puppet—a girl so bereft from losing everything and everyone
that she went mad. Your solution is to hide her in the depths of

the palace and hope no one notices. In the meantime, you and Ethelred run a military campaign to take over all of Avryn, sending your best troops north to invade Melengar just as the Nationalists invade from the south. Brilliant. I must say, with things so well in hand it's a wonder I was contacted at all."

"I'm not amused," Saldur told him.

"Nor should you be, for at this moment King Alric of Melengar is setting into motion plans to form an alliance with the Nationalists, trapping you in a two-front war, and bringing Trent into the conflict on their side."

"You know this?"

"It is what I would do. And with the wealth of Delgos and the might of Trent, your fledgling empire, with its insane empress, will crumble as quickly as it rose."

"More impressed now?" Guy asked.

"And what would you have us do to stave off this impending cataclysm?"

Merrick smiled. "Pay me."

❧

The grand, exalted empress Modina Novronian, ruler of Avryn and high priestess of the Church of Nyphron, sat sprawled on the floor, feeding her bowl of soup to Red, who expressed his gratitude by drooling on her dress. He rested his head on her lap and slapped his tail against the stone, his tongue sliding lazily in and out. The empress curled up beside the dog and laid her head on the animal's side. Amilia smiled. She was encouraged by seeing Modina interact with something, anything.

"Get that disgusting animal out of here and get her off the floor!"

Amilia jumped and looked up, horrified. Regent Saldur

entered the kitchen with Edith Mon, wearing a sinister smile. Amilia could not move. Several scullery maids rushed to the empress's side and gently pulled her to her feet.

"The very idea." He continued to shout as the maids busied themselves with smoothing out Modina's dress. "You," the regent growled, pointing at Amilia, "this is your doing. I should have known. What was I expecting when I put a common street urchin in charge of...of..." He trailed off, looking at Modina with an exasperated expression. "At least your predecessors didn't have her groveling with animals!"

"Your Grace, Amilia was—" Ibis Thinly began.

"Shut up, you oaf!" Saldur snapped at the stocky cook, and then returned his attention to Amilia. "Your service to the empress has ended, as well as your employment at this palace."

Saldur motioned to the empress's guard and then said, "Take her out of my sight."

The guard approached Amilia, unable to meet her eyes.

Amilia breathed in short, stifled gasps and realized she was trembling as the soldier approached. Not normally given to crying, Amilia could not help it, and tears began streaming down her cheeks.

"No," Modina said.

Spoken with no force, barely above a whisper, the single word cast a spell on the room. One of the cooking staff dropped a metal pot, which rang loudly on the stone floor. They all stared. The regent turned in surprise and then began to circle the empress, studying her with interest. The girl had a focused, challenging look as she glared at Saldur. The regent glanced from Amilia to Modina several times. He cocked his head from side to side, as if trying to work out a puzzle. The guard stood by awkwardly.

At length, Saldur put him at ease. "As the empress commands," Saldur said without taking his eyes off Modina. "It seems that I may have been a bit premature in my assessment of…" Saldur glanced at Amilia, annoyed. "What's your name?"

"A-Amilia."

He nodded as if approving the correct answer. "Your techniques are unusual, but certainly one can't argue with results."

Saldur looked back at Modina as she stood within the circle of maids, who parted at his approach. "She does look better, doesn't she? Color's improved. There's"—he motioned toward her face—"a fullness to her cheeks." He was nodding. He crossed his arms and with a final nod of approval said, "Very well, you can keep the position, as it seems to please Her Eminence."

The regent turned and headed out of the scullery. He paused at the doorway to look over his shoulder, saying, "You know, I was really starting to believe she was mute."

Chapter 7

The Jewel

Arista had always thought of herself as an experienced equestrian. Most ladies had never even sat in a saddle, but she had ridden since childhood. The nobles mocked, and her father scolded, but nothing could dissuade her. She loved the freedom of the wind in her hair and her heart pounding with the beat of the hooves. Before setting out, she had looked forward to impressing the thieves with her vast knowledge of horsemanship. She knew they would be awed by her skill.

She was wrong.

In Sheridan, Royce had found her a spirited bay mare to replace her exquisite palfrey. Since setting out, he had forced them over rough ground, fording streams, jumping logs, and dodging low branches—often at a trot. Clutching white-knuckled to the saddle, she had used all her skills and strength just to remain on the horse's back. Gone were her illusions of being praised as a skilled rider, and all that remained was the hope of making it through the day without the humiliation—not to mention the physical pain—of falling.

They rode south after leaving the university, following trails only Royce could find. Before dawn, they crossed the narrow headwaters of the Galewyr and proceeded up the embankment on the far side. Briars and thickets lashed at them. Unseen dips caught the horses by surprise, and Arista cried out once when her mount made an unexpected lunge across a washed-out gap. Their silence added to her humiliation. If she had been a man, they would have commented.

They climbed steadily, reaching such a steep angle that their mounts panted for air in loud snorts and on occasion uttered deep grunts as they struggled to scramble up the dewy slope. At last, they crested the hill, and Arista found herself greeting a chilly dawn atop the windswept Senon Uplands.

The Senon was a high, barren plateau of exposed rock and scrub bushes with expansive views on all sides. The horses' hooves clacked loudly on the barefaced granite until Royce brought them to a stop. His cloak fluttered with the morning breeze. To the east, the sunrise peered at them over the mist-covered forests of Dunmore. From this height, the vast wood looked like a hazy blue lake as it fell away below them, racing toward the dazzling sun. Arista knew that beyond it lay the Nidwalden River, the Parthaloren Falls, and the tower of Avempartha. Royce stared east for several minutes, and she wondered if his elven eyes could see that tiny pinnacle of his people in the distance.

In front of them and to the southwest lay the Warric province of Chadwick. Like everything else west of the ridge, it remained submerged in darkness. Down in the deep rolling valley, the predawn sky would only now be separating from the dark horizon. It would have appeared peaceful, a world tucked in bed before the first cock's crow, except for the hundreds of lights flickering like tiny fireflies.

"Breckton's camp," Hadrian said. "The Northern Imperial Army is not making very good time, it seems."

"We'll descend before Amber Heights and rejoin the road

well past Breckton," Royce explained. "How long do you figure before they reach Colnora?"

Hadrian rubbed the growing stubble of his beard. "Another three, maybe four, days. An army that size moves at a snail's pace, and I'm guessing Breckton isn't pleased with his orders. He's likely dragging his feet, hoping they'll be rescinded."

"You sound as if you know him," Arista said.

"I never met the man, but I fought under his father's banner. I've also fought against him, when I served in the ranks of King Armand's army in Alburn."

"How many armies have you served in?"

Hadrian shrugged. "Too many."

They pushed on, traversing the crest into the face of a fierce wind, which tugged at her clothes and caused her eyes to water. Arista kept her head down and watched her horse's hooves pick a path across the cracked slabs of lichen-covered rock. She clutched her cloak tight about her neck as the damp of the previous day's rain and sweat conspired with the wind to make her shiver. When they plunged back into the trees, the slow descent began. Once more the animals struggled. This time Arista bent backward, nearly to her horse's flanks, to keep her balance.

Although it was mercifully cooler than the day before, the pace was faster and more challenging. Finally, several hours after midday, they stopped on the bank of a small stream, where the horses gorged themselves on cool water and river grass. Royce and Hadrian grabbed packs and gathered wood. Exhausted, Arista as much fell as sat down. Her legs and backside ached. There were insects and twigs in her hair and a dusting of dirt covering her gown. Her eyes stared at nothing, losing their focus as her mind stalled, numb from fatigue.

What have I gotten myself into? Am I up to this?

They were below the Galewyr, in imperial territory. She had thrown herself into the fire, perhaps foolishly. Alric would be furious when he found her missing, and she could just imagine what Ecton would say. If they caught her— She stopped herself.

This is not helping.

She turned her attention to her escorts.

As during the hours on horseback, Royce and Hadrian remained quiet. Hadrian unsaddled the horses and gave them a light brushing while Royce set up a small cook fire. Watching the two of them was entertaining. Without a word, they would toss tools and bags back and forth. Hadrian blindly threw a hatchet over his shoulder and Royce caught it just in time to begin breaking up branches for the fire. Just as Royce finished the fire, Hadrian had a pot of water ready to place on it. For Arista, who had lived her life in public, among squabbling nobles and chattering castle staff, such silence was strange.

Hadrian chopped carrots and dropped them into the dented, blackened pot on the coals. "Are you ready to eat the best meal you've ever had, Highness?"

She wanted to laugh but did not have the strength. Instead, she said, "There are three chefs and eighteen cooks back at Essendon Castle that would take exception to that remark. They spend their whole lives perfecting elaborate dishes. You would be amazed at the feasts I've attended, filled with everything from exotic spices to ice sculptures. I highly doubt you'll be able to surpass them."

Hadrian smirked. "That might be," he replied, struggling to cut chunks of dry brine-encrusted pork into bite-sized cubes, "but I guarantee this meal will put them all to shame."

Arista removed the pearl-handled hairbrush from a pouch that hung at her side, and she tried in vain to untangle her hair. Eventually giving up, she sat and watched Hadrian drop wretched-looking meat into the bubbling pot. Ash and bits of twigs thrown up by the crackling fire landed in the mix.

"Master chef, debris is getting in your pot."

Hadrian grinned. "Always happens. Can't help it. Just be careful not to bite down too hard on anything or you might crack a tooth."

"Wonderful," she told him, then turned her attention to Royce, who was busy checking the horses' hooves. "We've come a long way today, haven't we? I don't think I've ever traveled so far so quickly. You keep a cruel pace."

"That first part was over rough ground," Royce mentioned. "We'll cover a lot more miles after we eat."

"After we eat?" Arista felt her heart sink. "We aren't stopping for the day?"

Royce glanced up at the sky. "It's hours until nightfall."

They mean for me to get back into the saddle?

She did not know if she could stand, much less ride. Virtually every muscle in her body was in pain. They could entertain any thoughts they wished, but she would not travel any farther that day. There was no reason to move this fast, or over such rough ground. Why Royce was taking such a difficult course, she did not understand.

She watched as Hadrian dished the disgusting soup he had concocted into a tin cup and held it out to her. There was an oily film across the top, through which green meat bobbed, everything seasoned with bits of dirt and tree bark. Most assuredly, it was the worst thing anyone had ever presented her to eat. Arista held the hot cup between her hands, grimacing and wishing she had eaten more of the meat pie back at Sheridan.

"Is this a...stew?" she asked.

Royce laughed quietly. "He likes to call it that."

"It's a dish I learned from Thrace," Hadrian explained with a reminiscent look on his face. "She's a much better cook than I am. She did this thing with the meat that— Well, anyway, no, it's not stew. It's really just boiled salt pork and vegetables. You don't get a broth, but it takes away the rancid taste of the salt and softens the meat. And it's hot. Trust me, you're going to love it."

Arista closed her eyes and lifted the cup to her lips. The steamy smell was wonderful. Before she realized it, she had devoured the entire thing, eating so quickly she burned her tongue. A moment later, she was scraping the bottom with a bit of hard bread. She looked for more and was disappointed to see Hadrian already cleaning the pot. Lying in the grass, she let out a sigh as the warmth of the meal coursed through her body.

"So much for ice sculptures." Hadrian chuckled.

Despite her earlier reluctance, she found new strength after eating. The next leg of the trip was over level ground, along the relative ease of a deer trail. Royce drove them as fast as the terrain allowed, never pausing or consulting a map.

After many hours, Arista had no idea where they were, nor did she care. The food faded into memory and she found herself once more near collapse. She rode bent over, resting on the horse's neck and drifting in and out of sleep. She could not discern between dream and reality and would wake in a panic, certain she was falling. Finally, they stopped.

Everything was dark and cold. The ground was wet and she stood shivering once more. Her guides went back into their silent actions. This time, to Arista's immense disappointment, no fire was made, and instead of a hot meal, they handed her strips of smoked meat, raw carrots, an onion quarter, and a triangle of hard, dry bread. She sat on the wet grass, feeling the moisture soak into her skirt and dampen her legs as she devoured the meal without a thought.

"Shouldn't we get a shelter up?" she asked hopefully.

Royce looked up at the stars. "It looks clear."

"But..." She was shocked when he spread out a cloth on the grass.

They mean to sleep right here—on the ground without even a tent!

Arista had three handmaids who dressed and undressed her daily. They bathed her and brushed her hair. Servants fluffed pillows and brought warm milk at bedtime. They tended the fireplace in shifts, quietly adding logs throughout the night. Sleeping in her carriage had been a hardship, sleeping on that ghastly cot in the dorm a torment—this was insane. Even peasants had hovels.

She wrapped her cloak tight against the night's chill.

Will I even get a blanket?

Tired beyond memory, she got on her hands and knees and feebly brushed a small pile of dead leaves together to act as a mattress. Lying down, she felt them crunch and crinkle beneath her.

"Hold on," Hadrian said, carrying over a bundle. He unrolled a canvas tarp. "I really need to make more of these. The pitch will keep the damp from soaking through." He handed her a blanket as well. "Oh, there's a nice little clearing just beyond those trees, just in case you need it."

Why in the world would I need a—

"Oh," she said, and managed a nod. Surely they would come upon a town soon. She could wait.

"Good night, Highness."

She did not reply as Hadrian went a few paces away and assembled his own bed from pine boughs. Without a tent, there was no choice but to sleep in her dress, which left her trapped in a tight corset. Arista spread out the tarp, removed her shoes, and lay down while pulling the thin blanket up to her chin. Though utterly miserable, she stubbornly refused to show it. After all, common women lived every day under similar conditions, so she could as well. The argument was noble but gave little comfort.

The instant she closed her eyes, she heard the faint buzzing. She was blinded by darkness, but the sound was unmistakable—a horde of mosquitoes descended. Feeling one on her cheek, she slapped at it and pulled the blanket over her head, exposing her feet. Curling into a ball, she buried herself under the thin wool shield. Her tight corset made breathing a challenge and the musty smell of the blanket, long steeped in horse sweat, nauseated her. Arista's frustration overflowed and tears slipped from her tightly squeezed eyes.

What was I thinking coming out here? I can't do this. Oh dear Maribor, what a fool I am. I always think I can do anything. I thought I could ride a horse—what a joke. I thought I was brave—look at me. I think I know better than anyone—I'm an idiot!

What a disappointment she was to those who loved her. She should have listened to her father and served the kingdom by marrying a powerful prince. Now that she was tarnished with the stain of witchery, no one would have her. Alric had stuck his neck out and given her a chance to be an ambassador. Her failure had doomed the kingdom. Now this trip—this horrible trip was just one more mistake, one more colossal error.

I'll go home tomorrow. I'll ask Royce to take me back to Medford and I'll formally resign as ambassador. I'll stay in my tower and rot until the empire takes me to the gallows.

Tears ran down her cheeks as she lay smothered by more than just the blanket until—mercifully in the cold, unforgiving night—she fell asleep.

❧

The songs of birds woke her.

Arista opened her eyes to sunlight cascading through the green canopy of leafy trees. Butterflies danced in brilliant shafts of golden light. The beams revealed a tranquil pond so placid it appeared as if a patch of sky had fallen. A delicate white mist hovered over the pool's mirrored surface like a scene from a fairy story. Circled by sun-dappled trees, cattails, and flowers, the pool was perfect—the most beautiful thing she had ever seen.

Where'd that come from?

Royce and Hadrian still slept under rumpled blankets, leaving her alone with the vision. She got up quietly, fearful of shattering the fragile beauty. Walking barefoot to the water's edge, she caught the warmth of the sun, melting the night's chill. She stretched, feeling the unexpected pride in the ache of a well-worked muscle. Crouching, Arista scooped a handful of water and gently rinsed away the stiff tears of the night before. In the middle of the pond, a fish jumped. She saw it only briefly as it flashed silver, then disappeared with a *plop!* Another followed and, delighted by the display, Arista stared in anticipation for the next leap, grinning like a child at a puppet show.

The mist burned away before sounds from the camp caught her attention, and Arista walked over to find the clearing Hadrian had mentioned. She returned to camp, brushed out her hair, and ate the cold pork breakfast waiting for her. When finished, she folded the blankets and rolled up the tarps, then stowed the food and refilled the water pouches. Arista mounted her mare, deciding at that moment to name her Mystic. Only after Royce had led them out of the little glade did she realize that no one had spoken a single word all morning.

They reached the road almost immediately, which explained the lack of a fire the night before and the unusual way Royce and Hadrian were dressed—in doublets and hose. Hadrian's swords were also conspicuously missing, stowed somewhere out of sight. How Royce had known the road was nearby baffled her. As they traveled with the warm sun overhead and the birds singing in the trees, Arista could scarcely understand what had troubled her the night before. She was still sore but felt a satisfaction in the dull pain that owed nothing to being a princess.

They had not gone far when Royce brought Mouse to a stop. A troop of imperial soldiers came down the road escorting a line of four large grain wagons—tall, solid-sided boxes with flat bottoms. Riders immediately rode forward, bringing a cloud of dust in their wake. An intimidating officer in bright armor failed to give his name but demanded theirs, as well as their destination and reason for traveling. Soldiers of his vanguard swept around behind the three with spears at the ready, horses puffing and snorting.

"This is Mr. Everton of Windham Village and his wife, and I am his servant," Royce explained quickly as he politely dismounted and bowed. His tone and inflections were formal and excessive, his voice nasal and high-pitched. Arista was amazed by how much like her fussy day steward he sounded. "Mr. Everton was—I mean, is—a respected merchant. We are on our way to Colnora, where Mrs. Everton has a brother whom they hope will provide temporary...er, I mean...they will be visiting."

Before they had left The Rose and Thorn, Royce had coached Arista on this story and the part she might have to play. In the safety of the Medford tavern, it had seemed like a plausible tale. But now that the moment had come and soldiers surrounded her, she doubted its chances of success. Her

palms began to sweat and her stomach churned. Royce continued to play his part masterfully, supplying answers in his
nonthreatening effeminate voice. The responses were specific-
sounding, but vague on crucial details.

"It's *your* brother in Colnora?" The officer confronted
Arista, his tenor harsh. No one had ever spoken to her in such
a tone. Even when Braga had threatened her life, he had been
more polite than this. She struggled to conceal her emotion.

"Yes," she said simply. Arista was remembering Royce's
instructions to keep her answers as short as possible and her
face blank. She was certain the soldiers could hear the pounding of her heart.

"His name?"

"Vincent Stapleton," she answered quickly and confidently,
knowing the officer would be looking for hesitation.

"Where does he live?"

"Bridge Street, not far from the Hill District," she replied.
This was a carefully rehearsed line. It would be typical for the
wife of a prominent merchant to boast about how near the
affluent section of the city her family lived.

Hadrian now played his part.

"Look here, I've had quite enough of you, and your imperial army. The truth of the matter is my estate has been overrun, used to quarter a bunch of brigands like you who I'm sure
will destroy my furniture and soil the carpets. I have some
questions of my own. Like when will I get my home back?" he
bellowed angrily. "Is this the kind of thing a merchant can
expect from the empress? King Ethelred never treated us like
this! Who's going to pay for damages?"

To Arista's great relief, the officer changed his demeanor.
Just as they had hoped, he avoided getting involved in complaints from evicted patrons and waved them on their way.

As the wagons passed, she was revolted by the sight visible

through the bars on the rear gates. The wagons did not hold captured soldiers, but elves. Covered in filth, they were packed so
tightly they were forced to stand, jostling into each other as the
wagon dipped and bounced over the rutted road. There were
females and children alongside the males, all slick with sweat
from the heat. Arista heard muffled cries as the wagons crawled
by at a turtle's pace. Some reached through the bars, pleading
for water and mercy. Arista was so sickened at the sight she forgot her fear, which only a moment before had consumed her.
Then a sudden realization struck her—she looked for Royce.

He stood a few feet away on the roadside, holding Mouse's
bridle. Hadrian was at his side, firmly gripping Royce's arm
and whispering in his ear. Arista could not hear what he said,
but guessed at the conversation. A few tense moments passed,
but then they turned and continued toward Colnora.

⁓

The street below drifted into shadow as night settled in. Carriages raced to their destinations, noisily bouncing along the
cobblestone. Lamplighters made their rounds in zigzag patterns, moving from lamp to lamp. Lights flickered to life in
windows of nearby buildings and silhouettes passed like
ghosts behind curtains. Shopkeepers closed their doors and
shutters while cart vendors covered their wares and harnessed
horses as another day's work ended.

"How long do you think?" Hadrian asked. He and Royce
had donned their usual garb and Hadrian once more wore his
swords. While Arista was used to seeing them this way, their
change in appearance and Royce's constant vigilance at the
window put her on edge.

"Soon," Royce replied, not altering his concentration on
the street.

They waited together in the small room at The Regal Fox Inn, the least expensive of the five hotels in the affluent Hill District. Once they had arrived, Royce had continued to pose as their servant by renting two rooms—one standard, the other small. He avoided inquiries about luggage and arrangements for dinner. The innkeeper had not pursued the matter.

When they were upstairs, Royce insisted they all remain in the standard room together. Arista noticed a pause after he said this, as if he expected an argument. This amused her, because the idea of sharing a comfortable room was infinitely better than any accommodations she had experienced so far. Still, she had to admit, if only to herself, that a week ago she would have been appalled by the notion.

Even the standard room was luxurious by most boarding-house standards. The beds were made of packed feathers and covered in smooth, clean sheets, overstuffed pillows, and heavy quilts. There were a full-length mirror, a large dresser, a wardrobe, a small writing table and chair, and an adjoining room for the washbasin and chamber pot. The room was equipped with a fireplace and lamps, but Royce left them unlit and darkness filled the space. The only illumination was from the outside streetlamps, which cast an oblong checkerboard image on the floor.

Now that they were off the road and in a more familiar setting, the princess gave in to curiosity. "I don't understand. What are we doing here?"

"Waiting," Royce replied.

"For what?"

"We can't just ride into the Nationalists' camp. We need a go-between. Someone to set up a meeting," Hadrian said. He sat at the writing desk across the room from her. In the growing darkness, he was fading into a dim ghostly outline.

"I didn't see you send any messages. Did I miss something?"

"No, but the messages were delivered nonetheless," Royce mentioned.

"Royce is kind of a celebrity here," Hadrian told her. "When he comes to town —"

Royce coughed intentionally.

"Okay, maybe not a celebrity, but he's certainly well known. I'm sure talk started the moment he arrived."

"Then we wanted to be seen?"

"Yes," Royce replied. "Unfortunately, the Diamond wasn't the only one watching the gate. Someone's watching our window."

"And he's not a Black Diamond?" Hadrian asked.

"Too clumsy. Has about the same talent for delicate work as a draft horse. The Diamond would laugh if he applied."

"Black Diamond is the thieves' guild?" she asked.

They both nodded.

While supposedly a secret organization, the Diamond was nevertheless well known. Arista heard of it from time to time in court and at council meetings. They were always spoken about with disdain by haughty nobles, even though they often used their services. The black market was virtually controlled by the Diamond, who supplied practically any commodity for anyone willing to pay the price.

"Can he see you?"

"Not unless he's an elf."

Hadrian and Arista exchanged glances, wondering if he had meant it as a joke.

Hadrian joined Royce at the window and looked out. "The one near the lamppost with his hand on his hilt? The guy shifting his weight back and forth? He's an imperial soldier, a veteran of the Vanguard Scout Brigade," Hadrian said.

Royce looked at him, surprised.

The light from the street spilled across Hadrian's face as he grinned. "The way he's shifting his weight is a technique taught to soldiers to keep from going footsore. That short sword is standard issue for a lightly armed scout and the gauntlet on his sword hand is an idiosyncrasy of King Ethelred, who insists all his troops wear them. Since Ethelred is now part of the New Empire, the fellow below is an Imp."

"You weren't kidding about serving in a lot of armies, were you?" Arista asked.

Hadrian shrugged. "I was a mercenary. It's what I did. I served anywhere the pay was good." Hadrian took his seat back at the table. "I even commanded a few regiments. Got a medal once. But I would fight for one army only to find myself going against them a few years later. Killing old friends isn't fun. So I kept taking jobs farther away. Ended up deep in Calis fighting for Tenkin warlords." Hadrian shook his head. "Guess you could say that was my low point. You really know you've—"

Hadrian was interrupted by a knock. Without a word, Royce crossed the room, taking up position on one side of the door while Hadrian carefully opened it. Outside, a young boy stood dressed in the typical poor clothing of a waif.

"Evening, sirs. Your presence is requested in room twenty-three," he said cheerily, and then, touching his thumb to his brow, he walked away.

"Leave her here?" Hadrian asked Royce.

Royce shook his head. "She comes along."

"Must you speak about me as if I'm not in the room?" Arista asked, but only with feigned irritation. She sensed the seriousness of the situation from the look on Royce's face and was not about to interfere. She was behind enemy lines. If she was caught, it was not certain what would happen. If she tried to claim a diplomatic status, it was doubtful the New Empire

would honor it. Ransoming Arista for Alric's compliance was
not out of the question—nor was a public execution.

"We're just going to walk in?" Hadrian asked skeptically.

"Yes, we need their help, and when one goes begging, it's
best to knock on the front door."

They lodged in room nineteen, so it was a short trip down
the hall and around a corner to room twenty-three. It was
conveniently isolated. There were no other doors off this hall,
only a stair, which likely led to the street. Royce rapped twice,
paused, then added three more.

The door opened.

"Come in, Duster."

The room was a larger, more luxurious suite with a chandelier brightly lighting the interior. No beds were visible as
they entered a parlor. Against the far wall were two doors,
which no doubt led to sleeping quarters. Dark green damask
fabric adorned the walls, and carpet covered the entire floor
except for the area around the marble fireplace. Four tall windows, each shrouded with thick velvet curtains, decorated the
outside wall. Several ornate pieces of furniture lined the room.
In the center stood a gaunt man with sunken cheeks and
accusing eyes. Two more men stood slightly behind him, while
another two waited near the door.

"Everyone, please take a seat," the thin man told them. He
remained standing until they all had sat. "Duster, let me get
right to the point. I made it clear on your last visit that you are
not welcome here, didn't I?"

Royce was silent.

"I was unusually patient then, but seeing as how you've
returned, perhaps politeness is not the proper tack to take
with you. Personally, I hold you in the highest regard, but as
First Officer, I simply cannot allow you to blatantly walk into
this city after having been warned." He paused, but when no

reaction came from Royce, he continued. "Hadrian and the princess are welcome to leave. Point of fact, I must insist the lady leave, as the death of a noblewoman would make things awkward. Shall I assume Hadrian will refuse?"

Hadrian glanced at Royce, who did not return his look, and then Hadrian shrugged. "I would hate to miss whatever show is about to start."

"In that case, Your Highness..." The man made a sweeping hand motion toward the door. "If you'll please return to your room."

"I'm staying," Arista said. It was only two words, but spoken with all the confidence of a princess accustomed to getting her way.

He narrowed his eyes at her.

"Shall I escort her, sir?" one of the men near the door offered with a menacing tone.

"Touch her and this meeting will end badly," Royce said barely above a whisper.

"Meeting?" The thin man laughed. "This is no meeting. This is retribution, and it'll most assuredly end very badly."

He looked back at Arista. "I've heard about you. I'm pleased to see the rumors are true."

Arista had no idea what he meant, but did not like a thug *knowing* about her. She was even more disturbed by his approval.

"Nevertheless, my men *will* escort you." He clapped his hands and the two doors to the adjoining rooms opened, as did the one behind them, leading to the hallway. Many well-armed men poured in.

"We're here to see the Jewel," Royce quietly said.

Immediately the thin man's expression changed. Arista watched as, in an instant, his face followed a path from confidence to confusion, then suspicion, and finally curiosity. He ran a bony hand through his thin blond hair. "What makes you think the Jewel will see you?"

"Because there's profit in it for him."

"The Jewel is already very wealthy."

"It's not that kind of profit. Tell me, Price, how long have you had the new gate guards? The ones in the imperial uniforms. For that matter, when did Colnora get a gate? How many others like them are roaming the city?" Royce sat back and folded his hands across his lap. "I should have been stopped the moment I entered Colnora, and under farmer Oslow's field over two hours ago. Why the delay? Why are there no watches posted on the Arch or Bernum Bridge? Are you really getting that sloppy, Price? Or are the Imps running the show?"

Now it was the thin man's turn to remain silent.

"The Diamond can't be happy with the New Empire flexing its muscle. You used to have full rein, and the Jewel his own fiefdom. But not anymore. Now he must share. The Diamond has been forced back into the shadows while the new landlord kicks up his heels in front of the fire in the house they built. Tell Cosmos I'm here to help with his little problem."

Price stared at Royce, and then his eyes drifted to Arista. He nodded and stood up. "You will, of course, remain here until I return."

"Why not?" Hadrian remarked, apparently undisturbed by the tension radiating in the room. "This is a whole lot better than our room. Are those walnuts over there?"

During the exchange and while Price was gone, Royce never moved. Four men who were the most menacing of those present watched him intently. There seemed to be a contest of wills going on, each waiting to see who would flinch first. Hadrian, in contrast, casually strode around the room, examining the various paintings and furnishings. He selected a chair with a padded footstool, put up his feet, and began eating from a bowl of fruits and nuts.

"This stuff is great," he said. "We didn't get anything like this in our room. Anyone else want some?" They ignored him. "Suit yourself." He popped another handful of walnuts into his mouth.

Finally, Price returned. He had been gone for quite a while, or perhaps it had just seemed that way to Arista as she had quietly waited. The Jewel had consented to the meeting.

A carriage waited for them in front of The Regal Fox. Arista was surprised when Royce and Hadrian surrendered their weapons before boarding. Price joined them in the carriage, while two of the guild members sat up top with the driver. They rolled south two blocks, then turned west and traveled farther up the hill, past the Tradesmen's Arch, toward the Langdon Bridge. Through the open window, Arista could hear the metal rims of the coach and the horses' hooves clattering on the cobblestone. Across from her the glare of tavern lights crawled across the face of Price, who sat eyeing her with a malevolent smile. The man was all limbs, with fingers that were too long and eyes sunk too deep.

"It would seem you're doing better these days, Duster," he said with his hands folded awkwardly in his lap, a jackal pretending to be civilized. "At least your clientele has improved." The Diamond's First Officer smiled a toothy grin and nodded at Arista. "Although rumor has it that Melengar might not be the best investment these days. No offense intended, Your Highness. The Diamond is as a whole—and I personally am—rooting for you, but as a businessman, one does have to face facts."

Arista presented him a pleasant smile. "The sun will rise tomorrow, Mr. Price. That is a fact. You have horrid breath and smell of horse manure. That is also a fact. Who will win this war, however, is still a matter of opinion, and I put no weight in yours."

Price raised his eyebrows.

"She's an ambassador and a woman," Hadrian told him. "You'd be cut less fencing with a Pickering, and stand a better chance of winning."

Price smiled and nodded.

Arista was unsure whether it was in approval or resentment; such was the face of thieves. "Who exactly are we going to see, or is that a secret?"

"Cosmos Sebastian DeLur, the wealthiest merchant in Avryn," Royce replied. "Son of Cornelius DeLur of Delgos, who's probably the richest man alive. Between the two of them, the DeLur family controls most of the commerce and lends money to kings and commoners alike. He runs the Black Diamond and goes by the moniker of the Jewel."

Price's hands twitched slightly.

As they reached the summit of the hill, the carriage turned into a long private brick road that ascended Bernum Heights, a sharply rising bluff that overlooked the river below. Protecting the palatial DeLur estate was a massive gate wider than three city streets, which opened at their approach. Elegantly dressed guards stood rigid while a stuffy administrative clerk with white gloves and a powdered wig marked their passing on a parchment. Then the carriage began its long serpentine ascent along a hedge- and lantern-lined lane. Unexpected breaks in the foliage revealed glimpses of an elegant garden with elaborate sculpted fountains. At the top of the bluff stood a magnificent white marble mansion. Three stories in height, it was adorned with an eighteen-pillar colonnade forming a half-moon entrance illuminated by a massive chandelier suspended at its center. This estate was built to impress, but what caught Arista's attention was the huge bronze fountain of three nude women pouring pitchers of water into a pool.

A pair of gold doors were opened by two more impeccably dressed servants. Another man, dressed in a long dark coat, led the way into the vestibule, filled with tapestries and more sculptures than Arista had ever seen in one place. They were led through an archway outside to an expansive patio. Ivy-covered lattices lined an open-air terrace decorated with a variety of unusual plants and two more fountains—once more of nude women, only these were much smaller and wrought of polished marble.

"Good evening, Your Highness, gentlemen. Welcome to my humble home."

Seated on a luxurious couch, a large man greeted them. He was not tall but of amazing girth. He looked to be in his early fifties and well on his way to going bald. He tied what little hair he had left with a black silk ribbon and let it fall in a tail down his back. His chubby face remained youthful, showing lines of age only at the corners of his eyes when he smiled, as he was doing now. He dressed in a silk robe and held a glass of wine, which threatened to spill as he motioned them over.

"Duster, how long has it been, my old friend? I can see now that I should have made you First Officer when I had the chance. It would have saved so much trouble for the both of us. Alas, but I couldn't see it then. I hope we can put all that unpleasantness behind us now."

"My business was settled the day Hoyte died," Royce replied. "Judging from our reception, I would say it was the Diamond that was having trouble putting the past behind them."

"Quite right, quite right." Cosmos chuckled. Arista determined he was the kind of man who laughed the way other people twitched, stammered, or bit their nails. "You won't let me get away with anything, will you? That's good. You keep me honest—well, as honest as a man in my profession can be." He chuckled again. "It's that pesky legend that keeps the guild on edge. You're quite the bogeyman. Not that Mr. Price here buys into any of that, you understand, but it's his responsibility to keep the organization running smoothly. Allowing you to stroll about town is like letting a man-eating tiger meander through a crowded tavern. As the tavern keeper, they expect me to maintain the peace."

Cosmos motioned toward Price with his goblet. "You knew Mr. Price only briefly when you were still with us, I think. A pity. You would like him if you met under different circumstances."

"Who said I didn't like him?"

Cosmos laughed. "You don't like anyone, Duster, with the exception of Hadrian and Miss DeLancy, of course. There are only those you put up with and those you don't. By the mere fact that I'm here, I can at least deduce I'm not on your short list."

"Short list?"

"I can't imagine your slate of targets stays full for very long."

"We both have lists. Names get added and names get erased all the time. It would appear Price added me to yours."

"Consider it erased, my friend. Now tell me, what can I get you to drink? Montemorcey? You always had a fondness for the best. I have a vintage stock in the cellar. I'll have a couple bottles brought up."

"That'd be fine," Royce replied.

Cosmos gave a slight glance to his steward, who bowed abruptly and left. "I hope you don't mind meeting in my little garden. I do so love the night air." Closing his eyes and tilting his head up, he took a deep breath. "I don't manage to get out nearly as often as I would like. Now please sit and tell me about this offer you bring."

They took seats opposite Cosmos on elaborate cushioned benches, the span between taken up by an ornate table whose legs were fashioned to look like powerful snakes, each different from the next, facing out with fanged mouths open. Behind them Arista could hear the gurgling of fountains and the late breeze shifting foliage. Below that was the deeper, menacing roar of the Bernum River, hidden from view by the balcony.

"It's more of a proposition, really," Royce replied. "The princess here has a problem you might be able to help with, and you have a problem she may be able to solve."

"Wonderful, wonderful. I like how this is starting. If you had said you were offering me the chance of a lifetime, I would have been doubtful, but arrangements of mutual benefit show you're being straightforward. I like that, but you were always blunt, weren't you, Duster? You could afford to lay your cards on the table, because you always had such excellent cards."

A servant with white gloves identical to those worn by the gate clerk arrived and silently poured the wine, then withdrew to a respectful distance. Cosmos waited politely for them each to take a taste.

"Montemorcey is one of the finest vineyards in existence, and my cellar has some of their very best."

Royce nodded his praise.

Hadrian sniffed the dark red liquid skeptically, then swallowed the contents in a single mouthful. "Not bad for old grape juice."

Cosmos laughed once more. "Not a wine drinker. I should have known. Wine is no potable for a warrior. Gibbons, bring Hadrian a pull from the Oak Cask and leave the head on it. That should be more to your liking. Now, Duster, tell me about our mutual problems?"

"Your problem is obvious. You don't like this New Empire crowding you."

"Indeed, I do not. They're everywhere and spreading. For each one you see in uniform, you can expect three more you don't. Tavern keepers and blacksmiths are secretly working for the Imperialists, passing information. It's impossible to run a proper guild as extensive and elaborate as the Black Diamond in such a restrictive environment. There is even evidence they have spies in the Diamond itself, which is most unsettling."

"I also happen to know that Degan Gaunt is your boy."

"Well, not mine, per se."

"Your father's, then. Gaunt is supported by Delgos, Tur Del Fur is the capital of Delgos, and your father is the ruler of Tur Del Fur."

Cosmos laughed again. "No, not the ruler. Delgos is a republic, remember. He's but one of a triumvirate of businessmen elected to lead the government."

"Ah-huh."

"You don't sound convinced."

"It doesn't matter. The DeLurs are backing Gaunt in the hopes of breaking the empire, so something that might help Gaunt would help you as well."

"True, true, and what are you bringing me?"

"An alliance with Melengar. The princess here is empowered to negotiate on behalf of her brother."

"Word has it Melengar is helpless and about to fall to Ballentyne's Northern Imperial Army."

"Word is mistaken. The empress recalled the northern army to deal with the Nationalists. We passed it near Fallon Mire. Only a token force remains to watch the Galewyr River. The army moves slowly but it'll reach Aquesta before Gaunt does. That will tip the scales in favor of the empire."

"What are you suggesting?"

Royce looked at Arista, indicating that she should speak now.

Arista set down her glass and gathered her thoughts as best she could. She was still befuddled from the day's ride and now the wine on an empty stomach caused her head to fog. She took a short breath and focused.

"Melengar still has a defensive force," the princess began. "If we use it to attack across the river and break into Chadwick, there would be nothing to stop us from sweeping across into Glouston. Once there, Marquis Lanaklin could raise an army from his loyal subjects and together we could march on Colnora. We can catch the empire in a vise with Melengar pushing from the north and the Nationalists from the south. The empire would have to either recommit the northern army, leaving the capital to Gaunt, or let us sweep across northern Warric unopposed."

Cosmos said nothing, but there was a smile on his face. He took a drink of his wine and sat back to consider their words.

"All we need you to do" — Royce spoke again — "is to set up a meeting between Gaunt and the princess."

"Once a formal agreement is struck between the Nationalists and Melengar," Arista explained, "I can take that to Trent. With the Nationalists on Aquesta's doorstep, and my brother ravaging northern Warric, Trent will be more than happy to join us. And with their help, the New Empire will be swept back into history, where it belongs."

"You paint a lovely picture, Your Highness," Cosmos said. "But is it possible for Melengar to break out of Medford? Will Lanaklin be able to raise a force quickly enough to fend off any counterattack the empire sends? I suspect you would say yes to both, but without the conviction that comes from knowing. Fortunately, these are not my concerns so much as they're yours. I'll contact Gaunt's people and arrange a meeting. It'll take a few days, however, and in the meantime it's not safe for you to stay in Colnora."

"What do you mean?" Royce asked.

"As I said, I fear it's possible the guild has been compromised. Mr. Price tells me imperial scouts were on hand when you passed through the gate, so it would only be wishful thinking to suppose your visit here was not observed. Given the situation, it'll not take a genius to determine what's happening. The next logical step will be to eliminate the threat. And, Duster, you're not the only Diamond alumnus passing through Warric."

Royce's eyes narrowed as he stared at Cosmos and studied the fat man carefully. Cosmos said nothing more on the subject, and strangely, Royce did not inquire further.

"We'll leave immediately," Royce said abruptly. "We'll head south into Rhenydd, which will carry us closer to Gaunt. I'll expect you to contact us with the meeting's place and time in three days. If by the morning of the fourth day we don't hear from you, we'll find our own way to Gaunt."

"If you don't hear from me by then, things will be very bad indeed," Cosmos assured them. "Gibbons, see that they have whatever is needed for travel. Price, arrange for them to slip out of town unnoticed, and get that message to Gaunt's people. Will you need to send a message back to Medford?" Cosmos asked the princess.

She hesitated briefly. "Not until I've reached an agreement with Gaunt. Alric knows the tentative plan and has already begun preparing the invasion."

"Excellent," Cosmos said, standing up and draining his glass. "What a pleasure it is to work with professionals. Good luck to all of you and may fortune smile upon us. Just remember to watch your back, Duster. Some ghosts never die."

◆

"Your horses and gear will be taken to Finlin's windmill by morning," Price told them as he rapidly led them out through the rear of the patio. His long gangly legs gave him the appearance of a wayward scarecrow fleeing across a field. Noticing Arista had trouble keeping up, he paused for her to catch her breath. "However, you three will be leaving by boat down the Bernum tonight."

"There'll be a watch on the Langdon and the South Bridge," Royce reminded him.

"Armed with crossbows and hot pitch, I imagine," Price replied, grinning. His face looked even more skull-like in the darkness. "But no worries, arrangements have been made."

The Bernum started as a series of tiny creeks that cascaded from Amber Heights and the Senon Uplands. They converged, creating a swift-flowing river that cut through a limestone canyon, forming a deep gorge. Eventually it spilled over Amber Falls. The drop took the fight out of the water, and from there on the river flowed calmly through the remaining ravine that divided the city. This put Colnora at the navigable headwater of the Bernum—the last stop for goods coming up the river, and a gateway for anyone traveling to Dagastan Bay.

After Arista had regained her breath, Price resumed rushing them along at a storm's pace. They ducked under a narrow ivy-covered archway and passed through a wooden gate, which brought them to the rear of the estate. A short stone wall, only a little above waist high, guarded the drop to the river gorge. Looking down, she could see only darkness, but across the expanse she could make out points of light and the silhouette of buildings. Price directed them to an opening and the start of a long wooden staircase.

"Our neighbor, Bocant, the pork mogul, has his six-oxen hoist," Price said, motioning to the next mansion over. Arista could just make out a series of cables and pulleys connected to a large metal box. Two lanterns, one hung at the top and another at the bottom, revealed the extent of the drop, which appeared to be more than a hundred feet. "But we have to make do with our more traditional, albeit more dangerous, route. Try not to fall. The steps are steep and it's a long way down."

The stairs were indeed frightening—a plummeting zigzag of planks and weathered beams bolted to the cliff's face. It looked like a diabolical puzzle of wood and rusting metal, which quaked and groaned the moment they stepped on it. Arista was certain she felt it sway. Memories of a tower collapsing while she clutched on to Royce flooded back to her. Taking a deep breath, she gripped the handrail with a sweaty palm and descended, sandwiched between Royce and Hadrian.

A narrow dock sat at the bottom and a shallow-draft rowboat banged dully against it with the river's swells. A lantern mounted on the bow illuminated the area with a yellow flicker.

"Put that damn light out, you fools!" Price snapped at the two men readying the craft.

A quick hand snuffed out the lantern and Arista's eyes adjusted to the moonlight. From previous trips to Colnora, she knew that the river was as congested as Main Street on Hospitality Row during the day, but in the dark it lay empty, the vast array of watercraft bobbing at various piers.

When the last of the supplies were aboard, Price returned their weapons. Hadrian strapped his on and Royce's white-bladed dagger disappeared into the folds of his cloak. "In you go," Price told them, putting one foot on the gunwale to steady the boat. A stocky, shirtless boatman stood in the center of the skiff and directed them to their seats.

"Which one of ya might be handy with a tiller?" he asked.

"Etcher," Price said, "why don't you take the tiller?"

"I'm no good with a boat," the wiry youth with a thin mustache and goatee replied as he adjusted the lay of the gear.

"I'll take the rudder," Hadrian said.

"And grateful I am to you, sir," the boatman greeted him cheerily. "Name's Wally... You shouldn't need to use it much. I can steer fine with just the oars, but in the current it's sometimes best not ta paddle a'tall. All ya needs to do is keep her in the center of the river."

Hadrian nodded. "I can do that."

"But of course you can, sir."

Royce held Arista's hand as she stepped aboard and found a seat beside Hadrian on a shelf of worn planking. Royce followed her and took up position near the bow next to Etcher.

"When did you order the supplies brought down?" Royce asked Price, who still stood with his foot on the rail.

"Before returning to pick you up at The Regal Fox. I like to stay ahead of things." He winked. "Duster, you might remember Etcher here from the Langdon Bridge last time you were in Colnora. Don't hold that against him. Etcher volunteered to get you safely to the mills when no one else cared for the idea. Now off you go." Price untied the bowline and shoved them out into the black water.

"Stow those lines, Mr. Etcher, sir," Wally said as he waited until they cleared the dock to lock the two long oars into place. With each stroke, the oars creaked quietly, and the skiff glided into the river's current.

The boatman sat backward as he pulled on the oars. Little effort was required as the current propelled them downstream. Wally pulled on one side or the other, correcting their course as needed. Occasionally he stroked both together, to keep them moving slightly faster than the water's flow.

"Blast," Wally cursed softly.

"What is it?" Hadrian asked.

"The lantern went out on the Bocant dock. I use it to steer by. Just my luck, any other night they leave it on. They use that hoisting contraption to unload boats. Sometimes the barges are late rounding the point, and in the darkness that lantern is their marker. They never know when the barges will arrive, so they usually just leave it on all night and—oh wait, it's back. Must have just blown out or something."

"Quiet down," Etcher whispered from the bow. "This is no pleasure cruise. You're being paid to row, not be a river guide."

Royce peered into their dark wake. "Is it normal for small boats to be on the river at night?"

"Not unless you're smuggling," Wally said in a coy tone that made Arista wonder if he had firsthand experience.

"If you don't keep your traps shut, someone will notice us," Etcher growled.

"Too late," Royce replied.

"What's that?"

"Behind us, there's at least one boat following."

Arista looked but could see nothing except the line the moon drew on the black surface of the water.

"You've got a fine pair of eyes, you do," Wally said.

"You're the one that saw them," Royce replied. "The light on the dock didn't go out. The other boat blocked it when they passed in your line of sight."

"How many?" Hadrian asked.

"Six, and they're in a wherry."

"They'll be able to catch us, then, won't they?" Arista questioned.

Hadrian nodded. "They race wherries down the Galewyr and here on the Bernum for prize money. No one races skiffs."

Despite this, Wally stroked noticeably harder, which, combined with the current, moved the skiff along at a brisk pace, raising a breeze in their faces.

"Langdon Bridge approaching," Etcher announced.

Arista saw it towering above them as they rushed toward it.

Massive pillars of stone blocks formed the arches supporting the bridge, whose broad span straddled the river eight stories above. She could barely make out the curved heads of the decorative swan-shaped streetlamps that lit the bridge, creating a line of lights against the starry sky.

"There are men up there," Royce said, "and Price wasn't kidding about them having crossbows."

Wally glanced over his shoulder and peered up at the bridge before regarding Royce curiously. "What are ya, part owl?"

"Stop paddling and shut up!" Etcher ordered, and Wally pulled his oars out of the water.

They floated silently, propelled by the river's current. In the swan lights, the men on the span soon became visible, even to Arista. A dark boat on a black river would be hard, but not impossible, to spot. The skiff started to rotate sideways as the current pushed the stern. A nod from Wally prompted Hadrian to compensate with the tiller and the boat straightened.

Light exploded into the night sky. A bright orange-and-yellow glow spilled onto the bridge from somewhere on the left bank. A warehouse was on fire. It burst into flame, spewing sparks skyward like a cyclone of fireflies. Silhouetted figures ran the length of the bridge and harsh shouts cut the stillness of the night.

"Now paddle!" Etcher ordered, and Wally put his back into it.

Arista used the opportunity to glance aft and now she also saw the wherry, illuminated by the fire from above. The approaching boat was a good fifteen feet in length and she guessed barely four feet across. Four men sat in two side-by-side pairs, each manning an oar. Besides the oarsmen, there were a man sitting in the stern and another at the bow with a grappling hook.

"I think they mean to board us," Arista whispered.

"No," Royce said. "They're waiting."

"For what?"

"I'm not sure, but I don't intend to find out. Give us as much distance as you can, Wally."

"Slide over, pal. Let me give you a hand," Hadrian told the boatman as he took up a seat beside him. "Arista, take the tiller."

The princess replaced Hadrian, grabbing hold of the wooden handle. She had no idea what to do with it and opted for keeping it centered. Hadrian rolled up his sleeves and, bracing his feet against the toggles, took one of the oars. Royce slipped off his cloak and boots and dropped them onto the floor of the boat.

"Don't do anything stupid," Etcher told him. "We've still got another bridge to clear."

"Just make sure you get them past the South Bridge and we'll be fine," Royce said. "Now, gentlemen, if you could put a little distance between us."

"On three," Wally announced, and they began stroking together, pulling hard and fast, so that the bow noticeably rose and a wake began to froth. Caught by surprise, Etcher stumbled backward and nearly fell.

"What the blazes are—" Etcher started when Royce leapt over the gunwale and disappeared. "Damn fool. What does he expect us to do, wait for him?"

"Don't worry about Royce," Hadrian replied as he and Wally stroked in unison. To Arista, the wherry did seem to drop farther back but perhaps that was only wishful thinking.

"South Bridge," Etcher whispered.

As they approached, Arista saw another fire blazing. This time it was a boat dock burning like well-aged kindling. The old South Bridge, which marked the city's boundary, was not nearly as high as the Langdon, and Arista could easily see the guards.

"They aren't going for it this time," Hadrian said. "They're staying at their posts."

"Quiet. We might slip by," Etcher whispered.

With oars held high, they all sat as still as statues. Arista found herself in command of the skiff as it floated along in the current. She quickly learned how the rudder affected the boat. The results felt backward to her. Pulling right made the bow swing left. Terrified of making a mistake, she concentrated on keeping the boat centered and straight. Up ahead, something odd was being lowered from the bridge. It looked like cobwebs or tree branches dangling. She was going to steer around it when she realized it stretched the entire span.

"They draped a net!" Etcher said a little too loudly.

Wally and Hadrian back paddled, but the river's current was the victor and the skiff flowed helplessly into the fishnet. The boat rotated, pinning itself sideways. Water frothed along the length, threatening to tip them.

"Shore your boat and don't move from it!" A shout echoed down from above.

A lantern lowered from the bridge revealed their struggles to free themselves from the mesh. Etcher, Wally, and Hadrian slashed at the netting with knives, but before they could clear it, two imperial soldiers descended and took up position on the bank. Each was armed with a crossbow.

"Stop now or we'll kill you where you stand," the nearest soldier ordered with a harsh, anxious voice. Hadrian nodded and the three dropped their knives.

Arista could not take her eyes off the crossbows. She knew those weapons. She had seen Essendon soldiers practicing with them in the yard. They pierced old helms placed on dummies, leaving huge holes through the heavy metal. These were close enough for her to see the sharp iron heads of the bolts—

the power to pierce armor held in check by a small trigger and pointed directly at them.

Wally and Hadrian maneuvered the boat to the bank and one by one they exited, Hadrian offering Arista his hand as she climbed out. They stood side by side, Arista and Hadrian in front, Wally and Etcher behind.

"Remove your weapons," one of the soldiers ordered, motioning toward Hadrian. Hadrian paused, his eyes shifting between the two bowmen, before slipping off his swords. One of the soldiers approached, while the other stayed back, maintaining a clear line of sight.

"What are your names?" the foremost soldier asked.

No one answered.

The lead guard took another step forward and intently studied Arista. "Well, well, well," he said. "Look what we have here, Jus. We done caught ourselves a fine fish, we have."

"Who is it?" Jus asked.

"This here is that Princess of Melengar, the one they say is a witch."

"How do you know?"

"I recognize her. I was in Medford the year she was on trial for killing her father."

"What's she doing here, ya think?"

"Don't know... What are you doing here?"

She said nothing, her eyes locked on the massive bolt heads. Made of heavy iron, the points looked sharp. Knight killers, Sir Ecton called them.

What will they do to me?

"The captain will find out," the soldier said. "I recognize these two as well." He motioned to Wally and Etcher. "I seen them around the city afore."

"Course you have." Wally spoke up. "I've piloted this river for years. We weren't doing nothin' wrong."

"If you've been on this river afore, then you knows we don't allow transports at night."

Wally did not say anything.

"I don't know that one, though. What's yer name?"

"Hadrian," he said, taking the opportunity to step forward as if to shake hands.

"Back! Back!" the guard shouted, bringing his bow to bear at Hadrian's chest. Hadrian immediately stopped. "Take one more step and I'll punch a hole clear through you!"

"So what's your plan?" Hadrian asked.

"You and your pals just sit tight. We sent a runner to fetch a patrol. We'll take you over to see the captain. He'll know what to do with the likes of you."

"I hope we don't have to wait long," Hadrian told them. "This damp night air isn't good. You could catch a cold. Looks like you have already. What do you think, Arista?"

"I ain't got no cold."

"Are you sure? Your eyes and nose look red. Arista, you agree with me, don't you?"

"What?" Arista said, still captivated by the crossbows. She could feel her heart hammering in her chest and barely heard Hadrian addressing her.

"I bet you two been coughing and sneezing all night, haven't you?" Hadrian continued. "Nothing worse than a summer cold. Right, Arista?"

Arista was dumbfounded by Hadrian's blathering and his obsession with the health of the two soldiers. She felt obligated to say something. "I—I suppose."

"Sneezing, that's the worst. I hate to *sneeze*."

Arista gasped.

"Just shut up," the soldier ordered. Without taking his eyes off Hadrian, he called to Jus behind him. "See anyone coming yet?"

"Not yet," Jus replied. "All of them off dealing with that fire, I 'spect."

Arista had never tried this under pressure before. Closing her eyes, she fought to remember the concentration technique Esrahaddon had taught her. She took deep breaths, cleared her mind, and tried to calm herself. Arista focused on the sounds around her—the river lapping against the boat, the wind blowing through the trees, and the chirping of the frogs and crickets. Then slowly she blocked each out, one by one. Opening her eyes, she stared at the soldiers. She saw them in detail now, the three-day-old whiskers on their faces, their rumpled tabards, even the rusted links in their hauberks. Their eyes showed their nervous excitement and Arista thought she even caught the musky odor of their bodies. Breathing rhythmically, she focused on their noses as she began to hum, then mutter. Her voice slowly rose as if in song.

"I said no—" The soldier stopped suddenly, wrinkling his nose. His eyes began to water and he shook his head in irritation. "I said no—" he began again, and stopped once more, gasping for air.

At the same time, Jus was having similar problems, and the louder Arista's voice rose, the greater their struggle. Raising her hand, she moved her fingers as if writing in the air.

"I—said—I—I—"

Arista made a sharp clipping motion with her hand and both of them abruptly sneezed in unison.

In that instant, Hadrian lunged forward and broke the closest guard's leg with a single kick to his knee. He pulled the screaming guard in front of him just as the other fired. The crossbow bolt caught the soldier square in the chest, piercing the metal ringlets of his hauberk and staggering both of them backward. Letting the dead man fall, Hadrian picked up his bow as the other guard turned to flee. *Snap!* The bow launched the bolt. The impact made a deep resonating *thwack!* and drove the remaining guard to the ground, where he lay dead.

Hadrian dropped the bow. "Let's move!"

They jumped back in the skiff just as the wherry approached.

It came out of the darkness, its long pointed shape no longer slicing through the water. Instead, it drifted aimlessly, helpless to the whims of the current. As it approached, it became apparent why. The wherry was empty. Even the oars were gone. As the boat passed by, a dark figure crawled out of the water.

"Why have you stopped?" Royce admonished, wiping his wet hair away from his face. "I would have caught up." Spotting the bodies halted his need for explanation.

Hadrian pushed the boat into the river, leaping in at the last instant. From above, they could hear men's voices. They finished cutting loose the net and, once free, slipped clear of the bridge. The current, combined with Wally's and Hadrian's pulling hard on the oars, sent them flying downriver in the dark of night, leaving the city of Colnora behind them.

CHAPTER 8

HINTINDAR

Arista woke feeling disoriented and confused. She had been dreaming about riding in her carriage. She sat across from both Sauly and Esrahaddon. Only, in her dream, Esrahaddon had hands and Sauly was wearing his bishop's robes. They were trying to pour brandy from a flask into a cup and were discussing something—a heated argument, but she could not recall it.

A bright light hurt her eyes, and her back ached from sleeping on something hard. She blinked, squinted, and looked around. Her memory returned as she realized she was still in the skiff coasting down the Bernum River. Her left foot was asleep, and dragging it from under a bag started the sensation of pins and needles. The morning sun shone brightly. The limestone cliffs were gone, replaced by sloping farmlands. On either side of the river, lovely green fields swayed gently in the soft breeze. The tall spiked grass might have been wheat, although it could just as easily have been barley. Here the river was wider and moved slower. There was hardly any current, and Wally was back to rowing.

"Morning, milady," he greeted her.

"Morning," Hadrian said from his seat at the tiller.

"I guess I dozed off," she replied, pulling herself up and adjusting her gown. "Did anyone else get any sleep?"

"I'll sleep when I get downriver," Wally replied, hauling on the oars, rocking back, then sitting up again. The paddle blades dripped and plunged. "After I drop you fine folks off, I'll head down to Evlin, catch a nap and a meal, then try to pick up some travelers or freight to take back up. No sense fighting this current for nothing."

Arista looked toward Hadrian.

"Some," he told her. "Royce and I took turns."

Her hair was loose and falling in her face. Her blue satin ribbon had been lost somewhere during the night's ride from Sheridan. Since then, she had been using a bit of rawhide provided by Hadrian. Even that was missing now, and she poked about her hair and found the rawhide caught in a tangle. While she worked to free it, she said, "You should have woken me. I would have taken a shift at the tiller."

"We actually considered it when you started to snore."

"I don't snore!"

"I beg to differ," Hadrian chided while chewing.

She looked around the skiff as each of them, even Etcher, nodded. Her face flushed.

Hadrian chuckled. "Don't worry about it. You can't be held accountable for what you do in your sleep."

"Still," she said, "it's not very ladylike."

"Well, if that's all you're worried about, you can forget it," Hadrian informed her with a wicked smirk. "We lost all illusions of you being prissy back in Sheridan."

How much better it was when they were silent.

"That's a compliment," he added hastily.

"You don't have much luck with the ladies, do you, sir?" Wally asked, pausing briefly and letting the paddles hang out like wings, leaving a tiny trail of droplets on the smooth surface of the river. "I mean, with compliments like that, and all."

Hadrian frowned at him, then turned back to her with a concerned expression. "I really did mean it as a compliment. I've never met a lady who would—well, without complaining you've been—" He paused in frustration, then added, "That little trick you managed back there was really great."

Arista knew Hadrian only brought up the sneezing spell to try to smooth things over, but she had to admit a sense of pride that she had finally contributed something of value to their trip. "That was the first practical application of hand magic I've ever performed."

"I really wasn't sure you could do it," Hadrian said.

"Who would have thought such a silly thing would come in handy?"

"Travel with us long enough and you'll see we can find a use for just about anything." Hadrian extended his hand. "Cheese?" he asked. "It's really quite good."

Arista took the cheese and offered him a smile but was disappointed he did not see it. His eyes had moved to the riverbank, and her smile faded as she ate self-consciously.

Wally continued to paddle in even strokes and the world passed slowly by. They rounded bend after bend, skirting a fallen tree, then a sandy point. It took Arista nearly an hour with her brush to finally work all the knots out of her hair. She retied its length with the rawhide into a respectable ponytail. Eventually a gap opened in the river reeds to reveal a small sandy bank that showed signs of previous boat landings.

"Put in here," Etcher ordered, and Wally deftly spun the boat to land beneath the shadow of a massive willow tree. Etcher leapt out and tied the bowline. "This is our stop. Let's get the gear off."

"Not yet," Royce said. "You want to check the mill sails first?"

"Oh yeah." Etcher nodded, looking a little embarrassed and a tad irritated. "Wait here," he said before trotting up the grassy slope.

"Sails?" Hadrian asked.

"Just over this rise is the millwright Ethan Finlin's windmill," Royce explained. "Finlin is a member of the Diamond. His windmill is used to store smuggled goods and also serves as a signal that can be seen from the far hills. If the mill's sails are spinning, then all is clear. If furled, then there's trouble. The position of the locked sails indicates different things. If straight up and down, like a ship's mast, it means he needs help. If the sails are cockeyed, it means stay away. There are other signals as well, but I'm sure they've changed since I was a member."

"All clear," Etcher notified them as he strode back down the hill.

They each took a pack, waved goodbye to Wally, and climbed up the slope.

Finlin's mill was a tall weathered tower that sat high on the crest of a grassy knoll. The windmill's cap rotated and currently faced into the wind, which blew steadily from the northeast. Its giant sails of cloth-covered wooden frames rotated slowly, creaking as they turned the great mill's shaft. Around the windmill were several smaller buildings, storage sheds, and wagons. The place was quiet and absent of customers.

They found their horses, as well as an extra one for Etcher, along with their gear in a nearby barn. Finlin briefly stuck his nose out of the mill and waved. They waved back, and Royce had a short talk with Etcher as Hadrian saddled their animals and loaded the supplies. Arista threw her own saddle on her mare, which garnered a smile from Hadrian.

"Saddle your own horse often, do you?" he asked as she reached under the horse's belly for the cinch. The metal ring at the end of the wide band swung back and forth, making catching it a challenge without crawling under the animal.

"I'm a princess, not an invalid."

She caught the cinch and looped the leather strap through it, tying what she thought was a fine knot, exactly like the one she used to tie her hair.

"Can I make one minor suggestion?"

She looked up. "Of course."

"You need to tie it tighter and use a flat knot."

"That's two suggestions. Thanks, but I think it'll be fine."

He reached up and pulled on the saddle's horn. The saddle easily slid off and came to rest between the horse's legs.

"But it *was* tight."

"I'm sure it was." Hadrian pulled the saddle back up and undid the knot. "People think horses are stupid—dumb animals, they call them—but they're not. This one, for instance, just out-smarted the Princess of Melengar." He pulled the saddle off, folded the blanket over, and returned the saddle to the animal's back. "You see, horses don't like to have a saddle bound around their chest any more than I suspect you enjoy being trussed up in a corset. The looser, the better, they figure, because they don't really mind if you slide off." He looped the leather strap through the ring in the cinch and pulled it tight. "So what she's doing right now is holding her breath, expanding her chest and waiting for me to tie the saddle on. When she exhales, it'll be loose. Thing is, I know this. I also know she can't hold her breath forever." He waited with two hands on the strap, and the moment the mare exhaled, he pulled, gaining a full four inches. "See?"

She watched as he looped the strap across, then through and down, making a flat knot that laid comfortably against the horse's side. "Okay, I admit it. This is the first time I've saddled a horse," she confessed.

"And you're doing wonderfully," he mocked.

"You are aware I can have you imprisoned for life, right?"

Royce and Etcher entered the barn. The younger thief grabbed his horse and left without a word.

"Friendly sorts, those Diamonds are," Hadrian observed.

"Cosmos seemed hospitable," Arista pointed out.

"Yeah, but that's how you might expect a spider to talk to a fly as she wraps him up."

"What an interesting metaphor," Arista noted. "You could have a future in politics, Hadrian."

He glanced at Royce. "We never considered that as one of the options."

"I'm not sure how it differs from acting."

"He never likes my ideas," Hadrian told her, then turned his attention back to Royce. "Where to now?"

"Hintindar," Royce replied.

"Hintindar? Are you serious?"

"It's out of the way and a good place to disappear for a while. Problem?"

Hadrian narrowed his eyes. "You know darn well there's a problem."

"What's wrong?" Arista asked.

"I was born in Hintindar."

"I've already told Etcher that's where we'll wait for him," Royce said. "Nothing we can do about it now."

"But Hintindar is just a tiny manorial village—some farms and trade shops. There's no place to stay."

"Even better. After Colnora, lodging in a public house might not be too smart. There must be a few people there that still know you. I'm sure someone will lend a hand and put us up for a while. We need to go somewhere off the beaten track."

"You don't honestly think anyone is still following us. I know the empire would want to stop Arista from reaching Gaunt, but I doubt anybody recognized her in Colnora — at least no one still alive."

Royce did not answer.

"Royce?"

"I'm just playing it safe," he snapped.

"Royce? What did Cosmos mean back there about you not being the only ex-Diamond in Warric? What was that talk of ghosts all about?" Royce remained silent. Hadrian glared at him. "I came along as a favor to you, but if you're going to keep secrets..."

Royce relented. "It's probably nothing, but then again — Merrick could be after us."

Hadrian lost his look of irritation and replied with a simple, "Oh."

"Anyone going to tell me who Merrick is?" Arista asked. "Or why Hadrian doesn't want to go home?"

"I didn't leave under the best of circumstances," Hadrian answered, "and haven't been back in a long time."

"And Merrick?"

"Merrick Marius, also known as Cutter, was Royce's friend once. They were members of the Diamond together, but they..." He glanced at Royce. "Well, let's just say they had a falling out."

"So?"

Hadrian waited for Royce to speak and, when he did not, answered for him. "It's a long story, but the gist of the matter is that Merrick and Royce seriously don't get along." He paused, then added, "Merrick is an awful lot like Royce."

Arista continued to stare at Hadrian until the revelation dawned on her.

"Still, that doesn't mean Merrick is after us," Hadrian

went on. "It's been a long time, right? Why would he bother with you now?"

"He's working for the empire," Royce said. "That's what Cosmos meant. And if there's an imperial mole in the Diamond, Merrick knows all about us by now. Even if there isn't a spy, Merrick could still find out about us from the Diamond. There are plenty who think of him as a hero for sending me to Manzant. I'm the evil one in their eyes."

"You were in Manzant?" Arista asked, stunned.

"It's not something he likes to talk about." Hadrian again answered for him. "So if Merrick is after us, what do we do?"

"What we always do," Royce replied, "only better."

⚭

The village of Hintindar lay nestled in a small sheltered river valley surrounded by gentle hills. A patchwork of six cultivated fields, outlined by hedgerows and majestic stands of oak and ash, decorated the landscape in a crop mosaic. Horizontal lines of mounded green marked three of the fields with furrows, sown in strips, to hold the runoff. Animals grazed in the fourth field and the fifth was cut for hay. The last field lay fallow. Young women were in the fields, cutting flax and stuffing it in sacks thrown over their shoulders, while men weeded crops and threw up hay.

The center of the village clustered along the main road near a little river, a tributary of the Bernum. Wood, stone, and wattle-and-daub buildings with shake or grass-thatched roofs lined the road, beginning just past the wooden bridge and ending halfway up the hillside toward the manor house. Between them were a variety of shops. From several buildings smoke rose, the blackest of which came from the smithy. Their horses announced their arrival with a loud hollow *clop clip clop* as they crossed the bridge. Heads turned, each villager nudging the next, fingers pointing in their direction. Those they passed stopped what they were doing to follow, keeping a safe distance.

"Good afternoon," Hadrian offered, but no one replied. No one smiled.

Some whispered in the shelter of doorways. Mothers pulled children inside and men picked up pitchforks or axes.

"This is where *you* grew up?" Arista whispered to Hadrian. "Somehow it seems more like how I would imagine Royce's hometown to be."

This brought a look from Royce.

"They don't get too many travelers here," Hadrian explained.

"I can see why."

They passed the mill, where a great wooden wheel turned with the power of the river. The town also had a leatherworker's shop, a candlemaker, a weaver, and even a shoemaker. They were halfway up the road when they reached the brewer.

A heavyset matron with gray hair and a hooked nose worked outside beside a boiling vat next to a stand of large wooden casks. She watched their slow approach, then walked to the middle of the road, wiping her hands on a soiled rag.

"That'll be fer enough," she told them with a heavy south-province accent.

She wore a stained apron tied around her shapeless dress and a kerchief tied over her head. Her feet were bare and her face was covered in dirt and sweat.

"Who are ya and what's yer business here? And be quick afore the hue and cry is called and yer carried to the bailiff. We don't stand fer troublemakers here."

"Hue and cry?" Arista softly asked.

Hadrian looked over. "It's an alarm that everyone in the

village responds to. Not a pretty sight." His eyes narrowed as he studied the woman. Then he slowly dismounted.

The woman took a step back and grabbed hold of a mallet used to tap the kegs. "I said I'd call the hue and cry and I meant it!"

Hadrian handed his reins to Royce and walked over to her. "If I remember correctly, *you* were the biggest troublemaker in the village, Armigil, and in close to twenty years, it doesn't seem much has changed."

The woman looked surprised, then suspicious. "Haddy?" she said in disbelief. "That can't be, can it?"

Hadrian chuckled. "No one's called me Haddy in years."

"Dear Maribor, how you've grown, lad!" When the shock wore off, she set the mallet down and turned to the spectators now lining the road. "This here is Haddy Blackwater, the son of Danbury the smithy, come back home."

"How are you, Armigil?" Hadrian said with a broad smile, stepping forward to greet her.

She replied by making a fist and punching him hard in the jaw. She had put all her weight into it, and winced, shaking her hand in pain. "Oww! Damned if ya haven't got a hard bloody jaw!"

"Why did you hit me?" Hadrian held his chin, stunned.

"That's fer running out on yer father and leaving him to die alone. I've been waiting to do that fer nearly twenty years."

Hadrian licked blood from his lip and scowled.

"Oh, get over it, ya baby! An' ya better keep yer eyes out fer more round here. Danbury was a damn fine man and ya broke his heart the day ya left."

Hadrian continued to massage his jaw.

Armigil rolled her eyes. "Come here," she ordered, and grabbed hold of his face. Hadrian flinched as she examined him. "Yer fine, for Maribor's sake. Honestly, I thought yer father made ya tougher than that. If I had a sword in me hand, yer shoulders would have less of a burden to carry, and the wee ones would have a new ball to kick around, eh? Here, let me get ya a mug of ale. This batch came of age this morning. That'll take the sting out of a warm welcome, it will."

She walked to a large cask, filled a wooden cup with a dark amber draft, and handed it to him.

Hadrian looked at the drink dubiously. "How many times have you filtered this?"

"Three," she said unconvincingly.

"Has His Lordship's taster passed this?"

"Of course not, ya dern fool. I just told ya it got done fermenting this morning. Brewed it day afore yesterday, I did, a nice two days in the keg. Most of the sediment ought to have settled and it should have a nice kick by now."

"Just don't want to get you into trouble."

"I ain't selling it to ya, now am I? So drink it and shut up or I'll hit ya again for being daft."

"Haddy? Is it really you?" A thin man about Hadrian's age approached. He had shoulder-length blond hair and a soft doughy face. He was dressed in a worn gray tunic and a faded green cowl, his feet wrapped in cloth up to his knees. A light brown dust covered him as if he had been burrowing through a sand hill.

"Dunstan?"

The man nodded and the two embraced, clapping each other on the shoulders. Wherever Hadrian patted Dunstan, a puff of brown powder arose, leaving the two in a little cloud.

"You used to live here?" a little girl from the gathering crowd asked, and Hadrian nodded. This touched off a wave of conversations among those gathering in the street. More people rushed over and Hadrian was enveloped in their midst. Eventually he was able to get a word in and motioned toward Royce and Arista.

"Everyone, this is my friend Mr. Everton and his wife, Erma."

Arista and Royce exchanged glances.

"Vince, Erma, this is the village brew mistress, Armigil, and Dunstan here is the baker's son."

"Just the baker, Haddy. Dad's been dead five years now."

"Oh—sorry to hear that, Dun. I've nothing but fond memories of trying to steal bread from his ovens."

Dunstan looked at Royce. "Haddy and I were best friends when he lived here—until he disappeared," he said with a note of bitterness.

"Will I have to endure a swing from you too?" Hadrian feigned fear.

"You should, but I remember all too well the last time I fought you."

Hadrian grinned wickedly as Dunstan scowled back.

"If my foot hadn't slipped..." Dunstan began, and then the two broke into spontaneous laughter at a joke no one else appeared to understand.

"It's good to have you back, Haddy," he said sincerely. He watched Hadrian take a swallow of beer, and then to Armigil he said, "I don't think it fair that Haddy gets a free pint and I don't."

"Let me give ya a bloody lip and ya can have one too." She smiled at him.

"Break it up! Break it up!" bellowed a large muscular man making his way through the crowd. He had a bull neck, a full dark beard, and a balding head. "Back to work, all of ya!"

The crowd groaned in displeasure but quickly quieted down as two horsemen approached. They rode down the hill, coming from the manor at a trot.

"What's going on here?" the lead rider asked, reining his horse. He was a middle-aged man with weary eyes and a strong chin. He dressed in light tailored linens common to a favored servant and on his chest was an embroidered crest of crossed daggers in gold threading.

"Strangers, sir," the loud bull-necked man replied.

"They ain't strangers, sir." Armigil spoke up. "This here's Haddy Blackwater, son of the old village smith—come fer a visit."

"Thank you, Armigil," he said. "But I wasn't speaking to you. I was addressing the reeve." He looked down at the bearded man. "Well, Osgar, out with it."

The burly man shrugged his shoulders and stroked his beard, looking uncomfortable. "She might be right, sir. I haven't had a chance to ask, what with getting the villeins back to work and all."

"Very well, Osgar, see to it that they return to work, or I'll have you in stocks by nightfall."

"Yes, sir, right away, sir." He turned, bellowing at the villagers until they moved off. Only Armigil and Dunstan quietly remained behind.

"Are you the son of the old smithy?" the rider asked.

"I am," Hadrian replied. "And you are?"

"I'm His Lordship's bailiff. It's my duty to keep order in this village and I don't appreciate you disrupting the villeins' work."

"My apologies, sir." Hadrian nodded respectfully. "I didn't mean—"

"If you're the smithy's son, where have you been?" The other rider spoke this time. Much younger-looking, he was better dressed than the bailiff, wearing a tunic of velvet and linen. His legs were covered in opaque hose, and his feet in leather shoes with brass buckles. "Are you aware of the penalty for leaving the village without permission?"

"I'm the son of a freeman, not a villein," Hadrian declared. "And who are you?"

The rider sneered at Hadrian. "I'm the imperial envoy to this village, and you would be wise to watch the tone of your voice. Freemen can lose that privilege easily."

"Again, my apologies," Hadrian said. "I'm only here to visit my father's grave. He died while I was away."

The envoy's eyes scanned Royce and Arista, then settled on Hadrian, looking him over carefully. "Three swords?" he asked the bailiff. "In this time of war an able-bodied man like this should be in the army fighting for the empress. He's likely a deserter or a rogue. Arrest him, Siward, and take his associates in for questioning. If he hasn't committed any crimes, he will be properly pressed into the imperial army."

The bailiff looked at the envoy with annoyance. "I don't take my orders from you, Luret. You forget that all too frequently. If you have a problem, take it up with the steward. I'm certain he will speak to His Lordship the moment he returns from loyal service to the empire. In the meantime, I'll administer this village as best I can for my lord—not for you."

Luret jerked himself upright in indignation. "As imperial envoy, I am addressed as *Your Excellency.* And you should understand that my authority comes directly from the empress."

"I don't care if it comes from the good lord Maribor himself. Unless His Lordship, or the steward in his absence, orders me otherwise, I only have to put up with you. I don't have to take orders from you."

"We'll see about that." The envoy spun and spurred his horse back toward the manor, kicking up a cloud of dust.

The bailiff shook his head with irritation, waiting for the dust to settle.

"Don't worry," he told them. "The steward won't listen to him. Danbury Blackwater was a good man. If you're anything like him, you'll find me a friend. If not, you had best make your stay here as short as possible. Keep out of trouble. Don't interfere with the villeins' work, and stay away from Luret."

"Thank you, sir," Hadrian said.

The bailiff then looked around the village in irritation. "Armigil, where did the reeve get off to?"

"Went to the east field, I think, sir. There is a team he has working on drainage up that way."

The bailiff sighed. "I need him to get more men working on bringing in the hay. Rain's coming and it'll ruin what's been cut if he doesn't."

"I'll tell him, sir, if he comes back this way."

"Thank you, Armigil."

"Sir?" She tapped off a pint of beer and handed it up to him. "While you're here, sir?" He took one swallow, then poured the rest out and tossed her back the cup.

"A little weak," he said. "Set your price at two copper tenents a pint."

"But, sir! It's got good flavor. At least let me ask three."

He sighed. "Why must you always be so damn stubborn? Let it be three, but make them brimming pints. Mind you, if I hear one complaint, I'll fine you a silver and you can take your case to the Steward's Court."

"Thank you, sir," she said, smiling.

"Good day to you all." He nodded and trotted off toward the east.

They watched him go, and then Dunstan started chuckling. "A fine welcome home you've had so far—a belt in the mouth and threat of arrest."

"Actually, outside the fact that everything looks a lot smaller, not much has changed here," Hadrian observed. "Just some new faces, a few buildings, and, of course, the envoy."

"He's only been here a week," Dunstan said, "and I'm sure the bailiff and the steward will be happy when he leaves. He travels a circuit covering a number of villages in the area and has been showing up here every couple of months since the New Empire annexed Rhenydd. No one likes him, for obvious reasons. He's yet to meet Lord Baldwin face to face. Most of us think Baldwin purposely avoids being here when the envoy comes. So Luret's list of complaints keeps getting longer and longer and the steward just keeps writing them down.

"So are you really here just to see your father's grave? I thought you were coming back to stay."

"Sorry, Dun, but we're just passing through."

"In that case, we had best make the most of it. What say you, Armigil? Roll a keg into my kitchen and I'll supply the bread and stools for toasts to Danbury and a proper welcome for Haddy?"

"He don't deserve it. But I think I have a keg round here that is bound to go bad if'n I don't get rid of it."

"Hobbie!" Dunstan shouted up the street to a young man at the livery. "Can you find a place for these horses?"

Dunstan and Hadrian helped Armigil roll a small barrel to the bakery. As they did, Royce and Arista walked their animals over to the stables. The boy cleared three stalls, then ran off with a bucket to fetch water.

"Do you think the envoy will be a problem?" Arista asked Royce once Hobbie had left.

"Don't know," he said, untying his pack from the saddle. "Hopefully we won't be here long enough to find out."

"How long will we be here?"

"Cosmos will move fast. Just a night or two, I imagine." He threw his bag over his shoulder and crossed to Hadrian's horse. "Have you decided what you'll say to Gaunt when you meet him? I hear he hates nobility, so I wouldn't start by asking him to kiss your ring or anything."

She pulled her own gear off Mystic and then, holding out

her hands, wiggled her bare fingers. "Actually, I thought I'd ask him to kidnap my brother." She smiled. "It worked for you. And if I can gain the trust and aid of a Royce Melborn, how hard can it be to win over a Degan Gaunt?"

They carried the gear across the street to the little white-washed shop with the signboard portraying a loaf of bread. Inside, a huge brick oven and a large wooden table dominated the space. The comforting scent of bread and wood smoke filled the air, and Arista was surprised the bakery wasn't broiling. The wattle-and-daub walls and the good-sized windows managed to keep the room comfortable. As Arista and Royce entered, they were introduced to Dunstan's wife, Arbor, and a host of other people whose names Arista could not keep up with.

Once word spread, freemen, farmers, and other merchants dropped by, grabbing a pint and helping themselves to a hunk of dark bread. There were Algar, the woodworker; Harbert, the tailor; and Harbert's wife, Hester. Hadrian introduced Wilfred, the carter, and explained how he used to rent Wilfred's little wagon four times every year to travel to Ratibor to buy iron ingots for his father's smithy. There were plenty of stories of the skinny kid with pimples who used to swing a hammer beside his father. Most remembered Danbury with kindness, and there were many toasts to his good name.

Just as the bailiff had predicted, it started to rain, and soon the villeins, released from work due to weather, dropped by to join the gathering. They slipped in, quietly shaking off the wetness. Each got a bit of bread, a pint to drink, and a spot to sit on the floor. Some brought steaming crocks of vegetable pottage, cheese, and cabbage for everyone to share. Even Osgar, the reeve, pressed himself inside and was welcomed to share the community meal. The sky darkened, the wind whipped up, and Dunstan finally closed the shutters as the rain poured.

They all wanted to know what had happened to Hadrian—where he had gone and what he had done. Most of them had spent their whole lives in Hintindar, barely crossing the river. In the case of the villeins, they were bound to the land and, by law, could not leave. For them, generations passed without their ever setting foot beyond the valley.

Hadrian kept them entertained with stories of his travels. Arista was curious to hear tales of the adventures he and Royce had shared over the years, but none of those came out. Instead, he told harmless stories of distant lands. Everyone was spellbound by stories about the far east, where the Calian people supposedly interbred with the Ba Ran Ghazel to produce the half-goblin Tenkin. Children gathered close to the skirts of their mothers when he spoke about the oberdaza—Tenkin who worshiped the dark god Uberlin and blended Calian traditions with Ghazel magic. Even Arista was captivated by his stories of far-off Dagastan.

With Hadrian the center of attention, few took notice of Arista, which was fine with her. She was happy just to be off her horse and in a safe place. The tension melted away from her.

The hot bread and fresh-brewed beer were wonderful. She was comfortable for the first time in days and reveled in the camaraderie of the bakery. She drank pints of beer until she lost track of the number. Outside, night fell and the rain continued. They lit candles, giving the room an even friendlier charm. The beer was infecting the group with mirth, and soon they were singing loudly. She did not know the words but found herself rocking with the rhythm, humming the chorus, and clapping her hands. Someone told a bawdy joke and the room burst into laughter.

"Where are you from?" Although it had been asked three times, this was the first instance that Arista had realized it was meant for her. Turning, she found Arbor, the baker's wife, sitting beside her. She was a petite woman with a plain face and short-cropped hair.

"I'm sorry," Arista apologized. "I'm not accustomed to beer. The bailiff said it was weak, but I think I would take exception to that."

"From yer mouth to his ears, darling!" Armigil said loudly from across the room. Arista wondered how she had heard from so far away, especially when she had thought she had spoken so softly.

Arista remembered Arbor had asked her a question. "Oh— right, ah...Colnora," the princess said at length. "My husband and I live in Colnora. Well, actually we are staying with my brother now, because we were evicted from our home in Windham Village by the Northern Imperial Army. That's up in Warric, you know—Windham Village, I mean, not the army. Of course, it could be—the army, I mean this time— not the village—because they could be there. Does that answer your question?"

The room was spinning slowly and it gave Arista the feeling she was falling, though she knew she was sitting still. The whole sensation made it difficult for her to concentrate.

"You were evicted? How awful." Arbor looked stricken.

"Well, yes, but it's not that great of a hardship, really. My brother has a very nice place in the Hill District in Colnora. He's quite well off, you know?" She whispered this last part into Arbor's ear. At least, she thought she did, but Arbor pulled back sharply.

"Oh really? You come from a wealthy family?" Arbor asked, rubbing her ear. "I thought you did. I was admiring your dress. It's very beautiful."

"This? Ha!" She pulled at the material of her skirt. "I got this old rag from one of my servants, who was about to throw it out. You should see my gowns. Now those are something, but yes, we're very wealthy. My brother has a virtual *army* of servants," she said, and burst out laughing.

"Erma?" someone said from behind her.

"What does your brother do?" Arbor asked.

"Hmm? Do? Oh, he doesn't *do* anything."

"He doesn't work?"

"Erma *dear*?"

"My brother? He calls it work, but it's nothing like what *you* people do. Did you know I slept on the ground just two nights ago? Not indoors either, but out in the woods. My brother never did that, I can tell you. You probably have, haven't you? But he hasn't. No, he gets his money from taxes. That's how all kings get their money. Well, some can get it from conquest. Glenmorgan got *loads* from conquest, but not Alric. He's never been to war—until now, of course, and he's not doing well at all, I can tell you."

"*Erma!*" Arista looked up to see Royce standing over her, his face stern.

"Why are you calling me that?"

"I think my wife has had a little too much to drink," he said to the rest of them.

Arista looked around to see several faces smirking in an effort to suppress laughter.

"Is there anywhere I can take her to sleep it off?"

Immediately several people offered the use of their homes, some even the use of their beds, saying they would sleep on the floor.

"Spend the night here," Dunstan said. "It's raining out. Do you really want to wander around out there in the dark? You can actually make a fine bed out of the flour sacks in the storeroom."

"How would you know that, Dun?" Hadrian asked,

chuckling. "The wife's kicked you out a few times?" This brought a roar of laughter from the crowd.

"Haddy, *you*, my friend, can sleep in the rain."

"Come along, Wife." Royce pulled Arista to her feet.

Arista looked up at him and winked. "Oh right, sorry. Forgot who I was."

"Don't apologize, honey," Armigil told her. "That's why we're drinking in the first place. Ya just got there quicker than the rest of us, is all."

❧

The next morning, Arista woke up alone and could not decide which hurt more, her head from the drink, or her back from the lumpy flour bags. Her mouth was dry, her tongue coated in some disgusting film. She was pleased to discover her saddlebags beside her. She pulled them open and grimaced. Everything inside smelled of horse sweat and mildew. She had brought only three dresses: the one worn through the rain, which was a wrinkled mess; the stunning silver receiving gown she planned to wear when she met Degan Gaunt; and the one she presently wore. Surprisingly, the silver gown was holding up remarkably well and was barely even wrinkled. She had brought it hoping to impress Gaunt, but recalling her conversation with Royce about how the Nationalist leader felt about royalty, she realized it was a poor choice. She would have been much better off with something simpler. It would at least have given her something decent to change into. She pulled off her dirt-stained garment, removed her corset, and pulled on the dress she had worn at Sheridan.

She stepped out of the storeroom and found Arbor hard at work kneading dough surrounded by dozens of cloth-covered baskets. Villagers entered and set either a bag of flour or a sackcloth of dough on the counter along with a few copper coins. Arbor gave them an estimated pickup time of either midday or early evening.

"You do this every day?" Arista asked.

Arbor nodded with sweat glistening on her brow as she used the huge wooden paddle to slide another loaf into the glowing oven. "Normally Dun is more helpful, but he's off with your husband and Haddy this morning. It's a rare thing, so I'm happy to let him enjoy the visit. They're down at the smithy if you're interested, or would you rather have a bite to eat?"

Arista's stomach twisted. "No, thank you. I think I'll wait a bit longer."

Arbor worked with a skilled hand born of hundreds, perhaps thousands, of repetitions.

How does she do it?

She knew the baker's wife got up every morning and repeated the same actions as the day before.

Where is the challenge?

Arista was certain Arbor could not read and probably had few possessions, yet she seemed happy. She and Dunstan had a pleasant home, and compared to that of those toiling in the fields, her work was relatively easy. Dunstan seemed a kind and decent man and their neighbors were good, friendly folk. While not terribly exciting, it was nonetheless a safe, comfortable life, and Arista felt a twinge of envy.

"What's it like to be wealthy?"

"Hmm? Oh—well, actually, it makes life easier but perhaps not as rewarding."

"But you travel and can see the world. Your clothing is so fine and you ride horses! I'll bet you've even ridden in a carriage, haven't you?"

Arista snorted. "Yes, I've certainly ridden in a carriage."

"And been to balls in castles where musicians played and the ladies dressed in embroidered gowns of velvet?"

"Silk, actually."

"Silk? I've heard of that but never seen it. What's it like?"

"I can show you." Arista went back into the storeroom and returned with the silver gown.

At the sight of the dress, Arbor gasped, her eyes wide. "I've never seen anything so beautiful. It's like—it's like…" Arista waited but Arbor never found her words. Finally, she said, "May I touch it?"

Arista hesitated, looking first at Arbor, then at the dress.

"That's okay," Arbor said quickly with an understanding smile. She looked at her hands. "I would ruin it."

"No, no," Arista told her. "I wasn't thinking that at all." She looked down at the dress in her arms once more. "What I was thinking was it was stupid for me to have brought this. I don't think I'll have a chance to wear it, and it's taking up so much space in my pack. I was wondering—would you like to have it?"

Arbor looked like she was going to faint. She shook her head adamantly, her eyes wide as if with terror. "No, I—I couldn't."

"Why not? We're about the same size. I think you'd look beautiful in it."

A self-conscious laugh escaped Arbor and she covered her face with her hands, leaving flour on the tip of her nose. "Oh, I'd be a sight, wouldn't I? Walking up and down Hintindar in *that*. It's awfully nice of you, but I don't go to grand balls or ride in carriages."

"Maybe one day you will, and then you'll be happy you have it. In the meantime, if you ever have a bad day, you can put it on and perhaps it'll make you feel better."

Arbor laughed again, only now there were tears in her eyes.

"Take it—really—you'd be doing me a favor. I do need the space." She held out the dress. Arbor reached toward it and gasped at the sight of her hands. She ran off and scrubbed them red before taking the dress in her quivering arms, cradling it as if it were a child.

"I promise to keep it safe for you. Come back and pick it up anytime, all right?"

"Of course," Arista replied, smiling. "Oh, and one more thing." Arista handed her the corset. "If you would be so kind, I never wish to see this thing again."

Arbor carefully laid the dress down and put her arms around Arista, hugging her close as she whispered, "Thank you."

৵

When Arista stepped out of the bakery into the sleepy village, her head throbbed, jolted by the brilliant sunlight. She shaded her eyes and spotted Armigil working in front of her shop, stoking logs under her massive cooker.

"Morning, Erma," Armigil called to her. "Yer looking a mite pale, lassie."

"It's your fault," Arista growled.

Armigil chuckled. "I try my best. I do indeed."

Arista shuffled over. "Can you direct me to the well?"

"Up the road four houses. You'll find it in front of the smithy."

"Thank you."

Following the unmistakable clanging of a metal hammer, Arista found Royce and Hadrian under the sun canopy in the smithy's yard, watching another man beating a bit of molten metal on an anvil. He was muscular and completely bald-headed, with a bushy brown mustache. If he had been in the bakery the previous night, Arista did not remember. Beside him was a barrel of water, and not far away was the well, a full bucket resting on its edge.

The bald man dropped the hot metal into his barrel, where it hissed. "Your father taught me that," the man said. "He was a fine smith—the finest."

Hadrian nodded and recited, "Choke the hammer after stroke, grip it high when drilling die."

This brought laughter from the smith. "I learned that one too. Mr. Blackwater was always making up rhymes."

"So this is where you were born?" Arista asked, dipping a community cup into the bucket of water and taking a seat on the bench beside the well.

"Not exactly," Hadrian replied. "I lived and worked here. I was actually born across the street there at Gerty and Abelard's home." He pointed at a tiny wattle-and-daub hovel without even a chimney. "Gerty was the midwife back then. My father kept pestering her so much that she took Mum to her house and Da had to wait outside in the rain during a terrible thunderstorm, or so I was told."

Hadrian motioned to the smith. "This is Grimbald. He apprenticed with my father after I left—does a good job too."

"You inherited the smithy from Danbury?" Royce asked.

"No, Lord Baldwin owns the smithy. Danbury rented from him, just as I do. I pay ten pieces of silver a year, and in return for charcoal, I do work for the manor at no cost."

Royce nodded. "What about personal belongings? What became of Danbury's things?"

Grimbald raised a suspicious eyebrow. "He left me his tools and if'n you're after them, you'll have to fight me before the steward in the manor court."

Hadrian raised his hands and shook his head, calming the burly man. "No, no, I'm not here after anything. His tools are in good hands."

Grimbald relaxed a bit. "Ah, okay, good, then. I do have something for you, though. When Danbury died, he made a list of all his things and who they should go to. Almost everyone in the village got a little something. I didn't even know the man could write until I saw him scribbling it. There was a letter and instructions to give it to his son, if he ever returned. I read it, but it didn't make much sense. I kept it, though."

Grimbald set down his hammer and ducked inside the shop, then emerged a few minutes later with the letter.

Hadrian took the folded parchment and, without opening it, stuffed the note into his shirt pocket and walked away.

"What's going on?" Arista asked Royce. "He didn't even read it."

"He's in one of his moods," Royce told her. "He'll mope for a while. Maybe get drunk. He'll be fine tomorrow."

"But why?"

Royce shrugged. "Just the way he is lately. It's nothing, really."

Arista watched Hadrian disappear around the side of the candlemaker's shop. Picking up the hem of her dress, she chased after him. When she rounded the corner, she found him seated on a fence rail, his head in his hands. He glanced up.

Is that annoyance or embarrassment on his face?

Biting her lip, she hesitated, then walked over and sat beside him. "Are you all right?" she asked.

He nodded in reply but said nothing. They sat in silence for a while.

"I used to hate this village," he offered at length, his tone distant and his eyes searching the side of the shop. "It was always so small." He lowered his head again.

She waited.

Does he expect me to say something now?

From down the street, she heard the rhythmic hammering

of metal as Grimbald resumed his work, the blows marking the passage of time. She pretended to straighten her skirt, wondering if it would be better if she left.

"The last time I saw my father, we had a terrible fight," Hadrian said without looking up.

"What about?" Arista gently asked.

"I wanted to join Lord Baldwin's men-at-arms. I wanted to be a soldier. He wanted me to be a blacksmith." Hadrian scuffed the dirt with his boot. "I wanted to see the world, have adventures—be a hero. He wanted to chain me to that anvil. And I couldn't understand that. I was good with a sword; he saw to that. He trained me every day. When I couldn't lift the sword anymore, he just made me switch arms. Why'd he do that if he wanted me to be a smith?"

A vision swept back to her of two faces in Avempartha: the heir she had not recognized—but Hadrian's face had been unmistakable as the guardian.

Royce didn't tell him? Should I?

"When I told him my plans to leave, he was furious. He said he didn't train me to gain fame or money. That my skills were meant for *greater things*, but he wouldn't say what they were.

"The night I left, we had words—lots of them—and none good. I called him a fool. I might even have said he was a coward. I don't remember. I was fifteen. I ran away and did just what he didn't want me to. I was gonna show him—prove the old man wrong. Only he wasn't. It's taken me this long to figure that out. Now it's too late."

"You never came back?"

Hadrian shook his head. "By the time I returned from Calis, I heard he'd died. I didn't see any point in returning." He pulled the letter out. "Now there's this." He shook the parchment in his fingers.

"Don't you want to know what it says?"

"I'm afraid to find out." He continued to stare at the letter as if it were a living thing.

She placed a hand on his arm and gave a soft squeeze. She did not know what else to do. She felt useless. Women were supposed to be comforting, consoling, nurturing, but she did not know how. She felt awful for him, and her inability to do anything to help just made her feel worse.

Hadrian stood up. With a deep breath, he opened the letter and began reading. Arista waited. He lowered his hand slowly, holding the letter at his side.

"What does it say?"

Hadrian held out the letter, letting it slip from his fingers. Before she could take it, the parchment drifted to the ground at her feet. As she bent to pick it up, Hadrian walked away.

∽

Arista rejoined Royce at the well.

"What was in the letter?" he asked. She held it out to Royce, who read it. "What was his reaction?"

"Not good. He walked off. I think he wants to be alone. You never told him, did you?"

Royce continued to study the letter.

"I can't believe you never told him. I mean, I know Esrahaddon told us not to, but I guess I just expected that you would anyway."

"I don't trust that wizard. I don't want me or Hadrian wrapped up in his little schemes. I couldn't care less who the guardian is, or the heir, for that matter. Maybe it *was* a mistake coming here."

"You came here on purpose? You mean this had nothing to do with— You came here for proof, didn't you?"

"I wanted something to confirm Esrahaddon's claim. I really didn't expect to find anything."

"He just told me his father trained him night and day in sword fighting and said his skills were *for greater things*. Sounds like proof to me. You know, you would have discovered that if you had just talked to him. He deserves the truth, and when he gets back, one of us needs to tell him."

Royce nodded, carefully refolding the letter. "I'll talk to him."

CHAPTER 9

THE GUARDIAN

The oak clenched the earth with a massive hand of gnarled roots unchanged by time. In the village, houses were lost to fires. New homes were built to accommodate growing families, and barns were raised on once vacant land, but on this hill time stood as still as the depths of Gutaria Prison. Standing beneath the tree's leaves, Hadrian felt young again.

Here, at this tree, Haddy had first kissed Arbor, the shoe-maker's daughter. He and Dunstan had been competing for years for her favor, but Haddy kissed her first. That had been what started the fight. Dun had known better. He had seen Haddy spar with his father, and witnessed Haddy beat the old reeve for whipping Willie, a villein friend of theirs. The reeve had been too embarrassed to report to the bailiff that a fourteen-year-old boy had bested him. Haddy's skill was no secret to Dunstan, but rage had overcome reason.

When Dunstan found out about Arbor, he had charged at Haddy, who instinctually sidestepped and threw him to the ground. Misfortune landed Dun's head on a fieldstone. He had lain unconscious with blood running from his nose and ears. Horrified, Haddy had carried him back to the village, convinced he had just killed his best friend. Dun recovered, but Haddy never would. He never spoke to Arbor again. Three days later, the boy known as Haddy had left for good.

Hadrian slumped to the ground and sat in the shade of the tree with his back to the old oak's trunk. When he had been a boy, this had been where he had always come to think. From here, he could see the whole village below and the hills beyond—hills that had called to him, and a horizon that had whispered of adventure and glory.

Royce and Arista would be wondering where he had gone. Hadrian was not usually self-indulgent on the job.

The job!

He unconsciously shook his head. This was Royce's job, not his. He had kept his part of the bargain, and all that remained was for Arista to reach the rendezvous. When she did, that would end the assignment and his career in the world of intrigue. Strange how the end brought him back to the beginning. Coming full circle could be a sign for him to make a fresh start.

Near the center of the village he could see the smithy, which was easy to pick out by its rising black smoke. He had worked those bellows for hours each day. Hadrian remembered the sound of the anvil and the ache in his arms. That had been a time when all he had known of the world had stopped at this tree, and Hadrian could not help wondering how different his life might have been if he had stayed. One thing was certain; he would have more calluses and less blood on his hands.

Would I've married Arbor? Had children of my own? A stout, strong son who would complain about working the bellows and come to this tree to kiss his first girl? Could I've found contentment making plowshares and watching Da smile as he taught his grandson fencing, like a commoner's version of the Pickerings? If I'd stayed, at this very moment, would I be sitting here thinking of my happy family below? Would Da have died in peace?

He sighed heavily. Regret was a curse without a cure, except to forget. He closed his eyes. He did not want to think. He fell asleep to the sound of songbirds and woke to the thunder of horses' hooves.

⤙

As night approached, Royce became worried. Once more they enjoyed the hospitality of the Bakers. Arbor was making a dinner of pottage while Dunstan ran a delivery of loaves to the manor. Arista offered assistance but appeared more a hindrance than a help. Arbor did not seem to mind. The two were inside, chatting and laughing, while Royce stood outside, watching the road with an uneasy feeling.

The village felt different to him. The evening had an edge, a tension to the air. Somewhere in the distance, a dog barked. He felt a nervous energy in the trees and an apprehension rising from the earth and rock. Before Avempartha, he had considered it intuition, but now he wondered. Elves drew power from nature. They understood the river's voice and the chatter of the leaves.

Did that pass to me?

He stood motionless, his eyes panning the road, the shops, the houses, and the dark places between. He was hoping to spot Hadrian returning, but felt something else.

"The cabbage goes in last," Arbor was telling Arista, her voice muffled by walls. "And cut it up into smaller pieces than that. Here, let me show you."

"Sorry," Arista said. "I don't have a lot of experience in a kitchen."

"It must be wonderful to have servants. Dun could never make that much money here. There aren't enough people to buy his bread."

Royce focused on the street. The sun had set and the twilight haze had begun to mask the village. He was looking at the candlemaker's shop when he spotted movement by the livery. When he looked closer, nothing was there. It could have been Hobbie coming to check the animals, but the fact that the image had vanished so quickly made him think otherwise.

Royce slipped into the shadows behind Armigil's brew shop and crept toward the livery. He entered from the rear, climbing to the loft. A fresh pile of hay cushioned his movements and muted his approach. In the dark, he could clearly see the back of a figure standing by the doorway, peering at the street.

"Move and die," Royce whispered softly in his ear.

The man froze. "Duster?" he asked.

Royce turned the man to face him. "Etcher, what are you doing here?"

"The meeting has been set. I've been sent to fetch you."

"That was fast."

"We got word back this morning and I rode hard to get here. The meeting is set for tonight at the ruins of Amberton Lee. We need to get going if we're going to make it in time."

"We can't leave right now. Hadrian is missing."

"We can't wait. Gaunt's people are suspicious—they think it could be an imperial trap. They'll back off if we don't stick to the plan. We need to leave now or the opportunity will pass."

Royce silently cursed to himself. It was his own fault for not having chased after Hadrian that afternoon. He almost had. Now there was no telling where he was. Etcher was right—the mission had to come first. He would leave word for Hadrian with the Bakers and get the princess to her meeting with Gaunt.

❧

The moist, steamy smell of the boiling cabbage and wood smoke filled the bakery. The candles Arista lit flickered with the opening of the door. Arbor was stirring the pot while Arista set the table. Both looked up, startled.

"Hadrian hasn't shown?"

"No," Arista replied.

"We need to get going," Royce told her.

"Now? But what about Hadrian?"

"He'll have to catch up. Get your things."

Arista hesitated only a moment and then crossed to the flour storage to gather her bags.

"Can't you even stay for dinner?" Arbor asked. "It's almost ready."

"We need to get moving. We have a—" Royce stopped as he heard the noisy approach of a horse and cart being driven fast down the road. It stopped just out front, so close they could hear the driver pull the hand brake. Dunstan came through the door a moment later.

"Hadrian's been arrested!" he announced hurriedly, and then he pointed at Royce and Arista. "The steward ordered your arrests as well."

"Their arrests?" Arbor said, shocked. "But why?"

"The bailiff was wrong. It looks like Luret has more influence than he thought," Royce muttered. "Let's get the horses."

"His Lordship's soldiers were just behind me as I started down the hill. They will be here in minutes," Dunstan said.

"My horse is down by the river," Etcher said. "It can carry two."

Royce was thinking quickly, calculating risks and outcomes. "You take her to the rendezvous on your horse, then," he told Etcher. "I'll see what I can do to help Hadrian. With any luck, we'll catch up to you. If we don't, it shouldn't matter." He looked at Arista. "From what I've heard of your *contact*, he will see to your safety even if he ultimately declines your offer."

"Don't worry about me." The princess rushed toward the door with her bags. "I'll be fine. Just make sure that Hadrian is okay."

Taking a bag and the princess's hand, Etcher pulled her out into the night and dodged into the shadows of the buildings.

Royce followed them out, caught hold of the eaves, and climbed up on the Bakers' shake roof, where he crouched in the shadow of the chimney, listening. He watched about half a dozen men with torches moving fast down the main street from the direction of the manor. They stopped first at the livery, then went to the Bakers'.

"Where are the strangers that rode in with the old blacksmith's son?" a loud voice he had not heard before demanded.

"They left hours ago," Dunstan replied.

Royce heard a grunt and a crash, followed by a scream from Arbor and the sound of furniture falling over.

"Their horses are still in the livery. We saw you race from the manor to warn them! Now where are they?"

"Leave him alone!" Arbor shouted. "They ran out when they heard you coming. We don't know where. They didn't tell us anything."

"If you're lying, you'll be arrested for treason and hanged, do you understand?"

There was a brief silence.

"Fan out in pairs. You two cover the bridge. You and you search the fields, and you two start going door-to-door. Until further notice, all citizens of Hintindar are to remain in their homes. Arrest anyone outside. Now move!"

The men, marked conveniently by their flaming torches,

scattered out of the bakery in all directions, leaving Royce to watch them scurrying about. He glanced across the dark fields. Etcher would have no trouble avoiding the foot search. Once they reached his horse, they would be gone. Arista was safely on her way, his job done. All he had to worry about now was Hadrian.

⇜

The manor house's jail was less a dungeon and more an old well. Forced to descend by a rope, Hadrian was left trapped at the bottom. He waited in silence, looking up at the stars. The rising moon cast a shaft of pale light that descended the wall, marking the slow passage of the night.

Cold spring water seeped in through the walls, leaving them damp and creating a shallow pool at the base. With his feet tiring, Hadrian eventually sat in the cold puddle. Jagged rocks hidden under the water added to his misery. In time, he was forced to stand again to fight the cold.

The moonlight was more than halfway down the wall when Hadrian heard voices and movement from above. Dark silhouettes appeared and the iron grate scraped as it slid clear. A rope lowered and Hadrian thought they had reconsidered. He stood up to take hold of it, but stopped when he saw another figure coming down.

"In ya go," someone at the top ordered, and laughed, his voice echoing. "We keep all our rats down there!"

The figure was nimble and descended quickly.

"Royce?" Hadrian asked. "They—they *captured you?*"

The rope was pulled up and the grate slid back in place.

"More or less," he replied, glancing around. "Not much on accommodations, are they?"

"I can't believe they caught you."

"It wasn't as easy as you'd think. They aren't very bright." Royce reached out and let his fingers run over the glistening walls. "Was this just a well that went dry?"

"Hintindar doesn't have much need for a big prison." Hadrian shook his head. "So you *let* them capture you?"

"Ingenious, don't you think?"

"Oh, brilliant."

"I figured it was the easiest way to find you." Royce shuffled his feet in the water, grimacing. "So what's your excuse? Did they come for you with an army of twenty heavily armored men?"

"They caught me sleeping."

Royce shot him a skeptical look.

"Let's just say I was put in a position where I'd have to kill people and I chose not to. This is my home, remember. I don't want to be known as a killer here."

"So it *is* good I didn't slit throats. I'm smarter than I thought."

"Oh yes, I can see the genius in your plan." Hadrian looked up. "How do you suggest we get out now?"

"Eventually, Luret will haul us out and hand us over to a press-gang, just as he threatened. We'll serve in the imperial army for a few days, learn what we can, and then slip away. We can report what we discover to Alric for an added bonus."

"What about Arista?"

"She's safely on her way to the rendezvous with Gaunt. Etcher arrived just before dark and I sent her with him. She'll likely stay with Gaunt, sending dispatches back to Melengar via messengers until Alric's forces join with the Nationalists."

"And if Gaunt turns her down?"

"It's in Gaunt's best interest to see to her safety. It's not like he's going to turn her over to the empire. She'll probably end up returning to Melengar by sea. Actually, it's better we aren't with her. If Merrick *is* out there, I'm sure he'll be more interested in me than her. So that job is complete."

"I guess there is that to be thankful for, at least."

Royce chuckled.

"What?"

"I'm just thinking about Merrick. He'll have no idea where I am now. My disappearance will drive him crazy."

Hadrian sat down.

"Isn't that water cold?" Royce asked, watching him and making an unpleasant face.

He nodded. "And the bottom has sharp rocks coated in a disgusting slime."

Royce looked up at the opening once more, then gritted his teeth and slowly eased himself down across from Hadrian. "Oh yeah, real comfortable."

They sat in silence for a few minutes, listening to the breeze flutter across the grating. It made a humming noise when it blew just right. Occasionally, a droplet of water would drip into the pool with a surprisingly loud *plop!* magnified by the chamber.

"You realize that with this job over, I'm officially retired."

"I assumed as much." Royce fished beneath him, withdrew a rock, and tossed it aside.

"I was thinking of returning here. Maybe Grimbald could use a hand, or Armigil. She's getting older now and probably would welcome a partner. Those barrels can be heavy and brewing beer has its perks."

Moonlight revealed Royce's face. He looked tense.

"I know you're not happy with this, but I really need a change. I'm not saying I'll stay here. I probably won't, but it's a start. I consider it practice for a peaceful life."

"And that's what you want, a peaceful life? No more dreams of glory?"

"That's all they were, Royce, just dreams. It's time I faced that and got on with my life."

Royce sighed. "I've something to tell you. I should have told you a long time ago, but...I guess I was afraid you'd do something foolish." He paused. "No, that's not true either. It's just taken me a while to see that you have the right to know."

"Know what?"

Royce looked around him. "I never thought I'd be telling you in a place like this, but I must admit it could be a benefit that they took your weapons." He pulled out Danbury's letter.

"How do you have that?" Hadrian asked.

"From Arista."

"Why didn't they take it when they grabbed you?"

"Are you kidding? I practically had to remind them to take my dagger. They don't seem too accustomed to thieves, much less ones that turn themselves in." Royce handed the note to Hadrian. "What did you think of when you read this?"

"That my father died filled with pain and regret. He believed the words of a selfish fifteen-year-old that he was a coward and wasted his life. It's bad enough I left him, but I had to paint that stain on him before leaving."

"Hadrian, I don't think this letter had anything to do with your leaving. I think it's due to your heritage. I think your father was trying to tell you something about your past."

"How would you know? You never met my father. You're not making any sense."

Royce sighed. "Last year in Avempartha, Esrahaddon was using a spell to find the heir."

"I remember. You told me that before."

"But I didn't tell you everything. The spell didn't find the heir exactly, but rather magical amulets worn by him and his guardian. Esrahaddon made the necklaces so he could locate the wearers and prevent other wizards from finding them. As

I told you, I didn't recognize the face of the heir. He was some guy with blond hair and blue eyes I'd never seen before."

"And this is important why?"

"I didn't know, at least not for certain, not really. I always thought Esra was using us. That's mainly why I never told you. I wanted to be sure it was true, and that's why I asked you to come and why I led us here."

Royce paused a moment, then asked, "Where did you get that necklace, the amulet you wear under your shirt?"

"I told you, my father…" Hadrian paused, staring at Royce, his hand unconsciously rising to his neck to feel the necklace.

"I didn't recognize the heir…but I did recognize the guardian. Your father had a secret, Hadrian—a *big* secret."

Hadrian continued to stare at Royce. His mind flashed back to his youth, to his gray-haired father, spending day after day toiling humbly on the anvil and forge, making harrows and plowshares. He recalled Danbury growling at him to clean the shop.

"No," Hadrian said. "My father was a blacksmith."

"How many blacksmiths teach their sons ancient Teshlor combat skills, most of which have been lost for centuries? Where did you get that big spadone sword you've carried on your back since I first met you? Was that your father's too?"

Hadrian slowly nodded and felt a chill raise the hairs on his arms. He had never told Royce about that. He had never told anyone. He had taken the sword the night he had left. He had needed his own blade. Da often had several weapons in his shop, but taking them would have cost his father money. Instead, he had taken the only weapon he felt his father would not miss. Da had kept the spadone hidden in a small compartment under the shop's fifth floorboard. Danbury had taken it out only once, a long time ago, when Hadrian's mother had still been alive. At the time, Hadrian was very young, and now the memory was hard to recall. His mother was asleep and Hadrian should have been as well, but something had woken him. Crawling out of bed, he had found his father in the shop. Da had been drinking Armigil's ale and was sitting on the floor in the glow of the forge. In his hands, he cradled the huge two-handed sword, talking to it as if it were a person. He was crying. In fifteen years of living with the man, Hadrian had seen him cry only that one time.

"I want you to do me a favor. Read this again, only this time pretend you hadn't run away. Read it as if you and your father were on great terms and he was proud of you."

Hadrian held the parchment up to the moonlight and read it again.

> Haddy,
> I hope this letter will find you. It's important that you know there is a reason why you should never use your training for money or fame. I should have told you the truth, but my pain was too great. I can admit to you now I'm ashamed of my life, ashamed of what I failed to do. I suppose you were right. I'm a coward. I let everyone down. I hope you can forgive me, but I can never forgive myself.
> love, Da

> Before you were born, the year ninety-two,
> lost what was precious, and that what was new.
> The blink of an eye, the beat of a heart,
> Out went the candle, and guilt was my part.

> A king and his knight went hunting a boar,
> A rat and his friends were hunting for love.

Together they fought, till one was alive.
The knight sadly wept, no king had survived.

The answers to riddles, to secrets and more,
Are found in the middle of legends and love.
Seek out the answer, and learn if you can
The face of regret, the life of a man.

"You realize a spadone is a knight's weapon?" Royce asked.

Hadrian nodded.

"And yours is a very old sword, isn't it?"

Hadrian nodded again.

"I would venture to guess it's about nine hundred years old. I think you're the descendant of Jerish, the Guardian of the Heir," Royce told him. "Although maybe not literally. The way I heard it, the heir has a direct bloodline but the guardian just needed to pass down his skills. The next in line didn't need to be his son, although I guess it's possible."

Hadrian stared at Royce. He did not know how to feel about this. Part of him was excited, thrilled, vindicated, and part of him was certain Royce was insane.

"And you kept this from me?" Hadrian asked, astonished.

"I didn't want to tell you until I knew for sure. I thought Esrahaddon might be playing us."

"Don't you think I would have thought of that too? What do you take me for? Have you worked with me for twelve years because you think I'm stupid? How conceited can you be? You can't trust me to make my own decisions, so you make them for me?"

"I'm telling you now, aren't I?"

"It took you a whole damn year, Royce!" Hadrian shouted at him. "Didn't you think I'd find this important? When I told you I was miserable because I felt my life lacked purpose—

that I wanted a cause worth fighting for—you didn't think that protecting the heir qualified?" Hadrian shook his head in disbelief. "You stuck-up, manipulative, lying—"

"I *never* lied to you!"

"No, you just concealed the truth, which to me is a lie, but in *your* twisted little mind is a virtue!"

"I knew you were going to take it this way," Royce said in a superior tone.

"How else would you expect me to take it? Gee, pal, thanks for thinking so little of me that you couldn't tell me the truth about my own life."

"That's not the reason I didn't tell you," Royce snapped.

"You just said it was!"

"I know I did!"

"So you're lying to me again?"

"Call me a liar one more time—"

"And what? What? You going to fight me?"

"It's dark in here."

"But there's no room for you to hide. You're only a threat until I get my hands on you. I just need to grab your spindly little neck. For all your quickness, once I get a grip on you, it's all over."

Without warning, cold water poured down on them. Looking up, Hadrian saw silhouetted figures.

"You boys, be quiet down there!" shouted a voice. "His Excellency wants a word with you."

One head disappeared from view and another replaced it at the opening's edge.

"I'm Luret, the imperial envoy of Her Eminence, the grand imperial empress Modina Novronian. Because of your involvement in escorting a member of the royal court of Melengar to Her Eminence's enemy, the Nationalists, the two of you are hereby charged with espionage and hitherto will be put to death by hanging in three days' time. Should, however, you wish to attempt to rescind that sentence to life in prison, I'd be willing to do so under the condition that you reveal to me the whereabouts of Princess Arista Essendon of Melengar."

Neither said a word.

"Tell me where she is, or you'll be hanged as soon as the village carpenter can build a proper gallows."

Again, they were silent.

"Very well, perhaps a day or two rotting in there will change your mind." He turned away and spoke to the jailor. "No food or water. It might help to loosen their tongues. Besides, there's really no sense in wasting it."

They waited in silence as the figures above moved away.

"How does he know?" Hadrian whispered.

A ghastly look stole over Royce's face.

"What is it?"

"Etcher. He's the mole in the Diamond."

Royce kicked the wall, causing a splash. "How could I've been so blind? He was the one who lit the lamp on the river, alerting the wherry behind us. The only reason he never thought to check the mill's sails was because it didn't matter to him. I bet he never even told Price where we were, so there would be no way for the Diamond to find us. There must be an ambush waiting at Amberton Lee, or somewhere along the way."

"But why take her there? Why not just turn Arista over to Luret?"

"I'd wager this is Merrick's game. He doesn't want some imperial clown like Luret getting the prize. She's a commodity which can be sold to the empire, or ransomed to Melengar for a profit. If Luret grabs her, he gets nothing."

"So why tell Luret about us at all?"

"Insurance. With the manor officials after us, we'd be

pressed for time and wouldn't question Etcher's story. I'm sure it was to hasten our departure and have us unprepared, but it turned out even better, because you were captured and I decided to stay behind to help you."

"And you sent Arista off alone with Etcher."

"She's on her way to Merrick, or Guy, or both. Maybe they'll keep her and demand Alric surrender Medford. He won't, of course. Pickering won't let him."

"I can't believe Alric sent her in the first place. What an idiot! Why didn't he pick a representative outside the royal court? Why did he have to send *her*?"

"He didn't send her," Royce said. "I doubt anyone in Medford has a clue where she is. She did this on her own."

"What?"

"She arrived at The Rose and Thorn unescorted. Have you *ever* seen her go anywhere without a bodyguard?"

"So why did you—"

"Because I needed an excuse to bring you here, to find out if what Esrahaddon showed me was true."

"So this is *my* fault?" Hadrian asked.

"No, it's everyone's fault: you for pushing so hard to retire, me for not telling you the truth, Arista for being reckless, even your father for never having told you who you really are."

They sat in silence a moment.

"So what do we do now?" Hadrian said at last. "Your original plan isn't going to work so well anymore."

"Why do I always have to come up with the plans, Mr. I'm-Not-So-Stupid?"

"Because when it comes to deciding how I should live my own life, I should be the one to choose—but when getting out of a prison, even as pathetic as it is, that's more your area of expertise."

Royce sighed and began to look around at the walls.

"By the way," Hadrian began, "what was the *real* reason you didn't tell me?"

"Huh?"

"A bit ago you said—"

"Oh." Royce continued to study the walls. He seemed a little too preoccupied by them. Just as Hadrian was sure he would not answer, Royce said, "I didn't want you to leave."

Hadrian almost laughed at the comment, thinking it was a joke, and then nearly bit his tongue. Thinking of Royce as anything but callous was difficult. Then he realized Royce never had a family and precious few friends. He had grown up an orphan on the streets of Ratibor, stealing his food and clothes and likely receiving his share of beatings for it. He had probably joined the Diamond as much from a desire to belong as a means to profit. After only a few short years, they had betrayed him. Hadrian realized at that moment that Royce did not see him as just his partner, but his family. Along with Gwen and perhaps Arcadius, Hadrian was the only one he had.

"You ready?" Royce asked.

"For what?"

"Turn around. Let's go back-to-back and link arms."

"You're kidding. We aren't going to do that again, are we?" Hadrian said miserably. "I've been sitting in cold water for hours. I'll cramp."

"You know another way to get up there?" Royce asked, and Hadrian shook his head. Royce looked up. "It isn't even as high as the last time and it's narrower, so it'll be easier. Stand up and stretch a second. You'll be fine."

"What if the guard is up there with a stick to poke us with?"

"Do you want to get out of here or not?"

Hadrian took a deep breath. "I'm still mad at you," he said, turning and linking arms back-to-back with Royce.

"Yeah, well, I'm not too happy with me either right now."

They began pushing against each other as they walked up the walls of the pit. Immediately Hadrian's legs began to protest the effort, but the strain on his legs was taken up some by the tight linking of their arms and the stiff leverage it provided.

"Push harder against me," Royce told him.

"I don't want to crush you."

"I'm fine. Just lean back more."

Initially the movement was clumsy and the exertion immense, but soon they fell into a rhythm.

"Step," Royce whispered. The pressure against each other was sufficient to keep them pinned.

"Step." They slid another foot up, scraping over the stony sides.

The water running down the walls gave birth to a slippery slime and Hadrian carefully placed his feet on the drier bricks and used the cracks for traction. Royce was infinitely better at this sort of thing, and likely impatient with their progress. Hadrian was far less comfortable and often pushed too hard. His legs were longer and stronger and he had to keep remembering to relax.

They finally rose above the level of the slime to where the rock was dry, and they moved with more confidence. They were now high enough that a fall would break bones. He started to perspire with the effort, and his skin was slicked with sweat. A droplet cascaded down his face and hung dangling on the tip of his nose. Above, he could see the grate growing larger, but it was still a maddening distance away.

What if we can't make it? How can we get back down besides falling?

Hadrian had to push the thought out of his mind and concentrate. Nothing good would come from anticipating failure.

Instead, he forced himself to think of Arista riding to her death or capture. They had to make it up—and quickly—before his legs lost all their strength. Already they shook from fatigue, buckling under the strain.

As they neared the top, Royce stopped calling steps. Hadrian kept his eyes on the wall where he placed his feet, but felt Royce tilting his head back, peering up. "Stop," Royce whispered. Panting for air, they steadied themselves, unlinked arms, and grabbed the grating. Letting their tortured legs fall loose, they hung for a minute. The release of the strain was wonderful, and Hadrian closed his eyes with pleasure as he gently swayed.

"Good news and bad news," Royce said. "No guards, but it's locked."

"You can do something about that, right?"

"Just give me a second."

He could feel Royce shifting around behind him. "Got it." There was another brief pause and Hadrian's fingers were starting to hurt. "Okay, we'll slide it to your left, ready? Feet up."

The grate was lighter than Hadrian had expected, and it easily slid clear. They hauled themselves out, rolling on the damp grass of the manor's lawn, and lay for a second catching their breath. They were alone in a darkened corner of the manor's courtyard.

"Weapons?" Hadrian asked.

"I'll check the house. You see about getting horses."

"Don't kill anyone," Hadrian mentioned.

"I'll try not to, but if I see Luret—"

"Oh yeah, kill him."

Hadrian worked his way carefully toward the courtyard stable. The horses started at his approach, snorting and bumping loudly into the stall dividers. He grabbed the first saddle and bridle he found and discovered they were familiar. Arista's bay mare, his horse, and Mouse were corralled with the rest.

"Easy, girl," Hadrian whispered softly as he threw the blankets on two of them. He buckled the last bridle around Mouse's neck when Royce came in carrying a bundle of swords.

"Your weapons, sir knight."

"Luret?" Hadrian asked, strapping his swords on.

Royce made a disappointed sound. "Didn't see him. Didn't see hardly anyone. These country folk go to bed early."

"We're a simple lot."

"Mouse?" Royce muttered. "I just can't seem to get rid of this horse, can I?"

❦

Arista discovered riding on the back of a horse was significantly less comfortable than riding in a saddle. Etcher added to her misery by keeping the horse at a trot. The hammering to Arista's body caused her head to ache. She asked for him to slow down but was ignored. Before long, the animal slowed to a walk on its own. It frothed and Arista could feel its sweat soaking her gown. Etcher kicked the beast until it started again. When the horse once more returned to a walk, Etcher resorted to whipping it with the ends of the reins. He missed and struck Arista hard across the thigh. She yelped, but that was also ignored. Eventually Etcher gave up and let the horse rest. She asked where they were going and why they needed to rush. Still, he said nothing—he never even turned his head. After a mile or two, he drove the animal into a trot once more. He acted as if she was not there.

With each jarring clap on the horse's back, Arista became increasingly aware of her vulnerability. She was alone with a strange man somewhere in the backwoods of Rhenydd, where any authority of law would seize her rather than him, regardless of what he did. All she knew about him—the only thing she could be certain of—was that he was morally dubious. While it was one thing to trust herself to Royce and Hadrian, it was quite another to leap onto the back of a horse with a stranger who took her off into the wilds. If she had thought about it, if there had been time to think, she might have declined to go, but now it was too late. She rode trusting the mercy of a dangerous man in a hostile land.

His silence did nothing to alleviate her fear. When it came to silence, Etcher put Royce to shame. He said nothing at all. The profession of thievery was not likely to attract gregarious types, but Etcher seemed an extreme case. He even refused to look at her. This was perhaps better than some alternatives. A man such as Etcher was likely acquainted only with sun-baked, easy women in dirty dresses. How appealing must it be to have a young noblewoman clutching to him alone in the wilderness—and a royal princess, at that.

If he attacks me, what can I do?

A good high-pitched scream would draw a dozen armed guards in Essendon Castle, but since leaving Hintindar, she had not seen a house or a light. Even if someone heard her, she would probably spend her life in an imperial prison once her identity was discovered. He could do anything he wanted with her. When he was done, he could either kill her or hand her over to imperial authorities, who would no doubt pay richly. No one would care if he delivered her bruised and bloodied. She regretted her fast escape without taking the time to think. She had nothing to defend herself with. Her small side pouch held only her father's hairbrush and a bit of coin. Her dagger was somewhere in the bundle of her bedding.

How long will it take me to find it in the dark?

She sighed.

Why must I always focus on the negative? The man has done nothing at all. So he's quiet, so what? He's risking his own life smuggling me to this meeting. He's nervous, watchful. Perhaps he's frightened too. Is it so odd he's not making small talk? I'm just scared, that's all. Everything looks bad when you're scared. Isn't it possible he's just shy around women? Cautious around noble ladies? Concerned anything he says or does could be misconstrued and lead to dangerous accusations? Obviously he has good cause to be concerned. I've already practically convicted him of a host of crimes he hasn't committed! Royce and Hadrian are honorable thieves. Why not Etcher as well?

The trail disappeared entirely and they rode across unmarked fields of windswept grass. They seemed to be heading toward a vague and distant hill. She spotted some structures silhouetted against the pallid sky. They entered yet another forest, this time through a narrow opening in the dense foliage, where Etcher was content to let the horse walk. Away from the wind it was quiet. Fireflies blinked around them and Arista listened to the clacking steps of their mount.

We're on a road?

Although it was too dark to see anything clearly, Arista recognized the sound of hooves on cobblestone.

Where are we?

When at last they cleared the trees, she could see the slope of a bald hill where the remains of buildings sat. Giant stones spilled and scattered to the embrace of grass, forming dark heaped ruins of arched doorways and pylons of rock. Like grave markers, they thrust skyward at neglected angles, the lingering cadavers and bleached bones of forgotten memories.

"What is this place?" Arista asked.

She heard a horse whinny and spotted the glow of a fire up the slope. Without a word, Etcher kicked the horse once more into a trot. Arista took solace in knowing the end of her ordeal was at hand.

Near the top, two men sat huddled amidst the ruins. A campfire flickered, sheltered from the wind by a corner section of weathered stone and rubble. One man was hooded, the other hatless, and immediately Arista thought of Royce and Hadrian.

Did they somehow arrive ahead of us?

As they drew closer, Arista realized she was wrong. These men were younger and both as large as, if not larger than, Hadrian. They stood at the horse's approach and Arista saw dark shirts, leather tunics, and broadswords hanging from thick belts.

"Running late," the hooded one said. "Thought you weren't going to make it."

"Are you Nationalists?" she asked.

The men hesitated. "Of course," the other replied.

They approached, and the hooded one helped her down from the horse. His hands were large and powerful. He showed no strain taking her weight. He had two days of beard and smelled of sour milk.

"Is one of you Degan Gaunt?"

"No," the hooded one replied. "He sent us ahead to see if you were who you said you were. Are you Princess Arista Essendon of Melengar?"

She looked from one face to the next, all harsh expressions. Even Etcher glared at her.

"Well, are you or aren't you?" he pressed, moving closer.

"Of course she is!" Etcher blurted out. "I have a long ride back, so I want my payment, and don't try to cheat me."

"Payment?" Arista asked.

Etcher once more ignored her.

"I don't think we can pay you for delivery until we know it's her, and we certainly aren't taking *your* word for it. She could be a whore from the swill yards of Colnora that you washed and dressed up—and did a piss-poor job of it, at that."

"She's pretending to be a commoner and she's dirty on account of the ride here."

The hooded man advanced even closer to study her. She backed up instinctively but not fast enough as he grabbed her roughly at the chin and twisted her face from side to side.

Infuriated, she kicked at him and managed to strike his shin.

The man grunted and anger flashed in his eyes. "You bloody little bitch!" He struck her hard across the face with the flat of his hand.

The explosion of pain overwhelmed her. She found herself on her hands and knees, gripping a spinning world with fists full of grass. Her face ached and her eyes watered.

The men laughed.

The humiliation was too much. "How dare you strike me!" she screamed.

"See?" Etcher said, pointing at her.

The hooded man nodded. "All right, we'll pay you. Danny, give him twenty gold."

"Twenty? The sentinel agreed to fifty!" Etcher protested.

"Keep your mouth shut or it'll be ten."

Arista panted on the ground, her breath coming in short stifled gasps. She was scared and rapidly losing herself to panic. She needed to calm down—to think. Through bleary eyes, she looked at Etcher and his horse. There was no chance of grabbing the animal and riding away. Etcher's feet were in the stirrups and her weight could never pull him off.

"Guy won't appreciate you pocketing thirty of the gold he sent with you."

They laughed. "Who do you really think he'll believe? You or us?"

Arista considered the fire. She could try to run to it and grab a stick. She concluded she would never make the distance. Even if she did, a stick would be useless against swords. They would only laugh at her.

"Take the twenty and keep your damn mouth shut, or you can ride away with nothing."

She thought about running. *It's downhill, and in the dark I could— No, I'm not fast enough and the hill has no cover.*

Arista would have to make it all the way to the forest before having the slightest hope of getting away, and Etcher could ride after her and drag her back. Afterward, they would beat and tie her, and then all hope would be lost.

"Don't even think about it, you little git," the hooded one was saying to Etcher.

Etcher spat in anger. "Give me the twenty."

The hooded man tossed a pouch that jingled and Etcher caught it with a bitter look.

Arista started to cry. Time was running out. She was helpless and there was nothing at all she could do. For all her royal rank, she could not defend herself. Nor was her education in the art of magic any help. All she could do was make them sneeze and that was not going to save her this time.

Where are Royce and Hadrian? Where is Hilfred? How could I be so stupid, so reckless? Isn't there anyone to save me?

Not surprisingly, Etcher left without a word to her.

"So this is what a princess looks like?" the hooded one said. "There's nothing special about you, is there? You look just as dirty as any wench I've had."

"I don't know," the other said. "She's better than I've seen. Throw me the rope over there. I wanna enjoy myself, not get scratched up."

She felt her blood go cold. Her body trembled. Tears streamed down her cheeks as she watched the man set off to fetch the rope.

No man had ever touched her before. No one dared to think in such terms. Doing so would mean death in Melengar. She had no midnight rendezvous, no casual affairs or castle romances. No boy had ever chanced so much as a kiss, but now...She watched as the man with the stubble beard came at her with a length of twine.

If only I'd learned something more useful than tickling noses and boiling water, I could—

Arista stopped crying. She did not realize it, but she had stopped breathing as well.

Can it work?

There was nothing else to try.

The man grinned expectantly as Arista closed her eyes and began to hum softly.

"Look at that. I think she likes the idea. She's serenading us."

"Maybe it's a noble ritual or something?"

Arista barely heard them. Once more, using the concentration method Esrahaddon had taught her, she focused her mind. She listened to the breeze swaying the grass, the buzz of the fireflies, the whine of the mosquitoes, and the song of the crickets. She could feel the stars and sense the earth below. There was power there. She pulled it toward her, breathing it in, sucking it into her body, drawing it to her mind.

"How you want her?"

"Wrists behind the back works for me, but maybe we should ask her how *she* likes it?" They laughed again. "Never know what might tickle a royal's fancy."

She was muttering, forming the words, drawing in the power, giving it form. She focused elements, giving them purpose and direction. She built the incantation as she had before, but now varied it. She pushed, altering the tone to shift the focus just enough.

The crickets stopped their song and the fireflies ceased their mating flashes. Even the gentle wind no longer blew. The only sound now was Arista's voice as it grew louder and louder.

Arista felt herself pulled to her feet as the man spun her and maneuvered her arms behind her back. She ignored him, concentrating instead on moving her fingers as if she were playing an invisible musical instrument.

Just as she felt the rough, scratchy rope touch her wrists, the men began to scream.

◦§

The ruins of Amberton Lee stood splintered on the hilltop. Pillars, steps of marble, and slab walls lay fractured and fallen. Only three trees stood near the summit of the barren hill, all of them dead, leafless corpses, like the rest of the ruins, still standing long after their time.

"There's a fire up there, but I only see Arista," Royce said.

"Bait?"

"Probably. Give me a head start. Maybe I can free her before they know something is up. If nothing else, I should spring whatever trap is waiting and then hopefully you can rush in and save the day."

It bothered Royce how quiet the hill was. He could hear the distant snorting and hoofing of horses and the crackle of the campfire, but nothing else. They had raced as fast as their horses could manage, and still Royce was afraid they would be too late. When riding, he had been certain she was dead.

Now he was confused. There was no doubt that the woman near the fire was Arista.

So where is Etcher? Where are those they intended to meet?

He crept carefully, slipping nimbly around a holly tree and up the slope. Half-buried stones and tilted rocks lay hidden beneath grass and thorns, making the passage a challenge. He circled once and found no sentries or movement.

He climbed higher and happened upon two bodies. The men were dead, yet still warm to the touch—more than warm, they felt...hot. There were no wounds, no blood. Royce proceeded up the last of the hill, advancing on the flickering fire. The princess sat huddled near it, quietly staring into the flames. She was alone and lacked even her travel bags.

"Arista?" he whispered.

She looked up lazily, drunkenly, as if her head weighed more than it should. The glow of the fire spilled across her face. Her eyes appeared red and swollen. A welt stood out on one of her cheeks.

"It's Royce. You all right?"

"Yes," she replied. Her voice sounded distant and weak.

"Are you alone?"

She nodded.

He stepped into the firelight and waited. Nothing happened. A light summer breeze gently brushed the hill's grass and breathed on the flames. Above them, the stars shone, muted only by the white moon, which cast nighttime shadows. Arista sat with the stillness of a statue, except for the hairbrush she turned over and over in her hands. As tranquil as the scene appeared, Royce's senses were tense. This place made him uneasy. The odd marble blocks, toppled and broken, rose out of the ground like teeth. Once more he wondered if somehow he was tapping into his elven heritage, sensing more than could be seen, feeling a memory lost in time.

He caught sight of movement down the slope and spotted Hadrian climbing toward them. He watched him pause for a moment near the bodies before continuing up.

"Where's Etcher?" Royce asked the princess.

"He left. He was paid by Luis Guy to bring me here, to deliver me to some men."

"Yeah. We found that out a bit late. Sorry."

The princess did not look well. She was too quiet. He expected anger or relief, but her stillness was eerie. Something had happened—something bad. Besides the welt, there was no sign of abuse. Her clothes were intact. There were no rips or tears. He spotted several blades of dead grass and a brown leaf tangled in her hair.

"You all right?" Hadrian asked as he crested the hill. "Are you hurt?"

She shook her head and one of the bits of grass fell out.

Hadrian crouched down next to her. "Are you sure? What happened?"

Arista did not answer. She stared at the fire and started to rock.

"What happened to the men down on the hill?" Hadrian asked Royce.

"Wasn't me. They were dead when I found them. No wounds either."

"But how—"

"I killed them," Arista said.

They both turned and stared at her.

"You killed two Seret Knights?" Royce asked.

"Were they seret?" Arista muttered.

"They have broken-crown rings," Royce explained. "There's no wound on either body. How did you kill them?"

She started trembling, her breaths drawn in staggered bursts. Her hand went to her cheek, rubbing it lightly with her fingertips. "They attacked me. I—I couldn't think of—I didn't know what to do. I was so scared. They were going to—and I was alone. I didn't have a choice. I didn't have a choice. I couldn't run. I couldn't fight. I couldn't hide. All I could do was make them sneeze and boil water. I didn't have a choice. It was all I could do." She began sobbing.

Hadrian tentatively reached toward her. She dropped the brush and took his hands, squeezing them tightly. She pulled at him and he wrapped his arms around her while she buried her face into the folds of his shirt. He gently stroked her hair.

Hadrian looked up at Royce with a puzzled expression and whispered, "She made them sneeze to death?"

"No," Royce said, glancing back over his shoulder in the direction of the bodies. "She boiled water."

"I didn't know—I didn't know if it would really work," she whispered between hitching breaths. "I—I had to change it. Switch the focus. Fill in the blanks on my own—invent a whole new spell. I was only guessing, but—but it felt right. The pieces fit. I felt them fit—I *made* them fit."

Arista lifted her head, wiped her eyes, and looked down the slope of the hill. "They screamed for a very long time. They were on the ground—writhing. I—I tried to stop it then, but I didn't know how and they just kept—they kept on screaming, their faces turning so red. They rolled around on the ground and clawed the dirt, they cried and their screams— they—they got quieter and quieter, then they didn't make any noise except—except they were hissing—hissing and I could see steam rising from their skin."

Tears continued to slip down her cheeks as she looked up at them. Hadrian wiped her face.

"I've never killed anyone before."

"It's okay," Hadrian told her, stroking the back of her head and clearing away the remainder of the grass and leaves. "You didn't want to do it."

"I know. It's just—just that I've never killed anyone before, and you didn't hear them. It's horrible, like part of me was dying with them. I don't know how you do it, Royce. I just don't know."

"You do it by realizing that if the situation was reversed and they succeeded, they wouldn't be crying."

Hadrian slipped a finger under her chin and tilted her face. He cleared the hair stuck to her cheeks and brushed his thumbs under her eyes. "It's okay. It wasn't your fault. You did what you had to. I'm just sorry I wasn't here for you."

Arista looked into his eyes for a moment, then nodded and took a clear deep breath and wiped her nose. "I'm really ruining your impression of me, aren't I? I get drunk, I wolf down food, I think nothing of sharing a room with you, and now I…"

"You've nothing to be ashamed of," Hadrian told her. "I only wish more princesses were as worthy of their title as you."

Royce made another survey of the hill and a thorough check of the seret, their horses, and their gear. He found symbol-emblazoned tunics, confirming their knightly identities, and a good-sized bag of gold, but no documents of any sort. He pulled the saddle and bridle off one horse and let it go.

"There's only the two?" Hadrian asked when he returned. "I expected more." He stirred the coals of the fire with a stick, brightening the hilltop. Arista looked better. She was eating a bit of cheese. Her face was washed, her hair brushed. She certainly was showing more resilience than he had expected.

"Gives you a whole new respect for Etcher, doesn't it?" Royce said.

"How do you mean?"

"He never planned to bring all of us here, just her. He's a lot brighter than I gave him credit for."

"He wasn't too smart," Arista told them. "The seret cheated him out of thirty gold Luis Guy had promised."

"So this was Guy's operation, not Merrick's," Hadrian said.

"Not sure," Royce responded. "Seems too sophisticated for Guy, but Merrick's plans don't fail." He looked at the princess. "Of course, not even Merrick could have anticipated what she did."

Hadrian stood up and threw away the stick, then looked at the princess. "You gonna be okay? Can you ride?"

She nodded rapidly and followed it with a sniffle. "I was pretty scared—really missed you two. You have no idea—no idea how happy I am to see you again." She blew her nose.

"I get that from a lot of women," Hadrian replied, grinning. "But I'll admit, you're the first princess."

She managed a slight smile. "So what do we do now? I haven't a clue where we are, and I'm pretty sure there isn't any meeting with Gaunt."

"There could be," Royce said. "But Cosmos doesn't know where we are to tell us. I'm sure Etcher never carried any message about Hintindar back to Colnora. I should have told Price before we left, but I didn't want to take chances. Just stupid, really. I was being too cautious."

"Well, you know I'm not going to argue," Hadrian told him. "It was withholding information that got us into this."

Arista looked at Royce questioningly.

"I told him," Royce said.

"No bruises?" she asked. "Not even a black eye?"

"We never got that far, but maybe later when we have more time," Hadrian said. "Turned out we had to hurry to save a woman who didn't need saving."

"I'm real glad you did."

"We should head to Ratibor," Royce said. "We aren't too far. We can reestablish connection with the Diamond there."

"*Ratibor?*" Hadrian said suddenly.

"Yeah, you know, dirty, filthy rat hole—the capital of Rhenydd? We've seen where you grew up, so we might as well stop by my hometown as well."

Hadrian started searching his clothing. "Hunting a boar!" he exclaimed as he pulled out the note from his father. He rushed toward the firelight. "'A king and his knight went hunting a boar; a rat and his friends were hunting for lore.' A rat and a boar—Ratibor! The king and his knight are my father and the heir, who must have traveled to Ratibor and were attacked by lore hunters." Hadrian pointed over his shoulder in the direction of the dead men. "Seret."

"What's the rest of it?" Royce asked, intrigued.

"'Together they fought, till one was alive. The knight sadly wept; no king had survived.'"

"So they fought, but only your father survived the battle and the heir was killed."

"No king had survived," Hadrian said. "An odd way to put that, isn't it? Why not say 'The king died'?"

"Because it doesn't rhyme?" Royce suggested.

"Good point."

"What comes next?" Arista asked.

"'The answers to riddles, to secrets and more, are found in the middle of Legends and Lore.'"

"There's more to the story, apparently," she said, "and you can find the answers in ancient lore? Maybe you should ask Arcadius."

"I think not," Royce said. "There's a street in Ratibor called Legends Avenue and another named Lore Street."

"Do they intersect?"

Royce nodded. "Just a bit south of Central Square."

"And what's there?"

"A church, I think."

"Royce is right. We need to get to Ratibor," Hadrian announced.

Arista stood up. "Trust me, I'm more than ready to leave this place. When I—" She stopped herself. "When I used the Art, I sensed something unpleasant. It feels..."

"Haunted," Royce provided, and she nodded.

"What is this place?" Royce asked Hadrian.

"I don't know."

"It's only a few miles from where you grew up."

Hadrian shrugged. "Folks in Hintindar never talked about it much. There are a few ghost stories and rumors of goblins and ghouls that roam the woods, that kind of thing."

"Nothing about what it was?"

"There was a children's rhyme I remember, something like,

Ancient stones upon the Lee,
dusts of memories gone we see.
Once the center, once the all,
lost forever, fall the wall."

"What's that supposed to mean?"

Hadrian shrugged again. "We used to sing it when playing Fall-the-Wall—it's a kids' game."

"I see," Royce lied.

"Whatever it used to be, I don't like it," Arista declared.

Royce nodded. "It almost makes me look forward to Ratibor—almost."

CHAPTER 10

REWARDS

The midday bell rang and Amilia stopped, uncertain of which way to go. As a kitchen servant, she was unfamiliar with areas reserved for nobles. Only on rare occasions had she filled in for sick chambermaids by servicing bedrooms on the third floor. She had worked as fast as possible to finish before the guests returned. Working with a noble present was a nightmare. They usually ignored her, but she was terrified of drawing attention. Invisibility was her best defense and it was easy to remain unseen in the steam and bustle of the scullery. In the open corridors, anyone could notice her.

This time she had no choice. Saldur had ordered her to his office. A soldier had found her on the way to breakfast and told her to report to His Grace at the midday bell. She lost her appetite and spent the rest of the morning speculating on what horrible fate awaited her.

The bell rang for the second time and Amilia began to panic. She had visited the regent's office only once, and since she had been under armed escort at the time, the route had been the last thing on her mind. She remembered going upstairs, but didn't recall the number of flights.

Oh, why didn't I leave earlier?

She passed the great hall, filled with long tables set with familiar plates and shining goblets, which she had washed each day—old companions all. They were friends of a simpler time, when the world had made sense. Back then she had woken each morning knowing every day would be as the one before. Now each day was filled with the fear of being discovered a failure.

On the far side of the hall, men entered, dressed in embroidered clothing rich in colors—nobles. They took seats, talking loudly, laughing, rocking back in chairs, and shouting for stewards to bring wine. She held the door for Bastion, who carried a tray of steaming food. He smiled gratefully at her as he rushed by, wiping his forehead with his sleeve.

"How do I get to the regent's office?" she whispered.

Bastion did not pause as he hurried past, but called back, "Go around the reception hall, through the throne room."

"Then what?"

"Just ask the clerk."

She headed down the corridor and around the curved wall of the grand stair toward the palace entrance. Workers propped the front doors open, granting entry to three stories of daylight, which revealed the cloud of dust they were building. Sweat-oiled men hauled in timber, mortar, and stone. Teams cut wood and marble. Workers scrambled up and down willowy ladders while pulleys hoisted buckets to scaffold-perched masons. All of them were working hard to reshape visitors' first impressions. She noticed with amazement that a wall had been moved and the ceiling was higher than the last time she had been here. The entrance was now more expansive and impressive than the darkened chamber it once had been.

"Excuse me?" a voice called. A thin man stood in the open doorway to the courtyard. He hesitated on the steps, dodging the passing workers. "May I enter?" He coughed, waving a handkerchief before his face.

Amilia looked at him and shrugged. "Why not? Everyone else is."

He took several tentative steps, glancing up fearfully, his arms partially raised as if to ward off a blow. A thin, brittle-looking man wearing a powdered wig, a brilliant yellow tunic, and striped orange britches, he stood taller than Amilia.

"Good day to you, my lady," he greeted her with a bow as soon as he had cleared the activity. "My name is Nimbus of Vernes and I have come to offer my services."

"Oh," she said with a blank stare. "I don't think—"

"Oh please, I beg of you, hear me out. I am a courtier formerly of King Fredrick and Queen Josephine of Galeannon. I am well versed in all courtly protocol, procedures, and correspondence. Prior to that, I was chamberlain to Duke Ibsen of Vernes, so I am capable of managing—" He paused. "Are you all right?"

Amilia swallowed. "I'm just in a hurry. I'm on my way to a very important meeting with the regent."

"Please forgive me, then. It is just that—well, I have—" He slouched his shoulders and sighed. "I am embarrassed to say that I am a refugee of the Nationalists' invasion and have nothing more than the clothes on my back and what little I have in this satchel. I have walked my way here and…I am a bit hungry. I was hoping I could find employment at the palace court. I am not suited for anything else," he said, dusting his shoulders clear of the snowy debris that drifted down from the scaffolds.

"I'm sorry to hear that, but I'm not—" She stopped when she saw his lip tremble. "How long has it been since you've eaten?"

"Quite some time, I am afraid. I have actually lost track."

"Listen," she told him. "I can get you something to eat, but you have to wait until after my meeting."

She thought he would cry then as he bit his lip and nodded several times, saying, "Thank you ever so much, my lady."

"Wait here. I'll be back soon...I hope."

She headed off, dodging the lathered men in leather aprons, and slipped past three others in robes, holding measuring sticks like staffs and arguing over lines on huge parchments spread across a worktable.

The throne room, which also showed signs of renovation, was nearly finished and only a few towers of scaffolding remained. The marble floor glistened with a luster, as did the mammoth pillars that held up the domed ceiling. Near the interior wall rose the dais, upon which stood the golden imperial throne, sculpted in the shape of a giant bird of prey. The wings spread into a vast circle of splayed feathers, which formed the chair's back. She passed through the arcade behind it to the administration offices.

"What do you want?" the clerk asked Amilia. She had never liked him. His face looked like a rodent's, with small eyes, large front teeth, and a brief smattering of black hair on a pale, balding head. The little man sat behind a formidable desk, his fingers dyed black from ink.

"I'm here to see Regent Saldur," she replied. "He sent for me."

"Upstairs, fourth floor," he said, dismissing her by looking back down at his parchments.

On the second floor, plaster covered the walls. On the third floor, she found paneling, and by the fourth level the paneling was a richly carved dark cherry wood. Lanterns became elegant chandeliers, a long red carpet ran the length of the corridor, and glass windows let in light from outside. She recalled how out of place Saldur had seemed when he had visited the kitchen. She looked down at her dirty smock and recognized the irony.

The door lay open and Regent Saldur stood before an arched window built from three of the largest pieces of glass she had ever seen. Birdsongs drifted in from the ward below as the regent read a parchment he held in the sunlight.

"You're late," he said without looking up.

"I'm sorry. I didn't know how to get here."

"Something you should understand: I'm not interested in excuses or explanations. I'm only interested in results. When I tell you to do something, I expect it'll be done exactly as I dictate, not sooner, not later, not differently, but *exactly* how I specify. Do you understand?"

"Yes, Your Grace." She felt considerably warmer than she had a moment earlier.

The regent walked to his desk and laid the parchment on it. He placed his fingertips together, tapping them against each other while studying her. "What's your name again?"

"Amilia of Tarin Vale."

"Amilia—a pretty name. Amilia, you impressed me. That is not easy to do. I appointed five separate women to the task of imperial secretary—ladies of breeding, ladies of pedigree. You are the first to show an improvement in Her Eminence. You have also presented me with a unique problem. I can't have a common scullery maid working as the personal assistant to the empress. How will that look?" He took a seat behind his desk, brushing out the folds of his robe. "It's conceivable that the empress could have died if not for whatever magic you performed. For this, you deserve a reward. I'm bestowing on you the diplomatic rank equal to a baroness. From this moment on, you will be known as Lady Amilia."

He dipped a quill into ink and scribbled his name. "Present

this to the clerk downstairs and he will arrange for you to obtain the necessary material for a better—Well, for a dress."

Amilia stared at him, unable to move, taking shallow breaths, not wanting to disturb anything. She was riding a wave of good fortune and feared the slightest movement could throw her into an unforgiving sea. He was not punishing her after all. The rest she could think about later.

"Have you nothing to say?"

Amilia hesitated. "Could the empress get a new dress as well?"

"You are now Lady Amilia, imperial secretary to Empress Modina Novronian. You can take whatever measures you feel are necessary to ensure the well-being of the empress."

"Can I take her outside for walks?"

"No," he said curtly. He then softened his tone and added, "As we both know, Modina is not well. I personally feel she may never be. But it's imperative that her subjects believe they have a strong ruler. Through her name, Ethelred and I are doing great things for the people out there." He pointed at the window. "But we can't hope to succeed if they discover their beloved empress does not have her wits about her. It's a difficult task that Novron has laid before us, to build a better world while concealing the empress's incapacitation, which brings me to your first assignment."

Amilia blinked.

"Despite all my efforts, word is getting out that the empress is not well. Since the public has never seen her, there is a growing rumor that she doesn't exist. We need to calm the people's fear. To this end, it will be your task to prepare Modina to give a speech upon the Grand Balcony in three days' time."

"What?"

"Don't worry, it's only three sentences." He picked up the

parchment he had been reading and held it out to her. "It should be a simple task. You got her to say one word. Now get her to say a few more. Have her memorize the speech and train her to deliver it—like an empress."

"But I—"

"Remember what I said about excuses. You are part of the nobility now, a person of privilege and power. I've given you means and with that comes responsibility. Now out with you. I've more work to do."

Taking the parchments, she turned and walked toward the door.

"And, Lady Amilia, don't forget that there were five imperial secretaries before you, and all of them were noble as well."

❧

"Well, if that don't put a stiff wind in your main," Ibis declared, looking at the patent of nobility Amilia showed him. Most of the kitchen staff gathered around the cook as he held the parchment up, grinning.

"It's awfully pretty," Cora pointed out. "I love all the fancy writing."

"Never had a desire to read before," Ibis said. "But I sure wish I could now."

"May I?" Nimbus asked. He carefully wiped his hands on his handkerchief and, reaching out, gently took the parchment. "It reads 'I, Modina, who am right wise empress, appointed to this task by the mercy of our lord Maribor, through my imperial regents, Maurice Saldur and Lanis Ethelred, decree that in recognition of faithful service and commission of charges found to our favor, Amilia of Tarin Vale, daughter of Bartholomew the carriage maker, be raised from her current station and shall belong to the unquestionable nobles of the Novronian Empire and will henceforth and forever be known as Lady Amilia of Tarin Vale.'" Nimbus looked up. "There is a good deal more, concerning the limitations of familial inheritance and nobility rights, but that is the essence of the writ."

They all stared at the cornstalk of a man.

"This is Nimbus," Amilia said, introducing him. "He's in need of a meal, and I was hoping you could give him a little something."

Ibis grinned and made a modest bow.

"Yer a lady now, Amilia. There isn't a person in this room who can say no to you. You hear that, Edith?" he shouted at the head maid as she entered. "Our little Amilia is a noble lady now."

Edith stood where she was. "Says who?"

"The empress and Regent Saldur, that's who. Says so right on this here parchment. Care to read it?"

Edith scowled.

"Oh, that's right. You can't read any more than I can. Would you like *Lady* Amilia to read it to you? Or how about her personal steward? He has an excellent reading voice."

Edith grabbed up a pile of linens from the bin and headed for the laundry, causing the cook to burst into laughter. "She's never given up spouting how you'd be back scrubbing dishes— or worse." Clapping his big hands, he turned his attention to Nimbus. "So, what would you like?"

"Anything, actually," Nimbus replied, his hands quivering, shaking the parchment he still held. "After several days, even shoe leather looks quite appetizing."

"Well, I'll get right on that, then."

"Can we clear a place for Nimbus to sit?" Amilia asked, and immediately Cora and Nipper were cleaning off the baker's table and setting it just as they had before.

"Thank you," Amilia said. "You don't need to go to this much trouble — but thank you, everyone."

"Pardon me, my lady," Nimbus addressed her. "If I may be so bold, it is not entirely proper for a lady of nobility to convey appreciation for services rendered by subordinates."

Amilia sat down beside him and sighed. She dropped her chin into her hands and grimaced. "I don't know how to be noble. I don't know anything, but I'm expected to teach Modina how to be an empress?" The contrast of fortune and pending disaster left her perplexed. "His Grace might as well kill me now." She took the parchment from Nimbus and shook it in her hand. "At least now that I'm noble, I might get a quick beheading."

Leif delivered a plate of stew. Nimbus looked down at the bowl and the scattering of utensils arrayed around him. "The kitchen staff is not very experienced in setting a table, are they?" He picked up a small two-prong fork and shook his head. "This is a shellfish fork, and it should be on the left of my plate...assuming I was eating shellfish. What I do not have is a spoon."

Amilia felt stupid. "I don't think anyone here knows what a fork is." She looked down incredulously at the twisted spindle of wire. "Even the nobility don't use them. At least, I've never washed one before."

"That would depend on where you are. They are popular farther south."

"I'll get you a spoon." She started to get up when she felt his hand on hers.

"Again," he said, "forgive my forwardness, but a lady does not fetch flatware from the pantry. And you *are* now in the nobility. You there!" He shouted at Nipper as the boy flew by with a bucket. "Fetch a spoon for Her Ladyship."

"Right away," the boy replied, setting the bucket down and running to the pantry.

"See?" he said. "It is not difficult, and takes just a bit of confidence and the right tone of voice."

Nipper returned with the spoon. It never touched the table. Nimbus took it right from his hand and began to eat. Despite his ravenous state, he ate slowly, occasionally using one of the napkins that he placed neatly on his lap to dab the corners of his mouth. He sat straight, in much the same way Lady Constance had—his chin up, his shoulders squared, his fingers placed precisely on the spoon. She had never seen anyone eat so...perfectly.

"You need not stay here," he told her. "While I appreciate the company, I am certain you have more important things to attend to. I can find my way out when I am finished, but I do wish to thank you for this meal. You saved my life."

"I want you to work for me," she blurted out. "To help me teach Modina to act like an empress."

Nimbus paused with a spoonful halfway to his mouth.

"You know all about being noble. You even said you were a courtier. You know all the rules and stuff."

"Protocol and etiquette."

"Yeah, those too. I don't know if I can arrange for you to be paid, but I might. The regent said I could take whatever steps necessary. Even if I can't, I can find you a place to sleep and see that you get meals."

"At the moment, my lady, that is a fortune, and I would consider it an honor if I could assist Her Eminence in any way."

"Then it's settled. You are officially the..."

"Imperial Tutor to Her Eminence, the Empress Modina?" Nimbus supplied.

"Right. And our first job is to teach her to give a speech on the Grand Balcony in three days."

"That does not sound too difficult. Has she done much public speaking?"

Amilia forced a smile. "A week ago she said the word *no*."

CHAPTER 11

RATIBOR

Entering the city of Ratibor at night, Arista thought it the most filthy, wretched place she could ever imagine. Streets lay in random, confusing lines, crisscrossing at intersections as they ran off at various odd angles. Refuse was piled next to every building, and narrow dirt thoroughfares were appalling mires of mud and manure. Wooden planks created a network of haphazard paths and bridges over the muck, forcing people to parade in lines like tightrope walkers. The houses and shops were as miserable as the roads. Constructed to fit in the spaces left by the street's odd, acute corners, buildings were shaped like wedges of cheese, giving the city a strange, splintered appearance. The windows, shut tight against the city's stench, were opaque with thick grime repeatedly splashed by passing wagons.

Ratibor reveled in its filth like a poor man who is proud of the calluses on his hands. Arista had heard of its reputation, but until experiencing it firsthand, she had not truly understood. This was a workingman's town, a struggling city where no quarter was expected or given. Here men bore poverty and misfortune as badges of honor, deriving dubious prestige from contests of woe over tankards of ale.

Idlers and vagabonds, hawkers and thieves moved along the plank ways, appearing and disappearing again into the shadows. There were children on the street—orphans, by the look—ragged and pitiful waifs covered in filth, crouching under porches. Small families also moved among the crowds. Tradesmen with their wives and children carried bundles or wheeled overfilled carts loaded with all their worldly possessions. All looked exhausted and destitute as they trudged through the city's maze.

The rain had started not long after they had left Amberton Lee, and poured the entire trip. She was soaked through. Her hair lay matted to her face, her fingers were pruned, and her hood collapsed about her head. Arista followed Royce as he led them through the labyrinth of muddy streets. The cool night wind blew the downpour in sheets, making her shiver. During the trip, she had looked forward to reaching the city. Although it was not what she had expected, anything indoors would be welcomed.

"Care for a raincoat, mum?" a hawker asked, holding up a garment for Arista to see. "Only five silver!" he continued as she showed no sign of slowing her horse. "How about a new hat?"

"Either of you gentlemen looking for companionship for the night?" called a destitute woman standing on a plank beneath the awning of a closed dry-goods shop. She flipped back her hair and smiled alluringly, revealing missing teeth.

"How about a nice bit of poultry for an evening meal?" another man asked, holding up a dead bird so thin and scraggly it was hardly recognizable as a chicken.

Arista shook her head, saying nothing except words to urge her horse forward.

Signs were everywhere—nailed to porch beams or attached to tall stakes driven into the mud. They advertised things like

ALE, CIDER, MEAD, WINE, NO CREDIT! and THREE-DAY-OLD PORK — CHEAP! But some were more ominous, such as BEGGARS WILL BE JAILED! and ALL ELVES ENTERING THE CITY MUST REGISTER AT THE SHERIFF'S OFFICE. This last poster's paint was still bright.

Royce stopped at a public house with a signboard of a grotesque cackling face and a scripted epitaph that read THE LAUGHING GNOME. The tavern stood three stories, a good size even by Colnora's standards, yet people still struggled to squeeze in the front door. Inside, the place smelled of damp clothes and wood smoke. A large crowd filled the common room such that Hadrian had to push his way through.

"We're looking for the proprietor," Royce told a young man carrying a tray.

"That would be Ayers. He's the gray-haired gent behind the bar."

"It's true, I tell you!" a young man with fiery red hair was saying loudly as he stood in the center of the common room. To whom he was speaking, Arista was not certain. It appeared to be everyone. "My father was a Praleon Guard. He served on His Majesty's personal retinue for twenty years."

"What does that prove? Urith and the rest of them died in the fire. No one knows how it started."

"The fire was set by Androus!" shouted the red-haired youth with great conviction. Abruptly, the room quieted. The young man was not content with this, however, and he took the stunned pause to press his point. "He betrayed the king, killed the royal family, and took the crown so he could hand the kingdom over to the empress. Good King Urith would never have accepted annexation into the New Empire, and those loyal to his name shouldn't either."

The crowd burst into an uproar of angry shouts.

In the midst of this outburst, the three of them reached the bar, where a handful of men stood watching the excitement with empty mugs in hand.

"Mr. Ayers?" Royce asked of a man and a boy as they struggled to hoist a fresh keg onto the rear dock.

"Who wants to know?" asked the man in a stained apron. A drop of sweat dangled from the tip of his red nose, his face flushed from exertion.

"We're looking to rent a pair of rooms."

"Not much luck of that. We're full up," Ayers replied, not pausing from his work. "Jimmy, jump up and shim it." The young lad, filthy with sweat and dirt, leapt up on the dock and pushed a wooden wedge under the keg, tilting it forward slightly.

"Do you know of availability elsewhere in the city?" Hadrian asked.

"Gonna be the same all over, friend. Every boardinghouse is full—refugees been coming in from the countryside for weeks."

"Refugees?"

"Yeah, the Nationalists have been marching up from the coast sacking towns. People been running ahead of them and most come here. Not that I mind—been great for business."

Ayers pulled a tap out of the old keg and hammered it into the face of the new barrel with a wooden mallet. He turned the spigot and drained a pint or two to clear the sediment. Wiping his hands on his apron, he began filling the demands of his customers.

"Is there no place to find lodging for the night?"

"I can't say that, just no place I know of," Ayers replied, and finally took a moment to wipe a sleeve over his face and clear the drop from his nose. "Maybe some folks will rent a room in their houses, but all the inns and taverns are packed. I've even started to rent floor space."

"Is there any left?" Hadrian asked hopefully.

"Any what?"

"Floor space. It's raining pretty hard out there."

Ayers lifted his head up and glanced around his tavern. "I've got space under the stairs that no one's taken yet. If you don't mind the people walking on top of you all night."

"It's better than the gutter," Hadrian said, shrugging at Royce and Arista. "Maybe tomorrow there will be a vacancy."

Ayers's face showed he doubted this. "If you want to stay, it'll be forty-five silver."

"Forty-five?" Hadrian exclaimed, stunned. "For space under the stairs? No wonder no one has taken it. A room at The Regal Fox in Colnora is only twenty!"

"Go there, then, but if you want to stay here, it'll cost you forty-five silver—in tenents. I don't take those imperial notes they're passing now. It's your choice."

Hadrian scowled at Ayers but counted out the money just the same. "I hope that includes dinner."

Ayers shook his head. "It doesn't."

"We also have three horses."

"Lucky you."

"No room at the stable either? Is it okay to leave them out front?"

"Sure...for another...five silver a horse."

They pushed and prodded their way through the crowd with their bags until they came to the wooden staircase. Beneath it, several people had discarded their wet cloaks on nail heads or on the empty kegs and crates stored there. Royce and Hadrian stacked the containers to make a cubby and threw the coats and cloaks on them. A few people shot them harsh looks—the owners of the cloaks, no doubt—but no one said anything, as it appeared most understood the situation. Looking around, Arista saw others squatting in corners

and along the edge of the big room. Some were families with
children trying to sleep, their little heads resting on damp
clothes. Mothers rubbed their backs and sang lullabies over
the racket of loud voices, shifting wooden chairs, and the
banging of pewter mugs. These were the lucky ones. She wondered about the families who could not afford floor space.

*How many are cowering outside under a boardwalk or in
a muddy alley somewhere in the rain?*

As they settled, Arista noticed the noise of the inn was not
simply the confusing sounds of forty unrelated conversations,
but rather one discussion voiced by several people with various opinions. From time to time one speaker would rise above
the others to make a point, and then drown in the response
from the crowd. The most vocal was the red-haired young man.

"No, he's not!" he shouted once more. "He's not a blood
relative of Urith. He's the brother of Urith's second wife."

"And I suppose you think his first wife was murdered so he
could be pushed into marrying Amiter, just so Androus could
become duke?"

"That's exactly what I'm saying!" the youth declared.
"Don't you see? They planned this for years, and not just here
either. They did it in Alburn, Warric... They even tried it in
Melengar, but they failed there. Did anyone see that play last
year? You know, *The Crown Conspiracy.* It was based on real
events. Amrath's children outsmarted the conspirators. That's
why Melengar hasn't fallen to the New Empire. Don't you see?
We're all the victims of a conspiracy. I've even heard that the
empress might not exist. The whole story of the Heir of Novron is a sham, invented to placate the masses. Do you really
think a farm girl could kill a great beast? It is men like
Androus who control us—evil, corrupt murderous men without an ounce of royal blood in their veins, or honor in their
hearts!"

"So what?" a fat man in a checked vest asked defiantly. "What do we care who rules us? Our lot is always the same. You speak of matters between blue bloods. It doesn't affect us."

"You're wrong! How many men in this city were pressed into the army? How many are off to die for the empress? How many sons have gone to fight Melengar, who has never been our enemy? Now the Nationalists are coming. They're only a few miles south. They will sack this city, just as they did Vernes, and why? Because we are now joined to the empire. Do you think your sons, brothers, and fathers would be off dying if Urith were still alive? Do you want to see Ratibor destroyed?"

"They won't destroy Ratibor!" the fat man shouted back. "You're just spouting rumors, trying to scare decent people and stir up trouble. Armies will fight, and maybe the city will change hands, but it won't affect *us*. We'll still be poor and still struggling to live, as we always have. King Urith had his wars and Viceroy Androus will have his. We work, fight, and die under both of them. That's our lot and treasonous talk like this will only get people killed."

"They will burn the city," an older woman in a blue kerchief said suddenly. "Just as they burned Kilnar. I know. I was there. I saw them."

All eyes turned to her.

"That's not true! It can't be," the fat man protested. "It doesn't make sense. The Nationalists have no cause to burn the cities. They would want them intact."

"The Nationalists didn't burn it," she said. "The empire did." This statement brought the room to stunned silence. "When the imperial government saw that the city would be lost, they ordered Kilnar to be torched to leave nothing for the Nationalists."

"It's true," said a man seated with his family near the kitchen. "We lived in Vernes. I saw the city guards burning the shops and homes there too."

"The same will happen here." The youth caught the crowd's attention once more. "Unless we do something about it."

"What can we do?" a young mother asked.

"We can join the Nationalists. We can give the city to them before the viceroy has a chance to torch it."

"This is treason," the fat man said. "You'll bring death to us all!"

"The empire took Rhenydd through deceit, murder, and trickery. I don't speak treason. I speak loyalty—loyalty to the monarchy. To sit by and let the empire rape this kingdom and burn this city *is* treason and, what's more, it's foolhardy cowardice!"

"Are you calling me a coward?"

"No, sir, I'm calling you a fool *and* a coward."

The fat man stood up indignantly and drew a dagger from his belt. "I demand satisfaction."

The youth stood and unsheathed a long sword. "As you wish."

"You would duel me sword against dagger and call me the coward?"

"I also called you a fool, and a fool it is who holds a dagger and challenges a man with a sword."

Several people in the room laughed at this, which only infuriated the fat man more. "Do you have no honor?"

"I'm but a poor soldier's son from a destitute town. I can't afford honor." Again, the crowd laughed. "I'm also a practical man, who knows it's more important to win than to die—for honor is something that concerns only the living. But understand this: if you choose to fight me, I'll kill you any way I can, the same way that I'll try to save this city and its people any way I can. Honor and allegiance be damned!"

The crowd applauded now, much to the chagrin of the fat man. Red-faced, he stood for a moment, then shoved his dagger back in his belt and abruptly stalked out the door into the rain.

"But how can we turn the city over to the Nationalists?" the old woman asked.

The youth turned to her. "If we raise a militia, we can raid the armory and storm the city garrison. After that, we'll arrest the viceroy. That will give us the city. The imperial army is camped a mile to the south. When the Nationalists attack, they will expect to retreat to the safety of the city walls. But when they arrive, they will find the gates locked. In disarray and turmoil, they will be routed and the Nationalists will destroy them. After that, we'll welcome the Nationalists in as allies. Given our assistance in helping them take the city, we can expect fair treatment and possibly even self-rule, as that is the Nationalists' creed.

"Imagine that," he said dreamily. "Ratibor, the whole city—the whole kingdom of Rhenydd—being run by a people's council, just like Tur Del Fur!"

This clearly caught the imagination of many in the room.

"Craftsmen could own their own shops instead of renting. Farmers would own their land and be able to pass it tax-free to their sons. Merchants could set their own rates and taxes wouldn't be used to pay for foreign wars. Instead, that money can be used to clean up this town. We could pave the roads, tear down the vacant buildings, and put all the people of the city to work doing it. We would elect our own sheriffs and bailiffs, but they would have little to do, for what crime could there be in a free city? Freemen with their own property have no cause for crime."

"I would be willing to fight for that," a man seated with his family near the windows said.

"For paved roads, I would too," said the elderly woman.

"I'd like to own my own land," another said.

Others voiced their interest and soon the conversation turned more serious. The level of the voices dropped and men clustered together to speak in small groups.

"You're not from Rhenydd, are you?" someone asked Arista.

The princess nearly jumped when she discovered a woman had slipped in beside her. She was not immediately certain that it was a woman, as she was oddly dressed in dark britches and a man's loose shirt. Arista initially thought she was an adolescent boy, due to her short blonde hair and dappled freckles, but her eyes gave her away. They were heavy and deep, as if stolen from a much older person.

"No," Arista said apprehensively.

The woman studied Arista, her old eyes slowly moving over her body as if she were memorizing every line of her figure and every crease in her dress. "You have an odd way about you. The way you walk, the way you sit. It's all very...*precise*, very...*proper*."

Arista was over being startled now and was just plain irritated. "You don't strike me as the kind of person who should accuse others of being odd," she replied.

"There!" the woman said excitedly, and wagged a finger. "See? Anyone else would have called me a mannish little whore. You have manners. You speak in subtle innuendo, like a...*princess*."

"Who are you?" Hadrian abruptly intervened, moving between the two. Royce also appeared from the shadows behind the strange woman.

"Who are *you*?" she replied saucily.

The door to The Laughing Gnome burst open and uniformed imperial guards poured in. Tables were turned over and drinks hit the floor. Customers nearest the door fell back in fear, cowering in the corners, or were pushed aside.

"Arrest everyone!" a man ordered in a booming voice. He was a big man with a potbelly, dark brows, and sagging cheeks. He kept his weight on his heels and his thumbs in his belt as he glared at the crowd.

"What's this all about, Trenchon?" Ayers shouted from behind the bar.

"You would be smart to keep your hole shut, Ayers, or I'll close this tavern tonight and have you in stocks by morning— or worse. Harboring traitors and providing a meeting place for conspirators will buy you death at the post!"

"I didn't do nothing!" Ayers cried. "It was the kid. He's the one that started all the talk, and that woman from Kilnar. They're the ones. I just served drinks like every night. I'm not responsible for what customers say. I'm not involved in this. It was them and a few of the others who were going along with it."

"Take everyone in for questioning," Trenchon ordered. "We'll get to the bottom of this. I want the ringleaders!"

"This way," the mannish woman whispered. Grabbing Arista's arm, she began to pull the princess away from the soldiers toward the kitchen.

Arista pulled back.

The woman sighed. "Unless you want to have a long talk with the viceroy about who you are and what you're doing here, you'll follow me now."

Arista looked at Royce, who nodded, but there was concern on his face. They grabbed up their bags and followed.

Starting at the main entrance, the imperial soldiers began hauling people out into the rain and mud. Women screamed and children cried. Those who resisted were beaten and thrown out. Some near the rear door tried to run, only to find more soldiers waiting.

The mannish woman plowed through the crowd into the tavern's kitchen, where a cook looked over, surprised. "Best look out," their guide said. "Trenchon is looking to arrest everyone."

The cook dropped her ladle in shock as they pressed by her, heading to the walk-in pantry. Closing the door, the woman revealed a trapdoor in the pantry's floor. They climbed down a short wooden stair into The Laughing Gnome's wine cellar. Several dusty bottles lined the walls, as did casks of cheese and containers of butter. The woman took a lantern that hung from the ceiling and, closing the door above, led them behind the wine racks to the cellar's far wall. There was a metal grate in the floor. She wedged a piece of old timber in the bars and pried it up.

"Inside, all of you," she ordered.

Above, they could still hear the screams and shouts, then the sound of heavy boots on the kitchen floor.

"Hurry!" she whispered.

Royce entered first, climbing down metal rungs that formed a ladder. He slipped into darkness and Hadrian motioned for the princess to follow. She took a deep breath as if going underwater and climbed down.

The ladder continued far deeper than Arista would have expected, and instead of the tight, cramped tunnel she anticipated, she found herself dropping into a large gallery. It was completely dark, except around the lantern, and the smell was unmistakable. Without pause or a word of direction, the woman walked away. They had no choice but to follow her light.

They were in a sewer far larger and grander than Arista had imagined possible after seeing the city above. Walls of brick and stone rose twelve feet to a roof of decorative mosaic tiles. Every few feet grates formed waterfalls that spilled from the ceiling, raining down with a deafening roar. Storm water frothed and foamed in the center of the tunnel as it churned around corners and broke upon dividers, spraying walls and staining them dark.

They chased the woman with the lantern as she moved quickly along the brick curb near the wall. Like ribs supporting the ceiling, thick stone archways jutted out at regular intervals, blocking their path. The woman skirted around these easily, but it was much harder for Arista in her gown to traverse the columns and keep her footing on the slick stone curb. Below her, the storm's runoff created a fast-flowing river of dirty water and debris that echoed in the chamber.

The corridor reached a four-way intersection. In the stone at the top corners were chiseled small notations. These read HONOR WAY going one direction and HERALD'S STREET going the other. The woman with the lantern never wavered, and turned without a pause, leading them down Honor Way at a breakneck pace. Abruptly, she stopped.

They stood on a curb beside the sewer river, which was like any other part of the corridor they had traveled except a bit wider and quieter.

"Before we go further, I must be certain," she began. "Allow me to make things easier by guessing the lady here is actually Princess Arista Essendon of Melengar. You are Hadrian Blackwater, and you're Duster, the famous Demon of Colnora. Am I correct?"

"That would make you a Diamond," Royce said.

"At your service." She smiled, and Arista thought how cat-like her face was, in that she appeared both friendly and sinister at the same time. "You can call me Quartz."

"In that case, you can assume you're correct."

"Thanks for getting us out of there," Hadrian offered.

"No need to thank me. It's my job and, in this particular

case, my happy pleasure. We didn't know where you were since leaving Colnora, but I was hoping you would happen by this way. Now follow me."

Off she sprang again, and Arista once more struggled to follow.

"How is this here?" Hadrian asked from somewhere behind Arista. "This sewer is incredible but the city above has dirt roads."

"Ratibor wasn't always Ratibor," Quartz shouted back. "Once it was something bigger. All that's been forgotten— buried like this sewer under centuries of dirt and manure."

They moved on down the tunnel until they came to an alcove, little more than a recessed area surrounded by brick. Quartz leaned up against a wooden panel and gave a strong shove. The back shifted inward slightly. She put her fingers in the crack and slid the panel sideways, exposing a hidden tunnel. They entered and traveled up a short set of steps to a wooden door. Light seeped around its cracks and voices could be heard from the other side. Quartz knocked and opened it, revealing a large subterranean chamber filled with people.

Tables, chairs, desks, and bunk beds stacked four high filled the room, lit by numerous candles that spilled a wealth of waxy tears. A fire burned in a blackened cooking hearth, where a huge iron pot was suspended by a swivel arm. Several large chests lay open, displaying sorted contents of silverware, candlesticks, clothes, hats, cloaks, and even dresses. Still other chests held purses, shoes, and rope. At least one was partially filled with coins, mostly copper, but Arista spotted a few silver and an occasional gold tenent sparkling in the firelight. This last chest they closed the moment the door opened.

A dozen people filled the room, all young, thin predators, each dressed in an odd assortment of clothing.

"Welcome to the Rat's Nest," Quartz told them. "Rats, let

me introduce you to the three travelers from Colnora." Shoulders settled, hands pulled back from weapons, and Arista heard a number of exhales. "The older gent back there is Polish." Quartz pointed over some heads at a tall, thin man with a scraggly beard and drooping eyes. He sported a tall black hat and a dramatic-looking cloak, like something a bishop would wear. "He's our fearless leader."

This comment drew a round of laughter.

"Damn you, Quartz!" a boy no older than nine cursed her.

"Sorry, Carat," she told him. "They just walked into the Gnome while I was there."

"We heard the Imps just crashed the Gnome," Polish said.

"Aye, they did." Quartz gleamed.

Eyes left them and focused abruptly on Quartz, who allowed herself a dramatic pause as she took a seat on a soft, beat-up chair, throwing her legs over the arm in a cavalier fashion. She obviously enjoyed the attention as the members of the room gathered around her.

"Emery was speeching again," she began like a master storyteller addressing an eager audience. "This time people were actually listening. He might have gotten something started, but he got under Laven's skin. Laven challenged him to a duel, but Emery says he'll fight sword to dagger, which really irks Laven and he storms out of the Gnome. Emery shoulda known to beat it then, but the dispute with Laven gets him in real good with the crowd, see, so he keeps going."

Arista noticed the thieves hanging on every word. They were enthralled as Quartz added to her tale's drama with sweeping arm gestures.

"Laven, being the bastard that he is, goes to Bailiff Trenchon, right? And returns with the town garrison. They bust in and start arresting everyone for treason."

"What'd Ayers do?" Polish asked excitedly.

"What could he do? He says, 'What's going on?' and they tell him to shut up, so he does."

"Anyone killed?" Carat asked.

"None that I saw, but I had to beat it out of there real quick like to save our guests here."

"Did they take Emery?"

"I suppose so, but I didn't see it."

Polish crossed the room to face them up close. He nodded as if in approval and pulled absently on his thin beard.

"Princess Arista," he said formally, and tipped his hat as he made a clumsy bow. "Please excuse the place. We don't often entertain guests of your stature here, and quite frankly, we didn't know when, or even if, you'd be coming."

"If we had known, we'd have at least washed the rats!" someone in the back shouted, bringing more laughter.

"Quiet, you reprobate. You must forgive them, milady. They're the lowest form of degenerates and their lifestyle only aggravates their condition. I try to elevate them, but as you can see, I've been less than successful."

"That's because you're the biggest blackguard here, Polish," Quartz shot at him.

Polish ignored the comment and moved to face Royce. "Duster?" he said, raising an eyebrow.

At the mention of that name, the whole room quieted and everyone pushed forward to get a better look.

"I thought he was bigger," someone said.

"That's not Duster," Carat declared, bravely stepping forward. "He's just an old man."

"Carat," Quartz said dismissively, "the cobbler's new puppy is old compared to you."

This brought forth more laughter and Carat kicked Quartz's feet off the chair's arm. "Shut up, freckle face."

"The lad makes a good point," Polish said.

"I don't have that many freckles," Quartz countered.

Polish rolled his eyes. "No, I meant just how do we really know this *is* Duster and the princess? Could be the Imps knew we were looking and are setting us up. Do you have any proof about who you are?"

As he said this, Arista noticed Polish let his hand drift casually to the long black dagger at his belt. Others in the room began to spread out, making slow but menacing movements. Only Quartz remained at ease on her chair.

Hadrian looked a bit concerned as Royce cast off his cloak, letting it fall to the floor. Eyes narrowed on him as they stared at the white-bladed dagger in his belt. Everyone waited anxiously for his next move. Royce surprised them by slowly unbuttoning his shirt and pulling it down to expose his left shoulder, revealing a scarred brand in the shape of an *M*.

Polish leaned forward and studied the scar. "The Mark of Manzant," he said, and his expression changed to one of wonder. "Duster is the only living man known to have escaped that prison."

They all nodded and murmured in awed tones as Royce put his cloak back on.

"He still doesn't look like no monster to me," Carat said with disdain.

"That's only because you've never seen him first thing in the morning," Hadrian told him. "He's an absolute fiend until he's had breakfast."

This brought a chuckle from the Diamonds and a reluctant smile from Carat.

"Now that that's settled, can we get to business?" Royce asked. "You need to send word to the Jewel that Etcher is a traitor and find out if a meeting has been set up with Gaunt."

"All in good time," Polish said. "First we have a very important matter to settle."

"That's right." Quartz came to life, leapt to her feet, and took a seat at the main table. "Pay up, people!"

There were irritated grumblings as the thieves reluctantly pulled out purses and counted coins. They each set stacks of silver in front of Quartz. Polish joined her and they started counting together.

"You too, Set," Quartz said. "You were down for half a stone."

When everyone was finished, Polish and Quartz divided the loot into two piles.

"And for being the one to find them?" she said, smiling at Polish.

Polish scowled and handed her a stack of silver, which she dropped into her own purse, now bulging and so heavy she needed to use two hands to hold it.

"You bet we wouldn't make it here?" Arista asked.

"Most everyone did, yes," Polish replied, smiling.

"'Cept Polish and I," Quartz said happily. "Not that I thought you'd make it either. I just liked the odds and the chance for a big payoff if you did."

"Great minds, my dear," Polish told her as he also put his share away. "Great minds, indeed."

Once his treasure was safely locked in a chest, Polish turned with a more serious look on his face. "Quartz, take Set and visit the Nationalists' camp. See if you can arrange a meeting. Take Degan Street. It'll be the safest now."

"Not to mention poetic," Quartz said, smiling at her own insight. She waved at Set, who grabbed his cloak. "I know exactly how much is in my trunk," Quartz told everyone as she dropped her purse in a chest. "It had best be there when I come back or I'll make sure *everyone* pays."

No one scoffed or laughed. Apparently, when it came to money, thieves did not make jokes.

"Yes, yes, now out with you two." Polish shooed them into the sewer, then turned to face the new guests. "Hmm, now what to do with you? We can't move around tonight with the city watch in a frenzy, besides which, the weather has been most unfriendly. Perhaps in the morning we can find you a safe house, but for tonight I'm afraid you'll all have to stay here in our humble abode. As you can see, we don't have the finest accommodations for a princess."

"I'll be fine," she said.

Polish looked at her, surprised. "Are you sure you *are* a princess?"

"She's becoming more human every day," Hadrian said, smiling at her.

"You can sleep over here," Carat told them, bouncing on one of the bunks. "This is Quartz's bed and the one below is Set's. They'll be out all night."

"Thank you," Arista told him, taking a seat on the lower berth. "You're quite the gentleman."

Carat straightened up at the comment and puffed up his chest, smiling back at Arista fondly.

"He's a miserable thief, behind on his accounts, is what he is," Polish admonished, pointing a finger. "You still owe me, remember?"

The boy's proud face dropped.

"I'm surprised they already named a street after Degan Gaunt," Arista mentioned, changing the subject. "I had no idea he was that popular."

Several people snickered.

"You got it backward," an older man with a craggy face said.

"The street wasn't named after Gaunt," Polish explained. "Gaunt's mother named him after the street."

"Gaunt is from Ratibor?" Hadrian asked.

Polish looked at him as if he had just questioned the existence of the sun. "Born on Degan Street. They say he was captured by pirates and that's where his life changed and the legend began."

Hadrian turned to Royce. "See? Being raised in Ratibor isn't always such a bad thing."

"Duster is from Ratibor? Where 'bouts did you live?"

Royce kept his eyes on his pack. "Don't you think you should send someone with that message about Etcher back to Colnora? The Jewel will want to know about him immediately, and any delay could get people killed."

Polish wagged a finger at Royce. "I remember you, you know. We never met, but I was in the Diamond back when you were. You were quite the bigwig, telling everyone what to do." Polish allowed himself a snicker. "I suppose that's a hard habit to break, eh? Still, practice makes perfect," Polish said, turning away. "There are dry blankets here you can use. We'll see about better arrangements in the morning."

Royce and Hadrian rooted around in their bags. Arista watched them enviously. Etcher had taken her bundle with him. Maybe he needed it as proof, or perhaps he had thought there could have been something of value in it. In any case, he had known she would not need it. Most likely, he had forgotten her pack was still on the horse. The loss was not great, a mangled and dirty dress, her nightgown and robe, her kris dagger, and a blanket. The only thing she still had with her was the only thing she cared about—the hairbrush from her father, which she took out. She attempted to tame the tangled mess that was her hair.

"You have such a way with people, Royce," Hadrian mentioned as he opened another pack.

Royce growled something Arista could not make out, and seemed overly focused on his gear.

"Where *did* you live, Royce?" Arista asked. "When you were here."

There was a long pause. Finally, he replied, "This isn't the first time I've slept in these sewers."

⌇

The sun had barely peeked over the horizon and already the air was hot, heavy with a stifling blanket of humidity. The rain had stopped but clouds lingered, shrouding the sun in a milky haze. The streets were filled with puddles, great pools of brown water, still as glass. A mongrel dog—thin and mangy—roamed the market, sniffing garbage. Flushing a rat, the mutt chased it to the sewers. Having lost it, he lapped from the brown water, then collapsed, panting. Insects appeared. Clouds of gnats formed over the larger puddles and biting flies circled the tethered horses. They fought them as best they could with a shake of the head, a stomp of the hooves, or a swish of the tail. Before long, people appeared. Most were women clad in plain dresses. The few men were shirtless, and everyone went about barefoot, their legs caked with mud to their knees. They opened shops and stands displaying a meager assortment of fruits, eggs, vegetables, and some meat, laid bare, to the flies' delight.

Royce had barely slept. Too wary to close his eyes for more than a few minutes at a time, he had given up. He rose sometime before dawn and made his way to the surface. He climbed on the bed of a wagon left abandoned in the mud and watched East End Square come alive. He had seen the sight before, only the faces were different. He hated this city. If it were a man, he would have slit its throat decades ago. The thought appealed to him as he stared at the muddy, puddle-filled square. Some problems were easily fixed by the draw of a knife, but others...

He was not alone.

Not long after first light, Royce spotted a boy lying under a cart in the mud, only his head visible above the ruts. For hours, the two remained aware of each other, but neither acknowledged it. When the shops began to open, the boy slipped from his muddy bed, crawled to one of the larger puddles, and washed some of the muck off. His hair remained caked with the gray clay, because he did not submerge his head. As the boy moved down the road, Royce saw he was nearly naked and kept a small pouch tied around his neck. Royce knew the pouch held all the boy's possessions. He imagined a small bit of glass for cutting, string, a smooth rock for hammering and breaking, and perhaps even a copper coin or two—it was a king's ransom that he would defend with his life, if it came to that.

The boy moved to an undisturbed puddle and drank deeply from the surface. Untouched rainwater was the best. Cleaner, fresher than well water, and much easier to get—much safer.

The boy kept a keen eye on him, constantly glancing over.

With his morning wash done, the lad crept around the cooper's shop, which was still closed. He hid himself between two tethered horses, rubbing their muddy legs. He glanced once more at Royce with an irritated look and then threw a pebble in the direction of the grocer. Nothing happened. The boy searched for another, paused, then threw again. This time the stone hit a pitcher of milk, which toppled and spilled. The grocer howled in distress and rushed to save what she could. As she did, the boy made a dash to steal a small sour apple and an egg. He made a clean grab and was back around the corner of the cooper's barn before the grocer turned.

His chest heaved as he watched Royce. He paused only a moment, then cracked the egg and spilled the gooey contents into his mouth, swallowing with pleasure.

Over the waif's right shoulder, Royce saw two figures

approaching. They were boys like him, but older and larger. One wore a pair of men's britches that extended to his ankles. The other wore a filthy tunic tied around his waist with a length of twine and a necklace made from a torn leather belt. The boy did not see them until it was too late. The two grabbed him by the hair and dragged him into the street, where they forced his face into the mud. The bigger boys wrenched the apple from his hand and ripped the pouch from his neck before letting go.

Sputtering, gasping, and blind, the boy struggled to breathe. He came up swinging and found only air. The kid wearing the oversized britches kicked him in the stomach, crumpling the boy to his knees. The one wearing the tunic took a turn and kicked the boy once, striking him in the side and landing him back in the mud. They laughed as they continued up Herald's Street, one holding the apple, the other swinging the neck pouch.

Royce watched the boy lying in the street. No one helped. No one noticed. Slowly the boy crawled back to his shelter beneath the wheel cart. Royce could hear him crying and cursing as he pounded his fist in the mud.

Feeling something on his cheek, Royce brushed away the wetness. He stood up, surprised his breathing was so shallow. He followed the plank walkway to the grocer, who smiled brightly at him.

"Terribly hot today, ain't it, sir?"

Royce ignored her. He picked out the largest, ripest apple he could find.

"Five copper if you please, sir."

Royce paid the woman without a word, then pulled a solid gold tenent from his pouch and pressed it sideways into the fruit. He walked back across the square. This time he took a different path, one that passed by the cart the boy lay under, and as he did, the apple slipped from his fingers and fell into the mud. Royce muttered a curse at his clumsiness and continued his way up the street.

*

As the day approached midmorning, the temperature grew oppressive. Arista was dressed in a hodgepodge of boyish clothes gleaned from the Diamond's stash. A shapeless cap hid most of her hair. A battered, oversized tunic and torn trousers gave her the look of a hapless urchin. In Ratibor, this nearly guaranteed her invisibility. Hadrian guessed it was more comfortable than her heavy gown and cloak.

The three of them arrived at the intersection of Legends and Lore. There had been a brief discussion about leaving Arista in the Rat's Nest, but after Hintindar, Hadrian was reluctant to have her out of his sight.

The thoroughfares of the two streets formed one of the many acute angles so prevalent in the city. Here a pie-shaped church dominated. Made of stone, the building stood out among its wooden neighbors, a heavy, overbuilt structure more like a fortress than a place of worship.

"Why a Nyphron church of all things?" Hadrian asked as they reached the entrance. "Maybe we got it wrong. I don't even know what I'm looking for."

Royce nudged Hadrian and pointed at the cornerstone. Chiseled into its face, the epitaph read:

ESTABLISHED 2992

"'Before you were born, the year ninety-two,'" he whispered. "I doubt it's a coincidence."

"Churches keep accounts concerning births, marriages,

and deaths in their community," Arista pointed out. "If there was a battle in which people died, there could be a record."

Pulling on the thick oak doors, Hadrian found them locked. He knocked and, when no response came, knocked again. He pounded with his fist, and then, just as Royce began looking for another way in, the door opened.

"I'm sorry, but services aren't until tomorrow," an elderly priest announced. He was dressed in the usual robes. He had a balding head and a wrinkled face that peered through the small crack of the barely opened door.

"That's okay. I'm not here for services," Hadrian replied. "I was hoping I could get a look at the church records."

"Records?"

Hadrian glanced at Arista. "I heard churches keep records on births and deaths."

"Oh yes, but why do you want to see them?"

"I'm trying to find out what happened to someone." The priest looked skeptical. "My father," he added.

Understanding washed over the priest's face and he beckoned them in.

As Hadrian had expected, it was oppressively dark. Banks of candles burned on either side of the altar and at various points around the worship hall, each doing more to emphasize the darkness than provide illumination.

"We actually keep very good records here," the priest mentioned as he closed the door behind them. "By the way, I'm Monsignor Bartholomew. I'm watching over the church while His Reverence Bishop Talbert is away on pilgrimage to Ervanon. And you are?"

"Hadrian Blackwater." He gestured to Royce and Arista. "These are friends of mine."

"I see. Then if you'll please follow me..." Bartholomew said.

Hadrian had never spent much time in churches. The darkness, opulence, and staring eyes of the sculptures unnerved him. He was at home in a forest or a field, a hovel or a fortress, but the interior of a church always made him uneasy. This one had a vaulted ceiling supported by marble columns and cinquefoil-shaped stonework and blind-tracery moldings common to Nyphron churches. The altar itself was an ornately carved wooden cabinet with three broad doors and a blue-green marble top. His mind flashed back to a similar cabinet in Essendon Castle that had concealed Magnus, a dwarf waiting to accuse him and Royce of Amrath's death. That incident had started his and Royce's long-standing employment with Medford's royal family.

On this one, more candles burned, and three large gilded tomes lay sealed. The sickly-sweet fragrance of salifan incense was strong. On the altar stood the obligatory alabaster statue of Novron. As always, he knelt, sword in hand, while the god Maribor loomed over him, placing a crown on his head, anointing his son the ruler of the world. All the churches Hadrian had visited had one, each a replica of the original sculpture preserved in the Crown Tower of Ervanon. They varied only in size and material.

Taking a candle, the priest led them down a narrow, curling stair. At the base, they stopped at a door, beside which hung an iron key on a peg. The priest lifted it off and twisted it in the large square lock until it clanked. The door creaked open and the priest replaced the key.

"Doesn't make much sense, does it? To keep the key there?" Royce pointed out.

The priest glanced back at it blankly. "It's heavy and I don't like carrying it."

"Then why lock the door?"

"Only way to keep it closed. And if left open, the rats eat the parchments."

Inside, the cellar was half the size of the church above and divided into aisles of shelves that stretched to the ceiling and were filled with thick leather-bound books. The priest took a moment to light a lantern that hung near the door.

"They're all in chronological order," he told them as the lantern revealed a low ceiling and walls made of small stacked stones quite unlike the larger blocks and bricks used in the rest of the church.

"About what time period are you looking for? When did your father die?"

"Twenty-nine ninety-two."

The priest hesitated. "Ninety-two? That was forty-two years ago. You age remarkably well. How old were you?"

"Very young."

The priest looked skeptical. "Well, I'm sorry. We have no records from ninety-two."

"The cornerstone outside says this church was built then," Royce said.

"And yet we do not have the records for which you ask."

"Why is that?" Hadrian pressed.

The priest shrugged. "Maybe there was a fire."

"*Maybe* there was a fire? You don't know?"

"Our records cannot help you, so if you'll please follow me, I'll show you out." The priest took a step toward the exit.

Royce stepped in his path. "You're hiding something."

"I'm doing nothing of the sort. You asked to see records from ninety-two—there are none."

"The question is, why?"

"Any number of reasons. How should I know?"

"The same way you knew there aren't any records here for

that date without even looking," Royce replied, his voice lowering. "You're lying to us, which again brings up the question of why."

"I'm a monsignor. I don't appreciate being accused of lying in my own church."

"And I don't appreciate being lied to." Royce took a step forward.

"Neither do I," Bartholomew replied. "You're not looking for anyone's father. Do you think I'm a fool? Why are you back here? That business ended decades ago. Why are you still at it?"

Royce glanced at Hadrian. "We've never been here before."

The priest rolled his eyes. "You know what I mean. Why is the seret still digging this up? You're Sentinel Thranic, aren't you?" He pointed at Royce. "Talbert told me about the interrogation you put him through—a bishop of the church! If only the Patriarch knew what his pets were up to, you would all be disbanded. Why do you still exist, anyway? The Heir of Novron is on her throne, isn't she? Isn't that what we're all supposed to believe? At long last, you found the seed of Novron and all is finally right with the world. You people can't accept that your mandate is over, that we don't need you anymore—if we ever did."

"We aren't seret," Hadrian told him, "and my friend here is definitely not a sentinel."

"No? Talbert described him perfectly—small, wiry, frightening, *like Death himself.* But you must have shaved your beard."

"I'm not a sentinel," Royce told him.

"We're just trying to find out what happened here forty-two years ago," Hadrian explained. "And you're right. I'm not looking for a record of my father's death, because I know he didn't die here. But he was here."

The monsignor hesitated, looking at Hadrian and shooting

furtive glances at Royce. "What was your father's name?" he asked at length.

"Danbury Blackwater."

The priest shook his head. "Never heard of him."

"But you know what happened," Royce said. "Why don't you just tell us?"

"Why don't you just get out of my church? I don't know who you are, and I don't want to. What happened, happened. It's over. Nothing can change it. Just leave me alone."

"You were there," Arista muttered in revelation. "Forty-two years ago—you were there, weren't you?"

The monsignor glared at her, his teeth clenched. "Look through the stacks if you want," he told them in resignation. "I don't care. Just lock up when you leave. And be sure to blow out the light."

"Wait." Hadrian spoke quickly as he fished his medallion out of his shirt and held it up toward the light. Bartholomew narrowed his eyes and then stepped closer to examine it.

"Where did you get that?"

"My father left it to me. He also wrote me a poem, a sort of riddle, I think. Maybe you can help explain it." Hadrian took out the parchment and passed it to the cleric.

After reading, the cleric raised a hand to his face, covering his mouth. Hadrian noticed his fingers tremble. His other hand sought and found the wall and he leaned heavily against it. "You look like him," the priest told Hadrian. "I didn't notice it at first. It's been over forty years and I only knew him briefly, but that's his sword on your back. I should have recognized that if nothing else. I still see it so often in my nightmares."

"So you knew my father, you knew Danbury Blackwater?"

"His name was Tramus Dan. That's what he went by, at least."

"Will you tell us what happened?"

He nodded. "There's no reason to keep it secret, except to protect myself, and perhaps it's time I faced my sins."

The monsignor looked at the open door to the stairs. "Let's close this." He stepped out, then returned, puzzled. "The key is gone."

"I've got it," Royce volunteered, revealing the iron key in his hand. Pulling the door shut, he locked it from the inside. "I've never cared for rooms I can be locked in."

Bartholomew took a small stool from behind one of the stacks and perched himself on it. He sat bent over with his head between his knees, as if he might be sick. They waited as the priest took several steadying breaths.

"It was forty-two years ago, next week, in fact," he began, his head still down, his voice quiet. "I had been expecting them for days and was worried. I thought they had been discovered, but that wasn't it. They were traveling slowly because she was with child."

"Who was?" Hadrian asked.

The monsignor looked up, confused. "Do you know the significance of that amulet you wear?"

"It once belonged to the Guardian of the Heir of Novron."

"Yes," the old man said simply. "Your father was the head of our order—a secret organization dedicated to protecting the descendants of Emperor Nareion."

"The Theorem Eldership," Royce said.

Bartholomew looked at him, surprised. "Yes. Shopkeepers, tradesmen, farmers—people who preserved a dream handed down to them."

"But you're a priest in the Nyphron Church."

"Many of us were encouraged to take vows. Some even tried to join the seret. We needed to know what the church was doing, where they were looking. I was the only one in Ratibor to receive the would-be emperor and his guardian.

The ranks of the Eldership had dwindled over the centuries. Few believed in it anymore. My parents raised me to believe in the dream of seeing the heir of Nareion returned to an imperial throne, but I never expected it would happen. I often questioned if the heir even existed, if the stories were just a myth. You see, the Eldership only contacted members if needed. You had a few meetings and years could go by without a word. Even then, messages were only words of encouragement reminding us to stay strong. We never heard a thing about the heir. There were no plans to rise up, no news of sightings, victories, or defeats.

"I was only a boy, a young deacon, recently arrived in Ratibor, assigned to the old South Square Church, when my father sent a letter saying simply 'He is coming. Make preparations.' I didn't know what to think. It took several readings before I even understood what 'he' meant. When I realized, I was dumbstruck. The Heir of Novron was coming to Ratibor. I didn't know exactly what I should do, so I rented a room at the Bradford's boardinghouse and waited. I should have found a better place. I should have..." He paused for a moment, dropped his head again to look at the floor, and took a breath.

"What happened?" Hadrian asked, keeping his voice calm, not wanting to do anything to stop the cleric from revealing his tale.

"They arrived late, around midnight, because his wife was about to give birth and their travel was slow. His name was Naron and he traveled with his guardian, Tramus Dan, and Dan's young apprentice, whose name I sadly can't recall. I saw them to their rooms at the boardinghouse and your father sent me in search of a midwife. I found a young girl and sent her ahead while I set out to find what supplies were needed.

"By the time I returned with my arms full, I saw a company of Seret Knights coming up the street, searching door-to-door.

I was horrified. I had never seen seret in Ratibor. They reached the boardinghouse before I could.

"They found it locked and beat on the door. There was no answer. When they tried to break in, your father refused them entry and the fight began. I watched from across the street. It was the most amazing thing I ever saw. Your father and his apprentice stepped out and fought back-to-back, defending the entrance. Knight after knight died until as many as ten lay dead or wounded on the street, and then came a scream from inside. Some of the seret must have found a way into the building from the back.

"The apprentice ran inside, leaving your father alone at the door to face the remainder of the knights. There must have been a dozen or more. By wielding two swords in the shelter of the entrance, he kept them at bay. He held them off for what felt like an eternity, and then Naron appeared at the doorway. He was mad with rage and drenched in blood. He pushed past Dan into the street. Your father tried to stop him, but Naron kept screaming, 'They killed her!' and threw himself into the crowd of knights, swinging his sword like a man possessed.

"Your father tried to reach Naron—to protect him. The seret surrounded Naron and I watched him die on their swords. I fell to my knees, the blankets, needle, and thread falling to the street. Your father, surrounded by his own set of knights, cried out and dropped his two swords. I thought they had stabbed him too. I expected to see him fall, but instead he drew the spadone blade from his back. The bloodshed I witnessed up to that point did not compare to what followed. Tramus Dan, with that impossibly long sword, began cleaving the seret to pieces. Legs, arms, and heads—explosions of blood. Even across Lore Street, I felt the spray carried on the wind like a fine mist on my face.

"When the last seret fell, Dan ran inside and emerged a

moment later with tears streaking down his cheeks. He went to Naron and cradled the heir, rocking him. I admit that I was too frightened to approach or even speak. Dan looked like Uberlin himself, bathed slick from head to foot in blood, that sword still at his side, his body shaking as if he might explode. After a time, he gently laid Naron on the porch. A few of the knights were still alive, groaning, twitching. He picked up the sword again and cut through them as if he were chopping wood. Then he picked up his weapons and walked away.

"I was too scared to follow, too terrified to even stand up, and I did not dare approach the house. As time passed, others arrived, and together we found the courage to enter. We found the younger swordsman—your father's apprentice—dead in the upper bedroom, surrounded by several bodies of seret. In the bed was a woman stabbed to death, her newborn child murdered in her arms. I never saw or heard anything of your father again."

They sat in silence for a few minutes.

"It explains a lot I never understood about my father," Hadrian finally said. "He must have wandered to Hintindar after that and changed his name. Dan—bury. Even his name was a riddle. So the line of Novron is dead?"

The old priest said nothing at first. He sat perfectly still except for his lips, which began to tremble. "It's all my fault. The seed of Maribor is gone. The tree, so carefully watered for centuries, has withered and died. It was all my fault. If only I had found a better safe house, or if I had kept a better watch." He looked up. The light from the lantern glistened off tears.

"The next day, more seret came and burned the boarding-house to the ground. I petitioned for this church to be built. The bishops never realized I was doing it as a testament—a monument to their memory. They thought I was honoring the fallen seret. So here I remained, upon their graves, guarding still. Yet now I protect not hope but a memory, a dream that, because of me, will never be."

✆

At noon, the ringing of the town bell summoned the citizens to Central Square. On their way back from the church, Arista, Hadrian, and Royce entered the square, barely able to see due to the gathered crowd. There they found twelve people locked in stocks. They all stood bent over with head and wrists locked, their feet and lower legs sunk deep in mud. Above each hung a hastily scrawled sign with the word *Conspirator* written on it.

The young, red-haired Emery was not in a stock, but instead hung by his wrists from a pole. Naked to the waist, his body was covered in numerous dark bruises and abrasions. His left eye was puffed and sealed behind a purple bruise, and his lower lip was split and stained dark with dried blood.

Next to him hung the older woman from The Laughing Gnome, the one who had mentioned that the Imperialists had burned Kilnar. Above both of them were signs reading TRAITOR. Planks circled the prisoners, and around them paced the sheriff of Ratibor. In his hands he held a short whip comprising several strands knotted at the ends, which he wagged threateningly as he walked. The whole city garrison had turned out to keep the angry crowd at bay. Archers were poised on roofs, and soldiers armed with shields and unsheathed swords threatened any who approached too close.

Many of the faces in the stocks were familiar to Arista from the night before. She was shocked to see mothers, who had sung their children to sleep on the floor of the tavern, now locked in stocks beside their husbands, sobbing. The children reached out for their parents from the crowd. The treatment of the woman from Kilnar disturbed her the most. Her only crime was telling the truth, and now she hung before the entire city, awaiting the whip. The sight was all the more terrifying because Arista knew it could have been her up there if Quartz had not intervened.

A regally dressed man in a judge's robe and a scribe approached the stocks. When they reached the center of the square, the scribe handed a parchment to the judge. The sheriff shouted for silence, and then the judge held up the parchment and began to read.

"'For the crimes of conspiracy against Her Royal Eminence the empress Modina Novronian, the New Empire, Maribor, and all humanity; for slander against His Excellency the empress's imperial viceroy; and for the general agitation of the lower classes to challenge their betters, it is hereby proclaimed good and right that punishment be laid immediately upon these criminals. Those guilty of conspiracy are hereby ordered to be flogged twenty lashes and spend one day in stocks, not to be released until sunset. Those guilty of treason will receive one hundred lashes and, if they remain alive, will be left hanging until they expire from want of food and water. Anyone attempting to help or lend comfort to any of these criminals will be likewise found guilty and receive similar punishment.'" He rolled up the parchment. "Sheriff Vigan, you may commence."

With that, he thrust the scroll into the hands of the scribe and promptly walked back the way he had come. With a nod from the sheriff, a soldier approached the first stock and ripped open the back of the young mother's dress. From somewhere in the crowd, a child screamed, yet without pause the sheriff swung his whip, even as the poor woman cried for mercy. The knots bit into the pale skin of her back and she howled and danced in pain. Stroke after stroke fell with the scribe standing by, keeping careful track. By the time it was done, her back was red and slick with blood. The sheriff took a break and handed the whip to a soldier, who performed similar punishment on her husband as the sheriff sat by, leisurely drinking from a cup.

The crowd, already quiet, grew deadly still as they came to the woman from Kilnar, who began screaming as they approached. The sheriff and his deputies took turns whipping her, as the day's heat made such work exhausting. The fatigue in their arms was evident by the wild swings that struck the woman high on her shoulders as well as low on her back, and even occasionally as low as her thighs. After the first thirty lashes, the woman stopped screaming and only whimpered softly. The whipping continued, and by the time the scribe counted sixty, the woman merely hung limp. A physician approached the post, lifted her head by her hair, and pronounced her dead. The scribe made a note of this. They did not remove her body.

The sheriff finally moved to Emery. The young man was not daunted after seeing the punishment carried out on the others, and made the bravest showing of all. He stood defiant as the soldier with the whip approached him.

"Killing me will not change the truth that Viceroy Androus is the real traitor and guilty of killing King Urith and the royal family!" he managed to shout before the first strokes of the whip silenced him. He did not cry out but gritted his teeth and only dully grunted as the knots turned his back into a mass of blood and pulpy flesh. By the last stroke, he also hung limp and silent, but everyone could see him breathing. The physician indicated such to the scribe, who dutifully jotted it down.

"Those people didn't do anything," Arista said as the crowd began to disperse. "They're innocent."

"You, of all people, know that isn't the point," Royce replied.

Arista whirled. She opened her mouth, hesitated, and then shut it.

"Alric had twelve people publicly flogged for inciting riots when the church was kicked out of Melengar," he reminded her. "How many of them were actually guilty of anything?"

"I'm sure that was necessary to keep the peace."

"The viceroy will tell you the same."

"This is different. Mothers weren't whipped before their children, and women weren't beaten to death before a crowd."

"True," Royce said. "It was only fathers, husbands, and sons who were whipped bloody and left scarred for life. I stand corrected. Melengar's compassion is astounding."

Arista glared at him but could say nothing. As much as she hated it, as much as she hated him for pointing it out, she realized what Royce said was true.

"Don't punish yourself over it," Royce told her. "The powerful control the weak. The rich exploit the poor. It's the way it's always been and how it always will be. Just thank Maribor you were born both rich and powerful."

"But it's not right," she said, shaking her head.

"What does *right* have to do with it? With anything? Is it right that the wind blows or that the seasons change? It's just the way the world is. If Alric hadn't flogged those people, maybe they would have succeeded in their revolt. Then you and Alric might have found yourselves beaten to death by a cheering crowd, because they would hold the power and you two would be weak."

"Are you really that indifferent?" she asked.

"I like to think of it as practical, and living in Ratibor for any length of time has a tendency to make a person *very* practical." He glanced sympathetically at Hadrian, who had been quiet since leaving the church. "Compassion doesn't make house calls to the streets of Ratibor—now or forty years ago."

"Royce…" Hadrian said, then sighed. "I'm going to take a walk. I'll see you two back at the Nest in a little while."

"Are you all right?" Arista asked.

"Yeah," he said unconvincingly, and moved away with the crowd.

"I feel bad for him," she said.

"Best thing that could have happened. Hadrian needs to understand how the world really works and get over his childish affection for ideals. You see Emery up there? He's an idealist and that's what eventually happens to idealists, particularly those that have the misfortune of being born in Ratibor."

"But for a moment he might have changed the course of this city," Arista said.

"No, he would only have changed who was in power and who wasn't. The course would remain the same. Power rises to the top like cream and dominates the weak with cruelty disguised as—and often even believed to be—benevolence. When it comes to people, there is no other possibility. It's a natural occurrence, like the weather, and you can't control either one."

Arista thought for a moment and glanced skyward. Then she said defiantly, "I wouldn't be so sure of that."

CHAPTER 12

MAKING IT RAIN

By the time Hadrian returned to the Rat's Nest, he could see Quartz had returned and there was trouble. Arista stood in the middle of the room with arms folded stubbornly, a determined look on her face. The rest watched her, happily entertained, while Royce paced with a look of exasperation.

"Thank Maribor you're back!" Royce said. "She's driving me insane."

"What's going on?"

"We're going to take control of the city," Arista announced.

Hadrian raised an eyebrow. "What happened to the meeting with Gaunt?"

"Not going to happen," Quartz answered. "Gaunt's gone."

"Gone?"

"Officially, he's disappeared," Royce explained. "Likely he's dead or captured. I'm certain Merrick is behind this somehow. It feels like him. He stopped us from contacting Gaunt and used both sides as bait for the other. Brilliant, really. Degan went to meet with Arista just as Arista went to meet him, and both walked into a trap. Arista avoided hers but it would appear that Gaunt was not so fortunate. The Nationalists are blaming Her Highness and Melengar, convinced that she's responsible. Even though the plan failed to catch the princess, there is no chance for an alliance. Definitely Merrick."

"Which is exactly why we need to prove ourselves to the Nationalists," Arista explained while Royce shook his head. She turned to face Hadrian. "If we take the city from the inside and hand it over to them, they'll trust us and we'll be able to get them to agree to an alliance. When you took this job, I reserved the right to change the objectives, and I'm doing so now."

"And how, *exactly*, do we *take* the city?" Hadrian asked carefully, trying to keep his tone neutral. He was usually inclined to side with Royce, and at face value Arista's idea did seem more than a little insane. On the other hand, he knew Arista was no fool and Royce often made choices based solely on self-interest. Beyond all that, he could not help admiring Arista, standing in a room full of thieves and opportunists, proclaiming such a noble idea.

"Just like Emery said at The Laughing Gnome," Arista began. "We storm the armory. Take weapons and what armor we can find. Then attack the garrison. Once we defeat them, we seal the city gates."

"The garrison in Ratibor is made up of what?" Hadrian asked. "Fifty? Sixty experienced soldiers?"

"At least that," Royce muttered disdainfully.

"Going up against hastily armed tailors, bakers, and grocers? You'd need to have half the population of the city backing you," he pointed out.

"Even if you could raise a rabble, scores of people will die and the rest will break and run," Royce added.

"They won't run," Arista said. "There's no place for them to go. We're trapped in a walled city. There can be no retreat. Everyone will have to fight to the death. After this afternoon's demonstration of the empire's cruelty, I don't think anyone will chance surrender."

Hadrian nodded. "But how do you expect to incite the city to fight for you? They don't even know you. You're not like Emery, with lifelong friends who will lay their lives on the line on your behalf. I doubt not even Polish here has a reputation that will elicit that kind of devotion—no offense."

Polish smiled at him. "You are quite right. The people rarely see me, and when they do, I'm thought of as a despicable brigand—imagine that."

"That's why we need Emery," Arista said.

"The kid dying in the square?"

"You saw the way the people listened," she said earnestly. "They believe in him."

"Right up until they were flogged at his side," Royce put in.

Arista stood straighter and spoke in a louder voice. "And even when they were, did you see the look in the faces of those people? In The Laughing Gnome, they already saw him as something of a hero—standing up for them against the Imperialists. When they flogged him, when he faced death and yet stood by his convictions, it solidified their feelings for him and his ideals. The Imperialists left Emery to die today. When they did, they made him a martyr. Just imagine how the people will feel if he survives! If he slipped out of the Imperialists' grasp just as everyone felt certain he was dead, it could be the spark that can ignite their hopes."

"He's probably already dead," Quartz said indifferently as she cleaned her nails with a dagger.

Arista ignored her. "We'll steal Emery from the post, spread the news that he's alive and that he asks everyone to stand up with him and fight—to fight for the freedom he promised them."

Royce scoffed but Hadrian considered the idea. He wanted

to believe. He wanted to be swept along with her passion, but his practical side, which had waged dozens of battles, told him there was little chance for success. "It won't work," he finally stated, "Even if you managed to take the city, the imperial army will just take it back. A few hundred civilians could overwhelm the city garrison, but they aren't going to stop an army."

"That's why we have to coordinate our attack with the Nationalists'. Remember Emery's plan? We'll shut the gates and lock them out. Then the Nationalists can crush them."

"And if you don't manage to close the gates in time? If the battle against the garrison doesn't go perfectly to plan?" Royce asked.

"It still won't matter," Arista said. "If the Nationalists attack the imperial army at the same time that we launch our rebellion, they won't be able to bother with us."

"Except the Nats won't attack without Gaunt," Polish said. "That's the reason they're still out there. Well, that and the three hundred heavy cavalry Lord Dermont commands along with the rest of his army. The Nats haven't ever faced an organized force. Without Gaunt, they have no one to lead them. They aren't disciplined troops. Just townsfolk and farmers Gaunt picked up along the way here. They'll run the moment they see armored knights."

"Who's in charge of Gaunt's army?" Hadrian asked. He had to admit Arista's plans were at least thought out.

"Some fat chap who goes by the name of Parker. Rumor has it he was a bookkeeper for a textile business. He used to be the Nats' quartermaster before Gaunt promoted him," Quartz said. "Not the brightest coin in the purse, if you understand me. Without Gaunt planning and leading the attack, the Nats don't stand a chance."

"You could do it," Arista said, looking squarely at Hadrian. "You've commanded men in battle before. You got a medal."

Hadrian rolled his eyes. "It wasn't as impressive as it sounds. They were only small regiments. Grendel's army was, well, in a word, pathetic. They refused to even wear helms, because they didn't like the way their voices echoed in their heads."

"But you led them in battle?"

"Yes, but—"

"And did you win or lose?"

"We won but—"

"Against a larger or smaller force?"

Hadrian stood silent, a beaten look on his face.

Royce turned toward him. "Tell me you aren't considering this nonsense."

Am I? But three hundred heavy cavalry!

Desperation slipped into Arista's voice. "Breckton's Northern Imperial Army is marching here. If the Nationalists don't attack now, the combined imperial forces will decimate them. That's what Lord Dermont is waiting for—that's his plan. If he sits and waits, then he will win. But if the Nationalists attack first, if he has no support, and nowhere to run…This may be our only chance. It's now or all will be lost.

"If the Nationalists are destroyed, nothing will stop the empire. They'll retake and punish all of Rhenydd for its disobedience, and that will include Hintindar." She paused, letting him consider this. "Then they will take Melengar. After that, nothing will stop them from conquering Delgos, Trent, and Calis. The empire will rule the world once more, but not like it once did. Instead of an enlightened rule uniting the people, it will be one of cruelty dividing them, headed not by a noble, benevolent emperor, but by a handful of greedy, power-hungry men who pull strings while hiding behind the shield of an innocent girl.

"And what about you, Royce?" She turned toward him.

"Have you forgotten the wagons? What do you think the fate of those and others like them will be when the New Empire rules all?

"Don't you see?" She addressed the entire room. "We either fight here and win, or die trying, because there won't be anything left if we fail. This is the moment. This is the crucial point where the future of yet unborn generations will be decided either by our action or inaction. For centuries to come, people will look back at this time and rejoice at our courage or curse our weakness." She looked directly at Royce now. "For we have the power. Here. Now. In this place. We have the power to alter the course of history and we will be forever damned should we not so much as try!"

She stopped talking, exhausted and out of breath.

The room was silent.

To Hadrian's surprise, it was Royce who spoke first. "Making Emery disappear isn't the hard part. Keeping him hidden is the problem."

"They'll tear the city apart looking, that's certain," Polish said.

"Can we bring him here?" Arista asked.

Polish shook his head. "The Imps know about us. They leave us alone because we don't cause much trouble and they enjoy the black market we provide. No, they'll most certainly come down here looking. Besides, without orders from the Jewel or the First Officer, I couldn't expose our operation to that much risk."

"We need a safe house where the Imps won't dare look," Royce said. "Someplace they won't even want to look. Is the city physician an Imperialist or a Royalist?"

"He's a friend of Emery, if that's any indication," Quartz explained.

"Perfect. By the way, Princess, conquering Ratibor wasn't

in our contract. This will most certainly cost you extra," Royce said.

"Just keep a tally," she replied, unable to suppress her smile.

"If this keeps up, we're going to own Melengar," Hadrian mentioned.

"What's this *we* stuff?" Royce asked. "You're retired, remember?"

"Oh? So *you'll* be leading the Nationalist advance, will you?"

"Sixty-forty?" Royce proposed.

⚜

Despite the recent rain, the public stable on Lords Row caught fire just after dark. More than two dozen horses ran through the streets. The city's inhabitants responded with a bucket brigade. Those unable to find a place in line stood in awe as the vast wooden building burned with flames reaching high into the night's sky.

With no chance of saving the stable, the town fought to save the butcher's shop next door. Men climbed on the roof and, braving the rain of sparks, soaked the shake shingles. Bucket after bucket doused the little shop as the butcher's wife watched from the street, terrified. Her face glowed in the horrific light. The townsfolk, and even some imperial guards, fought the fire for hours, until, at last, deprived of the shop next door, it burned itself out. The stable was gone. All that remained of it was charred and smoking rubble, but the butcher's shop survived with one blackened wall to mark its brush with disaster. The townsfolk, covered in soot and ash, congratulated themselves on a job well done. The Gnome filled with patrons toasting their success. They clapped their neighbors on the back and told jokes and stories of near death.

No one noticed Emery Dorn was missing.

The next morning, the city bell rang with the news. A stuffed dummy hung in his place. Guards swore they had not left their stations, but had no explanation. Sheriff Vigan, the judge, and various other city officials were furious. They stood in Central Square, shouting and pointing fingers at the guards, then at each other. Even Viceroy Androus interrupted his busy schedule to emerge from City Hall and personally witness the scene.

By midmorning, the Gnome filled with gossipers and happy customers, as if the town had declared a holiday, and Ayers was happily working up a sweat filling drinks.

"He was still breathing at sunset!" the cooper declared.

"He's definitely alive. Why free him if he was dead?" the grocer put forth.

"Who did it?"

"What makes you think *anyone* did it? That boy likely got away himself. Emery is a sly one, he is. We shoulda known the Imps couldn't kill the likes of him."

"He's likely down in the sewers."

"Naw, he's left the city. Nothing for him here now."

"Knowing Emery, he's in the viceroy's house right now, drinking the old man's brandy!"

This brought laughter to go with the round of ales Ayers dispensed. Ayers had his own thoughts on the matter—he guessed the guards had freed him. Emery was a great talker. Ayers had heard him giving speeches in the Gnome dozens of times, and the lad had always won over the crowd. He could easily imagine the boy talking all night to the men who were charged to watch him and convincing them to let him go. He wanted to mention his idea, but the keg was nearly empty and he was running low on mugs. He did not care much for the Imps personally, but they were great for business.

A loud banging at the tavern's entrance killed the laughter and people turned sharply. Ayers nearly dropped the keg he was lifting, certain the sheriff was leading another raid, but it was only Dr. Gerand. He stood at the open door, hammering the frame with his shoe to get their attention. Everyone breathed again.

"Come in, Doctor!" Ayers shouted. "I'll have another keg brought up."

"Can't," he replied. "Need to be keeping my distance from everyone for a while. Just want to let people know to stay clear of the Dunlaps' house. They've got a case of pox there."

"Is it bad?" the grocer asked.

"Bad enough," the physician said.

"All these new immigrants from down south are bringing all kinds of sickness with them," Ayers complained.

"Aye, that's probably what did it," Dr. Gerand said. "Mrs. Dunlap took in a boarder a few days back, a refugee from Vernes. It was that fella who first come down with the pox. So don't be going near the Dunlaps' place until you hear it's safe from me. In fact, I'd steer clear of Benning Street altogether. I'm gonna see if I can get the sheriff to put up some signs and maybe a fence or something to let people know to keep out. Anyway, I'm just going around telling folks, and I would appreciate it if you helped me spread the word before this gets out of hand."

By noon, the city guard was turning all the townsfolk out of their houses and shops, searching for the escaped traitor, and the very first place they looked was the Dunlaps' home. The five guards on duty the night Emery had disappeared were forced to draw lots, and one lone soldier went in. He came out after finding nothing but a couple of sick people, neither of whom was Emery. After making his report from a distance, he returned to the Dunlaps' to remain under quarantine.

The soldiers then tore through The Laughing Gnome, the marketplace, the old church, and even the scribe's office, leaving them all a mess. Squads of soldiers entered the sewers and came up soaked. They did not find the escaped traitor, but they did find a couple of chests that some said were filled with stolen silver.

There was no sign of Emery Dorn.

By nightfall, a makeshift wooden fence stood across Benning Street and a large whitewashed sign read

KEEP OUT!
Quarantined by order of the Viceroy!

Two days later, the soldier who had searched the Dunlaps' house died. He was seen covered with puss-filled boils in the yard. The doctor dug a hole while people watched from a distance. After that, no one went near Benning Street.

The city officials and those at the Gnome concluded Emery had left town or died—and was secretly buried somewhere.

～

Arista, Hadrian, and Royce waited silently just outside the entrance to the bedroom until the doctor finished. "I've taken the bandages off him," Dr. Gerand said. He was an elderly man with white hair, a hooknose, and bushy eyebrows that managed to look sad even when he smiled. "He's much better today. A whipping like he took…" He paused, unsure how to explain. "Well, you saw what it did to the poor lady that hung alongside him. He should have died, but he's young. He'll bounce back once he wakes up and starts eating. Of course, his back will be scarred for life and he'll never be as strong as he was—too much damage. The only concern I have is noxious humors causing an imbalance in his body, but honestly, that doesn't look like it'll be a problem. Like I said, the boy is young and strong. Let him continue to rest and he should be fine."

They followed the doctor downstairs, escorting him to the front door of the Dunlaps' home, where he bid them good night.

Pausing in the doorway, he looked back. "Emery is a good lad. He was my son's best friend. James was taken into the imperial army and died in some battle up north." He glanced at the floor. "Watching Emery on that post was like losing him all over again. Whatever happens now, I just wanted to say thank you." With that, the doctor left.

Arista had seen the insides of more commoners' homes over the past week than she had in her entire life. After visiting with the Bakers of Hintindar, she had assumed all families lived in identical houses, but the Dunlaps' home was nothing like the Bakers'. This one was two stories tall, with a solid wooden floor on both levels. The upper story created a thick-beamed ceiling to the lower one. While still modest and a bit cramped, it showed touches of care and a dash of prosperity, which Hintindar lacked. The walls were painted and decorated with pretty designs of stars and flowers, and the wood surfaces were buffed and stained. Knickknacks of glazed pottery and wood carvings lined shelves above the fireplace. Unlike Dunstan and Arbor's sparse home, the Dunlaps' house had a lot of furniture. Wooden chairs with straw seats circled the table. Another pair bookended a spinning wheel surrounded by several wicker baskets. Little tables held vases of flowers, and on the wall hung a cabinet with small doors and knobs. Kept neat, clean, and orderly, it was a house loved by a woman whose husband had been a good provider, but had rarely been home.

"Are you sure you don't want anything else?" Mrs. Dunlap

asked while clearing the dinner plates. She was an old, plump woman who always wore an apron and a matching white scarf and had a habit of wringing her wrinkled hands.

"We're fine," Arista told her. "And thank you again for letting us use your home."

The old woman smiled. "It's not so much a risk as you might think. My husband has been dead six years now. He proudly served as His Majesty Urith's coachman. Did you know that?" Her eyes sparkled as she looked off as if seeing him once more. "He was a handsome man in his driver's coat and hat with that red plume and gold broach. Yes, sir, a mighty fine-looking man, proud to serve the king, and had for thirty years."

"Was he killed with the king?"

"Oh no." She shook her head. "But he died soon after, of heartbreak, I think. He was very close to the royal family. Drove them everywhere they went. They gave him gifts and called him by his given name. Once, during a storm, he even brought the princes here to spend the night. The little boys talked about it for weeks. We never had children of our own, you see, and I think Paul—that's my husband—I think he thought of the royals as his own boys. It devastated him when they died in that fire—that horrible fire. Emery's father died in it too, did you know that? He was one of the king's body-guards. There was so much death that terrible, terrible night."

"Urith was a good king?" Hadrian asked.

She shrugged. "I'm just an old woman, what do I know? People complained about him all the time when he was alive. They complained about the high taxes, and some of the laws, and how he would live in a castle with sixty servants, dining on deer, boar, and beef all at the same meal while people in the city were starving. I don't know that there is such a thing as a good king. Perhaps there are just kings that are good enough." She looked at Arista and winked. "Perhaps what we need is less kings and more womenfolk running things."

Mrs. Dunlap went back to the work of straightening as they sat at the round dining table.

"Well," Royce began, looking at Arista, "step one of your rebellion is complete. So now what?"

She thought a moment, then said, "We'll need to circulate the story of Emery leading the coming attack. Play him up as a hero, a ghost that the empire can't kill."

"I've heard talk like that around town already," Royce said. "You were right about that, at least."

Arista smiled. Such a compliment from Royce was high praise.

"We need to use word of mouth," she continued, "to get the momentum for the revolt started. I want everyone to know it's coming. I want them to think of it as inevitable as the coming of dawn. I want them to believe it can't fail. I'll need leaders as well. Hadrian, keep an eye out for reliable men who can help lead the battle. Men others listen to and respect. I'll also need you to devise a battle plan to take the armory and the garrison for me. Unlike my brother, I never studied the art of war. They made me learn needlepoint instead. Do you know how often I've used needlepoint?"

Hadrian chuckled.

"It's also imperative that we get word to Alric to start the invasion from the north. Even if we take the city, Breckton can wait us out unless Melengar applies pressure. I would suggest asking the Diamond to send the message, but given how reliable they were last time and how utterly important this is— Royce, I need to ask you to carry the message for me. If anyone can get through and bring back help, it's you."

Royce pursed his lips, thinking, and then nodded. "I'll talk to Polish just the same and see if I can get him to part with one or two of his men to accompany me. You should write three messages to Alric. Each of us will carry one and split up if there's trouble. Three people will increase the odds that at least one will make it. And don't neglect to write an additional letter explaining how this trip south was all your idea. I don't want to bear the brunt of his anger when he finds out where you went. Oh, and, of course, an explanation of the fees to be paid," he said with a wink.

Arista sighed. "He'll want to kill me."

"Not if you succeed in taking the city," Hadrian said encouragingly.

"Speaking of which, after you complete the battle plan for the garrison, you'll need to see about reaching Gaunt's army and taking command of it. I'm not exactly sure how you're going to do that, but I'll write you a decree and declare you general-ambassador in proxy, granting you the power to speak on my behalf. I'll give you the rank of auxiliary marshal and the title of lord. That might just impress them and at least give you the legal right to negotiate and the credentials to command."

"I doubt royal titles will impress Nationalists much," Hadrian said.

"Maybe not, but the threat of the Northern Imperial Army should give you a good deal of leverage. Desperate men might be willing to cling to an impressive title in the absence of anything else."

Hadrian chuckled again.

"What?" she asked.

"Oh, nothing," he said. "I was just thinking that for an ambassador, you're a very capable general."

"No you weren't," she told him bluntly. "You're thinking that I'm capable for a *woman*."

"That too."

Arista smiled. "Well, it's lucky that I am, because so far I'm pretty lousy at being a woman. I honestly can't stand needlepoint."

"I suppose I should set out tonight for Melengar," Royce said. "Unless there's something else you need before I go?"

Arista shook her head.

"How about you?" he asked Hadrian. "Assuming you survive this stunt, what are you going to do now that you know the heir is dead?"

"Hang on, are you sure the heir is dead?" Arista broke in.

"You were there. You heard what Bartholomew said," Hadrian replied. "I don't think he was lying."

"I'm not saying that he was…It's just that…well, Esrahaddon seemed pretty convinced the heir was still alive when he left Avempartha. And then there's the church. They're after Esra, expecting him to lead them to the *real* heir. They so much as told me that when I was at Ervanon last year. So why is everyone looking if he's dead?"

"There's no telling what Esrahaddon is up to. As for the church, they pretended to look for the heir just as they're pretending they found her," Royce said.

"Perhaps, but there's still the image that we saw in the tower. He seemed like a living, breathing person to me."

Royce nodded. "Good point."

Hadrian shook his head. "There couldn't have been another child. My father would have known and searched for him…or *her*. No, Danbury knew the line ended or he wouldn't have stayed in Hintindar."

He glanced at Royce, then lowered his eyes. "In any case, if I survive, I won't be returning to Riyria."

Royce nodded. "You'll probably get killed, anyway. But… I suppose you're okay with that—as happy as a dog with a bone."

"How's that?"

"Nothing."

There was a pause, then Hadrian said, "It's not completely hopeless. It's just that damn cavalry. They'll cut down the Nationalists in a heartbeat. If only it would rain again."

"Rain?" Arista asked.

"Charging horses carrying heavy armored knights need solid ground. After the last few days, the ground has already dried. If I could engage them over tilled rain-drenched farmland, the horses will mire themselves and Dermont would lose his best advantage. But the weather doesn't look like it's gonna cooperate."

"So you would prefer it to rain nonstop between now and the battle?" Arista asked.

"That would be one sweet miracle, but I don't expect we'll have that kind of luck."

"Perhaps luck isn't what we need." Arista smiled at him.

⮟

The Dunlap household was dark except for the single candle Arista carried up the steps to the second floor. She had said her goodbyes to Royce and Hadrian. Mrs. Dunlap had gone to bed hours earlier and the house was quiet. This was the first time in ages she found herself alone.

How can this plan possibly work? Am I crazy?

She knew what her old handmaid, Bernice, would say. Then the old woman would offer her a gingerbread cookie as a consolation prize.

What will Alric say when Royce reaches him?

· Even if she succeeded, he would be furious that she had disobeyed him and gone off without telling anyone. She pushed those thoughts away, deciding to worry about all that later. They could hang her for treason if they wished, so long as Melengar was safe.

All estimates indicated Breckton would arrive in less than four days. She would have to control the city by then. She planned to launch the revolt in two days and hoped she would have at least a few days to recover, pull in supplies from the surrounding farms, and set up some defenses.

Royce would get through with the message. If he could get to Alric quickly, and if her brother moved fast, Alric could attack across the Galewyr in just a few days, and it would take only two or three days for word to reach Aquesta and new orders to be sent to Sir Breckton. She would need to hold him off at least that long. All this assumed they successfully took the city and defeated Lord Dermont's knights to the south.

Two days. How long does it normally take to plan a successful revolution?

Longer than two days, she was certain.

"Excuse me. Hello?"

Arista stopped as she passed the open door of Emery's bedroom. They had put him in the small room at the top of the stairs, in the same bed where the princes of Rhenydd had once slept on a stormy night. Emery had remained unconscious since they had stolen him from the post. She was surprised to see his eyes open and looking back at her. His hair was pressed from sleep, and a puzzled look was on his face.

"How are you feeling?" she asked softly.

"Terrible," he replied. "Who are you? And where am I?"

"My name is Arista and you're at the Dunlaps' on Benning Street." She set the candle on the nightstand and sat on the edge of the bed.

"But I should be dead," he told her.

"Awfully sorry to disappoint, but I thought you would be more helpful alive." She smiled at him.

His brow furrowed. "Helpful with what?"

"Don't worry about that now. You need to sleep."

"No! Tell me. I won't be a party to the Imperialists, I tell you!"

"Well, of course you won't. We need your help to take the city back *from* them."

Emery looked at her, stunned. His eyes shifted from side to side. "I don't understand."

"I heard your speech at The Laughing Gnome. It's a good plan, and we're going to do it in two days, so you need to rest and get your strength back."

"Who are 'we'? Who are you? How did you manage this?"

Arista smiled. "Practice, I guess."

"Practice?"

"Let's just say this isn't the first time I've had to save a kingdom from a traitorous murderer out to steal the throne. It's okay. Just go back to sleep. It will—"

"Wait! You said your name is *Arista*?"

She nodded.

"You're the Princess of Melengar!"

She nodded again. "Yes."

"But…but how…Why?" He started to push up on the bed with his hands and winced.

"Calm down," she told him firmly. "You need to rest. I mean it."

"I shouldn't be lying down in your presence!"

"You will if I tell you to, and I'm telling you to."

"I—I just can't believe…Why…why would you come here?"

"I'm here to help."

"You're amazing."

"And you're suffering from a flogging that would have killed any man with the good sense to know he should be dead. Now you need to go back to sleep this instant, and that's an order. Do you understand?"

"Yes, Your Majesty."

She smiled. "I'm not a ruling queen, Emery, just a princess. My brother is the king."

Emery looked embarrassed. "Your Highness, then."

"I would prefer it if you just called me Arista."

Emery looked shocked.

"Go ahead, give it a try."

"It's not proper."

"And is it proper that you should deny a princess's request? Particularly one who saved your life?"

He shook his head slowly. "Arista," he said shyly.

She smiled at him and, on an impulse, leaned over and kissed him on the forehead. "Good night, Emery," she said, and stepped back out of the room.

She walked back down the steps through the dark house and out the front door. The night was still. Just as Hadrian had mentioned, the sky was clear, showing a bountiful banquet of stars spilling across the vast blackness. Benning Street, a short lane that dead-ended at the Dunlaps' carriage house, was empty.

It was unusual for Arista to be completely alone outdoors. Hilfred had always been her ever-present shadow. She missed him and yet it felt good to be on her own facing the night. It had been only a few days since she had ridden out of Medford, but she knew she was not the same person who had left. She had always feared her life would be no more than that of a woman of privilege, helpless and confined. She had escaped that fate and entered into the more prestigious, but equally restricted, role of ambassador, which was nothing more than a glorified messenger. Now, however, she felt for the first time she was finding her true calling.

She began to hum softly to herself. The spell she had cast on the Seret Knights had worked, yet no one had taught her how to do it. She had invented the spell, drawing from a similar idea and her general knowledge of the Art and altering the incantation to focus on the blood of their bodies.

That's what makes it an art.

There was indeed a gap in her education, but it was because what was missing could not be taught. Esrahaddon had not held back anything. The gap was the reality of magic. Instructors could teach the basic techniques and methods, but a mastery of mechanical knowledge could never make a person an artist. No one could teach creativity or invention. A spark needed to come from within. It must be something unique, something discovered by the individual, a leap of understanding, a burst of insight, the combining of common elements in an unexpected way.

Arista knew it to be true. She had known it since killing the knights. The knowledge both excited and terrified her. The horrible deaths of the seret had only compounded that terrible realization. Now, however, standing alone in the yard under the blanket of stars and in the stillness of the warm summer night, she embraced her understanding and it was thrilling. There was danger, of course, both intoxicating and alluring, and she struggled to contain her emotions. Recalling the death cries of the knights and the ghastly looks on their faces helped ground her. She did not want to get lost in that power. In her mind's eye, the Art was a great beast, a dragon of limitless potential that yearned to be set free, but a mindless beast let loose upon the world would be a terrible thing. She understood the wisdom of Arcadius and the need to restrain the passion she now touched.

Arista set the candle down before her and cleared her mind to focus.

She reached out and pressed her fingers in the air as if gently touching the surface of an invisible object. Power vibrated like the strings of a harp as her humming became a chant. They were not the words that Esrahaddon had taught her. Nor was it an incantation from Arcadius. The words were her own. The fabric of the universe was at her fingertips, and she fought to control her excitement. She plucked the strings on her invisible harp. She could play individual notes or chords, melodies, rhythms, and a multitude of combinations of each. The possibilities of creation were astonishing, and so numerous were the choices that she was equally overwhelmed. It would clearly take a lifetime, or more, to begin to grasp the potential she now felt. That night, however, her path was simple and clear. A flick of her wrist and a sweep of her fingers, almost as if she were motioning farewell, and at that moment the candle blew out.

A wind gusted. The dry soil of the street whirled into a dust devil. Old leaves and bits of grass were buffeted about. The stars faded as thick, full clouds crept across the sky. She heard the sound ring off the tin roof. It sang on the metal, the chorus of her song, and then she felt the splatter of rain on her upturned and laughing face.

CHAPTER 13

MODINA

The ceiling of the grand imperial throne room was a dome painted robin's egg blue interspersed with white puffy clouds mimicking the sky on a gentle summer's day. The painting was heavy and uninspired, but Modina thought it was beautiful. She could not remember the last time she had seen the real sky.

Her life since Dahlgren had been a nightmare of vague unpleasant people and places she could not, and did not care to, remember. She had no idea how much time had passed since the death of her father. It did not matter. Nothing did. Time was a concern of the living, and if she knew anything, it was that she was dead. A ghost drifting dreamlike, pushed along by unseen hands, hearing disembodied voices—but something had changed.

Amilia had come, and with her, the haze and fog that Modina had been lost in for so long had begun to lift. She started to become aware of the world around her.

"Keep your head up, and do not look at them," Nimbus was telling her. "You are the empress and they are beneath you, contemptible and not worthy of even the slightest glance from your imperial eyes. Back straight. Back straight."

Modina, dressed in a formal gown of gold and white, stood on the imperial dais before an immense and gaudy throne. She scratched it once and discovered the gold was a thin veneer over dull metal. The dais itself was five feet from the ground, with sheer sides except for where the half-moon stairs provided access. The stairs were removable, allowing her to be set on display, the perfect unapproachable symbol of the New Empire.

Nimbus shook his head miserably. "It is not going to work. She is not listening."

"She's just not used to standing straight all the time," Amilia told him.

"Perhaps a stiff board sewn into her corset and laced tight?" a steward proposed timidly.

"Actually, that's not a bad idea," Amilia replied. She looked at Nimbus. "What do you think?"

"Better make it a *very* stiff board," Nimbus replied sardonically.

They waved over the royal tailor and seamstress and an informal meeting ensued. They droned on about seams, stays, and ties while Modina looked down from above.

Can they see the pain in my face?

She did not think so. There was no sympathy in their eyes, just awe—awe and admiration. They simultaneously marveled and quaked when in her presence. She had heard them whispering about *the beast* she had slain, and how she was the daughter of a god. To thousands of soldiers, knights, and commoners, she was something to worship.

Until recently, Modina had been oblivious to it all, her mind shut in a dark hole where any attempt to think caused such anguish she recoiled back into the dull safety of the abyss. Time dulled the pain, and slowly the words of nearby conversations seeped in. She began to understand. According to what she had overheard, she and her father were descendants of some legendary lost king. This was why only they could harm the beast. She had been anointed empress, but she was not certain what that meant. So far, it had meant pain and isolation.

Modina stared at those around her without emotion. She was no longer capable of feeling. There was no fear, anger, or hate, nor was there love or happiness. She was a ghost haunting her own body, watching the world with detached interest. Nothing that transpired around her held any importance—except Amilia.

Previously the people hovering around her were vague gray faces. They had spoken to her of ridiculous notions, the vast majority she could not begin to comprehend even if she wanted to. Amilia was different. She had said things to Modina that she could understand. Amilia had told stories of her own family and reminded Modina of another girl—a girl named Thrace—who had died and was just a ghost now. It was a painful memory, but Amilia managed to remind her about times before the darkness, before the pain, when there had been someone in the world who loved her.

When Saldur had threatened to send Amilia away, Modina had seen the terrible fear in the girl's eyes. She had recognized that fear. Saldur's voice was the screech of the beast, and at that moment, she had awoken from her long dream. Her eyes had focused, seeing clearly for the first time since that night. She would not allow the beast to win again.

Somewhere in the chamber, out of sight of the dais, a door slammed. The sound echoed around the marbled hall. Loud footsteps followed with an even louder conversation.

"I don't understand why I can't launch an attack against Alric on my own." The voice came from an agitated well-dressed man.

"Breckton's army will dispatch the Nationalists in no time.

Then he can return to Melengar, and you can have your prize, Archie," replied the voice of an older man. "Melengar isn't going anywhere, and it's not worth the risk."

The younger voice she did not recognize, but the older one she had heard many times before. They called him Regent Ethelred. The pair of nobles and their retinue came into view. Ethelred was dressed as she usually had seen him—in red velvet and gold silk. His thick mustache and beard betrayed his age, as both were steadily going gray.

The younger man walking beside him dressed in a stylish scarlet silk tunic with a high-ruffed collar, an elegant cape, and an extravagant plumed hat that matched the rest of his attire perfectly. He was taller than the regent, and his long auburn hair trailed down his back in a ponytail. They walked at the head of a group of six others: personal servants, stewards, and court officials. Four of the six Modina recognized, as she had seen the little parade before.

There was the court scribe, who went everywhere carrying a ledger. He was a plump man with long red cheeks and a balding head, and he always had a feathered quill behind each ear, making him look like a strange bird. His staunchly straight posture and odd strut reminded her of a quail parading through a field, and because she did not know the scribe's name, in her mind she dubbed him simply *The Quail*.

There was also Ethelred's valet, whom she labeled *The White Mouse*, as he was a thin, pale man with stark white hair, and his fastidious pampering seemed rodent-like. She never heard him speak except to say, "Of course, my lord." He continuously flicked lint from Ethelred's clothes and was always on hand to take a cloak or change the regent's footwear.

Then there was *The Candle*, so named because he was a tall, thin man with wild red curly hair and a drooping mouth that sagged like tallow wax.

The last of the entourage was a soldier of some standing. He wore a uniform that had dozens of brightly colored ribbons pinned to it.

"I would appreciate you using a formal address when we are in public," Archie pointed out.

Ethelred turned as if surprised to see they were not alone in the hall.

"Oh," he said, quickly masking a smile. Then, in a tone heavy with sarcasm, he proclaimed, "Forgive me, *Earl of Chadwick*. I didn't notice them. They're more like furniture to me. My point was, however, that we only suspect the extent of Melengar's weakness. Attacking them would introduce more headaches than it is worth. As it is, there is no chance Alric will attack us. He's a boy, but not so foolhardy as to provoke the destruction of his little kingdom."

"Is that..." Archibald stared up at Modina and stopped walking so that Ethelred lost track of him for a moment.

"The empress? Yes," Ethelred replied, his tone revealing a bit of his own irritation that the earl had apparently not heard what he had just said.

"She's...she's...beautiful."

"Hmm? Yes, I suppose she is," Ethelred responded without looking. Instead, he turned to Amilia, who, along with everyone else, was standing straight, her eyes looking at the floor. "Saldur tells me you're our little miracle worker. You got her eating, speaking, and generally cooperating. I'm pleased to hear it."

Amilia curtsied in silence.

"She'll be ready in time, correct? We can ill afford another fiasco like the one we had at the coronation. She couldn't even make an appearance. You'll see to that, won't you?"

"Yes, my lord." Amilia curtsied again.

The Earl of Chadwick's eyes remained focused on Modina,

and she found his expression surprising. She did not see the awe-inspired look of the palace staff, nor the cold, callous countenance of her handlers. His face bore a broad smile.

A soldier entered the hall, walking briskly toward them. The one with the pretty ribbons left the entourage and strode forward to intercept him. They spoke in whispers for a brief moment and then the other soldier handed over some parchments. Ribbon Man opened them and read them silently to himself before returning to Ethelred's side.

"What is it?"

"Your Lordship, Admiral Gafton's blockade fleet succeeded in capturing the *Ellis Far*, a small sloop, off the coast of Melengar. On board, they found parchments signed by King Alric granting the courier permission to negotiate with the full power of the Melengar crown. The courier and ship's captain were unfortunately killed in the action. The coxswain, however, was taken and persuaded to reveal the destination of the vessel as Tur Del Fur."

Ethelred nodded his understanding. "Trying to link up with the Nationalists, but that was expected. So the sloop sailed from Roe?"

"Yes."

"You're sure no other ship slipped past?"

"The reports indicate it was the only one."

While Ethelred and the soldier spoke and the rest of the hall remained still as statues, the Earl of Chadwick stared at the empress. Modina did not return his gaze, and it made her uncomfortable the way he watched her.

He ascended the steps and knelt. "Your Eminence," he said, gently taking her hand and kissing the ring she wore. "I am Archibald Ballentyne, twelfth Earl of Chadwick."

Modina said nothing.

"Archibald?" Ethelred's voice once more.

"Forgive my rude approach," the earl continued, "but I find I can't help myself. How strange it is that we haven't met before. I've been to Aquesta many times but never had the pleasure. Bad luck, I suppose. I'm certain you're very busy, and as I command a substantial army, I'm busy as well. Recent events have seen fit to bring my command here. It's not something I was pleased with. That is, until now. You see, I was doing very well conquering new lands for your growing empire, and having to stop I considered unfortunate. But my regret has turned to genuine delight as I've been blessed to behold your splendor."

"Archie!" Ethelred had been calling out to him for some time, but it was not until he used that name that the well-dressed man's attention finally left her. "Stop with that foolishness, will you? We need to get to the meeting."

The earl frowned in irritation.

"Please forgive me, Your Eminence, but duty calls."

⌁

The moment the practice had ended, they changed Modina back into her simple dress and she had been escorted to her cell. She thought there had been a time when two palace soldiers had walked with her everywhere, but now there was only one. His name was Gerald. That was all she knew about him, which was strange, because she saw him every day. Gerald escorted her wherever she went and stood guard outside her cell door. She assumed he took breaks, most likely late at night, but in the mornings, when she and Amilia went to breakfast, he was always there. She never heard him speak. They were quite a quiet pair.

When she reached the cell door, it was open, the dark interior waiting. He never forced her in. He never touched her. He merely stood patiently, taking up his post at the entrance. She hesitated before the threshold, and when she looked at Gerald, he stared at the floor.

"Wait." Amilia trotted up the corridor toward them. "Her Eminence is moving today."

Both Gerald and Modina looked puzzled.

"I've given up talking to the chamberlain," Amilia declared. She was speaking quickly and seemed to address them both at once. "Nimbus is right—I'm the secretary to the empress, after all." She focused on Gerald. "Please escort Her Eminence to her new bedroom on the east wing's fifth floor."

The order was weak, not at all in the voice of a noblewoman. It lacked the tenor of confidence, the power of arrogance. There was a space of time, a beat of uncertainty, when no one moved and no one spoke. Committed now, Amilia remained awkwardly stiff, facing Gerald. For the first time, Modina noticed the largeness of the man, the sword at his side, and the castle guard uniform. He was meticulous, every line straight, every bit of metal polished.

Gerald nodded and moved aside.

"This way, Your Eminence," Amilia said, letting out a breath.

The three of them walked to the central stairs as Amilia continued to speak. "I got her eating, I got her to talk—I just want a better place for her to sleep. How can they argue? No one is even on the fifth floor."

As they reached the main hall, they passed several surprised servants. One young woman stopped, stunned.

"Anna." Amilia caught her attention. "It is Anna, isn't it?"

The woman nodded, unable to take her eyes off Modina.

"The empress is moving to a bedroom on the fifth floor. Run and get linens and pillows."

"Ah—but Edith told me to scrub the—"

"Forget Edith."

"She'll beat me."

"No, she won't," Amilia said, and thought for a moment. With sudden authority, she continued. "From now on, you're working for the empress—her personal chambermaid. From now on, you report directly to me. Do you understand?"

Anna looked shocked.

"What do you want to do?" Amilia asked. "Defy Edith Mon or refuse the empress? Now get those linens and get the best room on the fifth floor in order."

"Yes, Your Eminence," she said, addressing Modina, "right away."

They climbed the stairs, moving quickly by the fourth floor. In the east wing, the fifth floor was a single long hall with five doors. Light entered from a narrow slit at the far end, revealing a dust-covered corridor.

Amilia looked at the doors for a moment. Shrugging, she opened one and motioned for them to wait as she entered. When she returned, she grimaced and said, "Let's wait for Anna."

They did not have to wait long. The chambermaid, chased by two young boys with rags, a broom, a mop, and a bucket, returned with an armload of linens. Anna panted for breath and her brow glistened. The chambermaid traversed the corridor and selected the door at the far end. She and the boys rushed in. Amilia joined them. Before long, the boys raced back out and returned hauling various items: pillows, a blanket, more water, brushes. Modina and Gerald waited in the hallway, listening to the grunts and bumps and scrapes. Before long, Anna exited covered in dirt and dust, dragging armloads of dirty rags. Then Amilia reappeared and motioned for Modina to enter.

Sunlight. She spotted the brilliant shaft spilling in, slicing across the floor, along a tapestry-covered wall, and over a massive bed covered in satin sheets and a host of fluffy pillows. There was even a thick carpet on the floor. A mirror and a washbasin sat on a small stand. A little writing desk stood next to a fireplace, and on the far wall was the open window.

Modina walked forward and looked out at the sky. Breathing in the fresh air, she fell to her knees. The window was narrow, but Modina could peer down into the courtyard below or look up directly into the blue of the sky—the real sky. She rested her head on the sill, reveling in the sunshine like a drought victim might douse herself with water. Until that moment, she had not noticed how starved she had been for fresh air and sunlight. Amilia might have spoken to her, but she was too busy looking at the sky to notice.

Smells were a treat. A cool breeze blew in, tainted by the stables below. For her, this was a friendly, familiar scent, hearty and comforting. Birds flew past. A pair of swallows darted and dove in aerial acrobatics as they chased each other. They had a nest in a crevice above one of the other windows that dotted the exterior wall.

She did not know how long she had knelt there. At some point, she realized she was alone. The door behind her had been closed and a blanket had been draped over her shoulders. Eventually she heard voices drifting up from below.

"We've spent more than enough time on the subject, Archibald. The case is closed." It was Ethelred's voice, coming from one of the windows just below hers.

"I know you're disappointed." She recognized the fatherly tone of Regent Saldur. "Still, you have to be mindful of the big picture. This isn't just some wild landgrab. This is an empire we are building."

"Two months at the head of an army and he acts as if he were a war-hardened general!" Ethelred laughed.

Another voice spoke, too softly or too distant from the window for her to hear. Then she heard the earl once again. "I've taken Glouston and the Rilan Valley through force of arms and thereby secured the whole northern rim of Warric. I think I've proved my skill."

"Skill? You let Marquis Lanaklin escape to Melengar and you failed to secure the wheat fields in Rilan, which burned. Those crops would have fed the entire imperial army for the next year, but now they're lost because you were preoccupied with taking an empty castle."

"It wasn't empty..." There was more said but the voices were too faint to hear.

"The marquis was gone. The reason for taking it went with him," the bellowing voice of Ethelred thundered. The regent must be standing very near the window, as she could hear him the best.

"Gentlemen," Saldur said, intervening, "water under the bridge. What's past is past. What we need to concern ourselves with is the present and the future, and at the moment both go by the same name—Gaunt."

Again, there were other voices speaking too faintly, their sounds fading to silence. All Modina could hear was the hoeing of servants weeding the vegetable garden below.

"I agree," Ethelred suddenly said. "We should have killed that bastard years ago."

"Calm yourself, Lanis," Saldur's voice boomed. Modina wasn't certain if he was using Ethelred's first name or addressing someone else whose voice was too distant for her to catch. "Everything has its season. We all knew the Nationalists wouldn't give up their freedom without a fight. Granted, we had no idea Gaunt would be their general or that he would prove to be such a fine military commander. We had assumed he was nothing more than an annoying anarchist, a lone voice in the wilderness, like our very own Deacon Tomas. His transformation into a skilled general was—I will admit—a bit unexpected. Nevertheless, his successes are not beyond our control."

"And what does that mean?" someone asked.

"Luis Guy had the foresight to bring us a man who could effectively deal with the problems of Delgos and Gaunt and I present him to you today. Gentlemen, let me introduce Merrick Marius." His voice began to grow faint. "He's quite a remarkable man...been working for us these...on a..." Saldur's voice drifted off, too far from the window.

There was a long silence, and then Ethelred spoke again. "Let him finish. You'll see."

Again, the words were too quiet for her to hear.

Modina listened to the wind as it rose and rustled distant leaves. The swallows returned and played again, looping in the air. From the courtyard below came the harsh shouts of soldiers in the process of changing guards. She had nearly forgotten about the conversation from below when she heard an abrupt communal gasp.

"Tur Del Fur? You're not serious?" an unknown voice asked in a stunned tone.

More quiet murmurings.

"...and as I said, it would mark the end of Degan Gaunt and the Nationalists forever." Saldur's voice returned.

"But at what cost, Sauly?" another voice floated in. Normally too far, it was now loud and clear.

"We have no other choice," Ethelred put in. "The Nationalists are marching north toward Ratibor. They must be stopped."

"This is insane. I can't believe you're even contemplating it!"

"We've done much more than contemplate. Nearly everything is in place. Isn't that so?" Saldur asked.

Modina strained to hear, but the voice that replied was too faint.

"We'll send it by ship after we receive word that all is set," Saldur explained. There was another pause, and then he spoke again. "I think we all understand that."

"I see no reason to hesitate any longer," Ethelred said. "Then we're all in agreement?"

A number of voices spoke their acknowledgment.

"Excellent. Marius, you should leave immediately..."

"There's just one more thing..." She had not heard this voice before and it faded, probably because the man speaking was walking away from the window.

Saldur's voice returned. "You have? Where? Tell us at once!"

More muffled conversation.

"Blast, man! I can assure you that you'll get paid," Ethelred said.

"If he's led you to the heir, he's no longer of any use. That's right, isn't it, Sauly? You and Guy have a greater interest in this, but unless you have an objection, I say be done with him at your earliest convenience."

Another long pause.

"I think the Nyphron Empire is good for it, don't you?" Saldur said.

"You're quite the magician, aren't you, Marius?" said Ethelred. "We should have hired your services earlier. I'm not a fan of Luis Guy or any of the Patriarch's sentinels, but it seems his decision to employ you was certainly a good one."

The voices drifted off, growing fainter until it was quiet.

Most of what she had heard held no interest for Modina— too many unknown names and places. She had only the vaguest notions of the terms *Nationalist*, *Royalist*, and *Imperialist*. Tur Del Fur was a famous city—someplace south—that she had heard of before, but Degan Gaunt was only a name. She was glad the talking was over. She preferred the quiet sounds of the wind, the trees, and the birds. They took her back to an earlier time, a different place. As she sat looking out at her sliver of the world, she found herself wishing she could still cry.

CHAPTER 14

THE EVE

Gill had a hard time seeing anything clearly in the pouring rain, but he was certain that a man was walking right at him. He felt for the horn hanging at his side and regretted trapping it underneath his rain smock that morning. During thirty watches, he had never needed it. He peered through the gray curtain—no army, just the one guy.

He was dressed in a cloak that hung like a soaked rag, his hood cast back, his hair slicked flat. No armor or shield, but two swords hung from his belt, and Gill spotted the two-handed pommel of a great sword on his back. The man walked steadily through the muddy field. He seemed to be alone and could hardly pose a threat to the nearly one thousand men bivouacked on the hill. If Gill sounded the alarm without cause, he would never hear the end of it. He was confident he could handle one guy.

"Halt!" Gill shouted over the drumming rain as he pulled his sword from its sheath and brandished it at the stranger. "Who are you, and what do you want?"

"I'm here to see Commander Parker," the man said, not showing any signs of slowing. "Take me to him at once."

Gill laughed. "Oh, aren't you the bold one?" he said,

extending the sword. The stranger walked right up to the tip, as if he meant to impale himself. "Stop or I'll run—"

Before Gill could finish, the man hit the flat face of the sword. The vibration ran down the blade, breaking Gill's grip. A second later, the man had the weapon and was pointing it at him.

"I gave you an order, picket," the stranger snapped. "I'm not accustomed to repeating myself to my troops. Look sharp or I'll have you flogged."

Then the man returned his sword, which only made matters worse.

"What's your name, picket?"

"Gill, ah, sir," he said, adding the *sir* in case this man was an officer.

"Gill, in the future when standing watch, arm yourself with a crossbow and never let even one man approach to within one hundred feet without putting a hole through him, do you understand?" The man did not wait for an answer. He walked past him and continued striding up the hill through the tall wet grass.

"Umm, yes, sir, but I don't have a crossbow, sir," Gill said as he jogged behind him.

"Then you had best get one, isn't that right?" the man called over his shoulder.

"Yes, sir." Gill nodded even though the man was ahead of him.

The man walked past scores of tents, heading toward the middle of the camp. Everyone was inside, away from the rain, and no one saw him pass. The tents were a haphazard array of rope and stick-propped canvas. No two were alike, as the soldiers had scrounged supplies as they moved. Most were cut from ship sails grabbed at the port in Vernes and again in Kilnar. Others made do with nothing but old bed linens, and in a few rare cases, actual tents were used.

The stranger paused at the top of the hill. When Gill caught up, he asked, "Which of these tents belongs to Parker?"

"Parker? He's not in a tent, sir. He's in the farmhouse down that way," Gill said, pointing.

"Gill, why are you off your post?" Sergeant Milford growled at him as he came out of his tent, blinking as the rain stung his eyes. He was wrapped in a cloak, his pale bare feet showing beneath it.

"Well, I—" Gill began, but the stranger interrupted.

"Who is this now?" The stranger walked right up to Milford and, scowling, stood with his hands on his hips.

"This here is Sergeant Milford, sir," Gill answered, and the sergeant looked confused.

The stranger inspected him and shook his head. "Sergeant, where in Maribor's name is your sword?"

"In my tent, but—"

"You don't think it necessary to wear your sword when an enemy army stands less than a mile away and could attack at any minute?"

"I was sleeping, sir!"

"Look up, sergeant!" the man said.

The sergeant tilted his head up, wincing as rain hit his face.

"As you can see, it's nearly morning."

"Ah—yes, sir. Sorry, sir."

"Now get dressed and get a new picket on Gill's post at once, do you understand?"

"Yes, sir. Right away, sir!"

"Gill!"

"Yes, sir!" Gill jumped.

"Let's get moving. I'm late as it is."

"Yes, sir!" Gill set off following once more, offering the sergeant a flummoxed shrug as he passed.

The main body camped on what everyone called Bingham

Hill, apparently after farmer Bingham, who grew barley and rye in the fields below. Gill heard there had been quite the hullabaloo when Commander Gaunt had informed Bingham the army would be using his farm and Gaunt would take his house for a headquarters. The pastoral home with a thatched roof and wooden beams found itself surrounded by a sea of congested camps. Flowers that had once lined the walkway had been crushed beneath a hundred boots. The barn housed the officers and the stable provided storage and was also used as a dispensary and tavern for those with rank. There were tents everywhere and a hundred campfires burned rings into the ground.

"Inform Commander Parker I'm here," the stranger told one of the guards on the porch.

"And who are you?"

"Marshal Lord Blackwater."

The sentry hesitated only a moment, then disappeared inside. He reemerged quickly and held the door open.

"Thank you, Gill. That will be all," the stranger said as he stepped inside.

⚜

"You're Commander Parker?" Hadrian asked the portly man before him, who was sloppily dressed in a short black vest and dirty white britches. An upturned nose sat in the middle of his soft face, which rested on a large wobbly neck.

He was seated before a rough wooden table littered with candles, maps, dispatches, and a steaming plate of eggs and ham. He stood up, pulling a napkin from his neck, and wiped his mouth. "I am, and you are Marshal Blackwater? I wasn't informed of—"

"Marshal *Lord* Blackwater," he said, correcting the man with a friendly smile, and handed over his letter of reference.

Parker took the letter, roughly unfolding it, and began reading.

Wavy wooden beams edged and divided the pale yellowing walls. Along these hung pots, sacks, cooking tools, and what Hadrian guessed to be Commander Parker's sword and cloak. Baskets, pails, and jugs huddled in corners, stacked out of the way on the floor, which listed downhill toward the fireplace.

After reading the letter, Parker returned to his seat and tucked his napkin back into his collar. "You're not really a lord, are you?"

Hadrian hesitated briefly. "Well, technically I am, at least for the moment."

"What are you when you're not a lord?"

"I suppose you could call me a mercenary. I've done a lot of things over the years."

"Why would the Princess of Melengar send a mercenary to me?"

"Because I can win this battle for you."

"What makes you think I can't win it?"

"The fact that you're still in this farmhouse instead of the city. You're very likely a good manager and quartermaster, and I'm certain a wonderful bookkeeper, but war is more than numbers in ledgers. With Gaunt gone, you might be a bit unsure of what to do next. That's where I can help you. As it happens, I have a great deal of combat experience."

"So you know about Gaunt's disappearance."

Hadrian did not like the tone in his voice. There was something there, something coy and threatening. Aggression was still his best approach. "This army has been camped here for days, and you've not launched a single foray at the enemy."

"It's raining," Parker replied. "The field is a muddy mess."

"Exactly," Hadrian said. "That's why you should be attacking. The rain will give you the upper hand. Call in your captains and I can explain how we can turn the weather to our advantage, but we must act quickly—"

"You'd like that, wouldn't you?" There was that tone again, this time more ominous. "I have a better idea. How about you explain to me why Arista Essendon would betray Degan?"

"She didn't. You don't understand. She's—"

"Oh, she most certainly did!" Parker rose to his feet and threw his napkin to the floor as if it were a gauntlet of challenge. "And you needn't lie any further. I know why. She did it to save her miserable little kingdom." He took a step forward and bumped the table. "By destroying Degan, she hopes to curry favor for Melengar. So what are your real orders?" He advanced, pointing an accusatory finger. "To gain our confidence? To lead this army into an ambush like you did with Gaunt? Was it you? Were you there? Were you one of the ones that grabbed him?"

Parker glanced at Hadrian's swords. "Or is it to get close enough to kill me?" he said, staggering backward. The commander knocked his head on a low-hanging pot, which fell with a brassy clang. The noise made Parker jump. "Simms! Fall!" he cried, and the two sentries rushed in.

"Sir!" they said in unison.

"Take his swords. Shackle him to a stake. Get him out of—"

"You don't understand. Arista isn't your enemy," Hadrian interrupted.

"Oh, I understand perfectly."

"She was set up by the empire, just as Gaunt was."

"So she's missing too?"

"No, she's in Ratibor right now planning a rebellion to aid your attack."

Parker laughed aloud at that. "Oh please, sir! You do need lessons in lying. A *princess* of Melengar organizing an uprising in Ratibor? Get him out of here."

One of the soldiers drew his sword. "Remove your weapons—now!"

Hadrian considered his options. He could run, but he would never get another opportunity to persuade them. Taking Parker prisoner would require killing Simms and Fall and destroy any hope of gaining their trust. With no other choice, he sighed and unbuckled his belt.

᪥

"Exactly how confident are you that Hadrian will succeed in persuading the Nationalists to attack tomorrow morning?" Polish asked Arista as they sat at the Dunlaps' table. Outside, it continued to storm.

"I have the same level of confidence in his success as I do in ours," Arista replied.

Polish smirked. "I keep forgetting you're a diplomat."

Eight other people sat around the little table, where the city lay mapped out with knickknacks borrowed from Mrs. Dunlap's shelves. Those present had been handpicked by Hadrian, Dr. Gerand, Polish, or Emery, who was back on his feet and eating everything Mrs. Dunlap put under his nose.

With Royce and Hadrian gone, Arista spent most of her time talking with the young Mr. Dorn. While he no longer stumbled over using her first name, the admiration in his eyes was unmistakable, and Arista caught herself smiling self-consciously. He had a nice face—cheerful and passionate—and while he was younger even than Alric, she thought him more mature. Perhaps that came from hardship and struggle.

Since he had regained consciousness, she had babbled on about the trials that had brought her there. He told her about how his mother's death had given him life and what it had been like to grow up as a soldier's son. They both shared memories of the fires that had robbed them of the ones they loved. She listened as he poured out his life's story of being an orphan with such intensity that it filled her eyes with tears. He had such a way with words, a means of inciting emotion and empathy. She realized Emery could have changed the world if only he had been born noble. Listening to him, to his ideals, to his passion for justice and compassion, she realized this was what she could expect from Degan Gaunt, a common man with the heart of a king.

"You must understand it's not entirely up to me," Polish told them. "I don't issue policy in the guild. I simply don't have the authority to sanction an outright attack, particularly when there is nothing to be gained. Even if victory were assured, instead of a rather wild gamble, my hands would still be tied."

"Nothing to be gained?" Emery said, stunned. "There is a whole city to be gained! Furthermore, if the imperial army is routed from the field, it's possible that all Rhenydd might fall under the banner of the Delgos Republic."

"I would also add," Arista said, "that defeating the Imperialists here would leave Aquesta open for assault by the remainder of the Nationalists, Melengar, and possibly even Trent—if I can swing their alliance. If Aquesta falls, Colnora will be a free city and certain powerful merchants could find themselves in legitimate seats of power."

"You are good. I'll grant you that, milady," Polish replied. "But there are many *if*s in that scenario, and the Royalists won't allow Colnora to be ruled by a commoner. Lanaklin would assume the throne of Warric and likely appoint his own duke to run the city."

"Well, the Diamond's position will certainly continue to decline if you fail to aid us and the New Empire's strength grows," Arista shot back.

Polish frowned and shook his head. "This is far beyond the

bounds of my mandate. I simply can't commit without orders from the Jewel. The Imps leave the Diamond alone, for the most part. They see us as inevitable as the rats in any sewer. As long as we don't make too much of a nuisance, they leave us to our scurrying. But if we do this, they will declare war. The Diamond will no longer be neutral. We'll be a target in every Imp city. Hundreds could be imprisoned or executed."

"We could keep your involvement a secret," Emery offered.

Polish laughed. "The winner chooses which secrets are kept, and which remain hidden, so I would have to insist on proof of your success before I could help you. We both know that is not possible. If your chances were that good, then you would not need my assistance in the first place. No, I'm sorry. My rats will do what we can, but joining in the assault is not possible."

"Can you at least see that the armory door is unlocked?" Emery asked.

Polish thought a moment and nodded. "That I can do."

"Can we get back to the plan?" Dr. Gerand asked.

Before leaving, Hadrian had outlined the details for a strategy to take the city. Emery's idea was a good one, but an idea simply was not the same as a battle plan and they were all thankful for Hadrian's advice. He had explained that surprise was their greatest tool and catching the armory unaware was their best tactic. After that, things would be more difficult. Their greatest adversary would be time. Securing the armory would be essential, and they must be quick in order to prepare for the attack by the garrison.

"I'll lead the men into the armory," Emery declared. "If I survive, I'll take my place in the square with the men at the weak point of the line."

Everyone nodded grimly.

Hadrian's plan further called for the men to form two straight lines—one before the other—outside the armory and to purposely leave a gap as a weak point. Professional soldiers would look for this kind of vulnerability, so the rebels could predetermine where the attack would fall the hardest. He warned that the men stationed there would suffer the highest number of casualties, but it would also allow the townsfolk to fold the line and generate a devastating envelopment maneuver, which would best utilize their superior numbers.

"I'll lead the left flank," Arista said, and everyone looked at her, stunned.

"My lady," Emery began, "you understand I hold you in the highest esteem, but a battle is no place for a woman and I would be sorely grieved should your life come into peril."

"My life will be in peril no matter where I am, so I may as well be of some use. Besides, this is all my idea. I can't stand by while all of you risk your own lives."

"You need fear no shame," Dr. Gerand told her. "You have already done more than we can hope to repay you for."

"Nevertheless," she said resolutely, "I'll stand with the line."

"Can you wield a sword too?" Perin the grocer asked. His tone was not mocking or sarcastic, but one of expectant amazement, as if he anticipated she would reply that she was a master sword fighter of some renown.

The miraculous survival of Emery was only one of the rallying points of the rebellion. Arista had overlooked the power of her own name. Emery pointed out that she and her brother were heroes to those wishing to fight the New Empire. Their victory over Percy Braga, immortalized in the traveling theater play, had inspired many throughout Apeladorn. All the recruiters had to do was whisper that Arista Essendon had come to Ratibor and that she had stolen Emery from death at the hands of the empire, and most people simply assumed victory was assured.

"Well," she said, "I certainly have just as much experience as most of the merchants, farmers, and tradesmen that will be fighting alongside me."

No one said anything for a long while, and then Emery stood up.

"Forgive me, Your Highness, but I cannot allow you to do this."

Arista gave him a harsh, challenging stare and Emery's face cringed, exposing that a mere unpleasant glance from her was enough to hurt him.

"And how do you plan to stop me?" she snapped, recalling all the times her father, brother, or even Count Pickering, had shooed her out of the council hall, insisting she would spend her time more productively with a needle in her hand.

"If you insist on fighting, I will not fight," he said simply.

Dr. Gerand stood up. "Neither will I."

"Nor I," Perin said, also rising.

Arista scowled at Emery. Again, her glare appeared to hurt the man, but he remained resolute. "All right. Sit down. You win."

"Thank you, my lady," Emery said.

"Then I'll lead the left flank, I suppose," Perin volunteered. He was one of the larger men at the table, stocky and strong.

"I'll take the right flank," Dr. Gerand said.

"That is very brave of you, sir," Emery told him, "but I'll ask Adam the wheeler to take that responsibility. He has fighting experience."

"And he's not an old man," the doctor said bitterly.

Arista knew the helplessness that he was feeling. "Doctor, your services will be required to tend to the injured. Once the armory is taken, you and I will do what we can for those that are wounded."

They went over the plan once more from beginning to end. Arista and Polish came up with several potential problems: What if too few people came? What if they could not secure the armory? What if the garrison did not attack? They made contingency plans until they were certain everything was accounted for.

As they concluded, Dr. Gerand drew forth a bottle of rum and called for glasses from Mrs. Dunlap. "Tomorrow morning we go into battle," he said. "Some of us at this table will not survive to see the sunset again." He lifted his glass. "To those who will fall and to our victory."

"And to the good lady who made it possible," Emery added as they all raised their glasses and drank.

Arista drank with the rest but found the liquor to have a bitter taste.

§

The princess lay awake in the tiny room across the hall from Mrs. Dunlap's bedroom. Smaller than her maid's quarters in Medford, it had just a small window and a tiny shelf to hold a candle. There was so little room between the walls and the bed that she was forced to crawl over the mattress to enter. She could not sleep. The battle to take the city would start in just a few hours and she was consumed by nervous energy. Her mind raced through precautions, running a checklist over and over again.

Have I done all I can to prepare?

Everything was about to change, for good or ill.

Will Alric forgive me if I die? She gave a bitter laugh. *Will he forgive me if I live?*

She stared at the ceiling, wondering if there was a spell to help her sleep.

Magic.

She considered using it in the coming battle. She toyed with the idea while tapping her feet together, anxiously listening to the rain patter the roof.

If I can make it rain, what else can I do? Could I conjure a phantom army? Rain fire? Open the earth to swallow the garrison?

She was certain of only one thing—she could boil blood. The thought sobered her.

What if I lose control? What if I boiled the blood of our men...or Emery?

When she had boiled the water at Sheridan, the nearby clothing had sizzled and hissed. Magic was not easy. Perhaps with time she could master it, but already she sensed her limitations. Now it was clear why Esrahaddon had given her the task of making it rain. Previously she had thought it an absurd challenge to attempt such an immense feat. Now she realized that making it rain was easy. The target was as broad as the sky and the action was natural—it was the equivalent of a marksman throwing a rock and trying to hit the ground. The process would be the same, she guessed, for any spell—the drawing of power, the focus, and the execution through synchronized movement and sound—but the idea of pinpointing such an unruly force to a specific target was daunting. She realized with a shudder that if Royce and Hadrian had been on the hill that night, they would have died along with the seret. There was no doubt she could defeat the garrison, but she might kill everyone in Ratibor in the process. She could possibly use the Art to draw down lightning or summon fire to consume the soldiers, but it would be like a first-year music student trying to compose and orchestrate a full symphony.

No, I can't take such a risk.

She turned her mind to more practical issues. Did they have enough bandages prepared? She had to remember to get a fire going to have hot coals for sealing wounds.

Is there anything else I can do?

She heard a soft rapping and pulled the covers up, as she wore only a thin nightgown borrowed from Mrs. Dunlap. "Yes?"

"It's me," Emery said. "I hope I didn't wake you."

"Come in, please," she told him.

Emery opened the door and stood at the foot of the bed, wearing only his britches and an oversized shirt. "I couldn't sleep and I thought maybe you couldn't either."

"Who would have guessed that waiting to see if you'll live or die would make it so hard to sleep?" She shrugged and smiled.

Emery smiled back and looked for a means to enter the room.

She sat up and propped two pillows behind her. "Just crawl on the bed," she told him, folding her legs and slapping the covers. He looked awkward but took her offer and sat at the foot of the mattress, which sank with his weight.

"Are you scared?" she inquired, and realized too late that it was not the kind of question a woman should ask a man.

"Are you?" he parried, pulling his knees up and wrapping his arms around them. He was barefoot and his toes shone pale in the moonlight.

"Yes," she said. "I'm not even going to be on the line and I'm terrified."

"Would you think me a miserable coward if I said I was frightened too?"

"I would think you a fool if you weren't."

He sighed and let his head rest on his knees.

"What is it?"

"If I tell you something, do you promise to keep it a secret?" he asked, keeping his head down.

"I'm an ambassador. I do that sort of thing for a living."

"I've never fought in a battle before. I've never killed a man."

"I suspect that is the case for nearly everyone fighting tomorrow," she said, hoping he would assume she included herself in that statement. She could not bear to tell him the truth. "I don't think most of these people have ever used a sword."

"Some have." He lifted his head. "Adam fought with Ethel-red's army against the Ghazel when Lord Rufus won his fame. Renkin Pool and Forrest, the silversmith's son, also fought. That's why I have them as leaders in the line. The thing is, everyone is looking to me like I'm a great war hero, but I don't know if I'll stand and fight or run like a coward. I might faint dead away at the first sight of blood."

Arista reached out, taking his hand in hers. "If there is one thing I'm certain of"—she looked directly into his eyes—"it's that you'll stand and fight bravely. I honestly don't think you could do anything else. It just seems to be the way you're made. I think your innate courage is what everyone sees and why they look up to you—like I do."

Emery bowed his head. "Thank you, that was very kind."

"I wasn't being kind, just honest." Suddenly feeling awkward, she released his hand and asked him, "How is your back?"

"It still hurts," he said, raising his arm to test it. "But I'll be able to swing a sword. I really should let you get to sleep." He scrambled off the bed.

"It was nice that you came," she told him, and meant it.

He paused. "I'll only have one regret tomorrow."

"And what is that?"

"That I'm not noble."

She gave him a curious look.

"If I were even a lowly baron and survived the battle, I would ride to Melengar and ask your brother for your hand. I would pester him until he either locked me up or surrendered you. I know that is improper. I know you must have dukes and princes vying for your affections, but I would try just the same. I would fight them for you. I would do anything...if only."

Arista felt her face flush and fought an urge to cover it with her hands. "You know, a common man whose father died in the service of his king, who was so bold as to take Ratibor and Aquesta, could find himself knighted for such heroics. As ambassador, I would point out to my brother that such an act would do well for our relationship with Rhenydd."

Emery's eyes brightened. They had never looked so vibrant or so deep. There was joy on his face. He took a step back toward the bed, paused, then slowly withdrew.

"Well, then," Emery said at last, "I shall need my sleep if I'm to be knighted."

"You shall indeed, *Sir* Emery."

"My lady," he said, and attempted a sweeping bow but halted partway with a wince and a gritting of his teeth. "Good night."

After he had left her room, Arista discovered her heart was pounding, her palms moist. How shameful. In a matter of hours, men would die because of her. By noon, she could be hanging from a post, yet she was flushed with excitement because a man showed an interest in her. How horribly child-ish...how infantile...how selfish...and how wonderful. No one had ever looked at her the way he just had. She remembered how his hand felt and the rustle of his toes on her bed covers—what awful timing she had.

She lay in bed and prayed to Maribor that all would be well. They needed a miracle, and immediately she thought of Hadrian and Royce. Isn't that what Alric always called them...his miracle workers? Everything would be all right.

CHAPTER 15

THE SPEECH

Amilia sat biting her thumbnail, or what little was left of it. "Well?" she asked Nimbus. "What do you think? She seems stiff to me."

"Stiff is good," the thin man replied. "People of high station are known to be reserved and inflexible. It lends an air of strength to her. It is her chin that bothers me. The board in her corset fixed her back, but her chin—it keeps drooping. She needs to keep her head up. We should put a high collar on her dress, something stiff."

"A little late for that now," Amilia replied, irritated. "The ceremony is in less than an hour."

"A lot can be done in that time, Your Ladyship," he assured her.

Amilia still found it awkward, even embarrassing, to be referred to as "Your Ladyship" or "my lady." Nimbus, who had always followed proper protocol, insisted on referring to her formally. His mannerisms rubbed off on the other members of the castle staff. Maids and pages, who only months earlier had laughed and made fun of Amilia, took to bowing and curtsying to her. Even Ibis Thinly had begun addressing Amilia as *Her Ladyship*. The attention was flattering, but it could also be fleeting. Amilia was a noble in name only. She could lose her title just as easily as it had been won—and that was exactly what would happen in less than an hour.

"All right, wait outside," she ordered. "I'll hand you the dress to take to the seamstress. Your Eminence, can I please have the gown?"

Modina raised her arms as if in a trance and two hand-maidens immediately went to work undoing the numerous buttons and hooks.

Amilia's stomach churned. She had done everything possible in the time allotted. Modina had been surprisingly cooperative and easily memorized and repeated the speech Saldur had provided, which was mercifully short and easy to remember. Modina's role was remarkably simple. She would step onto the balcony, recite the words, and withdraw. The whole process would only take a few minutes, yet Amilia was certain of an impending disaster.

Despite all the preparations, Modina simply was not ready. The empress had only recently showed signs of lucidity and managed to follow directions, but no more than that. In many ways, she reminded Amilia of a dog. Trained to sit and stay, a pup would do as it was told when the master was around, but how many could maintain their composure when left on their own? A squirrel passing by would break their discipline and off they would go. Amilia was not permitted on the balcony, and if anything unexpected happened, there was no telling how the empress would react.

Amilia took the elaborate gown to Nimbus. "Make it quick. I don't want to be here with an empress clad only in her undergarments when the bell strikes."

"I will run like the wind, my lady," he said with a forced smile.

"What are you doing out here?" Regent Saldur asked.

Nimbus made a hasty bow, then ran off with the empress's gown.

The regent was lavishly dressed for the occasion, which made him even more intimidating than usual. "Why aren't you in with the empress? There is less than an hour before the presentation."

"Yes, Your Grace, but there are some last-minute prep—"

Saldur took her angrily by the arm and dragged her inside the staging room. Modina was wrapped in a robe and the two handmaidens fussed with her hair. They both stopped abruptly and curtsied. Saldur took no notice.

"Must I waste my time impressing on you the importance of this day?" he said while roughly releasing her. "Outside this palace, all of Aquesta is gathering, as well as dignitaries from all over Warric and even ambassadors from as far away as Trent and Calis. It's paramount that they see a strong, competent empress. Has she learned the speech?"

"Yes, Your Grace," Amilia replied with a bowed head.

Saldur examined the empress in her disheveled robe and unfinished hair. He scowled and whirled on Amilia. "If you ruin this—if she falters—I'll hold you personally responsible. A single word from me and you'll never be seen again. Given your background, I won't even have to create an excuse. No one will question your disappearance. No one will even notice you're gone. Fail me, Amilia, and I'll see you deeply regret it."

He left, slamming the door behind him and leaving Amilia barely able to breathe.

"Your Ladyship?" the maid Anna addressed her.

"What is it?" she asked weakly.

"It's her shoe, milady. The heel has come loose."

What else could go wrong?

On any ordinary day, nothing like this would happen, but

that day, because her life depended on it, problems followed one upon another. "Get it to the cobbler at once and tell him if it isn't fixed in twenty minutes, I'll—I'll—"

"I will tell him to hurry, milady." Anna ran from the room, shoe in hand.

Amilia began to pace. The room was only twenty feet long, causing her to turn frequently, which made her dizzy, but she continued it anyway. Her body was reacting unconsciously while her mind flew over every aspect of the ceremony.

What if she leaps off the balcony?

The thought hit her like a slap. As absurd as it seemed, it was possible. The empress was not of sound mind. With the noise and confusion of thousands of excited subjects, Modina could become overwhelmed and simply snap. The balcony was not terribly high, only thirty feet or so. The fall might not kill the empress if she landed well. Amilia, on the other hand, would not survive the incident.

Sweat broke out on her brow as her pacing quickened.

There was no time to put up a higher rail.

Perhaps a net at the bottom? No, that won't help.

The problem was not the injury. It was the spectacle.

A rope?

She could tie a length around Modina's waist and hold it from behind. That way if she made any forward movement, Amilia could stop her.

Nimbus returned, timidly peeking into the room. "What is it, my lady?" he asked, seeing her expression.

"Hmm? Oh, everything. I need a rope and a shoe—but never mind that. What about the dress?"

"The seamstress is working as fast as she can. Unfortunately, I don't think there will be time for a test dressing."

"What if it doesn't fit? What if it chokes her so she can't even speak?"

"We must think positively, my lady."

"That's easy for you to say. Your life isn't dangling by a thread—perhaps literally."

"But surely, Your Ladyship, you cannot fear such repercussions merely from a dress alteration? We are civilized people, after all."

"I'm not certain what civilization you're from, Nimbus, but this one can be harsh to those who fail."

Amilia looked at Modina, sitting quietly, oblivious to the importance of the speech she was about to give. They would do nothing to her. She was the empress and the whole world knew it. If she disappeared, there would be an inquiry and the people would demand justice for the loss of their god-queen. Even people as well placed as Saldur could hang for such a crime.

"Shall I bring the headdress?" Nimbus asked.

"Yes, please. Anna fetched it from the milliner's this morning and likely left it in the empress's bedroom."

"And how about I bring a bite for you to eat, my lady? You haven't had anything all day."

"I can't eat."

"As you wish. I will be back as soon as I can."

Amilia went to the window. From this vantage point, she could just see the east gate, through which scores of people poured. Men, women, and children of all classes entered the outer portcullis. The gathering throng emitted a low murmur, like some gigantic beast growling just out of sight. There was a knock at the door and in stepped the seamstress with the gown in her arms as if it were a newborn baby.

"That was fast," Amilia said.

"Forgive me, Your Ladyship, it's not quite done, but the royal tutor just stopped by and said I should finish up here, where I can size it to Her Eminence's neck. It's not how things are done, you see. It's not right to make the great lady sit and wait on me like some dress dummy. Still, the tutor said if I didn't do as he said, then he—" She paused and lowered her voice to a whisper. "He said he'd have me horsewhipped."

Amilia put a hand over her mouth to hide a smile. "He was not serious about the whipping, I can assure you, but he was quite right. This is too important to worry about inconveniencing Her Eminence. Get to work."

They dressed her once more in the gown and the seamstress worked feverishly, stitching in the rest of the collar. Amilia had begun to resume her pacing when there was another knock on the door. With the seamstress and maids occupied, Amilia opened it herself and was startled to find the Earl of Chadwick.

"Good evening, Lady Amilia," he said, bowing graciously. "I was hoping for a word with Her Eminence prior to the commencement."

"This is not a good time, sir," she said. Amilia could hardly believe she was saying no to a noble lord. "The empress is indisposed at the moment. Please understand."

"But of course. My apologies. Perhaps I could have a word with you, then?"

"Me? Ah, well—yes, I suppose that would be all right." Amilia stepped outside, closing the door behind her.

Amilia expected the earl would make his issue known right then, but instead, he began to walk down the corridor, and it took a moment for her to realize he expected her to follow.

"The empress is well, I trust?"

"Yes, my lord," she said, glancing back at the door to the dressing room, which was getting farther and farther away.

"I'm pleased to hear that," the earl said, and then suddenly added, "How rude of me. How are *you* feeling, milady?"

"I'm as well as can be expected, sir."

If Amilia had not been so consumed with thoughts of the empress, she would have found it funny that an earl was embarrassed by not immediately inquiring about her own health.

"And it's beautiful weather for the festivities today, is it not?"

"Yes, sir, it is." She forced her voice to remain calm.

Nimbus, Anna, and the cobbler all appeared and rushed down the hall. Nimbus paused briefly, giving her a worried look before entering the dressing room.

"Allow me to be blunt," the earl said.

"Please do, sir." Amilia's anxiety neared the breaking point.

"Everyone knows you're the closest to the empress. She confides in no one but you. Can you—Have you—Does the empress ever speak of me?"

Amilia raised her eyebrows in surprise. Under ordinary circumstances, the earl's hesitancy could have seemed quaint and even charming, but at that moment, she prayed he would just get it out and be done with it.

"Please, I know I'm being terribly forward, but I'm a forward man. I would like to know if she has ever thought of me, and if so, is it to her favor?"

"My lord, I can honestly say she has never once mentioned you to me."

The earl paused to consider this.

"I'm not sure how I should interpret that. I'm certain she sees so many suitors. Can you do me a favor, milady?"

"If it is in my power, sir."

"Could you speak to her about gracing me with a dance this evening at the ball after the banquet? I would be incredibly grateful."

"Her Eminence won't be attending the ball or the banquet, sir. She never dines in public and has many matters that require her attention."

"Never?"

"I'm afraid not, sir."

"I see." The earl paused in thought as Amilia rapidly drummed the tips of her fingers together.

"If you please, sir, I do need to be seeing to the empress."

"Of course. Forgive me for taking up your valuable time. Still, if you should perhaps mention me to Her Eminence and let her know I would very much like to visit with her..."

"I will, Your Lordship. Now, if you'll excuse me..."

Amilia hurried back and found that the seamstress had finished the collar, which was tall and did indeed keep her chin up. The addition looked horribly uncomfortable. Modina, of course, didn't seem to care. The cobbler, however, was still working on her shoe.

"What's going on here?" she asked.

"The new heel he put on was taller than the other," Nimbus told her. "He tried to resize, but in his haste he overcompensated and now it is shorter."

Amilia turned to Anna. "How long do we have?"

"About fifteen minutes," she replied gloomily.

"What about the headdress? I don't see it."

"It was not in the bedroom, or hall, my lady."

Anna's face drained of color. "Oh dear Maribor, forgive me. I forgot all about it!"

"You forgot? Nimbus!"

"Yes, my lady?"

"Run to the milliner and fetch the headdress, and when I say run, I mean sprint, do you hear me?"

"At once, my lady, but I don't know where the milliner shop is."

"Get a page to escort you."

"The pages are all busy with the ceremony."

"I don't care! Grab one at sword point if necessary. Find one who knows the way and tell him it's by order of the empress and don't let anyone stop you. Now move!"

"Anna!" Amilia shouted.

"Yes, milady." The maid was trembling, in tears. "I'm so sorry, milady, truly I am."

"We don't have time for apologies or tears. Go to the empress's bedroom and fetch her day shoes. She'll have to wear them instead. Do it now!"

Amilia slammed the door behind them and gave it a solid kick in frustration. She leaned her forehead against the oak as she concentrated on calming down. The gown would cover the shoes. No one would know the difference. The headdress was another matter. They had worked on it for weeks and the regents would notice its absence. The milliner's shop was out in the city proper, and she had left it to Anna to pick up. She could really blame only herself. She should have asked about it earlier and was furious at her incompetence. She kicked the door once more, then turned around and slumped to the floor, her gown ballooning about her.

The ceremony would begin in minutes but there was still time. Modina's speech was scheduled to be last and Amilia was certain she would have at least another twenty, perhaps even thirty, minutes while the others addressed the crowd. Across from her, Modina sat stiff and straight in her royal gown of white and gold, her long neck held high by the new collar. There was something different about Modina. She was watching Amilia with interest. She was actually studying her.

"Are you going to be all right?" she asked the empress.

Immediately, the light in her eyes vanished and the blank stare returned.

Amilia sighed.

✑

Regent Ethelred spoke for nearly an hour from the balcony, which was decorated in colorful bunting, although Amilia hardly heard a word of what he said. Something about the grandness and might of the New Empire and how Maribor had ordained that it would unite all of humanity once again. He spoke of the New Empire's military successes in the north and the bloodless annexation of Alburn and Dunmore. He followed this with the news of an expected surplus in wheat and barley and an end to the elven problem. They would no longer be allowed to roam free, and instead of being turned into useless slaves, they would simply disappear. The New Empire was gathering wayward elves from all over the realm. How they would be disposed of, he did not say. The massive crowd below cheered their approval and their combined voices roared.

Amilia sat in the staging room, her arms wrapped about her waist. She could not even pace now. The empress herself appeared unconcerned by the approaching presentation and sat calmly as ever in her shimmering gown and massive head-dress, which mimicked a fanning peacock.

Nimbus had managed excellent time reaching the milliner, although in the process he had apparently terrified a young page with threats. They also had good fortune in that the ceremony had started late due to a last-minute dispute about the order of speakers. Amilia had managed to secure the head-dress on Modina just minutes before the first started.

The chancellor had spoken first, then Ethelred, and finally Saldur. With each word, Amilia felt it harder and harder to breathe. Finally, Ethelred's speech concluded and Saldur stepped forward for the formal introduction. The crowd hushed, as they knew the expected moment was at hand.

"Nearly a thousand years have passed since the breaking of the great Empire of Novron," he told the multitude below. "We stand here today as witnesses to the enduring power of Maribor and his promise to Novron that his seed will reign forever. Neither treachery nor time can break this sacred covenant. Allow me to introduce to you proof of this. Welcome with me now the once simple farm maid, the slayer of the elven beast, the Heir of Novron, the high priestess of the Nyphron Church, Her Most Serene and Royal Grand Imperial Eminence, Empress Modina Novronian!"

The crowd erupted in cheers and applause. Amilia could feel the vibration of their voices even where she sat. She looked at Modina, pleading and hopeful. The empress's face was calm as she stood up straight and gracefully walked forward, the train of her dress trailing behind her.

When she stepped upon the balcony—when the people finally saw her face—the noise of the crowd did the impossible. It exploded. The unimaginably boisterous cheering was deafening, like a continuous roll of thunder that vibrated the very stone of the castle. It went on and on and Amilia wondered if it would ever stop.

In the face of the tumult, surely Modina could not endure. What effect would this have on her fragile countenance? Amilia wished Saldur had allowed her to use the rope or accompany her onto the balcony. Amilia's only consolation was knowing that Modina was likely frozen, her mind retreating to that dark place she had so long lived in, the place she crawled to hide from the world.

Amilia prayed the crowd would quiet. She hoped Ethelred or Saldur would do something to silence them, but neither moved and the crowd continued to roar with no end in sight. Then something unexpected happened. Modina slowly raised her hands, making a gentle quieting motion. Almost immediately, the crowd fell silent. Amilia could not believe her eyes.

"My beloved and cherished loyal subjects." She spoke with a loud, clear, almost musical voice that Amilia had not heard at practice. "It is wonderful to finally meet you."

The crowd roared anew, even louder than before. Modina allowed them to cheer for a full minute before raising her hands and silencing them again.

"As some of you may have heard, I have not been well. The battle with Rufus's Bane left me weakened, but with the help of my closest friend, the grand imperial secretary, Lady Amilia of Tarin Vale, I am feeling much better."

Amilia stopped breathing at the mention of her name. That was not in the speech.

"I owe Amilia the greatest debt of gratitude for her efforts on my behalf, for I should not be here at all if not for her strength, wisdom, and kindness."

Amilia closed her eyes and cringed.

"While I am feeling better, I am still easily exhausted and I must keep my strength in order to devote it to ensuring our defense against invaders, a bountiful harvest, and our return to the glory and prosperity that was Novron's Empire," she finished with an elaborate wave of her hand, turned, and left the balcony with elegant grace and poise.

The crowd erupted once more into cheers, which continued long after Modina had returned inside.

"I swear I didn't tell her to say that." Amilia pleaded with Saldur.

"Because the empress publicly named you her friend and the hero of the realm, you've become famous," Saldur replied. "This will make it almost impossible for me to replace you— *almost*. But don't worry," he continued thoughtfully. "With such a fine display, I would be a fool to do anything other than praise you. I'm once more impressed. I wouldn't have expected this from you. You're more clever than I thought, but I should have guessed that already. I'll have to remember this. Good work, my dear. Good work, indeed."

"Yes, that was excellent!" Ethelred said. "We can now put the fiasco of the coronation behind us. I can't say I approve of the self-aggrandizement, Amilia, but seeing what you've done with her, I can't begrudge you a little recognition. In fact, we should consider rewarding her for a job well done, Sauly."

"Indeed," he replied. "We'll have to consider what that should be. Come, Lanis, let's proceed to the banquet." The two of them left, talking back and forth about the ceremony as they went.

Amilia moved to the empress's side, took her hand, and escorted her back to her quarters. "You'll be the death of me yet," she told her.

Chapter 16

The Battle of Ratibor

Hadrian sat in the rain. Heavy chains shackled his ankles and wrists to a large metal stake driven into the ground. All day, and throughout the night, he waited in the mud, watching the lazy movements of the Nationalist army. They were just as slow to decide his fate as they were to attack. Horses walked past, meals were called, and men grumbled about the rain and the mud. The gray light faded into night and regret consumed him.

He should have escaped, even if it had meant shedding blood. He might have been able to save Arista's life. He could have warned her that the Nationalists would not cooperate and would have her call off the attack. Now even if she succeeded, the victory would be short-lived and she would face the gallows or a beheading.

"Gill!" he shouted as he saw the sentry walking by in his soaked cloak.

"Ah yes!" Gill laughed, coming closer with a grin. "If it isn't the *grand marshal*. Not so grand now, are you?"

"Gill, you have to help me," he shouted over the roar of the rain. "I need you to get a message to—"

Gill bent down. "Now why would I help the likes of you? You made a fool out of me. Sergeant Milford weren't too pleased neither. He has me running an all-night shift to show his displeasure."

"I have money," Hadrian told him eagerly. "I could pay you."

"Really? And where is this money, in some chest buried on some distant mountain, or merely in another pair of pants?"

"Right here in the purse on my belt. I have at least ten gold tenents. You can have it all if you just promise me to take a message to Ratibor."

Gill looked at Hadrian's belt curiously. "Sure," he said. Reaching down, he untied the purse. He weighed it in his hands. The bouncing produced a jingle. He pulled open the mouth and poured out a handful of coins. "Whoa! Look at that. You weren't joshing. There's really gold in here. One, two, three…damn! Well, thank you, Marshal." He made a mock salute. "This will definitely take the sting out of having to stand two watches." He started to walk away.

"Wait!" Hadrian told him. "You need to hear the message."

Gill kept walking.

"You need to tell Arista not to attack," he shouted desperately, but Gill continued on his way, swinging the purse, until his figure was obscured by the rain.

Hadrian cursed and kicked the stake hard. He collapsed on his side, lost in frustration. He remembered the look on Arista's face, how hopeful she had been. It had never crossed her mind that he could fail. When he had first met the princess, he had thought she was arrogant and egotistical, like all nobles—grown-up brats, greedy and self-centered.

When did that change?

Images flooded back to him. He remembered her hanging out her wet undergarments at Sheridan. How stubbornly she had slept under the horse blanket that first night outside, crying herself to sleep. He and Royce had both been certain she would cancel the mission the next day. He saw her sleeping in the skiff that morning when they had drifted down the Bernum, and remembered how she had practically announced her identity to everyone when drunk in Dunstan's home. She had always been their patron and their princess, but somewhere along the way she had become more than that.

As he sat there, pelted with rain and helpless in the mud, he was tormented with visions of her death. He saw her lying facedown in the filthy street, her dress torn, her pale skin stained red with blood. The Imperialists would likely hoist her body above Central Square or perhaps drag it behind a horse to Aquesta. Maybe they would cut her head off and send it to Alric as a warning.

In a flash of anger and desperation, he began digging in the mud, trying to dislodge the stake. He dug furiously, pulled hard, then dug again—wrenching the stake back and forth. A guard spotted him and used a second stake on the chains connected to his wrists to stretch him out flat.

"Still trying to get away and cause mischief, are ya?" the guard said. "Well, that ain't gonna happen. You killed Gaunt. You'll die for that, but until then, you'll stay put." The guard spat in his face, but the effect was hardly what he sought, as the rain rinsed it away. It crushed Hadrian to know that it was Arista's rain washing him clean. Lying there, he saw the first sign of dawn lightening the morning sky and his heart sank further.

⚬

Emery could see the horizon as the faint light of dawn separated sky from building and tree. Rain still fell and the sound of crickets was replaced by early-morning stirrings. Merchants appeared on the street far earlier than usual, pushing carts and rolling wagons toward the West End Square. They neglectfully left them blocking the entrances from King's Street and Legends Avenue.

Other men came out of their homes and shops. Emery watched them appear out of the gray morning rain, coming one and two at a time, then gathering into larger groups as they wandered aimlessly around the square, drifting slowly, almost hesitantly, toward the armory. They wore heavy clothes and carried hoes, pitchforks, shovels, and axes. Most had knives tucked into their belts.

A pair of city guards working the end of the night shift— dressed only in light summer uniforms—had just finished their last patrol circuit. They stopped and looked around at the growing crowd with curious expressions. "Say there, what's going on here?"

"I dunno," a man said, and then moved away.

"Listen, what are you all doing here?" the other guard asked, but no one answered.

Barefoot and dressed in a white oversized shirt and a pair of britches that left his shins bare, Emery strode forward, feeling the clap of the sword at his side. "We're here to avenge the murder of our lord and sovereign, King Urith of Rhenydd!"

"It's him. It's Emery Dorn," the guard shouted. "Grab the bastard!"

The guards rushed forward, but they were too late to realize their peril as the groups closed around them, sweeping together like a flock of birds.

The soldiers hastily drew their swords and swung them. "Back! Get back! All of you! Back or we'll have the lot of you arrested!"

Hatred filled the faces of the crowd and excitement crept into their eyes. They jabbed at the soldiers with pitchforks and hoes. The guards knocked them away with swords.

For several minutes the crowd taunted with feints and

threats, and then Emery drew his blade. Mrs. Dunlap had found the sword for him. It had once belonged to her husband. In all his years of service, Paul Dunlap, carriage driver for King Urith, had never had occasion to draw it. The steel scraped as Emery pulled the blade from the metal sheath. With a grim expression and a set jaw, he pushed his way through the circle and faced the guards.

They were sweating. He could see the wetness on the upper lip of the closest man. The guard lunged, thrusting. Emery stepped to the side and hit the soldier's blade with his own, hearing the solid *clank* and feeling the impact in his hand. He took a step forward and swung. It felt good. It felt perfect, just the right move. The tip of his sword hit something soft and Emery watched as he sliced the man, cutting him across the chest. The soldier screamed, dropping his sword. He fell to his knees, his eyes wide in shock, clutching himself as blood soaked his clothes. The other guard tried to run, but the crowd held him back. Emery pushed past the wounded man and, with one quick thrust, stabbed the remaining guard through the kidney. Several cheered and began beating the wounded men, hacking them with axes and shovels.

"Enough," Emery shouted. "Follow me!"

The guards' weapons were taken and the crowd chased Emery to the flagstone building with the iron gate. By the time they arrived, Carat was already picking the lock. They killed those on duty only to discover most of the rest were still in their beds. A few had gotten to their feet before the mob arrived. They stabbed the first confused man through the ribs with a pitchfork, which he took with him when he fell. Emery stabbed another and an axe took a third's shoulder partway off, lodging there so that the owner had to kick his victim to pull the axe free. Swords and shields lined the walls and lay in pine boxes. Steel helms and chain hauberks sat on shelves.

The mob grabbed these as they passed, discarding their

tools of trade for tools of war. Only ten men guarded the armory and all died quickly, most beaten to death in their beds. The men cheered when they realized they had taken the armory without a single loss of life from their side. They laughed, howled, and jumped on tables, breaking plates and cups and whatever else they could find as they gleefully tested out their new weapons.

All around him, Emery could see the wild looks in the eyes of the men and realized he must wear a similar expression. His heart was pounding, his lungs pumping air. He felt no pain at all from his back now. He felt powerful, elated, and a little nauseous all at the same time.

"Emery! Emery!" He turned to see Arista pushing through the men. "You're too slow," she screamed at him. "The garrison is coming. Get them armed and formed up in the square."

As if pulled from a dream, Emery realized his folly. "Everyone out!" he shouted. "Everyone out—now! Form up on the square!"

⌁

Arista had already begun organizing those men who remained outside into two lines with their backs to the armory and their faces to the square.

"We need to get weapons!" Perin shouted at the princess.

"Stay in line!" she barked. "We'll have them brought out. You have to maintain the lines to stop the garrison from charging."

The men who stood in line holding only farm tools looked at her, terrified, as across the square, the first of the soldiers struggled to push away the wagons and carts that had been rutted in the mud. Before long, the men Emery had shooed out began taking their place in front of the line.

"Form up!" Emery shouted. "Two straight lines."

Arista ran back into the armory and began grabbing

swords and dragging them out. She spotted Carat stealing coins from a dead man's purse and shoved him against a wall. "Help me carry swords and shields out!"

"But I'm not allowed to," he said.

"You're not allowed to fight, but you can carry some swords, damn it. Just like you unlocked the door. Now do it!"

Carat seemed like he would say something and then gave in. He started pulling shields down from the walls. Dr. Gerand entered carrying bandages but discarded them quickly to help deliver weapons. On her way out, Arista saw a woman running in, her dress soaked from the rain, her long blonde hair pasted to her face so that she could barely see. The blonde stopped abruptly at Arista's approach.

"Let me help," she said to Arista. "You get more while I pass these out."

Arista nodded and handed over the weapons, then ran back inside.

Carat handed her the stack of shields he was carrying and she ran them down to the young woman, who in turn took them to the waiting line. When Arista came out again, she found that a line of older men and some women had formed up, and they were passing the weapons like a bucket brigade, with the young blonde adding more people to the line.

"More swords!" Arista shouted. "Helms and mail last."

Carat assembled weapons into manageable piles for the others to grab.

"No more swords!" The call soon came. "Send shields!"

The bell in Central Square began to ring, its tone sounding different that morning than on any other, perhaps due to the heavy rain or the pounding of blood in Arista's ears. Most men on the line held only a sword. Arista could see fear in every face.

She could hear Emery's voice drifting above the rain with each delivery. "Steady! Dress those lines. Tighten that formation." He barked the orders like a veteran commander. "No more than a fist's distance between your shoulders. Those with spears or pikes to the rear line. Those with shields to the front. Wait! Halt!" he shouted. "Forget that. Back in line. Just pass the spears back and hand the shields forward."

With the next delivery of weapons, Arista paused at the armory doorway and looked out across the square. The garrison had cleared the wagons from King's Street and a few soldiers entered. They looked briefly at the lines of townsfolk, then went to work to clear the other carts.

Emery stood in front of the troops. Everyone had a sword or a spear but most did not know how to wield them properly. Nearly every man in the front row had a wooden shield, but most simply held them in their hands. At least one man had his shield upside down.

"Adam the wheeler, front and center!" Emery shouted, and the middle-aged wheelwright stepped forward. "Take the left side and see that the men know how to wear their shields and hold their swords." Emery likewise called Renkin Pool and Forrest into action and set them to dressing the line.

"Keep your shield high," Adam was shouting. "Don't swing your sword—thrust it instead. That way you can maintain closer formations. Keep the line tight. The man next to you is a better shield than that flimsy bit of wood in your hands! Stay shoulder to shoulder!"

"Don't let them turn the flank!" Renkin was shouting on the other side of the line. "Those on the ends, turn and hold your shields to defend from a side assault. Everyone must move and work together!"

Helms and hauberks were coming out now and there were a few in the front row hastily pulling chain mail netting over their heads.

A surprising number of imperial soldiers had already

formed themselves into rows on the far side of the square. Each one was impeccably dressed in hauberk, helm, sword, and shield. They stood still, straight, and confident. Looking at Emery's men, Arista saw nervous movements and fear-filled eyes.

Four knights rode into the square. Two bore the imperial pennant at the ends of tall lances. On the foremost horse rode Sheriff Vigan. Beside him came Trenchon, the city's bailiff, splashing through the puddles. Hooked to Vigan's belt, in addition to his sword, was the whip. Vigan's face was stern and unimpressed by the hastily assembled, slightly skewed lines of peasants. He rode up and down, trotting menacingly, his mount throwing up clods of mud into the air.

"I know why you're here," Vigan shouted at them. "You're here because of one man." He pointed at Emery. "He has incited you to perform criminal acts. Normally, I would have each one of you executed for treason, but I can see it's the traitor Emery Dorn, and not you, who has caused this. You are victims of his poison, so I'll be lenient. Put down those stolen weapons, return to your homes, and I'll only hang the leaders that led you astray. Continue this and you'll be slaughtered to the last man."

"Steady, men," Emery shouted. "He's just trying to frighten you. He's offering you a deal because he's scared—scared of us because we stand before him, united and strong. He's scared because we do not cower before his threats. He's scared because, for the first time, he does not see sheep, he does not see slaves, he does not see victims to beat, but men. Men! Tall and proud. Men who are still loyal to their king!"

Vigan raised his hand briefly, then lowered it. There was a harsh crack followed immediately by a muffled *thwack!* Emery staggered backward. Blood sprayed those near him. A crossbow bolt was lodged in his chest. An instant later, the fiery red-haired boy fell into the mud.

The line wavered at the sight.

"No!" Arista screamed, and shoved through the men and collapsed in the mud beside Emery. Frantically she struggled to turn him over, to pull his face out of the muck. She wiped the mud away while blood vomited from his mouth. His eyes rolled wildly. He wheezed in short, halting gasps.

Everyone was silent. The whole world stopped.

Arista held Emery in her arms. She could see a pleading in his eyes as they found hers. She could feel his breath shortening with each wretched gasp. With each jerk of his body, she felt her heart breaking.

This can't be happening!

She looked into his eyes. She wanted to say something—to give him a part of her to take with him—but all she could do was hold on. As she squeezed him tightly, he stopped struggling. He stopped moving. He stopped breathing.

Arista cried aloud, certain her body would break.

Above her the sheriff's horse snorted and stomped. Behind her the men of the rebellion wavered. She heard them dropping weapons, discarding shields.

Arista took in a shuddering breath of her own and turned her face toward the sky. She raised one leg, then the other, pushing herself—willing herself—to her feet. As her shaking body rose from the mud, she drew Emery's sword in a tight fist, lifted the blade above her head, and glared at the sheriff.

She cried in a loud voice, "Don't—you—dare—break! *Hold the line!*"

✎

As Hadrian lay on his back, chained and stretched out in the mud, a shadow fell across his face and the rain stopped hitting him. He opened his eyes and, squinting, saw a man outlined in the morning light.

"What in Maribor's name are you doing here?"

The voice was familiar and Hadrian struggled to see the face lost in the folds of a hooded robe. All around him, rain continued to pour, splashing the mud puddles and grass, forcing him to blink.

The figure standing over him shouted, "Sergeant! Explain what goes on here. Why is this man chained?"

Hadrian could hear boots slogging through the mud. "It's Commander Parker's orders, sir." There was nervousness in his voice.

"I see. Tell me, Sergeant, do you enjoy being human?"

"What's that, sir?"

"I asked if you liked the human form. For example, do you find it useful to have two hands and two legs?"

"I, ah—well, I don't think I quite understand your meaning."

"No, you don't, but you will if this man isn't freed immediately."

"But, Lord Esrahaddon, I can't. Commander Parker—"

"Leave Parker to me. Get those chains off him, get him out of that mud, and escort him to the house immediately, or I swear you'll be walking on all fours within the hour, and for the rest of your life."

"Wizards!" the sergeant grumbled after Esrahaddon had left him. He pulled a key from his belt and struggled to open the mud-caked locks. "Get up," he ordered.

The sergeant led Hadrian back to the house. The chains were gone but his wrists were still bound by two iron manacles. Hadrian was cold and hungry and felt nearly drowned, but only one thought filled his mind as he watched the sun rising in the east.

Is there still time?

"And what about the wagons on the South Road?" Esrahaddon growled as Hadrian entered. The wizard stood in his familiar robe, which was, at that moment, gray and perfectly dry despite the heavy rain. Esrahaddon looked the same as he had in Dahlgren except for the length of his beard, which now reached to his chest, giving him a more wizardly appearance.

Parker was seated behind his table, a napkin tucked into his collar, another plate of ham and eggs before him.

Does he have the same meal brought to him each morning?

"It's the mud. They can't be moved, and I don't appreciate—" He paused when he spotted Hadrian. "What's going on? I ordered this man staked. Why are you bringing him here?"

"I ordered it," Esrahaddon told him. "Sergeant, remove those restraints and fetch his weapons."

"You?" Parker replied, stunned. "You are here only as an advisor. You forget I'm in command."

"Of what?" the wizard asked. "A thousand lazy vagabonds? This was an army when I left. I come back and it's a rabble."

"It's the rain. It doesn't stop."

"It's not supposed to stop," Hadrian burst out in frustration. "I tried to tell you. We need to attack Dermont now. Arista is launching a rebellion this morning in Ratibor. She'll seal the city so he can't retreat. We have to engage and defeat Dermont before he's reinforced by Sir Breckton and the Northern Imperial Army. They will be here any day now. If we don't attack, Dermont will enter the city and crush the rebellion."

"What nonsense." Parker pointed an accusing finger. "This man entered the camp claiming to be a marshal-at-arms who was taking command of *my* troops."

"He is, and he will," the wizard told him.

"He will not! He and the Princess of Melengar are both

responsible for the treachery that probably cost Degan his life. And we have had no news of any Northern—"

"Degan is alive, you idiot. Neither Hadrian nor Arista had anything to do with his abduction. Do as this man instructs or everyone will likely be dead or captured by the imperium in two days. You, of course"—the wizard glared at Parker—"will die much sooner."

Parker's eyes widened.

"I don't even know who he is!" Parker exclaimed. "I can't turn over command to a stranger I know nothing about. How do I know he's capable? What are his qualifications?"

"Hadrian knows more about combat than any living man."

"And am I to take your word? The word of a—a— sorcerer?"

"It was on my word that this army was formed—my direction that produced its victories."

"But you've been gone. Things have changed. Degan left me in charge and I don't think I can—"

Esrahaddon stepped toward the commander. As he did, his robe began to glow. A bloodred radiance filled the interior of the house, making Parker's face look like a plump beet.

"All right! All right!" Parker shouted abruptly to the sergeant, "Do as he says. What do I care!"

The sergeant unlocked Hadrian's hands, then exited.

"Now, Parker, make yourself useful for once," Esrahaddon said. "Go round up the regiment captains. Tell them that they will now be taking their orders from Marshal Blackwater, and have them gather here as soon as possible."

"Marshal *Lord* Blackwater," Hadrian said with a smile.

Esrahaddon rolled his eyes. "Do it now."

"But—"

"Go!"

Parker grabbed up his cloak and his sword and pulled his boots from under the table. He retreated out the door still holding them.

"Is he going to be a problem?" Hadrian asked, watching the ex-commander hop into the rain, grumbling.

"Parker? No. I just needed to remind him that he's terrified of me." Esrahaddon looked at Hadrian. "Marshal *Lord* Blackwater?"

"*Lord* Esrahaddon?" he replied, rubbing feeling back into his wrists.

The wizard smiled and nodded. "You still haven't said what you're doing here."

"A job—for Arista Essendon. She hired us to help her contact the Nationalists."

"And now she has you seizing control of my army."

"Your army? I thought this was Gaunt's."

"So did he. And the moment I'm away, Degan gets himself captured after putting that thing in charge. Royce with you?"

"Was—Arista sent him to contact Alric about invading Warric."

While eating Parker's ham and eggs, Hadrian provided Esrahaddon with further details about the rebellion and his plans for attacking Dermont. Just as he had finished the meal, there was a knock on the door. Five officers and the harried-looking sergeant who carried Hadrian's swords entered.

Esrahaddon addressed them. "As Parker no doubt informed you, this is Marshal Lord Blackwater, your new commander. Do anything he says, as if he were Gaunt himself. I think you'll find him a very worthy replacement for your general."

They nodded and stood at attention.

Hadrian got up, walked around the table, and announced, "We will attack the imperial position immediately."

"Now?" one said, astonished.

"I wish there was more time, but I've been tied up elsewhere. We'll launch our attack directly across that muddy field, where the Imps' three hundred heavy cavalry can't ride, and where their longbow archers can't see in this rain. Our lightly armored infantry must move quickly to overwhelm them. We'll close at a run and butcher them man to man."

"But they'll—" a tall gruff-looking soldier with a partial beard and mismatched armor started, then stopped himself.

"They'll what?" Hadrian asked.

"I was just thinking. The moment they see us advance, won't they retreat within the city walls?"

"What's your name?" Hadrian asked.

The man looked worried but held his ground. "Renquist, sir."

"Well, Renquist, you're absolutely right. That's exactly what they will try to do. Only they won't be able to get in. By then our allied forces will own the city."

"Allied forces?"

"I don't have time to explain. Don't strike camp, and don't use horns or drums to assemble. With luck, there's a good chance we can catch them by surprise. By now, they probably think we'll never attack. Renquist, how long do you estimate to have the men assembled and ready to march?"

"Two hours," he replied with more confidence.

"Have them ready in one. Each of you form up your men on the east slope, out of their sight. Three regiments of infantry in duel lines, senior commanders located at the center, left, and right flanks in that order. And I want light cavalry to swing to the south and await the call of the trumpet to sweep their flank. I want one contingent of cavalry—the smallest—that I'll command and hold in reserve to the north, near the city. At the waving of the blue pennant, begin crossing the field as quietly as possible. When you see the green flag, relay the signal and charge. We move in one hour. Dismissed!"

The captains saluted and ran back out into the rain. The sergeant handed over Hadrian's weapons and started to slip out quietly.

"Wait a moment." Hadrian halted him. "What's your name?"

The sergeant spun. "I was just following orders when I chained you up. I didn't know—"

"You've just been promoted to adjutant general," Hadrian told him. "What's your name?"

The ex-sergeant blinked. "Bently...sir."

"Bently, from now on you stick next to me and see that my orders are carried out, understand? Now, I'll need fast riders to work as messengers—three should do—and signal flags, a blue and a green one, as big as possible. Mount them on tall sticks and make certain all the captains have identical ones. Oh, and I need a horse!"

"Make that two," the wizard said.

"Make that three," Hadrian added. "You'll need one too, Bently."

The soldier opened his mouth, closed it, then nodded and stepped out into the rain.

"An hour," Hadrian muttered as he strapped on his weapons.

"You don't think Arista can hold out that long?"

"I was supposed to take control of this army yesterday. If only I had more time...I could have...I just hope it's not too late."

"If anyone can save Ratibor, it's you," the wizard told him.

"I know all about being the guardian to the heir," Hadrian replied.

"I had a feeling Royce would tell you."

Hadrian picked up the large spadone sword and looped the baldric over his head. He reached up and drew it out, testing the position of the sheath.

"I remember that weapon." The wizard pointed to the blade. "That's Jerish's sword." He frowned, then added, "What have you done to it?"

"What do you mean?"

"Jerish loved that thing—had a special cloth he kept in his gauntlet that he used to polish it—something of an obsession, really. That blade was like a mirror."

"It's seen nine hundred years of use," Hadrian told him, and put it away.

"You look nothing like Jerish," Esrahaddon said, then paused when he saw the look on Hadrian's face. "What is it?"

"The heir is dead—you know that, don't you? Died right here in Ratibor forty years ago."

Esrahaddon smiled. "Still, you hold a sword the same way Jerish did. Must be in the training somehow. Amazing how much it defines both of you. I never really—"

"Did you hear me? The bloodline ended. Seret caught up to them. They killed the heir—his name was Naron, by the way—and they killed his wife and child. My father was the only survivor. I'm sorry."

"My teacher, old Yolric, used to insist the world has a way of righting itself. He was obsessed with the idea. I thought he was crazy, but after living for nine hundred years, you perceive things differently. You see patterns you never knew were there. The heir isn't dead, Hadrian, just hidden."

"I know you'd like to think that, but my father failed and the heir died. I talked to a member of the Theorem Eldership who was there. He saw it happen."

Esrahaddon shook his head. "I've seen the heir with my own eyes, and I recognize the blood of Nevrik. A thousand years cannot mask such a lineage from me. Still, just to be sure, I performed a test that cannot be faked. Oh yes, the heir is alive and well."

"Who is it, then? I'm the guardian, aren't I? Or I'm supposed to be. I should be protecting him."

"At the moment, anonymity is a far better protection than swords. I cannot tell you the heir's identity. If I did, you would rush off and be a beacon to those watching." The wizard sighed. "And trust me, I know a great deal about being watched. In Gutaria they wrote down every word I uttered. Even now, at this very moment, every word I say is being heard."

"You sound like Royce." Hadrian looked around. "We're alone, surrounded by an army of Nationalists. Do you think Saldur or Ethelred have spies pressing an ear against this farmhouse?"

"Saldur? Ethelred?" Esrahaddon chuckled. "I'm not concerned with the imperial regents. They're pawns in this game. Haven't you wondered how the Gilarabrywn escaped Avempartha? Do you think Saldur or Ethelred could manage such a trick? My adversary is much more dangerous, and I'm certain he spends a great deal of time listening to what I say, no matter where I am. You see, I do not have the benefit of that amulet you wear."

"Amulet?" Hadrian touched his chest, feeling the metal circle under his shirt. "Royce said it prevents wizards like you from finding the wearer."

The wizard nodded. "Preventing clairvoyant searches was the primary purpose, but they are far more powerful than that. The amulets protect the wearers from all effects of the Art and have a dash of good fortune added in. Flip a coin wearing that, and it will come up the way you need it to more often than not. You've been in many battles and I'm sure in plenty of dangerous situations with Royce. Have you not considered yourself lucky on more than one occasion? That little bit of jewelry is extremely powerful. The level of the Art that went into making it was beyond anything I'd ever seen."

"I thought you made it."

"I did, but I had help. I could never have built them on my own. Yolric showed me the weave. He was the greatest of us. I could barely understand his instructions and wasn't certain I had performed the spell properly, but it appears I was successful."

"Still, you're the only one left in the world who can really do magic, right? So there's no chance anyone is magically listening."

"What about this rain? It's not *supposed* to stop? It would seem I'm not the only one."

"You're afraid of Arista?"

"No, just making a point. I'm not the only wizard in the world and I've already been far too careless. In my haste, I took chances that maybe I should not have, drawing too much attention, playing into others' hands. With so little time left—only a matter of months—it would be foolhardy to risk more now. I fear the heir's identity has already been compromised, but there is a chance I'm wrong and I'll cling to that hope. I'm sorry, Hadrian. I can't tell you just yet, but trust me, I will."

"No offense, but you don't seem too trustworthy."

The wizard smiled. "Maybe you *are* Jerish's descendant after all. Very soon I'll need Riyria's help with an extremely challenging mission."

"Riyria doesn't exist anymore. I've retired."

The wizard nodded. "Nevertheless, I'll require both of you, and as it concerns the heir, I presume you'll make an exception."

"I don't even know where I'll be."

"Don't worry, I'll find you both when the time comes. But for now, we have the little problem of Lord Dermont's army to contend with."

There was a knock at the door. "Horses ready, sirs," the new adjutant general reported.

As they stepped out, Hadrian spotted Gill walking toward him with his purse. "Good morning, Gill," Hadrian said, taking his pouch back.

"Morning, sir," he said, looking sick but making an effort to smile. "It's all there, sir."

"I'm a bit busy at the moment, Gill, but I'm sure we'll have a chance to catch up later."

"Yes, sir."

Hadrian mounted a brown-and-white gelding that Bently held for him. He watched as Esrahaddon mounted a smaller black mare by hooking the stub of his wrist around the horn. Once in the saddle, the wizard wrapped the reins around his stubs.

"It's strange. I keep forgetting you don't have hands," Hadrian commented.

"I don't," the wizard replied coldly.

Overhead, heavy clouds swirled as boys ran about the camp spreading the order to form up. Horses trotted, kicking up clods of earth. Carts rolled, leaving deep ruts. Half-dressed men darted from tents, slipping in the slick mud. They carried swords over their shoulders, dragged shields, and struggled to fasten helms. Hadrian and Esrahaddon rode through the hive of soggy activity to the top of the ridge, where they could see the lay of the land for miles. The city to the north, with its wooden spires and drab walls, stood as a ghostly shadow. To the south lay the forest, and between them a vast plain stretched westward. What had once been farmland was now a muddy soup. The field was shaped like a basin, and at its lowest point a shallow pond had formed. It reflected the light of the dreary gray sky like a steel mirror. On the far side, the hazy encampment of the imperial army was just visible through a thick curtain of rain. Hadrian stared but could make out only faint, shadowy shapes. Nothing indicated they knew what was about to happen. Below them on the east side of the slope, hidden from imperial view, the Nationalist army assembled into ranks.

"What is it?" Esrahaddon asked.

Hadrian realized he was grimacing. "They aren't very good soldiers," he replied, watching the men wander about, creating misshapen lines. They stood listless, shoulders slumped, heads down.

Esrahaddon shrugged. "There are a few good ones. We pulled in some mercenaries and a handful of deserters from the Imperialists. That Renquist you were so taken with, he was a sergeant in the imperial forces. Joined us because he heard nobility didn't matter in the Nationalist army. We got a few of those, but mostly they're farmers, merchants, or men who lost their homes or families."

Hadrian glanced across the field. "Lord Dermont has trained foot soldiers, archers, and knights—men who devoted their whole lives to warfare and trained since an early age."

"I wouldn't worry about that."

"Of course *you* wouldn't. I'm the one who has to lead this ugly rabble. I'm the one who must go down there and face those lances and arrows."

"I'm going with you," he said. "That's why you don't need to worry about it."

Bently and three other young men carrying colored flags rode up beside them. "Captains report ready, sir."

"Let's go," Hadrian told them, and trotted down to take

his place with a small contingent of cavalry. The men on horseback appeared even less capable than those on foot. They had no armor and wore torn, rain-soaked clothes. Except for the spears they held across their laps, they looked like vagabonds or escaped prisoners.

"Raise your lances!" he shouted. "Stay tight, keep your place, wheel together, and follow me." He turned to Bently. "Wave the blue flag."

Bently swung the blue flag back and forth until the signal was mimicked across the field, and then the army began moving forward at a slow walk. Armies never moved at a pace that suited Hadrian. When attacking with him, they crept with agonizing slowness. But when he was defending, they seemed to race at an unnatural speed. He patted the neck of his horse, which was larger and more spirited than old Millie. Hadrian liked to know his horse better before a battle. They needed to work as a team in combat, but he did not even know this one's name.

With the wizard riding at his right side, and Bently on his left, Hadrian crested the hill and began the long descent into the wet field. He wheeled his cavalry to the right, sweeping toward the city, riding the rim of the basin and avoiding the middle of the muck, which he left to the infantry. He would stay to the higher ground and watch the army's northern flank. This would also place him near the city gate, able to intercept any imperial retreat. After his company made the turn, he watched as the larger force of light-mounted lancers broke and began to circle left, heading to guard the southern flank. The swishing tails of their horses soon disappeared into the rain.

The ranks of the infantry came next. They crested the hill, jostling each other, some still struggling to get their helms on and shields readied. The lines were skewed, broken and wavy, and when they hit the mud, whatever mild resemblance they had to a formation was lost. They staggered and slipped forward as a mob. They were at least quiet. He wondered if it might be because most of them were half-asleep.

Hadrian felt his stomach twist.

This will not go well. If only I had more time to drill the men properly, then they would at least look like soldiers.

Success or failure in battle often hinged on impressions, decided in the minds of men before the first clash. Like bullies casting insults in a tavern, it was a game of intimidation—a game the Nationalists did not know how to play.

How did they ever win a battle? How did they take Vernes and Kilnar?

Unable to see the Imperialists' ranks clearly, he imagined them lined up in neat straight rows, waiting, letting his troops exhaust themselves in the mud. He expected a wall of glistening shields peaked with shining helms locked shoulder to shoulder, matching spears foresting above. He anticipated hundreds of archers already notching shafts to string. Lord Dermont would hold back the knights. Any fool could see the futility of ordering a charge into the muck. Clad in heavy metal armor, their pennants fluttering from their lances, the knights probably waited in the trees or perhaps around the wall of the city. They would remain hidden until just the right moment. That is what Hadrian would have done. When the Nationalists tried to flank, only Hadrian and his little group would stand in the way. He would call the charge and hope those behind him followed.

They were more than halfway across the field when he was finally able to see the imperial encampment. White tents stood in perfect rows, horses were corralled, and no one was visible.

"Where are they?"

"It's still very early," the wizard said, "and in a heavy rain no one likes to get up. It's so much easier to stay in bed."

"But where are the sentries?"

Hadrian watched in amazement as the mangled line of infantry cleared the muddy ground and closed in on the imperial camp, their lines straightening out a bit. He saw the heads of his captains. There was still no sign of the enemy.

"Have you ever noticed," Esrahaddon said, "how rain has a musical quality about it sometimes? The way it drums on a roof? It's always easier to sleep on a rainy night. There's something magical about running water that is very soothing, very relaxing."

"What did you do?"

The wizard smiled. "A weak, thin enchantment. Without hands it's very hard to do substantive magic anymore, but—"

They heard a shout. A tent flap fluttered, then another. More shouts cascaded, and then a bell rang.

"There, see?" Esrahaddon sighed. "I told you. It doesn't take much to break it."

"But we have them," Hadrian said, stunned. "We caught them sleeping! Bently, the green flag. Signal the charge. Signal the charge!"

❧

Sheriff Vigan scowled at Arista. Behind her, men picked up weapons and shuffled back into position.

"I told you to lay down your arms and leave," the sheriff shouted. "Not more than a few of you will be punished in the stocks, and only your leaders will be executed. The first has already fallen. Will you stand behind a woman? Will you throw away your lives for her sake?"

No one moved. The only sounds were those of the rain and the sheriff's horse and the jangling of his bridle.

"Very well," he said. "I'll execute the leading agitators one at a time if that's what it takes." He glanced over his shoulder and ominously raised his hand again.

The princess did not move.

She stood still and tall with Emery's sword above her head, his blood on her dress, and the wind and rain lashing her face. She glared defiantly at the sheriff.

Thwack!

The sound of a crossbow.

Phhump!

A muffled impact.

Arista felt blood spray her face, but there was no pain. Sheriff Vigan fell sideways into the mud. Polish stood in front of the blacksmith's shop, an empty crossbow in his hands.

Renkin Pool grabbed Arista by the shoulder and jerked her backward. Off balance, she fell. He stood over her, his shield raised. Another telltale _thwack_ and Pool's shield burst into splinters. The bolt continued into his chest. The explosion of blood and wood rained on her.

Another crossbow fired, this one handled by Adam. Trenchon screamed as the arrow passed through his thigh and continued into his horse, which collapsed, crushing Trenchon's leg beneath it. Another bow fired, then another, and Arista could see that during the pause, the blonde woman had hauled crossbows out of the armory and passed them throughout the ranks.

The garrison captain assumed command of the Imperialists. He gave a shout and the remainder of their bowmen fired across the square. Men in the line fell.

"Fire!" Adam shouted, and rebel bows gave answer. A handful of imperial soldiers dropped in the mud.

"Tighten the line!" Adam shouted. "Fill in the gaps where people fall!"

They heard a shout from across the field, then a roar as the garrison drew their swords and rushed forward. Arista felt the vibration of charging men. They screamed like beasts, their faces wild. They struck the line in the center. There was no prepared weak point—Emery and Pool were dead, the tactic lost.

She heard cries, screams, the clanging of metal against metal, and the dull thumps of swords against wooden shields. Soldiers pushed forward and the line broke in two. Perin was supposed to lead the left flank in a folding maneuver. He lay in the mud, blood running down his face. His branch of the line disconnected from the rest and quickly routed. The main line also failed, disintegrated, and disappeared. Men fought in a swirling turmoil of swords, broken shields, blood, and body parts.

Arista remained where she had collapsed. She felt a tugging on her arm and looked up to see the blonde woman again. "Get up! You'll be killed!" She had a hold on her wrist and dragged Arista to her feet. All around them men screamed, shouted, and grunted. Water splashed, mud flew, and blood sprayed. The hand squeezing her wrist hauled her backward. She thought of Emery lying in the mud and tried to pull away.

"No!" the blonde snapped, jerking her once more. "Are you crazy?" The woman dragged her to the armory entrance, but once she reached the door, Arista refused to go in any farther and remained at the opening, watching the battle.

The skill and experience of the garrison guards overwhelmed the citizens. They cut through the people of Ratibor and pushed them against the walls of the buildings. Every puddle was dark with blood, every shirt and face stained red. Mud and manure mixed and churned with severed limbs and blood. Everywhere she looked lay bodies. Dead men with open, lifeless eyes and those writhing in pain lay scattered across the square.

"We're going to lose," Arista said. "I did this."

The candlemaker, a tall thin man with curly hair, dropped his weapons and tried to run. Arista watched as six inches of sword came out of his stomach. She did not even know his name. A young bricklayer called Walter had his head crushed. Another man she had not met lost his arm.

Arista still held Emery's sword in one hand and clutched the doorframe with the other as the world spun around her. She felt sick and wanted to vomit. She could not move or turn away from the carnage. They would all die, and it was her fault. "I killed us all."

"Maybe not." The blonde caught Arista's attention and pointed at the far end of the square. "Look there!"

Arista saw a rush of movement coming up King's Street and heard the pounding of hooves. They came out of the haze of falling rain. Riding three and four abreast, horsemen charged into the square, shouting. One carried the pennant of the Nationalists, but the foremost brandished a huge sword, and she recognized him instantly.

Throwing up a spray of mud, Hadrian crossed the square. As he closed on the battle, he led the charge into the thickest of the soldiers. The garrison heard the cry and turned to see the band of horsemen rushing at them. Out front, Hadrian came at them like a demon, whirling his long blade, cleaving a swath through their ranks, cutting them down. The garrison broke and routed before the onslaught. When they found nowhere to retreat to, they threw down their weapons and pled for mercy.

Spotting Arista, Hadrian leapt to the ground and ran to her. Arista found it hard to breathe, and the last of her strength gave out. She fell to her knees, shaking. Hadrian reached down, surrounding her in his arms, and pulled her up.

"The city is yours, Your Highness," he said.

She dropped Emery's sword, threw her arms around his neck, and cried.

Chapter 17

Degan Gaunt

The rain stopped. The sun, so long delayed, returned full face to a bright blue sky. The day quickly grew hot as Hadrian made his way around the square through the many mud-covered bodies, searching for anyone who was still alive. Everywhere seemed to be the muffled wails and weeping of wives, mothers, fathers, and sons. Families pulled their loved ones from the bloody mire and carried them home to wash them for a proper burial. Hadrian stiffened when he spotted Dr. Gerand gently closing the lifeless eyes of Carat. Not far from him, Adam sat slumped against the armory. He looked as if he had merely walked over and sat down for a moment to rest.

"Over here!"

He spotted a woman with long blonde hair motioning to him. Hadrian quickly crossed to where she squatted over the body of an imperial soldier.

"He's still alive," she said. "Help me get him out of the mud. I can't believe no one saw him."

"Oh, I think they saw him," Hadrian replied as he gripped the soldier under his back and knees and lifted him.

He carried the man to the silversmith's porch and laid him

down gently as the woman ran to the well for a bucket of clean water.

Hadrian shed his own bloodstained shirt. "Here," he said, offering the linen to the woman.

"Thank you," she replied. She took the shirt and began rinsing it in the bucket. "Are you certain you don't mind me using this to help an imperial guard?"

"My father taught me that a man is only your enemy until he falls."

She nodded. "Your father sounds like a wise man," she said, and wrung the excess water from the shirt, then began to clean the soldier's face and chest, looking for the wound.

"He was. My name is Hadrian, by the way."

"Miranda," she replied. "Pleased to meet you. Thank you for saving our lives. I assume the Nationalists defeated Lord Dermont?"

Hadrian nodded. "It wasn't much of a battle. We caught them sleeping."

Pulling up the soldier's hauberk and tearing back his tunic, she wiped his skin and found a puncture streaming blood.

"I hope you aren't terribly attached to this shirt," she told Hadrian as she tore it in two. She used half as a pad, and the other half to tie it tight about the man's waist. "Let's hope that will stop the bleeding. A few stitches would help, but I doubt a needle could be spared for him right now."

Hadrian looked the man over. "I think he'll live, thanks to you."

This brought a shallow smile to her lips. She dipped her blood-covered hands in the bucket and splashed water on her face. Looking out across the square, she muttered, "So many dead."

Hadrian nodded.

Her eyes landed on Carat, a hand went to her mouth, and

her eyes started to tear. "He was such a help to us," she said. "Someone said he was a thief, but he proved himself a hero today. Who would have thought that thieves would stick out their necks? I saw their leader, Polish, shoot the sheriff."

Hadrian smiled. "If you ask him, he'll tell you you're mistaken."

"Thieves with hearts, who'd have thought?" she said.

"I'm not so sure I would go that far."

"No? Then where are the vultures?"

Hadrian looked up at the sky, then, realizing his own stupidity, shook his head. "You mean the looters?" He looked around. "You're right. I didn't even notice until now."

She nodded. Hadrian's medallion reflected the sunlight, catching her eye. Miranda pointed. "That necklace, where did you get it?"

"My father."

"Your father? Really? My older brother has one just like it."

Hadrian's heart raced. "Your brother has a necklace like this?"

She nodded.

Hadrian looked around the square, suddenly concerned. "Is he..."

She thought a moment. "I don't think so," she said. "At least, my heart tells me he's still alive."

Hadrian tried to control his racing thoughts. "How old is your brother?"

"I think he'd be about forty now, I guess."

"You guess?"

She nodded. "We never celebrated his birthday, which was always kind of strange. You see, my mother adopted him. She was the midwife at his birth and..." She hesitated. "Things didn't go well. Anyway, my mother kept an amulet just like yours and gave it to my brother as his inheritance the day he left home."

"What do you mean things didn't go well with the birth?" Hadrian asked.

"The mother died—that sort of thing happens, you know. Mothers die all the time in childbirth. It's not at all uncommon. It just happens. We should probably look for other wounded—"

"You're lying," Hadrian shot back.

She started to stand but Hadrian grabbed her arm. "This is very important. I must know everything you can tell me about the night your brother was born."

She hesitated but Hadrian held her tight.

"It wasn't her fault. There was nothing she could do. They were all dead. She was just scared. Who wouldn't be!"

"It's okay. I'm not accusing your mother of anything. I just need to know what happened." He held up his amulet. "This necklace belonged to my father. He was there that night."

"Your father, but no one…" He saw realization in her eyes. "The swordsman covered in blood?"

"Yes." Hadrian nodded. "Does your mother still live in the city? Can I speak to her?"

"My mother died several years ago."

"Do you know what happened? I have to know. It's very important."

She looked around, and when she was sure no one could overhear, she said, "A priest came to my mother one night looking for a midwife and took her to a boardinghouse, where a woman was giving birth. While my mother worked to deliver the baby, a fight started on the street. My mother had just delivered the first child—"

"First child?"

Miranda nodded. "She could see another was on the way, but men in black broke into the room. My mother hid in a wardrobe. The husband fought, but they killed his wife, child, and another man who came to help. The father took off his necklace—like the one you wear—and put it around the neck of the dead baby. There was still fighting on the street out front and the husband ran out of the room.

"My mother was terrified. She said there was blood everywhere, and the poor woman and her baby…But she summoned the courage to slip out of the wardrobe. She remembered the second child and knew it would die if she didn't do something. She picked up a knife and delivered it.

"From the window she saw the husband die, and the street was filled with a dozen bodies. A swordsman covered in blood was killing everyone. She didn't know what was happening. She was terrified and certain he would kill her too. With the second child in her arms, she took the necklace from the dead baby and fled. She pretended the baby was hers and never told anyone what really happened until the night she died—when she told me."

"Why did she take the necklace?"

"She said it was because the father meant it for his child."

"But you don't believe that?"

She shrugged. "Look at it." She pointed at his amulet. "It's made of silver. My mother was a very poor woman. But it's not like she sold it. In the end, she did give it to him."

"What's your brother's name?"

She looked puzzled. "I thought you knew. I mean, you were with the Nationalists, weren't you?"

"How would being with—"

"My brother is the leader of the Nationalist army."

"Oh." Hadrian's hopes sank. "Your brother is Commander Parker?"

"No, no, my name is Miranda Gaunt. My brother is Degan."

⚜

She had not fought or taken blows, but Arista felt battered and beaten. She sat in what until that morning had been the viceroy's office. A huge, gaudy chamber, it contained all that had survived the burning of the old royal palace. Night had fallen, heralding a close to the longest day she could recall. Memories of that morning were already distant, from another year, another life.

Outside, the flicker of bonfires bloomed in the square, where they had sentenced Emery to die. Die he did, but his dream survived, his promise fulfilled. She could hear the citizens of Ratibor singing and saw their shadows dance. They toasted Emery with mugs of beer and celebrated his victory with lambs on spits. A decidedly different gathering than the one the sheriff had planned.

Inside, Arista sat with a dozen men with concerned faces.

"We insist you take the crown of Rhenydd," Dr. Gerand repeated, his voice carrying over the others.

"I agree," Perin said. Since the battle, the big grocer, who had been designated to lead the failed left flank and was wounded in the fight, had become a figure of legend. He found himself thrust into the ad hoc city council, hastily composed of the city's most revered surviving citizens.

Several other heads nodded. She did not know them but guessed they owned large farms or businesses—commoners all. None of the former nobility remained after the imperial takeover and all the Imperialists were either dead or imprisoned. Viceroy Androus, evicted from his office, was relocated to a prison cell along with the city guards who had surrendered. A handful of other city officials and Laven, the man who had argued with Emery in the Gnome, waited to stand trial for crimes against the citizenry.

After the battle had ended, Arista had helped organize the treatment of the wounded. People kept returning to her, asking what to do next. She directed them to bury the bodies of those without families outside the city. There was a brief ceremony presided over by Monsignor Bartholomew.

The wounded and dying overwhelmed the armory, and makeshift hospitals were created in the Dunlaps' barn and rooms commandeered at the Gnome. People also volunteered their private homes, particularly those with beds recently made empty. With the work of cleaning up the dead and wounded under way, the question of what to do with the viceroy and the other imperial supporters arose, along with a dozen other inquiries. Arista suggested they form a council to decide what should be done. They did, and their first official act was to summon her to the viceroy's old office.

The decision was unanimous. The council had voted to appoint Arista ruling queen of the kingdom of Rhenydd.

"There is no one else here of noble blood," Perin said. He wore a bloodstained bandage around his head. "No one else who even knows how to govern."

"But Emery envisioned a republic," Arista told them. "A self-determining government, like they have in Delgos. This was his dream—the reason he fought, the reason he died."

"But we don't know how to do that," Dr. Gerand said. "We need experience and you have it."

"He's right." Perin spoke up again. "Perhaps in a few months we could hold elections, but Sir Breckton and his army are still on their way. We need action. We need the kind of leadership that won us this city, or come tomorrow, we'll lose it again."

Arista sighed and looked over at Hadrian, who sat near the window. As commander of the Nationalist army, he had also received an invitation.

"What do you think?" she asked.

"I'm no politician."

"I'm not asking you to be. I just want to know what you think."

"Royce once told me two people can argue over the same point and both can be right. I thought he was nutty, but I'm not so sure anymore, because I think you're both right. The moment you become queen, you'll destroy any chance of this becoming the kind of free republic Emery spoke of, but if someone doesn't take charge—and fast—that hope will die anyway. And they're right. If I were going to choose anyone to rule, it would be you. As an outsider, you have no bias, no chance of favoritism—you'll be fair. And everyone already loves you."

"They don't love me. They don't even know me."

"They think they do, and they trust you. You can give directions and people will listen. And right now, that's what is needed."

"I can't be queen. Emery wanted a republic, and a republic he will have. You can appoint me temporary mayor of Ratibor and steward of the kingdom. I'll administer only until a proper government can be established, at which time I'll resign and return to Melengar." She nodded more to herself than to any of them. "Yes, that way I'll be in a position to ensure it gets done."

The men in the room muttered in agreement. After addressing a few of the more pressing matters, the council filed out of City Hall into the square, leaving Arista and Hadrian alone. Outside, the constant noise of the crowd grew quiet and then exploded with cheers.

"You're very popular, Your Highness," Hadrian told her.

"Too popular. They want to commission a statue of me."

"I heard that. They want to put it in the West End Square, one of you holding up that sword."

"It's not over yet. Breckton is almost here, and we don't even know if Royce got through. What if he never made it? What if he did and Alric doesn't listen? He might not think it possible to take Ratibor, and refuse to put the kingdom at risk. We need to be certain."

"You want me to go?"

"No," she said. "I want you here. I *need* you here. But if Breckton lays siege, we'll eventually fall, and by then it'll be too late for you to get away. Our only hope is if Alric's forces can turn Breckton's attention away from us."

He nodded and his hand played with the amulet around his neck. "I suppose it doesn't matter where I go for a while."

"What do you mean?"

"Esrahaddon was in Gaunt's camp. He's been helping the Nationalists."

"Did you tell him about the heir?"

Hadrian nodded. "And you were right. The heir is alive. I think he's Degan Gaunt."

"Degan Gaunt is the heir?"

"Funny, huh? The voice of the common man is also the heir to the imperial throne. There was another child born that night. The midwife took the surviving twin. No one else knew. I've no idea how Esrahaddon figured it out, but that explains why he's been helping Gaunt."

"Where is Esrahaddon now?"

"Don't know. I haven't seen him since the battle started."

"You don't think . . ."

"Hmm? Oh no. I'm sure he's fine. He hung back when we engaged Dermont's forces. I suspect he's off to find Gaunt and will contact me and Royce once he does." Hadrian sighed. "I wish my father could have known he didn't fail after all.

"Anyway, I'll take care of things tonight before I leave. I'll put one of the regiment captains in charge of the army. There's a guy named Renquist who seems intelligent. I'll have him see to the walls, patch up the stonework, ready gate defenses, put up sentries, guards, and archers. He should know how to do all of that. And I'll put together a list of things you'll want to do, like bring the entire army and the surrounding farmers within the city walls and seal it up. You should do that right away."

"You'll be leaving in the morning, then?"

He nodded. "Doubt I'll see you again before I go, so I'll say goodbye now. You've done the impossible, Arista—excuse me—Your Highness."

"Arista is just fine," she told him. "I'm going to miss you." It was all she could say. Words were too small to express gratitude so immense.

He opened his mouth but hesitated. He smiled then and said, "Take care of yourself, Your Highness."

◆

In her dream, Thrace could see the beast coming for her father. He stood smiling warmly at her, his back to the monster. She tried to scream for him to run, but only a soft muffled moan escaped. She tried to wave her arms and draw his attention to the danger, but her limbs were heavy as lead and refused to move. She tried to run to him, but her feet were stuck, frozen in place.

The beast had no trouble moving.

It charged down the hill. Her poor father took no notice, even though the beast shook the ground as it ran. It consumed him completely with a single swallow, and she fell, as if pierced through the heart. She collapsed onto the grass, struggling to breathe. In the distance, the beast was coming for her now, coming to finish the job, coming to swallow her up—his legs squeaking louder and louder as he advanced.

She woke up in a cold sweat.

She was sleeping on her stomach in her feather bed with the pillow folded up around her face. She hated sleeping. Sleep always brought nightmares. She stayed awake as long as possible, many nights sitting on the floor in front of the little window, watching the stars and listening to the sounds outside. There was a whole symphony of frogs that croaked in the moat and a chorus of crickets. Fireflies sometimes passed by her tiny sliver of the world. But eventually, sleep found her.

The dream had been the same every night. She was on the hill, her father unaware of his impending death, and there was never anything she could do to prevent it. However, tonight's dream had been different. Usually it ended when the beast devoured her, but this time she had woken early, and something else was different. When the beast came that night, it had made a squeaking sound. Even for a dream, that seemed strange.

Then she heard it again. The sound entered through her window.

Squeak...squeak...squeak!

There were other noises too, sounds of men talking. They spoke quietly but their voices drifted up from the courtyard below. She went to the window and peered out. As many as a dozen men with torches drew a wagon whose large wooden wheels squeaked once with each revolution. The wagon was a large box with a small barred window cut in the side, like the kind that would hold a lion for a traveling circus. The men were dressed in black-and-scarlet armor. She had seen that armor before, while in Dahlgren.

One man stood out. He was tall and thin with long black hair and a short, neatly trimmed beard.

The wagon came to a stop and the knights gathered.

"He's chained, isn't he?" she heard one of them say.

"Why? Are you frightened?"

"He's not a wizard," the tall man scolded. "He can't turn you into a frog. His powers are political, not mystical."

"Come now, Luis, even Saldur said not to underestimate him. Legends speak of strange abilities. He's part god."

"You believe too much in church doctrine. We're the protectorate of the faith. We don't have to wallow in superstition like ignorant peasants."

"That sounds blasphemous."

"The truth can never be blasphemous, so long as it's tempered with an understanding of what's good and right. The truth is a powerful thing, like a crossbow. You wouldn't hand a child a loaded crossbow and say, 'Run and play,' would you? People get killed that way, tragedies occur. The truth must be kept safe, reserved only for those capable of handling it. This—this sacrilegious treasure in a box—is one truth above all that must be kept a secret. It must never again see the light of day. We will bury it deep beneath the castle. We will seal it in for all time and it will become the cornerstone on which we will build a new and glorious empire that will eclipse the previous one and wash away the sins of our forefathers."

She watched as they opened the rear of the wagon and pulled out a man. A black hood covered his face. Chains bound his hands and ankles, yet the men treated him carefully, as if he could explode at any minute.

With four men on either side, they marched him across the courtyard out of the sight of her narrow window.

She watched as they rolled the wagon back out and closed the gate behind them. Modina stared at the empty courtyard for more than an hour, until, at last, she fell asleep again.

అ

The carriage bounced through the night on the rough, hilly road, following a sliver of open sky between walls of forest. The jangle of harnesses, the thudding of hooves, and the crush of wheels dominated this world. The night's air was heavily scented with the aroma of pond water and a skunk's spray.

Arcadius, the lore master of Sheridan University, peered out the open window and hammered on the roof with his walking stick until the driver brought the carriage to a halt.

"What is it?" the driver shouted.

"This will be fine," the lore master replied, grabbing up his bag and slipping it over his shoulder.

"What is?"

"I'm getting out here." Arcadius popped open the little door and carefully climbed out onto the desolate road. "Yes, this is fine." He closed the door and lightly patted the side of the carriage as if it were a horse.

The lore master walked to the front of the coach. The driver sat on the raised bench with his coat drawn up around his neck, a formless sack hat pulled down over his ears. Between his thighs he trapped a small corked jug. "But there's nothing here, sir," he insisted.

"Don't be absurd; of course there is. You're here, aren't you? And so am I." Arcadius pulled open his bag. "And look, there are some nice trees and this excellent road we've been riding on."

"But it's the middle of the night, sir."

Arcadius tilted his head up. "And just look at that wonderful starry sky. It's beautiful, don't you think? Do you know your constellations, good man?"

"No, sir."

"Pity." He measured out some silver coins and handed them up to the driver. "It's all up there, you know. Wars, heroes, beasts, and villains, the past and the future spread above us each night like a dazzling map." He pointed. "That long, elegant set of four bright stars is Persephone, and she, of course, is always beside Novron. If you follow the line that looks like Novron's arm, you can see how they just barely touch—lovers longing to be together."

The driver looked up. "Just looks like a bunch of scattered dust to me."

"It does to a great many people. Too many people."

The driver looked down at him and frowned. "You sure you want me to just leave you? I can come back if you want."

"That won't be necessary, but thank you."

"Suit yourself. Good night." The carriage driver slapped the reins and the coach rolled out, circled in a field, and returned the way it had come. The driver glanced up at the sky twice, shaking his head each time. The carriage and the team rode away, the horses' clopping became softer and softer until it faded below the harsh shrill of nightly noises.

Arcadius stood alone, observing the world. It had been some time since the old professor had been out in the wild. He had forgotten how loud it was. The high-pitched trill of crickets punctuated the oscillating echoes of tree frogs, which peeped with the regular rhythm of a human heart. Winds rustled a million leaves, fashioning the voice of waves at sea.

Arcadius walked along the road, crossing the fresh grooves of the carriage wheels. His shoes on the dirt made a surprisingly large amount of noise. The dark had a way of drawing attention to the normally invisible, silent, and ignored. That was why

Michael J. Sullivan

nights were so frightening. Without the distraction of light, the doors to other senses were unlocked. To children, the dark spoke of the monster beneath the bed. To adults, it spoke of the intruder. To old men, it was the herald of death on its way.

"Long, hard, and rocky is the road we walk in old age," he muttered to his feet.

He stopped when he reached a post lurching at a crossroad. The sign declared RATIBOR to the right and AQUESTA to the left. He stepped off the road into the tall grass and found a fallen log to sit on. He pulled the shoulder strap of the sack over his head and set it down. Rummaging through the bag, he found a honeyed muffin, one of three he had pilfered from the dinner table at the inn. He was old, but his sleight of hand was still impressive. Royce would have been proud—less so if he found out that Arcadius had paid for the meal, which had included the muffins. Still, the big swarthy fellow at his elbow would have poached them if he had not acted first. Now it looked as if they would come in handy, as he had no idea when—

He heard hoofbeats long before he saw the horse. The sound came from the direction of Ratibor. As unlikely as it was for anyone else to be on that road at that hour, the lore master's heart nevertheless increased until, at last, the rider cleared the trees. A woman rode alone in a dark hood and cloak. She came to a stop at the post.

"You're late," he said.

She whirled around, relaxing when she recognized him. "No, I'm early. You are just earlier."

"Why are you alone? It's too dangerous. These roads are—"

"And who would you suggest I trust to escort me? Have you added to our ranks?"

She dismounted and tied her horse to the post.

"You could have paid some young lad. There must be a few in the city you trust."

"Those I trust would be of no aid, and those that could help, I don't trust. Besides, this isn't far. I couldn't have been on the road for more than two hours. And there's not much between Ratibor and here." Before she reached him, he started to rise. "You don't have to get up."

"How else can I give you a hug?" He embraced her. "Now tell me, how have you been? I was very worried."

"You worry too much. I'm fine." She drew back her hood, revealing long blonde hair, which she wore scooped back.

"The city has been taken?" Arcadius asked.

"The Nationalists have it now. They attacked and defeated Lord Dermont's forces in the field and the princess led a revolt against Sheriff Vigan in the city. Sir Breckton and the Northern Imperial Army arrived too late. With the city buttoned up and Dermont dead, Breckton's army turned around and headed back north."

"I passed part of his supply train. He's taking up a defensive position around Aquesta, I think. Hadrian and Arista? How are they?"

"Not a scratch on either," she replied. "Hadrian turned command of the Nationalist army over to a man named Renquist—one of the senior captains—and left the morning after the battle. I'm not sure where to."

"Did you have a chance to talk with him?"

She nodded. "Yes, I told him about my brother. Arcadius, do you know where Degan is?"

"Me?" He looked surprised. "No. The seret have him, I'm certain of that, but where is anyone's guess. They have gotten a whole lot smarter recently. It's like Guy has sprouted another head, and this one has a brain in it."

"Do you think they killed him?"

"I don't know, Miranda." The wizard paused, regretting his curt words, and looked at her sympathetically. "It's hard to fathom the imperial mind. We can hope they want him alive. Now that we've unleashed Hadrian, there's a good chance that he and Royce will save him. It could even be that Esrahaddon will connect the dots and send them."

"Esrahaddon already knows," Miranda said. "He's been with Degan for months."

"So he found out. Excellent. I thought he might. When he visited Sheridan, it was obvious he knew more than he let on."

"Maybe he and Hadrian are looking together—planned a place to meet up after the battle?"

The wizard stroked his chin thoughtfully. "Possible... probable, even. So those two are off looking for your brother. What about Arista? What is she doing?"

Miranda smiled. "She's running the city. The citizens of Ratibor were ready to proclaim her queen of Rhenydd, but she settled for mayor pro tem until elections can be held. She intends to honor Emery's dream of a republic in Rhenydd."

"A princess establishing the first republic in Avryn." Arcadius chuckled. "Quite the turn of events."

"The princess has cried a lot since the battle. I've watched her. She works constantly, settling disputes, inspecting the walls, appointing ministers. She falls asleep at her desk in City Hall. She cries when she thinks no one is looking."

"All that violence after so privileged a life."

"I think she might have been in love with a young man who was killed."

"In love? Really? That's surprising. She's never showed an interest in anyone. Who was he?"

"No one of note—the son of the dead bodyguard to King Urith."

"That's too bad," the wizard said sadly. "For all her privilege, she's not had an easy life."

"You didn't ask about Royce," she noted.

"I know about him. He arrived back in Medford not long before I set out. The next day, Melengar's army crossed the Galewyr. Alric has enlisted every able-bodied man and even a good deal of the boys. He's put Count Pickering, Sir Ecton, and Marquis Lanaklin in command. They broke through the little imperial force and at last report were sweeping south, causing a great deal of havoc. Another obstacle I had to travel around. Getting back to the university will take a month, I expect."

The wizard sighed and a look of concern passed over his face. "Two things still trouble me. First, Aquesta is threatened by an enemy army resting in Ratibor, and they aren't negotiating or evacuating. Second, there's Marius."

"Who?"

"Merrick Marius, also known as Cutter."

"Isn't he the one who put Royce in Manzant?"

"Yes, and now he's working for the New Empire. He's a wild card I hadn't expected." The old man paused. "You're certain that Hadrian believed everything you said?"

"Absolutely. His eyes nearly fell out of his head when I told him Degan was the heir." She sighed. "Are you sure we—"

"I'm sure, Miranda. Make no mistake. We're doing what's absolutely right and necessary. It's imperative that Royce and Hadrian never find out the truth."

BOOK IV

THE EMERALD STORM

Chapter 1

Assassin

Merrick Marius fitted a bolt into the small crossbow before slipping the weapon beneath the folds of his cloak. Smoke-thin clouds drifted across the sliver of moon, leaving him and Central Square shrouded in darkness. Looking for movement, he searched the filthy streets lined with ramshackle buildings, but found none. At this hour, the city was deserted.

Ratibor may be a pit, he thought, *but at least it's easy to work in.*

Conditions had improved since the Nationalists' recent victory. The imperial guards were gone, and without them the regular patrols had stopped. The town lacked even an experienced sheriff, as the new mayor refused to hire seasoned men or members of the military to administer so-called law and order. Instead, she had opted to make do with grocery clerks, shoemakers, and dairy farmers. Merrick thought her choices were ill-advised, but he expected such mistakes from an inexperienced noble. Not that he was complaining—he appreciated the help.

Despite this shortcoming, he admired Arista Essendon's accomplishments. In Melengar, her brother, King Alric, reigned, and as an unwed princess, she possessed no real power. Then she had come here and masterminded a revolt, and the surviving peasants had rewarded her with the keys to the city. She was a foreigner and a royal, yet they thanked her for taking rule over them. *Brilliant.* He could not have done better himself.

A slight smile formed at the edge of Merrick's lips as he watched her from the street. A candle still burned on the second floor of City Hall, even at this late hour. Her figure moved hazily behind the curtains as she left her desk.

It will not be long now, he thought.

Merrick shifted his grip on the weapon. Only a foot and a half long, with a bow span even shorter, it lacked the penetration strength of a traditional crossbow. Still, it would be enough. His target wore no armor, and he was not relying on the force of the bolt. Venden pox coated the serrated steel tip. A deplorable poison for assassination, it neither killed quickly nor paralyzed the victim. The concoction would certainly kill, but only after what he considered an unprofessional span of time. He had never used it before, and had only recently learned of its most important trait—venden pox was invulnerable to magic. Merrick had it on good authority that the most powerful spells and incantations would be useless against its venom. Given his target, this would prove to be essential.

Another figure entered Arista's room, and she sat abruptly. Merrick thought she had just received some interesting news and he was about to cross the street to listen at the window when the tavern door behind him opened. A pair of patrons exited, and by the sway of their steps and the volume of their voices, he could tell they had drained more than one mug that night.

"Nestor, who's that leaning against the post?" one said,

pointing in Merrick's direction. A plump man with a strawberry nose whose shape matched its color squinted in the dim light and staggered forward.

"How should I know?" said the other. The thin man's mustache still glistened with beer foam.

"What's he doing here at this time of night?"

"Again, how should I know, you git?"

"Well, ask him."

The tall man stepped forward. "Whatcha doing, mister? Holding up the post so the porch doesn't fall down?" Nestor snorted a laugh and doubled over with his hands on his knees.

"Actually," Merrick told them, his tone so serious it was almost grave, "I'm waiting to appoint the position of town fool to the person who asks me the stupidest question. Congratulations. You win."

The thin man slapped his friend on the shoulder. "See? I've been telling you all night how funny I am, and you haven't laughed once. Now I'm getting a new job...probably pays better than yours."

"Oh yeah, you're quite the entertainer," his friend assured him as they staggered off into the night. "You should audition at the theater. They're gonna be doing *The Crown Conspiracy* for the mayor. The day I see you on a stage—now *that* will be funny."

Merrick's mood turned sour. He had seen that play several years ago. While the two thieves depicted in it used different names, he was sure they portrayed Royce Melborn and Hadrian Blackwater. Royce had once been Merrick's best friend, back when the two of them were assassins for the Diamond. That friendship had ended seventeen years earlier on that warm summer night when Royce murdered Jade.

Although he had not been present, Merrick had imagined the scene countless times. That was before Royce had his white dagger, back when he had used a pair of curved, black-handled kharolls. Merrick knew Royce's technique well enough to picture him silently slicing through Jade with both blades at once. Merrick did not care that someone had set up Royce, or that he had not known his victim's identity when it happened. All Merrick knew was that the woman he loved was dead and his best friend had killed her.

Nearly two decades had passed, and still Jade and Royce haunted him. He could not think of one without the other, and he could not bear to forget. Love and hate welded together forever, intertwined in a knot too tight to untie.

Loud noises and shouts from Arista's room pulled Merrick back to the present. He checked his weapon, then crossed the street.

⊰

"Your Highness?" the soldier asked, entering the mayoral office.

Her hair a tangled mess and eyes wreathed in shadow, Princess Arista looked up from her cluttered desk. She took a moment to assess her visitor. The man in mismatched armor displayed an expression of unabated annoyance.

This is not going to go well, she thought.

"You sent for me?" he asked with only partially restrained irritation.

"Yes, Renquist," she said, her mind catching up with his face. She had hardly slept in two days and was having difficulty concentrating. "I asked you here to—"

"Princess, you can't be summoning me like this. I have an army to run and a war to win. I don't have time to chat."

"Chat? I wouldn't call you here if it wasn't important."

Renquist rolled his eyes.

"I need you to remove the army from the city."

"What?"

"It can't be helped. Your men are causing trouble. I'm getting daily reports of soldiers bullying merchants and destroying property. There has even been an accusation of rape. You must take your men out of the city where they can be controlled."

"My men risked their lives against the Imperialists. The least this lousy city can do is feed and house them. Now you want me to take away their beds and the roof over their heads as well?"

"The merchants and farmers refuse to feed them because they can't," Arista explained. "The empire confiscated the city's reserves when the Imperialists took control. The rains and the war destroyed most of this year's crops. The city doesn't have enough to feed its citizens, much less an army. Fall is here, and cold weather is on its way. These people don't know how they will survive the winter. They can't take care of themselves with a thousand soldiers raiding their shops and farms. We're thankful for your contribution in taking the city, but your continued presence threatens to destroy what you risked your lives to liberate. You must leave."

"If I force them back into camps with inadequate food and leaky canvas shelters, half will desert. As it is, many are talking of going home for the harvest season. I shouldn't have to tell you that if this army disappears, the empire will take this city back."

Arista shook her head. "When Degan Gaunt was in charge, the Nationalist army lived under similar conditions for months without it being a problem. The soldiers are becoming complacent here in Ratibor. Perhaps it's time you pressed on to Aquesta."

Renquist stiffened at the suggestion. "Gaunt's capture makes taking Aquesta all the more difficult. I need time to gather information and I'm waiting for reinforcements and supplies from Delgos. Attacking the capital won't be like taking Vernes or Ratibor. The Imperialists will fight to the last man to defend their empress. No. We need to stay here until I'm fully prepared."

"Wait if you must, but not here," she replied firmly.

"What if I refuse?" His eyes narrowed.

Arista put the parchments she was holding on the desk but said nothing.

"My army conquered this city," he told her pointedly. "You hold authority only because *I* allow it. I don't take orders from you. You're not a princess here, and I'm not your serf. My responsibility is to my men, not to this city and certainly not to you."

Arista slowly rose.

"I'm the mayor of this city," she said, her voice growing in authority, "appointed by the people. Furthermore, I'm steward and acting administrator of all of Rhenydd, again by the consent of those who live here. You and your army are here by *my* leave."

"You are a princess from Melengar! At least *I* was born in Rhenydd."

"Regardless of your personal feelings toward me, you'll respect the authority of this office and do as I say."

"And if I don't?" he asked coldly.

Renquist's reaction did not surprise Arista. He had been a career soldier serving with King Urith, as well as the imperial army, before joining the rebel Nationalists when Kilnar fell. When Gaunt had disappeared, Renquist had been appointed commander in chief, a position far higher in rank than he could ever have hoped for. Now he was finally realizing the power he possessed and starting to assert himself. She had hoped he would demonstrate the same spirit Emery had shown, but Renquist was not a commoner with the heart of a nobleman. If she did not take action now, Arista could find herself facing a military overthrow.

"This city just liberated itself from one tyrant, and I won't allow it to fall under the heel of another. If you refuse to obey me, I'll replace you as commander."

"And how will you do that?"

Arista revealed a faint smile. "Think hard…I'm sure you can figure it out."

Renquist continued to stare at her, and then his eyes widened in realization and fear flashed across his face.

"Yes," she told him, "the rumors about me are true. Now take your army out of the city before I feel a need to prove it. You have just one day to remove them. Scouts found a suitable valley to the north. I suggest you camp where the river crosses the road. It's far enough away to prevent further trouble. By heading north, your men will feel they're progressing toward the goal of Aquesta, thus helping morale."

"Don't tell me how to run my army," he snapped, although not as loudly, nor as confidently, as before.

"My apologies," she said with a bow of her head. "That was only a suggestion. The order to leave the city, however, is not. Good evening to you, sir."

Renquist hesitated, his breath labored, his hands balled into fists.

"I said, good evening, sir."

He muttered a curse and slammed the door as he left.

Exhausted, Arista slumped in her chair.

Why does everything have to be so hard?

Everyone wanted something from her now: food, shelter, assurances that everything would be all right. The citizens looked at her and saw hope, but Arista could see little herself. Plagued by endless problems and surrounded by people, she felt oddly alone.

Arista laid her head on her desk and closed her eyes.

Just a few minutes' catnap, she told herself. *Then I'll get up and figure out how to deal with the shortage of grain and look into the reports of the mistreatment of prisoners.*

Since she had become mayor, a hundred issues had demanded her attention, such as who should be entitled to harvest the fields owned by farmers who had been lost in battle. With food in short supply, and harsh autumn weather threatening, she needed a quick solution. At least these problems distracted her from thinking about her own loss. Like everyone in town, Arista remained haunted by the Battle of Ratibor. She bore no visible injury—her pain came from a memory, a face seen at night, when her heart ached as if pierced. It would never fully heal. There would always be a wound, a deformity, a noticeable scar for the rest of her life.

When she finally fell asleep, thoughts of Emery, held at bay during her waking hours, invaded her dreams. He appeared, as always, sitting at the foot of her bed, bathed in moonlight. Her breath shortened in anticipation of the kiss as he leaned forward, a smile across his lips. Abruptly he stiffened, and a drop of blood slipped from the corner of his mouth—a crossbow bolt protruding from his chest. She tried to cry out but could not make a sound. The dream had always been the same, but this time Emery spoke. "*There's no time left*," he told her, his face intent and urgent. "*It's up to you now.*"

She struggled to ask what he meant when—

"Your Highness." She felt a gentle hand jostle her shoulder.

Opening her eyes, Arista saw Orrin Flatly. The city scribe, who had once kept track of the punishment of rebels in Central Square, had volunteered to be her secretary. His cold efficiency had given her pause but eventually she had realized that there was no crime in doing one's job well. Her decision had proved sound and he had turned out to be a loyal, diligent worker. Still, waking to his expressionless face was disturbing.

"What is it?" she asked, wiping her eyes and feeling for the tears that should have been there.

"Someone is here to see you. I explained you were occupied, but he insists. He's very…" Orrin shifted uncomfortably. "…hard to ignore."

"Who is he?"

"He refused to give his name, but he said you knew him and claims his business is of utmost importance. He insists that he must speak to you immediately."

"Okay." Arista nodded drowsily. "Give me a moment and then send him in."

Orrin left, and in his absence, she smoothed the wrinkles from her dress to ensure her appearance was at least marginally presentable. Having lived the life of a commoner for so long, what Arista deemed acceptable had reached an appallingly low level. Checking her hair in a mirror, she wondered where the Princess of Melengar had gone and if she would ever return.

While she was inspecting herself, the door opened. "How may I help—"

Esrahaddon stood in the doorway, wearing the same flowing robe whose color Arista could never determine. His arms, as always, were lost in its shimmering folds. His beard was longer, and gray streaked his hair, making him appear older than she remembered. She had not seen the wizard since that morning on the bank of the Nidwalden River.

"What are *you* doing here?" she asked, her warm tone icing over.

"I'm pleased to see you as well, Your Highness."

After admitting the wizard, Orrin had left the doors open. With a glance from Esrahaddon, they swung shut.

"I see you're getting along better without hands these days," Arista said.

"One adapts to one's needs," he replied, sitting opposite her.

"I didn't extend an invitation for you to sit."

"I didn't ask for one."

Arista's own chair slammed into the backs of her legs, causing her to fall into it.

"How are you doing that with no hands or sound?" she asked, disarmed by her own curiosity.

"The lessons are over, or don't you remember declaring that at our last meeting?"

Arista hardened her composure once more. "I remember. I also thought I made it clear I never wanted to see you again."

"Yes, yes, that's all well and good, but I need your help to locate the heir."

"Lost him again, have you?"

Esrahaddon ignored her. "We can find him with a basic location spell."

"I'm not interested in your games. I have a city to run."

"We need to perform the spell immediately. We can do it right here, right now. I've a good idea where he is, but time is short and I can't afford to run off in the wrong direction. So clear your desk and we can get started."

"I have no intention of doing anything of the sort."

"Arista, you know I can't do this alone. I need your help."

The princess glared at him. "You should have thought of that before you arranged my father's murder. What I should do is order your execution."

"You don't understand. This is important. Thousands of lives are at stake. This is larger than your loss. It's larger than the loss of a hundred kings and a thousand fathers. You are not the only one to suffer. Do you think I enjoyed rotting in a prison for a thousand years? Yes, I used you and your father to escape. I did so out of necessity—because what I protect is more important than any single person. Now stop this foolishness. We're running out of time."

"I'm so happy to be of no service to you." She smirked. "I can't bring my father back, and I know I could never kill you, nor would you allow yourself to be imprisoned again. This is truly a gift—the opportunity to repay you for what you took from me."

Esrahaddon sighed and shook his head. "You don't really hate me, Arista. It's guilt that's eating you. It's knowing that you had as much to do with your father's death as I. But the church is the one to blame. They orchestrated the events so I would escape and hopefully lead them to the heir. They enticed you to Gutaria, knowing I would use you."

"Get out!" Arista got to her feet, her face flushed red. "Orrin! Guards!"

The scribe struggled with the door, and it opened a crack, but a slight glance from Esrahaddon slammed it again. "Your Highness, I'll get help," Orrin said, his voice coming from behind the door.

"You need to forgive yourself, Arista."

"*Get out!*" she screamed. With a wave of her hand, the office door burst open, nearly coming free from the hinges.

Esrahaddon got up and moved toward the door, adding, "You need to realize you didn't kill your father any more than I did."

After he left the room, Arista slammed the door and sat on the floor with her back against it. She wanted to scream, *It wasn't my fault!* even though she knew that was a lie. In the years since her father's death, she had hid from the truth, but she could hide no longer. As difficult as it was to admit, Esrahaddon was right.

᧦

Esrahaddon stepped out of City Hall into the darkness of Ratibor's Central Square. He looked back and sighed. He genuinely liked Arista. He wished he could tell her everything, but the risk was too great. Even though he was free of Gutaria Prison, he feared the church still listened to his conversations — not every word, as when he had been incarcerated, but Mawyndulë had the power to hear from vast distances. Therefore, Esrahaddon had to assume all conversations were suspect. A single slip, the casual mention of a name, and he could ruin everything.

Time was growing short but at least now there was no doubt that Arista *had* become a Cenzar. He had safely planted the seed, and the soil had proved fertile. He had begun to suspect her abilities on the morning of the Battle of Ratibor, when Hadrian had mentioned that the rain was not *supposed* to stop. He suspected Arista had cast the spell that had been instrumental to the Nationalists' victory. Since then, he had heard the rumors concerning the new mayor's *unnatural powers*. But it was only when she broke his locking charm, with just a simple wave of her hand, that he knew for certain that Arista finally understood the Art.

Aside from Arcadius and him, no human wizards remained, and the two of them were pitiful representatives of the craft. Arcadius was nothing but an old hack, what Cenzars used to refer to as a *faquin*, an elven term for the most inept magician — knowledge without talent. *Faquins* never managed to transition from materials-based alchemy to the kinetic true version of the Art.

Esrahaddon did not consider himself any better. Without his hands, he was as much a magical cripple as a physical invalid. Now, however, with Arista's birth into the world of wizardry, mankind once again possessed a true artist. She was still a novice, a mere infant, but given time, her talent would grow. One day she would become more powerful than any king, emperor, warrior, or priest.

Knowing that she could hold sway over all mankind was more than a little disturbing. During the Old Empire, safeguards had existed. The Cenzar Council had overseen wielders of the Art and ensured its proper use. They were all gone now. The other wizards, his brethren and even the lesser mages, were dead. With him essentially castrated, the church thought they had eliminated the Cenzar threat from the world. Now a true practitioner of the Art had returned, and he was certain no one understood the danger this simple princess posed.

He needed her, and though she did not know it yet, she needed him. He could explain the Art's source and how they had come to use it. The Cenzars had been the guardians, the preservers, and the defenders. They had kept secrets that would protect mankind when the *Uli Vermar* ended.

When Esrahaddon had learned the truth so long ago, he had felt relieved that it would not be his problem to face, as the day of reckoning was centuries away. How ironic that his imprisonment in the timeless vault of Gutaria had extended his life to this time. What had once been forever in the future was now but months away. He allowed himself a bitter laugh, then walked to the center of the square to sit and think.

His plan was so tenuous, so weak, but all the pieces were in their proper places. Arista just needed time to master her feelings and then she would come around. Hadrian knew he was the Guardian of the Heir, and he had proved himself worthy of that legacy. Then there was the heir, an unlikely choice to be sure, but one that somehow made perfect sense.

Yes, it'll be all right, he concluded. *Things always work out in the end. At least, that is what Yolric always used to say.*

Yolric had been the wisest of them all and had been passionate about the world's ability to correct itself. Esrahaddon's greatest fear when the Old Empire fell had been that Yolric might side with Venlin. That the emperor's descendant still lived proved Esrahaddon's master had not helped the Patriarch find the emperor's son when the boy had been taken into hiding. Esrahaddon allowed himself a grin. He missed old Yolric. His teacher would be dead now. He had been ancient even when Esrahaddon was a boy.

Esrahaddon stretched his legs and tried to clear his mind. He needed to rest, but rest had eluded him for centuries. Rest was enjoyed only by men of clear conscience, and he had too much innocent blood on his hands. Too many people had given their lives for him to fail now.

Remembering Yolric opened the door to his past, and through it emerged faces of people long dead: his family, his friends, and the woman he had hoped to marry. It seemed his life before the fall had been merely a dream, but perhaps his current state was the real dream, a nightmare that he was trapped in. Maybe one day he would wake and find himself back in the palace with Nevrik, Jerish, and his beloved Elinya.

Did she somehow survive the destruction of the city?

He wanted to believe so, no matter how unlikely. It pleased him to think that she had escaped the end, but even that thought gave him little comfort.

What if she believed what they said about me afterward? Did she marry someone else, feeling betrayed? Did Elinya die at an old age, hating me?

He needed to stop thinking this way. What he had told Arista was true: the sacrifices they made were insignificant when compared to the goal. He should try to get some sleep. He rose and headed back toward the inn. A cloud covered the moon, snuffing out what little light it cast. As it did,

Esrahaddon felt a stabbing pain in his back. Crying out in anguish, he fell to his knees. Twisting at the waist, he felt his robe stick to his skin with a growing wetness.

I'm bleeding.

"*Venderia*," he whispered, and instantly his robe glowed, lighting up the square. At the fringe of its radiance, he caught a glimpse of a man dressed in a dark cloak. At first he thought it might be Royce. He shared the same callous gait and posture, but this man was taller and broader.

Esrahaddon muttered a curse and four beams supporting the porch directly over the man exploded into splinters. The heavy roof collapsed just as the man stepped out from under it. The force of the crashing timbers merely billowed his cloak.

With sweat coating his face and a stabbing pain in his back, Esrahaddon struggled to rise and confront his attacker, who walked casually toward him. The wizard concentrated. He spoke again, and the dirt of the square whirled into a tornado, traveling directly toward his attacker. It engulfed the man, who burst into flames. Esrahaddon could feel the heat of the inferno as the pillar surged, bathing the square in a yellow glow. At its center, the figure stood wreathed in blue tongues of flame, but when the fire faded, the man continued forward, unharmed.

Reaching the wizard, he looked curiously at Esrahaddon — the way a child might study a strange bug before crushing it. He said nothing, but revealed a silver medallion that hung from a chain he wore around his neck.

"Recognize this?" the man asked. "Word is you made it. I'm afraid the heir won't need it any longer."

Esrahaddon gasped.

"If only you had hands, you might rip it from my neck. Then I'd be in real trouble, wouldn't I?"

The noise of the collapse, and the explosions of light, had

woken several people in nearby buildings. Candles were lit in windows and doors opened onto the square.

"The regents bid me to tell you that your services are no longer required." The man in the dark cloak smiled coldly. Without another word, he walked away, disappearing into the maze of dark streets.

Esrahaddon was confused. The bolt or dart lodged in his back did not feel fatal. He could breathe easily, so it had missed his lungs and was nowhere near his heart. He was bleeding but not profusely. The pain was bad, a deep burning, but he could still feel his legs and was certain he could walk.

Why did he leave me alive? Why would—poison!

The wizard concentrated and muttered a chant. It failed. He struggled with his handless arms to weave a stronger spell. It did not help. He could feel the poison now as it spread throughout his back. He was helpless without hands. Whoever the man in the cloak was, he knew exactly what he was doing.

Esrahaddon looked back at City Hall. He could not die— not yet.

⌇

The noise from the street caught Arista's attention. She still sat against the office door as voices and shouts drifted from the square. What had happened was unclear, but the words *he's dying* brought Arista to her feet.

She found a small crowd gathered on the steps outside. Within their center, an eerie pulsating light glowed, as if a bit of the moon had landed in Central Square. Drawing closer, Arista saw the wizard. The light emitted from his robe, growing bright, then ebbing, then brightening again in pace with his slow and labored breath. The pale light revealed a pool of blood. As Esrahaddon lay on his back, a bolt beside him, his face was almost luminous with a ghostly pallor, his lips a dark shade of blue. His disheveled sleeves exposed the fleshy stumps of his wrists.

"What happened here?" she demanded.

"We don't know, Your Highness," someone from the crowd replied. "He's been asking to see you."

"Get Dr. Gerand," she ordered, and knelt beside him, gently pulling down his sleeves.

"Too late," Esrahaddon whispered, his eyes locked intently on hers. "Can't help me—poison—Arista, listen—there's no time." His words came hurriedly between struggles to take in air. On his face was a look of determination mixed with desperation, like that of a drowning man searching for a handhold. "Take my burden—find..." The wizard hesitated, his eyes searching the faces gathered. He motioned for her to draw near.

When she placed her ear close to his mouth, he continued. "Find the heir—take the heir with you—without the heir everything fails." Esrahaddon coughed and fought to breathe. "Find the Horn of Gylindora—need the heir to find it— buried with Novron in Percepliquis—" He drew in another breath. "Hurry—at Wintertide the *Uli Vermar* ends—" Another breath. "They will come—without the horn everyone dies." Another breath. "Only you know now—only you can save...Patriarch...is the same..." The next breath never came. The next words were never uttered. The pulsating brilliance of his robe faded, leaving them all in darkness.

~§~

Arista watched the foul-smelling, chalk-colored smoke drift as the strand of blond hair smoldered. There was no breeze or draft in her office, yet the smoke traveled unerringly toward the northern wall, where it disappeared against the stone and mortar.

A spell of location required burning a part of a person. Hair was the obvious choice, but fingernails or even skin would work. The day after Esrahaddon's death, she had requested delivery of any personal belongings left behind by the missing leader of the Nationalist army. Parker had sent over an old pair of Degan Gaunt's worn muddy boots, a tattered shirt, and a woolen cloak. The boots had been useless, but the shirt and cloak held many treasures. Scraping the surfaces, she had retrieved dozens of blond hairs and hundreds of flakes of skin, which she carefully gathered and placed in a velvet pouch. At the time, she had convinced herself she merely wanted to see if the spell would work. When she had started the incantation, she had no intention of acting on the results. Now she was unsure what to do next.

To Esrahaddon, the heir had meant everything. Since leaving Gutaria, the wizard had dedicated his life to finding the emperor's descendant, even coercing Arista to assist him by casting a spell in Avempartha to identify the heir and his guardian. The guardian she had recognized immediately as Hadrian; however, the heir she had never seen before. The blond-haired image of a middle-aged man had been just a face until after the Battle of Ratibor, when she learned that he was Degan Gaunt, the leader of the Nationalists. There was no doubt that the New Empire was responsible for Gaunt's disappearance, and the smoke's color confirmed he was alive and held somewhere to the north within a few days' travel. She stared at the wall where the smoke disappeared.

"This is crazy," she said aloud to the empty room. *I can't possibly go in search of the heir. The empire has him and they'll kill me on sight. Besides, I'm needed here. Why should I care about Esrahaddon's obsession?*

If Arista wanted, she could declare herself high queen of Rhenydd and the citizenry would welcome her. She could permanently reign over a kingdom larger than Melengar and be rich as well as beloved. Long after her death, her name would endure in stories and songs—her image immortalized on statues and in books.

She glanced at the neatly folded robe on the corner of her desk. It had been delivered after Esrahaddon's burial. The sum of all the wizard's worldly possessions amounted to just this piece of cloth. He had devoted everything to his quest, and after nine hundred years, he had died without fulfilling his mission. The question of exactly what that mission had been nagged at her. Loyalty to the descendant of a boy ruler from a millennium ago could not have driven Esrahaddon so fanatically—she was missing something.

"They will come."

What did that mean? Who is coming?

"Without the horn everyone dies."

Everyone? Who is everyone? He couldn't have meant everyone, everyone—could he? Maybe he was just babbling. People do that when they're dying, don't they?

She remembered his eyes, clear and focused, holding on like...Emery. *"There's no time left. It's up to you now."*

"Only you know now—only you can save..." When Esrahaddon had spoken those words, she had not really listened, but now she could hear nothing else. She could not ignore the fact that the wizard had used his last breath to deliver to her the secrets he had carried for a thousand years. She felt that he had presented her with sparkling gems of immeasurable worth, but without his knowledge, they were nothing more than dull pebbles. While she could not unravel what he had been trying to say, it was impossible to ignore what had to be done. She had to leave. Once she discovered where Gaunt was

being held, she could send word to Hadrian and leave the rest to him. After all, he was the guardian, and Gaunt was his problem, not hers.

Arista stuffed the only possession she cared about, a pearl-handled hairbrush from Tur Del Fur, into a sack. She hastily wrote a letter of resignation and left it on the desk. Reaching the door, she paused and glanced back. Somehow, taking it seemed appropriate...almost necessary. She crossed the office and picked up the old wizard's robe. It hung, gray and dull, in her hands. No one had cleaned it, yet she found no stain of blood. Even more surprising, no hole marked the passage of the bolt. She wondered at this puzzle—even in death the man continued to be a mystery. Slipping the robe over her dress, she was amazed that it fit perfectly—despite the fact that Esrahaddon had been more than a foot taller than her. Turning her back on her office, she walked out into the night.

The autumn air was cold. Arista pulled the robe tight and lifted the hood. The material was unlike anything she had ever felt before—light, soft, yet wonderfully warm and comforting. It smelled pleasantly of salifan.

She considered taking a horse from the stables. No one would begrudge her a mount, but wherever she was going, it could not be too far, and a long walk suited her. Esrahaddon had indicated a need for haste, but it would be imprudent to rush headlong into the unknown. Walking seemed a sensible way to challenge the mysterious and unfamiliar. It would give her time to think. She guessed Esrahaddon would have chosen the same mode of travel. It just felt right.

Arista filled a water skin at the square's well and packed some food. Farmers, who objected to providing for the soldiers, always placed a small tribute on the steps of City Hall. Most she gave to the city's poor, which only resulted in more food appearing. She helped herself to a few rounds of cheese, two loaves of bread, and a number of apples, onions, and turnips. Hardly a king's feast, but it would keep her alive.

She slipped the full water bag over her shoulder, adjusted her pack, and headed for the north gate. She was conscious of the sound of her feet on the road and the noises of the night. How dangerous, even foolhardy, leaving Medford had been, even in the company of Royce and Hadrian. Now, just a few weeks later, she set out into the darkness by herself. She knew her path would lead into imperial territory, but she hoped that by traveling alone she would avoid attention.

"Your Highness!" the north gate guard said with surprise when she approached.

She smiled sweetly. "Can you please open the gate?"

"Of course, milady, but why? Where are you going?"

"For a walk," she replied.

The guard stared at her incredulously. "Are you certain? I mean…" He looked over her shoulder. "Are you alone?"

She nodded. "I assure you I'll be fine."

The guard hesitated briefly before relenting and drew back the bar. Putting his back against the giant oak doors, he slowly pushed one open.

"You need to be careful, milady. There is a stranger about."

"A stranger?"

"A fellow came to the gate just a few hours after sunset, wanting in—a masked man in a hood. I could see he was up to no good, so I turned him away. Likely as not, he's out there somewhere waiting for me to open at sunrise. Please be careful, Your Highness."

"Thank you, but I'm sure I'll be fine," she said while slipping past him. Once she was through, the gate closed behind her.

Arista stayed to the road, walking as quickly and quietly as she could. Now on her way, she felt exhilarated despite the dangers that lay ahead. Leaving Ratibor without farewells was for the best. They would have insisted she appoint a successor and remain for a time to counsel whoever was selected. While she did not feel enough urgency for a horse, she worried that too long of a delay would be a mistake. Besides, she could not risk an imperial spy discovering her plan and placing sentries to capture her.

In one way she felt safer on the road than in her office—she was confident no one knew where she was or where she was going. This thought was as comforting as the old wizard's robe. In the days following Esrahaddon's death, she had been concerned that she too might be a target. His assassin had escaped capture, the only trace was an unusually small crossbow discovered in an East End Square rain barrel. She felt certain that the killer was an agent of the New Empire, sent to eliminate a lingering threat. She was Esrahaddon's apprentice, who had helped defeat the church's attempt to take Melengar, and led the revolt in Ratibor. Surely those in power wanted her dead as well.

Before long, she spotted the flicker of a light not far off the road—a simple campfire burning low.

The man turned away at the gate? Could he be the assassin?

She kept her eyes on the fire while carefully walking past. She soon cleared a hill and the light disappeared behind it. After a few hours, the excitement of the adventure waned and she found herself yawning. With several hours until dawn, she pulled a blanket from her bag and found a soft place to lie.

Is this what each night was like for Esrahaddon?

She had never felt so alone. In the past, Hilfred had been her ever-present shadow, but her bodyguard had disappeared more than two years earlier after having suffered burns in her service. Most of all, she missed Royce and Hadrian, a common thief and an ex-mercenary. To them, she was nothing more than a wealthy patron, but to her, they were nothing less than her closest friends. She imagined Royce disappearing into the trees to search the area as he had at every camp. Even more, she wanted Hadrian there by her side. She pictured him with a lopsided grin, making that awful stew of his. He always made her feel safe. She remembered how he had held her on the hill of Amberton Lee and at the armory after the Battle of Ratibor. She had been soaked in rain, mud, and Emery's blood, and his arms had held her up. She had never felt so horrible and no one's embrace had ever felt so good.

"I wish you were here now," she whispered.

Lying on her back, she looked up at the stars, scattered like dust over the immense heavens. Seeing them, she felt even more alone. She closed her eyes and drifted off to sleep.

Chapter 2

The Empty Castle

Above Hadrian's head the wooden sign displaying a thorny branch and a faded bloom rocked in the morning breeze. It was weathered and worn, and it took imagination to determine that the flower depicted was a rose. The tavern it announced displayed the same haphazard charm of necessity as the other buildings along Wayward Street. The crooked length of the narrow road was empty. Autumn leaves scattering in the wind and the rocking sign marked the only movement.

The lack of activity surprised Hadrian. At this time of year, Medford's Lower Quarter usually bustled with vendors selling apples, cider, pumpkins, and hardwood. The air should be scented with wood smoke. Chimney sweeps should be dancing across rooftops as children watched in awe. Instead, the doors of several stores were nailed shut—and to his dismay, even The Rose and Thorn Tavern lay dormant.

Hadrian sighed as he tethered his horse. Skipping breakfast in exchange for an early start had left him eager for a hot meal eaten indoors. He had expected the war to take its toll and Medford to be affected, but he had never expected The Rose and Thorn to—

"Hadrian!"

He recognized the voice before turning to see Gwen, the lovely Calian native, who, in her sky-blue day dress, looked more like an artisan's wife than a madam. She swept down the steps of Medford House, one of the few open businesses. Prostitutes were always the first to arrive and the last to leave. Hadrian hugged her, lifting her small body. "We were worried about you," she said. "What took you so long?"

"What are you doing back at all?" Royce called as he stepped out onto the porch. The lithe and slender thief stood barefoot, wearing only black pants and a loose unbelted tunic.

"Arista sent me to make sure you made it all right and were able to convince Alric to send the army south."

"Took you long enough. I've been back for weeks."

Hadrian shrugged. "Well, Alric's forces laid siege to Colnora right after I arrived. It took me a while to find a way out."

"So, how did—"

"Royce, shouldn't we let Hadrian sit and eat?" Gwen interrupted. "You haven't had breakfast, have you? Let me grab a shawl, and I'll have Dixon fire the stove."

"How long has the tavern been closed?" Hadrian asked as Gwen disappeared back inside.

Royce raised an eyebrow and shook his head. "Not closed. Business has just been slow, so she opens for the midday meal."

"It's like a ghost town around here."

"A lot of people left, expecting an invasion," Royce explained. "Most who stayed were called to serve when the army moved out."

Gwen reappeared with a wrap around her shoulders and led them across the street to The Rose and Thorn. In the shadows of an alley, Hadrian spotted movement. Figures slept huddled amid piles of trash. Unlike Royce, who easily passed for human, these shabbily dressed creatures bore the unmistakable angled ears, prominent cheekbones, and almond eyes characteristic of elves.

"The army didn't want them," Royce commented, seeing Hadrian's stare. "No one wants them."

Dixon, the bartender and manager, was taking chairs off the tables when Gwen unlocked the doors. A tall, stocky man, he had lost his right arm several years earlier in the Battle of Medford.

"Hadrian!" he shouted in his booming voice. Hadrian instinctively held out his left hand to shake Dixon's. "How are you, lad? Gave them what for in Ratibor, eh? Where you been?"

"I stayed to sweep up," Hadrian replied with a wink and a smile.

"Denny in yet?" Gwen asked Dixon, stepping past him and rummaging through a drawer behind the bar.

"Nope, just me. I figured, why bother? All of you want breakfast? I can manage if you like."

"Yes," Gwen told him, "and make some extra."

Dixon sighed. "You keep feeding them and they'll just keep hanging around."

She ignored the comment. "Did Harry deliver the ale last night?"

"Yup."

"Three barrels, right?"

As Gwen talked with Dixon, Royce slipped his arm around her waist and gave her a gentle squeeze. That he loved her was no secret, but Royce had never even held Gwen's hand in public before. Seeing him with her, Hadrian noticed that his friend looked different. It took him a moment to realize what it was—Royce was smiling.

When Gwen followed Dixon into the pantry to discuss inventory, Royce and Hadrian resumed the task of pulling chairs off tables. Throughout the years, Hadrian had likely sat in each one and drunk from every wooden cup and pewter tankard hanging behind the bar. For more than a decade The Rose and Thorn had been his home, and it felt odd to be *just visiting*.

"So, have you decided what you'll do now?" Royce asked.

"I'm going to find the heir."

Royce paused, holding a chair inches above the floor. "Did you hit your head during the Battle of Ratibor? The heir is dead, remember?"

"Turns out he's not. What's more, I know who he is."

"But the nice priest told us the heir was murdered by Seret Knights forty years ago," Royce countered.

"He was."

"Am I missing something?"

"Twins," Hadrian told him. "One was killed, but the midwife saved the other."

"So who's this heir?"

"Degan Gaunt."

Royce's eyes widened and a sardonic grin crossed his face. "The leader of the Nationalist army, who is bent on the New Empire's destruction, is the imperial heir destined to rule over it? How ironic is that? It's also pretty unfortunate for you, seeing as how the Imps snatched him up."

Hadrian nodded. "Yeah, it turns out Esrahaddon's been helping him win all those victories in Rhenydd."

"Esrahaddon? How do you know that?"

"I found him in Gaunt's camp right before the Battle of Ratibor. Looks like the old wizard was planning to put Gaunt on the throne by force."

The two finished with the chairs and took seats at a table near the windows. Outside, a lone apple seller wheeled a cart past, presumably on her way to the Gentry Quarter.

"I hope you're not taking Esrahaddon's word about Gaunt

being the heir. You can never be sure exactly what he's up to,"
Royce said.

"No—well, yes—he confirmed the heir was alive, but I
discovered his identity through Gaunt's sister."

"So how do you plan to find Gaunt? Did either of them tell
you where he is?"

"No. I'm pretty sure Esrahaddon knows, or has a good idea,
but he wouldn't tell me, and I've not seen him since the battle.
He did say he would need us for a job soon. I think he'll want
help rescuing Gaunt. He hasn't been around here, has he?"

Royce shook his head. "I'm happy to say I haven't seen him.
Is that why you're in town?"

"Not really. I'm sure he can find me wherever I am. After
all, he found us in Colnora when he wanted us to come to
Dahlgren. I'm on my way to see Myron at the abbey. If anyone
knows about the history of the heir, he should. I was also given
a letter to drop off to Alric."

"A letter?"

"When I was stuck in Colnora during the siege, your old
friends helped get me out."

"The Diamond?"

Hadrian nodded. "Price arranged for me to slip away one
night in exchange for delivering the letter. He preferred risking my neck rather than one of his boys."

"What did it say? Who was it from?"

Hadrian shrugged. "How would I know?"

"You didn't read it?" Royce asked incredulously.

"No, it was for Alric."

"Do you still have it?"

Hadrian shook his head. "Delivered it to the castle on the
way in."

Royce dropped his face into his hands. "Sometimes, I
just…" Royce shook his head. "Unbelievable."

"What's wrong?" Gwen asked as she joined them.

"Hadrian's an idiot," Royce replied, his voice muffled by his hands.

"I'm sure that's not true."

"Thank you, Gwen. See? At least *she* appreciates me."

"So, Hadrian, tell me about Ratibor. Royce told me about the rebellion. How did it go?" Gwen asked with an excited smile.

"Emery was killed. Do you know who he was?"

Gwen nodded.

"So were a lot of others, but we took the city."

"And Arista?"

"She survived the fight but took the aftermath hard. She's become something of a heroine there. They put her in charge of the whole kingdom."

"She's a remarkable woman," Gwen said. "Don't you think so, Hadrian?" Before he could answer, a loud crash from the kitchen made her sigh. "Excuse me while I help Dixon."

She started to stand but Royce reached his feet first. "Sit," he said, kissing the crown of her head. "I'll help him. You two get caught up."

Gwen looked surprised but simply said, "Thank you."

Royce hurried off, shouting in an unusually good-natured tone, "Dixon! What's taking you so long? You've still got one hand, haven't you?"

Gwen and Hadrian both laughed, mirroring surprised expressions.

"So, what's new around here?" Hadrian asked.

"Not a whole lot. Albert came by last week with a job from a nobleman to place the earrings of a married woman in the bedchambers of a priest, but Royce declined it."

"Really? He loves plant jobs. And a priest? That's just easy money."

She shrugged. "I think with you retired, he's—"

Outside, an approaching clatter of hooves halted abruptly. A moment later, a man dressed as a royal courier, and walking with a distinct limp, entered the tavern. He paused at the doorway, looking puzzled.

"Can I help you?" Gwen asked as she stood.

"I have a message from His Majesty for the royal protectors. I was told they were here."

"I'll take that," Gwen said, stepping forward.

The courier stiffened and shook his head. "It's for the royal protectors only."

Gwen halted and Hadrian noticed her annoyed expression.

"You must be new." Rising to his feet, Hadrian held out his hand to the courier. "I'm Hadrian Blackwater."

The courier nodded smartly and pulled a waxed scroll from his satchel. He handed over the dispatch and departed. Hadrian sat back down and broke the falcon seal.

"It's a job, isn't it?" Gwen's expression darkened and she stared at the floor.

"It's nothing. Alric just wants to see us," Hadrian said. She looked up, her eyes revealing a troubled mix of emotions Hadrian could not decipher. "Gwen, what's wrong?" he pressed, his voice softening.

At length she replied, almost in a whisper, "Royce asked me to marry him."

Hadrian sat back in his chair. "Seriously?"

She nodded and hastily added, "I guess he thought that since you retired from Riyria, he would too."

"That's—why, that's wonderful!" Hadrian burst out as he leapt to his feet and hugged her. "Congratulations! He didn't even say anything. We'll be like family! It's about time he got around to this. I would have asked for your hand myself years ago, except I knew if I did, I'd wake up dead the next morning."

"When he asked me, it was as if—well, as if a wish I never dared ask for had come true. So many problems solved, so much pain eased. Honestly, I didn't think he ever would."

Hadrian nodded. "That's only because he's not only an idiot, he's blind as well."

"No. I mean, well—he's Royce."

"Isn't that what I just said? But yeah, he's really not the marrying type, is he? Clearly, you've had tremendous influence on him."

"You have too," she said, reaching out and taking hold of his hand. "There are times I hear him say things I know come from you. Things like *responsibility* and *regret*, words that were never part of his vocabulary before. I wonder if he even knows where he found them. When I first met you two, he was so withdrawn, so guarded."

Hadrian nodded. "He has trust issues."

"But he's learning. His life has been so hard. I know it has, abandoned and betrayed by those who should have loved him. He doesn't talk about it, at least not to me. But I know."

Hadrian shook his head. "Me either. Occasionally something might come up, but he usually avoids mentioning anything about his past. I think he's trying to forget."

"He's built so many defenses, but every year it's as if another wall has fallen. He even summoned the courage to tell me he's part elven. His fortress is dissolving, and I can see him peering out at me. He wants to be free. This is the next step— and I'm so proud of him."

"When will the wedding be?"

"We were thinking in a couple of weeks at the monastery, so Myron can preside. But we'll have to postpone, won't we?"

"Why do you say that? Alric just wants to see us. It doesn't mean—"

"He needs the two of you for a job," Gwen interrupted.

"No. He might *want us*, but we're retired. I have other things to do and Royce...well, Royce needs to start a new life—with you."

"You'll go, and you must take Royce with you." Her voice was filled with sadness and a hint of regret, emotions so unlike her.

Hadrian smiled. "Listen, I can't think of anything Alric could say that would get me to go, but if he does, I'll do the job on my own—as a wedding present. We don't even have to tell Royce the courier was here."

"No!" she burst out. "He *has* to go. If he doesn't, you'll die."

Hadrian's first impulse was to laugh, but that thought evaporated when he saw her face. "I'm not as easy to kill as all that, you know?" He winked at her.

"I'm from Calis, Hadrian, and I know what I'm talking about." Her gaze drifted off toward the windows, but her eyes were unfocused, as if she were seeing another place. "I can't be the one responsible for your death. The life we would have after..." She shook her head. "No, he *must* go with you," she repeated firmly.

Hadrian was not convinced but knew there was no reason to argue further. Gwen was not the type for debate. Most women he knew invited discussion and even enjoyed arguments, but not Gwen. There was clarity to her thinking that let you know she had already made her own journey to the inevitable conclusion and was just politely waiting there for you to join her. In her own way, she was much like Royce— except for the polite waiting.

"With you two gone, I'll have time to organize a first-rate wedding," she said, her voice strained as she blinked frequently. "It will take that long just to decide what color dress a former prostitute should wear."

"You know something, Gwen?" Hadrian began as he reached out and took her hand. "I've known a lot of women, but I've met only two I admire. Royce is a very lucky man."

"Royce is a man on the edge," she replied thoughtfully. "He's seen too much cruelty and betrayal. He's never known mercy." She gave his hand a squeeze. "*You* have to do this, Hadrian. You have to be the one to show him mercy. If you can do that, I know it will save him."

⁓

Royce and Hadrian entered Essendon Castle's courtyard, once the site of Princess Arista's witchcraft trial. Nothing remained of that unfortunate day except a slightly raised patch of ground where the stake and woodpile had stood. It had been just three years earlier, and the weather had been turning cold then too. That had been a different time. Amrath Essendon had only recently been murdered and the New Empire had been little more than an Imperialist's dream.

The guards at the gate nodded and smiled at them.

"I hate that," Royce muttered as they passed.

"What?"

"They didn't even think to stop us, and they actually smiled. They know us by sight now—*by sight*. Alric used to have the decency to send word discreetly and receive us unannounced. Now uniformed soldiers knock on the door in daylight, waving and saying, 'Hello, we have a job for you.'"

"He didn't wave."

"Give it time, he will be—waving and grinning. One day Jeremy will be buying drinks for his soldier buddies at The Rose and Thorn. They'll all be there, the entire sentry squad, laughing, smiling, throwing their arms over our shoulders and asking us to sing 'Calide Portmore' with them—'Once more, with gusto!' And at some point one particularly sweaty ox will give me a hug and say how *honored* he is to be in our company."

"*Jeremy?*"

"What? That's his name."

"You know the name of the soldier at the gate?"

Royce scowled. "You see my point? Yes, I know his name and they know ours. We might as well wear uniforms and move into Arista's old room."

They climbed the stone steps to the main entrance, where a soldier quickly opened a door for them and gave a slight bow. "Master Melborn, Master Blackwater."

"Hey, Digby." Hadrian waved as he passed. When he caught Royce scowling, he added, "Sorry."

"It's a good thing we're both retired. You know, there's a reason there are no famous *living* thieves."

Hadrian's heels echoed on the polished floor of the corridor as they walked. Royce's footsteps made no sound at all. They crossed the west gallery past the suits of armor and the ballroom. The castle appeared as empty as the rest of the city. As they approached the reception hall, Hadrian spotted Mauvin Pickering heading their way. The young noble looked thinner than Hadrian had remembered. There was a hollow cast to his cheeks, shadows beneath his eyes, but his hair was the same wild mess.

"About time," Mauvin greeted them. "Alric just sent me to look for you."

Two years had passed since his brother Fanen's death, and Mauvin still dressed in black. The haunted look in his eyes would be unnoticeable to most. Only those who had known him before the contest in Dahlgren would see the difference. That had been when Sentinel Luis Guy attacked Hadrian with a force of Seret Knights, and Mauvin and Fanen had taken up arms with him. The brothers had fought masterfully, as was the nature of Pickerings. Yet Mauvin had been unable to save his brother from the killing stroke. Before that day, Mauvin Pickering had been bright, loud, and joyful. He had worn a permanent smile and challenged the world with a wink and a laugh. Now he stood with his shoulders slumped and his chin dipped.

"You're wearing it again?" Hadrian gestured toward Mauvin's sword.

"They insisted."

"Have you drawn it?"

Mauvin looked at his feet. "Dad says it doesn't matter. If the need arises, he's certain I won't hesitate."

"And what do you think?"

"Mostly I try not to." Mauvin opened the doors to the hall and let them swing wide. He led Royce and Hadrian past the clerk and the door guards into the reception hall. Tall windows let in the late-morning light, casting bright spears on the parquet floor. The great tapestries still lay rolled in bundles against the wall, stacked in hope of a better day. In their places, maps with red lines covered by blue arrows pointing south plastered the walls.

Alone, Alric paced near the windows, his crowned head bowed and his mantle trailing behind him like—*like a king*, Hadrian thought. Alric looked up as they entered, and pushed the rim of the royal diadem back with his thumb.

"What took you so long?"

"We ate breakfast, Your Majesty," Royce replied.

"You ate break— Never mind." The king held out a rolled parchment. "I'm told you delivered this dispatch to the castle this morning?"

"Not me," Royce said. Unrolling it, he found two parchments and began reading.

"I did," Hadrian admitted. "I just arrived from Ratibor. Your sister has matters well in hand, Your Majesty."

Alric scowled. "Who sent this?"

"I'm not sure," Hadrian replied. "I got it from a man named Price in Colnora."

Royce finished reading and looked up. "I think you're about to lose this war," he said without bothering to add the expected *Your Majesty.*

"Don't be absurd. This is likely a hoax. Ecton is probably behind it. He enjoys seeing me make a fool of myself. Even if it's authentic, it's simply someone making wild claims to extort a bit of gold from the New Empire."

"I don't think so." Royce handed the letter to Hadrian.

King Alric—
Found this on a courier traveling from Calis to Aquesta. Sweepers bumped him in Alburn but he was more than he seemed. Three Diamonds dead. Bucket men caught him and found this letter addressed to the regents. The Jewel thought you'd like to know.

Esteemed Regents,

*T*he fall of Ratibor was unexpected and unfortunate but, as you know, not fatal. Thus far, I have delivered Degan Gaunt and eliminated the wizard Esrahaddon. This completes two-thirds of our contract, but the best is yet to come.

The <u>Emerald Storm</u> rests anchored in Aquesta Harbor, ready to sail. When you receive this message, place the payment on board along with the sealed orders I left. Once loaded, the ship will

*depart, the fortunes of war will shift, and your
victory will be assured. With the Nationalists
eliminated, Melengar is yours for the taking.*

*While I have all the time in the world, you, on
the other hand, might wish to make haste, lest the
flame you call the New Empire is snuffed out.*

Merrick Marius

"Merrick?" Hadrian muttered, and looked at Royce. "Is
this...?"

Royce nodded.

"You know this Marius?" Alric asked.

Again, Royce nodded. "Which is why I know you're in
trouble."

"And do you know who sent this?"

"Cosmos DeLur."

"Isn't Cosmos a wealthy merchant in Colnora?"

"He's also the leader of the thieves' guild known as the
Black Diamond."

Alric paused to consider this, then paced once more. "Why
would he send this to me?"

"The Diamond wants the Imps out of Colnora. I guess with
Gaunt gone, Cosmos thought you could make the best use of
this information."

Alric stroked his beard thoughtfully. "So who is this Merrick fellow? How do you know him?"

"We were friends when I was a member of the Diamond."

"Excellent. Find him and ask what this is all about."

Royce shook his head. "I have no idea where Merrick
is, and we're not on good terms anymore. He won't tell me
anything."

Alric sighed. "I don't care what kind of terms you're on.

Find him, resolve your differences, and get me the information I need."

Royce said nothing and Hadrian hesitantly added, "Merrick had Royce sent to Manzant after he mistakenly killed the woman Merrick loved."

Alric stopped pacing and stared. "Manzant Prison? But no one ever leaves Manzant."

"That was the plan. I was happy to disappoint him," Royce replied.

"Nowadays, Royce and Merrick have an unspoken agreement to stay out of each other's way."

"So how can I find out if this Merrick is just boasting, or if there is a real threat to Melengar?"

"Merrick doesn't boast. If he says he can turn the war in the New Empire's favor, he can. I suggest you take this seriously." Royce thought a moment. "If I were you, I'd send someone to deliver this message and then stow away on this ship and see where it leads."

"Fine. Do that, and let me know what you find out."

Royce shook his head. "We're retired. Only a week ago I came here and explained how—"

"Don't be ridiculous! You said to take his threat seriously, which is why I need my best—and that means you."

"Pick someone else," Royce said firmly.

"All right, how much do you want? It's land this time, right? Fine. As it happens, Baron Milborough of Three Fords was killed in battle a few weeks ago. He doesn't have any sons, so I'll grant you his estate if you succeed. Land, title—all of it."

"I don't want land. I don't want anything. *I'm retired.*"

"By Mar, man!" Alric shouted. "The future of the kingdom may depend on this. I'm the king and—"

Hadrian interrupted. "I'll do it."

"What?" Alric and Royce asked together.

"I said I'll go."

⅌

"You can't take this job," Royce told him as they walked back to The Rose and Thorn.

"I have to. If Esrahaddon is dead, Merrick is my only chance to find Gaunt. Do you think he really could have done it?"

"Merrick wouldn't lie to a client about a job."

"But Esrahaddon was a wizard. He's survived a thousand years—I can't imagine he could be murdered by a common killer."

"I just said it was Merrick. He's not common."

As the two walked through an empty Gentry Square, even the bells of Mares Cathedral were silent. Hadrian sighed. "Then I'm on my own in finding the heir now. If I follow the payment to Merrick, I'll be halfway to finding Gaunt."

"Hadrian." Royce placed a hand on his friend's arm, stopping them mid-step. "You're not up to this. You don't know Merrick. Think a minute. If he can kill a wizard, one who could create pillars of fire even without hands, what do you think your chances are? You're a good—no, you're a great—fighter, the best I've ever seen, but Merrick is a genius and he's ruthless. You go after him, he'll know, and he'll kill you."

They were across from Lester Furl's old haberdashery in Artisan Row, the shop that the monk Myron once worked in. The sign of the cavalier hat still hung out front, but the place was empty.

"Listen, I'm not asking you to come. I know you're marrying Gwen. Congratulations on that, by the way. And it's about time, I might add. This isn't your problem. It's mine. It's what

I was born to do. What my father trained me for. Protecting Gaunt, and finding a way to put him on the imperial throne— that's my destiny."

Royce rolled his eyes.

"I know you don't believe that, but I do."

"Gaunt could be dead already, you know? If Merrick killed Esrahaddon, he might have slit Gaunt's throat too."

"I still have to go. By now, even you must see that."

~§~

When they reached The Rose and Thorn, Gwen was waiting with anxious eyes. She stood on the porch, her arms crossed, clutching her shawl. The autumn wind brushed her skirt and hair. Behind her, within the darkened interior, patrons talked loudly around the bar.

"It's okay," Hadrian reassured her as they approached. "I'm taking the job, but Royce is staying. With luck I'll be back for—"

"Go with him," Gwen told Royce firmly.

"No—really, Gwen," Hadrian said, "it's nothing—"

"You have to go with him."

"What's wrong?" Royce asked. "I thought we were getting married. Don't you want to?"

Gwen closed her eyes, shaken. Then her hands clenched into fists and she straightened. "You *must* go. Hadrian will be killed if you don't—and then you…you…"

Royce took her in his arms on the steps of the tavern and held her as she began to cry.

"You have to go," Gwen said, her voice muffled by Royce's shoulder. "Nothing will be right if you don't. I can't marry you—I *won't* marry you—if you don't. Tell me you'll go, please, Royce, please…"

Royce gave Hadrian a puzzled glance and whispered, "Okay."

❦

"Here, I made this for you," Gwen said to Royce, holding out a folded bit of knitted cloth. They were in Gwen's room at the top of the stairs of Medford House and he had just finished packing.

He held it up. "A scarf?"

Gwen smiled. "Since I'm going to be married, I thought I should take up knitting. I hear that's what proper wives do for their husbands."

Royce started to laugh but stopped when he saw her expression. "This is important to you, isn't it? You realize you've always been better than all those ladies in the Merchant Quarter. Having a husband doesn't make them special."

"It's not that. It's just...I know you had a less than perfect childhood, and so did I. I want something *better* for our children. I want their lives—our home—to be perfect, or as much as possible for a pair such as us."

"I don't know. I've met dozens of aristocrats who had ideal childhoods and they turned out to be horrors. You, on the other hand, are the best person I've ever met."

She smiled at him. "That's nice, but I highly doubt you would approve of our daughter working here. And would you really want our son living the way you did as a boy? We can raise them right. Just because they grow up in a proper home doesn't mean they will turn out to be *horrors*. You'll be firm, and I'll be loving. You'll spank little Elias when he acts disrespectfully, and I'll kiss his tears and give him cookies."

"Elias? You've named our son already?"

"Would you prefer Sterling? I can't decide between the two.

But the girl's name is not negotiable—it's Mercedes. I've always loved that name.

"I'll sell this house and my other holdings. Combined with the money I banked for you, we'll never want for anything. We can live peaceful, happy, simple lives—I mean, if you want to live like that. Do you?"

He looked into her eyes. "Gwen, if it means being with you, I don't care where we are or what I do."

"Then it's settled." Gwen grinned and her eyes brightened. "It's what I've always dreamed of…the two of us in a small cottage somewhere safe and warm, raising a family."

"You make us sound like squirrels."

"Yes, exactly! A family of squirrels tucked in our cozy nest in some tree trunk while the troubles of the world pass us by." Her lower lip quivered.

Royce pulled her close and held her tight as she buried her face in his shoulder. He stroked her head, feeling her hair linger on his fingertips. For all Gwen's strength and courage, he was forever amazed at how fragile she could be. He had never known anyone like her, and he considered telling Hadrian that he had changed his mind. "Gwen—"

"Don't even think it," she told him. "We can't build a new life until you're done with the old one. Hadrian needs you, and I won't be blamed for his death."

"I could never blame you."

"I couldn't bear it if I felt you hated me, Royce. I'd rather be dead than let that happen. Promise me you'll go. Promise me you'll take care of Hadrian. Promise me you won't despair, and that you'll set things right."

Royce let his head lower until it rested on hers. He stood there, smelling the familiar scent of her hair as his own breathing tightened. "All right, but you have to agree to go to the abbey if things get bad like they did before."

"I will," she said. Her arms tightened around him. "I'm so scared," she whispered.

Surprised, Royce said, "You've always told me you were never frightened when I left on missions."

She looked up at him with tears in her eyes and a guilty expression on her face. "I lied."

CHAPTER 3

THE COURIER

Hadrian stood in the anteroom, waiting in line to deliver the dispatch. The clerk was a short, plump, balding man with ink-stained fingers and a spare quill behind each ear. He sat behind a formidable desk, scribbling on documents and muttering to himself, unconcerned with the growing line of people.

Hadrian and Royce had ridden to Aquesta, and Hadrian had volunteered to deliver the dispatch while Royce waited at a rendezvous with horses at the ready. Although Hadrian had performed jobs for many of the nobility, few here would know him by sight. Riyria had always conducted business anonymously, working through third parties, such as Viscount Albert Winslow, who fronted the organization and preserved their anonymity. He doubted that Saldur would recognize him, but Luis Guy certainly would. As a result, Hadrian kept a clear map of the nearest exit in his head and a count of the imperial guards between him and freedom.

The seat of the New Imperial Empire was busy. Members of the palace staff hurried by, entering and exiting through the many doors around him. They ran or walked as briskly as need dictated and dignity allowed. Some turned his way, but only briefly. As he knew from experience, the degree of attention someone paid others was inversely proportional to his or her status. The lord chamberlain and high chancellor passed without a glance, while the serving steward ventured a long look, and a young page stared curiously for nearly a full minute. Although Hadrian was invisible to those at the highest levels, he was becoming uncomfortable.

This is taking too long.

Two dispatch riders reached the front of the line, quickly dropped off their satchels, and left. A city merchant was next and had come to file a complaint. This took some time, as the clerk asked numerous questions and meticulously recorded each answer.

Next came the young, plain-looking woman directly ahead of Hadrian. "Tell the chamberlain I wish an audience," she said, stepping forward. She wore no makeup, leaving her face dull. Her hair, pulled back and drawn up in a net, did nothing to accentuate her appearance. She was pear-shaped, a feature made even more evident by her gown, which flared at the hips into a great hoop.

"The lord chamberlain is in a meeting with the regents and cannot be disturbed, Your *Ladyship.*"

The words were proper, but the tone was disrespectful. The inflection on *ladyship* sounded particularly sarcastic. The woman either did not notice or chose to ignore it.

"He's been ducking me for over a week," the woman said accusingly. "Something must be done. I need material for the empress's new dress."

"My records indicate that quite a large sum was spent on a gown for Modina recently. We're at war and have more important appropriations to make."

"That was for her presentation on the balcony. She can't walk around in that. I'm talking about a day dress."

"It was very expensive nonetheless. You don't want to take food from our soldiers' mouths just so the empress can have another pretty outfit, do you?"

"Another? She has two worn hand-me-downs!"

"Which is more than many of her subjects, isn't it?"

"The empire has spent a fortune remodeling this palace. Surely it won't break the imperial economy to buy a bit of cloth. She doesn't need silk. Linen will do. I'll have the seamstress—"

"I'm quite certain that if the lord chamberlain thought the empress needed another dress, he would provide one. Since he has not, she doesn't need it. Now, *Amilia*," he said brazenly, "if you don't mind, I have work to do."

The woman's shoulders slumped in defeat.

Footsteps echoed from behind them, and the small man's smug expression faltered. Hadrian turned and saw the farm girl he had once known as Thrace walking up, flanked by an armed guard. Her dress was faded and frayed, just as Amilia had said, but the young woman stood tall, straight, and unabashed. She motioned to the guard to wait as she moved to the front of the line to face the clerk.

"Lady Amilia speaks with my authority. Please do as she has requested," Thrace said.

The clerk looked confused. His bright eyes flickered nervously between the two.

Thrace continued, "I'm sure you do not wish to refuse an order from your empress, do you?"

The scribe lowered his voice, but his irritation still carried as he addressed Amilia. "If you think I'm going to kneel before your trained dog, you're mistaken. She's as insane as rumored. I'm not as ignorant as the castle staff, and I'm not going to be toyed with by common trash. Get out of here, both of you. I don't have time for foolishness this morning."

Amilia cringed openly, but Thrace did not waver. "Tell me, Quail, do you think the palace guards share your opinions of me?" She looked back at the soldier. "If I were to call him over and accuse you of…let's see…being a traitor, and then…let me think…order him to execute you right here, what do you think he would do?"

The clerk looked suspiciously at Thrace, as if trying to see behind a mask. "You wouldn't dare," he said, his eyes shifting between the two women.

"No? Why not?" Thrace replied. "You just said yourself that I'm insane. There's no telling what I might do, or why. From now on, you'll treat Lady Amilia with respect and obey her orders as if they come from the highest authority. Do you understand?"

The clerk nodded slowly.

As Thrace turned to leave, she caught sight of Hadrian and stopped as if she had run into an invisible wall. Her eyes locked on his and she staggered a step and stood, wavering.

Amilia reached out to support her. "Modina, what's wrong?"

Thrace said nothing. She continued to stare at him—her eyes filling with tears, her lips trembling.

The door to the main office opened.

"I don't want to hear another word about it!" Ethelred thundered as he, Saldur, and Archibald Ballentyne entered the anteroom together. Hadrian looked toward the hall window, estimating the number of steps it would take to reach it.

The old cleric focused on Thrace. "What's going on here?"

"I'm taking Her Eminence back to her room," Amilia replied. "I don't think she's feeling well."

"They were requesting material for a new dress," the clerk announced with an accusing tone.

"Well, obviously she needs one. Why is she still wearing that rag?" Saldur asked.

"The lord chamberlain refuses—"

"What do you need him for?" Saldur scowled. "Just tell the clerk to order what you require. You don't need to pester Bernard with such trivialities."

"Thank you, Your Grace," Amilia said, placing one arm around Thrace's waist and supporting her elbow with the other as she gently led her away. Thrace's eyes never left Hadrian, her head turning over her shoulder as they departed.

Saldur followed her gaze and looked curiously at Hadrian. "You look familiar," he said, taking a step toward him.

"Courier," Hadrian said, his heart racing. He bowed and held up the message like a shield.

"He's probably been here a dozen times, Sauly." Ethelred snatched the folded parchment and eyed it. "This is from Merrick!"

All three lost interest in Hadrian as Ethelred unfolded the letter.

"Your Lordships." Hadrian bowed, then turned and quickly walked away, passing Amilia and Thrace. With each step, he felt her stare upon his back, until he turned the corner, placing him out of her sight.

❧

"Any problems?" Royce asked when Hadrian met him outside.

"Almost. I saw Thrace," Hadrian said as they walked. "She doesn't look good. She's thin—real thin—and pale. She was begging for clothes from some sniveling little clerk."

Royce looked back, concerned. "Did she recognize you?"

Hadrian nodded. "But she didn't say anything. She just stared."

"I guess if she was planning to arrest us, she'd have done it by now," Royce said.

"Arrest us? This is Thrace we're talking about, for Maribor's sake."

"They've had her for more than a year—she's Empress Modina now."

"Yeah, but..."

"What?"

"I don't know," Hadrian said, remembering the look on Thrace's face. "She doesn't look well. I'm not sure what's going on in the palace, but it's not good. And I promised her father I'd look out for her."

Royce shook his head in frustration. "Can we focus on one rescue at a time? For a man in retirement, you're really busy. Besides, Theron's idea of success was to get his eldest son a cooper's shop. I think he *might* settle for his daughter being crowned empress. Now, let's get rid of these horses and make our way down to the wharf. We need to find the *Emerald Storm*."

CHAPTER 4

THE RACE

While not as large or as wealthy as Colnora, the imperial capital of Aquesta was the most powerful city in Avryn. The palace dated back to before the age of Glenmorgan and had originally been a governor's residence in the ancient days of the Novronian Empire. Scholars pointed to the gray rock of the castle's foundation with pride and boasted about how imperial engineers from Percepliquis had laid it. Here, at Highcourt Fields, great tournaments were held each Wintertide. The best knights from all of Apeladorn arrived to compete in jousting, fencing, and other contests of skill. These weeklong events included an ongoing feast for the nobles and provided healthy revenue for the merchants, who showed their wares along the streets. The city became a carnival of sights and sounds that attracted visitors for hundreds of miles.

Much of Aquesta's economic success came from possessing the largest and busiest saltwater port in Avryn. The docks were awash with all manner of sailing watercraft. Brigs, trawlers, grain ships, merchant vessels, and warships all anchored in its harbor. To the south lay the massive shipyard, along with rope, net, and sail manufacturers. The northern end of the bay held the wharf and its fish houses, livestock pens, lumberyards, and tar boilers. All the industries of the sea and sea-faring were represented.

"Which one is the *Emerald Storm*?" Hadrian asked, looking at the forest of masts and rigging that lined the docks.

"Let's try asking at the information office." Royce hooked his thumb at a tavern perched on the edge of the dock. The wooden walls were bleached white with salt, and the clapboards were warped like ocean waves. The door hung askew off leather hinges, and above it, a weathered sign in the shape of a fish announced THE SALTY MACKEREL.

The tavern had few windows, leaving the interior dim and smoky. Each tiny table had a melted candle, and a weak fire smoldered in a round brick hearth in the center of the room. Men, dressed in loose trousers, long checkered shirts, and wide-brimmed hats with glossy tops, packed the place. Many sat with pipes in their mouths and their feet on tables. Some stood leaning against posts. All heads turned when Hadrian and Royce entered, and Hadrian realized just how much they stood out in their tunics and cloaks.

"Hello." Hadrian smiled as he struggled to close the door. The wind whistled through and snuffed out the three candles nearest them. "Sorry, could use some better hinges."

"Iron hinges rust overnight here," the bartender said. The thin, crooked man wiped the counter with one hand while gathering empty mugs in the other. "What do you two want?"

"Looking for the *Emerald Storm*." Royce spoke up.

Neither took more than a step inside. None of the haggard faces looked friendly, and Hadrian liked the comfort of a nearby exit.

"Whatcha want with it?" another man asked.

"We heard it was a good ship, and we were wondering if there are any openings for sailors."

This brought a riotous round of laughter.

"And where be these sailors who be looking fer a job?" another voice bellowed from within the murky haze. "Certainly not two sand crabs like you."

More laughter.

"So what you're saying is you don't know anything about the *Emerald Storm*. Is that right?" Royce returned in a cutting tone that quieted the room.

"The *Storm* is an imperial ship, lad," the crooked man told them, "and it's all pressed up. They're only taking seasoned salts now—if there's any room left at all."

"If yer looking fer work, the fishery always needs gutters. That's about as close to seafaring work as is likely for you two."

Once more the room filled with boisterous laughter.

Hadrian looked at Royce, who shoved the door open and, with a scowl, stepped outside. "Thanks for the advice," Hadrian told everyone before following his partner.

They sat on the Mackerel's steps, staring at the line of ships across the street. Spires of wood draped with tethered cloth looked like ladies getting dressed for a ball. Hadrian wondered if that was why they always referred to ships as women.

"What now?" he asked softly.

Royce sat hunched with his chin on his hands. "Thinking," was all he said.

Behind them the door scraped open, and the first thing Hadrian noticed was a wide-brimmed hat with one side pinned up by a lavish blue plume.

The face beneath the hat was familiar, and Royce recognized the man immediately. "Wyatt Deminthal."

Wyatt hesitated as he locked eyes with Royce. He stood with one foot still inside. He did not look surprised to see them, but seemed to be merely questioning the wisdom of advancing, like a child who approached a dog that had unexpectedly growled. For a heartbeat no one said a word, and then Wyatt gritted his teeth and pulled the door shut behind him.

"I can get you on the *Storm*," he said quickly.

Royce narrowed his eyes. "How?"

"I'm the helmsman. They're short a cook and can always use another topman. She's ready to sail as soon as a shipment from the palace arrives."

"Why?"

Wyatt swallowed, and his hand absently drifted to his throat. "I know you saw me. You're here to collect, but I don't have the money I owe. Setting you up in Medford was nothing personal. We were starving, and Trumbul paid gold. I didn't know they were going to arrest you for the king's murder. I was just hiring you to steal the sword—that's all. A hundred gold tenents is a lot of money. And honestly—well, I've never saved that much in my life and I doubt I ever will."

"So you think getting us on the *Emerald Storm* is worth a hundred gold?"

Wyatt licked his lips, his eyes darting back and forth between them. "I don't know... is it?"

⚓

Royce and Hadrian crossed the busy street, dodging carts, and stepped onto weathered decking suspended by ropes. The boards bobbed and weaved beneath their feet. The two were dressed in loose-fitting duck-trousers, oversized linen shirts, tarpaulin hats with a bit of ribbon, and neckerchiefs tied in some arcane way that Wyatt had fussed with for some time to get right. They both carried large, heavy cloth seabags, in which they stowed their old clothes and Hadrian hid his three swords. Being unarmed left him feeling off balance and naked.

They snaked through the crowded dock, following Wyatt's directions to the end of the pier. The *Emerald Storm* was a smart-looking, freshly painted ship, with three masts, four decks, and the figurehead of a golden winged woman ornamenting the bow. Its sails were furled, and green pennants flew from each mast. A small army of men hoisted bags of flour and barrels of salted pork onto the deck, where the crew stowed the supplies. Shouts came from what appeared to be an officer, who directed the work, and another man, who enforced the orders with a stout rattan cane. Two imperial soldiers guarded the ramp.

"Do you have business here?" one asked at their approach.

"Yeah," Hadrian replied with an innocent, hopeful tone. "We're looking for work. Heard this ship was short on hands. We were told to speak with Mr. Temple."

"What's this here?" asked a short, heavyset man with threadbare clothes, bushy eyebrows, and a gruff voice worn to gravel from years of yelling in the salt air. "I'm Temple."

"Word is you're looking to put on a cook," Hadrian said pleasantly.

"We are."

"Well then, this is your lucky day."

"Ah-huh." Temple nodded with a sour look.

"And my friend here is an able—ah—topman."

"Oh, he is, is he?" Temple eyed Royce. "We have openings, but only for *experienced* sailors. Normally, I'd be happy to take on green men, but we can't afford any more landlubbers on this trip."

"But we are sailors—served on the *Endeavor*."

"Are you, now?" the ship's master asked skeptically. "Let me see yer hands."

The master examined Hadrian's palms, looking over the various calluses and rough places while grunting occasionally.

"You must have spent most of your time in the galley. You've not done any serious rope work." He examined Royce's hands and raised an eyebrow at him. "Have you *ever* been on a ship before? It's certain you've never handled a sheet or a capstan."

"Royce here is a—you know—" Hadrian pointed up at the ship's rigging. "The guy who goes up there."

The master shook his head and laughed. "If you two are seamen, then I'm the Prince of Percepliquis!"

"Oh, but they are, Mr. Temple," a voice declared. Wyatt exited the forecastle and came jogging toward them. A bright white shirt offset his tawny skin and black hair. "I know these men, old mates of mine. The little one is Royce Melborn, as fine a topman as they come. And the big one is, ah..."

"Hadrian." Royce spoke up.

"Right, of course. Hadrian's a fine cook—he is, Mr. Temple."

Temple pointed toward Royce. "This one's a topman? Are you joking, Wyatt?"

"No, sir, he's one of the best."

Temple looked unconvinced.

"You can have him prove it to you, sir," Hadrian offered. "You could have him race your best up the ropes."

"You mean up the *shrouds*," Wyatt said, correcting him.

"Yeah."

"You mean *aye*."

Hadrian sighed and gave up.

The master did not notice as he had been focused on Royce. He sized him up, then shouted, "Derning!" His strong, raspy voice carried well against the ocean wind. Immediately, a tall, thin fellow with leathery skin jogged over.

"Aye, sir?" he responded respectfully.

"This fellow says he can beat you in a race to loose the topsail and back. What do you think?"

"I think he's mistaken, sir."

"Well, we'll find out." The master turned back to Royce. "I don't actually expect you to beat Derning. Jacob here is one of the best topmen I've seen, but if you put in a good showing, the two of you will have jobs aboard. If it turns out you're wasting my time, well, you'll be swimming back. Derning, you take starboard. Royce, you have port. We'll begin after Lieutenant Bishop gives permission for us to get under way."

Mr. Temple moved toward the quarterdeck and Wyatt slid down the stair rail to Royce's side. "Remember what I taught you last night...and what Temple said. You don't need to beat Derning."

Hadrian clapped Royce on the back, grinning. "So the idea is to just free the sail and get back down alive."

Royce nodded and looked apprehensively up at the towering mast before him.

"Not afraid of heights, I hope." Wyatt grinned.

"All right, gentlemen!" Mr. Temple shouted, addressing the crew from his new position on the quarterdeck. "We're having a contest." He explained the details to the crew as Royce and Jacob moved to the base of the mainsail. Royce looked up with a grimace that drew laughter from the rest.

"Seriously, he isn't afraid of heights, is he?" Wyatt asked, looking concerned. "I mean, it looks scary, and well—okay, it is the first few times you go aloft, but it really isn't that hard if you're careful and can handle heights."

Hadrian grinned at Wyatt, but all he said was, "I think you're going to like this."

An officer appeared on the quarterdeck and stood beside the master. "You may set sail, Mr. Temple."

The master turned to the main deck and roared, "Loose the topsail!"

Royce appeared caught by surprise, not realizing this was

the order to begin the competition. As a result, Jacob got the jump on him, racing up the ratlines like a monkey. Royce turned but did not begin climbing. Instead, he watched Jacob's ascent for several seconds. The majority of the crew rooted for Jacob, but a few, perhaps those who had heard they would win a ship's cook if the stranger won, urged Royce to get climbing and called to him like a dog: "Go on, boy! Climb, you damn fool!" Some laughed, and a few made disparaging comments about his mother.

Royce finally seemed to work something out in his head and leapt to the task. He sprang, clearing the deck by several feet, and began to run, rather than climb, up the ratlines. It appeared as if Royce was defying gravity as he pumped his legs up the netting, showing no more difficulty than if he were running up a staircase. He had nearly caught up to Jacob by the time he reached the futtock shrouds. Here the webbing extended away from the mast, reaching toward the small wooden platform known as the masthead. Both men were forced to hang upside down using the ratlines, and Royce lost momentum without the ability to go no-handed.

Jacob swung around the masthead and jumped to the topmast shroud, where he ascended rapidly once more in monkey form. By the time Royce cleared the masthead, he was well behind Derning. He made up time when he could once again advance without crawling inverted. They reached the yard together and both ran out along the top of the narrow beam like circus performers. Seeing them balance a hundred feet above the deck drew gasps from some of the crew, who gaped in amazement. Royce stopped, pivoting to watch his opponent. Derning threw himself down across the yard, lying on his belly. He reached below for the gaskets to free the buntlines. Royce quickly imitated him, and together they worked their way across the arm. As they did, the sail came free, revealing its bright white face and dark green crown. It spilled down, whipping in the wind. Royce and Jacob lifted themselves back to their feet and moved to the end of the beam. They each grabbed the brace, the rope connected to the far end of the yardarm, and slid to the deck with the cheers of the crew in their ears. The two touched down together.

Mr. Temple shouted to restore order of the unruly crew. It did not matter who had won. The skillful display by both men had been impressive enough to earn their approval. Even Hadrian found himself clapping, and he noticed Wyatt was staring with his mouth open. Temple nodded at Hadrian and Wyatt.

"Stand by at the capstan!" Lieutenant Bishop shouted, returning order. "Loose the heads'ls, hands aloft, loose the tops'ls fore and aft!"

The crew scattered to their duties. A ring of men surrounded the wooden spoke wheel of the capstan, ready to raise the anchor. Wyatt moved quickly toward the ship's helm while the rest, Jacob included, climbed the shrouds of the three masts.

"And what are you two waiting for?" Mr. Temple asked after Hadrian had joined Royce. "You heard the lieutenant—get those sails loosed. Hadrian, take station at the capstan."

As they trotted to their duties, Mr. Temple gestured in Royce's direction and remarked to Wyatt, "No wonder he doesn't have rough hands. He doesn't use them!"

The ship's captain appeared on the quarterdeck. He stood beside the lieutenant, his hands clasped behind his back, chest thrust out, and chin set against the salty wind that tugged at the edges of his uniform. Of slightly less than average height, he seemed the opposite of the lieutenant. While Bishop was tall and thin, the captain was short and plump, with a double chin and long hanging cheeks, which quickly flushed red with

the wind. He watched the progress of the crew and then nodded to his first officer.

"Take her out, Mr. Bishop."

"Raise anchor!" the lieutenant bellowed. "Wheel hard
over!"

Hadrian found a place among those at the capstan and
pushed against the wooden spokes, rotating the large spool
that lifted the anchor from the bottom of the harbor. With the
anchor broken out, the wheel hard over, and the forecastle
hands drawing at the headsail sheets, the *Emerald Storm*
brought its bow around. As it gained steerage, it moved away
from the dock and into the clear of the main channel, and the
rigging crew dropped the remaining sails. The great canvases
quivered and flapped, snapping in the wind like three violent
white beasts.

"Hands to the braces!" Mr. Temple barked, and the men
took hold of the ropes, pulling the yards around until they
caught the wind. The sails plumed full as the sea breeze
stretched them taut. Hadrian could feel the deck lurch beneath
his feet as the *Emerald Storm* slipped forward through the
water, rudder balanced against sail pressure.

They traveled down the coast, passing farmers and workers, who paused briefly to look at the handsome vessel flying
by. At the helm, Wyatt spun the wheel, steering steadily out to
sea. The men on the braces trimmed the yards so not a sail
fluttered, sending the ship dashing through the waves as it
raced from shore.

"Course sou'west by south, sir," Wyatt said, updating
Temple, who repeated the statement to the lieutenant, who
repeated it to the captain, who in turn nodded his approval.

The men at the capstan dispersed, leaving Hadrian looking
around for something to do. Royce descended to the deck
beside him, neither one certain of his duty now that the ship

was under way. It did not matter much, as the lieutenant, the captain, and Temple were all busy on the quarterdeck. The other hands moved casually now, cleaning up the rigging, finishing the job of stowing the supplies, and generally settling in.

"Why didn't we ever consider sailing as a profession?" Hadrian asked Royce as he moved to the side and faced the wind. He took a deep, satisfying breath and smiled. "This is nice. A lot better than a sweaty, fly-plagued horse—and look at the land go by! How fast do you think we're going?"

"The fact that we're trapped here, with no chance of retreat except into the ocean, doesn't bother you?"

Hadrian glanced over the side at the heaving waves. "Well, not until now. Why do you always have to ruin everything? Couldn't you let me enjoy the moment?"

"You know me, just trying to keep things in perspective."

"Our course is south. Any clue where we might be going?"

Royce shook his head. "It only means we aren't invading Melengar, but we could be headed just about anywhere else." Someone arriving deck side caught his attention. "Who's this now?"

A man in red and black appeared from below and climbed the stair to the quarterdeck. He stood out from the rest of the crew by virtue of his pale skin and silken vestments, which were far too elegant for the setting and whipped about like streamers at a fair. He moved hunched over; his slumped shoulders reminded Hadrian of a crow shuffling along a branch. He sported a mustache and short goatee. His dark hair, combed back, emphasized a dramatically receding hairline.

"Broken-crown crest," Hadrian noted. "Seret."

"Red cassock," Royce added. "Sentinel."

"At least he's not Luis Guy. It'd be pretty hard to hide on a ship this size."

"If it was Guy"—Royce smiled wickedly—"we wouldn't need to hide."

Hadrian noticed Royce glance over the side of the ship at the water, which foamed and churned as it rushed past.

"If a sentinel is on board," Royce continued, "we can assume there are seret as well. They never travel alone."

"Maybe below."

"Maybe disguised in the crew," Royce cautioned.

To starboard, a sailor dropped his burden on the deck and wiped the sweat from his brow with a rag. Noticing them standing idle, he walked over.

"Yer good," he said to Royce. "No man's beaten Jacob aloft before."

The sailor was tan and thin, with a tattoo of a woman on his forearm and a ring of silver in his ear.

"I didn't beat him. We landed together," Royce said, correcting him.

"Aye, clever that. My name's Grady. What do they call you?"

"Royce, and this is Hadrian."

"Oh yeah, the cook." Grady gave Hadrian a nod, and then returned his attention. "Royce, huh? I'm surprised I haven't heard yer name before. With skills like you got, I woulda figured you'd be famous. What ships have you served on?"

"None around these waters," Royce replied.

Grady looked at him curiously. "Where, then? The Sound? Dagastan? The Sharon? Try me, I've been around a few places myself."

"Sorry, I'm really bad at remembering names."

Grady's eyebrows rose. "You don't remember the names of the ships you served on?"

"I would prefer not to discuss them."

"Aye, consider the subject closed." He looked at Hadrian. "You were with him, then?"

"We've worked together for some time."

Grady nodded. "Just forget I said anything. I won't be getting in the way. You can bank money on Grady's word, too." The man winked, then walked away, glancing back over his shoulder at them a few times as he went off, grinning.

"Seems like a nice sort," Hadrian said. "Strange and confusing, but nice. You think he knows why we're here?"

"Wish he did," Royce replied, watching Grady resume his work. "Then he could tell us. Still, I've found that when hunting Merrick, stranger things have been known to happen. One thing's for certain—this trip is going to be interesting."

Chapter 5

Broken Silence

Although it was early, Nimbus was already waiting outside the closed door of Amilia's office with armloads of parchments. He smiled brightly at her approach. "Good morning, Your Ladyship," he greeted her with as much of a bow as he could manage without spilling his burden. "Beautiful day, is it not?"

Amilia grunted in reply. She was not a morning person, and that day's agenda included a meeting with Regent Saldur. If anything was likely to ruin a day, that would do it. She opened her office door with a key kept on a chain around her neck. The office was a reward for the successful presentation of the empress nearly a month before.

Modina had been near death when Saldur had appointed Amilia imperial secretary to the empress. At that time, the young ruler had not spoken a word, was dangerously thin, and had an unwavering expression, which was never more than a blank stare. Amilia had provided her with better living conditions and worked hard to get her to eat. After several months, the girl had begun to improve. Modina had managed to memorize a short speech for the day of her presentation but abandoned the prepared text and publicly singled out Amilia, proclaiming her a hero.

No one had been more shocked than Amilia, but Saldur thought she had been responsible. Rather than exploding in anger, he congratulated her. Since that day, his attitude toward Amilia had changed—as if she had bought admission into the exclusive club of the deviously ambitious. In his eyes, she had not only been capable of manipulating the mentally unbalanced ruler, but willing to do so as well. This raised opinion of her had been followed by additional responsibilities and a new title: Chief Imperial Secretary to the Empress.

She took her directions from Saldur as Modina remained locked in the dark recesses of her madness. One of her new responsibilities was reading and replying to mail addressed to the empress. Saldur gave her the task as soon as he discovered she could read and write. Amilia also received the responsibility of being the empress's official gatekeeper. She decided who could, and who could not, have an audience with Modina. Normally a position of extreme power, hers was just a farce, because absolutely no one *ever* saw Modina.

Despite Amilia's grandiose new title, her office was a small chamber with nothing but an old desk and a pair of bookshelves. The room was cold, damp, and sparse—but it was hers. She was filled with pride each morning when she sat behind the desk, and pride was something Amilia was unaccustomed to.

"Are those more letters?" Amilia asked.

"Yes, I am afraid so," Nimbus replied. "Where would you like them?"

"Just drop them on the pile with the others. I can see now why Saldur gave me this job."

"It is a very prestigious task," Nimbus assured her. "You are the de facto voice of the New Empire as it relates to the people. What you write is taken as the word of the empress, and thus the voice of a god incarnate."

"So you're saying I'm the voice of god now?"

Nimbus smiled thoughtfully. "In a manner of speaking—yes."

"You have a crazy way of seeing things, Nimbus. You really do."

He was always able to cheer her up. His outlandishly colored clothes and silly powdered wig made her smile on even the bleakest of days. Moreover, the odd little courtier had a bizarre manner of finding joy in everything, blind to the inevitable disaster that Amilia knew lurked at every turn.

Nimbus deposited the letters in the bin beside Amilia's desk, then fished out a tablet and looked it over briefly before speaking. "You have a meeting this morning with Lady Rashambeau, Baroness Fargal, and Countess Ridell. They have insisted on speaking to you personally about their failed petitions to have a private audience with Her Supreme Eminence. You also have a dedication to make on behalf of the empress at the new memorial in Capital Square. That is at noon. Also, the material has arrived, but you still need to get specifications to the seamstress for the new dress. And, of course, you have a meeting this afternoon with Regent Saldur."

"Any idea yet what he wants to see me about?"

Nimbus shook his head.

Amilia slumped in her chair. She was certain Saldur's appointment had to do with Modina's berating of the clerk the previous day. She had no idea how to explain the empress's actions. That had been the only time since her speech that Modina had uttered a single word.

"Would you like me to help you answer those?" Nimbus asked with a sympathetic smile.

"No, I'll do it. Can't have both of us playing god, now can we? Besides, you have your own work. Tell the seamstress to meet me in Modina's chambers in four hours. That should give me time to reduce this pile some. Reschedule the ladies of the court meeting to just before noon."

"But you have the dedication at noon."

"Exactly."

"Excellent planning," Nimbus said, praising her. "Is there anything else I can do for you before I get to work?"

Amilia shook her head. Nimbus bowed and left.

The pile beside her got higher each day. She plucked a letter from the top and started working. While not a difficult job, the task was repetitious and boring, as she said the same thing in each reply.

The office of the empress regrets to inform you that Her Most Serene and Royal Grand Imperial Eminence, Empress Modina Novronian, will not be able to receive you due to time constraints caused by important and pressing matters of state.

She had replied to only seven of the letters when there was a soft knock at the office door. A maid hesitantly popped her head inside, the new girl. She had started only the day before, and she worked quietly, which Amilia appreciated. Amilia nodded an invitation, and the maid wordlessly slipped inside with her bucket, mop, and cleaning tools, taking great pains not to bang them against the door.

Amilia recalled her own days as a servant in the castle. As a kitchen worker, she had rarely cleaned rooms but occasionally had to fill in for a sick chambermaid. She used to loathe working in a room with a noble present. It always made her self-conscious and frightened. She could never tell what they might do. One minute they might seem friendly. The next they could be calling for you to be whipped. Amilia had never understood how they could be so capricious and cruel.

She watched the girl set about her work. The maid was on

her hands and knees, scrubbing the floor with a brush, the skirt of her uniform soaked with soapy water. Amilia had a stack of inquiries to attend to, but the maid distracted her. She felt guilty not acknowledging the girl's presence. It felt rude.

I should talk to her. Even as Amilia thought this, she knew it would be a mistake. This new girl saw her as a noble, the chief imperial secretary to the empress, and would be terrified if Amilia so much as offered a *good morning.*

Perhaps a few years older than Amilia, the girl was slender and pretty, although little could be determined, given her attire. She wore a loose-fitting dress with a canvas apron, her figure hidden, a mystery lost beneath the folds. All serving girls adopted the style except the foolish or ambitious. When you worked in the halls of those who took whatever they wanted, it was best to avoid notice.

Amilia tried to decide if the girl was married. After Modina's speech, the ban on servants leaving the castle had been lifted, and it was possible that the maid had a family in the city. She wondered if she went home to them each night, or, like Amilia, she had left everything, and everyone, to live in the castle. She likely had several children; pretty peasant girls married young.

Amilia chided herself for watching the maid instead of working, but something about the girl kept her attention. The way she moved and how she held her head seemed out of place. She watched her dab the brush in the water and stroke the floor, moving the brush from side to side like a painter. She spread water around but did little to free the dirt from the surface. Edith Mon would whip her for that. The headmistress was a cruel taskmaster. Amilia had found herself on the wrong end of her belt on a number of occasions for lesser infractions. For that reason alone, Amilia felt sorry for the poor girl. She knew all too well what she faced.

"Are they treating you well here?" Amilia found herself asking, despite her determination to remain silent.

The girl looked up and glanced around the room.

"Yes, you," Amilia assured her.

"Yes, milady," the maid replied, looking up.

She's looking right at me, Amilia thought, stunned. Even with her title, and a rank equivalent to baroness, Amilia still had a hard time returning the stare of even the lowest-ranking nobles, but this girl was looking right at her.

"You can tell me if they aren't. I know what it's like to—" She stopped, realizing the maid would not believe her. "I understand new servants can be picked on and belittled by the others."

"I'm getting along fine, milady," she said.

Amilia smiled, trying to set her at ease. "I didn't mean to suggest you weren't. I'm very pleased with you. I just know it can be hard sometimes when you start out in a new place. I want you to know that I can help if you're having trouble."

"Thank you," she said, but Amilia heard the suspicion in her voice.

Having a noble offer to help with bullying peers was probably a shock to the girl. If it had been her, Amilia would have thought it a trap of some kind, a test perhaps to see if she would speak ill of others. If she admitted to problems, the noble might have her removed from the palace. Under no circumstances would Amilia have admitted anything to a noble, no matter how kindly the woman might have presented herself.

Amilia instantly felt foolish. There was a division between nobles and commoners, and for good or ill, she was now on the other side. The conditioning that separated the two was far too entrenched for her to wipe away. She decided to stop tormenting the poor girl and return to her work. Just then, however, the maid put down the scrub brush and stood.

"You're Lady Amilia, is that right?"

"Yes," she replied, surprised at the sudden forwardness.

"You're the chief secretary to the empress?"

"How well informed you are. It's good that you're learning your way around. It took me quite some time to figure out—"

"How is she?"

Amilia hesitated. Interrupting was very inappropriate, and it was incredibly bold to inquire so bluntly about Her Eminence. Amilia was touched, however, by her concern for the welfare of Modina. Perhaps this girl was unaccustomed to interacting with the gentry. She was likely from some isolated village that had never seen a visiting noble. The unnerving way she held Amilia's stare revealed she had no experience with proper social etiquette. Edith Mon would waste no time beating those lessons into her.

"She's fine," Amilia replied. Then, as a matter of habit, she added, "She was ill, and still is, but getting better every day."

"I never see her," the maid went on. "I've seen you, the chancellor, the regents, and the lord chamberlain, but I never see her in the halls or at the banquet table."

"She guards her privacy. You have to understand that everyone wants time with the empress."

"I guess she gets around using secret passages?"

"Secret passages?" Amilia chuckled at the imagination of this girl. "No, she doesn't use secret passages."

"But I heard this palace is very old and filled with hidden stairs and corridors that lead to all kinds of secret places. Is that true?"

"I don't know anything about that," Amilia replied. "What got this into your head?"

The maid immediately put a hand over her mouth in embarrassment. Her eyes dropped to the floor in submission. "Forgive me, milady. I didn't mean to be so bold. I'll get back to my work now."

"That's all right," Amilia replied as the maid dunked her brush again. "What's your name, dear?"

"Ella, milady," the maid replied softly without pausing or looking up.

"Well, Ella, if you have problems or other questions, you have permission to speak to me."

"Thank you, milady. That is very kind of you."

Amilia returned to her own work and left the maid to hers. In a short time, the servant finished and gathered her things to leave.

"Goodbye, Ella," Amilia offered.

The maid smiled at the mention of her name and nodded appreciatively. As she walked out, Amilia glanced at her hands, which gripped the bucket handle and the mop, and was surprised to see long fingernails on them. Ella noticed her glance, shifted her grip to cover her nails, and promptly left the chamber.

Amilia stared after her awhile, wondering how a working girl could manage to grow nails as nice as hers. She put the thought out of her mind and returned to her letters.

∽

"You realize they're going to get wise," Amilia said after the seamstress had finished taking Modina's measurements and left the chamber.

The chief secretary moved around the empress's bedroom, straightening up. Modina sat beneath the narrow window, in the only patch of sunshine entering the room. This was where Amilia found her most often. She would sit there for hours, just staring outside, watching clouds and birds. It broke Amilia's heart a little each time she saw her longing for a world barred to her.

The empress showed no response to Amilia's comment. Her lucidity from the day before had vanished. The empress heard her, though. She was quite certain of that now.

"They aren't stupid," she went on as she fluffed a pillow. "After your speech and that incident with the clerk yesterday, I think it's only a matter of time. You would have been wiser to stay in your room and let me handle it."

"He wasn't going to listen to you." The empress spoke.

Amilia dropped the pillow.

Turning as casually as she could, she stole a glance over her shoulder to see Modina still looking out the window with her traditional vague and distant expression. Amilia slowly picked up the pillow and resumed her straightening. Then she ventured, "It might have taken a little time, but I'm certain I could have persuaded him to provide us with the material."

Amilia waited, holding her breath, listening.

Silence.

Just when she was certain it had been only one of her rare outbursts of coherency, Modina spoke again. "He never would have given in to you. You're scared of him, and he knows that."

"And you aren't?"

Again silence. Amilia waited.

"I'm not afraid of anything anymore," the empress finally replied, her voice distant and thin.

"Maybe not afraid, but it would bother you if they took the window away."

"Yes," Modina said simply.

Amilia watched as the empress closed her eyes and turned her face full into the light of the sun.

"If Saldur discovers your masquerade—if he thinks you've been just acting insane and misleading the regents for over a year—it might frighten him into locking you up where you can't do any harm. They could put you in a dark hole some-where and leave you there."

"I know," Modina said, her eyes still closed and head tilted upward. Immersed in the daylight, she appeared almost to glow. "But I won't let them hurt you."

The words took a moment to register with Amilia. She had heard them clearly enough, but their meaning came so unex-pectedly that she sat on the bed without realizing it. As she thought back, it should have been obvious, but not until that moment did she realize what Modina had done. The empress's speech had been for Amilia's benefit—to ensure that Ethelred and Saldur could not have her removed or killed. Few people had ever gone out of their way for Amilia. The concept that Modina—the crazy empress—had risked herself in this way was unimaginable. Such an event was as likely as the wind changing direction to suit her, or the sun asking her permis-sion to shine.

"Thank you," was all she could think to say. For the first time she felt awkward in Modina's presence. "I'm going to go now."

She headed for the door. As her hand touched the latch, Modina spoke again.

"It isn't completely an act, you know."

᪅

Waiting inside the regent's office, Amilia realized she had not heard a word in her meeting with the ladies or during the ded-ication later that morning. Dumbfounded by her conversation with Modina—by the mere fact that she had actually had a conversation with Modina—she registered little else. Her dis-traction, however, vanished the instant Saldur arrived.

The regent appeared imposing, as always, in his elegant

robe and cape of purple and black. His white hair and lined face lent him a grandfatherly appearance, but his eyes held no warmth.

"Afternoon, Amilia," he said, walking past her and taking a seat at his desk. The regent's office was dramatically opulent. Ten times larger than hers, it featured an elegant decor. A fine patterned rug covered the polished hardwood, and numerous end tables flanked couches and armchairs. On one table sat an elaborately carved chess set. The fireplace was an impressively wide hearth of finely chiseled marble. There were decanters of spirits on the shelves, along with thick books. Religious-themed paintings lined the spaces between the bookcases and windows. One illustrated the familiar scene of Maribor anointing Novron. The immense desk, behind which Saldur sat, was a dark mahogany polished to a fine luster and adorned with a bouquet of fresh flowers. The entire office was perfumed with the heady scent of incense, the kind Amilia had smelled only once before, when visiting a cathedral.

"Your Grace," Amilia replied respectfully.

"Sit down, my dear," Saldur said.

Amilia found a chair and mechanically sat. Every muscle in her body was tense. She wished Modina had not spoken to her that morning—then she could honestly plead ignorance. Amilia was no good at lying and had no idea how she should respond to Saldur's interrogation in order to bring the least amount of punishment to her and the empress. She was still debating what she might say when Saldur spoke.

"I've some news for you," he said, folding his hands on the surface of the desk and leaning forward. "It won't be public for several weeks, but you need to know now so you can begin preparations. I want you to keep this to yourself until I announce it, do you understand?"

Amilia nodded as if she understood.

"In almost four months, during the Wintertide celebrations, Modina will marry Regent Ethelred. I don't think I need to impress upon you the importance of this occasion. The Patriarch himself is personally coming to perform the ceremony. All eyes will be on this palace...and on the empress."

Amilia said nothing and barely managed another shallow nod.

"It's your charge to ensure that nothing embarrassing occurs. I've been very pleased with your work to date, and as a result I'm giving you an opportunity to excel further. I'm putting *you* in charge of arranging the ceremony. It'll be your responsibility to develop a guest list and prepare invitations. Go to the lord chamberlain for help with that. You'll also need to coordinate with the palace cooks for meals. I understand you have a good relationship with the head cook?"

Once more she nodded.

"Wonderful. There should be decorations, entertainment— music certainly, and perhaps a magician or a troupe of acrobats. The ceremony will take place here, in the great hall. That should make things a bit easier for you. You'll also need to have a wedding dress made—one worthy of the empress." Seeing the tension on her face, Saldur added, "Relax, Amilia, this time you only need to get her to say two words...*I do*."

CHAPTER 6

THE EMERALD STORM

As the ship lurched once more, Hadrian stumbled and nearly hit his head on the overhead beam. It would have been his third time that day. The lower decks of the *Emerald Storm* provided meager headroom and precious little light. An obstacle course of sea chests, ditty bags, crude wooden benches, tables that swung from ropes, and close to one hundred thirty men was crammed into the berth deck. Hadrian made his way aft, dodging the majority of the starboard watch, most of whom were asleep, swaying in hammocks strung from the same thick wooden crossbeams on which Hadrian had nearly cracked his skull. The clutter and the shifting of the ship were not the only things making Hadrian stagger. He had been feeling nauseated since sunset.

The *Emerald Storm* had been at sea for nearly fifteen hours, and the enigma of life aboard ship was slowly revealing itself. Hadrian had spent many years in the company of professional soldiers and recognized that each branch of the military held its own jargon, traditions, and idiosyncrasies, but he had never set foot on a ship. He knew he could be certain of only two things: he had a lot of learning to do, and he had little time to do it.

He had already picked up several important pieces of information, such as where to relieve himsclf, which, to his surprise, was at the head of the ship. A precarious experience, as he had to hang out over the sea at the base of the bowsprit. This might be second nature to sailors, and easy for Royce, but it gave Hadrian pause.

Another highly useful discovery was a cursory understanding about the chain of command. Hadrian determined that the officers—noblemen mostly—were skilled tradesmen and held a higher rank than the general seamen, but he could also tell there were substrata within these broad classes. There were different ranks of officers and even more subtle levels of seniority, influence, and jurisdiction. He could not expect to penetrate such a complex hierarchy on his first day, but he had managed to determine that the boatswain and his mates were the ones charged with making sure the seamen did their jobs. They were quite persuasive with their short rope whips and kept a keen eye on the crew at all times. Because of this, they were the ones he watched.

The ship's crew divided into two watches. While one worked the ship, the other rested, slept, or ate. Lieutenant Bishop had placed Royce on the starboard watch assigned to the maintop. His job was to work the rigging on the center mast. This put him under Boatswain Bristol Bennet and his three mates. Hadrian had seen their like before. Drunks, vagrants, and thugs, they would never have amounted to much on land, but aboard ship they held power and status. The chance to repay others for any mistreatment they had experienced made them cruel and quick to punish. Hadrian still waited to discover his watch assignment, but he hoped it would be the same as Royce's.

He had been lucky so far. This being the first day out, preparing meals had been little more than placing out fresh foods from the recent stay at port. Fruit, fresh bread, and salted meats were merely handed out with no cooking required. Consequently, Hadrian's talents remained untested, but time was running out. He knew how to cook, of course. He had prepared meals for years using little more than a campfire, but that had mainly been for him and Royce. He didn't know how to cook for an entire ship's crew. Needing to find out exactly what they expected drove him to wander in hopes of finding Wyatt.

"The Princess of Melengar rules there now," Hadrian heard a young lad say.

He didn't look to be much more than sixteen. He was a waif of a boy with thin whiskers, freckles darkened by days in the sun, and curly hair cut in a bowl-like fashion except for a short ponytail he tied with a black cord. He sat with Wyatt, Grady, and a few other men around a swaying table illuminated by a candle melted to the center of a copper plate. They were playing cards and the giant shadows they cast only made Hadrian's approach more disorienting.

"She doesn't rule Ratibor. She's the mayor," Wyatt said, correcting the boy as he laid a card on the pile before him.

"What's the difference?"

"She was appointed, lad."

"What's that mean?" the boy asked as he tried to decide which card to play, holding his hand so tight to his chest he could barely see the cards himself.

"It means she didn't just take over. The people of the city *asked* her to run things."

"But she can still execute people, right?"

"I suppose."

"Sounds like a ruler to me." With a wide grin, the boy laid a card indicating that he thought it was a surprisingly good play.

"Sounds like them people of Ratibor are dumb as dirt," Grady said gruffly. His expression betrayed his irritation at the boy's discard. "They finally get the yoke off their backs and right away they ask for a new one."

"Grady!" said a man with a white kerchief on his head. "I'm from Ratibor, you oaf!"

"Exactly! Thanks for proving me point, Bernie," Grady replied, slamming his play on the table so hard several surrounding seamen groaned in their hammocks. Grady laughed at his own joke and the rest at the table chuckled good-naturedly, except Bernie from Ratibor.

"Hadrian!" Wyatt greeted him warmly as the new cook staggered up to them like a drunk. "We were just talking about land affairs. Most of these poor sods haven't been ashore in over a year and we were filling them in on the news about the war."

"Which has been bloody cracking, seeing as how we didn't even know there was one," Grady said, feigning indignation.

"We were just in dock, though," Hadrian said. "I would have thought—"

"That don't mean nuttin'," one of the other men said. With next to no hair and few teeth, he appeared to be the oldest at the table, and possibly the entire ship. He had a silver earring that glinted with the candlelight and a tattoo of a mermaid that wrapped around his forearm. He too wore a white kerchief on his head. "Most of this here crew is pressed. The captain would be barmy to let them touch solid ground in a port. He and Mr. Bishop would be the only ones left to rig her!"

This brought a round of laughter and garnered irritated growls from those trying to sleep.

"You don't look so good," Wyatt mentioned to Hadrian.

He shook his head miserably. "It's been a long time since I've been on a ship. Does the *Storm* always rock so much?"

"Hmm?" Wyatt glanced at him, then laughed. "This? This here is nothing. You won't even notice it in a day or so." He watched the next man at the table play his card. "We're still in the sound. Wait until we hit the open sea. You might want to sit. You're sweating."

Hadrian touched his face and felt the moisture. "Funny, I feel chilled, if anything."

"Have a seat," Wyatt said. "Poe, give him your spot."

"Why me?" the young boy asked, insulted.

"Because I said so." Poe's expression showed that was not enough for him to give up one of the limited places. "And because I'm a quartermaster and you're a seaman, but even more importantly, because Mr. Bishop appointed you cook's mate."

"He did?" Poe asked, and blinked, a smile crossing his face.

"Congratulations," Wyatt said. "Now, you might want to make a good impression on your new boss and move your infernal arse!"

The boy promptly stood and pretended to clean the bench with an invisible duster. "After you, sir!" he said with an exaggerated bow.

"Does he know anything about cooking?" Hadrian asked dubiously, taking the seat.

"Sure, sure!" Poe declared exuberantly. "I know plenty. You just wait. I'll show ya."

"Good, I don't feel up to working with food yet." Hadrian let his head drop into his hands. The old man next to Wyatt tossed down his card and the whole group groaned in agony.

"You bloody bastard, Drew!" Grady barked at him, tossing what remained of his cards onto the pile. The others did the same.

Drew grinned, showing his few yellowed teeth, and

collected the tiny pile of silver tenents. "That's it for me, boys. Good night."

"Night, Drew, ya lousy Lanksteer!" Grady said, shooing him away as if he were a bug. "We can talk at breakfast, eh?"

"Sure, Grady," Drew said. "Oh, that reminds me. I heard something right funny tonight when I was reefing the tops'l. We're going to be taking on a passenger to help find the horn. How stupid are these landlubbers? It's only the most well-known point on the Sharon! Anyway, remind me at breakfast and I'll tell ya about it. It's a real hoot, it is. Night now."

Most of the rest of the men headed off, leaving just Wyatt, Grady, Poe, and Hadrian.

"You should turn in as well," Wyatt told Poe.

"I'm not tired," he protested.

"I didn't ask if you were tired, did I?"

"I want to stay up and celebrate my promotion."

"Off with ya before I report you for disobeying a superior."

Poe scowled and stomped off, looking for his hammock.

"You too, Grady," Wyatt told him.

The old seaman looked at Wyatt suspiciously, then leaned over and quietly asked, "Why you trying to get rid of me, Deminthal?"

"Because I'm tired of looking at that ugly scowl of yours, that's why."

"Codswallop!" he hissed. "You wanna be alone to talk about the you-know-what, don't ya? Both of you are in on it. I can tell, and that Royce fellow, he's in too. How many more you got, Wyatt? Room for another? I'm pretty good in a fight."

"Shut up, Grady," Wyatt told him. "Talk like that can get you hanged."

"Okay, okay," Grady said, holding up his palms. "Just letting you know, that's all." He got up and headed for his own hammock, casting several glances back over his shoulder, until he disappeared into the forest of swinging men.

"What was that all about?" Hadrian asked, hooking a thumb toward Grady's retreating figure.

"I don't know," Wyatt replied. "There's always one sailor on board any ship looking for a mutiny. Grady seems to be the *Emerald Storm's*. Ever since he signed on, he's been thinking there's a conspiracy going on—mostly because he wants there to be, I think. He has issues with authority, Grady does." Wyatt started gathering up the scattered deck of cards into a pile. "So, what's your story?"

"How do you mean?" Hadrian asked.

"Why are you and Royce here? I stuck my neck out getting you on board. I think I've a right to know why."

"I thought you got us aboard to pay off a debt."

"True, but I'm still curious why you wanted on the *Storm* in the first place."

"We're looking for a safer line of work and thought we'd try sailing," Hadrian offered. Wyatt's face showed he was not buying it. "We're on a job, but I can't tell you more than that."

"Does it have to do with the secret cargo?"

Hadrian blinked. "It's possible. What *is* the secret cargo?"

"Weapons. Steel swords, heavy shields, imperial-made crossbows, armor—enough to outfit a good-sized army. It came aboard at the last minute, hauled up in the middle of the night just before we sailed."

"Interesting," Hadrian mused. "Any idea where we're headed?"

"Nope, but that's not unusual. Captains usually keep that information to themselves, and Captain Seward doesn't even share that with me...and I'm the quartermaster."

"Quartermaster? I thought you were the helmsman."

"I'm guessing you've served in armies, haven't you?"

"A few, and the quartermaster is the supply officer."

"But on the sea, the quartermaster steers the ship, and as I mentioned, the captain hasn't even told me where we are going." Wyatt shuffled the cards absently. "So, you don't know where the ship is going, and you weren't aware of the cargo. This job didn't come with much in the way of information, did it?"

"What about you?" Hadrian turned the tables. "What are you doing here?"

"I could say I was working for a living, and for me it would actually make sense, but like you, I'm looking for answers."

"To what?"

"To where my daughter is." Wyatt paused a moment, his eyes glancing at the candle. "Allie was taken a week ago. I was out finding work, and while I was gone, the Imps grabbed her."

"Grabbed her? Why?"

Wyatt lowered his voice. "Allie is part elven, and the New Empire is not partial to their kind. Under a new law, anyone with even a drop of elf blood is subject to arrest. They've been rounding them up and putting them on ships, but no one can tell me where they've taken them. So here I am."

"But what makes you think this ship will go to the same place?"

"I take it you haven't ventured down to the waist hold yet?" He paused a second, then added, "That's the bottom of the ship, below the waterline. Ship stores are there, as well as livestock like goats, chickens, and cows. Sailors on report get the duty to pump the bilge. It's a miserable job on account of the manure mixing with the seawater that leaks in. It's also where—right now—more than a hundred elves are chained up in an area half this size."

Hadrian nodded with a grimace at the thought.

"You and Royce gave me a break once because of my daughter. Why was that?"

"That was Royce's call. You need to take that up with him. Although I wouldn't do it for a while. He's sicker than I am. I've never seen him so miserable, and this sea business is making him irritable. Well, more irritable than usual."

Wyatt nodded. "My daughter's the same way on water. Pitiful little thing, she's like a cat on a piece of driftwood. It takes her forever to get accustomed to the rocking." He paused a moment, looking at the candle.

"I'm sure you'll find her, don't worry." Hadrian glanced at the mass of men around him and lowered his voice to a whisper. "The job we're on is important, and we can't afford to be distracted, but if the situation presents itself, we'll help any way we can. Something tells me I won't have much trouble convincing Royce."

Hadrian felt the nausea rising in his stomach once more. His face must have betrayed his misery.

"Don't worry. Seasickness usually only lasts three days," Wyatt assured him as he put the cards in his breast pocket. "After that, both of you will be fine."

"If we can stay on board that long. I don't know anything about being a ship's cook."

Wyatt smiled. "Don't worry. I've got you covered. Poe will do most of the work. I know he looks young, but he'll surprise you."

"So how is it that I get an assistant?"

"As ship's cook, you rank as a petty officer. Don't get all excited, though. You're still under the boatswains and their mates, but it does grant you the services of Ordinary Seaman Poe. It also exempts you from the watches. That means so long as the ship's meals are on schedule, the rest of your time is your own. What you need to know is that breakfast is served promptly at the first bell of the forewatch." Wyatt paused. "That's the first time you'll hear a single bell toll after eight bells is rung just after the sun breaks above the horizon.

"So have Poe light the galley fires shortly after middle watch. He'll know when that is. Tell him to make skillygalee — that's oatmeal gruel. Don't forget biscuits. Biscuits get served at every meal. At eight bells, the men are piped to breakfast. Each mess will send someone to you with a messkid, sorta like a wooden bucket. Your job will be to dish out the food. Have Poe make some tea as well. The men will drink beer and rum at dinner and supper, but not at breakfast, and no one on board will risk drinking straight water."

"Risk?"

"Water sits in barrels for months, or years if a ship is on a long voyage. It gets rancid. Tea and coffee are okay 'cause they're boiled and have a little flavor. Coffee is expensive, though, and reserved for the officers. The crew and the midshipmen eat first. After that, Basil, the officers' cook, will arrive to make meals for the lieutenants and captain. Just stay out of his way.

"For dinner make boiled pork. Have Poe start boiling it right after Basil leaves. The salted meat will throw off a thick layer of fat. Half of that goes to the top captains to grease the rigging. The other half you can keep. You can sell it to tallow merchants at the next port for a bit of coin, but don't give it to the men. It will make you popular if you do, but it can also give them scurvy, and the captain won't like it. Have Poe boil some vegetables and serve them together as a stew, and don't forget the biscuits."

"So I tell Poe what to make and dish it out, but I don't actually do any cooking?"

Wyatt smiled. "That's the benefit of being a petty officer. Sadly, however, you only get a seaman's rate of pay. For supper, just serve what's left over from dinner, grog, and, of course, biscuits. After that, have Poe clean up, and like I said, the rest of the day is open to you. Sound easy?"

"Maybe, if I could stand straight and keep my stomach from doing backflips."

"Listen to Poe. He'll take good care of you. Now you'd best get back in your hammock. Trust me, it helps. Oh, and just so you know, you would have been wrong."

"About what?" Hadrian asked.

"About thinking sailing was a safer line of work."

⁓

It was still dark when the captain called, "All hands!"

A cold wind had risen, and in the dark hours before dawn, a light rain sprayed the deck, adding a wet chill to the seasick misery that had already deprived Hadrian of most of his sleep. During the night, the *Emerald Storm* had passed by the Isle of Niel and now approached the Point of Man. The point was a treacherous headland shoal that marked the end of Avryn Bay and the start of the Sharon Sea. In the dark, it was difficult to see the shoal, but the sound was unmistakable. From somewhere ahead there came the rhythmic, thundering boom of waves crashing against the point.

The below decks emptied as the boatswain and his mates roused all the men from both watches with their starter ropes, driving them up to stations.

"Bring her about!" shouted the captain from his perch on the quarterdeck. The dignified figure of Lieutenant Bishop echoed the order, which Mr. Temple repeated.

"Helm-a-lee!" shouted the captain. Once more the order echoed across the decks. Wyatt spun the ship's great wheel.

"Tacks and sheets!" Lieutenant Bishop barked to the crew.

cook, after all, but it seemed even a cook was expected to lend a hand on deck when necessary. He still felt ill, but Royce appeared worse. Hadrian watched as Boatswain Bristol, a big burly man, ordered him up the ropes, waving his short whip menacingly. Drained of color, Royce's face and hands stood out pale in the dark. His eyes were unfocused and empty. He reluctantly moved up the mainmast's ratlines, but he did not display any of the acrobatics of the previous day. Instead, he crawled miserably and hesitated partway up. He hovered in the wet rigging as if he might fall. From below, Bristol cursed at him until, at last, he moved upward once more. Hadrian imagined that the higher into the rigging Royce went, the more pronounced the sway of the ship would be. Between that, the slippery wet ropes, and the cold wind-driven rain, he did not envy his friend.

Several men were working the ropes that controlled the direction of the sails, but others, like him, remained idle, waiting in lines, which the boatswains formed. There was a tension evident in the silence of the crew. The booming of the headlands grew louder and closer, sounding like the pounding of a giant's hammer or the heartbeat of a god. They seemed to be flying blindly into the maw of some enormous unseen beast that would swallow them whole. The reality, Hadrian imagined, would not be much different should they come too close to the shoal.

Anticipating something, all eyes watched the figure of Captain Seward. Hadrian could tell by the feel of the wind and the direction of the rain that the ship was turning. The sails, once full and taut, began to flutter and collapsed as the bow crossed over into the face of the wind.

"Mains'l haul!" the captain suddenly shouted, and the crew cast off the bowlines and braces.

Seeing the movements, Hadrian realized the strategy. They were attempting a windward tack around the dangerous point, which meant the wind would be blowing the ship's hull toward the treacherous rocks even as they struggled to reset the sails to catch the wind from the other side. The danger came from the lack of maneuverability caused by empty sails during the tack. Without the wind driving the ship, the rudder could not push against the water and turn it. If the ship could not come about fully, it would not be able to catch the wind again, and it would drift into the shoal, which would shatter the timbered hull like an eggshell and cast the cargo and crew into a dark, angry sea.

Hadrian took hold of the rope in his line and, along with several others, pulled the yards round, repositioning the sails to catch the wind as soon as they were able. The rope was slick, and the wind jerked the coil so roughly that it took the whole line to pull the yards safely into position.

There was another deafening boom, and a burst of white spray shot skyward as the breaking water exploded over the port bow. The vessel was turning fast now, pulling away from the foam, struggling to get clear. No sooner had the bow cleared the wind than he heard the captain order: "Now! Meet her! Hard over!"

His voice was nearly lost as another powerful wave rammed the rocks just beside them, throwing the *Emerald Storm's* bow upward with a rough lurch that staggered them all. On the quarterdeck, Wyatt followed the order, spinning the wheel back, checking the swing before the ship could turn too far and lose its stern in the rocks.

Overhead, Hadrian heard a scream.

Looking up, he saw the figure of a man fall from the

mainsail rigging. His body landed a dozen steps away with a sickening thud. All eyes looked at the prone figure lying like a dark stain on the deck, but none dared move from their stations. Hadrian strained to see who it was. The man lay facedown, and in the dim light it was difficult to tell anything.

Is that Royce?

Normally he would never have questioned his friend's climbing skills, but with his sickness, the motion of the ship, and his inexperience, it was possible he could have slipped.

"Haul off all!" Mr. Temple shouted, ignoring the fallen man. The crew pulled on the sheets and braces, and once more captured the wind. The sails bloomed full, and Hadrian felt the lurch under his feet as the ship burst forward once more, heaving into the waves, now steering out to the open sea.

"Dr. Levy on deck!" Bishop shouted.

Hadrian rushed over the instant he could, but stopped short on seeing the tattoo of the mermaid on the dead man's forearm.

"It's Edgar Drew, sir. He's dead, sir!" Bristol shouted to the quarterdeck as he knelt next to the fallen man.

Several sailors gathered around the body, glancing upward at the mainsail shrouds, until the boatswain's mates took them to task. Hadrian thought he could see Royce up near the top yard, but in the dark he could not be sure. Still, he must have been close by when Drew fell.

The boatswain broke up the crowd and Hadrian, once more unsure of his duty, stood idle. The first light of dawn arrived, revealing a dull gray sky above a dull gray sea that lurched and rolled like a terrible dark beast.

"Cook!" a voice barked sharply.

Hadrian turned to see a young boy who was not much older than Poe but wearing the jacket and braid of an officer. He stood with a firm-set jaw and a posture so stiff he seemed made of wood. His cheeks were flushed red with the cool night air, and rainwater ran off the end of his nose.

"Aye, sir?" Hadrian replied, taking a guess it would be the right response.

"We are securing from all hands. You're free to fire the stove and get the meal ready."

Not knowing anything better to say, Hadrian replied, "Aye, aye." He turned to head for the galley.

"Cook!" the boy-officer snapped disapprovingly.

Hadrian pivoted as sharply as he could, recalling some of his military training. "Aye, sir?" he responded once more, feeling a bit stupid at his limited vocabulary.

"You neglected to salute me," he said hotly. "I'm putting you on report. What's your name?"

"Hadrian, sir. Blackwater, sir."

"I'll have the respect of you men even if I must flog you to obtain it! Do you understand? Now, let's see that salute."

Hadrian imitated the salute he had seen others perform by placing his knuckles to his forehead.

"That's better, seaman. Don't let it happen again."

"Aye, aye, sir."

It felt good to get down out of the rain and wind, and Poe met him on the way to the galley. The boy knew his way around the kitchen well, which was no doubt why Wyatt had suggested him. They fired up the stove and Hadrian watched Poe go to work cooking the morning oatmeal, adding butter and brown sugar in proper amounts and asking Hadrian to taste test it. Despite its name, the skillygalee was surprisingly good. Hadrian could not say the same about the biscuits, which were rock hard. Poe had not made them. He had merely fetched the round stones from the bread room, where boxes of them were stored. Hadrian's years of soldiering had made him familiar with hardtack, as they were known on land. The ubiquitous biscuits lasted forever but were never very filling. They were so hard that you had to soften them in tea or soup before eating them.

With the meal made, stewards from the mess arrived to gather their shares and carry them below.

Hadrian entered the berth deck, helping the mess steward carry the last of the servings. "Bloody show-off couldn't even make it up the lines," Jacob Derning was saying loudly. The men of the tops, and the petty officers, sat together at the tables as befitted their status on board, while others lay scattered with their copper plates amid the sacks and chests. Jacob looked like he was holding court at the center table. All eyes were on him as he spoke with grand gestures. On his head he wore a bright blue kerchief, as did everyone on the foretop crew.

"It's a different story with him when the sea's heaving and the lines are wet," Jacob went on. "You don't see him prancing then."

"He looked scared to me," Bristol the boatswain added. "Thought I was gonna have to go up and wallop him good to get him going again."

"Royce was fine," said a thin, gangly fellow with a white kerchief tied over his head and a thick blond walrus mustache. Hadrian did not know his name but recognized him as the captain of the maintop. "Just seasick, that's all. Once he was aloft, he reefed the tops'l just fine, albeit a bit oddly."

"Make excuses for him all ya want, Dime," Jacob told him, pointing a finger his way, "but he's a queer one, he is, and I find it more than a little dodgy that his first day aloft finds his fellow mate falling to his death."

"You suggesting Royce killed Drew?" Dime asked.

"I ain't saying nuttin', just think it's odd is all. Of course, you'd know better what went on up there, wouldn't you, Dime?"

"I didn't see it. Bernie was with him on the tops'l yard when he fell. He says Drew just got careless. I've seen it before. Fools like him skylarking in the sheets. Bernie says he was trying to walk the yard when the ship lurched 'cause of that burst from the shoal. He lost his footing. Bernie tried to grab him as he hung on to the yard, but the wetness made him slip off."

"Drew walking the yard in a rainstorm?" Jacob laughed. "Not likely."

"And where was Royce during all this?" Bristol asked.

Dime shook his head. "I dunno, didn't see him till later when he turned up at the masthead."

"Bernie was playing cards with him last night, wasn't he? I heard Drew walked away with a big pot."

"Now you're saying Bernie killed him?" a third fellow, with a red kerchief, asked. Hadrian had never seen him before but guessed he must be the captain of the mizzenmast, as the top captains, along with the boatswains, seemed to dine together at the same table.

"No, but I'm saying the cook was there and he and Royce are mates, aren't they? I think—" Jacob stopped short when he spotted Hadrian. "Bloody good thing you're a better cook than your mate is a topman or Mr. Temple's liable to chuck you both in the deep."

Hadrian said nothing. He looked around for Royce but did not find him, which was not too surprising, as he guessed his friend would not want to be anywhere near food.

"Might want to let your mate know I've asked Bristol here to have a word with Mr. Beryl about him."

"Beryl?" Bristol responded, puzzled. "I was gonna talk to Wesley."

"Bugger that," Jacob said. "Wesley's useless. He's a bleeding joke, ain't he?"

"I can't go over his head to Beryl," Bristol said defensively. "Wesley was watch officer when it happened."

"Are you barmy? What're you scared of? Think Wesley's gonna have at ya for going to Beryl? All Wesley will do is report you. That's all he ever does. He's a boy and hasn't grown a spine yet in that midshipman's uniform of his. Only reason he's on the *Storm* is 'cause his daddy is Lord Belstrad."

"We need to serve the midshipmen next," Poe reminded Hadrian, urgently tugging at his sleeve. "They mess in the wardroom aft."

Hadrian dropped off the messkid, hanging it from a hook the way he had seen Poe do, and gave Jacob one last glance only to find the fore captain grinning malevolently.

Far smaller and not much more comfortable than the crew's quarters, the midshipmen's mess was a tiny room aft on the berth deck that creaked loudly as the ship's hull lurched in the waves. Normally, Basil delivered the food he cooked for the officers, but this morning he was kept particularly busy working on the lieutenants' and captain's meal and had asked Poe and Hadrian for help in delivering the food to the midshipmen's mess.

"What are you doing in here?" the biggest midshipman asked abruptly as Hadrian and Poe entered. Hadrian almost answered when he realized the question was not addressed to him. Behind them, coming in late, was the young officer who had put Hadrian on report earlier. "You're supposed to be on watch, Wesley."

"Lieutenant Green relieved me a bit early so I could get some food while it was hot."

"So you've come to force yourself in on your betters, is that it?" the big man asked, and got a round of laughter from those with him. This had to be Beryl, Hadrian guessed. He was by far the oldest of the midshipmen—by ten years or more. "You're going to be nothing but a nuisance to the rest of us on this voyage, aren't you, boy? Here we thought we could have a quiet meal without you disturbing us. What did you do, whine to Green about how your stomach was hurting because we didn't let you have anything to eat last night?"

"No, I—" Wesley began.

"Shut it! I don't want to hear your sniveling voice. You there, cook!" Beryl snapped. "Don't serve Midshipman Wesley any food, not a biscuit crumb, do you understand?"

Hadrian nodded, guessing that Beryl somehow outranked Wesley despite both of them wearing midshipmen uniforms.

Wesley looked angry but said nothing. The boy turned away from the table toward his sea chest.

"Oh yes," Beryl said, rising from the table and walking across the room to Wesley. As he did, Hadrian noticed an old scar down the side of Beryl's face that looked to have nearly taken out his eye. "I've been meaning to go through your stuff to see if you had anything I might like."

Wesley turned, closing his chest abruptly.

"Open it, boy, and let me have a look."

"No, you have no right!"

Beryl's toadies at the table jeered the boy and laughed.

He took a step forward, and from his posture, Hadrian knew what was coming even if Wesley was oblivious. The big midshipman struck Wesley hard across the face. The boy fell over his sea chest onto his back. He rolled to his side, his face red with fury, but never got farther than his knees before Beryl struck him again, this time hard enough to spray blood from his nose. Wesley collapsed to the floor again with a wail of pain and lay crumbled in a ball, holding his face. The other midshipmen cheered.

Beryl sifted through the contents of Wesley's chest. "All that for nothing? I thought you were a lord's son. This is pathetic." He pulled a white linen shirt out and looked it over. "Well, this isn't too bad, and I could use a new shirt." He slammed the chest and returned to his breakfast.

Disgusted, Hadrian started to move to help Wesley but stopped when he saw Poe earnestly shaking his head. The young seaman took hold of Hadrian's arm and nearly dragged him back up to the main deck, where the sun had risen sufficiently enough to cause them to squint.

"Don't involve yourself in the affairs of officers," Poe told him earnestly. "They're just like nobles. Strike one and you'll hang for it. Trust me, I know what I'm talking about. My older brother Ned is the coxswain on the *Immortal*. The horror stories he's told me can turn one's stomach. Blimey, you act like you've never been on a ship before."

Hadrian did not say anything as he followed Poe back toward the galley.

"You haven't, have you?" Poe asked suddenly.

"So, who is this big fella? Is he Beryl?" Hadrian asked, changing the subject.

Poe scowled, then sighed. "Yep, he's the senior midshipman."

"So Beryl's a noble?"

"Don't know if he is or he ain't. Most are third or fourth sons, the ones not suited for the tournaments or monastic life who volunteer to serve, hoping they can one day manage a captain's rank, rule their own ship, and make some money. Most midshipmen only serve about five years before making lieutenant, but Beryl, he's been a midshipman for something like ten years now, I reckon. I guess it makes a man sorta cranky, being left behind like that. Even if he isn't a true blue-blooded noble, he's still an officer, and on this ship, that means the same thing."

❦

"Royce?" Hadrian whispered.

Royce lay in his hammock near the bow of the ship, his

head still covered with the white kerchief—the insignia of the maintop crew. He was shivering and wet, lying in soaked clothes.

"Royce," he repeated. This time, he shook his partner's shoulder.

"Do that again and I'll cut your hand off," he growled, his voice garbled and sickly.

"I brought you some coffee and bread. I put raisins in the bread. You like raisins."

Royce peered out from under his thin blanket with a vicious glare. He eyed the meal and promptly looked away with a grimace.

"Sorry, I just knew you hadn't eaten since yesterday." Hadrian put the tray down away from him. "They gave you extra duty, didn't they? You seemed to be up there longer than anyone else."

"Bristol kept me on station as punishment for being slow yesterday. How long was I up there?"

"Twelve hours at least. Listen, I thought we'd have a look around the forward hold. Wyatt tells me the seret are hiding a special cargo up there. If you can get your stomach under control, maybe you can open a few locks for me?"

Royce shook his head. "Not until this ship stops rolling. I stand up and the world spins. I've got to sleep. How come you're not sick?"

"I am, but not like you. I guess elven blood and water don't mix."

"It might," Royce said, disappearing back under his blanket. "If I don't start feeling better soon, I'll slit my wrists."

Hadrian took his blanket, laid it over the shivering form of Royce, and was about to head back up topside when he paused and asked, "Any idea what happened to Edgar Drew?"

"The guy that fell?"

"Yeah, some of the crew think he might have been murdered."

"I didn't see anything. Spent most of my time hugging the mast. I was pretty sick—still am. Get out of here and let me sleep."

It was late and the port watch was on duty, but most of them slept on deck or in the rigging. Only a handful had to remain alert during the middle watch: three lookouts aloft at the masthead, the quartermaster's mate who manned the wheel in Wyatt's absence, and the officer of the watch. Hadrian nearly ran into this last man as he came on deck.

"Mr. Wesley, sir," Hadrian said, shifting the tray so he could properly perform the salute.

Wesley's face was blotchy, his nose and eyes black and blue. Hadrian knew he was standing an additional watch. On his way to Royce, Hadrian had overheard Lieutenant Bishop questioning the midshipman about a brawl, but because Wesley had refused to divulge the name of his adversary, the young man took the punishment alone.

"Mr. Wesley, I thought you might like something to eat. I'm guessing you haven't had much today."

The officer glared at him a moment, then looked at the tray. As he saw the steam rising from the coffee cup, his mouth opened and abruptly shut. "Who sent you here? Was it Beryl? Is this supposed to be funny?"

"No, sir. I just know you didn't get to eat breakfast, and you've been on duty through the rest of the meals today. You must be starved."

"You were ordered not to feed me."

Hadrian shrugged. "I've also been ordered by the captain to see that the crew is fed and fit for duty. You've been up a long time. A man could fall asleep without something to help keep his eyes open."

Wesley looked back down. "That's coffee, isn't it?" the young midshipman asked, astonished. "There's not more than a few pounds of that on the entire ship, most of which is reserved for the captain."

"I did a bit of trading this afternoon with the purser and managed to get a couple cups' worth."

"Why offer it to me?"

Hadrian looked up at the night sky. "It's a cold night, and punishment for falling asleep can be severe."

Wesley nodded gravely. "On this ship, a midshipman is flogged."

"Do you think that's Beryl's plan, sir? For standing up to him this morning in front of the other officers, I mean."

"Maybe. Beryl is a tyrant of the worst order, and a libertine who squandered his family's fortune. I suspect Beryl would not even notice me, if it were not for my brother. By beating me he thinks he is superior to our family."

"Your brother is Sir Breckton Belstrad?"

Wesley nodded. "But the joke is on him. I am nothing like my brother, so besting me is no great accomplishment. If I were like him, I would not allow myself to be bullied by a lout like Beryl."

"Take the coffee and bread, sir," Hadrian said. "I can't say I care for Beryl, and if keeping you awake tonight gets under his skin, it'll make tomorrow all the better in my book. The orders of the captain override a senior midshipman's."

"I'll still have to put you on report for this morning. This kindness will not change that."

"I didn't expect it to, sir."

The midshipman studied Hadrian, his face betraying a new curiosity. "In that case, thank you," he said, taking the food.

∾

Dovin Thranic walked through the waist hold. Dark and
cramped, the ship's bottom deck reeked of animal dung and
salt water. A good four inches of liquid slime pooled along the
centerline gutter, forcing him to walk up the sides, hurdling
the futtock rider beams to keep his shoes dry. The next day he
would order Lieutenant Bishop to direct the detail of men to
work the bilge pump in the evening to ensure he did not need
to go through this every night. He was a sentinel of the Nyphron Church, presently one of only two men allowed to speak
personally with His Holiness the Patriarch, and yet here he
was crawling through sewage.

His unsettled stomach made the ordeal even more miserable. After several days of sleeping on board the *Emerald Storm*
while it was in dock, he thought he had gained his sea legs.
The initial wretchedness had subsided only to return now that
the ship was rolling at a different cadence on the open sea.
While not nearly as bad as before, his nausea was still a nuisance and would make his work less enjoyable.

Thranic carried no light but did not need one. The sentry's
lanterns at the far end of the hold gave sufficient illumination
for him to see. He passed several sentries, seret who stood rigidly at their stations, ignoring his approach.

"They seem quiet tonight. Have they been behaving?"
Thranic asked as he approached the cages.

"Yes, sir," the senior guard replied, breaking his statuesque
facade only briefly. "Seasickness. They're all under the weather."

"Yes," Thranic noted, not without a degree of revulsion.
He watched them. "They can see me, you know, even in the
dark. They have very good eyesight."

Because a response was not required, the seret remained
silent.

"I can see recognition on their faces, recognition and fear. This is my first trip to visit them, but already they know me. They can sense the power of Novron within me, and the evil in them instinctually cowers. It's like I'm a candle, and the light I give off pushes back their darkness."

Thranic stepped closer to the cages, each so densely packed the elves were forced to take turns standing and lying. Those standing pressed their filthy naked bodies against each other for support. Males, females, and children were jammed together tightly, creating a repugnant quivering mass of flesh. He watched with amusement as they whimpered and whined, struggling to move away from his approach.

"See? I am light, and the putrid blackness of their souls retreats before me." Thranic studied their faces, each gaunt and hollow from starvation. "They're disgusting creatures— unnatural abominations that never should have been. Their very existence is an insult. You feel it, don't you? We need to purge the world of the stain they cause. We need to do our best to clear the offense. We need to prove ourselves worthy."

Thranic was no longer looking at the elves. He was staring at his own hands. "Purification is never easy, but always necessary," he muttered pensively. "Fetch me that tall male with the missing tooth," Thranic ordered. "I'll begin with him."

Following the sentinel's direction, the guards ripped the elf from his cage and bound his elbows behind his back. Using a spare rigging pulley, they hoisted the unfortunate prisoner by his arms to the overhead beam. The effort pulled the elf's limbs from their sockets, causing him to scream in agony. His wails and the wretched look on his face caused even the seret to look away, but Thranic watched stoically, his lips pursed approvingly.

"Swing him," he said. The elf howled anew from the motion. The sentinel looked at the cages again. Inside, others were weeping. At his glance, one female pushed forward. "Why can't you leave us alone?"

Thranic searched her face with a look of genuine pity. "Maribor demands that the mistake of his brother be erased. I'm merely his tool."

"Then why not—why not just kill us and get it over with?" she cried at him, eyes wild. Thranic paused. He stared once more at his hands. He turned them over, examining both sides with a distant expression. He was silent for so long that even the seret turned to face him. Thranic looked back at the female, his eyes blurring and lips trembling. "One must scrub very hard to remove *some* stains. Take her next."

CHAPTER 7

ROTTEN EGGS

For Empress Modina, everything had changed a month ago, after she had stood on the balcony and addressed the citizens of the New Empire. Due to Amilia's constant chipping away at the regents' resolve, the empress now enjoyed an unprecedented degree of freedom within the palace, and she wandered freely, dressed in fresh new clothing.

She never went anywhere in particular, and oftentimes after returning she could not recall where she had been. Although she longed to feel grass beneath her feet, her permitted boundary did not extend past the palace walls. She was certain no guard would stop her if she tried to leave, but she feared Amilia would suffer the regents' wrath if she did, so she remained inside the keep.

Now Modina walked gracefully in her new dress, silent and pensive, the way an empress should. As she descended the curved stair, she felt the hem of her gown drag along the stone steps. The new dresses had also been Amilia's doing. Her secretary had personally supervised the imperial seamstress in their construction and curtailed any attempts the woman had tried to make to embellish them with lace or embroidery. Each was brilliant white and patterned after a simple, yet eloquent, design. Amilia had told the seamstress that the main goal was to create clothing that would make Modina feel as comfortable as possible, so the dressmaker focused on constructing plain but well-fitted garments and dispensed with utilizing stiff collars, tight bodices, or stays.

While the freedom and new dresses had been welcome changes, the most dramatic difference had been the way people reacted when seeing the empress. Since leaving her bedroom, Modina had passed two young women carrying a pile of linens and a page with an armful of assorted boots. He had dropped one the moment he spotted her, and the two girls chatted excitedly to each other. She had seen in their faces the same look that everyone wore: the belief that she was the Chosen One of Maribor.

When she had first come to the palace, everyone had avoided her the way one evades a dog known to bite. After her speech, those few members of the palace staff she chanced upon had looked at her with affectionate admiration and an unspoken understanding, as if acknowledging that they finally comprehended her previous behavior. The new gowns had the unintended effect of turning admiration into adoration, as the white purity and modest simplicity gave Modina an angelic aura. She had transformed from the mad empress to the saintly—although troubled—high priestess.

Everyone attributed Modina's recovery to Amilia's healing powers. What she had said on the balcony was the truth. Amilia had saved her, if *saved* was the right word. Modina did not feel saved.

Ever since Dahlgren, she had been drowning in overwhelming terrors that she could not face. Amilia had pulled her to shore, but no one could call her existence living. There had been a time, long, long ago, when she would have said that life carried hope for a better tomorrow, but for her, hope was a dream that had blown away on a midsummer's night. The horrors were all that remained, calling to her, threatening to pull her under again. It would be easy to give in, to close her eyes and sink to the bottom once more, but if pretending to live could help Amilia, then she would. Amilia had become a tiny point of light in a sea of darkness, the singular star Modina steered by, and it did not matter where that light led.

Like most afternoons, Modina wandered the sequestered halls and chambers like a ghost searching for something long forgotten. She heard that people with missing limbs felt an itching in a phantom leg or arm. Perhaps it was the same for her, as she struggled to scratch at her missing life.

The smell of food indicated she was near the kitchen. Modina did not recall the last time she had eaten, but she was not hungry. Ghosts did not get hungry, at least not for food. She had come to the bottom of the stairs. To the right, cupboards lined a narrow room holding plates, goblets, candles, and utensils. To the left, folded linens were stacked on shelves. Filled with laboring servants and steam, the place was hot and noisy.

Modina spotted the big elkhound sleeping in the corner of the kitchen and immediately recalled that his name was Red. She had not been down this way in a long time, not since Saldur had caught her feeding the dog. That was the first day since her father had died that she could remember clearly. Before that—nothing—nothing but...*rotten eggs*.

She smelled the rancid stench as she stood at the bottom of the steps. Modina glanced around with greater interest. That awful smell triggered a memory. There was a place, a small room that was cold, dark, and lacked any windows. She could almost taste it.

Modina approached a small wooden door. With a shaking hand, she pulled it open. Inside was a small pantry filled with sacks of flour and grain. This was not the room, but the smell was stronger there.

There was another place—small like this—small, dark, and evil. The thought came at her with the force of a forgotten nightmare. Black, earthy, and cold, a splashing and a ratcheting that echoed ominously, the wails of lost souls crying for mercy and finding none. She had been one of them. She had cried aloud in the dark until she could cry no more, and always the smell of dirt penetrated her nostrils and the dampness of the dirt floor soaked into her skin. A sudden realization jolted her.

I'm remembering my grave! I am dead. I am a ghost.

She looked at her hands—this was not life. The darkness closed in all around her, growing deeper, swallowing her, smothering her.

⌁

"Are you all right, Your Eminence?"

"Ya think she's sick again?"

"Don't be daft. She's just upset. You can see that well enough, can't ya?"

"Poor thing, she's so fragile."

"Remember who you're speaking of. That lass slew Rufus's Bane!"

"*You* remember who *you're* speaking of, *that lass* indeed! By Maribor's beard, she's the empress!"

"Out of my way," Amilia growled as she shooed the crowd like a yard full of chickens.

She was in no mood to be polite. Fear made her voice harsh, and it lacked the familiar tone of a fellow kitchen worker—it was the voice of an angry noblewoman. The servants scattered. Modina sat on the floor with her back against the wall. She was weeping softly with her hands covering her face.

"What did you do to her?" Amilia snapped accusingly while glaring at the lot of them.

"Nothing!" Leif said, defending them.

Leif, the butcher and assistant cook, was a scrawny little man with thick dark hair covering his arms and chest but absent from his balding head. Amilia had never cared for him, and the thought that he, or any of them, might have hurt Modina made her blood boil.

"No one was even near her. I swear!"

"That's right," Cora confirmed. The dairymaid was a sweet, simple girl who churned the butter each morning and always added too much salt. "She just sat and started crying."

Amilia knew better than to listen to Leif, but Cora was trustworthy. "All right," she told them. "Leave her be. Back to work, all of you."

They were slow to respond until Amilia gave them a threatening glare.

"Are you all right? What's wrong?" she asked, kneeling beside Modina.

The empress looked up and threw her arms around Amilia's neck as she continued to sob uncontrollably. Amilia held her, stroking her hair. She had no idea what was wrong, but needed to get the empress to her room. If word reached Saldur, or worse, if he wandered in—She tried not to think of it.

"It's okay, it's all right. I've got you. Try to calm down."

"Am I alive?" Modina asked with pleading eyes.

For the briefest of moments, Amilia thought she might be joking, but there were two things wrong with that. First, there was the look in Modina's eyes, and second, the empress *never* joked.

"Of course you are," she reassured her. "Now come. Let's get you to bed."

Amilia helped her up. Modina stood like a newborn fawn,

weak and unsure. As they left, excited whispering rose. *I'll have to deal with that right away*, she thought.

She guided Modina upstairs. Gerald, the empress's personal guard, gave them a concerned look as he opened the chamber door.

"Is she all right?" Gerald asked.

"She's tired," Amilia said, closing the door on him.

The empress sat on the edge of her bed, staring at nothing. This was not her familiar blank stare. Amilia could see her thinking hard about something.

"Were you sleepwalking? Did you have a nightmare?"

Modina thought a moment, then shook her head. "I remembered something." Her voice was faint and airy. "It was something bad."

"Was it about the battle?" This was the first time Amilia had brought up the subject. Details of Modina's legendary combat with the beast that had destroyed Dahlgren were always vague or clouded by so much dogma and propaganda that it was impossible to tell truth from fiction. Like any imperial citizen, Amilia was curious. The stories claimed Modina had slain a powerful dragon with a broken sword. Just looking at the empress, she knew that could not be true, but Amilia was certain something terrible had happened.

"No," Modina said softly. "It was afterward. I woke up in a hole, a terrible place. I think it was my grave. I don't like remembering. It's better for both of us if I don't try."

Amilia nodded. Since Modina had begun speaking, most of their conversations had centered on Amilia's life in Tarin Vale. On the few occasions when she asked Modina about her own past, the empress's expression darkened and the light in her eyes faded. She would not speak any more after that, sometimes for days. The skeletons in Modina's closet were legion.

"Well, don't think about it, then," Amilia told her in a soothing voice. She sat next to Modina on the edge of the bed and ran her fingers through the empress's hair. "Whatever it was, it's over. You're here with me now. It's getting late. Do you think you can sleep?"

The empress nodded, but her eyes remained troubled.

Once she was certain the empress was resting peacefully, Amilia crept out of her room. Ignoring Gerald's questioning looks, she trotted downstairs to the kitchen. If left to themselves, the scullions would start a wave of rumors certain to engulf the entire palace, and she could not afford to have this getting back to Saldur.

Amilia had not visited the kitchens for quite some time. The moist steamy cloud that smelled of onions and grease, once so familiar, was now oppressive. Eight people worked the evening shift. There were several new faces, mostly young boys fresh off the street and girls still smelling of farm manure. All of them worked perfunctorily, as they were engrossed in the conversation that rose above the sound of the boiling kettles and the clatter of pans. That all stopped when she entered.

"Amilia!" Ibis Thinly boomed the moment he saw her. The old sea cook was a huge barrel-chested man with bright blue eyes and a beard that wreathed his chin. Blood and grease stained his apron. He held a towel in one hand and a spoon in the other. Leaving a large pot on the stove, he strode over to her, grinning. "Yer a fine sight for weathering eyes, lass! How's life treating you, and why don't you visit more often?"

She rushed to him. Ignoring his filthy garment and all courtly protocol, she hugged the big man tight.

The water boy dropped both buckets and gasped aloud.

Ibis chuckled. "It's as if they plum forgot you used to work here. Like they think their old Amilia died er sumptin' and the chief imperial secretary to the empress grew outta thin air."

He put down the spoon and took her by the hand. "So, how are you, lassie?"

"Really good, actually."

"I hear you got a fancy place up there in the east wing with all the swells. That's sumptin' to be proud of, that is. Yer moving up in the world. There's no mistaking that. I just hope you don't forget us down here."

"If I do, just burn my dinner and I'll remember who the really important people are."

"Oh, speaking of that!" Ibis quickly used the towel to lift the steaming pot from the stove. "Don't want to be ruining the sauce for the chamberlain's quail."

"How are things here?"

"Same as always." He hoisted the pot onto the stone bench and lifted the lid, freeing a cloud of steam. "Nuttin' changes in the scullery, and you picked a fine time to visit. Edith ain't here. She's upstairs hollering at the new chambermaid."

Amilia rolled her eyes. "They should have dismissed that woman years ago."

"Don't I know it, but I only run the kitchen and don't have no say over what she does. Course, you being a swell an' all now, maybe—"

She shook her head. "I don't have any real power. I just take care of Modina."

Ibis used the spoon to taste the sauce before replacing the lid.

"Well now, I know you didn't come here to jaw with me about Edith Mon. This have sumptin' to do with the empress crying down here a bit ago? It wasn't the pea soup I made for her, was it?"

"No," Amilia assured him. "She loves your cooking, but yes, I did sort of want to explain things." She turned to face the rest of the staff and raised her voice. "I just wanted everyone to know the empress is okay. She heard some bad news today and it saddened her is all. But she's fine now."

"Was it about the war?" Nipper asked.

"I bet it had to do with the prisoners in Ratibor," Knob, the baker, speculated. "The princess from Melengar done executed them, didn't she? Everyone knows she's a witch and a murderess. She'd think nothing of slaughtering defenseless folk. That's why she was weeping, wasn't it? 'Cause she couldn't save them?"

"The poor dear," the butcher's wife declared. "She cares so much, it's no wonder she's so upset with everything she has to deal with. Thank Maribor she has you taking care of her, Lady Amilia. You're a mercy and then some, you are."

Amilia smiled and turned to Ibis. "Didn't she always used to yell at me about the way I cleaned her husband's knives?"

Ibis chuckled. "She also accused you of taking that pork loin a year ago last spring. Said you ought to be whipped. I guess she forgot about that. They all have, I 'spect. It's the dress, I think. Seeing you in a gown like this, even I have to fight the impulse to bow."

"Don't do that," she told him, "or I'll never come back here."

Ibis grinned. "It's good to see you again."

❦

In her dream, Modina saw the beast coming up behind her father. She tried to scream, but only a muffled moan escaped. She tried to run to him, but her feet were stuck in mud—thick, green, foul-smelling mud. The beast had no trouble moving as it charged down the hill toward him. To Modina's anguished amazement, Theron took no notice of the ground shaking from the monster's massive bulk. It consumed him in a single bite, and Modina collapsed in the dirt. The musty smell filled her nostrils as she struggled to breathe. She could feel the damp earth against her body. In the darkness, the sounds of splashing told her that the beast came for her too. All around, men and women cried and howled in misery and fear. The beast came for them all. Splashing, cranking, splashing, cranking, it was coming to finish the job, coming to swallow her up as well.

It was hungry. Very hungry. It needed to eat.

They all needed to eat, but there was never enough food. What little they had was a putrid gruel that smelled awful — like rotten eggs. She was cold, shivering, and weeping. She had cried so hard and for so long that her eyes no longer teared. There was nothing left to live for . . . or was there?

Modina woke in her darkened room shivering in a cold sweat.

The same dream haunted her each night, making her afraid to close her eyes. She got up and moved toward the moonlight of her window. By the time she reached it, most of the dream was forgotten, but she realized something had been different. Sitting in her usual place, she looked out over the courtyard below. It was late and everyone was gone except the guards on watch. She tried to remember her nightmare, but the only thing she could recall was the smell of rotten eggs.

CHAPTER 8

THE HORN

After the first few disorienting days, life aboard the *Emerald Storm* settled into a rigid pattern. Every morning began with the scrubbing of the upper deck, although it never had a chance to get dirty from one day to the next. Breakfast followed. The watches changed and the scrubbing continued, this time on the lower decks. At noon, Lieutenant Bishop or one of the other officers fixed their position using the sun and confirmed it with the captain. Afterward, the men drilled on the masts and yards, launching longboats, boarding and repelling, and practicing archery, the ballista, and hand-to-hand combat. Not surprisingly, Hadrian won high marks in sword fighting and archery, his display of skill not lost on Grady, who nodded knowingly.

From time to time, the men were drummed to the main deck to witness punishment. So far, there had been four floggings, but Hadrian knew the victims only by name. In the afternoon, the men received their grog, a mixture of rum and sugar water, and in the evening, the master-at-arms went about making certain all fires were out.

Most days were the same as the one before, with only a few exceptions. On make 'n' mend day, the captain granted the crew extra time in the afternoon to sew up rips in their clothing or indulge in hobbies such as wood carving or scrimshaw. On wash day, they cleaned their clothes. Because using freshwater was forbidden and there was no soap, shirts and pants usually felt better after a day working in the rain than they did after wash day.

By now, everyone knew his responsibilities and could perform them reasonably well. Hadrian and Royce were pleased to discover they were not the only novices aboard. Recently pressed men composed nearly a quarter of the crew. Many came from as far away as Alburn and Dunmore, and most had never seen the ocean before. The other men's bumbling presence, and Wyatt's assistance, masked Hadrian's and Royce's lack of experience. Now both knew the routine and their tasks well enough to pass on their own.

The *Emerald Storm* continued traveling due south, with the wind on its port quarter laying it over elegantly as it charged the following sea. It was a marvelously warm day. Either they had run so far south that the season had yet to change, or autumn had blessed them with one last breath of perfect weather. The master's mate and a yeoman of the hold appeared on deck at the ringing of the first bell to dispense the crew's grog.

About four days into the voyage, Royce finally found his sea legs. His color returned, but even after more than a week, his temper remained sour. One contributing factor was Jacob Derning's constant accusations about his culpability in Drew's death.

"After I slit his throat, I can just drop the body into the sea," Royce casually told Hadrian. They had collected their grog and the crew lay scattered about the top decks, relaxing in the bright sunshine. Royce and Hadrian found a cozy out-of-the-way space on the waist deck between the longboat and the bulkhead where the sailmaker and his mates had left a pile of excess canvas. It made for a luxurious deck bed from which to watch the clear blue sky with its decorative puffs of clouds.

"I'll dump him at night and he's gone for good. The body won't even wash up onshore, because the sharks will eat it. It's better than having your own personal vat of lye."

"Okay, one more time." Hadrian had become exhausted from the conversation. "You can't kill Jacob Derning. We have no idea what's going on yet. What if he's Merrick's contact? So until we know something—anything—you can't kill anyone."

Royce scowled and folded his arms across his chest in frustration.

"Let's get back to what we know," Hadrian went on.

"Like the fact that Bernie Defoe was once in the Black Diamond?" Royce replied.

"Really? Well, that's interesting. So let's see . . . We've got a cargo hold full of elves, enough weapons to outfit an army, a sentinel with a company of seret, a Tenkin, and an ex-Diamond. I think Thranic must be part of this. I doubt a sentinel is just taking a pleasure cruise."

"He does stand out like a knife in a man's back, which is why I doubt he's involved."

"Okay, let's put him in the maybe category. That leaves Bernie at the top of the list. Was he in the guild at the same time as you and Merrick?"

Royce nodded. "But we never worked with him—hardly even saw him. Bernie was a digger—specialized in robbing crypts mostly, and then he got into looking for buried treasure. Taught himself to read so he could search old books for clues. He found Gable's Corner and the Lyrantian Crypt, apparently buried somewhere out in Vilan Hills. Came back with some nice stuff and all these tall tales about ghosts and goblins. He ended up having some disagreement with the Jewel, and it wasn't long before he went independent. Never heard of him after that."

"But Merrick knew him, right?"

"Yeah."

"Think he recognized you?"

"I don't know. Maybe. He wouldn't let on if he had. He's no fool."

"Any chance he's turned a new leaf and taken up sailing for real?"

"About as likely as me doing it."

Hadrian eyed Royce for a heartbeat. "I put him at the top of the list."

"What about the Tenkin?"

"That's another strange one. He—"

"Land ho!" the lookout on the foremast shouted while pointing off the port bow. Royce and Hadrian got up and looked in the direction indicated. Hadrian could not make out much, just a thin gray line, but he thought he could see twin towers rising in the distance. "Is that…"

"Drumindor," Royce confirmed, glancing over his shoulder before sitting back down with his rum.

"Oh yeah? We're that far south? Been a while since we've been around here."

"Don't remind me."

"Okay, so the fortress wasn't the best of times, but the city was nice. You have to admit Tur Del Fur is better than Colnora, really. Beautiful climate, brightly painted buildings on an aqua sea, and it's a republic port. You've got to love an open city."

"Oh? Remember how many times you banged your head?"

Hadrian frowned at him. "You really do hate dwarves, don't you? Honestly, I'm surprised you let Magnus stay at the abbey. All right, so there's a bit too much dwarven architecture there, but it sure is built well. You've got to admit that, and you liked the wine, remember?"

Royce shrugged. "What were you going to say about the Tenkin?"

"Oh yeah. His name is Staul."

"Doesn't seem like the sailor type."

"No." Hadrian shook his head. "He's a warrior. Most Tenkin men are. Thing is, Tenkins never leave the Gur Em."

"The what?"

"You've never been to Calis, have you? The whole eastern half is a tropical forest, and the thickest part is a jungle they call the Gur Em. This is the first time I've ever seen a Tenkin outside of Calis, which makes me think Staul is an outcast."

"Doesn't sound like the type Merrick would be doing business with."

"So Bernie remains our number one." Hadrian thought a moment. "You think he had anything to do with Drew's death?"

"Maybe," Royce replied, taking a sip of rum. "He was on the mainmast that night, but I was too sick to pay attention. I wouldn't put it past Bernie to give him a little push. He'd need a reason, though."

"Drew and Bernie were both at a card game earlier that night. Drew won the pot and if Bernie is a thief…"

Royce shook his head. "Bernie wouldn't kill him over a gambling dispute. Not unless it was really big money. The coppers and silvers they were likely playing for wouldn't qualify. That doesn't mean he didn't kill him. It just wasn't about gambling. Anything else happen at the game?"

"Not really, although Drew did mention he was going to talk to Grady the next morning at breakfast about someone coming aboard to help find a horn. Drew thought it was kinda funny, actually. He seemed to think the horn was easy to find. He was going to go into more detail at breakfast."

"Maybe Drew overheard something Defoe preferred he hadn't. That's a more likely reason. But a horn?"

֍

They came across Wyatt at the ship's wheel. His plumed hat was off and his white linen shirt fluttered about his tan skin like a personal sail. He had the *Storm* tight over, playing the pressure of the rudder against the press of the wind. He was staring out at the headland with glassy eyes as they approached, but when he spotted them, he abruptly cast his head down at the binnacle and quickly wiped his face with the sleeve of his forearm.

"You all right?" Hadrian asked.

"Y-yeah," Wyatt croaked, then coughed to clear his throat. "Fine." He sniffed and wiped his nose.

"There's a good chance you'll find her," Royce assured him.

"See?" Hadrian said. "You've even got Mr. Cynical feeling optimistic about your chances. That's gotta count for something."

Wyatt forced a smile.

"Hey, we've got a question for you," Royce said. "Do you have any idea what the *horn* is?"

"Sure, you're looking right at it," Wyatt declared, gesturing toward the point. "That's the Horn of Delgos. As soon as we clear it, the captain will likely order the ship to weather round the point and then tack windward."

Royce frowned. "Let's assume for just a moment that I'm not an experienced sailor, shall we?"

Wyatt chuckled. "We're gonna make a left turn and head east."

"How do you know?"

Wyatt shrugged. "The horn is the farthest spit of land south. If we stay on this course, we'll sail into the open sea. There's nothing out there but whirlpools, Dacca, and sea serpents. If we weather round—er—turn left, we'll sail up the eastern coast of Delgos."

"And what's up that way?"

"Not much. These cliffs you see continue all the way round to Vandon, the only other sea port in Delgos. Besides being the headquarters for the Vandon Spice Company, it's also a haven for pirates, or more accurately *the* haven for pirates. We aren't going there either. The *Storm* is as fine a ship as they come, but the jackals would gather like a pack of wolves and dog her until we surrender, or they sink us."

"How does the spice company manage any trade, surrounded by pirates?"

"Who do you think runs the spice company?"

"Oh."

"Beyond that?" Royce asked.

"Dagastan Bay and the whole coast of Calis, with ports at Wesbaden and Dagastan. Then you drift out of civilization and into the Ba Ran Archipelago, and no one goes there, not even pirates."

"And you're sure this here is the horn?"

"Yep, every sailor who's ever been in the Sharon knows it. It'd be impossible to miss old Drumindor."

Though the coast was still many leagues off, the ancient dwarven edifice was clearly visible now, standing taller than anything Hadrian had ever seen. He smiled at the irony, knowing dwarves had built it. The massive towers were close to eight hundred feet from the raw rocky base, where waves crashed, to the top of the dome. It appeared to be equal parts fortification and monument. In some respects, it resembled two massive gears laid on their sides, huge cylinders with teeth jutting seaward. From the top of each tower, smoke rose. Midway up were fins—arced openings like gigantic teapot spouts that pointed toward the ocean. Between the twin towers was a single-span stone bridge connecting them like a lintel over the entrance of the harbor.

"Can't even miss her at night, the way she lights up. You should see her during a full moon when they blow the vents. It puts on quite a show. She's built on a volcano, and the venting prevents too much pressure from building up. Ships in the area often arrange to pass the point at the full moon just for the entertainment. But they also keep their distance. The dwarves that built that fortress sure knew what they were doing. No ship can enter Terlando Bay if the masters of Drumindor don't want them to. They can spew molten rock for hundreds of feet and burn a fleet of ships to drifting ash in minutes."

"We're familiar with how that works," Royce said coldly.

Wyatt cocked an eyebrow. "Bad experience?"

"We had a job there once," Hadrian replied. "A dwarf named Gravis was angry about humans desecrating what he considered a dwarven masterpiece. We had to get in to stop him from sabotaging it."

"You broke into Drumindor?" Wyatt looked impressed. "I thought that was impossible."

"Just about," Royce answered, "and we didn't get paid enough for the trouble it gave me."

Hadrian snorted. "*You?* I was the one who nearly died making that leap. You just hung there and laughed."

"How'd you get in? I heard that place is kept tighter than Cornelius DeLur's purse," Wyatt pressed.

"It wasn't easy," Royce grumbled. "I learned to hate dwarves on that job. Well, there and..." He trailed off, rubbing his left shoulder absently.

"It will be the harvest moon in a few weeks. Maybe we'll catch the show on the way back," Wyatt said.

The lookout announced the sighting of sails. Several ships clustered under the safety of the fort, but they were so far out that only their topsails showed.

"I would have expected the captain to have ordered a course change by now. He's letting us get awfully close."

"Drumindor can't shoot this far, can she?" Hadrian asked.

"No, but the fortress isn't the only danger," Wyatt pointed out. "It isn't safe for an imperial vessel to linger in these waters. Delgos isn't officially at war with us, but everyone knows the DeLurs support the Nationalists and—well—accidents can happen."

⇜

They continued sailing due south. Not until the point was well astern and nearly out of sight did the captain appear on the quarterdeck. Now they would discover which direction the *Emerald Storm* would go.

"Heave to, Mr. Bishop!" he ordered.

"Back the mains'l!" the lieutenant shouted, and the men sprang into action.

This was the first time Hadrian had heard these particular orders and he was glad that, as ship's cook, he was not required to carry them out. It did not take long for him to see what was happening. Backing the mainsail caused it to catch the wind on its forward side. If the foremast and mizzenmast were also backed, the ship would sail in reverse. Since they remained trimmed as they were, the force of the wind lay balanced between them, leaving the ship stationary on the water.

Once the ship was heaved to, the captain ordered a reading

on the ship's position, then disappeared once more into his cabin, leaving Lieutenant Bishop on the quarterdeck.

"So much for picking a direction," Hadrian muttered to himself.

They remained stationary for the rest of that day. At sunset, Captain Seward ordered lights hauled aloft, but nothing further slipped his lips.

Hadrian served supper, boiled salt pork stew again. Even he was tired of his menu, but the only complaints came from the recently pressed, who were not yet hardened to the conformities of life at sea. Hadrian suspected most of the veterans on board would demand salt pork and biscuits even on land, rather than break the routine.

"He is a murderer, that's why!"

Hadrian heard Staul shout as he entered the below deck with the last of the evening meals. The Tenkin was standing slightly crouched in the center of the crew's quarters. His dark tattooed body and rippling muscles were revealed as he removed his shirt. In his right hand he held a knife. A cloth wrapped his left fist. His chest heaved with excitement, a mad grin on his face and a sinister glare in his eyes.

In front of Staul stood Royce.

"He killed Edgar Drew. Everyone knows it. Now he'll be the one to die, eh?"

Royce stood casually, his hands loosely clasped before him as if he were just one of the bystanders—except his eyes never left the knife. Royce followed it as a cat might watch the movement of a string. It took Hadrian only a second to see why. Staul was holding the knife by the blade. On a hunch, Hadrian scanned the room and found Bernie Defoe standing behind and to Royce's left, a hand hidden behind his back.

Staul took his attention off Royce for a moment, but Hadrian noticed his weight shift to his rear foot and hoped his friend noticed as well. An instant later Staul threw the knife. The blade flew with perfect accuracy, only when it arrived, Royce was not there and the tip buried itself in a deck post.

All eyes were on Staul as he bristled with rage, shouting curses. Hadrian forced himself to ignore the Tenkin and searched for Bernie. He had moved. Spotting the glint of a blade in the crowd, he found him again. Bernie had slipped up behind Royce and lunged. Royce spun. Not taken in by the plot, he faced his old guild mate with the blade Staul had provided. Bernie halted mid-step, hesitated, and then backed away, melting into the crowd. Hadrian doubted anyone else noticed his involvement.

"Ah! You dance well!" Staul shouted, and laughed. "That is good. Perhaps next time you trip, eh?"

The excitement over, the crowd broke up. As they did, Jacob Derning muttered loud enough for everyone to hear, "Good to see I'm not the only one who thinks he killed poor Drew."

"Royce," Hadrian called, keeping his eyes focused on Jacob. "Perhaps you should take your meal up on the deck, where it's cooler."

⚜

"That was pleasant," Hadrian said after the two had safely reached the galley and closed the door behind them.

"What was?" Poe asked, dishing out the last of the stew for the midshipmen.

"Oh, nothing really. A few crewmen just tried to murder Royce."

"What?" Poe almost dropped the whole kettle.

"Now can I kill people?" Royce asked, stepping into the corner and putting his back against the wall. He had an evil look on his face.

"Who tried to murder him?"

"Bernie," Royce replied. "So what am I supposed to do now? Lie awake at night waiting for him and his buddies—I'm sorry, his *mates*—to knife me?"

"Poe, would it be possible for me and Royce to sleep in here at night?"

"In the galley? I suppose. Won't be too comfortable, but if Royce is always on time for his watch, and if you tell Mr. Bishop you want him to help with the nighttime boils, he might allow it."

"Great, I'll do that. While I'm gone, Poe, can you go below and get us a couple of hammocks that we can hang in here? Royce, maybe you can rig a lock for the door?"

"It's better than being bait."

❦

Royce worked both the second dogwatch and the first watch, which kept him aloft from sunset until midnight. By the time he returned, Hadrian had obtained permission for Royce to sleep in the galley. Poe had moved up what little gear they had and strung two hammocks between the walls of the narrow room.

"How is it?" Royce asked, entering the darkened galley and finding Hadrian hanging in the netting.

"Hmm?" he asked, waking up. "Oh, okay, I guess. The room is too narrow for me. I feel like I'm being bent in half, but it should be fine for you. How was your watch? Did you see Defoe?"

"Never took my eyes off old *Bernie*," he said, grinning and dodging a pot that hung from the overhead beam. Hadrian knew Royce must have enjoyed a bit of revenge on Bernie. If there was ever a place where Royce held an advantage, it was a hundred feet in the air, dangling from beams and ropes in the dark of night.

Hadrian shifted his weight, causing his hammock to swing. "What did you do?"

"Actually, I didn't do anything, but that was what drove him crazy. He's still sweating."

"So he did recognize you."

"Oh yeah, and it was like there were two moons out tonight, his face was so pale."

Royce checked the lines and the mountings of the hammock Poe had installed for him, and looked generally pleased with the work.

"To be honest, I'm surprised Bernie didn't suffer an accidental fall," Hadrian said.

Royce shook his head. "Two accidents off my mast is just bad planning. Besides, Bernie wasn't trying to kill me."

"Sure looked that way from where I was standing. And it seemed pretty organized too."

"You think so?" he asked, sitting on the crate of biscuits Poe had brought up for the morning's breakfast. "It's not how I would do it. First, why stage the fight in a room full of witnesses? If they had killed me, they would hang. Second, why attack me below? Like I said, the sea is the perfect place to dispose of a body, and the closer to the rail you get your victim, the easier it is."

"Then what do you think they were up to?"

Royce pursed his lips and shook his head. "I have no idea. If it's a diversion to rifle our belongings, why not hold it topside? For that matter, why bother with a diversion at all? There have been plenty of times while we were on deck to go through our stuff."

"You think it was just to intimidate us?"

"If it was, it wasn't Bernie's idea. Threatening to kill me but not finishing the job is famously fatal. He would know that."

"So Derning put them up to it?"

"Maybe, but...I don't know. Derning doesn't seem like someone Bernie would take orders from—especially not such stupid orders."

"Makes sense. So then—"

A muffled thump, like another body hitting the deck, brought them to their feet. Hadrian threw open the door of the galley and cautiously looked out.

The larboard watch was on duty, but rather than the typical watch-and-snooze routine, they were hard at work, running a boat drill. They had hoisted the longboat from the yard and had it over the side, where it bumped the gunwale once more before being lowered into the sea.

"Odd time for a lifeboat drill," Wyatt said, walking toward them from the shelter of the forecastle.

"Trouble sleeping?" Royce asked.

Wyatt beamed a grin. "Look who else is on duty," he told them, pointing at the quarterdeck, where Sentinel Thranic, Mr. Beryl, Dr. Levy, and Bernie Defoe stood talking.

They slipped around the forecastle, moving quickly to the bow. Looking over the rail, Hadrian saw six men rowing toward a nearby light.

"Another ship," Royce muttered.

"Really?"

"A small single-mast schooner. No flag."

"Is there anything in the longboat?" Hadrian asked. "If that's payment going to—"

Royce shook his head. "Just the crew."

They watched as the sound of the oars faded, then waited. Hadrian strained, peering into the darkness, but all he could see were the bobbing light of the little boat and the one marking its destination.

"Boat's coming back," Royce announced, "and there's an extra head now."

Wyatt squinted. "Who would they be picking up in the middle of the night from Delgos?"

They watched as the longboat returned. Just as Royce had said, there was an additional man—a passenger. Wrapped in ship's blankets, he was small and thin, with a long pasty face and wild, white hair. He looked to be very old, far too old to be any use as a sailor. He came aboard and spoke to Thranic and Dr. Levy at length. The old man's things were gathered and deposited beside him. One of the bags came loose and two weighty leather-bound books spilled onto the bleached deck. "Careful, my boy," the old man cautioned the sailor. "Those are one of a kind and, like me, are very old and sadly fragile."

"Gather his things and take them to Dr. Levy's quarters," Thranic ordered. Glancing toward the bow, he stopped abruptly. He glared at them, licking his thin lips in thought, then slowly approached. As he did, he held his dark cloak tight, his shoulders raised to protect his neck from the cold wind. Between this and his stooped back, he resembled a scavenger bird.

"What are all of you doing on deck? None of you are part of the larboard watch."

"Off duty, sir," Wyatt answered for them. "Just getting a bit of fresh air."

Thranic peered at Hadrian and took a step toward him. "You're the cook, aren't you?"

Without thinking, Hadrian felt at his side for the hilt of his absent sword. Something about the sentinel made him flinch. Sentinels were always scary, but this one was absolutely chilling. Returning his gaze was like staring into the eyes of restrained madness.

"You joined this voyage along with..." Thranic's eyes shifted to Royce. "This one—yes, the nimble fellow—the one so good at climbing. What's your name? Melborn, isn't it? Royce Melborn? I heard you were seasick. How odd."

Royce remained silent.

"Very odd, indeed."

"Sentinel Thranic?" the old man called, his weak voice barely making the trip across the deck. "I would rather like to get out of the damp wind, if I could." He coughed.

Thranic stared a moment longer at Royce, then pivoted sharply and left them.

"Not exactly the kind of guy you want taking an interest in you, is he?" Wyatt offered.

With the longboat back aboard, the captain appeared on the quarterdeck and ordered a new course—due east, into the wind.

CHAPTER 9

ELLA

A nother dispatch from Sir Breckton, sir," the clerk announced, handing a small scroll to the imperial chancellor. The elderly man returned to the desk in his little office and read the note. A scowl grew across his face.

"The man is incorrigible!" the chancellor burst out to no one, then pulled a fresh sheet of parchment and dipped his quill.

The door opened unexpectedly and the chancellor jumped. "Can't you knock?"

"Sorry, Biddings, did I startle you?" the Earl of Chadwick asked, entering with his exquisite floor-length cape trailing behind him. He had a pair of white gloves draped over one forearm as he bit into a bright red apple.

"You're always startling me. I think you get a sadistic pleasure from it."

Archibald smiled. "I saw the dispatch arrive. Is there any word from the *Emerald Storm*?"

"No, this is from Breckton."

"Breckton? What does he want?" Archibald sat in the armchair opposite the chancellor and rested his booted feet on a footstool.

"No matter how many times I tell him to wait and be patient, he refuses to grasp that we know more than he does. He wants permission to attack Ratibor."

Archibald sighed. "Again? I suppose you see now what I've had to put up with all these years. He and Enden are so headstrong I—"

"Were," the chancellor said, correcting him. "Sir Enden died in Dahlgren."

Ballentyne nodded. "And wasn't that a waste of a good man?" He took another bite and, with his mouth still full, went on. "Do you need me to write him personally? He's my knight, after all."

"What would help is to be able to tell him *why* he doesn't need to attack."

Archibald shook his head. "Saldur and Ethelred are still insisting on secrecy regarding the—"

The chancellor raised a hand, stopping him. Archibald looked confused and the chancellor pointed at the chambermaid on her knees scrubbing the floor near the windows of his office.

Archibald rolled his eyes. "Oh please. Do you really think the scrub girl is a spy?"

"I've always found it best to err on the side of caution. She doesn't have to be a spy to get you hanged for treason."

"She doesn't even know what we're talking about. Besides, look at her. It isn't likely she'll be bragging in some pub. You don't go out at night boasting in bars, do you, lass?"

Ella shook her head and refused to look up, so that her brown sweat-snarled hair continued to hang in her face.

"See!" Archibald said in a vindicated tone. "It's like censoring yourself because there is a couch or a chair in the room."

"I was referring to a more subtle kind of danger," Biddings

told him. "Should something happen. Something unfortunate with the plan, such that it fails—someone always has
to be blamed. How fortunate it would be to discover a
loquacious earl who had boasted details to even a mindless
chambermaid."

Archibald's smirk faded immediately.

"The third son of a dishonored baron doesn't rise to the
position of imperial chancellor by being stupid," Biddings
said.

"Point taken." Archibald glanced back at the scrub girl
with a new expression of loathing. "I had best return to Saldur's office or he'll be looking for me. Honestly, Biddings, I'm
really starting to detest staying in this palace."

"She still won't see you?"

"No, I can't get past her secretary. That Lady Amilia is a
sly one. Plays all innocent and doe-eyed, but she guards the
empress with ruthless determination. And Saldur and Ethelred are no help at all. They insist she plans to marry Ethelred.
It has to be a lie. I simply can't imagine Modina wanting that
old moose."

"Particularly when she could choose a young buck like
yourself?"

"Exactly."

"And your desire is true love, of course. You've given absolutely no thought about how marrying Modina would make
you emperor?"

"For a man who went from third baron's son to chancellor,
I'm surprised you can even ask me that."

"Archie!" bellowed the voice of Regent Saldur, echoing
down the hall outside the office.

"I'm in with Biddings!" Archibald shouted back through
the open door. "And don't call me—" He was interrupted by
the sudden rush of the scrub girl running, bucket in hand,

from the office. "Looks like she doesn't like Saldur any more than I do."

৵

Arista had spilled scrub water onto her skirt, causing it to plaster the rough material to her legs. Her thin cloth shoes made a disagreeable slapping noise as she ran down the corridor. The sound of Saldur's voice made her run faster.

That had been close, yet she wondered if even Saldur, who had known her since birth, would recognize her now. There was nothing magical about her transformation, but that did not make it any less impenetrable. She wore dirty rags, she lacked makeup, and her once lustrous hair was now a tangled mess. It had lightened, bleached by the same sun that had tanned her skin. Still, it was more than just her appearance. Arista had changed. At times, when she caught her own reflection, it took a moment to register that she was seeing herself and not some poor peasant woman. The bright-eyed girl was gone, and a dark, brooding spirit possessed her battered body.

More than anything else, the sheer absurdity of the situation provided the greatest protection. No one would believe that a sheltered, self-indulgent princess would willingly scrub floors in the palace of her enemy. She doubted even Saldur's mind would grant enough latitude to penetrate the illusion. Even if some people thought she looked familiar—and several seemed to—their minds simply could not bend that far. To conceive of the thought that Ella the scrub girl was the Princess of Melengar was as ridiculous as the idea that pigs could talk or that Maribor was not god. To entertain such a notion would require a mind open to new possibilities, and no one at the palace fit that description.

The only one she worried about, besides Saldur, was the

empress's secretary. She was not like the others—she noticed Arista. Amilia saw through her veneer with suspicious eyes. Saldur clearly surrounded the empress with his best and brightest, and Arista did all she could to avoid her.

On the road north from Ratibor, Arista had fallen in with a band of refugees fleeing to Aquesta, and they had arrived nearly a month earlier. The location spell had led her to the palace itself. Things grew more complicated after that. If she had been more confident in the magic, and her ability to use it, she might have returned to Melengar right away with the news that Gaunt was a prisoner in the imperial palace. As it was, she felt the need to see Degan for herself. She managed to obtain a job as a chambermaid, hoping to repeat the location spell inside the castle walls at various locations, only that was not working out. Closely watched by the headmistress, Edith Mon, she rarely found enough free time and privacy to cast the spell. On the few occasions she succeeded, the smoke indicated a direction, but the maze of corridors blocked any attempt to follow. Magically stymied, Arista sought to determine Gaunt's whereabouts by eavesdropping while at the same time learning her way around the grounds.

"What have ya done now?" Edith Mon shouted at Arista as she entered the scullery.

Arista had no idea what a hobgoblin looked like, but she guessed it probably resembled Edith Mon. She was stocky and strong. Her huge head sat on her shoulders like a boulder, crushing whatever neck she might have once had. Her face, pockmarked and spotted, provided the perfect foundation for her broad nose with its flaring nostrils, through which she breathed loudly, particularly when angry, as she was now.

Edith yanked the bucket from her hands. "Ya clumsy little wench! Ya best pray you spilled it only on yerself. If I hear ya left a dirty puddle in a hallway…"

Edith had threatened to cane her on three occasions but had been interrupted each time—twice by the head cook. Arista was not sure what she would do if it came to that. Scrubbing floors was one thing, but allowing herself to be beaten by an old hag was something else. If tried, she might discover there was more to her new chambermaid than she had thought. Arista often amused herself by contemplating which curse might be best for old Edith. At that moment, she was considering the virtues of skin worms, but all she said was "Is there anything else today?"

The older woman glared. "Oh! Ya think yer something, don't ya? Ya think yer better than the rest of us, that yer arse shines of silver. Well, it don't! Ya don't even have a family. I know you live in that alley with the rest of them runners. Yer one dodgy smile away from making yer meals whoring, so I'd be careful, sweetie!"

There were several snickers from the other kitchen workers. Some risked Edith's wrath by pausing in their work to watch. The scullery maids, charwomen, and chambermaids all reported to Edith. The others, like the cook, butcher, baker, and cupbearer, reported to Ibis Thinly but they sided with Edith—after all, Ella was the *new* girl. In the lives of those who lived in the scullery, seeing punishment administered was what passed for entertainment.

"Is that a yes or a no?" Arista asked calmly.

Edith's eyes narrowed menacingly. "No, but tomorrow ya start by cleaning every chamber pot in the palace. Not just emptying them, mind ya. I want them scrubbed clean."

Arista nodded and started to walk past her. As she did, cold water rained down as Edith emptied the bucket on her.

The room burst into laughter. "A shame it wasn't clean water. Ya could use a bath." Edith cackled.

The uproar died abruptly as Ibis appeared from out of the cellar.

"What's going on here?" The chief cook's booming voice drew everyone's attention.

"Nothing, Ibis," Edith answered. "Just training one of my girls is all."

The cook spotted Arista standing in a puddle, drenched from head to foot. Her hair hung down her face, dripping filthy water. Her entire smock was soaked through and the thin material clung indecently to her skin, causing her to fold her arms across her breasts.

Ibis scowled at Edith.

"What is it, Ibis?" Edith grinned at him. "Don't like my training methods?"

"No, I can't say I do. Why do you always have to treat them like this?"

"What are ya gonna do? Ya gonna take Ella under your wing like that tramp Amilia? Maybe this one will become archbishop!"

There was another round of laughter.

"Cora!" Ibis barked. "Get Ella a tablecloth to wrap around her."

"Careful, Ibis. If she ruins it, the chamberlain will have at you."

"And if Amilia hears you called her a tramp, you might lose your head."

"That little pretender doesn't have the piss to do anything against me."

"Maybe," the chief cook said, "but she's one of *them* now, and I'll bet that any noble who heard that you insulted one of their own — well, they might take it personally."

Edith's grin disappeared and the laughter vanished with it.

Cora returned with a tablecloth, which Ibis folded twice before wrapping around Arista's shoulders. "I hope you have another kirtle at home, Ella. It's gonna be cold tonight."

Arista thanked him before heading out the scullery door. It was already dark and, just as Ibis had predicted, cold. Autumn was in full swing, and the night air shocked her wet body. The castle courtyard was nearly empty, with only a few late carters dragging their wagons out through the main gate. A page raced between the stables and the keep, hauling armloads of wood, but most of the activity that usually defined the yard was absent. She passed through the great gates, where the guards ignored her, as they had done each evening. The moment she reached the bridge and stepped beyond the protection of the keep's walls, the full force of the wind struck her. She clenched her jaw to stifle a cry, hugged her body with fingers that were already turning red, and shivered so badly it was hard to walk.

Not skin worms. No. Not nearly bad enough.

"Oh dear!" Mrs. Barker exclaimed, rushing over as Arista entered Brisbane Alley. "What happened, child? Not that Edith Mon again?"

Arista nodded.

"What was it this time?"

"I spilled some wash water."

Mrs. Barker shook her head and sighed. "Well, come over to the fire and try and dry off before you catch your death."

She coaxed Arista to the communal fire pit. Brisbane Alley was literally the end of the road in Aquesta, a wretched little dirt patch behind Brickton's Tannery where the stench from the curing hides kept away any except the most desperate. Newcomers without money, relatives, or connections settled here. The lucky ones lived huddled under canvas sheets, carts, and the wagons they had arrived in. The rest simply huddled against the tannery wall, trying to block the wind as they slept. So had Arista—that is, until the Barkers adopted her.

Brice Barker worked shouting advertisements through the city streets for seven coppers a day. All of that went to buy food to feed three children and his wife. Lynnette Barker took in what sewing work she could find. When the weather turned colder, they had offered Arista a place under their wagon. She had known them for only a few weeks, but already she loved them like her own family.

"Here, Ella," Lynnette said, bringing an old kirtle for her to put on. The dress was little more than a rag, worn thin and frayed along the hem. Lynnette also brought Esrahaddon's robe. Arista went around the corner and slipped out of her wet things. Lynnette's dress did nothing to keep out the cold, but the robe vanquished the wet chill instantly in uncompromising warmth.

"That's really a wonderful robe, Ella," Lynnette told her, marveling at how the firelight made it shimmer and reflect colors. "Where did you get it?"

"A...friend left it to me when he died."

"Oh, I'm sorry," she said sadly. Her expression changed then from one of sadness to one of concern. "That reminds me, a man was looking for you."

"A man?" Arista asked as she folded the tablecloth. If anything happened to it, Edith would make Ibis pay.

"Yes, earlier today. He spoke to Brice while he was working on the street, and mentioned he was looking for a young woman. He described you perfectly, although oddly enough, he didn't know your name."

"What did he look like?" Arista hoped her concern was not reflected in her voice.

"Well," Lynnette faltered, "that's the thing. He wore a dark hood and a scarf wrapped about his face, so Brice didn't get a good look at him."

Arista pulled the robe tightly about her.

Is he here? Has the assassin managed to track me down?

Lynnette noticed the change in her and asked, "Are you in trouble, Ella?"

"Did Brice tell him I lived here?"

"No, of course not. Brice is many things, but he's no fool."

"Did he give a name?"

Lynnette shook her head. "You can ask Brice about him when he returns. He and Wery went to buy flour. They should be back soon."

"Speaking of that," Arista said, fishing coins out of her wet dress, "here's three copper tenents. They paid me this morning."

"Oh no. We couldn't—"

"Of course you can! You let me sleep under your wagon, and you watch my things when I'm at work. You even let me eat with you."

"But three! That's your whole pay, Ella. You won't have anything left."

"I'll get by. They feed me at the palace sometimes, and my needs are pretty simple."

"But you'll want a new set of clothes, and you'll need shoes come winter."

"So will your children, and you won't be able to afford them without an extra three coppers a week."

"No, no—we can't. It's very nice of you, but—"

"Ma! Ma! Come quick! It's Wery!" Finis, the Barkers' eldest son, raced down the street, shouting as he came. He looked frightened, his eyes filled with tears.

Lynnette lifted her skirt and ran, Arista chasing after her. They rushed to Coswall Avenue, where a crowd formed outside the bakery. Pushing past the crowd, they saw a boy lying unconscious on the cobblestone.

"Oh sweet Maribor!" Lynnette cried, falling to her knees beside her son.

Brice knelt on the stone, holding Wery in his arms. Blood soaked his hands and tunic. The boy's eyes were closed, his matted hair slick as if dipped in red ink.

"He fell from the baker's loft." Finis answered their unasked question, his voice quavering. "He was pulling one of them heavy flour bags down 'cause the baker said he'd sell us two cups for the price of one if he did. Pa and I told him to wait fer us, but he ran up, like he's always doing. He was pulling *real* hard. As hard as he could, and then his hands slipped. He stumbled backward and..." Finis was talking fast, his voice rising as he did until it cracked and he stopped.

"Hit his head on the cobblestones," declared a stranger who wore a white apron and held a lantern. Arista thought he might be the baker. "I'm real sorry. I didn't think the boy would hurt himself like this."

Lynnette ignored the man and pried her child from her husband, pulling Wery to her breast. She rocked him as if he were a newborn. "Wake up, honey," she whispered softly. Tears fell on Wery's blood-soaked cheeks. "Please, baby, oh for the love of Maribor, please wake up! Please, oh please..."

"Lynn, honey..." Brice started.

"*No!*" she shouted at him, and tightened her grip on the boy.

Arista stared at the scene. Her throat was tight, and her eyes were filling so quickly that she could not see clearly. Wery was a wonderful boy, playful, friendly. He reminded her of Fanen Pickering, which only made matters worse. But Fanen had died with a sword in his hand, and Wery was only eight and likely had never touched a weapon in his short life. She could not understand why such things happened to good people. Tears slipped down her cheeks as she watched the small figure of the boy dying in his mother's arms.

Arista closed her eyes, wiping the tears. When she opened them again, she noticed several people in the crowd backing away.

Her robe was glowing.

Giving off a pale light, the shimmering material illuminated those around her with an eerie white radiance. Lynnette saw the glow, and hope flooded her face. She looked up at Arista, her eyes pleading. "Ella, can...can you save him?" she asked with trembling lips and desperate eyes. Arista began to form the word *no*, but Lynnette quickly spoke again. "You can!" she insisted. "I know you can! I've always known there was something different about you. The way you talk, the way you act. The way you forget your own name, and that—*that robe*! You can save him. I know you can. Oh please, Ella." She paused and swallowed, shaking so hard it made Wery's head rock. "Oh, Ella, I know—I know it's so much more than three coppers, but he's my baby! You'll help him, won't you? Please, oh please, Ella."

Arista could not breathe. She felt her heart pounding in her ears and her body trembled. Everyone silently watched her. Even Lynnette stopped her pleading. Arista found herself saying through quivering lips, "Lay him down."

Lynnette gently lowered Wery's body, his limbs lifeless, his head tilted awkwardly to one side. Blood continued to seep from the boy's wound.

Arista knelt beside him and placed a hand on the boy's chest. He was still breathing, but it was so shallow, so weak. Closing her eyes, she began to hum. She heard the concerned mutterings of those in the crowd, and one by one, she tuned them out. Arista could sense the heartbeats of the men and women surrounding her, and she forced them out as well. She focused on the sound of the wind. Soft and gentle it blew, swirling between the buildings, across the street, skipping over stones. Above her she felt the twinkle of the stars and the smile of the moon. Her hand was on the body of the boy, but her fingers felt the strings of the instrument she longed to play.

The gentle wind grew stronger. The swirl became an eddy; the eddy, a whirlwind; and the whirlwind, a vortex. Her hair whipped madly, but she hardly noticed. Before her lay a void, and beyond that was a distant light. She could see him in the darkness, a dull silhouette before the brilliance, growing smaller as he traveled away. She shouted to him. He paused. She strummed the chords and the silhouette turned. Then, with all her strength, she clapped her hands together and the sound was thunder.

When she opened her eyes, the light from the robe had faded and the crowd was cheering.

Chapter 10

Fallen Star

S ail ho!" the lookout shouted from the masthead.

The *Emerald Storm* was now two weeks out of Aquesta, slipping across the placid waters of the Ghazel Sea. The wind remained blowing from the southwest. Since rounding the Horn of Delgos, they made slow progress. The ship was close hauled, struggling to gain headway into the wind. Mr. Temple kept the top crews busy tacking the ship round, wearing windward, and keeping their course by crossing back and forth, but Hadrian guessed that a quickly walking man could make faster progress.

It was midmorning, and seamen who were not in the rigging or otherwise engaged in the ship's navigation were busy scrubbing the deck with sandstone blocks or flogging it dry. All the midshipmen were on the quarterdeck taking instruction in navigation from Lieutenant Bishop. Hadrian heard the lookout's call as he returned to the galley after delivering the previous evening's pork grease. Making his way to the port side, he spotted a small white square on the horizon. Bishop immediately suspended class and took an eyeglass to see for himself, then sent a midshipman to the captain's cabin. The captain emerged so quickly that he was still adjusting his hat as he appeared on the quarterdeck. He paused for a moment, tugged on his uniform, and sniffed the air with a wrinkle of his nose.

"Lookout report!" he called to the masthead.

"Two ships, off the port bow, sir!"

Hadrian looked again, and just as the lookout had reported, he spotted a second sail now visible above the line of the water.

"The foremost is showing two squares—appears to be a lugger. The farther ship...I'm seeing two red lateen sails, single-decked, possibly a tartane. They're running with the wind and closing fast, sir."

"What flag are they flying?"

"Can't say, sir, the wind has them blowing straight at us."

Hadrian watched the ships approach, amazed at their speed. Already he could see them clearly.

"This could be trouble," Poe said.

Hadrian had been so intent on the ships that he had failed to notice his assistant appear beside him. The thin rail of a boy was busy tying the black ribbon in his ponytail as he stared out at the vessels.

"How's that?"

"Those red sails."

Hadrian looked back out across the water. "And why's that a problem?"

"Only the Dacca use them, and they're worse than any pirates you'll run across."

"Beat to quarters, Mr. Bishop," the captain ordered.

"All hands on station!" the lieutenant shouted. "Beat to quarters!"

Hadrian heard a drumroll as the boatswain and his mates cleared the deck. The midshipmen, dispersed to their stations, shouted orders to their crews.

"Come on!" Poe told him.

There was a pile of briquettes at the protected center of the forecastle. Hadrian ignited them with hot coals from the galley stove as soon as the surrounding deck had been soaked with seawater. Around it, archers prepped their arrows with oil. Seamen brought dozens of buckets of seawater, along with buckets of sand, and positioned them around the ship. It took only minutes to secure for battle, and then they waited.

The ships were closer and larger now, but still the flags they flew were invisible. The *Storm* remained deathly silent, the only sounds coming from the wind, the waves, and the creaking hull. A random gust fluttered the lugger's flag.

"They're flying the Gribbon of Calis, sir!" the lookout shouted.

"Mr. Wesley," the captain addressed the midshipman stationed on the quarterdeck. "You've studied signals?"

"Aye, sir."

"Take a glass and get aloft. Mr. Temple, run up our name and request theirs."

"Aye, aye, sir."

Still no one else moved or spoke. All eyes were on the approaching vessels.

"Lead vessel is the *Bright Star*. Aft vessel is..." Wesley hesitated. "Aft vessel isn't responding, sir."

"Two points aport!" the captain shouted abruptly, and Wyatt spun the wheel, weathering the ship as close to the wind as possible, heading them directly toward the lugger. The topmen went into action like a hundred spiders, crawling along the shrouds, working to grab every bit of wind possible.

"New signal from the *Bright Star*," Wesley shouted. "Hostile ship astern!"

Small streaks of smoke flew through the otherwise clear sky. The tartane was firing arrows at the *Bright Star*, but the shots fell short, dropping into the sea a good two hundred yards astern.

"Ready the forward ballista!" the captain ordered. A squad of men on the forecastle began to crank a small capstan, which ratcheted the massive bowstring into firing position. They lighted another brazier in advance of the stanchion as an incendiary bolt was loaded. Then they waited, once more watching the ships sail closer.

Everything about the Dacca ship was exotic. Made of dark wood, the vessel glittered with gold swirls artfully painted along the hull. It bore long decorative pendants of garish colors. A stylized image of a black dragon in flight adorned the scarlet mainsail, and on the bowsprit was the head of a ghoulish beast with bright emerald eyes. The sailors appeared as foreign as the ship. They were dark-skinned, powerful brutes wearing only bits of red cloth wrapped around their waists.

Poorly handled, the *Bright Star* lost the wind and its momentum. Behind it, the tartane descended. Another volley of arrows from the Dacca smoked through the air. This time several struck the *Bright Star* in the stern, but one lucky shot made it to the mainsail, setting it aflame.

Although victorious over the lugger, the tartane chose to flee before the approaching *Emerald Storm*. It came about and Hadrian watched Captain Seward ticking off the distance as the *Storm* inched toward it. Even after the time lost during the turn, the Dacca ship was still out of ballista range.

"Helm alee. Bring her over!" the captain shouted. "Tacks and sheets!"

The *Emerald Storm* swung round to the same tack as the tartane, but the *Storm* did not have the momentum under it, nor the nimbleness of the smaller ship. The tartane was the faster vessel, and all the crew of the *Emerald Storm* could do was watch as the Dacca sailed out of reach.

Seeing the opportunity lost, Captain Seward ordered the *Storm* heaved to and the longboats launched. The *Bright Star's* mainsail and mast burned like a giant torch. Stays and braces snapped and the screams of men announced the fall of the flaming canvas to the deck. Still, the ship's momentum carried it astern of the *Storm*. As it passed, they could see the terrified sailors struggling hopelessly to put out the flames that enveloped the deck. Before the longboats were in the water, the *Bright Star* was an inferno, and most of the crew were already in the sea.

The boats returned laden with frantic men. Nearly all were tawny-skinned, dark-eyed sailors dressed in whites and grays. They lay across the deck coughing, spitting water, and thanking Maribor, as well as any nearby crew member.

The *Bright Star* was an independent Wesbaden trader from Dagastan heading home to western Calis with a load of coffee, cane, and indigo. Despite the *Storm's* timely intervention, more than a third of the small crew perished. Some passed out in the smoke while fighting the flames, and others remained trapped below deck. The captain of the *Bright Star* perished, struck by one of the fiery arrows the Dacca had rained on his vessel. This left only twelve men, five of whom lay in Dr. Levy's care with burns.

Mr. Temple sized up the able-bodied survivors and added them to the ship's complement. Royce was back at work aloft as Hadrian finished serving dinner to the crew. Hadrian's easygoing attitude and generosity with the galley grease had won him several friends. There had been no more attempts on Royce's life, but they still did not know why Royce had been targeted, or by whom. For the moment, it was enough that Bernie, Derning, and Staul remained at a safe distance.

"Aye, this is Calis, not Avryn," Hadrian heard one of the new seamen say in a harsh, gravelly voice, as he brought down the last messkid. "The light of civilization grows weak like a candle in a high easterly wind. The farther east you go, the stronger the wind blows, till out she goes, and in the darkness ye stand!"

A large number of the off-watch clustered around an aft table, where three of the new sailors sat.

"Then there you are in the world of the savage," the Calian sailor went on. "A strange place, me lads, a strange place indeed. Harsh, violent seas and jagged inlets of black-toothed rock, gripped tight by dense jungle. The netherworld of the Ba Ran Ghazel, the heart of darkness is a place of misery and despair, the prison where Novron drove the beasties to their eternal punishment. They can't help but try to get out. They look at the coasts of Calis with hungry eyes and they find footholds. Like lichen, they slip in and grow everywhere. The Calians try to push them back, but it be like trying to swat a sky of flies or hold water in yer hands." He cupped his palms, pretending to lose something between his fingers.

"Goblin and man living so close together ain't natural," another said.

The first sailor nodded gravely. "But nothing in them jungles be natural. They have been linked for too long. The sons of Maribor and the spawn of Uberlin be warring one moment, then trading the next. Just to survive, the Calian warlords took to the ways of the goblins and spread the cursed practices of the Ba Ran to their own kin. Some of them are more goblin now than men. They even worship the dark god, burning tulan leaves and making sacrifices. They live like beasts. At night, the moon makes them wild, and in the darkness their eyes glow red!"

Several of the men made sounds of disbelief.

"It's the truth, me lads! Centuries ago, when the Old Empire fell, the eastern lords were abandoned to their fate. Left alone in the deep dark of the Calian jungles, they lost their humanity. Now the great stone fortresses along the Goblin Sea that once guarded the land from invasion be the home of Tenkin warlords—half-human, half-goblin monsters. They've turned their backs on the face of Maribor and embraced the ways of the Ghazel. Aye, me fellows, the state of Calis is a fearful one. So thankful we be for your daring act of kindness, for we'd be at the mercy of fate if ya hadn't pulled us from the sea. If it wasn't for your bravery, we'd surely be dead now...or worse."

"Wasn't much bravery needed," Daniels said. "The *Storm* could have whipped those buggers in a dead calm with half the crew drunk and the other half sick with the fever."

"Is that what you think?" Wyatt asked. Hadrian had not noticed him sitting silently in the gloom beyond the circle of the candle's light. "Is that what you *all* think?" His tone was oddly harsh—challenging. Wyatt sighed and, with an exasperated shake of his head, got up and climbed the ladder to the deck.

Having finished with the messkids, Hadrian followed. He found the helmsman on the forecastle. His hands gripped the rail as he stared at the shimmer of the new moon rolling on the back of the black sea.

"What's that all about?"

"We're in trouble and—" He paused, angrily motioning at the quarterdeck. Catching himself, he clenched his teeth, as if by doing so he could trap the words inside his mouth.

"What kind of trouble?" Hadrian glanced at the quarterdeck.

"The captain doesn't want me to say anything. He's a damn fool who won't listen to reason. I should disobey him and alter the ship's course right now. I could relieve Bliden on the wheel early and take us off course. No one would know until the reckoning is taken tomorrow at noon."

"Wesley would know." Hadrian pointed to the young man climbing to the quarterdeck on his nightly round as officer of the first watch. "He'd have you hauled to Mr. Bishop before you could blink."

"I could deal with Wesley if I had to. The deck is slippery, you know?"

"Now you're starting to sound like Royce. What's going on?"

"I suppose if I'm contemplating killing a midshipman, it hardly matters if I break captain's orders to keep quiet." Wyatt looked once again at the sea. "They're coming back."

"Who?"

"The Dacca. They didn't run. They're regrouping." He looked at Hadrian. "They dye their sails with the blood of their enemies. Did you know that? Hundreds of small ruddy boats line the coves and ports of their island. They know we're hugging the coast and sailing against the wind. Like wolves, they'll chase us down. Ten, twenty lateen-rigged tartanes will catch the wind that we can't. The *Storm* won't stand a chance."

"What makes you so sure? You could be wrong. The captain must have a good reason to stay on course."

"I'm not wrong."

CHAPTER 11

THE HOODED MAN

The hooded man walked away again.

Arista cowered deeper into the shadows under the tavern steps. She wanted to disappear, to become invisible. Her robe had turned a dingy brown, blending with the dirty wood. Drawing up the hood, she waited. It was *him*—the same man Lynnette had described. He was looking for her. She heard the sound of his boots on the cobblestone. They slowed, hesitated, and then grew louder.

He's coming back again!

The tall, dark figure appeared at the end of the alley for the third time. He paused. She held her breath. The streetlamps revealed a frightening figure dressed in a black hooded cloak and a thick scarf hiding his face. He wore an unseen sword— she could hear the telltale clap.

He took a tentative step toward her hiding place, then another, and then paused. The light's glare exposed white puffs issuing from his scarf. His head turned from side to side. He stood for several seconds, then pivoted so sharply his boot heel dug a tiny depression in the gravel, and walked away. After several tense minutes, Arista carefully crept out.

He was gone.

The first light of dawn rose in the east. If only she could make it back to the palace. At least there she would be safe from the assassin and away from the inevitable questions: "Who is she? How did she do it? Is she a witch?"

She had left Brisbane Alley before anyone thought to ask, but what about after? She had drawn too much attention, and—although she doubted anyone would connect the dots—the unabashed use of magic would cause a stir.

She removed the robe, carefully tucked it under the tavern steps, and set off toward the palace. The guards ignored her as usual, and she went about her tasks without incident. Throughout the day she had the good fortune to work relatively unnoticed, but by midday, news of the events of the night before had reached the palace. Everyone buzzed about the disturbance on Coswall Avenue. A boy had been brought back to life. By evening, rumors named the Witch of Melengar as the culprit. Luckily, no one suspected the scrub girl Ella of any more wrongdoing than failing to return the borrowed tablecloth.

Arista was exhausted and not merely from losing a night's sleep while avoiding the assassin. Saving Wery had drained her. After the day's work was over, she returned to the alley and retrieved the wizard's robe. She did not dare put it on, for fear someone might recognize it. Rolling it up and clutching it to her chest, she made her way to the edge of the broad avenue, unable to decide what to do next. Staying would be sheer stupidity. Looking down the broad length of Grand Avenue, she could see the front gates of the city. It felt like a lifetime since she had been home, and it would be so good to see a familiar face, to hear her brother's voice—to rest.

She knew she should leave. She should go that very minute, but she was so tired. The idea of setting out into the cold dark, alone and hungry, was too much to bear. She desperately needed a safe place to sleep, a hot meal, and a friendly face—

which meant just one thing: the Barkers. Besides, she could not leave without retrieving her pearl-handled hairbrush, the last remaining keepsake from her father.

Nothing had changed at the end of Brisbane Alley. The length was still dotted with small campfires and littered with bulky shadows of makeshift tents, carts, wagons, and barrels. People moved about in the growing dark. Some glanced at her as she passed, but no one spoke or approached her. She found the Barkers' wagon and, as always, a great tarp stretched out from it like a porch awning. One of the boys spotted her, and a moment later Lynnette rushed out. Without a word, she threw her arms around Arista and squeezed tightly.

"Come, have something to eat," she said, wiping her cheeks and leading Arista by the hand. Lynnette laid a pot on the fire. "I saved some just in case. I had to hide it, of course, or the vultures would have gobbled it all down. I wasn't sure you'd be back..."

The rest of the Barkers gathered around the fire. Finis and Hingus sat on the far side. Brice Barker, dressed in his usual white shirt and gray trousers, sat on an upturned crate, whittling a bit of wood. No one spoke. Arista took a seat on a wooden box, feeling awkward.

Is that apprehension in their eyes, or outright fear?

"Ella?" Lynnette finally asked in a small tentative voice. "Who are you?"

"I can't tell you that," she said after a long pause. She expected them to complain or press further. Instead, they all nodded silently, as if they had expected her answer, just as she had expected their question.

"I don't care who you are. You're always welcome at this fire," Brice said. He kept his eyes on the flames, but his words betrayed an emotion she had not expected. Brice, who made his living shouting in the streets all day, hardly ever spoke.

Lynnette dished out the bit of stew she had warmed up. "I wish there was more. If I had only known you'd be back."

"How is Wery?" Arista asked.

"He slept all night but was up most of the day running around, causing a nuisance as usual. Everyone who's seen him is saying the same thing—it was a miracle."

"Everyone?" Arista asked with concern.

"Folks been stopping by all day to see him and asking about you. Many said they had sick children or loved ones who are dying. One got so angry he knocked down the canvas and nearly upset the wagon before Finis brought Brice home to clear him out."

"I'm sorry."

"Oh, don't be! Please—no—don't ever be sorry," Lynnette pleaded. She paused, her eyes tearing again. "You won't be able to stay with us anymore, will you?"

Arista shook her head.

"The hooded man?"

"And others."

"I wish I could help," Lynnette said.

Arista leaned over and hugged her. "You have…more than you'll ever know. If I could just get a good night's sleep, then I—"

"Of course you can. Sleep in the wagon. It's the least we can do."

Arista was too exhausted to argue. She climbed up and, in the privacy of the cart, put the robe on to fight away the night's cold. She crawled across a lumpy bedding of coarse cloth that smelled of potatoes and onions, and laid her head down at last. It felt so good to close her eyes and let her muscles and mind go. She could hear them whispering outside, trying not to disturb her.

"She's a servant of Maribor," one of the boys said. She

could not tell which. "That's why she can't say. The gods never let them say."

"Or she could be Kile—a god disguised and doing good deeds," the other added. "I heard he gets feathers from Muriel's cloak for each one he does."

"Hush! She'll hear you," Lynnette scolded. "Go clean that pot."

Arista fell asleep to their whispers and woke to loud voices.

∗

"I told you, I don't know what you're talking about! I don't know anything about a witch." It was Brice's voice, and he sounded frightened.

Arista peered out from the wagon. An imperial soldier stood holding a torch, his way blocked by Brice. Behind him, farther up the alley, other soldiers pounded on the door to the tannery and forced their way into the other tents.

"Sergeant," the man in front of Brice called, "over here!"

Three soldiers walked fast, their armor jangling, hard boots hammering the cobblestone.

"Tear down this hovel and search it," the sergeant ordered. "Continue to do the same for all these places. They're an eyesore and should be removed anyway."

"Leave them alone," Arista said, stepping out of the wagon. "They haven't done anything."

"Ella!" Brice snapped. "Stay out of this."

The sergeant moved briskly toward Arista, but Brice stepped in the way.

"Leave my daughter alone," he threatened.

"Brice, no," Arista whispered.

"I'm only here for the witch," the soldier told them. "But if you insist, I'll be happy to torch every tent in this alley."

"She's no witch!" Lynnette cried, clutching Wery to her side. "She saved my baby. She's a servant of Maribor!"

The sergeant studied Arista briefly, sucking on his front teeth.

"Bind her!" he ordered.

Two of his men stepped forward with a length of rope and grabbed hold of Arista by her arms. They immediately cried out in pain, let go, and stumbled backward. Esrahaddon's robe glowed a deep pulsating red. The guards glared at her in fear, shaking their injured hands.

Seeing her chance, Arista closed her eyes and began to concentrate. She focused on blocking out the sounds of the street and on—

Pain exploded across her face.

She fell backward to the ground, where she lay dazed. Her eyesight darkened at the edges. A ringing wailed in her ears.

"We'll have none of that!" the sergeant declared.

She looked up through watery eyes, seeing him standing over her, rubbing his knuckles. He drew his sword and pointed it at Brice.

"I know better than to let you cast your spells, witch. Don't make another sound, and remove that robe. Do it now! I'll strip you naked if needed. Make no sudden moves or sounds, or I'll cleave off this man's head here and now."

Lynnette was somewhere to her right, and Arista heard her gasp in horror.

"The robe. Take it off!"

Arista wiggled out of the robe, leaving herself clothed only in Lynnette's thin kirtle. The sergeant sucked on his teeth again and stepped closer. "Are my men going to have any more trouble with you?" He lifted the point of his sword toward Brice once again.

Arista shook her head.

"Good. Bind her tightly. Wrap her wrists and fingers and find something to gag her with." The guards approached again and jerked her arms so roughly behind her back that she cried out.

"Please don't hurt her," Lynnette begged. "She didn't do anything wrong!"

They tied her wrists, wrapping the rope around her fingers, pulling until the skin pinched painfully. As they did, the sergeant ordered Lynnette to pick up the robe and hand it to him. One of the soldiers grabbed Arista by the hair, dragging her to her feet. Another took hold of one of her sleeves and ripped it off.

"Open yer mouth," he ordered, pulling Arista's head back. When she hesitated, the soldier slapped her across the face. Again she staggered, and might have fallen if not for the other guard, still holding her hair. The slap was not nearly as painful as the blow the sergeant had given, but it made her eyes water again. "Now open!"

He stuffed the material into her mouth, jamming it in so far Arista thought she would choke. He tied it in place by wrapping more rope around her head and wedging it between her lips. When they tied one final length around her neck, Arista feared they might hang her right there.

"Now, that should keep us safe," declared the sergeant. "We'll cut those hands off when we get to the palace, and after you've answered questions, I expect we'll take that tongue as well."

A crowd gathered as they dragged her away, and Arista could hear Lynnette weeping. As they reached Coswall, the patrons of the Bailey turned out to watch. The men stood on the porch, holding mugs. She heard the word *witch* muttered more than once as she passed by.

By the time they reached the square, she was out of breath and choking on the gag. When she lagged behind, the guard holding the leash jerked hard and she fell. Her left knee struck the cobblestone of Bingham Square and she screamed, but the sound came out as a muffled grunt. Twisting, she landed on her shoulder to avoid hitting her face. Lying on her side, Arista cried in agony from the pain shooting up her leg.

"Up!" the soldier ordered. The rope tightened on her throat, the rough cord cutting her skin. The guard growled, "Get up, you lazy ass!" He pulled harder, dragging her a few inches across the stones. The rope constricted. She heard the pounding of blood in her ears. "Up, damn you!"

She felt the rope cut into her neck. She could barely breathe. The pounding in her ears hammered like drums, pressure building.

"Bruce?" one of the guards called. "Get her up!"

"I'm trying!"

There was another tug and Arista managed to sit up, but she was light-headed now. The street tilted and wobbled. As darkness grew at the edges of her vision, it was becoming difficult to see. She tried to tell them she was choking. All that came out was a pitiful moan.

She struggled to reach her knees, but the dizziness worsened. The ground shifted and dipped. She fell, hitting her shoulder again, and rolled to her back. She looked up at the soldier holding the leash and pleaded with her eyes, but all she saw in reply was anger and disgust.

"Get up or—" He stopped. The soldier looked abruptly to his right. He appeared puzzled. He let go of the rope and took a step backward.

The cord loosened, the pounding eased, and she could breathe again. She lay in the street, her eyes closed, happy to be alive. The clang of metal and the scuffle of feet caught her attention. Arista looked up to see the would-be strangler collapse to the street beside her.

Standing an arm's length away, the hooded man loomed with a blood-coated sword. From his belt he drew a dagger and threw it. Somewhere behind her there was a grunt and then a sound like a sack of flour hitting the ground.

The hooded man bolted past her. She heard a cry of pain. Metal struck metal, then another grunt, this one followed by a gurgling voice speaking garbled words. Another clash, another cry. She twisted around, rolling to her knees. She found him again. He stood in the center of Bingham Square, holding his sword in one hand and a dagger in the other. Three bodies lay on the ground. Two soldiers remained.

"Who are you?" the sergeant shouted at him. "We are imperial soldiers acting on official orders."

The hooded man said nothing. He rushed forward, swinging his blade. He dodged to the right, and catching the sergeant's sword high, he stabbed the man in the neck with his dagger. As he did, the remaining soldier swung at him. The hooded man cried out, then whirled in rage. He charged the last soldier, striking at him, his overwhelming fury driving the guard back.

The soldier turned and ran. The hooded man gave chase. The guard nearly made it to the end of the street before he was cleaved in the back. Once the soldier collapsed, the man continued attacking his screaming victim, stabbing him until he fell silent.

Arista sat helpless, bound in the middle of the square as the hooded man turned. With his sword and cloak dripping blood, he came for her. He pulled Arista to her feet and into a narrow alley.

He was breathing hard, sucking wetly through the scarf. No longer having the strength, physical or mental, Arista did not resist. The world was spinning and the night slipped into the unreal. She did not know what was happening or why, and she gave up trying to understand.

He dragged her into a stable and pushed her against the rough-hewn wall. A pair of horses shifted fearfully, spooked by the smell of blood. He held her tightly and brought his knife to her throat. Arista closed her eyes and held her breath. She felt the cold steel press against her skin as he drew it, cutting the cord away. He spun her around, cut her wrists loose, and then the cord holding the gag fell free.

"Follow me, quickly," he whispered, pulling her along by the hand. Confused, she staggered after him. Something was familiar in that voice.

He led her through a dizzying array of alleys, around dark buildings, and over wooden fences. Soon she had no idea where they were. He paused in a darkened corner, holding a finger to his scarf-covered lips. They waited briefly, then moved on. The wind picked up, carrying an odor of fish, and Arista heard the sound of surf. Ahead she could see the naked masts of ships bobbing at anchor along the wharf. When he reached a particularly dilapidated building, he led her up a back stair into a small room and closed the door behind them.

She stood rigid near the door, watching him as he started a fire in an iron stove. Seeing his hands, his arms, and the tilt of his head—something was so familiar. With the fire stoked, he turned and took a step toward her. Arista shrank until her back was against the door. He hesitated and then nodded. She recognized something in his eyes.

Reaching up, he drew back his hood and unwrapped the scarf. The face before her was painful to look at. Deformed and horribly scarred, it appeared to have melted into a patchwork of red blotches. One ear was missing, along with his eyebrows and much of his hair. His mouth lacked the pale pink of lips. His appearance was both horrid and so welcome she could find no words to express herself. She broke into tears of joy and threw her arms around him, hugging as tightly as her strength allowed.

"I hope this will teach you not to run off without me, Your Highness," Hilfred told her.

She continued to cry and squeeze, her head buried in his chest. Slowly his arms crept up, returning her embrace. She looked up and he brushed strands of tear-soaked hair from her face. In more than a decade as her protector, he had never touched her so intimately. As if realizing this, Hilfred straightened up and gently escorted her to a chair before reaching for his scarf.

"You're not going back out?" she asked fearfully.

"No," he replied, his voice dropped a tone. "The city will be filled with guards. It won't be safe for either of us to venture in public for some time. We'll be all right here. There are no occupied buildings around, and I rented this flat from a blind man."

"Then why are you covering up?"

He paused a moment, looking at the scarf. "The sight of my face—it makes people...uncomfortable, and it's important that you feel safe and at ease. That's my job, remember?"

"And you do it very well, but your face doesn't make me uncomfortable."

"You don't find me...unpleasant to look at?"

Arista smiled warmly. "Hilfred, your face is the most beautiful thing I've ever seen."

∽

The flat Hilfred stayed in was very small, just a single room and a closet. The floor and walls were rough pine planks weathered gray and scuffed smooth from wear. There were a rickety table, three chairs, and a ship's hammock. The single window was hazy from the buildup of ocean salt, admitting only a muted gray light. Hilfred refused to burn a single candle after dark, for fear of attracting attention. The small stove kept the drafty shack tolerably warm at night, but before dawn it was extinguished to avoid the chance of someone seeing the smoke.

For two days they stayed in the shack, listening to the wind buffet the roof shingles and howl over the stovepipe. Hilfred made soup from clams and fish he bought from the old blind man. Other than that, neither of them left the little room. Arista slept a lot. It seemed like years since she had felt safe, and her body surrendered to exhaustion.

Hilfred kept her covered and crept around the flat, cursing to himself whenever he made a noise. On the night of the second day, she woke when he dropped a spoon. He looked at her sheepishly and cringed at the sight of her open eyes.

"Sorry, I was just warming up some soup. I thought you might be hungry."

"Thank you," she told him.

"Thank you?"

"Yes, isn't that what you say when someone does something for you?"

He raised what would have been his eyebrows. "I've been your servant for more than ten years, and you've never once said *thank you*."

It was the truth, and it hurt to hear it. What a monster she had been. "Well overdue, then, don't you think? Let me check your bandage."

"After you eat, Your Highness."

She looked at him and smiled. "I've missed you so," she said. Surprise crossed his face. "You know, there were times growing up that I hated you. Mostly after the fire—for not saving my mother—but later I hated the way you always followed me. I

knew you reported my every move. It's a terrible thing for a
teenage girl to have an older boy silently following her every
step, watching her eat, watching her sleep, knowing her most
intimate secrets. You were always silent, always watchful. Did
you know I had a crush on you when I was fourteen?"

"No," he said curtly.

"You were, what, a dashing seventeen? I tried everything
to make you jealous. I chased after all the squires at court,
pretending they wanted me, but none of them did. And you...
you were such the loathingly perfect gentleman. You stood by
stoically, and it infuriated me. I would go to bed humiliated,
knowing that you were standing just outside the door.

"When I was older, I treated you like furniture—still, you
treated me as you always had. During the trial—" She noticed
Hilfred flinch and decided not to finish the thought. "And
afterward, I thought you believed what they said and hated me."

Hilfred put down the spoon and sighed.

"What?" she asked, suddenly fearful.

He shook his head and a small sad laugh escaped his lips.
"It's nothing, Your Highness."

"Hilfred, call me Arista."

He raised his brow once more. "I can't. You're my princess,
and I'm your servant. That's how it's always been."

"Hilfred, you've known me since I was ten. You've followed me day and night. You've seen me early in the morning.
You've seen me drenched in sweat from fevers. I think you can
call me by my first name."

He looked almost frightened and resumed stirring the pot.

"Hilfred?"

"I'm sorry, Your Highness. I cannot call you by your given
name."

"What if I command you to?"

"Do you?"

"No." Arista sighed. "What is it with men who won't use my name?"

Hilfred glanced at her.

"I only knew him briefly," she explained, not knowing why. She had never spoken about Emery to anyone before. "I've lived so much of my life alone. It never used to bother me and there's never been anyone—until recently."

Hilfred looked down and stirred the soup.

"He was killed. Since then, I've felt this hole. The other night I was so scared. I thought—no, I was certain—I was going to my death. I lost hope and then you appeared. I could really use a friend—and if you called me by—"

"I can't be your friend, Your Highness," Hilfred told her coldly.

"Why not?"

There was a long pause. "I can't tell you that."

A loud silence filled the room.

Arista stood, clutching the blanket around her shoulders. She stared at Hilfred's back until it seemed her stare caused him to turn and face her. When he did, he avoided looking in her eyes. He set out bowls on the table. She stood before him, blocking his way.

"Hilfred, look at me."

"The soup is done."

"I'm not hungry. Look at me."

"I don't want it to burn."

"Hilfred."

He said nothing and kept his eyes focused on the floor.

"What have you done that you can't face me?"

He did not answer.

The realization dawned on her and devastated Arista. He was not there to save her. He was not her friend. The betrayal was almost too much to bear.

"It's true." Her voice quavered. "You do believe the stories they say about me: that I'm a witch, that I'm evil, that I killed my father over my lust for the throne. Are you working for Saldur, or someone else? Did you steal me from the palace guards for some political advantage? Or is this all some plan to—to control me, to get me to trust you and lure me into revealing something?"

Her words had a profound effect on him. He looked pained, as if rained on by blows. His face was strained, his jaw stiff.

"You could at least tell me the truth," she said. "I should think you owe that much to my father, if not to me. He trusted you. He picked you to be my bodyguard. He gave you a chance to make something of yourself. You've enjoyed the privilege of court life because of his faith in you."

Hilfred was having trouble breathing. He turned away from her and, grabbing his scarf, moved toward the door.

"Yes, go—go on!" she shouted. "Tell them it didn't work. Tell them I didn't fall for it. Tell Sauly and the rest of those bastards that—that I'm not the stupid little girl they thought I was! You should have kept me tied and gagged, Hilfred. You're going to find it harder to haul me off to the stake than you think!"

Hilfred slammed his hand against the doorframe, making Arista jump. He spun on her, his eyes fierce and wild in a way she had never seen before, and she stepped back.

"*Do you know why I saved you?*" he shouted, his voice broken and shaking. "Do you? Do you?"

"To—to hand me over and get—"

"No! No! Not now. Back *then*," he cried, waving his arm. "Years ago, when the castle was burning. Do you know why I saved you back then?"

She did not speak. She did not move.

"I wasn't the only one there, you know. There were others.

Soldiers, priests, servants, they all just stood watching. They knew you were inside, but not a single person did anything. They just watched the place burn. Bishop Saldur saw me running for the castle and actually ordered me to stop. He said it was too late, that I would die. I believed him. I truly did, but I went in anyway. Do you know why? *Do you?*" he shouted at her.

She shook her head.

"Because I didn't care! I didn't want to live...not if you died." Tears streamed down his scarred face. "But don't ask me to be your friend. That is far too cruel a torture. As long as I can maintain a safe distance, as long as...as long as there is a wall between us—even if it's only one of words—I can tolerate—I can *bear* it." Hilfred wiped his eyes with his scarf. "Your father knew what he was doing—oh yes, he knew *exactly* what he was doing when he appointed me your bodyguard. I would die a thousand times over to protect you. But don't ask me to be grateful to him for the life he's given me, for it's been one of pain. I wish I had died that night so many years ago, or at least in Dahlgren. Then it would be over. I wouldn't have to look at you. I wouldn't have to wake up every day wishing I had been born the son of a great knight, or you the daughter of a poor shepherd."

He covered his eyes and leaned his head against the threshold. Arista did not recall doing it, but somehow she had crossed the room. She took Hilfred's face in her hands, and rising up on her toes, she kissed his mouth. He did not move, but he trembled. He did not breathe, but he gasped.

"Look at me," she said, extending her arms to display her stained and torn kirtle. "A shepherd's daughter would pity me, don't you think?" She took his hand and kissed it. "Can you ever forgive me?"

He looked at her, confused. "For what?"

"For being so blind."

CHAPTER 12

SEA WOLVES

As it had for days, the *Emerald Storm* remained on its easterly course, making slow progress against a headwind that refused to shift. Maintaining direction required frequent tacking, which caused the top crews to work all night. Royce, as usual, had drawn the late shift. Getting this assignment was not Dime's fault. Royce had concluded that the mainmast captain was a fair man, but Royce was the newest member of a crew that rewarded seniority. He did not mind the shift. He enjoyed the nights he spent aloft. The air was fresh, and in the dark among the ropes, he was as comfortable as a spider in its web. This afforded Royce the opportunity to relax, think, and occasionally amuse himself by tormenting Bernie, who panicked anytime his old guild mate lost track of Royce.

Royce hung in the netting of the futtock shroud, his feet dangling over the open space—a drop of nearly a hundred feet. Above lay the dust of stars, while on the horizon the moon rose as a sliver—a cat's eye peering across the water at him. Below, lanterns flickered on the bow, quarterdeck, and stern, outlining the *Emerald Storm*. To his left, he could just make out the dark coast of Calis. Its thick vegetation was occasionally punctuated by a cliff or the brilliant white plume of a waterfall catching moonlight.

The seasickness was gone. He could not recall a more miserable time than his first week on board. The nausea and dizziness reminded him of being drunk—a sensation he hated. He had spent most of the first night hugging the ship's figurehead and vomiting off the bow. After four days, his stomach had settled, but he remained drained, and he tired easily. It had taken weeks to dull the memory of that misery, but nested in the rigging, looking out at the dark sea, he forgot it all. It surprised him just how beautiful the black waves could be, the graceful undulating swells kissed by the barefaced moon, all below a scattering of stars. Only one sight could surpass it.

What's she doing right now? Is she looking at the same moon and thinking of me?

Royce reached inside his tunic, pulled out the scarf, and rubbed the material between his fingers. He held it to his face and breathed deep. It smelled like her. He kept it hidden—his tiny treasure, soft and warm. On the nights of his sickness, he had lain in the hammock clutching it to his cheek as if it were a magic talisman to ward off misery. Only because of it had he been able to fall asleep.

The officers' deck hatch opened, and Royce spotted Beryl stepping out into the night air. Beryl liked his sleep and, being senior midshipman, rarely held the late watch. He stood glancing around, taking in the lay of the deck. He cast an eye up at the maintop, but Royce knew he was invisible in the dark tangles. Beryl spotted Wesley making his rounds on the forecastle and crossed the waist and headed up the stair. Wesley looked concerned at his approach but held his ground. Perhaps the boy would get another beating that night. Whatever torments Beryl had planned for Wesley were no concern of Royce's, and he thought it might be time to scare Bernie again.

"I won't do it," Wesley declared, drawing Royce's attention. Once more Beryl nervously looked upward.

Who are you looking for, Mr. Beryl?

Royce unhooked himself from the shrouds and rolled over for his own glance upward. As usual, Bernie was keeping his distance.

No threat there.

Royce climbed to the yard, walked to the end, and, just as he had done during the race with Derning, slid down the rope so he could hear them.

"I can make life on this ship very difficult for you," Beryl said, threatening Wesley. "Or have you forgotten your two days without sleep? There is talk that I'll be made acting lieutenant, and if you think your life is hard with my current rank, after my promotion it'll be a nightmare. And I'll see to it that any transfer is refused."

"I don't understand."

"You don't have to. In fact, it's better if you don't. That way you can sound sincere if the captain questions you. Just find him guilty of something. Misconduct, disrespect, I don't care. You put his buddy the cook on report for not saluting. Do something like that. Only this time it needs to be a flogging offense."

"But why me? Why can't *you* invent this charge?"

"Because if the accusation comes from you, the captain and Mr. Bishop will not question it." He grinned. "And if they do, it's your ass, not mine."

"And that's supposed to entice me?"

"No, but I'll get off your back. If you don't, you won't eat, you won't sleep, and you'll become very accident-prone. The sea can be dangerous. Midshipman Jenkins lost both thumbs on our last voyage when he slipped with a rope, which is strange, 'cause he didn't handle ropes that day. Invent a charge, make it stick, and get him flogged."

"And why do you want him whipped?"

"I told you. My friends want blood. Now do we have a deal?"

Wesley stared at Beryl and took a deep breath. "I can't misrepresent a man, and certainly not one under my command, simply to avoid personal discomfort."

"It will be a great deal more than discomfort, you little git!"

"The best I can do is to forget we had this conversation. Of course, should some unusual or circumstantial accusation be leveled against Seaman Melborn, I might find it necessary to report this incident to the captain. I suspect he will take a dim view of your efforts to advance insubordination on his vessel. It could be viewed as the seeds of mutiny, and we both know the penalty for that."

"You don't know who you're playing with, boy. As much as you'd like to think it, you're no Breckton. If I can't use you, I'll lose you."

"Is that all, Mr. Beryl? I must tack the ship now."

Beryl spat at the younger man's feet and stalked away. Wesley remained standing rigidly, watching him go. Once Beryl had disappeared below, Wesley gripped the rail and took off his hat to wipe the sweat from his forehead. He took a deep breath, replaced his hat, straightened his jacket, and then shouted in a clear voice, "Hands to the braces!"

Royce had dealt with many people in his life, from serfs to kings, and few surprised him. He knew he could always depend on their greed and weakness, and he was rarely disappointed. Wesley was the first person in years to astonish him. While the young midshipman could not see it, Royce offered him the only sincere salute he had bestowed since he had stepped aboard.

Royce ascended to the topsail to loose the yard brace in

anticipation of Wesley's next order when his eye caught an irregularity on the horizon. At night, with only the suggestion of a moon, it was hard for anyone to tell where the sky ended and the sea began. Royce, however, could discern the difference. At that moment, he noticed a break in the line. Out to sea, ahead of the *Storm*, a black silhouette broke the dusty star field.

"Sail ho!" he shouted.

"What was that?" Wesley asked.

"Sail off the starboard bow," he shouted, pointing to the southeast.

"Is there a light?"

"No, sir, a triangle-shaped sail."

Wesley moved to the starboard rail. "I don't see anything. How far out?"

"On the horizon, sir."

"The horizon?" Wesley picked up the eyeglass and panned the sea. The rest of the ship was silent except for the creaking of the oak timbers as they waited. Wesley muttered something as he slapped the glass closed and ran to the quarterdeck to pound on the captain's cabin. He paused and then pounded again.

The door opened to reveal the captain, barefoot in his nightshirt. "Mr. Wesley, have we run aground? Is there a mutiny?" The captain's steward rushed to him with his robe.

"No, sir. There's a sail on the horizon, sir."

"A what?"

"A triangular sail, sir. Over there." Wesley pointed while handing him the glass.

"On the horizon, you say? But how—" Seward crossed to the rail and looked out. "By Mar! But you've got keen eyes, lad!"

"Actually, the maintop crew spotted it first, sir. Sounded like Seaman Melborn, sir."

"I'll be buggered. Looks like *three* ships, Mr. Wesley. Call all hands."

"Aye, aye, sir!"

Wesley roused Bristol, who woke the rest of the crew. In a matter of minutes men ran to their stations. Lieutenant Bishop was still buttoning his coat when he reached the quarterdeck, followed by Mr. Temple.

"What is it, sir?"

"The Dacca have returned."

Wyatt, who was taking the helm, glanced over. "Orders, sir?" he asked coldly.

"Watch your tone, helmsman!" Temple snapped.

"Just asking, sir."

"Asking for a caning!" Mr. Temple roared. "And you'll get one if you don't keep a civil tongue."

"Shut up, the both of you. I need to think." Seward began to pace the quarterdeck, his head down. One hand played with the tie to his robe; the other stroked his lips.

"Sir, we only have one chance and it's a thin one at that," Wyatt said.

Mr. Temple took hold of his cane and moved toward him.

"Belay, Mr. Temple!" the captain ordered before turning his attention back to Wyatt. "Explain yourself, helmsman."

"At that range, with the land behind us, the Dacca can't possibly see the *Storm*. All they can see are the lanterns."

"Good god! You're right, put out those—"

"No, wait, sir!" Wyatt stopped him. "We *want* them to see the lanterns. Lower the longboat, rig it with a pole fore and aft, and hang two lanterns on the ends. Put ours out as you light those, then cast off. The Dacca will focus on it all night. We'll be able to bring the *Storm* about, catch the wind, and reach the safety of Wesbaden Bay."

"But that's not our destination."

"Damn our orders, sir! If we don't catch the wind, the Dacca will be on us by tomorrow night."

"*I'm* the captain of this ship!" Seward roared. "Another outburst and I'll not hold Mr. Temple's hand."

The captain looked at the waiting crew. Every eye was on him. He returned to pacing with his head down.

"Sir?" Bishop inquired. "Orders?"

"Can't you see I'm thinking, man?"

"Yes, sir."

The wind fluttered the sails overhead as the ship began to lose the angle on the wind.

"Lower the longboat," Seward ordered at last. "Rig it with poles and lanterns."

"And our heading?"

Seward tapped his lips.

"I shouldn't need to remind you, Captain Seward," Thranic said as he joined them on the quarterdeck, "that it's imperative we reach the port of Dagastan without delay."

Seward tapped his lips once more. "Send the longboat aft with a crew of four, and have them stroke for their lives toward Wesbaden. The Dacca will think we've seen them and will expect us to head that way, but the *Storm* will maintain its present course. There is to be no light on this ship without my order, and I want absolute silence. Do you hear me? Not a sound."

"Aye, sir."

Seward glanced at Wyatt, who shook his head with a look of disgust. The captain ignored him and turned to his lieutenant. "See to it, Mr. Bishop."

"Aye, aye, sir."

෴

"You should have tried for the longboat's crew," Wyatt whispered to Hadrian. "We all should have."

It was still dark, and the crescent moon had long since

fallen into the sea. As per the captain's orders, the ship was quiet. Even the wind had died, and the ship rocked, motionless and silent, in the darkness.

"You don't have a lot of faith in Seward's decision?" Hadrian whispered back.

"The Dacca are smarter than he is."

"You've got to at least give him the benefit of the doubt. They might think we turned and ran."

Wyatt muffled a laugh. "If you were captain and decided to make a run for it against faster ships in the dead of night, would you have left the lanterns burning? The lantern ruse only works if they think we *haven't* seen them."

"I hadn't thought of that," Hadrian admitted. "We'll know soon enough if they took the bait. It's getting lighter."

"Where's Royce and his eagle eyes?" Wyatt asked.

"He went to sleep after his shift. We've learned over the years to sleep and eat when you can, so you don't regret not doing so later."

They peered out across the water as the light increased. "Maybe the captain was right," Hadrian said.

"How do you mean?"

"I don't see them."

Wyatt laughed. "You don't see them because you can't see anything, not even a horizon. There's fog on the water. It happens this time of year."

It grew lighter, and Hadrian could see Wyatt was right. A thick gray blanket of clouds surrounded them.

Lieutenant Bishop climbed to the quarterdeck and rapped softly on the captain's door. "You asked to be awakened at first light, sir," he whispered.

The captain came out, fully dressed this time, and proudly strode to the bridge.

"Fog, sir."

The captain scowled at him. "I can see that, Mr. Bishop. I'm not blind."

"No, sir."

"Send a lad with a glass up the mainmast."

"Mr. Wesley," Bishop called softly. The midshipman came running. "Take this glass to the masthead and report."

"Aye, sir."

Captain Seward, rocking on his heels and staring out at the fog, stood with his hand fidgeting behind his back. "It looks promising so far, doesn't it, Mr. Bishop?"

"It does indeed, sir. The fog will help hide us all the more."

"What do you think now, helmsman?" the captain asked Wyatt.

"I think I'll wait for Mr. Wesley's report. If you don't mind, sir."

Seward folded his arms in irritation and began to pace, his short legs and plump belly doing little to impart the vision of a commanding figure.

Wesley reached the masthead and extended the glass.

"Well?" Seward called aloud, his impatience getting the better of him.

"I can't tell, sir. The fog is too thick."

"They say the Dacca can use magic to raise a fog when they want," Poe whispered to Hadrian as they watched. "They're likely using it to sneak up on us."

"Or maybe it's just because the air is cooler this morning," Hadrian replied.

Poe shrugged.

The crew stood around, silent and idle, for an hour before Mr. Temple ordered Hadrian to serve the morning meal. The men ate, then wandered the deck in silence, like ghosts in a misty world of white. The midday meal came and went as well, with no break in the mist that continued to envelop them.

Hadrian had just finished cleaning up when he heard Wesley's voice from the masthead shout, "Sail!"

Emerging from the hold, Hadrian felt a cool breeze as a wind moved the fog, parting the hazy white curtains veil after veil.

The single word left everyone on edge.

"Good Maribor, man!" Seward shouted up. "What kind of sail?"

"Red lateen sails, sir!"

"Damn!" Seward cursed. "How many?"

"Five!"

"Five? Five! How could there be five?"

"No, wait!" Wesley shouted. "Six to windward! And three more coming off the port bow."

The captain's face drained of color. "Good Maribor!"

Even as he spoke, Hadrian spotted the sails clustered on the water.

"Orders, Captain?" Wyatt asked.

Seward glanced around him desperately. "Mr. Bishop, lay the ship on the port tack."

Wyatt shook his head defiantly. "We need to grab the wind."

"Damn you!" Seward hesitated only a moment, then shouted, "So be it! Hard aport, helmsman. Bring her around, hard over!"

Wyatt spun the wheel, the chains cranking the rudder so that the ship started to turn. Mr. Temple barked orders to the crew. The *Emerald Storm* was sluggish, stalling in the futile wind. The ship slowed to a mere drift. Then the foresail fluttered, billowed, and started to draw, coming around slowly. The yards turned as the men ran aft with the lee braces. The mainsail caught the breeze and blew full. The ship creaked loudly as the masts took up the strain.

The *Storm* picked up speed and was halfway round and pointed toward the coast. Still, Wyatt held the wheel hard over. The wind pressed the sails and leaned the ship, dipping the beam dangerously low. Spray broke over the rail as men grabbed hold of whatever they could to remain standing as the deck tilted steadily upward. The captain glared at Wyatt as he grabbed hold of the mizzen shroud, yet he held his tongue.

Letting the wind take the ship full on with all sails set, Wyatt pressed the wheel, raising the ship on its edge. Bishop and Temple glanced from Wyatt to the captain and back again, but no one dared give an order in the captain's presence.

Hadrian also grabbed hold of a rail to keep from slipping down the deck. Holding tight, he worried that Wyatt might capsize the ship. The hull groaned from the strain, the masts creaked with the pressure, but the ship picked up speed. At first it bucked through the waves, sending bursts of spray over the deck, then faster it went until the *Storm* skipped the waves, flying off the crests with the wind squarely on its aft quarter. The ship made its tight circle and at last Wyatt let up, leveling the deck. The ship fell in direct line with the wind and the bow rose as the *Storm* ran with it.

"Trim the sails," the lieutenant ordered. The men set to work once more, periodically glancing astern to watch the approach of the ships.

"Mr. Bishop," Seward called. "Disburse weapons to the men and issue an extra ration of grog."

Royce was on his way aloft as the larboard crew came off duty. "How long do you think before they catch us?" he asked Hadrian, looking aft at the tiny armada of red sails chasing their wake.

"I don't know. I've never done this before. What do you think?"

Royce shrugged. "A few hours maybe."

"It's not looking good, is it?"

"And you wanted to be a sailor."

᠊᠊᠊᠊᠊

Hadrian went about the business of preparing for the evening meal, mindful that it might be the last the men would have. Poe, conspicuously absent, hastily entered the galley.

"Where you been?"

Poe looked sheepish. "Talking to Wyatt. Those Dacca ships are gaining fast. They'll be on us tonight for sure."

Hadrian nodded grimly.

Poe moved to help cut the salted pork, then added, "Wyatt has a plan. It won't save everyone—only a handful, really— and it might not work at all, but it's something. He wants to know if you're in."

"What about Royce?"

"Him too."

"What's the plan?"

"Sail!" they heard Mr. Wesley cry even from the galley. "Two more tartanes dead ahead!"

Poe and Hadrian, like everyone else aboard, scrambled to the deck to see Mr. Wesley pointing off the starboard bow. Two red sails were slipping out from hidden coves along the shore to block their retreat. Sailing nimbly against the wind, they moved to intercept the *Storm*.

"Clear the deck for action!" Seward shouted from the quarterdeck, wiping the sweat from his head.

Men scrambled across the ship, once more hauling buckets of sand and water. Archers took their positions on the forecastle, stringing their bows. Oil and hot coals were placed at the ready.

"We need to steer clear," the captain said. "Helm, bring her—"

"We need speed, *sir*," Wyatt interrupted.

The captain winced at the interruption. "Be mindful, Deminthal, or I'll skip the flogging I owe you and have you hanged!"

"With all due respect, you abdicated that privilege to the Dacca last night. All the sooner if I alter course now."

"By Maribor! Mr. Temple, take—" The captain stopped as he spotted the tartanes beginning to turn.

"See! They expected us to break," Wyatt told him.

Realizing their mistake, the Dacca fought to swing back, but it was too late. A hole had been created.

Seward grumbled and scowled at Wyatt.

"Sir?" Temple asked.

"Never mind. Steady as she goes, Mr. Bishop. Order the archers to take aim at the port-side ship! Perhaps we can slow them down if we can manage to set one afire."

"Aye, aye, sir!"

Hadrian rushed to the forecastle. Having proved himself one of the best archers on the ship, he was stationed at the center of the port side. He picked a strong, solid bow and tested the string's strength.

"The wind will set the arrows off a bit toward the bow," Poe mentioned, readying a bucket of glowing hot coals. "Might want to lead the target a bit, eh?"

"You're my squire now as well?"

Poe smiled and shook his head. "I've seen you in practice. I figure the safest place on this ship right now is here. I'll hand you the oiled arrows. You just keep firing."

The Dacca tartanes slipped through the waves, their red triangular sails billowing out sideways as they struggled on a tight tack to make the best use of the headwind. Dark figures scurried like ants across the decks and rigging of the smaller ships.

"Ready arrows!" Lieutenant Bishop shouted.

Hadrian fitted his first shaft in the string.

As the Dacca closed in on the *Storm*, they began to turn. Their yards swept round and their tillers cranked, pivoting much as Wyatt had, the action all the more impressive as both ships moved in perfect unison, like dancers performing simultaneous pirouettes.

"Light arrows!"

Hadrian touched the oil-soaked wad at the tip of the shaft to the pot of coals and it burst into flame. A row of men on the port side stood ready, a trail of soot-black smoke wafting aft.

"Take aim!" Bishop ordered as the Dacca ships came into range. On the deck of the tartanes, a line of flaming arrows mirrored their own. "Fire!"

Into the blue sky flew a staggered arc of fire trailing black smoke. At the same time, the Dacca launched their volley, and the arrows passed each other in midair. All around him, Hadrian heard pattering as they struck. The bucket brigade was running to douse the flames, and above them Royce dropped along a line to kick free one lodged in the masthead before it could ignite the mainsail.

Poe had another arrow ready. Hadrian fitted it, lit it with the pot, took aim, and sent it into the lower yard of their mainsail. To his right, he heard the loud *thwack* of the massive ballista, which sent forth a huge flaming missile. It struck the side of the tartane, splintering the hull and lodging there.

Hadrian heard a hissing fly past his ear. Behind him, the oil bucket splashed and the liquid ignited. Poe jumped backward as his trousers flamed. Grabbing a nearby bucket, Hadrian smothered the fire with sand.

Another volley rained, peppering the deck. Boatswain

Bristol, in the process of cranking the ballista for a second shot, fell dead with an arrow in his throat, his hair catching fire. Basil, the officers' cook, took one in the chest, and Seaman Bliden screamed as two arrows hit him, one in the thigh, and the other through his hand. Looking up, Hadrian saw this second volley came from the other ship.

Shaken but not seriously harmed, Poe found another oil bucket and brought it to Hadrian. As the two ships came closer, Hadrian found what he was looking for—a bucket at the feet of the archers. Leading his target, he held his breath, took aim, and released. The tartane's bucket exploded. Hadrian spotted a young Dacca attempt to douse the flames with water. Instantly the fire washed the deck. At that moment, the *Storm's* ballista crew, having loaded the weapon with multiple bolts this time, released a cruel hail on the passing Dacca. Screams bridged the gap between the ships as the *Storm* sailed on, leaving the burning ships in its wake.

Once more the crew cheered their victory, but it was hollow. Amid the blackened scorch marks left by scores of arrows, a dozen men lay dead on the deck. They had not slipped through the trap unscathed, and the red sails behind them were closer now.

✑

When night fell, the captain ordered the off-crew, including Hadrian and Royce, below deck to rest. On the way they grabbed their old gear from the galley, and the two took the opportunity to change into their cloaks and tunics. Hadrian strapped on his swords. It brought a few curious looks, but no one said a word.

Not a single man slept, and few even sat. Most paced with their heads bowed to avoid the short ceiling, but perhaps this time they were also praying. Many of the crew had appeared superstitious, but none religious—until now.

"Why don't we put inland?" Seaman Davis asked his fellow sailors. "The coast's only a few miles off. We could put in and escape into the jungle."

"Coral shoals ring the shores of Calis," Banner said, scraping the surface of the table with a knife. "We'd rip the bottom of the *Storm* a mile out, and the Dacca would have it. Besides, the captain ain't gonna abandon his ship and run."

"Captain Seward is an arse!"

"Watch yer mouth, lad!"

"Why? What's he gonna do that can be worse than the Dacca?"

To that, Banner had no answer. No one did. Fear spread through the crew—fear of certain death and the poison that comes from waiting idly for it. Hadrian knew from countless battles the folly of leaving men to stagnate with nothing else to occupy their thoughts.

The hatch opened and everyone looked up to see Wyatt and Poe.

"What's the word?" Davis asked.

"It won't be long now, men. Make ready what you need to. The captain will call general quarters soon, I expect."

Wyatt paused at the bottom of the ladder and spoke quietly with Grady and Derning. They nodded, then went aft. Wyatt motioned with his eyes for Hadrian and Royce to follow him forward. Only empty hammocks filled the cramped space, leaving them enough privacy to speak.

"So, what's this plan?" Royce whispered.

"We can't win a fight," Wyatt told them. "All we can hope to do is run."

"You said the *Storm* can't outrun them," Hadrian reminded him.

"I wasn't planning on outrunning them in the *Storm*."

Hadrian and Royce exchanged glances.

"The Dacca will want her and the cargo. That's why we made it through the blockade so easily. They were trying to slow us, not stop us. If I had followed Seward's orders, we'd all be dead now. As it is, I only bought us a few hours, but they were needed."

"Needed for what, exactly?" Royce asked.

"For darkness. The Dacca can't see any better at night than we can, and while they take the *Storm*, we'll escape. They'll bring as many of their ships alongside as they can to overwhelm our decks by sheer numbers. When they board us, a party of men I've handpicked will take one of the tartanes. We'll cut the ship free and, with luck, get clear of the *Storm* before they see us. In the darkness and the confusion of battle, it might work."

They both nodded.

Wyatt motioned to Hadrian. "I want you to lead the boarding party. I'll signal you from the quarterdeck."

"What are you going to be doing?" Royce asked.

"You mean what are *we* going to be doing? I didn't come all this way not to find Allie. You and I will use the distraction to break into the captain's quarters and steal any orders or parchments we find. Just watch me. You'll know when."

"What about the elves below?" Royce asked.

"Don't worry about them. The Dacca want the ship intact. In all likelihood, they will treat them better than the New Empire has."

"Who's in this team of yours?" Hadrian asked.

"Poe, of course, Banner, Grady—"

"All hands on deck!" Temple shouted from above as drums thundered.

"See you above, gentlemen," Wyatt said while heading for the hold.

The sky was black. Invisible clouds covered the stars and shrouded the sliver of moon. Darkness wrapped the sea, a shadowy abyss where only the froth at the bow revealed the presence of water. Behind them, Hadrian saw nothing.

"Archers to the aft deck!"

Hadrian joined the others at the railing, where they lined up, shoulder to shoulder, looking out across the *Emerald Storm's* wake.

"Light arrows!" came the order.

From across the water they heard a sound, and a moment later men around Hadrian screamed as arrows pelted the stern.

"Fire!" Bishop ordered.

They raised their bows and fired as one, launching their burning shafts blindly into the darkness. A stream of flame flew in a long arch, some arrows dying with a hiss as they fell into the sea, others striking wood, their light outlining a ship about three hundred yards behind them.

"There," Bishop shouted. "There's your target, men!"

They exchanged volley after volley. Men fell dead on both ships, thinning the ranks of archers. Small fires broke out on the tartane, illuminating it and its crew. The Dacca were short, stocky, and lean, with coarse long beards and wild hair. The firelight cast on them a demonic glow that glistened off their bare sweat-soaked skin.

When the tartane lay less than fifty yards astern, its mainmast caught fire and burned like a dead tree. The brilliant light exposed the sea in all directions and stifled the cheers of the *Storm's* crew when it revealed the positions of the rest of the Dacca fleet. Four ships had already slipped alongside them.

"Stand by to repel boarders!" shouted Seward. He drew his sword and waved it over his head as he ran to the safety of the forecastle walls.

"Raise the nets!" ordered Bishop. The rigging crew drew up netting on either side of the deck, creating an entangling barrier of rope webbing. Under command of their officers, men took position at the waist deck, cutlasses raised.

"Cut the tethers!" Mr. Wesley cried as hooks caught the rail.

The deck shook as the tartanes slammed against the *Emerald Storm's* hull. A flood of stocky men wearing only leather armor and red paint stormed over the side. They screamed in fury as swords met.

"Now!" Hadrian heard Wyatt shout at him.

He turned and saw the helmsman pointing to the tartane tethered to the *Storm's* port side near the stern, the first of the Dacca's ships to reach them. Most of its crew had already boarded the *Storm*. Poe, Grady, and others in Wyatt's team held back, watching Hadrian.

"Go!" Hadrian shouted and, grabbing hold of the mizzen's port-side brace, cut it free and swung out across the gulf, landing on the stern of the tartane.

The stunned Dacca helmsman reached for his short blade as Hadrian cut his throat. Two more Dacca rushed him. Hadrian dodged, using the move to hide the thrust. His broadsword drove deep into the first Dacca's stomach. The second man, seeing his chance, attacked, but Hadrian's bastard sword was in his left hand. With it he deflected a wild swing. Drawing the broadsword from the first Dacca's stomach, Hadrian brought it across, severing the remaining man's head.

With three bodies on the aft deck, Hadrian looked up to see Poe and the rest already in possession of the ship and in the process of cutting the tethers free. With the last one cut, Poe used a pole and pushed away from the *Storm*.

"What about Royce and Wyatt?" Hadrian asked, climbing down to the waist deck.

"They'll swim for it and we'll pick them up on the far side," Poe explained as he ran past him, heading aft. "But we need to get into the shadows now!"

Poe climbed the short steps to the tartane's tiny quarter-deck and took hold of the tiller. "Swing the boom!" he shouted in a whisper. "Trim the sails!"

"We know our jobs a lot better than you, boy!" Derning hissed at him. He and Grady were already hauling on the mainsail sheet, trying to tame the canvas that snapped above like a serpent, jangling the rigging rings against the mast. "Banner, Davis! Adjust the headsail for a starboard tack."

Hadrian had never learned the ropes, and he stood by uselessly while the others raced across the deck. Even if he had picked up anything about rigging, it would not have helped. The Dacca tartane was quite different in design. Besides being smaller, the hull was sloped like a fishing vessel, but with two decks. It had just two sails: a headsail supported on a forward-tilting mast and the mainsail. Both were triangular and hung from long curved yards that crossed the masts at angles so that the vessel's profile appeared like the heads of two axes cleaving through the air. The deck was dark wood. Glancing around, Hadrian wondered if the Dacca stained it with the same blood as the sails. After seeing the rigging ornamented with human skulls, it was an easy conclusion to make.

On the *Storm*, the battle was going badly. At least half the crew lay dead or dying. No canvas was visible, as the boarding party had made striking the sails a priority. The deck was awash in stocky, half-naked men who circled the forecastle with torches, dodging arrows as they struggled to breach the bulwark.

Poe pushed the tartane's tiller over, pointing the bow away from the *Storm*. The wind caught the canvas and the little ship glided gently away. With the sails on the *Emerald Storm* struck, the ship was dead in the water, and it was easy for them to circle it. Equally small crews remained to operate the other Dacca boarding ships, but that hardly mattered, as all eyes were on the *Storm*. As far as Hadrian could tell, no one noticed them.

"I'm bringing her around," Poe said. "Hadrian, stand by with that rope there, and everyone watch the water for Wyatt and Royce."

"Royce?" Derning questioned with distaste. "Why are we picking up the murderer? I can handle the rigging just fine."

"Because Wyatt said so," Poe replied.

"What if we can't find them? What if they die before they can get off the ship?" Davis asked.

"I'll decide that when it happens," Poe replied.

"You? You're barmy, boy. I'll be buggered if I'll take orders from a little sod like you! Bloody Davis here's got more years at sea than you and he's a git if there ever was one. If we don't find Deminthal after the first pass, you'll be taking orders from me."

"Like I said," Poe repeated, "I'll decide that when it happens."

Derning grinned menacingly, but Hadrian did not think Poe, being at the stern, could have seen it in the darkness.

◈

Royce wasted no time hitting the deck at the signal.

"We haven't got long," Wyatt told him. "The captain's quarters will be a priority."

He kicked the door open, shattering the frame.

Fully carpeted, the whole rear of the ship was one luxurious suite. Silk patterns in hues of gold and brown covered the walls, with matching upholstered furniture and a silk bedcover. A painting hung on one wall, showing a man bathed in sunlight, his face filled with rapture as a single white feather floated into his upraised hands. Silver lanterns swayed above vast stern windows that banked the far wall. The bed stood to one side with a large desk across from it.

Wyatt scanned the room quickly, then moved to the desk. He rifled the drawers. "He'll have put the orders in a safe place."

"Like a safe?" Royce asked, pulling a window drape aside to reveal a porthole-size compartment with a lock. "They always put them behind the drapes."

"Can you open it?"

Royce smirked. He pulled a tool from his belt and within seconds the little door swung open. Wyatt reached inside, grabbed the entire stack of parchments, and stuffed them into a bag.

"Let's get out of here," he said, making for the door. "Jump off the starboard side. Poe will pick us up."

They came out of the cabin into a world of chaos. Stocky men painted in red poured over the sides of the vessel. Each wielded short broad blades or axes that cut down everything before them. Only a handful of men stood on the waist deck. The rest had fallen back to the perceived safety of the forecastle. Those who tried to hold their ground died. Royce stepped out on the deck just in time to see Dime, his topsail captain, nearly cut in half by a cleaving blow from a Dacca axe.

Lieutenant Bishop and the other officers had been slow in reaching the castle, but now, as the Dacca flooded the deck, they were running full out to reach its walls. Stabbed in the back, Lieutenant Green collapsed. As he fell, he reached out, grabbing at anything. His hands found Midshipman Beryl running past and dragged him down as well. Beryl cursed and kicked Green off but got to his feet too late. The Dacca circled him.

"Help me!" he cried.

Royce watched as the crew ignored him and ran on—all but one. Midshipman Wesley ran back just in time to stab the nearest Dacca caught off guard by the sudden change in his fleeing prey. Wielding his sword with both hands, Wesley sliced horizontally across the chest of the next brute and kicked him aside.

"Beryl! This way, run!" he shouted.

Beryl lashed out at the Dacca, then ran to Wesley. They were quickly surrounded, and the Dacca drove them farther and farther away from the forecastle. An arrow from the walls saved Wesley from decapitation as the two struggled to defend themselves. Pushed by the overwhelming numbers, they retreated until their backs hit the rail.

A Dacca blade slashed Beryl's arm and then across his hip. He screamed, dropping his sword. Wesley threw himself between Beryl and his attacker. The young midshipman slashed wildly, struggling to defend the older man. Then Wesley was hit. He stumbled backward and reached out for the netting chains but missed them and fell overboard. Alone and unarmed, Beryl screamed as the Dacca swarmed him until they sent his head from his body.

No one noticed Wyatt or Royce creeping in the shadows around the stern, seeking a clear place to jump. They crouched just above the captain's cabin windows. Royce was about to leap when he spotted Thranic stepping out from the hold. The sentinel exited, a torch in hand, as if he merely wondered what all the noise was about. He led the seret to the main deck, where they quickly formed a wall around the sentinel. Seeing reinforcements, the Dacca rallied to an attack. They charged, only to die upon the serets' swords. The Knights of Nyphron were neither sailors nor galley slaves. They knew the use of arms and how to hold formation.

Gripping his bag to his chest, Wyatt leapt from the ship.

"Royce!" Wyatt shouted from the sea below.

Royce watched, impressed by the knights' courage and skill, as they battled the Dacca. It looked as if they might just turn the tide. Then Thranic threw his flaming brand into the ship's hold. A rush of air sounded, as if the ship were inhaling a great breath. A roar followed. A deep, resonating growl shook the timber beneath Royce's feet. Tongues of flame licked out of every hatch and porthole, the air filling with screams and cries. And in the flickering glow of burning wood and flesh, Royce saw the sentinel smile.

∽

Hadrian and the tiny crew of the stolen Dacca ship had only just reached the starboard side of the *Storm* when the area grew bright. The *Emerald Storm* was ablaze. Within little more than a minute, the fire had enveloped the deck. Men in the rigging had no choice but to jump. From that height, their bodies hit the water with a cracking sound. The rigging ignited, ropes snapped, and yards broke free, falling like flaming tree trunks. The darkness of the starless sea fell away as the *Emerald Storm* became a floating bonfire. Those near the rail leapt into the sea. Screams, cries, and the crackle and hiss of fire filled the night.

Looking over the black water, whose surface was alive with wild reflections, Hadrian spied a bit of sandy hair and a dark uniform. "Mr. Wesley, grab on!" Hadrian called, throwing a rope.

Hearing his name, Wesley turned, his face showing the same dazed expression as a man waking from a dream until he spotted Hadrian reaching out. He took the rope thrown and was reeled in like a fish and hoisted on deck.

"Nice to have you aboard, sir," Hadrian told him.

Wesley gasped for air and rolled over, vomiting seawater.

"From that, I assume you're happy to be here."

"Wyatt!" Poe shouted.

"Royce!" Hadrian called.

"Over there!" Derning said, pointing.

Poe turned the tiller and they sailed toward the sound of splashing.

"It's Bernie and Staul," Grady announced from where he stood on the bow.

The two wasted no time scrambling up the ship's ropes.

"More splashing over there!" Davis pointed.

Poe did not have to alter course, as the swimmers made good progress to them. Davis was the first to lend a hand. He reached out to help and a blade stabbed him in the chest before he was pulled overboard.

Hadrian saw them now—swarthy, painted brutes with long daggers, their wet, glistening skin shimmering with the light of the flames. They grabbed at the netting and scrambled like rats up the side of the tartane.

Hadrian drew his sword and lashed out at the nearest one, who dodged and stubbornly continued to climb. The Tenkin warrior, Staul, stabbed another in the face and the Dacca dropped backward with a cry and a splash. Bernie and Wesley joined in, thrashing wildly until the Dacca gave up and fell away into the darkness.

"Watch the other side!" Wesley shouted.

Staul and Bernie took positions on the starboard rail, but nothing moved.

"Any sign of Davis?" Hadrian asked.

"The man be dead now," Staul said. "Be more careful who you sail to, eh?"

"Bulard!" Bernie said, pointing ahead to more swimmers.

"And three more over there," Wesley announced, picking out faces in the tumultuous water. "One is Greig, the carpenter, and that's Dr. Levy, and there is ..."

Hadrian did not need Royce's eyes to identify the other man. The infernal light coming off the burning ship suited the face. Sentinel Thranic swam toward them, his hood thrown back and his pale face gleaming. Derning, Bernie, and Staul were bad enough. Now they had Dovin Thranic, of all people.

Thranic needed no help as he climbed nimbly up the side of the little ship, his cloak soaked, his face angry. If he were a dog, Hadrian knew he would be growling, and for that he was pleased. Bulard, the man who had come aboard in the middle of the night, looked even paler than before. The reason became obvious the moment he hit the deck and blood mingled with seawater. Levy went to him and applied pressure to the wound.

"Hadrian ... Poe!" Wyatt's voice carried from the sea below.

Poe steered toward the sound as the rest stood on their guard. This time there was no need. Wyatt and Royce were alone swimming for the boat.

"Where were you?" Wyatt asked, climbing aboard.

"Sorry, boss, but it's a big ocean."

"Not big enough," Derning said, looking over at what remained of the *Storm*, his face bright with the glow. "The Dacca are finally taking notice of us."

The mainmast of the *Emerald Storm*, burning like a tree-sized torch, finally cracked and fell. The forecastle walls blazed. Seward, Bishop, and the rest had either been lost to blades or burned alive. The *Storm* had blackened and cracked, allowing the ship to take on water. The hull listed to one side, sinking from the bow. As it did, the fire was still bright enough to see several of the Dacca on the nearest vessel pointing in their direction and shouting.

"Wheel hard over!" Wyatt shouted, running for the tiller. "Derning, Royce, get aloft! Hadrian, Banner—the mainsail braces. Grady to the headsail braces! Who else do we have here? Bernie, join Derning and Royce. Staul, help with the mainsail. Mr. Wesley, if it wouldn't be too much trouble, perhaps you could assist Grady on the forward braces. Bring her round east-nor'east!"

"That will put us into the wind again!" Grady said even as Wyatt brought the ship round.

"Aye, starboard tack. With fewer crew, and the same ship, we'll be lighter and faster."

They got the ship around and caught what wind they could.

"Here, Banner, take the tiller," Wyatt said as he scanned the deck. "We can dump some gear and lighten the load further. Who's that next to you?"

Wyatt stopped abruptly when he saw Thranic look up.

"What's he doing on board?" Wyatt asked.

"Is there a problem, helmsman?" Thranic addressed him.

"You fired the ship!" Wyatt accused. "Royce told me he saw you throw a torch in the hold. How many oil kegs did you break to get it to go up like that?"

"Five, I think. Maybe six."

"There were elves—they were locked in the hold—trapped down there."

"Precisely," Thranic replied.

"You bastard!" Wyatt rushed the sentinel, drawing his cutlass. Thranic moved with surprising speed and dodged Wyatt's attack, throwing his cloak around Wyatt's head and shoving the helmsman to the deck as he drew a long dagger.

Hadrian pulled his swords and Staul immediately moved to intercept him. Poe drew his cutlass, as did Grady, followed quickly by Defoe and Derning.

From the rigging above, Royce dropped abruptly into the

midst of the conflict, landing squarely between Thranic and Wyatt. The sentinel's eyes locked on him and smoldered.

"Mr. Wesley!" Royce shouted, keeping his eyes fixed on Thranic. "What are your orders, sir?"

At this everyone stopped. The ship continued to sail with the wind, but the crew paused. Several glanced at Wesley. The midshipman stood frozen on the deck, watching the events unfold around him.

"*His* orders?" Thranic mocked.

"Captain Seward, Lieutenants Bishop and Green, and the other midshipmen are dead," Royce explained. "Mr. Wesley is senior officer. He is, by rights, in command of this vessel."

Thranic laughed.

Wesley began to nod. "He is right."

"Shut up, boy!" Staul snapped. "It's time we took care of this business here."

Staul's words brought Wesley around. "I am no boy!" Turning to Thranic, he added, "What I am, *sir*, is the acting captain of this ship, and as such, you, and everyone else" — he glanced at Staul — "*will* obey my orders!"

Staul laughed.

"I assure you this is no joke, seaman. I also assure you that I will not hesitate to see you cut down where you stand, and anyone else who fails to obey me."

"And how do you plan to do that?" Staul asked. "This is not the *Emerald Storm*. You command no one here."

"I wouldn't say that." Hadrian flashed his familiar smile at Staul.

"Neither would I," Royce added.

"Me neither," Derning joined in, his words quickly echoed by Grady.

Wyatt got to his feet slowly. He glared at Thranic but said, "Aye, Mr. Wesley is captain now."

Poe, Banner, and Greig acknowledged with a communal "Aye."

What followed was a tense silence. Staul and Bernie looked at Thranic, who never took his gaze off Royce. "Very well, *Captain*," the sentinel said at length. "What are your orders?"

"I hereby promote Mr. Deminthal to acting lieutenant. Everyone will follow his instructions to the letter. Mr. Deminthal, you will confine your orders to saving this vessel from the Dacca and maintaining order and discipline. There are to be no executions and no disciplinary actions of any kind without my authorization. Is that clear?"

"Aye, sir."

"Petty Officer Blackwater, you are hereby appointed master-at-arms. Collect the weapons, but keep them at the ready. See to it Mr. Deminthal's and my orders are carried out. Understood?"

"Aye, sir."

"Mr. Grady, you are now boatswain. Dr. Levy, please take Mr. Bulard below so that he can be properly cared for. Let me know if there is anything you need. Mr. Derning will be top captain. Seamen Defoe and Melborn, report to him for duties. Mr. Deminthal, carry on."

"Your sword." Hadrian addressed Staul. The Tenkin hesitated but, after a nod from Thranic, handed the blade over. As he did, he laughed and cursed in the Tenkin language.

"You'd have found that a bit harder than you think," Hadrian replied to Staul, and he was rewarded with the Tenkin's shocked expression.

Wyatt had everything nonessential and not attached to the ship thrown overboard. Then he ordered silence and whispered the order to change tack. The boom swung over, catching the wind and angling the little ship out to sea. Well behind them, the last light of the *Emerald Storm* disappeared, swallowed by the waves. Not quite so far away, they could see lanterns bobbing on the following ships. From the shouts, it was clear they were displeased at losing their prize. All eyes faced astern, watching the progression of lanterns as the Dacca continued following their previous tack. After a while, two ships altered course but guessed incorrectly and turned westward. Eventually all the lanterns disappeared.

"Are they gone?" Hadrian heard Wesley whisper to Wyatt.

He shook his head. "They just put out the lanterns, but with luck they will think we're running for ground. The nearest friendly port is Wesbaden back west."

"For a helmsman, you're an excellent commander," the young man observed.

"I was a captain once," Wyatt admitted. "I lost my ship."

"Really? In whose service, the empire or a royal fleet?"

"No service. It was *my* ship."

Wesley looked astonished. "You were…a pirate?"

"Opportunist, sir. Opportunist."

～

Hadrian awoke to a misty dawn. A steady breeze pushed the tartane through undulating waves. All around them lay a vast and empty sea.

"They are gone," Wesley said, answering the unasked question. "We have lost them."

"Any idea where we are?"

"About three days' sail from Dagastan," Wyatt answered.

"Dagastan?" Grady muttered, looking up. "We're not headed there, are we?"

"That was my intention," Wyatt replied.

"But Wesbaden is closer."

"Unfortunately, I confess no knowledge of these coasts," Wesley said. "Do you know them well, Mr. Deminthal?"

"Intimately."

"Good. Then tell us, is Mr. Grady correct?"

Wyatt nodded. "Wesbaden is closer, but the Dacca know this and will be waiting in that direction. However, since it's impossible for them to be ahead of us, our present course is the safest."

"Despite our earlier differences, I agree with Mr. Deminthal," Thranic offered. "As it turns out, Dagastan was the *Storm's* original destination, so we must continue toward it."

"But Dagastan is much farther away from Avryn," Wesley said. "The *Storm's* mission was lost with her sinking. I have no way of knowing her original destination, and even if I did, I have no cargo to deliver. Going farther east only increases our difficulties. I need to be mindful of provisions."

"But you do have cargo," Thranic announced. "The *Storm's* orders were to deliver myself, Mr. Bulard, Dr. Levy, Bernie, and Staul to Dagastan. The main cargo is gone, but as an officer of the realm, it's your duty to fulfill what portion you can of Captain Seward's mission."

"With all due respect, Your Excellency, I have no way to verify what you say."

"Actually, you do." Wyatt pulled a bent and battered scroll from his bag. "These are Captain Seward's orders."

Wesley took the damp scroll and asked, "But how did you come by this?"

"I knew we'd need charts to sail by. Before I left the *Storm*, I entered the captain's cabin, and being in a bit of a hurry, I just grabbed everything on his desk. Last night I discovered I had more than just charts."

Wesley nodded, accepting this and, Hadrian thought, perhaps choosing not to inquire further. He paused a second before reading it. Most men were awake now and, having heard the conversation, watched Wesley with anticipation. When he finished, he looked over at Wyatt.

"Was there a letter?"

"Aye, sir," he said while handing over a sealed bit of parchment.

Wesley slipped it carefully into his coat without opening it. "We will maintain course to Dagastan. Being bound by imperial naval laws, I must do everything in my power to see the *Storm's* errand is fulfilled."

CHAPTER 13

THE WITCH OF MELENGAR

Modina stared out her window as usual, watching the world with no real interest. It was late and she feared sleep. It always brought the dreams, the nightmares of the past, of her father, and of the dark place. She sat up most nights, studying the shadows and the clouds as they passed over the stars. A line of moonlight crossed the courtyard below. She noted how it climbed the statues and the far gate wall, just like the creeping ivy. Once green, the plant was now a dreary red. It would go dormant, appearing to die, but would still hang on to the wall. It would continue its desperate grip on the stone even as it withered. For it, at least, there would be a spring.

The hammering at her chamber door roused her. She turned, puzzled. No one ever knocked except for Gerald, who always used a light tap. Amilia came and went frequently but never knocked. Whoever it was, they beat the door with a fury.

The pounding landed harder and with such violence that the door latch bounced with a distinct metallic clank as it threatened to break. It never occurred to her to ask who was there. It never crossed her mind to be fearful. She slid back the bolt, letting the door swing inward.

Standing outside was a man she vaguely recognized. His face was flushed, his eyes glassy, and the collar to his shirt lay open.

"There you are," he exclaimed. "At long last I am rewarded with your presence. Permit me to introduce myself again, in case you've forgotten me. I am Archibald Ballentyne, twelfth Earl of Chadwick." He bowed low, taking an awkward step when he lost his balance. "May I come in?"

The empress said nothing, and the earl took this as an invitation, pushing his way into the chamber. He held a finger to his lips. "Shh, we need to be quiet, lest someone discover I'm here." The earl stood wavering, his glazed eyes canvassing the full length of Modina's small body. His mouth hung partially open and his head moved up and down, as if trying to save his eyes the effort.

Modina was dressed only in her thin nightgown but did not think to cover herself.

"You're beautiful. I thought so from the first. I wanted to tell you before this, but they wouldn't let me see you." The earl pulled a bottle of liquor from his breast pocket and took a swallow. "After all, I'm the hero of your army, and it isn't fair that Ethelred gets to have you. You should be mine. I earned you!" the earl shouted, raising his fist.

Pausing, he looked toward the open door. After a moment, he continued, "What has Ethelred ever done? It was my army that saved Aquesta and would have crushed Melengar if they had let me. But they didn't want me to. Do you know why? They knew if I took Melengar, then I would be too great to hold back. They're jealous of me, you know. And now Ethelred is planning to take you, but you're mine. *Mine*, I say!" He shouted this last bit, then cringed. Once more he placed a finger to his lips. "Shh."

Modina watched the earl with mild curiosity.

"How can you want *him*?" He slammed his fist against his chest. "Am I not handsome? Am I not young?" He twirled around with his arms outstretched until he staggered. He steadied himself on the bedpost. "Ethelred is old, fat, and has pimples. Do you really want that? He doesn't care about you. He's only after the crown."

The earl took a moment to glance around the empty room. "Don't get me wrong," he said in a harsh whisper. He leaned in so close he had to put a hand on her shoulder to steady himself. "I want the crown, too—anyone saying different is a liar. Who wouldn't want to be emperor of the world, but"—he held up a wavering finger—"*I* would have loved you."

He paused, breathing hotly into her face. He licked his lips and caressed her skin through the thin nightgown. His hand left her shoulder and inched up her neck, his open fingers slipping into her hair. "Ethelred will never look at you like this." Archibald took her hand and placed it against his chest. "His heart will never pound like mine just by being near you. I want power. I want the throne, but I also want you." He looked into her eyes. "I love you, Modina. I love you and I want you for my own. You should be *my* wife."

He pulled her to him and kissed her on the mouth, pressing hard, pinching her lips to her teeth. She did not struggle—she did not care. He pulled back and searched her face. She did not respond except to blink.

"Modina?" Amilia called, entering the room. "What's going on?"

"Nothing," Ballentyne said sadly. He looked at Modina. He searched her face again. "Absolutely nothing at all."

He turned and left the room.

"Are you all right?" Amilia rushed to the empress, brushing her hair back and looking her over. "Did he hurt you?"

"Am I to marry Regent Ethelred?"

Amilia held her breath and bit her lip.

"I see. When were you going to tell me? On my wedding night?"

"I—I just learned about it recently. You had that incident in the kitchen and I didn't want to upset you."

"It doesn't upset me, Amilia, and thank you for stopping by."

"But I—" Amilia hesitated.

"Is there something else?"

"Ah—no, I just—You're different suddenly. We should talk about this."

"What is there to talk about? I'll marry Ethelred so he can be emperor."

"You'll still be empress."

"Yes, yes, there's no need to worry. I'm fine."

"You're never *fine*."

"No? It must be the good news that I'm to become a bride."

Amilia looked terrified. "Modina, what's going on? What's happening in that head of yours?"

Modina smiled. "It's okay, Amilia. Everything will be *fine*."

"Stop using that word! You're really frightening me," Amilia said, reaching toward her.

Modina pulled away, moving to the window.

"I'm sorry I didn't tell you myself. I'm sorry there was no guard at the door. I'm sorry you had to hear such a thing from the brandy-soaked breath of—"

"It's not your fault, Amilia. It's important to me that you know that. You're all that matters to me. It's amazing how worthless a life feels without someone to care for. My father understood that. At the time, I didn't, but now I do."

"Understand what?" Amilia asked, shaking.

"That living has no value—it's what you do with life that gives it worth."

"And what are you planning to do with your life, Modina?"

Modina tried to force another smile. She took Amilia's head in her hands and kissed her gently. "It's late. Goodbye, Amilia."

Amilia's eyes went wide with fear. She began shaking her head faster and faster. "No, no, no! I'll stay here. I don't want you left alone tonight."

"As you wish."

Amilia looked pleased for a moment, then fear crept back in. "Tomorrow I'll assign a guard to *watch* you."

"Of course you will," Modina replied.

⌒

True to her word, Amilia remained in Modina's chamber all night, but slipped out before dawn while the empress still slept. She went to the office of the master-at-arms and burst in on the soldier on duty, unannounced.

"Why wasn't there a guard outside the empress's door last night? Where was Gerald?"

"We couldn't spare him, milady. The imperial guard is stretched thin. We're searching for the witch, the Princess of Melengar. Regent Saldur has commanded me to use every man I have to find her."

"I don't care. I want Gerald back watching her door. Do you understand?"

"But, milady—"

"Last night the Earl of Chadwick forced his way into the empress's room. In her room! And has it occurred to you—to anyone—that the witch might be coming to kill the empress?"

A long pause.

"I didn't think so. Now, get Gerald back on his post at once."

Leaving the master-at-arms, Amilia roused Modina's chambermaid from her bunk in the dormitory. After the girl had dressed, she hurried her along to Modina's room.

"Anna, I want you to stay with the empress and watch her."

"Watch her, what for? I mean, what should I be watching for, milady?"

"Just make certain the empress doesn't hurt herself."

"How do you mean?"

"Just keep an eye on her. If she does anything odd or unusual, send for me at once."

᪈

Modina heard Anna enter the room quietly. She continued pretending to sleep. Near dawn she stretched, yawned, and walked over to the washbasin to splash water on her face. Anna was quick to hand her a towel and grinned broadly to have been of assistance.

"Anna, is it?" Modina asked.

The girl's face flushed, and her eyes lit up with joy. She nodded repeatedly.

"Anna, I'm starved. Would you please run to the kitchen and see if they can prepare me an early breakfast? Be a dear and bring it up when it's ready."

"I—I—"

Modina put on a pout and turned her eyes downward. "I am sorry. I apologize for asking so much of you."

"Oh no, Your Gloriousness, I'll get it at once."

"Thank you."

"You are most welcome, Your Worship."

Modina wondered if she kept her longer how many elaborate forms of address she might come up with. As soon as Anna left the room, Modina walked to the door, closed it, and slid the dead bolt. She walked toward the tall mirror that hung on the wall, picking up the pitcher from the water basin as she passed. Without hesitation, she struck the mirror, shattering both. She picked up a long shard of glass and went to her window.

"Your Eminence?" Gerald called from the other side of the door. "Are you all right?"

Outside, the sun was just coming up. The autumn morning light angled in sharp, slanted shafts across the courtyard below. She loved the sun and thought its light and warmth would be the only thing besides Amilia that she would miss.

She wrapped her gown around the end of the long jagged piece of glass. It felt cold. Everything felt cold to her. She looked down at the courtyard and breathed in a long breath of air scented with the dying autumn leaves.

The guard continued to bang on the door. "Your Eminence?" he repeated. "Are you all right?"

"Yes, Gerald," she said, "I'm *fine*."

Arista entered the palace courtyard, walking past the gate guards, hoping they could not hear the pounding of her heart.

This must be how Royce and Hadrian feel all the time. I'm surprised they don't drink more.

She shook from both fear and the early-morning chill. Esrahaddon's robe had been lost the night of Hilfred's rescue, leaving her with only Lynnette's kirtle.

Hilfred. He'll be furious if he reads the note.

It hurt her heart just to think of him. He had stood in her shadow for years, serving her whims, taking her abuse, trapped in a prison of feelings he could never reveal. Twice he had nearly died for her. He was a good man—a great man.

She wanted to make him happy. He deserved to be happy. She wanted to give him what he never thought possible, to fix what she had broken.

For three nights they had hid together, and every day Hilfred had tried to convince her to return to Melengar. At last she had agreed, telling him they would leave the next day. Arista had slipped out when Hilfred went to get supplies. If all went well, she would be back before he returned and they could leave as planned. If not—if something happened—the note would explain.

It had occurred to her, only the night before, that she had never cast the location spell in the courtyard. From there, the smoke would certainly locate the wing, and if lucky enough, she might even pinpoint Gaunt's window. The information would be invaluable to Royce and Hadrian and could mean the difference between a rescue and a suicide mission. And as much as she did not want to admit it, she owed Esrahaddon as well. If doing this small thing could save Degan Gaunt, a good man wrongly imprisoned; ease the wizard's passing; and vanquish her guilt, it would be worth the risk.

The gate guards paid little attention when she had entered. She took this as a good sign that no one had connected Ella the scrub girl to the Witch of Melengar. All she needed to do now was cast the spell and walk out again.

She crossed the inner ward to the vegetable garden. The harvest had come and gone, the plants were cleared, and the soil had been turned to await the spring. The soft earth would allow her to draw the circle and symbols required. She clutched the pouch of hair still in the pocket of her kirtle as she glanced around. Nothing looked amiss. The few guards on duty ignored her.

As casually as she could, she began drawing a circle by dragging her foot in the dirt. When she had finished, she moved on to the more tedious task of the runes, which was more time-consuming to do with her toe than with her hand and a bit of chalk. All the while, she worried that her drawing would be obvious from any number of upper-story windows.

She was just finishing the second to last rune when a guard exited the palace and walked toward her. Immediately she crouched, pretending to dig. If he questioned her, she could say that Ibis sent her to look for potatoes, or that she thought she might have dropped the pantry key when she was in the courtyard. She hoped he would just walk by. She needed to be the invisible servant this one last time. It quickly became apparent that he was specifically coming for her. As he closed the distance, her only thought was of Hilfred and how she wished she had kissed him goodbye.

—⁊—

Amilia was in her office, quickly going over instructions with Nimbus. They had ticked off only a few items for the wedding preparations. If she could give him enough to keep busy, she could return to Modina. The urgency pulled at her every minute she was away.

"If you get done with that, then come see me and I'll give you more to do," she told him curtly. "I have to get back to the empress. I think she might do something stupid."

Nimbus looked up. "The empress is a bit eccentric certainly, but, if I may, she has never struck me as stupid, my lady."

Amilia narrowed her eyes at him suspiciously.

Nimbus had been a good and faithful servant, but she did not like the sound of that. "You notice too much, I think, Nimbus. That's not such a good trait when working in the imperial palace. Ignorance is perhaps a better choice for survival."

"I am just trying to cheer you up," he replied, sounding a little hurt.

Amilia frowned and collapsed in her chair. "I'm sorry. I am starting to sound a bit like Saldur, aren't I?"

"You still have to work on making your veiled threats sound more ominous. A deeper voice would help, or perhaps toying with a dagger or swishing a glass of wine as you say it."

"I wasn't threatening you. I was—"

He cut her off. "I am just joking, my lady."

Amilia scowled, then pulled a parchment off her desk, crumpled it into a ball, and threw it at him. "Honestly, I don't know why I hired you."

"Not for my comedy, I sense."

Amilia gathered a pile of parchments, a quill, and a bottle of ink and headed for the door. "I'm going to be working from Modina's room today. Look there if you need me."

"Of course," he said as she left.

Not far down the hall, Amilia saw Anna walking by with a tray of food. "Anna," she called, rushing toward her. "I told you to stay with the empress!"

"Yes, milady, but..."

"But what?"

"The empress asked me to fetch her some breakfast."

A cold chill shot up Amilia's spine. The empress had *asked* her. "Has the empress ever spoken to you before?"

On the verge of tears, Anna shook her head. "No, milady, I was very honored. She even knew my name."

Amilia raced for the stairs, her heart pounding. Reaching the top and nearing the bedchamber, she feared what she would find. Nimbus was right, perhaps more than he knew. Modina was not stupid, and Amilia's mind filled with the many terrible possibilities. Arriving at the door, she pushed

Gerald aside and burst into the empress's room. She steeled herself, but what she saw was beyond her wildest imaginings.

Modina and Ella sat together on the empress's bed, hand in hand, chatting.

Amilia stood still, shocked. Both glanced up as she entered. Ella's face was fearful, but Modina's expression was calm as usual, as if expecting her.

"Ella?" Amilia exclaimed. "What are you doing—"

"Gerald," Modina interrupted, "from now on, no one—and I mean *no one*—is to enter without my say-so. Understood?"

"Of course, Your Eminence." Gerald looked down guiltily.

Modina waved her hand. "It's not your fault. I didn't tell you. Now please close the door."

He bowed and drew the door shut.

Amilia meanwhile stood silent. Her mouth was agape but no words came out.

"Sit down before you fall down, Amilia. I want to introduce you to a friend of mine. This is Arista, the Princess of Melengar."

Amilia tried to make sense out of the senselessness. "No, Modina, this is Ella—a scrub girl. What's going on?" Amilia asked desperately. "I thought—I thought you might be—" Her eyes went to the broken pitcher and shards of mirrored glass scattered across the corner of the room.

"I know what you thought," the empress said, looking toward the window. "That's another reason you should be welcoming Arista. If I hadn't seen her in the courtyard and realized—well—anyway, I want you two to be friends."

Amilia's mind was still whirling. Modina appeared more lucid than ever, yet she made no sense. Maybe she only sounded rational. Maybe the empress had cracked altogether. At any moment, she might introduce Red, the elkhound from the kitchen, as the Ambassador of Lanksteer.

"Modina, I know you think this girl is a princess, but just a week ago you also thought you were dead and buried, remember?"

"Are you saying you think I'm crazy?"

"No, no, I just…"

"Lady Amilia"—Ella spoke for the first time—"my name is Arista Essendon, and I *am* the Princess of Melengar. Your empress isn't crazy. She and I are old friends."

Amilia stood staring at the two of them, confused. Were they both insane? How could—*Oh sweet Maribor. It's her!* The long fingernails, the way she met Amilia's stare, the bold inquiries about the empress. Ella was the Witch of Melengar. "Get away from her!" Amilia yelled.

"Amilia, calm down."

"She's been posing as a maid to get to you."

"Arista's not here to harm me. You're not, are you?" she asked Ella, who shook her head. "There, you see? Now come here and join us. We have much to do."

"Thrace." Ella spoke, looking nervously at Modina. The empress raised a hand to stop her.

"The both of you need to trust me," Modina said.

Amilia shook her head. "But how can I? Why should I? This—this woman—"

"Because," the empress interrupted, "we have to help Arista."

Amilia would have laughed at the absurdity if Modina had not looked so serious. In all the time she had taken care of her, Amilia had never seen her so focused, so clear-eyed. She felt out of her element. The hazy Modina was gone, but she was still speaking nonsense. She had to make her understand, for her own good. "Modina, guards are looking for this woman. They've been combing the city for days."

"That's why she's going to stay here. It's the safest place.

Not even the regents will look for her in my bedroom. And it'll make helping her that much easier."

"Helping her? Helping her with what?" Amilia was nearly at the end of her own sanity just trying to follow this absurd conversation.

"We're going to help her find Degan Gaunt, the true Heir of Novron."

CHAPTER 14

CALIS

The port of Dagastan surprised first-time visitors from Avryn, who thought of everywhere else as less civilized or uncultured. Calis was generally held, by those who had never been there, to be a crude, ramshackle collection of tribal bands living in mud or wooden huts within a dense and mysterious jungle. It shocked most when they first laid eyes on the massive domes and elegant spires rising along the coast. The city was astonishingly large and well developed. Stone and gray-brick buildings sat densely packed on a graduated hillside rising from the elegant harbor that put Aquesta's wooden docks to shame. Here four long stone piers stretched into the bay, along which stately towers rose at regular intervals, facilitating the needs of the bustling trade center. Masts of more than a hundred ships, nearly all of them exotic merchant vessels, lined the harbor.

Hadrian remembered the city the moment it came into view. The heat of the ancient stones, the spice-scented streets, the exotic women—all memories of an impetuous youth that he preferred to forget. He had left the east behind without regret, and it was not without reservations that he found himself returning.

No bells rang in the towers along the harbor as they

entered. No alarm signaled as the bloodred sails of their Dacca-built tartane entered port. A pilot boat merely issued out and hailed them at their approach.

"*En dil dual lon duclim?*" the pilot called to them.

"I can't understand you," Wesley replied.

"What's name of your vessel? And name of captain?" the pilot repeated.

"Oh, ah—it doesn't have a name, I'm afraid, but my name is Wesley Belstrad."

The pilot jotted something on a handheld tablet, frowning. "Where you outing from?"

"We are the remaining crew of the *Emerald Storm*, Her Imperial Eminence's vessel out from the capital city of Aquesta."

"What your business and how long staying will you be?"

"We are making a delivery. I am not certain how long it will take."

The pilot finished asking questions and indicated they should follow him to a berth. Another official was waiting on the dock and asked Wesley to sign several forms before he would allow anyone to set foot on land.

"According to Seward's orders, we are to contact a Mr. Dilladrum. I will go ashore and try to locate him," Wesley announced. "Mr. Deminthal, you and Seaman Staul will accompany me. Seaman Blackwater, you will be in charge here until my return. See to it that the stores are secured and the ship buttoned down."

"Aye, sir." Hadrian saluted. The three disembarked and disappeared into the maze of streets.

"Wonderful luck we've had in picking up survivors, eh?" Hadrian mentioned to Royce as he met his partner on the raised aft deck of the ship.

The others remained at the waist or the bow, staring in fascination at the port around them. There was a lot to take in.

Unusual sounds drifted from the urban landscape. The jangle of bells, the ringing of a gong, shouts of merchants in a strange musical language, and above it all the haunting voice of a man singing in the distance.

Dockworkers moved cargo to and from ships. Most were dressed in robes with vertical stripes, their skin a tawny brown, their faces bearded. Bolts of shimmering silks and sheer cloth waited to be loaded, as did urns of incense and pots of fragrant oil, whose scents drifted on the harbor breeze. The stone masonry of the buildings was impressive. Intricate designs of flowers and geometric shapes adorned nearly all the constructions. Domes were the most common architectural style, some inlaid in gold, others in silver or in colorful tiles. The larger buildings displayed multiple domes, each featuring a central spire pointing skyward.

For the first time in three days they had found an opportunity to speak alone. "I thought you showed great restraint, and I was impressed with your diplomatic solution to our little civil war," Hadrian told Royce.

"I'm just watching your back, like Gwen asked." Royce took a seat on a thick pile of netted ropes.

"It was a stroke of brilliance appointing Wesley," Hadrian remarked. "I wish I had thought of it. I like that boy. Did you see the way he picked Staul and Wyatt to go with him? Wyatt knows the docks, and Staul knows the language and possibly the city. Perfectly sensible choices, but they're also the two who would make the most trouble out of his sight. He's a lot more like his brother than he thinks. It's a shame they were born in Chadwick. Ballentyne doesn't deserve them."

"It's not looking good. You know that, right?" Royce asked. "What with the weapons and Merrick's payment going down with the *Storm*, and everyone in charge now dead. I don't see where we go from here."

Hadrian took a seat on the railing beside Royce. Water lapped against the wooden hull of the tartane and seagulls cried overhead.

"But we still have Merrick's orders and that letter. What did it say?"

"I didn't read it."

"Weren't you the one who called me stupid because—"

"I never had a chance. Wyatt grabbed them first. Then there was this little incident with a burning ship and lots of swimming. Now Wesley has them and he's hardly slept. I've not had an opportunity."

"Then we'll have to stick to that letter until either you get a chance to take a peek or we solve this riddle. I mean, what is the empire doing sending weapons to Calis when they need them to fight the Nationalists?"

"Maybe bribing Calis to join the fight on their side?"

Hadrian shook his head. "Rhenydd could beat them in a war all by itself. There's no organization down here, no central authority, just a bunch of competing warlords. The whole place is corrupt, and they constantly fight each other. There is no way Merrick could convince enough leaders to go fight for the New Empire—most of these warlords have never even heard of Avryn. And what's with the elves? What were they doing with them?"

"I have to admit, I'd like to know that myself," Royce said.

Hadrian's glance followed Thranic as he came topside and lay among the excess canvas at the bow, his hood pulled down to block the light, his arms folded across his chest. He almost looked like a corpse in need of a coffin.

Hadrian gestured toward the sentinel. "So, what's going on between you and Thranic, anyway? He appears to *really* hate you—even more than most people."

Royce did not look in his direction. He sat nonchalantly,

pretending to ignore the world, as if they were the only two aboard. "Funny thing, that. I never met him, never heard of him until this voyage, and yet I know him rather well, and he knows me."

"Thank you, Mr. Esrahaddon. Can you provide me with perhaps a more cryptic answer?"

Royce smiled. "I see why he does it now. It's rather fun. I'm also surprised you haven't figured it out yet."

"Figured what out?"

"Our boy Thranic has a nasty little secret. It's what makes him so unpleasant and at the same time so dangerous. He would have killed Wyatt, might even have given you a surprise or two. With Staul added to the mix and Bernie slinking about, it wasn't a battle I felt confident in winning, even if I didn't have Gwen's voice echoing in my head."

"You aren't going to tell me, are you?"

"What would be the fun in that? This will give you something to do. You can try to guess, and I can amuse myself by insulting your intelligence. I wouldn't take too long, though. Thranic is going to die soon."

⨎

Wesley returned and trotted up the gangway to address them. "I want volunteers to accompany me, Sentinel Thranic, Mr. Bulard, Dr. Levy, and Seamen Staul and Defoe inland. We will be traveling deep into the Calian jungles. The journey will not be without significant risks, so I won't order anyone to follow me who doesn't want to go. Those who choose to stay behind will remain with the ship. Upon my return, we will sail for home, where you will receive your pay."

"Where in the jungle are you headed, Mr. Wesley?" Banner asked.

"I must deliver a letter to Erandabon Gile, who I am informed is a warlord of some note in these parts. I have met with Mr. Dilladrum, who has been awaiting our arrival and has a caravan prepared and ready to escort us. Gile's fortress, however, is deep in the jungles, and contact with the Ba Ran Ghazel is likely. Now, who is with me?"

Hadrian, who was one of the first to raise his hand, found it strange that he was among the majority. Wyatt and Poe did not surprise him, but even Jacob and Grady joined in after seeing the others. Only Greig and Banner abstained.

"I see," Wesley said with a note of surprise. "All right then, Banner, I'll leave you in charge of the ship."

"What are we to do while yer gone, sir?" Banner asked.

"Nothing," he told them. "Just stay with the ship and out of the city. Don't cause any trouble."

Banner smiled gleefully at Greig. "So we can just sleep all day if we want?"

"I don't care what you do, as long as you protect the ship and don't embarrass the empire."

Both of them could hardly contain their delight. "I'll bet the rest of you are wishing you hadn't raised your hands now."

"You realize there's only about a week's worth of rations below, right?" Wyatt mentioned. "You might want to eat sparingly."

A worried look crossed Banner's face. "You're gonna hurry back, right?"

≼

Wesley led them off the ship and into the city, setting a brisk pace and keeping a sharp eye on the line of men. The old man, Antun Bulard, was the only straggler, but this had more to do with his age than his wounds, which had turned out to be only superficial cuts.

Loud-colored tents and awnings lined the roads of Dagastan from the harbor to the square. Throngs filled the paved pathways as merchants shouted to the crowds, waving banners with unrecognizable symbols. Old men smoked pipes beneath the shelter of striped canopies as scantily dressed women with veiled faces stood provocatively on raised platforms, gyrating slowly to the beat of a dozen drummers, bell ringers, and cymbal players. There was too much happening to focus on any single thing. Everywhere one looked there were dazzling colors, tantalizing movements, intoxicating scents, and exciting music. Overwhelmed, the little parade of sailors marched in step with Mr. Wesley as he led them to their promised guide. He and his team were waiting along a paved avenue not far from the city's Grand Bazaar.

Dilladrum looked like an overweight beggar. His coat and dark britches were faded and poorly patched. Long, dirty hair burst out from under a formless felt hat as if in protest. His beard, equally mismanaged, showed bits of grass nested in its snarls. His face was dusky, and his teeth yellow, but his eyes sparkled in the afternoon sun. He stood on the roadside before a train of curious beasts. They appeared to be shrunken, shaggy horses. The animals were loaded with bundles and linked together by leads from one to the next. Six short, half-naked men helped Dilladrum keep the train under control. They wore only breechcloths of loose linen and clattering necklaces of colored stones. Like Dilladrum, they grinned brightly at the sailors' approach.

"Welcome, welcome, gentlemen," he warmly addressed them. "I am Dilladrum, your guide. Before we leave our fair city, perhaps you would like some time to peruse our fine shops? As per previous arrangements, I and my Vintu friends will be providing you with food, water, and shelter, but we'll be many days afield, and as such, some comforts as could be obtained in the bazaar might make your trek more pleasant. Consider our fine wines, liquors, or perhaps an attractive slave girl to make the camps more enjoyable."

A few eyes turned appraisingly toward the shops, where dozens of colorful signboards advertised in a foreign tongue. Music played—strange twanging strings and warbling pipes. Hadrian could smell lamb spiced with curry, a popular dish as he recalled.

"We will leave immediately," Wesley replied, louder than was necessary for merely Dilladrum to hear him.

"Suit yourself, good sir." The guide shrugged sadly. He made a gesture to his Vintu workers and the little men used long switches and yelping cries to urge the animals of the caravan forward.

As they did, one spotted Hadrian and paused in his work. His brows furrowed as he stared intently until a shout from Dilladrum sent him back to herding.

"What was that all about?" Royce asked. Hadrian shrugged, but Royce looked unconvinced. "You were here for what—five years? Anything happen? Anything you want to share?"

"Sure," he replied with a sarcastic grin. "Right after you fill me in on how you escaped from Manzant Prison and why you never killed Ambrose Moor."

"Sorry I asked."

"I was young and stupid," Hadrian offered. "But I can tell you that Wesley is right about the jungle being dangerous. We'll want to watch ourselves around Gile."

"You met him?"

Hadrian nodded. "I've met most of the warlords of the Gur Em, but I'm sure everyone's forgotten me by now."

As if overhearing, the train worker glanced over his shoulder at Hadrian once more.

≪≫

"Everywhere landward from Dagastan is uphill," Dilladrum was saying as the troop walked along the narrow dirt path through farmlands dotted by domed grass huts. "That is the way of the world everywhere, is it not? From the sea, we always need to go up. It makes the leaving that much harder, but the returning that much more welcome."

They walked two abreast, with Wesley and Dilladrum, Wyatt and Poe, Royce and Hadrian in front while Thranic's group followed behind the Vintu and the beasts. Having Thranic and his crew behind them was disconcerting, but it was better than walking with them. Dilladrum set a brisk pace for a portly little man, stepping lively and thrusting his bleached walking stick out with practiced skill. He bent the brim down on his otherwise shapeless hat to block the sun, making him look comical even while Hadrian wished he had a silly-looking hat of his own.

"Mr. Dilladrum, what exactly are your instructions concerning us?" Wesley inquired.

"I am contracted to safely deliver officers, cargo, and crew of the *Emerald Storm* to the Palace of the Four Winds in Dur Guron."

"Is that the residence of Erandabon Gile?"

"Ah yes, the fortress of the Panther of Dur Guron."

"Panther?" Wyatt asked.

Dilladrum chuckled. "It's what the Vintu call the warlord. They're a very simple folk, but very hard workers, as you can see. The Panther is a legend among them."

"A hero?" Wesley offered.

"A panther is not a hero to anyone. A panther is a great cat that hides himself in the jungle. He's a ghost to those who seek him, deadly to those he hunts, but to those he doesn't, he's merely a creature deserving of respect. The Panther does not concern himself with the Vintu, but stories of his valor, cruelty, and cunning reach them."

"You are not Vintu?"

"No. I'm Erbonese. Erbon is a region to the northwest, not far from Mandalin."

"And the Tenkin?" Wesley asked. "Is the warlord one of them?"

Dilladrum's expression turned dark. "Yes, yes. The Tenkin are everywhere in these jungles." He pointed to the horizon ahead of them. "Some tribes are more welcoming than others. Not to worry, my Vintu and I know a good route. We'll pass through one Tenkin village, but they're friendly and familiar to us, like the one you call Staul, yes? We'll make it safely."

As they climbed higher, they entered a great plain of tall grass that swayed enchantingly with the breeze. Climbing a large rock, they could see for miles in all directions except ahead, where a tall, forested ridge rose several hundred feet. They made camp just before sundown. Hardly a word passed between Dilladrum and the Vintu, but they immediately went to work setting up decorative tents with embroidered geometric designs and neatly bordered canopies. Cots and small stools were put out for each, along with sheets and pillows.

Cooked in large pots over an open fire, the evening meal was strong and spicy enough to make Hadrian's eyes water. He found it tasty and satisfying after weeks of eating the same tired pork stew. The Vintu took turns entertaining. Some played stringed instruments similar to a lute, others danced, and a few sang lilting ballads. The words Hadrian could not understand, but the melody was beautiful. Animal calls filled the night. Screeches, cries, and growls threatened in the darkness, always too loud and too close.

⤝

On their third day out, the landscape began to change. The level plains tilted upward and trees appeared more frequently. The forests that had lined the distance were upon them, and soon they were trudging under a canopy of tall trees whose massive roots spread out across the forest floor like the fingers of old men. At first it was good to be out of the sun, but then the path became rocky, steep, and hard to navigate. It did not last long, as they soon crested a ridge and began a sharp descent. On the far side of the ridge, they could see a distinct change in the flora. The undergrowth thickened, turning a deeper green. Larger leaves, vines, thickets of creepers, and needle-shaped blades encroached on the track, causing the Vintu to occasionally move ahead to chop a path.

The next day it began to rain, and while at times it poured and at others it only misted, it never ceased.

"They always seem content, don't they?" Hadrian mentioned to Royce as they sat under the canopy of their tent watching the Vintu preparing the evening meal. "It could be blazingly hot or raining like now, and they don't seem to care one way or the other."

"Are you now saying we should become Vintu?" Royce asked. "I don't think you can just apply for membership into their tribe. I think you need to be born into it."

"What's that?" Wyatt asked, coming out of the tent the three shared, wiping his freshly shaved face with a cloth.

"Just thinking about the Vintu and living a simple existence of quiet pleasures," Hadrian explained.

"What makes you think they're content?" Royce asked.

"I've found that when people smile all the time, they're hiding something. These Vintu are probably miserable—economically forced into relative slavery, catering to wealthy foreigners. I'm sure they would smile just as much while slitting our throats to save themselves another day of hauling Dilladrum's packs."

"I think you've been away from Gwen too long. You're starting to sound like the *old Royce* again."

Across the camp they spotted Staul, Thranic, and Defoe. Staul waved in their direction and grinned.

"See? Big grin," Royce mentioned.

"Fun group, eh?" Hadrian muttered.

"Yeah, they are a group, aren't they?" Royce nodded thoughtfully. "Why would a sentinel, a Tenkin warrior, a physician, a thief, and…whatever the heck Bulard is go into the jungles of Calis to visit a Tenkin warlord? And what's Bulard's deal?"

Wyatt and Hadrian shrugged in unison.

"Isn't that a bit odd? We were all on the same ship together for weeks, and we don't know anything about the man beyond the fact that he doesn't look like he's seen the sun in a decade. Perhaps if we found out, it would provide the common connection between the others and this Erandabon fellow."

"Bernie and Bulard share a tent," Hadrian pointed out.

"Hadrian, why don't you go chat with Bulard?" Royce said. "I'll distract Bernie."

"What about me?" Wyatt asked.

"Talk with Derning and Grady. They don't seem as connected to the others as I first thought. Find out why they volunteered."

The Vintu handed out dinner, which the *Storm's* crew ate sitting on stools the Vintu provided. Dinner consisted mostly of what appeared to be shredded pork and an array of unusual vegetables in a thick, hot sauce that needled the tongue.

After the meal, darkness descended on the camp and most retired to their tents. Antun Bulard was already in his, just like he always stayed in his cabin aboard ship. The light in Bulard and Bernie's tent flickered and the silhouettes of their heads bobbed about, magnified on the canvas walls. A few hours after dark, Bernie stepped out. An instant later, Royce swooped in.

✑

"How you been, *Bernie?*" Royce greeted him. "Going for a walk?"

"Actually, I was about to find a place to relieve myself."

"Good, I'll go with you."

"Go with me?" he asked nervously.

"I've been known to help people relieve themselves of a great many things." Royce put an arm around Bernie's shoulder as he urged him away from the tents. Once more Bernie flinched. "A little jumpy, aren't we?" Royce asked.

"Don't you think I have good reason?"

Royce smiled and nodded. "You have me there. I honestly still can't figure out what you were thinking."

The two were outside the circle of tents, well beyond the glow of the campfire, and still Royce urged him farther away.

"It wasn't my idea. I was just following orders. Don't you think I'd know better than to—"

"Whose idea was it?"

Bernie hesitated only a moment. "Thranic," he said, then hastily added, "but he just wanted you bloodied. Not dead, just cut."

"Why?"

"Honestly, I don't know."

They stopped in a dark circle of trees. Night frogs croaked

hesitantly, concerned by their presence. The camp was only a distant glow.

"Care to tell me what all of you are doing here?"

Bernie frowned. "You know I won't, even to save my life. It wouldn't be worth it."

"But you told me about Thranic."

"I don't like Thranic."

"So he's not the one you're afraid of. Is it Merrick?"

"Merrick?" Bernie looked genuinely puzzled. "Listen, I never faulted you for Jade's death or the war you waged on the Diamond. Merrick should have never betrayed you like that, not without first hearing your side of it."

Royce took a step forward. In the darkness of the canopy, he was certain Bernie could barely see him. Royce, on the other hand, could make out every line on Bernie's face. "What's Merrick's plan?"

"I haven't seen Merrick in years."

Royce drew out his dagger and purposely allowed it to make a metal scraping sound as it came free of its scabbard. "So you haven't seen him. Fine. But you're working for him, or someone else who's working for him. I want to know where he is and what he's up to, and you're going to tell me."

Bernie shook his head. "I—I really don't know anything about Marius or what he's doing nowadays."

Royce paused. Every line of Bernie's face revealed he was telling the truth.

"What have we here?" Thranic asked. "A private meeting? You've strayed a bit far from camp, dear boys."

Royce turned to see Thranic and Staul. Staul held a torch, and Thranic carried a crossbow.

"It's not safe to venture too far away from your friends, or didn't you think about that, Royce?" Thranic said, then fired the crossbow at Royce's heart.

∽

"Antun Bulard, isn't it?" Hadrian asked, sticking his head in the tent.

"Hmm?" Antun looked up. He was lying on his stomach, writing with a featherless quill worn to only a few inches in length. He had on a pair of spectacles, the top of which he peered over. "Why, yes, I am."

The old man was more than just pale—he was white. His hair was the color of alabaster, while his skin was little more than wrinkled quartz. He reminded Hadrian of an egg, colorless and fragile.

"I wanted to introduce myself." Hadrian slipped fully inside. "All this time at sea and we never had the opportunity to properly meet. I thought that was unfortunate, don't you?"

"Why, I—Who are you again?"

"Hadrian. I was the cook on the *Emerald Storm*."

"Ah, well, I hate to say it, Hadrian, but I was not impressed with your cooking. Perhaps a little less salt and some wine would have helped. Not that this is any great feast," he said, gesturing toward his half-eaten meal. "I'm too old for such rich foods. It upsets my stomach."

"What are you writing?"

"Oh, this? Just notes, really. My mind isn't what it once was, you see. I'll forget everything soon, and then where will I be? A historian who can't remember his own name. It really could come to that, you know. Assuming I live that long. Bernie keeps reassuring me I won't live out this trip. He's probably right. He's the expert on such things, after all."

"Really? What kind of things?"

"Oh, spelunking, of course. I'm told Bernie is an old hand at it. We make a good team, he and I. He digs up the past and I put it down, so to speak." Antun chuckled to himself until he coughed. Hadrian poured the man a glass of water, which he gratefully accepted.

After he had recovered, Hadrian asked, "Have you ever heard of a man called Merrick Marius?"

Bulard shook his head. "Not unless I have and then forgotten. Was he a king or a hero, perhaps?"

"No, I actually thought he might have been the man who sent you here."

"Oh no. Our mandate is from the Patriarch himself, though Sentinel Thranic doesn't tell me much. I'm not complaining, mind you. How often does a priest of Maribor have the opportunity to serve the Patriarch? I can tell you precisely—twice. Once when I was so much younger, and now that I'm nearly dead."

"I thought you were a historian. You're also a priest?"

"I know I don't look much like one, do I? My calling was the pen, not the flock."

"You've written books, then?"

"Oh yes, my best is still *The History of Apeladorn*, which I'm constantly having to append, of course."

"I know a monk at the Winds Abbey who'd love to meet you."

"Is that up north in Melengar? I passed through there once about twenty years ago." Antun nodded thoughtfully. "They were very helpful, saved my life if I recall correctly."

"So, you're on this trip to record what you see?"

"Oh no, that's only what I've been doing so far. As you can imagine, I don't get out much. I do most of my work in libraries and stuffy cellars, reading old books. I was in Tur Del Fur before setting off on this wonderful trip. This has been an excellent opportunity to record what I see firsthand. The Patriarch knows about my research on ancient imperial history, and that's why I'm here. Sort of a living, breathing version of my books, you see. I suppose they think that if they put in the right questions, out will pop the correct answers, like an oracle."

Hadrian was about to ask another question when Grady and Poe poked their heads in.

"Hadrian." Poe caught his attention.

"Well, isn't my tent the social center tonight?" Antun remarked.

"I'm kinda busy at the moment. Can this wait?" Hadrian asked.

"I don't think so. Thranic and Staul just followed Royce and Bernie into the jungle."

∽

Royce heard the click of the release and began to move even before the hiss of the string indicated the missile's launch. Still, his reflexes could not move faster than a flying bolt. The metal shaft pierced his side below the rib cage. The impact thrust him backward, where he collapsed in pain.

"Lucky we found you, Bernie," Thranic told the startled thief as he moved away from Royce's body. "He would have killed you. Isn't that what you said bucket men do? Now, don't you feel foolish for saying I couldn't protect you?"

"You could have hit me!" Bernie snapped.

"Stop being so dramatic. You're alive, aren't you? Besides, I heard the conversation. It didn't take much for you to give me up. In my profession, lack of faith is a terrible sin."

"In mine, it's all too often justified," Bernie snarled back.

"Get back to the camp before you're missed."

Bernie grumbled as he trotted back up the path. Thranic watched his retreat.

"We might have to do something about him," the sentinel

told the Tenkin. "Funny that you, my heathen friend, should be my stalwart ally in all this."

"Bernie, he thinks too much. Me? I am just greedy, and therefore trustworthy. We going to just leave the body?"

"No, it's too close to the path we'll be taking tomorrow, and I can't count on the animals eating him before we break camp. Drag him away. A few yards should be enough."

"Royce?" Hadrian shouted from behind them on the trail.

"Quickly, you idiot. They're coming!"

Staul rushed forward and, planting his torch in the ground, lifted Royce and ran with him into the jungle. He had traveled only a few dozen yards when he cursed.

Royce was still breathing.

"*Izuto!*" the Tenkin hissed, drawing his dagger.

"Too late," Royce whispered.

⌁

Hadrian led them into the trees the way Royce had gone earlier. Ahead he spotted the glow of a torch and ran toward it. Behind him Wyatt, Poe, Grady, and Derning followed.

"There's blood here," Hadrian announced when he got to the burning torch thrust in the ground. "Royce!"

"Spread out!" Wyatt ordered. "Sweep the grass and look for more blood."

"Over here!" Derning shouted, moving into the ferns. "There, up ahead. Two of them, Staul and Royce!"

Hadrian cut his way through the thick undergrowth to where they lay. Royce was breathing hard, holding his blood-soaked side. His face was pale, but his eyes remained focused.

"How ya doing, buddy?" Hadrian asked, dropping to his knees and carefully slipping an arm under his friend.

Royce didn't say anything. He kept his teeth clenched, blowing his cheeks out with each breath.

"Get his feet, Wyatt," Hadrian ordered. "Now lift him gently. Poe, get out front with the torch."

"What about Staul?" Derning asked.

"What about him?" Hadrian glanced down at the big Tenkin, whose throat lay open, slit from ear to ear.

When they returned to camp, Wesley ordered Royce to be taken to his tent, which was the largest, originally reserved for Captain Seward. He started to send Poe for Dr. Levy, but Hadrian intervened. Wesley appeared confused, but as Hadrian was Royce's best friend, he did not press the issue. The Vintu were surprisingly adept at first aid, and under Hadrian's watchful eye they cleaned and dressed the wound.

The bolt aimed at Royce's heart had entered and exited cleanly. He suffered significant blood loss, but no organ damage, nor broken bones. The Vintu sealed the tiny entry hole without a problem. The larger tearing of his flesh at the exit was another matter. It took a dozen bandages and many basins of water before they got the bleeding under control and Royce lay, sleeping calmly.

"Why wasn't I notified about this? I'm a physician, for Maribor's sake!"

Hadrian stepped outside the tent flap to find Levy arguing with Wyatt, Poe, Grady, and Derning, who, at Hadrian's request, guarded the entrance.

"Ah, Dr. Levy, just the man I wanted to see," Hadrian addressed him. "Where's your boss? Where's Thranic?"

Levy did not need to answer, as across the camp Thranic walked toward them alongside Wesley and Bernie.

Hadrian drew his sword at their approach.

"Put away your weapon!" Wesley ordered.

"This man nearly killed Royce tonight," Hadrian declared, pointing at Thranic.

"That's not the way he tells it," Wesley replied. "He said Seaman Melborn attacked and murdered Seaman Staul over accusations regarding Seaman Drew's death. Mr. Thranic and Seaman Defoe claim they were witnesses."

"We don't *claim* anything. We saw it," Thranic said coolly.

"And how do you *claim* this took place?" Hadrian asked.

"Staul confronted Royce, telling him he was going to Wesley with evidence. Royce warned him that he would never live to see the dawn. Then, when Staul turned to walk back to camp, Royce grabbed him from behind and slit his throat. Bernie and I expected such treachery from him, but we couldn't convince Staul not to confront the blackguard. So we followed. I brought a crossbow, borrowed from Mr. Dilladrum's supplies, for protection. I fired in self-defense."

"He's lying," Hadrian declared.

"Oh, were you there?" Thranic asked. "Did you see it happen as we did? Funny, I didn't notice your presence."

"Royce left the camp with Bernie, not Staul," Hadrian said.

Thranic laughed. "Is that the best you can come up with to save your friend from a noose? Why not say you saw Staul attack him unprovoked, or me, for that matter?"

"I saw Royce leave with Bernie too, and Thranic and Staul followed after them," Wyatt put in.

"That's a lie!" Bernie responded, convincingly offended. "I watched Royce leave with Staul. Thranic and I followed. I worked the topmast with Royce. I was there the night Edgar Drew died. Royce was the only one near him. They were having an argument. You all saw how agile he is. Drew never had a chance."

"Why didn't you report it to the captain?" Derning asked.

"I did," Bernie declared. "But because I didn't actually see him push poor Drew off, he refused to do anything."

"How convenient that Captain Seward is too dead to ask about that," Wyatt pointed out.

Thranic shook his head with a pitiful smile. "Now, Wesley, will you actually take the word of a pirate and a cook over the word of a sentinel of the Nyphron Church?"

"Your Excellency," Wesley said, turning to face Thranic. "You will address me as *Mr.* Wesley or *sir.* Is that understood?" Thranic's expression soured. "And *I* will decide whose word I will accept. As it happens, I am well aware of your personal vendetta against Seaman Melborn. Midshipman Beryl tried to convince me to bring false charges. Well, sir, I did not buckle to Beryl's threats, and I'll be damned if I will be intimidated by your title."

"*Damned* is a very good choice of words, *Mr.* Wesley."

"Sentinel Thranic," Wesley barked at him. "Be forewarned that if any further harm befalls Seaman Melborn that is even remotely suspicious, I will hold you responsible and have you executed by whatever means are at hand. Do I make myself clear?"

"You wouldn't dare touch an ordained officer of the Patriarch. Every king in Avryn—why, the regents themselves—would not oppose me. It's you who should be concerned about execution."

Wyatt, Grady, and Derning drew their blades and Hadrian took a step closer to Thranic.

"Stand down, gentlemen!" Wesley shouted. At his order, they paused. "You are quite correct, Sentinel Thranic. Your office does influence how I treat you. Were you an ordinary seaman, I would order you flogged for your disrespect. I am well aware that upon our return to Aquesta you could ruin my career, or perhaps have me imprisoned or hanged. But let me point out, sir, that Aquesta is a long way from here, and a dead man has difficulty requesting anything. It would be in my best interest, therefore, to see you executed here and now. It would be a simple matter to report you and Seaman Defoe lost to the dangers of the jungle."

Bernie looked worried and took a subtle step away from Thranic's side.

"I would have thought I could rely on your family's famous code of honor," Thranic said in a sarcastic tone.

"You can, sir, and you are, as indeed that is all that keeps you alive at this moment. It is also what you can count on to have you executed should you threaten Seaman Melborn again. Do I make myself clear?"

Thranic fumed but said nothing. He simply turned and walked away with Bernie following.

Wesley exhaled loudly and straightened his vest. "How is he doing?" he asked Hadrian.

"Sleeping at the moment, sir. He's weak, but should recover. And thank you, sir."

"For what?" Wesley replied. "I have a mission to accomplish, Seaman Blackwater. I cannot have my crew killing one another. Seamen Derning and Grady, take a few others and bring Mr. Staul's body back to camp. Let us not leave him to the beasts of this foul jungle."

CHAPTER 15

THE SEARCH

I think I saw him."

Arista woke at the sound. Disoriented, she did not know where she was at first. Turning over, she found Thrace illuminated by a streak of moonlight. The empress was dressed in her wispy, thin nightgown, which fluttered in the draft. She stood straight, hair loose, eyes lost to a vision beyond the window's frame.

Nearly a week had passed since Gerald had invited Arista to the empress's bedroom, and she wondered if being here was a sign that she was on the right path. If fate could speak, surely this would be how it would sound.

Thrace saw to her safety, guarding her like the mother of a newborn. Soldiers stood outside her door at all times, now in pairs, with strict orders to prevent the entry of anyone without permission. Only Amilia and Nimbus ever entered the chamber, and even they knocked. At Thrace's urging, Nimbus carried messages to Hilfred.

In her nightgown, Thrace looked almost like the girl from Dahlgren, but there was something different about her—akin to sadness, yet lacking even the passion for that. Often she would sit and stare at nothing for hours, and when she spoke, her words were dull and emotionless. She never laughed, cried, or smiled. In this way, she appeared to have successfully transformed from a lively peasant girl into a true empress—serene and unflappable.

Yet at what cost?

"It was late like this," Thrace said, looking out the window. Her voice sounded disconnected, as if she was in a trance. "I was having a dream, but a squeaking noise woke me. I came to the window and I saw them. They were in the courtyard below. Men with torches, as many as a dozen, wheeled in a sealed wagon. They were knights, dressed in black-and-scarlet armor, like those we saw in Dahlgren. They spoke of the man inside the box as if he were a monster, and even though he was hooded and chained, they were afraid. After they took him away, the wagon rolled back out of the courtyard." Thrace turned to face her. "I thought it was a dream until just now. I have a lot of unpleasant dreams."

"How long ago did this happen?"

"Three months, perhaps more."

Shivering, Arista sat up. The fire had long since died and the stone walls did nothing to keep the chill out. The window was open again. Regardless of what time of day it was, or how cold the temperature, Thrace insisted. Not with words—she rarely spoke—but each time Arista closed the window, the girl opened it again.

"That would coincide with Gaunt's disappearance. You never heard anything else about this prisoner?"

"No, and you would be surprised how much you hear when you're very quiet."

"Thrace, come—" The sudden tilt of Modina's head and the curious look on her face stopped Arista.

"No one calls me that anymore."

"A shame. I've always liked the name."

"Me too."

"Come back to bed. You'll catch a cold."

Thrace walked toward her, looking at where the mirror had once hung. "I'll need to get a new mirror before Wintertide."

≈

Dawn brought breakfast and morning reports from Amilia and Thrace's tutor. Nimbus was bright-eyed and cheery, bowing to both—a courtesy Amilia refused to extend to Arista. The chief imperial secretary looked haggard. The dark circles under her eyes grew deeper each day. Holding her jaw stiff and her fists clenched, she glared at Arista eating breakfast in Thrace's bed. Despite Amilia's obvious contempt, Arista could not help liking her. She recognized the same fierce protectiveness that Hilfred exhibited.

"They've stopped the search for the Witch of Melengar," Amilia reported, looking coldly at Arista. "They think she's headed to either Melengar or Ratibor. Patrols are still out, but no one really expects to find her."

"What about where Degan Gaunt might be held?" Arista asked.

Amilia glanced at Nimbus, who stepped up. "Well, my research at the Hall of Records is inconclusive. In ancient imperial times, Aquesta was a city called Rionillion, and a building of some significance stood on this site. Ironically, several parchments refer to it as a prison, but it was destroyed during the early part of the civil wars that followed the death of the last emperor. Later, in 2453, Glenmorgan the First built a fortress here as a defense against rebellions. That fortress is the very palace in which we now stand.

"None of the histories mention anything about a dungeon—odd, given the unrest. I've made a detailed search of nearly every section of the palace, interviewed chambermaids, studied old maps and plans, but I haven't uncovered a single mention of any kind."

"What does Aquesta do with criminals?" Arista asked.

"There are three jails in the city that deal with minor offenses and the Warric prison in Whitehead for harsher cases that don't result in execution. And then there is the infamous Manzant Prison and Salt Mine in Maranon for the most severe crimes."

"Perhaps it's not a dungeon or prison at all," Arista said. "Maybe it's merely a secret room."

"I suppose I could make some inquiries along those lines."

"What is it, Amilia?" Thrace asked, catching a thoughtful look on her secretary's face.

"What? Oh, nothing…" Amilia's expression switched to one of annoyance. "This is very dangerous. Asking all these questions and nosing about. It's risky enough ordering extra food with each meal. Someone will notice. Saldur is not a fool."

"But what were you thinking just now, Amilia?" Thrace repeated.

"Nothing."

"Amilia?"

The secretary frowned. "I just—Well, a few weeks ago you talked about a dark hole…"

"You think I was there—in this dungeon?"

"Don't, Modina. Don't think about it," Amilia begged. "You're too fragile."

"I have to try. If I can remember—"

"You don't *have* to do anything. This woman—she comes here—she doesn't care about you—or what might happen. All she cares about is herself. You've done more than enough.

If you won't turn her in, at least let me get her out of here and away from you. Nimbus and I—"

"No," Thrace said softly. "She needs us…and I need her."

᠃

"Dirt," Thrace said, and shivered.

Arista looked over. She was in the midst of trying to determine how to finish her latest letter to Hilfred when she heard the word. The empress had knelt before the open window since Amilia and Nimbus had left, but this was the first she had spoken.

"Damp, cold—terrible cold, and voices, I remember them—cries and weeping, men and women, screams and prayers. Everything was dark." Thrace wrapped her arms around herself and began to rock. "Splashing, I remember splashing, a hollow sound, creaking, a whirl, and the splash. Sometimes there were distant, echoing voices coming from above, falling out of a tunnel. The walls were stone, the door wood. A bowl—yes, every day a bowl—soup that smelled bad. There was so little to eat."

Thrace rocked harder, her voice trembling, her breath hitching.

"I could hear the blows and cries, men and women, day and night, screaming for mercy. Then I heard a new voice added to the wailing, and realized it was my own. I killed my family. I killed my brother, his wife, and little Hickory. I destroyed my whole village. I killed my father. I was being punished."

Thrace began to cry.

Arista moved to her, but the girl jumped at her touch and cowered away. Crawling against the wall and sobbing, she rubbed the stone with her hands, wetting it with her tears.

Fragile? Arista thought. Thrace had taken a blow that would have killed most people. No matter what Amilia believed, Thrace was not fragile. Yet even granite would crack if you hit it with a big enough hammer.

"Are you all right?" Arista asked.

"No, I keep searching but I can't find it. I can't understand the sounds. It's so familiar and yet..." She trailed off and shook her head. "I'm sorry, I wanted to help. I wanted—"

"It's okay, Thrace. It's okay."

The empress frowned. "You have to stop calling me that." She looked up at her. "Thrace is dead."

CHAPTER 16

THE VILLAGE

It was perpetually twilight. The jungle's canopy blocked what little sunlight managed to penetrate the rain clouds. A hazy mist shrouded their surroundings and intensified the deeper they pressed into the jungle. Exotic plants with stalks the size of men's legs towered overhead. Huge leaves adorned with intricate patterns and vibrant flowers of purple, yellow, and red surrounded the party. It all left Hadrian feeling small, shrunken to the size of an insect or crawling across the floor of a giant's forest.

Rain constantly plagued them. Water danced on a million leaves, sounding like thunder. When actual thunder cracked, it was the voice of a god. Everything was wet. Clothes stuck to their skin and hung like weights. Boots squished audibly with every step. Their hands were wrinkled like those of old men.

Royce rode on the back of a *gunguan*, what the Vintu called the pack ponies. He was awake but weak. A day had passed since the attack, because Wesley had insisted on burying Staul. Their new captain had proclaimed he would not allow the beasts to have a taste of any of his crew, and he insisted on a deep grave. No one had complained about the strenuous work of cutting through the thick mat of roots.

Hadrian doubted Wesley really cared about the fate of Staul's carcass, but the work granted Royce time to rest, kept the crew busy, and affirmed Wesley's commitment to them. Hadrian thought once again about the similarities between the midshipman and his famous brother.

Royce traveled wrapped in his cloak with the weight of the rain collapsing the hood around his head—not a good sign for Thranic and Bernie. Until then, Royce had played the part of the good little sailor, but with the reemergence of the hood, and the loss of his white kerchief, Hadrian knew that role had ended. They had not spoken much since the attack. Not surprisingly, Royce was in no mood for idle discussion. Hadrian guessed that by now his friend had imagined killing Thranic a dozen times, with a few Bernies thrown in here and there for variety. Hadrian had seen Royce wounded before and was familiar with the cocooning—only what would emerge from that cloak and hood would not be a butterfly.

Thranic, Defoe, and Levy traveled at the end of the train and Hadrian often caught them whispering. They wisely kept their distance, avoiding attention. Wesley led the party along with Dilladrum, who made a point of not taking sides or venturing anything remotely resembling an opinion. Dilladrum remained jolly as always and focused his attention on the Vintu.

Hadrian was most surprised with Derning. When Royce had been most vulnerable, his shipboard nemesis had come to his aid rather than taking advantage. Hadrian would have bet money that on the subject of Royce's guilt, Derning would have sided with Thranic. Wyatt had never had the chance to find out his reason for volunteering, but now more than ever Hadrian was convinced Derning was not part of Thranic's band. There was no doubt that Antun Bulard was a member of Thranic's troop, but the old man lacked the ruthlessness of the others. He was merely a resource. After showing an interest, Hadrian became Bulard's new best friend.

"Look! Look there." Bulard pointed to a brilliant flower blooming overhead. The old man took to walking beside Hadrian, sharing his sense of discovery along the way. "Gorgeous, simply gorgeous. Have you ever seen the like? I daresay I haven't. Still, that isn't saying much, now is it?"

Bulard reminded Hadrian of a long-haired cat, with his usually billowing robe and fluffy white hair deflated in the rain, leaving a remarkably thin body. He held up a withered hand to protect his eyes as he searched the trees.

"Another one of those wonderful long-beaked birds," the historian said. "I love the way they hover."

Hadrian smiled at him. "It's not that you don't mind the rain that amazes me. It's that you don't seem to notice it at all."

Bulard frowned. "My parchments are a disaster. They stick together, the ink runs, I haven't been able to write anything down, and as I mentioned at our first meeting, my head is no place to store memories of such wonderful things. It makes me feel like I've wasted my life locked in dusty libraries and scriptoriums. Don't do what I did, Hadrian. You're still a young man. Take my advice: live your life to the fullest. Breathe the air, taste the wine, kiss the girls, and always remember that the tales of another are never as wondrous as your own. I'll admit I was, well, concerned about this trip. No, I'll say it truthfully—I was scared. What does a man my age have to be afraid of, you wonder? Everything. Life becomes more precious when you have less of it to spare. I'm not ready to die. Why, look at all that I've never seen."

"You have seen horses before, and known women, right?" Hadrian asked with a wry grin.

Bulard looked at him curiously. "I'm a historian, not a monk."

Hadrian nearly tripped.

"I realize I don't look it now, but I was quite handsome once. I was married three times, in fact. Outlived all of them, poor darlings. I still miss them, you know—each one. My silly little mind hasn't misplaced their faces, and I can't imagine it ever will. Have you ever been in love, Hadrian?"

"I'm not sure. How do you tell?"

"Love? Why, it's like coming home."

Hadrian considered the comment.

"What are you thinking?" Bulard asked.

Hadrian shook his head. "Nothing."

"Yes, you were. What? You can tell me. I'm an excellent repository for secrets. I'll likely forget, but if I don't, well, I'm an old man in a remote jungle. I'm sure to die before I can repeat anything."

Hadrian smiled, then shrugged. "I was just thinking about the rain."

⤚

The trail widened, revealing a great, cascading waterfall and a dozen grass-thatched buildings clustered at the center of a small clearing. The domed-roof huts rested on high wooden stilts and were accessed by short stairs or ladders, depending on the size and apparent prestige of the structure. Occupying the very center of the clearing was a fire pit, surrounded by a ring of colorfully painted stones and wooden poles decorated in animal skins, skulls, and strings of bones, beads, and long vibrant feathers. The inhabitants were dark-haired, dark-eyed, umber-skinned men and women dressed in beautifully painted cloths and silks. They paused as Dilladrum advanced respectfully. Elder men met him before the fire ring, where they exchanged bows.

"Who are these people, do you suppose?" Bulard asked.

"Tenkins," Hadrian replied.

Bulard raised his eyebrows.

The village was familiar to Hadrian, though he had never been there. Hundreds of similar ones were scattered across the peninsula, mirror images of each other. The rubble of eastern Calis was the last standing residue of the Old Empire. After civil wars had torn apart the west, Calis still flew the old imperial banners and for centuries formed the bulwark against the advancing Ghazel horde. Time, however, was on the Ghazel's side. The last of the old world died when the ancient eastern capital, Urlineus, fell to the goblin hordes sweeping through the jungles. They might have overrun all of Avryn if not for Glenmorgan III.

Glenmorgan III had rallied the nobles and defeated the goblins at the Battle of Vilan Hills. The Ghazel fell back but were never driven off the mainland. Betrayed shortly after his victory, Glenmorgan III never finished his work of reestablishing the kingdom's borders. This task fell to lesser men, who squabbled over the spoils of war and were too distracted to stop the Ghazel from digging in. Urlineus, the last great city of the Old Empire, remained in the hands of the Ghazel, and Calis had never been the same.

Fractured and isolated, the eastern half of the country struggled against the growing pressure of the Ghazel nation in a maelstrom of chaos and confusion. Self-appointed warrior-kings fought against each other. Out of desperation, some enlisted the aid of the Ghazel to vanquish a rival. Ties formed, lines blurred, and out of this tenuous alliance were born the Tenkin—humans who had adopted the Ghazel's ways, traditions, and beliefs. For this, Calians ostracized the Tenkin, forcing their kind deeper into the jungles, where they lived on the borderlands between the anvil and the hammer.

Dilladrum returned. "This is the village of Oudorro. I've been here many times. Although Tenkin, they're a friendly and generous people. I've asked them to let us rest here for the night. Tomorrow morning we'll push on toward the Palace of the Four Winds. Beyond this point, travel will be much harder and unpleasant, so we'll need a good night's rest. I must caution you, however: please do nothing to offend or provoke these people. They're courteous but can be fierce if roused."

The physical appearance of the Tenkin always impressed Hadrian. Staul was a crude example of his kin, and these men were more what he remembered. Lean, bronzed muscles and strong facial features that looked hewn from blocks of stone were the hallmarks of the Tenkin warrior. Like the great cats of the jungle, they had bodies graceful in their strength and simplicity. The women were breathtaking. Long, dark hair wreathed sharp cheekbones and almond eyes. Their satin-smooth skin enveloped willowy curves. The "civilized" world never saw Tenkin women. A closely guarded treasure, they never left their villages.

The inhabitants showed neither fear nor concern at the procession of the foreigners. Most observed their arrival with silent curiosity. The women showed more interest, pressing forward to peer and talking among themselves.

"I thought Tenkins were grotesque," Bulard said with the casual manner and volume of a man commenting on animals. "I had heard they were abominations of nature, but these people are beautiful."

"A common misconception," Hadrian explained. "People tell tales that Tenkin are the result of interbreeding between Calians and Ghazel, but if you ever saw a goblin, you'd understand why that's not possible."

"I guess you can't believe everything you read in books. But don't spread that around, or I'll be out of a job."

When they reached the village center, the Vintu went about their work and began unpacking. They moved with stoic familiarity. The party waited, listening to the hiss of rain on the fire and the murmur of the crowd gathering around them. With an expectant expression, Dilladrum struggled to see over their heads. He exchanged looks with Wesley but said nothing. Soon a small elderly Tenkin dressed in a leopard wrap entered the circle. His skin was like wrinkled leather, and his hair like gray steel. He walked with a slow dignity and an upturned chin. Dilladrum smiled and the two spoke rapidly. Then the elderly Tenkin clapped his hands and shouted. The crowd fell back and he led the crew of the *Emerald Storm* into the largest of the buildings. It had four tree-sized pillars holding up a latticework of intertwined branches overlaid with thatch. The interior lacked partitions and stood as an open hall lined with tanned skins and pillows made from animal hides.

Waiting inside were four Tenkins. Three men and a woman sat upon a raised mound covered in luxurious cushions. Their leopard-clad guide bowed deeply to the four, then left. Outside, the rain increased and poured off the thatched roof.

Dilladrum stepped forward, bowed with his hands clasped before him, and spoke in Tenkin, which was a mix of the old imperial tongue and Ghazel. Hadrian had mastered a working knowledge of the language, but the isolation between villages had caused each to develop a slightly different dialect. While Hadrian missed a number of Dilladrum's words, he recognized that formal introductions were being made.

"This is Burandu," Dilladrum explained to the *Emerald Storm's* crew in Apelanese. "He is Elder." Dilladrum paused to think, then added, "Similar to the lord of a manor, but not quite. Beside him is Joqdan, his warlord—chief knight, if you will. Zulron is Oudorro's oberdaza." He gestured at a stunted, misshapen Tenkin, the only deformed one Hadrian had ever seen. "The closest thing to his office in Avryn might be a chief priest as well as doctor, and next to him is Fan Irlanu. You have no equivalent position for her. She's a seer, a visionary."

"Welcome, peoples of great Avryn." Burandu spoke haltingly in Apelanese. Despite his age, betrayed only by a head of startling white hair, he looked as strong and handsome as any man in the village. He sat adorned in a silk waistcloth and kilt, a broad necklace of gold, and a headdress formed from long, brightly colored feathers. "We are pleased to have you in our home."

"Thank you, sir, for granting us an invitation," Wesley replied.

"We enjoy company of those Dilladrum brings. Once brothers in ancient days—is good to sit, to listen, to find each other. Come, drink, and remember."

Zulron cast a fine powder over a brazier of coals. Flames burst forth, illuminating the lodge.

They all sat amid the pillows and hides. Royce found a place within the shadows against the rear wall. As always, Thranic and Bernie kept their distance from the rest of the party. They sat close to the four Tenkins, where the sentinel watched Zulron with great interest. Bulard invited Hadrian to sit beside him.

"This explains a great deal," said the old man, pointing to the decorations in the hut. "These are people lost in time. Do you see those decorated shields hanging from the rafter with the oil lamps? They used to do that in the ancient imperial throne room, and the leaders mirror the imperial body, represented by a king and his two councilors, always a wizard and a warrior. Although the seer is probably an addition of the Ghazel influences. She's lovely."

Hadrian had to agree: Fan Irlanu was stunning, even by

Tenkin standards. Her thin silk gown embraced her body with the intimacy of liquid.

Food and wine circulated as men carried in jugs and platters. "After eating," Burandu said to Wesley, "I ask you, Dilladrum, and your second to meet at my *durbo*. I discuss recent news on the road ahead. I fear the beasts are loose and you must be careful. You tell me of road just traveled."

Wesley nodded with a mouthful of food, then, after swallowing, added, "Of course, Your, ah..." He hesitated before simply adding, "Sir."

Bulard looked with suspicion at the sliced meat set before him. Hadrian chuckled, watching the old man push it around his plate. "It's pork. Wild pigs thrive in these jungles and the Tenkin hunt them. You'll find it a little tougher and gamier than what you're used to back home, but it's good—you'll like it."

"How do you know so much about them?" the old man asked.

"I lived in Calis for several years."

"Doing what?"

"You know, I still ask myself that." Hadrian stuffed a hunk of pork in his mouth and chewed, but Bulard's expression showed he did not understand. At last Hadrian gave in. "I was a mercenary. I fought for the highest bidder."

"You seem ashamed." Bulard tried a bit of fruit and grimaced. "The mercenary profession has a long and illustrious history. I should know."

"My father never approved of me using my training for profit. In a way, you might say he thought it sacrilegious. I didn't understand then, but I do now."

"So were you any good?"

"A lot of men died."

"Battles are sometimes necessary and men die in war—it

happens. You have nothing to be ashamed of. To be a warrior and live is a reward Maribor bestows on the virtuous. You should be proud."

"Except there was no war, just battles. No cause, just money. No virtue, just killing."

Bulard wrinkled his brows as if trying to decipher this and Hadrian got up before he could think of anything else to ask.

When the meal was over, three Tenkin boys held large palm branches over the heads of Burandu, Wesley, Dilladrum, and Wyatt as they ventured out into the rain. With the Elder gone, formalities relaxed. The Vintu headed out to resume camp preparations before all daylight was lost. Across the hall, Thranic and Levy spoke quietly with the oberdaza, Zulron, and all three left together. Poe, Derning, and Grady helped themselves to a jug of wine and reclined casually on the pillows.

Hadrian went over to sit beside Royce. "Wanna try the wine?"

"It's not time for drinking yet," the hood replied.

"How you feeling?"

"Not good enough."

"You need to get the dressing on your wound changed?"

"It can wait."

"Wait too long and it'll fester."

"Leave me alone."

"You should at least eat. The pork is good. Best meal you'll have for a while, I think. It'll help you heal."

There was no reply. They sat listening to the wind and rain on the grassy roof and low conversations punctuated by the occasional laugh and clink of ceramic cups.

"Are you aware you're being watched?" Royce asked. "The Tenkin on the dais, the one Dilladrum called Joqdan, the warlord. He's been staring at you since we entered. Do you know him?"

Hadrian looked at the bald, muscular man wreathed in a dozen bone necklaces. "Never seen him before. The woman next to him—she looks oddly familiar."

"She looks like Gwen."

"That's it. You're right. She does look just like her. Is Gwen from—"

"I don't know."

"I just assumed she was from Wesbaden. Everyone in Avryn who's from Calis is from there, but she could be from a village like this, huh?" Hadrian chuckled. "What an odd pairing you two make. Maybe Gwen's from this very village. That could be her sister up there, or cousin. You might be meeting the bride's family before the wedding, just like a proper suitor. You should brush your hair and take a bath. Make a good enough impression, and the two of you could settle down here. You'd look good bare-chested in one of those kilts."

Hadrian expected a cutting retort. All he heard from his friend was a harsh series of breaths. Looking over, he noticed the hood was drooping.

"Hey, you're really not doing too good, are you?"

The hood shook.

Hadrian placed a hand on Royce's back. His cloak was soaked and hot. "Damn it. I'll convince Wesley to extend our stay. In the meantime, let's get you dry and in a bed."

᜶

With a flaming brand, the oberdaza led Thranic and Levy toward a cliff wall at the edge of the village, where the great waterfall thundered. Somehow even the plunging water felt foul as it splattered against rocks, casting a damp mist. Thranic continually wiped the tainted wet from his face. Everything about the village was evil. Everywhere stood signs that these humans had turned their backs on Novron and embraced his enemy—the hideous feathers they wore, the symbolic designs in the pillows, the tattoos on their bodies. They did not whisper, but rather shouted, their allegiance to Uberlin. Thranic could not imagine a greater blasphemy, and yet the others were blind to their transgressions. Given the opportunity, Thranic would burn the whole village to ash and scatter the remains. He had tried to prepare himself for what to expect even before the *Emerald Storm* set sail, but now, surrounded by their poison, he longed to strike a blow for Novron. While he could not safely put a torch to this nest of vipers, there was another profanation he could rectify, one that these worshipers of Uberlin might even assist him with.

The powder the oberdaza used to ignite the braziers had caught his attention. The Tenkin witch doctor was also an alchemist. Zulron was not like the rest of the heathens. He lacked their illusionary facade, their glimmer of false beauty. One leg was shorter than its partner, causing Zulron to shuffle with a noticeable limp. One shoulder rode up, hugging his chin, while the other slipped low, dangling a weak and withered arm. He was singular in his wretched appearance, and this honest display of his evil made him more trustworthy than the rest.

As they reached the waterfall, Zulron led them along a narrow path around the frothing pool to a crack in the cliff face. Within the fissure was a cave. Its ceiling teemed with chattering bats and its floor was laden with guano.

"This is my storeroom and workshop," Zulron explained as he pushed deeper into the cavern. "It stays cooler here and is well protected from wind and rain."

"And what prying eyes can't see..." Thranic added, guessing at the truth of the matter. Years of dealing with tainted souls had left him with an understanding of evil's true nature.

Zulron paused only briefly, to cast a glance over his low-slung shoulder at the sentinel. "You see more clearly than the rest of your brethren."

"And you speak Apelanese better than yours."

"I'm not built for hunting. I rely on study and have learned much about your world."

"This is disgusting." Levy grimaced, carefully picking his path.

"Yes," the oberdaza agreed. He walked through the guano as if it were a field of spring grass. "But these bats are my gate-keepers, and their soil, my moat."

Soon the cave grew wide and the floor cleared of filth. In the center of the cavern was a domed oven built of carefully piled stones. Surrounding it were dozens of huge clay pots, bundles of browned leaves, and a vast pile of poorly stacked wood. On shelves carved from the stone walls rested hundreds of smaller ceramic jars and a variety of stones, crystals, and bowls.

Zulron reached into one of the pots and threw a handful of dust into the mouth of the oven. He thrust his torch at the base, and a fire roared to life, which he then fed with wood. When the oven was sated and he had finished lighting a number of oil lamps, he turned to Levy. "Let me see it."

The doctor set his pack on the floor and withdrew the bundle of bloody rags. Zulron took the bandages and studied each, even holding them to his nose and sniffing. "And you say these belong to the hooded one among you? It's his blood?"

"Yes."

"How was he wounded?"

"I shot him with a crossbow."

Zulron showed no surprise. "Did you not wish him dead? Or are you a poor hunter?"

"He moved."

Zulron raised a dark brow. "He is quick?"

"Yes."

"Sees well in the dark?"

"Yes."

"And you came by ship, yes? How did he fare on the water?"

"Poorly — very sick for the first four days, I hear."

"And his ears, are they pointed?"

"No. He has no elven features. This is why we need you to test the blood. You know the method?"

The oberdaza nodded.

Thranic felt a twinge of regret that this creature was so unworthy to Novron. He sensed a kinship of minds. "How long?"

Zulron rubbed the crusted bandages between his fingers. "Days with this. It is too old. If we had a fresh sample, it could be quick."

"Getting blood from him is nearly impossible," Levy grumbled.

"I will start the test with these, but I'll also see what I can do to get fresh blood. He will need treatment soon."

"Treatment?"

"The jungle does not abide the weak or the wounded for long. He will summon me or die."

"How much gold will you want?" Thranic asked.

Zulron shook his head. "I have no need for gold."

"What payment, then?"

"My reward will not come from you. I will reap my own reward, and it is no concern of yours."

∽

The Tenkin granted them the use of three sizable huts and Wesley divided his crew accordingly. The accommodations were surprisingly luxurious, subdivided by walls of wide woven ribbons that gave the impression of being inside a basket. Carpets of tight-threaded fibers inlaid with beautiful designs covered the floor. Peanut-shaped gourds hung from the rafters, burning oil that provided more than enough light.

Having convinced Wesley to linger in the village, Hadrian watched over Royce, who looked worse with each passing hour. Royce's skin burned and sweat poured down his forehead even as he shivered beneath two layers of blankets.

"You need to get better, pal," Hadrian told him. "Think of Gwen. Better yet, think what she'll do to me if I come back without you."

There was no reaction. Royce continued to shiver, his eyes closed.

"May enter?" a soft voice asked. Hadrian could see only the outline in the doorway, and for an instant he thought it was Gwen. "He grows worse, but you refused Zulron to see him."

"Your oberdaza has been keeping close company with the man who nearly killed my friend. I don't feel comfortable letting Zulron treat him."

"Will allow me? Am not skilled like Zulron, but know some things."

Hadrian nodded and waved her in.

"Am Fan Irlanu," she said, dipping her head into the hut while, outside, two other women waited in the rain with covered baskets.

"I'm Hadrian Blackwater, and this is my friend Royce."

She nodded, then knelt beside Royce and placed a hand to his forehead. "He has fever."

She motioned for the oil lamp and Hadrian pulled it down, then helped her open Royce's cloak and pull back his tunic to reveal the stained bandage, which she carefully removed.

Irlanu grimaced as she peeled back the cloth and studied the wound.

She shook her head. "It is the *shirlum-kath*," she said, pressing lightly on the skin around the wound, causing Royce to flinch in his sleep. "See here?" She scraped a long nail along the edge of the bloody wound and drew away a squirming parasite the size of a coarse hair. It twisted and curled on her fingertip. "They are eating him."

Fan Irlanu waved to the women outside, who entered and deposited their baskets beside her. She spoke briefly in Tenkin, ordering them to fetch other items, which Hadrian was unfamiliar with, and the two dashed from the hut.

"Can you help him?"

The woman nodded as she took out a stone mortar and began crushing bits of what looked to be dirt, leaves, and nuts with a pestle. "They common here with open wounds. Left alone, *shirlum-kath* will devour him. He die soon without help. I make poison for the *shirlum-kath*."

One of the women returned with a gourd and an earthen pot, in which Fan Irlanu mixed the contents of her mortar with oil, beating it until she had a thick, dark paste, which she spread over Royce's wound, packing it into the puncture. They turned him over and did the same to the exit wound. Then she placed a single large foul-smelling leaf over each and together they wrapped him in fresh cloth. Royce barely woke during the procedure. Groggy and confused, he soon passed out once more.

Fan Irlanu covered Royce back up with the blankets and nodded approvingly. "He will get better now, I think. I brew drinks—more poison for *shirlum-kath* and a tea for strength. When he wakes, make him drink both, eh? Then he feel better much faster."

Hadrian thanked her. As she left, he wondered why Royce always attracted beautiful women when he was near death.

⤝

When Royce woke the next morning, the fever was gone, and he was strong enough to curse. According to him, the draft Fan Irlanu had provided tasted worse than fermented cow dung, but he actually liked the tea. The following day, he was sitting up and eating. By the third, he was able to walk unassisted to the communal *ostrium* for his meals.

No one complained about the delay because the rain continued. Seeing Royce in the *ostrium* that morning, Grady winked and asked Hadrian if it might be possible for Royce to have a relapse.

"He is good?" Fan Irlanu asked, coming to them after the evening meal had concluded. Her movement was entrancingly graceful, her dress glistening like oil in the lamplight. All eyes followed her.

"No—but he's feeling a lot better," Hadrian replied. His mischievous grin left a puzzled expression on her face.

"My language is perhaps not—"

"I'm very good, thank you," Royce told her. "Apparently I owe you my life."

She shook her head. "Repay me by getting strong—ah, but I do have a favor to ask of your friend Hay-dree-on. Joqdan, warlord of the village, asks that he speak with you at the *sarap*."

"Me?" Hadrian asked, looking across to where the man in the bone necklaces sat. "Is it all right if Royce joins us? I'd like to keep an eye on him."

"But of course, if he is up to it."

Hadrian helped Royce to his feet, and as the rest watched with envious stares, the two followed Fan Irlanu out of the *ostrium*. The sun had not yet set, but for what little light the jungle permitted, it might just as well have. Oil lamps hung from branches, illuminating the path, decorating the village like a Summersrule festival. The rain still poured, so they left the lodge under the protection of palm branches. Hadrian knew *sarap* translated to "meeting place," or "talking place." In this case, it was a giant oudorro tree, from which, he had recently learned, the village took its name.

The tree was not as tall as it was round. Great green leaves thrived on many of its branches despite the center of the trunk's being completely hollow. The space within provided shelter from the rain and was large enough for the four of them. A small ornately decorated fire pit dominated the center of the floor and glowed with red coals. Around this they took seats on luxurious pillows of silk and satin. The interior walls were painted with various ocher and umber dyes smeared into the wood, apparently by stained fingers. The images depicted men and animals—twisted shapes of strange visions. There were also mysterious symbols and swirling designs. Illuminated by the glowing coals, the interior of the tree was eerily talismanic, creating a sensation that left Hadrian on edge.

Joqdan was already there. He had not waited for a boy with the palms, and his bare head and chest were slick with rain. They all exchanged bows respectfully.

"Pleased am I," Joqdan greeted them. "Mine speech...is, ah...not good as the learned. I warrior—do not speak to outsiders. You are"—he paused for a moment, thinking hard—"special. Am honored. Welcome you to Oudorro, Galenti. I..." He paused, thinking again, and quickly became frustrated and turned to Fan Irlanu.

"The warlord Joqdan regrets that language skills are not good enough to honor you, and he asks that I speak words," Fan Irlanu told them as she removed her wet wrap. "He says that he saw you fight in the arena at Drogbon. He has never forgotten it. To have such a legend here is great honor. You do not wear the laurel, so he thinks you do not wish be recognized. He has asked you here to pay proper respect in private."

Hadrian glanced briefly at Royce, who remained silent but attentive. "Thank you," he told Joqdan. "And he's right—I would prefer not to be recognized."

"Joqdan begs permission to ask a question of the great Galenti. He would like to know why you left."

Hadrian paused only a moment, then replied, "It was time to seek new battles."

The warlord of Oudorro nodded as Fan Irlanu translated his words.

At that moment, something about Fan Irlanu caught Royce's attention and he rapidly approached her. She did not move, although given the ominous manner of his advance, Hadrian guessed that most anyone else would have taken a step back.

"Where did you get that mark on your shoulder?" Royce asked, indicating a small swirling tattoo.

"That is the mark of a seer," Zulron declared, startling all of them as he entered.

Unlike the other men of the village, Zulron wore a full robe. Made from a shimmering cloth, it was open enough for them to see his misshapen body, covered in strange tattoos. The one that spread across his face resembled the web of a spider.

"Fan Irlanu is a vision-walker," he explained, staring admiringly at her. "It is a talent and a gift bestowed by Uberlin upon those endowed with the hot blood of the Ghazel. Few are born each age, and she is very powerful. She can see the depths of a heart and the future of a nation." He paused to run his fingers gingerly down the side of her cheek. "She can see all things except her own destiny."

"You don't suffer from a language barrier, I see," Hadrian said.

Zulron smiled. "I am the oberdaza. I know the movement of the stars in the Ba Ran and the books of your world. All mysteries are revealed to me."

"Is it true that you are a visionary?" Royce asked Fan Irlanu.

She nodded. "With the burning of the tulan leaves, I—"

"Give him a demonstration," Zulron interrupted, causing her to look sharply at him. "Read this one's future," he said, gesturing toward Royce.

A puzzled look crossed her face, but she nodded.

Joqdan put a firm hand to Zulron's shoulder and spun him around, but he spoke too quickly for Hadrian to understand. The two argued briefly, but all he caught was one word of Zulron's reply: *important*.

When Zulron turned back, his eyes fell on Hadrian, who he openly studied. "So, you are the legendary Galenti." He raised an eyebrow. "Looking at you, I would say Joqdan is mistaken, but I know Joqdan is never mistaken. Still, you don't look like the Tiger of Mandalin. I'd thought you would be much bigger." He turned abruptly back to Fan Irlanu. "The leaves, burn them."

As Fan Irlanu moved to a stone box, Zulron asked them to take seats around the glowing coals of the fire ring.

Hadrian took Royce aside. "Perhaps we should go. I can't say I like Mr. Witch Doctor's attitude much. Seems like he's up to something. The fact that he's been spending time with Thranic doesn't help."

Royce glanced at Fan Irlanu. "No, I want to stay."

"What's all this about?"

"The tattoo—Gwen has the same one."

Reluctantly, Hadrian sat.

Fan Irlanu returned with several large dry leaves. Even withered and brittle, they were a brilliant shade of red. She held them over the coals and muttered something while crushing the leaves and letting them fall onto the embers. Instantly a thick white smoke billowed. It did not rise, but pooled and drifted. Fan Irlanu used her hands to contain the smoke, wafting it, scooping it, swirling it into a cloud before her. Then she bent and breathed in the ashen mist. Repeatedly, she swept the smoke and inhaled deeply.

The last of the leaves burned away and the smoke faded. Fan Irlanu's eyes closed and she began swaying on her knees, humming softly. After a few minutes, she reached out her hands.

"Touch her," Zulron instructed Royce.

Royce hesitated briefly. He looked at her the way Hadrian had seen him eye an elaborate lock. The greater the potential treasure behind the door, the more tension showed in Royce's eyes, and at that moment he looked as if Fan Irlanu might hold the secret to a fortune. He reached out his fingers. At his touch, she took hold of him.

There was a pause, and then Fan Irlanu began to moan and finally shake her head, slowly at first but faster and faster the longer she held on. Her mouth opened and she groaned the way one might in a nightmare, struggling to speak but unable to form words. She jerked, her eyes shifting wildly under closed lids, her voice louder but saying nothing distinguishable.

Joqdan's face was awash with concern, making Hadrian wonder if something was wrong. Fan Irlanu continued to struggle. Joqdan started to move, but a quick glare from Zulron held him back. At last, the woman screamed and collapsed on the pillows.

"*Leave her alone!*" Zulron shouted in Tenkin.

Joqdan ignored him, rushing to her side. Fan Irlanu lay on the ground thrashing. She cried out and then became still.

Joqdan clutched her, whispering in her ear. He held her head and placed a hand near her mouth to feel for breath. "*You've killed her!*" he shouted at Zulron. Without another word, he lifted the seer in his arms and ran out into the rain.

"What's going on? What's happening?" Hadrian asked.

"Your friend is not human," the oberdaza declared. Zulron stepped up to face Royce. "Why are you here?"

"We're part of the crew of the *Emerald Storm*, on our way to deliver a message to the Palace of the Four Winds," Hadrian answered for him.

Zulron did not take his eyes off Royce. "For three thousand years the ancient legends have told of the Day of Reckoning, when the shadow from the north will descend to wash over our lands."

Derning, Grady, Poe, and Bulard entered. "What's going on?" Derning asked. "We heard a woman scream and saw the big guy carrying her away."

"There was an accident," Hadrian explained.

Both Derning and Grady immediately looked at Royce.

"We don't know what happened to her," Hadrian continued. "She was doing a kind of spiritual demonstration—reading Royce's fortune or something—and she collapsed."

"She collapsed?" Derning said.

"She was breathing tulan leaf smoke. Maybe it was a bad batch."

Zulron ignored their conversation and continued to glare at Royce. "The Ghazel legend, preserved by oral memory from the time of the first Ghazel-Da-Ra, tells of death and destruction, revenge unleashed, the Old Ones coming again. I have seen the signs myself. I watch the stars and know. To the north, there have been rumblings. Estramnadon is active, and Avempartha has been opened. Now here is an elf in my village, where one has never walked before."

"An elf?" Derning asked, puzzled.

"That is what killed Fan Irlanu," Zulron told them. "Or at the very least has driven her insane."

"What?" Hadrian exclaimed.

"It's not possible to use the sight on an elf. The lack of a soul offers up only infinity. For her it was like walking off a bottomless cliff. If she lives, she will never be the same."

"You're the village healer. Shouldn't you be trying to help her?"

"He wants her dead." Royce finally spoke. Then, looking at Zulron, he added, "You knew."

"What did he know?" Bulard asked, tense but fascinated. Grady and Derning also leaned forward.

"You knew I was elven, didn't you? But you told her—no, coerced her—to do a reading," Royce said.

Outside, there were sounds of commotion, running feet and raised voices. Hadrian heard Wesley saying something over the heated shouts of Tenkins.

"Why did you want her dead?"

"I did nothing. You are the one that killed her. And killing a member of the village, especially a seer, is an unpardonable crime. The punishment is death." Zulron gave a smile before stepping outside.

The rest of them followed to find a gathering crowd.

"There he is!" Thranic shouted the moment Royce stepped out of the tree. He pointed and said, "There's your *elf*! I warned you about him."

"He has slain our seer, Fan Irlanu!" Zulron announced, and repeated it in Tenkin.

Burandu, Wesley, and Wyatt pushed their way through the mob.

"Is this true?" Wesley asked quickly, his voice nervous.

"Which?" Royce asked.

"Are you an elf, and did you just kill Fan Irlanu?"

"Yes, and I'm not sure."

The crowd grew and Hadrian could pick out words such as *justice*, *revenge*, and *kill* among the many Tenkin shouts.

"By Mar, man!" Wesley said fiercely but quietly to Royce. "What is it with you? I should let you hang just for the amount of trouble you've caused." He took a breath. The crowd pressed in. Lightning flashed overhead while thunder boomed. "What do you mean when you say you're not sure?" Wesley asked. He was speaking quickly, wiping the rain from his face.

"*The murderer must pay for his crime, Burandu,*" Zulron declared in Tenkin. "*His soullessness has killed our beloved Fan Irlanu. The law demands justice!*"

"*Where is Joqdan?*" Burandu asked.

"*Paying his last respects to his dead would-be wife. If he was here, he would agree.*"

"*He lies! Zulron is to blame.*" Hadrian spoke in Tenkin, which drew surprised looks from everyone.

"What are they saying?" Wesley asked Hadrian.

"The oberdaza is pushing for our deaths and Burandu is buying it."

"*Bring them all!*" Burandu shouted.

The warriors of the village descended. Hadrian considered for a moment whether he should draw his swords, but decided against it. He shot a look at Royce to indicate he should not resist.

They were driven to the village center, where Dilladrum was shouting, "Let go of me! What are you doing?" When he saw Wesley, he asked, "What did you do? I told you not to offend them!"

"We didn't offend them," Hadrian explained. "We killed their beloved seer."

"What!" Dilladrum looked as if he was about to faint.

"Actually, it is a misunderstanding, but I am not sure we will get the chance to explain," Wesley put in.

"At least Thranic will die with us," Royce said loud enough for the sentinel to hear.

"A martyr's death is a fair price to rid the world of you and your kind."

Lightning flashed again, revealing the pallid faces of the crew in its stark light.

Grady was shoved to the ground, and he moved his hand toward his sword.

"Grady, don't!" Hadrian said.

"That is right," Wesley shouted. "No one draw weapons. They will slaughter us."

"They will anyway," Derning replied.

Poe and Hadrian pulled Grady back to his feet. All around them the ring of warriors formed a wall, behind which churned a crowd of shouting faces and raised fists. The rain-drenched mob pushed and cried, its words lost in a roar of hatred. Lightning flashed once more, and a single voice rang out, "*You knew!*"

Instantly the crowd fell silent and parted. Only the sound of rain disturbed the stillness as Fan Irlanu entered the circle. Joqdan, at her side, carried a deadly-looking spear, his eyes grim and focused on Zulron.

"*Burandu, it is not the stranger's fault. It was Zulron who asked that I do the reading. He knew this one had elven blood. But I am still alive!*"

"*But—no…How could you…*" Zulron stammered.

"*He is not an Old One,*" Fan Irlanu said. "*He is a* kaz! *There is humanity in him—footholds, Zulron, footholds!*"

"What's going on?" Wesley asked Hadrian. "Isn't she the one Royce killed? What's she saying?"

"She seems a mite upset," Grady said.

"But not at Royce," Poe remarked.

"Who, then?" Grady asked.

"Zulron has tried to kill me. I have known for some time his ambitions were great. I saw the treachery in his heart, but I never expected he would go so far."

"Joqdan, what say you? Is what Fan Irlanu says true?" Burandu addressed his warlord.

Joqdan thrust his spear into the chest of Zulron.

The long blade passed fully through the oberdaza's body. Those nearby jostled backward, everyone moving away. Joqdan advanced the length of his spear's shaft and gripped Zulron by the throat. Holding him with strong arms, he spat in the witch doctor's face. The light faded from the oberdaza's eyes, and Joqdan withdrew his spear as Zulron fell dead.

"I think that answers your question," Poe remarked.

Burandu looked down at the body, then up at Joqdan, and nodded. *"Joqdan is never wrong. I am pleased you are safe, Fan Irlanu,"* he said to her. Then the Elder addressed Wesley and the others. "Forgive the dishonor of evil Zulron. Judge us not by his actions. You too have such men in your world, eh?"

Wesley glanced at Thranic and Royce.

Burandu shouted to his warriors and they dispersed the crowd. Many paused to kiss Fan Irlanu, who stood weakly, leaning against Joqdan. She offered a strained smile, but Hadrian could see the paleness of her face and the effort in her breathing.

The Elder spoke briefly with Joqdan and Fan Irlanu, and then Joqdan lifted the seer once more and carried her to one of the smaller dwellings. Zulron's body was dragged away and with him went most of the Tenkin.

"That's it?" Grady asked.

"Wait," Dilladrum said as the leopard-skinned man approached. They spoke for a moment, and then Dilladrum returned. "The village of Oudorro asks our forgiveness for the misunderstanding and begs the honor to continue as our host."

They looked at one another skeptically.

"They are sincere."

Wesley sighed and nodded. "Thank them for their kindness, but we will be leaving in the morning."

"Kindness?" Derning muttered. "They nearly skinned us alive. We should get out now while we can."

"I see no advantage in venturing into these jungles at night," Wesley affirmed. "We will leave at first light."

"And what about Melborn?" Thranic said.

"You, Dr. Levy, and Seamen Blackwater and Melborn will come with me. The rest I order to quarters to get as much sleep as possible."

A young Tenkin trotted up to them and spoke to Dilladrum, his eyes watching Royce.

"What is it?" Wesley asked.

"Fan Irlanu has requested Royce and Hadrian."

Wesley nodded at them, but added, "Try not to start a war this time. You are to report to me directly after—by your honor, gentlemen."

Before Thranic could object, they both nodded and offered an "Aye, aye, sir."

❧

Fan Irlanu lay on a bed beneath a thin white sheet as a young girl patted her forehead with a damp cloth, rinsed repeatedly in a shallow basin. Joqdan remained at her side. His great spear, still covered in Zulron's blood, stood by the door.

"Is she really all right?" Hadrian asked.

"I be fine," Fan Irlanu replied. "It was terrible shock. Will take time."

"I'm sorry," Royce offered.

"I know," she told him. Her face was sympathetic to the point of sadness. "I *know* you are."

"You saw something?"

"Were I to touch Joqdan's hand with the tulan smoke in me, I could tell what he ate for his midday meal yesterday and what he eat tomorrow. If I touched Galenti's hand, I could name the woman he will marry and who will outlive the other. I could also tell the precise events that will surround his death. So clear is my sight that I can see a life in detail, but not you. You are mystery, a cloud. Looking into you is seeing a mountain range in thick fog—I can only see the high points with no means of connecting them. You are *kaz* in the Ghazel tongue—in your language a *mir*, yes?—mix of human and elven blood. This gives you long life." She paused to gather some strength, and Joqdan's brow furrowed further.

"Imagine looking down road, you see most things well, the trees, the rocks, the leaves. But with you, it is as if standing high in air, staring out at horizon—very few details. My sight can only span so far, and that not include life span of a *kaz*. There is too much."

"But you saw something."

"I saw many things. Too many," she told him. Her eyes were soft and comforting.

"Tell me," Royce said. "Please, I know a woman. She's very much like you, but something troubles her. She won't speak of it, and I think she has seen things like you have—things that trouble her."

"She is Tenkin?"

"I'm not sure, but she bears the same mark as you."

Fan Irlanu nodded. "I sent for you because of what I saw. I will tell you what I know and then I rest. I sleep for long time, and Joqdan will not let any disturb me. So I speak now. Am certain I will not see you again. I saw much but understood little—too much distance, too much time. Most are vague feelings that are hard to put in words, but what I sensed was powerful."

Royce nodded.

She paused a moment, thinking, then said, "Darkness surrounds you, death is everywhere, it stalks you, hunts you, and you feed upon it—blood begets blood—the darkness consumes you. In this darkness, I saw two lights beside you. One will blow out. The other flickers, but it must not go out. You must protect the flame against the storm.

"I saw a secret—it is, ah...it is hidden. This great treasure is covered. A man hides it, but a woman knows—she alone knows and so she prepares. She speaks in riddles that will be revealed—truth disguised for now. You will remember when the time comes. The path is laid out for you—in the dark."

Joqdan spoke something in Tenkin, but Fan Irlanu shook her head and pushed on.

"I saw great journey. Ten upon the road. She who wears the light will lead the way. The road goes deep into the earth and into despair. The voice of the dead guide your steps. You walk back in time. The three-thousand-year battle begins again. Cold grips the world, death comes to all, and a choice is before you. Alone stand you in the balance. Your weight will tilt the scales, but to which side is unclear. You must choose between darkness and light, and your choice will affect many." She paused, shaking her head slowly. "Like trees in a forest, like blades of grass—too many to count. And I fear that in the end you will choose the darkness and turn your back to the light."

"You said *she*. Who did you mean? Is it Gwen?" Royce questioned.

"I not know names. They mere feelings, glimpses of a dream."

"What is this secret?"

"I not know. It is hidden."

"When you say there are two lights and one blows out, does that mean someone will die?"

She nodded. "Think so—yes, feels that way. I sensed a loss, so great I still feel it." She reached out and touched Royce's hand and a tear slipped down her cheek. "Your road is one of great anguish."

Royce said nothing for a moment and then asked, "What is this great journey?"

She shook her head. "I wish knew more. Your life—whole life been pain and so much more lies ahead. Am sorry, but cannot tell more than that."

"She rests now," Joqdan told them. From his firm tone they knew it was time to go.

They walked out of the hut and found Wyatt watching out for them.

"Waiting up?" Hadrian asked.

"Didn't want you to step into the wrong hut by accident." He gave a wink.

"The rest bunked down?"

He nodded. "So, you're an elf," Wyatt said to Royce. "That explains a lot. What did the lady want?"

"To tell me my future."

"Good news?"

"It nearly killed her. What do you think?"

CHAPTER 17

THE PALACE OF THE FOUR WINDS

Thranic was furious. Wesley refused to take any action against Royce, and the sentinel railed that under imperial law all elves were subject to arrest. Wesley had little choice but to acknowledge this, but added that given their circumstances, he had neither a prison nor chains. He also pointed out that they were not within the bounds of the New Empire, and until they were, he was the sole judge of the law.

"It is my duty to see this mission to completion," Wesley told the sentinel. "A bound man will only be a hindrance to this effort, particularly when he is injured and exhibits no desire to flee."

Royce watched all this with an expression of mild amusement. Thranic went on relentlessly until finally Wesley gave in and approached Royce. "Will you give me your word you will not attempt to escape me or Sentinel Thranic before this mission is over?"

"On my word, sir," Royce replied. "There is nothing that could make me willingly leave Sentinel Thranic's side."

"There you have it," Wesley concluded, satisfied.

"He's an elf! What good is the word of an elf?" As Thranic straightened and rose above Wesley, the look on the sentinel's face caused him to take a step back. "As secretary of Erivan affairs, appointed by the Patriarch, it's my duty to purge the empire of their foul influence. I demand you place the elf under my authority at once!"

Wesley hesitated. The challenge of a sentinel broke the nerve of many kings, and Thranic was more intimidating than any other Hadrian had encountered. His hunched-vulture demeanor and piercing glare were more than daunting.

Hadrian was tense. He knew the sentinel was already dead, but would prefer his partner got to pick his own time and place. If Wesley agreed to surrender Royce, there would be a battle that would see one of them dead. Hadrian let his fingers slip slowly to the pommels of his swords and he marked the position of Bernie in anticipation.

Wesley locked his jaw and returned Thranic's glare. "He might be an elf, sir, but he is also one of *my* crew."

"Your crew? You no longer have a ship. You're nothing but a boy playing pretend captain!" the sentinel bellowed angrily.

Wesley stiffened.

"And what were you playing at in the hold of the ship, sir? Was that what you call administering your authority?"

This took Thranic by surprise.

"Oh yes, the officers knew of your nightly visits to the *cargo*. It is a small ship, sir, and the officers' bunks were just above. We heard you every night torturing them, and I fear a good deal more than that. I am no great fan of elves, but by Maribor, there are limits to the abuses conscience permits! No, sir, I do not think I will be turning Seaman Melborn over to your authority anytime soon. Even should I trust you to treat him honorably, I need all the hands I can get, and as we both know, you are not an honorable man."

"It's a pity to see such a young, promising lad throw his life away," Thranic fumed. "I'll see that you are executed for this."

"To do so, we must return to Avryn. Let us hope we both live to see that day."

⸏

At dawn the crew of the *Emerald Storm* left the village and once more plunged into the jungle, traveling northeast of the Oudorro Valley by a narrow, barely visible path. The rain had left the ground swamped, but it had stopped at last. On the third day, cliffs and chasms barred their path. They followed ridgelines where a stumble could send a man falling hundreds of feet, walked perilous rope bridges that spanned raging rivers, and followed rocky clefts down into dark valleys. In the lower ravines it was dark, even at midday. Trees created phantom images. Rocks looked like crouching animals, and stunted, gnarled bushes appeared like monsters in the mist.

Royce's health steadily improved, though his disposition remained unchanged. He was able to walk on his own most of the day, and thanks to Fan Irlanu's balm, his wounds no longer required a bandage.

They found the bodies on the fourth day out of Oudorro. Corpses, dressed in clothes similar to those of Dilladrum and the Vintu, lay on the path. Flies hovered, and the stench of decay lingered in the air. They had been dead for some time, and many were missing limbs or showed evidence of bites.

"Animals?" Wesley asked.

"Maybe." Dilladrum looked off toward the east. "But perhaps the Panther is not able to contain his beasts, just as Burandu told us."

"You're saying the Ghazel did this?"

Dilladrum paused to study the jungle around them. "Impossible to say, yet these bodies are weeks old and it's not like the jungle to let them rot. Animals don't like Ghazel and will avoid an area with their smell, even if it means passing up a free meal.

"This man is Hingara." Dilladrum pointed to the body of a swarthy little man in a red cap. "He's a guide, like me. He set out for the Palace of the Four Winds with a party like ours weeks ago. He was a good man. He knew the jungle well, and as you can see, his group was large—as many as thirty men in all. What kind of animal do you think would attack so large a company? A pack of wolves, perhaps? A pride of lions? No, they would never attack a party this large. And what animal could kill without leaving a single body of their own behind? Ghazel, on the other hand..."

"What about them?" Wesley asked.

"They're like ghosts. Hingara could not have seen them coming. Imagine beings as nimble and at ease in these jungles as monkeys, but possessing the strength and ferocity of tigers. They have the instinct of beasts but the intelligence of men. On a rainy day they can smell a human three leagues away. This was a safe path, but I fear things have changed."

"There are only about eighteen bodies here," Wesley observed. "If he set out with thirty men, where are the rest?"

Dilladrum let his sight settle on the naval officer. "Where, indeed."

Wesley grimaced as he looked at the dead. "Are you saying they took them to eat?"

"That's what they do." Dilladrum pointed to the torn and mutilated bodies. "They ate some on the spot in the fever following the battle, but I think they carried the rest back to their den, where I can only guess they feasted by barbecuing them on spits and drinking warmed blood from the men's skulls."

"You don't know that!" Wesley challenged.

Dilladrum shook his head. "As I said, I'm guessing. No one

truly knows what goes on in their camps any more than a deer knows what goes on in the dining halls of a king."

"You make it sound as if they're our betters."

"In these jungles, they are. Here they're the hunters and we're the prey. I told you the trip would be harder from now on. We'll burn no fire, cook no food, and pitch no tent. Our only hope of survival lies in slipping through unnoticed."

"Should we bury them?" Wesley asked.

"What the animals do not touch, neither should we. It would announce our presence to the whole jungle. It's also not wise to linger. We should press on with all haste."

⁂

They traveled steadily downward now, following a rapidly flowing river through a cleft in the mountains. The lower they went, the higher the canopy rose, and the darker their world became. They camped along a bank where the river swirled around a break of boulders. With no fire or tent, it was not much of a camp. They huddled on a bare sandy patch exposed by a shift in the river's bend, eating cold salted meat. Royce sat at the edge of the camp and watched Thranic watching him.

They had played this game each night since the village. Royce was certain Bernie had filled Thranic's head with numerous stories about his reign of terror against the Diamond. Thranic appeared aloof, but Royce was certain Bernie's words had wormed in nonetheless. Without Staul, and with Bernie no longer a trusted ally, Thranic was dramatically weakened. The sentinel's confrontation with Wesley had revealed Thranic's growing desperation—his failure another setback. The balance had shifted, he slipped from the hunter to the hunted, and with each day Royce grew stronger.

Royce enjoyed the game. He liked watching the shadows growing under Thranic's eyes as he got less and less sleep. He savored the way Thranic spun, his eyes searching rapidly for Royce, whenever an animal rustled branches behind him on the trail. Mental torture was never something Royce aimed for, but in Thranic's case he was making an exception.

Royce's quick turn had saved his life. Although he might have bled to death if Hadrian and the others had not found him, or died from fever if the Tenkin woman had not helped, the wound itself was relatively superficial. For several days he had portrayed being weaker than he was. He had pain when pressing on his side and was still experiencing some lack of movement, but for the most part he was his old self again.

Royce might have continued the game longer, but it was becoming too dangerous. Wesley's defiance had changed the playing field. The sentinel's options were diminishing. The ploy to force Wesley's hand had been his last civil gambit. As long as Wesley remained a legitimate leader, those like Wyatt, Grady, Derning, and Poe would side with him. Royce knew Thranic saw Wesley as a pawn blocking his forward movement, one that he would need removed. It was time to deal with the sentinel.

Royce curled up to sleep with the rest of them, but selected a place hidden by a small thicket of plants. In the darkness he lay there only briefly before leaving his blanket filled with brush and melted into the jungle.

Thranic had chosen to bed down near the river, which Royce thought considerate, since he intended to dispose of the sentinel's body in the strong current. Royce slipped around the outside of the camp until he came to where Bernie and Levy slept, but Thranic was missing.

❦

Thwack! A narrow tree trunk splintered.

At the last moment, Royce had moved. A crossbow bolt lodged itself in the wood where a second before he had been crouching.

Thranic struggled desperately to crank back the string on his weapon. "Did you think to find me in my bed?" he said. "Did you really think killing me would be that easy—*elf*?"

He cranked back on the gear.

"You shouldn't fear me so much. I'm here to help you. It's my responsibility to help all of you. I'll cleanse the darkness in your hearts. I'll free you of the burden of your disgusting, offensive life. You no longer need to be an affront to Maribor. I'll save you!"

"And who will save you?" Royce replied.

He was just a few feet from where he had been. Thranic glanced down to set the bolt in the track. He lifted the bow, but when he looked up, Royce was gone.

"What do you mean?" Thranic asked, hoping Royce would reveal his position.

"You see awfully well in the dark, Thranic," Royce said from his right.

Thranic turned and fired, but the bolt merely ripped through an empty thicket.

"Well, but not perfectly," Royce observed, appearing once more, but much closer. Thranic immediately began ratcheting back his bow.

He had two more bolts.

"You also managed to slip into the trees without me seeing you. And you crept up behind me. That's indeed remarkable. How old are you, Thranic? I'll bet you're older than you look."

The sentinel loaded the bolt and looked up, but once more Royce was gone.

"What are you driving at, elf?" Thranic asked, holding his crossbow at his hip. Backing against a tree, he peered around the jungle.

"We're alike, you and I," Royce said from behind him.

Thranic spun around. He saw movement slipping through the brush and fired. The shot went wide and he cursed. Thranic began cranking back the string once more.

"Is that why you do it?" Royce asked. "Is that why you torture elves? Tell me, are you purging them—or yourself?"

"Shut up!" Thranic's hand slipped on the gear and the string snapped back, slashing his fingers. He was shaking now.

"You can't kill the elf inside, so you torture and murder all those you find."

He was closer.

"I said shut up!"

"How much elven blood does it take to wash away the sin of *being* one yourself?"

Closer still.

"Damn you!" he screamed, fighting with the bow, which refused to cooperate with his shaking fingers.

He drew the string back again only to have it jump the track and snap free. He put a foot through the loop at the bow's nose and pulled. Now it was stuck. He pressed desperately on the ratchet handle. It refused to move. *Crack!* The winch snapped.

In horror, Thranic stopped breathing as he looked down. He struggled to pull the bowstring back with just the strength of his arms. He pulled with all his might, but he could not get it to the catch. He was giving Melborn too much time. He let the bow fall to the grass and drew his dagger.

He waited. He listened. He spun. He looked.

He was alone.

๑

"Get up." Hadrian woke to Royce's voice as his friend moved through the camp. He knew the tone and instantly got to his feet.

"What is it?"

"Company," Royce told him. "Wake everyone."

"What's happening?" Wesley asked groggily as the camp slowly came alive.

"Quiet," Royce whispered. He crouched with his dagger drawn, staring out into the darkness.

"Ghazel?" Grady asked.

"Something," Royce replied. "A lot of somethings."

The rest of them heard it now, twigs snapping and leaves rustling. They were all on their feet with weapons drawn.

"Backs to the river!" Wesley shouted.

Ahead of them a light appeared, then disappeared, and then another blinked. Two more flickered off to the right and left and sounds of movement grew louder and closer. Dovin Thranic stumbled back into camp, causing a brief alarm. Several people looked at him oddly but said nothing.

Everyone's attention remained on sounds from the trees.

Shadowy figures carried torches within the thick weave of the jungle. Slowly they climbed out of the brush and into the clearing around the riverbank. Twenty approached from all sides at once. At first, they appeared to be strange, monstrous beasts. When they fully entered the clearing, Hadrian saw that they were men: stocky, bull-necked brutes with white-painted faces, bone armor, and headdresses of long feathers. They moved with ease through the dense brush. In their hands were crude clubs, axes, and spears. The men circled in silence, creeping forward.

"*We come in peace!*" Hadrian heard Dilladrum shout in

Tenkin, his voice sounding weak. "*We have come to see War-lord Erandabon. We bear a message for him.*"

As they grew nearer, the men began hooting and howling, shaking their weapons. Some brandished teeth, while others beat their chests or stomped naked feet.

Dilladrum repeated his statement.

One of the larger men, who carried a decorated war axe, stepped forward and approached Dilladrum. "*What message?*" the Tenkin asked in a harsh, shallow voice.

"*It is a sealed letter,*" Dilladrum replied. "*To be given only to the warlord.*"

The man eyed each of them carefully. He grinned and then nodded. "*Follow.*"

Although it was the best they could expect, Dilladrum mopped his forehead with his sleeve as he explained the conversation to the party.

The Tenkin howled orders. Torches went out and the rest melted back into the jungle. The leader remained as they quickly broke camp. Then, with a motion for them to follow, he ran back into the trees, his torch lighting the way. He led them at a brisk pace that had everyone panting for breath—and Bulard near collapse. Dilladrum shouted forward for a rest or at least a slower pace. The only response was laughter.

"Our new friends aren't terribly considerate of an old man." Bulard panted in between wheezing inhales.

"That's enough!" Wesley shouted, and raised a hand for them to stop. The crew of the *Emerald Storm* needed little persuasion to take a break. The Tenkin and his torch continued forward, disappearing into the trees. "If he wants to keep jogging on without us, let him!"

"He's not," Royce commented. "He's hiding in the trees up ahead with his torch out. There are also several on either side of us, and more than a few to our rear."

Wesley looked around, then said, "I don't see anything at all."

Royce smiled. "What good is it having an elf in your crew if you can't make use of him?"

Wesley raised an eyebrow, looked back out into the trees, then gave up altogether. He pulled the cork from his water bag, took a swig, and passed it around. Turning his attention to the historian, who sat in the dirt doubled over, he asked, "How you doing, Mr. Bulard?"

Bulard's red face came up. He was sweating badly, his thin hair matted to his head. He said nothing, his mouth preoccupied with the effort of sucking in air, but he managed to offer a smile and a reassuring nod.

"Good," Wesley said, "let's proceed, but *we* will set the pace. Let's not have them exhausting us."

"Aye," Derning agreed, wiping his mouth after his turn at the water. "It would be just the thing for them to run us in circles until we collapse, then fall on us and slit our throats before we can catch our breaths."

"Maybe that's what happened to the others we spotted. Perhaps it was these blokes," Grady speculated.

"We're going somewhere," Royce replied. "I can smell the sea."

Hadrian had not noticed it until that moment, but he could taste the salt in the air. What he had assumed was wind in the trees he now realized was the voice of the ocean.

"Let's continue, shall we, gentlemen?" Wesley said, moving them out. As they started, the Tenkin's torch appeared once more and moved on ahead. Wesley refused to chase it, keeping them at a comfortable pace. The torch returned, and after a few more attempts to coax them, gave up. Instead, the man carrying it matched their stride.

Travel progressed sharply downward. The route soon

became a rocky trail that plummeted to the face of a cliff. Below they could hear the crashing of waves. As dawn approached, they could see their destination. A stone fortress rose high on a rocky promontory that jutted into the ocean and guarded a natural harbor hundreds of feet below. The Palace of the Four Winds looked ancient, weathered by wind and rain until it matched the stained and pitted face of the dark granite upon which it sat. The palace was built of massive blocks, and it was inconceivable that men could have placed such large stones. Displaying the same austerity as the Tenkin, it lacked ornamentation. Ships filled the large sheltered bay on the lee side of the point. There were hundreds, all with reefed black sails.

When they approached the great gate, their guide stopped. "*Weapons are not allowed past this point.*"

Wesley scowled as Dilladrum translated, but he did not protest. This was the custom even in Avryn. One did not expect to walk armed into a lord's castle. They presented their weapons and Hadrian noted that neither Thranic nor Royce surrendered any.

Thranic had been acting oddly ever since stumbling into camp. He had not said a word and his eyes never left Royce.

They entered the fortress, where a dozen well-equipped guards looked down from ramparts and many more lined their route. The exterior looked nearly ruined. Stone blocks had fallen and were left broken on the ground.

Inside, the castle decor was no more cheerful. Here, too, the withering decay of centuries of neglect had left the once-great edifice little more than a primordial cave. Roots and fungi grew along the corridor crevices, and dead leaves clustered in corners where the swirl of drafts deposited them. Dust, dirt, and cobwebs obscured the ancient decorative carvings, sculptures, and chiseled writings.

Over the walls, the Tenkin had strung crude banners, long pennants that depicted a white Tenkin-style axe on a black field. Just as in Oudorro, row upon row of shields hung from the ceiling like bats in a cavern. A huge fireplace occupied one whole side of the great chamber, a massive gaping maw of a hearth, in which an entire tree trunk smoldered. Upon the floor lay the skin of a tiger, whose head stared with gleaming emerald eyes and yellowing fangs. A stone throne stood at the far end of the hall. The base of the chair had cracked where a vine intertwined the legs, making it list. Its seat was draped in a thick piling of animal skins and on it sat a wild-eyed man.

His head sported a tempest of hair, long and black with streaks of white, jutting in all directions. Deep cuts and burns scarred his face. Thick brows overshadowed bright, explosive eyes, which darted about rapidly, rolling in his skull like marbles struggling to free themselves from the confines of his head. He was bare-chested except for an elaborate vest of small laced bones. His long fingers absently toyed with a large bloodstained axe lying across his lap.

"*Who is this?*" the warlord asked in Tenkin, his loud, disturbing voice echoed from the walls. "*Who is this that enters the hall of Erandabon unannounced and unheralded? Who treads Erandabon's forest like sheep to be gathered? Who dares seek Erandabon in his den, his holy place?*"

A strange assortment of people surrounded him, and all eyes were on the party as they entered. Toothless, tattooed men spilled drinks while women with matted hair and painted eyes swayed back and forth to unheard rhythms. One lounged naked upon a silk cushion, with a massive snake coiled about her body as she whispered to it. Beside her an old hairless man with yellow nails as long as his fingers painted curious designs on the floor, and everywhere the hall was choked with the smoke of burning tulan leaves, which smoldered in a central brazier.

In the darkest shadows were others. Hadrian could barely make them out through the fog of smoke and the flickering firelight. They clustered in the dark, making faint staccato chattering sounds like the whine of cicadas. Hadrian knew that sound well. He could not see them, merely the suggestion of movement cast in shadows upon stone. They shifted nervously, anxiously, like a pack of hungry dogs, their motions jittery and too fast to be human.

Dilladrum shooed Wesley forward. Wesley took a breath and said, "I am Midshipman Wesley Belstrad, acting captain of what remains of the crew of Her Imperial Eminence's ship the *Emerald Storm*, out of Aquesta. I have a message for you, Your Lordship." He bowed deeply. Hadrian found it comical that a lad of such noble bearing bowed before the likes of Erandabon Gile, who was just shy of a madman.

"Long Erandabon has waited for word." The man upon the throne spoke in Apelanese. "Long Erandabon has counted the moons and the stars. The waves crash, the ships approach and gather, the darkness grows, and still Erandabon waits. Sits and waits. Waits and sits. The great shadow is growing in the north. The gods come once more, bringing death and horror to all. The undying will crush the world beneath their step, and Erandabon is made to wait. Where is this message? Speak! Speak!"

Wesley took a step forward as he pulled the letter from his coat, but paused after noticing the broken seal. As he hesitated, an overly thin man dressed in feathers and paint snatched the letter away. He growled at Wesley like a dog showing his teeth. "Not approach the great Erandabon with unclean hands!"

The feathered man handed the message to the warlord,

who studied it for a moment, his eyes racing madly back and forth. A terrible grin grew across his face, and he tore the note into pieces and began eating them. It did not take long, and while he ate, no one said a word. With his final swallow, the warlord raised his hand and said, "*Lock them away.*"

Wesley looked stunned as Tenkin guards approached and grabbed him. "What's happening?" he protested. "We are officials of the Empire of Avryn! You cannot—"

Erandabon laughed as the guard dragged them down the hall.

"Wait!" another voice bellowed. "It was arranged!" Thranic deftly dodged the guards, advancing angrily on the warlord. "My team and I are to be given safe passage. I'm here to pick up a Ghazel guide to take us safely through Grandanz Og!"

Erandabon rose to his feet and raised his axe, halting Thranic mid-step. "Weapons did you bring? Food for the Many did you deliver to Erandabon?" the warlord shouted at him.

"It sank!" Thranic yelled back. "And the deal wasn't based on the weapons or the elves."

The chattering sounds from the darkness grew louder. The noise appeared to disturb even the Tenkin. The hairless man stopped drawing his designs and shuddered. The woman with the snake gasped.

Erandabon remained oblivious to the rise in their tenor as he gibbered in glee. "No! Based on the open gates of Delgos! What proof of this? What proof does Erandabon have? You wait here. You stay sealed and if Drumindor does not fall, *you* will be food for the Many! Erandabon decrees it! Who are you to defy Erandabon?"

"*Who are you to defy Erandabon?*" chanted the crowd. The warlord waved his hand in the air and the chattering grew loud again. The guards moved in with spears.

❧

"Now we know what the empire has been doing with the elves they've been rounding up," Royce muttered as he ran his fingers lightly along the length of the doorjamb.

The Tenkin had locked them in cells buried in the foundation of the fortress. There were no windows. The only light came from the small barred opening of the door, beyond which torches mounted in iron sconces flickered intermittently. Hadrian and Royce were fortunate enough to share a cell with Wyatt and Wesley, while the others were in similar cells within the same block. The sounds of their independent conversations echoed as indiscernible whispers.

"It's ghastly," Wesley said, collapsing on the stone floor and dropping his head in his hands. "Admittedly, I've never held any love for those of elven blood"—he gave Royce an apologetic glance—"but this—this is loathsome beyond human imagining. That the empire could sanction such a vile and dishonorable act is…is…"

"And now we also know what that fleet of ships in the bay is for," Hadrian said. "They're planning to invade Delgos, and it would appear we delivered the orders for them to attack."

"But Drumindor is impregnable from the sea," Wesley said. "Do you think this Erandabon fellow knows that? All those ships will be burned to cinders the moment they enter the bay."

"No, they won't," Royce said. "Drumindor has been sabotaged. When they vent at the next full moon, there will be an explosion, destroying it, and I suspect Tur Del Fur as well. After that, the armada can sail in unopposed."

"What?" Wesley asked. "You can't possibly know that."

Royce said nothing.

"Yes, he does," Hadrian said.

Realization crossed Wesley's face. "The seal was broken. You read the letter?"

Royce continued exploring the door.

"How is it going to explode?" Hadrian asked.

"The vents have been blocked."

"No..." Hadrian shook his head. "Only Gravis knew how to do that and he's dead."

"Merrick found out somehow. He's doing the same thing Gravis tried. He's blocked the portals. When they try to vent during the harvest moon, the gas and molten rock will have nowhere to go. The whole mountain will blow. And that's what Merrick meant about turning the tide of war for the empire. Delgos supports the Nationalists, funded largely by Cornelius DeLur. When they eliminated Gaunt, they cut off the rebellion's head. Now they will cut off its legs. Destroying Delgos will mean the New Empire will only need to deal with Melengar."

"But those ships we saw in the harbor were not just Tenkin. The vast majority were Ghazel," Hadrian pointed out. "Gile thinks he can use them as muscle, as his attack dogs, but goblins can't be tamed. He can't control them. The empire is handing Delgos over to the Ba Ran Ghazel. Once they entrench themselves, the goblins will become a greater threat to the New Empire than the Nationalists ever were."

"I doubt Merrick cares," Royce said.

"You stole the letter from me and read it?" Wesley asked Royce. "And you had us deliver it to the warlord knowing it would launch an invasion?"

"Are you saying you wouldn't have? Those were your orders, sanctioned by the regents themselves."

"But giving Delgos to that...that...insane man and the Ghazel, it's...it's..."

"It's your sworn duty as an officer of the New Empire."

Wesley stared, aghast. "My father used to say, 'A knight draws his sword for three reasons: to defend himself, to defend the weak, and to defend his lord,' but he always added, 'Never defend yourself against the truth, never defend the weakness in others, and never defend a lord without honor.' I don't see how anyone can find honor in feeding a child to goblins or handing over a nation of men to the Ghazel horde."

"Why did you let him deliver the letter?" Hadrian asked.

"I just read it tonight during the water break. It was my last chance to get a look. I figured if we showed up completely empty-handed, we'd be killed."

"I won't be party to this…this…atrocity! We must prevent Drumindor's destruction," Wesley announced.

"You realize interfering with this would be treason?" Royce told Wesley.

"By ordering the delivery of every man, woman, and child in Tur Del Fur into the bloodthirsty hands of the Ba Ran Ghazel, the empress has committed treason to her people. It is I who remain loyal…loyal to the cause of honor."

"It might comfort you to know that it's highly unlikely that Empress Modina gave this order," Hadrian told him. "We know her—met her before she became empress. She would never sanction anything like this. I was in the palace the day before we sailed from Aquesta, and she's not in charge. The regents are the ones behind this."

"One thing's for sure: if we foil Merrick's plan, we won't have to look for him anymore. He'll find us," Royce added.

"This is all my fault." Wesley sighed. "My first command, and look where it has led."

"Don't beat yourself up. You did fine." Hadrian patted him on the shoulder. "But your duty is done now. You completed the task your lord set for you. Everything after this is of your own choosing."

"Not much of a choice, I'm afraid," Wesley said, looking around their cell.

"How long before the harvest moon?" Hadrian asked.

"About two weeks, I would guess," Royce replied.

"It would take us too long to travel back by land. How long would it take us to get there by sea, Wyatt?" Hadrian asked.

"With the wind at our backs, we'd make the trip in a fraction of the time it took us to come out. Week and a half, maybe two."

"Then we still have time," Hadrian said.

"Time for what?" Wesley asked. "We are locked in the dungeon of a madman at the edge of the world. Merely surviving will be a feat."

"You are far too pessimistic for one so young," Royce told him.

Wesley let out a small laugh. "All right, Seaman Melborn, how do you propose we sneak down to the harbor, capture a ship loaded with Ghazel warriors, and sail it out of a bay past an armada when we can't even get out of this locked cell?"

Royce gave the door a gentle push and it swung open. "I unlocked it while you were ranting," he said.

Wesley's face showed his astonishment. "You're not just a seaman, are you?"

"Wait here," Royce said, slipping out.

He was gone for several minutes. They heard no sound. When he returned, Poe, Derning, Grady, Dilladrum, and the Vintu followed. Royce had blood on his dagger and a ring of keys in his hand.

"What about the others?" Wesley asked.

"Don't worry, I won't forget about them," Royce said with a devilish grin. When he left, the others followed. A guard lay dead in a pool of blood and Royce was already at the door of the last cell.

"We don't need to be released," Defoe said from behind the door. "I could open it myself if I wanted to get out."

"I'm not here to let you out," Royce said, opening the door.

Bernie backed up and drew his dagger.

"Stay out of this, Bernie," Royce told him. "So far you've just been doing a job. I get that, but stand between me and Thranic and it gets personal."

"Seaman Melborn!" Wesley snapped. "I can't let you kill Mr. Thranic."

Royce ignored him and Wesley appealed to Hadrian, who shrugged in response. "It's a policy of mine not to get in his way, especially when the other guy deserves it."

Wesley turned to Wyatt, whose expression showed no compassion. "He burned a shipload of elves and, for all I know, was responsible for taking my daughter. Let him die."

Dr. Levy stepped aside, leaving Thranic alone at the back of the cell with only his dagger for protection. By his grip and stance, Hadrian knew the sentinel was not a knife fighter. Thranic was sweating, his eyes tense as Royce moved in.

"Might I ask why you're killing Mr. Thranic?" Bulard asked suddenly, stepping between them. "Those of you intent on fleeing could make better use of your time than butchering a man in his cell, don't you think?"

"Won't take but a second," Royce assured him.

"Perhaps, perhaps, but I'm asking you not to. I'm not saying he doesn't deserve death, but who are you to grant it? Thranic will die, and quite soon, I suspect, given where we're headed. Regardless, our mission is vital not just to the empire, but to all of mankind, and we'll need him if we're to have any hope to complete it."

"Shut up, you old fool," the sentinel growled.

This caught Royce's attention, though he kept his eyes on Thranic. "What mission?"

"To find a very old and very important relic called the Horn of Gylindora that will be needed very soon, I'm afraid."

"The horn?" Hadrian repeated.

"Yes. Given our precarious situation, I don't think it wise to give you a history lesson just now, but suffice to say it's in all of our best interests to leave Thranic alive—for now."

"Sorry," Royce replied, "but you'll just have to make do without—"

The door to the cellblock opened and a pair of soldiers with meal plates stepped in. A quick glance at the dead guard and they ran.

Royce sprinted after them. Bernie quickly closed his cell door again.

"Go, all of you!" Bulard urged.

The party ran out of the cellblock and up the stairs. By the time they reached the top, the hallway was filled with loud voices.

"They got away," Royce grumbled.

"We gathered that from the shouting," Hadrian said.

They faced a four-way intersection of identical narrow stone corridors. Wall-mounted flames burned from iron cradles staggered at long intervals, leaving large sections of shifting shadows.

Royce glanced back toward the cellblock and cursed under his breath. "That's what I get for hesitating."

"Any idea which way now?" Wyatt asked.

"This way," Royce said.

He led them at a rapid pace, then stopped abruptly and motioned everyone into a doorway. Moments later a troop of guards rushed by. Wesley started forward and Royce hauled him back. Two more guards passed.

"*Now* we go," he told them, "but stay *behind* me."

Royce continued along the multitude of corridors and

turns, pausing from time to time. They climbed two more sets of stairs and dodged another group of soldiers. Hadrian saw the wonderment reflected in the party's faces at Royce's skill. It was as if he could see through walls or knew the location of every guard. For Hadrian it was nothing new, but even he was impressed at their progress, given that Royce was towing a parade.

A door unexpectedly opened and several Tenkins literally bumped into Dilladrum and one of the Vintu. Terrified, Dilladrum fled down a corridor, the Vintu following. The stunned Tenkins were not warriors and were just as scared as Dilladrum. They retreated inside. Royce shouted for Dilladrum to stop, but it was no use.

"Damn it!" Royce cursed, chasing after them. The rest of the crew raced to keep up as they ran blindly through corridor after corridor. Rounding a corner, Hadrian nearly ran into Royce, whose way was blocked by Tenkin warriors. The dead bodies of Dilladrum and the Vintu lay on the floor, blood pooling across the stone. Behind them, a small army cut off their retreat.

"*Who are you to defy Erandabon?*" chanted the crowd of Tenkin warriors.

"Get back!" Hadrian ordered, pushing Wesley and the others into a niche that afforded a small amount of defense. He pulled a torch from the wall and together with Royce formed a forward defense.

The Tenkin soldiers charged, screaming as they attacked.

Royce appeared to dodge the advance, but the foremost warrior fell dead. Hadrian drove the flame of his torch into the second Tenkin's face. Using his feet, Royce flipped the dead man's sword to Hadrian, who caught it in time to decapitate the next challenger.

Two Tenkins charged Royce, who simply was not where

they expected him to be when they arrived. His movements were a blur, and two more collapsed. Hadrian advanced as Royce kicked the dead men's weapons behind them to Wyatt, Derning, and Wesley. Hadrian stood at the center now.

Three attacked. Three fell dead.

The rest retreated, bewildered, and Hadrian picked up a second blade.

Clap! Clap! Clap!

The warlord walked toward them, applauding and grinning. "Galenti, it is you. So good to have you back!"

CHAPTER 18

THE POT OF SOUP

Amilia sulked in the kitchen, head in her hands, elbows resting on the baker's table. This was where it had all started, when Modina's former secretary had brought her to the kitchen for a lesson in table manners. Remembering the terror of those early days, she was staggered to realize those had been better times.

Now a witch hid in Modina's room, filling the empress's head with nonsense. She was a foreigner, the princess of an enemy kingdom, and yet she spent more time with Modina than Amilia did. She could be manipulating the empress in any number of ways. Amilia had tried to reason with Modina, but no matter what Amilia said, the girl remained adamant about helping the witch find Degan Gaunt.

Amilia preferred the old days, when Modina had left everything to her. Sitting there, she wondered what she should do. She wanted to go to Saldur and report the witch but knew that would hurt Modina. The empress might never recover from such a betrayal, especially by Amilia, whom she trusted implicitly. The loss would surely crush her fragile spirit, and Amilia saw disaster at the end of every path. She felt as if she were in a runaway carriage racing toward a cliff, with no way to reach the reins.

"How about I make you some soup?" Ibis Thinly asked her. The big man stood in his stained apron, stirring a large steaming pot, into which he threw bits of celery.

"I'm too miserable to eat," she replied.

"It can't be as bad as all that, can it?"

"You have no idea. She's become a handful and then some. I'm actually afraid to leave her alone. Every time I walk out of her room, I'm frightened something terrible will happen."

It was late and they were the only two in the scullery. Long shadows, cast by the flames of the cook's hearth, traced up the far wall. The kitchen was warm and pleasant, except for a foul smell coming from the bubbling broth Ibis cooked on the stove.

"Oh, it can't be as bad as all that. Come on, can't I interest you in some soup? I make a pretty mean vegetable barley, if I do say so myself."

"You know I love your food. It's just that my stomach is in knots. I noticed a gray hair in the mirror the other day."

"Oh please, you're still just a girl," Ibis laughed, then caught himself. "I guess I shouldn't speak to you that way, you being noble and all. I should be saying, 'Yes, Your Ladyship,' or in this case, 'No, no, Your Ladyship! If you'll allow me to be so bold as to speak plainly in your presence, I beg to differ, for I think you're purty as a pot!' That would be a more proper response."

Amilia smiled. "You know, I never have understood that saying of yours."

Ibis drew himself up in feigned offense. "I'm a cook. I like pots." He chuckled. "Have some soup. Something warm in your belly will help untie some of those knots, eh?"

She glanced at the pot he was stirring and grimaced. "I don't think so."

"Oh no, not this. Great Maribor, no! I'll make you something good."

Amilia looked relieved. "What is that you're making? It smells like rotten eggs."

"Soup, but it's barely fit for animals, made with all the worst parts of old leftovers. The smell comes from this horrid yellow powder I have to use. I try to dress it up as best I can. I throw some celery and spices in, just to ease my conscience."

"Who's it for?"

"I've no idea but in a little while a couple of guards will come by and take it. To be honest...I'm afraid to ask where it goes." He paused. "Amilia, what's wrong?"

Amilia stared at the big pot, her mouth partially open. Noise on the stairs caught her attention. Two men entered the kitchen. She knew them by sight. They were guards normally assigned to the east wing's fourth-floor hall—the administration corridor, where she and Saldur worked. They recognized her as well and took a moment to bow. Amilia graciously inclined her head in response. Their looks revealed they found this courtesy odd but appreciated it. Then they turned to Ibis.

"All done?"

"Just a sec, just a sec," he muttered. "You're early."

"We've been on duty since dawn," one of the guards complained. "This is the last job of the night. Honestly, I don't know why you put such effort into it, Thinly."

"It's what I do, and I want it done right."

"Trust me, no one is going to complain. Nobody cares."

"*I* care," Ibis remarked, his voice sharp enough to end the subject.

The guard shrugged his shoulders and waited.

"Who's the soup for?" Amilia asked.

The guard hesitated. "Not really supposed to talk about that, milady."

The other guard gave him a rough nudge. "She's the bloody secretary to the empress."

The first one blushed. "Forgive me, milady. It's just that Regent Saldur can be a little scary sometimes."

Amilia agreed in her head but externally remained aloof.

His friend slapped himself in the forehead, rolling his eyes. "Blimey, James, you're a fool. Forgive him, milady."

"What?" James looked puzzled. "What'd I say?"

The guard shook his head sadly. "You just insulted the regent and admitted you don't respect Her Ladyship all in one breath."

James's face drained of color.

"What's your name?" she asked the other guard.

"Higgles, milady." He swallowed hard and bowed again.

"Why don't *you* answer my question, then?"

"We takes the soup to the north tower. You know, the one 'tween the well and the stables."

"How many prisoners are there?"

The two guards looked at each other. "None that we know of, milady."

"So who is the soup for?"

He shrugged. "We just leave it with the Seret Knight."

"Soup's done," Ibis declared.

"Is that all, milady?" Higgles asked.

She nodded and the two disappeared out the door to the courtyard, each holding one of the pot's handles.

"Now, let me make *you* something," Ibis said, wiping his big hands on his apron.

"Huh?" Amilia asked, still thinking about the two guards. "No thanks, Ibis," she said, getting up. "There's something I need to do, I think."

◆

The lack of a cloak became painfully uncomfortable when Amilia was halfway across the inner ward. The weather had jumped from a friendly autumn of brightly colored leaves, clear blue skies, and crisp nights to the gray, icy cold of pre-winter. A half-moon glimmered through hazy clouds as she stepped through the vegetable garden, now no more than a graveyard of brown dirt. She approached the chicken coop carefully, trying to avoid disturbing the hens. There was nothing wrong with being out, no rules against wandering the ward at night, but at that moment she felt sinister.

She ducked into the woodshed just as James and Higgles passed by on their return journey. After several minutes, Amilia crept forward, slipped around the well, and entered the north tower—the *prison tower* as she now dubbed it.

Just as described, a Seret Knight, dressed in black armor with the red symbol of a broken crown on his chest, stood at attention. Decorated with a red feather plume, the helm he wore covered his face. He appeared not to notice her, which was odd, as all guards bowed to Amilia now. The seret said nothing as she stepped around him toward the stairs. She was shocked when he made no move to stop her.

Up she went, periodically passing cells. None of the doors were locked, and she pushed some open and stepped inside. Each room was small. Old, rotted straw lay scattered across the ground. Tiny windows allowed only a fraction of moonlight to enter. There were heavy chains mounted to the walls and the floor. Some rooms had a stool or a bucket, but most were bare of any furniture. Amilia felt uncomfortable while in the rooms—not just because of the cold, but because she feared she might end up in just such a place.

James and Higgles had been correct. The tower was empty.

She returned down the steps to the seret. "Excuse me, but what are you guarding? There is no one here."

He did not respond.

"Where did the soup go?"

Again, the seret stood mute. Unable to see his eyes through the helm, and thinking perhaps he was asleep while standing up, she took a step closer. The seret moved, and as fast as a snake, his hand grabbed hold of his sword and drew it partway from its scabbard, allowing the metal to hiss, a sound that echoed ominously in the stone tower.

Amilia fled.

᷒

"Are you going to tell her?" Nimbus asked.

The two were in Amilia's office, finishing the last of the invitation lists for the scribes to begin working on. Parchments were everywhere. On the wall hung a layout of the great hall, perforated with countless pinholes from the shifting of guest positions.

"No, I'll not add to that witch's arsenal of insanity with tales of mysterious disappearing pots of soup! I've worked for months to put Modina back together. I won't allow her to be broken again."

"But what if—"

"Drop it, Nimbus." Amilia shuffled through her scrolls. "I should never have told you. I went. I looked. I saw nothing. I can't believe I even did that much. Maribor help me. The witch even had me out in the dark chasing her phantoms. What are you grinning at?"

"Nothing," Nimbus said. "I just have this impression of you slinking around the courtyard."

"Oh, stop it!"

"Stop what?" Saldur asked as he entered unannounced.

The regent swept into her office and looked at each of them with a disarming smile.

"Nothing, Your Grace, Nimbus was merely having a little joke."

"Nimbus? Nimbus?" Saldur repeated while eyeing the man, trying to recall something.

"He's my assistant, and Modina's tutor, a refugee from Vernes," Amilia explained.

Saldur looked annoyed. "I'm not an idiot, Amilia, I know who Nimbus is. I was thinking about the name. The word is from the old imperial tongue. *Nimbus*, unless I'm mistaken, means 'mist' or 'cloud,' isn't that right?" He looked at Nimbus for acknowledgment, but Nimbus merely shrugged apologetically. "Well, anyway," Saldur said, addressing Amilia. "I wanted to know how things were proceeding for the wedding. It's only a few months away."

"I was just sending these invitations to the scribes. I've ordered them by distance, so those living the farthest away should have couriers leaving as early as next week."

"Excellent, and the dress?"

"I finally got the design decided. We're just waiting for material to be delivered from Colnora."

"And how is Modina coming along?"

"Fine, fine," she lied, smiling as best she could.

"She took the news of her wedded bliss well, then?"

"Modina receives all news pretty much the same way."

Saldur nodded at her pleasantly. "Yes, true...true." He appeared so grandfatherly, so kind and gentle. It would be easy to trust him if she had not seen firsthand the volcano that lurked beneath that warm surface. He brought her back to reality when he asked, "What were you doing in the north tower last night, my dear?"

She bit her tongue just in time to stop herself from replying with total honesty. "I bumped into some guards delivering soup there in the middle of the night, which I thought odd, because..."

"Because what?" Saldur pressed.

"Because there's no one in the tower. Well, besides a seret, who appears to be standing guard over nothing. Do you know what that's all about?" she asked, pleased with how she had managed to reinforce her innocence by casually turning the tables on the old man. She even considered batting her eyes but did not want to push it. Memories of Saldur ordering the guard to take her out of his sight still rang in her head. She did not know what that order had really meant, but she remembered the regret in the guard's eyes as he had approached her.

"Of course I do. I'm regent—I know *everything* that goes on."

"The thing is...that was quite a lot of soup for one knight. And it vanished, pot and all, in just a few minutes. But since you already know, I suppose it doesn't matter."

Saldur studied her silently for a moment. His expression was no longer the familiar one of condescension. She detected a faint hint of respect forming beneath his wrinkled brows.

"I see," he replied at length. He glanced over his shoulder at Nimbus, who was smiling back, as innocent as a puppy. To her chagrin, Amilia noticed that he did bat his eyes. Saldur took no apparent notice of his antics, then reminded her not to seat the Duke and Lady of Rochelle next to the Prince of Alburn before withdrawing from her office.

"That was creepy," Nimbus mentioned after Saldur left. "You poke your head in the tower and the next morning Saldur knows about it?"

Amilia paced the length of her office, which allowed her only a few steps each way before she had to turn, but it was better than standing still. Nimbus was right. Something strange was going on with the tower, something that Saldur himself kept careful watch over. She struggled to think of alternatives, but her mind kept coming back to one name—Degan Gaunt.

CHAPTER 19

GALENTI

The corridor outside the great hall in the Palace of the Four Winds was deathly silent as the small band remained huddled in the niche. All of the *Emerald Storm's* party now held swords salvaged from slain Tenkins, each one made from Avryn steel. Warriors took strategic positions, armed with imperial-crafted crossbows, while the bulk of the Tenkin fighters moved back to allow them clear lines of sight. Clustered in a tight group, Hadrian's party made an easy target.

Erandabon stepped forward, but not so far as to block the path of the archers. "Erandabon did not recognize you, Galenti! Many years it has been, but you have not lost your skill," he said, looking down at the bodies of his fallen warriors. "Why travel with such creatures as these, Galenti? Why suffer the humiliation? It would be the same for Erandabon to slither on the forest floor with the snakes or wallow with the pigs. Why do you do this? Why?"

"I came to see you, Gile," Hadrian replied. Instantly there was a gasp in the hall.

"Ha-ha!" the warlord laughed. "You use my Calian name, a crime for which the punishment is death, but I pardon you,

Galenti! For you are not like these." He waved his hand, gesturing vaguely. "You are in the cosmos with Erandabon. You are a star in the heavens shining nearly as bright as Erandabon. You are a brother and I will not kill you. You must come and feast with me."

"And my friends?"

Erandabon's face soured. "They have no place at the table of Erandabon. They are dogs."

"I'll not eat with you if they are ill-treated."

Erandabon's eyes moved about wildly in random circles, then stopped. "Erandabon will have them locked up again— safely this time—for their own good. Then you will eat with Erandabon?"

"I will."

He clapped his hands and warriors tentatively moved forward.

Hadrian nodded, and Royce and the others laid down their weapons.

❧

The balcony looked out over the bay from a dizzying height. Moonlight revealed the vast fleet of Ghazel and Tenkin ships anchored in the harbor. Dotted with lights, the vessels bobbed on soft swells. Distant shouts rose with the cool breeze and arrived as faint whispers. Like the rest of the castle, the balcony was a relic of a forgotten time. While perhaps beautiful long ago, the stone railing had weathered over centuries to a dull, vague reminder of its previous glory. A lush covering of vines blanketed it with blooming white flowers the way a cloth might disguise a marred table. Beneath their feet, once-stunning mosaic tiles lay dirty, chipped, and broken. Several oil lanterns circled the balcony but appeared to be more for decoration than illumination. On a stone table lay a massive feast of wild animals, fruits, and drink.

"Sit! Sit and eat!" Erandabon told Hadrian as several Tenkin women and young boys hurried about, seeing to their every need. Aside from the servants, the two were alone. Erandabon tore a leg from a large roasted bird and gestured with it toward the bay. "A beautiful sight, eh, Galenti? Five hundred ships, fifty thousand soldiers, and all of them under Erandabon's command."

"There are not fifty thousand Tenkin in all of Calis," Hadrian replied. He looked at the food on the table dubiously, wondering if elf was somewhere on the menu. He selected a bit of sliced fruit.

"No," the warlord said regretfully. "Erandabon must make do with the Ghazel. They are like ants spilling out of their island holes. Erandabon cannot trust them any more than Erandabon can trust a tiger, even if Erandabon raised it from a cub. They are wild beasts, but Erandabon needs them to reach the goal."

"And what is that?"

"Drumindor," he said simply, and followed the word with a swallow of wine, much of which spilled unnoticed down the front of his chin. "Erandabon needs a shelter from the storm, Galenti, a strong place, a safe place. For many moons the ants fight for Drumindor. They know it can stand against the coming wind. Time is running out, the sand spills from the glass, and they are desperate to flee the islands. Erandabon promises he can help them get it. He could have fifty thousand, perhaps a hundred thousand ants, Galenti. They are everywhere in the islands, but Erandabon will make do with these. Too many ants spoil a picnic, eh, Galenti?" He laughed.

A servant refilled the wineglass Hadrian had barely touched.

"What do you know about Merrick Marius?" Hadrian asked.

Erandabon spat. "He is dirt. He is pig. He is pig in dirt. He promise weapons...there is none. He promise food for the Many...and there is none. He makes it hard for Erandabon to control the ants. Erandabon wish he was dead."

"I might be able to help you with that, if you tell me where he is."

The warlord laughed. "Oh, Galenti, you do not fool Erandabon. You would do this for you, not for Erandabon. But it matters not. Erandabon does not know where he is."

"Do you expect him to visit again?" Hadrian pressed.

"No, there be no need. Erandabon will not be here long. This place is old. This is not good place for storm." He rolled a fallen block of granite from the balcony. "Erandabon and his ants will go to the great fortress, where even the Old Ones cannot reach us. Erandabon will watch the return of the gods and the burning of the world. You could have a seat beside Erandabon. You could lead the ants."

Hadrian shook his head. "Drumindor will be destroyed. There will be no fortress for you and your ants. If you release me and my friends, we can stop this from happening."

Erandabon roared a great laugh. "Galenti, you make big joke. You think Erandabon is dumb like the ants? Why do you try to tell Erandabon such lies? You will say anything to leave here with your dog friends."

He finished off the leg by ripping the meat from the bone and chewed it with an open mouth, spitting out bits of gristle.

"Galenti, you offer Erandabon so much help. You must see how great Erandabon is and wish to please. Erandabon likes this. Erandabon knows of something you can do."

"What is that?"

"There is a Ghazel chieftain—Uzla Bar." He spat on the

ground. "He defies Erandabon. He challenge Erandabon for control of the ants. Now, with no food for the Many, he be big problem. Uzla Bar attacks caravans from Avryn, stealing the weapons and the Many's food. He do this to weaken Erandabon in the eyes of the ants. Uzla Bar challenge Erandabon to fight. But Erandabon is no fool. Erandabon knows none of his warriors can win against the speed and strength of the Ba Ran Ghazel. But then the stars shine on Erandabon and bring you here."

"You want me to fight him?"

"The challenge is by Ghazel tradition. Erandabon has seen you fight this way. Erandabon think you can win."

"Who will I be fighting with? You?"

He shook his head and laughed. "Erandabon does not dirty his hands so."

"Your warriors?"

"Why should Erandabon risk his warriors? Erandabon need them to control the ants. Erandabon saw those dogs with you. They fight good. When choice is death, all dogs fight. If you lead the dogs, they will fight well. Erandabon has seen you win in the arena with worse dogs. And if you lose— Erandabon is same as before."

"And why would I do this?"

"Did you not offer to help Erandabon twice already?" He paused. "Erandabon can see you like your dogs. But you and them kill many of Erandabon's men. For that you must die. But...if you do this...Erandabon will let you live. Do this, Galenti. The heavens would be less bright without all its stars."

Hadrian pretended to consider the proposal in silence. He waited so long that Erandabon became agitated. It was obvious the warlord had nearly as much riding on this fight as Hadrian did.

"You answer Erandabon now!"

Hadrian remained quiet for a few moments longer and then said, "If we win, I want our immediate release. You won't hold us until the full moon. I want a ship—a small, fast ship—fully provisioned and waiting the moment the battle is won."

"Erandabon agrees."

"I also want you to look into finding an elven girl who is called Allie. She may have been brought with the last shipment from Avryn. If she's alive, I want her brought here."

Erandabon looked doubtful but nodded.

"I want my companions freed, treated well, and all of our weapons and gear returned to us immediately."

"Erandabon will have the dogs you fought with brought here so you can eat with them when Erandabon is done. Erandabon also give other weapons you might need."

"What about the others? The men that did not fight with me in the hall."

"They no kill Erandabon's men, so they no die. Erandabon have deal with them. They stay until deal is done. Deal goes good, they be let go. Deal no good, they be food for the Many. Is good?"

"Yes. I agree."

"Excellent, Erandabon is very happy. Erandabon get to see Galenti fight in arena once more." Erandabon clapped twice and warriors appeared on the balcony, each reverently carrying one of Hadrian's three swords. More approached with the rest of their gear. Erandabon took Hadrian's spadone and lifted it.

"Erandabon has heard of Galenti's famous sword. It is weapon of the ancient style."

"It's a family heirloom."

He gave it to Hadrian. "This..." the warlord said, picking

up Royce's dagger, "Erandabon has never seen such a weapon. Does it belong to the small one? The one who fought next to you?"

"Yes." Hadrian saw the greed in Erandabon's eyes. "That's Alverstone. You don't want to think of keeping *that* weapon."

"You no fight if Erandabon keeps?"

"That too," Hadrian told him.

"That one is a *kaz*?"

"Yes, and as you saw, he's a good fighter. I need him and his weapon." Hadrian strapped his swords back on, feeling more like himself again.

"So, the Tiger of Mandalin will fight for Erandabon."

"It looks that way," Hadrian said, then sighed.

⚜

"So how does this work?" Royce asked, checking over his dagger.

The sun had risen on a gray day. The seven of them ate together on the balcony. The food—leftovers from the warlord—was now suitable for the dogs.

Hadrian said, "The battle will be five against five. I was thinking Wesley and Poe ought to be the ones to sit out. They're the youngest—"

"We will draw lots," Wesley declared firmly.

"Wesley, you've never fought the Ba Ran Ghazel before. They're extremely dangerous. They're stronger than men—faster too. To disarm them you literally have to, well, disarm them."

"We will draw lots," Wesley repeated, and finding a dead branch he snapped seven twigs—two shorter than the others.

"I have to fight. It's part of the deal," Hadrian said.

Wesley nodded and tossed one of the long twigs away.

"I'm fighting too," Royce told him.

"We need to do this fairly," Wesley protested.

"If Hadrian fights, so do I," Royce declared.

Hadrian nodded. "So it will be between you five."

Wesley hesitated, then threw aside another twig and held his fist out. Wyatt pulled the first stick, a long one. Poe drew next and got the first short twig. He showed no emotion and simply stepped back. Grady drew—a long one. Derning drew last, receiving the other short stick, leaving the last long twig in Wesley's fist.

"When do we fight?"

"At sunset," Hadrian replied. "Ghazel prefer to fight in the dark. That gives us the day to plan, practice a few things, and take a quick nap before facing them."

"I don't think I can sleep," Wesley told them.

"Best give it a try anyway."

"I've never even seen a Ghazel," Grady admitted. "What are we talking about here?"

"Well," Hadrian began, "they have deadly fangs, and if given the chance, they will hold you down and rip with their teeth and claws. The Ghazel have no qualms about eating you alive. In fact, they relish it."

"So they're animals?" Wyatt asked. "Like bears or something?"

"Not really. They're also intelligent and proficient with weapons." He let this sink in a moment before continuing. "They're usually short-looking, but that's misleading. They walk hunched over and can stand up to our height, or taller. They are strong and fast and can see well in the dark. The biggest problem—"

"There's a bigger problem?" Royce asked.

"Yeah, funny that, but you see, the Ghazel are clan fighters, so they're organized. A clan is a group of five made up of a chief, a warrior, an oberdaza, a finisher, and a range. The chief is usually not as good of a fighter as the warrior. And don't confuse a Ghazel oberdaza with a Tenkin. The Ghazel version wields real magic, dark magic, and he should be the first one we target to kill. They won't know we're aware of his importance, so that might give us an edge."

"Leave him to me," Royce announced.

"The finisher is the fastest of the group, and it'll be his job to kill us while the warriors and oberdaza keep us busy. The range will be armed with a trilon—the Ghazel version of a bow—and maybe throwing knives as well. He'll likely stay near the oberdaza. The trilon isn't terribly accurate, but it's fast. His job won't be so much to kill us as to distract. You'll want to keep your shield arm facing him."

"Will we have shields?" Grady asked.

"Good point." Hadrian looked over the weapons provided. "No, I don't see any. Well, look at it this way: that's one less thing to worry about, right? The clan is well organized and experienced. They will communicate through clicks and chattering that will be gibberish to us, but they can understand everything we say. We'll use that to our advantage."

"How do we win?" Wyatt asked.

"By killing all of them before they kill all of us."

꿎

They spent the morning hours sparring and practicing. Luckily, they were all adept with basic combat. Wesley had trained with his brother and as a result was a far better swordsman than Hadrian had expected. Grady was tough and surprisingly fast. Wyatt was the most impressive. His ability with a cutlass showed real skill, the kind Hadrian recognized instantly as something he called *killing experience*.

Hadrian demonstrated some basic moves to counter likely scenarios. Most dealt with parrying multiple attacks, like those from both mouths and claws, something none of them had any training in. He also showed them how to use the trilon Erandabon had provided, and each took his turn, with Grady showing the most promise.

Hungry after the morning's practice, they sat to eat once more.

"So, what's our battle plan?" Wyatt asked.

"Wesley and Grady will stay to the rear. Grady, you're on the trilon."

He looked nervous. "I'll do the best I can."

"That's fine. Just don't aim anywhere near the rest of us. Ignore the battle in the center of the arena and concentrate your arrows on the oberdaza and the range. Keep them off balance as much as possible. You don't have to hit them, just keep them ducking.

"Wesley, you protect Grady. Wyatt, you and I will form the front and engage the warrior and chief. Just remember to say what I told you and stay away from him. Questions?"

"What about Royce?" Wyatt asked.

"He knows what to do," Hadrian said, and Royce nodded. "Anything else?"

If there was anything, no one spoke up, so they all bedded down for a nap. After the workout even Wesley managed to fall asleep.

◈

The arena was a large oval open-air pit surrounded by a stone wall, behind which tiers of spectators rose. Two gates at opposite ends provided entrance to opposing teams. Giant braziers mounted on poles illuminated the area. The dirt killing field, like everything else at the Palace of the Four Winds, had suffered from neglect. Large blocks of stone had fallen and small trees grew around them. Near the center a shallow muddy pool formed. A partially hidden rib cage glimmered eerily in the firelight, and a skull hung from a pike that protruded from the earth.

As Hadrian walked out, his mind reeled with memories. The scent of blood and the cheering crowd opened a door he had thought locked forever. He had been only seventeen the first time he had entered an arena, yet his training had made victory a certainty. He had been the more knowledgeable, the more skilled, and the crowds loved him. He had defeated opponent after opponent with ease. Larger, stronger men had challenged him and died. When he had fought teams of two and three, the results were always the same. The crowds had begun to chant his new name, Galenti — *killer.*

He had traveled throughout Calis, meeting with royalty, eating at banquets held in his honor, and sleeping with women who had been given in tribute. He had entertained his hosts with displays of skill and prowess. Eventually the battles had become macabre. Multiple strong men had not been enough to defeat him. They had tested him against Ghazel and wild animals. He had fought boars, a pair of leopards, and finally the tiger.

He had killed scores of men in the arena without a thought, but the tiger in Mandalin had been his last arena fight. Perhaps the blood he had spilled had finally soaked in, or he had grown older and had matured beyond his desire for fame. Even now he was unsure what was the truth and what he merely wanted to believe. Regardless, everything changed when the tiger died.

Each man he had battled had chosen to fight, but not the cat. As he had watched the regal beast die, for the first time he had felt like a murderer. In the stands above, the crowd had shouted, *Galenti!* The meaning had never sunk in until that moment. His father's words had reached him at last, but Danbury would die before Hadrian could apologize. Like the tiger, his father had deserved better.

Now, as he entered the arena, the crowd once again shouted the name—*Galenti!* They cheered and stomped their feet like thunder. "Remember, Mr. Wesley, stay back and guard Grady," Hadrian said as they gathered not far from where the skull hung.

The far gate opened and into the arena came the Ba Ran Ghazel. Hadrian could tell from his friends' shocked expressions that even after his description, they had never expected what now came toward them. Everyone had heard tall tales of hideous goblins, but no one really expected to see one—much less five, scurrying in full battle regalia illuminated by the flickering red glow of giant torch fires.

They were not human, not animal, nor anything at all familiar. They did not appear to be of the same world. Movements defied eyesight, and muscles flexed unnaturally. They drifted across the ground on all fours. Rather than walk, they skittered, their claws clicking on the stones in the dirt. Their eyes flashed in the darkness, lit from within, a sickly yellow glow rising behind an oval pupil. Muscles rippled along hunched backs and arms as thick as a man's thigh. Their mouths were filled with row upon row of needle-sharp teeth that spilled out each side as if there was not enough room to contain them.

The warrior and the chief advanced to the center. They were large, and even hunched over, they still towered above Hadrian and Wyatt. Behind them the smaller oberdaza, decorated in dozens of multicolored feathers, danced and hummed.

"I thought they were supposed to be smaller," Wyatt whispered to Hadrian.

"Ignore it. They're puffing themselves up like frogs—trying to intimidate you—make you think you can't win."

"They're doing a good job."

"The warrior is on the left, and the chief is on the right," Hadrian told him. "Let me take the warrior. You have the chief. Try to stay on his left side, swing low, and don't get too close. He'll likely kill you if you do. And watch for arrows from the range."

From the walls a flaming arrow struck the center of the field, and the moment it did, drums began to beat.

"That's our cue," Hadrian said, and walked forward along with Royce and Wyatt.

The Ghazel chief and warrior waited for them in the center. Each held a short curved blade and a small round shield. They hissed at Hadrian and Wyatt as they approached. Wyatt had his cutlass drawn, but Hadrian purposely walked to meet them with his weapons sheathed. This brought a look from Wyatt.

"It's my way of puffing up."

Before they reached the center of the arena, Hadrian had lost track of Royce, who veered away into a shadow beyond the glow of bonfires.

"When do we start?" Wyatt asked.

"Listen for the sound of the horn."

This comment was overheard by the chief, causing him to smile. He chattered to the warrior, who chattered back.

"They can't understand us, right?" Wyatt recited his line.

"Of course not," Hadrian lied. "They're just dumb animals. Remember, we want to draw them forward so Royce can slip up behind the chief and kill him. He's the one we need to kill first. He's their leader. Without him, they will all fall apart. Just step back as you fight, and he will follow you right into the trap."

More chattering.

Two more flaming arrows whistled and struck the ground.

"Get ready," Hadrian whispered, then very slowly he drew both swords.

≈

A horn sounded from the stands.

Wesley watched as Hadrian and the warrior slammed into each other, metal clanging. Wyatt, however, shuffled back like a dancer, his cutlass held up and ready. The chief stood still, sniffing the air.

Grady let loose the first of his arrows. He aimed at the distant pile of dancing feathers but greatly overshot. "Damn," he cursed, working to fit another in the string.

"Lower your aim," Wesley snapped.

"I never said I was a marksman, did I?"

Something hissed, unseen, by Wesley's ear. Grady fired a second shot. It landed too short, coming close to where Wyatt feinted, trying to persuade the chief to follow him.

Hissing whistled by again.

"I think they are shooting their arrows at us," Wesley said, turning just in time to see Grady collapse with a black shaft buried in his chest. He hit the ground, coughing and kicking. His hands struggled to reach the arrow. His fingers went limp, and his hands flapped on the ends of his wrists. He flailed on the dirt, spitting blood, struggling to breathe. A third arrow hissed and struck Grady in his boot. His leg struggled to recoil, but his foot was pinned to the ground.

Wesley stared in horror as Grady shuddered, then fell still.

≪

Royce was already close to the oberdaza when the horn sounded. The clash of steel let him know the fight was on. He had slipped around one of the shattered stone blocks, trying to find a position behind the witch doctor, when the air felt wrong. It was no longer blowing, but bouncing—hitting something unseen. A quick glance at the field revealed only four Ghazel: the chief, the warrior, the oberdaza, and the range. Royce ducked just in time to avoid a slit throat. He spun, cutting air with Alverstone. Turning, he found himself alone. On instinct, he dodged right. Something cut through his cloak. He thrust back his elbow and was rewarded with a solid, meaty thump. Then it was gone again.

Royce spun completely around, but he could see nothing.

In the center of the arena, Hadrian battled with the warrior while Wyatt taunted the chief, who was still reluctant to engage. The range fired arrow after arrow. Beside him, the oberdaza danced and sang.

Intuition told Royce to move again, only he was too late. Thick, heavy arms gripped him as the weight of a body drove him forward. His feet slipped and he fell, pulled down to the bloodstained earth. He turned his blade and stabbed, but it passed through thin air. He could feel clawed hands trying to pin him. Royce twisted like a snake, depriving his attacker of a firm grip. He repeatedly cut at the shadowy thing, but nothing connected. Then he felt the hot breath of the Ghazel finisher.

≪

Hadrian's stroke glanced off the Ghazel's shield. He thrust with his other sword but found it blocked by an excellent parry. The warrior was good. Hadrian had not anticipated his skill. He was strong and fast, but more importantly, more frighteningly, the Ghazel anticipated Hadrian's moves perfectly. The warrior stabbed and Hadrian dodged back and to the left. The Ghazel bashed his face with his shield, having started his swing even before Hadrian turned. It was as if his opponent were reading his mind. Hadrian staggered backward, putting distance between them to catch his breath.

Above, the crowd booed their displeasure with Galenti. Beside him, Wyatt was still playing with the chief. His ruse had bought the helmsman time. The chief was too afraid of Royce to engage, but it would not last long. Hadrian needed to finish his opponent quickly, only now he was not even certain he could win.

The warrior advanced and swung. Hadrian spun to the left. Once more the Ghazel anticipated his move and cut Hadrian across the arm. He staggered back and dodged behind a large fallen block, keeping it between him and his opponent.

The crowd booed and stomped their feet.

Something was very wrong. The warrior should not be this good. His form was bad, his strokes lacking expertise, yet he was beating him. The warrior attacked again. Hadrian took a step back and his foot caught on a rock and he stumbled. Once more the Ghazel appeared to foresee this and was ready with a kick that sent Hadrian into the dirt.

He lay flat on his back. The warrior screamed a cry of victory and raised his sword for a downward penetrating kill. Hadrian started to twist left to dodge the thrust, but at the last minute, while still concentrating his thoughts on turning left, he pulled back to center. The stroke of the warrior pierced the turf exactly where Hadrian would have been.

ᪿ

Grady was dead and the arrows were still coming.

Wesley was shaken. He had already failed in his duty. Not knowing what else to do, he picked up the trilon, fitted an arrow, and let it loose. Wesley was no archer. The arrow did not even fly straight, but spun wildly, falling flat on the ground not more than five yards ahead of him.

In the center of the field, Hadrian was avoiding his opponent and the chief had finally decided to engage Wyatt. Royce was in the distance, on the ground, wrestling with something invisible not far from where the oberdaza danced and chanted.

This was not going as planned. Grady was dead and Hadrian...Wesley saw the warrior raise his sword for the killing blow.

"No!" Wesley shouted. Just then, the sharp exploding pain from an arrow pierced his right shoulder, and he fell to his knees.

The world spun. His eyes blurred. He gasped for air and gritted his teeth as darkness threatened at the edges of his eyesight. In his ears, a deafening silence grew, swallowing the sounds of the crowd.

The oberdaza! The memory of Hadrian's instructions surfaced. *The Ghazel version wields real magic, dark magic, and he should be the first one we target to kill.*

Wesley clutched the hilt of his sword, fighting back, willing himself not to pass out. He ordered his legs to lift him. Shaking, wobbling, they slowly obeyed. His heart calmed, and his breathing grew deeper. The world came into focus once more and the roar of the crowd returned.

Wesley looked across the field at the witch doctor. He glanced at the trilon and knew he could never use it. He tried to raise the sword, but his right arm did not move. He shifted the pommel to the left. It felt awkward and clumsy, but it had strength. Listening to the sound of his heart pounding, he walked forward, slowly at first, but faster with each step. Another arrow hissed. He ignored it and began to jog. His feet pounded the moist, muddy ground. Wesley held his sword high like a banner. His hat flew off, his hair flowing in the breeze.

Another arrow landed just a step ahead of him and he snapped it as he ran. He felt a strange painful pulling and realized the wind was blowing against the feathers of the arrow that still protruded from his shoulder. He focused on the dancing witch doctor.

Out of the corner of his eye he saw the range put down his bow and run at him, drawing a blade. He was too late. Only a few more strides. The oberdaza danced and sang with his eyes closed. He could not see Wesley's charge.

Wesley never checked his pace. He never bothered to slow down. He merely lowered the point of his blade as if it were a lance and put on a last burst of speed—jousting like his famous brother—jousting on foot. Already the darkness was creeping in, tunneling his vision once more. His strength was running out, flowing away with his blood.

Wesley plowed into the oberdaza. The two collided with a loud *thrump!* They skidded together, then rolled apart. Wesley's sword was gone from his hands. The arrow in his shoulder had snapped. The taste of blood was in his mouth as he lay facedown, struggling to push himself up. A hot pain burst across his back, but it faded quickly as darkness swallowed him.

⚜

Royce twisted but could not break free of the claws that cut into his flesh, struggling to break his grip on Alverstone. He could not grab the shadow. Its body felt loose and slippery, as if it existed only where it wanted. Royce would get a partial grip and then it would dissolve.

Teeth grazed him as the Ghazel snapped, trying to rip his throat out. Each time, Royce knew to move. On the third attempt, he gambled and butted forward with his own head. There was a *thunk* and pain, but he was able to break free.

He looked around and once more the finisher was invisible.

Royce caught a glimpse of Wesley running across the field with his sword out in front of him, then dodged another attack. He avoided the blow but fell to the ground. Weight hit him once more. This time the claws got a better grip. Rear claws scraped along Royce's legs, pinning him, stretching him out, holding him helpless. He felt the hot breath again.

There was a noise of impact not far away and a burst of feathers.

Suddenly Royce saw yellow eyes, bright glowing orbs, inches away from his own. Fangs drenched with spit drooled on him.

"*Ad haz urba!*" the creature said, gibbering.

Alverstone was still in Royce's hand. He just needed a little movement from his wrist. He spat in the Ghazel's eye and twisted. Like cutting through ripe fruit, the blade severed the hand of the Ghazel at the wrist. With a howl, the finisher lost support and fell forward. Royce rolled him over, using two hands to restrain his remaining claw, pinning the Ghazel with his knees. The finisher continued to snap, snarl, and rake. Royce severed the goblin's other hand, and the beast shrieked in pain until Royce removed its head.

❧

The Ghazel warrior staggered suddenly, though Hadrian had not touched him. Trying to keep his distance, Hadrian was a good two sword lengths away, but the warrior clearly rocked as if struck. The Ghazel paused, confidence faded from his eyes, and he hesitated.

Hadrian looked over his shoulder to the hill and spotted Grady's body, but Wesley was gone. He looked over his opponent's shoulder and found Wesley on the ground. At his side, the oberdaza lay with the midshipman's cutlass buried in his chest. As Hadrian watched, the range stabbed Wesley in the back.

"Wesley! No!" he shouted.

Then Hadrian's eyes locked sharply on the warrior before him. "I only wish you could read my thoughts now," he said, sheathing both swords.

Confusion crossed the warrior's face until he saw Hadrian draw forth the large spadone from his back. Seizing the chance, the warrior swung. Hadrian blocked the stroke, which made the spadone sing. He followed this with a false swing, which the Ghazel nevertheless moved to dodge, setting himself off balance. Hadrian continued to spin, carrying the stroke round in a full circle. He leveled the blade at waist height. There was nowhere for the Ghazel to go, and the great sword cut the warrior in half.

Wyatt was fighting the chief now, their swords ringing like an alarm bell as they repeatedly clashed. Blow after blow drove Wyatt farther and farther backward until Hadrian thrust the spadone through the chief's shoulder blades.

With a roar like a violent wind, the crowd jumped to its feet, cheering and applauding.

Turning, Hadrian saw Royce kneeling beside Wesley's prone body. The range lay beside him. Hadrian ran to them as Wyatt checked on Grady.

Royce shook his head in silent reply to Hadrian's look.

"Grady is dead too," Wyatt reported when he reached them.

Neither said a word.

The gates opened and Erandabon entered with a bright smile. Poe and Derning followed him. Derning stared at Grady's body. Erandabon lifted his arms to the stands like a conquering hero as the crowd cheered even louder. He approached them, exuberant and delighted.

"Excellent! Excellent! Erandabon is very pleased!"

Hadrian strode forward. "Get us to that ship now. Give me time to think, and I swear I'll introduce you to Uberlin myself!"

Chapter 20

The Tower

Modina watched as Arista sat within the chalk circle on the floor of her bedroom, burning the hair. Together they watched the smoke drift.

"What's that awful smell?" Amilia said, entering and waving a hand in front of her face while Nimbus trailed behind her.

"Arista was performing a spell to locate Gaunt," Modina explained.

"She's doing magic—in here?" Amilia looked aghast, then added, "Did it work?"

"Sort of," Arista said with a decidedly disappointed tone. "He's somewhere directly northeast of here, but I can't pinpoint the exact location. That's always been the problem."

Amilia stiffened, her eyes glancing at Nimbus accusingly.

"I didn't say a word," he told her.

Amilia asked Arista, "If you find Degan Gaunt, what are you planning to do?"

"Help him escape."

"He's the general of an army poised to attack us." She turned to Modina. "I don't see why you're helping her—"

"I'm not trying to return him to his army," Arista cut in. "I need him to help me find something—something only the Heir of Novron can locate."

"So you…and Gaunt…will leave?"

"Yes," Arista told her.

"And what if you are caught? Will you betray the empress by revealing the aid she has provided you?"

"No, of course not. I would never do anything to harm her."

"Why are you asking this, Amilia?" Modina looked from her to Nimbus and back again. "What do you know?"

Amilia hesitated for only a moment, then spoke. "There is a Seret Knight standing guard in the north tower."

"I'm not familiar with your palace. Is that unusual?" Arista asked.

"There's nothing to guard there," Amilia explained. "It's a prison tower, but none of the cells hold prisoners. Yet last night I watched two fourth-floor guards deliver a pot of soup there."

"To the guard?"

"No," Amilia said, "they delivered the soup to the tower. Less than five minutes later, I arrived. The soup was gone, pot and all."

Arista stood. "They were feeding a prisoner, but you say there are no occupied cells in the tower? Are you sure?"

"Positive. Every door was open, and every cell vacant. It looked to have been that way for some time."

"I need to get in that tower," Arista declared. "I could burn a hair in one of the empty cells. If he's nearby, that could really tell us something."

"There is no way you are getting in that tower," Amilia told her. "You'd have to walk right past the knight. While the chief imperial secretary to the empress might get away with such a thing, I highly doubt the fugitive Witch of Melengar will."

"I bet Saldur could walk in and out of there without question, couldn't he?"

"Of course, but you aren't him."

Arista smiled.

She turned to the tutor. "Nimbus, I have a letter for Hilfred and another for my brother. I wrote them in the event something happened to me. I want to give them to you now, just in case. Don't deliver them unless you know I'm not coming back."

"Of course." He bowed.

Amilia rolled her eyes.

Arista handed the letters to Nimbus and, for no particular reason, gave him a kiss on the cheek.

"Just make certain when you are caught that you don't drag Modina into it," Amilia said, leaving with Nimbus.

"What are you planning to do?" Modina asked.

"Something I've never tried before, something I'm not even certain I can do. Modina, I don't know what will happen. I might do some strange things. Please ignore them and don't interfere, okay?"

Modina nodded.

Arista knelt and spread her gown out around her. She took a deep breath, closed her eyes, and tilted her head back. She took another deep breath, then sat still. She did not move for a long time. She sat breathing very slowly, very rhythmically. Her hands opened. Her arms lifted, as if floating on their own— pulled by invisible strings or rising on currents of air. She began to sway gently from side to side, her hair flowing back and forth. Soon she began to hum. The humming took on a melody, and the melody produced words Modina did not understand.

Then Arista began to glow. The light grew brighter with each word. Her dress turned pure white, her skin luminous. It soon hurt Modina's eyes to look at her, so she turned away.

The light went out.

"Did it work?" Modina asked. She turned back to face Arista and gasped.

෴

When Arista opened the door, the guard stared at her, stunned. "Your Grace! I didn't see you come in."

"You should be more watchful, then," Arista said, frightened by the sound of her own voice—so familiar and yet so different.

The guard bowed. "Yes, Your Grace. I will. Thank you, Your Grace."

Arista hurried down the stairs, self-conscious and fearful as she clutched three strands of hair in her left hand and a chunk of chalk in her right. She felt exposed, walking openly in the hallways after hiding for so long. She did not feel any different. Only by looking at her hands and clothing could she see evidence that the spell had worked. She was wearing imperial robes and her hands were those of an old man, with thick gaudy rings. Each servant or guard she passed nodded respectfully, saying softly, "Good afternoon, Your Grace."

Growing up with Saldur practically as her uncle had one advantage—she knew every line of his face, his mannerisms, and his voice. She was certain she could not perform a similar illusion with Modina, Amilia, or Nimbus, even if she had them in front of her for reference. This took more—she *knew* Saldur.

By the time she reached the first floor of the palace, she was gaining confidence. Only two concerns remained. What if she ran into the real Saldur, and how long would the spell last? Stumbling through what had to be an advanced magical technique, she had worked solely by intuition. She had known what she wanted and had a general idea how to go about it, but the result had been more serendipity than skill. So much of magic was guesswork and nuance. She was starting to understand that now and could not help being pleased with herself.

Unlike what she had managed in the past, this was completely new, something she had not even known was possible. Casting an enchantment on herself was a frightening prospect. What if there were rules against such things? What if the source of the Art forbade it and imposed harm on those who tried? She never would have attempted it under different circumstances, but she was desperate. Still, having done so, and succeeded, she felt thrilled. She had invented it. Perhaps no wizard had ever managed such a thing!

"Your Grace!" Edith Mon was caught by surprise, coming around a corner where they nearly collided. She carried a stack of sheets in her arms and nearly lost them. "Forgive me, Your Grace! I—I—"

"Think nothing of it, my dear." The *my dear* at the end of the sentence came out unconsciously—it just felt right. Hearing it sent a chill through her, which proved it was pitch-perfect. This might be fun if not for the mortal fear.

A thought popped into her head. "I've heard reports that you've been treating your staff poorly."

"Your Grace?" Edith asked, looking nervous. "I—I don't know what you mean."

Arista leaned toward her with a smile that she knew from experience would appear all the more frightening for its friendly, disarming quality. "You aren't going to lie to my face, are you, Edith?"

"Ah—no, sir."

"I don't like it, Edith. I don't like it at all. It breeds discontent. If you don't stop, I'll need to find a means of correcting your behavior. Do you understand me?"

Edith's eyes were wide. She nodded as if her head were hinged too tight.

"I'll be watching you. I'll be watching *very* closely."

With that, Arista left Edith standing frozen in the middle of the corridor, clutching her bundle of sheets.

The guards at the front entrance bowed and opened the doors for her. Stepping outside, her senses were alert for any sign of trouble. She could smell the bread in the ovens of the bakehouse. To her left, a boy chopped wood, and ahead of her, two lads shoveled out the stable, placing manure in a cart, no doubt for use in the garden. The afternoon air was cold and the manure steamed. She could see her breath puffing in steamy clouds as she marched between the brick chicken coop and the remnants of the garden.

She reached the north tower, opened the door, and entered. A Seret Knight with a deadly-looking sword strapped to his belt stood at attention. He said nothing and she did the same while looking about.

The tower was cylindrical, with arched windows that allowed light to stream in and gleam off the polished stone floor. A tall arched frame formed the entrance to the spiral stair. Across from it, a small fireplace provided heat for the guard. Covered in cobwebs, a wooden bench stood beside a small empty four-legged table. The only unusual thing was the stone of the walls. The rough-hewn rock of the upper portion of the tower was lighter in color than the more neatly laid, darker stone beneath.

The knight appeared uncomfortable at her silence.

"Is everything all right here?" Arista asked, going for the most neutral thing she could think of.

"Yes, Your Grace!" he replied enthusiastically.

"Very good," she said, and casually shuffled to the stairs and began to climb. She glanced behind her to see if the guard would follow, but he remained where he was without even looking in her direction.

She went up one flight and stopped at the first open cell. Just as Amilia had reported, it appeared to have been long abandoned. She checked to make certain the cell door would not lock, and then carefully closed it. She got on her knees, quickly drawing the circle and the runes.

She placed the blond hairs on the floor, lining them up in rows. Picking up several pieces of straw, she twisted them tightly into a rope stalk. She repeated the phrase she had used for weeks and instantly the top of the straw caught fire, becoming a tiny torch. She recited the location spell and touched the flame to one of the hairs. It heated up like a red coil and turned to ash. Arista looked for the smoke, but there was none. She glanced around the room, confused. She looked at the smoke coming off the straw. It drifted straight up. There was no wind, no draft of any kind in the cell.

She tried again with the second hair, this time putting out the straw, thinking its smoke might be interfering. Instead, she cast the burn spell directly on the hair, followed by the location incantation. The hair turned to ash without a trace of the familiar light gray smoke.

Was something about the tower blocking her spell? Could it be like the prison where they had kept Esrahaddon? The Old Empire had placed complicated runes on the walls, blocking the use of magic. She looked around. The walls were bare.

No, she thought, *I wouldn't be able to cast the burn spell if that were the case. For that matter, my Saldur guise would have failed the moment I entered.*

Looking down, she saw that there was only one hair left. She considered moving to a different room, and then the answer dawned on her. Reciting the spell once more, she picked up the last hair, held it between her fingers, and lit it.

There it is!

The smoke was pure white now and spilled straight down between her fingers like a trickle of water. It continued to fall until it met the floor, where it immediately disappeared.

She stood in the cell, trying to figure out what it meant. According to the smoke, Gaunt was very close and directly below her, but there was nothing down there. She considered that perhaps there might be a door in the fireplace, but concluded the opening was too small. There simply was nothing else below her except—the guard!

Arista gasped.

She checked her hands, reassured to see the wrinkled skin and ugly rings, and went back down the stairs to the base of the tower. The guard remained standing statue-like with his helm covering every trace of his features.

"Remove your helm," she ordered.

The knight hesitated only briefly, then complied.

She knew exactly what Degan Gaunt looked like from his image in Avempartha. The moment he removed his helm, her hopes disappeared. This was not the man she had seen in the elven tower.

She forgot herself for a moment and sighed in a most unSaldur-like way.

"Is there something wrong, Your Grace?"

"Ah—no, no," she replied quickly, and started to leave.

"I assure you, sir, I told her nothing of the prisoner. I refused to speak a single word."

Arista halted. She pivoted abruptly, causing her robes to sweep around her majestically. The dramatic motion had a visible impact on the guard and she finally understood why Saldur always did that.

"Are you certain?"

"Yes!" he declared, but doubt crossed his face. "Did she say differently? If she did, she's lying."

Arista said nothing but merely continued to stare at him. This was not an intentional act. She was simply trying to determine what to say next. She was not sure how to form her statement to get the knight to talk without being obvious. As she stood there, formulating her next words, the knight broke under her stare.

"Okay, I did threaten to unsheathe my sword, but I didn't. I was very careful about that. I only pulled it partway out. The tip never cleared the sheath, I swear. I just wanted to scare her off. She did not see anything. Watch." The knight pulled his sword and gestured toward the floor. "See? Nothing."

Arista's eye immediately focused on the large emerald in the pommel, and she bit her tongue to restrain herself. It all made sense. There was only one thing still to learn. To inquire was a gamble, but a good one, she thought. Arista asked, "Did Gaunt like his soup?"

She held her breath as she waited for his answer.

"He ate it, but none of them ever like it."

"Very good," she said, and left.

When Arista returned, Modina did not speak a word. After admitting her, the empress stood watching cautiously. Arista started to laugh, then rushed forward and gave her an unexpected hug. "We've found him!"

CHAPTER 21

DRUMINDOR

Led by a fast-walking Tenkin warrior, the few remaining members of the *Emerald Storm's* crew made their way down from the Palace of the Four Winds through a series of damp caves to the base of the blackened cliffs where the surf attacked the rock. In a tiny cove, a little sloop waited for them. Smaller and narrower than the Dacca vessel, the ship sported two decks but only a single mast. Wyatt rapidly looked the ship over, declaring it sound, and Poe checked for provisions, finding it fully stocked for a monthlong trip.

They quickly climbed aboard. Poe and Hadrian cast off while Wyatt grabbed the wheel. Derning and Royce ran up the mast and loosed the headsail, which billowed out handsomely. The power of the wind just off the point was so strong that the little sloop lurched forward, knocking Poe off his feet. He got up and wandered to the bow.

"Look at them. They're everywhere," he said, motioning at the hundreds of black sails filling the harbor like a hive of bees.

"Let's just hope they let us through," Derning said.

"We'll get through," Hadrian told them. He was seated on a barrel, holding Wesley's hat, turning it over and over.

Hadrian had refused to leave Wesley and Grady in Eranda-bon's hands. Their bodies had been brought aboard for a proper burial at sea. He kept Wesley's hat. He was not sure why.

"He was a good man," Royce said.

"Yes, he was."

"They both were," Derning added.

The tiny sloop was a bit hard to manage with just the five of them, but it would be ideal once they picked up Banner and Greig in Dagastan. It was a fast ship, and they were confident they could reach Tur Del Fur in time. The armada of Tenkin and Ghazel ships looked to be still gathering.

"Jacob, trim the foresail. I'm bringing her over two points," Wyatt snapped as he gripped the slick ship's wheel. "And everyone jump lively. We're in the Ba Ran Archipelago and this is no place for slow-witted sailors."

The moment they cleared the cove they understood Wyatt's warning. Here the sea was a torrent of wave-crashed cliffs and splintered islands of jagged rock. Towering crags rose from dense fog, and blind reefs of murderous coral lay in ambush. Currents coursed without reason, rogue waves crashed without warning, and everywhere the dark water teemed with sweeping triangles of black canvas—each emblazoned with white slashes that looked vaguely like a skull. The Ghazel ships spotted them the moment they cleared the point. Five abruptly changed course and swooped in.

The black ships of the Ba Ran Ghazel made the Dacca look like incompetent ferrymen as they channeled through the surf and flew across the waves.

"Run up the damn colors!" Wyatt shouted, but Royce was already hauling the black banner with white markings that stretched out long and thin.

There was a brief moment of tension as Hadrian watched

the approaching sails. He started to curse himself for trusting Erandabon Gile. But after the colors were hoisted, the sails peeled away like a shiver of sharks, swinging around to resume their earlier paths.

Wyatt cranked the wheel until they were headed for Dagastan, and ordered Royce to the top of the masthead to watch for reefs. No one spoke after that except for Royce, who shouted out obstacles, and Wyatt, who barked orders. It took only a few hours for them to clear the last of the jagged little islands, leaving both the archipelago and the black sails behind. The little sloop rolled easily as it entered the open waters of the Ghazel Sea.

The crew relaxed. Wyatt set a steady course. He leaned back against the rail, caught the sea spray in his hand, and wiped his face as he looked out at the ocean. Hadrian sat beside him, head bowed while he turned Wesley's hat over in his hands.

Erandabon had sent a messenger to Hadrian as they had left the arena. The search for Allie had produced no results. All previous shipments had been delivered to the Ghazel weeks earlier. He knew females, especially young ones, were considered a rare delicacy. She was dead, likely eaten alive by a high-ranking goblin who would have savored the feast by keeping the girl conscious as long as possible. For Ghazel, screams were a garnish.

Hadrian sighed. "Wyatt...I've something to tell you... Allie..."

Wyatt waited.

"As part of the deal, I made Gile investigate the whereabouts of your daughter. The results weren't good. Allie is dead."

Wyatt turned to gaze once more at the ocean. "You—you made that part of the deal? Asking about my daughter?"

"Yeah, Gile was a little put out, but—"

"What if he had said no?"

"I wasn't going to accept that answer."

"But he could have killed all of us."

Hadrian nodded. "She's your daughter. If I thought she was alive, trust me, Royce and I would be on it, even if that meant heading back into the Ba Ran Islands, but...well. I'm really sorry. I wish I could have done more." He looked down at the hat in his hands. "I wish I could have done a lot more."

Wyatt nodded.

"We can still save Tur Del Fur," Hadrian told him. "And we wouldn't have that chance without you. If we succeed, she won't have died in vain."

Wyatt turned to look at Hadrian. He opened his mouth, then stopped and looked away again.

"I know," Hadrian said, once more fidgeting with Wesley's hat. "I know."

~

Greig and Banner were pleased to see them. Nights living on the little Dacca ship were getting cold, and provisions were dangerously low. They had already resorted to selling nets and sails to buy food in town. They made a hasty sale of the Dacca ship, since the Tenkin vessel was far faster and already loaded.

Wyatt aimed the bow homeward, catching the strong autumn trade winds. The closer they came to home, the colder it got. The southern currents that helped warm Calis did not reach Delgos, and soon the wind turned biting. A brief rainstorm left a thin coat of ice on the sheets and deck rails.

Wyatt continued at the helm, refusing to sleep until he was near collapse. Hadrian concluded that, failing to find Allie,

Wyatt placed his absolution in saving Delgos instead. In a way, he was certain that they all did. Many good people had died along the trip, and they each felt the need to make those sacrifices mean something. Even Royce, suffering once more from seasickness, managed to climb to the top of the mainsail, where he replaced the Ghazel banner with Mr. Wesley's hat.

They explained to Greig and Banner the events of the previous weeks, as well as Merrick's plan and the need to reach Drumindor before the full moon. Each night they watched the moon rise larger on the face of the sea, indifferent to their race against time. Fortune and the wind were with them. Wyatt captured every breath, granting them excellent speed. Royce spotted red sails off the port aft twice, but they remained on the horizon and each time vanished quietly in their wake.

Shorthanded, and with Royce seasick, Hadrian volunteered for mast work. Derning spent the days teaching him the ropes. He would never be very good at it. He was too big, yet he managed to grasp the basics. After a few days he was able to handle most of the maneuvers without instruction. At night, Poe cooked while Hadrian sat practicing knots and watching the stars.

Instead of hugging the coast up to Wesbaden, they took a risk and sailed due west off the tip of Calis directly across Dagastan Bay. The gamble almost proved to be a disaster, as they ran into a terrible storm producing mountainous waves. Wyatt expertly guided the little sloop, riding the raging swells with half canvas set, never leaving the wheel. Seeing the helmsman's rain-lashed face exposed in a flash of lightning, Hadrian seriously began to wonder if Wyatt had gone mad. By morning, the sky had cleared and they could all see Wesley's hat still blowing in the wind.

The gamble paid off. Two days ahead of the harvest moon they rounded the Horn of Delgos and entered Terlando Bay.

❦

As they approached the harbor, the Port Authority stopped them. They did not care for the style of the ship or the black sails—Wesley's hat notwithstanding. As the ship was held directly under the terrifying smoking spouts of Drumindor, dock officers boarded and searched the vessel thoroughly before allowing them to pass below the bridge between the twin stone towers. Even then they were given an escort to berth fifty-eight, slip twenty-two of the West Harbor. Being familiar with the city and the Port Authority, Wyatt volunteered to notify the officials of the impending invasion and warn them to search for signs of sabotage.

"I'm off, mates," Derning announced as soon as they had the ship berthed. The topman had a small bundle over his shoulder.

"What about the ship and the stores?" Greig asked. "We're going to sell it—you'll get a share."

"Keep it—I've business to attend to."

"But what if we can't get..." Greig gave up as Derning trotted away into the narrow streets. "That seemed a bit abrupt—man's in a hurry to go somewhere."

"Or just glad to be back in civilization," Banner mentioned.

Tur Del Fur welcomed sailors like no other port. Brightly painted buildings with exuberant decorations welcomed them to a city filled with music and mirth. Most of the shops and taverns butted up against the docks, where loud signs fought for attention: THE DRUNKEN SAILOR — JOIN THE CREW! FRESH BEEF & POULTRY! PIPES, BRITCHES, & HATS! LADIES OF THE BAY (WE WRING THE SALT OUT!)

For recently paid sailors who might have been at sea for two or more years, they screamed *paradise*. The only oddity remained the size and shapes of the buildings. Whimsical western decorations could not completely hide the underlying history of this once-dwarven city. Above every door and threshold was the sign WATCH YOUR HEAD.

Seagulls cried above them as they crisscrossed a brilliant blue sky. Water lapped the sides of ships, which creaked and moaned like living beasts stretching after a long run.

Hadrian stepped onto the dock alongside Royce. "Feels like you're gonna fall over, doesn't it?"

"To answer your question from before...No, I don't think we should be sailors. I'd be happy never to see a ship again."

"At least you don't have to worry about land sickness."

"Still feels like the ground is pitching beneath me."

The five of them bought fresh-cooked fish from dock vendors and ate on the pier. They listened to the shanty tunes spilling out of the taverns and smelled the pungent fishy reek of the harbor. By the time Wyatt returned to the ship, he was red-faced angry.

"They're going through with the venting! They refused to listen to anything I said," he shouted, trotting up the quay.

"What about the invasion?" Hadrian asked. "Didn't you tell them about that?"

"They didn't believe me! Even Livet Glim, the port controller—and we were once mates! I shared a bunk with him for two years and the bloody bastard refuses to, as he puts it, 'Turn the entire port on its ear because one person thinks there might be an attack.' He says they haven't heard anything from any other ships, and they won't do a thing unless the armada is confirmed by other captains."

"It will be too late by then."

"I tried to tell them that, but they went on about how they *had* to regulate the pressure on the full moon. I went to every official in the city, but no one would listen. After a while, I think they became suspicious that *I* was up to something. I stopped when they threatened to lock me up. I'm sorry."

"Maybe if we all went?"

Wyatt shook his head. "It won't do any good. Can you believe this? After all we've been through, we get here and it won't change a single thing. Unless…" He looked directly at Hadrian.

"Unless what?" Poe asked.

Hadrian sighed and looked at Royce, who nodded.

"What am I missing?" Poe asked.

"Drumindor was built by dwarves thousands of years ago," Hadrian explained. "Those huge towers are packed with stone gears and hundreds of switches and levers. The Tur Del Fur Port Authority only knows what a handful of them actually do. They know how to vent the pressure and blow the spouts, and that's about it."

"We know how to shut it off," Royce said.

"Shut it off?" Poe asked. "How do you shut off a volcano?"

"Not the volcano—the system," Hadrian went on. "There's a master switch that locks the whole gearing system. Once dropped, the fortress doesn't build pressure anymore. The volcano just vents itself. It won't be able to stop the invasion, but it won't explode either."

"How does that help?"

"If nothing else, it'll prevent the instant destruction of this city. When the black sails appear, people might have time to evacuate, maybe even put up a defense. Once the system is shut down, Royce and I can crawl through the portals to find out what Merrick did. If we can get it fixed in time, we can raise the master switch and barbecue an armada of very surprised goblins."

"Can we help?" Banner asked.

"Not this time," Hadrian told him. "Can you four handle this ship alone?"

Wyatt nodded. "It will be tough with no topmen, but we'll work something out."

"Good, then you get out of here before the fleet comes in. You were a good assistant, Poe. Stick with Wyatt and you'll be a captain one day. This one we have to do alone."

❧

Legend held that dwarves had existed centuries before man walked the face of the world. Back in an age when they and the elves had fought for supremacy of Elan, dwarves had a powerful and honorable nation governed by their own kings with their own laws and traditions. That had been a golden age of great feats, wondrous achievements, and marvelous heroes. Then the elves won the war.

The strength of the dwarves had been shattered forever, and the emergence of men had destroyed what remained. Although dwarves had never been enslaved like the remnants of the elves, men distrusted and shunned the sons of Drome. Fearful of a unified dwarven kingdom, humans had forced the dwarves out of their homeland of Delgos into a shadowy existence of nomadic persecution. Despite the dwarves' skills in crafts, humans scattered them whenever they gathered in groups too large for comfort. For their own survival, dwarves had learned to hide. Those who could, adopted human ways and attempted to fit in. Their culture had been obliterated by centuries of careful erasure, little survived of their former glory except what stone could tell. Few dwarves, and even fewer humans, possessed the imagination to recall a day when dwarves had ruled half the world—unless, like Royce and Hadrian, they were staring up at Drumindor.

The light of the setting sun bathed the granite rock, making it shine like silver. Sheer walls towered hundreds of feet, rising out of the bedrock of the burning mountain's back. The twin towers stood joined by the thin line of what appeared from that distance to be a wafer-thin bridge. The tops of the towers smoldered quietly, leaking plumes of dark smoke out of every vent, creating a thin gray cloud that hovered overhead. Up close, the scope and mammoth size were breathtaking.

They had one night and the following day to accomplish the same magic trick they had performed many years earlier. By the time they purchased the necessary supplies it was dark. They slipped through the city of Tur Del Fur and hiked up into the countryside, following goat paths into the foothills that eventually led to the base of the great fortress itself.

"Is this where it was?" Royce asked, stopping and studying the base of the tower.

"How should I know?" Hadrian replied as his eyes coursed up the length of the south tower. Up close, it blocked everything else out, a solid wall of black rising against the light of the moon. "I can never understand why such small people build such gigantic things."

"Maybe they're compensating," Royce said, dropping several lengths of rope.

"Damn it, Royce. It's been eight years since we did this. I was in better shape then. I was younger, and if I recall, I vowed I would never do it again."

"That's why you shouldn't make vows. The moment you do, fate starts conspiring to shove them down your throat."

Hadrian sighed, staring upward. "That's one tall tower."

"And if the dwarves were still here maintaining it, it would be impregnable. Lucky for us, they've let it rot. You should be happy—the last eight years would only have eroded it further. It should be easier."

"It's granite, Royce. Granite doesn't erode much in eight years."

Royce said nothing as he continued to lay out coils of rope, checking the knots in the harnesses and slipping on his hand-claws.

"Do you recall that I nearly fell last time?" Hadrian asked.

"So don't step there this time."

"Do you remember what the nice lady in the jungle village told you? One light will go out?"

"We either climb this or let the place blow. We let the place blow and Merrick wins. Merrick wins, he gets away and you never find Degan Gaunt."

"I never thought you cared all that much if I ever found Gaunt." Hadrian looked up at the tower again. "At least not *that* much."

"Honestly? I don't care at all. This whole quest of yours is stupid. So you find Gaunt—then what? You follow him around being his bodyguard for the rest of your life? What if he's like Ballentyne? Wouldn't that be fun? Granted it'll be exciting, as I'm sure anyone with a sword will want to kill him, but who cares? There's no reward, no point to it. You feel guilt—I kinda get that. You ran out on your father and you can't say you're sorry anymore. So for that, you'll spend your life following this guy around being his butler? You're better than that."

"I think there was a compliment in there somewhere—so thanks. But if you're not doing this to help me find Gaunt, why are you?"

Royce paused. From a bag he drew out Wesley's hat. He must have fetched it down before they left the ship. "He stuck his neck out for me three times. The last one got him killed. There's no way this fortress is blowing up."

~

Even in the dark, Royce found handholds and spots to place his feet that Hadrian could never have spotted in the full light of day. Like a spider, he scaled the side of the tower, until he came to the base of the first niche. There he set his first anchor and dropped a rope to Hadrian. By the time Hadrian reached the foothold of that niche, Royce was already nailing in the next pin and sending down another coil. They continued this way, finding minute edges where several thousand years of erosion revealed the maker's seams in the rock. Centuries-old crevices and cracks allowed Royce to climb what had once been slick, smooth stone.

Two hours later, the trees below appeared like tiny bushes, and the cold, wintry winds buffeted them like barn swallows. They were only a third of the way up.

"It's time," Royce shouted over the howl of the wind. He anchored a pin, tied a rope to it, and climbed back down.

Hadrian groaned. "I hate this part!"

"Sorry, buddy, nothing I can do about it. The niches are all over that way." Royce gestured across to where the vertical grooves cut into the rock on the far side of a deep crevasse.

Royce tied the rope to his harness and linked himself to Hadrian.

"Now, just watch me," Royce told him, and taking hold of the rope, he sprinted across the stone face. Reaching the edge of the crevasse, he leapt, swinging out like a clock's pendulum. He cleared the gap by what looked like only a few inches. On the far side, he clung to the stone, dangling like a bug on a twig. He slowly pulled himself up and drove another pin. Then, after tying off the rope, he waved to Hadrian.

If Hadrian missed the jump, he would slip into the crevasse, where he would end up dangling helplessly, assuming the rope held him. The force of the fall could easily pop out the holding pin or even snap the rope. He took a deep breath of cold air, steadied himself, and began to run. On the far side, Royce leaned out for him. He reached the edge and jumped. The wind whistled past his face, blurring his vision as tears streaked across his cheeks. He struck the far side just short of the landing, bashing his head hard enough to see stars. He tasted blood and wondered if he had lost his front teeth even as his fingertips lost their tenuous hold and he began to fall. Royce tried to grab him, but was too late. Hadrian fell.

He dropped about three inches.

Hadrian dangled from the rope Royce had anchored the moment his partner landed. Hadrian groaned in pain while wiping blood from his face.

"See?" Royce shouted in his ear. "That went *much* better than last time!"

They continued scaling upward, working within the relative shelter of the vertical three-sided chimneys. They were too high now for Hadrian to see anything except the tiny lights of the port city. Everything else below was darkness. They rested for a time in the semi-sheltered niche and then climbed upward again.

Higher and higher, Royce led the way. Hadrian's hands were sore from gripping the rope and burned from the few times he had slipped. His legs, exhausted and weak, quivered dangerously. The wind was brutal. Gusting in an eddy caused by the chimney they followed, it pushed outward like an invisible hand trying to knock them off. The sun came up and

Hadrian was nearing the end of his endurance when they finally reached the bridge. They were slightly more than two-thirds of the way, but thankfully they did not need to reach the top.

What appeared from the ground to be a thin bridge was actually forty feet thick. They scrambled over the edge, hauled up their ropes, ducked into a sheltered archway, and sat in the shadows, catching their breath.

"I'd like to see Derning scale *that*," Royce said, looking down.

"I don't think anyone but you could manage it," Hadrian replied. "Nor is there anyone crazy enough to try."

Dozens of men guarded the great gates at the base of the tower, but no one was on the bridge. It was thought to be impossible for intruders to enter from the top, and the cold wind kept the workers inside. Royce gave the tall slender stone doors a push.

"Locked?" Hadrian asked.

Royce nodded. "Let's hope they haven't changed the combination."

Hadrian chuckled. "Took you eighteen hours last time, right after you told me, 'This will only take a minute.'"

"Remind me again why I brought you?" Royce asked, fanning his hands out across the embossed face of the doors. "Ah, here it is."

Royce placed his fingers carefully and pushed. A hundred tons of solid stone glided inward as if on a cushion of air, rotating open without a sound. Inside, an enormous cathedral ceiling vaulted hundreds of feet above them. Shafts of morning sunshine entered through distant skylights built into the dome overhead, revealing a complex world of bridges, balconies, archways, and a labyrinth of gears. Some gears lay flat, while others stood upright. Some were as small as a copper coin, and then there were those that were several stories tall and thicker than a house. A few rotated constantly, driven by steam created from the volcanically superheated seawater. The majority of the gears, particularly the big ones, remained motionless, waiting. Aside from the mechanisms, nothing else moved. The only sounds were the regular ratcheting rhythm and the whirl of the great machine.

Royce scanned the interior. "Nobody home," he said at length.

"Wasn't last time either. I'm surprised they haven't tightened security up more."

"Oh yeah, a single break-in after centuries is something to schedule your guards around."

"They'll be kicking themselves tomorrow."

They found the stairs—short, shallow steps built for little feet. Royce and Hadrian took them two and three at a time. Ducking under low archways, Hadrian nearly had to crawl through the entrance to the Big Room. This was the name Hadrian had given it the last time they had visited. The room itself was huge, but the name came from the master gear. It stood on edge and what they could see was as high as a castle tower, but most of its bulk sunk beneath the floor and through a wall, leaving only a quarter of the gear visible. Its edge was ringed with thick teeth like a castle battlement, only larger—much larger. It meshed with two other gears, which connected to a dozen more that joined the dwarven puzzle.

"The lock was at the top, right?" Royce asked.

"Think so—yeah, Gravis was up there when we found him."

"Okay, I'll handle this. Keep an eye out."

Royce leapt up to one of the smaller gears and walked up the teeth like they were a staircase. He jumped from one to the next until he reached the master gear. Harder to climb since the teeth were huge, but for Royce it was no problem. He was soon out of sight, and a few minutes later a loud stone-upon-stone sound echoed as a giant post of rock descended from the ceiling, settling in the valley between two teeth, locking the great gear.

When Royce returned, he was grinning happily.

"I'd love to see the look on Merrick's face when this place doesn't blow. Even if the Ghazel take the city, he'll be scratching his head for months. There's no way he can know about this master switch. Gravis only knew because it was his ancestor that designed the place."

"And we only know because we caught him in the act." Hadrian thought a moment. "Do you think Merrick might be nearby, waiting for the fireworks?"

Royce sighed. "Of course not. If it were me, I wouldn't be within a hundred miles of this explosion. I don't even want to be here now. Don't worry, I know him. The fact that this mountain doesn't explode will drive him nuts. All we have to do is drop the right hints to the wrong people and we won't have to look for him—he'll find us. Now come on. Let's see if we can find what's blocking the vents so we can put this back in place and cook some goblins."

CHAPTER 22

GOING HOME

Archibald Ballentyne stared out the window of the great hall. It looked cold. Brown grass, blowing dead leaves, clouds that looked heavy and full of snow, and geese that flew away before a veil of gray all reminded him the seasons had changed. Wintertide was less than two months away. He kicked the stone of the wall with his boot. It made a muffled thud and sent a pain up his leg, making him wince.

Why do I have to think of that? Why do I always have to think of that?

Behind him, Saldur, Ethelred, and Biddings debated something, but he was not listening. He did not care anymore. Maybe he should leave. Maybe he should take a small retinue and just go home to Chadwick and the sanctity of his Gray Tower. The palace would be a wreck by now, and he could busy himself with repairing the damage the servants had caused in his absence. Bruce had likely been dipping into his brandy store and the tax collectors would be behind in their duties. It would feel nice to be home for the holiday. He could invite a few friends and his sister over for— He stopped and considered kicking the wall again, but it had hurt enough last time.

Sleeping in a tent this time of year would be miserable.

Besides, what would the regents say? Moreover, what would they do in his absence? They treated him badly enough when he was here. How much worse would they conspire against him if he left?

He did not really want to be home. Ballentyne Castle could be a lonely place, all the more horrid in winter. He used to dream of how all that would change when he married, when he had a beautiful wife and children. He used to fantasize about Alenda Lanaklin. She was a pretty thing. He also often imagined taking the hand of King Armand's daughter, Princess Beatrice. She was certainly appealing. He had even spent many a summer evening watching the milkmaids in the field and contemplating the possibility of snatching one from her lowly existence to be the new Lady Ballentyne. How grateful she would be, how dutiful, how easily controlled. That had been before he had come to Aquesta—before he had met her.

Even sleep gave him no solace, as he dreamed about Modina now. He danced with her on their own wedding day. He despised waking up. Archibald did not even care about the title anymore. He would give up the idea of being emperor if he could have her. He even considered that he would give up being earl—but she was marrying *Ethelred*!

He refused to look at the regent. The fool cared nothing for her. How could he be so cold as to force a girl to marry him just for the political benefit? The man was a blackguard.

"Archie...Archie!" Ethelred was calling him.

He cringed at the mention of the name he hated and turned from the window with a scowl.

"Archie, you need to talk to your man Breckton."

"What's wrong with him now?"

"He's refusing to take my orders. He insists he serves only you. You need to set him straight on the lay of things. We can't have knights whose allegiance is strictly to their lords.

They have to recognize the supremacy of the New Empire and the chain of command."

"Seems to me that's what he's doing, observing the chain of command."

"Yes, yes, but it's more than that. He's becoming obstinate. I'm going to be the emperor in a couple of months and I can't have my best general requiring that I get your permission to give him an order."

"I'll speak with him," Archibald said miserably, mostly just so he could stop listening to Ethelred's voice. If the old bastard were not such an accomplished soldier, he would seriously consider challenging him, but Ethelred had fought in dozens of battles, while Archibald had engaged only in practice duels with blunt-tipped swords. Even if he wanted to commit suicide, he certainly would not give Ethelred the satisfaction.

"What about Modina?" Ethelred asked.

The mention of her name brought Archibald's attention back to the conversation.

"Will she be ready?"

"Yes, I think so," Saldur replied. "Amilia has been doing wonders with her."

"Amilia?" Ethelred tapped his forehead. "Isn't she the maid you promoted to Chief Imperial Secretary?"

"Yes," Saldur said, "and I've been thinking that after the wedding, I want to keep her on."

"We'll have no use for her *after* the wedding."

"I know, but I think I could use her elsewhere. She's proven herself to be both intelligent and resourceful."

"Do whatever you like with her. I certainly don't—"

"Queens always have need of secretaries, even when they have husbands," Archibald interrupted. "I understand you're going to assume total control of the New Empire, but she'll still need an assistant."

Ethelred looked at Saldur with a puzzled expression. "He doesn't know?"

"Know what?" Archibald asked.

Saldur shook his head. "I felt the fewer that knew, the better."

"After the wedding," Ethelred told Archibald, "once I'm crowned emperor, I'm afraid Modina will have an unfortunate accident—a fatal accident."

∽⑤

"It's all arranged," Nimbus reported. Arista paced the room and Modina sat alone on the bed. "I got the uniform to him, and tonight the farmer will smuggle Hilfred into the gate just before sunset in the hay cart."

"Will they check that?" Arista asked, pausing in her journey across the room.

"Not anymore, not since they called off the witch hunt. Things are business as usual again. They know the farmer. He's in and out every third day of the week."

Arista nodded and resumed her pacing.

"The same wagon will cart you all out at dawn. You'll go out through the city gates. There will be three horses waiting at the crossroads for you with food, water, blankets, and extra clothing."

"Thank you, Nimbus." Arista hugged the beanpole of a man, bringing a blush to his cheeks.

"Are you sure this will work?" Modina asked.

"I don't see why not," Arista said. "I'll do just what I did last time. I'll become Saldur, and Hilfred will be a fourth-floor guard. You're sure you took the right uniform?"

Nimbus nodded.

"I'll order the guard to open the entrance to the prison.

We'll grab Gaunt and leave. I'll instruct the seret to remain on duty and tell no one. Believing I'm Saldur, no one will know he's gone for hours, maybe even days."

"I still don't understand." Modina looked puzzled. "Amilia said there was a prison in the tower, but all the cells were empty."

"There is a secret door in the floor. A very cleverly hidden door, sealed with a gemlock."

"What's a gemlock?"

"A precious stone cut to produce a specific vibration that when held near the door trips the lock open. I used a magical variation on my tower door back home, and the church used a far more sophisticated version to seal the main entrance to Gutaria Prison. They're using the same thing here, and the key is the emerald in the pommel of the sword the Seret Knight wears."

"So, you'll make your escape tonight?" the empress asked.

Arista nodded. The empress looked down, a sadness creeping into her eyes. "What's wrong?" Arista asked.

"Nothing. I'm just going to miss you."

≪

Arista's stomach twisted as she looked out the window and watched the sun set.

Am I being foolish?

Her plan had always been to merely locate Gaunt, not break him out. Now that she knew exactly where he was, she could return home and have Alric send Royce and Hadrian to rescue him. Only that had been before—before she had found Hilfred, before she had been reunited with Thrace, and before she had known she could impersonate Saldur. It seemed like such an easy thing to do that leaving without Gaunt would be an unnecessary risk. The smoke verified that he still lived, but could she be sure that would be the case several weeks from then?

She was alone with Modina. They had not said a word to each other for hours. Something was troubling the empress—something more than usual. Modina was stubborn, and no force could move her once she decided on a course. Apparently the course she had decided on was not to talk.

The gate opened and the hay cart entered.

Arista watched intently. Nothing seemed amiss—no guards, no shouting, just a thick pile of hay and a slow-walking donkey pulling it. The farmer, an elderly man, parked the cart by the stables, unhitched his donkey, hitched it to a new cart, and led the animal out again. Staring at the cart, she could not help herself. The plan had been to wait until just before dawn, but she could not leave Hilfred lying there. She managed to restrain herself only until she saw the harvest moon begin to rise, and then she stood.

"It's time," she said.

Modina lifted her head.

Arista walked to the middle of the room and knelt.

"Arista, I…" Modina began hesitantly.

"What is it?"

"Nothing… Good luck."

Arista got up and crossed the room to hug her tightly. "Good luck to you too."

The empress shook her head. "You keep all of it—I'm not going to be needing any."

❧

Disguised as Regent Saldur, Arista traveled down the stairs, wondering what Modina had almost said. The excitement of the night, however, kept her thoughts jumping from one thing to the next. She discovered that she could remain in her disguise for a long time. It broke when she slept, but it would last beyond what she would need that night. This gave her greater confidence. Although she was still concerned about bumping into the real Saldur, the thought of seeing Hilfred again was overwhelming.

Her heart leapt at just the thought of traveling home to Melengar with Hilfred once more at her side. It had been a long and tiring road, and she wanted to be home. She wanted to see Alric and Julian and to sleep in her own bed. She vowed she would treat Melissa better and planned to give her maid a new dress for Wintertide. Arista was occupied with a long list of Wintertide presents for everyone when she stepped outside. The broad face of the harvest moon illuminated the inner ward, allowing her to see as clearly as if it were a cloudy day. The courtyard was empty as she crept to the wagon.

"Hilfred!" she whispered. There was no response, no movement in the hay. "Hilfred." She shook the wagon. "It's me, Arista."

She waited.

Her heart skipped a beat when the hay moved. "Princess?" it said hesitantly.

"Yes, it's me. Just follow." She led him into the stables and to the last stall, which was vacant. "We need to wait here until it's nearly dawn."

Hilfred stared at her dubiously, keeping a distance.

"How...?" he began, but faltered.

"I thought Nimbus explained I would appear like this."

"He did."

Hilfred's eyes traveled up and down her figure, a look on his face as if he had just tasted something awful.

"The rumors are true," she admitted, "at least the ones about me using magic."

"I've known that, but your hair, your face, your voice." He shook his head. "It's perfect. How do I know you're not the real Saldur?"

Arista closed her eyes, and in an instant Saldur disappeared and the Princess of Melengar returned.

Hilfred stumbled backward until he hit the rear of the stall, his eyes wide and his mouth open.

"It *is* me," she assured him. Arista took a step forward and watched him flinch. It hurt her to see this, more than she would have expected. "You need to trust me," she told him.

"How can I? How can I be certain it's really you, when you trade skins so easily?"

"Ask me a question that will satisfy you."

Hilfred hesitated.

"Ask me, Hilfred."

"I've been with you daily since I was a very young man. Give me the names of the first three women I fell in love with and the name of the one I lost because of the scars on my face."

She smiled and felt herself blush. "Arista, Arista, Arista, and no one."

He smiled. She did not wait for him. She knew he would never presume to take such a step on his own. She threw her arms around his neck and kissed him. She could feel the sudden shock in the tightening of his muscles, but he did not pull away. His body relaxed slowly and his arms surrounded her. He squeezed so that her cheek pressed against his, her chin resting on his shoulder.

"Maribor help me if you really are Saldur," Hilfred whispered in her ear.

She laughed softly and wondered if it was the first time she had done so since Emery died.

CHAPTER 23

THE HARVEST MOON

Royce and Hadrian began investigating the spouts, giant tunnels bored out of the rock through which molten lava would blast on its way to the sea. There were dozens, each one aiming in a different direction, their access to the mountain's core sealed off by gear-controlled portals. They climbed the interior until they reached the opening and the sky.

The sun was up and the sight below forced Hadrian's stomach into his mouth. They were well above the bridge level. The world looked very small and very far away. Tur Del Fur was a small cluster of petite buildings crouched in the elbow of a little cove. Beyond it rose mountains that looked like little hills. Directly below, the sea appeared like a puddle with tiny flashes of white. It took Hadrian a moment to realize they were the crests of waves. What he thought might be insects were gulls circling far below.

None of the spouts were blocked, none of the portals tampered with.

"Maybe it's in the other tower?" Hadrian asked after they had climbed out of the last tunnel.

Royce shook his head. "Even if that one is blocked, the pressure will vent here. Both have to be closed. It's not the spouts or the portals. It's something else—something we've overlooked—something that can seal all the exits at once to make the mountain boil over. There has to be another master switch, one that locks all the portals closed."

"How are we going to find that? Do you see how many gears are in here? And it could be any one. We should have brought Magnus."

"Sure, with him it would be easy to find—in a year or two. Look at this place!" Royce gestured at the breadth of the tower, where the sun's light pierced through skylights, spraying the tangled riddle of a million stone gears. Some spun, some whirled, some barely moved, and everywhere were levers. Like arrows peppering a battlefield, stone arms protruded. Just as the gears came in various sizes, so did the levers—some tiny and others the size of tree trunks. "It's a wonder they ever learned how to vent the core."

"Exactly," Hadrian said. "No one knows what most of this stuff does anymore. The Port Authority leaves it alone for fear they might destroy the world or something, right? So whatever Merrick did, it's a sure bet the folks in charge here don't know anything about it. It's got to be a lever that hasn't been moved in centuries, maybe even thousands of years. It might show signs of recent movement, right?"

"Maybe."

"So we just need to find it."

Royce stared at him.

"What?"

"We only have a few hours left, and you're talking about finding a displaced grain of sand on a beach."

"I know, and when you come up with something better, we'll try it. Until then, let's keep looking."

Hours passed and still they found nothing. Adding to the

dilemma was the interior of Drumindor itself, which was a maze of corridors, archways, and bridges. Often they could see where they wanted to go but could not determine how to get there. Luck remained on their side, however, as they saw precious few people. They spotted only a handful of workers and even fewer guards. All of them were easily avoided. The sunshine passing through the skylights shone with the brilliance of midday, then diminished as evening arrived, and they still had not achieved their goal.

Finally, they headed for the bottom of the tower.

Going there was their last resort, as the Drumindor defensive garrison fortified the first three floors. Approximately forty soldiers guarded the base, and they had a reputation for their harsh treatment of intruders. Still, whatever Merrick had done, he had most likely done it to the mechanism that controlled the lava's release. Descending yet another winding staircase, they paused in a sheltered alcove just outside a large chamber. Peering in, they saw it was similar to an interior courtyard, or a theater, with four gallery balconies ringing it stacked one upon another.

"There." Royce pointed to an opening in the room below, which radiated a yellow glow. "It has to be in there."

They crept down the stairs to the bottom. Elaborate square-cut designs of inlaid bronze and quartz lined the tiled floor. It picked up the glow coming from the open doorway on the far side. The air warmed dramatically as it blew in their faces, heavy with the smell of sulfur.

"This has to be it," Royce whispered.

They looked up at the stacked galleries of arched openings circling the walls above them, and slowly, carefully stepped forward together, crossing the shimmering tile, heading for the glowing doorway.

"Halt!" The command echoed through the chamber the moment they reached the center of the room. "Lie facedown, arms and legs spread."

They hesitated.

Twenty archers appeared, moving out from behind the pillars of the galleries with stretched bows aimed down on Royce and Hadrian from three sides. Pikemen entered the hall in an orderly march, boot heels clicking on the tile. They spread out, forming two lines. A dozen more armored men issued down the side corridor from the second-story gallery and proceeded in two-by-two formation to the bottom of the stairs, fanning out to block any retreat back the way they had come.

"Now, lie on your bellies, or we'll cut you down where you stand."

"We're not here to cause trouble. We're here—" Hadrian's words were cut short as an arrow hissed through the air and glinted off the stone less than a foot from them.

"Now!" the voice shouted.

They lay down.

The moment they did, troops from in front and behind entered, pinning them and stripping them of their weapons.

"You have to listen to us. There's an invasion coming—"

"We've heard all about your phantom armada, Mr. Blackwater, and you can give up that charade."

"It's real! They will be here tonight, and if you don't fix the tower, all of Delgos will be taken!"

"Bind them!"

They brought forth chains, tongs, and a brazier. Smiths arrived and went to work hammering manacles onto their wrists and legs.

"Listen to me!" Hadrian shouted. "At least check the pressure-release controls, see if something is wrong."

There was no reply except the smiths' hammers pounding the manacles closed.

"What's the harm in checking?" Hadrian went on. "If I'm wrong, what does it matter? If I'm right and you don't even look, you're sealing the fate of the Delgos Republic. Just humor me. If nothing else, it'll shut me up."

"Slitting your throat will do that too," the voice said. "But I'll send a worker if you two come quietly without resistance."

Hadrian was not certain what kind of resistance he expected them to give as the smith finished attaching another chain to his legs, but he nodded anyway.

The voice gave the order and the guards pulled them to their feet. Navigating stairs with hobbled legs was difficult. Hadrian nearly fell more than once, but soon they reached the main gate at the bottom of the fortress.

The gigantic doors of stone soundlessly swept open. Outside, the late-afternoon sun revealed a contingent of port soldiers waiting. The commander of the fortress guard stepped forward and spoke quietly with the Port Authority captain for some time.

"You don't think these guys are always waiting out here, do you?" Hadrian whispered to Royce. "We've been set up, haven't we?"

"It didn't tip you off when they called you by name?"

"Merrick?"

"Who else?"

"That's a bit far-fetched. How could he possibly expect us to be here? We didn't even know we would be here. He can't be that smart."

"He is."

A runner appeared, trotting up from the bottom of the tower, and reported to the commander with a sharp salute.

"Well?" the fortress commander asked.

The runner shook his head. "There is no problem with the pressure-release control — everything checked out fine."

"Take them away," the commander ordered.

ᖰ

The Tur Del Fur City Prison and Workhouse sat back, hidden on a hillside away from the dock, the shops, and the trades. It appeared as little more than a large stone box at the end of Avan Boulevard, with few windows and a spiked iron fence. Hadrian and Royce both knew it by reputation. Most offenders typically died within the first week due to execution, suicide, or brutality. The magistrate's role was merely to determine the manner of execution. Parole was not an option. Only those known to be serious threats went there. Petty thieves, drunks, and malcontents went to the more popular and lenient Portside Jail. For those in Tur Del Fur Prison, this was the end of the road, literally as well as figuratively.

Royce and Hadrian hung by their wrists with their ankles chained to the wall of cell number three, where they had spent the past few hours. The room was smaller than those in Calis. There was no window, stool, nor pot — not even straw. The room was little more than a small stone closet with a single metal door. The only light came from the gap between the door and its frame.

"You're awfully quiet," Hadrian said to the darkness.

"I'm trying to figure this out," Royce replied.

"Figure it out?" Hadrian laughed even though his arms and wrists burned like fire from the metal cutting into his skin. "We're hanging chained to a wall, awaiting execution, Royce. There's not that much to it."

"Not *that*. I want to know why we didn't find anything wrong with the spouts."

"Because there's a million levers and switches in there and we were looking for just one?"

"I don't think so. When we got to the bridge, what was it you said? You said you didn't think anyone could scale that fortress except me. I think you're right. I know Merrick couldn't. He's a genius, not an elf. I always outdid him when it came to anything physical."

"So?"

"So a thought has been nagging me since they brought us here. How could Merrick get into Drumindor to sabotage it?"

"He figured another way in."

"We spent weeks trying to do that, remember?"

"Maybe he bribed someone on the inside, or maybe he paid someone to break in."

"Who?" Royce thought a minute. "This is too important to trust to someone who *might* be able to do it—he would need someone he *knew* could do it."

"But how do you know someone can do something until they've actually—" Hadrian stopped himself as the realization hit. "Oh, that's not good."

"Throughout this whole thing we've been following two letters, both written by Merrick. The first we thought was intercepted and delivered to Alric, but what if it was *intentionally* sent to him? Everyone knows we work for Melengar."

"Which led us to the *Emerald Storm*," Hadrian said.

"Right. Where we got the next letter—the one to be delivered to that crazy Tenkin in the jungle, and it just happened to mention that Drumindor was set to blow."

"I'm not liking where this is heading," Hadrian muttered.

"And what if Merrick knew about the master gear?"

"That's impossible. Gravis is dead. Crushed, as I recall, under one of those big gears."

"Yes. *He* is dead, but Lord Byron isn't. He probably boasted about how he saved Drumindor by hiring two no-account thieves."

"It still seems too perfect." Hadrian tried to convince himself. "In retrospect, sure, it sounds like the pieces fall into place, but there are too many things that could have gone wrong along the way."

"Right. That's why he had someone on board the *Storm* making sure it all worked—Derning. Did you see the way he took off the moment we hit port? He knew what was coming and wanted to get away."

"I should have let you kill him."

Silence.

"You're nodding, aren't you?"

"I didn't say a word."

"Bastard," Hadrian grumbled.

"You know the worst thing?"

"I've got a pretty long list of *bad* things right now, and I'm not sure which one I would put on top. So I'll bite."

"We did exactly what Merrick *couldn't* do himself. He used us to disarm Drumindor."

"So he never sabotaged anything? That would explain why Gile laughed when I told him Drumindor was going to explode. He knew it wasn't. Merrick promised he would have it intact. Merrick's a bloody genius."

"I think I mentioned that once or twice."

"So now what?" Hadrian asked.

"Now nothing. He's beaten us. He's sitting somewhere with a warm cup of cider, smiling smugly with his feet up on the pile of money he's just been paid."

"We have to warn them to reengage the master gear."

"Go ahead."

Hadrian shouted until the little observation door opened, flooding the cell with light.

"We need to speak to someone. It's important."

"What is it?"

"We realized the mistake we made. We were tricked. You need to tell the commander at Drumindor that we locked the master gear. We can show him where it is and how to release it."

"You two never stop, do you? I'm not sure if you're really saboteurs or just plain nuts. One thing's for certain: we're going to find out how you got in, and then we're going to kill you."

The observation door closed, casting them back into darkness.

"That worked out really well," Royce said. "Feel better now?"

"Bastard."

CHAPTER 24

THE ESCAPE

Arista stayed in the corner of the stable, wrapped in Hilfred's arms most of the night. He stroked her hair and, from time to time, without any particular reason, kissed her passionately. It felt safe, and lying there, Arista realized two things. First, she was certain she could be content remaining in his arms forever. And second, she was not in love with Hilfred.

He was a good friend, a piece of home she missed so dearly that she drank him in with a desert-born thirst, but something was missing. She thought it strange that she had come to this conclusion while in his arms. Yet she knew it with perfect clarity. She did not love Hilfred and she had not loved Emery. She was not even certain what love was, what it should feel like, or if it existed at all.

Noblewomen rarely knew the men they married before their wedding day. Perhaps they grew to love their husbands in time, or merely grew to believe they did. At least she knew Hilfred loved her. He loved enough for both of them. She could feel it radiating off him like warmth from smoldering coals. He deserved happiness after waiting so long, after so much sacrifice, and she would make it up to him. Arista would return to Melengar and marry him. Alric would make him Archduke Reuben Hilfred. She laughed softly at the thought.

"What?"

"I just remembered your first name is Reuben."

Hilfred laughed, then pointed to his face. "I look like this, and you're making fun of my *name*?"

She took his face in her hands. "I wish you wouldn't do that. I think you're beautiful."

He kissed her again.

Periodically, Hilfred would peek out at the sky and check the position of the moon. Eventually he returned and said, "It's time."

She nodded, and once more Arista transformed into the morose visage of Regent Saldur.

"I still can't believe it," Hilfred told her.

"I know. I'm really starting to get the hang of this. Care to kiss me again?" she teased, and laughed at his expression. "Now remember, don't do anything. The idea is to just walk in and walk out. No fighting, understand?"

Hilfred nodded.

They stepped out of the stable. As they did, Arista looked up at Modina's window. Although it was dark, she was certain she saw her figure sitting framed within it. Once again she recalled Modina's final words, and regretted not asking her to come. Maybe she would have refused, but now it was too late. Arista wished she had at least asked.

Nipper came out of the kitchens, yawning and carrying two empty water buckets. He stopped short, surprised to see them.

She ignored him and headed directly to the tower.

Just as before, the Seret Knight stood at attention in the center of the room, his face hidden, his shoulders back, the jeweled sword at his side.

"I'm going to see Degan Gaunt. Open up."

The guard drew his sword.

There was a brief moment of terror when Arista's heart pounded so loudly she thought the seret might hear. She glanced at Hilfred and saw him flinch, his hand approaching his own weapon. Then the knight bent on one knee and lightly tapped the stone floor with the pommel. The stones immediately slid away, revealing a stair curving into the darkness.

"Shall I come with you, Your Grace?"

Arista considered this. She had no idea what was down there. It could be one cell or a maze of corridors. It might take her a long time to discover where Gaunt was. Just outside, she heard Nipper filling his buckets. The castle was already waking up.

"Yes, of course. Lead the way."

"As you wish, Your Grace." The knight pulled a torch from the wall and descended the steps.

It was dark inside. The stair was narrow and oppressive. Ahead, she could hear the sounds of faint weeping. The same heavy stones that made up the base of the tower formed the dungeon. Here, however, decorations adorned the walls. Nothing recognizable, merely abstract designs carved everywhere. Arista felt she had seen them before—not these exactly, but similar ones.

Then she felt it.

Like the snap of a twig or the crack of an egg, a tremor passed through her body—a sudden disconcerting break.

She looked down. The old man's hands were gone and she was seeing her own fingers and sleeves revealed in the flickering torchlight.

With his back turned, the knight continued to escort them. As he reached the bottom of the stairs, he began to turn, saying, "Your Grace, I—"

Before he was fully around, Hilfred shoved her aside.

He drew his sword just as the knight's eyes widened. As he drove his blade at the man's chest, the black armor turned the tip. It skipped off, penetrating the gap between the chest plate and the right pauldron, piercing the man's shoulder.

The knight cried out.

Hilfred withdrew his sword. The knight staggered backward, struggling to draw his own. Hilfred swung at the knight's neck. Blood exploded, spraying both of them. The seret made no further noise as he crumpled and fell.

"What happened?" Hilfred asked, picking up the torch.

"The walls," she said, touching the chiseled symbols. "They have runes on them like in Gutaria Prison. I can't do magic in here. Do you think anyone heard that?"

"I'm sure the kid fetching water did," he said. "Will he do anything?"

"I don't know. We should close the door," Arista said, picking up the sword with the emerald and looking up the long staircase at the patch of light at the top. What they had covered so casually minutes earlier now appeared so far — so dangerous. "I'll do it. You find Gaunt."

"No. I won't leave your side. There could be more guards. Forget the door. We'll find him together and get out of here." He took her left hand and pulled her along. Her right hand held on to the sword.

The hallways were narrow stone corridors without any light except what came from the torch they held. The ceiling arched to a peak not more than a foot above Arista's head, forcing Hilfred to stoop. Wooden doors, so short they looked more like livestock gates, began appearing on either side.

"Gaunt!" Hilfred yelled.

"Degan Gaunt!" Arista shouted.

They ran down the darkened passageways, pounding on

doors, calling his name, and peering inside. The hallway ended at a T-intersection. With only one torch, they had no option to split up, even if Hilfred could be convinced. They turned right and pressed on, finding more doors.

"Degan Gaunt!"

"Stop!" Arista stopped suddenly.

"Wha—"

"Shush!"

Very faintly—"Here!"

They trotted down the next corridor but reached a dead end.

"This place is a maze," Arista said.

They ran back and took another turn. They called again.

"Here! I'm here!" came the reply, louder now.

Running once more, they again met a solid wall. They retraced their steps, found another corridor that appeared to go in the right direction, and followed it as far as the hallway allowed.

"Degan!" she cried.

"Over here!" called a voice from the last door in the block.

When they reached it, Arista bent down and held up the torch. In the tiny grated window, she saw a pair of eyes. She grabbed the door handle and pulled—locked. She tried the gemstone but nothing happened.

"Damn it!" she cried. "The guard, he must have the key. Oh, how could I be so stupid? I should have searched him before we ran off."

Hilfred hammered the wooden door with his sword. The hard oak, nearly as solid as stone, gave up only sliver-size chips.

"We'll never get the door open this way. Your sword isn't doing anything! We have to go back for the keys."

Hilfred continued to strike the door.

"We'll be back, Degan!" Arista said before starting back down the hall, carrying the torch.

"Arista!" Hilfred shouted as he chased after her.

They rounded the corridors, turning left, then right, and then—

"Arista?" Saldur said, stunned, as they nearly ran into the regent. Around him were five Seret Knights with swords drawn and torches held high.

Hilfred pushed Arista back. "Run!" he told her.

Saldur stared at them for a moment, then shook his head. "There is nowhere to run to, dear boy. You're both quite trapped."

Saldur, his hair loose and wild, wore a white linen nightgown, over which he had pulled a red silk robe that he was still in the midst of tying about his waist. "So it was you after all. I would not have believed it. You've been very clever, Arista, but you've always been a clever girl, haven't you? Always poking your nose into places you shouldn't.

"And you, Hilfred, reunited with your princess once more, I see. It's a wonderfully gallant gesture to defend her with your life, but it's also futile, and where is the honor in futility? There's no other exit from this dungeon. These men are Seret Knights, highly skilled, brutally trained soldiers who will kill you if you resist."

Saldur took the torch from the lead seret, who now also drew a dagger. "You have wasted half your life protecting this foolish girl, whose stupidity and rash choices have dragged you through torment and fire. Put down your sword and back away."

Hilfred checked his grip and planted his feet.

"When I was fifteen, you told me I would die if I tried to save her. That night I ran into an inferno. If I didn't listen to you then, what makes you think I will now?"

Saldur sighed. "Don't make them kill you."

Hilfred stood his ground.

"Stop, please. I beg you!" Arista shouted. "Sauly, I'll do anything you ask. Please, just let him go."

"Persuade him to put down his sword and I will."

"Hilfred—"

"Not even if you order me to," he said, his voice grave. "There is no power in Elan capable of making me walk away from you—not now, not ever again."

"Hilfred..." she whispered as tears fell.

He glanced at her. In that moment of inattention, the seret saw an opening and slashed. Hilfred dodged.

Swords clashed.

"*No!*" Arista cried.

Hilfred swung for the throat again, but the knight ducked. Hilfred's blade struck the wall, kicking up sparks. The knight stabbed him in the side. Hilfred gasped and staggered but managed to lunge and thrust his sword at the knight's chest. Again the point of the blade deflected off the black armor, but this time he was not fortunate enough to connect.

Arista watched as a second knight lunged, driving his sword through Hilfred's stomach. The sword pierced his body, pushing out the back of his tunic.

"No! *No!*" she screamed, falling against the wall as her knees threatened to buckle.

With blood spilling from his lips, Hilfred struggled to raise his sword again. The foremost knight brought his own blade down, severing Hilfred's arm at the elbow with a burst of warm blood that splashed across Arista's face.

Hilfred collapsed to his knees. His body hitched.

"A-Aris..." he sputtered.

"Oh, Hilfred..." Arista whispered as her eyes burned.

The knights stood over him. One raised his sword.

"*Arista!*" he cried.

The knight's sword came down.

Arista collapsed as if the blade pierced them both. She slumped to the floor. She could not speak. She could not breathe. Her eyes locked on the dead body of Hilfred as a warm wetness pooling across the stone floor crept between her fingers.

"Hilfred." She mouthed the word. She had no breath left to speak it.

Saldur sighed. "Get him out of here."

"What about her?"

"She went through so much trouble to get in, so let's find her a nice permanent room."

CHAPTER 25

INVASION

"What do you think is going to happen?" Hadrian asked Royce as they hung in the dark.

"The fleet will come in and there will be no pressure to fire the spouts. The Ghazel will land without opposition and slaughter everyone. Eventually they'll reach here, break in, and butcher us."

"No," Hadrian said, shaking his head. "See, that's where you're wrong. The Ghazel will eat us alive, and they'll take their time savoring every moment. Trust me."

They hung in silence.

"What time do you think it is?" Hadrian asked.

"Close to sunset. It was pretty late when they brought us in."

Silence.

They could hear the random movements of guards on the other side of the door, muffled conversation, the slide of a chair, occasional laughter.

"Why does this always happen?" Royce asked. "Why are we always hanging on a wall, waiting to die by slow vivisection? I just want to point out that this was your idea—*again*."

"I've been waiting for that. But I believe I told you not to come." Hadrian shifted in his chains and sighed. "I don't suppose there's much chance of a beautiful princess coming in here and saving us again."

"That card's been dealt."

"I wish I had met Gaunt," Hadrian said at length. "It would have been nice to actually meet the man, you know? My whole life was fated to protect this guy and I never even saw him."

They were quiet for a time, and then Royce made a *hmm* sound.

"What?"

"Huh? Oh—nothing."

"You're thinking something. What is it?"

"Just interesting that you think Arista is beautiful."

"Don't you?"

"She's okay."

"You're blinded by Gwen."

Hadrian heard Royce sigh. There was a silence, and then he said, "She already named our children. Elias if we had a boy—or was it Sterling? I forget—and Mercedes if a girl. She even took up knitting and made me a scarf."

"For what it's worth, I'm sorry I dragged you into this."

"She wanted me to go, remember? She said I had to protect you. I had to save your life."

Hadrian looked over at him. "Good job."

Chairs moved in the outer office, footsteps, a banging door, agitated voices. Hadrian caught snippets of the conversation.

"...black sails...a dark cloud on the ocean..."

"No, someone else..."

A chair turned over and hit the floor. More hurried footsteps. Silence.

"Sounds like the fleet is in." Hadrian waited, watching the door to their cell. "They left us for dead, didn't they? We told them this would happen. We came all this way to try and save them. You'd think they'd have the decency to let us out when they saw we were right."

"Probably think we're behind it. We're lucky they didn't just kill us."

"Not sure that's lucky. A nice, quick decapitation is kind of appealing right now."

"How long do you think before the Ba Ran find us?" Royce asked.

"You in a hurry?"

"Yeah, actually. If I have to be eaten, I would sort of like to get it over with."

Hadrian heard the sound of breaking glass.

"Ah, well, that didn't take long, did it?" Royce muttered miserably.

Footsteps shuffled in the outer room. There was a pause, and then the steps started again, coming closer. There were sounds of a struggle and a muffled cry. Hadrian braced himself and watched the door as it opened. What stood in the doorway shocked him.

"You boys ready to go?" Derning asked.

"What are *you* doing here?" they both said in unison.

"Would you prefer me to leave?" Derning smiled. Noticing the riveted manacles, he grimaced. "Thorough buggers, aren't they? Hang on. I saw some tools out here."

Royce and Hadrian looked at each other, bewildered.

"Okay, so he's not a beautiful princess. But it works for me."

There were sounds of slamming and an "Aha!" Then Derning returned with a hammer and a chisel.

"The Ghazel fleet arrived and Drumindor isn't working, but it didn't blow up either, so I guess we have you to thank for that," Derning told them as he went to work on the manacle pins.

"Don't mention it. And I'm not just saying that. I really mean...don't mention it," Hadrian said with a wince.

"Now half the folks—the smart half—are running. The others are going to try to fight. That means we don't have much time to get out of here. I have horses and provisions waiting just outside town. We'll take the mountain road north. I'll ride with you as far as Maranon and then I'll be going my own way."

"But I still don't get why you're here," Royce said as Derning finished with one of the metal bracelets. "Don't you work for Merrick?"

"Merrick Marius?" Derning laughed. "That's funny. Grady and I were convinced you two worked for Marius." Derning finished cracking open the manacles on Royce, then turned to Hadrian. "We work for Cornelius DeLur. You might know him—big fat guy, father of Cosmo. He pretty much runs this country—or owns it, depending on your viewpoint. Imagine my surprise yesterday when I checked in and found out you worked for Melengar. DeLur got a big kick out of that. The old fat man has a sick sense of humor sometimes."

"I'm confused. Why were you on the *Storm*?"

"When the Diamond found a message from Merrick, Cosmos thought it was important enough to relay to his daddy, and Cornelius sent us to check out what was going on. Grady and I started as sailors and are still well known on the Sharon. We were so sure Royce killed Drew, which is why we thought you two were mixed up with Merrick. We thought it had something to do with that horn comment that Drew made."

"Bernie killed him," Royce said simply.

"Yeah, we figured that out. And, of course, that horn thing

had nothing to do with Merrick. That was all Thranic's group. When we heard you had been arrested, it wasn't too hard to find ya."

He finished freeing Hadrian, who rubbed his wrists.

"Come on, most of your gear is out here." He pulled Alverstone out of his belt and handed it to Royce. "Took this off one of the guards. I think he thought it was pretty."

Outside their cell the tiny jail office was empty except for two guards. One looked dead but the other might have just been unconscious. They found their possessions in a series of boxes set aside in a room filled with all manner of impounded items.

Outside, dawn rose and people were running with bundles in their arms. Mothers held crying children to their breasts. Men struggled to push overfilled carts uphill. Down in the harbor they could see a forest of dark masts. Drumindor stood a mute witness to the sacking of the city.

Derning led them up refugee-choked streets. Fights broke out. Roads were blocked, and finally Derning resorted to the roofs. They scaled balconies and leapt alleys, trotting across the clay-tiled housetops until they cleared the congestion. They dropped back to the street and soon reached the city's eastern gate. Hundreds of people were rushing by with carts and donkeys—women and children mostly, traveling with boys and old men.

Derning stopped just outside the gates, looking worried. He whistled and a bird call answered in response. He led them off the road and up an embankment.

"Sorry, Jacob," said a spindly youth, emerging with four horses. "I figured it was best to wait out of sight. If anyone saw me with these, I wouldn't keep them for long."

From the crest of the hill they could see the bay far below. Smoke rose thickly from the buildings closest to the water.

"We weren't able to stop it," Derning said, looking at the refugees fleeing the city, "but between you defusing the explosion and my reporting to Cornelius so he could raise the alarm, it looks like we saved a lot of lives."

They mounted up and Hadrian took one last look at Tur Del Fur as the flames, fanned by the morning's sea breeze, swept through the streets below.

Chapter 26

Payment

Merrick entered the great hall of the imperial palace. Servants were hanging Wintertide decorations, which should have given the room a festive feel, but to Merrick it was still just a dreary chamber with too much stone and too little sunlight. He had never cared for Aquesta, and regretted that it would be the capital of the New Empire—an empire whose security he had ensured. He would have preferred Colnora. At least it had glass streetlamps.

"Ah! Merrick," Ethelred greeted him. The regents, Earl Ballentyne, and the chancellor were all gathered around the great table. "Or should I call you Lord Marius?"

"You should indeed," Merrick replied.

"You bring good news, then?"

"The best, Your Lordship—Delgos has fallen."

"Excellent!" Ethelred applauded.

Merrick reached the table and pulled off his gloves, one finger at a time. "The Ghazel invaded Tur Del Fur five days ago, meeting only a weak resistance. They took Drumindor and burned much of the port city."

"And the Nationalist army?" Ethelred asked, sitting down

comfortably in his chair with a smile stretching across his broad face.

"As expected, the army packed up and went south the moment they heard. Most have family in Delgos. You can retake Ratibor at will. You won't even need the army. A few hundred men will do. Breckton can turn his attention north to Melengar and begin plans for the spring invasion of Trent."

"Excellent! Excellent!" Ethelred cheered. Saldur and the chancellor joined in his applause, granting each other smiles of relief and pleasure.

"What happens when the Ghazel finish with Delgos and decide to march north?" the Earl of Chadwick asked. Seated at the far end of the table, he did not appear to share his companions' gaiety. "I'm told there's quite a lot of them and hear they're fearsome fighters. If they can destroy Delgos, what assurance do we have they won't attack us?"

"I'm certain the Nationalists will halt their ambitions in the short term, milord," Merrick replied. "But even if not, we face no threat from the Ba Ran Ghazel. They're a superstitious lot and expect some sort of world-ending catastrophe to beset them shortly. They want Drumindor as a refuge, not as a base for launching attacks. This will buy the time you need to take Melengar, Trent, and possibly even western Calis. By then the New Empire will be supreme and the Nationalists a memory. The remaining residents of Delgos, those once-independent merchant barons, will beg for imperial intervention against the Ghazel and eagerly submit to your absolute rule. The empire of old will be reforged."

The earl scowled and sat back down.

"You are indeed a marvel and deserving of your new title and station, Lord Marius."

"Because you already have Gaunt and Esrahaddon is dead, I believe that finishes my employment obligations."

"For now," Ethelred told him. "I won't let a man of your talents get away that easily. Now that I've found you, I want you in my court. I'll make it worth your loyalty."

"Actually, I already spoke with His Grace about the position of Magistrate of Colnora."

"Magistrate, eh? Want your own city, do you? I like the idea. Think you can keep the Diamond under your thumb? I suppose you could—certainly, why not? Consider it done, Lord Magistrate, but I insist you do not take your post until after Wintertide. I want you here for the festivities."

"Ethelred is getting married and crowned emperor," Saldur explained. "The Patriarch will be coming to perform the ceremony himself, and if that's not enough, we will be burning a famous witch."

"I wouldn't miss it."

"Excellent!" Ethelred grinned. "I trust accommodations in the city are to your liking? If not, tell the chamberlain and he'll find a more suitable estate."

"The house is perfect. You are too kind, my lord."

"I still don't see why you don't simply stay in the palace."

"It's easier for me to do business if I'm not seen here too frequently. And now, if you'll forgive me, I must—"

"You aren't leaving?" Ethelred asked, disappointed. "You just got here. With news like this, we have to celebrate. Don't doom me to merrymaking with the likes of an old cleric and a melancholy earl. I'll call for wines and beef. We'll get some entertainment, music, dancers, and women if you'd like. How do you like your women, Marius? Thin or plump, light or dark, saucy or docile? I assure you, the lord chamberlain can fill any order."

"Alas, my lord, I have some remaining business to which I must attend."

Ethelred frowned. "Very well, but you must show up for Wintertide. I insist."

"Of course, my lord."

Merrick left while the imperial rulers exchanged congratulatory accolades. Outside, a new carriage waited, complete with four white horses and a uniformed driver. On the seat rested the package from the city constable. Merrick had offered brandy in trade and the man had leapt at the opportunity. A bottle of fine liquor in return for the worthless remnants of the defunct witch hunt was the sort of good fortune that the sheriff was unaccustomed to receiving. Unwrapping the package, Merrick ran his fingers over the shimmering material of the robe.

The carriage traveled up The Hill and turned on Heath Street, one of the more affluent neighborhoods in the city. The homes, though not terribly large, were tasteful and elegant. A servant waited dutifully to remove his cloak and boots while another stood by with a warm cup of cider. Merrick no longer drank wine, ale, or spirits, and was amused to see this accommodation taken into account. He sat in the drawing room, surrounded by burgundy furnishings and dark wood paneling, sipping his drink and listening to the pop of the fireplace.

A knock sounded at the door. He nearly rose to answer when he spotted one of his new servants trotting to the foyer.

"Where is she, Merrick?" he heard an angry voice shout.

A moment later the valet led two men into the drawing room.

"Please have a seat, both of you." Merrick reclined in his soft chair, warming his hands with his cup. "Would either of you care for a drink before we conduct business? My servants can bring you whatever you like, but I must say the cider is especially good."

"I said, where is she?"

"Relax, Mr. Deminthal, your daughter is fine and I'll bring her down shortly. You fulfilled your end of the bargain brilliantly, and I always honor my commitments. I merely wish to go over a few details. Only a formality, I assure you. First, let me congratulate you, Wyatt. May I call you Wyatt? You've done an excellent job. Poe's report gave you extremely high marks.

"He tells me you were instrumental in getting Royce and Hadrian on board, and even after the unexpected sinking of the *Emerald Storm*, your quick thinking saved the ship's orders and the mission. I'm especially impressed by how you won over Royce's trust—no small feat, I might add. You must be a very convincing fellow, as demonstrated by how you persuaded the Port Authority that Royce and Hadrian were in Tur Del Fur to destroy Drumindor. I'm convinced it's only by your skill and intelligence that the operation was such a wonderful success."

Merrick took a sip from his cider and sat back with a grin. "I have just one question. Do you know where Royce and Hadrian are now?"

"Dead. By the Ghazel or the Tur Del Fur officials, whoever got them first."

"Hmm, I doubt that. Royce is not easy to kill. He has gotten out of much more difficult situations before. I would say he leads a charmed life, but I know all too well what kind of life he's lived. Still, I wouldn't even trust Death to bind him long."

"I want my daughter—now," Wyatt said quietly through clenched teeth.

"Of course, of course. Mr. Poe, would you be so kind as to run up and bring her down? Third door on the left." Merrick handed him a key. "Seriously, Wyatt, you're a very capable man. I could use you."

"Do you think I *liked* doing this? How many hundreds of people are dead because of me?"

"Don't think of it that way. Think of it as a job, an assignment, which you performed with panache. I don't see talent such as yours often, and I could find other uses of your skills. Join with me and you'll be well compensated. I'm working on another project now, for an even more lucrative employer, and I'm in a position to make a great many good things happen for you. You and your daughter can live like landed gentry. How would you like your own estate?"

"You kidnapped my daughter. The only business I'm interested in doing with you is arranging your death."

"Don't be so dramatic. Ah, see? Here she is now. Safe and sound."

Poe escorted a little girl down the steps. She was around ten years old, her light-brown hair was tied in a bow, and she wore an elegantly tailored blue dress with fine leather shoes.

"Daddy!" she shouted.

Wyatt rushed over, throwing his arms around her. "Did they hurt you, honey?"

"No, I'm okay. They bought me this pretty dress and got me these shoes! And we played games."

"That's good, honey." Turning to Merrick, Wyatt asked, "What about Elden?"

"He's fine, still in Colnora. Waiting for you, I presume. Wyatt, you really need to consider my offer, if for no other reason than your own safety."

Wyatt spun on him. "I did your job! You sat there and told me I did it *brilliantly*! Why are you still threatening us?"

Merrick looked at the girl. "Poe, take Allie in the kitchen. I think there are some cookies she might like."

Wyatt held her to him.

"Don't worry, she'll be right back."

"Do you like cookies?" Poe asked her. The little girl grinned, bobbing her head. She looked up at her father.

Wyatt nodded. "It's okay, go ahead. Hurry back, honey."

Poe and Allie left the room hand in hand.

"I'm not threatening you. As I already said, I'm very pleased with your skills. I'm merely trying to protect you. Consider for a moment, what if Royce is not dead? He'll put two and two together, if he hasn't already. You should be afraid of what he'll do to you—and your daughter. Royce will probably kill Allie first and make you watch."

"He's not like that."

Merrick released a small chuckle. "Oh, sir, you have no idea what Royce is like. I'll grant you that his association with Hadrian Blackwater has tempered him greatly. Twelve years with that idealistic dreamer have made him practically human, but I *know* him. I know what lurks beneath. I've seen things that make even my hardened heart shudder. Get his anger up, and you'll unleash a demon that no one can control. Believe me, he's *like that* and so much more. Nothing is beyond him."

Allie returned with a handful of sugar cookies. Taking her other hand, Wyatt headed for the door. He paused at the threshold and looked back. "Merrick, if what you say about Royce is true, then shouldn't *you* be the one who's afraid?" Wyatt walked out, closing the door behind him.

Merrick sipped his cider again, but it had gone cold.

GLOSSARY OF TERMS AND NAMES

ADAM: Wheeler from Ratibor

ADDIE WOOD: Mother of Thrace/Modina, wife of Theron, killed in Dahlgren

ALBERT WINSLOW: Landless viscount used by Riyria to arrange assignments from the gentry

ALBURN: Kingdom of Avryn ruled by King Armand and Queen Adeline, member of the New Empire

ALENDA LANAKLIN: Daughter of Marquis Victor Lanaklin and sister of Myron the monk

ALGAR: Woodworker in Hintindar

ALLIE: Daughter of Wyatt Deminthal

ALRIC BRENDON ESSENDON: King of Melengar, son of Amrath, brother of Arista

ALVERSTONE: \al-ver-stone\ Dagger used by Royce

AMBERTON LEE: Hill with old ruins not far from Hintindar

AMBROSE MOOR: Administrator of the Manzant Prison and Salt Works

AMILIA: Carriage maker's daughter from the small village of Tarin Vale

AMITER: Second wife of King Urith, sister of Androus

AMRATH ESSENDON: \am-wrath\ Deceased king of Melengar, father of Alric and Arista

AMRIL: \am-rill\ Countess that Arista cursed with boils

ANDROUS: Viceroy of Ratibor

ANNA: Chambermaid of Empress Modina

ANTUN BULARD: Historian and author of *The History of Apeladorn*, passenger on the *Emerald Storm*

APELADORN: \ah-pell-ah-dorn\ Four nations of man, consisting of Trent, Avryn, Delgos, and Calis

APELANESE: Language spoken throughout the four kingdoms of men

AQUESTA: \ah-quest-ah\ Capital city of the kingdom of Warric, seat of power for the New Empire

ARBOR: Baker in Hintindar, married to Dunstan, shoemaker's daughter

ARCADIUS VINTARUS LATIMER: Professor of Lore at Sheridan University

ARCHIBALD BALLENTYNE: Earl of Chadwick, commander of Sir Breckton, promised providence of Melengar for service to the New Empire

ARISTA ESSENDON: Princess of Melengar, daughter of Amrath, sister of King Alric

ARMAND: King of Alburn, married to Adeline

ARMIGIL: Brew mistress of Hintindar

ART, THE: Magic, generally feared due to superstition

ARVID MCDERN: Son of Dillon McDern from Dahlgren

AVEMPARTHA: Ancient elven tower, home of Gilarabrywn, which attacked Dahlgren

AVRYN: \ave-rin\ Central and most powerful of the four nations of Apeladorn, located between Trent and Delgos

AYERS: Proprietor of The Laughing Gnome in Ratibor

BACKING: Rigging a sail such that it catches the wind from its forward side; having both backed and regular rigged sails can render a ship motionless

BAILIFF: Officer who is employed to make arrests and administer punishments

BALDWIN: Lord whose landholdings include Hintindar

BALLENTYNE: \bal-in-tine\ Ruling family of the earldom of Chadwick

BANNER: Crew member of the *Emerald Storm*

BA RAN ARCHIPELAGO: Island of the goblins

BA RAN GHAZEL: Goblins of the sea

BARKERS: Refugee family living in Brisbane Alley of Aquesta; father Brice, mother Lynnette, sons Finis, Hingus, and Wery

BARTHOLOMEW: Carriage maker of Tarin Vale, father of Amilia

BARTHOLOMEW: Priest in Ratibor

BASIL: Officers' cook on the *Emerald Storm*

BASTION: Servant in the imperial palace

BATTLE OF MEDFORD: Skirmish that occurred during Princess Arista's witch trial

BATTLE OF RATIBOR: Skirmish between Nationalists and Imperialists

BELINDA PICKERING: Extremely attractive wife of Count Pickering, mother of Lenare, Mauvin, Fanen, and Denek

BELSTRADS: \bell-straads\ Noble family from Chadwick, including Sir Breckton and Wesley

BENTLY: Sergeant in the Nationalist army

BERNARD: Lord Chamberlain of the imperial palace

BERNICE: Former handmaid of Princess Arista, killed in Dahlgren

BERNIE DEFOE: Topsail crew member of the *Emerald Storm*, former member of the Black Diamond thieves' guild

BERNUM HEIGHTS: Wealthiest residential district in Colnora

BERNUM RIVER: Waterway that bisects the city of Colnora

BERYL: Senior midshipman on the *Emerald Storm*

BETHAMY: King reputed to have had his horse buried with him

BIDDINGS: Chancellor of the imperial palace

BISHOP: Lieutenant aboard the *Emerald Storm*

BLACK DIAMOND, THE: International thieves' guild centered in Colnora

BLACKWATER: Last name of Hadrian and his father, Danbury

BLINDEN: Quartermaster's mate on the *Emerald Storm*

BLYTHIN CASTLE: Castle in Alburn

BOATSWAIN: Petty officer who controls the work of other seamen on a ship

BOCANT: Family who built a lucrative industry from pork, second wealthiest merchants in Colnora

BOTHWICKS: Family of peasant farmers from Dahlgren

BRAGA, PERCY: See Percy Braga

BRECKTON: Sir Breckton Belstrad, son of Lord Belstrad, brother of Wesley, commander of the Northern Imperial Army, knight of Chadwick, considered by many to be the best knight of Avryn

BRIGHT STAR, THE: Ship sunk by Dacca

BRISTOL BENNET: Boatswain on the *Emerald Storm*

BRODRIC ESSENDON: Founder of the Essendon dynasty

BUCKET MEN: Term for assassin used by the Black Diamond thieves' guild

BULARD, ANTUN: See Antun Bulard

BURANDU: \bur-and-dew\ Lord of the Tenkin village of Oudorro

BYRNIE: Long (usually sleeveless) tunic of chain mail worn as defensive armor

CALIAN: \cal-lay-in\ Pertaining to the nation of Calis

CALIANS: Residents of the nation of Calis, darker in skin tone, with almond-shaped eyes

CALIDE PORTMORE: Folk song often sung while drinking

CALIS: \cal-lay\ Southern- and easternmost of the four nations of Apeladorn, considered exotic; in constant conflict with the Ba Ran Ghazel

CAPSTAN: Spoked wheel on a ship that turns to raise the anchor

CARAT: Young member of the Black Diamond thieves' guild

CASWELL: Family of peasant farmers from Dahlgren

CENZARS: \sen-zhar\ Wizards of the Old Novronian Empire

CHAMBERLAIN: Someone who manages the household of a king or nobleman

COLNORA: \call-nor-ah\ Largest and wealthiest city of Avryn, merchant-based, grew from a rest stop at a central crossroads from various major trade routes

CONSTANCE, LADY: Noblewoman, fifth imperial secretary to Empress Modina

CORA: Dairymaid at the imperial palace

CORNELIUS DELUR: Rich businessman, rumored to finance Nationalists and involved in black market, father of Cosmos

COSMOS SEBASTIAN DELUR: Son of Cornelius, also known as the Jewel, head of the Black Diamond thieves' guild

COXSWAIN: Helmsman of a racing ship

CRANSTON: Professor at Sheridan University, tried and burned for heresy

CRIMSON HAND: Thieves' guild operating out of Melengar

CROWN CONSPIRACY, THE: Play reputed to be based on the murder of King Amrath, follows the exploits of two thieves and the Prince of Melengar

CROWN TOWER: Home of the Patriarch, center of the Nyphron Church

CUTTER: Moniker used by Merrick Marius when a member of the Black Diamond thieves' guild

DACCA: Fierce seafaring people who live on the island of Dacca, south of Delgos

DAGASTAN: Major and easternmost trade port of Calis

DAHLGREN: \dall-grin\ Remote village on the bank of the Nidwalden River, destroyed by Gilarabrywn

DANBURY BLACKWATER: Father of Hadrian

DANTHEN: Woodsman from Dahlgren

DAREF, LORD: Noble of Warric, associate of Albert Winslow

DARIUS SERET: Founder of the Seret Knights

DAVENS: Squire who Arista had a youthful crush on

DAVIS: Crew member of the *Emerald Storm*

DEACON TOMAS: Priest of Dahlgren, witnessed destruction of Gilarabrywn, proclaimed Thrace Wood as the Heir of Novron

DEFOE, BERNIE: See Bernie Defoe

DEGAN GAUNT: Leader of the Nationalists, sister of Miranda

DELANCY, GWEN: See Gwen DeLancy

DELANO DEWITT: Alias used by Wyatt Deminthal when he framed Hadrian and Royce for King Amrath's death

DELGOS: One of the four nations of Apeladorn. The only republic in a world of monarchies, Delgos revolted against the Steward's Empire after Glenmorgan III was murdered and after surviving an attack by the Ba Ran Ghazel with no aid from the empire.

DELORKAN, DUKE: Nobleman from Calis

DELUR: Family of wealthy merchants

DEMINTHAL, WYATT: See Wyatt Deminthal

DENEK PICKERING: Youngest son of Count Pickering

DENNY: Worker at The Rose and Thorn

DERMONT, LORD: General of imperial army

DERNING, JACOB: Maintop captain on the *Emerald Storm*

DEVON: Monk of Tarin Vale, taught Amilia to read and write

DEWITT, DELANO: See Delano DeWitt

DIGBY: Guard at Essendon Castle

DILLADRUM: Erbonese guide, hired to take crew of the *Emerald Storm* to Palace of the Four Winds

DILLNARD LINROY: Royal Financier of Melengar

DIME: Crew member of the *Emerald Storm*

DIOYLION: \die-e-leon\ *The Accumulated Letters of Dioylion*, a very rare scroll

DIXON TAFT: Bartender and manager of The Rose and Thorn Tavern, lost an arm in the Battle of Medford

DOVIN THRANIC: Sentinel of Nyphron Church aboard the *Emerald Storm*

DREW, EDGAR: See Edgar Drew

DR. GERAND: Physician in Ratibor

DR. LEVY: Physician aboard the *Emerald Storm*

DROME: God of the dwarves

DRONDIL FIELDS: Count Pickering's castle, once the fortress of Brodric Essendon, the original seat of power in Melengar

DRUMINDOR: Dwarven-built fortress located at the entrance to Terlando Bay in Tur Del Fur, can utilize lava from nearby volcano for its defense

DRUNDEL: Peasant family from Dahlgren consisting of Mae, Went, Davie, and Firth

DUNLAP, PAUL: Former carriage driver of King Urith, dead

DUNMORE: Youngest and least sophisticated kingdom of Avryn, ruled by King Roswort; member of the New Empire

DUNSTAN: Baker in Hintindar, childhood friend of Hadrian, married to Arbor

DURBO: Tenkin dwelling

DUR GURON: Easternmost portion of Calis

DUSTER: Moniker used by Royce while a member of the Black Diamond

ECTON, SIR: Chief knight of Count Pickering and military general of Melengar

EDGAR DREW: Old seaman on the *Emerald Storm*, died in a fall

EDITH MON: Head maid in charge of the scullery and chamber servants in the imperial palace

EDMUND HALL: Professor of geometry at Sheridan University, reputed to have found Percepliquis, declared a heretic by the Nyphron Church, imprisoned in the Crown Tower

ELAN: The world

ELDEN: Large man, friend of Wyatt Deminthal

ELINYA: Esrahaddon's girlfriend

ELLA: Cook at Drondil Fields

ELLA: Maid at imperial palace

ELLIS FAR, THE: Melengarian ship

ELVEN: Pertaining to elves

EMERALD STORM, THE: Ship of the New Empire, captained by Seward

EMERY DORN: Young revolutionary living in Ratibor

EMPRESS MODINA: See Modina, Empress

ENDEN, SIR: Knight of Chadwick, considered second best to Breckton

ERANDABON GILE: Panther of Dur Guron, Tenkin Warlord, madman

ERBON: Region of Calis northwest from Mandalin

EREBUS: Father of the gods, also known as Kile

ERIVAN: \ear-ah-van\ Elven Empire

ERMA EVERTON: Alias used by Arista while in Hintindar

ERVANON: \err-vah-non\ City in northern Ghent, seat of the Nyphron Church, once the capital of the Steward's Empire as established by Glenmorgan I

ESRAHADDON: \ez-rah-hod-in\ Wizard, former member of the Cenzar, convicted of destroying the Old Empire, sentenced to imprisonment, held in Gutaria

ESSENDON: \ez-in-don\ Royal family of Melengar

ESSENDON CASTLE: Home of ruling monarchs of Melengar

ESTRAMNADON: \es-tram-nah-don\ Believed to be the capital or at least a very sacred place in the Erivan Empire

ESTRENDOR: \es-tren-door\ Northern wastes

ETCHER: Member of the Black Diamond thieves' guild

ETHELRED, LANIS: \eth-el-red\ Former king of Warric, co-regent of New Empire, Imperialist

EVERTON: Alias used by Arista, Hadrian, and later Royce

EVLIN: City along the banks of the Bernum River

FALINA BROCKTON: Real name of Emerald, waitress at The Rose and Thorn Tavern

FALQUIN: Professor at Sheridan University

FANEN PICKERING: \fan-in\ Middle son of Count Pickering, killed by Luis Guy

FAN IRLANU: Visionary of Oudorro, seer, fortune-teller

FAQUIN: Inept magician who uses alchemy rather than channeling the Art

FAULD, THE ORDER OF: \fall-ed\ Post-imperial order of knights dedicated to preserving the skill and discipline of the Teshlor Knights

FENITILIAN: Monk of Maribor, made warm shoes

FERROL: God of the elves

FINILESS: Noted author

FINISHER: Stealthy Ghazel fighter

FINLIN, ETHAN: Member of the Black Diamond, stores smuggled goods, owns windmill

FLETCHER: Maker of arrows

FORECASTLE: Raised portion in the bow of a ship containing living quarters of senior crew members

FORREST: Ratibor citizen with fighting experience, son of a silversmith

GAFTON: Imperial admiral

GALEANNON: \gale-e-an-on\ Kingdom of Avryn, ruled by Fredrick and Josephine, member of the New Empire

GALENTI: \ga-lehn'-tay\ Calian nickname attributed to Hadrian

GALEWYR RIVER: \gale-wahar\ Marks the southern border of Melengar and the northern border of Warric and reaches the sea near the fishing village of Roe

GALIEN: \gal-e-in\ Archbishop of the Nyphron Church

GALILIN: \gal-ah-lin\ Province of Melengar formerly ruled by Count Pickering

GAUNT, DEGAN: See Degan Gaunt

GEMKEY: Gem that opens a gemlock

GEMLOCK: Dwarven invention that seals a container or entrance and can only be opened with a precious gem of the right type and cut

GENTRY SQUARE: Affluent district of Melengar

GERALD BANIFF: Primary bodyguard of Empress Modina

GERTY: Midwife in Hintindar who delivered Hadrian, married to Abelard

GHAZEL: \gehz-ell\ Ba Ran Ghazel, the dwarven name for goblins, literally: Sea Goblins

GHAZEL SEA: Southern body of water east of the Sharon Sea

GHENT: Ecclesiastical holding of the Nyphron Church, member of New Empire

GILARABRYWN: \gill-lar-ah-bren\ Elven beast of war; one escaped Avempartha and destroyed village of Dahlgren before being killed by Thrace

GILL: Sentry in the Nationalist army

GINLIN: \gin-lin\ Monk of Maribor, winemaker, refused to touch a knife

GLAMRENDOR: \glam-ren-door\ Capital of Dunmore

GLENMORGAN: 326 years after the fall of the Novronian Empire, this native of Ghent reunited the four nations of Apeladorn; founder of Sheridan University; creator of the great north-south road; builder of the Ervanon palace (of which only the Crown Tower remains)

GLENMORGAN II: Son of Glenmorgan. When his father died young, the new and inexperienced emperor relied on church officials to assist him in managing his empire. They in turn took the opportunity to manipulate the emperor into granting sweeping powers to the church and nobles loyal to the church. These leaders opposed defending Delgos against the invading Ba Ran Ghazel in Calis and the Dacca in Delgos, arguing the threat would increase dependency on the empire.

GLENMORGAN III: Grandson of Glenmorgan. Shortly after assuming the stewardship, he attempted to reassert control over the realm his grandfather had created by leading an army against the invading Ghazel that had reached south-eastern Avryn. He defeated the Ghazel at the First Battle of Vilan Hills and announced plans to ride to the aid of Tur Del Fur. Fearing his rise in power, in the sixth year of his reign, his nobles betrayed and imprisoned him in Blythin Castle. Jealous of his popularity and growing strength, and resentful of his policy of stripping the nobles and clergy of their power, the church charged him with heresy. He was found guilty and executed. This began the rapid collapse of what many called the Steward's Empire. The church later claimed the nobles had tricked them, and condemned many, most of whom reputedly ended their lives badly.

GLOUSTON: Province of northern Warric bordering on the Galewyr River, formerly ruled by Marquis Lanaklin, invaded and taken over by the New Empire

GNOME, THE: Nickname of The Laughing Gnome Tavern

GRADY: Seaman on the *Emerald Storm*

GRAVIS: Dwarf who sabotaged Drumindor

GREAT SWORD: Long sword designed to be held with both hands

GREEN: Lieutenant on the *Emerald Storm*

GREIG: Carpenter aboard the *Emerald Storm*

GRELAD, JERISH: See Jerish Grelad

GRIBBON: Flag of Mandalin Calis

GRIGOLES: \gry-holes\ Author of *Grigoles Treatise on Imperial Common Law*

GRIMBALD: Blacksmith in Hintindar

GRONBACH: Dwarf, fairy-tale villain

GRUMON, MASON: \grum-on\ Blacksmith in Medford, worked for Riyria, died in Battle of Medford

GUARDIAN OF THE HEIR: Teshlor, protector of the Heir of Novron

GUNGUAN: Vintu pack ponies

GUR EM: Thickest part of the jungle in Calis

GUTARIA: \goo-tar-ah\ Secret Nyphron prison designed to hold Esrahaddon

GUY, LUIS: See Luis Guy

GWEN DELANCY: Calian prostitute and proprietor of Medford House and The Rose and Thorn Tavern in Medford, girlfriend of Royce Melborn

HADDY: Childhood nickname of Hadrian

HADRIAN BLACKWATER: Mercenary, one-half of Riyria

HALBERD: Two-handed pole used as a weapon

HANDEL: Master at Sheridan University, originally from Roe, proponent to have Delgos's Republic officially recognized

HARBERT: Tailor in Hintindar, husband of Hester

HARVEST MOON: Full moon nearest the fall equinox

HEIR OF NOVRON: Direct descendant of demigod Novron, destined to rule all of Avryn

HELDABERRY: Wild-growing fruit often used to make wine

HESLON: Monk of Maribor, great cook

HIGHCOURT FIELDS: Once the site of the supreme noble judicial court of law in Avryn, location of Wintertide games

HILFRED, REUBEN: Former bodyguard of Princess Arista, severely burned in Dahlgren

HILL DISTRICT: Affluent neighborhood in Colnora

HIMBOLT: Baron of Melengar

HINGARA: Calian guide, died in jungles of Gur Em

HINTINDAR: Small manorial village in Rhenydd, home of Hadrian Blackwater

HOBBIE: Stableboy in Hintindar

HORN OF DELGOS: Landmark used by sailors to determine the southernmost tip of Delgos

HORN OF GYLINDORA: Item Esrahaddon indicates is buried in Percepliquis

HOUSE, THE: Nickname used for Medford House

HOYTE: Onetime First Officer of the Black Diamond, set up Royce to kill Jade, sent Royce to Manzant Prison, killed by Royce

IBIS THINLY: Head cook of the imperial palace

IMP: Slang for Imperialist

IMPERIALISTS: Political party that desires to unite all the kingdoms of men under a single leader who is the direct descendant of the demigod Novron

IMPERIAL PALACE: Seat of power of the New Empire

IMPERIAL SECRETARY: Caretaker of Empress Modina, charged with making her publically presentable

JACOB DERNING: See Derning, Jacob

JADE: Assassin in the Black Diamond, girlfriend of Merrick, mistakenly killed by Royce

JENKINS TALBERT: Squire in Tarin Vale

JEREMY: Guard at Essendon Castle

JERISH GRELAD: Teshlor Knight, first Guardian of the Heir, protector of Nevrik

JERL, LORD: Nobleman, neighbor of the Pickerings known for his prize-winning hunting dogs

JEWEL, THE: Head of the international Black Diamond thieves' guild, also known as Cosmos DeLur

JIMMY: Tavern worker at The Laughing Gnome

JOQDAN: \jok-dan\ Warlord of the Tenkin village of Oudorro

JULIAN TEMPEST: Chamberlain of the kingdom of Melengar

KAZ: Calian term for anyone with mixed elven and human blood

KENDELL, EARL: Nobleman of Melengar, loyal to Alric Essendon

KHAROLL: Long dagger

KILE: Name used by Erebus when sent to Elan, performs good deeds in the form of a man

KILNAR: City in the south of Rhenydd

KNOB: Baker at the imperial palace

KRINDEL: Prelate of the Nyphron Church and historian

KRIS DAGGER: Weapon with a wavy blade, sometimes used in magic rituals

LAMBERT, IGNATIUS: Chancellor of Sheridan University

LANAKLIN: Once ruling family of Glouston, currently in exile in Melengar, opposes the New Empire

LANDONER: Professor at Sheridan University, tried and burned for heresy

LANKSTEER: Capital city of the Lordium kingdom of Trent

LAUGHING GNOME, THE: Tavern in Ratibor

LAVEN: Citizen of Ratibor

LEIF: Butcher at the imperial palace

LENARE PICKERING: Daughter of Count Pickering and Belinda, sister of Mauvin, Fanen, and Denek

LINGARD: Capital city of Relison, kingdom of Trent

LINROY, DILLNARD: See Dillnard Linroy

LIVET GLIM: Port Controller at Tur Del Fur

LONGWOOD: Forest in Melengar

LOTHOMAD THE BALD: King of Lordium, Trent, expanded territory following the collapse of the Steward's Reign, pushing south through Ghent into Melengar, where Brodric Essendon defeated him in the Battle of Drondil Fields in 2545

LOWER QUARTER: Impoverished section of the city of Medford

LUGGER: Small fishing boat rigged with one or more lugsails

LUIS GUY: Sentinel of the Nyphron Church, killed Fanen Pickering

LURET: Imperial envoy to Hintindar

MAGNUS: Dwarf, killed King Amrath, sabotaged Arista's Tower, discovered entry into Avempartha, rebuilding Winds Abbey

MANDALIN: \man-dah-lynn\ Capital of Calis

MANZANT: \man-zahnt\ Infamous prison and salt mine, located in Manzar, Maranon; Royce Melborn is the only prisoner to have been released from it

MARANON: \mar-ah-non\ Kingdom in Avryn, ruled by Vincent and Regina, member of the New Empire, rich in farmland

MARES CATHEDRAL: Center of the Nyphron Church in Melengar, formerly run by Bishop Saldur

MARIBOR: \mar-eh-bore\ God of men

MARIUS, MERRICK: See Merrick Marius

MAUVIN PICKERING: \maw-vin\ Eldest of Count Pickering's sons, friends since childhood with Essendon royal family, bodyguard to King Alric

MAWYNDULË: Powerful wizard

McDERN, DILLON: Blacksmith of Dahlgren

MEDFORD: Capital of Melengar

MEDFORD HOUSE: Brothel run by Gwen DeLancy and attached to The Rose and Thorn

MELENGAR: \mel-in-gar\ Kingdom in Avryn, ruled by the Essendon royal family, only Avryn kingdom independent of the New Empire

MELENGARIANS: Residents of Melengar

MELISSA: Head servant of Princess Arista, nickname Missy

MERCS: Mercenaries

MERCY: Young girl under the care of Arcadias

MERLONS: Solid section between two crenels in a crenellated battlement

MERRICK MARIUS: Former member of the Black Diamond, alias Cutter, master thief and assassin, former best friend of Royce, known for his strategic thinking, boyfriend of Jade

MESSKID: Container used to transport meals aboard a ship, resembles bucket

MILBOROUGH: Melengarian baron, died in battle

MILFORD: Sergeant in the Nationalist army

MILLIE: Formerly Hadrian's horse, died in Dahlgren

MIR: Person with both elven and human blood

MIRANDA GAUNT: Sister of Degan Gaunt

MIZZENMAST: Third mast from the bow in a vessel having three or more masts

MODINA, EMPRESS: Ruler of the New Empire, previously Thrace Wood of Dahlgren

MON, EDITH: See Edith Mon

MONTEMORCEY: \mont-eh-more-ah-sea\ Excellent wine imported through the Vandon Spice Company

MOTTE: Man-made hill

MOUSE: Royce's horse, named by Thrace, gray mare

MR. RINGS: Baby raccoon, pet of Mercy

MURIEL: Goddess of nature, daughter of Erebus, mother of Uberlin

MYRON LANAKLIN: Sheltered monk of Maribor with indelible memory, son of Victor, sister of Alenda

MYSTIC: Name of Arista's horse

NAREION: \nare-e-on\ Last emperor of the Novronian Empire

NARON: Heir of Novron who died in Ratibor in 2992

NATIONALISTS: Political party led by Degan Gaunt that desires rule by the will of the people

NATS: Nickname of the Nationalists

NEST, THE: Nickname of the Rat's Nest

NEVRIK: \nehv-rick\ Son of Nareion, the heir who went into hiding, protected by Jerish Grelad

NEW EMPIRE: Second empire uniting most of the kingdoms of man, ruled by Empress Modina, administered by co-regents Ethelred and Saldur

NIDWALDEN RIVER: Marks the eastern border of Avryn and the start of the Erivan realm

NIMBUS: Tutor to the empress, assistant to the imperial secretary, originally from Vernes

NIPPER: Young servant assigned primarily to the kitchens of the imperial palace

NOVRON: Savior of mankind, demigod, son of Maribor, who defeated the elven army in the Great Elven Wars, founder of the Novronian Empire, builder of Percepliquis, husband of Persephone

NOVRONIAN: \nov-ron-e-on\ Pertaining to Novron

NYPHRON CHURCH: The worshipers of Novron and Maribor

NYPHRONS: \nef-rons\ Devout members of the church

OBERDAZA: \oh-ber-daz-ah\ Tenkin or Ghazel witch doctor

OLD EMPIRE: Original united kingdoms of man, destroyed one thousand years in the past after the murder of Emperor Nareion

ORRIN FLATLY: Ratibor city scribe

OSGAR: Reeve of Hintindar

OSTRIUM: Tenkin communal hall where meals are served

OUDORRO: Friendly Tenkin village in Calis

PALACE OF THE FOUR WINDS: Home of Erandabon Gile in Dur Guron

PARKER: Quartermaster of Nationalist army

PARTHALOREN FALLS: \path-ah-lore-e-on\ The great cataracts on the Nidwalden near Avempartha

PATRIARCH: Head of the Nyphron Church who lives in the Crown Tower of Ervanon

PAULDRON: A piece of armor covering the shoulder

PERCEPLIQUIS: \per-sep-lah-kwiss\ The ancient city and capital of the Novronian Empire, named for the wife of Novron, destroyed and lost during the collapse of the Old Empire

PERCY BRAGA: Former Archduke and Lord Chancellor of Melengar, expert swordsman, uncle-in-law to Alric and Arista, killed by Count Pickering, commissioned the murder of King Amrath

PERIN: Grocer from Ratibor

PERSEPHONE: Wife of Novron

PICKERING: Noble family of Melengar and rulers of Galilin. Count Pickering is known to be the best swordsman in Avryn and believed to use a magic sword.

PICKILERINON, SEADRIC: Noble who shortened the family name to Pickering

PLESIEANTIC INCANTATION: \plass-e-an-tic\ A method used in the Art to draw power from nature

POE: Cook's assistant aboard the *Emerald Storm*

POLISH: Head of the Black Diamond thieves' guild in Ratibor

PRALEON GUARD: \pray-lee-on\ Bodyguards to the king in Ratibor

PRICE: First Officer of the Black Diamond thieves' guild

QUARTZ: Member of the Ratibor thieves' guild

RATIBOR: Capital of the kingdom of Rhenydd, home to Royce

RAT'S NEST, THE: Hideout of the Black Diamond thieves' guild in Ratibor

RED: Old elkhound, large dog frequently found in kitchen of imperial palace

REEVE: Official who supervises serfs and oversees the lands for a lord

REGAL FOX INN, THE: Least expensive tavern in affluent Hill District in Colnora

REGENT: Someone who administers a kingdom during the absence or incapacity of the ruler

RENDON, BARON: Nobleman of Melengar

RENIAN: \rhen-e-ahn\ Childhood friend of Myron the monk

RENKIN POOL: Citizen of Ratibor with fighting experience

RENQUIST: Soldier in the Nationalist army

RENTINUAL, TOBIS: History professor at Sheridan University, built catapult to fight Gilarabrywn

RHELACAN: \rell-ah-khan\ Great sword given to Novron by Maribor, forged by Drome, enchanted by Ferrol, used to defeat and subdue the elves

RHENYDD: Poor kingdom of Avryn, now part of the New Empire

RILAN VALLEY: Fertile land that separates Glouston and Chadwick

RIONILLION: \ri-on-ill-lon\ Name of the city that first stood on the site of Aquesta but was destroyed during the civil wars that occurred after the fall of the Novronian Empire

RIYRIA: \rye-ear-ah\ Elvish for *two*, a team or a bond, name used to collectively refer to Royce Melborn and Hadrian Blackwater

RONDEL: Common type of stiff-bladed dagger with a round handgrip

ROSE AND THORN, THE: Tavern in Medford run by Gwen DeLancy, used as a base by Riyria

ROSWORT: King of Dunmore

ROYALISTS: Political party that favors rule by independent monarchs

ROYCE MELBORN: Thief, one-half of Riyria

RUFUS: Ruthless northern warlord, intended emperor for the New Empire, killed by a Gilarabrywn in Dahlgren

RUFUS'S BANE: Name given to the Gilarabrywn slain by Thrace/Modina

RUSSELL BOTHWICK: Farmer from Dahlgren

SALDUR, MAURICE: Former bishop of Medford, former friend and advisor to the Essendon family, co-regent of the New Empire

SALIFAN: \sal-eh-fan\ Fragrant wild plant used in incense

SALTY MACKEREL, THE: Tavern in the shipping district of Aquesta

SARAP: Meeting place, or talking place, in the Tenkin language

SAULY: Nickname of Maurice Saldur, used by those closest to him

SENON UPLANDS: Highland plateau overlooking Chadwick

SENTINEL: Inquisitor generals of the Nyphron Church, charged with rooting out heresy and finding the lost Heir of Novron

SERET: \sir-ett\ Knights of Nyphron. The military arm of the church, first formed by Lord Darius Seret, commanded by Sentinels.

SET: Ratibor member of the Black Diamond thieves' guild

SEWARD: Captain of the *Emerald Storm*

SHARON SEA: Southern body of water west of the Ghazel Sea

SHERIDAN UNIVERSITY: Prestigious institution of learning, located in Ghent

SHIP'S MASTER: Highest non-officer, in charge of running the daily working of the ship

SHIRLUM-KATH: Small, parasitic worm found in Calis, can infect untreated wounds

SIWARD: Bailiff of Hintindar

SKILLYGALEE: \Skil`li-ga-lee\ A kind of thin, weak broth or oatmeal porridge

SPADONE: Long two-handed sword with a tapering blade and an extended flange ahead of the hilt allowing for an extended variety of fighting maneuvers. Due to the length of the handgrip and the flange, which provides its own barbed hilt, the sword provides a number of additional hand placements, permitting the sword to be used similarly to a quarterstaff, as well as a powerful cleaving weapon. The spadone is the traditional weapon of a skilled knight.

STAUL: Tenkin warrior aboard the *Emerald Storm*

SUMMERSRULE: Popular midsummer holiday celebrated with picnics, dances, feasts, and jousting tournaments

TABARD: A tunic worn over armor usually emblazoned with a coat of arms

TALBERT, BISHOP: Head of Nyphron Church in Ratibor

TARIN VALE: Hometown of Amilia

TARTANE: Small ship used for fishing and coastal trading; single mast, large sail

TEK'CHIN: One of the fighting disciplines of the Teshlor Knights, preserved by the Knights of the Fauld and handed down to the Pickerings

TEMPLE: Ship's master of the *Emerald Storm*, second in command

TENENT: Most common form of semi-standard international currency. Coins of gold, silver, and copper stamped with the likeness of the king of the realm where it was minted.

TENKIN: Community of humans living in the manner of Ghazel and suspected of having Ghazel blood

TERLANDO BAY: Harbor of Tur Del Fur

TESHLORS: Legendary knights of the Novronian Empire, greatest warriors ever to have lived

THEOREM ELDERSHIP: Secret society formed to protect the heir

THERON WOOD: Father of Thrace Wood, farmer of Dahlgren, killed by Gilarabrywn

THRACE WOOD: Daughter of Theron and Addie, name changed to Modina by regents, crowned empress of the New Empire, killed Gilarabrywn in Dahlgren

THRANIC, DOVIN: See Dovin Thranic

TIGER OF MANDALIN: Moniker given to Hadrian while in Calis

TILINER: Superior side sword used frequently by mercenaries in Avryn

TOLIN ESSENDON: Son of Brodric, moved the Melengar capital to Medford, built Essendon Castle, also known as Tolin the Great

TOPMEN: Members of a ship's crew that work high up in the rigging and sails

TORSONIC: Torque-producing, as in the cable used in crossbows

TRAMUS DAN: Guardian of Naron

TRENCHON: City bailiff of Ratibor

TRENT: Northern mountainous kingdoms not yet controlled by the New Empire

TRILON: Small, fast bow used by Ghazel

TRUMBUL, BARON: Mercenary, hired by Percy Braga to kill Prince Alric

TULAN: Tropical plant found in southeastern Calis, used in religious ceremonies, leaves are dried and burned as offerings to the god Uberlin, smoke of the leaves produce visions when inhaled

TUR: Small legendary village believed to have once been in Delgos, site of the first recorded visit of Kile, mythical source of great weapons

TUR DEL FUR: Coastal city in Delgos, on Terlando Bay, originally built by dwarves

UBERLIN: The god of the Dacca and the Ghazel, son of Erebus and his daughter, Muriel

ULI VERMAR: Obscure reference used by Esrahaddon

URITH: Former king of Ratibor, died in a fire

URLINEUS: Last of the Novronian Empire cities to fall, located in eastern Calis, constantly attacked by Ghazel. After collapse it became the gateway for the Ghazel into Calis.

UZLA BAR: Ghazel chieftain, challenging Erandabon Gile for control of Ghazel

VALIN, LORD: Elderly knight of Melengar known for his valor and courage but lacking strategic skills

VANDON: Port city of Delgos, home to the Vandon Spice Company, pirate haven, grew into a legitimate business center when Delgos became a republic

VELLA: Kitchen servant in the imperial palace

VENDEN POX: Poison impervious to magic remedies

VENLIN: Patriarch of the Nyphron Church during the fall of the Novronian Empire

VERNES: Port city at the mouth of the Bernum River

VIGAN: Sherriff of Ratibor

VILLEIN: Person who is bound to the land and owned by the feudal lord

VINCE EVERTON: Alias used by Royce Melborn while in Hintindar

VINTU: Native tribe of Calis

WANDERING DEACON OF DAHLGREN: Name that refers to Deacon Tomas

WARRIC: Kingdom of Avryn, once ruled by Ethelred, now part of the New Empire

WATCH OFFICER: Officer of the watch, in charge during a particular shift, responsible for everything that transpires during this time

WESBADEN: Major trade port city of Calis

WESLEY: Son of Lord Belstrad, brother of Sir Breckton, junior midshipman on the *Emerald Storm*

WESTBANK: Newly formed province of Dunmore

WESTERLANDS: Unknown frontier to the west

WHERRY: Light rowboat, used for racing or transporting goods and passengers on inland waters and harbors

WICEND: \why-send\ Farmer in Melengar, name of the ford that crosses the Galewyr into Glouston

WIDLEY: Professor at Sheridan University, tried and burned for heresy

WILFRED: Carter in Hintindar

WINDS ABBEY: Monastery of the Monks of Maribor, rebuilt by Myron Lanaklin after being burned

WINSLOW, ALBERT: See Albert Winslow

WINTERTIDE: Chief holiday, held in midwinter, celebrated by feasts and games of skill

WITCH OF MELENGAR: Derogatory title attributed to Princess Arista

WYATT DEMINTHAL: Quartermaster and helmsman of the *Emerald Storm*, father of Allie

WYLIN: \why-lynn\ Master-at-arms at Essendon Castle

WYMAR, MARQUIS: Nobleman of Melengar, member of Alric's council

YOLRIC: Teacher of Esrahaddon

ZULRON: Deformed oberdaza of Oudorro

extras

meet the author

Michael J. Sullivan

After finding a manual typewriter in the basement of a friend's house, Michael J. Sullivan inserted a blank piece of paper and typed *It was a dark and stormy night and a shot rang out*. He was just eight. Still, the desire to fill the blank page and see where the keys would take him next wouldn't let go. As an adult, Michael spent ten years developing his craft by reading and studying authors such as Stephen King, Ayn Rand, and John Steinbeck, to name just a few. He wrote ten novels, and after finding no traction in publishing, he quit, vowing never to write creatively again.

Michael discovered forever is a very long time and ended his writing hiatus ten years later. The itch returned when he decided to write books for his then thirteen-year-old daughter, who was struggling in school due to dyslexia. Intrigued by the idea of a series with an overarching story line, yet told through individual self-contained episodes, he created the Riyria Revelations. He wrote the series with no intention of publishing it. After presenting his book in manuscript form to his daughter, she declared that it had to be a "real book" in order for her to be able to read it.

So began his second adventure on the road to publication, which included drafting his wife to be his business manager, signing with a small independent press, and creating a publishing company. He sold more than sixty thousand books as a self-published author and leveraged this success to achieve mainstream publication through Orbit (the fantasy imprint of Hachette Book Group) as well as foreign translation rights including French, Spanish, Russian, German, Polish, and Czech.

Born in Detroit, Michigan, Michael presently lives in Fairfax, Virginia, with his wife and three children. He continues to fill the blank pages with three projects under development: a modern fantasy, which explores the relationship between good and evil; a literary fiction piece profiling a man's descent into madness; and a medieval fantasy, which will be a prequel to his best-selling Riyria Revelations series.

Find out more about the author at www.michaelsullivan-author .com and his blog www.riyria.blogspot.com.

introducing

**If you enjoyed
RISE OF EMPIRE,
look out for**

HEIR OF NOVRON

Volume Three of the Riyria Revelations

by Michael J. Sullivan

CHAPTER 1

AQUESTA

Some people are skilled, and some are lucky, but at that moment Mince realized he was neither. Failing to cut the merchant's purse strings, he froze with one hand still cupping the bag. He knew the pickpocket's creed allowed for only a single touch, and he had dutifully slipped into the crowd after two earlier attempts. A third failure meant they would bar him from another meal. Mince was too hungry to let go.

With his hands still under the merchant's cloak, he waited. The man remained oblivious.

Should I try again?

The thought was insane, but his empty stomach won the battle over reason. In a moment of desperation, Mince pushed caution aside. The leather seemed oddly thick. Sawing back and forth, he felt the purse come loose, but something was not right. It took only an instant for Mince to realize his mistake. Instead of purse strings, he had sliced through the merchant's belt. Like a hissing snake, the leather strap slithered off the fat man's belly, dragged to the cobblestones by the weight of his weapons.

Mince did not breathe or move as the entire span of his ten disappointing years flashed by.

Run! the voice inside his head screamed as he realized there was a heartbeat, perhaps two, before his victim—

The merchant turned.

He was a large, soft man with saddlebag cheeks reddened by the cold. His eyes widened when he noticed the purse in Mince's hand. "Hey, you!" The man reached for his dagger, and surprise filled his face when he found it missing. Groping for his other weapon, he spotted them both lying in the street.

Mince heeded the voice of his smarter self and bolted. Common sense told him the best way to escape a rampaging giant was to head for the smallest crack. He plunged beneath an ale cart outside The Blue Swan Inn and slid to the far side. Scrambling to his feet, he raced for the alley, clutching the knife and purse to his chest. The recent snow hampered his flight, and his small feet lost traction rounding a corner.

"Thief! Stop!" The shouts were not nearly as close as he had expected.

Mince continued to run. Finally reaching the stable, he ducked between the rails of the fence framing the manure pile. Exhausted, he crouched with his back against the far wall. The boy shoved the knife into his belt and stuffed the purse down his shirt, leaving a noticeable bulge. Panting amidst the steaming piles, he struggled to hear anything over the pounding in his ears.

"There you are!" Elbright shouted, skidding in the snow and catching himself on the fence. "What an idiot. You just stood there—waiting for the fat oaf to turn around. You're a moron, Mince. That's it—that's all there is to it. I honestly don't know why I bother trying to teach you."

Mince and the other boys referred to thirteen-year-old Elbright as the Old Man. In their small band only he wore an actual cloak, which was dingy gray and secured with a tarnished metal broach. Elbright was the smartest and most accomplished of their crew, and Mince hated to disappoint him.

Laughing, Brand arrived only moments later and joined Elbright at the fence.

"It's not funny," Elbright said.

"But—he—" Brand could not finish as laughter consumed him.

Like the other two, Brand was dirty, thin, and dressed in mismatched clothing of varying sizes. His pants were too long and snow gathered in the folds of the rolled-up bottoms. Only his tunic fit properly. Made from green brocade and trimmed with fine supple leather, it fastened down the front with intricately carved wooden toggles. A year younger than the Old Man, he was a tad taller and a bit broader. In the unspoken hierarchy of their gang, Brand came second—the muscle to Elbright's brains. Kine, the remaining member of their group, ranked third, because he was the best pickpocket. This left Mince unquestionably at the bottom. His size matched his position, as he stood barely four feet tall and weighed little more than a wet cat.

"Stop it, will ya?" the Old Man snapped. "I'm trying to

teach the kid a thing or two. He could have gotten himself killed. It was stupid—plain and simple."

"I thought it was brilliant." Brand paused to wipe his eyes. "I mean, sure it was dumb, but spectacular just the same. The way Mince just stood there blinking as the guy goes for his blades. But they ain't there 'cuz the little imbecile done cut the git's whole bloody belt off! Then..." Brand struggled against another bout of laughter. "The best part is that just after Mince runs, the fat bastard goes to chase him, and his breeches fall down. The guy toppled like a ruddy tree. *Wham.* Right into the gutter. By Mar, that was hilarious."

Elbright tried to remain stern, but Brand's recounting soon had them all laughing.

"Okay, okay, quit it." Elbright regained control and went straight to business. "Let's see the take."

Mince fished out the purse and handed it over with a wide grin. "Feels heavy," he proudly stated.

Elbright drew open the top and scowled after examining the contents. "Just coppers."

Brand and Elbright exchanged disappointed frowns and Mince's momentary elation melted. "It felt heavy," he repeated, mainly to himself.

"What now?" Brand asked. "Do we give him another go?"

Elbright shook his head. "No, and all of us will have to avoid Church Square for a while. Too many people saw Mince. We'll move closer to the gates. We can watch for new arrivals and hope to get lucky."

"Do ya want—" Mince started.

"No. Give me back my knife. Brand is up next."

The boys jogged toward the palace walls, following the trail that morning patrols had made in the fresh snow. They circled east and entered Imperial Square. People from all over Avryn were arriving for Wintertide, and the central plaza bustled with likely prospects.

"There," Elbright said, pointing toward the city gate. "Those two. See 'em? One tall, the other shorter."

"They're a sorry-looking pair," Mince said.

"Exhausted," Brand agreed.

"Probably been riding all night in the storm," Elbright said with a hungry smile. "Go on, Brand, do the old helpful stableboy routine. Now, Mince, watch how this is done. It might be your only hope, as you've got no talent for purse cutting."

&

Royce and Hadrian entered Imperial Square on ice-laden horses. Defending against the cold, the two appeared as ghosts shrouded in snowy blankets. Despite wearing all they had, they were ill-equipped for the winter roads, much less the mountain passes that lay between Ratibor and Aquesta. The all-night snowstorm had only added to their hardship. As the two drew their horses to a stop, Royce noticed Hadrian breathing into his cupped hands. Neither of them had winter gloves. Hadrian had wrapped his fingers in torn strips from his blanket, while Royce opted for pulling his hands into the shelter of his sleeves. The sight of his own handless arms disturbed Royce as they reminded him of the old wizard. The two had learned the details of his murder while passing through Ratibor. Assassinated late one night, Esrahaddon had been silenced forever.

They had meant to get gloves, but as soon as they had arrived in Ratibor, they saw announcements proclaiming the Nationalist leader's upcoming execution. The empire planned to publicly burn Degan Gaunt in the imperial capital of Aquesta as part of the Wintertide celebrations. After Hadrian and Royce had spent months traversing high seas and dark jungles seeking Gaunt, to have found his whereabouts tacked up to every tavern door in the city was as much a blow as a blessing. Fearing some new calamity might arise to stop them from finally reaching him, they left early the next morning, long before the trade shops opened.

Unwrapping his scarf, Royce drew back his hood and looked around. The snow-covered palace took up the entire southern side of the square, while shops and vendors dominated the rest. Furriers displayed trimmed capes and hats. Shoemakers cajoled passers-by, offering to oil their boots. Bakers tempted travelers with snowflake-shaped cookies and white-powdered pastries. And colorful banners were everywhere announcing the upcoming festival.

Royce had just dismounted when a boy ran up. "Take your horses, sirs? One night in a stable for just a silver each. I'll brush them down myself and see they get good oats too."

Dismounting and pulling back his own hood, Hadrian smiled at the boy. "Will you sing them a lullaby at night?"

"Certainly, sir," the boy replied without losing a beat. "It will cost you two coppers more, but I do have a very fine voice, I does."

"Any stable in the city will quarter a horse for five coppers," Royce challenged.

"Not this month, sir. Wintertide pricing started three days back. Stables and rooms fill up fast. Especially this year. You're lucky you got here early. In another two weeks, they'll be stocking horses in the fields behind hunters' blinds. The only lodgings will be on dirt floors, where people will be stacked like cordwood for five silvers each. I know the best places and the lowest costs in the city. A silver is a good price right now. In a few days it'll cost you twice that."

Royce eyed him closely. "What's your name?"

"Brand the Bold they call me." He straightened up, adjusting the collar of his tunic.

Hadrian chuckled and asked, "Why is that?"

"'Cuz I don't never back down from a fight, sir."

"Is that where you got your tunic?" Royce asked.

The boy looked down as if noticing the garment for the first time. "This old thing? I got five better ones at home. I'm just wearing this rag so I don't get the good ones wet in the snow."

"Well, Brand, do you think you can take these horses to The Bailey Inn at Hall and Coswall and stable them there?"

"I could indeed, sir. And a fine choice, I might add. It's run by a reputable owner charging fair prices. I was just going to suggest that very place."

Royce gave him a smirk. He turned his attention to two boys who stood at a distance, pretending not to know Brand. Royce waved for them to come over. The boys appeared hesitant, but when he repeated the gesture, they reluctantly obliged.

"What are your names?" he asked.

"Elbright, sir," the taller of the two replied. This boy was older than Brand and had a knife concealed beneath his cloak. Royce guessed he was the real leader of their group and had sent Brand over to make the play.

"Mince, sir," said the other, who looked to be the youngest and whose hair showed evidence of having recently been cut with a dull knife. The boy wore little more than rags of stained, worn wool. His shirt and pants exposed the bright pink skin of his wrists and shins. Of all his clothing, the item that fit best was a torn woven bag draped over his shoulders. The same material wrapped his feet, secured around his ankles by twine.

Hadrian checked through the gear on his horse, removed his spadone blade, and slid it into the sheath, which he wore on his back beneath his cloak.

Royce handed two silver tenents to the first boy, then, addressing all three, said, "Brand here is going to have our horses stabled at the Bailey and reserve us a room. While he's gone, you two will stay here and answer some questions."

"But, ah, sir, we can't—" Elbright started, but Royce ignored him.

"When Brand returns with a receipt from the Bailey, I will pay *each* of you a silver. If he doesn't return, if instead he runs off and sells the horses, I shall slit both of your throats and hang you on the palace gate by your feet. I'll let your blood drip into a pail, then paint a sign with it to notify the city that Brand the Bold is a horse thief. Then I'll track him down, with the help of the imperial guard and *other connections* I have in this city, and see he gets the same treatment." Royce glared at the boy. "Do we understand each other, Brand?"

The three boys stared at him with mouths agape.

"By Mar! Not a very trusting fellow, are ya, sir?" Mince said.

Royce grinned ominously. "Make the reservation under the names of Grim and Baldwin. Run along now, Brand, but do hurry back. You don't want your friends to worry."

Brand led the horses away while the other two boys watched him go. Elbright gave a little shake of his head when Brand looked back.

"Now, boys, why don't you tell us what is planned for this year's festivities?"

"Well…" Elbright started, "I suspect this will be the most memorable Wintertide in a hundred years on account of the empress's marriage and all."

"Marriage?" Hadrian asked.

"Yes, sir. I thought everyone knew about that. Invitations went out months ago, and all the rich folk, even kings and queens, have been coming from all over."

"Who's she marrying?" Royce asked.

"*Lard* Ethelred," Mince said.

Elbright lowered his voice. "Shut it, Mince."

"He's a snake."

Elbright growled and cuffed him on the ear. "Talk like that will get you dead." Turning back to Royce and Hadrian, he said, "Mince has a bit of a crush on the empress. He's not too pleased with the old king, on account of him marrying her and all."

"She's like a goddess, she is," Mince declared, misty-eyed. "I seen her once. I climbed to that roof for a better view when she gave a speech last summer. She shimmered like a star, she did. By Mar, she's beautiful. Ya can tell she's the daughter of Novron. I've never seen anyone so pretty."

"See what I mean? Mince is a bit crazy when it comes to the empress," Elbright apologized. "He's got to get used to Regent Ethelred running things again. Not that he ever really stopped, on account of the empress being sick and all."

"She was hurt by the beast she killed up north," Mince explained. "Empress Modina was dying from the poison, and healers came from all over, but no one could help. Then Regent Saldur prayed for seven days and nights without food or water. Maribor showed him that the pure heart of a servant girl named Amilia from Tarin Vale had the power to heal the empress. And she did. Lady Amilia has been nursing the empress back to health and doing a fine job." He took a breath, his eyes brightened, and a smile grew across his face.

"Mince, enough," Elbright said.

"What's all this about?" Royce asked, pointing at bleachers that were being built in the center of the square. "They aren't holding the wedding out here, are they?"

"No, the wedding will be at the cathedral. Those are for folks to watch the execution. They're gonna kill the rebel leader."

795

"Yeah, that piece of news we heard about," Hadrian said softly.

"Oh, so you came for the execution?"

"More or less."

"I've got our spots all picked out," Elbright said. "I'm gonna have Mince go up the night before and save us a good seat."

"Hey, why do I have to go?" Mince asked.

"Brand and I have to carry all the stuff. You're too small to help and Kine's still sick, so you need to —"

"But you have the cloak and it's gonna be cold just sitting up there."

The two boys went on arguing, but Royce could tell Hadrian was no longer listening. His friend's eyes scanned the palace gates, walls, and front entrance. Hadrian was counting guards.

⌘

Rooms at the Bailey were the same as at every inn — small and drab, with worn wooden floors and musty odors. A small pile of firewood was stacked next to the hearth in each room but never enough for the whole night. Patrons were forced to buy more at exorbitant prices if they wanted to stay warm. Royce made his usual rounds, circling the block, watching for faces that appeared too many times. He returned to their room confident that no one had noticed their arrival — at least, no one who mattered.

"Room eight. Been here almost a week," Royce said.

"A week? Why so early?" Hadrian asked.

"If you were living in a monastery for ten months a year, wouldn't you show up early for Wintertide?"

Hadrian grabbed his swords and the two moved down the hall. Royce picked the lock of a weathered door and slid it open. On the far side of the room, two candles burned on a small table set with plates, glasses, and a bottle of wine. A man, dressed in velvet and silk, stood before a wall mirror, checking the tie that held back his blond hair and adjusting the high collar of his coat.

"Looks like he was expecting us," Hadrian said.

"Looks like he was expecting someone," Royce clarified.

"What the—" Startled, Albert Winslow spun around. "Would it hurt to knock?"

"What can I say?" Royce flopped on the bed. "We're scoundrels and thieves."

"Scoundrels certainly," Albert said, "but thieves? When was the last time you two stole anything?"

"Do I detect dissatisfaction?"

"I'm a viscount. I have a reputation to uphold, which takes a certain amount of income—money that I don't receive when you two are idle."

Hadrian took a seat at the table. "He's not dissatisfied. He's outright scolding us."

"Is that why you're here so early?" Royce asked. "Scouting for work?"

"Partially. I also needed to get away from the Winds Abbey. I'm becoming a laughingstock. When I contacted Lord Daref, he couldn't lay off the Viscount Monk jokes. On the other hand, Lady Mae does find my pious reclusion appealing."

"And is she the one who..." Hadrian swirled a finger at the neatly arranged table.

"Yes. I was about to fetch her. I'm going to have to cancel, aren't I?" He looked from one to the other and sighed.

"Sorry."

"I hope this job pays well. This is a new doublet and I still owe the tailor." Blowing out the candles, he took a seat across from Hadrian.

"How are things up north?" Royce asked.

Albert pursed his lips, thinking. "I'm guessing you know about Medford being taken? Imperial troops hold it and most of the provincial castles except for Drondil Fields."

Royce sat up. "No, we didn't know. How's Gwen?"

"I have no idea. I was here when I heard."

"So Alric and Arista are at Drondil Fields?" Hadrian asked.

"King Alric is but I don't think the princess was in Medford. I believe she's running Ratibor. They appointed her mayor, or so I've heard."

"No," Hadrian said. "We just came through there. She was governing after the battle but left months ago in the middle of the night. No one knows why. I just assumed she went home."

Albert shrugged. "Maybe, but I never heard anything about her going back. Probably better for her if she didn't. The Imps have Drondil Fields surrounded. Nothing is going in or out. It's only a matter of time before Alric will have to surrender."

"What about the abbey? Has the empire come knocking?" Royce asked.

Albert shook his head. "Not that I know of. But like I said, I was already here when the Imperialists crossed the Galewyr."

Royce got up and began to pace.

"Anything else?" Hadrian asked.

"Rumor has it that Tur Del Fur was invaded by goblins. But that's only a rumor, as far as I can tell."

"Not a rumor," Hadrian said.

"Oh?"

"We were there. Actually, we were responsible."

"Sounds...interesting," Albert said.

Royce stopped his pacing. "Don't get him started."

"Okay, so what brings you to Aquesta?" Albert asked. "I'm guessing it's not to celebrate Wintertide."

"We're going to break Degan Gaunt out of the palace dungeon, and we'll need you for the usual inside work," Royce said.

"Really? You do know he's going to be executed on Wintertide, don't you?"

"Yeah, that's why we need to get moving. It would be bad if we were late," Hadrian added.

"Are you crazy? The palace? At Wintertide? You've heard about this little wedding that's going on? Security might be a tad tighter than usual. Every day I see a line of men in the courtyard, signing up to join the guard."

"Your point?" Hadrian asked.

"We should be able to use the wedding to our advantage," Royce said. "Anyone we know in town yet?"

"Genny and Leo arrived recently, I think."

"Really? That's perfect. Get in touch. They'll have rooms in the palace for sure. See if they can get you in. Then find out all you can, especially about where they're keeping Gaunt."

"I'm going to need money. I was only planning to attend a few local balls and maybe one of the feasts. If you want me inside the palace, I'll have to get better clothes. By Mar, look at my shoes. Just look at them! I can't meet the empress in these."

"Borrow from Genny and Leo for now," Royce said. "I'm going to leave for Medford tonight and return with funds to cover our expenses."

"You're going back? Tonight?" Albert asked. "You just got here, didn't you?"

The thief nodded.

"She's okay," Hadrian assured Royce. "I'm sure she got out."

"We've got nearly a month to Wintertide," Royce said. "I should be back in a week or so. In the meantime, learn what you can, and we'll formulate a plan when I return."

"Well," Albert grumbled, "at least Wintertide won't be boring."

DeWitt had told Hadrian he had left the sword behind the altar, and they headed toward it.

As they approached the first set of pews, both men froze in mid-step. Lying there, facedown in a pool of freshly spilled blood, was the body of a man. The rounded handle of a dagger protruded from his back. While Royce made a quick survey for Pickering's sword, Hadrian checked the man for signs of life. The man was dead, and the sword was nowhere to be found. Royce tapped Hadrian on the shoulder and pointed at the gold crown that had rolled to the far side of a pillar. The full weight of the situation registered with both of them—it was time to leave.

They headed for the door. Royce paused only momentarily to listen to ensure the hall was clear. They slipped out of the chapel, closed the door, and moved down the hall toward the bedroom.

"*Murderers!*"

The shout was so close and so terrifying that they both spun with weapons drawn. Hadrian had his bastard sword in one hand, his short sword in the other. Royce held a brilliant white-bladed dagger.

Standing before the open chapel door was a bearded dwarf.

"*Murderers!*" the dwarf cried again, but it was not necessary. Footfalls could already be heard, and an instant later, soldiers, with weapons drawn, poured into the hallway from both sides.

BOOKS BY MICHAEL J. SULLIVAN

THE RIYRIA REVELATIONS

Theft of Swords
Rise of Empire
Heir of Novron

THEFT OF SWORDS

Volume One of the
Riyria Revelations

MICHAEL J. SULLIVAN

www.orbitbooks.net

Orbit
Hachette Book Group
1290 Avenue of the Americas, New York, NY 10104
www.HachetteBookGroup.com

First Edition: November 2011

Orbit is an imprint of Hachette Book Group, Inc. The Orbit name
and logo are trademarks of Little, Brown Book Group Limited.

Library of Congress Cataloging-in-Publication Data
Sullivan, Michael J.
    Theft of swords / Michael J. Sullivan. — 1st ed.
        p. cm.
    Summary: "Two thieves in the wrong place at the wrong time are
on the run in this fast-paced adventure fantasy"—Provided by
publisher.
    ISBN 978-0-316-18774-9
    I. Title.

    PS3619.U4437T47 2011
    813'.6—dc22

                                        2011008814

Printing 21, 2023

Printed in the United States of America

To my wife, Robin, my partner in life and in the adventure of making this series, whose hard work and dedication made it all possible

To my daughter Sarah, who would not read the story until it was published

To Steve Gillick for his feedback, and Pete DeBrule, who started this whole thing

And to the members of Dragonchow, my original fan club

CONTENTS

KNOWN REGIONS OF THE WORLD OF ELAN

Estrendor: Northern wastes
Erivan Empire: Elvenlands
Apeladorn: Nations of man
Ba Ran Archipelago: Islands of goblins
Westerlands: Western wastes
Dacca: Isle of south men

NATIONS OF APELADORN

Avryn: Central wealthy kingdoms
Trent: Northern mountainous kingdoms
Calis: Southeastern tropical region ruled by warlords
Delgos: Southern republic

KINGDOMS OF AVRYN

Ghent: Ecclesiastical holding of the Nyphron Church
Melengar: Small but old and respected kingdom
Warric: Most powerful of the kingdoms of Avryn
Dunmore: Youngest and least sophisticated kingdom
Alburn: Forested kingdom
Rhenydd: Poor kingdom
Maranon: Producer of food. Once part of Delgos, which was
   lost when Delgos became a republic
Galeannon: Lawless kingdom of barren hills, the site of
   several great battles

The Gods

Erebus: Father of the gods
Ferrol: Eldest son, god of elves
Drome: Second son, god of dwarves
Maribor: Third son, god of men
Muriel: Only daughter, goddess of nature
Uberlin: Son of Muriel and Erebus, god of darkness

Political Parties

*Imperialists: Those wishing to unite mankind under a single
  leader who is the direct descendant of the demigod
  Novron*
*Nationalists: Those wishing to be ruled by a leader chosen
  by the people*
*Royalists: Those wishing to continue rule by individual,
  independent monarchs*

THE WORLD OF ELAN

Elan

N E S W

Eastern coastline drawn
from ancient imperial text

BA RAN
Archipeligo

GOBLIN
SEA

C A L I S

Em
Gur
Dur Guron
Mandalin
Dagastan

GHAZEL
SEA

E R I V A N
elvenlands

Avempartha

Nidwalden River

Dalgreth

Rolunche
Westbacken

Vilan Hills

Galeannon

Lingard

Dunmore

Glamrendor

A L B U R N

Alburn
Caten
Rochelle

Ervanon

Ghent

Sheridan

Melengar

T R E N T

Lankster

Hintindar

Wicend Abbey

Drondil Fields
Galilin

Chadwick
Bramstrad
Roe

Colnora

W A R R I C

Amberton Lee

Hargrove River

Kilnar

R h e n y d d

Vernes

Vandon

D E L G O S

M a r a n o n

Manzar

Dagastan
Bay

T i e r r e

Tur Del Fur

Raibor

Aquesta

SHARON
SEA

W E S T E R L I N S

The Lost Lands

THE
SOUND

Wilecia islands

DETAIL OF AVRYN

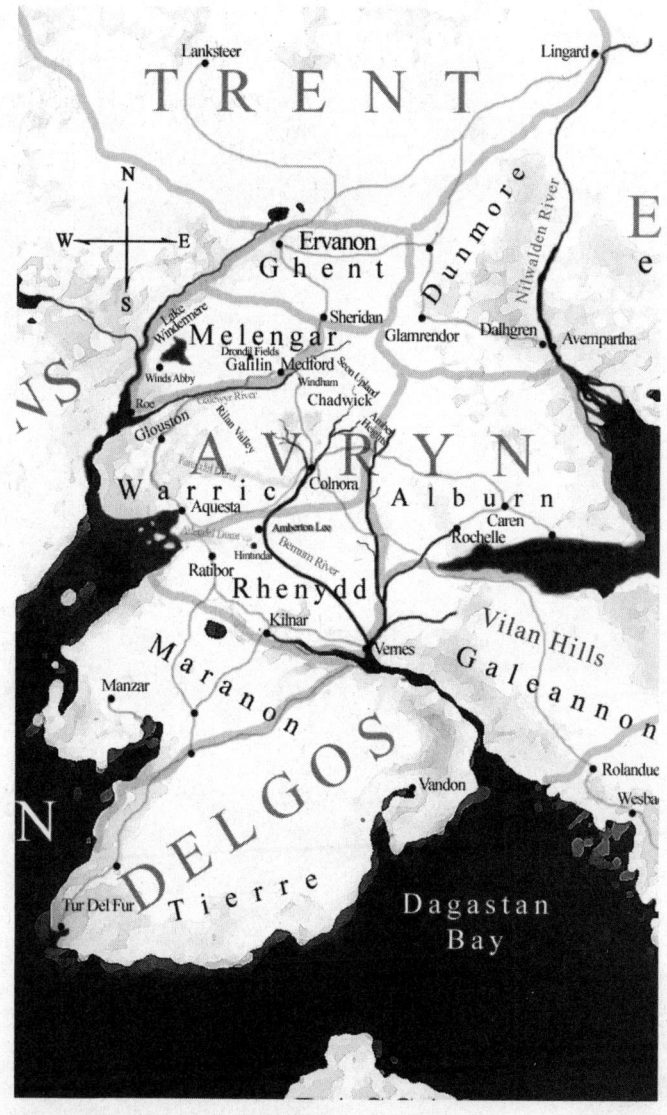

BOOK I

THE CROWN CONSPIRACY

Chapter 1

Stolen Letters

Hadrian could see little in the darkness, but he could hear them—the snapping of twigs, the crush of leaves, and the brush of grass. There were more than one, more than three, and they were closing in.

"Don't neither of you move," a harsh voice ordered from the shadows. "We've got arrows aimed at your backs, and we'll drop you in your saddles if you try to run." The speaker was still in the dark eaves of the forest, just a vague movement among the naked branches. "We're just gonna lighten your load a bit. No one needs to get hurt. Do as I say and you'll keep your lives. Don't—and we'll take those, too."

Hadrian felt his stomach sink, knowing this was his fault. He glanced over at Royce, who sat beside him on his dirty gray mare with his hood up, his face hidden. His friend's head was bowed and shook slightly. Hadrian did not need to see his expression to know what it looked like.

"Sorry," he offered.

Royce said nothing and just continued to shake his head.

Before them stood a wall of fresh-cut brush blocking their way. Behind lay the long moonlit corridor of empty road. Mist pooled in the dips and gullies, and somewhere an unseen stream trickled over rocks. They were deep in the forest on the old southern road, engulfed in a long tunnel of oaks and ash whose slender branches reached out over the road, quivering and clacking in the cold autumn wind. Almost a day's ride from any town, Hadrian could not recall passing so much as a farmhouse in hours. They were on their own, in the middle of nowhere—the kind of place people never found bodies.

The crush of leaves grew louder until at last the thieves stepped into the narrow band of moonlight. Hadrian counted four men with unshaven faces and drawn swords. They wore rough clothes, leather and wool, stained, worn, and filthy. With them was a girl wielding a bow, an arrow notched and aimed. She was dressed like the rest in pants and boots, her hair a tangled mess. Each was covered in mud, a ground-in grime, as if the whole lot slept in a dirt burrow.

"They don't look like they got much money," a man with a flat nose said. An inch or two taller than Hadrian, he was the largest of the party, a stocky brute with a thick neck and large hands. His lower lip looked to have been split about the same time his nose was broken.

"But they've got bags of gear," the girl said. Her voice surprised him. She was young, and—despite the dirt—cute, and almost childlike, but her tone was aggressive, even vicious. "Look at all this stuff they're carrying. What's with all the rope?"

Hadrian was uncertain if she was asking him or her fellows. Either way, he was not about to answer. He considered making a joke, but she did not look like the type he could charm with a compliment and a smile. On top of that, she was pointing the arrow at him and it looked like her arm might be growing tired.

"I claim the big sword that fella has on his back," flat-nose said. "Looks right about my size."

"I'll take the other two he's carrying." This came from one with a scar that divided his face at a slight angle, crossing the bridge of his nose just high enough to save his eye.

The girl aimed the point of her arrow at Royce. "I want the little one's cloak. I'd look good in a fine black hood like that."

With deep-set eyes and sunbaked skin, the man closest to Hadrian appeared to be the oldest. He took a step closer and grabbed hold of Hadrian's horse by the bit. "Be real careful now. We've killed plenty of folks along this road. Stupid folks who didn't listen. You don't want to be stupid, do you?"

Hadrian shook his head.

"Good. Now drop them weapons," the thief said. "And then climb down."

"What do you say, Royce?" Hadrian asked. "We give them a bit of coin so nobody gets hurt."

Royce looked over. Two eyes peered out from the hood with a withering glare.

"I'm just saying, we don't want any trouble, am I right?"

"You don't want my opinion," Royce said.

"So you're going to be stubborn."

Silence.

Hadrian shook his head and sighed. "Why do you have to make everything so difficult? They're probably not bad people — just poor. You know, taking what they need to buy a loaf of bread to feed their family. Can you begrudge them that? Winter is coming and times are hard." He nodded his head in the direction of the thieves. "Right?"

"I ain't got no family," flat-nose replied. "I spend most of my coin on drink."

"You're not helping," Hadrian said.

"I'm not trying to. Either you two do as you're told, or we'll gut you right here." He emphasized this by pulling a long dagger from his belt and scraping it loudly against the blade of his sword.

A cold wind howled through the trees, bobbing the branches and stripping away more foliage. Red and gold leaves flew, swirling in circles, buffeted by the gusts along the narrow road. Somewhere in the dark an owl hooted.

"Look, how about we give you half our money? *My half.* That way this won't be a total loss for you."

"We ain't asking for half," the man holding his mount said. "We want it all, right down to these here horses."

"Now wait a second. Our horses? Taking a little coin is fine but horse thieving? If you get caught, you'll hang. And you know we'll report this at the first town we come to."

"You're from up north, ain't you?"

"Yeah, left Medford yesterday."

The man holding his horse nodded and Hadrian noticed a small red tattoo on his neck. "See, that's your problem." His face softened to a sympathetic expression that appeared more threatening by its intimacy. "You're probably on your way to Colnora—nice city. Lots of shops. Lots of fancy rich folk. Lots of trading going on down there, and we get lots of people along this road carrying all kinds of stuff to sell to them fancy folk. But I'm guessing you ain't been south before, have you? Up in Melengar, King Amrath goes to the trouble of having soldiers patrol the roads. But here in Warric, things are done a bit differently."

Flat-nose came closer, licking his split lip as he studied the spadone sword on his back.

"Are you saying theft is legal?"

"Naw, but King Ethelred lives in Aquesta and that's awfully far from here."

"And the Earl of Chadwick? Doesn't he administer these lands on the king's behalf?"

"Archie Ballentyne?" The mention of his name brought

chuckles from the other thieves. "Archie don't give a rat's ass what goes on with the common folk. He's too busy picking out what to wear." The man grinned, showing yellowed teeth that grew at odd angles. "So now drop them swords and climb down. Afterward, you can walk on up to Ballentyne Castle, knock on old Archie's door, and see what he does." Another round of laughter. "Now unless you think this is the perfect place to die—you're gonna do as I say."

"You were right, Royce," Hadrian said in resignation. He unclasped his cloak and laid it across the rear of his saddle. "We should have left the road, but honestly—I mean, we are in the middle of nowhere. What were the odds?"

"Judging from the fact that we're being robbed—pretty good, I think."

"Kinda ironic—Riyria being robbed. Almost funny even."

"It's not funny."

"Did you say Riyria?" the man holding Hadrian's horse asked.

Hadrian nodded and pulled his gloves off, tucking them into his belt.

The man let go of his horse and took a step away.

"What's going on, Will?" the girl asked. "What's Riyria?"

"There's a pair of fellas in Melengar that call themselves that." He looked toward the others and lowered his voice a bit. "I got connections up that way, remember? They say two guys calling themselves Riyria work out of Medford and I was told to keep my distance if I was ever to run across them."

"So what you thinking, Will?" scar-face asked.

"I'm thinking maybe we should clear the brush and let them ride through."

"What? Why? There's five of us and just two of them," flat-nose pointed out.

"But they're Riyria."

"So what?"

"So, my *associates* up north—they ain't stupid, and they told everyone never to touch these two. And my associates ain't exactly the squeamish types. If they say to avoid them, there's a good reason."

Flat-nose looked at them again with a critical eye. "Okay, but how do you know these two guys are them? You just gonna take their word for it?"

Will nodded toward Hadrian. "Look at the swords he's carrying. A man wearing one—maybe he knows how to use it, maybe not. A man carries two—he probably don't know nothing about swords, but he wants you to think he does. But a man carrying three swords—that's a lot of weight. No one's gonna haul that much steel around unless he makes a living using them."

Hadrian drew two swords from his sides in a single elegant motion. He flipped one around, letting it spin against his palm once. "Need to get a new grip on this one. It's starting to fray again." He looked at Will. "Shall we get on with this? I believe you were about to rob us."

The thieves shot uncertain glances to each other.

"Will?" the girl asked. She was still holding the bow taut but looked decidedly less confident.

"Let's clear the brush out of their way and let them pass," Will said.

"You sure?" Hadrian asked. "This nice man with the busted nose seems to have his heart set on getting a sword."

"That's okay," flat-nose said, looking up at Hadrian's blades as the moonlight glinted off the mirrored steel.

"Well, if you're sure."

All five nodded and Hadrian sheathed his weapons.

Will planted his sword in the dirt and waved the others

over as he hurried to clear the barricade of branches blocking the roadway.

"You know, you're doing this all wrong," Royce told them.

The thieves stopped and looked up, concerned.

Royce shook his head. "Not clearing the brush—the robbery. You picked a nice spot. I'll give you that. But you should have come at us from both sides."

"And, William—it is William, isn't it?" Hadrian asked.

The man winced and nodded.

"Yeah, William, most people are right-handed, so those coming in close should approach from the left. That would've put us at a disadvantage, having to swing across our bodies at you. Those with bows should be on our right."

"And why just one bow?" Royce asked. "She could have only hit one of us."

"Couldn't even have done that," Hadrian said. "Did you notice how long she held the bow bent? Either she's incredibly strong—which I doubt—or that's a homemade greenwood bow with barely enough power to toss the arrow a few feet. Her part was just for show. I doubt she's ever launched an arrow."

"Have too," the girl said. "I'm a fine marksman."

Hadrian shook his head at her with a smile. "You had your forefinger on top of the shaft, dear. If you had released, the feathers on the arrow would have brushed your finger and the shot would have gone anywhere but where you wanted it to."

Royce nodded. "Invest in crossbows. Next time stay hidden and just put a couple bolts into each of your targets' chests. All this talking is just stupid."

"Royce!" Hadrian admonished.

"What? You're always saying I should be nicer to people. I'm trying to be helpful."

"Don't listen to him. If you do want some advice, try building a better barricade."

"Yeah, drop a tree across the road next time," Royce said. Waving a hand toward the branches, he added, "This is just pathetic. And cover your faces for Maribor's sake. Warric isn't that big of a kingdom and people might remember you. Sure Ballentyne isn't likely to bother tracking you down for a few petty highway robberies, but you're gonna walk into a tavern one day and get a knife in your back." Royce turned to William. "You were in the Crimson Hand, right?"

Will looked startled. "No one said nothing about that." He stopped pulling on the branch he was working on.

"Didn't need to. The Hand requires all guild members to get that stupid tattoo on their necks." Royce turned to Hadrian. "It's supposed to make them look tough, but all it really does is make it easy to identify them as thieves for the rest of their lives. Painting a red hand on everyone is pretty stupid when you think about it."

"That tattoo is supposed to be a hand?" Hadrian asked. "I thought it was a little red chicken. But now that you mention it, a hand does make more sense."

Royce looked back at Will and tilted his head to one side. "Does kinda look like a chicken."

Will clamped a palm over his neck.

After the last of the brush was cleared, William asked, "Who are you, really? What exactly is Riyria? The Hand never told me. They just said to keep clear."

"We're nobody special," Hadrian replied. "Just a couple of travelers enjoying a ride on a cool autumn's night."

"But seriously," Royce said. "You need to listen to us if you're going to keep doing this. After all, we're going to take your advice."

"What advice?"

Royce gave a gentle kick to his horse and started forward

on the road again. "We're going to visit the Earl of Chadwick, but don't worry—we won't mention you."

✦

In his hands Archibald Ballentyne held the world, conveniently contained within fifteen stolen letters. Each parchment had been penned with meticulous care in a fine, elegant script. He could tell the writer believed that the words were profound and that their meaning conveyed a beautiful truth. Archibald felt the writing was drivel, yet he agreed with the author that they held a value beyond measure. He took a sip of brandy, closed his eyes, and smiled.

"Milord?"

Reluctantly Archibald opened his eyes and scowled at his master-at-arms. "What is it, Bruce?"

"The marquis has arrived, sir."

Archibald's smile returned. He carefully refolded the letters, tied them in a stack with a blue ribbon, and returned them to his safe. He closed its heavy iron door, snapped the lock in place, and tested the seal with two sharp tugs on the unyielding bolt. Then he headed downstairs to greet his guest.

When Archibald reached the foyer, he spied Victor Lanaklin waiting in the anteroom. He paused for a moment and watched the old man pacing back and forth. Watching him brought Archibald a sense of satisfaction. While the marquis enjoyed a superior title, the man had never impressed the earl. Perhaps Victor had once been lofty, intimidating, or even gallant, but all his glory had been lost long before, shrouded under a mat of gray hair and a hunched back.

"May I offer you something to drink, Your Lordship?" a mousy steward asked the marquis with a formal bow.

"No, but you can get me your earl," he commanded. "Or shall I hunt for him myself?"

The steward cringed. "I'm certain my master will be with you presently, sir." The servant bowed again and hastily retreated through a door on the far side of the room.

"Marquis!" Archibald called out graciously as he made his entrance. "I'm so pleased you have arrived—and so quickly."

"You sound surprised," Victor replied with a sharp voice. Shaking a wrinkled parchment clasped in his fist, he continued, "You send a message like this and expect me to delay? Archie, I demand to know what is going on."

Archibald concealed his disdain at the use of his childhood nickname, *Archie*. This was the moniker his dead mother had given him and one of the reasons he would never forgive her. When he was a youth, everyone from the knights to the servants had used it, and Archibald had always felt demeaned by its familiarity. Once he became earl, he made it law in Chadwick that anyone referring to him by the name would suffer the lash. Archibald did not have the power to enforce the edict on the marquis, and he was certain Victor used it intentionally.

"Please do try to calm down, Victor."

"Don't tell me to calm down!" The marquis's voice echoed off the stone walls. He moved closer, his face mere inches from the younger man's, and glared into his eyes. "You wrote that my daughter Alenda's future was at stake and spoke of evidence. Now I must know—is she, or is she not, in danger?"

"She is most certainly," the earl replied calmly, "but nothing imminent, to be sure. There is no kidnapping plot nor is anyone planning to murder her, if that's what you fear."

"Then why send me this message? If you've caused me to run my carriage team to near collapse while I worried myself sick for nothing, you'll regret—"

Holding up his hand, Archibald cut the threat short. "I

assure you, Victor, it's not for nothing. Nevertheless, before we discuss this further, let us retire to the comfort of my study, where I can show you the evidence I mentioned."

Victor glowered at him but nodded in agreement.

The two men crossed the foyer, passed through the large reception hall, and veered off through a door that led to the living quarters of the castle. As they traversed various hallways and stairways, the atmosphere of their surroundings changed dramatically. In the main entry, fine tapestries and etched stonework adorned the walls, and the floors were made of finely crafted marble. Yet beyond the entry, no displays of grandeur were found, leaving barren walls of stone the predominate feature.

By architectural standards, or any other measures, Ballentyne Castle was unremarkable and ordinary in every respect. No great king or hero had ever called the castle home. Nor was it the site of any legend, ghost story, or battle. Instead, it was the perfect example of mediocrity and the mundane.

After several minutes navigating the various hallways, Archibald stopped at a formidable cast-iron door. Impressive oversized bolts secured the door at its hinges, but no latch or knob was visible. Flanking either side of it stood two large well-armored guards bearing halberds. Upon Archibald's approach, one rapped three times. A tiny viewing window opened, and a moment later, the hall echoed with the sharp sound of a bolt snapping back. As the door opened, the metal hinges screamed with a deafening noise.

Victor's hands moved to defend his ears. "By Mar! Have one of your servants tend to that!"

"Never," Archibald replied. "This is the entrance to the Gray Tower—my private study. This is my safe haven and I want to hear this door's opening from anywhere in the castle, which I can."

Behind the door, Bruce greeted the pair with a deep and

stately bow. Holding a lantern before him, he escorted the men up a wide spiral staircase. Halfway up the tower, Victor's pace slowed and his breathing appeared labored.

Archibald paused courteously. "I must apologize for the long ascent. I really don't notice it anymore. I must have climbed these stairs a thousand times. When my father was the earl, this was the one place I could go to be alone. No one ever bothered to take the time or effort to reach the top. While it may not reach the majestic height of the Crown Tower at Ervanon, it's the tallest tower in my castle."

"Don't some people come merely to see the view?" Victor speculated.

The earl chuckled. "You would think so, but this tower has no windows, which is what makes it the perfect location for my private study. I added the doors to protect the things dear to me."

Reaching the top of the stairs, they encountered another door. Archibald removed a large key from his pocket, unlocked it, and gestured for the marquis to enter. Bruce resumed his normal post outside the study and closed the door.

The room was large and circular with an expansive ceiling. The furnishings were sparse: a large disheveled desk, two cushioned chairs near a small fireplace, and a delicate table between them. A fire burned in the hearth behind a simple brass screen, illuminating most of the study. Candles, which lined the walls, provided light to the remaining areas and filled the chamber with a pleasant, heady aroma of honey and salifan.

Archibald smiled when he noticed Victor eyeing the cluttered desk overflowing with various scrolls and maps. "Don't worry, sir. I hid all the truly incriminating plans for world

domination prior to your visit. Please, do sit down." Archibald
indicated the pair of chairs near the hearth. "Rest yourself
from your long journey while I pour us a drink."

The older man scowled and grumbled, "Enough of the tour
and formalities. Now that we are here, let's get on with it.
Explain what this is all about."

Archibald ignored the marquis's tone. He could afford to
be gracious now that he was about to claim his prize. He
waited while the marquis took his seat.

"You are aware, are you not, that I have shown an interest
in your daughter, Alenda?" Archibald asked, walking to the
desk to pour two glasses of brandy.

"Yes, she's mentioned it to me."

"Has she mentioned why she refuses my advances?"

"She doesn't like you."

"She hardly knows me," countered Archibald with a raised
finger.

"Archie, is this why you asked me here?"

"Marquis, I would appreciate your addressing me by my
proper name. It's inappropriate to call me *that*, since my father
is dead and I now hold title. In any case, your question does
have a bearing on the subject. As you know, I'm the twelfth
Earl of Chadwick. Granted, it's not a huge estate, and Ballentyne isn't the most influential of families, but I'm not without
merit. I control five villages and twelve hamlets, as well as the
strategic Senon Uplands. I currently command more than
sixty professional men-at-arms, and twenty knights are loyal
to me—including Sir Enden and Sir Breckton, perhaps the
two greatest living knights. Chadwick's wool and leather
exports are the envy of all of Warric. There is even talk of the
Summersrule Games being held here—on the very lawn you
crossed to enter my castle."

"Yes, Archie—I mean, *Archibald*—I'm well aware of Chadwick's status in the world. I don't need a commerce lesson from you."

"Are you also aware that King Ethelred's nephew has dined here on more than one occasion? Or that the Duke and Duchess of Rochelle have asked to dine with me at Wintertide this year?"

"Archibald, this is quite tiresome. What exactly is your point?"

Archibald frowned at the marquis's lack of awe. Carrying over the glasses of brandy, he handed one to Victor and took the remaining seat. He paused a moment to sip his liquor.

"My point is this. Given my position, my stature, and my promising future, it makes no sense for Alenda to reject me. Certainly, it's not because of my appearance. I'm young, handsome, and wear only the finest imported fashions made from the most expensive silks to be found. The rest of her suitors are old, fat, or bald—in several cases all three."

"Perhaps looks and wealth are not her only concerns," replied Victor. "Women don't always think about politics and power. Alenda is the kind of girl who follows her heart."

"But she will also follow her father's wishes. Am I correct?"

"I don't understand your meaning."

"If you told her to marry me, she would. You could *order* her."

"So, this is why you coerced me into coming here? I'm sorry, Archibald, but you have wasted your time and mine. I have no intention of forcing her to marry anyone, least of all you. She would hate me for the rest of her life. I care more about my daughter's feelings than the political implications of her marriage. I happen to cherish Alenda. Of all my children, she is my greatest joy."

Archibald took another sip of brandy and considered Victor's remarks. He decided to approach the subject from a different direction. "What if it were for her own good? To save her from what would be certain disaster."

"You warned me of danger to get me here. Are you finally ready to explain, or do you prefer to see if this old man can still handle a blade?"

Archibald disregarded what he knew was an idle threat. "When Alenda repeatedly declined my advances, I reasoned something must be amiss. There was no logic to her rebuffs. I have connections and my star is rising. Then I discovered the real reason for your daughter's refusal—she is already involved with someone else. Alenda is having an affair, a secret affair."

"I find that difficult to believe," Victor declared. "She has not mentioned anyone to me. If someone caught her eye, she would tell me."

"It's little wonder she's kept his identity from you. She's ashamed. She knows that their relationship will bring disgrace to your family. The man she is entertaining is a mere commoner without a single drop of noble blood in his veins."

"You're lying!"

"I assure you, I'm not. The problem goes further than that, I'm afraid. His name is Degan Gaunt. You've heard of him, haven't you? He's quite famous. He's the leader of that Nationalist movement out of Delgos. You know that down south he has stirred up all kinds of emotions with his fellow commoners. They are all intoxicated with the idea of butchering the nobility and establishing self-rule. He and your daughter have been rendezvousing at Windermere near the monastery. They meet when you are away and occupied with matters of state."

"That is ridiculous. My daughter would never—"

"Don't you have a son there?" Archibald inquired. "At the abbey, I mean. He's a monk, isn't he?"

Victor nodded. "My third son, Myron."

"Perhaps he has been helping them. I've made inquiries and it seems that your son is a very intelligent fellow. Perhaps he is masterminding liaisons for his beloved sister and carrying their correspondences. This looks very bad, Victor. Here you are, the marquis of a staunchly Imperialist king, and your daughter is involved with a revolutionary and meeting him in the Royalist kingdom of Melengar while your son sets the whole thing up. Many could assume it's a family plot. What would King Ethelred say if he knew? We both know you're loyal, but others may have their doubts. While I realize this is nothing more than the misguided affections of an innocent girl, her escapades could ruin your family's honor."

"You *are* insane," Victor shot back. "Myron went to the abbey when he was barely four years old. Alenda has never even spoken to him. This whole fabrication is an obvious attempt to have me pressure Alenda into marrying you and I know why. You don't care about her. You want her dowry, the Rilan Valley. That piece of land borders ever so nicely against your own and that's what you are really after. Well, that and the opportunity to raise your own standing by marrying into a family that's above yours both socially and politically. You are pathetic."

"Pathetic, am I?" Archibald set down his glass and produced a key on a silver chain from inside his shirt. He rose and crossed the room to a tapestry depicting a Calian prince on horseback abducting a fair-haired noblewoman. He drew it back, revealing a hidden safe. Inserting the key, he opened the small metal door.

"I have a stack of letters written in your precious daughter's own hand that proves what I've been saying. They tell of her undying love for her disgusting revolutionary peasant."

"How did you get these letters?"

"I stole them. When I was trying to determine who my rival was, I had her watched. She was sending letters that led a path to the abbey and I arranged to have them intercepted." From the safe, Archibald brought forth a stack of parchments and dropped them in Victor's lap. "There!" he declared triumphantly. "Read what your daughter has been up to and decide for yourself whether or not she would be better off marrying me instead."

Archibald returned to his seat and lifted his brandy glass victoriously. He had won. In order to avoid political ruin, Victor Lanaklin, the great Marquis of Glouston, would order his daughter to marry him. The marquis had no choice. If word of this reached Ethelred, it was even possible Victor could face charges for treason. Imperialist kings demand that their nobles mirror their political attitudes and devotion to the church. While Archibald doubted that Victor was really a Royalist or Nationalist sympathizer, any appearance of impropriety would be enough reason for their king to express his displeasure. At the very least, Victor faced crippling embarrassment from which the House of Lanaklin might never recover. The only sensible course for the marquis was to agree to the marriage.

Finally, Archibald would have the borderland, and perhaps in time, he would control the whole of the marchland. With Chadwick in his right hand and Glouston in his left, he would have power at court that would rival that of the Duke of Rochelle.

Looking down at the old, gray-haired man in his fine traveling clothes, Archibald almost felt sorry for him. Once, long ago, the marquis had enjoyed a reputation for cleverness and fortitude. Such distinction came with his title. The marquis was no mere noble, nor was he a simple sheriff of the land, like an earl or a count. Victor had been responsible for guarding the king's borders. This was a serious duty, which required a capable leader, an ever-vigilant man tested in battle. However, times had changed, and peaceful neighbors now bordered Warric, such that the great guard had become complacent, and his strength had withered from lack of use.

As Victor opened the letters, Archibald contemplated his future. The marquis was right. He was after the land that came with his daughter. Still, Alenda was attractive, and the thought of forcing her to his bed was more than a little appealing.

"Archibald, is this a joke?" Victor questioned.

Startled from his thoughts, Archibald set down his drink. "What do you mean?"

"These parchments are blank."

"What? Are you blind? They're—" Archibald stopped when he saw the empty pages in the marquis's hand. He grabbed a handful of letters and tore them open, only to find still more blank parchments. "This is impossible!"

"Perhaps they were written in disappearing ink?" Victor smirked.

"No...I don't understand...These aren't even the same parchments!" He rechecked the safe but found it empty. His confusion turned to panic and he tore open the door, calling anxiously for Bruce. The master-at-arms rushed in, his sword at the ready. "What happened to the letters I had in this safe?" Archibald shouted at the soldier.

"I—I don't know, my lord," Bruce replied. He sheathed his weapon and stood at attention before the earl.

"What do you mean, you don't know? Have you left your post at all this evening?"

"No, sir, of course not."

"Did anyone, anyone at all, enter my study during my absence?"

"No, my lord, that's impossible. You hold the only key."

"Then where in Maribor's name are those letters? I put

them there myself. I was reading them when the marquis arrived. I was only gone a few minutes. How could they disappear like that?"

Archibald's mind raced. He had held them in his hands only moments ago. He had locked them in the safe. He was convinced of that fact.

Where had they gone?

Victor drained his glass and stood. "If you don't mind, *Archie*, I'll be leaving now. This has been a tremendous waste of my time."

"Victor, wait. Don't go. The letters are real. I assure you I had them!"

"But of course you did, Archie. The next time you plan to blackmail me, I suggest you provide a better bluff." He crossed the room, passed through the door, and disappeared down the stairs.

"You had better consider what I said, Victor," Archibald yelled after him. "I'll find those letters. I will! I'll bring them to Aquesta! I'll present them at court!"

"What do you want me to do, my lord?" Bruce asked.

"Just wait, you fool. I have to think." Archibald ran his trembling fingers through his hair as he began to pace around the room. He reexamined the letters closely. They were indeed a different grade of parchment than the ones he had read so many times before.

Despite his certainty he had placed the letters in the safe, he began pulling out the drawers and riffling through the parchments on his desk. Archibald poured himself another drink and crossed the room. Ripping the screen from the fireplace, he probed the ashes with a poker to search for any telltale signs of parchment remains. In frustration, Archibald threw the blank letters into the fire. He drained his drink in one long swallow and collapsed into one of the chairs.

"They were just here," Archibald said, puzzled. Slowly, a solution began to form in his mind. "Bruce, the letters must have been stolen. The thief could not have gotten far. I want you to search the entire castle. Seal every exit. Don't let anyone out. Not the staff or any of the guards—no one leaves. Search everyone!"

"Right away, my lord," Bruce responded, and then paused. "What about the marquis, my lord? Shall I stop him as well?"

"Of course not, you idiot, he doesn't have the letters."

Archibald stared into the fire, listening to Bruce's footsteps fade away as he ran down the tower stairs. Alone, he had only the sound of the crackling flames and a hundred unanswered questions. He racked his brain but could not determine exactly how the thief had managed it.

"Your Lordship?" The timid voice of the steward roused him from his thoughts. Archibald glared up at the man who poked his head through the open door, causing the steward to take an extra breath before speaking. "My lord, I hate to disturb you, but there seems to be a problem down in the courtyard that requires your attention."

"What kind of problem?" Archibald snarled.

"Well, my lord, I was not actually informed of the details, but it has something to do with the marquis, sir. I have been sent to request your presence—respectfully request it, that is."

Archibald descended the stairs, wondering if perhaps the old man had dropped dead on his doorstep, which would not be such a terrible thing. When he reached the courtyard, he found the marquis alive but in a furious temper.

"There you are, Ballentyne! What have you done with my carriage?"

"Your what?"

Bruce approached Archibald and motioned him aside. "Your

Lordship," he whispered in the earl's ear. "It seems the marquis's carriage and horses are missing, sir."

Archibald held up a finger in the direction of the marquis. With a raised voice, he replied, "I'll be with you in a moment, Victor." Then he returned his attention to Bruce and whispered, "Did you say *missing*? How is that possible?"

"I don't know exactly, sir, but you see, the gate warden reports that the marquis and his driver, or rather two people he thought were them, have already passed through the front gate."

Suddenly feeling quite ill, Archibald turned back to address the red-faced marquis.

Chapter 2

Meetings

Several hours after nightfall, Alenda Lanaklin arrived by carriage at the impoverished Lower Quarter of Medford. The Rose and Thorn Tavern lay hidden among crooked-roofed hovels on an unnamed street, which to Alenda appeared to be little more than an alley. A recent storm had left the cobblestones wet, and puddles littered the street. Passing carriages splashed filthy water on the pub's front entrance, leaving streaks of grime on the dull stone and weathered timbers.

From a nearby doorway, a sweaty, shirtless man with a bald head emerged carrying a large copper pot. He unceremoniously cast the pot's contents, the bony remains of several stewed animals, into the street. Immediately, half a dozen dogs set upon the scraps. Wretched-looking figures, dimly lit by the flickering light from the tavern's windows, shouted angrily at the canines in a language that Alenda did not recognize. Several of them threw rocks at the scrawny animals, which yelped and darted away. They rushed to what the animals had left behind and stuffed the remnants into their mouths and pockets.

"Are you *sure* this is the right place, my lady?" Emily asked, taking in the scene. "Viscount Winslow couldn't have meant for us to come here."

Alenda reexamined the curled thorny branch with a single bloom painted on the warped signboard above the door. The red rose had faded to gray, and the weathered stem looked like a coiled snake. "This has to be it. I don't think there's more than one tavern called The Rose and Thorn in Medford."

"I just can't believe he'd send us to such a — a place!"

"I don't like it any more than you do, but this is what was arranged. I don't see how we have a choice," Alenda replied, surprised by how brave she sounded.

"I know you're tired of hearing this, but I still think this is a mistake. We shouldn't be dealing with *thieves*. You can't trust them, my lady. Mark my words: these people you hired will steal from you just like they steal from everyone else."

"Nevertheless, we're here now, so we might as well get on with it." Alenda opened the door of the carriage and stepped out onto the street. As she did, she noticed with concern that several of those loitering nearby were watching her intently.

"That'll be a silver tenent," the driver told her. He was a gruff, elderly man who had not shaved in days. His narrow eyes were framed with so many wrinkles that Alenda wondered how he could see to drive the carriage.

"Oh, well, you see, I was expecting to pay you at the end of our journey," Alenda explained. "We're only stopping here for a short while."

"If you want me to wait, it'll cost ya extra. And I want the money ya owe me now, in case ya decide not ta come back."

"Don't be absurd. I can assure you we will be coming back."

The man's expression was as pliable as granite. He spit over the side of the carriage at Alenda's feet.

"Oh! Well, really!" Alenda pulled a coin from her bag and handed it to the driver. "Here, take the silver, but don't wander off. I'm not exactly sure how long we'll be, but as I told you, we *will* return."

Emily exited the carriage and took a moment to adjust Alenda's hood and to ensure her ladyship's buttons were secure. She brushed the wrinkles out of Alenda's cloak and then repeated the procedure on herself.

"I wish I could tell that stupid driver who I am," Alenda whispered. "Then I'd tell him a few more things."

The two women were dressed in matching woolen cloaks, and with their hoods up, little more than their noses were visible. Alenda scowled at Emily and brushed her fidgeting hands away.

"You're being such a mother hen, Emmy. I'm sure women have come into this establishment before."

"Women, yes, but I doubt any ladies have."

As they entered the narrow wooden doorway of the tavern, the pungent odor of smoke, alcohol, and a scent that Alenda had previously smelled only in a privy assaulted them. The din of twenty conversations fighting each other for supremacy filled the room while a fiddler worked a lively tune. Before a bar, a small crowd danced, hammering their heels loudly on the warped wooden floor, keeping time to the jig. Glasses clinked, fists pounded on tables, and people laughed and sang far louder than Alenda thought dignified.

"What do we do now?" Emily's voice emanated from the depths of her woolen hood.

"I suppose we look for the viscount. Stay close to me."

Alenda took Emily's hand and led the way, weaving through the tables and dodging the dancers and a dog that was gleefully licking up spilled beer. Never in her life had Alenda been in such a place. Vile-looking men surrounded her. Most were dressed in rags, and more than a few were shoeless. She spotted only four women in the place; all were barmaids dressed indecently in tattered gowns with plunging necklines. Alenda thought their manner of dress invited men to paw at them. A toothless, hairy beast grabbed one of the barmaids around her waist. Dragging her to his lap, he ran his hands along the length of her body. Alenda was shocked to see the girl giggle instead of scream.

At last, Alenda spotted him. Viscount Albert Winslow was dressed not in his typical doublet and hose but in a simple cloth shirt, wool pants, and a neatly tailored suede vest. His apparel was not entirely without noble adornment; he was sporting a lovely, if not ostentatious, plumed hat. He sat at a small table with a stocky, black-bearded man dressed in cheap work clothes.

On their approach, Winslow stood and pulled out chairs for them. "Welcome, ladies," he said with a cheerful smile. "So glad you were able to meet me this evening. Please sit down. May I order you both something to drink?"

"No, thank you," Alenda replied. "I was hoping not to stay very long. My driver is not a considerate man, and I would like to conclude our business before he decides to strand us here."

"I understand and, might I say, very wise of you, Your Ladyship. But I'm sad to say your delivery has not yet arrived."

"It hasn't?" Alenda felt Emily give her hand a squeeze of support. "Is there something wrong?"

"Unfortunately, I don't know. You see, I'm not privy to the inner workings of this operation. I don't concern myself with such trifles. You should understand, however, this wasn't an easy assignment. Any number of things could have transpired that might create delays. Are you sure there's nothing I may order for you?"

"Thank you, no," Alenda replied.

"At least take a seat, won't you?"

Alenda glanced at Emily, whose eyes were awash with concern. They sat down, and as they did, she whispered to Emily, "I know, I know. I shouldn't deal with thieves."

"Make no mistake, Your Ladyship," the viscount said in reassurance. "I would not waste your time, money, or risk your station if I didn't have the utmost confidence in the outcome."

The bearded man seated at the table chuckled softly. He was dark and seedy with skin as tan as leather. His huge hands were calloused and dirty. Alenda watched as he tipped his mug to his lips. When he withdrew the cup, droplets of ale ran unchecked through his whiskers and dripped onto the table-top. Alenda decided she did not like him.

"This is Mason Grumon," Winslow explained. "Forgive me for not introducing him sooner. Mason is a blacksmith here in Medford's Lower Quarter. He's...a friend."

"Those chaps you hired are very good," Mason told them. His voice reminded Alenda of the sound her carriage wheels made traveling over crushed stone.

"Are they?" Emily asked. "Could they steal the ancient treasures of Glenmorgan from the Crown Tower of Ervanon?"

"What's that?" Winslow asked.

"I once heard a rumor about thieves who stole treasure from the Crown Tower of Ervanon and replaced it the very next night," Emily explained.

"Why would anyone do such a thing?" Alenda asked.

The viscount chuckled softly. "I'm sure that's merely a legend. No sensible thief would behave in such a way. Most people don't understand the workings of thieves. The reality is that most of them steal to line their pockets. They break into homes or waylay travelers on the open road. Your bolder variety might kidnap nobles and hold them for ransom. Sometimes, they even cut off a finger of their victim and send it to a loved one. It helps to prove how dangerous they are and reinforces that the family should take their demands seriously. In general, they are an unsavory lot to be sure. They care only about making a profit with as little effort as possible."

Alenda felt another squeeze on her hand. This one was so tight it caused her to wince.

"Now, your better class of thief, they form guilds, sort of like masons' or woodworkers' guilds, although far more hush-hush, you understand. They are very organized and make a business out of thievery. They stake out territories where they maintain a monopoly on pilfering. Oftentimes, they have arrangements with the local militia or potentate that allow them to work relatively unmolested for a fee, as long as they avoid certain targets and abide by accepted rules."

"What kind of rules could be acceptable between officers of a province and known criminals?" Alenda asked skeptically.

"Oh, I think you'd be quite surprised to discover the number of compromises made to maintain a smoothly functioning kingdom. There is, however, one more type of malefactor—the freelance contractor or, to put it bluntly, thief-for-hire. These rogues are employed for a particular purpose, such as obtaining an item in the possession of a fellow noble. Codes of honor, or *fear of embarrassment*," he said with a wink, "force some nobles and wealthy merchants to seek out just such a professional."

"So, they'll steal anything for anyone?" Alenda asked. "The ones you hired for me, I mean."

"No, not anyone—only those who are willing to pay the number of tenents equal to the job."

"Then it doesn't matter if the client is a criminal or a king?" Emily chimed in.

Mason snorted. "Criminal or king, what's the difference?" For the first time during their meeting, he produced a wide grin that revealed several missing teeth.

Disgusted, Alenda turned her attention back to Winslow. He was looking in the direction of the door, straining to see above the tavern patrons. "You'll have to excuse me, ladies," he said, abruptly standing up. "I need another drink, and the waitstaff seems preoccupied. Look after the ladies, won't you, Mason?"

"I'm not a bloody wet nurse, you daffy old sod!" Mason shouted after the viscount as he left the table and moved off through the crowd.

"I'll—I'll not have you referring to Her Ladyship in such a way," Emily declared boldly to the smith. "She's no infant. She's a noblewoman of title, and *you* had best remember your place."

Mason's expression darkened. "This *is* my place. I live five bloody doors down. My pa helped build this infernal pub. My brother works here as a ruddy cook. My mother used ta work here as a cook too, up until she died being hit by one of yer fancy noble carriages. This is *my* place. *You're* the one who needs to be remembering yours." Mason slammed his fist down on the table, causing the candle, and the ladies, to jump.

Alenda pulled Emily close. *What have I gotten myself into?* She was starting to think Emily was right. She should never have trusted that no-account Winslow. She really did not know anything about him except that he attended the Aquesta Autumn Gala as a guest of Lord Daref. Of all people, she should have learned by now that not all nobles are noble.

They sat in silence until Winslow returned without a drink. "Ladies, if you'll please follow me?" The viscount beckoned.

"What is it?" Alenda asked, concerned.

"Just, please, come with me, this way."

Alenda and Emily left the table and followed Winslow through the haze of pipe smoke and the obstacle course of dancers, dogs, and drunks to the back door. The scene behind the tavern made everything they had endured so far appear virtuous. They entered an alley that was almost beyond comprehension. Trash lay scattered everywhere, and excrement, discarded from the windows above, mixed with mud in a wide-open trench. Wooden planks, serving as bridges, crisscrossed the foul river of slime, causing the ladies to hold their gowns above their ankles as they shuffled forward.

A large rat darted from a woodpile to join two more in the sewage trough.

"Why are we in an alley?" Emily whispered in a quavering voice to Alenda.

"I don't know," Alenda answered, trying desperately to control her own fear. "I think you were right, Emmy. I should never have dealt with these people. I don't care what the viscount says. People like *us* simply shouldn't do business with people like *them*."

The viscount led them through a wooden fence and around a pair of shanties to a poor excuse for a stable. The shelter was little more than a shack with four stalls, each filled with straw and a bucket of water.

"So good to see you again, Your Ladyship." A man out front addressed her.

Alenda could tell it was the big one of the pair, but she could not remember his name. She had seen them only briefly through an arranged meeting by the viscount, which had been on a lonely road on a night darker than this. Now, with the moon more than half-full and his hood thrown back, she could make out his face. He was tall, rugged in feature and dress but not unkind or threatening in appearance. Wrinkles, which might have come from laughter, tugged at the edges of his eyes. Alenda thought his demeanor was remarkably cheerful, even friendly. She could not help thinking he was handsome, which was not the reaction she had expected to have about anyone she might meet in such a place. He was dressed in dirt-stained leather and wool and was well armed. On his left side, he had a short sword with an unadorned hilt.

On his right was a similarly plain, longer, wider sword. Finally, slung on his back was a massive blade, nearly as tall as he was.

"My name is Hadrian, in case you have forgotten," he said, and followed the introduction with a suitable bow. "And who is this lovely lady with you?"

"This is Emily, my maid."

"A maid?" Hadrian feigned surprise. "For one so fair, I would have guessed her to be a duchess."

Emily inclined her head, and for the first time on this trip, Alenda saw her smile.

"I hope we didn't keep you waiting too long. The viscount tells me he and Mason were keeping you company?"

"Yes, they were."

"Did Mr. Grumon tell you the tragic tale of his mother being run down by an insensitive royal carriage?"

"Why, yes, he did. And I must say—"

Hadrian held up his hands in mock defense. "Mason's mother is alive and well. She lives on Artisan Row in a home considerably nicer than the hovel where Mason resides. She has never been a cook at The Rose and Thorn. He tells that story to every gentleman or lady he meets to put them on the defensive and make them feel guilty. You have my apologies."

"Well, thank you. He was rather rude and I found his comments more than a little disturbing, but now..." Alenda paused. "Did you—I mean, do you have...Were you able to get them?"

Hadrian smiled warmly; then, turning, he called over his shoulder in the direction of the stable.

"Royce?"

"If you knew how to tie a proper knot, I wouldn't be taking so long," said a voice from inside. A moment later, the other half of the pair emerged and joined them.

Alenda's memory of him was easier to recall, because he

was the more disturbing of the two. He was smaller than Hadrian and possessed elegant features, dark hair, and dark eyes. He was dressed in layers of black with a knee-length tunic and a long flowing cloak that gathered about him like a shadow. Not a single weapon was visible. Despite his smaller size and apparent unarmed state, Alenda feared this man. His cold eyes, expressionless face, and curt manner had all the warmth of a predator.

From his tunic, Royce drew forth a bundle of letters bound with a blue ribbon. Handing them to her, he said, "Getting to those letters before Ballentyne presented them to your father wasn't easy. As far as races go, it was very close but ultimately successful. You might want to burn those before something like this happens again."

She stared at the package as a smile of relief crossed her face. "I—I can't believe it! I don't know how you did it, or how to thank you!"

"Payment would be nice," Royce replied.

"Oh, yes, of course." She handed the bundle to Emily, untied the purse from her waist, and handed it to the thief. He quickly scanned the contents, snapped the purse closed, and tossed it to Hadrian, who slipped it in his vest as he headed for the stables.

"You'd better be careful. It's a dangerous game you and Gaunt are playing," Royce told her.

"You read my letters?" she asked fearfully.

"No. I'm afraid you didn't pay us that much."

"Then how did you know—"

"We overheard your father and Archibald Ballentyne talking. The marquis appeared not to believe the earl's accusations, but I'm certain he did. Letters or no letters, your father will be watching you closely now. Still, the marquis is a good man. He'll do the right thing. My guess is he's so relieved

Ballentyne doesn't have proof to take to court that your affair won't bother him much. However, as I said, you'd better be more careful in the future."

"How would the likes of *you* know anything about my father?"

"Oh, I'm sorry. Did I say your father? I meant the other marquis, the one with the appreciative daughter."

Alenda felt as though Royce had slapped her.

"Making friends again, Royce?" Hadrian asked as he led two horses from the stable. "You'll have to forgive my friend. He was raised by wolves."

"Those are my father's horses!"

Hadrian nodded. "We left the carriage behind a bramble patch by the river bridge. By the way, I think I might have stretched out one of your father's doublets. I put it and the rest of his things back in the carriage."

"You were wearing my father's clothes?"

"I told you," Royce repeated, "it was close, very close."

⊰

They called it the Dark Room because of the business conducted in it, but the little back room at The Rose and Thorn was anything but gloomy. Several candles set in sconces on the walls and on the meeting table, along with a nice-sized fire burning in the hearth, gave off a warm, friendly light. A row of copper pots, reminders of the days when the Dark Room doubled as kitchen storage, hung from an exposed wooden beam. There was room for only one table and a handful of chairs, but it was more than enough for their purposes.

The door opened, and a small party filed in. Royce poured himself a glass of wine, took a seat near the fire, removed his boots, and wriggled his toes before the hearth. Hadrian, Viscount Albert Winslow, Mason Grumon, and a pretty young woman opted for chairs at the meeting table. Gwen, the owner of the tavern, always prepared a fine feast when they returned from a job, and that night was no exception. The evening's selections included a pitcher of ale, a large roast, a loaf of freshly baked sweet bread, boiled potatoes, a cloth-wrapped cask of white cheese, carrots, onions, and the big pickles from the barrel normally kept behind the bar. For Royce and Hadrian, she spared no expense, which included the black bottle of Montemorcey wine she had imported all the way from Vandon. Gwen always kept it on hand because it was Royce's favorite. Despite how appealing everything looked, Hadrian showed no interest in any of it. He focused his attention on the woman.

"So, how did it go last night?" Emerald asked, sitting atop Hadrian's lap and pouring him a frothy stein of the inn's home brew. Her real name was Falina Brockton, but all the girls who worked at the tavern, or Medford House next door, went by monikers for their own safety. Emerald, a bright and cheery waif, was the senior barmaid at The Rose and Thorn and one of only two women allowed in the Dark Room when a meeting was in session.

"It was cold," he told her, encircling her waist with his arms. "As was the ride here, so I desperately need warming." He pulled her to him and began kissing her neck as a sea of brunette waves engulfed him.

"We did get paid, didn't we?" Mason asked.

The blacksmith had started to prepare a heaping plate almost the instant he sat down. Mason was the son of the former preeminent Medford metalworker. He had inherited his father's shop but had lost it through a gambling habit coupled with bad luck. Forced out of Artisan Row, he landed in the Lower Quarter, where he fashioned horseshoes and nails, making enough to pay for his forge, drinks, and the occasional meal. For Royce and Hadrian, he offered three benefits: he was cheap, he was local, and he was solitary.

"We did indeed. Alenda Lanaklin paid us the full fifteen gold tenents," Royce said.

"Quite the haul," Winslow declared, happily clapping his hands.

"And my arrows? How'd they work?" Mason asked. "Did they anchor in the tiles?"

"They anchored just fine," Royce said. "Getting them out was the problem."

"The release failed?" Mason asked, concerned. "But I thought—well, I'm no fletcher. Ya shoulda gone to a fletcher. Told ya that, didn't I? I'm a smith. I work with steel, not wood. That fine-toothed saw I made—that worked, didn't it? That's a smithing product, by Mar! But not the arrows and, for sure, not ones like you wanted. No, sir. I done said ya shoulda gotten a fletcher and ya shoulda."

"Relax, Mason," Hadrian said, emerging from Emerald's mane. "Of the two, the anchor was the most important, and it worked perfectly."

"A'course it did. The arrow tips are metal, and I know metal. I'm just disappointed the rope release didn't work. How did ya get the rope down? Ya didn't leave it there, did ya?"

"Couldn't, the guard would have spotted it on his next pass," Royce said.

"So, how'd ya do it?"

"Personally, I would like to know how you did the whole thing," Winslow said. Like Royce, he was sitting back with his feet up and mug in hand. "You never let me in on the details of these operations."

The Viscount Albert Winslow came from a long line of

landless gentry. Years ago, one of his ancestors had lost the family fief. Now all that remained was his title. This was enough to open doors closed to the peasantry or merchant class and was a step better than the common baronage. When Royce and Hadrian had first met him, he was living in a barn in Colnora. The pair invested a little money on clothes and a carriage, and he aptly performed the delicate duties of liaison to the nobles. With an allowance funded by them, the viscount attended every ball, gala, and ceremony, patrolling the political landscape for business opportunities.

"You're too visible, Albert," Hadrian explained. "Can't afford to have our favorite noble hauled to some dungeon where they cut off your eyelids or pull off your fingernails until you tell them what we're up to."

"But if they torture me, and I don't know the plan, how will I save myself?"

"I'm sure they'll believe you after the fourth nail or so," Royce said with a wicked grin.

Albert grimaced and took another long drink of his ale. "But you can tell me now, can't you? How did you get past the iron door? When I met with Ballentyne, I had the impression a dwarf with a full set of tools couldn't get it open. It didn't even have a lock to pick, or a latch to lift."

"Well, your information was very helpful," Royce said. "That's why we avoided it completely."

The viscount looked confused. He started to speak but instead remained silent and cut himself a piece of the roast beef.

Royce took a sip of his wine, and when he did, Hadrian took over the tale. "We scaled the exterior of the east tower, or rather Royce did, and he dropped me a rope. It wasn't as tall but it was the closest to the one we were interested in. We used Mason's arrows to connect the two towers and, with our knees wrapped around the rope, inched our way across the length hand over hand."

"But there are no windows in the tower," Albert protested.

"Who said anything about using a window?" Royce interjected. "The arrows anchored in the taller tower's roof."

"Yep, like I said, that was quality craftsmanship," Mason said proudly.

"So, that gets you to the tower, but how did you get in? Through the chimney?" Albert inquired.

"No, it was too small, and last night there was a fire burning," Hadrian said. "So we used Mason's second little tool, a small saw, and cut the roof on a bevel. All in all, the night was going pretty much according to plan, until Archibald decided to visit his study. We figured he'd have to leave eventually, so we waited."

"We should have just slipped down, cut his throat, and taken the letters," Royce insisted.

"But we weren't being paid for that, were we?" Hadrian reminded him. Royce rolled his eyes in response. Ignoring him, Hadrian continued. "As I was saying, we lay there waiting and the wind on the top of that tower was bitter. The bastard must have sat in that room for two hours."

"You poor thing," Emerald purred, and nuzzled him like a cat.

"The good news was he actually looked at the letters while we were watching him through the cuts, so we knew right where the safe was. Then a carriage came into the courtyard, and you'll never guess who it was."

"The marquis arrived while you were on the roof?" Albert asked with his mouth full of roast beef.

"Yep—that's when our timetable got really tricky. Archibald left the tower to meet the marquis, and we made our move."

"So," Emerald said, guessing, "you opened the roof like the top of a pumpkin."

"Exactly. I lowered Royce into the study. He picked the safe, dumped the dummy letters, and I hauled him back up. Just as we replaced the roof section, Archibald and Victor walked in. We waited to make sure they did not hear us. Incredibly, he presented the letters right there and then. I must say, it was hilarious watching Archibald's reaction when he discovered the blank replacements. Things got pretty loud at this point, so we decided we better take the chance and rappelled down the tower to the courtyard below."

"That's amazing. I was telling Alenda sometimes problems occur during a job, but I had no idea I was telling the truth. We should have charged her extra," Albert interjected.

"It crossed my mind," Royce replied, "but you know Hadrian. Still, we've made a nice profit on both sides of this one."

"But wait, you didn't explain how you got the rope off the side of the tower if my releases didn't work."

Royce sighed. "Don't ask."

"Why not?" The smith looked from one to the other. "Is it a secret?"

"They want to know, Royce," Hadrian said with a wide grin.

Royce frowned. "He shot it off."

"He did what?" Albert asked, sitting up so abruptly his feet hit the floor with a clap.

"Hadrian used another arrow to cut the rope at the roofline."

"But that's impossible," Albert declared. "No man can shoot the width of a rope at—what was it?—two hundred feet maybe, in total darkness!"

"There *was* a moon," Royce said, correcting him. "Let's not make more out of this than it already is. You forget I have to work with him. Besides, it's not like he did it in a single shot."

"How many arrows?" Emerald inquired.

"What's that, sweetie?" Hadrian asked, wiping foam from his mouth with his sleeve.

"How many arrows did it take for you to cut the rope, silly?"

"Be honest," Royce told him.

Hadrian scowled. "Four."

"Four?" Albert said. "It was much more impressive when I imagined it as one lone shot, but still—"

"Do you think the earl will ever figure it out?" Emerald asked.

"The first time it rains, I imagine," Mason said.

There was a triple tap on the door and the stocky smith pushed back his chair and crossed the room. "Who is it?" he asked.

"Gwen."

Sliding the dead bolt free, he opened the door, and an exotic-looking woman with long, thick black hair and dazzling green eyes entered.

"A fine thing when a woman can't get access to her own back room."

"Sorry, gal," Mason said, closing the door behind her, "but Royce would skin me alive if I ever opened the door without asking first."

Gwen DeLancy was an enigma of the Lower Quarter. An immigrant to Avryn from the distant nation of Calis, she survived in the city as a prostitute and fortune-teller. Her dark skin, almond-shaped eyes, and high cheekbones were uniquely foreign. Her talent for eye makeup and an eastern accent made her an alluring mystery that the nobles found irresistible. Yet Gwen was no simple whore. In three short years, she turned her fortunes around, buying up shop rights in the district. Only nobles could own land, but merchants traded the rights to operate a business. Before long, she owned or possessed an interest in a sizable section of Artisan Row and most of the Lower Quarter. Medford House, commonly known as the House, was her most lucrative establishment. Despite its back-alley location, gentry from far and near frequented this expensive brothel. Gwen had a reputation for being discreet, especially with the identities of men who could not afford to be seen frequenting a brothel.

"Royce," Gwen said, "a potential customer visited the House earlier this evening. He was quite anxious to speak to one of you. I set up a meeting for tomorrow evening."

"Know him?"

"I asked the girls. None of them have ever seen him before."

"Was he serviced?"

Gwen shook her head. "No, he was just after information about thieves for hire. Funny how a man always expects prostitutes to know everything when he is looking for answers, but assumes a girl will take *his* secrets to her grave."

"Who talked to him?"

"Tulip. She said he was foreign, dark-skinned, and she mentioned an accent. He might be from Calis, but I didn't bump into him, so I can't tell you for sure."

"Was he alone?"

"Tulip didn't mention any companions."

"Want me to talk to him?" Albert asked.

"Nah, I'll do it," Hadrian said. "If he's poking around these parts, he'll probably be looking for someone more like me than you."

"If you like, Albert, you can be here tomorrow and watch the door for strangers," Royce added. "I'll keep an eye on the street. Has there been anyone new hanging around?"

"It has been pretty busy, and there are a few people I don't recognize. There are four right now in the main bar," Gwen mentioned, "and there was a different party of five a few hours ago."

"She's right," Emerald confirmed. "I waited on the five."

"What were they like? Travelers?"

Gwen shook her head. "Soldiers, I think. They weren't dressed like it but I could tell."

"Mercs?" Hadrian asked.

"I don't think so. Mercenaries are usually troublesome, grabbing the girls, shouting, picking fights—you know the type. These guys were quiet, and one was a noble, I think. At least, some of the others referred to him as Baron something— Trumbul, I think it was."

"I saw some like that up on Wayward Street yesterday," Mason said. "Mighta been as many as twelve."

"Anything going on in town?" Royce asked.

They looked at one another doubtfully.

"Do you think it has anything to do with those rumors about killings out near the Nidwalden River?" Hadrian asked. "Maybe the king is calling up support from other nobles."

"Are you talking about the elves?" Mason asked. "I heard about that."

"Me too," Emerald said. "They say elves attacked a village or something. I heard they slaughtered everyone—some even while they slept."

"Who said that? That doesn't sound right," Albert commented. "I've never known an elf to look a man in the eye, much less attack one."

Royce grabbed his boots and cloak and headed for the door. "You've never known an elf, Albert," he said as he abruptly left.

"What'd I say?" Albert asked, staring at everyone with an innocent expression.

Emerald shrugged.

Hadrian took out Alenda's purse and tossed it at the viscount. "I wouldn't worry about it. Royce can be moody at times. Here, divvy out the profits."

"Royce is right, though," Emerald said. She appeared pleased that she knew something they did not. "The elves that attacked the village were *wild* elves, full-bloods. The half-breeds from around here are nothing but a bunch of lazy drunks."

"A thousand years of slavery can do that to a person," Gwen pointed out. "Can I have my cut, Albert? I have to get back to work. We've got a bishop, the magistrate, and the Brotherhood of Barons visiting the House tonight."

✍

Hadrian was still sore from the previous day's exertion when he took a seat at an empty table near the bar and observed the patrons of the Diamond Room. The name came from its odd, stretched rectangle shape, caused by how the addition fit into the space at the end of Wayward Street. Hadrian knew or was familiar with almost everyone in the room. Lamplighters, carriage drivers, tinkers, they were the usual late crowd who came in after work for a meal. They all had the same tired, worn-out, dirty look about them as they sat with their heads bowed over their plates. Each was dressed in a coarse work shirt and poor-fitting britches gathered at the waist like the mouth of a sack. They chose this room because it was quieter, and they could eat in peace. One individual, however, stood out.

He sat alone at the far end of the room, his back to the wall. His table remained bare except for the standard tavern candle. He had not bought a drink or a plate. He wore a wide-brimmed felt hat with one side pinned up by a lavish blue plume. His doublet, worn over a brilliant gold satin waist shirt, was made of rich black and red brocade with stuffed shoulders. At his side was a saber attached to a fine studded-leather girdle matching his high black riding boots. Whoever he was, he was not hiding. Hadrian noted beneath the table a bundle on which he rested one boot at all times.

Once Royce sent Emerald over with the news that the street was clear of associates, Hadrian got up and walked the length of the room, stopping before the empty chair in front of the stranger.

"Care for some company?" he asked.

"That depends," the man replied, and Hadrian noted the slight saucy accent of a Calian native. "I'm looking for a representative of an organization called Riyria. Do you speak for that group?"

"That depends on what you want," Hadrian replied with a small grin.

"In that case, please sit down."

Hadrian took the seat and waited.

"My name is Baron Delano DeWitt, and I'm looking to hire men of talent. I was told there were a few in the area that could be had for a price."

"What kind of talents are you looking to buy?"

"Procurement skills," DeWitt said simply. "I have an item I need to make disappear. If at all possible, I would prefer it to disappear completely. But it has to happen tonight."

Hadrian smiled. "Sorry, I'm quite certain Riyria won't work under such tight constraints. Too dangerous. I hope you understand."

"I'm sorry about the timing. I tried to reach your organization last night, but I was told you were unavailable. I'm in a position to make it worth the risk."

"Sorry, but they have very strict rules." Hadrian started to get up.

"Please, listen. I have asked around. Those who know the

pulse of this city tell me there is a pair of independent professionals who take on such jobs if the price is right. How they
manage to work with impunity outside of the organized guilds
is a matter of speculation, but the fact remains that they do.
This is a testament to their reputation, is it not? If you know
these men, the members of this Riyria, I beg you, implore
them to assist me."

Hadrian considered the man. Initially, he had thought him
to be another of the many self-absorbed nobles looking for a
chuckle at some royal banquet. Now, however, the man's
demeanor changed. There was a hint of desperation in his voice.

"What's so important about this item?" Hadrian asked as
he eased back into his seat. "And why does it have to disappear tonight?"

"Have you heard of Count Pickering?"

"Master swordsman, winner of the Silver Shield and the
Golden Laurel? He has an incredibly beautiful wife named…
Belinda, I think. I've heard he has killed at least eight men in
duels because of how they have looked at her, or so the legend
goes."

"You're unusually well informed."

"Part of the job," Hadrian admitted.

"In a contest of swords, the count has only been beaten by
Braga, the Archduke of Melengar, and that was in an exhibi-
tion tournament on the one day he didn't have his sword. He
was forced to use a replacement."

"Oh, right," Hadrian said as much to himself as to DeWitt.
"He's the one with the special rapier he won't duel without, at
least not in a real fight."

"Yes! The count is very superstitious about it." DeWitt said
nothing more for a moment and looked uncomfortable.

"Did you stare at the count's wife too long?" Hadrian
inquired.

The man nodded and bowed his head. "I've been challenged to a duel tomorrow at noon."

"And you want Riyria to steal the count's sword." It was a statement, not a question, but DeWitt nodded again.

"I'm with the retinue of Duke DeLorkan of Dagastan. We arrived in Medford two days ago, part of a trade negotiation hosted by King Amrath. They held a feast for our arrival and Pickering was there." The baron wiped his face nervously. "I've never been to Avryn before—for Maribor's sake, I didn't know who he was! I didn't even know she was his wife until I was slapped in the face with a glove."

Hadrian sighed. "That is not an easy job. Taking a prized sword from the bedside of—"

"Ah—but I have made it easier," DeWitt told him. "The count, like me, is staying with the king for the negotiations. His quarters are very near my duke's. Earlier this evening, I slipped into his room and took his sword. There were so many people around I panicked and dropped it in the first open door I found. It must be removed from the castle before he notices it's missing, since a search will surely find it."

"So, where is it now?"

"The royal chapel," he said. "It's not guarded and is just down the hall from an empty bedroom with a window. I can make certain the window will be open tonight. There are also ivy vines just outside the wall below the window. It should be a simple thing really."

"Then why don't *you* do it?"

"If thieves are caught with the sword, all that will happen is the loss of their hands, but if *I* am caught, my reputation will be destroyed!"

"I can see the reason for your concern," Hadrian said sardonically, but DeWitt appeared oblivious.

"Exactly! Now, seeing as how I have done most of the work, it doesn't sound so bad, does it? Before you answer, let me add this to the proposal."

With some strain, the baron pulled the bundle from beneath his foot and placed it on the table. A metallic jingle rustled when the saddlebag settled on the wood. "Inside you'll find one hundred gold tenents."

"I see," Hadrian responded, staring at the bag and trying to breathe at an even pace. "And you are paying up front?"

"Of course, I'm not a fool. I know how these things work. I'll pay you half now and half when I get the sword."

Hadrian took another controlled breath, nodding and reminding himself to stay calm. "So, you're offering *two hundred* gold tenents?"

"Yes," DeWitt said with a look of concern. "As you can see, this is very important to me."

"Apparently, if the job is as easy as you say."

"Then you think they will do it?" he asked eagerly.

Hadrian sat back in his chair just as DeWitt leaned forward anxiously. DeWitt looked like a man set before a judge, awaiting sentencing on a murder charge.

Royce would kill him if he agreed. One of the basic rules they had established for Riyria was that they would not take jobs on short notice. They needed time to do background checks, verify stories, and case potential targets. Still, DeWitt's only crime was choosing the wrong moment to look at a beautiful woman, and Hadrian knew he held the man's life in his hands. There was no chance he could hire anyone else. As DeWitt had mentioned, no independent thieves other than them would dare take a job in a guild city. The officers of the Crimson Hand would not allow any of their boys to do it, for the same reason Hadrian felt he ought to turn it down. On the

other hand, Hadrian was not really a thief and was not familiar with all their various deliberations. Royce was the one who
had grown up on the streets of Ratibor, picking pockets to
survive. He was the professional burglar, the ex-member of
the infamous Black Diamond Guild. Hadrian was a warrior, a
soldier who preferred his battles to be fair and in the daylight.

Hadrian was never completely comfortable with most of
the tasks they did for nobles. They wanted to embarrass a
rival, to hurt an ex-lover, or to increase their standing in the
strange and twisted world of high-stakes politics. The gentry
hired them because they possessed fortunes and could afford
to pay for their games. To them, that was what life was—one
big chess match with real knights, kings, and pawns. There
was no good or evil, no right or wrong. It was all just politics.
A game within a game with its own set of rules and no values.
Their squabbles, however, did provide a fertile field for them
to harvest profits. Not only were the nobles rich and petty,
they were also dim-witted. How else could Royce and Hadrian
receive payment from the Earl of Chadwick to intercept letters
Alenda Lanaklin sent to Degan Gaunt only to turn around
and double their profit by stealing them back? They had simply asked Albert to contact Alenda with the news Ballentyne
had her letters and an offer to help get them back. Their business was profitable but ugly. Just another game he played in a
world where heroes were legends and honor was a myth.

He tried to rationalize that what he and Royce did was not
that horrible. After all, Alenda could certainly afford it. People
like Mason and Emerald needed the money more than a
wealthy marquis's daughter. Besides, perhaps it taught her a
valuable lesson that might save her father's reputation and
lands. Yet it was still just a way of lying to himself. Trying to
convince his conscience that what he was doing was right, or
at least not wrong. He desired to do a job with merit, one with

which he could actually save a man's life, one with intentions that resembled what he remembered as virtuous.

"Sure," he said.

⚜

When Hadrian finished speaking, the silence in the Dark Room was thick with anticipation. Only three men were present and when Hadrian stopped, both he and Albert turned their attention to Royce. As expected, the thief did not look pleased and began slowly shaking his head even before he spoke. "I can't believe you took this job," he scolded.

"Look, I know it's short notice, but his story checks out, right?" Hadrian asked. "You followed him back to the castle. He is a guest of King Amrath. He didn't make any side trips. I can verify he appears to be from Calis, and none of Gwen's girls heard anything to contradict his claims. The job looks clean."

"*Two hundred gold tenents* to slip a sword out an open window—you don't find that suspicious?" Royce asked with a tone of amazed disbelief.

"Personally, I would call it a dream come true," Albert mentioned.

"Maybe they do things differently in Calis. It's pretty far away," Hadrian argued.

"It's not *that* far," Royce shot back. "And how is it this DeWitt is walking around with that much coin? Does he always travel to international trade meetings carrying bags bursting with gold? Why did he bring it?"

"Maybe he didn't. Maybe he sold a valuable ring tonight, or perhaps he obtained a loan using the good name of the Duke DeLorkan. It's even possible that he got it from the duke himself. I'm certain the two of them didn't ride up here on a couple of ponies. The duke likely travels in a huge caravan of wagons. To them, several hundred gold coins might not be unusual."

Hadrian's voice became more serious. "You weren't there. You didn't see this guy. He's facing a virtual execution tomorrow. How much is gold worth if you're dead?"

"We just got done with a job. I was hoping to take a few days off, and now you've signed us up for a new one." Royce sighed. "You say DeWitt was scared?"

"He was sweating."

"So, that's what this is really about. You want to take the job because it's for a good cause. You think risking our necks is worth it so long as we can pat ourselves on the back afterward."

"Pickering will kill him—you know it. And he's not the first."

"He won't be the last either."

Hadrian sighed and, folding his arms across his chest, sat back in his chair. "You're right; there will be others. So imagine we pinch the sword and get rid of the damn thing. The count never sees it again. Think of all the happy men who could finally look at Belinda without fear."

Royce chuckled. "So now it's a public service?"

"And there is the two hundred gold tenents," Hadrian added. "That's more money than we've made all year. Cold weather is coming, and with that coin, we could sit out the winter."

"Well, at least now you are talking some sense. That would be nice," Royce admitted.

"And it's only a couple hours of work, just a quick climb and grab. You're the one always telling me how poorly guarded Essendon Castle is. We'll be done and in bed before dawn."

Royce bit his lower lip and grimaced, refusing to look at his partner.

Hadrian saw his opening and pressed his advantage. "You remember how cold it was on top of that tower. Just think how cold it will be in a few months. You can spend the winter safe and warm, eating richly and drinking your favorite wine. Then of course" — Hadrian leaned closer — "there's the snow. You know how you hate the snow."

"All right, all right. Grab the gear. I'll meet you in the alley."

Hadrian smiled. "I knew there was a heart in there somewhere."

⁓

Outside, the night was even colder than it had been. A slick frost formed on the roads. Winter snows would indeed be falling soon. Despite what Hadrian thought, Royce did not actually hate snow. He liked the way it blanketed the Lower Quarter, dressing it up in an elegant white gown. Nevertheless, its beauty came with a cost; tracks remained in snow and made his job much harder. Hadrian was right: after that night they would have enough cash set aside to spend the whole winter in quiet hibernation. With that much money, they could even consider opening a legitimate business. He thought about it every time they scored big, and he and Hadrian had discussed it on more than one occasion. A year ago, they had talked seriously about opening a winery, but it did not suit them. That was always the problem. Neither could think of any lawful business that was right for them.

He stopped in front of Medford House at the end of Wayward Street and across the street from The Rose and Thorn Tavern. The House was nearly as large as the tavern, which Gwen considered linking with by building extensions so customers could move back and forth freely without exposing themselves to the elements, or public scrutiny. Gwen DeLancy was a genius. Royce had never known anyone like her. She was clever and intelligent beyond reason, and she was more open and sincere than anyone he had ever met. She was a paradox to him, an impossible mystery he could not solve—she was an honest person.

"I thought you might stop by," Gwen said, stepping out onto the porch of the House and wrapping a cape about her shoulders. "I was watching for you through the doorway."

"You have good eyes. Most people never see me when I walk a dark street."

"You must have wanted to be seen, then. You were coming to visit me, weren't you?"

"I just wanted to be sure you received your portion of the payment last night."

Gwen smiled. As she did, Royce could not help noticing how beautifully her hair shimmered in the moonlight.

"Royce, you know you don't have to pay me. I'd give you anything you asked for."

"No," Royce insisted. "We use your place as a base. It's dangerous, and for that, you get a part of the profit. We've been over this."

She stepped closer and took his hand. Her touch was soothingly warm amidst the chilling air. "I also wouldn't own The Rose and Thorn if it wasn't for you. There's a very good chance I wouldn't even be alive."

"I have no idea what you speak of, Your Ladyship," Royce said as he performed a formal bow. "I can prove I wasn't even in town that night."

She stared at him with the same smile. He loved to see her happy, but now her brilliant green eyes searched for something, and Royce turned away, letting go of her hand.

"Listen, Hadrian and I are taking that job. We have to do it tonight, so I need to—"

"You're a strange man, Royce Melborn. I wonder if I'll ever really know you."

Royce paused and then softly said, "You already know me better than any woman should, more than is safe for either of us."

Gwen stepped toward him again, her heeled shoes crunching on the frosty ground, her eyes intense with pleading. "Be careful, won't you?"

"I always am."

With his cloak billowing in the wind, he walked away. She watched him until he entered a shadow and was gone.

Chapter 3

Conspiracies

The crowned falcon standard flew from the highest tower of Essendon Castle, marking the presence of the king. The castle was the royal seat of the kingdom of Melengar, and although not especially large or powerful, it was nevertheless an old and respected realm. The castle, an imposing structure of elaborate gray walls and towers, stood at the center of the capital city of Medford, forming the hub of the four distinct quarters of Gentry Square, Artisan Row, the Common Quarter, and the Lower Quarter. Like most cities in Avryn, Medford lay behind the protection of a strong outer wall. Nevertheless, the castle also had its own fortifications partitioning it from the general city. This inner wall, crowned with crenellated parapets where skilled archers kept watch from behind stone merlons, did not completely encircle the castle. Instead, it connected to a large, imposing keep that served as its rear barrier. The height of the keep and the wide moat surrounding its base kept the king's home well protected.

During the day, merchants wheeled carts to the castle wall and positioned themselves on either side of the gate, forming a tent city of bustling vendors, entertainers, and lenders who sought to do business with the castle inhabitants. This wave of local commerce receded at sunset, as citizens could not pass within fifty feet of the walls from dusk until dawn. This restriction was enforced by royal archers, who were trained to fire at those who ventured too close at night. Pairs of guards, dressed in chain mail with steel helms bearing the falcon standard of Melengar, patrolled the perimeter of the castle. They walked casually, with thumbs in their sword belts, often discussing events of the day or their off-duty plans.

Royce and Hadrian watched the pace of the guard's routine for an hour before moving toward the rear of the keep. Just as DeWitt had explained, negligent gardeners had ignored a spider-work of thick-stemmed vines tracing their way up the stone. Unfortunately, the vines did not reach as high as the windows. On this frosty late-autumn night, the swim across the moat was bone-chillingly cold. The ivy, however, proved to be quite reliable, and the climb was as easy as ascending a ladder.

"I now know why DeWitt didn't want to do this himself," Hadrian whispered to Royce as they hung from the ivy. "After being frozen in that water, I think if I fell right now, I would shatter on impact."

"Just imagine how many chamber pots are dumped into it each day," Royce mentioned as he drove a small ringed spike into the seam between two stone blocks.

Hadrian looked up at the many windows he presumed led to bedrooms, and cringed at the implications. "I could have lived without that bit of insight." He pulled a strap harness from his satchel and fastened it to the eyelet of the spike's ring.

"Just trying to take your mind off the cold," Royce said, tapping in another spike.

Although tedious and tense, the process was surprisingly

fast, and they reached the lowest window before the guards completed their circuit. Royce tested the shutter, which was open, as promised. He pulled it gently back, just a hair, and peered inside. A moment later, he climbed in and waved Hadrian up.

A small bed draped in a burgundy canopy took up the center of one wall. A dresser with a washbasin stood beside it. The only other piece of furniture was a simple wooden chair. A modest tapestry of hounds hunting deer covered much of the opposite wall. Everything was neat but sterile. There were no boots near the door and no cloak thrown across the chair, and the bedcovers showed no wrinkles. The room was unused.

Hadrian remained silent near the window as Royce moved across the room to the door. He watched as the thief's feet tested the surface of the floor before committing his weight. Royce mentioned once how he had been in an attic on a job when he hit a weak board and fell through the bedroom ceiling. This floor was stone, but even stones sometimes had loose mortar or contained hidden traps or alarms. Royce made it to the door, where he crouched and paused to listen. He motioned a sign for walking with his hand and then began counting on his fingers for Hadrian to see. There was a pause, and then he repeated the signal. Hadrian crossed the room to join his friend and the two sat waiting for several minutes in silence.

Eventually Royce lifted the latch with gloved hands but did not open the door. Outside they could hear the heavy footfalls of hard boots on stone, first one set, and then a second. As the steps faded, Royce opened the door slightly and peered out. The hall was empty.

Before them lay a narrow hallway lit by widely spaced torches, whose flames cast flickering shadows, which created an illusion of movement on the walls. They entered the hall,

quietly closed the door behind them, and quickly moved
approximately fifty feet to a set of double doors, adorned with
gilded hinges and a metal lock. Royce tried the doors and then
shook his head. He knelt and pulled a small kit of tools from
his belt pouch while Hadrian moved to the far side of the hall.
From where Hadrian stood, he could see the length of the corridor in both directions as well as a portion of the stairs that
entered from the right. He stood ready for any trouble, which
came sooner than he had expected.

A noise echoed in the corridor and Hadrian could hear the
faint sound of hard heels on stone coming in their direction.
Still on his knees, Royce worked the lock as the steps grew
closer. Hadrian moved his hand to the hilt of his sword when
at last the thief quickly opened the door. Trusting to luck that
the room was empty, the two slipped inside. Royce softly closed
the door behind them, and the footsteps passed without pause.

They were in the royal chapel. Banks of candles burned on
either side of the large room. Supporting a glorious vaulted
ceiling, marble columns rose near the chamber's center. Four
rows of wooden pews lined either side of the main aisle.
Cinquefoil-shaped adornments and blind-tracery moldings
common to the Nyphron Church decorated the walls. Alabaster statues of Maribor and Novron stood behind the altar.
Novron, depicted as a strong, handsome man in the prime of
his youth, was kneeling, sword in hand. The god Maribor,
sculpted as a powerful, larger-than-life figure with a long
beard and flowing robes, loomed over Novron, placing a
crown upon the young man's head. The altar itself consisted
of a wooden cabinet with three broad doors and a rose-colored
marble top. Upon it, two more candles burned and a large
gilded tome lay open.

DeWitt had told Hadrian he had left the sword behind the

altar, and they headed toward it. As they approached the first set of pews, both men froze in mid-step. Lying there, face-down in a pool of freshly spilled blood, was the body of a man. The rounded handle of a dagger protruded from his back. While Royce made a quick survey for Pickering's sword, Hadrian checked the man for signs of life. The man was dead, and the sword was nowhere to be found. Royce tapped Hadrian on the shoulder and pointed at the gold crown that had rolled to the far side of a pillar. The full weight of the situation regis-tered with both of them—it was time to leave.

They headed for the door. Royce paused only momentarily to listen to ensure the hall was clear. They slipped out of the chapel, closed the door, and moved down the hall toward the bedroom.

"Murderers!"

The shout was so close and so terrifying that they both spun with weapons drawn. Hadrian had his bastard sword in one hand, his short sword in the other. Royce held a brilliant white-bladed dagger.

Standing before the open chapel door was a bearded dwarf.

"Murderers!" the dwarf cried again, but it was not neces-sary. Footfalls could already be heard, and an instant later, soldiers, with weapons drawn, poured into the hallway from both sides.

"Murderers!" The dwarf continued pointing at them. "They've killed the king!"

Royce lifted the latch to the bedroom door and pushed, but the door failed to give way. He pulled and then pushed again, but the door would not budge.

"Drop your weapons, or we'll butcher you where you stand!" a soldier ordered. He was a tall man with a bushy mustache that bristled as he gritted his teeth.

"How many do you think there are?" whispered Hadrian.

The walls echoed with the sounds of more soldiers about to arrive.

"Too many," Royce replied.

"Be a lot less in a minute," Hadrian assured him.

"We won't make it. I can't get the door open; we have no exit. I think someone spiked it from the inside. We can't fight the entire castle guard."

"Put them down now!" the soldier in charge shouted, and took a step closer while raising the level of his sword.

"Damn." Hadrian let his blades drop. Royce followed suit.

"Take them," the soldier barked.

᷄

Alric Essendon awoke, startled by the commotion. He was not in his room. The bed he was lying in was a fraction of the size and lacked the familiar velvet canopy. The walls were bare stone, and only a small dresser and wash table decorated the space. He sat up, rubbing his eyes, and soon realized where he was. He had accidentally fallen asleep, apparently several hours ago.

He looked over at Tillie, her bare back and shoulder exposed above the quilt. Alric wondered how she could sleep with all the shouting going on. He rolled out of bed and felt around for his nightshirt. Determining his clothing from hers was easy to do even in the dark. Hers was linen; his was silk.

Awakened by his movement, Tillie groggily asked, "What's wrong?"

"Nothing, go back to sleep," Alric replied.

She could sleep through a hurricane, but his leaving always woke her. That he had fallen asleep was not her fault, but he blamed her just the same. Alric hated waking up here. He hated Tillie even more and was conscious of the paradox.

Throughout the day, her need for him attracted Alric, but in the morning, it repulsed him. Of all the castle servants, however, she was by far the prettiest. Alric did not care for the noble ladies his father invited to court. They were haughty and considered their virginity more valuable than the crown. He found them dull and irritating. His father thought differently. Alric was only nineteen, but already his father was pressuring him to pick a bride.

"You'll be king someday," Amrath told him. "Your first duty to the kingdom is to sire an heir." His father spoke of marriage as if it were a profession, and that was how Alric saw it as well. For him, this, or any other form of work, was best avoided—or at least postponed as long as possible.

"I wish you could spend the whole night with me, my lord," Tillie babbled at him as he pulled his nightshirt over his head.

"Then you should be grateful I dozed as long as I did." With his toes he felt along the floor for his slippers, and finding them, he slid his feet into the warm fleece lining.

"I am, my lord."

"Good night, Tillie," Alric said as he reached the door and stepped outside.

"Good—" Alric closed the door before she finished.

Tillie usually slept with the other maids, in a dorm near the kitchens. Alric brought her to the little vacant bedroom on the third floor of the castle for privacy. He did not like taking girls to his room—his father's bedroom was right next door. The vacant room was on the north side of the castle, and because it received less sunlight, it was always cooler than the royal chambers. He pulled his nightshirt tight and shuffled down the corridor toward the stairs.

"I've checked all the upper floors, Captain. He's not there," Alric heard someone say from just up the steps. By the speaker's curt tone, Alric guessed him to be a sentry. He spoke to them rarely, but when he did, they were always abrupt, as if words were a commodity in short supply.

"Continue the search, down to the prisons if necessary. I want every room examined, each pantry, cabinet, and wardrobe. Do you understand?"

Alric knew that voice well; it was Wylin, the captain of the guard.

"Yes, sir, right away!"

Alric heard the sentry trotting down the steps, and he saw the soldier stop abruptly the moment he met Alric's gaze. "I found him, sir!" the soldier shouted with a hint of relief.

"What's going on, Captain?" Alric called out even as Wylin and three other castle guards rushed down the steps.

"Your Royal Highness!" The captain knelt briefly, bowing his head, and then rose abruptly. "Benton!" he snapped at the solider. "I want five more men here protecting the prince *right now*. Move!"

"Yes, sir!" The soldier snapped a salute and ran back up the stairs.

"Protecting me?" Alric said. "What's going on?"

"Your father's been murdered."

"My father? What?"

"His Majesty, the king—we found him in the royal chapel stabbed in the back. Two intruders are in custody. The dwarf Magnus confirmed it. He saw them murder your father, but he was powerless to stop them."

Alric heard Wylin's voice, but he could not understand the words. They did not make sense. *My father is dead?* He had just spoken with him before he had gone to Tillie's room, not more than a few hours ago. *How could he be dead?*

"I must insist that you remain here, Your Highness, under heavy guard until I finish sweeping the castle. They may not be alone. I'm presently conducting a—"

"Insist what you like, Wylin, but get out of my way. I want to see my father!" Alric demanded, pushing past him.

"King Amrath's body has been taken to his bedroom, Your Highness."

His body!

Alric did not want to hear any more. He ran up the steps, his slippers flying off his feet.

"Stay with the prince!" Wylin shouted after him.

Alric reached the royal wing. In the corridor there was a crowd, which moved aside at his approach. As he reached the chapel, its door lay open with several of the chief ministers gathered inside.

"My prince!" he heard his uncle Percy call, but he did not stop. He was determined to reach his father.

He couldn't be dead!

He rounded the corner, passed his own room, and rushed into the royal suite. Here the double doors were open as well. Several ladies in nightgowns and robes stood just outside weeping loudly. Inside, a pair of older women busied themselves wringing out pink-stained linens in a washbasin.

To the side of the bed stood his sister, Arista, dressed in a burgundy and gold gown. Her arms wrapped around the bedpost, which she gripped so tightly that her fingers were white. She stared at the figure on the mattress with eyes that were dry but wide with horror.

On the pale white sheets of the royal bed lay King Amrath Essendon. He still wore the same clothes Alric had seen him in before he had retired for the night. His face was pale and his eyes were closed. Near the corner of his lips, there was a tiny tear of dried blood.

"My prince—I mean, Your Royal Majesty." His uncle corrected himself as he followed Alric into the bedchamber. His uncle Percy had always looked older than his father had—his hair was very gray, his face wrinkled and drooping; however, he possessed the trim, elegant build of a swordsman. He was still in the process of tying up his robe as he entered. "Thank Maribor you are safe. We thought you might have met a similar fate."

Alric was at a loss for words. He just stood staring at the still body of his father.

"Your Majesty, do not worry. I'll take care of everything. I know how hard this must be. You're still a young man and—"

"What are you talking about?" Alric looked at him. "Take care of what? What are you taking care of?"

"A number of things, Your Majesty. There is the securing of the castle, the investigation as to how this happened, the apprehension of those responsible, arrangements for the funeral and, of course, the eventual coronation."

"Coronation?"

"You are king now, Sire. We will need to arrange your crowning ceremony, but that, of course, can wait until we have everything else settled."

"But I thought—Wylin told me the murderers have been captured."

"He captured two of them. I'm just making certain there aren't any more."

"What will happen to them?" He looked back at the still form of his father. "The killers, what will happen to them?"

"That is up to you, Your Royal Majesty. Their fate is yours to decide, unless you would prefer I handle the matter for you, since it can be quite unpleasant."

Alric turned to his uncle. "I want them to die, Uncle Percy. I want them to suffer horribly and then die."

"Of course, Your Majesty, of course. I assure you they will."

❧

The dungeons of Essendon Castle lay buried two stories beneath the earth. Groundwater seeped through cracks in the walls and wet the face of the stone. Fungus grew in the mortar between stone blocks, and mold coated the wood of doors, stools, and buckets. The foul, musty smell mixed with the stench of decay, and the corridors echoed with the mournful cries of doomed men. Despite the rumors told in Medford's taverns, the castle dungeons had a limited capacity. Needless to say, the prison staff found room for the king-killers. They moved prisoners to provide Royce and Hadrian with their own private cell.

News of the king's death did not take long to spread, and for the first time in years, the prisoners had something exciting to talk about.

"Who woulda thought I'd outlast old Amrath," a gravelly voice muttered. He laughed, but the laughter quickly broke into a series of coughs and sputters.

"Any chance the prince might review our sentences on account of all this?" a weaker, younger voice asked. "I mean, it's possible, isn't it?"

This question was met with a lengthy silence, more coughing, and a sneeze.

"The guard said they stabbed the bastard in the back right in his own chapel. What does that say about his piety?" a new, bitter voice questioned. "Seems to me he was asking for a bit too much from the man upstairs."

"The ones that done it are in our old cell. They moved me and Danny out to make room. I saw them when they shifted us—two of them, one big, the other little."

"Anyone know them? Maybe they was trying to break some of us out and got sidetracked, eh?"

"Gotta have some pretty big brass ones to kill a king in his own castle. They won't get a trial, not even one for show. I'm surprised they've lived this long."

"Gonna want a public torture before the execution. Things been quiet a long time. Haven't had a good torture in years."

"So why ya think they did it?"

"Why don't you ask 'em?"

"Hey, over there? You conscious in that cell of yours? Or did they beat you stupid?"

"Maybe they're dead."

They were not dead but neither were they talking. Royce and Hadrian stood chained to the far wall of their cell, their ankles locked in stocks, and their mouths gagged with leather muzzles. They had been there only for the better part of an hour, but already the strain on Hadrian's muscles was painful. The soldiers had removed their gear, cloaks, boots, and tunics, leaving them with nothing but their britches to fight the damp chill of the dungeon.

They hung listening to the rambling conversations of the other inmates. The conversation halted at heavy approaching footfalls. The door to the cellblock opened and banged against the interior wall.

"Right this way, Your Royal Highness—I mean, Your Royal Majesty," the voice of the dungeon warden said rapidly.

A metal key twisted in the lock, and the door to their cell creaked open. Four royal bodyguards led the prince and his uncle, Percy Braga, inside. Hadrian recognized Braga, the Archduke and Lord Chancellor of Melengar, but he had never seen Alric before. The prince was young, perhaps no more than twenty. He was short, thin, and delicate in appearance with light brown hair that reached to his shoulders and only the ghost of a beard. His stature and features must have come from his mother, because the former king had been a bear of a man. He wore only a silk nightshirt with a massive sword strapped comically to his side by an oversized leather belt.

"These are the ones?"

"Yes, Your Majesty," Braga replied.

"Torch," Alric commanded, snapping his fingers impatiently as a soldier pulled one from the wall bracket and held it out for him. Alric scowled at the offer. "Hold it near their heads. I wish to see their faces." Alric peered at them. "No marks? They haven't been whipped?"

"No, Your Majesty," Braga said. "They surrendered without a fight and Captain Wylin thought it best to lock them up while he searched the rest of the castle. I approved his decision. We can't be certain these two acted alone in this."

"No, of course not. Who gave the order to gag them?"

"I don't know, Your Majesty," Braga replied. "Do you wish their gags removed?"

"No, Uncle Percy—oh, I can't call you that anymore, can I?"

"You're the king now, Your Majesty. You can call me whatever you wish."

"But it isn't dignified, not for a ruler, but *Archduke* is so formal—I'll call you Percy, is that all right?"

"It's not my place to approve of your decisions any longer, Sire."

"Percy it is, then, and no, leave their gags on. I have no desire to hear their lies. What will they say except that they didn't do it? Captured killers always deny their crimes. What choice do they have? Unless they wish to take their last few moments of life to spit in the face of their king. I won't give them the satisfaction of that."

"They could tell us if they were working alone or for someone else. They could even tell us who that person or persons might be."

Alric continued to study them. His eyes focused on a twisted mark in the shape of an M on Royce's left shoulder. He squinted and then, out of frustration, snatched the torch from a guard and held it so close to Royce's face that he winced. "What is this here? Like a tattoo but not quite."

"A brand, Your Majesty," Braga replied. "It's the Mark of Manzant. It would seem this creature was once an inmate of Manzant Prison."

Alric looked puzzled. "I didn't think inmates were released from Manzant, and I wasn't aware anyone has ever escaped."

Braga appeared puzzled as well.

Alric then moved to inspect Hadrian. When he observed the small silver medallion that hung around Hadrian's neck, the prince lifted it, turned it over with mild curiosity, and then let it go with disdain.

"It doesn't matter," Alric said. "I really don't think they look like the type to volunteer information. In the morning have them hauled out to the square and tortured. If they say anything of merit, have them beheaded."

"If not?"

"If not, quarter them slowly. Draw their bowels into the sun and have the royal surgeon keep them alive as long as possible. Oh, and before you do, make certain heralds have time to make several announcements. I want a crowd for this. People need to know the penalty for treason."

"As you wish, Sire."

Alric started for the door and then stopped. He turned and struck Royce across the face with the back of his hand. "He was my father, you worthless piece of filth!" The prince walked out, leaving the two hanging helplessly awaiting the dawn.

❧

Hadrian could only guess how long they had been hanging against the wall; perhaps two or three hours had passed. The faceless voices of the other inmates grew less frequent until they stopped entirely, silenced with boredom or sleep. The muzzle covering Hadrian's mouth became soaked with spit and he found it difficult to breathe. His wrists were sore where the shackles rubbed and his back and his legs ached. To make matters worse, the cold tightened his muscles, making the strain even more painful. Not wanting to look at Royce, he alternated between closing his eyes and staring at the far wall. He did his best to avoid thinking about what would happen when daylight came. Instead, his mind was full of thoughts of self-incrimination—this was his fault. His insistence on breaking rules landed them where they were. Their death was on his hands.

The door opened, and once more, a royal guard, this time accompanied by a woman, entered the cell. She was tall, slender, and dressed in a gown of burgundy and gold silk, which shimmered like fire in the torchlight. She was pretty, with auburn hair and fair skin.

"Remove their gags," she ordered briskly.

The jailers rushed to unbuckle the straps and pull off the muzzles. "Now leave us, all of you."

The jailers promptly exited.

"You too, Hilfred."

"Your Highness, I'm your bodyguard. I need to stay to—"

"They are chained to the wall, Hilfred," she snapped, and then took a breath to calm herself. "I'm fine. Now please leave and guard the door. I want no interruptions by anyone. Do you understand?"

"As you wish, Your Highness." The guard bowed and stepped out, closing the door behind him.

She moved forward, carefully studying the two of them. On her belt was a jeweled kris dagger. Hadrian recognized the long wavy blade as the type used by eastern occultists for magical enchantments. Presently he was more concerned with its other use—as a deadly weapon. She toyed with the dragon-shaped hilt as if she might draw it forth and stab them at any moment.

"Do you know who I am?" she asked Hadrian.

"Princess Arista Essendon," Hadrian replied.

"Very good." She smiled at him. "Now, who are you? And don't bother lying. You'll be dead in less than four hours, so what is the point?"

"Hadrian Blackwater."

"And you?"

"Royce Melborn."

"Who sent you here?"

"A man by the name of DeWitt," Hadrian replied. "He's a member of Duke DeLorkan's group from Dagastan, but we weren't sent to kill your father."

"What were you sent to do?" Her painted nails clicked along the silver handle of the dagger, her eyes intent on them.

"To steal Count Pickering's sword. DeWitt said the count challenged him to a duel here last night at a dinner party."

"And what were you doing in the chapel?"

"That's where DeWitt said he hid the sword."

"I see…" She paused a moment as her mask of stone wavered. Her lips began to tremble, and tears welled in her eyes. She turned away from them, trying to compose herself. Her head was bowed and Hadrian could see her small body lurching.

"Listen," Hadrian said, "for what it's worth, we didn't kill your father."

"I know," she said, still facing away from them.

Royce and Hadrian exchanged glances.

"You were sent here tonight to take the blame for the murder. Both of you are innocent."

"Are you—" Hadrian began, but stopped. For the first time since their capture, he felt hopeful but thought better of it. He turned to Royce. "Is she being sarcastic? You can usually tell better than I."

"Not this time," Royce said, his face tense.

"I just can't believe he's really gone," Arista muttered. "I kissed him good night—it was only a few hours ago." She took a deep breath and straightened before turning to face them. "My brother has set plans for the two of you. You'll be tortured to death this morning. They're building a platform where you'll be drawn and quartered."

"We have already heard the details from your brother," Royce said dismally.

"He is the king now. I can't stop him. He is determined to see you punished."

"You could talk to him," Hadrian offered hopefully. "You could explain that we're innocent. You could tell him about DeWitt."

Arista wiped her eyes with the insides of her wrists. "There is no DeWitt. There was no dinner party here last night, no duke from Calis, and Count Pickering hasn't visited this castle in months. Even if any of that were true, Alric wouldn't believe me. Not a person in this castle will believe me. I'm just an emotional girl. They'll say, 'She's distraught. She's upset.' I can do no more to stop your execution today than I could do to save my own father's life last night."

"You knew he was going to die?" Royce asked.

She nodded, fighting the tears again. "I knew. I was told he would be killed, but I didn't believe it." She paused for a moment to study their faces. "Tell me, what would you do to get out of this castle alive before morning?"

The two glanced at each other in stunned silence.

"I'm thinking anything," Hadrian said. "How about you, Royce?"

His partner nodded. "I'd have to say I'm good with that."

"I can't stop the execution," Arista explained, "but I can see to it that you get out of this dungeon. I can return your clothes and weapons, and I can tell you a way to reach the sewers that run under this castle. I think they will take you out of the city. You should know that I have never personally explored them."

"I—I wouldn't think so," Hadrian said, not really certain he was hearing everything correctly.

"It's imperative that when you escape, you leave the city."

"I don't think that will be a problem," Hadrian explained. "We'd probably do that anyway."

"And one more thing, you must kidnap my brother."

There was a pause as they both stared at her.

"Wait, wait, hold on. You want us to *kidnap* the Prince of Melengar?"

"Technically, he's the King of Melengar now," Royce said, correcting him.

"Oh, yeah. I forgot," Hadrian muttered.

Arista walked back to the cell door, peeked out the window, and then returned.

"Why do you want us to kidnap your brother?" Royce asked.

"Because whoever killed my father will kill Alric next, and before his coronation, I imagine."

"Why?"

"To destroy the Essendon line."

Royce stared at her. "Wouldn't that place you at risk as well?"

"Yes, but the threat to me will not be serious as long as Alric is thought to be alive. He is the crown prince. I'm only the silly daughter. Besides, one of us has to stay here in order to run the kingdom and find my father's murderer."

"And your brother couldn't do that?" Hadrian asked.

"My brother is convinced *you* killed him."

"Oh, right—you have to forgive me. A minute ago I was about to be executed, and now I'm going to kidnap a king. Things are changing a bit fast for me."

"What are we supposed to do with your brother once we've gotten him out of the city?" Royce asked.

"I need you to take him to Gutaria Prison."

"I've never heard of the place," Royce said. He looked at Hadrian, who shook his head.

"I'm not surprised; few people have," Arista explained. "It's a secret ecclesiastical prison maintained exclusively by the Church of Nyphron. It lies on the north side of Windermere Lake. You know where that is?"

They both nodded.

"Travel around the edge of the lake; there is an old road that rises up between some hills; just follow it. I need you to take my brother to see a prisoner named Esrahaddon."

"And then what?"

"That's it," she said. "Hopefully, he will be able to explain everything to Alric well enough to convince him of what is going on."

"So," Royce said, "you want us to escape from this prison, kidnap the king, cross the countryside with him in tow while dodging soldiers who I assume might not accept our side of the story, and go to another secret prison so that he can visit an inmate?"

Arista did not appear amused. "Either that, or you can be tortured to death in four hours."

"Sounds like a really good plan to me," Hadrian declared. "Royce?"

"I like any plan where I don't die a horrible death."

"Good. I'll have two monks come in to give you last rites. I'll have your chains removed and the stocks opened so you can kneel. You'll take their frocks, lock them in your place, and silence them with the gags. Your things are right outside in the prison office. I'll tell the warden that you're taking them for the poor. I'll have my personal bodyguard, Hilfred, escort you to the lower kitchens. They won't be active for another hour or so. You should have the place to yourselves. A grate near the basin lifts out for sweeping debris into the sewer. I'll speak to my brother and convince him to meet me at the kitchens alone. I assume you are capable fighters?"

"He is." Royce bobbed his head toward Hadrian.

"My brother isn't, so you should be able to subdue him easily. Be certain not to hurt him."

"This is likely a really stupid question for me to ask," Royce said, "but what makes you think we won't just kill your brother, leave his body in the sewer to rot, and then just disappear?"

"Nothing," she replied. "Like you, I simply don't have a choice."

The monks posed little problem, and once dressed in their frocks, with hoods carefully drawn, Hadrian and Royce slipped out of their cell. Hilfred stood waiting just outside and quickly escorted them as far as the entrance to the kitchens, where, without a word, he left them alone. Royce, who had always had better night vision, led the way through the dark labyrinth of massive pots and piled plates. Dressed as they were with loose sleeves and long, disabling robes, they navigated this sea of potential disaster, where one wrong move could topple a ceramic stack and cause alarm.

So far Arista's plan was a success. The kitchen was empty. They shed their clerical garb in favor of their own clothes and gear. They located the central basin, under which was a massive iron grating. Although it was heavy, they were able to move it out of position without making too much noise. They were pleasantly surprised to find some iron rungs leading into the void. In the depths below, they could hear the trickle of water. Hadrian found a pantry filled with vegetables and felt around until he located a burlap sack filled with potatoes. He quietly dumped out the spuds, shook the sack as clean as he could, and then rooted around for twine.

They were still a long way from free, but the future was looking considerably better than it had only minutes before. Although Royce had not said a word, the fact that Hadrian was responsible bothered him. As he and Royce waited there together, the guilt and silence became overpowering.

"Aren't you going to say, *I told you so?*" Hadrian whispered.

"What would be the point in that?"

"Oh, so you're saying that you're going to hang on to this and throw it at me at some future, more personally beneficial moment?"

"I don't see the point in wasting it now, do you?"

They left the door to the kitchen slightly ajar, and before long, the distant glow of a torch appeared and Hadrian could hear approaching voices. At this signal, they took their positions. Royce took a seat at the table with his back to the entryway. He put the hood of his cloak up and pretended to hunch over a plate of food. Hadrian stood to one side of the door, holding his short sword by the blade.

"For Maribor's sake, why here?"

"Because I'm offering the old man a plate of food and a place to wash."

Hadrian recognized the voices of Alric and Arista and surmised they were now just outside the kitchen door.

"I don't see why we had to leave the guards, Arista. We don't know we—there might be other assassins."

"That's why you need to talk to him. He says he knows who hired the killers, but he refuses to talk to a woman. He said he will only deal with you, and only if you are alone. Listen, I'm not sure who to trust at this point, and you don't know either. We can't be sure who's responsible and some of the guards could be involved. Don't worry, he's an old man and you're a skilled swordsman. We have to find out what he has to say. Don't you want to know?"

"Of course, but what makes you think he has any clue?"

"I don't know anything for certain. But he's not asking for money, just a fresh start. That reminds me, here are some clothes to give him." There was a brief pause. "Look, he seems trustworthy to me. I think if he was lying, he would request gold or land."

"It's just so . . . strange. Hilfred's not even with you. It's as if you're walking around without a shadow. It's unnerving is what it is. Just coming down here with you, it's—well, you and I, we—you know. We're brother and sister, yet we hardly see each other. In the last few years, I think I've only spoken to you a dozen times, and then only when we visit Drondil Fields on holiday. You always lock yourself up in that tower, doing who knows what, but now—"

"I know, it's strange," Arista replied. "I agree. It's like the night of the fire all over again. I still have nightmares about that evening. I wonder if I'll have nightmares about tonight."

Alric's voice softened. "That's not really my point. It's just that we've never gotten along, not really. But now, well, you're the only family I have left. It seems strange to be saying it, but I suddenly find that matters to me."

"Are you saying you want to be friends?"

"Let's just say I want to stop being enemies."

"I didn't know we were."

"You've been jealous of me ever since Mother told you elder daughters don't get to be queen as long as little brothers are around to be king."

"I have not!"

"I don't want to fight. Maybe I do want to be friends. I'm the king now, and I'll need your help. You're smarter than most of the ministers, anyway. Father always said so. And you've had university training; that's more than I've had."

"Trust me, Alric, I'm more than your friend. I'm your big sister, and I'll look out for you. Now go in there and see what this man has to say."

As Alric entered the kitchen, Hadrian brought the hilt of his sword down on the back of his head. The prince collapsed to the floor with a dull thud. Arista rushed in.

"I said not to hurt him!" she scolded.

"He would be screaming for the guard right now otherwise," Hadrian explained. He tied a gag around the prince's mouth and placed the sack over his head. Royce was already up from his seat and securing Alric's ankles with twine.

"He's all right, though?"

"He'll live," Hadrian told her as he secured the hands and arms of the unconscious prince.

"Which is a whole lot more than he had in store for us," Royce added, pulling tight the noose around the prince's ankles.

"Keep in mind he was certain you killed his father," the princess said. "How would you react?"

"I never knew my father," Royce replied indifferently.

"Your mother, then."

"Royce is an orphan," Hadrian explained as they continued to wrap the prince in twine. "He never knew either of his parents."

"I suppose that explains a lot. Well then, imagine how you'll treat the person who sent you to the chapel tonight, once you find him. I doubt you'll be very charitable when coming face to face with him. In any case, you gave your word. Please do as I ask, and take good care of my brother. Don't forget I spared your lives tonight. I'm hoping that fact will keep you to your word."

She held out the bundle dropped by her brother. "Here is a set of clothes that should fit him. They used to belong to the steward's son, and I always thought he looked about the same size as Alric. Oh, and remove his ring but keep it safe. It bears the royal seal of Melengar and is proof of his identity. Without it, unless you encounter someone who knows his face, Alric is just another peasant. Return it to him when you reach the prison. He'll need it to get in."

"We'll hold up our end of the bargain," Hadrian told her as he and Royce moved the bundled body of the prince toward the open basin. Royce pulled the opulent dark blue ring from Alric's finger and stuffed it in his breast pocket. He then climbed to the bottom of the cistern. Using the rope tied around Alric's ankles, Hadrian lowered him headfirst to Royce. Once the prince was down, Hadrian grabbed the torch and dropped it to Royce. Then he entered the hole and dragged the grating back into position. At the bottom of the ladder was a five-foot-wide, four-foot-high arched tunnel in which a shallow river of filth flowed.

"Remember," the princess whispered through the metal grid. "Go to Gutaria Prison and speak to Esrahaddon. And please, keep my brother safe."

❦

An incomprehensible series of mumbles emitted from the prince under the potato sack. While they were not certain exactly what he was saying, Royce and Hadrian could tell the prince was doing his best to shout and was decidedly displeased with his situation.

The cold water backing up from the Galewyr River into the sewer had woken him. They were waist deep in it now and while the smell was better, the temperature was not. As they looked out through the end of the cistern, the first pale light of dawn revealed the difference between the forested horizon and the sky. Night was melting away fast, and they could hear the Mares Cathedral bell ringing for early service. The whole city would be waking soon.

Hadrian calculated they were below Gentry Square, not far from Artisan Row, where the city met the river. Determining their location was an easy guess, because it was the only section of town with covered sewers. A metal grate blocked their exit, and Hadrian was relieved to find hinges and a lock sealing it instead of bolts. Royce made quick work of the lock, and the rusted hinges surrendered to a few solid kicks from Hadrian. With the way clear, Royce went out to scout while Hadrian sat at the mouth of the sewer with Alric.

The prince had worked his gag loose, and Hadrian could recognize his words now. "I'll have you flailed to death! Release me this instant."

"You'll be quiet," Hadrian replied, "or I'll let you go into the river and we'll see how well you tread water with your hands and feet tied."

"You wouldn't dare! I'm the King of Melengar, you swine!"

Hadrian kicked Alric's legs out from under him, and the

prince fell facedown. After allowing him to struggle for a few moments, Hadrian pulled him up. "Now keep your mouth shut or I might leave you to drown next time." Alric coughed and sputtered but did not speak another word.

Royce returned, having slipped into the sewer soundlessly. "We are right on the river. I found a small boat by a fisherman's dock and took the liberty of commandeering it in His Majesty's name. It's just down the slope in a stand of reeds."

"No!" the prince protested, and shook his shoulders violently. "You must release me. I'm the king!"

Hadrian gripped him by the throat and into his ear whispered, "What did I tell you about talking? Not a sound or you swim."

"But—"

Hadrian dunked the prince again, pulled him up for a short breath, and dunked him once more. "Not another sound," Hadrian growled.

Alric sputtered, and Hadrian, dragging the prince with him, followed Royce down the slope.

The craft was little more than an oversized rowboat, bleached by the sun and filled with nets and small painted buoys. The heavy smell of fish from the boat helped mask the stench of sewage. A tarp, stretched to form a little tent used to store gear or to serve as a shelter, covered the bow. They stuffed the prince underneath, pinning him there with the nets and buoys.

Hadrian pushed off the bank with a long pole he found in the boat. Royce used the wooden rudder to steer the small craft as the river did the work of propelling them downstream. Near the headwaters, the current of the Galewyr was strong, and forward momentum was no problem. They found themselves working to keep the boat in the center of the river as they moved swiftly westward. Just as the sky was turning from a charcoal gray to dull steel, they passed under the shadow of the city of Medford. From the river, they could see the great tower of Essendon Castle, its falcon standard flying at half-mast for the dead king. The flag was a good sign, but how long would it be before they discovered the prince was missing and they removed it?

The river marked the southern edge of the city, skirting along Artisan Row. Large two-story warehouses of gray brick lined the bank, and great wooden wheels jutted out into the river, catching the current to power the millstones and lumberyards. Because the shallow waters of the Galewyr prevented the passage of deep-keeled ships, numerous docks serviced flat-bottomed barges that brought goods from the small seaport village of Roe. There were also piers built by the fishing industry, which led directly to fish markets, where pulleys raised large nets and dumped them onto the cutting floor. In the early morning light, the gulls had already begun to circle the docks where fishermen had started to clear the lines on their skiffs. No one paid particular attention to the two men in a small boat drifting down the river. Nevertheless, they stayed low in the boat until the last signs of the city disappeared behind the rising banks of the river.

The day's light grew strong, as did the pull of the current. Rocks appeared and the river trench deepened. Neither Royce nor Hadrian was an expert boatman, but they did their best dodging the rocks and shallows. Royce remained at the tiller while Hadrian, on his knees, used the long wooden pole to push the bow clear of obstacles. A few times, they glanced off unseen boulders, and the hull lurched abruptly with a deep unpleasant thud. When it did, they could hear the prince whimper, but otherwise he remained quiet and their trip was a smooth one.

In time, the full face of the sun rose overhead, and the river widened considerably and settled into a gentle flow with sandy banks and rich green fields beyond. The Galewyr divided two kingdoms. To the south lay Glouston, the northern marchland of the kingdom of Warric. To the north was Galilin, the largest province in Melengar, administered by Count Pickering. At one time, the river had been a hotly disputed division between two uneasy warlords, but those days were gone. Now it was a peaceful fence between good neighbors and both banks remained lovely, untroubled pastoral scenes of the late season, filled with hay mounds and grazing cows.

The day became unusually warm. Because it was so late in the year, there were few insects about. The cicadas' drone had disappeared, and even the frogs were quiet. The only sound that remained was that of the soft gentle breeze through the dry grasses. Hadrian reclined across the boat with his head on the bundle of the steward's son's old clothes and his feet on the gunwale. His cloak and boots were off and his shirt was open. Similarly, Royce lay with his legs up, idly guiding the boat. The sweet scent of wild salifan was strong in the air, the fragrance more pungent after the plants' surviving the year's first frost. Except for the lack of food, the day was turning out to be quite wonderful and would have been even if they had not just escaped a horrible death hours before.

Hadrian tilted his head back to catch the full light of the sun on his face. "Maybe we should be fishermen."

"Fishermen?" Royce asked dubiously.

"This is pretty nice, isn't it? I never realized how much I like the sound of water lapping against a boat before. I'm enjoying this: the buzzing of a dragonfly, the sight of the cattails, and the bank drifting lazily by."

"Fish don't just jump into the boat, you know?" Royce

pointed out. "You have to cast nets, haul them in, gut the fish, cut off their heads, and scale them. You don't just get to drift."

"Putting it that way makes it sound oddly more like work." Hadrian scooped a handful of water from the river and splashed it on his warm face. He ran his wet fingers through his hair and sighed contentedly.

"You think he's still alive?" Royce asked, nodding his head toward Alric.

"Sure," Hadrian replied without bothering to look. "He's probably sleeping. Why do you ask?"

"I was just pondering something. Do you think a person could smother in a wet potato bag?"

Hadrian lifted his head and looked over at the motionless prince. "I really hadn't thought about it until now." He got up and shook Alric, but the prince did not stir. "Why didn't you mention something earlier!" he said, drawing his dagger. He cut through the ropes and pulled the bag clear.

Alric lay still. Hadrian bent down to check if he was breathing. Just then, the prince kicked Hadrian hard, knocking him back toward Royce. Alric began feverishly untying his feet, but Hadrian was back on him before he cleared the first knot. He slammed Alric to the deck, pinning his hands over his head.

"Hand me the twine," Hadrian barked to Royce, who was watching the wrestling match with quiet amusement. Royce casually tossed him a small coil, and when Hadrian at last had the prince secured, he sat back down to rest.

"See," Royce said, "*that's* more like fishing; only fish don't kick, of course."

"Okay, so it was a bad idea." Hadrian rubbed his side where the prince had hit him.

"By brutalizing me, the two of you have sentenced yourselves to death! You know that, don't you?"

"That's a bit redundant, don't you think, Your Majesty?"

Royce inquired. "Seeing as how you already sentenced us to death once today."

The prince rolled onto his side, tilting his head back, squinted against the brilliant sunlight.

"You!" he shouted, amazed. "But how did you—Arista!" His eyes narrowed in anger. "Not jealous, is she! My dear sister is behind all this! She hired you to kill my father, and now she plans to eliminate me so she can rule!"

"The king was *her* father as well. Besides, if we wanted to kill you, don't you think you'd already be dead?" Royce asked. "Why would we go to all the trouble of hauling you down this river? We could have slit your throat, weighed you down with rocks, and dumped you hours ago. I might add that such a fate would still be considerably better than what you had planned for us."

The prince considered this for a moment. "So it's ransom, then. Do you intend to sell me to the highest bidder? Did she promise you a profit from my sale? You're both fools if you believe that. Arista will never allow it. She'll see me dead. She has to in order to secure her seat on the throne. You won't get a copper!"

"Listen, you little royal pain in the ass, we didn't kill your father. In fact, for what it's worth, I thought old Amrath was a fair king, as far as they go. We also aren't ransoming or selling you."

"Well, you certainly aren't trussing me up like a pig to get in my good graces. Now exactly what *are* you doing with me?" The prince struggled against his bonds but eventually settled down.

"If you really want to know, we are trying to save your life. As strange as that may seem," Hadrian said.

"You're what?" Alric asked, stunned.

"Your sister seems to think someone residing in the

castle—the same lot that killed your father—is plotting to kill everyone in the royal family. Because you would be the next likely target, she freed us to smuggle you out for your own safety."

Alric pulled his legs up under him and worked his way to a sitting position with his back resting up against the pile of white-and-red striped buoys. He stared at the two of them for a moment. "If Arista didn't hire you to kill my father, then exactly what were you doing in the castle tonight?"

Hadrian provided a quick summary of his meeting with DeWitt, to which the prince listened without interruption.

"And then Arista came to you in the dungeon with this story, asking you to abduct me to keep me safe?"

"Trust me," Hadrian said. "If there was another way to get out of there, we would have left you."

"So you actually believe her? You're dumber than I thought," Alric said, shaking his head. "Don't you see what she's doing? She's out to have the kingdom for herself."

"If that were so, why would she have us kidnap you?" Royce asked. "Why not just have you killed like your father?"

Alric thought a moment, his eyes drifting to the floor of the boat, and then he nodded. "She most likely tried." He looked back at them. "I wasn't in my room last night. I slipped out for a rendezvous and fell asleep until I heard the noise. It's very likely an assassin was sent for me but I wasn't there. After that, I had a guard with me at all times until Arista convinced me I had to come alone to the kitchen. I should have known she was betraying me."

He swung his bound legs into the mound of nets. "I just never thought she could be so cold as to kill our father, but that's how she is, you see. She's extremely clever. She told you this story about a traitor, and it was believable because it was true. She only lied about not knowing who it was. Once her assassin missed me, she used you. It was more likely that you'd agree to a kidnapping rather than murder, so she set you up."

Royce did not answer but glanced at Hadrian.

"There was this boat," the prince went on, looking around him, "perfect for your needs waiting at the river's edge."

Alric dipped his head at the tarp next to him. "How nice to have a boat with a cover like this to hide me under. With a nice boat, and a river, you wouldn't be tempted to stray off the water. You can't go upstream from the city. The headwaters are too rough. You have to go toward the sea. She knows exactly where we are, and where we'll be. Did she say where to take me? Is it somewhere down this river?"

"Lake Windermere."

"Ah, the Winds Abbey? It's not far from Roe, and this river travels toward it. How convenient! Of course, we'll never make it," the prince told them. "She'll have killers waiting along the bank. They will murder us. She'll say you two killed me, just as you killed my father. And, of course, her guards killed you when you tried to flee. She'll have a wonderful burial for me and my father. The next day she will call Bishop Saldur to perform her coronation."

Royce and Hadrian sat in silence.

"Do you need more proof?" the prince went on. "You say this fellow that hired you was called DeWitt? You said he was from Calis? Arista returned from a visit there only two months ago. Perhaps she made some new friends. Perhaps she promised them land in Melengar in return for help with a troublesome father and brother who stood between her and the crown."

"We need to get off this river," Royce told Hadrian.

"You think he's right?" Hadrian asked.

"Doesn't matter at this point. Even if he's wrong, the owner of this boat will report it stolen. When news leaks out that the prince is missing, they will connect the two."

Hadrian stood up and looked downstream. "If I were them, I would send a group of riders down the riverbank in case we stopped and another set of riders running fast down the Westfield road to catch us at Wicend Ford. It would only take them three or four hours."

"Which means they could already be there," Royce concluded.

"We need to get off this river," Hadrian said.

◈

The boat came into view of Wicend Ford, a flat, rocky area where the river widened abruptly and became shallow enough to cross. Farmer Wicend had built a small stock shelter of split rails close to the water, allowing his animals to graze and drink unattended; it was a pretty spot. Thick hedges of heldaberry bushes lined the bank, and a handful of yellowing willows bent so low toward the river that their branches touched the water and created ripples and whimsical whirlpools along the surface.

The moment the boat entered the shallows, hidden archers launched a rain of arrows from the bank. One struck the gunwale with a thud. A second and third found their target in the royal falcon insignia emblazoned on the back of the prince's robe. The figure in the robe fell from view into the bottom of the boat. More arrows found their marks in the chest of the tillerman, who dropped into the water, and the pole man, who merely slumped to one side.

From behind the screen of bushes and willows, six men emerged, dressed in browns, dirty greens, and autumn golds. They entered the river, waded out, and caught the still drifting boat.

"It's official, we're dead," Royce declared comically. "Interestingly enough, the first arrows hit Alric."

The three of them were lying concealed in the tall field grass atop the eastern hill overlooking the river upstream of the ford. Less than a hundred yards to their right lay the Westfield road. From there, the road ran along the riverbank all the way to Roe, where the river joined the sea.

"Now do you believe me?" the prince asked.

"It only proves that someone is indeed trying to kill you and that they are not us. They're not soldiers either, or at least they aren't in uniform, so they could be anyone," Royce told them.

"How can he see so much—the arrows, their clothing? I can only see movement and color from this distance," Alric said.

Hadrian shrugged.

The prince was now dressed in the clothes of the steward's son: a loose-fitting gray tunic, worn and faded wool knee-length britches, brown stockings, and a tattered, stained wool cloak, which was too long. He wore on his feet a pair of shoes that were little more than soft leather bags tied at his ankles. Although the prince was no longer bound, Hadrian kept hold of a rope tethered around his waist. Hadrian also carried the prince's sword for him.

"They're moving in on the boat," Royce announced.

All Hadrian could really see were shadowy movements under the trees until one of the men stepped out into the sunlight to grab the bow of the boat.

"It won't be long before they discover they've only killed three bushels of thickets wrapped in old clothes," Hadrian told Royce. "So I'd be quick."

Royce nodded and promptly trotted down the slope.

"What's he doing?" Alric asked in shock. "He'll get himself killed and us as well!"

"That's one opinion," Hadrian said. "Just sit tight."

Royce slipped into the shade of the trees, and Hadrian immediately lost sight of him. "Where'd he go?" the prince asked with a puzzled look on his face.

Once more Hadrian shrugged.

Below them, the men converged on the boat, and Hadrian heard a distant shout. He could not make out the words, but he saw someone holding up the Alric-bush complete with arrows. Two of the men remained with the boat while the others waded toward the bank. Just then, Hadrian caught sight of movement in the trees, a train of tethered horses trotting up the slope toward him and Alric. From the bank came shouts of alarm and cursing as the distant figures struggled to race across the field and up the hill.

When the horses drew nearer, Hadrian spotted Royce crouched down, hanging between the two foremost animals. He caught two of the horses, pulled the bridle off one, and quickly tied a lead line to the other horse's halter. He ordered Alric to mount. Angry shouts erupted as the archers spotted them. Two or three stopped to fit arrows but their uphill shots fell short. Before they could close the distance, the three mounted and galloped toward the road.

Royce led them a mile northwest to where the Westfield and Stonemill roads intersected. Here Hadrian, and by default Alric, rode west. Royce, leading the train of captured horses, stayed behind to cloud their tracks and then rode north. An hour later he caught up with them with only the horse he rode. They turned off the road into an open field and headed away from the river but still moved generally westward.

The horses had built up a solid sweat and were puffing for air. When the men reached the hedgerow lands, they slowed their pace. Eventually they reached the thickets, and there they stopped and dismounted. Alric found a spot clear of thornbushes and sat down, fussing with his tunic, which did not hang on him quite right. Royce and Hadrian took the opportunity to search the animals. There were no markings, symbols, parchments, or emblems of any kind to identify the attackers. Moreover, except for a spare crossbow and a handful of bolts left on Hadrian's mount, they wore only saddles.

"You'd think they would have some bread at least. Who travels without water?" Hadrian complained.

"They clearly didn't expect to be out long."

"Why do you still have me tethered?" the prince asked, irritated. "This is extremely humiliating."

"I don't want you getting lost," Hadrian replied with a grin.

"There's no reason to drag me around any further. I accept that you did not kill my father. My cunning sister merely fooled you. It's quite understandable. She's very intelligent. She even fooled me. Now, if you don't mind, I would like to return to my castle so I can deal with her before she consolidates her power and has the whole army turned out to hunt me down. As for you two, you can go wherever Maribor dictates. I really don't care."

"But your sister said—" Hadrian began.

"My sister just tried to have us all killed back there, or weren't you paying attention?"

"We have no proof it was her. If we let you return to Essendon, and she is right, you'll be walking to your death."

"And what proof do we have it wasn't her? Do you still intend to escort me to wherever she told you to take me? Don't you think she'll have another trap waiting? I see my death far more probable on the road there than on any other road. Look, this is my life; I think it's fair for me to decide. Besides,

what do you care if I live or die? I was about to have you two
tortured to death. Remember?"

"You know" — Royce paused a moment — "he's got a point
there."

"We promised her," Hadrian reminded him, "and she
saved our lives. Let's not forget that."

Alric threw his hands up and rolled his eyes. "By Mar! You
are thieves, aren't you? It's not as if you have a sense of honor
to contend with. Besides, she was also the one who betrayed
you and put your lives in danger in the first place. Let's not
forget *that*!"

Hadrian ignored the prince. "We don't know she is responsible, and we *did* promise."

"Another good deed?" Royce asked. "You'll remember
where the last one ended us?"

Hadrian sighed. "There it is! Didn't have to save it too long,
did you? Yes, I did screw up, but that isn't to say I'm wrong
this time. Windermere is only, what, ten miles from here? We
could be there by nightfall. We could stop at the abbey. Monks
have to help wayward travelers. It's in their doctrine or code
or whatever. We could really use some food, don't you think?"

"They also might know something about the prison,"
Royce speculated.

"What prison?" Alric asked, nervously getting to his feet.

"Gutaria Prison — it's where your sister told us to take you."

"To lock me up?" the prince asked fearfully.

"No, no. She wants you to talk to someone there, some guy
called...Esra — oh, what was it?"

"Haddon, I think," Hadrian said.

"Whatever. Do you know anything about this prison?"

"No, I've never heard of it," Alric replied. "Although it
sounds like the kind of place unwanted royals go to disappear
when a conniving sister steals her brother's throne."

Royce's horse butted against his shoulder, prompting him to rub its head while contemplating the situation. "I'm too tired to think clearly. I doubt any of us can make an intelligent decision at this point, and given the stakes, we don't want to be hasty. We'll go as far as the abbey at least. We'll talk to them and see what they can tell us about the prison. Then we'll decide what to do from there. Does that sound fair?"

Alric sighed heavily. "If I must go, can I at least be given the dignity of controlling my own horse?" There was a pause before he added, "I give you my word as king. I'll not try to escape until we reach this abbey."

Hadrian looked at Royce, who nodded. He then pulled the crossbow from behind his saddle. He braced it against the ground, pulled the string to the first notch, and loaded a bolt.

"It's not that we don't trust you," Royce said as Hadrian prepared the bow. "It's just that we've learned over the years that honor among nobles is usually inversely proportionate to their rank. As a result, we prefer to rely on more concrete methods for motivations—such as self-preservation. You already know we don't want you dead, but if you have ever been riding full tilt and had a horse buckle under you, you understand that death is always a possibility, and broken bones are almost a certainty."

"There's also the danger of missing the horse completely," Hadrian added. "I'm a good shot, but even the best archers have bad days. So to answer your question—yes, you can control your own horse."

～

They traveled at a moderate but steady pace for the remainder of the day. Royce guided them through fields, hedgerows, and forested trails. They stayed off the roads and away from the villages until at last there were no more of either. Even the farms disappeared as the land lost its tame face and they entered the wild highlands of Melengar. The ground rose, and forests grew thicker, with fewer passable routes. Ravines led to bogs at their bottoms, and hills sloped up into cliffs. This rough country, the western third of Melengar, lacked farmable land and remained unsettled. The area was home to wolves, elk, deer, bears, outlaws, and anyone seeking solitude, such as the monks of the Winds Abbey. Civilized men shunned it, and superstitious villagers feared its dark forests and rising mountains. Myths abounded about water nymphs luring knights to watery graves, wolf men devouring the lost, and ancient evil spirits that appeared as floating lights in the dense forest enticing children to their dark caves under the earth. Regardless of the legions of potential supernatural dangers, enough natural obstacles made the route one to avoid.

Hadrian never questioned his partner's choice of path or direction. He knew why Royce stayed clear of the Westfield road, which provided a clear and easy path along the riverbank to the fishing village of Roe. Despite its isolation at the mouth of the Galewyr, Roe had grown from a sleepy little dock into a thriving seaport. While it held the promise of food, lodging, and imagined safety, it would likely be watched. The other easy option was to travel north up the Stonemill road—the route Royce pretended to take by leaving enough tracks to hopefully mislead anyone who followed into thinking they were headed for Drondil Fields. Each path held obvious benefits, which anyone looking for them would understand as well. As a result, they plodded and hacked their way through the wilds, following whatever animal trails they could find.

After a particularly arduous fight through a dense segment

of forest, they came out unexpectedly on a ridge that afforded a magnificent view of the setting sun, which bathed the valley of Windermere and was reflected by the lake. Lake Windermere was one of the deepest in all of Avryn. Because it was too deep to support plant life, it was nearly crystal clear. The water shimmered in the folds and crevices of the three surrounding hills that shaped it in the form of a stretched, jagged triangle. The hills rose above the tree line, showing bald, barren peaks of scrub and stone. Hadrian could just make out a stone building on the top of the southernmost hill. Aside from Roe, the Winds Abbey was the only sign of civilization for miles.

The party aimed toward the building and descended into the valley, but night caught up with them before they were halfway there. Fortunately, a distant light from the abbey provided them a beacon. The weariness of being up for two stress-filled days combined with hard travel and no food was taking its toll on Hadrian, and he assumed the same was true of Royce, though his partner showed it less. The prince looked the worst. Alric rode just ahead of Hadrian. His head would droop lower and lower with each stride of his horse until he would nearly fall from his saddle. He would catch himself, straighten, and then the process would begin again.

Despite the warm day, night brought with it a bitter chill, and in the soft light of the rising moon, the breath of men and horses began to fog the crisp night air. Above, the stars shone like diamond dust scattered across the heavens. In the distance, the call of owls and the shrill static of crickets filled the valley. Had the party not been so exhausted and hungry, they might have described the trip that night as beautiful. Instead, they merely gritted their teeth and focused on the path ahead.

They began climbing the south hill as Royce led them with

uncanny skill along a switchback trail that only his keen eyes could see. The thin, worn clothes of the steward's son were a miserable defense against the cold, and soon the prince was shivering. To make matters worse, as they climbed higher, the temperature dropped and the wind grew. Soon trees began to shrink to stunted shrubs and the earth changed to lichen- and moss-covered stone. At last, they reached the steps of the Winds Abbey.

Clouds had moved in, and the moon was no longer visible. In the darkness, they could see very little except the steps and the light they had followed. They dismounted and approached the gate. A stone arch set within a peaked nave lay open on a porch of rock hewn from the hill itself. There was no longer the sound of crickets, nor of hooting owls; only the unremitting wind broke the silence.

"Hello?" Hadrian called. After a time, Hadrian called again. He was about to try a third time when he saw a light move within. Like a dim firefly weaving behind unseen trees, it vanished behind pillars and walls, reappearing closer each time. As it drew near, Hadrian saw that the strange will-o'-the-wisp was a small man in a worn frock holding a lantern.

"Who is it?" he asked in a soft, timid voice.

"Wayfarers," Royce answered. "Cold, tired, and hoping for a place to rest."

"How many are you?" The man poked his head out and swung the lantern about. He paused to study each face. "Just the three?"

"Yes," Hadrian replied. "We've been traveling all day with no food. We were hoping to take advantage of the famous hospitality of the legendary Monks of Maribor. Do you have room?"

The monk hesitated and then said, "I—I suppose." He stepped back to allow them entrance. "Come in, you can—"

"We have horses," Hadrian interrupted.

"Really? How exciting," the monk replied, sounding impressed. "Oh, I would like to see them, but it's very late and—"

"No, I just meant, is there somewhere we can stable them for the night? A barn or perhaps a shed?"

"Oh, I see." The monk paused, tapping his lip thoughtfully. "Ah, well, we had a lovely stable, mostly for cows, sheep, and goats, but that's not going to work tonight. We also had some animal pens where we kept pigs, but that really won't do either."

"I suppose we could just tie them up outside somewhere if that's all right," Hadrian said. "I think I remember a little tree or two."

The monk nodded, appearing relieved to have the issue resolved. After they stacked the saddles on the porch, the little man led them through an opening into what appeared to be a large courtyard.

With only the bleak glow of the monk's lantern, Hadrian could not see far beyond the stone walkway and was too tired for a tour even if the monk had been inclined to show off his home. The abbey had a heavy smell of smoke that conjured visions of warm crackling hearths where beds might be.

"We didn't mean to wake you," Hadrian said softly.

"Oh, not me," the monk said. "I actually don't sleep much. I was busy with a book, right in the middle of a sentence when I heard you. Most unnerving. It's a rare thing to hear someone in the middle of the day around here, much less a dark night."

Columns of freestanding stone rose beneath a cloudy sky, and various black silhouetted statues dotted the space. The smoky smell was stronger, but the only thing that appeared to be burning was the lantern in the monk's hand. They reached a small set of stone steps and he led the way down into what appeared to be a rough-hewn stone cellar.

"You can stay here," the monk told them.

The three stared at the tiny hovel, which Hadrian thought looked less inviting than the cells below Essendon Castle. Inside, it was very cramped, filled with piles of neatly stacked wood, tied bundles of twigs and heather, two wooden barrels, a chamber pot, a little table, and a single cot. No one said a word for a moment.

"It's not much, I know," the monk said regretfully, "but at the moment, it's all I can offer you."

"We'll make do, then, thank you," Hadrian assured him. He was so tired he did not care as long as he could lie down and be out of the wind. "Can we perhaps get a few blankets? As you can see, we really don't have any supplies with us."

"Blankets?" The monk looked concerned. "Well, there is one here." He pointed at the cot, where a single thin blanket lay neatly folded. "I truly am sorry I can't offer you any more. You can keep the lantern if you like. I know my way around without it." The monk left them without another word, perhaps fearful they would ask for something else.

"He didn't even ask us our names," the prince said.

"And wasn't that a pleasant surprise," Royce pointed out as he moved around the room with the lantern. Hadrian watched him take a thorough inventory of what little was there: a dozen or so bottles of wine hidden in the back, a small sack of potatoes under some straw, and a length of rope.

"This is intolerable," Alric said in disgust. "Surely an abbey of this size has better accommodations than this pit."

Hadrian found an old pair of burlap shoes that he cleared out before he lay down on the cellar floor. "I actually have to agree with the royal one there. I heard great things about the hospitality of this abbey. We do appear to be getting the dregs."

"Question is, why?" Royce said. "Who else is here? It would need to be several groups or a tremendously large party to turn us out to this hovel. Only nobility travel with such large retinues. They might be looking for us. They might be associated with those archers."

"I doubt it. If we were in Roe, I think we'd have more reason for concern," Hadrian said as he stretched and then yawned. "Besides, anyone who is here has turned in for the night and is probably not expecting any late arrivals."

"Still, I'm going to get up early and look around. We might need to make a hasty departure."

"Not before breakfast," Hadrian said, sitting on the floor and kicking off his boots. "We need to eat and I know abbeys are renowned for their food. If nothing else, you can steal some."

"Fine, but His Highness should not move about. He needs to keep a low profile."

Standing in the middle of the cellar with a sickened look on his face, Alric said, "I can't believe I'm being subjected to this."

"Consider it a vacation," Hadrian suggested. "For at least one day you get to pretend you are nobody, a common peasant, the son of a blacksmith perhaps."

"No," Royce said, preparing his own sleeping space but keeping his boots on. "They might expect him to know things like how to use a hammer. And look at his hands. Anyone could tell he was lying."

"Most people have jobs that require the use of their hands, Royce," Hadrian pointed out. He spread his cloak over himself and turned on his side. "What could a common peasant do that monks wouldn't know the first thing about and wouldn't cause calluses?"

"He could be a thief or a whore."

They both looked at the prince, who cringed at his prospects. "I'm taking the cot," Alric said.

Chapter 4

Windermere

The morning arrived cold and wet. A solid gray sky cast a steady curtain of rain on the abbey. The deluge streamed down the stone steps and pooled in the low pocket of the entryway. When the growing puddle reached Hadrian's feet, he knew it was time to get up. He turned over on his back and wiped his eyes. He had not slept well. He felt stiff and groggy, and the cold morning air chilled him to the bone. He sat up, dragged a large hand down the length of his face, and looked around. The tiny room appeared even more dismal in the drab morning light than it had the night before. He moved back away from the puddle and looked for his boots. Alric had the benefit of the cot, yet he did not appear to have fared much better. Despite having a blanket wrapped tightly around him, he lay shivering. Royce was nowhere to be seen.

Alric opened one eye and squinted at Hadrian as he pulled his big boots on.

"Good morning, *Your Highness*," Hadrian said in a mocking tone. "Have a pleasant sleep?"

"That was the worst night I have ever endured," Alric snarled through clenched teeth. "I have never felt such misery as this damp, freezing hole. Every muscle aches; my head is throbbing, and I can't stop my teeth from chattering. I'm going home today. Kill me if you must, but nothing short of my death will stop me."

"So that would be a no?" Hadrian got to his feet, rubbed his arms briskly, and looked out at the rain.

"Why don't you do something constructive and build a fire before we die of the cold?" the prince grumbled, pulling the thin blanket over his head and peering out as if it were a hood.

"I don't think we should build a fire in this cellar. Why don't we just run over to the refectory? That way we can warm up and get food at the same time. I'm sure they have a nice roaring fire. These monks get up early, probably been laboring for hours making fresh bread, gathering eggs, and churning butter just for the likes of us. I know Royce wants you to stay hidden, but I don't think he expected winter would arrive so soon, or so wet. I think if you keep your hood raised, we should be fine."

The prince sat up with an eager look. "Even a room with a door would be better than this."

"That may be," they heard Royce say from somewhere outside, "but you won't find it here."

The thief appeared a moment later, his hood up and his cloak slick with rain. Once he ducked in out of the downpour, he snapped it like a dog shaking his fur. This sent a spray of water at Hadrian and Alric. They flinched and with a grimace the prince opened his mouth to speak but he stopped short. Royce was not alone. Behind him followed the monk from the night before. He was soaked. His wool frock sagged with the weight of the water, and his hair laid plastered flat on his head. His skin was pale, his purple lips quivered, and his fingers were wrinkled as if he had been swimming too long.

"I found him sleeping outside," Royce said as he quickly grabbed an armful of the stacked wood. "Myron, take off that robe. We need to get you dry."

"Myron?" Hadrian said with an inquisitive look. "Myron

Lanaklin?" Hadrian thought the monk nodded in reply, but he was shivering so hard it was difficult to tell.

"You know each other?" Alric asked.

"No, but we are familiar with his family," Royce said. "Give him the blanket."

Alric looked shocked and held tightly to his covering.

"Give it to him," Royce insisted. "It's *his* blanket. This fool gave us his home to stay in last night while he huddled in a wind-lashed corner of the cloister and froze."

"I don't understand," Alric said, reluctantly pulling the blanket off his shoulders. "Why would you sleep outside in the rain when—"

"The abbey burned down," Royce told them. "Anything that wasn't stone is gone. We weren't walking through a court-yard last night—that was the abbey. The ceiling is missing. The outer buildings are nothing but piles of ash. The whole place is a gutted ruin."

The monk slipped out of his robe, and Alric handed the blanket to him. Myron hurriedly pulled it around his shoulders and, sitting down, drew his knees up to his chest, wrapping them in the folds as well.

"What about the other monks?" Hadrian asked. "Where are they?"

"I—I bu-buried them. In the garden mostly," Myron said through chattering teeth. "The gr-ground is softer there. I don't th-think they will mind. We all lo-loved the garden."

"When did this happen?"

"Night before last," Myron replied.

Shocked by the news, Hadrian did not want to press the monk further and a silence fell over the room. Royce built a fire near the entrance using various pieces of wood and some oil from the lantern. As it grew, the stone walls reflected the heat, and soon the room began to warm.

No one said anything for a long time. Royce prodded the fire with a stick, churning the glowing coals so that they sparked and spit. They each sat watching the flames, listening to the fire pop and crackle while outside the wind howled and the rain lashed the hilltop. Without looking at the monk, Royce said in a somber voice, "You were all locked in the church when it was burned, weren't you, Myron?"

The monk did not reply. His gaze remained focused on the fire.

"I saw the blackened chain and lock in the ash. It was still closed."

Myron, his arms hugging his knees, began to rock slowly.

"What happened?" Alric asked.

Still Myron said nothing. Several minutes passed. At last, the monk looked away from the fire. He did not look at them, but instead, he stared at some distant point outside in the rain. "They came and accused us of treason," he said with a soft voice. "There were maybe twenty of them, knights with helms covering their faces. They rounded us up and pushed us into the church. They closed the big doors behind us. Then the fire started.

"Smoke filled the church so quickly. I could hear my brothers coughing, struggling to breathe. The abbot led us in prayer until he collapsed. It burned very quickly. I never knew it contained so much dry wood. It always seemed to be so strong. The coughing got quieter and less frequent. Eventually, I couldn't see anymore. My eyes filled with tears, and then I passed out. I woke up to rain. The men and their horses were gone and so was everything else. I was under a marble lectern in the lowest nave, and all my brothers were around me. I looked for other survivors but there were none."

"Who did this?" Alric demanded.

"I don't know their names, or who sent them, but they were dressed in tunics with a scepter and crown," Myron said.

"Imperialists," Alric concluded. "But why would they attack an abbey?"

Myron did not reply. He merely stared out the window at the rain. A long time passed; finally Hadrian asked in a comforting voice, "Myron, you said they charged you with treason. What did they accuse you of doing?"

The monk said nothing. He just sat huddled in his blanket and stared. Alric finally broke the silence. "I don't understand. I gave no orders to have this abbey destroyed, and I can't believe my father did either. Why would Imperialists carry out such an act, especially without my knowledge?"

Royce cast a harsh and anxious look at the prince.

"What?" Alric asked.

"I thought we discussed the importance of keeping a low profile."

"Oh, please." The prince waved a hand at the thief. "I don't think it will get me killed if this monk knows I'm the king. Look at him. I've seen drowned rats more formidable."

"King?" Myron muttered.

Alric ignored him. "Besides, who is he going to tell? I'm heading back to Medford this morning anyway. Not only do I have a traitorous sister to deal with, but apparently there are things going on in my kingdom that I know nothing about. I need to address this."

"It might not have been one of your nobles," Royce said. "I wonder...Myron, did it have anything to do with Degan Gaunt?"

Myron shifted nervously in his seat as an anxious look came over his face. "I need to string a clothesline to dry my robe," he said while getting up.

"Degan Gaunt?" Alric inquired. "That deranged revolutionary? Why do you bring him up?"

"He's one of the leaders of the Nationalist movement, and he's rumored to be around this area," Hadrian confirmed.

"The Nationalist movement—ha! A grandiose name for that rabble." Alric sneered. "They're more like the peasant party. Those radicals want the commoners to have a say in how they're ruled."

"Perhaps Degan Gaunt was using the abbey for more than just a romantic rendezvous," Royce speculated. "Maybe he was meeting with Nationalist sympathizers as well. Perhaps your father did know, or it could have had something to do with his death."

"I'm going to gather some water to make us some breakfast. I'm sure you are all hungry," Myron said as he finished hanging his robe and began collecting various pots to set out in the rain.

Alric took no notice of the monk as he focused on Royce. "My father never would have ordered such a heinous attack! He'd be more upset at the Imperialists invading the abbey than the Nationalist revolutionaries using it for meetings. Those revolutionaries' dreams are just that, but the Imperialists are organized. They have the church behind them. My family has always been steadfast Royalists, believers in the god-given right for a king to rule through his nobles and in the independent sovereignty of each kingdom. Our greatest fear isn't from some rabble thinking they can organize and overthrow the rule of law. Our concern is that one day the Imperialists will find the Heir of Novron and demand all the kingdoms of the four nations of Apeladorn pledge fealty to a new empire."

"Yes, you prefer things exactly the way they are," Royce observed. "But being the king, that doesn't seem terribly surprising."

"You are no doubt a staunch Nationalist, in favor of lopping the heads off all the nobles, and the redistribution of their lands, to peasants, and letting them all have a say in how they are ruled," Alric told Royce. "That would solve all the problems of the world, wouldn't it? And that would certainly be in *your* favor."

"Actually," Royce said, "I don't have any political leanings. They get in the way of my job. Noble or commoner, people all lie, cheat, and pay me to do their dirty work. Regardless of who rules, the sun still shines, the seasons still change, and people still conspire. If you must place labels on attitudes, I prefer to think of myself as an individualist."

"And that's why the Nationalists will never organize enough to be a real threat."

"Delgos seems fairly well run and it's a republic—ruled by the people."

"They're nothing but a bunch of shopkeepers down there."

"They might be a bit more than that."

"It doesn't matter. What does is—why do Imperialists care so much about a few revolutionaries having meetings in Melengar?"

"Maybe Ethelred thought his marquis was plotting to help them—how did you put it?—lop off all the nobles' heads."

"Lanaklin? Are you serious? Victor Lanaklin isn't a Nationalist. Nationalists are commoners trying to steal power from the nobles. Lanaklin is an Imperialist, like all those Warric nobles. They're religious fanatics who want a single government under the control of the Heir of Novron. They think he will miraculously unite everyone and usher in some mythical age of paradise. It's as much wishful thinking as the Nationalists' dreams."

"Maybe this whole thing was just a romantic affair," Hadrian suggested.

Alric sighed and shook his head in resignation. He stood up and held his hands out to the fire. "So how long before breakfast is ready, Myron? I'm starving."

"I'm afraid I don't have much to offer you," Myron said. He set up a small elevated grate over the fire. "I have a few potatoes in a bag in the corner."

"That's all you have, isn't it?" Royce asked.

"I'm very sorry," Myron replied, looking sincerely pained.

"No, I mean those potatoes are all the food *you* have. If we eat them, you'll be left with nothing."

"Oh, well." He shrugged off the comment. "I'll manage somehow. Don't worry about me," he said optimistically.

Hadrian retrieved the bag, looked in it, and then handed it to the monk. "There are only eight potatoes in here. How long were you planning to stay?"

Myron did not answer for a while, until at last he said to no one in particular, "I'm not going anywhere. I have to stay. I have to fix it."

"Fix what, the abbey? That's an awfully big job for one man."

He shook his head. "The library, the books. That's what I was working on last night when you arrived."

"The library is gone, Myron," Royce reminded him. "The books were all burned. They're ash now."

"I know. I know," he said, brushing his wet hair back from his eyes. "That's why I have to replace them."

"How are you going to do that?" Alric asked with a smirk. "Rewrite all the books from memory?"

Myron nodded. "I was working on page fifty-three of *The History of Apeladorn* by Antun Bulard when you came." Myron went over to a makeshift desk and brought out a small box. Inside were about twenty pages of parchment and several curled sheets of thin bark. "I ran out of parchment. Not much survived the fire but the bark works all right."

Royce, Hadrian, and Alric shuffled through them. Myron wrote with small meticulous lettering, which extended to the edge of the page in every direction. No space was wasted.

The text was complete, including page numbers not placed at the end of the parchments but where the pages would have ended in the original document.

Staring at the magnificently rendered text, Hadrian asked, "How could you remember all of this?"

Myron shrugged. "I remember all the books I read."

"And did you read all the books in the library here?"

Myron nodded. "I had a lot of time to myself."

"How many were there?"

"Three hundred eighty-two books, five hundred twenty-four scrolls, and one thousand two hundred thirteen individual parchments."

"And you remember every one?"

Myron nodded once more.

They all sat back, staring at the monk in awe.

"I was the *librarian*," Myron said as if that would explain it all.

"Myron," Royce suddenly said, "in all those books did you ever read anything about a place called Gutaria Prison or a prisoner called Esra...haddon?"

Myron shook his head.

"I suppose it's unlikely anyone would write anything down concerning a secret prison," Royce said, looking disappointed.

"But it was mentioned a few times in a scroll and once in a parchment. On the parchment, however, the name Esrahaddon was altered to *prisoner* and Gutaria was listed as *The Imperial Prison*."

"Maribor's beard!" Hadrian exclaimed, looking at the monk in awe. "You really did memorize the whole library, didn't you?"

"Why 'imperial prison'?" Royce asked. "Arista said it was ecclesiastical."

Myron shrugged. "Maybe because in imperial times the

Church of Nyphron and the empire were linked. *Nyphron* is
the ancient term for *emperor*, derived from the name of the
first emperor, Novron. So, the Church of Nyphron is the *worshipers of the emperor* and anything associated with the
empire could also be considered part of the church."

"That's why members of the Nyphron Church are so intent
on finding the heir," Royce added. "He would be their god, so
to speak, and not merely a ruler."

"There were several very interesting books on the Heir of
the Empire," Myron said excitedly. "And speculation as to
what happened to him —"

"What about the prison?" Royce asked.

"Well, that's a subject which isn't mentioned much at all.
The only direct reference was in a very rare scroll called *The
Accumulated Letters of Dioylion*. The original copy came
here one night about twenty years ago. I was only fifteen at the
time, but I was already the library assistant when a priest,
wounded and near death, brought it. It was raining then,
much as it is now. They took him to the healing rooms and
told me to watch after his things. I took his satchel, which was
soaked, and inside I found all sorts of scrolls. I was afraid the
water might damage them, so I opened them up to dry. While
they lay open, I couldn't resist reading them. I usually can't
resist reading anything.

"Although he didn't look much better two days later, the
priest left and took his scrolls. No one could convince him to
stay. He seemed frightened. The scrolls themselves were several correspondences made by Archbishop Venlin, the head of
the Nyphron Church at the time of the breaking of the empire.
One of them was a post-imperial edict for the construction of
the prison, which is why I thought the document was so
important historically. It revealed the church exercised gov-
ernmental control immediately following the disappearance

of the emperor. I found it quite fascinating. It was also curious that the building of a prison had such high priority, considering the turmoil of that period. I now realize it was a very rare scroll, but of course, I didn't know that back then."

"Wait a minute," Alric interrupted. "So this prison was built—what—nine hundred years ago and exists in my kingdom and I don't know anything about it?"

"Well, based on the date of the scroll, it would have been started...nine hundred and ninety-six years, two hundred and fifty-four days ago. The prison was a massive undertaking. One letter in particular spoke of recruiting skilled artisans from around the world to design and build it. The greatest minds and the most advanced engineering went into its creation. They carved the prison out of solid rock from the face of the mountains just north of the lake. They sealed it not only with metal, stone, and wood but also with ancient and powerful enchantments. In the end, when it was finished, it was believed to be the most secure prison in the world."

"They must have had some really nasty criminals back then to go to so much trouble," Hadrian said.

"No," Myron replied matter-of-factly, "just one."

"One?" Alric asked. "An entire prison designed to hold just one man?"

"His name was Esrahaddon."

Hadrian, Royce, and Alric shared looks of surprise.

"What in the world did he do?" Hadrian asked.

"According to everything I read, he was responsible for the destruction of the empire. The prison was specifically designed to hold him."

They looked incredulously at the monk.

"And exactly how is he responsible for wiping out the most powerful empire the world has ever known?" Alric asked.

"Esrahaddon was once a trusted advisor to the emperor,

but he betrayed him, killing the entire imperial family, except, of course, for the one son who managed to miraculously escape. There are even stories that he destroyed the capital city of Percepliquis. The empire fell into chaos and civil war after the emperor's death. Esrahaddon was captured, tried, and imprisoned."

"Why not just execute him?" Alric asked, generating icy glares from the thieves.

"Is execution your answer to every problem?" Royce sneered.

"Sometimes it's the best solution," Alric replied.

Myron retrieved the pots from outside and combined the water into one. He added the potatoes and placed the pot over the fire to cook.

"Then Arista has sent us to bring her brother to see a prisoner who is over a thousand years old. Does anyone else see a problem with that?" Hadrian asked.

"See!" Alric exclaimed. "Arista is lying. She probably picked up the name Esrahaddon in her studies at Sheridan University and didn't realize when he lived. There is no way Esrahaddon could still be alive."

"He might be," Myron said casually, stirring the potatoes in the pot over the fire.

"How's that?" Alric queried.

"Because he's a wizard."

"When you say he was a wizard," Hadrian asked, "do you mean that he was a learned man of wisdom or that he could do card tricks and sleight of hand or maybe he was able to brew a potion to help you sleep? Royce and I know a man like that, and he is a bit of all three, but he can't hold off death."

"According to the accounts I have read," Myron explained, "wizards were different back then. They called magic 'the Art.' Most of the knowledge of the empire was lost when it fell. For instance, the ancient skills of Teshlor combat, which made warriors invincible, or the construction techniques that could create vast domes, or the ability to forge swords that could cut stone. Like these, the art of true magic was lost to the world with the passing of the true wizards. Reports say in the days of Novron, the Cenzars—that's what they called wizards—were incredibly powerful. There are stories of them causing earthquakes, raising storms, even blacking out the sun. The greatest of these ancient wizards formed into a group called the Great Cenzar Council. Members were part of the inner circle of government."

"Really," Alric said thoughtfully.

"Did you ever read anything about exactly where the prison was located?" Royce asked.

"No, but there was a bit about it in Mantuar's *Thesis on Architectural Symbolism in the Novronian Empire*. That's the parchment I mentioned where the name Esrahaddon was changed. Stuffed on a back shelf for years, I found it one day while clearing an old portion of the library. It was a mess, but it mentioned the date of construction, and a bit about the people commissioned to build it. If I hadn't first read *The Accumulated Letters of Dioylion*, I never would have made the connection between the two, because, as I said, it never mentioned the name of the prison or the prisoner."

"I don't understand how this prison could exist in Melengar without my knowing about it," Alric said, shaking his head. "And how does Arista know about it? And why does she want me to go there?"

"I thought you determined she was sending you there to kill or imprison you," Hadrian reminded him.

"That certainly makes more sense to me than a thousand-year-old wizard," Royce said.

"Maybe," Alric muttered, "but..." The prince, his eyes searching the ground before him for answers, tapped a finger on his lips. "Consider this: if she really wanted me dead, why choose such an obscure place? She could have sent you to this monastery and had a whole army waiting, and no one would hear a scream. It's unnecessarily complicated to drag me to a hidden place no one has heard of. Why would she mention this Esrahaddon or Gutaria at all?"

"Now you think she's telling the truth?" Royce asked. "Do you think there really is a thousand-year-old man waiting to talk to you?"

"I wouldn't go that far, but—well, consider the possibilities if he does exist. Imagine what I could learn from a man like that, an advisor to the last emperor."

Hadrian chuckled at the comment. "You're actually starting to sound like a king now."

"It might merely be the warmth of the fire or the smell of boiling potatoes, but I'm starting to think it might be a good idea to see where this leads. And look, the storm is breaking. The rain will be stopping soon, I think. What if Arista isn't trying to kill me? What if there really is something there I need to discover, something that has to do with the murder of our father?"

"Your father was killed?" Myron asked. "I'm so sorry."

Alric took no notice of the monk. "Regardless, I don't like this ancient prison existing in my kingdom without my knowledge. I wonder if my father knew about it, or his father. Perhaps none of the Essendons were aware of it. A thousand years would predate the founding of Melengar by several centuries. The prison was built when this land still lay contested during the Great Civil War. If it's possible for a man to live for a thousand years, if this Esrahaddon was an advisor to the last emperor, I think I should like to speak to him. Any noble in Apeladorn would give his left eye for a chance to speak to a true imperial advisor. Like the monk said, so much knowledge was lost when the empire fell, so much forgotten over time. What might he know? What advantage would a man like that be to a young king?"

"Even if he's just a ghost?" Royce asked. "It's unlikely there is a thousand-year-old man in a prison north of this lake."

"If the ghost can speak, what's the difference?"

"The difference is I liked this idea a lot better when you *didn't* want to go," Royce said. "I thought Esrahaddon was some old baron your father exiled who had put a contract out on you, or maybe the mother of an illegitimate half brother who was imprisoned to keep her quiet. But this? This is ridiculous!"

"Let's not forget you promised my sister." Alric smiled. "Let's eat. I'm sure those potatoes are done by now. I could eat them all."

Once more Alric drew a reproachful look from Royce.

"Don't worry about the potatoes," Myron told him. "There are more in the garden, I'm sure. These ones I found while digging in the—" He stopped himself.

"I'm not worried, monk, because you are coming with us," Alric told him.

"Wha—what?"

"You obviously are a very knowledgeable fellow. I'm sure you'll come in handy, in any number of situations that may lie before us. So you'll serve at the pleasure of your king."

Myron stared back. He blinked two times in rapid succession, and his face suddenly went pale. "I'm sorry, but I—I can't do that," he replied meekly.

"Maybe it would be best if you came with us," Hadrian told him. "You can't stay here. Winter is coming and you'll die."

"But you don't understand," Myron protested with increasing

anxiety in his voice, and shook his head adamantly. "I—I can't leave."

"I know. I know." Alric raised his hand to quell the protest. "You have all these books to write. That's a fine and noble task. I'm all for it. More people need to read. My father was a big supporter of the university at Sheridan. He even sent Arista there. Can you imagine that? A girl at the university? In any case, I agree with his views on education. Look around you, man! You have no parchment and likely little ink. If you do write these tomes, where will you store them? In here? There is no protection from the elements; they will be destroyed and blown to the wind. After we visit this prison, I'll take you back to Medford and set you up to work on your project. I'll see to it you have a proper scriptorium, perhaps with a few assistants to aid you in whatever it is you need."

"That is very kind but I can't. I'm sorry. You don't really understand—"

"I understand perfectly. You're obviously Marquis Lanaklin's third son, the one he sent away to avoid the unpleasant dividing of his lands. You're rather unique—a learned monk, with an eidetic mind, and a noble as well. If your father doesn't want you, I certainly could use you."

"No," Myron protested, "it's not that."

"What is it, then?" Hadrian asked. "You're sitting here, cold and wet in a stone and dirt hole, wrapped in only a blanket, looking forward to a grand feast consisting of a couple of boiled potatoes, and your king is offering to set you up like a landed baron and you're protesting?"

"I don't mean to be ungrateful, but I—well, I've never left the abbey before."

"What do you mean?" Hadrian asked.

"I've never left. I came here when I was four years old. I've never left—ever."

"Surely you've traveled to Roe, the fishing village?" Royce asked. Myron shook his head. "Never to Medford? What about the surrounding area? You've at least gone to the lake, to fish or just for a walk?"

Myron shook his head again. "I've never been off the grounds. Not even to the bottom of the hill. I'm not quite sure I can leave. Just the thought makes me nauseous." Myron checked the dryness of his robe. Hadrian could see his hand was shaking even though he had stopped shivering some time ago.

"So that's why you were so fascinated by the horses," Hadrian said mostly to himself. "But you have seen horses before, right?"

"I have seen them from the windows of the abbey when on rare occasions we would receive visitors who had them. I've never actually touched one. I've always wondered what it would be like to sit on one. In all the books, they talk about horses, jousts, battles, and races. Horses are very popular. One king—King Bethamy—he actually had his horse buried with him. There are many things I have read about that I've never seen—women, for one. They are also very popular in books and poems."

Hadrian's eyes widened. "You've never seen a woman before?"

Myron shook his head. "Well, some books did have drawings which depicted them, but—"

Hadrian hooked a thumb at Alric. "And here I thought the prince lived a sheltered life."

"But you've at least seen your sister," Royce said. "She's been here."

Myron did not say anything. He looked away and set about removing the pot from the fire and placing the potatoes on plates.

"You mean she came here to meet with Gaunt and never even tried to see you?" Hadrian asked.

Myron shrugged. "My father came to see me once about a year ago. The abbot had to tell me who he was."

"So you weren't a part of the meetings here at all?" Royce observed. "You weren't hosting them? Making arrangements for them?"

"*No!*" Myron screamed at them, and he kicked one of the empty pots across the room. "*I—don't—know—anything— about—letters—and—my—sister!*" He backed up against the cellar wall as tears welled up in his eyes, and he panted for breath. No one said a word as they watched him standing there, clutching his blanket and staring at the ground.

"I'm—I'm sorry. I shouldn't have yelled at you. Forgive me," Myron said, wiping his eyes. "No, I've never met my sister, and I saw my father only that once. He swore me to silence. I don't know why. Nationalists—Royalists—Imperialists—I don't know about any of it." There was a distance in the monk's voice, a hollow painful sound.

"Myron," Royce began, "you didn't survive because you were under a stone lectern, did you?"

The tears welled up once again and the monk's lips quivered. He shook his head. "At first, they made us watch while they beat the abbot bloody," Myron said, his voice choked and hitched in his throat. "They wanted to know about Alenda and some letters. He finally told them my sister was sending messages disguised in the form of love letters, but she wasn't meeting anyone. That was just a fabrication. The letters were arranged by my father and being picked up by a messenger from Medford. After they found out about my father's visit, that's when they started questioning me." Myron swallowed and took a ragged breath. "But they never hurt me. They didn't even touch me. They asked if my father was siding with the Royalists and plotting with Melengar against Warric and the church. They wanted to know who else was involved. I didn't say a word. I didn't know anything. I swear I didn't. But I could have said something. I could have lied. I could have said, 'Yes, my father is a Royalist and my sister is a traitor!' But I didn't. I never opened my mouth. Do you know why?"

Myron looked at them with tears running down his cheeks. "I didn't tell them because my father made me swear to be *silent*." He paused a moment then said, "I watched *in silence* as they sealed the church. I watched *in silence* as they set it on fire. And *in silence*, I listened to my brothers' screams. It was my fault. I let my brothers die because of an oath I made to a man who was a stranger to me." Myron began to cry uncontrollably. He slid down the wall into a crumpled ball on the dirt, his arms covering his face.

Hadrian finished serving the potatoes but Myron refused to eat. Hadrian stored two spuds away in the hopes that Myron might want them later.

By the time the measly meal ended, the monk's robe was dry, and he dressed. Hadrian approached him and placed his hands on Myron's shoulders. "As much as I hate to say it, the prince is right. You have to come with us. If we leave you here, you'll likely die."

"But I—" He looked frightened. "This is my home. I'm comfortable here. My brothers are here."

"They're all dead," Alric said bluntly.

Hadrian scowled at the prince and then turned to Myron. "Listen, it's time to move on with your life. There's a lot more out there besides books. I would think you'd want to see some of it. Besides, your *king*"—he said the last word sarcastically—"needs you."

Myron sighed heavily, swallowed hard, and nodded in agreement.

૭

The rain lightened, and by midday, it stopped completely. After they packed Myron's parchments and whatever supplies they could gather from the abbey's remains, they were ready to leave. Royce, Hadrian, and Alric waited at the entrance of the abbey, but Myron did not join them. Eventually Hadrian went looking and found the monk in the ruined garden. Ringed by soot-stained stone columns, it would have formed the central courtyard among all the buildings. There were signs of flower-beds and shrubs lining the pathway of interlocking paving stones now covered in ash. At the center of the cloister, a large stone sundial sat on a pedestal. Hadrian imagined that before the fire, this sheltered cloister had been quite beautiful.

"I'm afraid," Myron told Hadrian as he approached. Staring at the burnt lawn, the monk was sitting on a blackened stone bench, his elbows on his knees, his chin on his palms. "This must seem strange to you. But everything here is so familiar. I could tell you how many blocks of stone make up this walkway or the scriptorium. I can tell you how many win-dowpanes were in the abbey, the exact day of the year, and time of day, the sun peaks directly over the church. How Brother Ginlin used to eat with two forks because he vowed never to touch a knife. How Brother Heslon was always the first one up and always fell asleep during vespers."

Myron pointed across from them at a blackened stump of a tree. "Brother Renian and I buried a squirrel there when we were ten years old. A tree sprouted the following week. It grew white blossoms in spring, and not even the abbot could tell what species it was. Everyone in the abbey called it the Squir-rel Tree. We all thought it was a miracle and that perhaps the squirrel was a servant of Maribor who was thanking us for taking such good care of his friend."

Myron paused a moment and used the long sleeves of his robe to wipe his face as he stared at the stump. He pulled his gaze away and looked once more at Hadrian. "I could tell you how in winter the snow could get up to the second-story windows, and it was like we were all squirrels living in this cozy burrow, all safe and warm. I could tell you how each one of us was the very best at what we did. Ginlin made wine so light it evaporated on your tongue, leaving only the taste of wonder. Fenitilian made the warmest, softest shoes. You could walk out in the snow and never know you left the abbey. To say Heslon could cook is an insult. He would make steaming plates of scrambled eggs mixed with cheeses, peppers, onions, and bacon, all in a light spicy cream sauce. He'd follow this with rounds of sweet bread—each topped with a honey-cinnamon drizzle—smoked pork rounds, salifan sausage, flaky powdered pastries, freshly churned sweet butter, and a ceramic pot of dark mint tea. And that was just for breakfast."

Myron smiled, his eyes closed, with a dreamy look on his face.

"What did Renian do?" Hadrian asked. "The fellow you buried the squirrel with? What was his specialty?"

Myron opened his eyes but was slow to answer. He looked back at the stump of the tree across from them and he said softly, "Renian died when he was twelve. He caught a fever. We buried him right there, next to the Squirrel Tree. It was his favorite place in the world." He paused, taking a breath that was not quite even. A frown pulled at his mouth, tightening his lips. "There hasn't been a day that has gone by since then that I haven't said good morning to him. I usually sit here and tell him how his tree is doing. How many new buds there were, or when the first leaf turned or fell. For the last few days I've had to lie, because I couldn't bring myself to tell him it was gone."

Tears fell from Myron's eyes, and his lips quivered as he looked at the stump. "All morning I've been trying to tell him goodbye. I've been trying…" He faltered and paused to wipe his eyes. "I've been trying to explain why I have to leave him now, but you see, Renian is only twelve, and I don't think he really understands." Myron put his face in his hands and wept.

Hadrian squeezed Myron's shoulder. "We'll wait for you at the gate. Take all the time you need."

When Hadrian emerged from the entrance, Alric barked at him, "What in the world is taking so bloody long? If he's going to be this much trouble, we might as well leave him."

"We aren't leaving him, and we'll wait as long as it takes," Hadrian told them. Alric and Royce exchanged glances but neither said a word.

Myron joined them only a few minutes later with a small bag containing all his belongings. Although he was obviously upset, his mood lightened at the sight of the horses. "Oh my!" he exclaimed. Hadrian took Myron by the hand like a young child and led him over to his speckled white mare. The horse, its massive body moving back and forth as the animal shifted its weight from one leg to another, looked down at Myron with large dark eyes.

"Do they bite?"

"Not usually," Hadrian replied. "Here, you can pat him on the neck."

"It's so…*big*," Myron said with a look of terror on his face. He moved his hand to his mouth as if he might be sick.

"Please, just get on the horse, Myron." Alric's tone showed his irritation.

"Don't mind him," Hadrian said. "You can ride behind me. I'll get on first and pull you up after, okay?"

Myron nodded but the look on his face indicated he was

anything but okay. Hadrian mounted and then extended his arm. With closed eyes, Myron reached out, and Hadrian pulled him up. The monk held on tightly and buried his face in the large man's back.

"Remember to breathe, Myron," Hadrian told him as he turned the horse and began to walk back down the switch-back trail.

The morning started cold but it eventually warmed some. Still, it was not as pleasant as it had been the day before. They entered the shelter of the valley and headed toward the lake. Everything was still wet from the rain, and the tall fields of autumn-browned grass soaked their feet and legs as they brushed past. The wind came from the north now and blew into their faces. Overhead, a chevron of geese honked against the gray sky. Winter was on its way. Myron soon overcame his fear and picked his head up to look about.

"Dear Maribor, I had no idea grass grew this high. And the trees are so tall! You know, I had seen pictures of trees this size but always thought the artists were just bad at proportion."

The monk began to twist left and right to see all around him. Hadrian chuckled. "Myron, you squirm like a puppy."

Lake Windermere appeared like gray metal pooling at the base of the barren hills. Although it was one of the largest lakes in Avryn, the fingers of the round cliffs hid much of it from view. Its vast open face reflected the desolate sky and appeared cold and empty. Except for a few birds, little moved on the stony clefts.

They reached the western bank. Thousands of fist-sized rocks, rubbed smooth and flat by the lake, made a loose cobblestone plain where they could walk and listen to the quiet lapping of the water. From time to time, rain would briefly fall. They would watch it come across the surface of the lake, the crisp horizon blurring as the raindrops broke the stillness, and then it would stop while the clouds above swirled undecidedly.

Royce, as usual, led the small party. He approached the north side of the lake and found what appeared to be the faint remains of a very old and unused road leading toward the mountains beyond.

Myron's wriggling was finally subsiding. He sat behind Hadrian but did not move for quite some time. "Myron, are you okay back there?" Hadrian asked.

"Hmm? Oh, yes, I'm sorry. I was watching the way the horses walk. I've been observing them for the last few miles. They are fascinating animals. Their back feet appear to step in exactly the same place their front feet left an instant before. Although, I suppose they aren't feet at all, are they? Hooves! That's right! These are hooves! *Enylina* in Old Speech."

"Old Speech?"

"The ancient imperial language. Few people outside the clergy know it these days. It's something of a dead language. Even in the days of the empire it was only used in church services, but that has gone out of style and no one writes in it anymore."

Hadrian felt Myron rest his head against his back, and for the rest of the ride watched to make sure that Myron did not doze off and fall.

✥

They turned away from the lakeside and started into a broad ravine that became rocky as they climbed. The more they progressed, the more apparent it was to Alric that they were traveling on what had once been a road. The path was too smooth to be wholly natural, and yet over time, rocks had fallen from the heights and cracks had formed where weeds forced themselves out of the crevices. Centuries had taken their toll, but there remained a faint trace of something ancient and forgotten.

Despite the cold, the intermittent rain, and the strange circumstance of his being there, Alric was not nearly as miserable as he let on. There was an odd tranquility to the trip that day. Not often had the prince traveled so simply in such inclement weather and he found it captivating by its sheer strangeness. The vast silence, the muted light, the haunting clip-clop of the horses' hooves, everything suggested adventure in a fashion he had never experienced before. His most daring escapades had always been organized and catered by servants. He had never been on his own like this, never truly in danger.

When he had found himself bound in the boat, he had been furious. No one had ever treated him with such disregard. Striking a member of the royal family was punishable by death, and because it was, most avoided even touching him. To be trussed up like an animal was humiliating beyond his comprehension. It had never occurred to him that he could come to harm. He had fully expected to be rescued at any moment. That prospect had dimmed dramatically as they had traveled into the deep forests on their way to Windermere.

He had been serious when he had said it was the worst night of his life, but in the morning when the rain let up, and after the meal, he found what he could describe only as a second wind. The prospect of seeking out this mysterious prison and its reputed inmate smacked of real adventure. Perhaps more than anything, it kept his mind occupied. He was busy trying to stay alive and determine the identity of a killer, which kept him from dwelling on the death of his father.

On occasion while riding, when no one spoke for a time and silence took hold, his mind would touch on his father's death. He would be back in the royal bedchamber seeing his father's pale face and that tiny tear of dried blood near the corner of his lips. Alric expected to feel something. He expected to cry but that never happened. He felt nothing and wondered what that meant.

Back at the castle, everyone would be wearing black and the halls would be filled with the sounds of weeping—just like when his mother had died. No music, no laughter, and it had seemed like more than a month without the sun shining. He was relieved, almost happy, when the period of mourning ended. Part of him felt guilty for that, and yet it was as if a terrible weight had been lifted. That was how it would be if he were at the castle—solemn faces, weeping, and the priests passing a candle for him to walk around the casket with while they chanted. He had done that as a child and hated it. Alric was glad he was not there, trapped and drowning in that well of sorrow that he could not tap. He would deal with it all the next day, but for today he was grateful to be on a distant road with no one of importance for company.

Royce drew his horse to a stop. They were alone, since the others had a tendency to lag behind, as their horse carried two.

"Why are we stopping?" Alric asked.

"It's leveling off, so we're probably close. Have you forgotten that this might be a trap?"

"No," the prince said. "I'm quite aware of that fact."

"Good, then in that case, farewell, Your Majesty," Royce told him.

Alric was stunned. "You're not coming?"

"Your sister only asked us to bring you here. If you want to get yourself killed, that's your affair. Our obligation is complete."

Instantly Alric felt foolish for his earlier misguided satisfaction in being alone with strangers. He could not afford to lose his only guides or he would never find his way back. After only a moment's thought, he said, "Then I suppose this is a perfect time to tell you I'm officially bestowing the title of *royal protectors* on you and Hadrian, now that I'm certain you aren't trying to kill me. You'll be responsible for defending the life of your king."

"Really? How thoughtful of you, Your Highness." Royce grinned. "I suppose this is a good time to tell you I don't serve kings—unless they pay me."

"No?" Alric smiled wryly. "All right then, consider it this way. If I live to return to Essendon Castle, I'll happily rescind your execution orders and forgive your unlawful entry of my castle. However, if I die out here or am taken captive and locked away in this prison, you'll never be able to return to Medford. My uncle has already labeled you murderers of the highest order. I'm sure there are already men searching. Uncle Percy might seem like a courtly old gentleman, but believe me, I've seen his ugly side and he can be quite scary. He's the best swordsman in Melengar. Did you know that? So if sovereign loyalty isn't good enough for you, you might consider the practical benefits of keeping me alive."

"The ability to convince others that your life is worth more than theirs must be a prerequisite for being king."

"Not a prerequisite but it certainly helps," Alric replied with a grin.

"It will still cost you," Royce said, and the prince's grin faded. "Let's say one hundred gold tenents."

"One hundred?" Alric protested.

"Do you think your life is worth less? Besides, it's what DeWitt promised, so that seems fair. But there's one other thing. If we're going to be your protectors, you'll have to do as I say. I can't safeguard you if you don't and since we aren't just risking your silly little life, but my future as well, I'll have to insist."

Alric huffed. He did not like the way they treated him. They should feel honored to do his bidding. Besides, he was granting them absolution of serious crimes, and instead of showing gratitude, the man demanded payment. This type of behavior was just what he expected from thieves. Still, he needed them. "Like all good rulers, it's understood there are times when we must listen to skilled advisors. Just remember who I am and who I'll be when we get back to Medford."

As Hadrian and Myron caught up, Royce said, "Hadrian, we've just been promoted to royal protectors."

"Does it pay more?"

"Actually, it does. It also weighs less. Give the prince back his sword."

Hadrian handed the huge sword of Amrath to Alric, who slipped the broad leather baldric over one shoulder and strapped on the weapon. The sword was too big for him and he felt a bit foolish, but at least he thought it looked better now that he was dressed and mounted.

"The captain of the guard took this off my father and handed it to me—was it only two nights past? It was Tolin Essendon's sword, handed down from king to prince for seven hundred years. We are one of the oldest unbroken families in Avryn."

Royce dismounted and handed the reins of his horse to Hadrian. "I'm going to scout up ahead and make sure there are no surprises waiting." He left with surprising swiftness in a hunched run. He entered the shadows of the ravine and vanished.

⤚

"How does he do that?" Alric asked.

"Creepy, isn't it?" Hadrian said.

"How did he do what?" Myron stared at a cattail he had plucked just before they left the lakeside. "These things are marvelous, by the way."

They waited for several minutes, and at the sound of a bird's song, Hadrian ordered them forward. The road curved left and then right until they could once again see the lake, which was now far below and looked like a large bright puddle. The road began to narrow and at last stopped. To either side, hills rose at a gradual slope, but directly in front of them the path ended at a straight, sheer cliff extending upward several hundred feet.

"Are we in the wrong place?" Hadrian asked.

"It's supposed to be a *hidden* prison," Alric reminded them.

"I just assumed," Hadrian said, "being up here in the middle of nowhere was what was meant by *hidden*. I mean, if you didn't know the prison was here, would you come to such a place?"

"If this was made by the best minds of what was left of the empire," Alric said, "it's likely to be hard to find and harder to enter."

"Legends hold it was mostly constructed by dwarves," Myron explained.

"Lovely," Royce said. "It's going to be another Drumindor."

"We had issues getting into a dwarf-constructed fortress in Tur Del Fur a few years back," Hadrian explained. "It wasn't pretty. We might as well get comfortable; this could take a while."

Royce searched the cliff. The stone directly before the path was exposed, as if recently sheared off, and while moss and small plants grew among the many cracks elsewhere, none were found anywhere near the cliff face.

"There's a door here; I know it," the thief said, running his hands lightly across the stone. "Damn dwarves. I can't find a hinge, crack, or seam."

"Myron," Alric asked, "did you read anything about how to open the door to the prison? I've heard tales about dwarves having a fondness for riddles, and sometimes they make keys out of sounds, words that when spoken unlock doors."

Myron shook his head as he climbed down off the horse.

"Words that unlock doors?" Royce looked at the prince skeptically. "Are these fairy tales you're listening to?"

"An invisible door sounds like a fairy tale to me," Alric replied. "So it seems appropriate."

"It's not invisible. You can see the cliff, can't you? It's merely well hidden. Dwarves can cut stone with such precision you can't see a gap."

"You do have to admit, Royce," Hadrian said, "what dwarves can do with stone is amazing."

Royce glared over his shoulder at him. "Don't talk to me."

Hadrian smiled. "Royce doesn't much care for the wee folk."

"Open in the name of Novron!" Alric suddenly shouted with a commanding tone, his voice echoing between the stony slopes.

Royce spun around and fixed the prince with a withering stare. "Don't do that again!"

"Well, *you* weren't making any progress. I just thought perhaps since this was, or is, a church prison, maybe a religious command would unlock it. Myron, is there some standard religious saying to open a door? You should know about this. Is there such a thing?"

"I'm not a priest of Nyphron. The Winds Abbey was a monastery of Maribor."

"Oh, that's right," Alric said, looking disappointed.

"I mean, I know *about* the Church of Nyphron," Myron

clarified, "but since I'm not a member, I'm not privy to any secret codes or chants or such."

"Really?" Hadrian said. "I thought you monks were just sort of like the poorer, younger brother of the Nyphron Church."

Myron smiled. "If anything, we'd be the older but still the poorer brother. Worshiping Emperor Novron is a relatively recent event that began a few decades after the emperor's death."

"So you monks worship Maribor while the Nyphrons worship Novron?"

"Close," the monk said, "the Nyphron Church also worships Maribor but they just put more emphasis on Novron. The main difference comes down to what you are looking for. We monks believe in a personal devotion to Maribor—seeking his will in quiet places. It's through ancient rituals, and in this silence, that he speaks to us in our hearts. We're striving to know Maribor better.

"The Church of Nyphron, on the other hand, focuses on trying to understand Maribor's will. They believe the birth of Novron demonstrates Maribor's desire to take a direct hand in controlling the fate of mankind. As such, they are very involved in politics. You're familiar with the story of Novron, aren't you?"

Hadrian pursed his lips. "Um...he was the first emperor and defeated the elves in some war a long time ago. I'm not sure why that makes him a god."

"He's not, actually."

"Then why do so many people worship him?"

"Novron is believed to be the son of Maribor, sent to aid us in our darkest hour. There are six actual gods. Erebus is the father of all of the gods and he made the world of Elan. He brought forth three sons and a daughter. The eldest son,

Ferrol, is a master of magic and created the elves. His second son is Drome, the master craftsman who created the dwarves. The youngest is Maribor and he, of course, created man. It was Erebus's daughter, Muriel, who created the animals, birds, and the fish in the sea."

"That's five."

"Yes, there is also Uberlin, the son of Erebus and Muriel."

"The god of darkness," Alric put in.

"Yeah, I've heard of him, but wait—are you saying the father had a child with his own daughter?"

"It was a terrible mistake," Myron explained. "Erebus forced himself on Muriel while in a drunken rage. Their union resulted in the birth of Uberlin."

"That must have been awkward at family gatherings— raping your own daughter and all," Hadrian said.

"Quite. In fact, Erebus's original sons, Ferrol, Drome, and Maribor, slew him because of the incident. When Uberlin tried to defend his father, all three turned on him and imprisoned their nephew, or would that be *brother*? I guess it's really both, isn't it? Well, anyway, they locked Uberlin in the depths of Elan. Even though he was born through a terrible violation, Muriel was heartbroken to lose her only son and refused to speak to her brothers again."

"So now we're back to five gods."

"Not exactly. Many people believe that a god is immortal and cannot die. There are some cults that believe Erebus still lives and wanders Elan as a man searching for forgiveness for his crime."

The day was growing dark and the wind picked up, heralding another possible storm. The horses started to become spooked, so Hadrian went to check on them. Alric got up and walked around, rubbing his legs and muttering about being saddle sore.

"Myron?" Hadrian called over. "Would you like to help me unsaddle them? I don't think we'll be leaving soon."

"Of course," the monk said eagerly. "Now, how do I do that?"

Together, Hadrian and Myron relieved the animals of their saddles and packs and stowed the gear under a small rock ledge. Myron summoned the courage every so often to stroke their necks. Once everything was put away, Hadrian suggested Myron gather some grass for the animals while he went to check on Royce.

His partner sat on the path, staring at the cliff. Occasionally, the thief would get up, examine a portion of the wall, and sit back down, grumbling.

"Well? How's it going?"

"I hate dwarves," Royce replied.

"Most people do."

"Yes, but I have a reason. The bastards are the only ones that can make boxes I can't open."

"You'll open it. It won't be pretty, and it won't be soon, but you'll open it. What I don't understand is why would Arista send us here knowing that we couldn't get in?"

Royce sat on his haunches, his cloak draped out around him. His eyes remained focused but he was frustrated. "I can't even see anything. If I could even find just a crack, then maybe...but how can I break a lock when I can't even find the door?"

Hadrian gave him a reassuring pat on the shoulder before returning to Myron, who had finished feeding the horses and had joined Alric, sitting over by the cliff's wall.

"How's it coming?" Alric asked with a bit of annoyance in his voice.

"Nothing yet, just leave him be. Royce will figure it out. It just takes some time." Hadrian turned his attention back to

Myron. "I was thinking about what you were saying before. If Uberlin is considered a god, why did you say Novron is not? After all, they're both children of gods, right?"

"Well, no, technically he's a demigod, part god, part human. You see, Maribor sent Novron to—well, let me jump back a bit. Okay, so Ferrol was the oldest and when he created the elves, they spread, albeit slowly, across all of Elan. When Drome came along, he granted his children control of the underground world. This left no place for Maribor's children. So mankind was forced to struggle in the most wretched corners left to us."

"So the elves got all the good places, and we got stuck with the dregs? That doesn't sound very fair," Hadrian said.

"Well, our ancestors weren't happy about that either. Not to mention humans reproduce much more quickly than elves, who have a much longer life span. This made conditions rather crowded and it only got worse when the dwarves were driven to the surface."

"Driven? By who?"

"You remember what I said about the gods locking Uberlin in the underworld? Well, he created his own race, just like Drome, Maribor, and Ferrol."

"Ah...the goblins. I can see how they would make things less *homey* down there."

"Exactly. Between mankind's growing numbers and the emergence of the dwarves, our ancestors were being crushed. So they begged Maribor for help. He heard their pleas and tricked his brother Drome into forging the great sword Rhelacan. Then he convinced his other brother Ferrol to enchant the weapon. All he needed was a warrior to wield it, so he came to Elan in disguise and slept with a mortal woman. Their union produced Novron the Great. He united all the tribes of mankind and led them in a war against the elves.

Armed with the Rhelacan, Novron was victorious and so began mankind's dominance, led by Novron, who had united all of humanity."

"Okay, that makes sense, but when did we start worshiping Novron as a god?"

"That occurred after his death. The Church of Nyphron was established to pay homage to Novron as the savior of mankind. The newly formed church became the official religion of the empire, but farther away from the imperial capital of Percepliquis, people remembered the old ways and continued to worship Maribor as they always had."

"And that would be you, the Monks of Maribor, I mean?"

Myron nodded.

During their discussion, storm clouds continued to form, filling the sky and darkening the ravine. What light remained was an odd hue, adding a sense of the surreal to the landscape. Soon the wind began gusting through the pass, blowing dirt into the air. In the distance echoed the low rumble of thunder.

"Any luck with the door, Royce?" Hadrian called over. He sat resting with his back against the cliff, his legs outstretched, and he tapped the tips of his boots together. "Because it looks like we're in for another cold, wet night, only this time we won't have any shelter."

Royce muttered something indiscernible.

Down below, framed by the walls of the ravine, the surface of the lake shone like a mirror facing the sky. Every now and then it would flash brilliantly as lightning flickered in the distance.

Royce grumbled again.

"What's that?" Hadrian asked.

"I was just thinking about what you said earlier. Why *would* Arista send us here if she knew we couldn't get in? She must have thought we could; maybe to her it was obvious."

"Maybe it's magic," Alric said, pulling his cloak tighter.

"Enough with the enchanted words," Royce told him. "Locks are mechanical. Believe me. I know a thing or two on the subject. Dwarves are very clever and very skilled, but they don't make doors that unlock because of a sound."

"I just brought it up because Arista could do some, so maybe getting in was easy for her."

"Do some what?" Hadrian asked.

"Magic."

"Your sister is a witch?" Myron asked, disturbed.

Alric laughed. "You could certainly say that, yes, but it has little to do with her magical prowess. She went to Sheridan University for a few years and learned magical theory. It never amounted to much, but she was able to do a few things. For instance, she magically locks the door to her room, and I think she made the countess Amril sick over some dispute about a boy. Poor Amril was covered in boils for a week."

Royce looked over at Alric. "What do you mean, magically locks her door?"

"There's never been a lock on it, but no one can open it but her."

"Did you ever see your sister unlock her door?"

Alric shook his head. "I wish I had."

"Myron," Royce said, "did you ever read anything about unusual locks or keys? Maybe something associated with dwarves?"

"There's the tale of *Iberius and the Giant*, where Iberius uses a key forged by dwarves to open the giant's treasure box, but it wasn't magical—just big. There's also the Collar of Liem, from the *Myth of the Forgotten*, which refused to unlock until the wearer was dead—I guess that doesn't help much, does it? Hmm...let me think...perhaps it has something to do with gemlocks."

"Gemlocks?"

"They're not magical either but they were invented by dwarves. They're gems that interact with other stones to create subtle vibrations. Gemlocks are generally used when several people need to open the same locked container. All they need is a matching gem. For particularly valuable containers, the lock might require a specific cut, which modifies the resonance. Truly gifted gemsmiths could make a lock that actually changed with the seasons, allowing different gems to unlock it at different times of the year. This is what gave rise to the idea of birthstones, because certain stones have more strength at certain times. I've—"

"That's it," Royce interrupted.

"What's it?" Alric asked. Royce reached into his breast pocket and pulled out a dark blue ring. Alric jumped to his feet. "That's my father's ring. Give it to me!"

"Fine," Royce said, tossing it toward the prince. "Your sister told us to return it to you when we got to the prison."

"She did?" Alric looked surprised. He slipped the ring on his finger, and like his sword, it did not quite fit and spun around from the weight of the gem. "I thought she took it. It has the royal seal. She could have used it to muster the nobles, to make laws, or to announce herself as steward. With it, she could have taken control of everything."

"Maybe she *was* telling the truth," Hadrian suggested.

"Let's not make snap judgments," Royce cautioned. "First, let's see if this works. Your sister said you would need the ring to get into the prison. I thought she meant to identify you as the king, but I think she meant it a bit more literally. If I'm correct, touching the stone with the ring will cause giant doors to open."

They all gathered at the cliff face close to Alric in anticipation of the dramatic event.

"Go ahead, Alric—do it."

He turned the ring so the gem was on top, made a fist, and attempted to touch it to the cliff. As he did, his hand disappeared into the rock. Alric recoiled, wheeling backward with a cry.

"What happened?" Royce asked. "Did it hurt?"

"No, it just felt sort of cold but I can't touch it."

"Try it again," Hadrian said.

Alric did not look at all happy with the suggestion but nodded just the same. This time he pressed farther, and the whole party watched as his hand disappeared into the wall up to his wrist before he withdrew it.

"Fascinating," Royce muttered, feeling the solid stone of the cliff. "I didn't expect that."

"Does that mean he has to go in alone?" Hadrian asked.

"I'm not sure I want to enter solid stone by myself," Alric said with fear in his voice.

"Well, you may have no choice," Royce responded, "assuming you still want to talk to the wizard. But let's not give up yet. Give me the ring a moment."

Despite his earlier desire for the ring, Alric now showed no concern at handing it over. Royce slipped it on, and when he pressed his hand to the cliff face, it passed into the mountainside just as easily as Alric's had. Royce pulled his hand back; then he took the ring off, and holding it in his left hand, he reached out with his right. Once more, his hand passed through the stone.

"So you don't have to be the prince, and you don't have to be wearing it. You only need to be touching it. Myron, didn't you say something about the gem creating a vibration?"

Myron nodded. "They create a specific resonance with certain stone types."

"Try holding hands," Hadrian suggested.

Alric and Royce did so, and this time, both could penetrate the stone.

"That's it," Royce declared. "One last test. Everyone join hands. Let's make sure it works with four." They all joined hands and each was able to pierce the surface of the cliff. "Everyone, make sure you remove your hands before breaking the chain."

"Okay, we need to make some decisions before we go any further. I've seen some unusual things before but nothing like this. I don't have a clue what will happen to us if we go in there. Well, Hadrian, what do you think?"

Hadrian rubbed his chin. "It's a risk, to be sure. Considering some of the choices I've made recently, I'll leave this one up to you. If you think we should go, then that's good enough by me."

"I have to admit," Royce responded, "my curiosity is piqued, so if you still want to go through with this, Alric, we'll go with you."

"If I had to go in alone, I would decline," Alric said. "But I'm also curious."

"Myron?" Royce asked.

"What about the horses? Will they be all right?"

"I'm sure they will be fine."

"But what if we don't come back? They'll starve, won't they?"

Royce sighed. "It's us or them. You'll have to choose."

Myron hesitated. Lightning and thunder tore through the sky, and it began to rain. "Can't we just untie them, so in case we don't—"

"I don't intend to make plans based on our expected deaths. We'll need the horses when we come out. They're staying—are you?"

The wind sprayed rain into the monk's face as he stole one

last look at the horses. "I'll go," he said finally. "I just hope they'll be all right."

"Okay," Royce told them, "this is how we'll do it. I'll go first, wearing the ring. Alric comes in behind me, then Myron, and Hadrian will take up the rear. When we get inside, we break the chain in reverse order: Hadrian first, then Myron, and Alric last. Enter in the same place I do, and don't pass me. I don't want anyone setting off any traps. Any questions?"

All but Myron shook their heads. "Wait a second," he said as he trotted off toward where they had stored their gear. He gathered the lantern and tinder kit he had brought from the abbey and paused a moment to pet the horses' wet noses one more time. "I'm ready now," he said when he returned to the party.

"All right, here goes, everyone hang on and follow me," Royce said as they rejoined their chain and moved forward. One by one, they passed through the rock cliff. Hadrian was last. When the barrier reached his shoulder, he took a deep breath as if he were swimming, and with that, Hadrian dipped his head inside the stone.

CHAPTER 5

ESRAHADDON

They entered into total darkness. The air was dry, still, and stale. The only sound came from the rainwater dripping from their clothes. Hadrian took a few blind steps forward to make sure he was completely through the barrier before releasing Myron's hand. "See anything, Royce?" he asked in a whisper so quiet it could scarcely be heard.

"No, not a thing. Everyone stay still until Myron gets the lantern lit."

Hadrian could hear Myron fiddling in the dark. He tilted his head, searching in vain for anything to focus on. There was nothing. He could have had his eyes closed. Myron scraped the tiny metal lever on his tinder pad, and a burst of sparks flashed on the monk's lap. In the flare, Hadrian saw faces glaring from the darkness. They appeared briefly and vanished with the dying brilliance.

No one moved or spoke as Myron scraped the pad again. This time the tinder caught fire, and the monk lit the wick of the lantern. The light revealed a narrow hallway, only five feet wide, and a ceiling that was so high it was lost in darkness. Lining both walls were carvings of faces, as if people standing on the other side of a gray curtain were pressing forward to peer at them. Seemingly caught in a moment of anguish frozen forever in stone, their terrible ghastly visages stared at the party with gaping mouths and wild eyes.

"Pass up the light," Royce ordered softly.

As the lantern moved from Myron to Royce, its light shone on more faces. To Hadrian, it seemed as if they screamed at the intruders, but the corridor remained still and silent. Some of the figures had eyes wide with fear, while others' eyes were shut tight, perhaps to avoid seeing something too frightening to look at.

"Someone certainly had a morbid taste in decorating," Royce said, taking the lantern.

"I'm just thankful they're only carvings. Imagine if we could hear them," Alric said.

"What makes you think they're carvings?" Hadrian asked, reaching out to gingerly touch the nose of a woman with glaring eyes. He half expected warm skin and was grateful when his fingers met cold stone. "Maybe they let go of their gemstones too soon."

Royce held the lantern up high. "The passage keeps going."

"More faces?" Alric asked.

"More faces," the thief confirmed.

"At least we're out of the rain," Hadrian said, trying to sound cheerful. "We could still be back..." When he turned around, he was shocked. The corridor extended behind them seemingly without end. "Where's the wall we just came through?" He took a step and reached out. "It's not an illusion. The hallway keeps going." Turning back, Hadrian saw Royce pressing on the sides of the corridor. Unlike with the wall outside, his hand did not penetrate the surface.

"Well, this is going to make matters difficult," the thief muttered.

"There must be another way out, right?" Alric asked, his voice a bit shaky.

The thief looked back, then forward, and sighed. "We might as well travel in the direction we entered. Here, Alric, take your ring back, although I'm not sure what good it will do you in here."

Royce led them down the corridor. He checked and tested anything that appeared suspicious. The passage went on for what seemed like eternity. Despite the hallway's appearing perfectly straight and level, Hadrian began to wonder if the dwarves had built in an imperceptible curve that made it loop back onto itself to form a circle. He also worried about the amount of oil left in Myron's lantern. It would not be long before they were cast back into utter darkness.

The lack of variation in their surroundings made it impossible to judge exactly how long they had been walking. After a while, something luminescent appeared in the distance. A tiny light bobbed and weaved. As the light drew closer, the echo of sharp, deliberate footsteps accompanied it. At last, Hadrian could discern the figure carrying a lamp. He was tall and trim and wore a long-hooded hauberk. Over this was a scarlet and gold tabard that shimmered in the lamplight. The tabard was marked with a regal coat of arms depicting a celestial crown and a jeweled scepter above a shield divided into quarters and supported on either side by combatant lions. At his side he wore a polished sword with decorative detailing, and on his head, a pointed silver helm exquisitely etched with gold ivy trim. Below the helm were a pair of dark eyes and an even darker look.

"Why are you here?" His tone was reproachful and threatening.

There was a pause before Royce replied. "We are here to see the prisoner."

"*That* is not allowed," he responded firmly.

"Then Esrahaddon is still alive?" asked Alric.

"*Do not speak that name!*" thundered the sentry. He cast a tense look over his shoulder into the darkness. "Not here, not *ever* here. You should not have come."

"That may be but we are here and we need to see Esra — the prisoner," Royce replied.

"That will not be possible."

"Make it possible," Alric ordered. His voice was loud and commanding. He stepped out from behind the others. "I'm King Alric of Melengar, lord of this land wherein you stand. You will not tell me what *is* and what *is not* possible within the boundaries of my own kingdom."

The sentry took a step back and eyed Alric critically. "You lack a crown, *King*."

Alric drew his sword. Despite its size, he handled it smoothly and extended the point at the sentry. "What I lack in a crown, I more than make up for in a sword."

"A sword will not avail you. None who dwell here fear death any longer." Hadrian could not tell whether it was the weight of the sentry's words or the weight of the sword but Alric lowered his blade. "Do you have proof of your rank?"

Alric extended a clenched hand. "This is the seal of Melengar, symbol of the House of Essendon and emblem of this realm."

The sentry stared at the ring and nodded. "If you are the reigning sovereign of the realm, you do have the right to enter. But know this: there is magic at work here. You will do well to follow me closely." He turned and led them back the way he had come.

"Do you recognize the emblem on the guard?" Hadrian whispered to Myron as they followed him.

"Yes, that's the coat of arms of the Novronian Empire, worn by the Percepliquis Imperial City Guard. It's very old."

Their guide led them out of the corridor filled with faces,

and Hadrian was grateful to be free of it. The hallway opened into a massive cavern with a vaulted ceiling carved from natural stone and supported by pillars of the same. Torches lining the walls revealed a magnificent expanse. It appeared large enough to hold all of Medford. They traversed it by crossing narrow bridges that spanned chasms and traveling through open arches that rose like great trees whose branches supported the mountain above.

There was no visible sign of wood, fabric, or leather. Everything—chairs, benches, desks, tables, shelves, and doors—was made of stone. Huge fountains hewn from rock gurgled with water from unseen springs. The walls and floors lacked the adornment of tapestries and carpets. Instead, carved into virtually every inch of the stone were intricate markings—strange symbols of elaborate twisted designs. Some of them were chiseled with a rough hand, while others were smoothly sculpted. At times, from the corner of his eye, Hadrian thought he saw the carved markings change as he passed them. Looking closely, he discovered it was not an illusion. The shifts were subtle, like the movement of cobwebs in the wake of their passing.

They moved deeper, and their escort did not pause or waver. He walked at a brisk pace, which at times caused Myron, who had the shortest legs, to trot in order to keep up. Their footfalls bounced off the hard walls throughout the stone chamber. The only other sounds Hadrian heard were voices, distant whispers of hidden conversations, but they were too faint for him to make out the words. Whether the sounds were from inhabitants around an unseen corner, or the result of some trick of the stone, was impossible to tell.

Farther in, sentinels began to appear, standing guard along their path. Most were dressed identically to their guide, but others, found deeper in the prison, wore black armor with a simple white emblem of a broken crown. Sinister-looking helms hid their faces as they stood at perfect attention. None of them moved or said a word.

Hadrian asked Myron about the emblem these men wore.

"The crest is used by the ancient order of the Seret Knights," the monk explained quietly. "They were first formed eight hundred years ago by Lord Darius Seret, who had been charged by Patriarch Linnev with the task of finding the lost Heir of Novron. The broken crown is symbolic of the shattered empire, which they seek to restore."

Finally they reached what Hadrian assumed was their final destination. They entered an oval chamber with an incredibly tall door dominating the far wall. Carved of stone, it stood wreathed in a glittering array of fine spiderweb-like designs, which appeared organic in nature. Like the veins of a leaf or the delicate, curling tendrils of sprawling roots, the doorframe spread out until its artistry was lost in the shadows. On either side of the door stood dramatic obelisks covered with runes cut deep in beveled stone. Between these and the door, blue flames burned in braziers mounted on high pedestals.

A man sat on a raised chair behind a six-foot-tall stone desk that was exquisitely sculpted with intricate patterns of swirling lines. On two sides of the worktable, barrel-thick candles twice the height of a man burned. So many melted wax tears streaked down their sides that Hadrian thought they might once have been as tall as the great door.

"Visitors," their guide announced to the clerk, who, until then, had been busy writing in a massive book with a black feathered quill. The man looked up from his work. His gray beard hung all the way to the floor. Deeply lined with wrinkles, his face looked like the bark of an ancient tree.

"What are your names?" the clerk asked.

"I'm Alric Brendon Essendon, son of Amrath Essendon,

King of Melengar, Lord of the Realm, and I demand an audience with the prisoner."

"The others?" The clerk motioned toward the rest.

"They are my servants, the royal protectors and my chaplain."

The clerk rose from his seat and leaned forward to examine each party member in more detail. He looked into the eyes of each for a moment before he resumed his seat. He dipped his feather quill and turned to a new page. After a few moments of writing, he asked, "Why do you wish to see the prisoner?" With his quill poised, he waited for a reply.

"My business is not your concern," Alric answered in a kingly voice.

"That may be; however, this prisoner *is* my concern, and if you have dealings with him, it *is my business*. I must know your purpose, or I will not grant you entry, king or not."

Alric stared at the clerk for some time before relenting. "I wish to ask him questions concerning the death of my father."

The clerk considered this a moment, then scratched his quill on the page of the great book. When he finished, he looked up. "Very well. You may enter the cell but you must obey our rules. They are for your own safety. The man to whom you wish to speak is no ordinary man. He is a thing, an ancient evil, a demon that we have successfully trapped here. Above all else, we are dedicated to keeping him confined. As you might imagine, he very much desires to escape. He is cunning and perpetually tests us. Constantly he is looking for a weakness, a break in a line, or a crack in the stone.

"First, proceed directly down the path to his confinement; do not tarry. Second, stay in the gallery; do not attempt to descend to his cage. Third—and this is the most important—do nothing he asks. No matter how insignificant it may sound. Do not be fooled by him. He is intelligent and cunning. Ask him your questions; then leave. Do not deviate from these rules. Do you understand?" Alric nodded. "Then may Novron have mercy on you."

Just then, the great doors split along the central seam and slowly started to open. The loud grinding of stone on stone echoed until at last the doors stood wide. Beyond them lay a long stone bridge that spanned an abyss. The bridge was three feet wide and as smooth as glass, and it appeared no thicker than a sheet of parchment. At the far end of the span rose a column of black rock. An island-like tower, its only visible connection to the world was the delicate bridge.

"You may leave your lantern. You will have no need for it," the clerk stated. Royce nodded but kept the lantern nevertheless.

As they stepped through the doorway, Hadrian heard a sound like singing, a faint mournful song as if a thousand voices joined in a somber dirge. The sad, oppressive music brought to mind the worst memories of his life and filled him with a misery so great it sapped his resolve. His feet felt weighted, his soul chilled. Moving forward became an effort.

Once the party crossed the threshold, the great doors began to close, shutting with a thundering boom. The chamber was well lit, although the source of the light was not apparent. It was impossible to judge the height or the depth of the chasm. Both stretched into seeming emptiness.

"Are other prisons like *this?*" Myron asked, his voice quavering as they began to inch their way across the bridge.

"I would venture to guess this is unique," Alric replied.

"Trust me, I know prisons," Royce told them. "This *is* unique."

The party fell into silence during the crossing. Hadrian was in the rear, concentrating on the placement of his feet. Part-way across he paused and glanced up briefly to check on the others. Myron was holding his arms out at his sides like a tightrope walker. Alric, half crouching, reached out with his hands as if he might resort to crawling at any minute. Royce, however, strode casually forward with his head tilted up, and he frequently turned from side to side to study their surroundings.

Despite its appearance, the bridge was solid. They successfully crossed it to a small arched opening into the black tower. Once off the bridge, Royce turned to face Alric. "You were fairly free about revealing your identity back there, Your Majesty," he said, reproaching the monarch. "I don't recall discussing a plan where you walk in and blurt out, 'Hey, I'm the new king, come kill me.' "

"You don't actually think there are assassins in here, do you? I know I thought this was a trap, but look at this place! Arista never could have arranged this. Or do you honestly think others will be able to slip in the same cliff door we entered through?"

"What I think is that there is no reason to take unnecessary chances."

"Unnecessary chances? Are you serious? You don't consider crossing a slick, narrow bridge over a gorge, which is who knows how deep, a risk? Assassins are the least of our worries."

"Are you always this much trouble to those guarding you?"

Alric's only response was a look of disdain.

The archway led to a narrow tunneled corridor, which eventually opened into a large round room. Arranged like an amphitheater, the gallery contained descending stairs and stone benches set in rings, each lower than the one before it, which focused all attention on the recessed center of the room. At the bottom of the steps was a balcony, and twenty feet below it lay a circular stage. Once they descended the stairs,

Hadrian could see the stage was bare except for a single chair and the man who sat upon it.

An intense beam of white light illuminated the seated figure from high above. He did not appear terribly old, with only the start of gray entering his otherwise dark shoulder-length hair. Dark, brooding eyes gazed out from beneath a prominent forehead. No facial hair marred his high cheekbones, which surprised Hadrian, because the few wizards and magicians he knew about all wore long beards as a mark of their profession. He wore a magnificent robe, the color of which Hadrian could not quite determine. The garment shimmered somewhere between dark blue and smoky gray, but where it was folded or creased, it looked to be emerald green or at times even turquoise. The man sat with the robe gathered around him, his hands, lost in its folds, placed on his lap. He sat still as a statue, giving no indication he was aware of their presence.

"What now?" Alric whispered.

"You talk to him," Royce replied.

The prince looked around thoughtfully. "That man down there can't really be a thousand years old, can he?"

"I don't know. In here, anything seems possible," Hadrian said.

Myron looked around the room and up toward the unseen ceiling, a pained expression on his face. "That singing—it reminds me of the abbey, of the fire, as if I can hear them again—screaming." Hadrian gently put a hand on Myron's shoulder.

"Ignore it," Royce told the monk, and then turned to glare at Alric. "You have to talk to him. We can't leave until you do. Now go ahead and ask him what you came here to find out."

"What do I say? I mean, if he is, you know, really a wizard of the Old Empire, if he actually served the last emperor, how do I approach him?"

"Try asking what he's been up to," Hadrian suggested. That was met by a smirk from Alric. "No, seriously, look down there. It's just him and a chair. He has no books, no cards, nothing. I nearly went crazy with boredom cooped up in The Rose and Thorn last winter during a heavy snowfall. How do you suppose he's spent *a thousand years* just sitting in that chair?"

"And how do you not go insane, listening to that sound all that time?" Myron added.

"Okay, I've got something." Alric turned to address the wizard. "Excuse me, sir." The man in the chair slowly raised his head and blinked in response to the bright light from above. He looked weary, his eyes tired. "Sorry to disturb you. I'm Alric Ess—"

"I know well who art thee," Esrahaddon interrupted. His tone was relaxed and calm, his voice gentle and soothing. "Where be thy sinlister?"

"My what?"

"Thy *sinlister*, Arista?"

"Oh, my *sister*."

"*Sis-ter*," the wizard repeated carefully, and sighed, shaking his head.

"She's not here."

"Why doth not she come?"

Alric looked first to Royce and then to Hadrian.

"She asked us to come in her place," Royce responded.

Looking at the thief, the wizard asked, "And who art thee?"

"Me? I'm nobody," Royce replied.

Esrahaddon narrowed his eyes at the thief and raised one eyebrow. "Perhaps, perhaps not."

"My sister instructed me to come here and speak with you," Alric said, drawing the wizard's attention back to him. "Do you know why?"

" 'Tis I who bade her send thee."

"Neat trick since you're locked in here," Hadrian observed.

"*Neat?*" Esrahaddon questioned. "Dost thou intend 'twas a clean thing? For I see no filth upon the matter." The four men responded with looks of confusion. " 'Tis not a point upon which to dwell. Arista hath in habit graced me with her presence fair for a year and more, though difficult be it to determine the passage of the sun within this darkened hole. A student of the Art she fancies herself, but schools for wizards thy world abides not. A desert of want drove her to seek my counsel. She bade me teach those skills now long forgotten. Within these walls am I locked, as time skips across fingertips untethered, with naught but the sound of mine own voice to pose comfort. So did I acquiesce for pity's sake. Tidings of the new world thy princess did provide. In return, I imparted gifts upon her—gifts of knowledge."

"Knowledge?" Alric asked, concerned. "What kind of knowledge?"

"Trifles. Be not long ago thy father suffered ill? A henth bylin did I instruct her to create." They all looked at him, puzzled. Esrahaddon's gaze left them. He appeared to search for something. "By another name did she fix it. 'Twas…" His face strained with concentration until at last he scowled and shook his head.

"A healing potion?" Myron asked.

The wizard eyed the monk carefully. "Indeed!"

"You taught her to make a potion to give to my father?"

"Frightening, yes? To have such a devil as I administering potions to thy king. Yet no poison did I render nor death impart. Likeminded was she and did challenge me thus, so each did we drink from the same cup to prove it free of mischief. No horns did we grow nor deaths impart, but thy liege fared well upon the taking."

"That doesn't explain why Arista sent me here."

"Death upon thy house hast come?"

"How do you know that? Yes, my father was murdered," Alric said.

The wizard sighed and nodded. "I forewarned a curse so dreadful hung above thy family's fate, but ear thy sister hast not. Still, I beckoned her to send thee forth should death imperil or accident belay the ruling House of Essendon."

Esrahaddon looked deliberately at Hadrian, Royce, and then Myron. "Innocents accused thy fellows be? For I counseled her thus—trustworthy only are those assigned blame for deeds most foul."

"So, do you know who killed my father?"

"A name I have not nor clairvoyant am I. Yet clear is the bow from which the arrow flew. Thy father died by the hand of man in league with the adversary that holds me fast."

"The Nyphron Church," Myron muttered softly, yet still the wizard heard and his eyes narrowed once more at the monk.

"Why would the Church of Nyphron wish to kill my father?"

"For deaf and blind be the passions of men once scent is sniffed. Watchful are they and listen well these walls, for while act benign and intent charitable my jailors believed my hand did point the way and thy father the Heir of Novron be."

"Wait a minute," Alric interrupted, "the church doesn't want to murder the heir. Their whole existence revolves around restoring him to the throne and creating the New Imperial Era."

"A thousand years renders not truth from lie. Death called for and death sought for the blood of god. 'Tis reason true that sealed away am I."

"And why is that?"

"Alone, muzzled and buried deep, chained to a stone-lined grave I am kept. For witness to this counterfeit of the truth I stand, the only lamp in a ceaseless night. The church, that bastion of faith, the wicked serpent whose fangs did wretch the life from the emperor and his family—all save one. Should heir be found, evidence shall I hold and such proof against slander wield. For 'tis I who fought to save our lord."

"The way we heard the story, *you* were the one who killed the imperial family and are responsible for the destruction of the entire empire," Hadrian said.

"From whence did such tale arise? From the adder tongue of mitered serpents? Dost thou truly believe such power resides in one man?"

"What makes you think they killed the emperor?" Alric inquired.

" 'Tis not a question nor guess. 'Tis no supposition I extol but memory—as clear as yesterday. I *know*. 'Twas there and 'twas I who delivered the emperor's only son from death at pious hands."

"So you are telling us that you lived at the time of the emperor. Do you expect us to believe that you are over nine hundred years old?" Royce asked.

"Thou speak of doubt, but none have I. A question posed and a question answered."

"That's *just* an answer like this is *just* a prison," Royce countered.

"I still don't understand what all this has to do with my father. Why would the church kill him?"

"Kept alive by powers of enchantment am I, for I alone the heir can find. These serpents watch and hope to see me slip and cast into their hands the fruit of Novron. An interest upon him did I show. By kindness did I suggest deference toward thy father, and in haste to rid burdened souls of traceable guilt did the church slay thy king. Mores the blood to stain red hands. Never did I expect—but wonder nonetheless at their vicious thirst, so to Arista did I warn of perils and portents dark."

"And that's why you wanted me brought here? To explain this to me? To make me understand?"

"Nay! I did send summons but for a path of another course."

"And what is that?"

The wizard looked up at them, his expression revealing a hint of amusement. "Escape."

No one said anything. Myron took the moment to sit down on the stone bench behind him and whispered to Hadrian, "You were right. Life outside the abbey *is* much more exciting than books."

"You want us to help you to escape?" Royce asked incredulously. He held out his hands and looked around the black stone fortress. "From *here*?"

" 'Tis necessary."

" 'Tis also impossible. I have gotten out of a number of difficult situations in my time but nothing like this."

"And thou art aware of little. Measures thou see art but trifles. Walls, guards, and the abyss stand least among the gauntlet. Lo what works of magic ensnare me! Magical locks claim all the doors here as smoke and dream they vanish with passage. The bridge into the bargain, for it hath withered hence. Look and ye will find it so—'tis gone."

Royce raised an eyebrow skeptically. "Alric, I need your ring." The prince handed it to the thief, who climbed the steps and disappeared into the tunnel. He returned a few minutes later and gave the ring back to Alric. A slight nod of his head confirmed what Hadrian already suspected.

Hadrian turned his attention back to the wizard and

Esrahaddon continued. "More to the misery and serious still art the runes that line these prison walls. Magic defends this offending stone, which neither force of blow nor whit of wizardry shall let slip the portal of this hateful cage. 'Tis what thou hear as twisted euphony, this mournful wailing that plagues the ear. Within this spellbound grasp of symbols no new conjuration may manifest. Moreover, what more to trip hope and plague mind but that time itself lies captive in this hateful grip, suspended thus immobile. 'Tis why the years but wave in passing as they flee, never touching this cave nor inhabitants therein. In joining me, thou hast not aged one wink nor shall thou hunger nor thirst—lest no more than when thou entered. Shocking O this feat, this masterwork of mountainous achievement, built for one soul."

"Huh?" Alric asked.

"He says that no magic can be performed in here and... and...time does not pass," Myron explained.

"I don't believe that," Alric challenged.

"Put hand to thy breast and search for the meter of thy heart."

Myron inched his fingers across his chest and let out a tiny squeak.

"And with all these obstacles you expect us to help you escape?" Hadrian said.

The wizard replied with an impish grin.

"Although I'm dying to ask how," Royce said, "I'm even more compelled to ask why. If they went through this much effort to seal you in here, it seems to me they might have had a good reason. You've told us what we came to hear. We're done. So why would we be foolish enough to try and help you escape?"

"Little choice exists for the choosing."

"We have a great many choices," Alric countered bravely. "I'm the king and rule here. It's you who is powerless."

"Oh, 'tis not I that bars thy path, O prince. Thou under-stand rightly, helpless am I—a prisoner of weakness bound. 'Tis our jailors with whom thou need set thy argument. While every note in our words be measured and writ, I pray thee call out for release and greet the silence sure to follow. Shout, and hear the echo run unanswered. Trapped with me by walls or death they seek to claim thee."

"But if they are listening, they know I'm not the heir," Alric said, but the courage in his voice had melted away.

"Call out, and see which truth prevails."

Alric's concern showed on his face as he looked first to Hadrian and then to Royce. "He may be right," the thief said quietly.

Concern turned to panic and the prince began to shout commands for their release. There was no response, no sound of the great door opening or of approaching protectors to escort them to the exit. Everyone except the wizard looked worried. Alric wrung his hands, and Myron stood and held on to the rail of the balcony as if letting go would allow the world to spin away from him.

"It was a trap after all," Alric said. He turned to Royce. "My apologies for doubting your sound paranoia."

"Even I didn't expect this. Perhaps there's another way out." Royce took a seat on one of the observation benches and assumed the same contemplative look he had worn when he was trying to determine how to get inside the prison.

Everyone remained silent for some time. Finally, Hadrian approached Royce and whispered, "Okay, buddy, this is where you tell me you have this wonderfully unexpected plan to get us out of here."

"Well, I do have one, but it seems almost as frightening as the alternative."

"What's that?"

"We do what the wizard says."

They looked down at the man casually seated in the chair. His robe looked a slightly different shade of blue now. Hadrian waved the others over and explained Royce's plan.

"Could this be a trick?" Alric asked quietly. "The clerk did warn us not to do anything he said."

"You mean the nice clerk who took away our bridge and refuses to let us out?" Royce replied. "I'm not seeing an alternative, but if any of you have another idea, I'm willing to hear it."

"I'd just like to feel my heart again," Myron said, holding his palm to his chest and looking sick. "This is very disturbing. I almost feel like I'm actually dead."

"Your Majesty?"

Alric looked up at the thief with a scowl. "I just want to say for the record that as far as royal protectors go, you're not very good."

"It's my first day," Royce replied dryly.

"And already I'm trapped in a timeless prison. I shudder to think what might have happened if you had a whole week."

"Listen, I don't see we have a choice here," Royce told the group. "We either do what the wizard says and hope he can get us out, or we accept an eternity of sitting here listening to this dreadful singing."

The mournful wail of the music was so wretched that Hadrian knew listening to it would eventually drive him mad. He tried to ignore it, but as it did for Myron, it brought him unpleasant memories of places and people. Hadrian saw the disappointment on his father's face when he had left to join the military. He saw the tiger covered in blood, gasping for breath as it slowly died, and he heard the sound of hundreds chanting the name: *Galenti!* He had reached his conclusion. Anything was better than staying there.

Royce stood and returned to the balcony, below which the wizard waited calmly. "I assume if we help you escape, you'll see to it we get out as well?"

"Indeed."

"And there is no way to determine if you are telling the truth right now?"

The wizard smiled. "Alas, nay."

Royce sighed heavily. "What do we have to do?"

"Precious little. Thy prince, this wayward and recent king, need but recite a bit of poetry."

"*Poetry?*" Alric pushed past Hadrian to join Royce at the balcony. "What poetry?"

The wizard stood up and kicked his chair to one side to reveal four stanzas of text crudely scratched into the floor.

" 'Tis amazing what beauty time may grant," the wizard said with obvious pride. "Speak, and it wilt be so."

Hadrian silently read the lines brightly illuminated by the beam of the overhead light.

AS LORD OF THIS REALM AND KEEPER OF KEYS,
A DECREE WAS MADE AND COUNCILMAN SEIZED.

UNJUSTLY, I SAY, AND THE TIME 'TIS NIGH
TO OPEN THE GATE AND LET HIS SOUL FLY.

BY VIRTUE OF GIFT GRANTED TO ME,
BY RIGHTFUL BIRTH, THE SOVEREIGN I BE.

HEREBY I PROCLAIM THIS ROYAL DECREE,
ESRAHADDON THE WIZARD, THIS MOMENT IS FREE.

"How is that possible?" Alric asked. "You said spells don't work here."

"Indeed, and thou art no spell-caster. Thou art but granting freedom as the law allows the rightful ruler of this land—laws of control laid down before the birth of Melengar, laws built on assumptions false concerning the longevity of power and who might, in due course of time, wield it—at this moment, in this place, 'tis thee. Thou art the rightful and undisputed ruler of this land, and as such, the locks art thine to open. For here latch and bolt be forged with words of enchantment—words that in time hath changed their meaning.

"This gaol raised upon ground once claimed by imperial might, in absence of emperor slain did bend knee alone to the Nyphron Church Patriarch. Now within these walls never a grain of sand did drop to mark the passage of time but without thunder of war did rumble. Armies marched and lands divided, the empire lost to warlords' whim. Then through bloody strife did these hills birth Melengar, realm sovereign under lordly king. What privilege once reserved alone only for a mitered head hast now fallen to thee. To thee, good King of Melengar, who has the power to right wrong so long omit. Nine centuries of dust hast buried wit, dear king, for these jailers hath forgotten how to read their own runes!"

In the distance, Hadrian heard the grinding of stone on stone. Outside the cell, the great door was opening. "Speak those words, my lord, and thou will end nine hundred years of wrongful imprisonment."

"How does this help?" Alric asked. "This place is filled with guards. How does this get us out?"

The wizard smiled a great grin. "Thy words will cast aside the barrier enchantment and allow me the freedom to use the Art once more."

"You'll cast a spell. You'll disappear!"

Footsteps thundered on the bridge, which had apparently reappeared. Hadrian ran up the gallery stairs to look down the tunnel. "We have guards coming! And they don't look happy."

"If you're going to do this, you'd better make it fast," Royce told Alric.

"They've swords drawn," Hadrian shouted. "Never a good sign."

Alric glared down at the wizard. "I want your word you won't leave us here."

"Gladly given, my lord." The wizard inclined his head respectfully.

"This better work," Alric muttered, and began reading aloud the words on the floor below.

Royce raced to join Hadrian as he positioned himself at the mouth of the tunnel. Hadrian planned to use its confined space to limit the advantage of the guard's numbers and planted his feet while Royce took up position slightly behind him. In unison, they drew their weapons, preparing for the impending onslaught. At least twenty men stormed the gallery. Hadrian could see their eyes and recognized what burned there. He had fought numerous battles and he knew the many faces of combat. He had seen fear, recklessness, hatred, even madness. What came at him now was rage—blind, intense rage. Hadrian studied the lead man, estimating his footfalls to determine which leg his weight would land on when he came within striking range. He did the same with the man behind him. Calculating his attack, he raised his swords, but the prison guards stopped. Hadrian waited with his swords still poised, yet the guards did not advance.

"Let us away," he heard Esrahaddon say from behind. Hadrian whirled around and discovered the wizard was no longer on the stage below. Instead, he moved casually past Hadrian, navigating around the stationary guards. "Come, come," Esrahaddon called.

Without a word, the group hurried after the wizard. He led them through the tunnel and across the newly extended bridge. The prison was oddly silent, and it was then that Hadrian realized the music had stopped. The only remaining sound was their footfalls against the hard stone floor.

"Be at ease for perils past but tarry not and follow well," Esrahaddon told them reassuringly.

They did as instructed, and no one said a word. To pass the clerk, who stood peering through the great door, they needed to come within inches of his anxiety-riddled face. As Hadrian attempted to slip by without bumping him, he saw the man's eye move. Hadrian stiffened. "Can they see or hear us?"

"Nay. A ghostly breath is all thee be, a chill and swirl of air to their percept."

The wizard led them without hesitation, making turns, crossing bridges, and climbing stairs with total confidence.

"Maybe we're dead?" Myron whispered, glaring at each frozen guard he passed. "Maybe we're *all* dead now. Maybe we're ghosts."

Hadrian thought Myron might be on to something. Everything was so oddly still, so empty. The fluid movement of the wizard and his billowing robe, which now emitted a soft silvery light far brighter than any lantern or torch, only heightened the surreal atmosphere.

"I don't understand. How is this possible?" Alric asked, stepping around a pair of black-suited guards who watched the third bridge. He waved his hand before the face of one of them, who did not respond. "Is this your doing?"

" 'Tis the *ithinal*."

"Huh?"

"A magic box. Power to alter time eludes the grasp of man, for too vast be the scope and too great the field. Yet enclose the space, confine the effect, and tame the wild world within.

Upon these walls, my colleagues of old wove enchantments complex. Designed to affect magic and time, I had but to ever so slightly adjust a fiber or two within the weave to throw us out of phase."

"So, the guards can't see us, but that doesn't explain why they are just standing there," Hadrian said. "We disappeared, and you're free. Why are they not searching? Shouldn't they be locking doors to trap us?"

"Within these walls, locked art the sands of time for all but us."

"You turned it inside out!" Myron exclaimed.

Esrahaddon looked with an appraising eye over his shoulder at the monk. " 'Tis thrice thou hast impressed me. What did thou say thy name was?"

"He didn't," Royce answered for him.

"Thou dost not trust people easily, my black-hooded friend? 'Tis quite wise. Careful should be the dealings with the wise and wizards." Esrahaddon winked at the thief.

"What does he mean by 'turning it inside out'?" Alric asked. "So, time has stopped for them while we are free?"

"Indeed. Though time still moves, 'tis very slowly paced. Unaware will they remain sealed in an instant lost."

"I'm starting to see now why they were afraid of you," Alric said.

"Nine hundred years did I spend imprisoned for saving the son of a man we all swore our lives to serve and protect. Exceedingly kind is the reward I bestow, for there art worse moments in which for all eternity to be trapped."

They reached the great stair that led to the main entrance corridor and began the long, exhausting climb up the stone steps. "How did you stay sane?" Hadrian asked. "Or did time slip by in an instant like it is for them?"

"Slip it did but not so fast when measured in centuries.

Each day a battle did I fight. Patience is a skill learned as a practitioner of the Art. Yet times there were that...well, who can say what it means to be sane?"

When they approached the hall of faces, Esrahaddon looked down its length and paused. Hadrian noticed the wizard stiffen. "What is it?" he asked.

"Those faces, frozen thus, art the workers who built this gaol. Came I to this place during the final walling. Tented city did wreathed the lake. Hundreds of artisans with families came to the call to do their part for their fallen emperor. Such was the character of His Imperial Majesty. They all mourned his passing, and few in the vast and varied empire would not gladly give their lives for him. Labeled the betrayer, I beheld hatred in their eyes. Proud were they to be the builders of my tomb."

The wizard's gaze moved from face to face. "I recognize some—the stonecutters, sculptors, cooks, and wives. The church, for fear of secrets slipped from lips innocent, sealed them so. All before thee, ensnared by a lie. How many dead? How much lost to hide one secret, which even a millennium hast not erased?"

"There's no door down there," Alric warned the wizard.

Esrahaddon looked up at Alric as if awoken from a dream. "Be not a fool. Thou didst enter through it," he said, and promptly led them down the corridor at a brisk walk. "Thou wert merely out of phase with it."

Here, in the darkest segment of the prison, Esrahaddon's robe grew brighter still, and he looked like a giant firefly. In time, they came to a solid stone wall, and without hesitation or pause, Esrahaddon walked through it. The rest quickly followed.

The bright sunlight of a lovely, clear autumn morning nearly blinded them the moment they passed through the barrier. Blue sky and the cool fresh air were a welcome change.

Hadrian took a deep breath and reveled in the scent of grass and fallen leaves, a smell he had not even noticed prior to entering the prison. "That's strange. It should be nighttime and raining, I would think. We couldn't have been in there more than a few hours. Could we?"

Esrahaddon shrugged and threw his head back to face the sun. He stood and took long deep breaths of air, sighing contentedly with each exhale. "Unexpected be the wages of altering time. 'What morrow be it?' 'tis better to ask. This day, the next, or one after. 'Tis possible tens or hundreds did fly past." The wizard appeared amused at the shock on their faces. "Worry not, 'tis likely only hours hast thee skipped."

"That's rather unnerving," Alric said. "Losing time like that."

"Verily, for nine hundred years have I lost. Everyone I knew is dead, the empire gone, and who knows in what state the world is left. Should what thy sister reports prove true, much hath changed in the world."

"By the way," Royce mentioned, "no one uses the words 'tis or hath anymore and certainly not thou, thy, or verily."

The wizard considered this a moment, then nodded. "In my day, classes oft did speak different in forms of speech. Assumed I did that ye were of a lower station or, in the case of the king, poorly educated."

Alric glared. "It's you who sound strange, not us."

"Indeed. Then I shall need to speak as all of—you—do. Even though—it is—crude and backward."

Hadrian, Royce, and Myron began the task of saddling the horses, which remained standing where they had left them. Myron smiled, obviously happy to be with the animals once again. He petted them while eagerly asking how to tie a cinch strap.

"We don't have an extra horse and Hadrian is already

Michael J. Sullivan

riding double," Alric explained. He glanced at Royce, who showed no indication of volunteering. "Esrahaddon will have to ride with me, I suppose."

"Unnecessary will that be, for my own way I shall go."

"Oh no you're not. You're coming back with me. I have a great deal to speak with you about. You were an advisor to the emperor and are obviously very gifted and knowledgeable. I have great need for someone such as you. You'll be my royal counselor."

"Nay, 'twill..." He sighed, then continued. "No, *it will* come as a shock to—*you*—but I did not escape to help with *your* little problems. Matters more pressing I must attend to, and too long from them have I been."

The prince appeared taken aback. "What matters could you possibly have after nine hundred years? After all, it's not as if you have to get home to tend to your livestock. If it's a matter of compensation, you'll be well paid and live in as much luxury as I can afford. And if you are thinking you can make more elsewhere, only Ethelred of Warric is likely to offer as much, and trust me, you don't want to work for the likes of him. He's a dogmatic Imperialist and a loyal church supporter."

"I do not seek compensation."

"No? Look at you. You have nothing—no food, no place to sleep. I think you should consider your situation a bit more before refusing me. Besides, gratitude alone should compel you to help me."

"Gratitude? Has the meaning of this word changed as well? In my day, this meant to show appreciation for a favor."

"And it still does. I saved you. I released you from that place."

Esrahaddon raised an eyebrow. "Didst thou help me escape as favor to me? I think not. Thou—*you* freed me to save *yourself*. I owe *you* nothing, and if I did, I repaid *you* when I brought *you* out."

"But the whole reason I came here was to gain your assistance. I'm inheriting a throne handed down by blood! Thieves abducted and dragged me across the kingdom in my first few days as king. I still don't know who killed my father or how to find them. I'm in great need of help. You must know hundreds of things the greatest minds of today have never known—"

"Thousands at least but I am still not going with *you*. *You* have a kingdom to secure. My path lies elsewhere."

Alric's face grew red with frustration. "I insist you return with me and become my advisor. I can't just let you wander off. Who knows what kind of trouble you could cause? You're dangerous."

"Yes indeed, dear prince," the wizard said, and his tone grew serious. "So allow me to grant thee a bit of free counsel—use not the word *insist* with regards to me. Thou hast but only a small spill to contend with; do not tempt a deluge."

Alric stiffened.

"How long before the church starts hunting you?" Royce asked casually.

"What dost…" The wizard sighed. "What do *you* mean?"

"You locked things up nicely in the prison so no one will know you escaped. Of course, if we were to return and start bragging about how we broke you out, that might start inquiries," Hadrian said.

The wizard leveled his gaze at him. "Is it a threat you make?"

"Why would I do that? As you already know, I have nothing to do with this. Not to mention it would be pretty stupid of me to threaten a wizard. The thing is, though, the king here, he is not as bright as I am. He very well might get drunk and tell stories at the first tavern he arrives at, as nobles often do." Esrahaddon glanced at Alric, whose red face now turned pale. "Fact is, we came all this way to find out who killed Alric's father, and we really don't know much more than we did before we set out."

Esrahaddon chuckled softly. "Very well. Prithee, impart how 'tis—*it is*—*your* father died."

"He was stabbed with a knife," Alric explained.

"What kind of knife?"

"A common rondel military dagger." Alric held his hands about a foot apart. "About this long. It had a flat blade and a round pommel."

Esrahaddon nodded. "Where was he stabbed?"

"In his private chapel."

"Where physically?"

"Oh, in the back, upper left side, I think."

"Were there any windows or other doors in the chapel?"

"None."

"Who found the body?"

"These two." Alric pointed at Royce and Hadrian.

The wizard smiled and shook his head. "Nay, beside them, who announced the death of the king? Who raised the alarm?"

"That would be Captain Wylin, my master-at-arms. He was on the scene very quickly and apprehended them."

Hadrian thought about the night King Amrath had been killed. "No, that's not right. There was a dwarf there. He must have come around the corner of the hallway just as we left the room. He probably saw the king's body lying on the floor of the chapel and shouted. Right after he yelled, the soldiers came and surprisingly fast, I might add."

"That was just Magnus," Alric said. "He's been doing stonework about the castle for months."

"Didst thee—*you*—see this dwarf approach from the corridor?" the wizard asked.

"No," Hadrian replied, and Royce confirmed that with a shake of his head.

"And when *you* entered the chapel from the doorway, was the body of the king visible?"

Hadrian and Royce shook their heads.

"That solves it, then," the wizard said as if everything was perfectly clear. The party stared back at him in confusion. Esrahaddon sighed. "The dwarf killed Amrath."

"That's not possible," Alric said, challenging him. "My father was a big man, and the dagger thrust was downward. A dwarf couldn't possibly have stabbed him in the upper back."

"Your father was in his chapel, as any pious king, kneeling with head bowed. The dwarf killed him as he prayed."

"But the door was locked when we entered," Hadrian said. "And there was no one in the room besides the king."

"No one you could *see*. Did the chapel have an altar with a cabinet?"

"Yes, it did."

"They did a millennium ago as well. Religion changes slowly. The cabinet was likely too small for a man but could easily accommodate a dwarf. After he killed the king, he locked the door and waited for you two to find the body." Esrahaddon paused. "That cannot be right *you — two — to?*" He rolled his eyes and shook his head. "If this hast been done to language, I fear to know the fate of all else.

"With door locked, a night guard or cleaning steward would not find the body prematurely. Only a skilled thief would be able to enter, which I assume at least one of you is." He looked directly at Royce as he said the last part. "After you left, the dwarf crept out, opened the door, and sounded the alarm."

"So, the dwarf is an agent of the church?"

"No." The wizard sighed with a look of frustration. "Not a dwarf alive who would carry a common dagger. The traditions of dwarves change even slower than religion. Given the dagger he was by the one who hired him. Find that person and you will find the true killer."

Stunned, everyone looked at the wizard. "That's incredible," Alric said.

"Nay, not so difficult to determine." The wizard inclined his head toward the cliff. "Escape *was hard*. Speaking as you do *is hard*. Determining the murderer of King Amrath was... was...soft?"

"Soft?" Hadrian asked. "You mean easy."

"How be it that easy forms the opposite of hard? Sense this makes not."

Hadrian shrugged. "And yet, it is."

Esrahaddon looked frustrated. "Alas. Now, this is as much assistance as I shall lend in this matter. Therefore, I will be on my way. As I have said, I have affairs to attend. My help was sufficient to prevent any loose tongues?"

"You have my hand on it," Alric said, reaching out.

The wizard looked down at Alric's open palm and smiled. "Thy word is enough." He turned away and without so much as a parting gesture began walking down the slope.

"You're going to walk? You know, it's a long way to anywhere from here," Hadrian yelled after him.

"I am looking forward to the trip," the wizard replied without glancing back. Following the ancient road, he rounded the corner and slipped out of sight.

The remaining party members mounted their horses. Myron seemed more comfortable with the animals now and climbed confidently into his seat behind Hadrian. He even neglected to hold on until they began down the ravine back in the direction from which they had come. Hadrian expected they would pass Esrahaddon on the way down, but they reached the bottom of the ravine without seeing him.

"Not your run-of-the-mill fellow, is he?" Hadrian asked. He was continuing to look around for any signs of the wizard.

"The way he was able to get out of that place makes me wonder exactly what we did here today by letting him out," Royce said.

"No wonder the emperor was so successful." Alric frowned and knotted the ends of his reins. "Although I can tell it didn't come without aggravation. You know, I don't extend my hand often, but when I do, I expect it to be accepted. I found his reaction quite insulting."

"I'm not sure he was being rude by not shaking your hand. I think it's just because he couldn't," Myron told them. "Shake your hand, that is."

"Why not?"

"In *The Accumulated Letters of Dioylion*, they told a bit about Esrahaddon's incarceration. The church had both of his hands cut off in order to limit his ability to cast spells."

"Oh," Alric said.

"Why do I get the impression this Dioylion fellow didn't die a natural death?" Hadrian asked.

"He's probably one of those faces in the hallway." Royce spurred his horse down the slope.

CHAPTER 6

REVELATIONS BY MOONLIGHT

"I heard you were looking for me, Uncle?" Princess Arista swept into his office. She was followed by her bodyguard, Hilfred, who dutifully waited by the door. Still dressing in clothing mourning her father's death, she wore an elegant black gown with a silver bodice. Standing straight and tall with her head held high, she maintained her regal air.

The Archduke Percy Braga rose as she entered. "Yes, I have some questions for you." He resumed his seat behind the desk. Her uncle was dressed in black as well. His doublet, cape, and cap were dark velvet, causing his gold chain of office to stand out more than usual. His eyes looked weary from lack of sleep, and a thickening growth of stubble shadowed his face.

"Do you, now?" she said, glaring at him. "Since when does the lord chancellor summon the acting queen to answer *his* questions?"

Percy raised his eyes to meet hers. "There is no proof your brother is dead, Arista. You are not queen yet."

"No proof?" She walked over to Braga's chart table, where maps of the kingdom lay scattered everywhere. They were littered with flags marking where patrols, garrisons, and companies were deployed. She picked up the soiled robe she saw there; it bore the Essendon falcon crest. Poking her fingers through the holes cut in the back, she threw it on his desk. "What do you call this?"

"A robe," the archduke responded curtly.

"This is my brother's, and these holes look as though a dagger or arrow would fit through them nicely. Those two men who murdered my father killed Alric as well. They dumped his body in the river. My brother is dead, Braga! The only reason I have not already ordered my coronation is that I'm observing the appropriate mourning period. That time will soon be over, so you should mind how you speak to me, Uncle, lest I forget we are family."

"Until I have his body, Arista, I must consider your brother alive. As such, he is still the rightful ruler, and I'll continue to do everything in my power to find him regardless of your interference. I owe that much to your father, who entrusted me with this position."

"In case you haven't noticed, my father is dead. You should pay more attention to the living, or you won't be the Lord Chancellor of Melengar for long."

Braga started to say something and then stopped to take a calming breath. "Will you answer my questions or not?"

"Go ahead and ask. I'll decide after I hear them." She casually walked back to the chart table and sat on it. She crossed her long legs at the ankles and absently studied her fingernails.

"Captain Wylin reports that he has completed his interviews with the dungeon staff." Braga got up and moved from behind his desk to face Arista. In his hand, he held a parchment, which he glanced at for reference. "He indicates you visited the prisoners after your brother and I left them. He says you brought two monks with you who were later found gagged and hanging in place of the prisoners. Is that true?"

"Yes," she replied without embellishment. The archduke

continued to stare at her, the silence growing between them. "I'm a superstitious woman by nature, and I wanted to be certain they had last rites so their ghosts didn't remain after their execution."

"There is a report you ordered the prisoners unchained?" Braga took another step closer to her.

"The monks told me the prisoners needed to kneel. I saw no danger in it. They were in a cell with an army of guards just outside."

"They also reported you entered with the monks and had the door closed behind you." The archduke took another step. He was now uncomfortably close, studying her manners and expression.

"Did they also mention I left before the monks did? Or that I wasn't there when the brutes grabbed them?" Arista pushed off the desk, causing her uncle to step back. She casually slipped past him and walked to the window, which looked down at the castle courtyard. A man was chopping and stacking wood for the coming winter. "I'll admit it wasn't the smartest thing I've ever done, but I never thought they would escape. They were just two men!" She continued to stare out the window absently. Her gaze drifted from the woodcutter to the trees, which had lost all their leaves. "Now, is that all you wanted to know? Do I have the chancellor's permission to return to my duties as queen of this realm?"

"Of course, my dear." Braga's tone turned warmer. The princess left the window and moved toward the exit. "Oh, but there is one last thing."

Arista paused at the doorway and glanced over her shoulder. "What is it?"

"Wylin also reports the dagger used to kill your father is missing from the storeroom. Do you have any idea where it might be?"

She turned to face him. "Are you now accusing me of stealing?"

"I'm simply asking, Arista," the archduke huffed in irritation. "You don't need to be so obstinate with me. I'm merely trying to do my job."

"Your job? I think you are doing much more than your job. No, I don't know anything about the dagger, and stop pestering me with accusations thinly veiled as inquiries. Do it again and we shall soon see who rules here!"

Arista stormed out of Braga's office, leaving Hilfred to jog a step to keep up with her. She promptly crossed the keep to the residences. Asking Hilfred to stand guard, she rushed up the steps of her personal tower. She entered her room, slammed the door shut, and locked it with a tap from the gemstone in her necklace.

Breathing heavily, she paused a moment, with her back pressed against the door. She tried to steady herself. She felt as if the room were swaying like a young tree in a breeze. She had been feeling that way often lately. The world seemed to be constantly swirling around her. Yet this was her sanctuary, her refuge. Here was the one place she felt safe, where she kept her secrets, where she could practice her magic, and where she dreamed her dreams.

Although she was a princess, her room was very modest. She had seen the bedrooms of the daughters of earls, and even one baroness had a finer abode. By comparison, hers was quite small and austere. It was, however, by her own choice. She could have her pick of the larger, more ornately decorated bedrooms in the royal wing, but she chose the tower for its isolation and the three windows, which afforded a view of all the lands around the castle. Thick burgundy drapes extended from ceiling to floor, hiding the bare stone. She had hoped they might keep the chill out as well but unfortunately they did not. Winter nights were often brutally cold despite her efforts to keep the little fireplace roaring. Still the soft presence of the drapes made it seem warmer just the same. Four giant pillows rested on a tiny canopy bed. There was no room for a larger one. Next to the bed was a small table with a pitcher inside a washbasin. Beside it stood a wardrobe, which had been passed down to her from her mother along with her hope chest. The solidly made trunk with a formidable lock sat at the foot of her bed. The only other pieces of furniture in the room were her dressing table, a mirror, and a small chair.

She crossed the room and sat at her dressing table. The mirror, which stood beside it, was of lavish design. The looking glass was clearer than most and was framed on either side by two elegant swans swimming away from one another. This too had once belonged to her mother. She fondly remembered nights sitting before it, watching its reflection as her mother brushed her hair. On the table, she kept her collection of hairbrushes. She had many, one from each of the kingdoms her father had visited on matters of state, including a pearl-handled brush from Wesbaden and an ebony one with fine fish-bone teeth from the exotic port city of Tur Del Fur. Looking at them now brought back memories of days when her father would return home with a hand hidden behind his back and a twinkle in his eye. Now the swan mirror and the brushes were all that remained of her parents.

With a sudden sweep of her hand, she threw the brushes across the room. *Why had it come to this?* She cried softly; it did not matter. She had work yet to do. There were things she had started that must now be finished. Braga was getting more suspicious each day—time was running out.

She unlocked and opened her hope chest. From inside, she removed the bundle of purple cloth she had hidden there. How ironic, she thought, for her to have used that cloth. Her father had wrapped the last hairbrush he had given her in it. She laid the bundle on her bed and carefully unfolded it to reveal the rondel dagger. The blade was still stained with her father's blood.

"Only one more job left for you to do," she told the knife.

❧

The Silver Pitcher Inn was a simple cottage located on the outskirts of the province of Galilin. Fieldstone and mortar composed the lower half, while whitewashed oak beams supported a roof of thick field thatch, gone gray with time. Windows divided into diamond panes of poor-quality glass underscored by heldaberry bushes lined the sides. Several horses stood tied to the posts out front, with still more visible in the small stable to the side.

"Seems like a busy place for so far out," Royce observed.

Traveling east, they had ridden all day. Just as before, the trip through the wilds proved exhausting. As the evening light had faded, they had reached the farmland of Galilin. They passed through tilled fields and meadows until at last they stumbled onto a country lane. Because none of them knew for certain where they were, they decided to follow the road to a landmark. To their pleasant surprise, the Silver Pitcher Inn was the first building they found.

"Well, Majesty," Hadrian said, "you should be able to find your way back to the castle from here, if that's still your destination."

"It's about time I got back," Alric told him, "but not before I eat. Does this place have decent food?"

"Does it matter?" Hadrian chuckled. "I'd be happy for a bit of three-day-ripe field mouse at this point. Come on, we can have a last meal together, which, since you have no money on you, I'll be paying for. I hope you'll let me deduct it from my taxes."

"No need. We'll tack it on to the job as an additional expense," Royce interjected. He looked at Alric and added, "You haven't forgotten you still owe us one hundred tenents, have you?"

"You'll get paid. I'll have my uncle set the money aside. You can pick it up at the castle."

"I hope you don't mind if we wait a few days, just to make sure."

"Of course not." The prince nodded.

"And if we send a representative to pick up the money for us?" Royce asked. Alric stared at him. "One who has no idea how to find us in case he is captured?"

"Oh please, aren't you being just a tad bit too cautious now?"

"No such thing," Royce replied.

"Look!" Myron shouted suddenly, pointing at the stable.

All three of them jumped fearfully at the sudden outburst.

"There's a *brown* horse!" the monk said in amazement. "I didn't know they came in brown!"

"By Mar, monk!" Alric shook his head in disbelief, a gesture Royce and Hadrian mirrored.

"Well, I didn't," Myron replied sheepishly. His excitement, however, was still evident when he added, "What other colors do they come in? Is there a green horse? A blue one? I would so love to see a blue one."

Royce went inside and returned a few minutes later. "Everything looks all right. A bit crowded, but I don't see anything too out of the ordinary. Alric, be sure to keep your hood up and either spin your ring so the insignia is on the inside of your hand, or better yet, remove it altogether until you get home."

Just inside the inn was a small stone foyer, where several

cloaks and coats hung on a forest of wall pegs. A handful of walking sticks of various shapes and sizes rested on a rack to one side. Above, a shelf held an assortment of tattered hats and gloves.

Myron stood just inside the door, gaping at his surroundings. "I read about inns," he said. "In *Pilgrims' Tales*, a group of wayward travelers spend a night at an inn, where they decided to tell stories of their journeys. They made a wager for the best one. It's one of my favorites, although the abbot didn't much care for my reading it. It was a bit bawdy. There were several accounts about women in those pages and not in a wholesome fashion either." He scanned the crowd excitedly. "Are there women here?"

"No," Hadrian replied sadly.

"Oh. I was hoping to see one. Do they keep them locked up as treasures?"

Hadrian and the others just laughed.

Myron looked at them, mystified, then shrugged. "Even so, this is wonderful. There's so much to see! What's that smell? It's not food, is it?"

"Pipe smoke," Hadrian explained. "It probably was not a popular activity at the abbey."

A half dozen tables filled the small room. A slightly askew stone fireplace with silver tankards dangling from mantel hooks dominated one wall. Next to it stood the bar, which was built from rough and unfinished tree logs complete with bark. Some fifteen patrons lined the room, a handful of whom watched the group enter with passing interest. Most were rough stock, woodsmen, laborers, and traveling tinkers. The pipe smoke came from a few gruff men seated near the log bar, and a cloud of it hovered at eye level throughout the room, producing an earthy smell that mingled with that of the burning wood of the fireplace and the sweet scent of baking bread.

Royce led them to an open round table near the window, where they could see the horses outside.

"I'll order us something," Hadrian volunteered.

"This is a beautiful place," Myron declared, his eyes darting about the room. "There is so much going on, so many conversations. Speaking at meals wasn't allowed at the abbey, so it was always deathly silent. Of course, we got around that rule by using sign language. It used to drive the abbot crazy, because we were supposed to be focusing on Maribor, but there are times when you simply have to ask someone to pass the salt."

No sooner had Hadrian reached the bar than he felt someone press up behind him menacingly.

"You should be more careful, my friend," a man whispered softly.

Hadrian turned slowly and chuckled when he saw who it was. "I don't have to, Albert. I have a shadow who watches my back." Hadrian gestured toward Royce, who had slipped up behind the viscount.

Albert, who wore a dirty, tattered cloak with the hood pulled up, turned to face a scowling Royce. "I was just making a joke."

"What are you doing here?" Royce whispered.

"Hiding—" Albert started, but he fell quiet when the bartender came over with a pitcher of foaming beer and four mugs.

"Have you eaten?" Hadrian asked.

"No." Albert looked longingly at the pitcher.

"Could I get another mug and another plate of supper?" Hadrian asked the hefty man behind the bar.

"Sure thing," the bartender responded as he added another mug. "I'll bring the food over when it's ready."

They returned to the table with the viscount trailing them. Albert looked curiously at Myron and Alric for a moment.

"This is Albert Winslow, an acquaintance of ours," Hadrian explained as Albert pulled a chair over to their table. "These are—"

"Clients," Royce cut in quickly, "so no business talk, Albert."

"We've been out of town...traveling, the last few days," Hadrian said. "Anything been going on in Medford?"

"A lot," Albert said quietly as Hadrian poured the ale. "King Amrath is dead."

"Really?" Hadrian feigned surprise.

"The Rose and Thorn has been shut down. Soldiers tore through the Lower Quarter. A bunch of folks were rounded up and sent to prison. There's a small army surrounding Essendon Castle and the entrances to the city. I got out just in time."

"An army around the castle? What for?" Alric asked.

Royce motioned for him to calm down. "What about Gwen?"

"She's okay—I think," Albert replied, looking curiously at Alric. "At least she was when I left. They questioned her and roughed up a few of her girls but nothing more than that. She's been worried about you. I think she expected you to return from...traveling...days ago."

"Who are 'they'?" Royce asked, his voice several degrees colder.

"Well, a lot of them were royal guards, but they had a whole bunch of new friends as well. Remember those strangers in town we talked about a few days ago? They were marching with some of the royal guards, so they must be working for the crown prince, I would think." Again, Albert glanced at Alric. "They were combing the entire city and asking questions about a pair of thieves operating out of the Lower Quarter. That's when I made myself scarce. I left town and headed west. It was the same all over. Patrols are everywhere. They have been ripping apart inns and taverns, hauling people into the streets. I've stayed one step ahead of them so far. Last thing I heard, a curfew was ordered after nightfall in Medford."

"So, you just kept heading west?" Hadrian asked.

"Until I got here. This is the first place I came to that hadn't been ransacked."

"Which would explain the large turnout," Hadrian mentioned. "Mice leave a sinking ship."

"Yeah, a lot of people decided Medford wasn't so friendly anymore," Albert explained. "I figured I would stick around here for a few days and then start back and test the waters as I go."

"Has there been any word concerning the prince or princess?" Alric asked.

"Nothing in particular," the viscount responded. He took a drink, his eyes lingering on the prince.

The rear door to the inn opened and a slim figure entered. He was filthy, dressed in torn rags and a hat that looked more like a sack. He clutched a small purse tightly to his chest and paused for only a moment, his eyes darting around the room nervously. He walked quickly to the rear of the bar, where the innkeeper filled a sack of food in exchange for the purse.

"What do we have here?" asked a burly fellow from one of the tables as he got to his feet. "Take off the hat, elf. Show us them ears."

The ragged pauper clung to his bag tightly and looked toward the door. When he did, another man from the bar moved to block his path.

"I said take it off!" the burly man ordered.

"Leave him alone, Drake," the innkeeper told him. "He just came in for a bit of food. He ain't gonna eat it here."

"I can't believe you sell to *them*, Hall. Haven't you heard they're killing people up in Dunmore? Filthy things." Drake reached out to pull the hat off but the figure aptly dodged his reach. "See how they are? Fast little things when they want to be, but lazy bastards if you try to put 'em to work. They ain't nothing but trouble. You let 'em in here, and one day they'll end up stabbing you in the back and stealing you blind."

"He ain't stealing anything," Hall said. "He comes in here once a week to buy food and stuff for his family. This one has a mate and a kid. Poor things are barely alive. They're living in the forest. It's been a month since the town guard in Medford drove them out."

"Yeah?" Drake said. "If he lives in the forest, where's he getting the money to pay for the food? You stealing it, ain't you, boy? You robbing decent people? Breaking into farms? That's why the sheriffs drive 'em out of the cities, 'cause they're all thieves and drunks. The Medford guard don't want 'em on their streets, and I don't want 'em on ours!"

A man standing behind the vagabond snatched his hat off, revealing thick matted black hair and pointed ears.

"Filthy little elf," Drake said. "Where'd you get the money?"

"I said leave him be, Drake," Hall persisted.

"I think he stole it," Drake said, and pulled a dagger from his belt.

The unarmed elf stood fearfully still, his eyes darting back and forth between the men who menaced him and the door to the inn.

"Drake?" Hall said in a lower, more serious tone. "You leave him be, or I swear you'll never be served here again."

Drake looked up to see Hall, who was considerably larger than he, holding a butcher knife.

"You wanna go find him in the woods later, that's your business. But I won't have no fighting in my place." Drake put the dagger away. "Go on, get out," Hall told the elf, who carefully moved past the men and slipped back out the door.

"Was that really an elf?" Myron asked, astonished.

"They're half-breeds," Hadrian replied. "Most people don't believe pure-blood elves exist anymore."

"I actually pity them," Albert said. "They were slaves back in the days of the empire. Did you know that?"

"Well, actually, I—" Myron started, but he stopped short when he saw the slight shake of Royce's head and the look on his face.

"Why pity them?" Alric asked. "They were no worse off than the serfs and villeins we have today. And now they are free, which is more than the villeins can say."

"Villeins are bound to the land, true, but they aren't slaves," Albert said, correcting him. "They can't be bought and sold; their families aren't torn apart, and they aren't bred like livestock and kept in pens or butchered for entertainment. I heard they used to do that to the elves, and sure, they're free now, but they aren't allowed to be part of society. They can't find work, and you just saw what they have to go through just to get food."

Royce's expression had grown colder than usual, and Hadrian knew it was time to change the subject. "You wouldn't know it to look at him," he said, "but Albert here is a nobleman. He's a viscount."

"Viscount Winslow?" Alric said. "Of what holding?"

"Sad to say, none," Albert replied before taking a large drink of ale. "Granddad, Harlan Winslow, lost the family plot when he fell out of favor with the King of Warric. Although, truth be told, I don't think it was ever anything to boast about. From what I heard, it was a rocky patch of dirt on the Bernum River. King Ethelred of Warric gobbled it up a few years ago.

"Ah, the stories my father told me of Grandfather's trials

and tribulations trying to live with the shame of being a land-less noble. My dad inherited a little money from him, but he squandered it trying to keep up the pretense he was still a wealthy nobleman. I myself have no problem swallowing my pride if it will fill my stomach." Albert squinted at Alric. "You look familiar. Have we met before?"

"If we did, I'm certain it was in passing," Alric replied.

The meal arrived and chewing replaced conversation. The food was nothing special: a portion of slightly overcooked ham, boiled potatoes, cabbage, onions, and a loaf of old bread. Yet after nearly two days of eating only a few potatoes, Hadrian considered it a feast. As the light outside faded, the inn boy began lighting the candles on each table, and they took the opportunity to order another pitcher.

While sitting there relaxing, Hadrian noticed Royce repeat-edly looking out the window. After the third glance, Hadrian leaned over to see what was so compelling. With the darkness outside, the window was like a mirror. All he could see was his own face.

"When was The Rose and Thorn raided?" Royce asked.

Albert shrugged. "Two or three days ago, I guess."

"I meant, what time of day?"

"Oh, evening. At sunset, I believe, or just after. I suppose they wanted to catch the dinner crowd." Albert paused and sat up suddenly as his expression of contentment faded into one of concern. "Oh—ah...I hate to eat and run, but if it's all right with you boys, I'm going to make myself scarce again." He got up and exited quickly through the rear door. Royce glanced outside again and appeared agitated.

"What is it?" Alric asked.

"We have company. Everyone stay calm until we see which way the wind is blowing."

The door to the Silver Pitcher burst open, and eight men

dressed in byrnie with tabards bearing the Melengar falcon poured into the room. They flipped over a few tables near the door, scattering drinks and food everywhere. Soldiers brandishing swords glowered at the patrons. No one in the inn moved.

"In the name of the king, this inn and all its occupants are to be searched. Those resisting or attempting to flee will be executed!"

The soldiers broke into groups. One began pulling men from their tables and shoved them against the wall, forming a line. Others charged up the steps to the loft, while a third set descended into the tavern's cellar.

"I do an honest business here!" Hall protested as they pushed him up against the wall with the rest.

"Keep your mouth shut or I'll have this place torched," a man entering said. He did not wear armor, nor the emblem of Melengar. Instead, he was dressed in fine practical clothing of layered shades of gray.

"It was a pleasure having your company, gentlemen," Alric told those at the table, "but it seems my escort is here."

"Be careful," Hadrian told him as the prince stood up.

Alric moved toward the center of the room, pulled back his hood, and stood straight with his chin held high. "What is it you are looking for, good men of Melengar?" he asked in a loud clear voice that caught the attention of everyone in the room.

The man in gray spun around, and when he saw Alric's face, he showed a surprised smile. "Well! We are looking for you, Your Highness," he said with a gracious bow. "We were told you were kidnapped, possibly dead."

"As you can see, I'm neither. Now release these good people."

There was a brief hesitancy on the part of the soldiers, but the man in gray nodded, and the men stood at attention. The man in gray moved promptly to Alric. He looked the prince up and down with a quizzical expression. "Your choice of dress is a bit unorthodox, is it not, Your Majesty?"

"My choice of dress is none of your concern, sir..."

"It's Baron, Your Highness, Baron Trumbul. Your Majesty is needed back at Essendon Castle. Archduke Percy Braga ordered us to find you and escort you there. He has been worried about your welfare, considering all the recent events."

"As it happens, I was heading that way. You can, therefore, please the archduke and me by providing escort."

"Wonderful, my lord. Do you travel alone?" Trumbul looked at the others still seated at the table.

"No," Alric replied, "this monk is with me, and he will be returning to Medford as well. Myron, say goodbye to those nice people and join us." Myron stood up and with a smile waved at Royce and Hadrian.

"Is that all? Just the one?" The baron glanced at the remaining two of the party.

"Yes, just the one."

"Are you certain? It was rumored you might have been captured by two men."

"My dear baron," Alric replied sternly, "I think I would remember such a thing as that. And the next time you take it upon yourself to question your king, it may be your last. It's lucky for you that I find myself in a good mood, having just eaten and being too tired to take serious offense. Now give the innkeeper a gold tenent to pay for my meal and your disruption."

No one moved for a moment, and then the baron said, "Of course, Your Majesty. Forgive my impudence." He nodded to a soldier, who pulled a coin from his purse and flipped it toward Hall. "Now, Your Highness, shall we be going?"

"Yes," Alric replied. "I hope you have a carriage for me. I have had my fill of riding, and I'm hoping to sleep the rest of the way back."

"I'm sorry, Your Majesty, we do not. We can commandeer one just as soon as we reach a village, and hopefully some better clothes for you as well."

"That will have to do, I suppose."

Alric, Myron, Trumbul, and the troops left the inn. There was a brief discussion only partially heard through the open door as they arranged mounts. Soon the sound of hooves retreated into the night.

"That was Prince Alric Essendon?" Hall asked, coming over to their table and trying to see out their window. Neither Royce nor Hadrian replied.

After Hall returned to the bar, Hadrian asked, "Do you think we should follow them?"

"Oh, don't start that. We did our good deed for this month—two, in fact, if you count DeWitt. I'm content to just sit here and relax."

Hadrian nodded and drained his mug of ale. They sat there in silence while he stared out the window, drumming his fingers restlessly on the table.

"What?"

"Did you happen to notice the weapons that patrol was wearing?"

"Why?" Royce asked, irritated.

"Well, they were wearing Tiliner rapiers instead of the standard falchion swords carried by the Medford Royal Guard. The rapiers had steel rather than iron tangs but unmarked pommels. Either the Royal Armory has upgraded their standards or those men are hired mercenaries, most likely from eastern Warric. Not exactly the kind of men you'd hire to augment a search party for a lost Royalist king. And if I'm not mistaken, Trumbul is the name of the fellow Gwen pointed out as being suspicious in The Rose and Thorn the night before the murder."

"See," Royce said, irritated, "this is the problem with these good deeds of yours; they never end."

∽

The moon was rising as Arista placed the dagger on her windowsill. While it would still be some time before the moonbeams would reach it, all the other preparations were ready. She had spent all day working on the spell. In the morning, she had gathered herbs from the kitchen and garden. To find a mandrake root of just the right size had required nearly two hours. The hardest step, however, had been slipping down to the mortuary to clip a lock of hair from her father's head. By evening, she had been grinding the mixture with her mortar and pestle while she muttered the incantations needed to bind the elements. She had sprinkled the resulting finely ground powder on the stained blade and had recited the last words of the spell. All that was required now was the moonlight.

She jumped when a knock on her door startled her. "Your Highness? Arista?" the archduke called to her.

"What is it, Uncle?"

"Can I have a word with you, my dear?"

"Yes, just a minute." Arista drew the curtain shut, hiding the blade on the sill. She placed her mortar and pestle in her trunk and locked it. Dusting off her hands, she checked her hair in the mirror. She went to the door, and with a tap of her necklace, she opened it.

The archduke entered, still dressed in his black doublet, his thumbs hooked casually in his sword belt. His heavy chain of office shimmered in the firelight from Arista's hearth. He looked around her bedroom with a critical expression. "Your father never did approve of you living up here. He always wanted you down with the rest of the family. I actually think it hurt him a bit that you chose to separate yourself like this, but you have always been a solitary person, haven't you?"

"Does this visit have a point?" she asked with irritation as she took a seat on her bed.

"You seem very curt with me lately, my dear. Have I done something to offend you? You are my niece, and you did just lose your father and possibly your brother. Is it so impossible to believe I'm concerned for your welfare? That I'm worried about your state of mind? People have been known to do... unexpected things in moments of grief—or anger."

"My state of mind is fine."

"Is it?" he asked, raising an eyebrow. "You have spent most of the last few days in seclusion up here, which cannot be healthy for a young woman who has just lost her father. I would think you would want to be with your family."

"I no longer have a family," she said firmly.

"*I* am your family, Arista. I'm your uncle, but you don't want to see that, do you? You want to see me as your enemy. Perhaps that's how you deal with your grief. You spend all your time in this tower, and when you do step out of this stronghold of yours, it's only to attack me for my attempts to find your brother. I don't understand why. I have also asked myself why I've not seen you cry at the loss of your father. You two were quite close, weren't you?"

Braga moved to the dresser with the swan mirror and paused as he stepped on something. He picked up a silver-handled brush lying on the floor. "This brush is from your father. I was with him when he bought this one. He refused to have a servant select it. He personally went to the shops in Dagastan to find just the right one. I honestly think it was the highlight of the trip for him. You should take more care with things of such importance." He replaced it on the table with the other brushes.

He returned his attention to the princess. "Arista, I know you were afraid he was going to force you to marry some old, unpleasant king. I suspect the thought of being imprisoned within the invisible walls of marriage terrified you. But despite what you might have thought, he *did* love you. Why do you not cry for him?"

"I can assure you, Uncle, I'm perfectly fine. I'm just trying to keep busy."

Braga continued to move around her small room, studying it in detail. "Well, that's another thing," he said to her. "You're very busy, but you are not trying to find your father's killer? I would be, if I were you."

"Isn't that *your* job?"

"It is. I have been working continuously without sleep for days, I assure you. Much of my focus, however, as you should know, has been on finding your brother in the hopes of saving his life. I hope you can understand my priorities. You, on the other hand, seem to do little despite being the *acting queen*, as you call yourself."

"Did you come here to accuse me of being lazy?" Arista asked.

"Have you been lazy? I doubt it. I suspect you've been hard at work these last few days, perhaps weeks."

"Are you suggesting I killed my father? I ask only because *that* would be a very dangerous thing to suggest."

"I'm not suggesting anything, Your Highness. I'm merely trying to determine why you have shown so little sadness at the passing of your father and so little concern for the welfare of your brother. Tell me, dear niece, what were you doing in the oak grove this afternoon, returning with a covered basket? I also heard you were puttering around the kitchen pantry."

"You've had me followed?"

"For your own good, I assure you," he said with a warm, reassuring tone, patting her on the shoulder. "As I said, I'm concerned. I have heard stories of some who took their own lives after a loss such as yours. That's why I watch you. However, in your case, it was unnecessary, wasn't it? Taking your own life is not at all what you have been up to."

"What makes you say that?" Arista replied.

"Picking roots and pilfering herbs from the kitchen sounds more like you were working on a recipe of some kind. You know, I never approved of your father sending you to Sheridan University, much less allowing you to study under that foolish magician Arcadius. People might think you a witch. Common folk are easily frightened by what they don't understand, and the thought of their princess as a witch could be a spark that leads to a disaster. I told your father not to allow you to go to the university, but he let you leave anyway."

The archduke walked around the bed, absently smoothing her coverlets.

"Well, I'm glad my father didn't listen to you."

"Are you? I suppose so. Of course, it really didn't matter. It wasn't such a terrible thing. After all, Arcadius is harmless, isn't he? What could he teach you? Card tricks? How to remove warts? At least, that was all I thought he could teach you. But as of late, I have become…concerned. Perhaps he did teach you something of value. Perhaps he taught you a name… *Esrahaddon?*"

Arista looked up sharply and then tried to mask her surprise.

"Yes, I thought so. You wanted to know more, didn't you? You wanted to learn real magic, only Arcadius doesn't know much himself. He did, however, know someone who did. He told you about Esrahaddon, an ancient wizard of the old order who knows how to unlock the secrets of the universe and control the primordial powers of the elements. I can only imagine your delight in discovering such a wizard was imprisoned right here in your own kingdom. As princess, you have the authority to see the prisoner, but you never asked for your father's permission, did you? You were afraid he might say no. You should have asked him, Arista. If you had, he would have told you that no one is allowed in *that* prison. The church explained it all to Amrath the day of his coronation. He learned how dangerous Esrahaddon is and what he can do with innocent people like you. That monster taught you real magic, didn't he, Arista? He taught you black magic, am I right?" The archduke narrowed his eyes, his voice losing even the pretense of warmth.

Arista did not reply. She sat in silence.

"What did he teach you? I wonder. Certainly not party tricks or sleight of hand. He probably didn't show you how to call down lightning or how to split the earth, but I'm sure he taught you simple things—simple yet useful things—didn't he?"

"I have no idea what you're talking about," she said as she started to stand. Her voice betrayed a hint of fear. She wanted to put distance between the two of them. Crossing to the dressing table, she picked up a brush and began running it through her hair.

"No? Tell me, my dear, what happened to the dagger that killed your father and still bears his blood?"

"I told you I don't know anything about that." She watched him in the mirror.

"Yes, you did say that, didn't you? But somehow I find that hard to believe. You are the only person who might have a purpose for that blade—a dark purpose. A very evil purpose."

Arista whirled on him, but before she could speak, Braga

went on. "You betrayed your father. You betrayed your brother. Now you would betray me as well and with the same dagger! Did you really think me such a fool?"

Arista looked toward the window and could see, even through the heavy curtain, the moonlight had finally reached it. Braga followed her glance and a puzzled expression washed over his face. "Why does only one window have its curtains drawn?"

He turned, grabbed the drape, and threw it back, revealing the dagger bathed in moonlight. He staggered at the sight of it, and Arista knew the spell had worked its magic.

⁕

They had not gone far, only a handful of miles. The traveling was slow and the lack of sleep combined with his full stomach made Alric so drowsy he feared he might fall from the saddle. Myron did not look much better, riding along behind a guard, his head drooping. They traveled down a lonely dirt lane past a few farms and over footbridges. To the left lay a harvested cornfield, where empty brown stalks were left to wither. To the right stood a dark woodland of oak and hemlock, their leaves long since scattered to the wind; their naked branches reached out over the road.

It was another cold night, and Alric swore to himself he would never take another night ride as long as he lived. He was dreaming of curling up in his own bed with a roaring fire and perhaps a warmed glass of mulled wine when the baron ordered an unexpected halt.

Trumbul and five soldiers rode up beside Alric. Two of the men dismounted and took hold of the bridles of the prince's and Myron's horses. Four additional men rode ahead, beyond

Alric's sight, while three others turned and rode back the way they had come.

"Why have we stopped?" Alric asked, yawning. "Why have the men split up?"

"It's a treacherous road, Your Majesty," Trumbul explained. "We need to take precautions. Vanguards and rear guards are necessary when escorting one such as you, during times such as these. Any number of dangers might exist out here on dark nights. Highwaymen, goblins, wolves—there's no way to know what you might come across. There's even the legend of a headless ghost that haunts this road, did you know that?"

"No I didn't," the prince said. He did not care for the casual tone the baron was suddenly taking with him.

"Oh yes, they say it's the ghost of a king who died at this very spot. Of course, he wasn't really a king, just a crown prince who might have worn the crown one day. You see, as the tale goes, the prince was returning home one night in the company of his brave soldiers when one of them took it upon himself to chop the poor bastard's head off and put it in a sack." Trumbul paused as he pulled a burlap bag off his horse and held it up to the prince. "Just like this one here."

"What are you playing at, Trumbul?" Alric inquired.

"I'm not playing at all, Your Royal High-and-Mightiness. I just realized I don't need to return you to the castle to be paid; I only need to return part of you. Your head will do fine. It saves the horse the effort of carrying you the entire way, and I have always had a fondness for horses. So whatever I can do to help them, I try to do."

Alric spurred his mount, but the man with the reins held it firmly, and the horse only pivoted sharply. Trumbul took advantage of the animal's sudden lurch and pulled the prince to the ground. Alric attempted to draw his sword, but

Trumbul kicked him in the stomach. With the wind knocked out of him, Alric doubled over in the dirt, laboring to breathe.

Trumbul then turned his attention to Myron, who sat in his saddle with a look of shock as the baron approached him.

"You look familiar," Trumbul said as he pulled Myron roughly off the horse. He held the monk's head toward the moonlight. "Oh yes, I remember. You were the not-so-helpful monk at the abbey we burned. You probably don't remember me, do you? I was wearing a helm with a visor that night. We all were. Our employer insisted that we hide our faces." He stared at the monk, who had tears welling in his eyes. "I don't know if I should kill you or not. I was originally told to spare your life so you could deliver a message to your father, but you don't seem to be heading that way. Besides, keeping you alive was related to that job, and unfortunately for you, we have already been paid for its completion. So it seems what I do is completely at my discretion."

Without warning, Myron kicked the baron in the knee with such force that it broke the baron's grip on the monk, who leapt over a fallen log and bolted into the darkness of the trees, snapping twigs and branches as he ran into the night. Screaming in pain, the baron collapsed to the ground. "Get him!" he yelled, and two soldiers chased after Myron.

A commotion erupted in the trees. Alric heard Myron's cry for help, followed by the sound of a sword drawn from a scabbard. Another scream ended as quickly as it began, cut abruptly short. The silence returned. Still holding his leg, Trumbul cursed the monk. "That will teach the little wretch!"

"You all right, Trumbul?" asked the guard holding Alric's horse.

"I'm fine, just give me a second. Damn, that little monk kicked hard."

"He won't be kicking anyone anymore," another soldier added.

The baron slowly climbed to his feet and tested his leg. He walked over to where Alric lay and drew his sword. "Grab him by the arms and hold him tight. Make sure he doesn't cause me any trouble, boys."

The guard Myron had been riding behind dismounted and took Alric's left arm while another secured his right. "Just make sure you don't hit us by accident," he said.

Trumbul grinned in the moonlight. "I never do anything by accident. If I hit you, you've done something to deserve it."

"If you kill me, my uncle will hunt you down no matter where you try to hide!"

Trumbul chuckled at the young prince. "Your uncle is the one who will pay us for your head. He wants you dead."

"What? You lie!"

"Believe what you will." The baron laughed. "Turn him over so I get a clear stroke at the back of his neck. I want a pretty trophy. I hate it when I end up having to hack and hack."

Alric struggled but the two soldiers were stronger than he was. They twisted the prince's arms behind his back, forced him to his knees, and shoved his head to the ground.

There was the sound of snapping twigs from the thick brush by the side of the road. "It took you two a long time to kill that little monk," Trumbul said. "But you got back just in time for the night's finale."

The two soldiers holding Alric twisted his arms harder to keep him from moving. The prince struggled with all his strength, screaming into the dirt. "No! Stop! You can't! Stop!" His efforts were useless. The soldiers each had a firm grip, and years of wielding swords and shields in battle had turned their arms to steel. The prince was no match for them.

Alric waited for the blow. Instead of hearing Trumbul's blade whistling through the night air, he heard an odd gurgle, then a thud. The guards loosened their hold on him. One let go entirely, and Alric heard his rapid footfalls as he sprinted away. The other hauled the prince up, holding him tightly from behind. The baron lay dead on the ground. Two men stood on either side of the body. In the darkness, Alric saw only silhouettes, but they did not match the men who had chased Myron into the trees. The one nearest the baron held a knife, which seemed to glow with an eerie radiance in the moonlight. Next to him stood a taller, broader man, who held a sword in each hand.

Again the sound of twigs snapping came from the woods nearby.

"Everyone, over here!" shouted the soldier who still shielded himself with Alric.

The two guards holding the horses dropped the reins and drew their swords. Their faces, however, betrayed their fear.

Myron climbed out of the woods and stood in the moonlight, his rapid breath forming little clouds in the cold night air.

Alric heard Royce's voice: "Your friends aren't coming. They're already dead."

The two guards wielding swords looked at each other, then raced down the road in the direction of the Silver Pitcher Inn. The last remaining soldier, holding Alric, looked around wildly. As Royce and Hadrian took a stride toward him, he cursed abruptly, let go of the prince, and bolted.

Alric could not stop shaking as he wiped the tears and dirt from his face. Hadrian and Royce helped him to his feet. He stood on wobbly legs and looked at those around him.

"They were going to kill me," he said. "They were going to *kill me!*" he screamed.

He abruptly pushed Royce and Hadrian away and, drawing his father's sword, drove it deep into the torso of the dead

Trumbul. He staggered and stood there gasping, staring at the dead body before him, his father's sword swaying back and forth, the tip buried in the baron's back.

Soon men approached from both directions of the road. Many were from the Silver Pitcher Inn and carried crude weapons. Some of them were wet with blood but none appeared injured. Two of them led the horses that Royce, Hadrian, and Alric had been using since the Wicend Ford. There was also a thin figure in tattered rags wearing a shapeless hat. He bore only a heavy stick.

"Not a single one got past us," Hall declared as he approached the small group. "One tried to duck us, but the half-breed found him. I can see now why you asked him to come. Bastard can see better than an owl in the dark."

"As promised, you can keep the horses and everything on them," Hadrian said. "But make sure you bury these bodies tonight or you might find trouble in the morning."

"Is that really the prince?" one of the men asked, staring at Alric.

"Actually," Hadrian said, "I think you are looking at the new King of Melengar."

There was a quiet murmur of interest, and a few went through the bother of bowing, although Alric did not notice. He had retrieved his sword and was now searching Trumbul's body.

The men gathered in the road to look over the captured animals, weapons, and gear. Hall took charge and began to divvy up the loot as best he could.

"Give the elf one of the horses," Royce told him.

"What?" the innkeeper asked, stunned. "You want us to give *him* a horse? Are you sure? I mean, most of these men don't have a good horse."

Drake quickly cut in. "Listen, we all fought equally tonight.

He can have a share like everyone, but that miserable filth ain't walking off with no horse."

"Don't kill him, Royce," Hadrian said hurriedly.

The prince looked up to see Drake backing up as Royce took a step toward him. The thief's face was eerily calm but his eyes smoldered.

"What does the king say?" Drake asked quickly. "I mean—he is the king and all, right? Technically, them is his horses, right? His soldiers was a ridin' 'em. We should ask him to decide—okay?"

There was a pause while Alric stood up and faced the crowd. The prince felt sick. His legs were weak, his arms hurt, and he was bleeding from scrapes on his forehead, chin, and cheek. He was covered in dirt. He had come within seconds of death and the fear from it was still with him. He noticed Hadrian move away to where Myron was. The monk was crying off to his right, and Alric knew he was a hair away from joining him, but he was the king. He clenched his teeth and looked at them. A score of dirty, blood-splattered faces looked back. He stood there unable to think clearly. His mind was still on Trumbul. He was still furious and humiliated. Alric glanced at Royce and Hadrian and then looked back at the crowd.

"Do whatever these two men tell you to do," he said slowly, clearly, coldly. "They are my royal protectors. Any man who willfully disobeys them will be executed." There was silence in the wake of his voice. In the stillness, Alric pulled himself onto his horse. "Let's go."

Hadrian and Royce exchanged looks of surprise and then mounted. The monk was quiet now and walked in a daze. Hadrian pulled Myron up behind him.

As they started down the road, Royce stopped his horse near Hall and Drake and quietly told them both, "See to it the half-breed gets a horse and keeps it, or when I return, I'll hold everyone in this hamlet accountable—and for once, it will be legal."

The four rode along in silence for some time. Finally, Alric hissed, "It was my own uncle." Despite his efforts, his eyes began to water.

"I've been thinking about that," Hadrian mentioned. "The archduke stands next in line for the throne after you and Arista. But being family, I figured he'd be just as big a target as you, only he's not a blood uncle, is he? His last name is Braga, not Essendon."

"He married my mother's sister."

"Is she alive?"

"No, she died years ago, in a fire." Alric slammed his fist on the saddle's pommel. "He taught me the blade! He showed me how to ride. He's my uncle and he is trying to kill me!"

Nothing was said for a while, and then Hadrian finally asked, "Where are we going?"

Alric shook his head as if coming out of a dream. "What? Oh, to Drondil Fields, Count Pickering's castle. He is—was—one of my father's most trusted nobles and our closest friends. He's also the most powerful leader in the kingdom. I'll raise an army from there and march on Medford within the week. And Maribor help the man, or uncle, who tries to stop me!"

✍

"Is this what you wanted to see?" the archduke asked Arista, picking up the dagger. He held it out so she could read the name Percy Braga clearly spelled out on the blade in her father's blood. "It looks like you have indeed learned a thing or two from Esrahaddon. This, however, proves nothing. I certainly didn't stab your father with it. I wasn't even near the chapel when he was killed."

"But you ordered it. You might not have driven the dagger into his body, but you were the one responsible." Arista wiped the tears from her eyes. "He trusted you. We all trusted you. You were part of our family!"

"There are some things more important than family, my dear—secrets, terrible secrets which must remain hidden at all costs. As hard as it may be for you to believe, I do care for you, your brother, and your—"

"Don't you dare say it!" she shouted at him. "You murdered my father."

"It was necessary. If you only knew the truth, you'd understand what is truly at stake. There are reasons why your father had to die and Alric as well."

"And me?"

"Yes, I'm afraid so. But these matters must be handled delicately. One murder is not unusual, and Alric's disappearance has actually been a great help. If things had occurred the way they were planned, it would have looked much more suspicious. I suspect your brother will meet death in some quiet remote area far from here. I had originally planned for you to die accidently in an unfortunate accident, but you have provided me with a better approach. It'll be easy to convince others you hired those two thieves to kill your father and your brother. You see, I already planted the seeds that something was amiss. The night your father was killed, I had Captain Wylin and a squad of men at the ready. I'll simply explain that having failed the double murder, you sought to correct matters by freeing the killers. We have several witnesses who can attest to the arrangements you made that evening. I'll announce your trial at once and call all the nobles to court. They'll hear of your treachery, your betrayals, and your foul acts. They'll learn how education and witchcraft turned you into a power-craving murderess."

"You won't dare! If you put me before the nobles, I'll tell them the truth."

"That will be difficult, since you'll be gagged. After all"—he looked at his name glistening on the blade—"you're a witch and we can't allow you to cast spells on us. I would have your tongue cut out now except that it might look suspicious, since I haven't yet called for the trial."

Braga looked around the bedroom once more and nodded. "I was wrong. I do approve of your choice of quarters after all. I had other plans for this tower once, but now I think it will be the perfect place for you to await the trial in isolation. With the amount of time you've spent here by yourself, practicing your crafts, no one will notice a difference."

He walked out, taking the dagger with him. As he left, she saw a bearded dwarf with a hammer in hand standing outside the door. When it closed, she heard pounding and knew she had been locked in.

CHAPTER 7

DRONDIL FIELDS

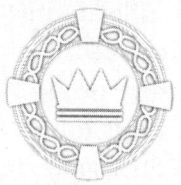

The four rode on through most of the night. They finally stopped when Myron toppled from the horse after falling asleep behind Hadrian. Leaving the horses saddled, they slept only briefly in a thicket. Soon they were back on the road, traveling through an orchard of trees. Each plucked an apple or two and ate the sweet fruit as they rode. There was little to see until the sun rose. Then a few workers began to appear. An older man drove an oxcart filled with milk and cheese. Farther down the lane, a young girl carried a basket of eggs. Myron watched her intently as they passed by, and she looked up at him, smiling self-consciously.

"Don't stare, Myron," Hadrian told him. "They will think you're up to something."

"They are even prettier than horses," the monk remarked, glancing back repeatedly over his shoulder as the girl fell behind them.

Hadrian laughed. "Yes, they are, but I wouldn't tell *them* that."

Ahead, a hill rose, and on top of it stood a castle. The structure was nothing like Essendon Castle—it looked more like a fortress than a house of nobility.

"Drondil Fields," Alric said. The prince had barely said anything since his ordeal the night before. He did not complain about the long ride or the cold night air. Instead, he rode in silence with his eyes fixed on the path that lay ahead.

"Odd name for a castle," Hadrian mentioned.

"Brodic Essendon built it during the wars following the fall of the Steward's Reign," Myron said. "His son, Tolin the Great, finished the work, defeated Lothomad the Bald, and proclaimed himself the first king of Melengar. They fought the battle on fields that belonged to a farmer named Drondil and later this whole area became known as Drondil Fields, or so the story goes."

"Who was Lothomad?" Hadrian asked.

"He was the King of Trent. After Glenmorgan III was executed, Lothomad seized his chance and sent his armies south. Ghent and Melengar would both be part of Trent today if it wasn't for Tolin Essendon."

"That's why they called him the Great, I assume."

"Exactly."

"Nice design. The five-pointed star shape makes it impossible to find a blind wall to scale."

"It's the strongest fortress in Melengar," Alric said.

"What brought the Essendons to Medford, then?" Royce asked.

"After the wars," Myron explained, "Tolin felt it was depressing living in such a gloomy fortress. He built Essendon Castle in Medford and entrusted Galilin to his most loyal general, Seadric Pickilerinon."

"Seadric's son was the one who shortened his name to Pickering," Alric added.

Hadrian noticed a distant look on Alric's face, a melancholy smile on his lips.

"My family has always been close to the Pickerings. There's

no direct blood relation, but Mauvin, Fanen, and Denek have always been like my brothers. We almost always spend Wintertide and Summersrule with them."

"I'll bet the other nobles aren't too happy about that," Royce said. "Particularly those who actually *are* blood relatives."

Alric nodded. "Nothing has ever come of their jealousies, though. No one would dare challenge a Pickering. They have a legendary family tradition with swords. Rumor has it that Seadric learned the ancient art of Tek'chin from the last living member of the Knights of the Order of the Fauld."

"Who?" Hadrian asked.

"The way I heard it—the way Mauvin told me—was that they were a post-imperial brotherhood who tried to preserve at least part of the ancient skills of the Teshlor Knights."

"And who were they?"

"Teshlors?" Alric glanced over at him, stunned. "The Teshlors are the greatest warriors who ever lived. They once guarded the emperor himself. But I guess like everything else, their techniques were lost with the fall of the empire. Still, what Seadric learned from the Order of the Fauld, and I guess it was just a tiny fraction of what the Teshlors knew, made him a legend. That knowledge has been faithfully passed from father to son for generations, and that secret gives the Pickerings an uncanny advantage in combat."

"We are well acquainted with that little bit of trivia," Hadrian muttered. "But like I was saying, it's a nice design for a fortress, except for those trees." He gestured toward the orchard. "That grove would provide good cover for an attacking army."

"This hill never used to look like it does now," Alric explained. "It used to be cut clear. The Pickerings planted this orchard only a couple of generations ago. Same with those rosebushes and rhododendrons. Drondil Fields hasn't seen warfare in five hundred years. I suppose the counts didn't see the harm in some fruit, shade, and flowers. The great fortress of Seadric Pickilerinon is now little more than a country estate."

They came up to the entrance and Alric led them in without pausing.

"Here now, hold on there!" an overweight gate warden ordered. He was holding a pastry in one hand and a pint of milk in the other. His weapon lay at his side. "Where do you think you're all going, riding up here as if this were your fall retreat?"

Alric pulled back his hood, and the warden dropped both his pastry and milk. "I—I'm sorry, Your Highness." He stumbled, snapping to attention. "I had no idea you were coming today. No one said anything to me." He wiped his hands and brushed the crumbs from his uniform. "Is the rest of the royal family coming as well?" Alric ignored him, continuing through the gate and across the plank bridge into the castle. The others followed him without a word as the astonished warden stared after them.

Like the outside of the castle, the interior courtyard showed little resemblance to its fortress heritage. The courtyard was an attractive garden of neatly trimmed bushes and the occasional small, carefully pruned tree. Colorful banners of greens and gold hung to either side of the keep's portico, rippling in the morning breeze. The grass looked carefully tended, although it was mostly yellow now with winter dormancy. Carts and wagons, most filled with empty bushel baskets possibly used to harvest the fruit, lay beneath a green awning. A couple of apples still lay in the bottom of one of them. A stable of horses stood near a barn where cows called for their morning milking. A shaggy black and white dog gnawed a bone at

the base of the fieldstone well, and a family of white ducks followed each other in a perfect line as they wandered freely,
quacking merrily as they went. Castle workers scurried about
their morning chores, fetching water, splitting wood, tending
animals, and quite often nearly stepping on the wandering
ducks.

Near a blacksmith shed, where a beefy man hammered a
glowing rail of metal, two young men sparred with swords in
the open yard. Each of them wore a helm and carried a small
heater shield. A third sat with his back to the keep steps. He
was using a slate and a bit of chalk to score the match. "Shield
higher, Fanen!" the taller figure shouted.

"What about my legs?"

"I won't be going after your legs. I don't want to lower my
sword and give you the advantage, but you need to keep the
shield high to deflect a downstroke. That's where you're vulnerable. If I hit you hard enough and you aren't ready, I can
drive you to your knees. Then what good will your legs be?"

"I'd listen to him, Fanen," Alric yelled toward the boy.
"Mauvin's an ass, but he knows his parries."

"Alric!" The taller boy threw off his helm and ran to
embrace the prince as he dismounted. At the sound of Alric's
name, several of the servants in the courtyard looked up in
surprise.

Mauvin was close to Alric in age but was taller and a good
deal broader in the shoulders. He sported a head of wild dark
hair and a set of dazzling white teeth, which shone as he
grinned at his friend.

"What are you doing here, and by Mar, what are you
dressed up as? You look frightful. Did you ride all night? And
your face—did you fall?"

"I have some bad news. I need to speak to your father
immediately."

"I'm not sure he's awake yet, and he is awfully cranky if you wake him early."

"This can't wait."

Mauvin stared at the prince and his grin faded. "This is no casual visit, then?"

"No, I only wish it was."

Mauvin turned toward his youngest brother and said, "Denek, go wake Father."

The boy with the slate shook his head. "I'm not going to be the one."

Mauvin started toward his brother. "Do it now!" he shouted, scaring the young boy into running for the keep.

"What is it? What's happened?" Fanen asked, dropping his own helm and shield on the grass and walking over to embrace Alric as well.

"Has any word reached you from Medford in the last several days?"

"Not that I know of," Mauvin replied, his face showing more concern now.

"No riders? No dispatches for the count?" Alric asked again.

"No, Alric, what is it?"

"My father is dead. He was murdered in the castle by a traitor."

"What!" Mauvin gasped, taking a step back. It was a reaction rather than a question.

"That's not possible!" Fanen exclaimed. "King Amrath dead? When did this happen?"

"To be honest, I'm not sure how long it has been. The days following his murder have been confusing, and I've lost track of the time. If word has yet to reach here, I suspect it hasn't been more than a few days."

All the workers stopped what they were doing and stood

around listening intently. The constant ringing of the black-smith's hammer ceased and the only sounds in the courtyard were the distant mooing of a cow and the quacking of the ducks.

"What's this all about?" Count Pickering asked as he stepped out of the castle, holding up an arm to shield his squinting eyes from the morning's bright sun. "The boy came in panting for air and said there was an emergency out here."

The count, a slim, middle-aged man with a long, hooked nose and a well-trimmed prematurely gray beard, was dressed in a gold and purple robe pulled over his nightshirt. His wife, Belinda, came up behind him, pulling on her robe and peering out into the courtyard nervously. Hadrian took advantage of Pickering's sun-blindness to chance a long look. She was just as lovely as rumor held. The countess was several years younger than her husband, with a slender, stunning figure and long golden hair, which spilled across her shoulders in a way she would never normally show in public. Hadrian now understood why the count guarded her jealously.

"Oh my," Myron said to Hadrian as he twisted to get a better view. "I don't even think of horses when I look at her."

Hadrian dismounted and helped Myron off the horse. "I share your feelings, my friend, but trust me, that's one woman you *really* don't want to stare at."

"Alric?" the count said. "What in the world are you doing here at this hour?"

"Father, King Amrath has been murdered," Mauvin answered in a shaky voice.

Shock filled Pickering's face. He slowly lowered his arm and stared directly at the prince. "Is this true?"

Alric nodded solemnly. "Several days ago. A traitor stabbed him in the back while he was at prayer."

"Traitor? Who?"

"My uncle, the archduke and lord chancellor—Percy Braga."

✧

Royce, Hadrian, and Myron followed their noses to the kitchen after Alric had left for a private meeting with Count Pickering. There they met Ella, a white-haired cook who was all too happy to provide them with a hearty breakfast in order to have first chance at any gossip. The food at Drondil Fields was far superior to the meal they had eaten at the Silver Pitcher Inn. Ella brought wave upon wave of eggs, soft powdered pastries, fresh sweet butter, steaks, bacon, biscuits, peppered potatoes, and gravy along with a jug of apple cider and an apple pie baked with maple syrup for dessert.

They ate their fill in the relative quiet of the kitchen. Hadrian repeated little more than what Alric had already revealed in the courtyard; however, he did mention that Myron had lived his life in seclusion at the monastery. Ella seemed fascinated by this and questioned the monk mercilessly on the subject. "So, you never saw a woman before today, love?" Ella asked Myron, who was finishing the last of his pie. He was eating heartily and there was a ring of apples and crust around his mouth.

"You're the first one I've ever spoken to," Myron replied as if he were boasting a great achievement.

"Really?" Ella said with a smile and feigned bashfulness. "I'm so honored. I haven't been a man's first in years." She laughed but Myron only looked at her, puzzled.

"You've a lovely home," Myron told her. "It looks very... sturdy."

She laughed again. "It's not mine, ducky, I just work here. It belongs to the nobles, like all the nice places do. Us normal folk, we lives in sheds and shacks and fights over what they throw away. We're sorta like dogs that way, aren't we? Course, I ain't complaining. The Pickerings aren't a bad lot. Not as snooty as some of the other nobles, who think the sun rises and falls because it pleases them. The count won't even have a chambermaid. He doesn't let no one help him dress neither. I've even seen him fetch water for himself more than once. He's downright daft, that one. His boys take after him too. You can see it in the way they saddle their own horses. That Fanen, why, just the other day I seen him swinging a smith's hammer. He was having Vern show him how to mend a blade. Now I asks you, how many nobles you see trying to learn the blacksmith trade? Can I get anyone another cup of cider?"

They all shook their heads and took turns yawning.

"Lenare, now she takes after her mother. They're a pair, they are. Both are pretty as a rose and smell just as sweet, but they do has their thorns. The temper those two have is frightful. The daughter is worse than the mother. She used to train with her brothers and was beating the stuffing out of Fanen until she discovered she was a lady and they don't do such things."

Myron's eyes closed and his head drooped, and suddenly the chair toppled as the monk fell over. He woke with a start and struggled to his knees. "Oh, I'm terribly sorry, I didn't mean to—"

Ella was so busy laughing she couldn't answer and simply waved her hand at him. "You've had a long night, dear," she finally managed to say. "Let me set you up in the back before that chair bucks you off again."

Myron hung his head and said quietly, "I have the same problem with horses."

❦

Alric told his story to the Pickerings over breakfast. As soon as he finished, the count shooed his sons out and called for his staff to begin arranging for a full-scale mobilization of Galilin. While Pickering dispatched orders, Alric left the great hall and began wandering through the corridors of the castle. This was the first time he had been alone since his father's death. He felt as though he was caught up in the current of a river, whisked along by the events unfolding around him. Now it was time to take control of his destiny.

Alric saw few people in the corridors. Aside from the occasional suit of armor or painting on the wall, there was little to distract his thoughts. Drondil Fields, though smaller than Essendon, felt larger due to its horizontal layout, which sprawled across the better part of the hilltop. Where Essendon Castle had several towers and lofty chambers that rose many stories high, Drondil Fields was only four stories at its tallest point. Because it was a fortress, fireproofing was essential, so the roof was made of stone rather than wood, requiring thick walls to support its weight. Because the windows were small and deep, they let in little light, which made the interior cave-like.

He remembered running through these corridors as a child, chasing Mauvin and Fanen. They had held mock battles, which the Pickerings had always won. He had always trumped them by bringing up that he would be king someday. At the age of twelve, it had been wonderful to be able to taunt a friend who had bested him with "Sure, but I'll be king. You'll have to bow to me and do as I say." The thought that in order for him to become king his father would have to die had never really occurred to him. He had no idea what being the king really meant.

I am king now.

Being king had always been something he had imagined to be far, far in the future. His father had been a strong man, and Alric had looked forward to many years as prince of the realm. Only a few months ago, at the Summersrule Festival, he and

Mauvin had made plans to go on a yearlong trip to the four corners of Apeladorn. They had wanted to visit Delgos, Calis, and Trent and even planned to seek the location of the fabled ruined city of Percepliquis. To discover and explore the ancient capital of the Old Novronian Empire had been a childhood dream of theirs. They wanted to find fortune and adventure in the lost city. Mauvin hoped to discover the rest of the lost arts of the Teshlor Knights, and Alric was going to find the ancient crown of Novron. While they had mentioned the trip to their fathers, neither one had brought up Percepliquis. It hardly mattered, given that no one knew where the lost city was, but it was considered heresy even to search for the ancient capital of the Old Empire. Still, walking the fabled halls of Percepliquis was probably the boyhood dream of every youth in Apeladorn. For Alric, though, his adolescence was over.

I am king now.

Dreams of endless days of reckless adventures, exploring the frontier while drinking bad ale, sleeping beneath the open sky, and loving nameless women, blew away like smoke in the wind. In their place came visions of stone rooms filled with old men with angry faces. He had only occasionally watched his father hold court, listening while the clergy and the nobles demanded fewer taxes and more land. One earl had even demanded the execution of a duke and the custody of his lands for the loss of one of his prized cows. Alric's father sat, in what Alric felt must have been dull misery, as the court secretary read the many petitions and grievances on which the king was required to rule. As a child, Alric had thought being king meant doing whatever he wished. But over the years, he saw what it really meant—compromise and appeasement. A king could not rule without the support of his nobles and the nobles were never happy. They always wanted something and expected the king to deliver.

I am king now.

To Alric, being king felt like a prison sentence. He would spend the rest of his life in service to his people, his nobles, and his family, just as his father had done. He wondered if Amrath had felt the same way when his own father had died. It was something he had never considered before. Amrath as a man and the dreams he might have sacrificed were foreign concepts to the young prince. He wondered if his father had been happy. When Alric remembered him, the images that came to mind were his bushy beard and bright smiling eyes. His father had smiled a great deal. Alric wondered if it was due to his enjoyment of being king or because being with his son gave him a much-needed break from the affairs of state. Alric felt a sudden longing to see his father once more. He wished he had taken time to sit and talk with him, man to man, to ask for his father's council and guidance in preparation for this day. He felt completely alone and uncertain about whether he could live up to the tasks that lay before him. More than anything, he just wished he could disappear.

⁓

The shrill ring of clashing metal awakened Hadrian. After Ella's breakfast, he had wandered into the courtyard. The weather was turning distinctly colder but he found a place to nap on a soft patch of lawn that caught the full face of the sun. He thought he had closed his eyes for only a moment, but when he opened them again, it was well past noon. Across the yard the Pickering boys were back at sparring.

"Come at me again, Fanen," Mauvin ordered, his voice muffled by his helm.

"Why? You're just going to whack me again!"

"You have to learn."

"I don't see why," Fanen protested. "It's not like I'm planning a life in the soldiery or the tournaments. I'm the second son. I'll end up at some monastery stacking books."

"Second sons don't go to abbeys; third sons do." Mauvin lifted his visor to grin at Denek. "Second sons are the spares. You've got to be trained and ready in case I die from some rare disease. If I don't, you'll get to roam the lands, fending for yourself. That means a life as a mercenary or on the tournament circuit. Or if you are lucky, you'll land a post as a sheriff, a marshal, or master-at-arms for some earl or duke. These days, it's almost as good as a landed title, really. Still, you won't get those jobs, or last long as a merc or swordsman, unless you know how to fight. Now come at me again and this time pivot, step, and lunge."

Hadrian walked over to where the boys were fighting and sat on the grass near Denek to watch. Denek, who was only twelve years old, glanced at him curiously. "Who are you?"

"My name is Hadrian," he replied as he extended his hand. The boy shook it, squeezing harder than was necessary. "You're Denek, right? The Pickerings' third son? Perhaps you should speak with my friend Myron, seeing as how I hear you are monastery-bound."

"Am not!" he shouted. "Going to the monastery, I mean. I can fight as well as Fanen."

"I wouldn't be surprised," Hadrian said. "Fanen is flat-footed, and his balance is off. He's not going to improve much either, because Mauvin is teaching him, and Mauvin is favoring his right and rocks back on his left too much."

Denek grinned at Hadrian and then turned to his brothers. "Hadrian says you both fight like girls!"

"What's that?" Mauvin said, whacking aside Fanen's loose attack once more.

"Oh, ah, nothing," Hadrian said, trying to recant, and

glared at Denek, who just kept grinning. "Thanks a lot," he told the boy.

"So, you think you can beat me in a duel?" Mauvin asked.

"No, it's not that. I was just explaining I didn't think Denek here would have to go to the monastery."

"Because we fight like girls," Fanen added.

"No, no, nothing like that."

"Give him your sword," Mauvin told Fanen.

Fanen threw his sword at Hadrian. It dove point down in the sod not more than a foot before his feet. The hilt swayed back and forth like a rocking horse.

"You're one of the thieves Alric told us about, aren't you?" Mauvin swiped his sword deftly through the air in a skillful manner that he had not used in his mock battles with his brother. "Despite this great adventure you all have been on, I don't recall Alric mentioning your great prowess with a blade."

"Well, he probably just forgot," Hadrian joked.

"Are you aware of the legend of the Pickerings?"

"Your family is known to be skillful with swords."

"So you *have* heard? My father is the second-best swordsman in Avryn."

"He's the best," Denek snapped. "He would have beaten the archduke if he had his sword, but he had to use a substitute, which was too heavy and awkward."

"Denek, how many times do I have to tell you, when speaking of one's reputation, it does not boost your position to make excuses when you lose a contest. The archduke won the match. You need to face that fact," Mauvin admonished. Turning his attention back to Hadrian, he said, "Speaking of contests, why don't you pick up that blade, and I'll demonstrate the Tek'chin for you."

Hadrian picked up the sword and stepped into the dirt ring

where the boys had been fighting. He made a feint, followed by a stab, which Mauvin easily deflected.

"Try again," Mauvin said.

Hadrian tried a slightly more sophisticated move. This time he swung right and then pivoted left and cut upward toward Mauvin's thigh. Mauvin moved with keen precision. He anticipated the feint and knocked the blade away once more.

"You fight like a street thug," Mauvin commented.

"Because that's what he is," Royce assured them as he approached from the direction of the keep, "a big, dumb street thug. I once saw an old woman batter him senseless with a butter churn." He shifted his attention to Hadrian. "*Now* what have you gotten yourself into? Looks like this kid will hand you a beating."

Mauvin stiffened and glared at Royce. "I would remind you that I'm a count's son, and as such, you will refer to me as *lord*, or at least *master*, but not *kid*."

"Better watch out, Royce, or he'll be after you next," Hadrian said, moving around the circle, looking for an opening. He tried another attack but that, too, was blocked.

Mauvin moved in now with a rapid step. He caught Hadrian's sword hilt-to-hilt, placed a leg behind him, and threw Hadrian to the ground.

"You're too good for me," Hadrian conceded as Mauvin held out a hand to help him to his feet.

"Try him again," Royce shouted.

Hadrian gave him an irritated look and then noticed a young woman entering the courtyard. It was Lenare. She wore a long gown of soft gold, which nearly matched her hair. She was as lovely as her mother and walked over to join the group.

"Who is this?" she asked, motioning at Hadrian.

"Hadrian Blackwater," he said with a bow.

"Well, Mr. Blackwater, it appears my brother has beaten you."

"It would appear so," Hadrian acknowledged, still dusting himself off.

"It's nothing to be ashamed of. My brother is a very accomplished swordsman—too accomplished, in fact. He has a nasty tendency to chase away any would-be suitors."

"They are not worthy of you, Lenare," Mauvin said.

"Try him again," Royce repeated. There was a perceptible note of mischief in his voice.

"Shall we?" Mauvin asked politely with a bow.

"Oh, please do," Lenare bade him, clapping her hands in delight. "Don't be afraid. He won't kill you. Father doesn't like them to actually hurt anyone."

With an evil smirk directed toward Royce, Hadrian turned to face Mauvin. This time he made no attempt to defend himself. He stood perfectly still, holding his blade low. His gaze was cool and he stared directly into Mauvin's eyes.

"Put up a guard, you fool," Mauvin told him. "At least *try* to defend yourself."

Hadrian raised his sword slowly, more in response to Mauvin's request than as a move to defend. Mauvin stepped in with a quick flick of his blade designed to set Hadrian off his footing. He then pivoted around behind the larger man and sought to trip him up once more. Hadrian, however, also pivoted and, swinging a leg, caught Mauvin behind the knees, dropping him to the dirt.

Mauvin looked curiously at Hadrian as he helped him to his feet. "Our street thug has some surprises, I see," Mauvin muttered with a smile.

This time, Mauvin struck at Hadrian in a fast set of sweeping attacks, most of which never caught anything but air as

Hadrian avoided the strokes. Mauvin moved in a flurry, his blade traveling faster than the eye could follow. The steel rang now as Hadrian caught the strokes with his blade, parrying them aside.

"Mauvin, be careful!" Lenare shouted.

The battle rapidly escalated from friendly sparring to serious combat. The strokes moved faster, harder, and closer. The shrill ring of the blades began to echo off the courtyard walls. The grunts and curses became grimmer. The match went on for some time, the two fighting toe to toe. Suddenly Mauvin executed a brilliant maneuver. Feinting left, he swung right, following through the stroke and spinning fully around, exposing his back to Hadrian. Seeing his opponent vulnerable, Hadrian made the obvious riposte, but Mauvin miraculously caught his blade instinctively without seeing it. Pivoting again, Mauvin brought his own sword to Hadrian's undefended side. Before he could finish the blow, however, Hadrian closed the distance between them and Mauvin's swing ran behind the larger man's back. Hadrian trapped the boy's sword arm under his own and raised his sword to the boy's throat. There was a gasp from Mauvin's siblings. Royce simply chuckled with sinister relish. Releasing his grip, Hadrian set Mauvin free.

"How did you do that?" Mauvin asked. "I performed a flawless Vi'shin Flurry against you. It's one of the most advanced maneuvers of the Tek'chin. No one has ever countered it before."

Hadrian shrugged. "First time for everything." He threw the sword back toward Fanen. It pierced the earth between the boy's feet. Unlike the previous time, it dove in edge first, so the hilt did not swing.

With his eyes on Hadrian and an expression of awe on his

face, Denek turned to Royce and said, "That must have been an awfully wicked old lady and a big butter churn."

&

"Alric?"

The prince had wandered into one of the castle storerooms and was sitting on the thick sill of a barrel-vaulted window, looking out at the western hills. The sound of his friend's voice roused him from deep thoughts, and it was not until then that he realized he was crying.

"Sorry," Mauvin said, "but Father's been looking for you. The local nobles have started to arrive, and I think he wants you to talk to them."

"It's okay," Alric said, wiping his cheeks and glancing longingly once more out the window at the setting sun. "I've been here longer than I thought. I guess I lost track of the time."

"It's easy to do in here." Mauvin walked around the room and took a bottle of wine out of a crate. "Remember the night we snuck down here and drank three of these?"

Alric nodded. "I was really sick."

"So was I, and yet we still managed to make the stag hunt the next day."

"We couldn't let anyone know we were drinking."

"I thought I was going to die, and when we got back, it turned out Arista, Lenare, and Fanen had already turned us in the night before."

"I remember."

Mauvin studied his friend carefully. "You'll make a good king, Alric. And I'm sure your father would be proud."

Alric did not say anything for a moment. He picked up a bottle from the crate and felt its weight in his hand. "I'd better get back. I have responsibilities now. I can't hide down here drinking wine like the old days."

"I suppose we could if you really wanted to." Mauvin grinned devilishly.

Alric smiled and threw his arms around him. "You're a good friend. I'm sorry we'll never get to Percepliquis now."

"It's all right; besides, you never know. We might get there someday."

As they left the storeroom, Alric dusted off his hands dirt that he had picked up from Mauvin's back during their embrace. "Is Fanen getting so good now that he was able to put you in the dirt?"

"No, it was the thief you brought with you, the big one. Where did you find him? His skill at sword fighting is unlike anything I've ever seen. It's actually rather remarkable."

"Really? Coming from a Pickering, that's high praise indeed."

"I'm afraid the Pickering legend won't last long at this rate: Father loses to Percy Braga, and now I get thrown in the dirt by a common ruffian. How long will it be before we are being challenged for our land and title by the other nobles without fear?"

"If your father had his sword that day..." Alric paused. "Why didn't your father have his sword?"

"Misplaced it," Mauvin said. "He was certain it was in his room, but the next morning, it was gone. A steward found it later the same day laying somewhere strange."

"Well, sword or no, I can tell you, Mauvin, I think your father is still the best swordsman in the kingdom."

∽

Royce, Hadrian, and Myron continued to enjoy the hospitality of the Pickerings with a hearty lunch as well as supper served to them in the warm comfort of Ella's kitchen. They spent most of the day napping, recovering lost sleep from the previous days. By nightfall, they were beginning to feel like themselves again.

Hadrian had a newfound shadow as Denek followed him wherever he went. After supper, Denek asked Hadrian, Royce, and Myron to come watch the marshaling of the troops from one of his favorite spots. The boy led them to the parapet above the main gate. From there, they could see both the grounds outside the castle and inside the courtyard without being underfoot.

Around early evening people began to arrive. Small groups of knights, barons, squires, soldiers, and village officials trickled in and formed camps outside the castle. Tall poles bearing the banners of various noble houses stood in the courtyard, signaling their presence in accordance with their sworn duty. By moonrise, eight standards and about three hundred men gathered in camps around bonfires. Their tents littered the hillside and extended throughout the orchards.

Vern, along with five other blacksmiths from various villages, worked late, sharing his forge and anvil. They were hammering out last-minute requests. The rest of the courtyard was equally active, with every lamp lit and each shop busy. Leatherworkers adjusted saddle stirrups and helms. Fletchers fashioned bundles of arrows, which they stacked like cordwood against the stable wall. Woodcutters created large rectangular archer shields. Even the butchers and bakers worked hard, preparing sack meals from smoked meats, breads, onions, and turnips.

"The green one with the hammer on it is Lord Jerl's banner," Denek told them. The weather had turned sharply cold again, and his breath created a frosty fog. "I spent a summer at their estate two years ago. It's right on the edge of the

Longwood Forest, and they love to hunt. They must have two dozen of the realm's best hounds. It's where I learned to shoot a bow. I bet you know how to shoot a bow real well, don't you, Hadrian?"

"I've been known to hit the forest from the field on occasion."

"I bet you could outshoot any of Jerl's sons. He's got six, and they all think they are the best marksmen in the province. My father never taught us archery. He said it didn't make sense because we would never be fighting in ranks. He taught us to concentrate on the sword. Although I don't know what good it will do me if I'm sent to a monastery. I'll be stuck doing nothing but reading all day."

"Actually, there is a great deal more than that to do in an abbey," Myron explained, pulling the blanket around his shoulders tighter. "In spring, most of your time will be spent gardening, and in autumn, there is the harvest, preserving, and brewing. Even in winter, there is the mending and cleaning. Of course the bulk of your time is spent in prayer, either communal in the chapel or silently in the cloister. Then there is—"

"I think I'd rather be a foot soldier," Denek sighed with a grimace. "Or maybe I could join you two and become a thief! It must be a wonderfully exciting life running all over the world, accomplishing dangerous missions for king and country."

"You'd think that, wouldn't you?" Hadrian muttered softly.

Below them, a single rider quickly approached the front gate.

"Isn't that the banner of Essendon?" Royce asked, pointing to the falcon flag the rider carried.

"Yeah," Denek said, surprised. "It's the king's standard. He's a messenger from Medford."

They looked at each other, puzzled, as the messenger entered the castle and did not reemerge. They went on talking with Myron, who was trying in vain to convince Denek life in the monastery was not bad at all, when Fanen came running up the parapet.

"There you are!" he shouted at them. "Father has half the castle turned out looking for you."

"Us?" Hadrian asked.

"Yes." Fanen nodded. "He wants to see the two thieves in his chambers right away."

"You didn't steal the silver or anything, did you, Royce?" Hadrian asked.

"I would bet it has more to do with your flirting with Lenare this afternoon and threatening Mauvin just to show off," Royce retorted.

"That was your fault," Hadrian said, jabbing his finger at him.

"It's nothing like that," Fanen said, interrupting them. "The princess Arista is going to be executed for treason tomorrow morning!"

❦

Once, long ago, the great hall of Drondil Fields had been the site of the first court of Melengar. It was there that King Tolin had drafted and signed the Drondil Charter, officially bringing the kingdom into existence. Now, old and faded, the parchment was mounted on one wall in a place of honor. Around it, massive burgundy drapes hung, tied back by gold cords with silken tassels. Today the hall served as the council chambers of Count Pickering; Royce and Hadrian hesitantly entered the hall.

At a long table in the center of the room sat a dozen men

dressed in the finery of nobles. Hadrian recognized most of the men and could make some good guesses at the identities of those he did not know. There were earls, barons, sheriffs, and marshals; the leadership of eastern Melengar sat assembled before them. At the head of the table was Alric, and at his right was Count Pickering. Standing behind the count was Mauvin, and as Hadrian and Royce entered, Fanen took up position next to his brother. Alric was dressed in fine clothes, no doubt borrowed from one of the Pickerings. Less than a day had passed since Hadrian had last seen the prince, but Alric looked much older than he remembered.

"Have you told them why they were summoned?" Count Pickering asked his son.

"I told them the princess was to be executed," Fanen replied. "Nothing more."

"I've been summoned by Archduke Percy Braga," Count Pickering explained, holding up the dispatch, "to report to Essendon Castle as witness for the immediate trial of Princess Arista on the grounds of witchcraft, high treason, and murder. He has accused her of killing not only Amrath but also Alric." He dropped the dispatch on the table and slammed his hand down on it in disgust. "The blackguard means to have the kingdom for his own!"

"It's worse than I feared." Alric summarized for the thieves: "My uncle planned to kill me and my father and then blame both murders on Arista. He will execute her and take the kingdom for himself. No one will be the wiser. He'll fool everyone into thinking he is the great defender of the realm. I'm sure his plan will work. Even I was suspecting her only a few days ago."

"It's true. It has long been rumored that Arista has dabbled in the arcane arts," Pickering confirmed. "Braga will have no trouble finding her guilty. People are afraid of what they don't understand. The thought of a woman with magical powers is terrifying to old men in comfortable positions. Even without the fear of witchery, most nobles are uncomfortable with the thought of a woman monarch. The verdict will be assured. Her sentence will be handed down quickly."

"But if the prince was to arrive," Baron Enild said, "and show he's alive, then—"

"That's exactly what Braga wants," Sir Ecton declared. "He can't find Alric. He's searched for days and couldn't locate him. He wants to draw him out before Alric has a chance to gather an army against him. He's counting on the prince's youth and lack of experience. He wants to manipulate the prince to react with emotion instead of reason. If he can't find Alric, he will lure the prince to him."

"Less than half our forces have mustered so far," Pickering grumbled despairingly. He walked to the great map of Melengar, which hung opposite the ancient charter, and slapped the western half of the map. "Our most powerful knights are the farthest from here, and because they have the most men to rally, it will take them longer to report. I don't expect them for another eight hours, maybe as long as sixteen.

"Even if we resign ourselves to employing only Galilin's forces, the earliest we could be ready to attack wouldn't be until tomorrow evening. By then Arista will be dead. I could march with what troops I have, leaving orders for the others to follow, but doing so would risk the whole army by dividing our forces. We cannot jeopardize the realm for the sake of one woman, even though she is the princess."

"Judging from the mercenaries we encountered at the inn," Alric told them, "I suspect the archduke anticipates an assault and has strengthened his forces with purchased arms loyal only to him."

"He will likely have scouts and ambushes prepared," Ecton

said. "At first sight of our march, he will tell the other nobles assembled for the trial that we are working for Arista and that they need to defend Essendon against us. There is simply no way for us to march until we have more forces."

"Waiting," Alric said sadly, "will surely see Arista burned at the stake. Now, more than ever, I feel guilty for not trusting her. She saved my life. Now hers is in jeopardy, and there is little I can do about it." He looked at Hadrian and Royce. "I can't simply sit idly by and let her die. But to act prematurely would be folly."

The prince stood and walked over to the thieves. "I have inquired about you two since we arrived. You've been holding out on me. I thought you were common thieves. So imagine my surprise when I discovered you two are famous." He glanced around at the other nobles in the room. "Rumor has it you two are unusually gifted agents known for taking difficult, sometimes nearly impossible, assignments of sabotage, theft, espionage, and even, on rare occasions, assassinations. Don't bother denying it. Many in this room have already confided in me that they have used your services in the past."

Hadrian looked at Royce and then around at the faces of the men before them. He nodded uncomfortably. Not only were some of the men past clients, some had been targets as well.

"They tell me you are independents and are not aligned with any established guilds. It's no small feat to operate with such autonomy. I have learned more in a few hours from them than I did after days riding with you. What I do know, however—what I discovered for myself—is that you saved my life twice, once to honor a promise to my sister and once for no reason I can discern. Last night, you challenged the might of the Lord Chancellor of Melengar and came to my aid against a superior force of trained killers. No one asked you to, no one would have faulted you for letting me die. You could expect no reward for saving me, and yet you did it. Why?"

Hadrian looked at Royce, who stood silent. "Well," he began as he glanced at the floor, "I guess—we'd just grown kind of fond of you, I suppose."

Alric smiled and addressed the room. "The life of the Prince of Melengar—the would-be king—was saved, not by his army, not by his loyal bodyguards, nor by a grand fortress—but by two treacherous, impudent thieves who didn't have the good sense to ride away."

The prince stepped forward and placed a hand on each of their shoulders. "I'm already deeply in your debt and have no right to ask, but I must beg you now to display the same poor judgment once again. Please save my sister and you can name whatever price you wish."

&

"Another last-minute, good-deed job," Royce grumbled as he stuffed supplies into his saddlebag.

"True," Hadrian said, slinging his sword belt over his shoulder, "but this is at least a *paying* job."

"You should have told him the real reason we saved him from Trumbul—because we wouldn't see the hundred tenents otherwise."

"That was *your* reason. Besides, how often do we get to do royal contracts? If word gets around, we'll be able to command top salaries."

"If word gets around, we'll be hanged."

"Okay, good point. But remember, she did save our skins. If Arista hadn't helped us out of the dungeon, we'd be ornaments for the Medford Autumn Festival right now."

Royce paused and sighed. "I didn't say we weren't doing it,

did I? Did I say that? No I didn't. I told the little prince we'd do it. Just don't expect me to be happy about it."

"I just want to make you feel better about your decision," Hadrian said. Royce glared at him. "Okay, okay, I'll see about the horses now." He grabbed his gear and headed for the courtyard, where a light snow was starting to fall.

Pickering had provided the thieves with two of his swiftest stallions and any supplies they thought they might need. Ella had a late-night snack and a sizable travel meal prepared for them. They took heavy woolen cloaks to brace against the cold and dark scarves that they wrapped around the lower half of their faces to keep the chill of the wind off their cheeks.

"I hope we will meet again soon," Myron told them as they prepared their mounts. "You two are the most fascinating people I have ever met, although I suppose that isn't saying a lot, is it?"

"It's the thought that counts," Hadrian told him, and gave the monk a bear hug, which caught the little man by surprise. As they climbed into their saddles, Myron bowed his head and muttered a soft prayer.

"There," Hadrian told Royce, "we've got Maribor on our side. Now you can relax."

"Actually," Myron said sheepishly, "I was praying for the horses. But I *will* pray for you as well," he added hastily.

Alric and the Pickerings came out to the courtyard to see them off. Even Lenare joined them, wrapped in a white fur cape. The fluffy muffler was wrapped so high on her shoulders that it hid the lower portion of her face. Only her eyes could be seen.

"If you can't get her out," Pickering said, "try to stall the execution until our forces can arrive. Once they do, however, you'd better have her secured. I'm certain Braga will kill her out of desperation. Oh, and one more thing: don't try to fight

Braga. He's the best swordsman in Melengar. Leave him for me." The count slapped the elegant rapier he wore at his side. "This time I'll have my own sword, and the archduke will feel its sting."

"I'll be leading the attack on Essendon," Alric informed them. "It's my duty as ruler. So if you do reach my sister and if I should fall before the end of this, let her know I'm sorry for not trusting her. Let her know..." He faltered for a moment. "Let her know I loved her and I think she will make a fine queen."

"You'll tell her yourself, Your Majesty," Hadrian assured him.

Alric nodded and then added, "And I'm sorry about what I said to you before. You two are the best royal protectors I could ever hope for. Now go. Save my sister or I'll have you both thrown back in my dungeon!"

They bowed respectfully in their saddles, then turned their horses and urged them into a gallop. They rode out the gate into the cold black of night.

CHAPTER 8

TRIALS

The morning of Arista Essendon's trial arrived along with the first snow. Despite not having slept, Percy Braga did not feel the least bit tired. Having set the wheels in motion the previous morning by sending the trial announcements, he had a hundred details demanding his personal attention. He was just rechecking his witness list when there was a knock at the door to his office and a servant entered.

"I'm sorry to disturb you, sir," the man said with a bow. "Bishop Saldur is here. He told me you wanted to see him?"

"Of course, of course, send him in," the archduke replied.

The elderly cleric entered, wearing his dress robes of black and red. Braga crossed the room and kissed his ring as he bowed. "Thank you for seeing me so early, Your Grace. Are you hungry? May I arrange for some breakfast?"

"No, thank you, I've already eaten. At my age, one tends to wake early whether one wants to or not. What exactly did you want to see me about?"

"I just wanted to make sure you didn't have any questions about your testimony today. We could go over it now if you do. I've scheduled some time."

"Ah, I see," the bishop replied, nodding slowly. "I don't

think that will be necessary. I have a clear understanding of what is required."

"Wonderful, then I think everything is in order."

"Excellent," the bishop said, and glanced toward the decanter. "Is that brandy I see?"

"Yes, would you like some?"

"Normally I wouldn't indulge so early, but this is a special occasion."

"Absolutely, Your Grace."

The bishop took a seat near the fire as Braga poured two glasses of brandy and handed one to him. "To the new Melengar regime," the archduke proposed. The crystal rang clear, like a bell, as their glasses touched. Then each took a deep drink.

"There's just something about a bit of brandy on a snowy day," Saldur remarked with a tone of satisfaction in his voice. The cleric had white hair and gentle-looking eyes. Sitting in the glow of the fire, casually cupping the glass in his wrinkled hand, he appeared the quintessential kindhearted grandfather. Braga knew better. He could not have risen to his present position without being ruthless. As bishop, Saldur was one of the chief officers of the Nyphron Church and the ranking clergy in the kingdom of Melengar. He worked and resided in the great Mares Cathedral, an edifice just as imposing as, and certainly more beloved than, Essendon Castle. As far as influence was concerned, Braga estimated that of the nineteen bishops who comprised the leadership of the faithful, Saldur must be in the top three.

"How long before the trial?" Saldur asked.

"We'll begin in about an hour or so."

"I must say, you've handled this very well, Percy." Saldur smiled at him. "The church is quite pleased. Our investment in you was substantial, but it would appear we made a wise choice. When dealing with timetables as long as we are, it's difficult to be sure we've put the right people in place. Each of these annexations needs to be handled delicately. We don't want anyone suspecting us of stacking the deck the way we are. When the time comes, it has to appear as if all the monarchies voluntarily accept the formation of the New Empire. I must admit, I had some doubts about you."

Braga raised an eyebrow. "I'm surprised to hear you say that."

"Well, you didn't look as though you had the makings of a king when we arranged your marriage to Amrath's sister. You were a scrawny, pretentious, little—"

"That was nearly twenty years ago," Braga protested.

"True enough. However, at the time, all I noticed about you was your skill with a sword and your staunch Imperialist view. I was afraid that being so young, you might—well, who knew if you'd stay loyal? But you proved me wrong. You've grown into an able administrator, and your ability to adapt in the face of unexpected events, like this sudden timetable shift Arista caused, proves your capability to manage problems effectively."

"Well, I'll admit it hasn't gone exactly as I planned. Alric's escape was unexpected. I clearly underestimated the princess, but at least she was good enough to provide me a convenient means to implicate her."

"So, exactly what are you planning to do about Arista's little brother? Do you know where he is?"

"Yes, he is at Drondil Fields. I have several reports of the mustering of Galilin. Troops are converging at Pickering's castle."

"And you're not concerned about that?"

"Let's just say I wish I could have caught the little brat before he reached Pickering. But I'll be turning my attentions to him as soon as I conclude with his sister. I hope to take care of him before he can bolster too much support. He's been quite elusive. He slipped through my fingers at the Wicend Ford. Not only did he escape but he also took horses from my men. I thought he would be easy to find, and I had scores of troops watching every road, valley, and village, but for several days he just vanished."

"And that's when he got through to Pickering?"

"Oh, no," Braga said. "I actually managed to catch him. A patrol picked him up at the Silver Pitcher Inn."

"Then I don't understand. Why isn't he here?"

"Because my patrol never came back. An advance rider brought the news Alric was captured, but the rest of them disappeared. I investigated and heard some amazing rumors. According to my reports, two men traveling with the prince organized the locals and staged an ambush on the men bringing Alric in."

"Do you know who these two men were who came to Alric's aid?"

"I have no names, but the prince called them his royal protectors. I'm certain, however, they're the same two thieves I set up to take the blame for Amrath's death. Somehow, the prince has managed to retain their services. He must have offered them riches, perhaps even land and title. The boy is more clever than I thought. But no matter, I have made adequate arrangements for him and his friends. I've been bolstering the ranks of the Melengar army for the last several weeks with mercenaries loyal to my money. Amrath never knew. One of the perks of being the lord chancellor is not having to get the royal seal on all orders."

There was another knock at the door, and the servant once again entered. "The Earl of Chadwick is here to see you, my lord."

"Archibald Ballentyne? What is he doing here? Get rid of him."

"No, wait," the bishop said, intervening. "I asked the earl to come. Please send him in." The servant bowed and left, closing the door behind him.

"I wish you had discussed this with me," Braga said. "Forgive me, Your Grace, but I have too much going on today to entertain a visit from a neighboring noble."

"Yes, yes. I know you are quite busy, but the church has its own matters to attend to. As you well know, you're not the only kingdom we administer to. The Earl of Chadwick possesses a certain interest to us. He is young, ambitious, and easily impressed by success. It will do him good to see firsthand just what kinds of things are possible with the right *friends*. Besides, having an ally on your southern border has benefits for you as well."

"Are you suggesting I try and sway him away from King Ethelred?"

"Ethelred is a good Imperialist, I admit, but there can be only one emperor. There's no reason it couldn't be you, assuming you continue to prove yourself worthy. Ballentyne has many assets that could help in that endeavor."

"I'm not even king yet and you're talking emperor?"

"The church hasn't lasted for three thousand years by not thinking ahead. Ah, here he is. Come in, come in, Archibald." Archibald Ballentyne entered, brushing the snow from his cloak and stomping his feet. "Toss your cloak aside and come to the fire. Warm up, lad. The carriage ride must have been a cold one."

Archibald crossed the room and kissed the ring of the still seated bishop. "Good morning, Your Grace," he said, then turned and bowed graciously to the archduke. "My lord."

He swept off his cloak and shook it out carefully. Perplexed, he looked around. "Your servant left before taking my cloak."

"Just throw it anywhere," Braga instructed.

The earl looked at him, aghast. "This is imported damask with gold thread embroideries." Just then, the servant reentered with a large comfortable chair. "Ah, there you are. Here, take this, and for Maribor's sake, don't hang it from a peg." He passed his cloak to the servant, who bowed and left.

"Brandy?" Braga asked.

"Oh, good lord, yes," Archibald replied. Braga handed him a glass, the bottom of which was filled with a smoky amber liquid.

"I appreciate your coming, Archibald," the bishop said. "I'm afraid we won't have much time to talk just now; there is quite a bit of turmoil in Melengar today. But as I was telling Braga, I thought it might be beneficial for the three of us to have a quick chat."

"I'm always at your service, of course, Your Grace. I appreciate any opportunity to meet with you and the new King of Melengar," Archibald said nonchalantly. Saldur and Braga exchanged looks. "Oh, come now, it can hardly be a secret. You are the archduke and lord chancellor. With King Amrath and the prince dead, if you execute Arista, you'll wear the crown. It's really rather nicely done. I commend you. Murder in broad daylight, right before the nobles—they'll cheer you on as you steal their crown."

Braga stiffened. "Are you accusing me of—"

"Of course not," the earl said, stopping him. "I accuse no one. What care do I have for the affairs of Melengar? My liege is Ethelred of Warric. What happens in your kingdom is none of my affair. I was merely offering my *sincere* congratulations"—he raised his glass and nodded at the bishop—"to both of you."

"Do you have a name for this game, Ballentyne?" Braga asked tentatively as both he and Saldur watched the young earl closely.

Archibald smiled again. "My dear gentlemen, I'm playing no game. I'm being truthful when I say I'm simply in awe. All the more because of my own recent failure. You see, I tried a gamble myself, to increase my station, only it was less than successful."

Braga became quite amused with this primly dressed earl. He understood what the bishop saw in him and he was curious now. "I'm very sorry to hear you suffered difficulties. Exactly what were you attempting?"

"Well, I acquired some letters and tried to blackmail the Marquis of Glouston into marrying his daughter to me so I could obtain his Rilan Valley. I had the messages locked in my safe in my private tower and was prepared to present them to Victor in person. Everything was perfect but—*poof*." Archibald made an exploding gesture with his fingers. "The letters vanished. Like a magic trick."

"What happened to them?" Saldur asked.

"They were stolen. Thieves sawed a hole in the roof of my tower and, in just a matter of minutes, slipped in and snatched them from underneath my very nose."

"Impressive," Saldur said.

"Depressing is what it was. They made me look like a fool."

"Did you catch the thieves?" Braga asked.

Archibald shook his head. "Sadly, no, but I finally figured out who they are. It took me days to reason it out. I did not tell anyone I possessed those letters. So the only ones who could have taken them are the same thieves which I hired in the first place. Cunning devils. They call themselves Riyria. I'm not sure why they stole them; perhaps they planned to charge me twice, but I won't give them the satisfaction, of course. I'll hire someone else to intercept the next set from the Winds Abbey."

"So, the letters you had were correspondences between the Marquis of Glouston and King Amrath?" Saldur asked.

Archibald looked at the bishop, surprised. "Interesting

guess, Your Grace. No, they were love letters between his daughter and her Nationalist lover, Gaunt. I planned to have Alenda marry me instead to spare Victor the embarrassment of his daughter being involved with a commoner."

Saldur chuckled.

"Have I said something funny?"

"You had more in your hands than you knew," Saldur informed him. "Those weren't love letters, and they weren't to Degan Gaunt."

"With all due respect, Your Grace, I had the letters in my possession. They were addressed to him."

"I'm sure they were, but that was merely a precaution against someone like you discovering them. It was quite clever, actually. It makes a fine diversion should someone intercept the letters. Degan Gaunt as a lover, I suspect, is meant to represent Lanaklin's desire for revolution against Ethelred. If the marquis stated his opinions openly, he would risk execution. Those letters were actually coded messages from Victor Lanaklin sent by Alenda to a messenger of King Amrath. The Marquis of Glouston is a traitor to his kingdom and the Imperialist cause. Had you realized, you could have had all of Glouston and Victor's head as a wedding gift."

"How do you know?"

"Archduke Braga learned of the meetings when the late king asked him to pay the messenger directly and without record. He of course told me."

Archibald stood silent and then swallowed the rest of his brandy in one mouthful. "But wait, why tell you?"

"Because as a good Imperialist, Percy here knows the importance of keeping the church informed of such things."

Archibald looked at Braga, puzzled. "But you're a Royalist, aren't you? I mean, how could the Lord Chancellor of Melengar be an Imperialist?"

"How indeed?" Saldur asked with a smile.

"By marrying into the royal family," Braga pointed out.

"The church has been surreptitiously placing Imperialists in key positions near the throne of nearly every Royalist kingdom in Avryn and even a few in the nations of Trent and Calis," Saldur explained. "Through unusual accidents, these men have managed to find themselves rulers of most of those realms. The church feels that when the heir is finally found, it will help make a smoother transition if all the various kingdoms are already prepared to pledge their allegiance."

"Incredible."

"Indeed. I must warn you, however, that you won't be able to obtain additional letters. There will be no more meetings at the Winds Abbey. Regrettably, I was forced to ask the archduke to teach the monks a lesson for hosting such meetings. The abbey was burned along with the monks."

"*You* killed your fellow shepherds of Maribor's flock?" Archibald asked Saldur.

"When Maribor sent Novron to us, it was as a warrior to destroy our enemies. Our god is not squeamish at the sight of spilled blood, and it's often necessary to prune weak branches to keep the tree strong. Killing the monks was a necessity, but I did spare one, the son of Lanaklin, so he could return home and let his father know the deaths were on his hands. We can't have Royalists organizing against us, can we?" Saldur smiled at him. The elderly cleric took another sip of his drink, the moment passed, and once more Braga observed the persona of the saintly grandfather.

"So, you were after Glouston, Archibald?" Braga said, refilling the earl's glass. "Perhaps I misjudged you. Tell me, my dear earl, were you more upset you lost the land or Alenda?"

Archibald waved his hand in the air as if he were shooing a fly. "She was merely an added benefit. It's the land I wanted."

"I see." Braga glanced at Saldur, who smiled and nodded. "You may still get it." Braga resumed speaking to the earl. "With me on the throne of Melengar, I'll want a strong Imperialist ally guarding my southern border with Warric."

"King Ethelred would call that treason."

"And what would you call it?"

Archibald smiled and drummed his fingernails on the beautiful cut crystal of the royal brandy glass, making it ring with a pleasant song. "Opportunity."

Braga sat back down and stretched out his feet to the fire. "If I help you obtain the marchland from Lanaklin, and you throw your allegiance to me, Melengar will replace Warric as the strongest kingdom in Avryn. Similarly, *Greater* Chadwick will be its most powerful province."

"That's assuming Ethelred doesn't declare war," Archibald warned. "Kings often frown upon losing a quarter of their realm, and Ethelred is not the type to take such an action without retaliation. He enjoys fighting. What's more, he's good at it. He has the best army in Avryn now."

"True," Braga said. "But he has no able general to command it. He doesn't have anyone near the talent of your Sir Breckton. That man is gifted when it comes to leading men. If you broke with Warric, could you count on his loyalty to you?"

"Breckton's loyalty to me is unwavering. His father, Lord Belstrad, is a chivalrous knight of archaic dimensions. He beat those values into his sons. Neither Breckton nor his brother—what's his name, the younger Belstrad boy, who went to sea— *Wesley*, would dishonor themselves by opposing a man they have sworn their allegiance to. I do admit, however, their honor can be an inconvenience. I remember once a servant dropped my new fustian hat in the mud, and when I commanded Breckton to cut off the clumsy oaf's hand in punishment, he refused. Breckton went on for twenty minutes explaining the code of chivalry to me. Oh yes, my lord, he is indeed loyal to House Ballentyne, but I would rather have a less loyal man who simply obeys without question. It's entirely possible that should I break with Warric, Breckton might refuse to fight at all, but I'm certain he would not oppose me. Personally, I would be more concerned with Ethelred himself. He is a fine commander in his own right."

"True," Braga acknowledged, "but so am I. I would welcome him engaging me personally. I already have a standing veteran army and a number of mercenaries at the ready. I'll be able to muster superior numbers should that prove necessary. The result will be that he would lose all of Warric, and that could provide me the keys to the rest of Avryn and, perhaps, all of Apeladorn."

This time Archibald chuckled. "My, but I do appreciate your ability to *think big*. I can see there would be many advantages to my joining with you. Do you really have your sights on the title of emperor?"

"Why not? If I'm poised to conquer, the Patriarch will be eager to throw his allegiance to me, just as the church did with Glenmorgan. If I promise certain rights to the church, he may even declare me the heir. Then no one will stand against me. In any case, this is for another day. We are getting ahead of ourselves." Braga turned his attention toward the bishop. "I want to thank you, Your Grace, for arranging this meeting. It was very educational. But now it's nearly midmorning, and I think it's time to get Arista's trial under way. I would, however, like to invite you to stay, Archibald. As it turns out, I think I may be able to offer you a gift to show you my commitment to you as a newfound friend of Melengar."

"I'm flattered, my lord. I'd welcome the opportunity to spend time with you, and I'm sure whatever gift you may have will be a generous one."

"You mentioned the thieves who spoiled your move against Victor Lanaklin called themselves Riyria?"

"Yes, I did. Why do you ask?"

"Well, it appears we share a common interest in these two rogues. They have also been a rather painful thorn in my own side. As you already discovered, they pay no respect to people who hire them, and are willing to turn against their employers. I, too, hired them for a task and now find them working against me. I have reason to believe they may be coming here today, and I have set plans in motion to capture them. If they do indeed make an appearance, I'll try them along with Arista. It's quite possible all three will be burning at the stake by early evening."

"You are, indeed, most generous, my lord," Archibald replied with a nod of his head and a smile on his lips.

"I thought you might enjoy that. You mentioned when you arrived that Alric is dead, and that's indeed the notion I've been circulating. Unfortunately, it's not so—that is, not yet. Arista actually arranged for those thieves to smuggle Alric out of this castle on the night of Amrath's death. I believe he has hired them and they will attempt to save her. Evidence indicates they used the sewers to exit the castle, so I've taken extra precautions there. The grate in the kitchen has been sealed, and Wylin, the captain of the castle guard, waits with his best men hidden to close the river grate behind them. I even failed to post guards near there, to make it more enticing. With luck, the fool of a prince might actually play the boyish hero and come with them. If he does—checkmate!"

Archibald nodded with obvious pleasure. "You really are very impressive."

Braga raised his glass in tribute. "To me."

"To you." Archibald drank to Braga's health.

There was a loud pounding on the door. "Come!" Braga called, irritated.

"Lord Chancellor!" One of Braga's hired soldiers burst into the room. His cheeks and nose were red, his armor dripping wet. On his head and shoulders a small bit of snow remained.

"Yes? What is it?"

"The wall guard reports footprints in the snow leading to the river near the sewers, my lord."

"Excellent," Braga replied, draining his glass. "Take eight men and support Captain Wylin from the river. I don't want them escaping. Remember, if the prince is with them, kill him on sight. Don't let Wylin stop you. Either way, I want the thieves alive. Lock them in the dungeons and gag them as before. I'll use them as further incriminating evidence against Arista and burn the whole lot together." The soldier bowed and left.

"Now, gentlemen, as I was saying, let's join the magistrate and the other nobles. I'm anxious to get this trial under way." They all stood, and walking three abreast, they exited the large double doors as one.

ക

The morning sun, magnified by the snow, entered the river grate as a stark white light. The wintry radiance splintered along the glistening ceiling, revealing ancient stone caked in mildew and moss. The frozen sweat of the sewer walls reflected the light, bouncing it back and forth until at last it scattered into the all-consuming darkness. In the gloom, the soldiers waited, crouching and cold. Their feet were ankle-deep in filthy cold water, which streamed between their legs, running from the castle drains to the river. For the better part of four hours, they lingered in silence, but now they could hear the sound of footsteps approaching. The sloshing of the dirty water echoed off the sewer walls, and the distant movement of shadows played upon the stone.

With a motion of his hand, Wylin ordered his troop to hold their position and maintain their silence. He wanted to be certain the rear guard was in place and his prey was in sight before he made his move. There were many avenues in the sewers where two men could run and hide in the dark. He did not want to be chasing the rats through a maze of tunnels. Not only was it unpleasant down there, but Wylin knew the archduke wanted the thieves for the morning festivities and would not be pleased with a long delay.

Soon they came into view. Two men—one tall and broad, the other shorter and slimmer—dressed in warm winter cloaks with hoods pulled high, rounded the corner slowly, pausing from time to time to look about.

"Remind me to compliment His Majesty on the quality of his sewers," one of them mentioned in a mocking tone.

"At least the slime is warmer than the river," the other replied.

"Yeah, too bad this is happening on the coldest day of the year. Why couldn't it be the middle of summer?"

"That would be warmer for sure, but could you imagine the smell?"

"Speaking of smell, do you think we're getting close to the kitchen yet?"

"You're the one leading; I can't see a thing in here."

Wylin waved his arm. *"Move in, now! Take them!"*

The castle guard rushed from their positions in an adjoining tunnel and charged the two men. From behind, more soldiers raced forward, blocking any retreat. The troops encircled the two, swords drawn and shields at the ready.

"Careful," Wylin said, "the archduke says they are full of surprises."

"I'll show you surprises," one of the soldiers from the rear said, and, stepping forward, struck the tall one with the pommel of his sword, dropping him to the ground. Another used his shield and the second man fell unconscious.

Wylin sighed and glared at his ranks, then shrugged. "I was planning on letting them walk but this works too. Chain 'em, gag 'em, and drag 'em to the dungeons. And for Maribor's sake, get their heads up before they drown. Braga wants them alive." The soldiers nodded and went to work.

∽

"This hearing of the High Court of Melengar has been assembled in good order to review allegations made against the princess Arista Essendon by the Lord Chancellor, the Archduke of Melengar, Percy Braga." The strong voice of the chief magistrate boomed across the chamber. "Princess Arista stands duly accused of treason against the crown, the murder of her father and brother, and the practicing of witchcraft."

The largest room in the castle, the Court of Melengar had a cathedral ceiling, stained-glass windows, and walls rimmed in emblems and shields of the noble houses of the kingdom. Bench seats and balconies were overflowing with spectators. The nobles and the city's affluent merchants pressed in to see the royal trial of the princess. Outside, many common people had been gathering since dawn and waited in the snow as runners reported the proceedings. A wall of armor-clad soldiers held them at bay.

The court itself was a boxed set of bleachers composed of

tiered armchairs, where the ranking nobles of the kingdom sat. Several of the seats were vacant but enough had arrived to serve Braga's purpose. Still frosty with the morning chill, most of the court wore fur wraps as they waited for the fire in the great hearth to warm the room. At the front stood the empty throne, its vacancy looming like an ominous specter before the court. Its presence was a stark reminder of the gravity and scope of the trial. The verdict could decide who would sit there next and control the reins of the kingdom.

"This judicial court, comprised of men of good standing and sound wisdom, will now hear the allegations and the evidence. May Maribor grant them wisdom."

The chief magistrate took his seat and a heavyset man with a short beard wreathing his small mouth stood up. He was dressed in expensive-looking robes that flowed behind him as he paced before the jury, eyeing each man carefully.

"Lords of the Court," the lawyer said, addressing the bleachers with a dramatic sweep of his arm. "Your noble personages have by now learned that our good king Amrath was murdered seven days past in this very castle. You may also be aware Prince Alric is missing, presumed abducted and murdered. But how could such things as these happen within a king's own castle walls? A king *might* be murdered. A prince *might* be abducted. But both in the same night and one after the other? How is this possible?"

The crowd quieted as they struggled to hear.

"How is it possible that two killers slipped inside the castle unnoticed, stabbed the king to death, and, despite being caught and locked in the dungeon, were able to escape? This in itself is incredible, because the cell in which they were locked was heavily guarded by skilled soldiers. Not only were they imprisoned, they were also chained by their wrists and ankles to the wall. But what is beyond amazing, what is beyond belief, is that after managing their miraculous escape, the two did not flee! No, indeed! Informed while in captivity that they would be drawn and quartered at dawn—a most painful and gruesome death, to be certain—for their most heinous crime, these two killers remained in a castle filled with hundreds of soldiers ready to thrust them back into their cell. Rather than flee for their lives, instead they sought out the prince, the most heavily guarded and high-profile personage in the castle, and kidnapped him! I ask you again, how is this possible? Were the castle guards asleep? Were they so totally incompetent as to let the killers of the king walk out? Or could it be that the assassins had help?

"Could a guard have done this? A foreign spy? Even a trusted baron or earl? No! None of them would have the authority to enter the dungeon to *see* the killers of the king, much less free them. Nay, gracious lords, no person in the castle that night had the authority to enter those jails so easily, save one—Princess Arista! Being the daughter of the victim, who could deny her the right to spit in the faces of the men who murdered her father so brutally? Only she wasn't there to defile the killers; she came to help them finish the job she started!"

The crowd murmured.

"This is an outrage!" an elderly man protested from the bleachers. "To accuse the poor girl of her father's death... You should be ashamed! Where is she? Why is she not present to dispute these claims?"

"Lord Valin," the lawyer addressed him, "we are honored to have you with us today. This court will call the princess forth shortly. She is not here for the presenting of facts, as it is a tedious and unpleasant matter, and this court does not want the princess to endure it. Likewise, those called to testify can speak freely, without the presence of their future queen, should she be found innocent. And there are still other, more unpleasant reasons, upon which I will elaborate in due time."

This did not appear to change Lord Valin's mood, but he made no further protest and sat back down.

"The court of Melengar calls Reuben Hilfred to testify."

The lawyer paused as the big soldier, still dressed in ring mail and the tabard of the falcon, stood before the court. His stance was proud and straight, but his expression was anything but pleased.

"Hilfred," the lawyer addressed him, "what is your position here at Essendon Castle?"

"I am personal bodyguard to Princess Arista," he told the court in a loud clear voice.

"Tell us, Reuben, what is your rank?"

"I am sergeant-at-arms."

"That's a fairly high rank, isn't it?"

"It is a respected position."

"How did you attain this rank?"

"I was singled out for some reason."

"For some reason? For some reason?" the lawyer repeated, laughing gaily. "Is it not true you were recommended for promotion by Captain Wylin for your years of consistent and unwavering loyalty to the crown? Moreover, is it not true that the *king himself* appointed you to be his daughter's personal bodyguard after you risked your life and saved Arista from the fire that killed the queen mother? Were you not also presented with a commendation for bravery by the king? Are not all these things true?"

"Yes, sir."

"I sense in you a reluctance to be here, Reuben. Am I correct?"

"Yes, sir."

"It is because you are loyal to your princess, and you do

not wish to be a part of anything which might harm her. That is an admirable quality. Still, you are also an honorable man, and as such, you must speak truthfully in your testimony before this court. So tell us, Reuben, what happened the night the king was murdered?"

Hilfred shifted his weight uncomfortably from one foot to the other and then took a breath and spoke. "It was late, and the princess was asleep in her bed. I was on post at the tower stairs when the king was found. Captain Wylin ordered me to check on Princess Arista. Before I reached her door, she came out, startled by the noise."

"How was she dressed?" the lawyer asked.

"In a gown, I am not sure which."

"But she was dressed? Was she not? Not in a robe or nightclothes?"

"Yes, she was dressed."

"You have spent years guarding Arista. Have you ever known her to sleep in her gowns?"

"No."

"Never?"

"Never."

"But I assume you have no doubt stood outside her door when she went to dress for meals or to change after traveling. Does she have servants to help her dress?"

"Yes."

"How many?"

"Three."

"And how long is the fastest you recall her dressing?"

"I am not certain."

"Make a guess; the court will not hold you to the exact time."

"Perhaps twenty minutes."

"Twenty minutes with three servants. That is actually quite

fast, considering all the ties and toggles that require lacing for most ladies' clothing. Now how long would you say it was between the discovery of the king's body and the time the princess came out of her room?"

Hilfred hesitated.

"How long?" the lawyer persisted.

"Perhaps ten minutes."

"Ten minutes, you say? And when she came out of her room, how many servants were with her?"

"None that I saw."

"Amazing! The princess woke up unexpectedly in the dark and managed to dress herself fully in a lavish gown in ten minutes without the help of a single servant!"

The lawyer paced the floor, his head down in thought, a finger tapping his lips. He paused with his back to Hilfred. Then, as if a sudden thought occurred to him, he spun abruptly.

"Tell us, how did she take the news of the king's death?"

"She was shocked."

"Did she weep?"

"I am sure she did."

"But did you *see* her?"

"No."

"Then what happened?"

"She went to Prince Alric's chambers to find him and was surprised he was not there. She then—"

"Please stop there just a minute. She went to *Alric's* chambers? She learns her father is murdered and her first inclination is to go to her brother's room? Did you not find it odd she did not immediately rush to her father's side? After all, no one had suggested any harm had come to Alric, had they?"

"No."

"What happened next?"

"She went to view her father's body, and Alric arrived."

"After the prince sentenced the prisoners to death, what did the princess do?"

"I do not understand what you mean," Hilfred replied.

"Is it true she went to visit them?" the lawyer questioned.

"Yes, she did."

"And were you with her?"

"I was asked to wait outside the cell."

"Why?"

"I do not know."

"Has she often asked you to wait outside when she is speaking with people?"

"Sometimes."

"Often?"

"Not often."

"Then what happened?"

"She called for monks to give last rites to the murderers."

"She called for monks?" the lawyer repeated with a clear note of skepticism in his voice. "Her father is murdered and she is concerned about the *murderers'* souls? Why did she call for two monks? Was one not sufficient to do the job for both? For that matter, why not call the castle priest?"

"I do not know."

"And did she also order the murderers unchained?"

"Yes, to be able to kneel."

"And when the monks entered the cell, did you go with them?"

"No, again she asked me to remain outside."

"So the monks could enter but not her trusted bodyguard? Not even when the known killers of her father were unchained and free? Then what?"

"She came out of the cell. She wanted me to stay behind and escort the monks to the kitchens after they were done giving last rites."

"Why?"

"She did not say."

"Did you ask?"

"No, sir. As a man-at-arms, it is not my place to question the orders from a member of the royal family."

"I see, but were you pleased with these orders?"

"No."

"Why?"

"I was fearful more assassins might be in the castle, and I did not wish the princess to be out of my sight."

"In point of fact, wasn't Captain Wylin in the process of searching the castle for additional threats, and didn't he make everyone aware he felt the castle was unsafe?"

"He did."

"Did the princess explain to you where she was going so you could find her after performing your duty to the monks?"

"No."

"I see. And how do you know the two you escorted to the kitchens were the monks? Did you see their faces?"

"Their hoods were up."

"Did they have their hoods up when they entered the cell?"

Hilfred thought a moment and then shook his head. "I do not think so."

"So, on a night when her father is killed, she orders her personal bodyguard to leave her unprotected and to escort two monks down to the empty kitchens—two monks who decided suddenly to pull their hoods up inside the castle, hiding their faces? And what about the murderers' possessions? Where were they?"

"They were in the custody of the cell warden."

"And what did she say to the warden concerning them?"

"She told him she was going to have the monks take them for the poor."

"And did they take them?"

"Yes."

The lawyer softened his address. "Reuben, you do not strike me as a fool. Fools don't rise to the rank and position you have achieved. When you heard the killers escaped, and the monks were found chained in their place, did it cross your mind that maybe the princess had arranged it?"

"I assumed the killers attacked the monks after the princess left the cell."

"You did not answer my question," the lawyer said. "I asked if it crossed your mind."

Reuben said nothing.

"Did it?"

"Perhaps, but only briefly."

"Let us turn our attention to more recent events. Were you present during the conversation between Arista and her uncle in his study?"

"Yes, but I was asked to wait outside."

"To wait just outside the door, correct?"

"Yes."

"Therefore, could you hear what transpired inside?"

"Yes."

"Is it true the princess entered the archduke's office, where he was diligently working at locating the prince, and informed him that Prince Alric was clearly dead and that no search was needed? That he would make a better use of his time"—he paused here and turned to face the nobles—"*to begin preparations for her coronation as our queen!*"

There was a decidedly unpleasant murmur from the crowd, and a few of the court whispered and nodded to one another.

"I do not remember her using those words."

"Did she, or did she not, indicate the archduke should stop looking for Alric?"

"Yes."

"And did she threaten the archduke, insinuating she would soon hold her coronation, and once she was queen, he might find he was no longer the lord chancellor?"

"I believe she did say something to that effect, but she was angry—"

"That will be all, Sergeant-at-arms. That is all I asked. You can step down." Hilfred began to leave the witness box when the lawyer spoke again. "Oh, I am sorry—just one last thing. Have you ever seen or heard the princess cry over the loss of her father or brother?"

"She is a very private woman."

"Yes or no?"

Hilfred hesitated. "No, I have not."

"I am prepared to call the cell warden to corroborate the testimony of Hilfred if the court feels his account of the events is not truthful," the lawyer told the magistrates.

They conferred in whispers, and then the chief magistrate replied, "That will not be necessary. The word of the sergeant-at-arms is recognized as honorable and we will not question it here. You may proceed."

"I am sure you are as perplexed as I was," the lawyer said, addressing the bleachers in a sympathetic voice. "Many of you know her. How could this sweet girl attack her own father and brother? Was it just to gain a throne? It is not like her, is it? I ask you to bear with me. The reason should become quite clear in a moment. The court calls Bishop Saldur to testify."

Eyes from the gallery swept the room, looking for the cleric, as the old man slowly stood up from his seat and approached the witness box.

"Your Grace, you have been in this castle on many occasions. You know the royal family extremely well. Can you shed some light on Her Highness's motivations?"

"Gentlemen," Bishop Saldur spoke to the court and judges in his familiar warm and humble tone, "I have watched over the royal family for years and this recent tragedy is heartbreaking and dreadful. The accusation the archduke brings against the princess is painful to my ears, for I feel almost like a grandfather to the poor girl. However, I cannot hide the truth, which is…she *is* dangerous."

This brought a round of whispers between the spectators.

"I can assure each of you she is no longer the sweet innocent child whom I used to hold in my arms. I have seen her, spoken to her, watched her in her grief—or rather, the lack of grief—for her father and brother. I can tell you truly, her lust for knowledge and power has caused her to fall into the arms of evil." The bishop paused, dropping his head into his hands and shaking it. He looked up with a remorse-filled face and said, "It's the result of what happens when a woman is educated and, in Arista's case, introduced to the wicked powers of black magic."

A collective gasp issued from the crowd.

"Against my advice, King Amrath allowed her to attend the university, where she studied sorcery. She opened herself up to the forces of darkness, and it created in her a craving for power. Education planted an evil seed in her, and it flowered into the horrible deaths of her father and her brother. She is no longer a princess of the realm but a *witch*. This is evident by the fact she hasn't wept for her father. You see, as a learned bishop of the church, I know—witches cannot cry."

The crowd gasped again. Braga heard a man say, "I knew it!" from somewhere in the gallery.

The lawyer called Countess Amril to the court, and she testified that two years earlier, Arista had hexed her when she had told the squire Davens that the princess fancied him. Amril went on to describe how she had suffered horribly of sickness and boils for days as a result.

Next the lawyer called the monks, who, like Countess Amril, were eager to relate how they had been ill-used by the princess. They told how she had insisted the thieves be unchained, despite their assurance it was not necessary, and explained they had been attacked the moment she had left the room.

The crowd's reaction grew louder, and even Lord Valin looked troubled.

Percy Braga observed the audience with satisfaction from his seat at the rear of the magistrates. The faces of the gentry were filling with anger. He had successfully coaxed the spark into a flame, and the flame would soon be a blaze.

In the crowd, he spotted Wylin moving in the wings toward him.

"We have them, my lord," Wylin reported in a whisper. "They are gagged and locked in the dungeon. A little banged up by two of my overzealous men but alive."

"Excellent, and has there been any movement on the roads? Has there been any indication nobles loyal to the traitor Arista may attack?"

"I don't know, sir. I came directly from the sewers."

"Very well, get to the gate and sound the horn if you see anything. I'm concerned there may be an assault from Pickering of Drondil Fields. Oh, and if you see that wretched little dwarf, tell him it's time to bring the princess down."

"Of course, Your Lordship." Wylin pulled a small parchment rolled into a tube from his tabard. "I was passed this on my way in. It just arrived via messenger addressed to you." Braga took the missive from Wylin and the master-at-arms left with a bow.

Braga grinned at the ease of it all. He wondered if the princess in her distant tower prison could sense her coming death. Her own beloved citizens would soon be begging — nay, demanding — her execution. He had yet to present the storeroom administrator who would attest to the stolen dagger that had later been found in Arista's possession. And then, of course, there were now the thieves. He would hold them until the last and drag them out to the floor gagged and chained. The mere sight of them was likely to start a riot. He would have Wylin explain how he apprehended them trying to save the princess. The magistrates would have no choice but to rule against Arista and grant him the throne.

He would still have to deal with the possibility of Alric's attacking, but that could not be helped now. He was certain he would defeat Alric. Several of the more disgruntled eastern lords had already agreed to join him the moment he was crowned king. Once the trial was complete, and Arista dead, he planned to hold the coronation. By the next day, he would marshal the kingdom. Alric would cease to be a prince and become a fugitive.

"The court calls storage clerk Kline Druess," the lawyer was saying, "who was in charge of keeping the knife used to kill the king."

More damning evidence, Braga thought as he unrolled the scroll that Wylin had presented him. It had no seal, no emblem of nobility, only a simple string tie. He read the message, which was as simple as its package.

> *You missed us in the sewers.*
> *We now have the princess.*
> *Your time is growing short.*

The archduke crumpled the note in his fist and glared around at the numerous faces in the crowd, wondering if whoever had written it was watching him. His heart began beating faster, and he stood up slowly, trying not to draw attention to himself.

The lawyer caught sight of his movement and gave him a

curious look. Braga dismissed his concern with a slight wave of his hand. He left the court, forcing himself to walk slowly and calmly. The moment he passed through the chamber doors and out of sight of the crowd, he trotted through the castle halls, his cape whipping behind him. In his fist, he held on to the note, crushing it.

It isn't possible, he thought. *It can't be!* Hearing footfalls approaching rapidly from behind, he stopped and spun, drawing his sword.

"Is there a problem, Braga?" Archibald Ballentyne inquired. He held his hands up defensively before the point of the archduke's blade. Braga silently threw the crumpled note at him and resumed his march toward the dungeon.

"It's those thieves, those damned thieves," the Earl of Chadwick called out as he ran after Braga. "They're demons! Magicians! Evil mages! They are like smoke, appearing and disappearing at will."

Archibald caught up with Braga and they descended the stairs to the detention block, where the door guard dodged aside just in time to avoid the archduke. After trying the door and finding it locked, Braga hammered on it. The warden promptly left his desk and brought his keys for the red-faced archduke.

"My lord, I—"

"Open the cell to the prisoners Wylin's men just brought in. Do it now!"

"Yes, my lord." Fumbling with his great ring of keys, the warden moved quickly to the cell hall. Two castle guards stood watch to either side of a door and promptly stepped aside at his approach.

"Have you two been here since the prisoners were brought in?" Braga asked the guards.

"Aye, my lord," the guard on the left replied. "Captain

Wylin ordered us to stand guard and to allow absolutely no admittance to anyone except him or you."

"Very good," he said. Then, to the warden, he added, "Open it."

The warden unlocked the door and entered the cell. Inside, Braga saw two men chained to the wall, stripped to their waists with gags in their mouths. They were not the same men he had seen the night of the king's murder.

"Remove the gags," Braga ordered the warden. "Who are you? What are you doing here?"

"M-m-my name's Bendent, Your Lordship. I'm just a street sweeper from Kirby's End—honest. We weren't doing nothing wrong!"

"What were you two doing in the sewers under this castle?"

"Hunting rats, sir," the other one said.

"*Rats?*"

"Yes, sir, honest, we was. We was told there was a big event here in the castle this morning and the castle kitchen was complaining about rats climbing up from the sewers. 'Cause of the cold, you see, sir. We was told we'd get paid a silver tenent for every rat we done killed and brought out—only..."

"Only what?"

"Only we never seen no rats, Your Lordship."

"Before we found any, we were knocked out by soldiers and brought here."

"See? What did I tell you?" Archibald told Braga. "They took her already. They stole her right from under your nose just like they took my letters!"

"They couldn't have. There's no way to get up to Arista's tower. It's too high, and it can't be climbed."

"I'm telling you, Braga, these men are skilled. They scaled my Gray Tower well enough, and it's one of the tallest there is."

"Trust me, Archibald. Arista's tower can't be climbed."

"But they did it," Ballentyne insisted. "I didn't think it was possible when they did it to me either, not until I opened the safe and my prize was gone. Now your prize is gone, and what will you do with that crowd out there when you have no princess to burn?"

"It's just not possible," Braga repeated, pushing Ballentyne out of his way. "You two," he said to the guards, still standing outside the cell as he walked out, "come with me and bring one of those gags. It's time the princess came down for her court appearance."

Braga led them through the castle and up six flights of stairs to the residence level. The hallway here was empty. All the servants were gathered with the others, listening to the proceedings of the trial.

They passed the royal chapel and continued up the hallway to the next door. Braga threw it open and shouted, "Magnus!" Inside, a dwarf with a braided brown beard and a broad flat nose lay on a bed. He was dressed in a blue leather vest, large black boots, and a bright orange puffed-sleeve shirt that made his arms appear huge.

"Is it time?" the dwarf asked. Hopping off the bed, he yawned and rubbed his eyes.

"Is there any chance someone could have gotten up in her tower and stolen Arista out of there?" Braga asked urgently.

"None whatsoever," the dwarf said with a tone of total confidence. Braga looked back and forth between Ballentyne and the dwarf, scowling.

"I have to know for certain. Besides, she needs to come down for the burning, and I must get back to the trial. You'll have to fetch her. Take these guards with you. One of them has a gag. Make sure they use it before bringing her down." To the guards the archduke added, "The princess has been corrupted by dark magic; she's a witch and can play tricks with your mind, so don't let her talk to you. Get her and bring her to the court." The guards nodded and the dwarf led them down the hallway in the direction of the tower.

"Archibald, go get Wylin, the captain of the guards. He's stationed at the castle gate. Tell him to come to the royal residence wing and provide assistance guarding the princess. I can't take any chances. Do you understand me?"

"I'll do as you say, Percy, but I'm sure she is already gone," Archibald insisted. "These bastards are incredible. They're like ghosts, and they have no fear at all. They work right under your nose, steal you blind, and then have the audacity to send you a note *telling* you what they have done!"

Braga paused in thought. "Yes, why *did* they do that?" he asked himself. "If they took her, why let me know? And if they didn't, they must have suspected I would immediately check to..." He glanced over his shoulder in the direction the dwarf had gone then turned back to Archibald. "Get Wylin up here, *now*!"

Braga ran up the hallway, following the dwarf and the two guards. They were just entering the north corridor, which led directly to the tower, when he caught up to them.

"Stop where you are!"

The dwarf turned around with a puzzled expression on his face. The guards responded differently. The larger of the two pivoted, drawing his sword, and moved to block the archduke's passage.

◈

"Time to move, Royce," Hadrian said, casting off his helm. The standard-issue sword of the castle guard felt heavy and awkward in his grip.

Royce removed his helm as well as he moved past the dwarf, running quickly down the hall.

"Stop him, you fool!" Braga ordered the dwarf, but he was too slow to react. The thief was already far down the hall and the small dwarf ran after him. Braga drew his own sword and turned his attention to Hadrian.

"Do you know who I am? I know we met in the dungeon recently when you were hanging in chains, but are you aware of my reputation? I'm Archduke Percy Braga, Lord Chancellor of Melengar and, more importantly, the winner of the title of Grand Circuit Tournament Swords Master for the last five years in a row. Do you have any titles? Any ribbons won? Any awards bestowed? Are there trophies shelved for your handling of a sword? I have bested the best in Avryn, even the famous Pickering and his magic rapier."

"The way I heard it, he didn't have his sword the day you two dueled."

Braga laughed. "That sword story is just that—a legend. He uses it as an excuse to account for his losses or when he is afraid of an opponent. His sword is just a common rapier with a fancy hilt."

Braga moved in and swiped at Hadrian in a savagely fast attack that drove him backward. He struck again and Hadrian had to leap backward to avoid being slashed across the chest.

"You're fast. That's good. It'll make this more interesting. You see, Mr. Thief, I'm sure you have the situation all wrong. You may be under the impression that you are holding me at bay while your friend races to rescue the damsel in distress. How noble for a commoner like yourself. You must entertain dreams of being a knight to be so idealistic." Braga lunged, dipped, and slashed. Hadrian fell back again, and once more,

Braga smiled and laughed at him. "The truth is, you are not holding me at all. I'm holding you."

The archduke feinted left and then short-stroked toward Hadrian's body. He dodged the attack, but it put him off balance and off guard. Although Braga's stroke missed, it allowed him the opportunity to punch the hilt of his sword hard into Hadrian's face, throwing him back against the corridor wall. His lip began to bleed. Immediately, Braga lashed out again, but Hadrian had moved, and the archduke's sword sparked across the stone wall.

"That looked like it hurt."

"I've had worse," Hadrian said. He was panting slightly, his voice less confident.

"I must admit, you two have been quite impressive. Your reputation is certainly well earned. It was very clever of you to slip into the sewers behind those rat catchers and use them as decoys. It was also intelligent of you to send that note causing me to direct you right to the princess but your genius ended there. You see, I can kill you whenever I want, but I want you alive. I need at least one person to execute. The mob will insist on that. In a few moments, Wylin and a dozen guards will come up here, and you'll be taken to the stake. Meanwhile, your friend, whom you are sure is rescuing Arista, will be the instrument of her death and his as well. You could run and warn him, but—oh, that's right—you are keeping me at bay, aren't you?"

Braga grinned and attacked again.

᠂᠊᠊

Royce reached a door at the end of the hall and was not surprised to find it locked. He pulled his tools from his belt. The lock was traditional, and he had no trouble picking it. The door swung open, but immediately Royce knew something was wrong. He felt, more than heard, a click as the door pulled back. His instincts told him something was not right. He looked up the spiral stairs that disappeared around the circle of the tower. Nothing looked amiss, but years of experience told him otherwise.

He tentatively put a foot on the first step and nothing happened. He moved to the second, and the third, inching his way up. Listening for any telltale sounds, he searched for wires, levers, and loose tiles. Everything appeared safe. Behind him down the hallway, he could hear the faint sounds of swordplay as Hadrian entertained the archduke. He needed to hurry.

He moved up five more steps. There were small windows, no more than three feet tall and only a foot wide, just enough to allow light to pass through but nothing else. The winter sun revealed the staircase in a washed-out brilliance. Weight, rather than mortar, held the smooth stone walls together. The steps were likewise made of solid blocks of stone also fitted with amazing artisanship so that a sheet of parchment could not slip between the cracks.

Royce moved up to the ninth step, and as he shifted his weight to the higher stone block, the tower shook. In reaction, he instinctively started to step back, and then it happened. The previous eight steps collapsed. They broke and fell out of sight into an abyss below him. Royce shifted his weight forward again just in time to avoid falling to his death and took another off-balance step upward. The moment he did, the previous step broke away and fell. The tower rumbled again.

"Your first mistake was picking the lock," Magnus told him.

Royce could hear the dwarf's voice from the doorway below. When he turned, he could see the dwarf standing just outside the door in the castle's corridor. He stood there, spinning a door key tied to a string around his index finger, winding and unwinding it. He absently stroked the hair of his beard.

"If you open the door without using the key, it engages the trap," Magnus explained with a grin.

The dwarf began to pace slowly before the open door like a professor addressing a class. "You can't jump the hole you made to get back here. It's already too far. And, in case you are wondering, the bottom is a long way down. You started climbing this tower on the sixth floor of the castle, and the base of the tower extends to the bedrock below the foundation. I also added plenty of jagged rocks at the bottom, just for fun."

"You made this?" Royce asked.

"Of course—well, not the tower. It was here already. I spent the last half year hollowing it out like a stone-eating termite." He grinned. "There's very little material left in it. All those solid-looking blocks of rock you see are parchment-thin. I left just the right amount of structure in place. The inside looks like a spiderweb made of stone rather than thread. Tiny strands of rock in a latticework of a classic crystalline matrix—strong enough to hold the tower up but extremely fragile if the right thread is broken."

"And I take it each time I take a step up, the previous one will fall?"

The dwarf's grin widened. "Beautiful, isn't it? You can't go down, but if you go up, you'll get into an even worse situation. The steps work as a horizontal support for the vertical planes. Without the steps to steady the structure, it will twist on itself and fall. Before you reach the top, the entire tower will collapse once enough supports fall away. Don't let my talk about hollow walls put you too much at ease. It's still stone, and the full weight of this tower remains immense. It will very easily crush you, and the lady at the top, should the fall and the sharp rocks at the bottom not manage to do the job. You've already weakened the structure to where it might fall on its own now. I can hear it with the blowing of the wind—the tiny little cracks and pops. All stone makes sounds as it grows, shrinks, twists, or erodes—it's a language I understand very well. It tells me stories of the past and of the future, and right now, this tower is singing."

"I hate dwarves," Royce muttered.

CHAPTER 9

RESCUERS

The water pitcher and basin hit the floor and shattered. The crash jolted Arista, who sat on her bed, disoriented and confused. The room was shaking. All summer the tower had felt strange but nothing like this. She held her breath—waiting. Nothing happened. The tower stopped moving.

Tentatively, she slipped off the bed, crept gingerly toward the windows, and looked out. She saw nothing to explain the tremor. Outside, the world was blanketed white by a fresh layer of snow that was still falling and she wondered if it was snow sliding from the tower's eves that made the room shake. It did not seem likely nor did that matter.

How much time do I have left?

She looked down. The crowd still circled the front gate of the castle. There must have been more than a hundred people there, all pressing for news of her trial. Around the perimeter of the castle, three times the usual number of guards patrolled in full armor. Her uncle was not taking any chances. Perhaps he thought the people of the city might rise up against him rather than see their princess burned? She knew better. No one cared if she lived or died. While she knew all the lords, earls, and barons by name and had sat down with them for dozens of meals, she knew they were not her friends. She did not have any friends. Braga was right; she spent too much time in her tower. No one really knew her. She lived a solitary life, but this was the first time she ever really felt alone.

She had spent all night trying to determine exactly what words she would use when brought before the court. In the end, she concluded there was little she could do or say. She could accuse Braga of the murder of her father, but she had no proof. He was the one with all the evidence on his side. After all, she had released the two thieves and was responsible for Alric's disappearance.

What was I thinking?

She had handed her brother over to two unknown thugs. Alric had personally explained his intent to torture them and she had left him to their mercy. Arista felt sick whenever she imagined them laughing at her expense as they drowned poor Alric in the river. Now they were likely halfway to Calis or Delgos, taking turns wearing the royal signet ring of Melengar. When the scouts had returned with Alric's robe, she had been certain he was dead, and yet there was no body.

Is it possible Alric still lives?

No, she reasoned, it was far more likely Braga kept Alric's corpse hidden. Revealing it before her trial would allow her to make a bid for the throne. Once the trial was over, once she was found guilty and burned, he would miraculously reveal its discovery. It was very possible Braga had Alric's body locked away in one of the rooms below her or somewhere in the vault.

It was all her fault. If she had not interfered, perhaps Alric might have taken charge and discovered Braga's treachery. Perhaps he could have saved both of them. Perhaps she was nothing more than a foolish girl after all. At least her death would put an end to the questions and the guilt consuming her. She closed her eyes and once more felt the unsteadiness of the world around her.

⊷

The Galilin host was now a full five hundred strong as it marched through the wintry landscape. Sixty knights dressed in full armor carried lances adorned with long forked banners. They flicked like serpents' tongues in the numbing wind. When they were back at Drondil Fields, Myron had overheard Alric arguing with the other nobles, about marching too soon. Apparently, they were still missing the strength of several lords, and leaving when they did was a risk. Pickering had finally agreed to Alric's demands and convinced the others once Barons Himbolt and Rendon arrived, bringing another score of knights. To Myron, the force was impressive at any size.

At the head of the line rode Prince Alric, Myron, Count Pickering, and his two eldest sons, as well as the land-titled nobles. Following them were the knights, who rode together in rows four abreast. An entourage of squires, pages, and footmen traveled behind them. Farther back were the ranks of the common men-at-arms: strong, stocky brutes dressed in chain and steel with pointed helms, plate metal shin guards, and metal shank boots. Each was equipped with a kite shield, a short broad-blade sword, and a long spear. Next in line were the archers, in leather jerkins and woolen cloaks that hid their quivers. They marched holding their unstrung bows as though they were mere walking sticks. At the rear came the artisans, smiths, surgeons, and cooks, pulling wagons that hauled the army's supplies.

Myron felt foolish. After hours on the road, he was still having trouble keeping his horse from veering to the left into Fanen's gelding. He was starting to get the hang of the stirrups, but he still had much to learn. The front toe guard, which prevented his feet from resting on the soles, frustrated him. The Pickering boys took him under their wing and explained how only the ball of the foot was to rest on the stirrup brace. This provided better control and prevented a foot from catching in the event of a fall. They also told him how tight stirrups helped to hold his knees to the horse's sides. All Pickering's horses were leg trained and could be controlled by the feet, thighs, and knees. They were taught this way so that knights could fight with one hand on a lance or sword and the other on a shield. Myron was working on this technique now, squeezing his thighs, trying to persuade the horse to steer right, but it was no use. The more he used his left knee, the more his right knee also squeezed to compensate. The result was confusion on the part of the animal, and it wandered over and brushed against Fanen's mount once again.

"You need to be more firm," Fanen told him. "Show her who's in charge."

"She already knows—*she* is," Myron replied pathetically. "I think I should just stick with the reins. It's not like I'll be wielding a sword and shield in the coming battle."

"You never know," Fanen said. "Monks of old used to fight a lot, and Alric said you helped save his life by fighting against those mercenaries who attacked him in the forest."

Myron frowned and dropped his gaze. "I didn't fight anyone."

"But I thought—"

Myron shook his head. "I should have, I suppose. They were the ones who burned the abbey. They were the ones who killed...but..." He paused. "I would have died if Hadrian and Royce hadn't saved me. The king just assumed that I fought and I never bothered to tell the truth. I really have to stop doing that."

"Doing what?"

"Lying."

"That's not lying. You just didn't correct him."

"It amounts to the same thing. The abbot once told me that lying was a betrayal to one's self. It's evidence of self-loathing. When you are so ashamed of your actions, thoughts, or intentions, you lie rather than accepting yourself for who you really are—or, in this case, pretend something happened when it didn't. The idea of how others see you becomes more important than the reality of you. It's like when a man would rather die than be thought of as a coward. His life is not as important to him as his reputation. In the end, who is braver? The man who dies rather than be thought of as a coward or the man who lives willing to face who he really is?"

"I'm sorry, you lost me there," Fanen said with a quizzical look.

"It doesn't matter. But the prince asked me along as a chronicler of events, not as a warrior. I think he wants me to record what happens today in a book."

"Well, if you do, please leave out the way Denek threw a fit at not being allowed to come. It will reflect badly on our family."

Everything they passed was new to Myron. He had seen snow, of course, but only in the courtyard and cloister at the abbey. He never had seen how it settled on a forest or glittered on the edges of rivers and streams. They were traveling through populated country now, passing village after village; each one larger than the one before. Myron could only stare in fascination at the many different types of buildings, animals, and people he saw along the way. Each time they came into a town, the villagers came out to stare at them. They scurried out of their homes, aroused by the ominous *thrump, thrump, thrump* of the soldiers marching. Some summoned the courage to ask where they were going, but the men said nothing, under strict orders to maintain silence.

Children ran to the edge of the road, where parents quickly pulled them back. Myron had never seen a child before—at least, not since he had been one. It was not uncommon for a boy to be sent to the abbey at ten or twelve, but rarely, if ever, was one sent before the age of eight. The smallest of the children fascinated Myron, and he watched them in amazement. They were like short drunk people, loud and usually dirty, but all were surprisingly cute and looked at him in much the same way that he looked at them. They would wave, and Myron could not help waving back, although he assumed it was not very soldierly to do so.

The war host moved surprisingly fast. The foot soldiers, responding in unison to orders, alternated between periods of double-time marching and a more relaxed stride, which was only slightly slower. Each of them wore a grim face, without a smile among them.

For hours, they marched. No one interfered; there were no advance formations lying in ambush, no challenges along the road. To Myron, the trip felt more like an exciting parade than the preparation for an ominous battle. Finally, he saw his first glimpse of Melengar in the distance. Fanen pointed out the great bell tower of Mares Cathedral and the tall spires of Essendon Castle, where no standard flew.

A vanguard rode up and reported a strong force entrenched around the city. The nobles ordered their regiments to form ranks. Flags relayed messages, archers strung their bows, and the army transformed themselves into blocks of men. In long lines of three across, they moved as one. The archers were summoned forward and moved ahead just behind the foot soldiers.

Ordered to the rear, Myron and Fanen rode with the cooks to watch and listen. From his new vantage point, Myron noticed part of the army had broken away from the main line and was moving to the right side of the city. When the ranks of men reached the rise, which left them visible to the castle walls, a great horn sounded in the distance.

One of their own answered the castle horn, and the Galilin archers released a barrage of arrows upon the defenders. The shafts flew and appeared to hang briefly in the air like a dark cloud. As they fell, Myron could hear the distant cries of men. He watched with anticipation as the mounted knights broke into three groups. One stayed on the road, while the other two took up flanking positions on either side. The main line increased their pace to a brisk walk.

⤚

When they heard the horn, Mason Grumon and Dixon Taft led their mob up Wayward Street, effectively emptying the Lower Quarter. It was the sign Royce and Hadrian had told them to wait for—the signal to attack.

Ever since the two thieves had woken them in the middle of the night, they had spent their time organizing the resistance in the Lower Quarter of Medford. They spread news of Amrath's assassination by the archduke, of the innocence of the princess, and of the return of the prince. Those not moved by loyalty or justice were enticed by the chance to strike back at their betters. It was not difficult to convince the poor and the destitute to take up arms against the soldiery who policed them. In addition, there were those hoping for a possibility to do a little looting, or perhaps receive some reward from the crown if they prevailed.

They armed themselves with pitchforks, axes, and clubs.

Makeshift armor was constructed by strapping whatever thin metal they could find under their clothing. In most cases, this meant commandeering a baking sheet from their wives. They had the numbers, but they looked like a pathetic lot. Gwen had roused the Artisan Quarter, which provided not only strong workers but a few swords, bows, and bits of armor. With the city guards ordered to the perimeter and most of the Gentry Quarter at the trial, there was no one to stop them from openly organizing.

With Dixon at his side, Mason marched at the head of the commoner procession, his smithing hammer in one hand and a rough-hewn shield he had beaten together that morning in the other. Years of frustration and resentment steamed to the surface as the smith strode forward. Anger born from the life he had been denied overwhelmed him. When he could not pay the taxes on his late father's shop, the city sheriff and his guards had come. When he refused to leave, they had beaten him unconscious and thrown him into the gutter of Wayward Street. Mason blamed the guards for most of his life's misfortunes. The beating had weakened his shoulders, and for years afterward, wielding his hammer was so painful he could work only a few hours each day. This, and his gambling habit, kept him in poverty. Of course, he never really considered the gambling to be the real problem; it was the guards who were responsible. It did not matter to him that the soldiers and the sheriff who had beaten him were no longer with the guard. That day was his chance to fight back, to repay in kind for the pain he had endured.

Neither he nor Dixon was a warrior or even athletic, but they were large men with broad chests and thick necks, and the crowd followed behind them as if the citizens of the Lower Quarter were plowing the city with a pair of yoked oxen. They turned onto Wayward Street and marched unchallenged into the Gentry Quarter. Compared to the Lower Quarter, it was like another world. The streets were paved with decorative tile work and lined with metal horse hitches. Along the avenue, enclosed streetlamps and covered sewers accentuated the care taken for the comfort of the privileged few. Marking the center of the Gentry Quarter was a large spacious square. The great Essendon Fountain, with its statue of Tolin on a rearing horse above the pluming water, was its main landmark. Across from it, Mares Cathedral rose. In its towers high above, bells chimed loudly. They passed the fine three-story stone-and-brick houses, with their iron fences and decorative gates. That the stables here looked better than the house Mason lived in was not lost on him. The trip through the square only added fuel to the fire that was sweeping across the city.

When they reached Main Street, they saw the enemy.

The sound of the horn brought Arista to the window once more. What she saw amazed her. In the distance, at the edge of her sight, she could see banners rising above the naked trees. Count Pickering was coming, and he was not alone. There was a score of flags, representing most of the western provinces. Pickering was marching on Medford with an army.

Is it on my account?

She pondered the question and concluded the answer was no. Of all the nobles, she knew the Pickerings the best, but she doubted the count marched for her. The more likely explanation was that news of Alric's death had reached him, and he was challenging Braga for the crown. Arista doubted Pickering had given any thought to her. He merely saw his opportunity and he was reaching for it. The fact that she might still live was only a technicality. No one wanted a woman as their ruler. If Pickering won, he would force her abdication of the throne in favor of himself or perhaps Mauvin. She would be sent away, or locked up, but she would never be truly free. At least if Pickering won, Braga would never sit on the throne—but she did not like Pickering's chances. She was no tactician and certainly not a general but even she could see that the forces marching up the road lacked the numbers for a castle siege. Braga had his forces well entrenched. Looking at the courtyard below, she realized the attack was distracting everyone.

Perhaps this time it will be different.

She rushed to her door and with a tap of her necklace unlocked it. She grabbed the latch and pushed. As usual, the door refused to budge. "Damn that dwarf," she said aloud to herself. She pushed violently against the door, throwing her entire weight, such that it was, against it. The door did not give way.

There was another rumble, and her room shook once more. Dust fell from the rafters. *What is going on?* She staggered as the tower swayed like a ship at sea. She did not know what else to do. Terrified and bewildered, she returned to the illusionary safety of her bed. She sat there, hugging her knees, hardly breathing, her eyes darting at the slightest sound. The end was coming. One way or another, she was certain the end was coming soon.

⁊

The prince was new to combat and unsure what to expect. He had hoped that merely assembling a massive force would cause the city's defenders to surrender. The reality was altogether different. When they reached Medford, they found trenches built outside the walls filled with spearmen. His archers had launched three flights of arrows but still the defenders remained steadfast. Using shields, they fended off much of the barrage and sustained little noticeable damage.

Who are they? Alric wondered. *Are my own soldiers standing between me and my home? What lies has Braga spread among the guards? Or are they all hired men? Did my gold pay for those lines of pointed steel?*

Alric sat on one of Pickering's horses draped with a caparison hastily adorned with rough sewn images of the Melengar falcon. The animal was as restless as its rider, shuffling its hooves and snorting great clouds of frosty fog. Alric held the reins with his right hand, his left holding his woolen cloak tight about his neck. His eyes rose above the heads of the spearmen to look on the city of his birth. The walls and towers of Medford appeared faint and dreamlike through the falling snow. The vision slowly faded into white as an eerie silence muffled the world.

"Your Majesty," Count Pickering spoke, breaking the stillness.

"Another flight?" Alric proposed.

"Arrows will not conquer your city."

Alric nodded solemnly. "The knights, then — send them in."

"Marshal!" the count shouted. "Order the knights to break that line!"

Gallant men in shining armor spurred their steeds and charged forward with banners dancing overhead. A whirlwind of snow launched into the sky at their passing and obscured them from view. They vanished from sight but Alric listened to the thunder of their hooves.

The clash was dreadful. Alric felt it as much as heard it. Metal shrieked and men cried out, and until that moment, Alric had never known it was possible for horses to scream.

When the cloud of snow settled, the prince could at last see the bloody spectacle. Spears braced in the dirt pierced the breasts of man and mount. Horses collapsed, throwing the knights to the ground where they lay, like turtles struggling to right themselves. Spearmen drew forth short swords and thrust downward, punching their sharp points into eye slits and the armor gaps at the armpit or groin.

"This is not going as well as I hoped," Alric complained.

"Battle rarely ever does, Your Majesty," Count Pickering assured him. "But this is a large part of what being king means. Your knights are dying. Are you going to leave them to their fate?"

"Should I send in the foot soldiers?"

"If I were you, I certainly would. You need to break a hole in that wall, and you'd better do so before your men decide you're incompetent and vanish into the forests around them."

"Marshal!" Alric shouted. "Marshal Garret, order the foot soldiers to engage immediately!"

"Yes, Sire!"

A horn sounded and the men roared forward into battle. Alric watched as steel cut through flesh. The footmen fared better than the knights, but the defensive position of the city soldiers took a toll. Alric could hardly bear to watch. Never before had he seen such a sight—there was so much blood. The white snow was gone, stained pink and in some desperate places turned to a dark red. Littering the grounds were body parts—arms severed, heads split open, and legs chopped off. The wall of men blended in a whirling mass of flesh, dirt, blood, and an endless cacophony of screams.

"I can't believe this is happening," Alric said, sounding and feeling sick. "This is my city. These are my people. My men!" He turned to Count Pickering. "I'm killing my own men!" He was shaking now, his face red, and tears filled his eyes.

Hearing the shrieks and cries, he squeezed the pommel of his saddle until his hands hurt. He felt helpless.

I am king now.

He did not feel like a king. He felt like he had on the road near the Silver Pitcher when those men had held him facedown in the dirt. The tears were now streaming down his cheeks.

"Alric! Stop it!" Pickering snapped at him. "You mustn't let the men see you crying!"

Fury flared in Alric, and he spun on the count. "No? *No?* Look at them! They are dying for me. They are dying on *my* order! I say they do have a right to see their king! They *all* have a right to see their king!"

Alric wiped the tears from his cheeks and gathered his reins. "I'm tired of this. I'm tired of having my face put in the dirt! I won't stand it. I'm tired of being helpless. That's my city, built by my ancestors! If my people choose to fight, then by Maribor, I want them to know it's me they fight!"

The prince put on his helm, drew his father's large sword, and spurred his horse forward, not at the trench but at the castle gate itself.

"Alric, no!" Pickering shouted after him.

∽

Mason rushed forward and drove his hammer through the helmet of the first guard he saw. Grinning with delight at his good fortune, he gathered the man's sword and looked up.

The mob had reached the main gate of the city. The great four-towered barbican of gray stone rose above them like a monstrous beast. It swarmed with soldiers shocked at the sight of the city rising against them. Surprise and the accompanying panic bought the mob time to clear the streets and reach the gatehouse. Mason heard Dixon shout, "For Prince Alric!" but the prince was the last thing on the smith's mind.

Mason picked out his next target—a tall guard absorbed in a swinging match with a street sweeper from Artisan Row. Mason stabbed the guard in the armpit and listened to him scream as he twisted the blade. The street sweeper grinned at the smith and Mason grinned back.

He had killed only two men but already Mason was slick with blood. His tunic felt heavy as it stuck to the skin of his chest and he could not tell if sweat or tears of blood dripped down his face. The grin he had shown to the sweeper remained glued to his lips by the thrill and elation.

This is freedom! This is living!

His heart thundered and his head swam as if he were drunk. Mason swung his sword again, this time at a man already down on one knee. His swing was so strong the blade cut halfway through his victim's neck. He kicked the dead man aside and cried aloud in his victory. He spoke no words; words were valueless at such a moment. He shouted the fury that pounded in his heart. He was a man again, a man of strength, a man to be feared!

A horn sounded and Mason looked up once more. A captain of the castle guard was on the ramparts shouting orders, rallying his troops. They responded to the call and fell back into ranks, struggling to defend the gate even as the mob closed in.

Mason stepped through the muddy, blood-soaked ground, now slick beneath his feet. He looked about and picked a new target. A castle guard with his back to the smith was in the process of retreating to the sound of his captain's voice. The smith aimed at the guard's neck, attempting to cleave off his head. His inexperience with a sword caused him to aim too high and the blade glanced off the man's helmet, ringing it loudly. He raised the sword for another blow when the man unexpectedly turned around.

Mason felt a sharp, burning pain in his stomach. In an instant, all the strength and fury drained from him. He let go his sword. He saw, rather than felt, himself drop to his knees. He looked down at the source of the pain and watched the soldier withdraw a sword from his stomach. Mason could not believe what he was seeing.

How could all that steel come out of me?

The smith felt a warm wetness on his hands as he instinctively pressed them to the wound. He tried as best he could to contain his organs as the blood flowed through a gash at least a foot wide. He no longer felt his legs, and lay helpless when, to his horror, he saw the soldier swing again—this time at his head.

⁓

Alric charged the castle barbican. Immediately, Count Pickering, Mauvin, and Marshal Garret led the reserve knights in behind him. Arrows rained down from the parapets above the great gates. One deflected off Alric's visor, and another struck deep into the horn of his saddle. One hit Sir Sinclair's horse in the flank, causing it to rear unexpectedly, but the knight remained mounted. Countless more struck the ground harmlessly. The enraged prince rode directly to the gate and, standing up in his stirrups, shouted, "I am Prince Alric Brendon Essendon! Open this gate in the name of your king!"

Alric was not certain anyone had heard him as he stood there, his sword raised high over his head. Furthermore, if they had heard him, there was no reason to believe another arrow would not whistle down and end his life. Behind the prince, the remaining knights fanned out around him as the marshal attempted to build a wall around his monarch.

Another arrow did not fly but neither did the gate open.

"Alric," Count Pickering shouted, "you must fall back!"

"I am Prince Alric Essendon! Open the gate *now*!" he demanded again, and this time, he removed his helm and threw it aside, backing his horse into full view of the ramparts.

Alric and the others waited. Count Pickering and Mauvin stared at the prince in terror and tried to persuade him to come away from the gate. Nothing happened for several tense moments as the prince and his bodyguards sat outside waiting, staring up at the parapets. From inside they heard the sounds of fighting.

A shout came from atop the walls of the city. "The prince! Open the gate! Let him in! It's the prince!" More shouts, a scream, and then suddenly the massive gate split open, and the great doors pulled back. Inside was a mass of confusion as uniformed guards fought a horde of citizens dressed up like tinkers, wearing makeshift armor or stolen helms.

Alric did not pause. He spurred his mount and drove into the crowd. Mauvin, Count Pickering, Sir Ecton, and Marshal Garret struggled to form a personal defense for their king, but there was little need. At the sight of him, the defenders laid down their weapons. Word that the prince was alive spread, and those who saw him charging toward the castle, brandishing his father's sword, roared with cheers.

❦

Royce heard the horn wail as he stood trapped on the steps of the tower. "Sounds like a fight outside," Magnus mentioned. "I wonder who will win." The dwarf scratched his beard. "For that matter, I wonder who is fighting."

"You don't take much interest in your employer's business, do you?" Royce said, studying the walls. When he tried to tap a spike into a seam, the stone broke like an eggshell. The dwarf was telling the truth about that.

"Only if it's necessary for the job. By the way, I wouldn't do that again. You were lucky you didn't hit a binding thread."

Royce cursed under his breath. "If you want to be helpful, why not just tell me how to get up and back?"

"Who said I was trying to be helpful?" The dwarf grinned at him wickedly. "I just spent half a year on this project. I don't want you to topple the whole thing in the first few minutes. I want to savor the moment."

"Are all dwarves this morbid?"

"Think of it as having built a sandcastle and wanting the pleasure of seeing it fall to a wave. I'm on the edge of my toes waiting to see exactly how and when it will finally collapse. Will it be a misstep, a loss of balance, or something amazing and unexpected?"

Royce drew his dagger and held it by the blade for the dwarf to see. "Are you aware I could put this through your throat where you stand?"

It was a false threat, as he would not dare throw away such a vital tool at this moment. Still, he expected a reaction of fear, or at least a mocking laugh. Instead, the dwarf did neither. He glared at the dagger, his eyes wide.

"Where did you get that blade?"

Royce rolled his eyes in disbelief. "I'm a little busy here. If you don't mind." He resumed his study of the steps. He observed the way they curved up and around the central trunk of the tower, how the steps above formed the ceiling to the ones below. He looked up ahead and then behind him.

"The step I am on doesn't collapse if I'm on it," Royce said to himself, but loud enough for the dwarf to hear. "It only falls if I step on the next one."

"Yes, quite ingenious, isn't it? As you might imagine, I'm quite proud of my work. I originally designed it to be an instrument of Arista's death. Braga hired me to set it up to look like an accident. A decrepit old tower in the royal residence collapses, and the poor princess is crushed in the process. Unfortunately, after Alric escaped, he changed his mind and decided to have her executed instead. I thought I would never get to see the fruits of all my hard work, but then you came along. How nice of you."

"All traps have weaknesses," Royce said. He looked ahead at the steps and smiled suddenly. Crouching, he leapt forward not one but two steps. The step in the middle slipped from its position and fell, but the step he had started from remained. "With no following step," Royce observed, "that step is now secure from breaking, isn't it?"

"Very clever," the dwarf replied, clearly disappointed.

Royce continued to leap two steps at a time until he moved around the circle out of sight of the dwarf. As he did, Magnus shouted, "It'll do you no good. The gap at the bottom is much too far for you to jump. You are still trapped!"

Arista was crouched on her bed when she heard someone out-side her door. It was probably that dreadful little dwarf or Braga himself coming to take her to the trial. She could hear a scraping and an occasional thud. She remembered too late that she had not resealed the door with her gemlock. As she moved toward the door, it swung open. To her surprise, it was neither Braga nor the dwarf. Instead, there in the doorway was one of the thieves from the dungeon.

"Princess," was all Royce said, entering with a respectful though brief nod in her direction. He quickly moved past her and seemed to be looking for something; his eyes roamed over the walls and ceiling of her bedroom.

"You? What are *you* doing here? Is Alric alive?"

"Alric's fine," Royce said as he moved about the room. He

looked out the windows and examined the material of the drapes. "Well, that's not going to work."

"Why are you here? How did you get here? Did you see Esrahaddon? What did he say to Alric?"

"I'm a bit busy just now, Your Highness."

"Busy? Doing what?"

"Saving you but I'll admit I'm not doing very well at the moment." Without asking permission, Royce opened her wardrobe and began sifting through her clothes. Then he rifled through her dresser drawers.

"What do you want with my *clothes*?"

"I'm trying to figure a way out of here. I suspect this tower is going to collapse in a few minutes, and if we don't get out soon, we'll die."

"I see," she said simply. "Why can't we just go down the stairs?" She got up and crept to the doorway. "Sweet Maribor!" she cried as she saw every other step missing.

"We can leap those but the last six or seven steps at the bottom are totally gone. It's too far to jump to the corridor. I was hoping maybe we could jump out the window to the moat, but that looks like instant death."

"Oh," was all she could utter. A scream was growing in her and she covered her mouth with her hand, holding it back. "You're right. You're not doing very well."

Royce looked under her bed and then stood up. "Wait a minute, you're a sorceress, aren't you? Esrahaddon taught you magic. Can you get us down? Levitate us, or turn us into birds or something?"

Arista smiled awkwardly. "I was never able to learn much from Esrahaddon and certainly not self-levitation."

"Can you levitate a board or stone we could jump to?"

Arista shook her head.

"And the bird thing?"

"Even if I could, which I can't, we'd stay birds, because I couldn't turn us back after changing, now could I?"

"So magic is out," Royce said, and began pulling the feather-stuffed mattress off Arista's bed, revealing the rope net beneath it. "Okay, then help me untie your bed."

"The rope isn't long enough to reach the bottom of the tower," Arista told him.

"It doesn't have to be," he replied, pulling the rope through the holes in the bed frame.

The tower shuddered, and dust cascaded from the rafters. Arista held her breath for a moment, her heart pounding in anticipation of a sudden plummet, but the tower steadied itself once more.

"Clearly we are running out of time." Royce coiled the length of rope over his shoulder and headed toward the door.

Arista paused only a moment to look back at the dressing table and the brushes her father had given her, and then moved to what remained of the stairs.

"You're going to have to jump down. The steps that are still there should be very sturdy and it should be easier than jumping up. Just be sure you don't over jump, but if you do, I'll try to catch you." With that, he sprang down two steps so gracefully that she felt embarrassed for her own lack of confidence.

Arista stood on the landing and rocked back and forth, focusing on the first step. She leapt and landed on it a little too far forward. Waving her arms madly, she teetered on the edge, struggling desperately against falling. Royce held out his hands, ready to catch her, but she regained her balance. Shaking slightly, she took a deep breath.

"Don't over jump!" he reminded her.

No kidding, she thought. *As if I haven't already learned that lesson.*

The second jump was easier, and the third better still. Soon she developed a rhythm and moved down the steps at a brisk pace following Royce, who almost danced his way down. They were nearly to the bottom when Royce stopped.

"Keep going," he told her. "Stop when you reach the last step and wait there."

She nodded as he pulled the rope from around his shoulder and began tying it to the step he stood on. Arista continued to jump her way down, reminding herself not to be overconfident. When she saw the open expanse at the bottom, her remaining confidence fled. The gaping hole, which fell away into darkness, was enough to shake her back into terror.

"Well, well, princess!" the dwarf called to her. He stood in the open doorway of the corridor, grinning, showing a mouthful of yellowed teeth. "I really didn't expect to see you again. Where's the thief? Did he fall to his death?"

"You disgusting little beast!" she cried at him.

The tower shifted once more. Its shuddering caused Arista to stagger a bit on the step and her heart to pound in fear. Clouds of dust and bits of rock rained down, clattering off the walls and steps. Arista cowered, covering her head with her arms, until the shaking stopped and the debris settled.

"This old tower, she's almost ready to fall," the dwarf told her with a manic glee in his voice. "Such a pity to be so close to safety and yet still so very far. If only you were a frog, you might leap it. As it is, you still don't have a way out."

A coil of rope fell from the heights above. Suspended by a stair, the rope dangled midway between the princess and the dwarf. Along the slender line, Royce descended like a spider. When he reached a point level with Arista, he stopped and began to swing.

"Now *that* is impressive!" the dwarf exclaimed, and nodded, showing his approval.

Royce swung onto the step next to Arista and tied the rope around his own waist. "All we have to do is swing across. Just hang on to me."

The princess gladly threw her arms around the thief's shoulders and squeezed tight, as much out of fear as for safety.

"You might have actually made it," the dwarf said. "For that you have my respect, but you must understand I have a reputation to uphold. I can't have someone walking around boasting they escaped one of my traps." Then, without warning, he abruptly closed the door, sealing them in.

⋘

Hadrian heard the wail of a horn as he faced Braga in the corridor of the royal residence. "I think it will be quite some time until Wylin and the castle guards arrive," he said, taunting the archduke. "I suspect the master-at-arms has more on his mind than responding to the demands of an earl from Warric to report to the royal residence when his castle is being stormed."

"More's the pity for you, as I no longer have the luxury of keeping you alive," Braga said as he lunged once more.

He swiped at Hadrian with lightning-fast cuts. Hadrian danced away from Braga, retreating farther and farther down the hall. The archduke showed perfect form, his weight centered on his back foot while only the toe of his front foot touched the ground, his back straight, his sword arm outstretched, and his other arm raised in a graceful bent L. Even the fingers of his free hand were elegantly posed as if they were holding up an invisible wineglass. His long black hair, peppered with lines of gray, cascaded down to his shoulders, and not a trace of perspiration was on his brow.

Hadrian in contrast acted clumsy and unsure. The Melengar sword was far inferior to any of his own blades. The tip wavered as he tried to hold it steady with both hands. He inched backward, working to keep a distance between them.

The archduke lunged again. Hadrian parried and then dove past Braga, barely avoiding a return slice, which nicked a wall sconce. He took the opportunity to run down the hallway and slip into the chapel. "Are we playing hide-and-seek now?" Braga said, goading him.

Braga entered and crossed swiftly to the altar, where Hadrian stood. When the archduke swung at him, Hadrian stepped back, ducked a swiping stroke, and then leapt clear of a slash. Braga's attacks glanced off the statue of Novron and Maribor, taking part of the god's first three fingers off. Hadrian now stood before the wooden lectern, keeping his eyes on the archduke while he awaited the next attack.

"It's so poetic of you to choose to die in the same room as the king," Braga said. He swung right, and Hadrian glanced the stroke aside. Braga pivoted on his back foot and swung his sword overhead in a powerful downward stroke. Expecting this attack, counting on it, Hadrian dove and slid across the polished marble floor on his stomach in the direction of the chapel door.

Hadrian got to his feet and turned in time to see Braga's stroke had sliced into the vertical grain of the lectern. His swing had been so forceful that the blade was now wedged in the wood and the archduke struggled to free it. Taking advantage of his distraction, Hadrian ran to the door, slipped out, and closed it behind him. Driving his sword into the jamb, he wedged it shut.

"That should hold you for a while," Hadrian said to himself, pausing to catch his breath.

❧

"That little worm!" Arista spat through clenched teeth at the closed door.

The tower shuddered again, and this time larger pieces fell. One block of stone plummeted down, taking out a step only a few feet from them. Both shattered on impact and fell into the abyss of the tower's foundation. With the loss of those blocks, the tower came free and began to twist and topple.

"Hang on!" Royce shouted as he pushed off the step. The two flew across the gap to the door. He grabbed hold of the large iron door ring, and they each found footholds on the ledge of the doorjamb.

"He locked it," Royce informed her. He looped one arm through the door ring and removed his lock-picking tools from his belt. With his free hand, he worked the lock. A deep, resonating thunder shook the castle, and suddenly the rope tied to Royce went slack. The thief dropped his tools and pulled out his dagger. He cut the rope around his waist just as the stone slab attached to it passed them heading down. The rest of the tower was collapsing now.

Royce drove his dagger deep into the wooden door for another handhold as the tower fell around them. Walls hollowed out by the dwarf splintered into shards, which burst and flew in all directions. Rocks and stone pummeled them as Royce and Arista cowered under the scant protection of the narrow stone arch of the doorframe.

A fist-size stone struck Arista's back. She lost her tenuous foothold and screamed as she fell. In an instant, Royce grabbed her. Grasping blindly, he caught the back of her dress and a substantial amount of hair. "I can't hold you!" he shouted.

He felt her sliding down his body, the back of her dress

tearing. Royce gave up his own toehold, hanging by his arm hooked through the door ring, so that he could wrap his legs around her. The princess's fingers clawed his body frantically, and when they finally found his belt, she latched on.

Royce was temporarily blinded by a cloud of dust and powdered stone. When it settled, he found they were dangling in the brilliant sunlight on what was now an exterior wall of the castle's keep. The debris of the tower fell into the moat, making a pile of broken rocks seventy feet below. The crowd of trial watchers screamed and gasped, pointing up at them. "It's the princess!" a voice shouted.

"Can you reach the ledge?" Royce asked.

"No! If I try, I'll fall. I can't—"

Royce felt her slipping again and tried to tighten his leg hold on her, but he knew it would not be enough.

"Oh no! My fingers—I'm slipping!"

Royce's arm, crooked in the ring, was wrenching his shoulder badly. His other hand, which gripped Arista's dress and hair, was slowly losing hold. She was sliding down once again; soon he would lose her altogether. Royce felt a tug on his arm. The door opened, and a strong hand reached out and grabbed Arista.

"I've got you," Hadrian told her as he hauled the princess up. Then he pulled the door open wide, dragging Royce into the hallway with it.

They lay on the floor exhausted and covered in bits of rock. Royce got to his feet and dusted off his clothes. "I thought I felt it unlock," he said, getting up and retrieving his dagger from the face of the door.

Hadrian stood in the threshold, looking out at the clearing blue sky. "Well, Royce, I love what you've done with the place."

"Where's the dwarf?" Royce asked, looking around.

"I didn't see him."

"And Braga? You didn't kill him, did you?"

"No. I locked him in the chapel but it won't hold. Which reminds me, could I borrow your sword? You're not going to use it, anyway."

Royce handed him the falchion sword that had been part of his castle guard disguise. Hadrian took the weapon, slipped it from its sheath, and weighed it in his hand. "I tell you, these swords are terrible. They are heavy and have all the balance of a drunken three-legged dog trying to take a piss." He then looked at Arista and added, "Oh, excuse me, Your Highness. How are you doing, Princess?"

Arista got to her feet. "Much better now."

"For the record, we're even, right?" Royce asked her. "You saved us from prison and a horrible death, and now we've saved you."

"Fine," she agreed, wiping the dust from her torn dress. "But I would like to point out my rescue of you was far less death defying." She ran a hand through her disheveled hair. "That really hurt, you know."

"Falling would have hurt more."

A loud bang echoed from down the hall.

"Gotta go," Hadrian told them. "His Lordship is loose."

"Be careful," Arista shouted after him. "He's a renowned swordsman!"

"I'm really tired of hearing that," Hadrian grumbled as he started back up the hall. He had not gone far when Braga rounded the corner, coming toward them.

"So, you got her out!" Braga bellowed. "I'll just have to kill her myself, then."

"You'll have to get by me first, I'm afraid," Hadrian told him.

"That won't be a problem."

The archduke charged Hadrian, swinging at him in a fury.

Braga hammered stroke after stroke on him in a rage. Hadrian fought to deflect the fierce blows, which fell so fast they whistled in the air. The look on Braga's reddening face was one of hatred as he continued to pummel Hadrian.

"Braga!" Alric shouted from the far end of the hall.

The archduke spun, panting for air.

∽

Hadrian saw the prince standing at the far end of the corridor. He was dressed in plate armor and a white tabard marred by a spattering of blood. Alric's hand rested on the hilt of his sheathed sword, and at his side were the Pickerings and Sir Ecton. Each wore a grim and dangerous look.

"Put down your weapon," the prince ordered in a powerful voice. "It's over. This is my kingdom!"

"You filthy little creature!" Braga cursed at the prince. He turned his attention away from Hadrian and began walking toward Alric. Hadrian did not follow. Instead, he joined Royce and Arista to watch.

"Did you think I was after your precious little kingdom?" Braga bellowed. "Is that what you think? I was trying to save the *world*, you fools! Can't you see it? Look at him!" The archduke pointed at the prince. "Look at the little maggot prince!" He turned and pointed back at Arista. "And her, too! Just like their father; they aren't human!" Braga, his face still red from the fight, continued down the corridor toward Alric. "You would have filth rule you all, but not me. Not while there is breath in this body!"

Braga charged forward, raising his sword as he moved. When he came within reach of Alric, he brought it down toward the prince. Before Alric could react, the attack was deflected. An elegant rapier caught Braga's blade mid-stroke.

Count Pickering held Braga's sword in the air, and Sir Ecton pulled the prince out of harm's way.

"You have your sword, I see. So there will be no excuse for you this time, dear count," Braga said.

"There will be no need for one. You are a traitor to the crown, and in memory of my friend Amrath, I'll end this."

Blades flashed. Pickering was as much a master of fencing as Braga, and the two moved elegantly, their swords appearing as extensions of their bodies. Reaching for their weapons, Mauvin and Fanen started forward, but Ecton stopped them. "This is your father's fight."

Pickering and Braga fought to kill. Sword strokes swept faster than the eye could follow, their deadly blades whistling a song to each other, crashing in chorus. The incredibly lustrous blade of Pickering's rapier caught the faint light in the corridor and glowed as it streaked through the air. It flashed and sparked when steel met steel.

Braga lunged, nicked Pickering's side, and, sweeping back, cut him shallowly across the chest. Pickering barely blocked a second stab with a quick parry, which allowed him an overhead stroke. Braga raised his sword to block, but Pickering ignored the defense. He swung down with force and speed, streaking light from his sword.

Hadrian instinctually cringed. The high, overpowered stroke would leave Pickering vulnerable, open to a fatal riposte by Braga. Then the metal of the swords clashed. A brilliant spark flared as, incredibly, Pickering's blade sheared Braga's sword in two. The count's stroke continued unabated into the archduke's throat. The lord chancellor collapsed to the floor, his head rolling a foot away.

Mauvin and Fanen rushed to their father's side, beaming with obvious pride and relief. Alric ran down the hall to where his sister stood between the two thieves. "Arista!" he shouted as he threw his arms around her. "Thank Maribor you're all right!"

"You aren't angry with me?" she asked, pulling away from him with surprise in her voice.

Alric shook his head. "I owe you my life," he said, hugging her again. "And as for you two—" he began, looking at Royce and Hadrian.

"Alric," Arista interrupted, "it was not their fault. They didn't kill Father, and they didn't want to kidnap you. It was my doing. I was the one who forced them. They didn't do anything."

"Oh, you are quite wrong there, my dear sister. They did a *great* deal." Alric smiled and placed a hand on Hadrian's shoulder. "Thank you."

"You're not going to charge us for the tower, I hope," Hadrian said. "But if you are, it was Royce's fault and should come out of his share."

Alric chuckled.

"My fault?" Royce growled. "Find that little bearded menace and take your payment out of *his* stubby little hide."

"I don't understand," Arista replied, looking confused. "You wanted them executed."

"You must be mistaken, dear sister. These two fine men are the royal protectors of Essendon, and it appears they have done a fine job today."

"Your Lordship." Marshal Garret appeared in the hall and approached the count, glancing only briefly at the dead body of Braga. "The castle has been secured and the mercenaries are slain or have fled. It would appear the castle guard is still loyal to the House of Essendon. The nobles are anxious to hear about the state of affairs and are waiting in the court."

"Good," the count replied. "Tell them His Majesty will

address them soon. Oh, and send someone to clean this mess up, will you?" The marshal bowed and left.

Alric and his sister walked hand in hand down the corridor toward the others. Hadrian and Royce followed behind them. "Even now it's hard for me to believe him capable of such treachery," Alric said, looking down at Braga's body. A large puddle of blood stretched across the floor of the hallway and Arista lifted the hem of her dress as she passed.

"What was all that ranting about us not being human?" Arista asked.

"He was clearly insane," Bishop Saldur said, approaching with Archibald Ballentyne in tow. Although Hadrian had never met the bishop in person, he knew who he was. Saldur greeted the prince and princess with a warm smile and fatherly expression. "It's so good to see you, Alric," he said, placing his hands on the boy's shoulders. "And my dear Arista, no one is more pleased than I about your innocence. I must beg your forgiveness, my dear, as I was misled by your uncle. He planted seeds of doubts in my mind. I should have followed my heart and realized you could not possibly have done the things he accused you of." He gently kissed her on one cheek and then the other.

The bishop looked down at the blood-soaked body at their feet. "I fear the guilt of killing the king was too much for the poor man, and in the end, he lost his mind completely. Perhaps he was certain you were dead, Alric, and seeing you in the hallway, he took you for a ghost or a demon back from the grave to haunt him."

"Perhaps," Alric said skeptically. "Well, at least it's over now."

"What about the dwarf?" Arista asked.

"Dwarf?" Alric replied. "How do you know about the dwarf?"

"He was the one who set the trap in the tower. He nearly killed me and Royce. Does anyone know where he has gotten to? He was just here."

"He's responsible for far more than that. Mauvin, run and tell the marshal to organize a search immediately," Alric instructed.

"Right away." Mauvin nodded and ran off.

"I, too, am pleased you are all right, Your Highness," Archibald told the prince. "I was told you were dead."

"And were you here to pay your respects to my memory?"

"I was here by invitation."

"Who invited you?" Alric asked, and looked at the slain corpse of Braga. "Him? What dealings do an Imperialist earl from Warric and a traitorous archduke have in Melengar?"

"It was a cordial visit, I assure you."

Alric glared at the earl. "Get out of my kingdom before I have you seized as a conspirator."

"You wouldn't dare," Archibald returned. "I'm a vassal of King Ethelred. Seize me or even treat me roughly and you risk war—a struggle Melengar can ill afford, particularly now, with an inexperienced boy at the helm."

Alric drew his sword, and Archibald took two steps back. "Escort the earl out before I forget Melengar has a treaty of peace with Warric."

"Times are changing, Your Highness," Archibald called to the prince as guards led him away. "The New Empire is coming, and there is no place for an archaic monarchy in the new order."

"Is there no way I can throw him in the dungeon, even for a few days?" Alric asked Pickering. "Can I try him as a spy perhaps?"

Before Pickering could reply, the bishop Saldur spoke. "The earl is quite right, Your Highness. Any hostile act made against Ballentyne would be considered by King Ethelred to be an act of war against Chadwick. Just consider how you would respond if Count Pickering here were hanged in Aquesta. You wouldn't stand for it any more than he would. Besides, the earl is all bluster. He is young and merely trying to sound important. Forgive him his youth. Have you not made errors in judgment as well?"

"Perhaps," Alric muttered. "Still, I can't help but suspect that snake is up to no good. I just wish there was some way I could teach him a lesson."

"Your Highness?" Hadrian said, stopping him. "If you don't mind, Royce and I have friends in the city we'd like to check on."

"Oh, yes, of course, go right ahead," Alric responded. "But there is the matter of payment. You've done me a great service," he said, looking fondly at his sister. "I intend to honor my word. You can name your price."

"If it's all right, we'll get back to you on that," Royce said.

"I understand." The prince revealed a hint of concern. "But I do hope you'll be reasonable in your request and not bankrupt the kingdom."

"You should address the court," Pickering told Alric.

Alric nodded and he, Arista, and Mauvin disappeared down the stairs. Pickering lingered behind with the two thieves.

"I think there's a chance that boy will actually make a decent king," he mentioned once the prince was too far away to hear. "I had my doubts in the past, but he seems to have changed. He is more serious, more confident."

"So, the sword is magic after all." Hadrian motioned toward the rapier.

"Hmm?" Pickering looked down at the sword he wore at his side and grinned. "Oh, well, let's just say it gives me an edge in a battle. That reminds me, why were you letting Braga beat you?"

"What do you mean?"

"I saw you fighting when we first came up. Your stance was defensive, your strokes all parries and blocks. You never once attacked."

"I was frightened," Hadrian lied. "Braga has won so many awards and tournament competitions, and I haven't won any."

Pickering looked puzzled. "But not being noble born, you aren't allowed to enter a tournament."

Hadrian pursed his lips and nodded. "Now that you mention it, I suppose you're right. You'd best see to your wounds, Your Lordship. You're bleeding on your nice tunic."

Pickering glanced down and looked surprised to see the slice Braga had given him across the chest. "Oh, yes, well, it doesn't matter. The tunic is ruined from the cut anyway, and the bleeding seems to have stopped."

Mauvin returned and trotted over to them. He stood next to his father, his arm around his waist. "I have soldiers looking for the dwarf but so far no luck." Despite the bad news, Mauvin was smiling broadly.

"What are you grinning at?" his father asked.

"I knew you could best him. I did doubt it for a time, but deep down I knew."

The count nodded and a thoughtful expression came over his face. He looked at Hadrian. "After so many years of doubt, it was fortuitous I had the opportunity and good fortune to defeat Braga, particularly with my sons watching."

Hadrian nodded and smiled. "That's true."

There was a pause as Pickering studied his face and then he placed a hand on Hadrian's shoulder. "To be quite honest, I for one am very pleased you're not noble, Mr. Hadrian Blackwater, quite pleased indeed."

"Are you coming, Your Lordship?" Sir Ecton called, and the count and his sons headed off.

"You didn't really hold back on Braga so Pickering could kill him, did you?" Royce asked after the two were left alone in the hallway.

"Of course not. I held off because it's death for a commoner to kill a noble."

"That's what I thought." Royce sounded relieved. "For a minute, I wondered if you'd gone from jumping on the good-deed wagon to leading the whole wagon train."

"Sure the gentry appear all nice and friendly, but if I'd killed him, even though they wanted him dead anyway, you can be sure they wouldn't be patting me on the back, saying, 'Good job.' No, it's best to avoid killing nobles."

"At least not where there are witnesses," Royce said with a grin.

As they headed out of the castle, they heard Alric's voice echoing: "...was a traitor to the crown and responsible for the murder of my father. He attempted to murder me and to execute my sister. Yet, due to the wisdom of the princess and the heroism of others, I am standing here before you."

This was followed by a roar of applause and cheers.

CHAPTER 10

CORONATION DAY

Seventy-eight people had died, and over two hundred bore wounds from what became known as the Battle of Medford. The timely attack by the citizenry at the gate had precipitated the prince's entrance into the city, and arguably had saved his life. Once news of Alric's return spread through the city, all resistance ended. This restored peace but not order. For several hours after the battle, roving gangs took the opportunity to loot shops and storehouses, mostly along the riverfront. A shoemaker died defending his cobbler shop, and a weaver was badly beaten. In addition to the general thieving, the sheriff, his two deputies, and a moneylender were murdered. Many believed there were those who took advantage of the chaos to settle old scores. The killers were never identified, and no one bothered to look for the looters. In the end, no one was even arrested; it was enough that the violence was over.

Most of the snow that had fallen the day of the battle had melted over the next few days, leaving only dirty patches hiding in the shadows. Still, for the most part, the weather remained decidedly cold. Autumn was officially finished, and winter had arrived. In the freezing winds, a silent crowd stood outside the royal crypt for hours as they removed Amrath's body for the official state funeral. Many others were buried the same day. The funerals provided a cleansing of the entire city's grief, followed by a weeklong period of mourning.

Among the dead was Wylin, the captain of the guard of Essendon Castle. He had fallen while directing the defenses at the castle gate. It was never determined if Wylin had been a traitor or had merely been deceived by the archduke's lies. Alric gave him the benefit of the doubt and granted him burial with full honors. Although Mason Grumon died, Dixon Taft, manager of The Rose and Thorn, survived the battle with only the loss of his right arm just above the elbow. He might have died, along with many others, except for the efforts of Gwen DeLancy and her girls. Prostitutes, it turned out, made excellent nurses. The maimed and wounded who lacked family to care for them filled Medford House for weeks. When word of this reached the castle, food, supplies, and linens were sent.

News spread throughout Melengar of Alric's heroic charge on the fortified gates. How he had survived the hail of arrows, only to bravely fling off his helm and dare them a second time—it made for great barroom stories. Few had thought much of the son of Amrath prior to the battle, but now he became a hero in the eyes of many. A somewhat lesser-known tale gained popularity a few days later as it, too, circulated through the city's taverns. This outlandish yarn described how two criminals, falsely accused of the king's murder, had escaped a torturous death by abducting the prince. The story grew with each telling, and soon these same thieves were said to have gone on a rollicking trip through the countryside with the prince, returning just in time to save the princess from the tower seconds before it collapsed. Some even claimed to have helped the thieves save the prince from a roadside execution, while others insisted they personally saw the princess and one of the criminals dangling from the side of the castle after the collapse of the tower.

Despite extensive searches, the dwarf whose hand had actually killed the king escaped. Alric posted a reward notice offering one hundred gold tenents on every crossroad sign and on the door of every tavern and church in the realm. Patrols rode the length of every road, searching barns, storehouses, mills, and even under the spans of bridges, yet he was not found.

Following the week of mourning, work began on repairing the castle. Crews cleared away the debris, and architects estimated at least a year to rebuild the lost tower. Though the falcon flag flew above the castle, the city saw little of Prince Alric. He remained sequestered within the halls of power, buried under hundreds of obligations. Count Pickering, acting as a counselor, remained in the castle along with his sons. He assisted the young prince in his efforts to assume his father's role.

One month to the day after the burial of King Amrath, the prince's coronation took place. By that time, the snows had returned and the city was white once more. Everyone came to the ceremony, yet only a fraction could fit inside the expansive Mares Cathedral, where the coronation took place. The majority caught a brief glimpse of their new monarch when he rode in an open carriage back to the castle or as he stood on the open balcony while trumpets blared.

It was a full day of celebration with minstrels and street performers hired to entertain the citizenry. The castle even provided free ale and rows upon rows of tables filled with all manner of food. In the evening, which came sooner with the shortening of the days, people crammed into the local taverns and inns, which were full of out-of-town visitors. The locals retold the stories of the Battle of Medford and the now famous legend of *Prince Alric and the Thieves*. These stories were still popular and showed no sign of going out of fashion. The day was long and eventually even the lights in the public houses winked out.

One of the few buildings still burning a candle was in the Artisan Quarter. It had originally been a haberdashery, but the previous owner, Lester Furl, had died in the battle the month before. Some said the plumed hat he had worn that day had caught the attention of an axe. Since then, the wooden sign of the ornate cavalier hat had still hung above the door, but no hats were for sale in the window. Even late into the night, the light was always on; however, no one was ever seen entering or exiting the shop. A small man in a simple robe greeted those nosy enough to knock. Behind him, visitors saw a room filled with the dried, hairless skins of animals. Most soaked in tubs or were stretched out on frames. There were pumice stones, needles and thread, and folded sheets of vellum piled neatly along the walls. The room also contained three desks with upright tops over which large sheets of parchment lay with carefully written text. Bottles of ink rested on shelves and in open drawers. The man was always polite, and when asked what he sold in his shop, he would reply, "Nothing." He simply wrote books. Because few people could read, most inquiries ended there.

The fact was there were very few books in the shop.

Myron Lanaklin sat alone in the store. He had written half a page of *Grigoles Treatise on Imperial Common Law* and then just stopped. The room was cold and silent. He stood up, walked to the shop window, and looked out at the dark, snowy street. In a city with more people than he had seen before in his lifetime, he felt utterly alone. A month had passed, but he had finished only half of his first book. He found himself spending most of his time just sitting. In the silence, he imagined he could hear the sound of his brothers speaking the evening vespers.

He avoided sleep because of the nightmares. They had started the third night he slept in the shop and were terrible. Visions of flames and sounds of pleading coming from his own mouth as the voices of his family died in the inferno. Every night they died again, and every day he awoke on the cold floor of the tiny room in a world more silent and isolated than the abbey had ever been. He missed his home and the mornings he spent with Renian.

Alric made good on his promise. The new King of Melengar provided him the shop rent-free and all the materials needed for making his books. Never was there a mention of cost. Myron should have been happy, but he felt more lost each day. Although he had more food than ever before, and no abbot to restrict his diet, he ate little. His appetite dwindled along with his desire to write.

When he had first arrived at the shop, he had felt obligated to replace the books, but as the days slipped by, he sat alone and confused. How could he *replace* the books? They were not missing. No shelf lay bare; no library stood wanting. What would he do if he ever completed the project? What would he do with the books? What would become of them? What would become of him? They had no home, and neither did he.

Myron sat down on the wooden floor in the corner, pulling his legs to his chest, and rested his head against the wall. "Why did I have to be the one who lived?" he muttered to the empty room. "Why did I have to be left behind? Why is it I'm cursed with an indelible memory, so that I can recall every face, every scream, every cry?"

As usual, Myron wept. There was no one to see, so he let the tears run unchecked down his cheeks. He cried there on the floor in the flickering candlelight and soon fell asleep.

The knock on the door startled him and he stood up. He could not have been asleep long; the candle still burned. Myron moved to the door and, opening it a crack, peered out. On the stoop outside, two men in heavy winter cloaks stood waiting.

"Myron? Are you going to let us in or leave us to freeze?"

"Hadrian? Royce!" Myron exclaimed as he threw open the door. He embraced Hadrian immediately and then turned to Royce and paused, deciding a handshake would suit him better.

"So it's been a while," Hadrian said, kicking the snow off his boots. "How many books have you finished?"

Myron looked sheepish. "I've had a little trouble adjusting but I'll get them done. Isn't this place wonderful?" he said, trying to sound sincere. "It was very generous of His Majesty to provide all this for me. I've enough vellum to last years, and ink? Well, don't get me started. As Finiless wrote, 'More could not be gotten though the world be emptied to the breath of time.'"

"So you like it here?" Hadrian asked.

"Oh, I love it, yes. I really couldn't ask for anything more." The two thieves exchanged looks, the meaning of which Myron could not discern. "Can I get either of you something—tea, perhaps? The king is very good to me. I even have honey to sweeten it."

"Tea would be nice," Royce said.

Myron moved to the counter to fetch a pot. "So what are you two doing out so late?" he asked, then laughed at himself. "Oh, never mind, I guess this isn't late for *you*. I suppose you work nights."

"Something like that," Hadrian said. "We just got back from a trip to Chadwick. We are heading back to The Rose and Thorn but wanted to stop by here on the way and deliver the news."

"News? What kind of news?"

"Well, I thought it might be good news, but now I'm not so sure."

"Why's that?" the monk asked, pouring water into the pot.

"Well, it would mean leaving here."

"It would?" Myron turned suddenly, spilling the water.

"Well, yes, but I suppose if you're really attached to this place, we could—"

"To go where?" Myron asked anxiously, setting down the pitcher, forgetting the tea.

"Well," Hadrian began, "Alric offered us whatever we wanted as payment for saving his sister, but seeing as how Arista saved our life first, it didn't seem right asking for money, or land, or anything personal like that. We got to thinking just how much was lost when the Winds Abbey was destroyed. Not just the books, mind you, but the safe haven for those lost in the wilderness. So we asked the king to rebuild the abbey just like it was."

"Are—are you serious?" Myron stammered. "And did he say yes?"

"To be honest, he sounded relieved," Royce said. "I think he felt as if there was a dagger dangling over his head for a month. I suppose he was afraid we'd ask for something ridiculous like his firstborn or the crown jewels."

"We might have, if we hadn't already stolen them." Hadrian chuckled, and Myron was not sure if he was joking or not.

"But if you really like this place..." Hadrian said, whirling his finger in the air. "I suppose we—"

"No! No—I mean, I think you are right. The abbey should be rebuilt for the sake of the kingdom."

"Glad you feel that way, because we need you to help the builders design it. I'm assuming you could draw a few floor plans and maybe some sketches?"

"Certainly, down to the finest detail."

Hadrian chuckled. "I bet you can. I can see you're going to drive the royal architect to drink."

"Who will be the abbot? Has Alric contacted the Dibben Monastery already?"

"He sent out a messenger this morning as one of his first acts as king. You're going to have a few guest monks trickling in over the winter, and this spring all of you'll have a great deal of work to do."

Myron was grinning widely.

"About that tea?" Royce inquired.

"Oh yes, sorry." He returned to pouring water into the pot. Stopping once more, he turned back to the thieves, and his grin faded.

"I would so much love to return to my home and see it rise again. But..." Myron paused.

"What is it?"

"Won't the Imperialists simply come back? If they hear the abbey is there again—I don't think I could..."

"Relax, Myron," Hadrian said. "That's not going to happen."

"But how can you be sure?"

"Trust me, the Imperialists won't advocate another foray into Melengar," Royce assured the monk. The smile on the thief's face made Myron think of a cat, and he was happy not to be a mouse.

⋄

In the hours before dawn, the Lower Quarter was quiet. Dampened by the snow, the only sound came from the muffled hoof falls of mounts as they moved slowly up the alley to The Rose and Thorn.

"Do you need any of the money?" Royce asked Hadrian.

"I have enough. Deposit the rest with Gwen. What does that come to now?"

"Well, we're in pretty good shape. We have our share of the fifteen gold tenents for returning Alenda's letters, and the twenty from Ballentyne for stealing them in the first place, plus DeWitt's one hundred, and Alric's one hundred. You know, one day we're going to have to find DeWitt—and *thank him* for that job." Royce grinned.

"Do you think it was fair asking for the money along with the abbey?" Hadrian asked. "I have to admit the guy was starting to grow on me, and I hate to think we took advantage of him."

"The hundred was for going into Gutaria with him," Royce reminded him. "The abbey was for saving his sister. We didn't ask for *anything* Alric didn't agree to in advance. And he did say anything, so we could easily have asked for land and noble rank."

"Why didn't we?"

"Oh? So you would like to be the count Blackwater, would you?"

"It might have been nice," Hadrian said, sitting up straighter in his saddle. "And you could be the infamous marquis Melborn."

"Why infamous?"

"Would you prefer notorious? Nefarious, perhaps?"

"What's wrong with *beloved*?"

Neither could hold a straight face at the thought.

"Come to think of it, we failed to bill the good king for saving him from Trumbul. Do you think—"

"It's too late, Royce," Hadrian told him.

Royce sighed, disappointed. "So, I think he wasn't too put out, all things considered. Besides, we *are* thieves, remember?

Anyway, the bottom line is, we won't be starving this winter."

"Yes, we've been good little squirrels, haven't we?" Hadrian said.

"Maybe this spring we can start that fishing enterprise you wanted."

"I thought you wanted the winery."

Royce shrugged.

"Well, you keep thinking. I'm going to go wake up Emerald and let her know I'm back. It's too cold to sleep alone tonight."

Royce passed the tavern and dismounted at Medford House. For some time, he stood, just staring at the top window, while his feet grew colder and colder in the snow.

"You *are* going to come up, aren't you?" Gwen asked from the doorway. She was still dressed and as pretty as ever. "Isn't it awfully cold out there?"

Royce smiled at her. "You waited up."

"You said you'd be coming back tonight."

Royce pulled his saddlebag off his horse and carried it up the steps. "I have another deposit to make."

"Is that why you were standing in the snow for so long? You were trying to decide whether or not to trust me with your money?"

Her words stung him. "No!"

"Then why were you standing there so long?"

Royce hesitated. "Would you prefer me if I were a fisherman, or perhaps a winemaker?"

"No," she said. "I prefer you as you are."

Royce took her hand. "Wouldn't you be better off with a nice farmer or rich merchant? Someone you can raise children with, someone you can grow old with, someone who will stay at home and not leave you alone and wondering."

She kissed him.

"What was that for?"

"I'm a prostitute, Royce. There aren't many men who consider themselves unworthy of me. I love you as you are and always will no matter what path you choose. If I did have the power to change anything, it would be to convince you of that."

He put his arms around her, and she pulled him close. "I missed you," she whispered.

∽

Archibald Ballentyne woke with a start.

He had fallen asleep in the Gray Tower of Ballentyne Castle. The fire had burned out, and the room was growing cold. It was also dark, but the dim glow of the faint orange embers in the hearth gave a little light. There was an odd and unpleasant odor in the air, and he felt the weight of something large and round on his lap. He could not make it out in the darkness. It seemed like a melon wrapped in linen. He stood up and set the object in his chair. He moved aside the brass screen and, taking two logs from the stack nearby, placed them on top of the hot coals. He prodded the embers with a poker, blew on them, and coaxed the fire back to life. As he did, the room filled with light once more.

He set the poker back to its stand, replaced the screen, and dusted his hands off. As he turned around, he looked at the chair he had been sleeping in and immediately pinwheeled backward in horror.

There on his seat was the head of the former archduke of Melengar. The cloth, which was covering it, had partially fallen away, revealing a large portion of what had once been Braga's face. The eyes were rolled back, leaving white and milky orbs in their sockets. The yellowed skin, stretched and leathery, was shriveled. A host of some kind of worms moved in the gaping mouth, slithering in a heaving mass, which made it almost appear as if Braga's tongue was trying to speak.

Archibald's stomach twisted in knots. Too frightened to scream, he looked around the room for intruders. As he did, he saw writing on the wall. Painted in what appeared to be blood, in letters a foot tall, were the words:

NEVER INTERFERE WITH MELENGAR AGAIN
BY ORDER OF THE KING
...AND US

BOOK II

AVEMPARTHA

Chapter 1

Colnora

As the man stepped out of the shadows, Wyatt Deminthal knew this would be the worst, and possibly the last, day of his life. Dressed in raw wool and rough leather, the man was vaguely familiar, a face seen briefly by candlelight over two years earlier, a face Wyatt had hoped he would never see again. The man carried three swords, each one battered and dull, the grips sweat-stained and frayed. Taller than Wyatt by nearly a foot, with broader shoulders and powerful hands, he stood with his weight distributed across the balls of his feet. He locked his eyes on Wyatt the way cats stare at mice.

"Baron Delano DeWitt of Dagastan?" It was not a question but an accusation.

Wyatt felt his heart shudder. Even after he recognized the face, a part of him—the optimist that had somehow managed to survive after all these dreadful years—still hoped the man was only after his money. But with the sound of those words, that hope died.

"Sorry, you must be mistaken," he replied to the man blocking his path, trying his best to sound friendly, care-free—guiltless. He even tried to mask his Calian accent to further the charade.

"No, I'm not," the man insisted as he crossed the width of the alley, moving closer, eating up the comforting space between them. His hands remained in full view, which was more worrisome than if they had rested on the pommels of his swords. Even though Wyatt wore a fine cutlass, the man had no fear of him.

"Well, as it happens, my name is Wyatt Deminthal. I think, therefore, that you must be mistaken."

Wyatt was pleased he had managed to say all this without stammering. With great effort, he concentrated on relaxing his body, letting his shoulders droop, resting his weight on one heel. He even forced a pleasant smile and glanced around casually as an innocent man might.

They faced each other in the narrow, cluttered alley only a few yards from where Wyatt rented a loft. It was dark. A lantern hung a few feet behind him, mounted on the side of the feed store. He could see its flickering glow, the light glistening in puddles the rain had left on the cobblestone. Behind him, he could still hear the music of the Gray Mouse Tavern, muffled and tinny. Voices echoed in the distance, laughter, shouts, arguments; the clatter of a dropped pot followed the cry of an unseen cat. Somewhere a carriage rolled along, its wooden wheels clacking on wet stone. It was late. The only people on the streets were drunken men, whores, and those with business best done in the dark.

The man took another step closer. Wyatt did not like the look in his eyes. They held a hard edge, a serious sense of resolve, but it was the hint of regret he detected that jarred Wyatt the most.

"You're the one who hired me and my friend to steal a sword from Essendon Castle."

"I'm sorry. I really have no idea what you are talking about. I don't even know where this *Essendon* place is. You must have me confused with some other fellow. It's probably the hat." Wyatt took off his wide-brimmed cavalier and showed it to the man. "See, it's a common hat in that anyone can buy one, but uncommon at the same time, as few people wear them these days. You most likely saw someone in a similar hat and just assumed it was me. An understandable mistake. No hard feelings, I can assure you."

Wyatt placed his hat back on, tilting it slightly down in front and cocking it a bit to one side. In addition to the hat, he wore an expensive black and red silk doublet and a short flashy cape; however, the lack of any velvet trimming, combined with his worn boots, betrayed his station. The single gold ring piercing his left ear revealed even more; it was his one concession, a memento to the life he had left behind.

"When we got to the chapel, the king was on the floor. Dead."

"I can see this is not a happy story," Wyatt said, tugging on the fingers of his fine red gloves—a habit he had when nervous.

"Guards were waiting. They dragged us to the dungeons. We were nearly executed."

"I'm sorry you were ill used, but as I said, I'm not DeWitt. I've never heard of him. I'll be certain to mention you should our paths ever cross. Who shall I say is looking?"

"Riyria."

Behind Wyatt, the feed store light winked out and a voice whispered in his ear, "It's elvish for *two*."

His heartbeat doubled, and before he could turn, he felt the sharp edge of a blade at his throat. He froze, barely allowing himself to breathe.

"You set us up to die." The voice behind him took over. "You brokered the deal. You put us in that chapel so we would take the blame. I'm here to repay your kindness. If you have any last words, say them now, and say them quietly."

Wyatt was a good cardplayer. He knew bluffs and the man behind him was not bluffing. He was not there to scare, pressure, or manipulate him. He was not looking for information; he knew everything he wanted to know. It was in his voice, his tone, his words, the pace of his breath in Wyatt's ear—he was there to kill him.

"What's going on, Wyatt?" a small voice called.

Down the alley, a door opened and light spilled forth, outlining a young girl, whose shadow ran across the cobblestones and up the far wall. She was thin with shoulder-length hair and wore a nightgown that reached to her ankles, exposing bare feet.

"Nothing, Allie—get back inside!" Wyatt shouted, his accent fully exposed.

"Who are those men you're talking to?" Allie took a step toward them. Her foot disturbed a puddle, which rippled. "They look angry."

"I won't allow witnesses," the voice behind Wyatt hissed.

"Leave her alone," Wyatt begged. "She wasn't involved. I swear. It was just me."

"Involved in what?" Allie asked. "What's going on?" She took another step.

"Stay where you are, Allie! Don't come any closer. Please, Allie, do as I say." The girl stopped. "I did a bad thing once, Allie. You have to understand. I did it for us, for you, Elden, and me. Remember when I took that job a few winters back? When I went up north for a couple of days? I—I did the bad thing then. I pretended to be someone I wasn't and I almost got some people killed. That's how I got the money for the winter. Don't hate me, Allie. I love you, honey. Please just get back inside."

"No!" she protested. "I can see the knife. They're going to hurt you."

"If you don't, they'll kill us both!" Wyatt shouted harshly, too harshly. He had not wanted to do it, but he had to make her understand.

Allie was crying now. She stood in the alley, in the shaft of lamplight, shaking.

"Go inside, honey," Wyatt told her, gathering himself and trying to calm his voice. "It will be all right. Don't cry. Elden will watch over you. Let him know what happened. It will be all right."

She continued to sob.

"Please, honey, you have to go inside now," Wyatt pleaded. "It's all you can do. It's what I need you to do. Please."

"I—love—you, Da—ddy!"

"I know, honey. I know. I love you too, and I'm *so sorry.*"

Allie slowly stepped back into the doorway, the sliver of light diminishing until the door snapped shut, leaving the alley once more in darkness. Only the faint blue light from the cloud-shrouded moon filtered into the narrow corridor where the three men stood.

"How old is she?" the voice behind him asked.

"Leave her out of this. Just make it quick—can you give me that much?" Wyatt braced himself for what was to come. Seeing the child had broken him. He shook violently, his gloved hands in fists, his chest so tight it was difficult to swallow and hard to breathe. He felt the metal edge against his throat and waited for it to move, waited for it to drag.

"Did you know it was a trap when you came to hire us?" the man with three swords asked.

"What? *No!*"

"Would you still have done it if you knew?"

"I don't know—I guess—yes. We needed the money."

"So, you're not a baron?"

"No."

"What, then?"

"I was a ship's captain."

"Was? What happened?"

"Are you going to kill me anytime soon? Why all the questions?"

"Each question you answer is another breath you take," the voice from behind him spoke. It was the voice of death, emotionless, and empty. Hearing it made Wyatt's stomach lurch as if he were looking over the edge of a high cliff. Not seeing his face, knowing that he held the blade that would kill him, made it feel like an execution. He thought of Allie, hoped she would be all right, then realized—she would see him. The thought struck with surprising clarity. She would rush out after it was over and find him on the street. She would wade through his blood.

"What happened?" the executioner asked again, his voice instantly erasing all other thoughts.

"I sold my ship."

"Why?"

"It doesn't matter."

"Gambling debts?"

"No."

"Why, then?"

"What difference does it make? You're going to kill me anyway. Just do it!"

He had steadied himself. He was ready. He clenched his teeth, shut his eyes. Still, the killer delayed.

"It makes a difference," the executioner whispered in his ear, "because Allie is not your daughter."

The blade came away from Wyatt's neck.

Slowly, hesitantly, Wyatt turned to face the man holding the dagger. He had never seen him before. He was smaller than his partner, dressed in a black cloak with a hood that shaded his features, revealing only hints of a face—the tip of a sharp nose, highlight of a cheek, end of a chin.

"How do you know that?"

"She saw us in the dark. She saw my knife at your throat as we stood deep in shadow across the length of twenty yards."

Wyatt said nothing. He did not dare move or speak. He did not know what to think. Somehow, something had changed. The certainty of death rolled back a step, but its shadow lingered. He had no idea what was happening and was terrified of making a misstep.

"You sold your ship to buy her, didn't you?" the hooded man guessed. "But from whom, and why?"

Wyatt stared at the face beneath the hood—a bleak landscape, a desert dry of compassion. Death was there, a mere breath away; an utterance remained all that separated eternity from salvation.

The bigger man, the one with three swords, reached out and placed a hand on his shoulder. "A lot is riding on your answer. But you already knew that, didn't you? Right now you're trying to decide what to say, and of course, you're trying to guess what we want to hear. Don't. Go with the truth. At least that way, if you're wrong, your death won't have been because of a lie."

Wyatt nodded. He closed his eyes again, took a deep breath, and said, "I bought her from a man named Ambrose."

"Ambrose Moor?" the executioner asked.

"Yes."

Wyatt waited but nothing happened. He opened his eyes. The dagger was gone and the three-sword man was smiling at him. "I don't know how much that little girl cost, but it was the best money you ever spent."

"You aren't going to kill me?"

"Not today. You still owe us one hundred tenents, for the balance on that job," the man in the hood told him coldly.

"I—I don't have it."

"Get it."

Light burst into the alley as the door to Wyatt's loft flew open with a bang and Elden charged out. He held his mammoth two-headed axe high above his head as he strode toward them with a determined look.

The man with three swords rapidly drew two of them.

"Elden, *no!*" Wyatt shouted. "They're not going to kill me! Just stop."

Elden paused, his axe held aloft, his eyes looking back and forth between them.

"They're letting me go," Wyatt assured him, then turned to the two men. "You are, aren't you?"

The hooded man nodded. "Pay off that debt."

As the men walked away, Elden moved to Wyatt's side and Allie ran out to hug him. The three returned to the loft and slipped inside the doorway. Elden took one last look around, then closed the door behind them.

∽

"Did you see the size of that guy?" Hadrian asked Royce, still glancing over his shoulder as if the giant might try to sneak up on them. "I've never seen anyone that big. He had to be a good seven feet tall, and that neck, those shoulders, and that axe! It would take two of me just to lift it. Maybe he isn't human; maybe he's a giant, or a troll. Some people swear they exist. I've met a few who say they have seen them personally."

Royce looked at his friend and scowled.

"Okay, so it's mostly drunks in bars who say that, but that doesn't mean it's not possible. Ask Myron, he'll back me up."

The two headed north toward the Langdon Bridge. It was quiet here. In the respectable hill district of Colnora, people were more inclined to sleep at night than to carouse in taverns. This was the home of merchant titans, affluent businessmen who owned houses grander than many of the palatial mansions of upper nobility.

Colnora had started out as a meager rest stop at the intersection of the Wesbaden and Aquesta trade routes. Originally, a farmer named Hollenbeck and his wife had watered caravans there and granted room in their barn to the traders in return for news and goods. Hollenbeck had an eye for quality and always picked the best of the lot.

Soon his farm became an inn and Hollenbeck added a store and a warehouse to sell what he acquired to passing travelers. The merchants deprived of first pick bought plots next to his farm and opened their own shops, taverns, and roadhouses. The farm became a village, then a city, but still, the caravans gave preference to Hollenbeck. Legend held that the reason was their fondness for his wife, a wonderful woman who, in addition to being uncommonly beautiful, sang and played the mandolin. It was said she baked the finest cobblers of peach, blueberry, and apple. Centuries later, when no one could accurately place the location of the original Hollenbeck farm, and few remembered there had ever been such a farmer, they continued to remember his wife—Colnora.

Over the years the city flourished, until it became the largest urban center in Avryn. Shoppers found the latest style in clothes, the most exquisite jewelry, and the widest variety of exotic spices from hundreds of shops and marketplaces. In addition, the city was home to some of the best artisans and boasted the finest, most popular inns and taverns in the country. Entertainers had long congregated there, prompting Cosmos DeLur, the city's wealthiest resident and patron of the arts, to construct the DeLur Theatre.

Crossing the district, Royce and Hadrian halted abruptly

in front of the theatre's large white painted board. It depicted the silhouette of two men scaling the outside of a castle tower and read:

THE CROWN CONSPIRACY
HOW A YOUNG PRINCE AND TWO THIEVES SAVED A KINGDOM
EVENING SHOWS DAILY

Royce raised an eyebrow while Hadrian slipped the tip of his tongue along his front teeth. They glanced at each other, but neither said a word before continuing on their way.

Leaving the hill district, they continued along Bridge Street as the land sloped downward toward the river. They passed rows of warehouses—mammoth buildings emblazoned with company brands like royal crests. Some were simply initials, usually the new businesses that had no sense of themselves. Others bore trademarks, like the boar's head of the Bocant Company, an empire whose genesis had been pork, or the diamond symbol of DeLur Enterprises.

"You realize he'll never be able to pay us the hundred?" Hadrian asked.

"I just didn't want him to think he was getting off easy."

"You didn't want him to think Royce Melborn went soft at the sight of a little girl's tears."

"She wasn't just *any* girl, and besides, he saved her from Ambrose Moor. For that alone he earned one life."

"That's something that has always puzzled me. How is it Ambrose is still alive?"

"I've been sidetracked, I suppose," Royce said in his *let's not talk about it* tone, and Hadrian dropped the subject.

Of the city's three main bridges, the Langdon was the most ornate. Made from cut stone, it was lined every few feet by large lampposts fashioned in the shapes of swans, which, when lit, gave the bridge a festive look. Now, however, with the lights out, the stone was wet and appeared oily and dangerous.

"Well, at least we didn't spend the last month looking for DeWitt for nothing," Hadrian said sarcastically as they crossed the bridge. "I would have thought—"

Royce stopped walking and abruptly raised his hand. Both men looked around and, without a word, drew their weapons as they moved back to back. Nothing seemed amiss. The only sound was the roar of the tumultuous waters that rushed and churned below them.

"Impressive, Duster," a man said, addressing Royce, as he stepped out from behind one of the bridge lampposts. His skin was pale, and his body so slender and bony that he swam in his loose britches and shirt. He looked like a corpse someone forgot to bury.

Behind them, Hadrian noted three more men crawling onto the span. They all had similar appearances, thin and muscular, each in dark-colored clothes. They circled like wolves.

"What tipped you off we were here?" the thin man asked.

"I'm guessing it was your breath, but body odor really can't be ruled out," Hadrian replied with a grin while noting their positions, their movements, and the direction of their eyes.

"Mind yer mouth, bub," the tallest of the four threatened.

"To what do we owe this visit, Price?" Royce asked.

"Funny, I was about to ask you the same," the thin man replied. "This is our city, after all, not yours—not anymore."

"Black Diamond?" Hadrian asked.

Royce nodded.

"And you would be Hadrian Blackwater," Price noted. "I always thought you'd be bigger."

"And you're a Black Diamond. I always thought there were more of you."

Price smiled, held his gaze long enough to suggest a threat, and returned his attention to Royce. "So what are you doing here, Duster?"

"Just passing through."

"Really? No business?"

"Nothing that would interest you."

"Well now, you see, that's where you're wrong." Price stepped away from the swan lamppost and began slowly circling them as he talked. The wind blowing down the river whipped his loose shirt like a flag at mast. "The Black Diamond is interested in everything that happens in Colnora, most particularly when it involves you, Duster."

Hadrian leaned over and asked, "Why does he keep calling you *Duster*?"

"That was my guild name," Royce replied.

"*He* was a Black Diamond?" asked the youngest-looking of the four. He had round, chubby cheeks blown red and blotchy and a narrow mouth wreathed by a thin mustache and goatee.

"Oh yes, that's right, Etcher, you've never heard of Duster before, have you? Etcher is new to the guild, only been with us, what—six months? Well, you see, not only was Duster a Diamond, he was an officer, bucket man, and one of the most notorious members in the guild's history."

"Bucket man?" Hadrian asked.

"Assassin," Royce explained.

"He's a legend, this one is," Price went on, pacing around the stone bridge, carefully avoiding the puddles. "Wonder boy of his day, he rose through the ranks so fast it unnerved people."

"Funny," Royce said, "I only remember one."

"Well, when the First Officer of the guild is nervous, so is everyone else. You see, back then the Jewel had a man named Hoyte running the show. He was an ass to most of us—a good thief and administrator, but an ass just the same. Duster here had a lot of support from the lower ranks and Hoyte was concerned Duster might replace him. He began ordering Duster on the most dangerous jobs—jobs that went suspiciously bad. Still, Duster always escaped unscathed, making him even more a hero. Rumors began circulating we might have a traitor in the guild. Rather than being concerned, Hoyte saw this as an opportunity."

Price paused in his orator's trek around the bridge and stopped in front of Royce. "You see, at that time there were three bucket men in the guild and all of them good friends. Jade, the guild's only female assassin, was a beauty who—"

"Is this going somewhere, Price?" Royce snapped.

"Just giving Etcher a little background, Duster. You wouldn't begrudge me the chance to educate my boys, would you?" Price smiled and returned to his casual pacing, slipping his thumbs into the loose waistline of his pants. "Where was I? Oh yes, Jade. It happened right over there." He pointed back across the bridge. "That empty warehouse with the clover symbol on its side. That's where Hoyte set them up, pitting one against the other. Then, like now, bucket men wore masks to prevent being marked." Price paused and looked at Royce with feigned sympathy. "You had no idea who she was until it was over, did you, Duster? Or did you know and kill her anyway?"

Royce said nothing but glared at Price with a dangerous look.

"The last of the three bucket men was Cutter, who was understandably upset to learn Duster murdered Jade, since Cutter and Jade were lovers. The fact that his friend was responsible made it personal, and Hoyte was happy to let Cutter settle the score.

"But Cutter didn't want Duster dead. He wanted him to

suffer and insisted on something more elaborate, more pain-ful. The man is a strategic mastermind—our best heist planner—and arranged for Duster to be apprehended by the city guard. Cutter traded a few favors and, with some money, bought a trial that resulted in Duster going to Manzant Prison. The hole no one ever comes back from. Escape was thought to be impossible—only somehow Duster managed it. You know, we still don't know how you got out." He paused, giving Royce a chance to reply.

Again, Royce remained silent.

Price shrugged. "When Duster escaped, he returned to Colnora. First, the magistrate who presided over his trial was found dead in his bed. Then the false witnesses—all three on the same night—and finally the lawyer. Soon, one by one, members of the Black Diamond started disappearing. They turned up in the strangest places: the river, the city square, even the steeple of the church.

"After losing more than a dozen members, the Jewel made a deal. He gave Hoyte to Duster, who forced him to confess publicly. Then Duster killed Hoyte and left his body in the Hill Square Fountain—it was pure artistry. It stopped the war, but the wounds were too deep to forgive. Duster left, only to reemerge years later working out of Crimson Hand territory up north. But you're not a member, are you?"

"I don't have much use for guilds anymore," Royce replied coldly.

"And who's that?" Etcher asked, pointing at Hadrian. "Duster's servant? He's carrying enough weapons for the both of them."

Price smiled at Etcher. "That's Hadrian Blackwater, and I wouldn't point at him—you're likely to lose that arm."

Etcher looked at Hadrian skeptically. "What? He's some kind of master swordsman? Is that it?"

Price chuckled. "Sword, spear, arrow, rock, whatever is at hand." He turned to Hadrian. "The Diamond doesn't know as much about you, but there are a lot of rumors. One says you were a gladiator. Another reports you were a general in a Calian army—successful, too, if the stories can be trusted. There's even one tale circulating that you were the enslaved courtier of an exotic eastern queen."

Some of the other Diamonds, including Etcher, chuckled.

"As much fun as this trip down memory lane has been, Price, do you have a reason for stopping us?"

"You mean beyond entertainment? Beyond harassment? Beyond reminding you that this is a Black Diamond–controlled city? Beyond informing you that unguilded thieves like yourselves are not allowed to practice here, and that you personally are not welcome?"

"Yeah, that's what I meant."

"Actually, there is one more thing. There's a girl looking for you two."

Royce and Hadrian glanced at each other curiously.

"She's been going around asking about two thieves named Hadrian and Royce. Now, as entertaining as it has been to hear your names publicly advertised, it's embarrassing for the Black Diamond to have anyone asking for thieves in Colnora that are not members of our guild. People are apt to get the wrong impression about this city."

"Who is she?" Royce asked.

"No idea."

"Where is she?"

"Sleeping under the Tradesmen's Arch on Capital Boulevard, so I think we can rule out her being a noble debutante or a rich merchant's daughter. Since she is traveling alone, I think you can also rule out the possibility that she is here to kill you or have you arrested. If I had to guess, I should think she is looking to hire you. I must say, if she is typical of the kind of patrons you two attract, I would consider a more traditional line of work. Perhaps there's a pig farm you might be able to get a job at—at least you would be keeping the same level of company."

Price's tone and expression dropped to a serious level. "Find her and get her, and yourselves, out of our city by tomorrow night. You might want to hurry. Cleaned up, she could be pretty and might fetch a fair price or at least provide several minutes of pleasure for someone. I suspect the only reason she hasn't been touched so far is that she's been dropping your names everywhere. Around here, Royce Melborn is still something of a bogeyman."

Price turned to leave and his mocking tone returned. "It's actually a shame you can't stay around; the theatre is showing a play about a couple of thieves lured into being accused of murdering the King of Medford. It's loosely based on the real murder of Amrath several years ago." Price shook his head. "Completely unrealistic. Can you imagine a seasoned thief being lured into a castle to steal a sword to save a man from a duel? Authors!"

Price continued to shake his head as he and the other thieves left Hadrian and Royce on the bridge and headed down the streets on the far bank.

"Well, that was pleasant, don't you think?" Hadrian said as they retraced their steps, heading back up the hill toward Capital Boulevard. "Nice bunch of guys. I feel a little disappointed they only sent four."

"Trust me, they were plenty dangerous. Price is the Diamond's First Officer, and the other two quiet ones were bucket men. There were also six more, three on each side of the bridge, hiding under the ambush lip, just in case. They weren't taking any chances with us. Does that make you feel better?"

"Much, thanks." Hadrian rolled his eyes. "Duster, huh?"

"Don't call me that," Royce said, his tone serious. "Don't ever call me that."

"Call you what?" Hadrian asked innocently.

Royce sighed, then smiled at him. "Walk faster; apparently, we have a client waiting."

⊸

She awoke to a rough hand on her thigh.

"Whatcha got in the purse, honey?"

Disoriented and confused, the girl wiped her eyes. She was in the gutter beneath the Tradesmen's Arch. Her hair was a filthy tangle of leaves and twigs, her dress a tattered rag. She clutched a tiny purse to her chest, the drawstring tied around her neck. To most passing by, she might appear as a bundle of trash discarded on the side of the road, or a pile of cloth and twigs absently left behind by the street sweepers. Still, there were those who were interested even in piles of trash.

The first thing she saw when her eyes could focus was the dark, haggard face and gaping mouth of a man crouching over her. She squealed and tried to crawl away. A hand grabbed her by the hair. Strong arms forced her down, pinning her wrists to her sides.

She felt his hot breath on her face and it smelled of liquor and smoke. He tore the tiny purse from her fingers and pulled it from around her neck.

"No!" She wrenched a hand free and reached out for it. "I need that."

"So do I." The man cackled, slapping her hand aside. Feeling the weight of coins in the bag, he smiled and stuffed the small pouch in his breast pocket.

"No!" she protested.

He sat on her, pinning her to the ground, and ran his fingers down her face, along her lips, stopping at her neck. Slowly they circled her throat and he gave a little squeeze. She gasped, struggling to breathe. He pressed his lips hard against hers, so hard she could tell he was missing teeth. The rough stubble of his whiskers scratched her chin and cheeks.

"Shush," he whispered. "We're only getting started. You need ta save your strength." He lifted off, pushing himself up to his knees, and reached for the buttons of his britches.

She struggled, clawing at him, kicking. He pinned her arms under his knees and her feet found only air. She screamed. The man replied by slapping her hard across the face. The shock left her stunned, staring blindly while he returned to work on his buttons. The pain did not hit her yet, not fully. It was there welling up, fire hot on her cheek. Through watering eyes, she saw him on top of her as if viewing the scene from a distance. Individual sounds were lost, replaced by a dull hum. She saw his cracked, peeling lips moving, his throat muscles shifting, long gangly cords, but never heard the words. She freed one arm, but it was captured and stuffed back down out of sight once more.

Behind him, she could see two figures approaching. Somewhere inside her, a thread of hope came alive, and she managed a weak whisper: "Help me."

The foremost man drew a massive sword and, holding it by the blade, swung the pommel. Her attacker fell sprawling across the gutter.

The man with the sword knelt down beside her. He was merely an outline against the charcoal sky, a phantom in the dark.

"May I be of assistance, milady?" She heard his voice—a nice voice. His hand found hers and he pulled her to her feet.

"Who are you?"

"My name is Hadrian Blackwater."

She stared at him. "Really?" she managed, refusing to let go of his hands. Before she realized it, she began to cry.

"What'd you do to her?" the other man asked, coming up behind them.

"I—I don't know."

"Are you squeezing her hand too hard? Let her go."

"I'm not holding her. She's holding me."

"I'm sorry. I'm sorry." Her voice quavered. "I just never thought I would ever find you."

"Oh, okay. Well, you did." He smiled at her. "And this fellow here is Royce Melborn."

She gasped and threw her arms around the smaller man's neck, hugging him tight and crying even harder. Royce stood awkward and stiff while Hadrian peeled her off.

"So I get the impression you're glad to see us; that's good," Hadrian told her. "Now, who are you?"

"I'm Thrace Wood of Dahlgren Village." She was smiling. She could not help herself. "I have been looking for you for a very long time."

She staggered.

"Are you all right?"

"I'm a little dizzy."

"When was the last time you had anything to eat?"

Thrace stood thinking, her eyes shifting back and forth as she tried to remember.

"Never mind." Hadrian turned to Royce. "This was once your city. Any ideas where we can get help for a young woman in the middle of the night?"

"It's a shame we aren't in Medford. Gwen would be great for this sort of thing."

"Well, isn't there a brothel here? After all, we're in the trade capital of the world. Don't tell me they don't sell *that*."

"Yeah, there's a nice one on South Street."

"Okay, Thrace is it? Come with us, we'll see if we can get you cleaned up and perhaps a bit of food in you."

"Wait." She knelt down beside the unconscious man and pulled her purse from his pocket.

"Is he dead?" she asked.

"Doubt it. Didn't hit him that hard."

Rising, she felt light-headed and darkness crept in from the edges of her vision. She hovered a moment like a drunk, began to sway, and finally collapsed. She woke only briefly and felt arms gently lifting her. Through a dull buzzing she heard the sound of a chuckle.

"What's so funny?" she heard one of them say.

"This is the first time, I suspect, anyone has ever visited a whorehouse and brought his own woman."

CHAPTER 2

THRACE

"Shines up purty as a new copper piece, that one does," Clarisse noted as the three looked through the doorway at Thrace, waiting in the parlor. Clarisse was a large rotund woman with rosy cheeks and short pudgy fingers that had a habit of playing with the pleats of her skirt. She and the other women of the Bawdy Bottom Brothel had done wonders with the girl. Thrace was clothed in a new dress. It was cheap and simple—a brown linen kirtle over a white smock with a starched brown bodice—but still decidedly more fetching than the rag she had worn. She hardly resembled the ragamuffin they had met the night before. In addition to giving her a bed to sleep in, the women had scrubbed, combed, and fed her. Her lips and eyes were even painted and the results were stunning. She was a young beauty with startling blue eyes and golden hair.

"Poor girl was in awful shape when you dropped her off. Where'd you find her?" Clarisse asked.

"Under the Tradesmen's Arch," Hadrian replied.

"Poor thing." The large woman shook her head sadly. "You know, if she needs a place, I'm sure we could put her on the roster. She'd get a bed to sleep in, three meals a day, and with her looks she could do well for herself."

"Something tells me she's not a prostitute," Hadrian told her.

"None of us are, honey. Not until you find yourself sleeping under the Tradesmen's Arch, that is. You shoulda seen her at breakfast. She ate like a starved dog. Course she wouldn't touch a thing till we convinced her that the food was free, given by the chamber 'a commerce to visitors of the city as a welcome. Maggie came up with that one. She's a hoot, she is. That reminds me, the bill for the room, dress, food, and general cleanup comes to sixty-five silver. We threw in the makeup for free, 'cause Delia just wanted to see how she'd look, on account she says she's never worn it 'afore."

Royce handed her a gold tenent.

"Well, well, you two really need to drop by more often, and next time without the girl, eh?" She winked. "Seriously, though, what's the story with this one?"

"That's just it; we don't know," Hadrian replied.

"But I think it's time we found out," Royce added.

Not nearly as nice as Medford House back home, the Bawdy Bottom Brothel was decorated with gaudy red drapes, rickety furniture, pink lampshades, and dozens of pillows. Everything had tassels and fringe, from the threadbare carpets to the cloth edging adorning the top of the walls. It was old, weathered, and worn but at least it was clean.

The parlor was a small oval room just off the main hall with two bay windows that looked out on the street. It contained two love seats, a few tables crowded with ceramic figures, and a small fireplace. Seated on one of the love seats, Thrace waited, her eyes darting about as if she were a rabbit in an open field. The moment the two men entered, she leapt from her seat, knelt, and bowed her head.

"Hey! Watch it, that's a new dress," Hadrian said with a smile.

"Oh!" She scrambled to her feet, blushing, then curtsied and bowed her head once more.

"What's she doing?" Royce whispered to Hadrian.

"Not sure," he whispered back.

"I'm trying to show the proper reverence, Your Lordships," she whispered to both of them while keeping her head down. "I'm sorry if I'm not very good at it."

Royce rolled his eyes and Hadrian began to laugh.

"Why are you whispering?" Hadrian asked her.

"Because you two were."

Hadrian chuckled again. "Sorry, Thrace—ah, your name is Thrace, right?"

"Yes, my lord, Thrace Annabell Wood of Dahlgren Village." She awkwardly curtsied again.

"Okay, well—Thrace." Hadrian struggled to continue with a straight face. "Royce and I are not lords, so there is no need to bow or curtsy."

The girl looked up.

"You saved my life," she told them in such a solemn tone Hadrian stopped laughing. "I don't remember a lot of last night, but I remember that much. And for that you deserve my gratitude."

"I would settle for an explanation," Royce said, moving to the windows. He began closing the drapes. "Straighten up, for Maribor's sake, before a sweeper sees you, thinks we're noble, and marks us. We're already on thin ice here as it is. Let's not add to it."

She stood up straight, and Hadrian could not help staring. Her long yellow hair, now free of twigs and leaves, shimmered in waves over her shoulders. She was a vision of youthful beauty and Hadrian guessed she could not be more than seventeen.

"Now, why have you been looking for us?" Royce asked, closing the last curtain.

"To hire you to save my father," she said, untying the purse from around her neck and holding it up with a smile. "Here. I have twenty-five silver tenents. Solid silver stamped with the Dunmore crown."

Royce and Hadrian exchanged looks.

"Isn't it enough?" she asked, her lips starting to tremble.

"How long did it take you to save up this money?" Hadrian asked.

"All my life. I saved every copper I was ever given, or earned. It was my dowry."

"Your dowry?"

She lowered her head, looking at her feet. "My father is a poor farmer. He would never—I decided to save for myself. It's not enough, is it? I didn't realize. I'm from a very small village. I thought it was a lot of money; everyone said so, but..." She looked around at the battered love seat and faded curtains. "We don't have palaces like this."

"Well, we really don't—" Royce began in his usual insensitive tone.

"What Royce is about to say," Hadrian interrupted, "is we really don't know yet. It depends on what you want us to do."

Thrace looked up, her eyes hopeful.

Royce just glared at him.

"Well, it does, doesn't it?" Hadrian shrugged. "Now, Thrace, you say you want us to save your father. Has he been kidnapped or something?"

"Oh no, nothing like that. As far as I know he's fine. Although I have been away a long time looking for you. So I'm not sure."

"I don't understand. What do you need us for?"

"I need you to open a lock for me."

"A lock? To what?"

"A tower."

"You want us to break into a tower?"

"No. I mean—well, yes, but it isn't like—it's not illegal.

The tower isn't occupied; it has been deserted for years. At least I think so."

"So you just want us to open a door to an empty tower?"

"Yes!" she said, nodding vigorously so that her hair bounced.

"Doesn't sound too hard." Hadrian looked at Royce.

"Where is this tower?" Royce asked.

"Near my village on the west bank of the Nidwalden River. Dahlgren is very small and has only been there a short time. It's in the new province of Westbank, in Dunmore."

"I've heard about that place. It's supposedly being attacked by elven raiders."

"Oh, it's not the elves. The elves have never caused us any trouble."

"I knew it," Royce said to no one in particular.

"Leastways, I don't think so," Thrace went on. "We think it's a beast of some kind. No one has ever seen it. Deacon Tomas says it's a demon, a minion of Uberlin."

"And your father?" Hadrian asked. "How does he fit into this?"

"He's going to try and kill the beast, only..." She faltered and looked at her feet once more.

"Only you think it will kill him instead?"

"It has killed fifteen people and over eighty head of livestock."

A freckle-faced woman with wild red hair entered the parlor dragging a short potbellied man who looked like he had shaved for the occasion, his face nicked raw. The woman was laughing, walking backward as she hauled him along with both hands. The man stopped short when he saw them. His hands slipped through hers and she fell to the wooden floor with a hollow thud. The man looked from the woman to them and back, frozen in place. The woman glanced over her shoulder and laughed.

"Oops," was all she could manage. "Didn't know it was taken. Give us a hand up, Rubis."

The man helped her to her feet. She paused to give Thrace a long appraising look, then winked at them. "We do good work, don't we?"

"That was Maggie," Thrace told them after the woman hauled her man back out again.

Hadrian moved to the sofa and gestured for Thrace to sit. She sat gingerly and straight, not allowing her back to touch the rear of the sofa, and carefully smoothed out her skirt.

Royce remained on his feet. "Does Westbank have a lord? Why isn't he doing something about this?"

"We had a fine margrave," she said. "A brave man with three good knights."

"Had?"

"He and his knights rode out to fight the beast one evening. Later, all that was found was bits and pieces of armor."

"Why don't you just leave?" Royce asked.

Thrace's head drooped and her shoulders slouched a bit. "Two nights before I left to come here, the beast killed everyone in my family except for me and my father. We weren't home. My father had worked late in the fields and I went to look for him. I—I accidentally left the door open. Light attracts it. It went right for our house. My brother, Thad, his wife, and their son were all killed.

"Thad—he was the joy of my father's life. He was the reason we moved to Dahlgren in the first place—so he could become the town's first cooper." Tears welled in her eyes. "Now they're all gone and my father has nothing left but his grief and the beast that brought it. He'll see it dead, or die himself before the month is out. If I had only closed the door... If I had just checked the latch..."

Her hands covered her face and her slender body quivered. Royce gave Hadrian a stern look, shaking his head very slightly and mouthing the word *no*.

Hadrian scowled and placed his hand on her shoulder and brushed the hair away from her eyes. "You're going to ruin all your pretty makeup," he said.

"I'm sorry. I really don't want to be such a bother. These aren't your problems. It is just that my father is all I have left and I can't bear the thought of losing him too. I can't reason with him. I asked him to leave, but he won't listen."

"I can see your problem, but why us?" Royce asked coldly. "And how does a farmer's daughter from the frontier know our names and how to find us in Colnora?"

"A crippled man told me. He sent me here. He said you could open the tower."

"A cripple?"

"Yes. Mr. Haddon told me the beast can't—"

"Mr. Haddon?" Royce interrupted.

"Uh-huh."

"This Mr. Haddon...he wouldn't be missing his hands, would he?"

"Yes, that's him."

Royce and Hadrian exchanged glances.

"What exactly did he say?"

"He said the beast can't be harmed by weapons made by man, but inside Avempartha there is a sword that can kill it."

"So, a man with no hands told you to find us in Colnora and hire us to get a sword for your father from a tower called *Avempartha*?" Royce asked.

The girl nodded.

Hadrian looked at his partner. "Don't tell me...it's a dwarven tower?"

"No…" Royce replied, "it's elvish." He turned away with a thoughtful expression.

Hadrian returned his attention to the girl. He felt awful. It was bad enough that her village was so far away, but now they faced an elven tower. Even if she offered them a hundred gold tenents, he would not be able to convince Royce to take the job. She was so desperate, so in need of help. His stomach knotted as he considered the words he would say next.

"Well," Hadrian began reluctantly, "the Nidwalden River is several days' travel over rough ground. We'd need supplies, for what—a six-, seven-day trip? That's two weeks there and back. We'd need food and grain for the horses. Then you'd have to add in time at the tower. That's time we could be doing other jobs, so that right there is money lost. Then there is the danger involved. Risk of any kind can bump our price and a mass-murdering phantom-demon-beast that can't be harmed by weapons has got to be classified as a risk."

Hadrian looked into her eyes and shook his head. "I hate to say it, and I'm very sorry, but we can't take—"

"Your money," Royce abruptly interjected as he spun around. "It's too much. To take the full twenty-five silver for this job… Ten really seems like more than enough."

Hadrian raised an eyebrow and stared at his partner but said nothing.

"Ten silver each?" she asked.

"Ah—no," Hadrian replied, keeping his eyes on Royce. "That would be together. Right? Five each?"

Royce shrugged. "Since I'll be doing the actual lock picking, I think I should get six, but we can work that out between us. It's not something she needs to be concerned about."

"Really?" Thrace asked, looking as if she might explode with happiness.

"Sure," Royce replied. "After all… we're not thieves."

∾

"Want to explain why we are taking this job?" Hadrian asked, shielding his eyes as they stepped outside. The sky was a perfect blue, the morning sun already working to dry the lingering puddles from the night before. All around them people rushed to market. Carts loaded with spring vegetables and tarp-covered barrels sat trapped behind three wagons mounded high with hay. Out of the crowd in front of them, a fat man charged forward with a flapping chicken gripped tightly under each arm. He danced around the puddles, dodging people and carts and offering a muttered "Excuse me," as he pressed by.

"She's paying us ten silver for a job that has already cost us a gold tenent," Hadrian continued after successfully skirting the chicken man. "It will cost us several more before we're done."

"We're not doing it for the money," Royce informed him as he cut a path through the crowd.

"Obviously, but why are we doing it? I mean, sure, she's cute as a button and all, but unless you're planning on selling her, I don't see the angle here."

Royce looked over his shoulder, displaying an evil grin. "I never even considered selling her. That could defray the costs considerably."

"Forget I brought it up. Just tell me why we're doing this."

Royce led them out of the crowd toward Ognoton's Curio Shop, whose window exhibited hookahs, porcelain animal figurines, and jewelry boxes with brass latches. They ducked around the side into the narrow bricked space between it and a confectioner shop that was offering free samples of hard candy.

"Don't tell me you haven't wondered what Esrahaddon has

been doing," Royce whispered. "That wizard was imprisoned for nine hundred years, then disappears the day we break him out and we don't hear a word about him until now? The church must know, and yet the Imperialists haven't launched search parties or posted notices. I would think that if the most dangerous man alive was on the loose, there might be a bit more of a commotion.

"Two years later he turns up in a tiny village and invites us to come visit. On top of that, he picks the elven frontier and Avempartha as the meeting place. Don't you want to find out what he wants?"

"What is this Avempartha?"

"All I know is that it's old. Real old. Some kind of ancient elven citadel. Which also begs the question, wouldn't you like to get a peek inside? If Esrahaddon thinks there's value in opening it, I'm guessing he's right."

"So we're going after ancient elven treasure?"

"I have no idea, but I'm sure there is something valuable in there. But for that we need supplies and we need to get out of town before Price lets loose the hounds."

"Well, as long as you promise not to sell the girl."

"I won't—if she behaves herself."

~§

Hadrian felt Thrace leaning again, this time gazing at a two-story country home of stucco and stone with a yellow thatch roof and orange clay chimney. It was surrounded by a waist-high wall overgrown with lilacs and ivy.

"It's so beautiful," she whispered.

It was early afternoon and they were only a few miles out of Colnora, traveling east along the Alburn road. The country lane twisted through the tangle of tiny villages that comprised the hill region surrounding the city, little hamlets where poor farmers worked their fields alongside the summer cottages of the idle rich, who for three months a year pretended to be country squires. Royce rode beside them or trotted forward as congestion demanded. His hood was up despite the pleasant weather. Thrace rode behind Hadrian on his bay mare, her legs dangled off one side, bobbing to the rhythm of the horse's stride.

"It's a different world here," she said. "A paradise, really. Everyone is wealthy. Everyone a king."

"Colnora does all right, but I wouldn't go that far."

"Then how do you explain all the grand houses? The horse carts have metal rims on their wheels. The vegetable stands overflow with bushels of onions and green peas. In Dahlgren all we have are footpaths and they are an awful mess after a rain, but here you have such wide roads and they even have names on posts. And back there a farmer was wearing gloves—gloves on his hands—while working. In Dahlgren, even the church deacon doesn't own fancy gloves, and he certainly wouldn't work in them if he did. You all are so rich."

"Some of them are."

"Like you two."

Hadrian laughed.

"But you have nice clothes and beautiful horses."

"She's not much of a horse really."

"No one in Dahlgren but the lord and his knights own horses, and yours are so pretty. I especially like her eyes—such long lashes. What's her name?"

"I call her Millie, after a woman I once knew who had the same habit of not listening to me."

"Millie is a pretty name. I like it. What about Royce's horse?"

Hadrian frowned and looked over at him. "I don't know. Royce, did you ever name her?"

"What for?"

Hadrian glanced back at Thrace, who returned an appalled look.

"How about..." She paused, shifting and twisting as she scanned the roadside. "Lilac, or Daisy? Oh wait, no, how about Chrysanthemum?"

"*Chrysanthemum?*" Hadrian repeated. As funny as it might be to have Royce riding a Chrysanthemum, or even a Lilac or Daisy, he had to point out that flower names just did not fit Royce's short, dirty gray mare. "How about Shorty or Sooty?"

"No!" Thrace scolded him. "It will make the poor animal feel awful."

Hadrian chuckled. Royce ignored the conversation. He clicked his tongue, kicked the sides of his horse, and trotted forward to avoid an approaching wagon, but remained there even after the road was clear.

"How about Lady?" Thrace asked.

"It seems a bit haughty, don't you think? She's not exactly a prancing show horse."

"Then it will make her feel better. Give her confidence."

They were coming upon a stream where honeysuckle and raspberry bushes crowned the heads of smooth granite banks with brilliant springtime green. A gristmill stood at the edge, its great wheel creaking and dripping. A pair of small square windows, like dark eyes, created a face in the stone exterior beneath the steeply peaked wooden roof. A low wall separated the mill from the road and on it rested a white and gray cat. Its green eyes opened lazily and blinked at them. When they drew closer, the cat decided they had come close enough and leapt from the wall, darting across the road into the thickets.

Royce's horse reared and whinnied, dancing across the dirt. As the horse shuffled backward, Royce cursed and tight-

ened the reins, pulling her head down and forcing her to turn
completely around.

"Ridiculous!" Royce complained once the horse was under
control. "A thousand-pound animal terrified by a five-pound
cat; you'd think she was a mouse."

"Mouse! That's perfect," Thrace shouted, causing Millie's
ears to twist back.

"I like it," Hadrian agreed.

"Oh, good lord," Royce muttered, shaking his head as he
trotted forward again.

As they rode farther east, the country estates became
farms, rosebushes became hedges, and fences that divided
fields gave way to mere tree lines. Still Thrace pointed out
curiosities, like the unimagined luxury of covered bridges and
the ornately decorated carriages that still occasionally thundered by.

The road climbed higher and soon they lost the shade as
the land opened up into vast fallow fields of goldenrod, milkweed, and wild salifan. Flies dogged them in the heat and the
drone of cicadas whined. Thrace at last grew quiet and laid
her head against Hadrian's back. He became concerned she
might fall asleep and topple off, but occasionally she would
stir to look about or swat at a fly.

Higher and higher they climbed until they reached the top
of Amber Heights. The prominent highland stood out as a
bald spot of short grass and bare rock. Part of a long ridge
that ran along the eastern edge of Warric, it served as the border between the kingdom of Warric and the kingdom of
Alburn. Alburn was the third most powerful and prosperous
kingdom in Avryn, after Warric and Melengar. Most of its
lands were deeply forested and its coast was often subjected to
attacks by the Ba Ran Ghazel, who made lightning assaults,

abducting the unfortunate and burning what they could not
carry. Its ruler, King Armand, had only recently gained the
throne, after the unexpected death of the old king. While King
Reinhold had been a Royalist, Hadrian had the impression the
new king was an Imperialist sympathizer, if not an open supporter, which was unfortunate for Melengar, whose list of
allies seemed to grow shorter each day.

Amber Heights was a curiosity even to the local residents
due to the standing stones, the massive blue-gray rocks carved
into uniquely fluid shapes. They appeared almost organic in
their rounded curves, like a series of writhing serpents burrowing in and out of the hilltop. Hadrian did not have the
slightest idea what purpose the stones might have originally
served. He doubted anyone did. Remnants of campfires were
scattered around the stones, etched with messages of true love
or the occasional slogan: "Maribor Is God!" "Nationalists
Are Barmy," "The Heir Is Dead," and even "Gray Mouse
Tavern—it's all downhill from here." Reaching the crest, they
could all see the city of Colnora spread out behind them, while
to the northeast lay the endless miles of dense and untamed
woodland where the kingdoms of Alburn and Dunmore
blurred together. To Hadrian the forest appeared as an ocean
of unbroken green—miles and miles of rugged wilderness, on
the other side of which lay a tiny village called Dahlgren.

Because the wind on the hilltop was cool and strong enough
to drive off the flies, it made a perfect place to break for a midday meal. They ate salted pork, hard dark bread, onions, and
pickles. It was the kind of meal Hadrian would loathe to eat in
a town, but it seemed somehow wonderful on the road, where
his appetite was greater and options were fewer. He watched
Thrace sitting on the grass, nibbling on a pickle, being careful
not to stain her new dress. She gazed off with a faraway look,
inhaling the air in deep appreciative breaths.

"What are you thinking?" he asked.

She smiled at him a bit self-consciously and he thought he noticed a sadness about her. "I was just thinking how wonderful it is here. How nice it would be to live on one of those farms we passed. We wouldn't need anything grand, not even a house—my father can build a house all by himself and he can turn any soil. There's nothing he can't do once he sets his mind to it, and once he sets his mind, there's no changing it."

"Sounds like a great guy."

"Oh, he is. He's very strong, very determined."

"I'm surprised he would allow you to set off alone across the country like you did."

Thrace smiled.

"You didn't walk all the way, did you?"

"Oh no, I got a ride with a peddler and his wife who stopped in Dahlgren. They refused to spend a second night and let me ride in the back of their wagon."

"Have you done much traveling before?"

"No. I was born in Glamrendor, the capital of Dunmore. My family worked a tenant farm for His Lordship there. We moved to Dahlgren when I was about nine, so I've never been out of Dunmore until now. I can't even say I remember all that much of Glamrendor. I do recall it was dirty, though. All the buildings were made of wood, and the roads very muddy—at least that's how I remember it."

"Still that way," Royce mentioned.

"I can't believe you had the courage to just go off like that," Hadrian said, shaking his head. "It must have been a shock leaving Dahlgren and a few days later finding yourself in the largest city in the world."

"Oh, it was," she replied, using her pinky finger to draw away a number of hairs that had blown into her mouth. "I felt foolish when I realized just how hard it was going to be to find you. I expected it would be like back home, where I would be able to walk up to anyone and they would know who you were. There are a lot more people in Colnora than I expected. To be honest, there's a lot more of everything. I looked and looked and I thought I would never find you."

"I expect your father will be worried."

"No he won't," she said.

"But if—"

"What are these things?" she asked, pointing at the standing stones with her pickle. "These blue stones. They're so odd."

"No one knows," Royce replied.

"Were they made by elves?" she asked.

Royce cocked his head and stared at her. "How did you know that?"

"They look a bit like the tower near my village—the one I need you to open. Same kind of stone—at least, I think so. The tower looks bluish too, but it might be because of the distance—ever notice how things get blue in the distance? I suppose if we could actually get near it, we might find it was just a common gray, you know?"

"Why can't you get near it?" Hadrian asked.

"Because it's in the middle of the river."

"Can't you swim?"

"You would have to be a real strong swimmer. The tower is built on a rock that hangs over a waterfall. Beautiful falls—really high, you know? Lots of water going over. On sunny days, you can see rainbows in the mist. Of course, it's very dangerous. At least five people have died—only two are for sure, the other three are just guesses, because—" She paused when she saw the looks on their faces. "Is something wrong?"

"You might have said something earlier," Royce replied.

"About the waterfall? Oh, I thought you knew. I mean, you

acted like you knew the tower when I mentioned it before. I'm sorry."

They ate in silence for a few moments. Thrace finished her lunch and walked around looking at the stones, her dress billowing behind her. "I don't understand," she finally said, raising her voice over the wind. "If the Nidwalden is the border, why are there elven stones here?"

"This used to be elven land," Royce explained. "All of it. Before there was a Colnora, or a Warric, it was part of the Erivan Empire. Most don't like to acknowledge that; they prefer to think that men always ruled here. It bothers them. Funny thing is many of the names we use are elvish. Ervanon, Rhenydd, Glamrendor, Galewyr, and Nidwalden are all elven. The very name of this country, Avryn, means *green fields*."

"Try and tell that to someone in a bar sometime and see how fast you get cracked in the head," Hadrian mentioned, drawing looks from both of them.

While they finished eating, Thrace stood among the great stones, staring west, her hair and dress whipping about. Her sight rose to the horizon, out beyond Colnora, beyond the blue hills to the thin line of the sea. She looked so small and delicate he half expected the wind to carry her away like some golden leaf, and then he noticed the look in her eyes. She was little more than a child and yet her eyes were older—the glow of innocence and the sparkle of wonder were absent. There was a weight to her face, a determination in her gaze. Whatever childhood she had known had long since abandoned her.

They finished their food, packed up, and set off again. Descending the far side of the heights, they continued to follow the road for the remainder of the day, but as sunset neared, the road narrowed to little more than a simple trail. Farmhouses still appeared from time to time, but they were less frequent. The forest grew thicker and the road darker.

As sunlight faded, Thrace grew very quiet. There was nothing to see or point out anymore but Hadrian guessed it was more than that. Mouse skipped a stone into a windblown pile of the past year's leaves and Thrace jumped, grabbing his waist. She dug her nails in deep enough to make him wince.

"Shouldn't we find shelter?" she asked.

"Not much chance of that out here," Hadrian told her. "From this point on we'll be leaving civilization behind. Besides, it's a lovely evening. The ground is dry and it looks like it will be warm."

"We're sleeping outside?"

Hadrian turned around to see her face. Her mouth was open slightly, her forehead creased, her eyes wide and looking up at the sky. "We're still a long way from Dahlgren," he assured her. She nodded but held on to him tighter.

They stopped at a clearing near a little creek that flowed over a series of rocks, making a friendly rushing sound. Hadrian helped Thrace down and pulled the saddles and gear off the horses.

"Where's Royce?" Thrace asked in a whispered panic. She stood with her arms folded across her chest, looking around anxiously.

"It's okay," Hadrian told her as he pulled the bridle off Millie's head. "He always does a bit of scouting whenever we stop for the night. He'll circle the area making sure we're alone. Royce hates surprises."

Thrace nodded but remained huddled, as if standing on a stone amidst a raging river.

"We'll be sleeping right over there. You might want to clear it some. A single stone can ruin a night's sleep. I ought to know; it seems whenever I sleep outside, I always end up with a stone under the small of my back."

She walked into the clearing and gingerly bent over, tossing

aside branches and rocks, nervously glancing skyward and jumping at the slightest sound. By the time Hadrian had the horses
settled, Royce had returned. He carried an armload of small
branches and a few shattered logs, which he used to build a fire.

Thrace stared at him, horrified. "It's so bright," she
whispered.

Hadrian squeezed her hand and smiled. "You know, I bet
you're a wonderful cook, aren't you? I could make us dinner,
but it would be miserable. All I know how to do is boil potatoes. How about you give it a try? What do you say? There are
pots and pans in that sack over there and you'll find food in
the one next to it."

Thrace nodded silently and, with one last glance upward,
shuffled over to the packs. "What kind of meal would you
like?"

"Something edible would be a pleasant surprise," Royce
said, adding more wood.

Hadrian threw a stick at him. The thief caught it and
placed it on the fire.

She dug into the packs, going so far as to stick her head
inside, and emerged moments later with an armload of items.
She borrowed Hadrian's knife and began cutting vegetables
on the bottom of a turned-up pan.

It grew dark quickly, the fire becoming the only source of
light in the clearing. The flickering yellow radiance illuminated the canopy of leaves around them, creating the feel of a
woodland cave. Hadrian picked out a grassy area upwind
from the smoke and laid out sheets of canvas coated in pitch.
It blocked the wetness that would otherwise soak in. The
treated fabric was something they had come up with after
years on the road. But they did not have time to make one for
Thrace. He sighed, threw Thrace's blankets on his canvas,
and went in search of pine boughs for his own bed.

When dinner was ready, Royce called for Hadrian. He returned to the fire, where Thrace was dishing out a thick broth of carrots, potatoes, onions, and salted pork. Royce was sitting with a bowl on his lap and a smile on his face.

"You don't have to be that happy," Hadrian told him.

"Look, Hadrian—food."

They ate mostly in silence. Royce made a few comments about things they should pick up when they passed through Alburn, such as another length of rope and a new spoon to replace the cracked one. Hadrian mostly watched Thrace, who refused to sit near the fire; she ate alone on a rock in the shadows near the horses. When they finished, she stole away to the river to wash the pot and wooden bowls.

"Are you all right?" Hadrian asked, finding her along the stony bank.

Thrace was crouched on a large moss-capped rock, her gown tucked tight around her ankles, as she washed the pot and bowls by scooping up what sand she could find and scrubbing them with her fingers.

"I'm fine, thank you. I'm just not used to being out at night."

Hadrian settled down beside her and began cleaning his bowl.

"I can do that," she said.

"So can I. Besides, you're the customer, so you should get your money's worth."

She smirked at him. "I'm not a fool, you know. Ten silver won't even cover the feed for the horses, will it?"

"Well, what you have to understand is Mouse and Millie are very spoiled. They only eat the best grain." He winked. She could not help smiling back.

Thrace finished the pot and the other bowls and they walked back to camp.

"How much farther is it?" she asked, replacing the pot and bowls in the sack.

"I'm not sure. I've never been to Dahlgren, but we made good time today, so maybe only another four days."

"I hope my father is all right. Mr. Haddon said he would try to convince him to wait until I returned before hunting the beast. I hope he did. As I said, my father is a very stubborn man and I can't imagine anyone changing his mind."

"Well, if anyone can, I suspect that Mr. Haddon could," Royce remarked, prodding the coals of the fire with a long stick. "How did you meet him?"

Thrace found the bed Hadrian had laid out for her near the fire and sat down on her blanket. "It was right after my family's funeral. It was very beautiful. The whole village turned out. Maria and Jessie Caswell hung wreaths of wild salifan on the markers. Mae Drundel and Rose and Verna McDern sang the 'Fields of Lilies,' and Deacon Tomas said a few prayers. Lena and Russell Bothwick held a reception at their house. Lena and my mother were very close."

"I don't remember you mentioning your mother; was she—"

"My mother died two years ago."

"I'm sorry. Sickness?"

Thrace shook her head.

No one spoke for a while, then Hadrian said, "You were telling us how you met Mr. Haddon—"

"Oh yeah, well, I don't know how many funerals you've been to, but it starts to feel...smothering. All the weeping and old stories. I snuck out. I was just wandering, really. I ended up at the village well and there he was...a stranger. We don't get many of those, but that wasn't all. He had on this robe that shimmered and kinda seemed to change colors from time to time, but the big thing was he had no hands. The poor man was trying to get himself a drink of water, struggling with the bucket and rope.

"I asked his name and then, oh, I don't know, I did something stupid like starting to cry and he asked me what was wrong. The thing was, at that moment, I wasn't crying because my brother and his wife just died. I was crying because I was terrified my father would be next. I don't know why I told him. Maybe because he was a stranger. It was easy to talk to him. It all just spilled out. I felt stupid afterward, but he was very patient. That's when he told me about the weapon in the tower and about you two."

"How did he know where we were?"

Thrace shrugged. "Don't you live there?"

"No...we were visiting an old friend. Did he talk oddly? Did he use *thee* and *thou* a lot?"

"No, but he spoke a bit more educated than most. He said his name was Mr. Esra Haddon. Is he a friend of yours?"

"We only met him briefly," Hadrian explained. "Like you, we helped him with a little problem he was having."

"The question is, why is he keeping tabs on us?" Royce asked. "And how, since I don't recall dropping our names and he couldn't have known we would be going to Colnora."

"All he told me is that you were needed to open the tower and if I left right away, I could find you there. Then he arranged for me to ride with the peddler. He's been very helpful."

"Rather amazing, isn't it, for a man who can't even get himself a cup of water," Royce muttered.

CHAPTER 3

THE AMBASSADOR

Arista stood at the tower window, looking down at the world below. She could see the roofs of shops and houses. They appeared as squares and triangles of gray, brown, and red pierced by chimneys left dormant on the warm spring day. The rain had washed through, leaving the world below fresh and vibrant. She watched the people walking along the streets, gathering in squares, moving in and out of doorways. Occasionally a shout reached her ears, soft and faint. Most of the noise came from directly below in the courtyard, where a train of seven coaches had just arrived and servants were loading trunks.

"No. No. No. Not the red dress!" Bernice shouted at Melissa. "Novron, protect us. Look at that neckline. Her Highness has a reputation to protect. Put that in storage, or better yet—burn it. Why, you might as well salt her, put a garnish behind her ear, and hand her over to a pack of starving wolves. No, not the dark one either; it's nearly black—it's spring, for Maribor's sake. Where's your head? The sky blue gown, yes, that one can stay. Honestly, it's a good thing I'm here."

Bernice was an old plump woman with a doughlike face

that sagged at the cheeks and doubled at the chin. The color of her hair was unknown, as she always wrapped it in a barbette veil that looped her head from crown to neck. To this she added a tall cloth filet that made it seem like the top of her head was flat. She stood in the center of Arista's bedroom, flailing her arms and shouting amidst the chaotic maelstrom that she had created.

Piles of clothes lay everywhere except in Arista's wardrobes. Those stood empty, waiting with doors wide, as Bernice sorted each gown, boxing the winter dresses for storage. In addition to Melissa, Bernice had drafted two other girls from downstairs to assist in the packing. Bernice had filled one chest but still her bedroom remained carpeted in gowns, and Arista already had a headache from all the shouting.

Bernice had been one of her mother's handmaids. Queen Ann had kept several. Drundiline, a beautiful woman, had been her secretary and close friend. Harriet ran the residence, organizing the cleaning staff, seamstresses, and laundry. Nora, whose lazy eye always made it impossible to tell who she was actually looking at, handled the children. Arista remembered how she would tell her fairy tales at bedtime about greedy dwarves who kidnapped spoiled princesses, but a dashing prince always saved them in the end. In all, Arista could remember no fewer than eight maids, but she could not remember Bernice.

She had come to Essendon Castle nearly two years earlier, only a month after Arista's father, King Amrath, had been murdered. Bishop Saldur explained that she had served the queen and was the only maid to survive the fire that had killed her mother so many years earlier. He mentioned Bernice had been away for years, suffering from melancholy and sickness, but after Amrath's death, she insisted on returning to care for her beloved queen's daughter.

"Oh, Your Highness," Bernice said, holding two separate

pairs of Arista's shoes, "I do wish you would come away from that window. The weather may look pleasant, but drafts are not something to toy with. Trust me, I know all about it—intimately. Pray you never have to go through what I did—the aches, the pains, the coughing. Not that I'm complaining, of course; I'm still here, aren't I? I'm blessed with the gift of seeing you grow into a lady, and Maribor willing, I will see you as a bride. What a fine bride you'll make! I hope King Alric picks a husband for you soon. Who knows how long I have left, and we don't want people gossiping about you any more than they already are."

"People are gossiping?" Arista turned and sat on the open windowsill.

Watching her on the edge, Bernice panicked and froze in place, her mouth opening and closing with silent protests, both hands waving the shoes at her. "Your Highness," she managed to gasp, "you'll fall!"

"I'm fine."

"No. No, you're not." Bernice shook her head frantically. "Please. I beg of you."

She dropped the shoes, planted her feet, and reached out her hand as if standing on the edge of a precipice. "Please."

Arista rolled her eyes, stood up, and walked away from the window. She crossed the room to her bed, which lay beneath several layers of clothes.

"No, wait!" Bernice shouted again. She shook her hands at the wrists as if trying to dry them. "Melissa, clear Her Highness a place to sit."

Arista sighed and ran a hand through her hair while she waited for Melissa to gather the dresses.

"Careful now, don't wrinkle them," Bernice cautioned.

"I'm sorry, Your Highness," Melissa told her as she gathered an armful. She was a small redhead with dark green eyes who had served Arista for the past five years. The princess got the distinct impression the maid's apology did not refer to the mess on the bed. Arista fought to keep from laughing and a smile emerged. It only made matters worse when she saw Melissa grinning as well.

"The good news is the bishop delivered a list of potential suitors to His Majesty this morning," Bernice said, and Arista no longer had any trouble quelling laughter, the smile disappeared as well. "I'm hoping it will be that nice prince Rudolf, King Armand's son." Bernice was raising her eyebrows and grinning mischievously like some deranged pixie. "He's very handsome—many say dashing—and Alburn is a very nice kingdom—at least so I have heard."

"I've been there and I've met him. He's an arrogant ass."

"Oh, that tongue of yours!" Bernice clasped her hands to the sides of her face and gazed upward, mouthing a silent prayer. "You must learn to control yourself. If anyone else had heard you—thankfully, we're the only two here."

Arista glanced at Melissa and the other two girls busy sorting through her things. Melissa caught her look and shrugged.

"All right, so you aren't certain about Prince Rudolf, that's fine. How about King Ethelred of Warric? You can't do better than him. The poor widower is the most powerful monarch in Avryn. You would live in Aquesta and be queen of the Wintertide festivals."

"The man has to be in his fifties. Not to mention he's an Imperialist. I'd slit my throat first."

Bernice staggered backward and threw one hand to her own neck while the other reached for the wall.

Melissa snickered and tried to cover it with a pretend cough.

"I think you're done here, Melissa," Bernice said. "Take the chamber pot when you go."

"But the sorting isn't—" Melissa protested.

Bernice gave her a reproachful look.

Melissa sighed. "Your Highness," she said, and curtsied to Arista, then picked up the chamber pot and left.

"She didn't mean anything by it," Arista told Bernice.

"It doesn't matter. Respect must be maintained at all times. I know I'm only an old crazy woman who doesn't matter to anyone, but I can tell you this: if I were here—if I had been well enough to help raise you after your mother died, people wouldn't be calling you a witch today."

Arista's eyes widened.

"Forgive me, Your Highness, but that's the truth of it. With your mother gone, and me away, I fear you were brought up poorly. Thank Maribor I came back when I did, or who knows what would become of you? But no worries, my dear, we have you on the right track now. You'll see, everything will work out once we find you a suitable husband. All that nonsense from your past will soon be forgotten."

❧

Her dignity, as well as the length of her gown, prevented Arista from running down the stairs. Hilfred trotted behind her, struggling to keep up with the sudden burst of speed. She had caught her bodyguard by surprise. She had surprised herself. Arista had had every intention of walking calmly up to her brother and politely asking if he had gone mad. The plan had worked fine up until she passed the chapel; then she started moving faster and faster.

The good news is the bishop delivered a list of potential suitors to His Majesty this morning.

She could still see the grin on Bernice's face and hear the perverse glee in her words, as if she were a spectator at the foot of a gallows waiting for the hangman to kick the bucket.

*I'm hoping it will be that nice prince Rudolf, King Armand's
son.*

It was hard to breathe. Her hair broke loose from the ribbon and flew behind her. As Arista rounded the turn near the
ballroom, her left foot slipped out from under her and she
nearly fell. Her shoe came off and spun across the polished
floor. She left it, pressing on, hobbling forward like a wagon
with a broken wheel. She reached the west gallery. It was a
long, straight hallway lined with suits of armor, and here she
picked up speed. Jacobs, the royal clerk, spotted her from his
perch outside the reception hall and jumped to his feet.

"Your Highness!" he exclaimed with a bow.

"Is he in there?" she barked.

The little clerk with the round face and red nose nodded.
"But His Majesty is in a state meeting. He's requested that he
not be disturbed."

"The man is already disturbed. I'm just here to beat some
sense into his feeble little brain."

The clerk cringed. He looked like a squirrel in a rainstorm.
If he had had a tail, it would have been over his head. Behind
her she heard Hilfred's familiar footsteps approach.

She turned toward the door and took a step.

"You can't go in," Jacobs told her, panicking. "They are
having a state meeting," he repeated.

The soldiers who stood to either side of the door stepped
forward to block her.

"Out of my way!" she yelled.

"Forgive us, Your Highness, but we have orders from the
king not to allow anyone entrance."

"I'm his sister," she protested.

"I am sorry, Your Highness; His Majesty—he specifically
mentioned you."

"He—what?" She stood stunned for a moment, then spun

on the clerk, caught wiping his nose with a handkerchief. "Who's in there with him? Who's in this *state meeting*?"

"What's going on?" Julian Tempest, the lord chamberlain, asked as he rushed out of his office. His long black robe with gold hash marks on the sleeve trailed behind him like the train of a bride. Julian was an ancient man who had been Lord Chamberlain of Essendon Castle since before she was born, perhaps even before her father was born. Normally he wore a powdered wig that hung down past his shoulders like the floppy ears of an old dog, but she had caught him by surprise and all he had on was his skullcap, a few tufts of white hair sticking out like seed silk from a milkweed pod.

"I want to see my brother," Arista demanded.

"But—but, Your Highness, he's in a state meeting; surely it can wait."

"Who is he meeting with?"

"I believe Bishop Saldur, Chancellor Pickering, Lord Valin, and, oh, I'm not sure who else." Julian glanced at Jacobs for support.

"And what is this meeting about?"

"Why, actually, I think it has to do with"—he hesitated—"your future."

"My future? They are determining my life in there and I can't go in?" She was livid now. "Is Prince Rudolf in there? Lanis Ethelred, perhaps?"

"Ah...I don't know—I don't think so." Again he glanced at the clerk, who wanted no part of this. "Your Highness, please calm down. I suspect they can hear you."

"Good!" she shouted. "They should hear me. I want them to hear me. If they think I am going to just stand here and wait for the verdict, to see what they will decide my fate to be, I—"

"Arista!"

She turned to see the doors to the throne room open. Her

brother, Alric, stood trapped behind the guards, who quickly stood aside. He was wearing the white fur mantle Julian insisted he drape over his shoulders at all state functions and the heavy gold crown, which he pushed to the back of his head. "What is your problem? You sound like a raving lunatic."

"I'll tell you what my problem is. I'm not going to let you do this to me. You are not going to send me off to Alburn or Warric like some—some—state commodity."

"I'm not sending you to Warric or Alburn. We've already decided you are going to Dunmore."

"Dunmore?" The word hit her like a blow. "You're joking. Tell me you're joking."

"I was going to tell you tonight. Although, I thought you'd take it better. I figured you'd like it."

"Like it? Like it! Oh yeah, I love the idea of being used as a political pawn. What are they giving you in return? Is that what you were doing in there, auctioning me off?" She rose on her toes, trying to get a look over her brother's shoulders to see who he was hiding in the throne room. "Did you have them bidding on me like a prized cow?"

"Prized cow? What are you talking about?" Alric glanced behind him self-consciously and closed the doors. He waved at Julian and Jacobs, shooing them away. In a softer voice he said, "It will give you some respect. You'll have genuine authority. You won't be just *the princess* anymore and you'll have something to do. Weren't you the one that said you wanted to get out of your tower and contribute to the well-being of the kingdom?"

"And—and this is what you thought of?" She was ready to scream. "Don't do this to me, Alric, I beg of you. I know I've been an embarrassment. I know what they say about me. You think I don't hear them whispering *witch* under their breath? You think I don't know what was said at the trial?"

"Arista, those people were coerced. You know that." He glanced briefly at Hilfred, who stood beside her, holding the lost shoe.

"I'm just saying I know about it. I'm sure they complain to you all the time." She gestured toward the closed door behind him. She did not know whom she meant by *they* and hoped he did not ask. "But I can't help what people think. If you want, I'll come to more events. I'll attend the state dinners. I'll take up needlepoint. I'll make a damn tapestry. Something cute and inoffensive. How about a stag hunt? I don't know how to make a tapestry, but I bet Bernice does—she knows all that crap."

"*You're* going to make a tapestry?"

"If that's what it takes. I'll be better—I will. I haven't even put the lock on my door in the new tower. I haven't done a thing since you were crowned, I swear. Please don't sentence me to a life of servitude. I don't mind being just a princess—I don't."

He looked at her, confused.

"I mean it. I really do, Alric. Please, don't do this."

He sighed, looking at her sadly. "Arista, what else can I do with you? I don't want you living like a hermit in that tower for the rest of your life. I honestly think this is for the best. It will be good for you. You might not see it now but—don't look at me like that! I am king and you'll do as I tell you. I need you to do this for me. The kingdom needs you to do this."

She could not believe what she was hearing. Arista felt tears working their way forward. She locked her jaw, squeezing her teeth together, breathing faster to stave them off. She felt feverish and a little light-headed. "And I suppose I am to be shipped off immediately. Is that why the carriages are outside?"

"Yes," he said firmly. "I was hoping you would be on your way in the morning."

"Tomorrow?" Arista felt her legs weaken, the air empty from her lungs.

"Oh, for Maribor's sake, Arista—it's not like I'm ordering you to marry some old coot."

"Oh—well! I am so pleased you are looking out for me," she said. "Who is it, then? One of King Roswort's nephews? Dearest Maribor, Alric! Why Dunmore? Rudolf would have been misery enough, but at least I could understand an alliance with Alburn. But Dunmore? That's just cruel. Do you hate me that much? Am I that horrible that you must marry me to some no-account duke in a backwater kingdom? Even Father wouldn't have done that to me—why—why are you laughing? Stop laughing, you insensitive little hobgoblin!"

"I'm not marrying you off, Arista," Alric managed to get out.

She narrowed her eyes at him. "You're not?"

"God, no! Is that what you thought? I wouldn't do that. I'm familiar with the kind of people you know. I'd find myself floating down the Galewyr again."

"What, then? Julian said you were deciding my fate in there."

"I have—I've officially appointed you Ambassador of Melengar."

She stood silent, staring at him for a long moment. Without turning her head, she shifted her eyes and grabbed her shoe from Hilfred. Leaning on his shoulder, she slipped it back on.

"But Bernice said Sauly brought a list of eligible suitors," she said tentatively, cautiously.

"Oh yes, he did," Alric said, and chuckled. "We all had a good laugh at that."

"We?"

"Mauvin and Fanen are here." He hooked his thumb at the door. "They're going with you. Fanen plans to enter the contest the church is organizing up in Ervanon. You see, it was supposed to be this big surprise, but you ruined everything as usual."

"I'm sorry," she said, her voice quavering unexpectedly. She threw her arms around her brother and hugged him tight. "Thank you."

The front wheels of the carriage bounced in a hole, followed abruptly by the rear ones. Arista nearly struck her head on the roof and lost her concentration, which was frustrating, because she was certain she was on the verge of recalling the name of Dunmore's Secretary of the Treasury. It started with a Bon, a Bonny, or a Bobo—no, it could not be Bobo, could it? It was something like that. All these names, all these titles, the third baron of Brodinia, the Earl of Nith—or was it the third baron of Nith and the Earl of Brodinia? Arista looked at the palm of her hand, wondering if she could write them there. If caught, it would be an embarrassment not just for herself, but for Alric, and all of Melengar as well. From now on, everything she did, every mistake, every stumble would not just hurt her, it would reflect poorly on her kingdom. She had to be perfect. The problem was she did not know how to be perfect. She wished her brother had given her more time to prepare.

Dunmore was a new kingdom, only seventy years old, an overgrown fief reclaimed from the wilderness by ambitious nobles with only passing pedigrees. It had none of the traditions or refinement found in the rest of Avryn, but it did have a plethora of mind-numbing titled offices. She was convinced King Roswort created them the way a self-conscious man might overdecorate a modest house. He certainly had more ministers than Alric, with titles twice as long and uniquely vague, such as the Assistant Secretary of the Second Royal Avenue Inspection Quorum. *What does that even mean?* And then there was the simply unfathomable, since Dunmore was landlocked, Grandmaster of the Fleet! Nevertheless, Julian had provided her with a list and she was doing her best to memorize it, along with a tally sheet of their imports, exports, trade agreements, military treaties, and even the name of the king's dog. She laid her head back on the velvet upholstery and sighed.

"Something wrong, my dear?" Bishop Saldur inquired from his seat directly across from her, where he sat pressing his fingers together. He stared at her with unwavering eyes that took in more than her face. She would have considered his looks rude if he had been anyone else. Saldur—or Sauly, as she always called him—had taught her the art of blowing dandelions that had gone to seed when she was five. He had shown her how to play checkers and pretended not to notice when she climbed trees or rode her pony at a gallop. For commencement on her sixteenth birthday, Sauly had personally instructed her on the Tenets of the Faith of Nyphron. He was like a grandfather. He always stared at her. She had given up wondering why.

"There's too much to learn. I can't keep it all straight. The bouncing doesn't help either. It's just that"—she flipped through the parchments on her lap, shaking her head—"I want to do a good job, but I don't think I will."

The old man smiled at her, his eyebrows rising in sympathy. "You'll do fine. Besides, it's only Dunmore." He gave her a wink. "I think you'll find His Majesty King Roswort an unpleasant sort of man to deal with. Dunmore has been slow to gain the virtues that the rest of civilization has learned to enjoy. Just be patient and respectful. Remember that you'll be standing in *his* court, not Melengar, and there you are subject to his authority. Your best ally in any discussion is silence. Learn to develop that skill. Learn to listen instead of speaking and you'll weather many storms. Also, avoid promising anything. Give the impression you are promising, but never actually say the words. That way Alric always has room to maneuver. It is a bad practice to tie the hands of your monarch."

"Would you like something to drink, my lady?" Bernice asked, sitting beside Arista on the cushioned bench, guarding a basket of travel treats. She sat straight, her knees together, hands clutching the basket, thumbs rubbing it gently. Bernice beamed at her, fanning deep lines from the corners of her eyes. Her round pudgy cheeks were forced too high by a smile too broad—a condescending smile, the sort displayed to a child who had scraped her knee. At times Arista wondered if the old woman was trying to *be* her mother.

"What have you got in there, dear?" Saldur asked. "Anything with a bite to it?"

"I brought a pint of brandy," she said, and then hastily added, "in case it got cold."

"Come to think of it, I feel a bit chilled," Saldur said, rubbing his hands up and down his arms, pretending to shiver.

Arista raised an eyebrow. "This carriage is like an oven," she said while pulling on the high dress collar that ran to her chin. Alric had emphasized that she needed to wear properly modest attire, as if she had made a habit of strolling about the castle in bosom-baring scarlet tavern dresses. Bernice took this edict as carte blanche to imprison Arista in antiquated costumes of heavy material. The sole exception was the dress for her meeting with the King of Dunmore. Arista wanted all the help she could get to make a good impression and decided to wear the formal reception gown that had once belonged to her mother. It was simply the most stunning dress Arista had ever seen. When her mother had worn it, every head had turned. She had looked so impressive, so magnificent—every bit the queen.

"Old bones, my dear," Saldur told her. "Come, Bernice, why don't you and I share a little cup?" This brought a self-conscious smile to the old lady's face.

Arista pulled the velvet curtain aside and looked out the window. Her carriage was in the middle of a caravan consisting of wagons and soldiers on horseback. Mauvin and Fanen were somewhere out there, but all she could see was what the window framed. They were in the kingdom of Ghent, although Ghent had no king. The Nyphron Church administered the region directly and had for several hundred years. There were few trees in this rocky land and the hills remained a dull brown, as if spring were tardy—off playing in other realms and neglecting its chores here. High above the plain a hawk circled in wide loops.

"Oh dear!" Bernice exclaimed as the carriage bounced again. *Oh dear!* was as close as Bernice ever came to cursing. Arista glanced over to see that the jostling was making the process of pouring the brandy a challenge. Sauly with the bottle, Bernice with the cup, their arms shifting up and down, struggling to meet in the middle like in some test-of-skill at a May Fair—a game that was designed to look simple but ultimately embarrassed the players. At last, Sauly managed to tip the bottle and they both cheered.

"Not a drop lost," he said, pleased with himself. "Here's to our new ambassador. May she do us proud." He raised the cup, took a large mouthful, and sat back with a sigh. "Have you been to Ervanon before, my dear?"

Arista shook her head.

"I think you'll find it spiritually uplifting. Honestly, I am surprised your father never brought you here. It is a pilgrimage every member of the Church of Nyphron needs to make once in their life."

Arista nodded, failing to mention her late father had not been terribly devout. He had been required to play his part in the religious services of the kingdom, but often skipped them if the fish were biting, or if the huntsmen reported spotting a stag in the river valley. Of course, there had been times when even he had sought solace. She had long wondered about his death. Why had he been in the chapel the night that miserable dwarf had stabbed him? More importantly, how had her uncle Percy known he would be there and used this knowledge to plot his death? It puzzled her until she realized he had not been there praying to Novron or Maribor—he had been talking to *her*. It had been the anniversary of the fire. The date Arista's mother had died. He had probably visited the chapel every year and it bothered Arista that her uncle knew more about her father's habits than she did. It also disturbed her that she had never thought to join him.

"You'll have the privilege of meeting with His Holiness the Archbishop of Ghent."

She sat up, surprised. "Alric never mentioned anything about that. I thought we were merely passing through Ervanon on our way to Dunmore."

"It is not a formal engagement, but he is eager to see the new Ambassador of Melengar."

"Will I be seeing the Patriarch as well?" she asked, concerned. Not being prepared for Dunmore was one thing, but meeting the Patriarch with no preparation would be devastating.

"No." Saldur smiled like a man amused by a child's struggle to take her first steps. "Until the Heir of Novron is found, the Patriarch is the closest thing we have to the voice of god. He lives his life in seclusion, speaking only on rare occasions. He is a very great man, a very holy man. Besides, we can't keep you too long. You don't want to be late for your appointment with King Roswort in Glamrendor."

"I suppose I'll miss the contest, then."

"I don't see how," the bishop said after taking another sip, which left his lips glistening.

"If I push on to Dunmore, I won't be in Ervanon to see—"

"Oh, the contest won't be held in Ervanon," Saldur explained. "Those broadsides you've no doubt seen only indicated that contestants are to *gather* there."

"Then where will it be?"

"Ah, well now, that's something of a secret. Given the gravity of this event, it is important to keep things under control, but I can tell you this: Dunmore will be on the way. You'll stop there long enough to have your audience with the king and then you'll be able to continue on to the contest with the rest of them. Alric will most assuredly want to have his ambassador on hand for this momentous occasion."

"Oh, wonderful, I would like that—Fanen Pickering is competing. But does that mean you won't be coming?"

"That will be up to the archbishop to decide."

"I hope you can. I'm sure Fanen would appreciate as many people as possible cheering him on."

"Oh, it's not a competition. I know all those heralds are promoting it that way, which is unfortunate, because the Patriarch did not intend it so."

Arista stared at him, confused. "I thought it was a tournament. I saw an announcement declaring the church was hosting a grand event, a test of courage and skill, the winner to receive some magnificent reward."

"Yes, and all of that's true but misleading. Skill will not be needed so much as courage and... Well, you'll find out."

He tipped the cup and frowned, then looked hopefully at Bernice.

Arista stared at the cleric a moment longer, wondering what all that meant, but it was clear Sauly would not be adding anything further on the topic. She turned back to the window, peering out once more. Hilfred trotted beside the carriage on his white stallion. Unlike Bernice, her bodyguard was unobtrusive and silent. He was always there, distant, watchful, respectful of her privacy, or as much as a man who was required to follow her everywhere could be. He was always in sight of her but never looking—the perfect shadow. It had always been that way, but since the trial, he had been different. It was a subtle change but she sensed he had withdrawn from her. Perhaps he felt guilty for his testimony, or maybe, like so many others, he believed some of the accusations brought against her. It was possible Hilfred thought he was serving a witch. Maybe he even regretted saving her life from the fire that night. She threw the curtain shut and sighed.

It was dark by the time the caravan arrived in Ervanon. Bernice had fallen asleep, her head hanging limp over the basket, which threatened to fall. Saldur had nodded off as well, his head drooping lower and lower, popping up abruptly only to droop again. Through her window, Arista felt the cool, dewy night air splash across her face as she craned her neck to look ahead. The sky was awash in stars, giving it a light dusty appearance, and Arista could see the dark outline of the city rising on the great hill. The lower buildings were nothing more than shadows, but from within them rose a singular finger. The Crown Tower was unmistakable. The alabaster battlements that ringed the top appeared like a white crown floating high in the air. The ancient remnant of the Steward's

Empire was distinctive as the tallest structure ever made by man. Even at a distance it was awe-inspiring.

Surrounding the city were campfires, flickering lights scattered across the flats like a swarm of resting fireflies. As they approached, she heard voices, shouts, laughter, arguments rising up from the many camps along the roadside. They were the contestants, and there must be hundreds of them. Arista saw only glimpses as the carriage rolled past. Faces were illuminated by the glow of firelight. Silhouetted figures carried plates; men and boys sat on the ground laughing, tipping cups to their mouths. Tents filled the spaces in between and lines of tethered horses and wagons lay in the shadows.

The wheels and hooves of her carriage began a loud click-clack as they rolled onto cobblestone. They entered through a gate and all she could see were torches illuminating the occasional wall, or a light in a nearby window. Arista was disappointed. She had learned about the city's history at Sheridan University and looked forward to seeing the ancient seat that had once ruled the world. In the power vacuum left after the fall of the ancient Novronian Empire, civil wars broke out and the people divided along their old Apelanese ethnic lines, forming the four nations of Apeladorn: Trent, Avryn, Calis, and Delgos. Within each of these, various warlords struggled for supremacy, battling their neighbors for land and power. After more than three hundred years of warfare, only one ruler ever managed to make a serious attempt at unifying the four nations into one empire again. Glenmorgan of Ghent ended the era of civil wars and, through brilliant and brutal conquests, unified Trent, Avryn, Calis, and Delgos under one banner once more. The Church of Nyphron threw its support behind him but reminded the people that Glenmorgan was not the Heir of Novron by naming him the Defender of the Faith and Steward to the Heir. They solidified the union by establishing the church's base in Ervanon and built their great cathedral alongside Glenmorgan Castle.

The Steward's Reign did not last. According to Arista's professor, Glenmorgan's son was ill suited to the task he inherited, and the Steward's Empire ended only seventy years after it began, collapsing with the betrayal of Glenmorgan III by his nobles. It was not long before Calis and Trent broke away and Delgos declared itself a republic.

Ervanon was mostly ruined in the warfare that followed, but in the aftermath, the Patriarch moved into the last remaining piece of Glenmorgan's great palace—the Crown Tower. From then on, the tower and the city became synonymous with the church and recognized as the holiest place in the world behind the ancient—but lost—Novronian capital of Percepliquis itself.

The carriage stopped with a jerk that rocked the inhabitants, waking Saldur and causing the old maid to gasp when her basket spilled to the floor.

"We've arrived," Saldur said with a groggy voice as he wiped his eyes, yawned, and stretched.

The coachman locked the brake, climbed down, and opened the door. A rush of cool damp air flooded inside and chilled Arista. She stepped out, stiff and weak, her head hazy. It felt strange to be standing still. They were at the very base of the massive Crown Tower. She looked up and doing so made her dizzy. Even at that dark hour, the top stood out brightly against the night sky. The tower rested on a domed crest known as Glenmorgan's Rise, which was the highest point for miles. Even though she didn't climb a step, it appeared as if she stood at the top of the world as she looked beyond the ancient wall and down to the sprawling valley below.

She yawned and shivered and instantly Bernice was there, throwing a cloak over her shoulders and buttoning it. Sauly

took longer getting out of the carriage. He slowly extended
each thin leg, stretching them out and testing his weight.

"Your Grace." A boy appeared. "I hope you had a pleasant
journey. The archbishop asked me to tell you he is waiting in
his private chambers for the princess."

Arista was stunned. "Now?" She turned to the bishop.
"You don't expect me to meet him with a day's coating of road
dust and sweat on me. I look a fright, smell like a pig, and I'm
exhausted."

"You look lovely as always, my lady," Bernice cooed while
stroking the princess's hair. It was a habit that Arista particularly disliked. "I'm sure the archbishop, being a spiritual man,
will be looking at your soul, not your physical person."

Arista gave Bernice a quizzical look, then rolled her eyes.

Servants dressed in clerical frocks appeared around them,
hauling luggage, breaking down the harnesses, and watering
the horses.

"This way, Your Grace," the boy said, and led them into
the tower.

They entered a large rotunda with a polished marble floor
and columns that divided the center from a walkway that encircled the wall. As if from a great distance, she could hear
soft singing. Dozens of voices, perhaps a choir, were rehears-
ing. Flickering light from unseen lamps bounced off polished
surfaces. Their footsteps echoed loudly.

"Couldn't I see him in the morning?"

"No," Saldur said, "this is a very important matter."

Arista furrowed her brow and pondered this. She had taken
for granted that visiting the archbishop was just a formality,
but now she was not so sure. As part of Percy Braga's plot to
usurp the kingdom of Melengar, he had placed her on trial for
her father's death. Barred from attending the proceedings, she
later heard rumors of testimony others had given, including

her beloved Sauly. If the stories were true, Sauly had denounced her not only for killing her father, but also for witchery. She had never spoken to the bishop about the allegations, nor had she demanded an explanation from Hilfred. Percy Braga was to blame for all of it. He had tricked everyone. Hilfred and Sauly had only done what they had thought best for the sake of the kingdom. Still, she could not help wondering if perhaps she had been the one fooled.

According to the church, witchery and magic of any kind were an abomination to the faith. *If Sauly thought I was guilty, might he take steps against me?* She considered it incredible that the bishop, who had been like a family member to her, who always seemed so kind and benevolent, could do such a thing. On the other hand, Braga had been her actual uncle, and after nearly twenty years of loyal service, he had murdered her father and tried to kill her and Alric as well. His desire for power knew no loyalties.

She was increasingly aware of Hilfred's presence coming up the stairs behind her. Normally giving her a comfortable feeling of security, it now seemed threatening. *Why is it he never looks at me?* Perhaps she was wrong. Perhaps it was not guilt or dislike; perhaps it was a matter of distancing himself. She heard farmers who raised cows for milking often named them Bessie or Gertrude, but those same farmers never named the beef cows, those destined for slaughter.

Arista's mind began to race. Were they leading her to a locked cell in yet another tower? Would they execute her, the way the church had executed Glenmorgan III? Would they burn her at a stake and later justify it as a purifying act for the crime of heresy? What would Alric do when he found out? Would he declare war on the church? If he did, all the other kingdoms would turn against him. He would have no choice but to accept the edict of the church.

They reached a door and the bishop asked Bernice to go and prepare the princess's room for her arrival. He asked Hilfred to wait outside while he led Arista in and closed the door behind her.

It was a surprisingly small room, a tiny study with a cluttered desk and only a few chairs. Wall sconces revealed old thick books, parchments, seals, maps, and clerical vestments for various occasions.

Two men waited inside. Seated behind the desk was the archbishop, an old man with white hair and wrinkled skin. He sat wrapped in a dark purple cassock with an embroidered shoulder cape and a golden stole that hung around his neck like an untied scarf. He had a long and pallid face, made longer by his unkempt beard, which, when he was seated as he was, reached to the floor. Similarly, his eyebrows were whimsically bushy. On a high wooden seat he sat bent in a hunched posture, giving the impression he was leaning forward with interest.

Searching through the clutter was another, much younger, thin little man, with long fingers and darting eyes. He, too, was pale, as if he had not seen the sun in years. His long black hair pulled back in a tight tail gave him the stark and intense look of a man consumed by his work.

"Your Holiness Archbishop Galien," Saldur said after they had entered, "may I introduce the princess Arista Essendon of Melengar."

"So pleased you could come," the old cleric told her. His mouth, which had lost many of its teeth, frequently sucked in his thin lips. His voice was windy, with a distinctive rasp. "Please, take a seat. I assume you had a rough day bouncing around in the back of a carriage. Dreadful things, really. They tear up the roads and shake you to a frazzle. I hate getting in one. It feels like a coffin and at my age you are wary of getting into boxes of any kind.

But I suppose I must endure it for the sake of the future, a future I won't even see." He unexpectedly winked at her. "Can I offer you a drink? Wine, perhaps? Carlton, make yourself useful, you little vagabond, and get Her Highness a glass of Montemorcey."

The little man said nothing but moved rapidly to a chest in the corner. He pulled a dark bottle from the contents and drew out the cork.

"Sit down, Arista," Saldur whispered in her ear.

The princess selected a red velvet chair in front of the desk and, brushing out her dress, sat down stiffly. She was not at ease but made an effort to control her growing fear.

Carlton presented her with a glass of red wine on an engraved silver platter. She considered that it might be drugged or even poisoned, but dismissed this notion as ridiculous. *Why poison or drug me? I already made the fatal error of blindly blundering into your web.* If Hilfred had defected to their side, she had only Bernice to protect her against the entire armed forces of Ghent. She was already at their mercy.

Arista took the glass, nodded at Carlton, and sipped.

"The wine is imported through the Vandon Spice Company in Delgos," the archbishop told her. "I have no idea where Montemorcey is, but they do make incredible wine. Don't you think?"

"I must apologize," Arista blurted out nervously. "I was unaware I was coming directly here. I assumed I would have a chance to freshen up after the long trip. I am generally more presentable. Perhaps I should retire and meet you tomorrow?"

"You look fine. You can't help it. Lovely young princesses are blessed that way. Bishop Saldur did the right thing bringing you here immediately, even more than he knows."

"Has something happened?" Saldur asked.

"Word has come down"—he looked up and pointed at the ceiling—"literally, that Luis Guy will be traveling with us."

"The sentinel?"

Galien nodded.

"That might be good, don't you think? He'll bring a contingent of seret, won't he? And that will help maintain order."

"I am certain that's the Patriarch's mind as well. I, however, know how the sentinel works. He won't listen to me and his methods are heavy handed. But that's not what we are here to discuss."

He paused a moment, took a breath, and returned his attention to Arista. "Tell me, my child, what do you know of Esrahaddon?"

Arista's heart skipped a beat but she said nothing.

Bishop Saldur placed his hand on hers and smiled. "My dear, we already know that you visited him in Gutaria Prison for months and that he taught you what he could of his vile black magic. We also know that Alric freed him. Yet none of that matters now. What we need to know is where he is and if he has contacted you since his release. You are the only person he knows who might trust him and therefore the only one he might reach out to. So tell us, child, have you had any communication with him?"

"Is this why you brought me here? To help you locate an alleged criminal?"

"He *is* a criminal, Arista," Galien said. "Despite what he told you, he is—"

"How do you know what he told me? Did you eavesdrop on every word the man said?"

"We did," he replied passively.

The blunt answer surprised her.

"My dear girl, that old wizard told you a story. Much of it is actually true; only he left out a great deal."

She glanced at Sauly, whose fatherly expression looked grim as he nodded his agreement.

"Your uncle Braga wasn't responsible for the murder of your father," the archbishop told her. "It was Esrahaddon."

"That's absurd," Arista scoffed. "He was in prison at the time and couldn't even send messages."

"Ah—but he could, and he did—through you. Why do you think he taught you to make the healing potion for your father?"

"Besides curing him of sickness, you mean?"

"Esrahaddon didn't care about Amrath. He didn't even care about you. The reality is he needed your father dead. Your mistake was going to him. Trusting him. Did you think he would be your friend? Your sage old tutor, like Arcadius? Esrahaddon is no tame beast, no honorable gentleman. He is a demon and he is dangerous. He used you to escape. From the moment you visited him, he calculated your use as a tool. To escape he needed the ruling monarch to come and release him. Your father knew who and what he was, so he would never do it. But Alric, because of his ignorance, would. So he needed your father dead. All Esrahaddon had to do was make the church believe your father was the heir. He knew it would cause us to act against him."

"But why would the church want the heir dead? I don't understand."

"We'll get to that in due time. But suffice it to say his interest in you and your father got our attention. It was the healing potion Esrahaddon had you create that sealed your father's fate. It tainted his blood to appear as if he was a descendent of the imperial bloodline. When Braga learned this, he followed what he thought was the church's wishes and put plans in motion to remove Amrath and his children."

"Are you saying that Braga was working for the church when he had my father murdered?"

"Not directly—or officially. But Braga was devout in his beliefs. He acted rashly, not waiting for the church *bureaucracy*, as he used to call it. Both the bishop and I speak for the whole church when we tell you we are truly sorry for the tragedy that occurred. Still, you must understand we did not orchestrate it. It was the design of Esrahaddon that set the wheels of your father's fate in motion. He used the church just as he used you."

Arista glared at the archbishop and then at Sauly. "You knew about this?"

The bishop nodded.

"How could you allow Braga to kill my father? He was your friend."

"I tried to stop it," Sauly told her. "You must believe me when I tell you this. The moment the test was done, and your father implicated, I called for an emergency council of the church, but Braga couldn't be stopped. He refused to listen to me and said I was wasting valuable time."

Fears of her own murder fled and anger filled the vacuum. She stood up, fists clenched, her eyes filled with hate.

"Arista, I know you are upset, and have every right to be, but let me explain further." The archbishop waited for her to sit down again. "What I am about to tell you is the most highly guarded secret of the Church of Nyphron. This information is strictly reserved for top-ranking members of the clergy. I am trusting you with this information because we need your help and I know you'll not extend it unless you understand why." He took the glass of wine, sipped it, then leaned forward and spoke to Arista in a quiet tone. "In the last few years of the empire, the church uncovered a dark and twisted scheme whose goal was no less than to enslave all of humanity. The conspiracy led directly to the emperor. Only the church could save mankind. We killed the emperor and tried to eliminate his bloodline, but the emperor's son was aided by Esrahaddon. His heritage contains the power to raise the demons of the past and once more bring humanity to the brink. For this reason, the church has sought to find the heir and destroy the lineage whose existence is a knife at the throat of all of us. After so long, the heir might not even be aware of his power, or even who he is. But Esrahaddon knows. If that wizard finds the heir, he can use him as a weapon against us. No one will be safe."

The archbishop looked at her carefully. "Esrahaddon was once part of the high council. He was one of the key members in the effort to save the empire from the conspirators, but at the last moment, he betrayed the church. Instead of a peaceful transition, he callously caused a civil war that destroyed the empire. The church cut off his hands and locked him away for nearly a millennium. What do you think he'll do if he has the chance to exact revenge? Whatever humanity he might have possessed died in Gutaria Prison. What remains is a powerful demon bent on our destruction—revenge for revenge's sake; he is mad with it. He is like a wildfire that will consume all if not stopped. As a princess of a kingdom, you must understand—sacrifices must be made to ensure the future of the realm. We deeply regret the error that occurred in respect to your father but hope you'll come to understand why it happened, accept our apologies, and help us prevent the end of all that we know.

"Esrahaddon is an incredibly intelligent madman bent on destroying everyone. The heir is his weapon. If he finds him before we do, if we cannot prevent him from reawakening the horror we managed to put to sleep centuries ago, then all this—this city, your kingdom of Melengar, all of Apeladorn will be lost. We need your help, Arista. We need you to help us find Esrahaddon."

The door opened abruptly and a priest entered.

"Your Grace," he said, out of breath, "the sentinel is calling the curia to order."

Galien nodded and looked back at Arista. "What say you, my dear? Can you help us?"

The princess looked at her hands. Too much was whirling in her head: Esrahaddon, Braga, Sauly, mysterious conspiracies, healing potions. The one image that remained steadfast was the memory of her father lying on his bed, his face pale, blood soaking the covers. It had taken so long to put the pain behind her, and now…had Esrahaddon killed him? Had they? "I don't know," she muttered.

"Can you at least tell us if he has contacted you since his escape?"

"I haven't seen or heard from Esrahaddon since before my father's death."

"You understand, of course," the archbishop told her, "that be this as it may, you are the most likely person he would trust and we would like you to consider working with us to find him. As Ambassador of Melengar you could travel between kingdoms and nations and never be suspected. I also understand that right now you may not be ready to make such a commitment, so I won't ask; but please consider it. The church has let you down grievously; I only request that you give us a chance to redeem ourselves in your eyes."

Arista drained the rest of her wine and slowly nodded.

᠅

"Do you think she is telling the truth?" the archbishop asked him. There was a faint look of hope on his face, clouded by an overall expression of misery. "There was a great deal of resistance in her."

Saldur was still looking at the door Arista had exited. "*Anger* would be a more accurate word, but yes, I think she was telling the truth."

He did not know what Galien had expected. Had he thought Arista would embrace him with open arms after they admitted to killing her father? The whole idea was absurd, desperate measures from a man sinking in quicksand.

"It was worth it," the archbishop said without any conviction.

Saldur played with a loose thread on his sleeve, wishing he had taken the remainder of Bernice's bottle with him. He had never cared much for wine. More than anything, the tragedy of Braga's death was the loss of a great source of excellent brandy. The archduke had really known his liquor.

Galien stared at him. "You're quiet," the archbishop said. "You think I was wrong, of course. You said so, didn't you? You were very vocal about it at our last meeting. You were watching her every move. You have that—that—" The old man waved his hand toward the door as if this would make his fumbling clearer. "That old handmaid monitoring her every breath. Isn't that right? And if Esrahaddon had contacted her, we would have known and they would be none the wiser, but now..." The archbishop threw up his hands, feigning disgust in a sarcastic imitation of Saldur.

Saldur continued to fiddle with the thread, wrapping it around the end of his forefinger, winding it tighter and tighter.

"You're too arrogant for your own good," Galien accused him defensively. "The man is an imperial wizard. What he is capable of is beyond your comprehension. For all we know, he may have been visiting her in the form of a butterfly in the garden or a moth that entered her bedroom window each night. We had to be sure."

"A butterfly?" Saldur said, genuinely amazed.

"He's a wizard. Damn you. That's what they do."

"I highly doubt—"

"The point is we didn't know for sure."

"And we still don't. All I can say is I don't think she was lying, but Arista is a clever girl. Maribor knows she has proven that already."

Galien lifted his empty wineglass. "Carlton!"

The servant looked up. "I'm sorry, Your Grace, but I can't say I know her well enough to offer much of an opinion."

"Good god, man. I'm not asking you about her; I want more wine, you fool."

"Ah," Carlton said, and headed for the bottle, then pulled the cork out with a dull, hollow pop.

"The problem is that the Patriarch blames me for Esrahaddon's disappearance," Galien continued.

For the first time since Arista's departure, Saldur leaned forward with interest. "He's told you this?"

"That's just it; he's told me nothing. He only speaks to the sentinels now. Luis Guy and that other one—Thranic. Guy is unpleasant, but Thranic..." He trailed off, shaking his head and frowning.

"I've never met a sentinel."

"Consider yourself lucky. Although your luck, I think, is running out on that score. Guy spent all morning upstairs in a long meeting with the Patriarch." He played with the empty glass, running his finger around the rim. "He's in the council hall right now, giving his address to the curia."

"Shouldn't we be there?"

"Yes," he said miserably, but he made no effort to move.

"Your Grace?" Saldur asked.

"Yes, yes." He waved at him. "Carlton, get me my cane."

◆

Saldur and the archbishop entered to the sound of a man's booming voice. The grand council chamber was a three-story circular room encompassing the entire width of the tower. It was lined in thin ornate columns set in groups of two that represented the relationship between Novron, the Defender of Faith, and Maribor, the god of man. Between each set was a tall thin window, which provided the room with a complete panoramic view of the surrounding countryside. Seated in circular rows, radiating out from the center, gathered the curia, the college of chief clerics of the Nyphron Church. The other eighteen bishops were present to hear the words of the Patriarch as spoken by Luis Guy.

Sentinel Luis Guy, a tall thin man with long black hair and disquieting eyes, stood in the center of the room. He was sharp; that was Saldur's first impression of the man, clean, ordered, focused, both in manner and looks. His hair was very black yet his skin was light, providing a striking contrast. His mustache was narrow, his beard short and severe, trimmed to a fine point. He dressed in the traditional red cassock, black cape, and black hood, with the symbol of the broken crown neatly embroidered on his chest. Not a hair or a pleat was out of place. He stood straight, his eyes not scanning the crowd but glaring at them.

"...the Patriarch feels that Rufus has the strength to persuade the Trent nobles and the church will deliver the rest. Remember, this isn't about picking the best horse. The Patriarch must choose the one that can win the race and Rufus is the most likely candidate. He's a hero to the south and a native of the north. He has no visible ties to the church. Crowning him emperor will immediately stifle a large segment of the population that might otherwise oppose us. While Rufus may not cause Trent and Calis to submit to the New Empire, it should prevent them from uniting against us. In their hesitation we shall find the time to consolidate the whole of Avryn under one emperor. After which time, we shall systematically, one-by-one, force Trent, then Calis to join or face invasion. Given the vastly superior wealth and power of Avryn, it is more than likely they will submit without a fight—all the more so with Rufus as emperor."

"You speak as if the unification is already complete," Bishop Tildale of Dunmore said. "But Avryn has eight kingdoms and only Dunmore, Ghent, and Warric are Imperialist. What about the Royalists? They aren't going to accept this without a fight. It's not like the time of Glenmorgan, when all he faced were a handful of warlords—these are kings with lands and titles that they've held for generations. The kingdoms of Alburn and Melengar are old and proud realms. Even King Urith of Rhenydd, as poor as he is, will not simply take a knee to Rufus merely because we say so. And what about Maranon? Their fields supply most of Avryn with the food we eat. If King Vincent resists, he could starve us into submission. And Galeannon? King Fredrick has often threatened to cede to Calis, where he could be the strong leader of a weak pack rather than a weak leader of a strong one. If we insist on his giving up what little independence he has, we could lose him."

"I can assure you King Fredrick will bow before the imperial throne when the time comes," the bishop of Galeannon announced.

"And you needn't worry about Maranon's wheat fields," the bishop of Maranon said.

"As you can see, the Royalist problem has been eliminated," Guy assured them. "It has taken nearly a generation, but the church has managed to successfully insert loyal Imperialists in key positions in each kingdom, with the minor exception of Melengar, where our plans did not proceed as expected. This failure will easily be mitigated by its singularity. Once Rufus is declared emperor, all the other kingdoms will pledge allegiance and Melengar will be alone. They will capitulate or face a war with the rest of Avryn. So yes, with just a few minor issues, the unification of Avryn has indeed already been accomplished. We just have not made this fact public."

This caused a murmur throughout the chamber.

"I knew we were progressing successfully on this project," Saldur told the archbishop, "but I had no idea we were so far along."

"Braga's appointment as king of Melengar was to be the final step," Galien replied with a disappointed tone. Of all the kingdoms the church had prepared for the coming New Empire, only Saldur's had failed.

"And the Nationalists?" the Prelate of Ratibor asked. "They have been growing in number. You can't simply ignore them."

"The Nationalists will be an issue," Guy admitted. "For years now the seret have been watching Gaunt and his followers. They are being funded by the DeLur family and several other powerful merchant cartels in the Republic of Delgos. Delgos has enjoyed its freedom for too long to be convinced of the advantages of a central authority. They already fear the very idea of a unified empire. So yes, we know they will fight. They will need to be defeated on the battlefield, which is another reason why the Patriarch has selected Rufus. He's a ruthless warlord. He'll crush the Nationalists as his first act as emperor. Delgos will fall soon after."

"Do we have the troops to take Delgos?" Prelate Krindel, the resident historian, asked. "Tur Del Fur is defended by a dwarven fortress. It held out against a two-year siege by the Dacca."

"I have been working on that very problem and I think I'll have a — unique — solution."

"And what might that be?" Galien asked suspiciously.

Luis Guy looked up. "Ah, Archbishop, so good of you to join us. I sent word we were beginning nearly an hour ago."

"Do you plan to spank me for being tardy, Guy? Or are you simply trying to avoid my question?"

"You are not ready to hear the answer to that question," the sentinel replied, which brought a reproachful look from the archbishop. "You would not believe me if I told you and certainly would not approve. But when the time comes, and it is necessary, then rest assured the fortress of Drumindor will fall, and Delgos along with it."

The archbishop frowned at the slight, but before he could comment, Saldur spoke up. "What about the common people? Will they embrace a new emperor?" he asked.

"I have traveled the length and breadth of the four nations, promoting the contest. Heralds have announced it from Dagastan in the south to Lanksteer in the north; all of Apeladorn is aware of the event. In the marketplaces, taverns, and castle courts, anticipation is high. Once we announce the true intent of the contest, the people will be beside themselves. Gentlemen, these are exciting times. It is no longer a question of if, but when the New Empire will rise. The groundwork is laid. All we need to do is bestow the crown."

"And King Ethelred of Warric?" Galien asked. "Is he on board?"

Guy shrugged. "He isn't pleased with giving up his throne to become a viceroy, but few of the monarchs are, even those we placed in power. It is amazing how quickly rulers become accustomed to being called Your Majesty. Yet he has been assured that for being the first to take off his crown, he will be first in line in the new order. It is very likely he will assume the role of regent, administering the empire on behalf of Lord Rufus as the new emperor is away handling any uprisings. I also suggested that he might remain as chief council. He appeared satisfied with that."

"I still don't like handing over power to Rufus and Ethelred," Saldur said.

"We won't be," Galien assured him. "The church will be in control. They are the faces, but we are the mind. The church will have a permanent appointee in the palace of the New Empire who will be charged with overseeing the construction of the new order." He looked to Guy. "Did the Patriarch mention this to you?"

"He did."

"And did he say if he would accept this responsibility himself?"

"Due to his advanced age, the Patriarch will not be taking on this burden but will instead select someone from this council who will be empowered to act autonomously on behalf of the entire church. That person will be appointed co-regent alongside Ethelred at least for the duration of the reconstruction phase."

"Such a man would be immensely powerful," the archbishop said. Saldur could tell from his tone—perhaps everyone could—that he knew it would not be him. "Would that person be you?"

Guy shook his head. "My task, as my father before me, and his before that, is to find the Heir of Novron. The Patriarch has asked me to assist in these matters concerning the immediate establishment of the empire, which I am happy to do, but I'll not be deterred from my life's goal."

"Who will it be, then?"

"His Holiness has not yet decided. I suspect he will wait to see how events with the contest play out." There was a pause as they waited for Guy to speak again. "This is a historic moment. All that we have worked for, all that has been carefully nurtured for centuries, is about to bear fruit. We now stand at the threshold of a new dawn for mankind. What began nearly a millennium ago will conclude with this generation. May Novron bless our hands."

"He's impressive," Saldur told Galien.

"You think so?" the archbishop replied. "Good, because you're coming with us."

"To the contest?"

He nodded. "I need someone to counterbalance Guy. Perhaps you can be just as big a pain to him as you've been to me."

ᥬ

Arista hesitated outside the door, holding a single candle. Inside, she could hear Bernice shuffling about, turning down the bed, pouring water into the basin, laying out Arista's bed clothes in that ghastly nursemaid way of hers. As tired as she was, Arista had no desire to open that door. She had too much to think about and could not bear Bernice just now.

How many days?

She tried counting them in her head, ticking them off, tracking her memories of those muddled times between the death of her father and the death of her uncle; so much had happened so quickly. She still remembered the pale white look of her father's face as he lay on the bed, a single tear of blood on his cheek, and the dark stain spreading across the mattress beneath him.

Arista glanced awkwardly at Hilfred, who stood behind her. "I'm not ready to go to bed yet."

"As you wish, my lady," he said quietly, as if understanding her need not to alert the nurse-beast within.

Arista began walking aimlessly. She traveled down the hallway. This simple act gave her a sense of control, of heading toward something instead of being swept along. Hilfred followed three paces behind, his sword clapping against his thigh, a sound she had heard for years, like the swing of a pen-dulum ticking off the seconds of her life.

How many days?

Sauly had known Uncle Percy would kill her father. He knew before it happened! How long in advance did he know? Was it hours? Days? Weeks? He said he had tried to stop him. That was a lie—it had to be. Why not expose him? Why not just tell her father? But maybe Sauly had. Maybe her father refused to listen. Was it possible Esrahaddon really had used her?

The dimly lit hall curved as it circled around the tower. The lack of decoration surprised Arista. Of course, the Crown Tower was only a small part of the old palace, a mere corner staircase. The stones were old hewn blocks set in place centu-ries earlier. They all looked the same—dingy, soot-covered, and yellow, like old teeth. She passed several doors, then came to a staircase and began climbing. It felt good to exert her legs after being idle so long.

How many days?

She remembered her uncle searching for Alric, watching her, having her followed. If Saldur had known about Percy, why had he not intervened? Why had he allowed her to be locked in the tower and put through that dreadful trial? Would Sauly have allowed them to execute her? If he had just spoken up, if he had backed her, she could have called for Braga's imprisonment. The Battle of Medford could have been avoided and all those people would still be alive.

*How many days before Braga's death did Saldur know…
and do nothing?*

It was a question without an answer. A question that echoed in her head, a question she was not certain she wanted answered.

And what was all this about the destruction of humanity? She knew they thought she was naïve. *Do they think I am ignorant as well?* No one person had the power to enslave an entire race. Not to mention the very idea that this threat emanated from the emperor was absurd. The man had already been the ruler of the world!

The stairs ended in a dark circular room. No sconces, torches, nor lanterns burned. Her little candle was the only source of illumination. Followed by Hilfred, Arista exited the stairs. They had entered the alabaster crown near the tower's pinnacle. An immediate sense of unease washed over her. She felt like a trespasser on forbidden grounds. There was nothing to give her that impression except perhaps the darkness. Still, it felt like exploring an attic as a child — the silence, the shadowy suggestion of hidden treasures lost to time.

Like everyone, she had grown up hearing the tales of Glenmorgan's treasures and how they lay hidden at the top of the Crown Tower. She even knew the story about how they had been stolen yet returned the following night. There were many stories about the tower, tales of famous people imprisoned at its top. Heretics like Edmund Hall, who had supposedly discovered the entrance to the holy city Percepliquis and paid by spending the remainder of his life sealed away — isolated where he could tell no one of its secrets.

It was here. It was all here.

She walked the circle of the room. The sounds of her footsteps echoed sharply off the stone, perhaps because of the low ceiling, or maybe it was just her imagination. She held up her candle and found a door at the far side. It was an odd door. Tall and broad, not made of wood as the others in the tower, nor was it made of steel or iron. This door was made of stone, one single solid block that looked like granite and appeared out of place beside the walls of polished alabaster.

She looked at it, perplexed. There was no latch, knob, or hinges. Nothing to open it with. She considered knocking.

What good will it do to knock on granite except to bloody my knuckles? Placing her hand on the door, she pushed, but nothing happened. Arista glanced at Hilfred, who stood silently watching her.

"I just wanted to see the view from the top," she told him, imagining what he might be thinking.

She heard something just then, a shuffle, a step from above. Tilting her head, she lifted the candle. Cobwebs lined the underside of the ceiling, which was made of wood. Clearly someone or something was up there.

Edmund Hall's ghost!

The idea flashed through her mind and she shook her head at her foolishness. Perhaps she should go and cower in bed and have Auntie Bernice read her a nice bedtime story. Still, she had to wonder. What lay behind that very solid-looking door?

"Hello?" a voice echoed, and she jumped. From below Arista saw the glow of another light rising, the sound of steps climbing. "Is someone up here?"

She had an instant desire to hide and she might have tried if there had been anything to hide behind and Hilfred had not been with her.

"Who's there?" A head appeared, coming around the curve of the steps from below. It was a man—a priest of some sort by the look of him. He wore a black robe with a purple ribbon that hung down from either side of his neck. His hair was thin, and from that angle, Arista could see the beginning of a bald spot on the back of his head, a tanned island in a sea of graying hair. He held a lantern above his head and squinted at her, looking puzzled.

"Who are you?" he asked in a neutral tone. It was neither threatening nor welcoming, merely curious.

She smiled self-consciously. "My name is Arista, Arista from Melengar."

"Arista from Melengar?" he said thoughtfully. "Might I ask what you are doing here, Arista from Melengar?"

"Honestly? I was—ah—hoping to get to the top of the tower to see the view. It's my first time here."

The priest smiled and began to chuckle. "You are sightseeing, then?"

"Yes, I suppose so."

"And the gentleman with you—is he also sightseeing?"

"He is my bodyguard."

"Bodyguard?" The man paused in his approach. "Do all young women from Melengar have such protection when they travel abroad?"

"I am the Princess of Melengar, daughter of the late king Amrath and sister of King Alric."

"Aha!" the priest said, entering the room and walking the curve toward them. "I thought so. You were part of the caravan that arrived this evening, the lady who came in with the Bishop of Medford. I saw the royal carriage, but didn't know what royalty it contained."

"And you are?" she asked.

"Oh yes, I'm very sorry, I am Monsignor Merton of Ghent, born and raised right down below us in a small village called Iberton, a stone's throw from Ervanon. Wonderful fishing in Iberton. My father was a fisherman, by the way. We fished year-round, nets in the summer and hooks in the winter. Teach a man to fish and he'll never go hungry, I always say. I suppose in a way that's how I came to be here, if you get my meaning."

Arista smiled politely and glanced back at the stone door.

"I'm sorry but that door doesn't go to the outside, and I'm afraid you can't get to the top." He tilted his head toward the ceiling and lowered his voice. "That's where *he* lives."

"He?"

"His Holiness, Patriarch Nilnev. The top floor of this tower is his sanctuary. I come up here sometimes to just sit and listen. When it is quiet, when the wind is still, you can sometimes hear him moving about. I once thought I heard him speak, but that might have just been hopeful ears. It is as if Novron himself is up there right now, looking down, watching out for us. Still, if you like, I do know where you can get a good view. Come with me."

The monsignor turned and descended back down the stairs. Arista looked one last time at the door, then followed.

"When does he come out?" Arista asked. "The Patriarch, I mean."

"He doesn't. At least not that I have ever seen. He lives his life in isolation—better to be one with the Lord."

"If he never comes out, how do you know he's really up there?"

"Hmm?" Merton glanced back at her and chuckled. "Oh, well, he does speak with people. He holds private meetings with certain individuals, who bring his words to the rest of us."

"And who are these people? The archbishop?"

"Sometimes, though lately his decrees have come down to us by way of the sentinels." He paused in their downward trek and turned to look at her. "You know about them, I assume?"

"Yes," she told him.

"Being a princess, I thought you might."

"We actually haven't had one visit Melengar for several years."

"That's understandable. There are only a few left and they have a very wide area to cover."

"Why so few?"

"His Holiness hasn't appointed any new ones, not since he ordained Luis Guy. I believe he was the last."

This was the first good news Arista had heard all day. The sentinels were notorious watchdogs of the church. Originally charged with the task of finding the lost heir, they commanded the famous order of the Seret Knights. These knights enforced the church's will—policing layman and clergy alike for any signs of heresy. When the seret investigated, it was certain someone would be found guilty, and usually anyone who protested would find themselves charged as well.

Monsignor Merton led her to a door two floors down and knocked.

"What is it?" an irritated voice asked.

"We've come to see your view," Merton replied.

"I don't have time for you today, Merton. Go bother someone else and leave me be."

"It's not for me. The princess Arista of Medford is here, and she wants to see a view from the tower."

"Oh no, really," Arista told him, shaking her head. "It's not that important. I just—"

The door popped open and behind it stood a fat man without a single hair on his head. He was dressed all in red, with a gold braided cord around his large waist. He was wiping his greasy hands on a towel and peering at Arista intently.

"By Mar! It is a princess."

"Janison!" Merton snapped. "Please, that's no way for a prelate of the church to speak."

The fat man scowled at Merton. "Do you see how he treats me? He thinks I am Uberlin himself because I like to eat and enjoy an occasional drink."

"It is not I that judges you, but our lord Novron. May we enter?"

"Yes, yes, of course, come in."

The room was a mess of clothes, parchments, and paintings that lay on the floor or leaned on baskets and chests. A desk stood at one end and a large flat, tilted table was at the other. On it were stacks of maps, ink bottles, and dozens of quills. Nothing appeared to be in its place or even to have one.

"Oh—" Arista nearly said *dear* but stopped short, realizing she had almost imitated Bernice.

"Yes, it is quite the sight, isn't it? Prelate Janison is less than tidy."

"I am neat in my maps and that's all that matters."

"Not to Novron."

"You see? And, of course, I can't retaliate. How can anyone hope to compete with His Holiness Monsignor Merton, who heals the sick and speaks to god?"

Arista, who was following Merton across the wretched room toward a curtain-lined wall, paused as a memory from her childhood surfaced. Looking at Merton, she recalled it. "You're the savior of Fallon Mire?"

"Aha! Of course he didn't tell you. It would be too prideful to admit he is the chosen one of our lord."

"Oh stop that." It was Merton's turn to scowl.

"Was it you?" she asked.

Merton nodded, sending Janison a harsh stare.

"I heard all about it. It was some years ago. I was probably only five or six when the plague came to Fallon Mire. Everyone was afraid because it was working its way up from the south and Fallon Mire was not very far from Medford. I remember my father spoke of moving the court to Drondil Fields, only we never did. We didn't have to because the plague never moved north of there."

"Because *he* stopped it," Janison said.

"I did not!" Merton snapped. "Novron did."

"But he sent you there, didn't he? Didn't he?"

Merton sighed. "I only did what the lord asked of me."

Janison looked at Arista. "You see? How can I hope to compete with a man whom god himself has chosen to hold daily conversations with?"

"You actually heard the voice of Novron telling you to go save the people of Fallen Mire?"

"He directed my footsteps."

"But you talk to him too," Janison pressed, looking at Arista. "He won't admit that, of course. Saying so would be heresy and Luis Guy is just downstairs. He doesn't care about your miracle." Janison sat down on a stool and chuckled. "No, the good monsignor here won't admit that he holds little conversations with the lord, but he does. I've heard him. Late at night, in the halls, when he thinks everyone else is asleep." Janison raised his voice an octave as if imitating a young girl. "*Oh Lord, why is it you keep me awake with this headache when I have work in the morning? What's that? Oh, I see, how wise of you.*"

"That's enough, Janison," Merton said, his voice serious.

"Yes, I'm certain it is, Monsignor. Now take your view and leave me to my meal."

Janison picked up a chicken leg and resumed eating while Merton threw open the drapes to reveal a magnificent window. It was huge, nearly the width of the room, divided only by three stone pillars. The view was breathtaking. The large moon revealed the night as if it were a lamp one could reach out and touch, hanging among a scattering of brilliant stars.

Arista placed a hand on the windowsill and peered down. She could see the twisting silver line of a river far below, shimmering in the moonlight. At the base of the tower, campfires circled the city, tiny flickering pinpricks like stars themselves. Looking straight down, she felt dizzy and her heartbeat quickened. Wondering how close she was to the top of the tower, she looked up and counted three more levels of windows above her, to the alabaster crown of white.

"Thank you," she told Merton, and nodded toward Janison.

"Rest assured, Your Highness. He is up there."

She nodded but was not certain if he was referring to god or the Patriarch.

CHAPTER 4

DAHLGREN

For five days, Royce, Hadrian, and Thrace made their way north through the nameless sea of trees that made up the eastern edge of Avryn, a region disputed by both Alburn and Dunmore. Each laid claim to the vast, dense forest between them, but until the establishment of Dahlgren, neither appeared in any hurry to settle the land. The great forest, referred to merely as either the East or the Wastes, remained uncut, untouched, unblemished. The road they traveled, once a broad lane as it had plowed north out of Alburn, quickly became two tracks divided by a line of grass, and finally squeezed down to a single dirt trail that threatened to vanish entirely. No fences, farms, nor wayside inns broke the woodland walls, nor did travelers cross their path. Here in the northeast, maps were vague, with few markings, and went entirely blank past the Nidwalden River.

At times, the beauty of the forest was breathtaking, even spiritual. Monolithic elms towered overhead, weaving a lofty tunnel of green. It reminded Hadrian of the few times he had poked his head into Mares Cathedral in Medford. The long-trunked trees arched over the trail like the buttresses of the great church, forming a natural nave. Delicate shafts of muted light pierced the canopy at angles as if entering through a gallery of windows far above. Along the ground, fans of finely fingered ferns grew up from the past year's brown leaves, creating a soft swaying carpet. A choir of birds sang in the unseen heights, and from the bed of brittle leaves came the rustle of squirrels and chipmunks like the coughs, whispers, and shifts of a congregation. It was beautiful yet disturbing, like swimming out too far, delving into unknown, unseen, and untamed places.

Over the last days, travel became increasingly difficult. The recent spring storms had dropped several trees across the trail, which blocked the route as formidably as any castle gate. They dismounted and struggled through the thick brush as Royce searched for a way around. Hours passed yet they failed to rejoin the road. Scratched and sweaty, they led their horses across several small rivers and on one occasion faced a sharp drop. Looking down from the rocky cliff, Hadrian offered Royce a skeptical look. Usually Hadrian didn't question Royce's sense of direction or his choice of path. Royce had an unerring ability to find his way in the wilderness, a talent proven on many occasions. Hadrian tilted his head up. He could not see the sun or sky; there was no point of reference—everything was limbs and leaves. Royce had never let him down, but they had never been in a place like this before.

"We're all right," Royce told them, a touch of irritation in his voice.

They worked their way down, Royce and Thrace leading the horses on foot while Hadrian cleared a path. When they reached the bottom, they found a small stream, but no trail. Again, Hadrian glanced at Royce, but this time the thief made no comment as they pressed on along the least dense route.

"There," Thrace said, pointing ahead to a clearing revealed by a patch of sun that managed to sneak through the canopy.

A few more steps revealed a small road. Royce looked at it for a moment, then merely shrugged, climbed back on his horse, and kicked Mouse forward.

They emerged from the forest as if escaping from a deep cave, into the first open patch of direct sun they had seen in days. In the glade, beside a rough wooden wellhead, stood a child among a herd of eight grazing pigs. The child, no more than five years old, held a long, thin stick, and an expression of wonder was on the little round face, covered in sweat-trapped dirt. Hadrian had no idea if it was a boy or a girl, as the child displayed no definite indication of either, wearing only a simple smock of flax linen, dirty and frayed with holes and rips so plentiful they appeared by design.

"Pearl!" Thrace called out as she scrambled off Millie so quickly the horse sidestepped. "I'm back." She walked over and tousled the child's matted hair.

The little girl—Hadrian now guessed—gave Thrace little notice and continued to stare at them, eyes wide.

Thrace threw out her arms and spun around. "This is Dahlgren. This is home."

Hadrian dismounted and looked around, puzzled. They stood on a small patch of close-grazed grass beside a well constructed of ill-fitted planks with a wooden bucket, wet and dripping, resting on a rail. Two other rutted trails intersected with the one they followed, forming a triangle with the well at its center. On all sides, the forest surrounded them. Massive trees of dramatic size still blocked the sky, except for the hole above the clearing, through which Hadrian could see the pale blue of the late-afternoon sky.

Hadrian scooped a handful of water from the bucket to wash the sweat from his face and Millie nearly shoved him aside as she pushed her nose into the bucket, drinking deeply.

"What's with the bell?" Royce asked, climbing down off Mouse and gesturing toward the shadows.

Hadrian looked over, surprised to see a massive bronze bell hanging from a rocker arm, which in turn hung from the lower branch of a nearby oak. Hadrian guessed that if it had been on the ground, Royce could have stood inside it. A rope dangled, with knots tied at several points along its length.

"That's different," he said, walking toward it. "How does it sound?"

"Don't ring it!" Thrace exclaimed. Hadrian pivoted his eyebrows up. "We only ring it for emergencies."

He looked back at the bell, noting the relief images of Maribor and Novron, along with lines of religious script circling its waist. "Seems sort of extravagant for...well..." He looked around at the empty clearing.

"It was Deacon Tomas's idea. He kept saying, 'A village isn't a village without a church, and a church isn't a church without a bell.' Everyone pitched in a little. The old margrave matched what we had and ordered it for us. The bell was finished long before we had time to build the church. Mr. McDern took his oxen and fetched it all the way from Ervanon. When he got back, we had no place to put it and he needed his wagon. It was my father's idea to hang it here and use it as an alarm until the church went up. That was a week before the attacks started. At the time no one had any idea how much use we'd get out of it." She stared at the huge bell for a moment and then added, "I hate the sound of that bell."

A gusty breeze rustled the leaves and threw a lock of hair in her face. She brushed it back and turned away from the oak and the bell. "Over there"—she pointed across the rutted path—"is where most of us live." Hadrian spotted structures hidden in shadow within a shallow dip, behind a blind of goldenrod and milkweed. They were small wooden-framed buildings plastered with wattle and daub—a mixture of mud, straw, and manure. The roofs were thatch, the windows no more than holes in the walls. Most lacked doors, making do with curtains across the entrances, which fluttered with the wind, revealing dirt floors. Beside one, he spotted a vegetable garden that managed to catch a sliver of sun.

"That's Mae and Went Drundel's place there in front," Thrace said. "Well, I guess it's just Mae's now. Went and the boys...they...were taken not long ago. To the left, the one with the garden is the Bothwicks'. I used to babysit Tad and the twins, but Tad's old enough now to watch the twins himself. They are like family really. Lena and my mother were very close. Behind them, you can just see the McDerns' roof. Mr. McDern is the village smith and the owner of the only pair of oxen. He shares them with everyone, which makes him popular come spring. To the right, the place with the swing is the Caswells'. Maria and Jessie are my best friends. My father hung that swing for us not long after we moved here. I spent some of the best days of my life on that swing."

"Where's your place?" Hadrian asked.

"My father built our house a ways down the hill." She gestured toward a small trail that ran to the east. "It was the best house—best farm, really—in the village. Everyone said so. There's almost nothing left now."

Pearl was still staring at them, watching every move.

"Hello," Hadrian said to her with a smile, bending down on his haunches, "my name is Hadrian, and this is my friend Royce." Pearl glared and took a step back, brandishing the stick before her. "You don't talk much, do you?"

"Her parents were both killed two months ago while planting," Thrace told them, looking at the girl with sympathetic eyes. "It was daylight, and like everyone else, they thought they were safe, but it was a stormy day. The clouds had darkened the sky." Thrace paused, then added, "A lot of people have died here."

"Where is everyone else?" Royce asked.

"They'll all be in the fields now, bringing in the first cutting of hay, but they'll be coming back soon; it's getting late. Pearl minds the pigs for the entire village, don't you, Pearl?" The girl nodded fiercely, holding her stick with both hands and keeping a wary eye on Hadrian.

"What's up there?" Royce asked. He had moved down off the green and was looking up the trail as it ran north.

Hadrian followed, leaving Millie with the bucket, her tail swishing vigilantly against a handful of determined flies. Moving past a stand of spruce, Hadrian could see a hill cleared of trees rising just a few hundred yards away. On its crest rested a stockade-style wall of hewn logs and, in the center, a large wooden house.

"That's the margrave's castle. The deacon Tomas has taken on the responsibility of steward until the king appoints a new lord. He's very nice and I don't think he'd mind you using the stables, considering there aren't any other horses in the village. For now just tie them to the well, I guess, and we can go see my father.

"Pearl, watch their stuff, and keep the pigs away. If Tad, Hal, or Arvid comes back before I do, have them take the horses up to the castle and ask the deacon if they can stable them there, okay?"

The little girl nodded.

"Does she talk?" Hadrian asked.

"Yes, just not very often anymore. C'mon, I'll take you to—to what used to be my home. Dad's probably there. It's not far and a pretty pleasant walk." She began leading them east along a footpath that ran downhill behind the houses. As they circled around, Hadrian got a better look at the village. He could see more houses, all of them tiny things, most likely single rooms with lofts. There were other, smaller structures, a few crated feed bins built on stilts to keep clear of rodents and what looked to be a community outhouse; it too lacked a solid door.

"I'll ask the Bothwicks to take you in while you're here. I'm staying with them myself; they—" Thrace stopped. Her hands flew to her face as she sucked in a sudden breath and her lips started to quiver.

Beside the path, not far from the house with the swing, two wooden markers stood freshly driven into the earth. Carved into them were the names Maria and Jessie Caswell.

❧

The Wood farm appeared down the footpath. Several acres lay cleared of trees, most at the bottom of a hill where lush wheat grew in perfectly straight rows. A low stone wall built from carefully stacked rocks ran the perimeter. It was a beautiful field of rich dark earth, well turned, well planted, and well drained.

The homestead itself stood on the rise overlooking the field. The house was a ruined shell, its roof gone, thatch scattered across the yard, blown by the wind. Only a few timbers remained—splintered poles jutting up like broken bones punching through skin. The lower half of the building and the chimney were both made of irregularly shaped fieldstone and remained mostly intact. Some stones lay in piles where they had slipped from their stacks, but the majority appeared eerily untouched.

Little things caught Hadrian's attention. Mounted beneath one window hung a flowerbox with a scallop edge and the image of a deer carved into it. The front door, made of solid oak, did not reveal a single peg or visible joint. The stones that created the walls, in alternated colors of gray, rose, and tan, were each chipped to a fine flat profile. The curved walkway was bordered with bushes trimmed to resemble a hedge.

Theron Wood sat amidst the ruins of his home. The big farmer, with dark leathery skin, had a short mangle of forgotten gray hair that crowned a face cut by wind and sun. He looked like a part of the earth itself, a gnarled trunk of a great tree with a face like a weathered cliff. Holding a grass cutter between his legs, he rested on the remaining wall of his home, slowly dragging a sharpening stone along the length of the huge curved scythe blade. Back and forth the stone scraped while the man stared down at the green field below, an expression on his face Hadrian could describe only as one of contempt.

"Daddy! I'm back." Thrace ran to the old farmer, hugging him around his neck. "I missed you."

Theron endured the squeeze and glared at them. "Are these the ones, then?"

"Yes. This is Hadrian and Royce. They've come all the way from Colnora to help. They can get the weapon Esra told us about."

"I have a weapon," the farmer growled, and resumed sharpening his blade. The sound was cold and grating.

"This?" Thrace asked. "Your grass cutter? The margrave had a sword, a shield, and armor and he—"

"Not this, I have another weapon, much bigger, much sharper."

Puzzled, she looked around. The old man offered no insight.

"I don't need what lies in that tower to kill the beast."

"But you promised me."

"And I am a man of my word," he replied, and drew the stone along the edge of the blade once more. "The waiting only made my weapon sharper." He dipped the stone into a bucket of water that sat beside him. He raised it back to the blade but paused and said, "Every day I wake up, I see Thad's broken bed and Hickory's cradle. I see the shattered barrel that Thad made, the fields I planted for him—growing despite me. Best season in a decade. I woulda reaped more than enough to pay for the contract and tools. I woulda had extra. I coulda built him a shop. I might even have afforded a sign and real glass windows. He coulda had a planed wooden door with hinges and studs. His shop woulda been better than any house in the village. Better than the manor. People would walk by and stare, wondering what great man owned such a business. How great an artisan was this town's cooper that he could manage such a fine store?

"Those bastards back in Glamrendor who wouldn't let Thad hang a shingle, they would never have seen the like. It woulda had a shake roof and scalloped eaves, a hard oak counter, and iron hooks to hold lanterns for when he needed to work late at night to complete all his orders. His barrels would be stacked in a storage shed beside the shop. A beautiful barn-size one, and I would paint it bright red so no one could miss it. I woulda got him a wagon too, even if I had to build it myself. That way he could send orders all over Avryn—back to Glamrendor too. I woulda driven them there myself just to see the shock and anger on their faces.

" 'Morning!' I'd say, grinning like a lipless crocodile. Here's another fine delivery of barrels from Thaddeus Wood, the best cooper in Avryn. They'd cringe and curse. Yep, that boy o' mine, he's no farmer, no sir. Starting with him, the Woods were gonna be artisans and shopkeepers.

"This village, it'd have grown. People woulda moved in

and started businesses of their own, only Thad's woulda always been the first, the biggest, and the best. I'd have seen to that. Soon this here woulda been a city, a fine city, and the Woods the most successful family—a merchant family giv'n money to the arts and riding around in fine carriages. This here house woulda been a true mansion, 'cause Thad woulda insisted, but I wouldn't care 'bout that, no sir. I'd have been content just watching Hickory grow up, seeing him learn to read and write—appointed magistrate, maybe. My grandson in the black robes! Yes sir, Magistrate Wood is going to court in a fine carriage and me standing there watching him.

"I see it. Every morning I get up; I sit; I look down Stony Hill and I see all of it. It's right there, right in that field growing in front of me. I haven't hoed. I haven't tilled, but look at it. The best crop I ever grew getting taller every day."

"Daddy, please come back with us to the Bothwicks'. It's getting late."

"This is my home!" the old man shouted, but not at her. His eyes were still on the field. He scraped the blade again. Thrace sighed.

There was a long silence.

"You and your friends go. I swore not to seek it, but there is always a chance it might come to me."

"But, Daddy—"

"I said take them and go. I don't need you here."

Thrace glanced at Hadrian. There were tears in her eyes. Her lips trembled. She stood for a moment, wavering, then abruptly broke and ran back up the path toward town. Theron ignored her. The old farmer tilted the blade of his grass cutter to the other side and resumed sharpening. Hadrian watched him for a moment, the sounds of the stone on metal drowning out Thrace's fading sobs. He never looked up, not at Hadrian, not to glance down the trail. The man was indeed a rock.

Hadrian found Thrace only a few dozen yards up the trail. She was on her knees, crying. Her small body jerked, her hair rocking with the movement. He placed his hand gently on her shoulder. "Your father is right. That weapon of his is very sharp."

Royce caught up with them, carrying a fractured piece of wood. He looked down at Thrace with an uncomfortable expression.

"What's up?" Hadrian asked before Royce said anything callous.

"What do you think of this?" Royce replied, holding out the scrap, which might have been part of the house framing. The beam was wide and thick, good strong oak taken from the trunk of a well-aged tree. The piece bore four deeply cut gouges.

"Claw marks?" Hadrian took the wood and placed his hand against the board with his fingers splayed out. "Giant claw marks."

Royce nodded. "Whatever it is, it's huge. So how come no one has seen it?"

"It gets very dark here," Thrace told them, wiping her cheeks as she stood. A curious expression crossed her face and she walked to where a yellow-flowered forsythia grew at the base of a maple tree. Taking a hesitant step, Thrace bent down and drew back what Hadrian thought was a wad of cloth and old grass. As she carefully cleaned away the leaves and sticks, he saw it was a crude doll with thread for hair and X's sewn for eyes.

"Yours?" Hadrian ventured.

She shook her head but did not speak. After a moment, Thrace replied, "I made this for Hickory, Thad's son. It was his Wintertide gift, his favorite. He carried it everywhere." Plucking the last bits of grass from the doll, she rubbed it.

"There's blood on it." Her voice quavered. Clutching the doll to her chest, she said softly, "He forgets—they were my family too."

✍

Royce guessed it was still early evening when they returned to the village common, but already the light was fading, the invisible sun quickly consumed by the great trees. The little girl and her herd of pigs were gone, and so were their horses and gear. In their place, they found a host of people rushing about with an urgency that left him uneasy.

Men crossed the clearing carrying hoes, axes, and piles of split wood over their shoulders. Most were barefoot, dressed in sweat-stained tunics. Women came behind, carrying bundles of twigs, reeds, thick marsh grasses, and stalks of flax. They too traveled barefoot, with their hair pulled up, hidden under simple cloth wraps. Royce could see why Thrace had made such a big deal out of the dress they had bought her, as all the village women wore simple homemade smocks of the same natural off-white color, lacking any adornment.

They looked hot and tired, focused on reaching the shelter of their homes and dumping their burdens. As the three approached the village, one boy looked up and stopped. He had a long-handled hoe across his shoulders, his arms threaded around it.

"Who's that?" he said.

This got the attention of those nearby. An older woman glared, still clutching her bag of twigs. A bare-chested man with thick, powerful arms lowered his pack of wood, holding tight to his axe. The topless man glanced at Thrace, who was still wiping her red eyes, and advanced on them, shifting the axe to his right hand.

"Vince, we got visitors!" he shouted.

A shorter, older man with a poorly kept beard turned his head and dropped his bundle as well. He looked at the boy who had first spotted them. "Tad, go fetch your pa." The boy hesitated. "Go now, son!"

The boy ran off toward the houses.

"Thrace, honey," the old woman said, "are you all right?"

The bearded man glared at them. "What they do to you, girl?"

As the men advanced, Royce and Hadrian moved together, each one looking expectantly at Thrace. Royce's hand slipped into the folds of his cloak.

"Oh no!" Thrace burst out. "They didn't do anything."

"Doesn't look like nothing. Disappear for weeks and you pop up crying, dressed like—"

Thrace shook her head. "I'm fine. It's just my father."

The men stopped. They kept a wary eye on the strangers but shot looks of sympathy at Thrace.

"Theron's a fine man," Vince told her, "a strong man. He'll come around, you'll see. He just needs some time."

She nodded, but it was forced.

"Now, who might you two be?"

"This is Hadrian and Royce," Thrace finally got around to saying, "from Colnora in Warric. I asked them here to help. This is Mr. Griffin, the village founder."

"Came out here with an axe, a knife, and not much else. The rest of these poor souls were foolish enough to follow, on account I told them life was better, and they was stupid enough to believe me." He extended his hand. "Just call me Vince."

"I'm Dillon McDern," the big bare-chested man said. "I'm the smith round here. Figure you fellas might want to know that. You got horses, right? My boys say they took two up to the manor a bit ago."

"This is Mae," Vince said, presenting the old woman. She nodded solemnly. Now that it was clear that Thrace was all right, the old woman slouched, and the look in her eyes became dull and distant as she turned away with her bundle of twigs.

"Don't mind her. She's—well, Mae's had it hard lately." He glanced at Dillon, who nodded.

The boy sent running returned with another man. Older than McDern, younger than Griffin, thinner than both, he dragged his feet as he walked, squinting despite the dim light. In his hands he held a small pig, which struggled to escape.

"Why'd you bring your pig, Russell?" Griffin asked.

"Boy said you needed me—said it was an emergency."

Griffin glanced at Dillon, who looked back and shrugged. "You find emergencies often call for pigs, do you?"

Russell scowled. "I just got hold of her. She gets riled up with Pearl all day, hard as can be to catch her. No way I'm letting her go with night coming on. What is it? What's the emergency?"

"Turns out there ain't one. False alarm," Griffin said.

Russell shook his head. "By Mar, Vince, scare a body to death. Next you'll be swinging from the bell rope just to see folks faint."

"Twarn't on purpose." He dipped his head at Royce and Hadrian. "We thought these fellas were up to something."

Russell looked at them. "Visitors, eh? Where'd you two come from?"

"Colnora," Thrace answered. "I invited them. Esra said they could help my father. I was hoping you'd let them stay with us."

Russell looked at her and sighed heavily, a frown pulling hard at the corners of his mouth.

"Oh, well—ah, that's okay, I guess," Thrace said, stumbling, looking embarrassed. "I can ask Deacon Tomas if he'll—"

"Of course they can stay with us, Thrace. You know better than to even ask." Tucking the pig under one arm, he placed his hand to the side of her face and rubbed her cheek. "It's just that, well, Lena and me—we was sure you were gone for good. Figured you'd found a new home, maybe."

"I'd never leave my father."

"No. No, I s'pose you wouldn't. You and your pa—you're alike that way. Rocks, the both of you, and Maribor help the plow that finds either of you in its path."

The pig made an attempt to escape, twisting, kicking its legs, and squealing. Russell caught it just in time. "Need to get back. The wife will be after me. C'mon, Thrace, and bring your friends." He led them toward the clump of tiny houses. "By Mar, girl, where'd you get that dress?"

Royce remained where he was as the rest started to go. Hadrian gave him a curious look but continued ahead with the others. Royce remained on the trail, unmoving, watching the villagers racing the light: fetching water, hanging out clothes, gathering animals. Pearl wandered past the well, her herd of pigs reduced to only two. Mae Drundel came out of her house, her kerchief pulled free, her gray hair hanging. Unlike the rest, she walked slowly. She crossed to the side of her home, where Royce noticed three markers like those of the Caswells'. She stood for a moment, knelt down for a time, then walked slowly back inside. She was the last villager to disappear indoors.

That left only Royce and the man at the well.

He was no farmer.

Royce had spotted him the moment they had returned, his long slender frame leaning silently against the side of the well-head, resting in shadow where he nearly faded into the background. The man's hair hung loose to his shoulders, dark with a few threads of gray. He had high cheekbones and deep brooding eyes. His long enveloping robe shimmered with the last rays of sunlight. He sat motionless. This was a man comfortable with waiting and well versed in patience.

He did not look old, but Royce knew better. He had not changed much in the two years since Royce, Hadrian, a young prince Alric, and a monk named Myron had aided his escape from Gutaria Prison. The color of his robe was different, yet still not quite discernible. This time Royce guessed it shimmered somewhere between a turquoise and a dark green. As always, the sleeves hung down, hiding the absence of his hands. He also bore a beard, but that, of course, was new.

They watched each other, staring across the green. Royce walked forward, crossing the distance between them in silence. Two ghosts meeting at a crossroad.

"It's been a while—Esra is it? Or should I call you Mr. Haddon?"

The man tilted his head, lifting his eyes. "I am delighted to see you as well, Royce."

"How do you know my name?"

"I'm a wizard, or did you miss that from our last meeting?"

Royce paused and smiled. "You know, you're right; I might have. Perhaps you should write it down for me lest I forget again."

Esrahaddon raised an eyebrow. "That's a bit harsh."

"How do you know who I am?"

"Well, I did see *The Crown Conspiracy* while in Colnora. I found the sets pathetic and the orchestration horrible, but the story was good. I particularly loved the daring escape from the tower, and the little monk was hilarious—by far my favorite character. I was also pleased there was no wizard in the tale. I wonder who I should thank for that oversight—certainly not you."

"They also didn't use our real names. So again, how do you know it?"

"How would you find out your name, if you were me?"

"I'd ask people that would know. So who did you ask?"

"Would *you* tell me?"

Royce frowned. "Do you ever answer a question with an answer?"

"Sorry, it's a habit. I was a teacher most of my free life."

"Your speech has changed," Royce observed.

"Thank you for noticing. I worked very hard. I sat in many taverns over the last two years and listened. I have a talent for languages; I speak several. I don't know all the colloquial terms yet, but the general grammar wasn't hard to adjust to. It is the same language, after all; the dialect you speak is merely...less sophisticated than what I was used to. It's like talking with a crude accent."

"So you found out who we were by asking around and watching bad plays and you picked up the language by listening to drunks. Now tell me, why are you here, and why do you want us here?"

Esrahaddon stood up and slowly walked around the well. He looked at the ground where the last light of the sun spilled through the leaves of a poplar tree.

"I could tell you that I am hiding here and that would sound plausible. I could also say that I heard about the plight of this village and came here to help, because that's what wizards do. Of course, we both know you won't believe those answers. So let's save time. Why don't *you* tell me why I am here? Then you can try and judge by my reaction if you are correct or not, since that's what you're planning to do anyway."

"Were all wizards as irritating as you are?"

"Much worse, I'm afraid. I was one of the youngest and nicest."

A young man—Royce thought his name was Tad—trotted

over with a bucket. "It's getting late," he said with a harried look, filling his bucket with water. A few yards away Royce spotted a woman struggling to pull a stubborn goat into a house as a small boy pushed the animal from behind.

"Tad!" a man shouted, and the boy at the well turned abruptly.

"Coming!"

He smiled and nodded at each of them, grabbed his bucket of water, and ran back the way he came, spilling half the contents in the process.

They were alone again.

"I think you're here because you need something from Avempartha," Royce told the wizard. "And I don't think it is a sword of demon-slaying either. You're using this poor girl and her tormented father to lure me and Hadrian here to turn a knob you obviously can't manage."

Esrahaddon sighed. "That's disappointing. I thought you were smarter than that, and these constant references to my disability are dull. I am not *using* anyone."

"So you are saying there really is a weapon in that tower?"

"That is exactly what I am saying."

Royce studied him for a moment and scowled.

"Can't tell if I am lying or not, can you?" Esrahaddon smiled smugly.

"I don't think you're lying, but I don't think you're telling the truth either."

The wizard's eyebrows rose. "Now that's better. There might be hope for you yet."

"Maybe there is a weapon in that tower. Maybe it can help kill this…whatever it is they have here, but maybe you also conjured the beast in the first place as an excuse to drag us here."

"Logical," Esrahaddon said, nodding. "Morbidly manipulative, but I can see the reasoning. Only, if you recall, the attacks on this village started while I was still imprisoned."

Royce scowled again. "So why are you here?"

Esrahaddon smiled. "Something you need to understand, my boy, is that wizards are not fonts of information. You should at least know this much—the farmer Theron and his daughter would be dead today if I hadn't arrived and sent her to fetch you."

"All right. Your purpose here is none of my business. I can accept that. But why am *I* here? You can tell me that much, can't you? Why go to the bother of finding out our names and locating us—which was really impressive, by the way—when you could have gotten any thief to pick your lock and open the tower for you?"

"Because not just anyone will do. You are the only one I know who can open Avempartha."

"Are you saying I am the only thief you know?"

"It helps if you actually listen to what I say. You are the only one I know who can open Avempartha."

Royce glared at him.

"There is a monster here that kills indiscriminately," Esrahaddon told him with great and unexpected seriousness. "No weapon made by man can harm it. It comes at night and people die. Nothing will stop it except the sword that lies in that tower. You need to find a way inside and get that sword."

Royce continued to stare.

"You are right. That is not the whole truth, but it is the truth nonetheless and all that I am willing to explain...for now. To learn more you need to get inside."

"Stealing swords," Royce muttered mostly to himself. "Okay, let's take a look at this tower. The sooner I see it, the sooner I can start cursing."

"No," the wizard replied. He looked back at the ground, where the sun had already faded. He glanced up at the darkening sky. "Night is coming and we need to get indoors. In the morning we will go, but tonight we hide with the rest."

Royce considered the wizard for a moment. "You know, when I first met you, there was all this talk about you being this scary wizard that could call lightning and raise mountains and now you can't even fight a little monster, or open an old tower. I thought you were more powerful than this."

"I was," Esrahaddon said, and for the first time the wizard held up his arms, letting his sleeves fall back, revealing the stumps where his hands should have been. "Magic is a little like playing the fiddle. It's damn hard to do without hands."

⌇

Dinner that evening was a vegetable pottage, a weak stew consisting of leeks, celery, onions, and potatoes in a thin broth. Hadrian took only a small portion that was far from filling, but he found it surprisingly tasty, filled with a mixture of unusual flavors that left a burning sensation in his mouth.

Lena and Russell Bothwick made good on their promise to put them up for the night, a kindness made all the more generous when they discovered how cramped the little house was. The Bothwicks had three children, four pigs, two sheep, and a goat they called Mammy, all of whom clustered in the single open room. Mosquitoes joined them as well, taking over the night shift from the flies. It was hard to breathe in the house filled with smoke, the scent of animals, and the steam from the stew pot. Royce and Hadrian staked out a bit of earth as near the open doorway as possible and sat on the floor.

"I didn't know the first thing about farming," Russell Bothwick was saying. Like most men in the village, he was dressed in a frayed and flimsy shirt that hung to his knees, belted around the waist with a length of twine. There were large dark circles under his eyes, another trait consistent with the other inhabitants of Dahlgren. "I was a candle maker back in

Drismoor. I worked as a journeyman in a trade shop on Hithil Street. It was Theron who kept us alive our first year here. We woulda starved or froze to death if not for Theron and Addie Wood. They took us under their wing and helped build this house. It was Theron that taught me how to plow a field."

"Addie was my midwife when I had the twins," Lena said while ladling out bowls, which Thrace handed to the children. The twin girls and Tad, exiled to the loft, looked down from their beds of straw, chins on hands, eyes watchful. "And Thrace here was our babysitter."

"There was never a question about taking her in," Russell said. "I only wish Theron would come too, but that man is stubborn."

"I just can't get over how beautiful that dress is," Lena Bothwick said again, looking at Thrace and shaking her head. Russell grumbled something, but since he had a mouthful of stew, no one understood him.

Lena scowled. "Well, it is."

She stopped talking about it but continued to stare. Lena was a gaunt woman with light brown hair cut straight and short, giving her a boyish look. Her nose came to a point so sharp it looked like it could cut parchment. She had a rash of freckles and no eyebrows to speak of. The children all took after her, each sporting the same cropped hairstyle, son and daughters alike, while Russell had no hair at all.

Thrace entertained them with stories of her adventure to the big city, of the sights and number of people she found there. She explained that Hadrian and Royce had taken her to a lavish hotel. This brought worried looks from Lena but she relaxed as more details were revealed. Thrace raved about her bath in a hot-water tub with perfumed soap and about how she had spent the night in a huge feather bed under a solid beamed roof. She never mentioned the Tradesmen's Arch, or what happened underneath it.

Lena was mesmerized to the point of nearly letting the remainder of the stew boil over. Russell continued to grunt and grumble his way through the meal. Esrahaddon sat with his back to the side wall between Lena's spinning wheel and the butter churn. His robe was now a dark gray. He was so quiet he could have been just a shadow. During dinner, Thrace spoon-fed the wizard.

How must that feel? Hadrian thought while watching them. *What is it like to have held so much power and now be unable to even hold a spoon?*

After dinner, while helping Lena clean up, Thrace was placing the washed bowls on a shelf and called out, "I remember this plate." A smile appeared on her face as she spotted the only ceramic dish in the house. The pale white oval with delicate blue traceries lay carefully tucked in a back corner of the cupboard with all the other treasured family heirlooms. "I remember when I was little, Jessie Caswell and I—" She stopped and the house quieted. Even the children stopped fussing.

Lena stopped cleaning the dishes and put her arms around Thrace, pulling her close. Hadrian noticed lines on the woman's face he had not seen previously. The two stood before the bucket of dirty water and silently cried together. "You shouldn't have come back," Lena whispered. "You should have stayed in that hotel with those people."

"I can't leave him." Hadrian heard Thrace's small voice muffled by Lena's shoulder. "He's all I have left."

Thrace pulled back and Lena struggled to offer her a smile.

It was dark outside now. From his vantage point at the doorway, Hadrian could not see much of anything—a tiny patch of moonlight scattered here and there. Fireflies blinked, leaving trails of light. The rest was lost in the vast black of the forest.

Russell pulled over a stool to sit across from Royce and Hadrian. Lighting a long clay pipe with a thin sliver of wood, he commented, "So, you two are here to help Theron kill the monster?"

"We'll do what we can," Hadrian replied.

Russell puffed hard on his pipe to ensure it lit, and then crushed the burning tip of the wooden sliver into the dirt floor. "Theron is over fifty years old. He knows the sharp end of a pitchfork from the handle, but I don't 'spect he's ever held a sword. Now you two look to me like the kind of fellas that have seen a fight up close, and Hadrian here not only has a sword—he's got three. A man carries three swords, he, like as not, knows how to use 'em. Seems to me a couple fellas like you could do more than just help an old man get himself killed."

"Russell!" Lena reprimanded him. "They're our guests. Why don't you scald them with hot water while you're at it?"

"I just don't want to see that damn fool kill himself. If the margrave and his knights didn't stand a chance, how well will Theron do out there? An old man with that scythe of his. What's he trying to prove? How brave he is?"

"He's not trying to prove anything," Esrahaddon said suddenly, and his voice silenced the room like a plate dropping. "He's trying to kill himself."

"What?" Russell asked.

"He's right," Hadrian said, "I've seen it before. Soldiers—career soldiers—brave men just reach a point where it's all too much. It can be anything that sets them off—one too many deaths, a friend dying, or even something as trivial as a change in the weather. I knew a man once who led charges in dozens of battles. It wasn't until a dog he befriended was butchered for food that he gave up. Of course, a fighter like that can't surrender, can't just quit. He needs to go out swinging. So they rush in unguarded, picking a battle they can't win."

"Then I needn't have wasted your time," Thrace said. "If my father doesn't want to live, whatever is in the tower can't save him."

Hadrian regretted speaking and added, "Every day your father is alive, there is the chance he can find hope again."

"Your father will be fine, Thrace," Lena told her. "That man is tough as granite. You'll see."

"Mom," one of the kids from the loft called.

Lena ignored the child. "You shouldn't listen to these people talking about your father that way. They don't know him."

"Mom."

"Honestly, telling a poor girl something like that right after she's lost her family."

"Mom!"

"What on earth is it, Tad?" Lena nearly screamed at the child.

"The sheep. Look at the sheep."

Everyone noticed it then. Crowded into the corner of the room, the sheep had been quiet through the meal. A content woolly pile that Hadrian had forgotten was there. Now they pushed each other, struggling against the wooden board Russell had put up. The little bell around Mammy's neck rang as the goat shifted uneasily. One of the pigs bolted for the door and Thrace and Lena tackled it just in time.

"Kids. Get down here!" Lena shouted in a whisper.

The three children descended the ladder with precision movements, veterans of many drills. Their mother gathered them near her in the center of the house. Russell got off his stool and doused the fire with the wash water.

Darkness enveloped them. No one spoke. Outside, the

crickets stopped chirping. The frogs fell silent an instant later. The animals continued to shift and stomp. Another pig bolted. Hadrian heard its little feet skitter across the dirt floor in the direction of the door. Beside him he felt Royce move; then there was silence.

"Here, someone take this," Royce whispered. Tad crawled toward the sound and took the pig from him.

They waited.

The sound began faint and hollow. A puffing, thought Hadrian, like bellows stoking a furnace. It grew nearer, louder, less airy—deep and powerful. The sound rose overhead and Hadrian instinctively looked up, but found only the darkness of the ceiling. His hands moved to the pommels of his swords.

Thrump. Thrump. Thrump.

They sat huddled in the darkness, listening, as the sound withdrew, then grew louder once more. A pause—total silence. Inside the house, even the noise of breathing vanished.

Crack!

Hadrian jumped at the loud burst that sounded as if a tree across the common exploded. Snapping, tearing, splintering, a war of violent noise erupted. A scream. A woman's voice. The shriek cut across the common, hysterical and frantic.

"Oh dear Maribor! That's Mae," Lena cried.

Hadrian leapt to his feet. Royce was already up.

"Don't bother," Esrahaddon told them. "She's dead, and there's nothing you can do. The monster cannot be harmed by your weapons. It—"

The two were out the door.

Royce was quicker and raced across the common toward the little house of Mae Drundel. Hadrian could not see a thing and found himself blindly chasing Royce's footfalls.

The cries stopped—a harsh, abrupt end.

Royce halted and Hadrian nearly plowed through him.

"What is it?"

"Roof is ripped away. There's blood all over the walls. She's gone. It's gone."

"It? Did you see something?"

"Through a patch in the canopy—just for a second, but it was enough."

CHAPTER 5

THE CITADEL

R oyce and Esrahaddon left at first light, following a small
trail out of the village. Ever since they had arrived in
Dahlgren, Royce had noticed a distant sound, a dull, constant
noise. As they approached the river, the sound grew into a
roar. The Nidwalden was massive—an expanse of tumultuous green water flowing swiftly, racing by and bursting against
rocks. Royce stood for a moment just staring. He spotted a
branch out in the middle, a black and gray fist of leaves bobbing helplessly against the current. It sped along, riding through
gaps in the boulders, ripping over rocks, until it vanished into
a cloud of white. In the center, he saw something tall rising up,
most of it lost in the mist and tree branches that extended over
the water.

"We need to go farther downriver," Esrahaddon explained
as he led Royce to a narrower trail that hugged the bank. River
grass grew along the edge, glistening with dew, and songbirds
sang shrill melodies in the soft morning breeze. Even with the
thundering river, and the vivid memory of a roofless home and
bloodstained walls, the place felt tranquil.

"There she is," Esrahaddon said reverently as they reached
a rocky clearing that afforded them an unobstructed view of

the river. It was wide and the water rushed by with a furious strength, then disappeared over the edge of a sudden fall.

They stood very near the ridge of the cataract and could see the white mist rising from the abrupt drop like a fog. Out in the middle of the river, at the edge of the falls, a massive shelf of bedrock jutted out like the prow of a mighty ship that ran aground just before toppling over the precipice. On this fearsome pedestal rose the citadel of Avempartha. Formed entirely of stone, the tower burst skyward from the rock shelf. A bouquet of tall, slender shards stretched upward like splinters of crystal or slivers of ice, its base lost in the billowing white clouds of mist and foam. At first sight it looked to be a natural stone formation, but a more careful study revealed windows, walkways, and stairs carefully integrated into the architecture.

"How am I supposed to get out there?" Royce asked, yelling over the roar, his cloak whipping and snapping like a snake.

"That would be problem number one," Esrahaddon shouted back, offering nothing more.

Is this some kind of test, or does he really not know?

Royce followed the river over the bare rocks to the drop. Here the land plummeted more than two thousand feet to the valley below. What stood before him was a vision of unsurpassed beauty. The falls were magnificent. The sheer power of the titanic surge was hypnotizing. The massive torrent of blue-green water spilled and sparkled into the billowing white bejeweled mist, the voice of the river thundering in his ears, rattling his chest. Beyond it, to the south, was an equally breathtaking vision. Royce could see for miles and marked the remaining passage of the river as it wound like a long shiny snake through the lush green landscape to the Goblin Sea.

Esrahaddon moved to a more sheltered escarpment farther inland and behind a brace of upward-thrust granite that blocked him from the gusting wind and spray. Royce climbed toward him when he noticed a depressed line in the trees running away from the river. A course of trees stood shorter than those around them, creating a trench in the otherwise uniform canopy. He made his way down to the forest floor and found that what he thought might be a gully was instead a section of younger growth. More importantly, the line was perfectly straight. Old vines and thornbushes masked unnatural mounds. He dug away some of the undergrowth and swept layers of dirt and dead leaves back until he touched flat stone.

"Looks like there might have been a road here," he shouted up to the wizard.

"There was. A great bridge once reached out across the river to Avempartha."

"What happened to it?"

"The river," the wizard told him. "The Nidwalden does not abide the efforts of man for long. Most of it likely washed away, leaving the remains to fall."

Royce followed the buried road to the river's edge, where he stood looking at the tower across the violent expanse. A vast gray volume rushed by him, its speed concealed by its size. The dark gray became a swirling translucent green as it reached the edge. The moment it fell, the water burst into white foam, billions of flying droplets, and all he could hear was the thundering roar.

"Impossible," he muttered.

He returned to where the wizard stood and sat down on the sun-warmed rock, looking at the distant tower that rose up in the haze where rainbows played.

"Do you want me to open that thing?" the thief asked with all seriousness. "Or is this some kind of game?"

"It's no game," Esrahaddon replied as he sat leaning against a rock, folding his arms, and closed his eyes.

It irritated Royce how comfortable he looked. "Then you'd better start saying more than you have so far."

"What do you want to know?"

"Everything—everything you know about it."

"Well, let's see, I was here once a very long time ago. It looked different then, of course. For one thing Novron's bridge was still up and you could walk right out to the tower."

"So the bridge was the only way to reach it?"

"Oh no, I don't think so. At least, it wouldn't make any sense if that were the case. You see, the elves built Avempartha before mankind walked on the face of Elan. No one—well, no human—knows why or what for. Its location here on the falls, facing south toward what we call the Goblin Sea, suggests perhaps the elves might have employed it as a defense against the Children of Uberlin—I believe you call them by the dwarven name, the Ba Ran Ghazel—*goblins of the sea*. But that seems unlikely, as the tower predates them as well. There might have even been a city here at one time. So little is left of their achievements in Apeladorn, but the elves had a fabulous culture rich in beauty, music, and the Art."

"When you say *the Art*, you mean magic?"

The wizard opened a single eye and frowned at him. "Yes, and don't give me that look, as if magic is dirty or vile. I have seen that too many times since I escaped."

"Well, magic isn't something people consider a good thing."

Esrahaddon sighed and shook his head with a stern look. "It is demoralizing to see what has happened to the world during my years of incarceration. I stayed alive and sane because I knew that one day I would be able to do my part to protect humanity, but now I discover it's almost no longer worth the effort. When I was young, the world was an incredible place. Cities were magnificent. Your Colnora wouldn't even rank as a slum in the smallest city of my time. We had indoor plumbing—spigots would pump water right into people's homes. There were extensive, well-maintained sewer systems that kept the streets from smelling like cesspools. Buildings were eight and nine stories tall, and some reached as high as twelve. We had hospitals where the sick were treated and actually got better. We had libraries, museums, temples, and schools of every kind.

"Mankind has squandered its inheritance from Novron. It's like having gone to sleep a rich man and waking up a pauper." He paused. "Then there's what you so feebly call magic. The Art separated us from the animals. It was the greatest achievement of our civilization. Not only has it been forgotten, it is now reviled. In my day, those who could weave the Art, and summon the natural powers of the world to their bidding, were considered agents of the gods—sacrosanct. Today they burn you if you accidentally guess tomorrow's weather.

"It was very different then. People were happy. There were no poor families living on the streets. No destitute hopeless peasants struggling to find a meal, or forced to live in hovels with three children, four pigs, two sheep, and a goat, where the flies in the afternoon are thicker than the family's evening stew."

Esrahaddon looked around sadly. "As a wizard, my life was devoted to the study of truth and the application of it in the service of the emperor. Never had I managed to find more truth or serve him more profoundly than when I came here. And yet, in many ways I regret it. Oh, if only I had stayed home. I would be long dead, having lived a happy, wonderful life."

Royce smiled at him. "Wizards aren't a font, I thought."

Esrahaddon scowled.

"Now, what about the tower?"

The wizard looked back at the elegant spires rising above

the mist. "Avempartha was the site of the last battle of the Great Elven Wars. Novron drove the elves back to the Nidwalden, but they held on by fortifying their position in the tower. Novron was not about to be stopped by a little water, and ordered the building of the bridge. It took eight years and cost the lives of hundreds, most of whom went over the falls, but in the end, the bridge was completed. It took Novron another five years after that to take the citadel. The act was as much symbolic as it was strategic and it forced the elves to accept that nothing would stop Novron from wiping them off the face of Elan. A very curious thing happened then, something that's still unclear. Novron is said to have obtained the Horn of Gylindora and with it forced the unconditional surrender of the elves. He ordered them to destroy their war agents and machines and to retreat across the river—never to cross it again."

"So there was no bridge until Novron built one? Not on either side?"

"No, that was the problem. There was no way to reach the tower."

"How did the elves get there?"

"Exactly." The wizard nodded.

"So you don't know?"

"I'm old, but not that old. Novron is farther in the past for me than my day is to you."

"So there is an answer to this puzzle. It's just not obvious."

"Do you think Novron would have spent eight years building a bridge if it was?"

"And what makes you think I can find the answer?"

"Call it a bunch."

Royce looked at him curiously. "You mean *hunch*?"

The wizard looked irritated. "Still a few holes in my vocabulary, I suppose."

Royce stared out at the tower in the middle of the river and considered why jobs involving stealing swords were never simple.

᷈

The service they held for Mae Drundel was somber and respectful, although to Hadrian it felt rehearsed. There were no awkward moments, no stumbling over words or miscues. Everyone was well versed in his or her role. Indeed, the remaining residents of Dahlgren were about as professional about funerals as mourners could be without being paid.

Deacon Tomas said the only customized portion of the service, when he mentioned her devotion to her late family and her church. Mae was the last of them to pass. Her sons had died of sickness before their sixth year and her husband had been killed by the beast less than five months earlier. In his eulogy, Tomas publicly shared what nearly everyone was thinking—that even though Mae's death was terrible, perhaps for her it was not so bad. Some even reported that she had left an inviting candle in her window for the past two nights.

As usual, there was nobody to bury, so they merely drove a whitewashed stake into the ground with her name burned into it. It stood next to the stakes marked DAVIE, FIRTH, and WENT DRUNDEL.

Everyone turned out for the service except Royce and Esrahaddon. Even Theron Wood made a showing to pay his respects. The old farmer looked even more haggard and miserable than he had the day before and Hadrian suspected he had been awake all night.

After the service ended, the village shared their midday dinner. The men placed a row of tables, end to end, across the village common, and each family brought a dish. Smoked fish, black pudding (a sausage made from pig's blood, milk, animal fat, onions, and oatmeal), and mutton were the most popular.

Hadrian stood back, leaning against a cedar tree, watching the others form lines.

"Help yourself," Lena told him.

"There doesn't look like there is a lot here. I have provisions in my bag," he assured her.

"Nonsense—we'll have none of that—everyone eats at a wake. Mae would want it that way, and what else is a funeral for if not to pay respects to the dead?"

She glared at him until he nodded and began looking about the tables for a plate.

"So those are your horses I have up in the castle stables?" a voice said, and he turned to see a plump man in a cleric frock. He was the first person who did not look in desperate need of a meal. His cheeks were rosy and large, and when he smiled, his eyes squinted nearly shut. He did not look terribly old, but his hair was pure white, including his short beard.

"If you are Deacon Tomas, then yes," Hadrian replied.

"I am indeed, and think nothing of it. I get rather lonely up on the hill at night all by myself with all those empty rooms. You hear every sound at night, you know. The wind slapping a shutter, the creak of rafters—it can be quite unnerving. Now at least I can blame the noises I hear on your horses. Being way down in the stables, I doubt I could hear them, but I can pretend, can't I?" The deacon chuckled to himself. "But honestly, it can be miserable up there. I'm used to being with people, and the isolation of the manor house is such a burden," he said while heaping his plate full of mutton.

"It must be awful for you. But I'll bet there is good food. Those nobles really know how to fill a storehouse, don't they?"

"Well, yes, of course," the deacon replied. "As a matter of fact, the margrave had put by a remarkable amount of smoked meats, not to mention ale and wine, but I only take what I need, of course."

"Of course," Hadrian agreed. "Just looking at you, I can tell that you're not the kind of man to take advantage of a situation. Did you supply the ale for the funeral?"

"Oh no," the deacon replied, aghast. "I wouldn't dare pillage the manor house like that. Like you just said, I am not the kind of man to take advantage of a situation and it's not my stores to give, now is it?"

"I see."

"Oh my, look at the cheese," said the deacon, scooping up a wedge and shoving it in his mouth. "Have to admit one thing," he spoke with his mouth full, "Dahlgren can really throw a funeral."

When they reached the end of the tables, Hadrian looked for a place to sit. The few benches were filled with folks eating off their laps.

"Up, you kids!" the deacon shouted at Tad and Pearl. "You don't need to be taking up a bench. Go sit on the grass." They frowned but got up. "You there, Hadrian is it? Come sit here and tell me what brings a man who owns a horse and three swords to Dahlgren. I trust you aren't noble or you'd have knocked on my door last night."

"No, I'm not a noble, but that brings up a question. How did you inherit the manor house?"

"Hmm? Inherit? Oh, I didn't inherit anything. It is merely my station as a public servant to help in a crisis like this. When the margrave and his men died, I knew I had to administer to this troubled flock and watch after the king's interests. So I endure the hardships and do what I can."

"Like what?"

"What's that?" the deacon asked, tearing into a piece of mutton, which left his lips and cheeks shiny with grease.

"What have you done to help?"

"Oh—well, let's see...I keep the house clean, the yard maintained, and the garden watered. You really have to keep after those weeds, you know, or the whole garden would be swallowed up and not a single vegetable would survive. And oh—the toll it takes on my back. I've never had what you would call a good back as it is."

"I meant about the attacks. What steps have you taken to safeguard the village?"

"Well now," the deacon said, chuckling, "I'm a cleric, not a knight. I don't even know how to hold a sword properly and I don't have an army of knights at my disposal, do I? So aside from diligent prayer, I'm not in a position where I can really *do* anything about that."

"Have you considered letting the villagers stay in the manor at night? Whatever this creature is, it doesn't have much trouble with thatched roofs, but the manor has what looks to be a sturdy roof and some thick walls."

The deacon shook his head, still smiling at Hadrian as an adult might look at a child who just asked why there must be poor people in the world. "No, no, that wouldn't do at all. I am quite certain the next lord of the house would not appreciate having a whole village taking over his home."

"But you are aware that the responsibility of a lord is to protect his subjects? That is why his subjects pay him a tax. If the lord isn't willing to protect them, why should they honor him with money, crops, or even respect?"

"You might not have noticed," the deacon replied, "but we are between lords at the moment."

"So then, you don't intend to continue taxing these people for the time they are without protection?"

"Well, I didn't mean that—"

"So you do intend to uphold the responsibility of a steward?"

"Well, I—"

"Now, I can understand your hesitation to overstep your authority and open the manor house to the village, so I am certain you'll want to take the other option."

"Other option?" The cleric was holding another slice of mutton to his mouth but sat too distracted to bite.

"Yes, as steward and acting lord, it falls on you to protect this village in his stead, and since inviting them into the house at night is out of the question, then I presume you'll be taking to the field to fight the beast."

"Fight it?" He dropped the mutton on his lap. "I don't think—"

Before he could say any more, Hadrian went on. "The good news is that I can help you there. I have an extra sword if you are missing one, and since you have been so kind as to let me board my horse at the stable, I think the least I can do is lend her to you for the fight. Now, I have heard that some people have determined where the lair of the beast is, so it really seems a simple matter of—"

"I—I don't recall saying that lodging the people in the manor at night was out of the question," the deacon said loudly to interrupt Hadrian. Several heads turned. He lowered his voice and added, "I was merely stating that it was something I had to consider carefully. You see, the mantle of leadership is a heavy one indeed, and I need to weigh the consequences of every act I make, as they can break as well as mend. No, no, you can't rush into these things."

"That is very understandable and very wise, I might add," Hadrian agreed, keeping his voice loud enough for others to hear him. "But the margrave was killed well over two weeks ago, so I am certain you have come to a decision by now?"

The deacon caught the interested looks of several of the villagers. Those who had finished their meals wandered over.

One was Dillon McDern, who was taller than the rest and stood watching them.

"I—ah."

"Everyone!" Hadrian shouted. "Gather round, the deacon wants to talk with us about the defense of the village."

The crowd of mourners, plates in hand, turned and gathered in a circle around the well. All eyes turned to Deacon Tomas, who suddenly looked like a defenseless rabbit caught in a trap.

"I—um—" the deacon started, then slumped his shoulders and said in a loud voice, "In light of the recent attacks on houses, everyone is invited to spend nights in the protection of the castle."

The crowd murmured to each other and then Russell Bothwick called out, "Will there be enough room for everyone?"

The deacon looked as if he was about to reconsider when Hadrian stood up. "I'm sure there's plenty of room in the house for all the women and children and most of the married men. Those single men, thirteen or older, can spend the night in the stables, smokehouse, and other outbuildings. Each of them has stronger walls and roofs than any of the village homes."

The inhabitants of the village began to cluster now in earnest.

"And our livestock? Do we abandon them to the beast?" another farmer asked. Hadrian did not recognize him. "Without the livestock we'll have no meat, no wool, or field animals for work."

"I've got Amble and Ramble to think of," McDern said. "Dahlgren would be in a sorry state if'n I let sumpin' happen to those oxen."

Hadrian jumped to the rim of the well, where he stood above them with one arm on the windlass. "There's plenty of room inside the stockade walls for all the animals where they will be safer than they have been in your homes. Remember there is safety in numbers. If you sit alone in the dark, it is easy for anything to kill you, but the creature will not be so bold as to enter a fenced castle with the entire village watching. We can also build bonfires outside the walls for light."

This brought gasps. "But light draws the creature!"

"Well, from what I can see, it doesn't have difficulty finding you in the dark."

The villagers looked from Hadrian to Deacon Tomas and back again.

"How do you know?" someone asked from the crowd. "How do you know any of this? You're not from here. How do you know anything?"

"It's a demon from Uberlin!" someone Hadrian did not recognize shouted.

"You can't stop it!" a woman on the right yelled. "Grouping together could just make killing us that much easier."

"It doesn't want to kill you all at once and it isn't a demon," Hadrian assured the villagers.

"How do you know?"

"It kills only one or two, why? If it can tear apart Theron Wood's house, or rip the roof off Mae Drundel's home in seconds, it could easily destroy this whole village in one night, but it doesn't. It doesn't because it isn't trying to kill you all. It's killing for food. The beast isn't a demon; it's a predator." The villagers considered this, and while they paused, Hadrian continued, "What I have heard about this creature is that no one has ever seen it and no victim has survived. Well, that doesn't surprise me at all. How do you expect to survive when you sit alone in the dark just waiting to be eaten? No one has ever seen it because it doesn't want to be seen. Like any predator, it conceals itself until it springs, and like a predator, it hunts the weakest prey; it looks for the stray, the young, the old, or the sick. All of you have been dividing yourselves up into tidy little meals. You've made yourselves too convenient to resist. If we group together, it might prefer to hunt a deer or a wolf that night instead of us."

"What if you're wrong? What if no one has seen it because it is a demon and can't be seen? It could be an invisible spirit that feeds on terror. Isn't that right, Deacon?"

"Ah—well—" the deacon began.

"It could be, but it isn't," Hadrian assured them.

"How do you know?"

"Because my partner saw it last night."

This caught the group by surprise and several conversations broke out at once. Hadrian spotted Pearl sitting on the grass staring at him. Several asked questions at once and Hadrian waved at them to quiet down.

"What did it look like?" a woman with a sunburned face and a white kerchief over her head asked.

"Since I didn't see it, I would prefer Royce tell you himself. He'll be back before dark."

"How could he have seen anything in the dark?" one of the older farmers asked skeptically. "I looked outside when I heard the scream and it was as black as the bottom of that well yer standing on. There's no way he could have seen anything."

"He saw the pig!" Tad Bothwick shouted.

"What's that, boy?" Dillon McDern asked.

"The pig, in our house last night," Tad said excitedly. "It was all dark and the pig ran, but he saw it and caught him."

"That's right," Russell Bothwick recalled. "We had just put the fire out and I couldn't see my hand in front of my face, but this fellow caught a running pig. Maybe he did see something."

"The point is," Hadrian went on, "we'll all stand a better chance of survival if we stick together. Now, the deacon has graciously invited all of us to join him behind the protection of walls and a solid roof. I think we should listen to his wisdom and start making plans to resettle and gather wood before the evening arrives. We still have plenty of time to build up strong bonfires."

They were looking at Hadrian now and nodding. There were still those who looked unconvinced, but even the skeptics appeared hopeful. Small groups were forming, talking, planning.

Hadrian sat back down and ate. He was not a fan of blood pudding and stayed with the smoked fish, which was wonderful.

"I'll bring the oxen over," he heard McDern say. "Brent, you go bring yer wagon and fetch yer axe too."

"We'll need shovels and Went's saw," Vince Griffin said. "He always kept it sharp."

"I'll send Tad to fetch it," Russell announced.

"Is it true?" Hadrian looked up from his plate to see Pearl standing before him. Her face was just as dirty as it had been the day before. "Did yer friend—did he really catch a pig in the dark?"

"If you don't believe me, you can ask him tonight."

Looking over the little girl's head, he spotted Thrace. She was sitting alone on the ground down the trail past the Caswells' graves. He noticed her hands wiping her cheeks. He set his empty plate on the table, smiled at Pearl, and walked over. Thrace did not look up, so he crouched down beside her. "What is it?"

"Nothing." She shook her head, hiding her face with her hair.

Hadrian glanced around the trail and then back up at the villagers. The women were putting away the uneaten food as the men gathered tools, all of them chattering quickly.

"Where's your father? I saw him earlier."

"He went back home," she said, sniffling.

"What did he say to you?"

"I told you, it's all right." She stood up, brushed off her dress, and wiped her eyes. "I should help with the cleaning. Excuse me."

~§

Hadrian entered the clearing and once more faced the remains of the Woods' farmhouse. The roofing poles listed to one side; the framing was splintered; the thatch was scattered. *This is what shattered dreams look like.* The farm seemed cursed, haunted by ghosts, only one of the ghosts was not at home. There was no sign of the old farmer, and the scythe rested, abandoned, up against the ruined wall. Hadrian took the opportunity to peer inside at the shattered furniture, broken cupboards, torn clothes, and bloodstains. A single chair stood in the center of the debris, beside a wooden cradle.

Theron Wood came up from the river a few moments later, carrying a shoulder yoke with two buckets full of water hanging from the ends. He did not hesitate when he spotted Hadrian standing before the ruins of his house. He walked right by. He set the buckets down and began pouring the water into three large jugs.

"You back again?" he asked without looking up. "She told me she paid you silver to come here. Is that what you do? Take advantage of simple girls? Steal their hard-earned money, then eat their village's food? If you came here to see if you can squeeze more coins out of me, you're gonna be disappointed."

"I didn't come here for money."

"No? Then why did you?" he asked, tipping the second bucket. "If you really are here to get that club or sword or whatever that crazy cripple thinks is in the tower, shouldn't you be trying to swim the river right now?"

"My partner is working on that as we speak."

"Uh-huh, he's the swimmer, is he? And what are you, the guy that squeezes the money out of poor miserable farmers? I've seen your kind before, highwaymen and cheats—you scare people into paying you just to live. Well, that's not gonna work this time, my friend."

"I told you I didn't come here for money."

Theron dropped the bucket at his feet and turned. "So why did you come here?"

"You left the wake early and I was concerned you might not have heard the news that everyone in the village is going to spend the night inside the castle walls."

"Thanks for the notice." He turned back and corked the jugs. When he finished, he looked up, annoyed. "Why are you still here?"

"What exactly do you know about combat?" Hadrian asked.

The farmer glared at him. "What business is it of yours?"

"As you pointed out, your daughter paid my partner and me good money to help you kill this monster. He's working on providing you with a proper weapon. I am here to ensure you know how to use it when it gets here."

Theron Wood ran his tongue along his teeth. "You're fixin' to educate me, are you?"

"Something like that."

"I don't need any training." He picked up his buckets and yoke and began walking away.

"You don't know the first thing about combat. Have you ever even held a sword?"

Theron whirled on him. "No, but I plowed five acres in one

day. I bucked half a cord of wood before noon. I survived being caught eight miles from shelter in a blizzard and I lost my whole damn family in a single night! Have *you* done any of that?"

"Not your *whole* family," Hadrian reminded him.

"The ones that mattered."

Hadrian drew his sword and advanced on Theron. The old farmer watched his approach with indifference.

"This is a bastard sword," Hadrian told him, and dropped it at the farmer's feet and walked half a dozen steps away. "I think it suits you rather well. Pick it up and swing at me."

"I have more important things to do than play games with you," Theron said.

"Just like you had more important things to do than take care of your family that night?"

"Watch yer mouth, boy."

"Like you were watching that poor defenseless grandson of yours? What was it really, Theron? Why were you really working so late that night? And don't give me this bull about benefitting your son. You were trying to get some extra money this year for something *you* wanted. Something you felt you needed so badly you let your family die."

The farmer picked up the sword, puffing his cheeks and rocking his shoulders back, his breath hissing through his teeth. "I didn't let them die. It wasn't me!"

"What did you trade them for, Theron? Some fool's dream? You didn't give a damn about your son; it was all about you. You wanted to be the grandfather of a magistrate. You wanted to be the big man, didn't you? And you'd do anything to make that dream come true. You worked late. You weren't there. You were out in the field when it came, because of your dream, your desires. Is that why you let your son die? You never cared about them at all. Did you? All you care about is yourself."

The farmer charged Hadrian with the sword in both hands and swung at him. Hadrian stepped aside and the wild swing missed, but the momentum carried the farmer around and he fell to the dirt.

"You let them die, Theron. You weren't there like a man is supposed to be. A man is supposed to protect his family, but what were you doing? You were out in the fields working on what *you* wanted. What *you* had to have."

Theron got up and charged again. Once more Hadrian stepped aside. This time Theron managed to remain standing and delivered more wild swings. Hadrian drew his short sword and deflected the blows. The old farmer was in a rage now and struck out maniacally, swinging the sword like an axe with single, hacking strokes that stole his balance. Soon Hadrian did not need to parry anymore and merely side-stepped out of the way. Theron's face grew redder with each miss. Tears filled his eyes. At last, the old man collapsed to the dirt, frustrated and exhausted.

"It wasn't me that killed them," he yelled. "It was *her*! She left the light on. She left the door open."

"No, Theron." Hadrian took the sword from the farmer's limp hands. "Thrace didn't kill your family and neither did you—the beast did." He slipped his sword back in its sheath. "You can't blame her for leaving a door open. She didn't know what was coming. None of you did. Had you known, you would have been there. Had your family known, they would have put out the light. The sooner you stop blaming innocent people and start trying to fix the problem, the better off everyone will be.

"Theron, that weapon of yours may be mighty sharp, but what good is a sharp weapon when you can't hit anything or, worse, hit the wrong target? You don't win battles with hate. Anger and hate can make you brave, make you strong, but they also make you stupid. You end up tripping over your own two feet." Hadrian stared down at the old man. "I think that's enough for today's lesson."

&

Royce and Esrahaddon returned less than an hour before sunset and found a parade of animals driving up the road. It looked like every animal in the village was on the move and most of the people were out along the edges with sticks and bells, pots and spoons, banging away, herding the animals up the hill toward the manor house. Sheep and cows followed each other fine enough, but the pigs were a problem, and Royce spotted Pearl with her stick, masterfully bringing up the rear.

Rose McDern, the smithy's wife, was the first to spot them and suddenly Royce heard "He's back!" excitedly repeated among the villagers.

"What's going on?" Royce asked Pearl, purposely avoiding the adults.

"Movin' the critters to the castle. We all stay'n there tonight, they says."

"Do you know where Hadrian is? You remember, the man I arrived with? Thrace was riding with him?"

"The castle," Pearl told him, and narrowed her eyes at the thief. "You really catch a pig in the dark?"

Royce looked at her, puzzled. Just then, a pig darted up the road and the girl was off after it, waving her long switch in the air.

The castle of the Lord of Westbank was a typical motte-and-bailey fortress, with the great manor house built on a steep man-made hill, surrounded by a wall of sharp-tipped wooden logs that enclosed the outbuildings. A heavy gate barred the entrance. A halfhearted attempt at a moat ringed it but amounted to nothing more than a shallow ditch. Cut trees left about forty yards of sharpened stumps in all directions.

A group of men worked at the tree line, cutting pines. Royce was still a bit vague on names but he recognized Vince Griffin and Russell Bothwick working a dual-handled saw. Tad Bothwick and a few other boys raced around, trimming branches with axes and hatchets. Three girls tied the branches into bundles and stacked them on a wagon. Dillon McDern and his sons used his oxen to haul the logs up the hill to the castle, where more men labored to cut and split the wood.

Royce found Hadrian splitting logs near the stockade gate. He was naked to the waist except for the small silver medallion that dangled from his neck as he bent forward to place another wedge. He had a solid sweat worked up along with a sizable pile of wood.

"Been meddling, have you?" Royce asked, looking around at the hive of activity.

"You must admit they didn't have much in the way of a defense plan," Hadrian said, pausing to wipe the sweat from his forehead.

Royce smiled at him. "You just can't help yourself, can you?"

"And you? Did you find the doorknob?"

Hadrian picked up a jug and downed several swallows, drinking so quickly some of the water dripped down his chin. He poured some in his palm and rinsed his face, running his fingers through his hair.

"I didn't even get close enough to see a door."

"Well, look on the bright side"—Hadrian smiled—"at least you weren't captured and condemned to death this time."

"That's the bright side?"

"What can I say? I'm a glass-half-full kinda guy."

"There he is," Russell Bothwick shouted, pointing. "That's Royce over there."

"What's going on?" Royce asked as throngs of people suddenly moved toward him from the field and the castle interior.

"I mentioned that you saw the thing and now they want to know what it looks like," Hadrian explained. "What did you think? They were coming to lynch you?"

He shrugged. "What can I say? I'm a glass-half-empty kinda guy."

"Half empty?" Hadrian chuckled. "Was there ever any drink in that glass?"

Royce was still scowling at Hadrian when the villagers crowded around them. The women wore kerchiefs over their hair, dark and damp where they crossed their foreheads. Their sleeves were rolled up, their faces smudged with dirt. Most of the men, like Hadrian, were topless, wood shavings and pine needles sticking to their skin.

"Did you see it?" Dillon asked. "Did you really get a look at it?"

"Yes," Royce replied, and several people murmured.

"What did it look like?" Deacon Tomas asked. The priest stood out from the crowd, looking fresh, clean, and rested.

"Did it have wings?" Russell asked.

"Did it have claws?" Tad asked.

"How big was it?" Vince Griffin asked.

"Let the man answer!" Dillon thundered, and the rest quieted.

"It does have wings and claws. I saw it only briefly because it was flying above the trees. I caught sight of it through a small opening in the leaves, but what I saw was long, like a snake, or lizard, with wings and two legs that—that were still clutching Mae Drundel."

"A lizard with wings?" Dillon repeated.

"A dragon," a woman declared. "That's what it is. It's a dragon!"

"That's right," Russell said. "That's what a winged lizard is."

"There's supposed to be a weak spot in their armor near the armpit, or whatever a dragon has for an armpit," a woman with a particularly dirty nose explained. "I heard an archer once killed a dragon in mid-flight by hitting him there."

"I heard you weaken a dragon by stealing its treasure hoard," a bald-headed man told them all. "There was a tale where this prince was trapped in the lair of a dragon and he threw all the treasure into the sea and it weakened the beast so much the prince was able to kill him by stabbing him in the eye."

"I heard that dragons were immortal and couldn't be killed," Rose McDern said.

"It's not a dragon," Esrahaddon said with a tone of disgust. He stepped out from the crowd and they turned to face him.

"Why do you say that?" Vince Griffin asked.

"Because it isn't," he replied confidently. "If it was a dragon whose wrath you had incurred, this village would have been wiped from the face of Elan months ago. Dragons are very intelligent beings, far more than you or even I, and more powerful than we can begin to comprehend. No, Mrs. Brockton, no archer ever killed a dragon by shooting him in a soft spot with an arrow. And no, Mr. Goodman, stealing a dragon's treasure doesn't weaken it. In fact, dragons don't have treasures. What exactly would a dragon do with gold or gems? Do you think there is a dragon store somewhere? Dragons don't believe in possessions, unless you count memories, strength, and honor as possessions."

"But that's what he said he saw," Vince countered.

The wizard sighed. "He said he saw a snake or lizard with wings and two legs. That should have been your first clue." The wizard turned to Pearl, who had finished driving the last of the pigs into the courtyard of the castle and had run back out to join the crowd. "Tell me, Pearl, how many legs does a dragon have?"

"Four," the child said without thinking.

"Exactly. This is not a dragon."

"Then what is it?" Russell asked.

"A Gilarabrywn," Esrahaddon replied casually.

"A—a what?"

"Gil...lar...ah...brin," the wizard pronounced slowly, mouthing the syllables carefully. "Gilarabrywn, a magical creature."

"What does that mean? Does it cast spells like a witch?"

"No, it means it's unnatural. It wasn't born; it was created—conjured, if you will."

"That's just crazy," Russell said. "How gullible do you think we are? This thingamabob—whatever you called it—killed dozens of people. It ain't no made-up thing."

"No, wait," Deacon Tomas said, intervening, waving to them from deep in the sea of villagers. They backed away to reveal the cleric standing with his hand still up in the air, his eyes thoughtful. "There *was* a beast known as the Gilarabrywn. I learned about it in seminary. In the Great Elven Wars they were tools of the Erivan Empire, beasts of war, terrible things that devastated the landscape and slaughtered thousands. There are accounts of them laying waste to cities and whole armies. No weapon could harm them."

"You know your history well, Deacon," Esrahaddon said. "The Gilarabrywn were devastating instruments of war—intelligent, powerful, silent killers from the sky."

"How could such a thing still be alive after so long?" Russell asked.

"They aren't natural. They can't die a normal death, because they really aren't alive as we understand living to be."

"I think we're going to need more wood," Hadrian muttered.

As the sun set, the farmers provisioned the castle for the night. The children and women gathered beneath the great beams of the manor house while the men worked to the last light of day building the woodpiles. Hadrian had organized effective teams for cutting, dragging, and tying the stacks such that by nightfall they had six great piles surrounding the walls and one in the center of the yard itself. They doused the piles in oil and animal fat to make the lighting faster. It was going to be a long night and they did not want the fires to burn out, nor would it do to have them lit too late.

"Hadrian!" Thrace yelled as she ran frantically through the courtyard.

"Thrace," Hadrian said, working to the last minute on the courtyard woodpile. "It's dark. You should be in the house."

"My father's not here," she cried. "I've looked everywhere around the castle. No one saw him come in. He must still be at home. He's out there alone, and if he's the only one alone tonight—"

"Royce!" Hadrian shouted, but it was unnecessary, as Royce was already leading their saddled horses out of the stable.

"She found me first," the thief said, handing him Millie's reins.

"That damn fool," Hadrian said, grabbing his shirt and weapons and pulling himself up on the horse. "I told him about coming to the castle."

"So did I," she said, her face a mask of fear.

"Don't worry, Thrace. We'll bring him back safe."

They spurred the animals and rode out the gate at a gallop.

❧

Theron sat in the ruins of his house on a wooden chair. A small fire burned in a shallow pit just outside the doorway.

The sky was finally dark and he could see stars. He listened to the night music of the crickets and frogs. A distant owl began its hunt. The fire snapped and popped, and beneath it all, the distant roaring of the falls. Mosquitoes entered the undefended house. They swarmed, landed, and bit. The old man let them. He sat as he had every night, staring silently at memories.

His eyes settled on the cradle. Theron remembered building the little rocker for his first son. He and Addie had decided to name their firstborn Hickory—a good, strong, durable wood. Theron had hunted the forest for the perfect hickory tree and found it one day on a hill, bathed in sunlight as if the gods had marked it. Each night Theron had carefully crafted the cradle and finished the wood so it would last. All five of his children had slept in it. Hickory died there before his first birthday from a sickness for which there was no name. All his sons had died young, except for Thad, who had grown to be a fine man. He had married a sweet girl named Emma, and when she had given birth to Theron's grandson, they had named him Hickory. Theron remembered thinking that it seemed as if the world was finally trying to make up for the hardships in his life—that somehow the unwarranted punishment of his firstborn's premature death was healed through the life of his first grandson. But it was all gone now. All he had left was the blood-sprayed bed of five dead children.

Behind the cradle lay one of Addie's two dresses. It was a terrible, ugly thing, stained and torn, but to his watering eyes it looked beautiful. She had been a good wife. For more than thirty years she had followed him from one dismal town to the next as he had tried to find a place he could call his own. They had never had much, and many times, they had gone hungry, and on more than one occasion nearly froze to death. In all that time, he had never heard her complain. She had mended his clothes and his broken bones, made his meals, and looked after him when he was sick. She had always been too thin, giving the biggest portions of each meal to him and their children. Her clothes had been the worst in the family. She never found time to mend them. She had been a good wife and Theron could not remember ever having said he loved her. It had never seemed important before. The beast had taken her too, plucked her from the path between the village and the farm. Thad's Emma had filled the void, making it easy to move on. He had avoided thinking about her by staying focused on the goal, but now the goal was dead, and his house had caved in.

What must it have been like for them when the beast came? Were they alive when it took them? Did they suffer? The thoughts tormented the farmer as the sounds of the crickets died.

He stood up, his scythe in his hands, preparing to meet the darkness, when he heard the reason for the interruption of the night noises. Horses thundered up the trail and the two men Thrace had hired entered the light of the campfire in a rush.

⁂

"Theron!" Hadrian shouted as he and Royce arrived in the yard of the Woods' farm. The sun was down, the light gone, and the old man had a welcome fire burning—only not for them. "Let's go. We've got to get back to the castle."

"You go back," the old man growled. "I didn't ask you to come here. This is my home and I'm staying."

"Your daughter needs you. Now get up on this horse. We don't have much time."

"I'm not going anywhere. She's fine. She's with the Bothwicks. They'll take good care of her. Now get off my land!"

Hadrian dismounted and marched up to the farmer, who stood his ground like a rooted tree.

"My god, you're a stubborn ass. Now either you're going to get on that horse or I'll put you on it."

"Then you'll have to put me on it," he said, setting his scythe down and folding his arms across his chest.

Hadrian looked over his shoulder at Royce, who sat silently on Mouse. "Why aren't you helping?"

"It's really not my area of expertise. Now, if you want him dead—that I can do."

Hadrian sighed. "Please get on the horse. You're going to get us all killed staying out here."

"Like I said, I never asked you to come."

"Damn," Hadrian cursed as he removed his weapons and hooked them on the saddle of his horse.

"Careful," Royce leaned over and told him. "He's old, but he looks tough."

Hadrian ran full tilt at the old farmer and tackled him to the ground. Theron was larger than Hadrian, with powerful arms and hands made strong by years of unending work, but Hadrian was fast and agile. The two grappled in a wrestling match that had them rolling in the dirt grunting as each tried to get the advantage.

"This is so stupid," Hadrian muttered, getting to his feet. "If you would just get on the horse..."

"You get on the horse. Get out of here and leave me alone!" Theron yelled at them as he struggled to catch his breath, standing bent over, hands resting on his knees.

"Maybe you can help me this time?" Hadrian said to Royce.

Royce rolled his eyes and dismounted. "I didn't expect you'd have so much trouble."

"It's not easy to subdue a person bigger than you and not hurt him in the process."

"Well, I think I found your problem, then. Why don't we try hurting him?"

When they turned back to face Theron, the farmer had a good-size stick in his hand and a determined look in his eyes.

Hadrian sighed, "I don't think we have a choice."

"Daddy!" Thrace shouted, running into the ring of firelight, her face streaked with tears. "Daddy," she cried again, and reaching the old man, threw her arms around him.

"Thrace, what are you doing here?" Theron yelled. "It's not safe."

"I came to get you."

"I'm staying here." He pulled his daughter off and pushed her away. "Now you take your hired thugs and get back to the Bothwicks right now. You hear me?"

"No," Thrace cried at him, her arms raised, still reaching. "I won't leave you."

"Thrace," he bellowed, his huge frame towering over her, "I am your father and you'll do as I say!"

"No!" she shouted back at him, the firelight shining on her wet cheeks. "I won't leave you to die. You can whip me if you want, but you'll have to come back to the castle to do it."

"You stupid little fool," he cursed. "You're gonna get yourself killed. Don't you know that?"

"*I don't care!*" Her voice ran shrill, her hands crushed into fists, arms punched down at her sides. "What reason do I have to live if my own father—the only person I have left in the world—hates me so much he would rather die than look at me?"

Theron stood stunned.

"At first," she began in a quavering voice, "I thought you wanted to make sure no one else was killed, and then I thought maybe it was—I don't know—to put their souls to rest. Then I thought you wanted revenge. Maybe the hate was eating you up. Maybe you had to see it killed. But none of that's true. You just want to die. You hate yourself—you hate me. There's nothing in this world for you anymore, nothing you care about."

"I don't hate you," Theron said.

"You do. You do because it was my fault. I know what they meant to you—and I wake up every morning with that." She wiped the tears enough to see. "If it was me, it would have been just like it was with Mom—you would have driven a stick into Stony Hill with my name on it and the next day gone back to work. You would have driven the plow and thanked Maribor for his kindness in sparing your son. I should have been the one to die, but I can't change what happened and your death won't bring him back. Nothing will. Still, if all I can do now—if all that's left for me—is to die here with you, then that's what I'll do. I won't leave you, Daddy. I can't. I just can't." She fell to her knees, exhausted, and in a fragile voice said, "We'll all be together again, at least."

Then, as if in response to her words, the wood around them went silent once more. This time the crickets and frogs stopped so abruptly the silence seemed suddenly loud.

"No," Theron said, shaking his head. He looked up at the night sky. "*No!*"

The farmer grabbed his daughter and lifted her up. "We're going." He turned. "Help us."

Hadrian pulled Millie around. "Up, both of you." Millie stomped her hooves and started to pull and twist, nostrils flaring, ears twitching. Hadrian gripped her by the bit and held tight.

Theron mounted the horse and pulled Thrace up in front of him, then, with a swift kick, he sent Millie racing up the trail back toward the village. Royce leapt on the back of Mouse and, throwing out a hand, swung Hadrian up behind him even as he sent the horse galloping into the night.

The horses needed no urging as they ran full out with the
sweat of fear dampening their coats. Their hooves thundered,
pounding the earth like violent drumbeats. The path ahead
was only slightly lighter than the rest of the wood and for
Hadrian it was often a blur as the wind drew tears from his
eyes.

"Above us!" Royce shouted. Overhead they heard a rush of
movement in the leaves.

The horses made a jarring turn into the thick of the
wood. Invisible branches, leaves, and pine boughs slapped
them, whipped them, beat them. The animals raced in blind
panic. They drove through the underbrush, glancing off tree
trunks, bouncing by branches. Hadrian felt Royce duck and
mimicked him.

Thrump. Thrump. Thrump.

He could hear a slow beating overhead, a dull, deep pumping. A blast of wind came from above, a massive downdraft of
air. Along with it came the frightening sounds of cracking,
snapping, splintering. The treetops shattered and exploded.

"Log!" Royce shouted as the horses jumped.

Hadrian kept his seat only by virtue of Royce's agile grab.
In the darkness, he heard Thrace's scream, a grunt, and a
sound like an axe handle hitting wood. The thief reined
Mouse hard, wrestling with her, pulling the animal's head
around as she reared and snorted. Hadrian could hear Millie
galloping ahead.

"What's going on?" Hadrian asked.

"They fell," Royce growled.

"I can't see them." Hadrian leapt down.

"In the thickets, there to your right," Royce said, climbing off
Mouse, who was in a panic, thrashing her head back and forth.

"Here," Theron said, his voice labored, "over here."

The farmer stood over his daughter. She lay unconscious, sprawled and twisted. Blood dripped from her nose and mouth.

"She hit a branch," Theron said; his voice was shaking, frightened. "I—I didn't see the log."

"Get her on my horse," Royce commanded. "Theron, take her and ride for the manor. We're close. You can see the light of the bonfires burning."

The farmer made no protest. He climbed on Mouse, who was still stomping and snorting. Hadrian picked up Thrace. A patch of moonlight showed a dark blemish on her face, a long wide mark. He lifted her. Her head fell back, limp; her arms and legs dangled free. She seemed dead. He handed her to Theron, who cradled his daughter to his chest and held her tight. Royce let loose the bit, and the horse thundered off, racing for the open field, leaving Royce and Hadrian behind.

"Think Millie's around?" Hadrian whispered.

"I think Millie is already an appetizer."

"I suppose the good news is that she bought Thrace and Theron safe passage."

They slowly moved to the edge of the wood. They were very close to where Dillon and his boys had been hauling logs earlier that day. They could see three of the six bonfires blazing away, illuminating the field.

"What about us?" Royce asked.

"Do you think the Gilarabrywn knows we're still in here?"

"Esrahaddon said it was intelligent, so I presume it can count."

"Then it will come back and find us. We have to reach the castle. The distance across the open is about—what? Two hundred feet?"

"About that," Royce confirmed.

"I guess we can hope it's still munching on Millie. Ready?"

"Run spread out so it can't get both of us. Go." The grass was slick with dew and filled with stumps and pits. Hadrian got only a dozen yards before falling on his face.

"Stay behind me," Royce told him.

"I thought we were spreading out?"

"That's before I remembered you're blind."

They ran again, dodging in and out, as Royce picked the path up the hillside. They were nearly halfway across when they heard the bellows again.

Thrump. Thrump. Thrump.

The sound rushed toward them. Looking up, Hadrian saw something dark pass across the face of the rising moon, a serpent with batlike wings gliding, arcing, circling like a hawk hunting mice in a field.

The bellows stopped.

"It's diving!" Royce shouted.

A massive burst of wind blew them to the ground. The bonfires were instantly snuffed out. A second later, a loud rumble shook the earth and a monolithic wall of green fire exploded in a great ring, surrounding the entire hill. Astounding flames, thirty feet high, flashed up like trees of light spewing intense heat.

No longer having any trouble seeing his way, Hadrian jumped to his feet and sped to the gate, Royce on his heels. Behind them the flames roared. Above them they heard a chilling scream.

Dillon, Vince, and Russell slammed the gate shut the instant they were inside. The bonfire in the courtyard, which had been unlit so far, startled everyone as it exploded into a brilliant blue-green flame, reaching like a pillar into the sky. Once more from the darkness above, the Gilarabrywn screamed at them.

The emerald inferno slowly burned down. The flames lost

their green color and diminished until only natural flames remained. The fires crackled and hissed, sending storms of sparks skyward. The men in the courtyard stared upward, but there were no further signs of the beast, only darkness and the distant sound of crickets.

CHAPTER 6

THE CONTEST

I can assure you, Your Royal Majesty," Arista said in her most congenial voice, "there will be no change in foreign or domestic policy under King Alric's reign. He will continue to pursue the same agenda as our father—upholding the dignity and honor of the House of Essendon. Melengar will continue to remain your friendly neighbor to the west."

Arista stood before the King of Dunmore in her mother's best dress—the stunning silver silk gown. Forty buttons lined the sleeves. Dozens of feet of crushed velvet trimmed the embroidered bodice and full skirt. The rounded neckline clung to her shoulders. She stood erect, chin high, eyes forward, hands folded.

King Roswort, who sat on his throne wearing furs that looked to have come from wolves, drained his cup and belched. He was short and immensely fat. His round pudgy face sagged under its own weight, gathering at the bottom and forming three full chins. His eyes were half closed, his lips were wet, and she was certain she could see a bit of spittle dribbling down through the folds of his neck. His wife, Freda, sat beside him. She, too, was large, but thin by comparison. Whereas the king seeped liquid, she was dry as a desert—in both looks and manner.

The throne room was small with a wooden floor and beams that supported a lofty cathedral ceiling. Protruding from the walls were heads of stags and moose, each covered in enough dust to make its fur look gray. Near the door stood the famous nine-foot stuffed bear named Oswald, its claws up, mouth open, snarling. Dunmore legend held that Oswald killed five knights and an unknown number of peasants before King Ogden—King Roswort's grandfather—slew him with nothing more than a dagger. That had been seventy years earlier, when Glamrendor was just a frontier fort, and Dunmore little more than a forest with trails. Roswort himself could not claim such glory. He had abandoned the hunting traditions of his sires in favor of courtly life, and it showed.

The king held up his cup and shook it.

Arista waited and the king yawned. Somewhere behind her, loud heels crossed the throne room. There was a muttering, then the heels again, followed by the snapping of fingers. Finally, a figure approached the dais, thin and delicate—an elf. He was dressed in a rough woolen uniform of dull brown. Around his neck was a heavy iron collar that was riveted in place. He approached with a pitcher and filled the king's cup, then backed away. The king drank, tipping the cup too high, wine dribbling down, leaving a faint pink line and a droplet dangling from his stubbly whiskers. He belched again, this time more loudly, and sighed with contentment. The king looked back at Arista.

"But what about this matter of Braga's death?" Roswort asked. "Do you have evidence to show that he was involved in this so-called conspiracy?"

"He tried to kill me."

"Yes, so you say, but even if he did, he had good reason, it seems. Braga was a good and devout Nyphron and you are—after all—a witch."

Arista squeezed her hands together. It was not for the first time and her fingers were starting to ache. "Forgive me, Your Royal Majesty, but I fear you may be misinformed on that subject."

"Misinformed? I have—" He coughed, coughed again, then spat on the floor beside the throne. Freda glared rigidly at the elf until he stepped over and wiped it up with the bottom of his tunic.

"I have very good information gatherers," the king went on, "who tell me both Braga and Bishop Saldur brought you to trial to answer charges of witchcraft and the murder of your father. Immediately afterwards Braga was dead, decapitated, and accused of the very charges he leveled against you. Now you come before us as Ambassador of Melengar—a woman. I fear this is all too convenient for my tastes."

"Braga also accused me of killing His Royal Majesty King Alric, who appointed me to this office, or do you also deny his existence?"

The royal eyebrows rose. "You are young," he said coldly. "This is your first audience as ambassador. I'll ignore your affront—this time. Insult me again, and I'll have you expelled from my kingdom."

Arista bowed her head silently.

"It does not bode well with us that the throne of Melengar was taken by blood. Nor that House Essendon pays only lip service to the church. Also, your kingdom's tolerance for elves is disgusting. You let the vile beasts run free. Novron never meant for this to be. The church teaches us that the elf is a disease. They must be broken into service or vanquished altogether. They are like rats and Melengar is the woodpile next door. Yes, I have no doubt that Alric will continue his father's policies. Both were born with blinders. Changes are coming and I can already see that Melengar is too foolish to bend with the wind. All the better for Dunmore, I think."

Arista opened her mouth, but the king held up a finger.

"This interview is over. Go back to your brother and tell him we fulfilled the favor of seeing you and were not impressed."

The king and queen stood together and walked out through the rear archway, leaving Arista facing two empty wooden chairs. The elf, which stood nearby, watched her intently but said nothing. She half considered going on with the rest of her prepared speech. The level of futility would remain; empty thrones could not be any less responsive and most certainly would be more polite.

She sighed. Her shoulders drooped. *Could it have gone any worse?* She turned and walked out, listening to her beautiful dress rustling.

She stepped outside the castle gate and looked down at the city. Deep baked ruts scarred the uneven dirt roads, so rough and littered with rocks they appeared as dry riverbeds. Sun bleached the tight rows of similarly framed wooden buildings to a pale gray. Most of the residents wore drab colors, clothes made of undyed wool or linen. Dozens of people with weary faces sat on corners or wandered about aimlessly with hands out. They appeared invisible to those walking by. It was Arista's first visit to Glamrendor, the capital of Dunmore. She shook her head and muttered softly, "We have seen you too."

Despite the meager offerings, the city was bustling, but she suspected few of those rushing by were locals. It was easy to tell the difference. Those from out of town wore shoes. Wagons, carriages, coaches, and horses flowed through the center of the capital that morning, all heading east. The church had opened the contest to all comers, common and noble alike. It was their shot at glory, wealth, and fame.

Her own coach waited, flying the Melengar falcon, and Hilfred stood holding the door. Bernice sat inside with a tray of sweets on her lap and a smile on her lips. "How did it go, my dear? Were you impressive?"

"No, I wasn't impressive, but we are also not at war, so I should thank Maribor for that kindness." She sat opposite Bernice, making certain to pull the full length of her gown inside the door before Hilfred closed it.

"Have a gingerbread man?" Bernice asked, holding up the tray with a look of pity that included pushing out her lower lip. "He is bound to steal the pain away."

"Where is Sauly?" she asked, eyeing the man-shaped cookies.

"He said he had some things to speak to the archbishop about and would ride in His Grace's coach. He hoped you did not mind."

Arista did not mind and only wished Bernice had joined him. She was tired of the constant company and missed the solitude of her tower. She took a cookie and felt the carriage rock as Hilfred climbed up with the driver. The coach lurched and they were off, bouncing over the rutted road.

"These are stale," Arista said with a mouthful of gingerbread that was hard and sandy.

Bernice looked horrified. "I'm so sorry."

"Where did you get them?"

"A little bakery up—" She started to point out the window, but the movement of the carriage confused her. She looked around, then gave up and put her hand down again. "Oh, I don't know now, but it was a very nice shop and I thought you might need—you know—something to help you feel better after the meeting."

"*Need* them?"

Bernice nodded her head with a forced smile, and reaching out, she patted the princess's hand and said, "It's not your fault, dear. It really isn't fair of His Majesty to put you in this position."

"I should stay in Medford and receive suitors," Arista guessed.

"Exactly. This just isn't right."

"Neither is this cookie." She placed the gingerbread man back on the tray minus the leg she had bitten off. She then sat raking her tongue with her upper teeth like a cat with hair in its mouth.

"At least His Royal Majesty must have been impressed by how you looked," Bernice said, eyeing her with pride. "You're beautiful."

Arista gave her a sidelong glance. "The dress is beautiful."

"Of course it is, but—"

"Oh dear Maribor!" Arista cut her off as she glanced out the window. "How many are there now? It will be like traveling with an army."

As the carriage reached the end of town, she saw the masses. There could be as many as three hundred men standing behind the banners of the Nyphron Church. They all waited in a single line, but they could not have been more different—the muscular, scrawny, tall, and short. All ranks were represented: knights, soldiers, nobles, and peasants. Some wore armor, some silk, others linen or wool. They sat on chargers, draft horses, ponies, mules, or inside coaches, open-air carriages, wagons, and buckboards. They appeared a strange and unlikely assortment, but each bore the same smile of expectation and excitement, all eyes looking east.

Arista's first official session as ambassador was finished. As bad as it had been, it was over. With Sauly gone, she could shelve thoughts of church and state, guilt and blame. Stress that had smothered her for days evaporated and at last she was able to feel the growing excitement that bubbled all around her.

From everywhere people rushed to join the growing train.

Some arrived with nothing but a small linen bag tucked under one arm, while others led their own personal train of packhorses.

There were those who commanded multiple wagons loaded with tents, food, and clothes. One well-dressed merchant carried velvet upholstered chairs and a canopy bed on top of a wagon.

A loud banging hammered the roof of the coach, shocking both of them. Gingerbread men flew. "Oh dear!" Bernice gasped. A moment later Mauvin Pickering's head appeared in the window, looking down and inside from the back of his horse so that his dark hair hung wildly.

"So how did it go?" He grinned mischievously. "Do I need to prepare for war?"

Arista scowled.

"That good, huh?" Mauvin went on, heedless of the commotion he had caused. "We'll talk later. I have to find Fanen before he starts dueling someone. Hiya, Hilfred. This is going to be great. When was the last time we were all camping together? See ya."

Bernice was fanning herself with both hands, staring up at the roof of the coach, her mouth slack. Seeing her and the little army of gingerbread men scattered on the benches, in the curtains, on the floor, and in her lap, Arista could not help smiling.

"You were right, Bernice. The cookies did cheer me up."

⚜

"See him?" Fanen pointed to the man in the brown suede doublet. "That's Sir Enden, possibly the greatest living knight after Sir Breckton."

After another day's travel that left her drowsy, Arista was

at the Pickerings' camp, hiding from Bernice. The two boys shared an elegant single-peak tent of alternating gold and green stripes, which they had pitched at the eastern edge of the main camp. The three sat out front under the scallop-edged canopy held up by two tall wooden poles. On the left flew the gold falcon on the red field of the House of Essendon, on the right the gold sword on the green field of the House of Pickering. It was a modest camp compared to most of the nobles'. Some looked like small castles and took hours for a team of servants to erect. The Pickerings traveled lightly, carrying everything they needed on their stallions and two packhorses. They did not have tables or chairs and Arista sprawled in a modest gown on a sheet of canvas. If Bernice saw, the old woman would have a heart attack.

Arista did not mind. She thought it was wonderful to lie back and stretch out under the sky. It reminded her of Summersrule when they were kids. At night the adults would dance and the children would lie on the south hill at the Pickerings' home of Drondil Fields, counting the falling stars and fireflies. It had been all of them then—Mauvin, Fanen, Alric, even Lenare—back before the boys' sister became too much of a lady. She remembered the feel of the cool night breeze rushing over her, the sensation of grass on her bare feet, the vast spray of stars above, and the faint melody of the band as it played "Calide Portmore," the Galilin folk song.

"And there, see the large man in the green tunic? That's Sir Gravin; he's a quester. He does most of his work for the Church of Nyphron. You know—recovering artifacts, slaying monsters, those kinds of things. He's known to be one of the greatest adventurers alive. He's from Vernes; that's all the way down near Delgos."

"I know where Vernes is, Fanen," Arista replied.

"That's right, you have to know all that stuff now, don't you?" Mauvin said. "Your High Exulted Ambassadorship." The elder Pickering offered an elaborate seated bow.

"Laugh now—just you wait," she told him. "You'll get yours—one day you'll be marquis. Then it won't be all fun and games. You'll have responsibilities, mister."

"I won't," Fanen said sadly.

If not for his being three years younger, Fanen could be Mauvin's twin. Both had the dashing Pickering features: sharp angled faces, dark thick hair, bright white teeth, and sweeping shoulders that tapered to narrow, athletic waists. Fanen was just leaner and a bit shorter, and unlike Mauvin, whose hair was always a frightful mess, Fanen kept his neatly combed.

"That's why you need to win this thing," Mauvin told his brother. "And, of course, you will, because you're a Pickering, and Pickerings never fail. Look at that guy over there. He doesn't stand a chance."

Arista did not bother sitting up. He had been doing this all night—pointing out people and explaining how he could tell by the way they walked or wore their swords that Fanen could best them. She had no doubt he was right; she was just tired of hearing it.

"What is the prize for this contest?" she asked.

"They haven't said yet," Fanen muttered.

"Gold, most likely," Mauvin replied, "in the form of some award, but that's not what makes it valuable. It's the prestige. Once Fanen takes this trophy, he will have a name; well, he already has the Pickering name, but he hasn't any titles yet. Once he does, opportunities will open up for him. Of course, it could be land. Then he'd be set."

"I hope so; I certainly don't want to end up at a monastery."

"Do you still write poetry, Fanen?" Arista asked.

"I haven't—in a while."

"It was good—what I remember, at least. You used to write all the time. What happened?"

"He learned the poetry of the sword. It will serve him far better than the pen," Mauvin answered for him.

"Who's that?" Fanen asked, pointing to the west.

"That's Rentinual," Mauvin replied, "the self-proclaimed genius. Get this. He's brought this thing, a huge contraption, with him."

"Why?"

"He says it's for the contest."

"What is it?"

Mauvin shrugged. "Don't know, but it's big. He keeps it covered under a tarp and wails like a girl whenever the wagon team bounces it through a rut."

"Say, isn't that Prince Rudolf?"

"Where?" Arista popped her head up, moving to her elbows. Mauvin chuckled. "Just kidding. Alric told us about... your misunderstanding."

"Have you met Rudolf?" she asked.

"Actually, I have," Mauvin said. "The man has donkeys wondering why they got stuck with him as a namesake." It took a second, then Fanen and Arista broke into laughter, dragging Mauvin with them. "He's a royal git, that's certain, and I'd have been plenty upset if I thought I was facing a life kissing that ass. Honestly, Arista, I'm surprised you didn't turn Alric into a toad or something."

Arista stopped laughing. "What?"

"You know, put a hex on him. A week as a frog would—what's wrong?"

"Nothing," she said, lying back down and turning onto her stomach.

"Hey—look—I didn't mean anything."

"It's okay," she lied.

"It was just a joke."

"Your first joke was better."

"Arista, I know you're not a witch."

A long uncomfortable silence followed.

"I'm sorry," Mauvin offered.

"Took you long enough," she said.

"It could have been worse." Fanen spoke up. "Alric could have forced you to marry Mauvin."

"That's really sick," Arista said, rolling over and sitting up. Mauvin looked at her with hurt, surprised eyes. She shook her head. "I just meant it would be like marrying a brother. I've always thought of you all as family."

"Don't tell Denek," Mauvin replied. "He's had a crush on you for years."

"Seriously?"

"Oh, and don't tell him I told you either. Uh—better yet, just forget I said that."

"What about those two?" Fanen asked abruptly, pointing toward a massive red and black striped tent from which two men had just exited. One was huge, with a wild red mustache and beard. He wore a sleeveless scarlet tunic with a green draped sash and a metal cap with several dents in it. The other man was tall and thin, with long black hair and a short trimmed beard. He was dressed in a red cassock and black cape with the symbol of a broken crown on his chest.

"I don't think you want to mess with either of them," Mauvin finally said. "That's Lord Rufus of Trent, Warlord of Lingard, a clan leader and veteran of dozens of battles against the wild men of Estrendor, not to mention being the hero of the battle of Vilan Hills."

"That's Rufus?" Fanen muttered.

"I've heard he's got the temperament of a shrew and the arm of a bear."

"Who's the other guy, the one with the broken crown standard?" Fanen asked, pointing at the other man.

"That, my dear brother, is a sentinel, and let's just hope this is the closest either of us ever get to one."

While Arista was watching the two men, she saw a silhouette appear against the light of the distant campfire—very short, with a long beard and puffy sleeves.

"By the way, I want to start early tomorrow, Fanen," his brother said. "I want to get out ahead of the train. I'm tired of eating dust."

"Anyone know exactly where we are going?" Fanen asked. "It feels like we are traveling to the end of the world."

Arista nodded. "I heard Sauly talking about it with the archbishop. I think it is a little village called Dahlgren."

She looked back, trying to find the figure once more, but it was gone.

CHAPTER 7

OF ELVES AND MEN

Thrace lay on the margrave's bed in the manor house, her head carefully wrapped in strips of cloth. Her hair was bunched and snarled, blond strands slipping out between the bandages. Purple and yellow bruises swelled around her eyes and nose. Her upper lip puffed up to twice its size and a line of dark dried blood ran its length. Thrace coughed and mumbled but never spoke, never opened her eyes.

And Theron never left her side.

Esrahaddon ordered Lena to boil feverfew leaves in a big pot of apple cider vinegar. She did as he instructed. Everyone did now. After the previous night, the residents of Dahlgren treated the cripple with newfound respect and looked at him with awe and a bit of fear. It was Tad Bothwick and Rose McDern who had seen him raise the green fire that had chased away the beast. No one said the word *witch* or *wizard*. No one had to. Soon the steam from the pot filled the room with a pungent flowery odor.

"I'm so sorry," Theron whispered to his daughter.

The coughing and mumbling had stopped and she lay still as death. He held her limp hand to his cheek, unsure if she could hear him. He had been saying that for hours, begging her to wake up. "I didn't mean it. I was just so angry. I'm sorry. Don't leave. Please come back to me."

He could still hear the sound in the dark of his daughter's cry, cut horribly short by a muffled crack. If it had been a tree trunk or a thicker branch, Theron guessed, she would have died instantly. As it was, she still might die.

No one but Lena and Esrahaddon dared enter the room that Theron filled with his grief. They all expected the worst. Blood had covered the girl's face and her father's shirt by the time they arrived at the manor. Skin white, lips an odd bluish hue, Thrace had not moved nor opened her eyes. Esrahaddon had whispered to her and instructed them to take the girl to the manor and keep her warm. It was the kind of thing one did for the dying, making them as comfortable as possible. Deacon Tomas had prayed for her and remained on hand to bless her departing soul.

In the past year, the village of Dahlgren had seen many deaths. Not all were by the beast. There were the normal accidents and sicknesses, and in the winter, wolves hunted the area. There were also some unexplained disappearances. Often attributed to the beast, they could just as likely have been the result of getting lost in the forest or accidentally falling in the Nidwalden. In no more than a year, over half the village's population had perished or gone missing. Everyone knew someone who had died, and nearly every family had lost at least one member. The people of Dahlgren had grown accustomed to death. He was a nightly visitor, a guest at every breakfast table. They knew his face, the sound of his voice, the way he walked, his peculiar habits. He was always there. If it were not for the mess he left, they might neglect to notice him altogether. No one expected Thrace to survive.

The sun came up, casting a dull light into the room where Theron wept for his daughter. The last of his family was leaving him. Only now he realized how much she meant to him. Thoughts came, uninvited, to his mind. Time and time again, it had been she who had always come for him. He remembered the night the beast attacked his farm, when he was coming home late. Only she had braved the darkness to search for him. It was Thrace, a young girl, little more than a child, who had traveled alone halfway across Avryn and spent her life savings to bring him help. Then, the previous night, when his stubbornness had kept him at the farm, she had come to him in the darkness, running alone through the forest, ignoring the dangers. There had been only one thought in her mind—to save him. She had succeeded. She had deprived the beast of his flesh, but more than that, she had pulled him back into the world of the living. She had ripped the black veil away from his eyes and freed his heart from the weight of guilt, but the price had been her life.

Tears ran down his cheeks. They hung on his upper lip. He kissed his daughter's hand, leaving a wet spot, an offering, an apology.

How could I have been so blind?

The even, constant breaths his daughter took slowed with each inhale, less frequent, shorter than the one before. He listened to their descent, like the sound of footsteps receding, walking away, growing fainter, quieter.

He clutched her hand, kissing it repeatedly and rubbing it to his wet cheek. It felt like his heart was being ripped out through his chest.

At last, the regular pace of her breathing stopped.

Theron sobbed. "Oh, god."

"Daddy?" He jerked his head up. His daughter's eyes were open. She was looking at him. "Are you all right?" she whispered.

His mouth opened but he could not speak. His tears continued to flow, and like a barren bit of land seeing water for the first time in years, a smile of joy grew on his face.

⌀

Swift clouds moved across a capricious sky as growing winds and the portents of a coming storm marked the new day. Royce sat on the rock ledge where the cliff met the river and the spray of the falls dampened the stone. His feet and legs were soaked from a morning spent trekking through the damp forest underbrush. His eyes stared out across the ridgeline of the falls at the promontory rock and the towering citadel that sat tantalizingly upon it. He thought that perhaps there might be a tunnel running under the river. He looked for an access in the trees but found nothing. He was getting nowhere.

After almost two days, he was no closer to his goal. The tower still lay out of reach. Unless he could learn to swim the current, walk on water, or fly, he had no chance of traversing the gulf that lay between.

"They're over there right now, you know," Esrahaddon said.

Royce had forgotten about the wizard. He had arrived some time earlier, mentioning only that Thrace had survived, was awake, and looked to make a full recovery. After that, he took a seat on a rock and spent the next hour or so staring across the river much as Royce had done all day.

"Who?"

"The elves. They're on their side of the river looking back at us. They can see us, I suspect, even at this range. They are surprising like that. Most humans consider them inferior—lazy, filthy, uneducated creatures—but the fact is they are superior to humans in nearly every way. I suppose that's why humans are so quick to denounce them; they are unwilling to concede that they may be second best.

"Elves are truly remarkable. Just look at that tower. It's fluid and seamless, as if growing right out of the rock. How elegant. How perfect. It fits into the landscape like a thing of nature, a natural wonder, only it isn't. They created it using skills and techniques that our best masons couldn't begin to understand. Just imagine how glorious their cities must be! What wonders those forests across the river must hold."

"So you have never crossed the river?" Royce asked.

"No man ever has, and no man is ever likely to. The moment a man touches that far shore, he will fall dead. The thread by which the fate of man hangs is a thin one indeed."

"How's that?"

Esrahaddon only smiled. "Did you know that no human army ever won a battle against the elves before the arrival of Novron? At that time, elves were our demons. The Great Library of Percepliquis had reams on it. Once we even thought they were gods. Their life span is so long that no one noticed them aging. Their death rites are so secret no human has ever seen an elven corpse.

"They were the firstborn, the Children of Ferrol, great and powerful. In combat, they were feared above all things. Sickness could be treated. Bears and wolves could be hunted and trapped. Storms and droughts prepared for. But nothing, nothing could stand before the elves. Their blades broke ours, their arrows pierced our armor, their shields were impenetrable, and, of course, they knew the Art. Imagine a sky darkened with a host of Gilarabrywn. And they are only one of their weapons. Even without all that, without the Art, their speed, eyesight, hearing, balance, and ancient skills are all beyond the abilities of man."

"If that's true, how come they're over there and we're sitting here?"

"It is all because of Novron. He showed us their weaknesses. He taught mankind how to fight, how to defend, and he taught us the art of magic. Without it we were naked and helpless against them."

"I still don't see how we won," Royce challenged. "Even with that knowledge, they still seem to have the advantage."

"True, and in an even fight we would have lost, but it wasn't even. You see, elves live for a very long time. I don't think any human actually knows how long, but they live for many centuries at least. There may be elves right now watching us that remember what Novron looked like. But no people can live that long and reproduce quickly. Elves have few children and a birth for them is quite significant. Birth and death in the elven world are rare and holy things.

"Imagine the devastation and misery it must have been for them during the wars. No matter how many battles they won against us, each time their numbers were fewer than before. While we humans recovered our losses in a generation, it would take a millennium for the elves. They were consumed—drowned, if you will—in a flooding sea of humanity." Esrahaddon paused, then added, "Only now Novron is gone. There will be no savior this time."

"This time?"

"What do you think keeps them over there? These are their lands. To us it seems eons ago, but to them it is just yesterday when they walked this side of the river. By now, their numbers have likely recovered."

"What keeps them on that side of the river, then?"

"What keeps anyone from what they want? Fear. Fear of annihilation, fear that we would destroy them utterly, but Novron is dead."

"You mentioned that," Royce pointed out.

"I told you before that mankind has squandered the legacy of Novron, and it has done so at its own peril. Novron brought magic to man, but Novron is gone, and the magic forgotten. We sit here like children, naked and unarmed. Mankind is inviting the wrath of a race so far beyond us they won't even hear our cries. The elves' ignorance of our weakness and this fragile agreement between the Erivan Empire and a dead emperor is all that remains of humanity's defense."

"It's a good thing they don't know, then."

"That's just it," the wizard told him. "They are learning."

"The Gilarabrywn?"

Esrahaddon nodded. "According to Novron's decree, the banks of the river Nidwalden are *ryin contita*."

"Off limits to everyone," Royce roughly translated, garnering a faint smile from the wizard. "I can read and write too."

"Ah, a truly educated man. So as I was saying, the banks of the river Nidwalden are *ryin contita*."

A look of realization washed over the thief's face. "Dahlgren is in violation of the treaty."

"Exactly. The decree also stipulates that elves are forbidden to take human lives, except should they cross the river. It says nothing about humans killed through benign actions. If I release a boulder, it could roll anywhere, but odds are it will roll downhill. If houses and people are downhill, it may destroy them, but it isn't me that's killing them; it is the boulder and the unfortunate fact they live downhill from it."

"And they are watching what we do, how we deal with it. They are sizing up our strengths and weaknesses. Much like you are doing with me."

Esrahaddon smiled. "Perhaps," he said. "There is no way to be certain if they are responsible for the beast's presence, but one thing is certain: they are watching. When they see we are helpless against one Gilarabrywn, if they feel the treaty is broken, or when it runs out, fear will no longer be a deterrent."

"Is that why you are really here?"

"No." The wizard shook his head. "It plays a part, but the war between the elves and man will come despite any action I can take. I am merely trying to lessen the blow and give humanity a fighting chance."

"You might begin by teaching some others to do what you did last night."

The wizard looked at the thief. "What do you mean?"

"Coy doesn't suit you," Royce told him.

"No, I suppose not."

"I thought you couldn't do your art without your hands?"

"It is very hard and takes a great deal of time and it isn't very accurate. Imagine trying to write your name with your toes. I began working on that spell before you arrived here, thinking it would come in handy at some point. As it was, the flame wall nearly consumed you two. It was supposed to be several yards farther away, and last for hours instead of minutes. With hands I could have..." He trailed off. "No sense going there, I suppose."

"Were you really that powerful before?"

Esrahaddon showed him a wicked smile. "Oh, my dear boy, you couldn't begin to imagine."

⌾

Word of Thrace's recovery quickly spread through the village. She was still a little groggy, but remarkably sound. She could see clearly, all her teeth were in her head, and she had an appetite. By midmorning, she was sitting up, eating soup. That day there was a decidedly different look in the villagers' eyes. The unspoken thought in every mind was the same—the beast had attacked and no one had died.

Most had seen the winged beast outlined in the brilliant green flames that night. Alongside each of them that morning walked a strange companion, a long-lost friend who had returned unexpectedly—hope.

They got busy at dawn preparing more wood fires. They had a system down now and were able to build up the piles with just a few hours' work. Suspecting that the beast—obviously able to see well in the dark—might not be able to see through thick smoke, Vince Griffin suggested they use smudge pots. For centuries, farmers had used smudge pots to drive off insects that threatened to devour their crops, and Dahlgren was no different. Old pots were promptly gathered and filled as if a cloud of locusts was on its way. At the same time, Hadrian, Tad Bothwick, and Kline Goodman began surveying the outbuildings of the lower bailey for the best shelters.

Hadrian busied himself organizing small groups of men. One group started to expand the cellar they had found in the smokehouse, and another went to work digging a tunnel with the idea of trying to capture the beast. A huge serpent chasing a man might follow him into a tunnel, but if the tunnel gradually narrowed, they might be able to seal the exits before it realized its mistake. No weapon made by man might be able to slay it, but Hadrian guessed there were no restrictions on imprisoning the beast.

Deacon Tomas was far from delighted with all the digging, cutting, and burning inside the castle grounds, but already it was clear that the villagers had found a new leader in Hadrian. Tomas remained quietly indoors caring for Thrace.

"Hadrian?"

He was washing at the well in the village, where he could find some privacy, when he looked up to see Theron.

"Been doing some digging, I see," the farmer said. "Dillon mentioned you had them making a tunnel. Pretty smart thinking."

"The odds of it working are slim," Hadrian explained, dousing his face with handfuls of water. "But at least it's a shot."

"Listen," the farmer began with a pained look on his face, and then said nothing.

"Thrace is doing well?" Hadrian asked after a minute or so.

"She's great, as solid as her old man," he said proudly, thumping his own chest. "It'll take more than a tree to break her. That's the thing about us Woods. We might not look like it, but we're a strong lot. It might take us a while, but we come back, and when we do, we're stronger than ever. Thing is, we need something—you know—a reason. I didn't have one—at least, I didn't think I did. Thrace showed me different."

They stood facing each other in an awkward silence.

"Listen," Theron said again, and once more paused. "I'm not used to being beholden to anyone, you see. I've always paid my own way. I got what I have by work and lots of it. I don't ask anyone's help and I don't apologize for the way I am, see?"

Hadrian nodded.

"But—well, a lot of what you said yesterday was true. Only today, some things are different—you follow? Thrace and me, we're gonna be leaving this place just as soon as she's able. I'm figuring a couple of days' rest and she'll be okay to travel. We'll head south, maybe to Alburn or even Calis; I hear it stays warm longer there, better growing season. Anyway, that still leaves a few nights we'll be here. A few more nights we'll have to live under this shadow. I'm not gonna lose my little girl the way I lost the others. Now, I know an old farmer like me ain't much good to her swinging a scythe or a pitchfork against that thing, but if it comes to that, it would be good if I knew how to fight proper. That way if it comes calling before we leave, at least there will be a chance. Now, I haven't got much, but I do have some silver set aside and I was wondering if your offer to teach me how to fight was still good."

"First, we need to get something straight," Hadrian told him sternly. "Your daughter already paid us in full to do whatever we could to help you, so you keep your silver for the trip south or I won't teach you a thing. Agreed?"

Theron hesitated, then nodded.

"Good. Well, I suppose we can begin right now if you're ready."

"Should we get your swords?" Theron asked.

"That would be a problem, considering I put my swords on Millie last night and no one has seen her since, but that shouldn't matter for now."

"Should I cut sticks, then?" the farmer asked.

"No."

"What, then?"

"How about sitting down and just listening? There's a lot to learn before you're ready to swing at anything."

Theron looked at Hadrian skeptically.

"You want me to teach you, right? If I said I wanted you to teach me to be a great farmer in a few hours, what would you say?"

Theron nodded in submission and sat down on the dirt not far from where Hadrian had first met Pearl. Hadrian slipped his shirt on, took a bucket, turned it over, and sat down in front of him.

"As with everything, fighting takes practice. Anything can look easy if you're watching someone who's mastered whatever it is they are doing, but what you don't see is the hours and years of effort that go into perfecting their craft. I am sure you can plow a field in a fraction of the time it would take me for this very reason. Sword fighting is no different. Practice will allow you to react without thought to events, and even to anticipate those events. It becomes a form of foresight, the ability to look into the future and know exactly what your opponent will do even before he does. Without practice, you'll need to think too much. When fighting a more skilled opponent, even a split second of hesitation can get you killed."

"My opponent is a giant snake with wings," Theron said.

"And it has killed more than a score of men. Most certainly a more skilled opponent, wouldn't you say? So practice is paramount. The question is, what do you need to practice?"

"Swinging a sword, I should think."

"True, but that's only a small part of it. If it were merely swinging a sword, everyone with two legs and at least one arm would be experts. No, there is much more to it. First, there is concentration, and that means more than just paying attention to the fight. It means not worrying about Thrace or thinking about your family, the past, or the future. It means focusing on what you are doing beyond all else. It might sound easy, but it isn't. Next comes breathing."

"Breathing?" Theron asked dubiously.

"Yeah, I know we breathe all the time, but sometimes we stop breathing or stop breathing correctly. Ever get startled and discover you were holding your breath? Ever find yourself panting when you're really nervous or frightened? Some people can actually pass out that way. Trust me, in a real fight, you'll be scared, and unless you train, you'll end up breathing shallow or not at all. Less air saps your body of strength and makes it hard to think clearly. You'll become tired and slow, something you can't afford in a battle."

"So how do you breathe correctly?" Theron asked, still with a hint of sarcasm.

"You have to breathe deep and slow even before you need

to, before your exertion demands it. At first, it will be a conscious thought and it will feel counterproductive, even distracting. But over time, it will become second nature. It is also good to keep in mind that you have the most strength for a blow on an exhale. It adds power and focus to a stroke. Sometimes actually yelling or shouting helps. I'll want you to do that during your training. I want to hear it when you swing. Later on, it won't be necessary, although sometimes it can help to startle your opponent." Hadrian paused briefly and Theron noted the faint hint of a smile tug at his lips.

"Next comes balance, and that means more than not falling down. Sadly, humans only have two feet. That's only two points to support us. Pick up one and you are vulnerable. This is why you want to keep your feet on the ground. That doesn't mean you don't move, but when you move, you slide your feet rather than pick them up. You need to keep your weight forward, your knees slightly bent, and your balance on the balls of your feet rather than in your heels. Drawing your feet together reduces your two points of balance to one, so keep your feet apart, about shoulder width.

"Timing is, of course, very important. I warn you now, you'll be terrible at it to begin with, as timing improves with experience. You saw from swinging at me yesterday how frustrating it can be to swing and miss. Timing is what allows you to hit, and not only to hit, but also to do damage. You'll learn to see patterns in movement. You'll know when to expect an opening, or a weakness. Frequently you can anticipate an attack by watching how your opponent moves—the placement of his feet, the look in his eyes, a telltale drop of his shoulder, the tightening of a muscle."

"But I'm not fighting a person," Theron interrupted. "And I don't even think it has a shoulder."

"Even animals give signs about what they will do. They

hunch up, twist and shift their weight, just like people. Such signals do not have to be obvious. Most skilled fighters will try to mask their intentions or, worse, purposely try to mislead you. They want to confuse your timing, throw you off balance, and make an opening for themselves. Of course, this is exactly what you want to do to them. If done well, your opponent sees the false move, but not the attack. The result—in your case—is a headless flying serpent.

"The last thing to learn is the hardest. It can't be taught. It can barely be explained. It is the idea that the fight—the battle—doesn't really exist so much in your hands or your feet, but in your head. The real struggle is in your own mind. You must know you are going to win before you start the fight. You have to see it, smell it, and believe it utterly. It is a form of confidence, but you must guard against overconfidence. You have to be flexible—able to adapt in an instant and never allow yourself to give up. Without this, nothing else is possible. Unless you believe you'll win, fear and hesitation will hold you down while your opponent kills you. Now, let's get a couple of stout sticks and we will see how well you listened."

That night they lit the bonfires once more and everyone stayed sheltered in either the manor house or the cellar of the smokehouse. Royce and Hadrian were the only two moving outside and even they remained in the shelter of the smokehouse doorway, watching the night by bonfire light.

"How's Thrace doing?" Royce asked, his eyes on the sky.

"Great considering the fact that she broke a tree branch with her head," Hadrian replied as he sat on a barrel, cleaning a mutton bone of the last of its meat. "I even heard she was walking around asking to help with dinner." He shook his head and smiled. "That girl, she's something, that's for sure. Hard to imagine it seeing her under that arch in Colnora, but she's tough. The real change is in the old man. Theron says they plan on leaving in a day or two, as soon as Thrace can travel."

"So we're out of a job?" Royce feigned disappointment.

"Why, were you getting close?" Hadrian asked, throwing the bone away and wiping his hands on his vest.

"Nope. I can't figure out how to reach it."

"Tunnel?"

"I thought of that, but I've been over every inch of the forest and the rocks and there's nothing; no cave, no sunken dell, nothing that could be confused with a tunnel. I'm completely stumped on this."

"What about Esra? Doesn't the wizard have any ideas?"

"Maybe, but he's being elusive. He's hiding something. He wants access to that tower but won't say why and avoids direct questions about it. Something happened to him here years ago. Something he doesn't want to talk about. But maybe I can get him to open up more tomorrow if I let him know the Woods no longer require our services and that there is no reason for me to try anymore."

"Don't you think he'll see through that?"

"See through what?" Royce asked. "Honestly, I'm giving it one more try tomorrow and if I can't find something, I say we head out with Theron and Thrace."

Hadrian was silent.

"What?" Royce asked.

"I just hate to run out on them like that. I mean, they're starting to turn it around now."

"You do this all the time. You get these lost causes under your skin—"

"I'd like to remind you, coming here was your idea. I was in the process of declining the job, remember?"

"Well, a lot can happen in a day; maybe I'll find a way in tomorrow."

Hadrian stepped to the doorway and peered out. "The forest is loud. Looks like our friend isn't coming to visit us tonight. Maybe Esrahaddon's flames singed its wings and it's dining on venison this evening."

"The fires won't keep it away forever," Royce said. "According to the wizard, the fires didn't hurt it; they just confused it—bright lights do that, apparently. Only the sword in the tower can actually harm it. It will be back."

"Then we'd best take advantage of its absence and get a good night's sleep."

Hadrian went down into the cellar, leaving Royce staring out at the night sky and the gathering clouds that crossed the stars. The wind was still up, whipping the trees and battering the fires. He could almost smell it: change was in the air and it was blowing their way.

CHAPTER 8

MYTHS AND LEGENDS

Royce stood on the bank of the river in the early morning light, trying to skip stones out toward the tower. None of them made more than a single jump before the turbulent water consumed them. His most recent idea for reaching the tower centered on building a small boat and launching himself upriver in the hopes of landing on the rocky parapet before the massive current washed him over the falls. Although there was no clear landing ground for such an attempt, it might be possible if he caught the current just right and landed against the rock. The force of the water would likely smash the boat or drive it under when it met the wall, but he might be able to scramble onto the precipice before going over. The problem was even if he managed to perform this harrowing feat, there was no way back.

He turned to see the wizard walking up the river trail. Perhaps to keep an eye on him but more likely to be on hand should he discover the entrance.

"Morning," the wizard said. "Any epiphanies today?"

"Just one. There is no way to reach that tower."

Esrahaddon looked disappointed.

"I have exhausted all the possibilities I can think of.

Besides, Theron and Thrace are going to be leaving Dahlgren. I no longer have a reason to bang my head against this tower."

"I see," Esrahaddon said, staring down at him. "What about the welfare of the village?"

"Hardly my problem. This village shouldn't even be here, remember? It's a violation of the treaty. It would be best if all these people left."

"If we allow it to be wiped out, it could be seen as a sign of weakness and invite the elves to invade."

"And allowing the village to survive is breaking the treaty, resulting in the same possibility. Fortunately for me, I am not wearing a crown. I am not the emperor, or a king, so it's not something I need to deal with."

"You're just going to leave?"

"Is there a reason for me to stay?"

The wizard raised an eyebrow and looked long at the thief. "What do you want?" he asked at length.

"Are you proposing to pay me now?"

"We both know I have no money, but still you want something from me. What is it?"

"The truth. What are you after? What happened here nine hundred years ago?"

The wizard studied Royce for a moment and looked down at his feet. After a few minutes, he nodded. He walked over to a beech log that lay across the granite rock, and sat down. He looked out toward the water and the spray as if searching for something in the mist, something that was not there.

"I was the youngest member of the Cenzars. We were the council of wizards that worked directly for the emperor. The greatest wizards the world had ever seen. There was also the Teshlors, comprised of the greatest of the emperor's knights. Tradition dictated that a mentor from each council was to serve as teacher and full-time protector to the emperor's son and heir. Because I was the youngest, it fell to me to be Nevrik's Cenzar instructor, while Jerish Grelad was picked from the Teshlors. Jerish and I didn't get along. Like most of the Teshlors, he held a distrust of wizards, and I thought little of him and his brutish, violent ways.

"Nevrik, however, brought us together. Like his father, the emperor Nareion, Nevrik was a breed apart, and it was an honor to teach him. Jerish and I spent nearly all our time with Nevrik. I taught him lore, books, and the Art, while Jerish instructed him in the schools of combat and warfare. Though I still felt the practice of physical combat was beneath the emperor and his son, it was very clear that Jerish was as devoted to Nevrik as I was. In that middle ground, we found a foothold where we could stand together. When the emperor decided to break tradition and travel here to Avempartha with his son, we went along."

"Break tradition?"

"It had been centuries since an emperor had spoken directly to the elves."

"After the war, there wasn't tribute paid or anything like that?"

"No, all contact was severed at the Nidwalden, so it was a very exciting time. No one really knew what to expect. I personally knew very little about Avempartha beyond the historical account of how it was the site of the last battle of the Great Elven Wars. The emperor met with several top officials of the Erivan Empire in the tower while Jerish and I attempted, without much luck, to continue Nevrik's studies. The sight of the waterfall and the elven architecture was too much to compete with for the attention of a twelve-year-old boy.

"It was around dusk, nearly night. Nevrik had been pointing things out to us all day, reveling in the fact that neither Jerish nor I could identify any of the elven things he found. For example, there were several sets of elven clothes made of a shimmering material that we couldn't name drying in the sun. This was, of course, the first time in centuries that humans had met with elves, placing us at a distinct disadvantage. Nevrik delighted in stumping his teachers, so when he asked about the *thing* he saw flying toward the tower, I thought he saw a bird, or a bat, but he said it was too large and that it looked like a serpent. He mentioned it had flown into one of the high windows of the tower. Nevrik was so adamant about it that we all went back inside. We had just started up the main staircase when we heard the screams.

"It sounded like a war was being fought above us. The personal bodyguards of the emperor—a detachment of Teshlors—were fighting off the Gilarabrywn, protecting the emperor as they fled down the stairs. I saw groups of elves throwing themselves at the creature, dying to protect our emperor."

"The elves were?"

Esrahaddon nodded. "I was amazed by the sight. The whole scene is still so vivid to me even after nearly a thousand years. Still, nothing the knights or the elves could do stopped the attacking beast, which seemed determined to kill the emperor. It was a terrible battle, with knights falling on the stairs and dying upon the wet steps, elves joining them. The emperor ordered us to get Nevrik to safety.

"Jerish grabbed the boy and dragged him out of the tower kicking and screaming, but I hesitated. I realized that once outside, the flying beast would be able to swoop down and kill at will. The Art could not defeat it. The creature was magic and without the key to unlock the spell, nothing I could do would alter that enchantment. A thought came to me, and as the emperor exited the door, I cast an enchantment of binding—not on the beast, but on the tower, trapping the Gilarabrywn inside. Those knights and elves still inside died, but the beast was trapped."

"Where did it come from? What caused the thing to attack?"

Esrahaddon shrugged. "The elves insisted they knew nothing of the attack, and that they had no idea where the Gilarabrywn came from, except that one Gilarabrywn had been left unaccounted for after the wars. They assumed it destroyed. They mentioned a militant society, a growing movement of elves within the Erivan Empire that sought to incite a war. It was speculated they were responsible. The elven lords apologized and assured us they would investigate the matter fully. The emperor, convinced that to retaliate or even make the incident public was unwise, chose to ignore the attack and returned home."

"So what's this about a weapon?"

"The Gilarabrywn is a conjured creature, a powerful magic endowed with a life of its own beyond the existence of its creator. The creature is not truly alive; it cannot reproduce, grow old, or appreciate existence, but it also cannot die. It can, however, be dispelled. No enchantment is perfect; every magic has a seam where the weave can be unraveled. In the case of the Gilarabrywn, the seam is its name. Whenever a Gilarabrywn is created, so is an object—a sword, etched with its name. It is used to control the beast and, if necessary, destroy it. According to the elves, at the end of the war they placed all the Gilarabrywn swords in the tower, per Novron's orders. At that time all the swords were accounted for and all but one was notched to show their associated beast was destroyed."

Royce got up to stretch his legs. "Okay, so the elven lords held one of their monsters back just in case, or this militant group hid one to cause trouble. The elven leaders tell you all the swords are in there. Maybe they are, or maybe they aren't, and they just want—"

"It's in there," Esrahaddon interrupted.

"You saw it?"

"We were given a tour when we first arrived. Near the top is a sort of memorial to the war. All the swords are on display."

"All right, so there is a sword," Royce said, "but that's not why you want in. You didn't come here to save Dahlgren. Why are you really here?"

"You didn't allow me to finish," Esrahaddon replied, sounding every bit like the wise teacher letting his student know to be patient. "The emperor believed he had prevented a war with the elves and returned home, but what waited for him was an execution. While we were away, the church, under the leadership of Patriarch Venlin, planned the emperor's assassination. The attack came on the steps of the palace during a celebration commemorating the anniversary of the empire's founding. Jerish and I escaped with Nevrik. I knew that many of the Cenzars and the Teshlors were involved in the church's plot and that they would find us, so Jerish and I came up with a plan—we hid Nevrik and I created two talismans. One I gave to Nevrik and the other to Jerish. These amulets would hide them from the clairvoyant search the Cenzars were certain to make, but allow me to find them. Then I sent them away."

"And you?" Royce asked.

"I stayed behind. I tried to save the emperor." He paused, looking far away. "I failed."

"So what happened to the heir?" Royce asked.

"How should I know? I was locked up in a prison for nine hundred years. Do you think he wrote me? Jerish was supposed to take him into hiding." The wizard allowed himself a grim smile. "We both thought it would only be for a month or so."

"So you don't even know if an heir exists anymore?"

"I'm pretty confident the church didn't kill him or they would have killed me shortly thereafter, but what became of Jerish and Nevrik I don't know. If anyone could have kept

Nevrik alive, it would have been Jerish. Despite his age, he was one of the best knights the emperor had. The fact that he trusted his son to his care was testament to that. Like all Teshlor knights, Jerish was a master of all the schools of combat; there wouldn't have been a man alive who could beat him in battle, and he would have died before surrendering Nevrik. They would both be dead now, of course—time would have seen to that. So would their great-great-grandchildren if they had any. I suspect Jerish would have known the need to perpetuate the line and would have settled down somewhere quiet and encouraged Nevrik to marry and have children."

"And wait for you?"

"What's that?"

"That was the plan, wasn't it? They run and hide and you stay behind and find them when it was safe?"

"Something like that."

"So you had a way to contact them. A way to locate the heir? Something to do with the amulets."

"Nine hundred years ago I would have said yes, but finding their descendants now is probably a fool's dream. Time can destroy so many things."

"But you are trying nevertheless."

"What else is there for an old crippled outlaw to do?"

"Care to tell me how you plan to find them?"

"I can't do that. I've already told you more than I should have. The heir has enemies and, as fond as I have grown of you, that kind of secret stays with me. I owe that much to Jerish and Nevrik."

"But something in that tower is part of it. That's why you want to get inside." Royce thought a moment. "You sealed that tower just before you went to prison, and since the Gilarabrywn was only recently released, you can be almost certain that the interior of that tower hasn't been touched in all that time. It's the only place that's still the same as the day you left it. There's something in there you saw that day, or something you left there—something you need to find the heir."

"It is a shame you aren't as good at deciphering a way to get into the tower."

"About that," Royce said. "You mentioned that the emperor met with the elves in the tower. They aren't allowed on this bank, right?"

"Correct."

"And there was no bridge on their side of the river, right?"

"Again correct."

"But you never saw how they entered the tower?"

"No."

Royce thought a moment, then asked, "Why were the stairs wet?"

Esrahaddon looked at him, puzzled. "What's that?"

"You said earlier that when the knights were fighting off the Gilarabrywn, they died on the wet steps. Was it blood?"

"No, water, I think. I remember how the stairs were wet when we were climbing up, because it made the stone so slippery I nearly fell. Some of the knights did fall; that's why I remember it."

"And you said the elves had clothes drying in the sun?"

Esrahaddon shook his head. "I see where you are going with this, but not even an elf can swim to the tower."

"That may be true, but then why were they wet? Was it a hot day? Could they have been swimming?"

Esrahaddon raised his eyebrows incredulously. "In that river? No, it was early spring and still cold."

"Then how'd they get wet?"

Royce heard a faint sound behind him. He started to turn but stopped himself.

"We're not alone," he whispered.

∽

"When you lunge, step in with the leg on your weapon side; it will give you more reach and better balance," Hadrian told Theron.

The two were at the well again. They had gotten up early and Hadrian was putting Theron through some basic moves using two makeshift swords they had created out of rake handles. To his surprise, Theron was spryer than he looked, and despite his size, the old man moved well. Hadrian had gone over the basics of parries, ripostes, flèches, presses, and the lunge, and they were now working on a compound attack comprising a feint, a parry, and a riposte.

"Cuts and thrusts must follow one upon the other without pause. The emphasis is always on speed, aggression, and deception. And everything is kept as simple as possible," Hadrian explained.

"I'd listen to him. If anyone knows stick fighting, it's Hadrian."

Hadrian and Theron turned to see two equestrians riding into the village clearing, each leading a pack pony laden with poles and bundles. They were young men not much older than Thrace, but dressed like young princes, in handsome doublets and hose complete with box-pleated frill and lace edging.

"Mauvin! Fanen?" Hadrian said, astonished.

"Don't look so surprised." Mauvin gave his horse rein to graze on the common's grass.

"Well, that's a little hard at this point. What in Maribor's name are you two doing here?"

Just then a procession of musicians, heralds, knights, wagons, and carriages emerged from the dense forest. Long banners of red and gold streamed in the morning light as standard-bearers preceded the march, followed by the plumed imperial guards of the Nyphron Church.

Hadrian and Theron moved aside against the trees for safety as the grand parade of elegantly draped stallions and gold-etched white carriages rolled in. There were well-dressed clergy and chain-mailed soldiers, knights with their squires leading packhorses laden with fine sets of shining metal armor. There were nobility with standards from as far away as Calis and Trent, but also commoners, rough men with broad swords and scarred faces, monks in tattered robes, and woodsmen with long bows and green hoods. Such an assortment of diverse characters made Hadrian think of a circus he had once seen, although this column of men and horses was far too grim and serious to be a carnival. Bringing up the rear echelon was a group of six riders in black and red with the symbol of a broken crown on their chests. At their head rode a tall thin man with long black hair and a short trimmed beard.

"So they've finally decided to do something about this," Hadrian said. "I'm impressed the church would go to such an effort to save a little village so far out that even its own king doesn't care. But that still doesn't explain why you two are here."

"I'm hurt." Mauvin feigned a chest pain. "Granted, I'm only here to help Fanen, but I might try my hand as well. Although, if you're going to be competing, it looks as if we shouldn't have bothered with the trip."

Theron whispered to Hadrian, "Who are these people? And what is he talking about?"

"Ah—sorry, this is Mauvin and Fanen Pickering, sons of Count Pickering of Galilin in Melengar, who are apparently very lost. Mauvin, Fanen, this is Theron Wood; he's a farmer."

"And he's paying you for lessons? Smart idea, but how did you two get here ahead of the rest of us? I didn't see you at any of the camps. Oh, what am I thinking? You and Royce probably had no trouble discovering the location of the contest."

"Contest?"

"Royce was probably hiding under the archbishop's desk as he set up the rules. So will it be swords? If it's swords, Fanen has a real chance to win, but if it's a joust, well…" He glanced at his brother, who scowled. "He's really not that good. Do you know how the eliminations will work? I can't imagine they will pit noble against commoner, which means Fanen won't be competing with you, so—"

"You're not here to slay the Gilarabrywn? Are you saying these people are here for that stupid contest?"

"Gilarabrywn? What's a Gilarabrywn? Is that like Oswald the bear? Heard about him coming through Dunmore. Terrorized villages for years until the king killed him with just a dagger."

The entourage traveled past them without pause up toward the manor house. One of the coaches separated from the group just after it cleared the well. It stopped, and a young well-dressed woman exited and ran to them, holding the edge of her skirt up to avoid the dirt.

"Hadrian!" she cried with a bright smile.

Hadrian bowed, and Theron joined him.

"Is this your father, Hadrian?" she asked.

"No, Your Highness. May I present Theron Wood of Dahlgren Village. Theron, this is Her Royal Highness Princess Arista of Melengar."

Theron stared at Hadrian, shocked. "You really get around, don't you?"

Hadrian smiled awkwardly and shrugged.

"Hey, Arista," Fanen said. "Guess what. Hadrian says the contest is to kill a beast."

"I didn't say that."

"Which is just fine by me, because if Hadrian was going to be competing, I think I would have to withdraw. But now, a hunt is a much different story. You know luck is often a deciding factor in these things."

" 'These things'?" Arista laughed at him. "Attended several beast-slaying contests, have you, Fanen?"

"Bah!" Fanen scoffed. "You know what I mean. Sometimes you are just in the right place at the right time."

Mauvin shrugged. "Doesn't sound like much of a contest for noblemen, really. If it turns out to be true, I'll be disappointed. Slaughtering a poor animal is no good use for a Pickering's sword."

"Say, did you also hear what the prize will be?" Fanen asked. "The way they've been selling this contest in every square, church, and tavern across Avryn, it has to be big. Will it just be a gold trophy, or is it land? I'm hoping to get an estate out of this. Mauvin will inherit our father's title, but I have to fend for myself. What does this animal look like? Is it a bear? Is it big? Have you seen it?"

Hadrian and Theron exchanged stunned looks.

"What is it?" Fanen asked. "It's not dead already?"

"No," Hadrian said. "It's not dead already."

"Oh good."

"Your Highness!" A woman's voice came from the carriage still lingering up the trail. "We need to be going—the archbishop will be waiting."

"I'm sorry," she told them. "I have to go. It was good seeing you again." She waved and ran back to her waiting carriage.

"We should probably be going too," Mauvin said. "We want to get Fanen's name as near to the top of the list as we can."

"Wait," Hadrian told them. "Don't enter the contest."

"What?" they both said.

"We rode days to get here for this," Fanen complained.

"Take my advice. Turn around right now and head back home. Take Arista with you too and anyone else you can convince to go. If it is a competition to kill the Gilarabrywn, don't sign up. You don't want to fight this thing. I'm serious. You don't know what you're dealing with. If you try and fight this creature, it will kill you."

"But you think you can kill it?"

"I'm not fighting it. Royce and I were just here doing a job for Theron's daughter and we were about to leave."

"Royce is here too?" Fanen asked, looking around.

"Do your father a favor and leave now."

Mauvin frowned. "If you were anyone else, I would take your tone as insolent. I might even call you a coward and a liar, but I know you're neither." Mauvin sighed and rubbed his chin thoughtfully. "Still, we did ride an awfully long way to just turn around. You say you were preparing to leave? When will that be?"

Hadrian looked at Theron.

"Another two days, I think," the old farmer told Hadrian. "I don't want to go until I know Thrace will be okay."

"Then we will stay here for that long and see for ourselves what's what. If it turns out to be as you say, we will leave with you. Is that fair, Fanen?"

"I don't see why you can't go and I stay. After all, I'm the one going to enter the contest."

"No one is going to kill that thing, Fanen," Hadrian told him. "Listen, I have been here for 3 nights. I have seen it and I know what it can do. It's not a matter of skill or courage. Your sword won't harm it; no one's will. Fighting that creature is nothing more than suicide."

"I'm not deciding yet," Fanen declared. "We aren't even certain what the contest is. I won't sign up right away, but I'm not leaving either."

"Do me a favor, then," Hadrian told them. "At least stay indoors tonight."

⁌

Something, or someone, was in the thickets.

Royce left Esrahaddon and moved away to the river's edge, careful not to look in the direction of the sound. He descended from the rocks to the depression near the river and slipped into the trees, circling back. Something was there and it was working hard to be quiet.

At first, Royce caught a glimpse of orange and blue through the leaves and almost thought it was nothing more than a bluebird, but then it shifted. It was far too large to be a bird. Royce drew closer and saw a light brown braided beard, a broad flat nose, a blue leather vest, large black boots, and a bright orange shirt with puffed sleeves.

"Magnus!" Royce greeted the dwarf loudly, causing him to stumble and fall out of the bramble. He slipped backward off the little grassy ledge and fell on his back on the bare rock not far from where Esrahaddon sat. With the wind knocked out of him, the dwarf lay gasping for breath.

Royce leapt down and placed his dagger to the dwarf's throat.

"A lot of people have been looking for you," Royce told him menacingly. "I have to admit, I rather wanted to see you again myself to thank you for all the help you gave me in Essendon Castle."

"Don't tell me this is the dwarf that killed King Amrath of Melengar," Esrahaddon said.

"His name is Magnus, or at least that's what Percy Braga called him. He's a master trap builder and stone carver, isn't that right?"

"It's my business!" the dwarf protested, still struggling for air. "I'm a craftsman. I take jobs the same as you. You can't fault a guy for working."

"I almost died due to your work," Royce told him. "And you killed the king. Alric will be very pleased when I tell him I finally eliminated you. And as I recall, there's a price on your head."

"Wait—hang on!" Magnus shouted. "It was nothing personal. Can you tell me you never killed anyone for money, Royce?"

Royce hesitated.

"Yes, I know who you are," the dwarf told him. "I wanted to find out who beat my trap. You used to work for the Black Diamond, and not as a delivery boy either. It was my job, I tell you. I don't care about politics, or Braga, or Essendon."

"I suspect he's telling the truth," Esrahaddon said. "I've never known a dwarf to care at all for the affairs of humans beyond the coin they can obtain."

"See, he knows what I am saying. You can let me go."

"I said you were telling the truth, not that he should let you live. In fact, now that I can see you have been eavesdropping on our conversations, I have to encourage the notion of ending your life. I can't be sure how much you heard."

"What?" the dwarf cried.

"After slitting his throat, you can just roll his little body off the ledge here." The wizard stepped up and looked over the cliff.

"No," Royce replied, "it will be better to toss him off the falls. He's not that heavy; his body will likely carry all the way to the Goblin Sea."

"Do you need his head?" Esrahaddon asked. "To take back to Alric?"

"It would be nice, but I'm not carrying a severed head for a week while traveling through those woods. It would draw every fly for miles and it would stink after a few hours. Trust me, I speak from experience."

The dwarf looked at both of them in horror.

"No! No!" he shouted in panic as Royce pressed his blade to his neck. "I can help you. I can show you how to get to the tower!"

Royce looked at the wizard, who appeared skeptical.

"For the love of Drome. I'm a dwarf. I know stone. I know rock. I know where the tunnel to the tower is."

Royce relaxed his dagger.

"Let me live and I'll show it to you." He turned his head toward Esrahaddon. "And as for what I heard, I care nothing about the affairs of wizards and men. I'll never say a word. If you know dwarves, well, then you know we're a lot like stone when we choose to be."

"So there *is* a tunnel," Royce said.

"Of course there is."

"Before I decide," Royce asked, "what are you doing here?"

"I was finishing another job, that's all."

"And what was this job?"

"Nothing sinister, I just made a sword for a guy."

"All the way out here? Who is this person?"

"Lord Rufus somebody. I was hired to come here to make it. I was told he would meet me. Honest, no traps, no killings."

"And how are you still alive? How did you get out of Melengar? How is it you haven't been caught?"

"My employer is very powerful."

"This Rufus guy?"

"No. I'm making the sword for him, but Rufus isn't my employer."

"So who is?"

Royce heard footfalls. Someone was running up the trail. Thinking it might be the dwarf's associates, he slipped behind

Magnus. He gripped his hair, pulled his head back, and prepared to slit his throat.

"Royce!" Tad Bothwick shouted up to them from down
near the water.

"What is it, Tad?" he asked cautiously.

"Hadrian sent me. He says you should come back to the
village right away, but that Esra should steer clear."

"Why?" the wizard asked.

"Hadrian said to tell you that the Church of Nyphron just
arrived."

"The church?" Esrahaddon muttered. "Here?"

"Is there a Lord Rufus with them?" Royce asked.

"Could be. There's a whole lot of fancy folk around. Must
be at least one lord in the bunch."

"Any idea why they're here, Tad?"

"Nope."

"You might want to make yourself scarce," Royce told the
wizard. "Someone might have mentioned your name. I'll go
see what's happening. In the meantime"—he looked down at
the dwarf—"it would appear your employer has just arrived.
Your death sentence has been suspended. This kindly old man
is going to watch you this afternoon, and you're going to stay
right here. Then later you're going to show us where this tunnel is, and if you're telling the truth about knowing, then you
live. Anything short of that and you're going over the falls in
two pieces. Agreed? Good." He looked back at the wizard.
"Want me to tie him up or just hit him over the head with a
rock?" Royce asked, panicking the dwarf again.

"Won't be necessary. Magnus here looks like the honorable
type. Besides, I can still manage a few surprisingly unpleasant
things. Do you know what it is like to have live ants trapped
inside your head?"

The dwarf did not move or speak. Royce searched him. He

found a belt under his clothes with little hammers and some rock-shaping tools and a dagger. Royce looked at the dagger, surprised.

"I tried copying it," the dwarf told him nervously. "It's not very good; I was working from memory."

Royce compared it to his own dagger. The two were very similar in design, though the blades were clearly different. Royce's weapon was made of an almost translucent metal that shimmered in the light, while Magnus's dagger seemed dull and heavy by comparison. The thief threw the dagger over the cliff.

"That's a magnificent weapon you have," the dwarf told him, mesmerized by the blade that a moment before had been at his throat. "It's a Tur blade, isn't it?"

Royce ignored him and spoke to Esrahaddon. "Keep an eye on him. I'll be back later."

✧

Arista took her seat on the balcony above the entrance to the great hall of the manor house, along with the entourage of the archbishop, which included Sauly and Sentinel Luis Guy. It was a very small balcony, created of rough logs and thick ropes, where only a few could fit, but Bernice managed to squeeze her way in and remained standing just behind her. Bernice's hovering out of sight was as irritating as a mosquito in the dark.

Arista had no idea what was going on—few people appeared to.

When they had arrived, everything was in chaos. The lord of the manor was apparently dead and the place was filled with peasants. They were promptly chased out. Luis Guy and his seret established order and assigned quarters based on rank. She was given a cramped but private room on the second level. It was a ghastly place, lacking even a single window. A bear rug lay on the floor, the head of a moose looked down at her from above the bed, and a coatrack made from deer antlers hung from the wall. Bernice was busy unpacking her clothes from the trunk when Sauly stopped by, insisting Arista join him on the balcony. At first, she thought the contest might be starting, but it was common knowledge it would begin at nightfall.

A trumpeter stepped up to the rail and blared a fanfare on his horn. Below, in the courtyard, a crowd formed. Men rushed over, some holding drinks or half-eaten meals. One man trotted up still buttoning his pants. The growing audience created a mass of heads and shoulders bunched together, all staring up at them.

The archbishop slowly stood up. Dressed in full regalia of long embroidered robes, he spread his arms in a grand gesture and spoke, his raspy voice barely adequate to the task.

"It is time to announce the details of this event and reveal the profound happening that you, the devoted of Novron, are about to take part in, an event so monumental that its conclusion will see the world altered forever."

Several people in the back complained they could not hear, but the archbishop ignored them and went on. "I know some of you came believing this contest was to be a battle of swords or lances, like some Wintertide tournament. Instead, what you will see is nothing less than a miracle. Some of you will die, one will succeed, and the rest will bear witness to the world.

"A terrible evil haunts this place. Here on the Nidwalden River, at the edge of the world, there is a beast. Not a great bear like Oswald that terrorized Glamrendor. This creature is none other than the legendary Gilarabrywn, a horror not seen since the days of Novron himself. A monster so terrible that even in those days of heroes and gods, only Novron, or one of his blood, could slay it. It will be your task, your challenge, to slay the creature and save this poor village from the ancient curse."

A murmur broke out among those gathered, and the archbishop raised his hands to quiet them. "Silence. For I have not yet told you of the reward!"

He waited as the mob grew quiet, many pushing closer to hear.

"As I said, the Gilarabrywn is a beast that only Novron or one of his bloodline can slay, and as such, he that succeeds in vanquishing this terror can be none other than the heir to the imperial crown, the long-lost Heir of Novron!"

The reaction was surprisingly quiet. There were no cheers, no shouts of jubilation. The crowd as a whole appeared stunned. They remained staring, as if expecting more. The archbishop in turn looked around, equally bewildered by the hesitancy of the congregation.

"Did he just say the winner would be the heir?" Arista asked, looking at Sauly, who appeared as if he'd just smelled something unpleasant. He smiled at her and, standing up, whispered in the archbishop's ear. The older man took his seat and Bishop Saldur addressed the crowd.

"For centuries the church has struggled to find the true heir, to restore the bloodline of our holy lord Novron the Great." Sauly's voice was loud and warm and carried well on the pine-scented afternoon air. "We have searched, but all we had to guide us were old books and rumors. Speculation, really, hopes and dreams. There has never been a means of finding him, no absolute method to determine where the heir was, or who he may be. Many have falsely claimed to be his descendent, many unworthy men have striven to take that lofty crown, and the church has sat helpless.

"Still, we have faith he is out there. Novron would not allow his own blood to die. We know he lives. He may be oblivious to who he is. A thousand years have passed since his disappearance, and who of us can accurately trace our lineage back to the days of the Old Empire? Who knows if one of us might have an ancestor who went to his grave with a terrible secret? A terrible, wonderful secret.

"The Gilarabrywn is a miracle Novron has sent. It is a tool to show us his son. He has confided this to the Patriarch and told His Holiness that he should hold a contest and if he did, the heir would be among the contestants, the truth of his lineage, oblivious even to himself.

"So you see, you—any one of you—may be the Heir of Novron, possessor of divine blood—a god. Have any of you sensed a power within? A belief in your own worth beyond that of others? This is your chance to prove to all of Elan that you are no fool, no mere man. Place your name upon the roster, ride out at nightfall, slay the beast, and you will become our divine ruler. You will not be a mere king, but *emperor*, and all kings will bow to you. You will take the imperial throne in Aquesta. All loyal Imperialists and the full force of the church will support you as we usher in a new age of order that will bring peace and harmony to the land. All you need do is destroy one lonely beast.

"What say you?"

This time the crowd cheered. Saldur glanced briefly at the archbishop and stepped away from the balcony to take a seat.

❧

When Royce reached Dahlgren, the village was in turmoil. People were everywhere. Most of the villagers were heading toward the common well. There were plenty of new faces, all of them men, most carrying some sort of weapon. Royce found Hadrian mobbed by villagers at the well. None of them looked happy.

"Where do we go now?" Selen Brockton asked, in tears.

Hadrian once more stepped up on the well, standing over the crowd and looking like he wanted to break something. "I don't know, Mrs. Brockton. Home, I guess—for now, at least."

"But our home has a thatched roof."

"Try digging cellars and getting as low as possible."

"What's going on?" Royce asked.

"The Archbishop of Ghent has arrived and moved into the manor house. He and his clergy, as well as a few dozen nobles, have taken over the castle and driven everyone else out. Well, except for Russell, Dillon, and Kline, whom he ordered to fill in the shelter and the tunnel we were digging, saying they could repair the damages or hang for destruction of property. Good old Deacon Tomas, he stands there nodding and saying, 'I told them not to do it, but they wouldn't listen.' They kept most of the livestock too, saying it was in the castle, so it belonged to the manor. Now everyone blames me for losing their animals."

"What about the bonfires?" Royce asked. "We could still build one here in the commons."

"No good," Hadrian told him. "His Lordship declared it unlawful to cut trees in the area and confiscated the oxen with the rest of the animals."

"Did you tell him what will happen when the sun goes down?"

"I can't tell him anything." Hadrian threw up his hands, running his fingers through his hair as if he might start pulling it out. "I can't get past the twenty-odd soldiers he has at the castle gate. Which is a good thing too or I might kill the guy."

"Why is the church here at all?"

"That's the kicker," Hadrian told him. "You know that competition the church has been announcing? Turns out that contest is to slay the Gilarabrywn."

"What?"

"They intend to send contestants out to fight the thing at nightfall, and if they die, they'll send the next one. They've got a damn list nailed to the castle gate."

"It's all right, it's all right," Deacon Tomas shouted.

Everyone turned to see the cleric coming down the trail from the castle, approaching the crowd at the well. He walked with his hands raised as if in blessing. On his face he had a great smile, which turned his eyes into half-moons. "Everything is going to be fine," he told them in a loud confident voice. "The archbishop has come to help us. They are going to kill the beast and save us from this nightmare."

"What about our livestock?" Vince Griffin asked.

"They will need most of them to feed the troops, but what isn't used will be returned after the beast has been slain."

The crowd grumbled.

"Now, now, what price do you put on safety? What price do you put on the lives of your children? Are a pig and a cow worth the lives of your children? Your wife? Consider it a tithe and be thankful the church has come to Dahlgren to save us. No one else has. The King of Dunmore ignored us, but your church has responded by sending not just some knight or margrave, but the Archbishop of Ghent himself. Soon the beast will be dead and Dahlgren will be a place of happiness once more. If that means one year of no meat, and plowing without an ox, surely that's not too high a price to pay. Now, everyone, please, back to your homes. Stay out of their way and let them do their work."

"What about my daughter?" Theron growled, and pushed forward, looking like he might kill the deacon.

"It's all right, I've spoken with the archbishop and Bishop Saldur; they have agreed to let her stay. They have moved her to a smaller room, but—"

"They won't let me in to see her!" the old farmer snapped.

"I know, I know," Tomas said in a soothing voice. "But I can. I just came down to explain things. I am heading right back, and I promise you, I'll stay by her side and watch over her until she is well."

Hadrian slipped out of the crowd that now shifted around the deacon. He turned to Royce with a bitter look. "Tell me you found a way into the tower."

Royce shrugged. "Maybe. We'll need to check it out tonight."

"Tonight?" Hadrian asked. "Shouldn't such things be done in the daylight? When we can both see and things with complicated names aren't flying around?"

"Not if I'm right."

"And if you're wrong?"

"If I'm wrong, we'll both certainly die—most likely by being eaten."

"The thing is, I know you're not kidding. Did I mention I lost my weapons?"

"With any luck we won't need them. What we will need, however, is a good length of rope, sixty feet at least," Royce told him. "Lanterns, wax, a tinderbox—"

"I'm not going to like this, am I?" Hadrian asked miserably.

"Not at all," Royce replied.

CHAPTER 9

TRIALS BY MOONLIGHT

Back in bed," the man shouted. "Back in bed this instant!" Arista was wandering the hallway of the manor house, as much to get to know her surroundings as to evade Bernice, who was insisting she take a nap. Initially she thought the yelling was directed at her, and while she put up with Bernice and her pampering, she was certainly not about to allow anyone to address her in such a manner as this brassy fellow seemed to be doing. She was no longer in her native kingdom of Melengar, where she was princess of the realm, but she was still a princess and an ambassador and no one had the right to speak to her like that.

With a fury in her countenance, she marched forward and, turning a corner, spotted a middle-aged man and a young girl. The girl was dressed only in her nightgown, her face battered and bruised. He held her wrist, attempting to drag her into a bedroom.

"Unhand her!" Arista ordered. "Hilfred! Guards!"

The man and girl both looked at her, bewildered.

Hilfred raced around the corner and in an instant stood with sword drawn between his princess and the source of her anger.

"I said get your filthy hands off her this instant, or I'll have them removed at the wrists."

"But I—" the man began.

From the other direction, two imperial guards arrived. "Milady?" the guards greeted her.

Hilfred said nothing but merely pointed his sword at the man's throat.

"Take this wretch into custody," Arista ordered. "He's forcing himself on this girl."

"No, no, please," the girl protested. "It was my fault. I—"

"It is not your fault." Arista looked at her with pity. "And you needn't be afraid. I can see to it that he never bothers you, or *anyone*, again."

"Oh dear Maribor, protect me," the man prayed.

"Oh no, you don't understand," the girl said. "He wasn't hurting me. He was trying to help me."

"How's that?"

"I had an accident." She pointed to the bruises on her face. "Deacon Tomas was taking care of me, but I was feeling better today and wanted to get up and walk, but he thought it best if I stay in bed another day. He is really only trying to look out for me. Please don't hurt him. He's been so kind."

"You know this man?" Arista asked the guards.

"He was cleared for entrance by the archbishop as the deacon of this village, my lady, and he was indeed attending to this girl, who is known as Thrace." Tomas, with his eyes wide with fear and Hilfred's sword steady at his throat, nodded as best he could and attempted a friendly though strained smile.

"Well," Arista said, pursing her lips, "my mistake, then." She looked at the guards. "Go back about your business."

"Princess." The guards bowed briskly, turned, and walked back the way they had come.

Hilfred slowly sheathed his sword.

She looked back at the two. "My apologies, it's just that—that—well, never mind." She turned away, embarrassed.

"Oh no, Your Highness," Thrace said, attempting as best she could to curtsy. "Thank you so much for coming to my aid, even if I didn't actually need it. It is good to know that someone as great as you would bother to help a poor farmer's daughter." Thrace looked at her in awe. "I've never met a princess before. I've never even seen one."

"I hope I'm not too much of a disappointment, then." Thrace was about to speak again but Arista beat her to it. "What happened to you?" She gestured at her face.

Thrace reached up, running her fingers over her forehead. "Is it that bad?"

"It was the Gilarabrywn, Your Highness," Tomas explained. "Thrace and her father, Theron, were the only two to ever survive a Gilarabrywn attack. Now please, my dear girl, please get back in bed."

"But really, I am feeling much better."

"Let her walk with me a bit, Deacon," Arista said, softening her tone. "If she feels worse, I'll get her back to bed."

Tomas nodded and bowed.

Arista took Thrace by the arm and led her up the hallway, Hilfred walking a few steps behind. They could not travel far, only thirty yards or so; the manor house was not a real castle. It was built from great rough-cut beams—some with the bark still on—and she guessed there were only about eight bedrooms. In addition, there were a parlor, an office, and the great hall, with a high ceiling and mounted heads of deer and bears. It reminded Arista of a cruder, smaller version of King Roswort's residence. The floor was made of wide pine planks, and the outer walls were thick logs. Nailed along them were iron lanterns holding flickering candles that cast semicircles of quivering light, for even though it was midafternoon, the interior of the manor was dark as a cave.

"You're so kind," the girl told her. "The others treat me... as if I don't belong here."

"Well, I'm glad you are here," Arista replied. "Other than my handmaiden, Bernice, I think you are the only other woman here."

"It is just that everyone else was sent back home and I feel so out of place, like I'm doing something wrong. Deacon Tomas says I'm not. He says I'm hurt and I need time to recover and that he'll see to it no one bothers me. He's been very nice. I think he feels as helpless as everyone else around here. Maybe taking care of me is a battle he feels he can win."

"I misjudged the deacon," Arista told her, "and you. Are all farmers' daughters in Dahlgren so wise?"

"Wise?" Thrace looked embarrassed.

Arista smiled at her. "Where is your family?"

"My father is in the village. They won't let him in to see me, but the deacon is working on that. I don't think it matters, as we will be leaving Dahlgren as soon as I can travel, which is another reason I want to get my strength back. I want to get away from here. I want us to find a new place and start fresh. I'll find a man, get married, have a son, and call him Hickory."

"Quite the plan, but how are you feeling—really?"

"I still have headaches and to be honest I'm getting a little dizzy right now."

"Maybe we should head back to your bedroom, then," Arista said, and they turned around.

"But I am feeling so much better than I was. That's another reason why I got up. I haven't been able to thank Esra. I thought he might be in the halls here somewhere."

"Esra?" Arista asked. "Is he the village doctor?"

"Oh no, Dahlgren's never had a doctor. Esra is—well, he's a very smart man. If it hadn't been for him, both me and my father would be dead by now. He was the one who made the medicine that saved me."

"He sounds like a great person."

"Oh, he is. I try to pay him back by helping him eat. He's very proud, you understand, and he would never ask, so I offer and I can see he appreciates it."

"Is he too poor to afford food?"

"Oh no, he just doesn't have any hands."

◈

"Tur is a myth," Esrahaddon was saying to the dwarf as Royce and Hadrian arrived at the falls.

"Says you," Magnus replied.

The wizard and the dwarf sat on the rocky escarpment facing each other, arguing over the roar. The sun, having dropped behind the trees, left the two in shadow, but the crystalline spires atop Avempartha caught the last rays of dying red light.

Esrahaddon sighed. "I'll never understand what it is about religion that causes otherwise sensible people to believe in fairy tales. Even in the world of religion, Tur is a parable, not a reality. You're dealing with myths based on legends based on superstitions and taking it literally. That is very undwarf-like. Are you certain you don't have some human blood in your ancestry?"

"That's just insulting." Magnus glared at the wizard. "You deny it, but the proof is right before you. If you had dwarven eyes, you could see the truth in that blade." Magnus gestured at Royce.

"What's this all about?" Hadrian asked. "Hello, Magnus, murder anyone lately?"

The dwarf scowled.

"This dwarf insists that Royce's dagger was made by Kile," Esrahaddon explained.

"I didn't say that," the dwarf snapped. "I said it was a Tur blade. It could have been made by anyone from Tur."

"What's Tur?" Hadrian asked.

"A misguided cult of lunatics that worship a fictitious god. They named him Kile, of all things. You'd think they could have at least come up with a better name."

"I've never heard of Kile," Hadrian said. "Now, I'm not a religious scholar, but if I remember what a little monk once told me, the dwarven god is Drome, the elvish god is Ferrol, and the human god is Maribor. Their sister, the goddess of flora and fauna, is...Muriel, right? And her son, Uberlin, is the god of darkness. So how does this Kile fit in?"

"He's their father," Esrahaddon explained.

"Oh right, I forgot about him, but his name isn't Kile, it's... Erebus or something, isn't it? He raped his daughter and his sons killed him, but he's not really dead? It didn't make a lot of sense to me."

Esrahaddon chuckled. "Religion never does."

"So who is Kile?"

"Well, the Cult of Tur, or Kile, as it is also known, insists that a god is immortal and cannot die. This deranged group of people appeared during the imperial reign of Estermon II and began circulating this story that Erebus had been drunk, or whatever equivalent there is to a god, when he raped his daughter, and he was ashamed for what he did. The story goes that Erebus allowed his children—the gods—to believe they had killed him. Then he came to Muriel in secret and begged her forgiveness. She told her father that she wasn't ready to forgive him and would only do so after he did penance. She said he had to do good deeds throughout Elan, but as a commoner, not as a god or even a king. For each act of sacrifice and kindness that she approved of, she would grant him a feather from her marvelous robe, and when her robe was gone, she would forgive and welcome him home.

"The Kile legend says that ages ago a stranger came to a poor village called Tur. No one knows where it was, of course, and over the centuries its location has changed in response to various claims, but the most common legend places it in Delgos, because it was being regularly attacked by the Dacca and, of course, because of the similarity in names to the port city of Tur Del Fur. The story goes that this stranger called himself Kile and, entering into Tur and seeing the terrible plight of the desperate villagers, taught them the art of weapon making to help in their defense. The weapons he taught them to make were reputed to be the greatest in the world, capable of cleaving through solid iron as if it were soft wood. Their shields and armor were light and yet stronger than stone. Once he taught them the craft, they used it to defend their homes. After driving off the Dacca, legend says there was a thunderclap on a cloudless day, and from the heavens, a single white feather fell into Kile's hands. He wept at the gift and bid them all farewell, never to be seen again. At least not by the residents of Tur. Throughout the various reigns of different emperors, there always seemed to be at least one or two stories of Kile appearing here and there, doing good deeds and obtaining his feather. The legend stood out beyond all others because the poor village of Tur was now famous for its great weaponry."

"I've never heard of a town by that name."

"You aren't the only one," Esrahaddon said. "So the myth

experts added a page to their story, as so often happens with these ridiculous tales when they crash into the face of reality. Supposedly, the village was inundated with requests for arms. The Turists didn't feel it was right to make weapons for just anyone, so they only made a few, and only for those who had a just and good need. Powerful kings, however, decided to take the god-given craft secrets for themselves and prepared to battle for control of the village. On the day of the battle, however, the armies marched in to discover that the village of Tur—all its inhabitants and buildings—was gone. Not a trace was left of their existence except for a single white feather that came from no known bird."

"Convenient," Hadrian said.

"Exactly," the wizard replied. "One mystery covered by another, but never any real evidence. Still it doesn't stop people from believing."

"For your information," Magnus spoke up, "Tur Del Fur was once a dwarven city, and in my tongue, its name means Village of Tur, and there are legends among my people of it once having been the source of great craftsmen who knew the secrets of folding metal and making great swords.

"Any dwarf in Elan would give his beard for the secrets of Tur, or even the chance to study a Tur blade."

"And you think Alverstone is a Tur blade?" Hadrian asked.

"What did you call it?" Magnus asked, his beady eyes abruptly focusing on him.

"Alverstone, that's what Royce calls his dagger," Hadrian explained.

"Don't encourage him," Royce said, his eyes fixed on the tower.

"Where did he get this Alverstone?" the dwarf asked, lowering his voice.

"It was a gift from a friend," Hadrian said, "right?"

"Who? And where did the friend get it from?" the dwarf persisted.

"You are aware I can hear you?" Royce told them; then, seeing something, he pointed toward Avempartha. "There, look."

They all scrambled up to peer at the outline of the fading tower. The sun was down now and night was upon them. Like great mirrors, the river and the tower captured the starlight and the luminous moon. The mist from the falls appeared as an eerie white fog skirting the base. Near the top of the spires, a dark shape spread its wings and flew down along the course of the river. It wheeled and circled back over the falls, catching air currents and rising higher until, with a flap of its massive wings, the beast headed out over the trees above the forest, flying toward Dahlgren.

"That's its lair?" Hadrian asked incredulously. "It lives in the tower?"

"Convenient, isn't it," Royce remarked, "that the beast resides at the same place as the one weapon that can kill it."

"Convenient for whom?"

"I guess that remains to be seen," Esrahaddon said.

Royce turned to the dwarf. "All right, my little mason, shall we head to the tunnel? It's in the river, isn't it? Somewhere underwater?"

Magnus looked at him, surprised.

"I am only guessing, but from the look on your face, I must be right. It's the only place I haven't looked. Now, in return for your life, you'll show us exactly where."

✧

Arista stood with the Pickerings on the south stockade wall watching the sunset over the gate. The wall provided the best view of both the courtyard and the hillside beyond while keeping them above the turmoil. Below, knights busied themselves dressing in armor; archers strung their bows, horses decorated in caparisons shifted uneasily, and priests prayed to Novron for wisdom. The contest was about to commence. Beyond the wall the village of Dahlgren remained silent. Not a candle was visible. Nothing moved.

Another scuffle broke out near the gate where the list of combatants hung on the hitching post. Arista could see several men pushing and swinging, rising dust.

"Who is it this time?" Mauvin asked. The elder Pickering leaned back against the log wall. He was in a simple loose tunic and a pair of soft shoes that day. This was the Mauvin she most remembered, the carefree boy who had challenged her to stick duels back when she stood a foot taller and could overpower him, in the days when she had a mother and father and her greatest challenge was making Lenare jealous.

"I can't tell," Fanen replied, peering down. "I think one is Sir Erlic."

"Why are they fighting?" Arista asked.

"Everyone wants a higher place on the list," Mauvin replied.

"That doesn't make sense. It doesn't matter who goes first."

"It does if the person in front of you kills the beastie before you get a chance."

"But they can't. Only the heir can kill the beast."

"You really think that?" Mauvin asked, turning around, grasping the sharpened points of the logs, and peering down the outside of the wall. "No one else does."

"Who's first on the list?"

"Well, Tobis Rentinual was."

"Which one is he?" she asked.

"He's the one we told you about with the big mysterious wagon."

"There"—Fanen pointed down in the courtyard—"the foppish-looking one leaning against the smokehouse. He has a shrill voice and a superior attitude that makes you want to throttle him."

Mauvin nodded. "That's him. I peeked under his tarp; there's this huge contraption made of wood, ropes, and pulleys. He managed to find the list first and sign his name. No one had a problem with it when they thought the contest was a tournament. Everyone was just itching to have a go at him, but now, well, the thought of Tobis as emperor has become a communal fear."

"What do you mean *was*?"

"He got bumped," Fanen said.

"Bumped?"

"Luis Guy's idea," Mauvin explained. "The sentinel decreed that those farther down on the list could move up via combat. Those unsatisfied with their place could challenge anyone for their position to a fight. Once issued, the challenged party could trade positions on the list or enter into combat with the challenger. Sir Enden of Chadwick challenged Tobis, who gave up his position. Who could blame him? Only Sir Gravin had the courage to challenge Enden, but several others drew swords against one another for lesser spots. Most expected the duels would be by points, but Guy declared battles over only when the opponent yielded, so they have gone on for hours. Many have been injured. Sir Gravin yielded only after Enden pierced his shoulder. He's announced he's withdrawing and will be leaving tomorrow, and he's not the only one. Several have already left wrapped in bandages."

Arista looked at Fanen. "You aren't challenging?"

Mauvin chuckled. "It was kinda funny. The moment Guy made the announcement, everyone looked at us."

"But you didn't challenge?"

Fanen scowled and glared at Mauvin. "He won't let me. And my name is near the bottom."

"Hadrian Blackwater told us not to sign up," Mauvin explained.

"So?" Fanen stared at his brother.

"So the one man here who could take that top spot without breaking a sweat doesn't even have his name on the list. Either he knows something we don't, or he thinks he does. That's worth waiting out the first night at least. Besides, you heard Arista; it doesn't matter who goes first."

"You know who else isn't on the list?" Fanen asked. "Lord Rufus."

"Yeah, I saw that. Thought he'd be the one to challenge Enden—it would have been worth the trip just to see that duel. He's not even out in the yard with the rest."

"He's been with the archbishop a lot."

From their elevated position, Arista scanned the courtyard below. The light was gone from the yard, the walls and trees casting the interior in shade. Men went around lighting torches and mounting them. There were hundreds assembled within the grounds and more outside all gathered into small groups. They talked; some shouted. She could hear laughter and even a bit of singing—she could not tell the song, but by its rhythm, she guessed it was a bawdy tavern tune. There was a lot of toasting going on. Dark figures in the failing light, broad, powerful men slamming cups together with enough force to spill foam. Above it all, on a wooden platform raised in the center of the yard, stood Sentinel Luis Guy. He was high enough to catch the last rays of the sun and the last breaths of the evening wind. The light made his red cassock look like fire and the wind blowing his cape lent him an ominous quality.

She looked back at the brothers. Mauvin had his mouth open, struggling to clear something from a back tooth with his forefinger. Fanen had his head up, looking at the sky. She was glad they were with her. It was a little bit of home in the wilderness and she imagined the smell of apples.

Arista and Alric had spent summer months at Drondil Fields to escape the heat of the city. She remembered how they used to climb the trees in the orchard outside the country castle and have apple fights in early autumn. The rotten apples would burst on the branches and spray pulp, soaking them until they all smelled like cider. Each tree a sovereign castle, they would make alliances. Mauvin always teamed with Alric, shouting, "My king! My king!" Lenare paired with Fanen, wanting to protect her younger brother from the "brutes," as she called them. Arista always remained on her own, fighting both groups. Even when Lenare stopped climbing trees, it became the boys against the girl. She did not mind. She did not notice. She did not even think about it until now.

There was so much in her head. So much she needed to sort out. It had been hard to think bouncing around in the coach with Bernice staring at her. She desperately wanted to talk to someone, if only to hear her own words aloud. The idea that Sauly was a conspirator was growing in her mind despite her reluctance to accept it. If Sauly could betray her father, who could be trusted? Could Esrahaddon? Had he used her to escape? Was he responsible for her father's death? Now it seemed the old wizard was nearby, somewhere just outside the walls perhaps, spending the night in one of the village houses. She did not know what to do, or who to trust.

Mauvin found what he was looking for and flicked it from his finger over the wall.

She opened her mouth to speak, hesitating to find the

proper words to say. The whole trip there she had planned to discuss the issues raised at Ervanon with the Pickerings; well, Mauvin, at least. She closed her mouth and bit her lip, once more thinking back to the long-ago orchard and the smell of apples.

"There you are, Your Highness," Bernice said, rushing to her with a shawl for her shoulders. "You shouldn't be out so late; it's not proper."

"Honestly, Bernice, you should have had children when you had the chance. This preoccupation with pampering me has got to stop."

The older woman only smiled warmly. "I'm just looking after you, dear. You need looking after. This foul place is full of rough men. There is little but thin walls and the grace of the archbishop separating them from your virtue. A lady such as yourself is a strong temptation, and given the untamed surroundings of this wilderness, it could easily drive many a good man to acts of rashness." She glanced suspiciously at the brothers, who looked back sheepishly. "And there are more than a few here who I couldn't even describe as good men. In a great castle with a proper retinue, men can be kept at bay by holding them in awe of royalty, but here, my lady, in this barbaric, feral landscape, they will surely lose their heads."

"Oh, Bernice, please."

"Here we go," Fanen said excitedly.

As the last of the sun's light faded, the gates opened and Sir Enden and his retinue of two squires and three pages rode out, torches flaming. They trotted to the open plain, where the knight prepared to do battle.

A shout rose from the crowd just then and Arista looked up to see a dark shadow sweep across the moonlit sky. It drifted in like a hawk, a silhouette of wings and tail. The crowd murmured and gasped as it circled the castle briefly, moving hesitantly before having its attention caught by torches waved by Sir Enden's entourage on the hillside.

It folded its wings and dove, falling out of the sky like an arrow aimed at the knight of Chadwick. Torches moved frantically and Arista thought she saw Sir Enden level his lance and charge forward. There were screams, cries of anguish and terror, as one by one the torches in the field went out.

"Next!" shouted Luis Guy.

⋙

The dwarf led them up the river path to where the moon revealed a large rock protruding out toward the water. To Hadrian it looked vaguely like the dull tip of a broad spear. Magnus thumped the dirt with his boot, then pointed toward the river. "We go in here. Swim straight down about twenty feet—there's an opening in the bank. The tunnel runs right under us, curves down, and then runs under the river to the tower."

"You can tell all that with your foot?" Royce asked.

Hadrian looked at Esrahaddon. "How are you at swimming?"

"I can't say I've had the opportunity since..." he said, lifting his arms. "But I can hold my breath a good long time. Drag me if necessary."

"Let me go first," Royce announced, his eyes on Magnus. He threw his coil of rope on the ground and tied one end around his waist. "Feed this out to me, but hang on to it. I don't know how swift the current is."

"There is no current here," Magnus told them. "There's an underwater shelf that juts out, creating an eddy. It's like a little pond down there."

"You'll forgive me if I don't take your word for it. Once I am down I'll give three tugs indicating that it's safe to follow. Tie off the end and follow the line down. If, on the other hand, I jump in and the rope runs out like you just caught a marlin, haul me back so I can personally kill him."

The dwarf sighed.

Royce slipped off his cloak, and with Hadrian holding the rope, he descended into the river as if he were rappelling off the side of a wall. He dropped and vanished under the dark water. Hadrian felt the rope slip out gradually from between his fingers. At his side, Magnus showed no signs of concern. The dwarf stood with his head cocked back, looking up at the sky. "What do you suppose it's doing tonight?" he asked.

"Eating knights would be my guess," Hadrian replied. "Let's just hope they keep the thing busy."

Deeper and deeper, the rope trolled out; then it stopped. Hadrian watched where the line entered the water; it made a little white trail as it cut the current.

Tug. Tug. Tug.

"That's it. He's in," Hadrian announced. "You next, little man."

Magnus glared at him. "I'm a dwarf."

"Get in the river."

Magnus walked to the edge. Holding his nose and pointing his toes, he jumped and disappeared with a plop.

"That leaves you and me," Hadrian said, tying the end of the rope to a birch tree that leaned a bit out toward the river. "You go first—I'll follow—see how well you do. If need be, I'll pull you through."

The wizard nodded, and for the first time since Hadrian had known him, he looked unsure of himself. Esrahaddon took three deep breaths, rapidly blowing each out; on the fourth inhale, he held it and jumped feetfirst. Hadrian leapt in right after.

The water was cold—not icy or breathtaking, but colder than expected. The immediate shock caught Hadrian off guard for an instant. He kicked out with his feet, pointed his head down, and began to swim along the rope. Magnus had been right about the current. The water was still as a pond. He opened his eyes. Above him, there was a faint blue-gray shimmer; below, it was black. Panic gripped Hadrian when he realized he could not see Esrahaddon. Almost in response, a faint light appeared directly below him. The wizard's robe gave off a blue-green glow as he swam, paddling with his feet and stroking with his arms. Despite the lack of hands, he made good headway.

The light from the robe revealed the riverbank and the rope running down. It disappeared inside a dark hole. He watched the wizard slip through, and with his lungs starting to burn, followed him. Once inside, he kicked upward, and almost together their heads emerged from a quiet pool in a small cave.

Royce had the other end of the rope tied to a rock. There was a lantern burning beside him. The single flame easily illuminated the room. The chamber was a natural cave with a tunnel leading out. Magnus stood off to the side, either studying the cavern walls or just keeping his distance from Royce.

When Esrahaddon surfaced, Royce hauled him out. "You might have had an easier time swimming if you'd taken off—" Royce stopped as he saw the wizard's robe. It was dry.

Hadrian climbed out of the pool, feeling the river water drizzle down his body. He could hear the drops echoing in the cave like a rainstorm, but Esrahaddon was exactly as he had been before entering the river. With the exception of his hair and beard, he was not even damp.

Hadrian and Royce exchanged glances but said nothing. Royce picked up his lantern. "Coming, short stuff?"

The dwarf grumbled and, taking hold of his beard with both hands, twisted a bit of water out. "You realize, my friend, dwarves are an older and far more accomplished—"

"Less chatter, more walking," Royce interrupted, pointing at the tunnel. "You lead. And you're not my friend."

Traveling forward, they entered into a new world. The walls were smooth and seamless, as if cut by the flow of water. The glossy surface magnified the light from Royce's lantern, making the curved interior surprisingly bright.

"So where are we?" Hadrian asked.

"Under the bank, not far below where we were standing before entering the water," Magnus told him. "The tunnel here corkscrews down."

"Incredible," Hadrian said, looking about him in amazement at the sparkling walls. "It's as though we're on the inside of a diamond."

Just as the dwarf had predicted, the tunnel curved around and around, sloping down. Right about the time Hadrian lost all sense of direction, it stopped spinning and ran straight. It was not long before they could hear and feel the thunder of the falls. It vibrated through the stone. Here the ceiling and walls seeped water. A thousand years of neglect had allowed stalactites of crystal to form on the ceiling, and jagged mounds of mineral deposits on the floor.

"This is a bit disturbing," Hadrian remarked, noticing a buildup of water on the floor that was getting deeper as they moved forward.

"Bah!" Magnus muttered, but failed to add anything more.

They slogged through the water, dodging stone spikes. Examining the walls, Hadrian noticed designs carved into them. Etchings of geometric shapes and patterns lined the corridor. Some of the more delicate lines were faded, missing, perhaps lost to the erosion of a billion water droplets. No words were visible and there were no recognizable symbols. The etching appeared to be nothing more than decorative. Above, almost lost in the growing stone, were brackets for what might have once been banner poles, and on the side walls he spotted mountings for lamps. Hadrian tried to imagine how the tunnel looked before the time of Novron, when multicolored banners and rows of bright lamps might have illuminated the causeway. It was not long before the tunnel pitched upward again and they could all see a faint light.

The tunnel ended at a stairway going up. The steps curved and were wide enough for them to take two strides before climbing the next step. When they reached the top, the star-filled sky was above them once more, and before long, they stood aboveground on the outcropping of rock that made up the base of the citadel. A strong wind met them. The gale was damp, filled with a wet mist. They stood at the end of a short stone bridge spanning a narrow crevasse, beyond which stood the spires of the monolithic tower. It loomed above them so high it was impossible to see the top.

More stairs awaited them on the far side and they moved at a slow but even pace, staying single file, even though the stairs were wide enough for two, or even three, to walk abreast. They climbed five sets of steps, zigzagging in a half circle around the outside of the tower. As they started their sixth flight, Royce waited until they had moved to the lee of the citadel, then called a halt for them to catch their breath. Below, the roar of the falls boomed, but from their perch, protected from the wind, the night seemed still. There were no sounds, no crickets or owls, just the deep voice of the river and the howl of the wind.

"This is ridiculous," Royce shouted over the roar. "Where's the damn door? I don't like being so exposed."

"It's just up ahead, not too much farther," Esrahaddon replied.

"How long do we have?" Hadrian asked, looking at the wizard, who shrugged in reply.

"Does it return here directly after killing, or does it enjoy the night?" Royce inquired. "I should think having been locked up in this tower for nine hundred years, it would want to spend some time flying about."

"It isn't a person, or an animal. It's a conjuration, a mystic embodiment of power. It mimics life and understands threats to its existence, certainly, but I doubt it has any concept of pleasure or freedom. Like I said, it's not alive."

"Then why does it eat?" Royce asked.

"It doesn't."

"Then why is it killing a person or two a night?"

"I've wondered that myself. It should attempt to fulfill its last instructions, and that was clearly to kill the emperor. It is possible that not finding its target, and not able to travel far from this tower—conjurations are often limited to a specific distance from their creator or point of origin—it might be trying to lure him here. It could have deduced that the emperor would not tolerate the slaughter of his people and would come to aid the village."

"Regardless, we'd better be quick," Hadrian concluded.

The wind resumed as they circled around. It whistled in their ears and buffeted their steps. The damp clothes chilled them despite the hard work of the march. Above, the spires still rose far into the night sky, and they all felt a grim sense of drudgery when they reached yet another short bridge, which ended abruptly at a solid wall.

Hadrian watched Royce sigh in disappointment as he looked at the dead end.

"I thought you said there was a door." Royce addressed the wizard.

"There was, and is."

Hadrian did not see a door. There was what appeared to be a faint outline of a door's frame etched in the wall in front of them, but it was solid stone.

Royce grimaced. "Another invisible stone portal?"

"Don't waste your time," Magnus told him. "You'll never open it. Trust me, I'm a dwarf. I spent hours trying to get in and nothing. That stone is enchanted and impenetrable. Crossing the river to get here was nothing compared to opening that door."

Royce turned to the dwarf with a puzzled look in his eyes. "You've been here? You tried to enter the tower. Why?"

"I told you, I was doing a job for the church."

"You said you made Lord Rufus a sword."

"I did, but the archbishop didn't want just any sword made for him. He wanted a replica of a sword, an elvish sword. He gave me a bunch of old drawings, which I used to make it. They were pretty good, with dimensions and material listed, but it's not like being able to examine the real thing." The dwarf's stare lingered on Royce suggestively. "I was told others of the same type could be found inside this tower. I came out here and spent all day climbing around, but never found a way in. No doors or windows, just things like this."

"This sword you made," Esrahaddon said. "Did it have writing on the blade?"

"Yep," Magnus replied. "They were real insistent that the inscription on the replica was exactly like that in the books."

"That's it," Esrahaddon muttered. "The church isn't here because of me, and they aren't here to find the heir; they're here to *make* an heir."

"Make an heir? I don't get it," Hadrian said. "I thought you said they wanted the heir dead."

"They do, but they are going to make a puppet. This Rufus has been picked to replace the true heir. There is a legend that only the bloodline of Novron can kill a Gilarabrywn. They will use this creature's death as undisputed proof that their boy is the true heir. Not only will it provide them legitimate means to dictate laws to the kings, but it will also hinder my efforts to reinstate the real heir to power. Who will believe an old outlawed wizard when their boy slew a Gilarabrywn? They will let a few bumpkins try to fight only to die, in order to prove the invincibility of the beast. Then this Rufus will step up, and with his sword etched with the name, he'll slay it and become emperor. With Rufus as their figurehead, the church will return to power and reform the empire. Excellent move, I must say. I'll admit I hadn't expected it."

"A few moderate kings might have something to say about that," Hadrian replied.

"And they know that as much as you do. They have a plan to deal with it, I'm sure."

"So do we still need to get inside?" Hadrian asked.

"Oh yes," the wizard told them. "Now more than ever." He chuckled. "Just imagine if before their boy Rufus slays this beast, another contestant slays it first."

The dwarf snorted. "Bah! I told you, you aren't getting through that door. It's solid stone."

The wizard considered the archway once more. "Open it, Royce."

Royce looked skeptical. "Open what? That's a wall. There's

no latch, no lock, not even a seam. Anyone have a gem we can try?"

"This isn't a gemlock," the wizard explained.

"I agree and I would know," Magnus told them.

"Try opening it anyway," the wizard insisted, staring at Royce. "That's why I brought you here, remember?"

Royce looked at the wall before him and scowled. "How?"

"Use your instincts. You opened the door to my prison and it had no latch either."

"I was lucky."

"You might be lucky again. Try."

Royce shrugged. He stepped forward and placed his hands lightly on the stone, letting his fingertips drift across the surface, searching by feel for what his eyes might not be able to see.

"This is a waste of time," Magnus said. "This is clearly a very powerful lock and without the key there is no way to open it. I know these things. I've *made* these things. They are designed to prevent thieves like him from entering."

"Ah," Esrahaddon said to the dwarf, "but you underestimate Royce. He is no ordinary lock picker. I sensed it the moment I first saw him. I know he can open it." The wizard turned to Royce, who was quickly showing signs of exasperation. "Stop *trying* to open it and just open it. Don't think about it. Just do it."

"Do what?" he asked, irritated. "If I knew how, don't you think I would have opened it by now?"

"That's just it; don't think. Stop being a thief. Just open the door."

Royce glared at the wizard. "Fine," he said as he pushed his palm against the stone wall and pulled it back with a look of shock on his face.

Esrahaddon's expression was one of sheer delight. "I knew it," the wizard said.

"Knew what? What happened?" Hadrian asked.

"I just pushed." Royce laughed at the absurdity.

"And?"

"What do you mean, *and*?" Royce asked, pointing at the solid wall.

"And what happened? Why are you smiling?" Hadrian studied the wall for something he missed, a tiny crack, a little latch, a keyhole, but he saw nothing. It was the same as it had always been.

"It opened," Royce said.

Hadrian and the dwarf looked at Royce, puzzled. "What are you talking about?"

Royce looked back over his shoulder as if that would make everything clear. "Are you both blind? The door is standing wide open. You can see there's a corridor that—"

"They can't see it," the wizard interrupted.

Royce looked from the wizard to Hadrian. "You can't see that the door is standing open now? You can't see this huge, three-story double door?"

Hadrian shook his head. "It looks just like it always has."

Magnus nodded his agreement.

"They can't see it because they can't enter," the wizard explained. Hadrian watched Royce look up, following the wizard's glance, and Royce's eyes widened.

"What?" Hadrian asked.

"Elven magic. Designed to prevent enemies from passing through these walls. All they see, and all they will encounter, is solid stone. The portal is closed to them."

"You can see it?" Royce asked Esrahaddon.

"Oh yes, quite plainly."

"So why is it we can see it and they can't?"

"I already told you, it is magic to stop enemies from entering. As it happens, I was invited into this tower nine hundred years ago. It was abandoned immediately after my visit, so I am guessing there was no one to revoke that permission." He looked back at what Hadrian still saw as solid stone. "I don't think I could have opened it, though, even if I had hands. That's why I needed you."

"Me?" Royce said; then a sudden shocked realization filled his expression and he glared at the wizard before him. "So you knew?"

"I wouldn't be much of a wizard if I didn't, now would I?"

Royce looked self-consciously at his own feet, then slowly turned to look cautiously at Hadrian, who only smiled. "You knew too?"

Hadrian frowned. "Did you really think I could work with you all these years and not figure it out? It is a little obvious, you know."

"You never said anything."

"I figured you didn't want to talk about it. You guard your past jealously, pal, and you have many doors on which I don't knock. Honestly, there were times I wondered if you knew."

"Knew what? What's going on?" Magnus demanded.

"None of your business," Hadrian told the dwarf, "but it does leave us with a parting of the ways, doesn't it? We can't come in, and I can tell you I am not fond of sitting here on the doorstep waiting for the flying lizard to come home."

"You should go back," Esrahaddon told them. "Royce and I can go on from here alone."

"How long will this take?" Hadrian asked.

"Several hours, a day perhaps," the wizard replied.

"I had hoped to be gone before it returned," Royce said.

"Not possible. Besides, this shouldn't be a problem for you, of all people. I am certain you have stolen from occupied homes before."

"Not ones where the owner can swallow me in a single bite."

"So we'll have to be extra quiet now, won't we?"

CHAPTER 10

LOST SWORDS

I thought last night went well," Bishop Saldur stated, slicing himself a wedge of breakfast cheese. He sat at the banquet table in the great hall of the manor along with Archbishop Galien, Sentinel Luis Guy, and Lord Rufus. The lofty cathedral ceiling of bound logs did little to elevate the dark, oppressive atmosphere caused by the lack of natural light. The entire manor had few windows and made Saldur feel as if he were crouching in an animal's den, some woodchuck's burrow or beaver's lodge. The thought that this miserable hovel would see the birth of the New Empire was a disappointment, but he was a pragmatic man. The method was irrelevant. All that mattered was the final solution. Either it worked or it did not—this was the only measure of value. Aesthetics could be added later.

Right now they needed to establish the empire. Mankind had drifted too long without a rudder. A firm hand was what the world needed, a solid grip on the wheel with a keen set of eyes that could see into the future and direct the vessel into clear, tranquil waters. Saldur envisioned a world of peace through prosperity, and security through strength. The feudal system so prevalent across the four nations held them back, chaining the kingdoms to a poverty of weakness and divided interests. What they needed was a centralized government with an enlightened ruler and a talented, educated bureaucracy overseeing every aspect of life. It was impossible to imagine the many goals that could be accomplished with the entire strength of mankind under one yoke. They could revolutionize farming, its fruits distributed evenly at a price that even the poorest could afford, vanquishing hunger. Laws could be standardized, eliminating arbitrary punishment by vindictive tyrants. Knowledge from the corners of the land could be gathered into a single repository where great minds could learn and develop new ideas, new techniques. They could improve transportation with standardized roads and they could clear the stench of cities with standardized sewage systems. If all this had to begin here in this little wood hut on the edge of the world, it was a small price to pay. "How many died?" he asked.

The archbishop shrugged and Rufus did not bother looking up from his plate.

"Five contestants were killed by the beast last night." Luis Guy answered his question as he plucked a muffin off the table with the point of his dagger.

The Knight of Nyphron continued to impress Saldur. He was a sword manifested in the form of a man—sharp, pointed, cutting, and just as elegant in appearance. He always stood straight, shoulders back, chin up, eyes focused directly on his target, his face a hard chiseled mask of contention, daring, almost begging for a confrontation from anyone fool enough to challenge him. Even after days in the wilderness, not a thread lay out of place. He was a paragon of the church, the embodiment of the ideal.

"Only five?"

"After the fifth was ripped in two, few were eager to step forward, and while they hesitated, the beast flew off."

"Do you think five deaths are sufficient to prove the beast is invincible?" Galien asked, looking at all of them.

"No, but we may have no choice. After last night, I'm not certain any more will volunteer," Guy replied. "The previously witnessed enthusiasm for the hunt has waned."

"And will you be ready, Lord Rufus? If no one else steps forward?" the archbishop asked, turning to the rough warrior seated at the end of the table.

Lord Rufus looked up. He was taking full advantage of the meal, chewing on a mutton leg that slicked his unruly beard with grease. His eyes stared at them from beneath the heavy hedges of his bushy red eyebrows. He spit a bit of bone out. "That depends," he said. "This sword the dwarf made, can it cut the beastie's hide?"

"We had our scribes check the dwarf's work against the ancient records," Saldur replied. "They match perfectly with the markings recorded on previous weapons that were capable of killing beasts of this kind."

"If it can cut it, I'll kill it." Rufus grinned a greasy smile. "Just be ready to crown me emperor." He bit into the leg again and ripped a large hunk of dark meat off, filling his mouth.

Saldur could hardly believe the Patriarch had chosen this oaf to be the emperor. If Guy was a sword, Rufus was a mallet, a blunt instrument of dull labor. Being a native of Trent, he would ensure the loyalty of the unruly northern kingdoms that most likely could not be gained any other way. That would easily double their strength going in. There was also his popularity, which extended down through Avryn and Calis. This reduced the number of protests against him. The fact that he was a renowned warrior would certainly help him in his first obstacles of killing the Gilarabrywn and crushing any opposition offered by the Nationalists. The problem, as Saldur saw it, was that Rufus, a rough, unreasonable dolt, had not only the heart of a warrior, but the mind as well. His answer to every problem was beating it to death. It would be hard to control him, but it made little sense to worry about the headaches of administrating an empire before one even existed. They needed to create it first and worry about the quality of the emperor later. If Rufus became a problem, they could merely ensure that once he had a son, and once that son was safe in their custody, Rufus could meet an untimely end.

"Well then," Galien said. "It would seem everything is in hand."

"Is that all you called me here for?" Guy asked with a tone of irritation.

"No," Galien replied, "I received some unexpected news this morning and I thought you might like to hear of it, Luis, as I suspect it will interest you very much. Carlton, will you ask the deacon Tomas to come in?"

Galien's steward, Carlton, who was busy pouring watered-down wine, promptly left the table and opened the door to the hallway. "His Grace will see you now."

In walked a plump, pudgy man in a priest's frock. "Luis Guy, Lord Rufus, let me introduce Deacon Tomas of Dahlgren Village. Tomas, this is Lord Rufus, Sentinel Guy, and you already know Bishop Saldur, of course."

Tomas nodded with a nervous smile.

"What's this all about?" Guy asked as if Tomas was not there.

"Go ahead, Tomas, tell the sentinel what you told me."

The deacon shifted his feet and avoided eye contact with anyone in the room. When he spoke, his voice was so soft they strained to hear him. "I was just mentioning to His Grace how I had stepped up and handled things here in the absence of the margrave. It has been hard times in this village, hard indeed, but I tried my best to keep the great house in order. It wasn't my idea that they should invade the place, I tried to stop them, but I am only one man, you see. It was impossible—"

"Yes, yes, tell him about the cripple," the archbishop put in.

"Oh, certainly. Ah yes, Esra came to live here, I don't know, about a month ago, he—"

"Esra?" Guy said, and glanced abruptly at the archbishop and Saldur, who both smiled knowingly at him.

"Yes," Deacon Tomas replied. "That's his name. He never said too much, but the villagers are a good lot and they took turns feeding him, as the poor man was in dire straits missing both hands as he is."

"Esrahaddon!" Guy hissed. "Where is the snake?"

The sudden violent reaction of the sentinel shocked Tomas, who took a step back.

"Ah, well, I don't know, he comes and goes, although I remember he was around the village a lot more before the two strangers arrived."

"Strangers?" Guy asked.

"Friends of the Wood family, I think. At least, they arrived with Thrace and spend a lot of time with her and her father. Since they got here, Esra spends most of his days off with the quiet one—Royce, I think they call him."

"Royce Melborn and Hadrian Blackwater, the two thieves that broke the wizard out of Gutaria, and Esrahaddon are all here in this village?" Saldur and Galien nodded at Luis.

"Very curious, isn't it?" the archbishop commented. "Perhaps we focused on the wrong hound when we approached Arista. It looks as if the old wizard has put his trust in the two thieves instead. The real question is, why would they all be here? It can't be coincidence that he turns up in this little backwater village at the precise moment when the emperor is about to be crowned."

"He couldn't know our plans," Guy told him.

"He *is* a wizard; they are good at discovering things. Regardless, you might want to see if you can determine what he's up to."

"Remember to keep your distance," Saldur added. "We don't want to tree this fox until we know he's led us to his den."

❧

Hadrian folded the blanket twice in length, then rolled it tight, buckling the resulting cloth log with two leather straps. He had all the gear left to them on the ground in neat piles. They still had all their camping gear, food, and feed. Royce had his saddle, bridle, and bags, but Hadrian had lost his tack along with his weapons when Millie had disappeared. It would be impossible to ride double and haul the gear. They would have to load Mouse up with everything and walk the trip home.

"There you are."

Hadrian looked up to see Theron striding from the direction of the Bothwicks', heading for the well with an empty bucket in his hand.

"We didn't see you around last night. Was worried something happened to you."

"Looks like everyone had a lucky night," Hadrian said.

"Everyone in the village—yeah. But I don't think them fellas up at the castle did so well. We heard a lot of shouting and screaming and they ain't celebrating this morning. My guess is their plan to kill the beast didn't go as hoped." The farmer scanned the piles. "Packing, eh? So you're leaving too?"

"I don't see why not. There's nothing keeping us here anymore. How's Thrace?"

"Doing well, rubbing elbows with the nobility, she tells me. She's walking around just fine; the headaches are mostly gone. We'll be on our way tomorrow morning, I expect."

"Good to hear it," Hadrian said.

"Who's your friend?" Theron motioned to the dwarf seated a few feet away in the shade of a poplar tree.

"Oh yeah. Theron, meet Magnus. He's not so much a friend as an associate." He thought about that and added, "Actually, he's more like an enemy I'm keeping an eye on."

Theron nodded, but with a puzzled look, and the dwarf grumbled something neither caught.

"What about my lesson?" Theron asked.

"Are you kidding? I don't really see the point in a lesson if you're both leaving tomorrow."

"You have something else to do? Besides, the road is a dangerous place and it wouldn't hurt to know a few more tricks, or is this your way of saying you want money now?"

"No." Hadrian waved his hand at the farmer. "Grab the sticks."

By noon, the sun was hot and Hadrian had worked up a sweat sparring with Theron, who was showing real improvement. Magnus sat on an overturned well bucket, watching the two with interest. Hadrian explained proper form, how to obtain penetrating thrusts and grips, which was hard using only rake handles.

"If you hold the sword with both hands, you lose versatility and reach, but you gain tremendous power. A good fighter knows when to switch from two hands to one and vice versa. If you are defending against someone with longer reach, you'd better be using one hand, but if you need to drive your sword deep through heavy armor—assuming you aren't holding a shield in your off hand—grip the pommel with both palms and thrust. Remember to yell as you do, like I taught you before. Then drive home the blow using all your power. A solid breastplate won't stop a sword thrust. They aren't designed to. Armor prevents a swing or a slice, and can deflect the point of a thrust; that's why professional fighters wear smooth, unadorned armor. You always see these princes and dukes with all their fancy gilded breastplates and light thin metal heavily engraved—it's like walking around in a death trap. Of course, they don't really fight. They have knights do that for them. They just walk around and look pretty. So the idea is when you thrust, you aim for a crease, groove, or seam in the armor, something that will catch and hold the tip. The armpits are excellent targets, or up under the nose guard. Drive a four-foot sword up under a nose guard and you don't have to worry much about a counterattack."

"How can you teach that poor fellow anything without swords?"

They both turned to see Mauvin Pickering walking toward them in his simple blue tunic. Gone was the dapper lord of Galilin; instead, he looked much like the boy Hadrian had first seen at Drondil Fields. In his hands, he carried two swords, and slung over his back were two small round shields.

"I saw you from the walls and thought you might like to borrow these," he said, handing a sword and shield to Theron, who accepted them awkwardly. "They are my and Fanen's spares."

Theron eyed the young man suspiciously, then looked to Hadrian.

"Go ahead," Hadrian told him, wiping the sweat from his brow with his sleeve. "He's right. You should know the feel of the real thing."

When Theron appeared confused by how to hold the shield, Mauvin began instructing him, showing the farmer where his arm slipped through the leather straps.

"See, Hadrian? It helps to actually teach your pupil how to put on a real shield; unless, of course, you expect he'll be spending all of his time warring against maple trees. Where are your weapons, anyway?"

Hadrian looked sheepish. "I lost them."

"Don't you carry enough for five people?"

"I've had a bad week."

"And who might you be?" Mauvin asked, looking at the dwarf.

Hadrian started to answer, then stopped himself. Alric had likely told Mauvin all about the dwarf who had murdered his father. "Him? He's...nobody."

"Okay..." Mauvin laughed, raising his hand and waving. "Pleased to meet you, Mr. Nobody." He then went and sat on the edge of the well, where he folded his arms across his chest. "Go on. Show me what he's taught you."

Hadrian and Theron returned to fighting, but slower now, as the sharp swords made Theron nervous. He soon became frustrated and turned to Mauvin, scowling.

"You any good with these things?"

The young man raised an eyebrow in surprise. "My dear sir, weren't we already introduced? My name is Mauvin Pickering." He grinned.

Theron narrowed his eyes in confusion, glanced at Hadrian, who said nothing, then faced the boy once more. "I asked if you knew how to use a sword, son, not your name."

"But—I—oh, never mind. Yes, I have been trained in the use of a sword."

"Well, I spent all my life on farms, or in villages not much bigger than this one, and I've never had much chance to see fellas beating each other with blades. It might help if'n I was to see what I'm s'posed to be doing. You know, all proper like."

"You want a demonstration?"

Theron nodded. "I have no way of knowing if Hadrian here even knows what he's doing."

"All right," Mauvin said, flexing his fingers and shaking his hands as he walked forward. He had a bright smile on his face, as if Theron had just invited him to play his favorite game.

The two paired off. Magnus and Theron took seats in the dirt and watched as Mauvin and Hadrian first walked through the basic moves and then demonstrated each at actual combat speed. Hadrian would explain each maneuver and comment on the action afterward.

"See there? Mauvin thought I was going to slice inward toward his thigh and dropped his guard briefly. He did that because I told him to by suggesting with a dip of my shoulder that this was my intention, so before I even started my stroke, I knew what Mauvin was going to do, because I was the one dictating it. In essence I knew what he would do before he did and in a battle that's very handy."

"Enough of the lessons," Mauvin said, clearly irritated at being the illustration of a fencing mistake. "Let's show him a real demonstration."

"Looking for a rematch?" Hadrian asked.

"Curious if it was luck."

Hadrian smiled and muttered, "Pickerings."

He took off his shirt and, wiping his face and hands, threw it on the grass and raised his sword to ready position. Mauvin lunged and immediately the two began to fight. The swords sang as they cut the air so fast their movements blurred. Hadrian and Mauvin danced around on the balls of their feet, shuffling in the dirt so briskly that a small cloud rose to knee height.

"By Mar!" the old farmer exclaimed.

Then abruptly they stopped, both panting from the exertion.

Mauvin glared at Hadrian with a look that was both amazed and irritated. "You're playing with me."

"I thought that was the point. You don't really want me to kill you?"

"Well no, but—well, like he said—by Mar! I've never seen anyone fight like you do; you're amazing."

"I thought you both were pretty amazing," Theron remarked. "I've never seen anything like that."

"I have to agree," Magnus chimed in. The dwarf was on his feet, nodding his head.

Hadrian walked over to the well and poured half a bucket over himself, then shook the water from his hair.

"Seriously, Hadrian," Mauvin asked, "where did you learn it?"

"From a man named Danbury Blackwater."

"Blackwater? Isn't that your name?"

Hadrian nodded and a melancholy look stole over his face. "He was my father."

"Was?"

"He died."

"Was he a warrior? A general?"

"Blacksmith."

"Blacksmith?" Mauvin asked in disbelief.

"In a village not much bigger than this. You know, the guy who makes horseshoes, rakes, pots."

"Are you telling me a village blacksmith knew the secret disciplines of the Teshlors? I recognized the Tek'chin moves, the ones my father taught me. The rest I can only assume were from the other lost disciplines of the Teshlors."

Mauvin drew blank stares from everyone.

"The Teshlors?" He looked around—more stares. He rolled his eyes and sighed. "Heathens, I'm surrounded by ignorant heathens. The Teshlors were the greatest knights ever to have lived. They were the personal bodyguards of the emperor. It's said they were taught the Five Disciplines of Combat from Novron himself. Only one of which is the

Tek'chin, and the knowledge of the Tek'chin alone is what has made a legend out of the Pickering dynasty. Your father clearly knew the Tek'chin, and apparently other Teshlor disciplines that I thought had been lost for nearly a thousand years, and you're telling me he was a blacksmith? He was probably the greatest warrior of his time. And you don't know what your father did before you were born?"

"I assume the same thing he did afterward."

"Then how did he know how to fight?"

Hadrian considered this. "I just assumed he picked it up serving in the local army. Several of the men in the village served His Lordship as men-at-arms. I assumed he saw combat. He used to talk like he had."

"Did you ever ask him?"

The thunder of hooves interrupted them as three men on horseback entered the village from the direction of the margrave's castle. The riders were all in black and red with the symbol of a broken crown on their chests. At their head rode a tall thin man with long black hair and a short trimmed beard.

"Excellent swordsmanship," the lead man said. He rode right up to Hadrian and reined in his animal roughly. The black stallion was draped in a scarlet and black caparison complete with braided tassels, a scarlet headpiece with a foot-tall black plume spouting from his head. The horse snorted and stomped. "I was wondering why the son of Count Pickering wasn't partaking in the combat today, but I see now you found a worthier partner to spar against. Who would this delightful warrior be and why haven't I seen you at the castle?"

"I'm not here to compete for the crown," Hadrian said simply, slipping on his shirt.

"No? Pity, you certainly appear to be worthy of a chance. What's your name?"

"Hadrian."

"Ah, good to meet you, Sir Hadrian."

"Just Hadrian."

"I see. Do you live here, *just* Hadrian?"

"No."

The horseman seemed less than pleased with the curt answer and nudged his horse closer in a menacing manner. The animal puffed out a hot moist breath into Hadrian's face. "Then what are you doing here?"

"Just passing through," Hadrian replied in his usual amiable manner. He even managed a friendly little smile.

"Really? Just passing through Dahlgren? To where in the world, might I ask, is Dahlgren on the way?"

"Just about everywhere, depending on your perspective, don't you think? I mean, all roads lead somewhere, don't they?" He was tired of being on the defensive and took a verbal swing. "Is there a reason you're so interested?"

"I'm Sentinel Luis Guy and I'm in charge of managing the contest. I need to know if everyone participating is listed."

"I already told you I wasn't here for the contest."

"So you did," Guy said, and slowly looked around at the others, taking particular notice of Magnus. "You are just passing through, you said, but perhaps those traveling with you wish to be listed on the roll."

A feint, perhaps? Hadrian decided to parry anyway. "No one I'm with will want to be on that list."

"No one you're with?"

Hadrian gritted his teeth. It *was* a feint. Hadrian mentally scolded himself.

"So you're not alone?" the sentinel observed. "Where are the others?"

"I couldn't tell you."

"No?"

Hadrian shook his head—fewer words, smaller chance of mistakes.

"Really? You mean they could be washing over the falls right now and you couldn't care less?"

"I didn't say that," Hadrian replied, irritated.

"But you see no need to know where they are?"

"They're grown men."

The sentinel smiled. "And who are *these men*? Please tell me so that I might inquire of them later perhaps."

Hadrian's eyes narrowed as he realized too late his mistake. The man before him was clever—too clever.

"Did you forget their names too?" Luis Guy inquired, leaning forward in his saddle.

"No." Hadrian tried to hold him off while he struggled to think.

"Then what are they?"

"Well," he began, wishing he had his own swords rather than a borrowed one. "Like I said, I don't know where *both* of them are. Mauvin is here, of course, but I have no idea where Fanen has gotten to."

"Surely you are mistaken. The Pickerings traveled with me and the rest of the entourage," Guy pointed out.

"Yes, they *were*, but they are planning on returning home with me."

Guy's eyes narrowed. "So you are saying that you traveled all the way out here *alone*—passing through, as you put it—and just happened to join up with the Pickerings?"

Hadrian smiled at the sentinel. It was weak, clumsy, and the fencing equivalent of dropping his sword and tackling his opponent to the ground, but it was all he could do.

"Is this true, Pickering?"

"Absolutely," Mauvin replied without hesitation.

Guy looked back at Hadrian. "How convenient for you," he said, disappointed. "Well, then don't let me keep you from your practice. Good day, gentlemen."

They all watched as the three men rode off toward the river trail.

"That was creepy," Mauvin remarked, staring off in their direction. "It can never be good when any sentinel takes an interest in you, much less Luis Guy."

"What's his story?" Hadrian asked.

"I really only know rumors. He's a zealot for the church, but I know many even in the church who are scared of him. He's the kind of person that can make kings disappear. He's also rumored to be obsessed with finding the Heir of Novron."

"Aren't all seret?"

"According to church doctrine, sure. But he really is, which explains why he's here."

"And the two with him?"

"Seret, the Knights of Nyphron, they are the sentinel's personal shadow army. They're answerable to no king or nation, just to sentinels and the Patriarch."

Mauvin looked at Hadrian. "You might want to keep that sword. It looks like a bad time to be without your weapons."

∽

Although he had put his lantern out long before the creature's return, Royce could see just fine. Light permeated the walls of Avempartha, seeping through the stone as if it were smoky glass. It was daylight outside, of that he was certain, as the color of light had changed from dim blue to soft white.

As the sun rose, the interior of the citadel became an illuminated world of wondrous color and beauty. Ceilings stretched in tall, airy arches, meeting hundreds of feet above the floor and giving the illusion of not being indoors at all but rather in a place where the horizon was merely lost in mist. The roar of the nearby cataracts, tamed by the walls of the tower, was a soft, muffled, undeniably soothing hum.

Thin gossamer banners hung from the lofty heights. Each shimmered with symbols Royce did not understand. They might have been standards of royalty, rules of law, directions to halls, or meaningless decorations. All Royce knew was that even in the wake of a thousand years, the detailed patterns still appeared fluid and vibrant. It was artistry beyond mortal hands, born of a culture unfathomable. Being the only elven structure Royce had ever entered, it was his only glimpse into that world and it felt oddly peaceful. Still and silent, it was beautiful. Although it looked nothing like anything Royce had ever seen, his reason fought against the growing sensation that somehow all this was familiar. Royce felt calm as he wandered the corridors. The very shapes and shadows touched chords in his mind he never realized were there. It all spoke to him in a language he could not understand. He caught only a word or a phrase in an avalanche of sensations that both mystified and captivated him as he wandered aimlessly, like a man blinded by a dazzling light.

He walked from room to room, up stairs and across balconies, following no conscious course, but merely moving, staring, and listening. Royce noticed with concern that every movement he made was recorded clearly in centuries of dust that blanketed the interior. Still, he was fascinated to discover that where he disturbed the dust, the floor revealed a glossy surface as clear as still water.

Passing through the various chambers, he felt as if he were in a museum, lost in a moment of frozen time. Plates were still out before empty chairs, some fallen on their sides—overturned in the confusion and alarm of nearly a millennium earlier. Books lay open to pages someone had been reading nine hundred years before, yet Royce knew that even to that person who had sat there so long ago, this place, this tower, had been ancient. Aside from its dramatic history, by its age alone Avempartha would be a monument—a sacred structure—to the elves, a link to an ancient era. This was not a citadel. He did not know how he knew, but he was certain this was something far more than a mere fortress.

Esrahaddon had left Royce almost immediately after entering the tower and pointing him in the direction he was now following. He had told Royce that he would find the sword he sought somewhere above the entrance, but that the wizard's path led elsewhere. It had been hours now since they had parted, and the light outside was already starting to dim. Royce still had not found the sword. Sights, sounds, and smells sidetracked him. It was too much to process at once, too much to classify, and soon he found himself lost.

He started to follow his trail in reverse when he discovered his footprints overlapped, leaving him a path that moved in circles. He was starting to become concerned when he heard a new sound. Unlike everything he had encountered so far, this noise was disturbing. It was the thick rhythmical resonance of heavy breathing.

Every path open to the thief was marred with his own tracks except one. This led to yet another stair, where the breathing was louder. How many floors up Royce had wandered, he was not certain, but he knew he had not come across any swords. Slowly, and as silently as he could, he began to creep upward.

He had not gone more than five steps when he spotted his first sword. It lay blanketed in dust on a step beside a bony form. What cloth there might have been was gone, but the armor remained. Farther up, he spotted another and yet another. There were two different types of bodies—humans in broad heavy breastplates and greaves, and elves in delicate blue armor. This was the last stand, the last defense to protect the emperor. Elves and men fallen one upon the other.

Royce reached down and slid his thumb along the flat of the blade at his feet. As the dust wiped clear, the amazing shine of the elven steel glimmered as if new, but no etching was on it. Royce looked up the stairs and reluctantly stepped over the bodies as he continued his climb.

The breathing grew louder and deeper, like wind blowing through an echoing cavern. A room lay ahead, and with the silence of a cat's shadow, Royce crept inside. The chamber was round with yet another staircase leading up. As he entered, he could feel and smell fresh air. Tall thin windows allowed unfettered shafts of light into the room, but Royce felt that somewhere above him a much larger window lay.

At last, Royce found a rack of elven swords mounted ceremoniously to the wall in ornate cases. Divided from the rest of the room by a delicate chain, the area appeared as a memorial, a remembrance set aside in honor. A plaque on a pedestal stood before the rack and on the walls were numerous lines of elven script carved into the stone. Royce knew only a few words and those before him had been written with such flair and embellishment that he was at a loss to recognize even a single word, although he was certain he recognized several letters.

On the rack were dozens of swords. They all appeared to be identical, and without having to touch them, Royce could see the etchings clearly cut into the blades and the notches hewn into the metal. One spot remained vacant.

With a silent sigh, he steadied himself and began to climb upward once more. With each step, the air grew fresher; currents banished dust to the cracks and corners. Along the stair, more openings and hallways appeared to either side, but Royce had a hunch and continued to climb, moving toward the sound of breathing.

At last, the steps ended and Royce looked up at open sky. Above him was a circular balcony with sculpted walls like petals on a flower. Statues that had once lined this open-air pavilion lay in broken heaps on the floor. At their center rested the malevolent sleeping figure of the Gilarabrywn, an enormous black-scaled lizard with wings of gray membrane and bone. It lay curled, its head on its tail, its body heaving with deep, long breaths. Muscular claws were armed with four twelve-inch-long black nails; encrusted with dried blood, they left deep groves in the surface of the floor where they scraped in the beast's sleep. Long sharp fangs protruded from beneath leathery lips, as did a row of frightening teeth that followed no visible scheme but seemed to mesh together like a wild fence of needles. Ears lay back upon its head, its eyes cloaked by broad lids, beneath which pupils darted about in a fretful slumber, of what dark visages Royce could not begin to imagine. The long tail, barbed at the end with a saber-like bone, twitched.

Royce caught himself staring and cursed at his own stupidity. It was a sight, to be certain, but this was no time to be distracted. Focus was all that separated him from certain death.

He had always hated places with animals. Hounds bellowed at the slightest sound or smell. He had managed to step past many a sleeping dog, but there had been a few that managed to sense him without warning. He mentally gripped himself and pulled his eyes away from the giant to study the rest of the room. It was a shambles, broken fixtures and rubble. On closer study, however, Royce noticed that the rubble held terrible treasures. He recognized torn bits of Mae Drundel's dress, matted with dark stains; and tangled within its folds was a bit of scalp and a long lock of gray hair. Other equally disturbing items lay around him. Arms, feet, fingers, hands, all cast aside like shrimp tails. He spotted Millie, Hadrian's bay mare, or rather one of her rear legs and her tail. Not too far away he was stunned to see Millie's saddle and Hadrian's swords. Luckily, they were within easy reach.

As he began to move around the pile, inching his way with the slow discipline of a mantis on the hunt, he saw something. The bodies and torn clothes lay atop the pile of bones and stone. But deep beneath, on the bottom stratum of built-up sediment, Royce caught the singular glint of mirrored steel. It was only a tiny patch, no larger than a small coin, which was what he initially took it for, but its brilliance was unmistakable. It possessed the same gleam as the swords on the stairs and in the rack below.

Barely breathing—each movement keyed to a painfully slow pace that might defy even a direct look—Royce stole closer to the beast and his vile treasure trove. He slipped his hand under the strands of Millie's tail and meticulously began to draw forth the blade.

It came loose with little effort or sound, but even before he had it free, Royce knew something was wrong. It was not heavy enough. Even given that elven blades might weigh dramatically less, it was ridiculously light. He soon realized why as he drew forth only part of a broken blade. Seeing the etching on the unnotched metal, Royce realized his hunch was correct. This Gilarabrywn was no animal, no dumb beast trained to kill. This conjured demon was self-aware enough to realize it had only one mortal fear in this world—a blade with its name on it. It took precautions. The monster had broken the blade, severing the name and rendering it useless. He could not see the other half of the sword, but it seemed obvious to him where it lay. The remainder of the sword rested in the one place from which Royce could not steal it—beneath the sleeping body of the Gilarabrywn itself.

CHAPTER 11

GILARABRYWN

It was nearing dusk when Royce, hauling three swords over his shoulder, found Hadrian and Magnus waiting at the well. The village was empty, its inhabitants holed up in their hovels, and the night was quiet except for the faint sounds of distant activity coming from the castle.

"It's about time," Hadrian said, jumping to his feet at Royce's approach.

"Here's your gear." Royce handed Hadrian his weapons. "Be careful next time where you stow it. I do have more important things to do than be your personal valet."

Hadrian happily took the swords and belts and began strapping them on. "I was starting to worry the church had grabbed you."

"Church?" Royce asked.

"Luis Guy was harassing me earlier."

"The sentinel?"

"Yeah. He was asking about my partners and rode off toward the river and I haven't seen him come back. I got the impression he might be fishing for Esra. Where is Esra, anyway? Did you leave him at the river?"

"He didn't stop back here?" Royce asked. They shook their

heads. "Doesn't mean anything; he'd be a fool to come back to the village. He's likely hiding in the trees."

"Assuming he didn't get swept away by the river," Hadrian said. "Why did you leave him?"

"He left me with a very *don't follow me* attitude, which under normal circumstances would ensure that I followed him, but I had other things on my mind. Before I knew it, the sun was going down. I thought he had already left."

"So did you find anything valuable inside? Gems? Gold?"

Royce suddenly felt stupid. "You know, it never even crossed my mind to look."

"What?"

"I completely forgot about it."

"So what did you do in there all day?"

Royce pulled the bare half blade from his belt. It gleamed even in the faint light. "All the other swords were in a neat display case, but I found this buried almost directly under the Gilarabrywn's foot."

"Its foot?" Hadrian said, stunned. "You saw it?"

Royce nodded with a grimace. "And trust me—it isn't a sight you want to see drunk or sober."

"You think *it* broke the blade?"

"Kinda makes you wonder, doesn't it?"

"So where's the other piece?"

"I'm guessing it's sleeping on it, but I wasn't about to try and roll it over to look."

"I'm surprised you didn't wait until it left."

"With our client leaving in the morning, what's the point? If it was an easy grab—if I could see it and didn't have to spend hours digging through…well, stuff—fine, but I'm not about to risk my neck for Esra's personal war with the church. Besides, remember the hounds in Blythin Castle?"

Hadrian nodded with a sick look on his face.

"If it can smell scents, I didn't want to be around when it wakes up. The way I see it, Thrace has her father, Esra has access to the tower, and Rufus will rid the village of the Gilar-abrywn. I say our work here is done." Royce looked at the dwarf, then back at Hadrian. "Thanks for keeping an eye on him." He drew his dagger.

"Wha—wait!" The dwarf backpedaled as Royce advanced. "We had a deal!"

Royce grinned at him. "Do I really look trustworthy to you?"

"Royce, you can't," Hadrian said.

The thief looked at him and chuckled. "Are you kidding? Look at him. If I can't slit his throat in ten seconds, tops, I'll buy you a beer as soon as we get back to Alburn. Tell me when you're ready to count."

"No, I meant he's right. You made a bargain with him. You can't go back on it."

"Oh please. This little...dwarf...tried to kill me and damn near succeeded, and you want me to let him go because I said I would? Hey, he lived a whole day longer for helping us. That's plenty reward."

"*Royce!*"

"*What?*" The thief rolled his eyes. "You aren't serious? He killed Amrath."

"It was a job, and you aren't a member of the royal guard. He upheld his end just as agreed. And there's no benefit to killing him."

"Enjoyment," Royce said. "Enjoyment and satisfaction are benefits."

Hadrian continued to glare.

Royce shook his head and sighed. "All right, okay, he can live. It's stupid, but he can live. Happy?"

Royce looked up at the great motte of the castle, where already the torches of that night's contestants were assembling. "It's nearly dark; we need to get inside. Where's the best seat for this dinner theatre I hear they've been holding at the castle? And when I say *best*, I mean *safest*."

"We still have an open invitation to the Bothwicks'. Theron is there now and we've been—"

A screeching cry from the direction of the river cut through the night.

"What in the land of Novron's ghost is that?" Magnus asked.

"You think maybe lizard wings found out his rattle was stolen?" Hadrian asked apprehensively.

Royce looked back toward the trees and then at his friend. "I think we'd better find a better place to hide tonight than the Bothwicks'."

"Where?" Hadrian asked. "If it comes looking for that blade, it will rip every house apart until it finds it, and we already know the local architecture doesn't pose much of a challenge. It's gonna kill everyone in the village."

"We could run them all to the castle; there might still be time," Royce suggested.

"No good," Hadrian countered. "The guards won't let us in. The forest, maybe?"

"The trees only slow it down. It won't stop it any more than the houses."

"Damn it." Hadrian looked around desperately. "I should have built the pit out in the village."

"What about the well here?" the dwarf asked, peering into the wooden-rimmed hole.

Royce and Hadrian looked at each other.

"I feel so stupid right now," Royce said.

Hadrian ran to the bell, grabbed hold of the dangling rope,

and began to pull it. The bell, intended for the future church of Dahlgren, raised the alarm.

"Keep ringing it," Hadrian yelled at Magnus as he and Royce raced to the houses, sweeping their cloth drapes aside and banging on the frames.

"Get out. Everyone out," they yelled. "Your houses won't protect you tonight. Get in the well. Everyone in the well now!"

"What's going on?" Russell Bothwick asked, peering out into the darkness.

"No time to explain," Hadrian shouted back. "Get in the well if you want to live."

"But the church? They are supposed to save us," Selen Brockton said, huddling in a blanket in the arch of her doorway.

"Are you willing to bet your life? You're all gonna have to trust me. If I am wrong, you'll spend one miserable night, but if I am right and you don't listen, you'll all die."

"That's good enough for me," Theron said, storming out of the Bothwick house, buttoning his shirt, his massive figure and loud harsh voice commanding everyone's attention. "And it had better be good enough for the lot of you too. Hadrian has done more to save this village from death in the past few days than all of us—and all of them—combined. If he says sleep in the well tonight, then by the beard of Maribor that's what I'll do. I don't care if the beast was known to be dead. I'd still do it, and any of you who refuse, why, you deserve to be eaten."

The inhabitants of Dahlgren ran to the well.

Loops were tied into the rope for footholds, and while the well was wide enough to lower four or even five people at a time, because they did not trust the strength of the windlass, they lowered them in groups of only twos and threes, depending on weight.

Although people moved quickly and orderly, obeying

Hadrian's instructions without argument, the process was excruciatingly slow. Magnus volunteered to go in and drive pegs into the walls to form footholds. Young Hal, Arvid, and Pearl, being too small to go down first, raced around the village fetching more shafts of wood for the dwarf to drive into the sides. Tad Bothwick went down and worked with Magnus, feeding him the wooden spikes as the little dwarf built makeshift platforms.

"Whoa, mister." Tad's voice echoed out of the mouth of the well. "I ain't never seen no one use a hammer like that. It took six weeks to build up these walls, and I swear you look like you coulda done it in six hours."

Outside, Hadrian, Theron, Vince, and Dillon did the work of lowering villagers in. Hadrian lined them up, sending women and children down first into the darkness, where only a single candle that Tad held for Magnus revealed anything below.

"How long?" Hadrian asked as they waited to lower the next set down.

"It would have been here by now if it had flown the moment we heard it," Royce replied. "It must be searching the tower. That gives us some time, but I don't know how much."

"Get up in a tree and yell when you see it."

When everyone was in, Hadrian lowered Theron and Dillon, leaving only Hadrian, Vince, and Royce aboveground, where they waited for Magnus to finish the last set of wall pegs. Up in a poplar tree, Royce stood out on a thin branch, scanning the sky while listening to the dwarf hammering the last stakes into place.

"Here it comes!" he shouted, spotting a shadow darting across the stars.

Seconds later the Gilarabrywn screamed from somewhere above the dark canopy of leaves and the three cringed, but nothing happened. They stood still, staring into the darkness around them, listening. Another cry ripped through the night. The Gilarabrywn flew straight for the torches of the manor house.

Royce spotted it in the night sky flying over the hill where the next challenger for the crown prepared to meet the beast. It descended, then rose once more. It issued another screech; then the beast let loose a roar and fire exploded from its mouth. Instantly, everything grew brighter as fire engulfed the hillside.

"That's new," Hadrian declared nervously as he watched the ghastly sight. The crowd of challengers lost their lives with hardly the time to scream. "Magnus, hurry!"

"All set. Go! Climb down," the dwarf shouted back.

"Wait!" Tad cried. "Where's Pearl?"

"She's looking for wood," Vince said. "I'll get her."

Hadrian grabbed his arm. "It's too dangerous; get in the well. Royce will go."

"I will?" Royce asked, surprised.

"It's lousy being the only one to see in the dark sometimes, isn't it?"

Royce cursed and ran off, pausing in homes and sheds to call the little girl's name as loudly as he dared. It got easier to see his way as the light from the hill grew larger and brighter. The Gilarabrywn screamed repeatedly and Royce looked over his shoulder to see the castle walls engulfed in flames.

"Royce," Hadrian shouted, "it's coming!"

Royce gave up stealth. "Pearl!" he yelled aloud.

"Here!" she screamed, darting out from the trees.

He grabbed the little girl up in his arms and raced for the well.

"Run, damn it!" Hadrian shouted, holding the rope for them.

"Forget the rope. Get down and catch her."

While Royce was still sprinting across the yard, Hadrian slid down the coil.

Thrump. Thrump. Thrump.

Hugging Pearl close to his chest, Royce reached the well and jumped. The little girl screamed as they fell in together. An instant later, there came a loud unearthly scream and a terrible vibration as the world above the well erupted in a brilliant light accompanied by a thunderous roar.

⌁

Arista paced the length of the little room, painfully aware of Bernice's head turning side to side, following her every move. The old woman was smiling at her; she always smiled at her, and Arista was about ready to gouge her eyes out. She was used to her tower, where even Hilfred gave her space, but for more than a week, she had been subjected to constant company—Bernice, her ever-present shadow. She had to get out of the room, to get away. She was tired of being stared at, of being watched after like a child. She walked to the door.

"Where are you going, Highness?" Bernice was quick to ask.

"Out," she said.

"Out where?"

"Just out."

Bernice stood up. "Let me get our cloaks."

"I am going alone."

"Oh no, Your Highness," Bernice said, "that's not possible."

Arista glared at her. Bernice smiled back. "Imagine this, Bernice: you sit back down and I walk out. It is possible."

"But I can't do that. You are the princess and this is a dangerous place. You need to be chaperoned for your own safety. We'll need Hilfred to escort us, as well. Hilfred," she called.

The door popped open and the bodyguard stepped in, bowing to Arista. "Did you need something, Your Highness?"

"No—yes," Arista said, and pointed at Bernice, "keep her here. Sit on her, tie her up, hold her at sword point if you must, but I am leaving and I don't want her following me."

The old maid looked shocked and put both hands to her cheeks in surprise.

"You're going out, Your Highness?" Hilfred asked.

"Yes, yes, I am going out!" she exclaimed, throwing her arms up. "I may roam the halls of this cabin. I may go to watch the contest. Why, I might even leave the stockade altogether and wander into the forest. I could get lost and die of starvation, eaten by a bear, tumble into the Nidwalden and get swept over the falls—but I'll do so alone."

Hilfred stood at attention. His eyes stared back at hers. His mouth opened and then closed.

"Is there something you want to say?" she asked, her tone harsh.

Hilfred swallowed. "No, Your Highness."

"At least take your cloak," Bernice insisted, holding it up.

Arista sighed, snatched it from her hands, and walked out.

The moment she left, regret set in. Storming down the corridor, dragging the cloak, she paused. The look on Hilfred's face left her feeling miserable. She recalled having a crush on him as a girl. He was the son of a castle sergeant, and he used to stare at her from across the courtyard. Arista had thought he was cute. Then one morning she had awoken to fire and smoke. He saved her life. Hilfred had been just a boy, but he had run into the flaming castle to drag her out. He spent two months suffering from burns and coughing fits that caused him to spit up blood. For weeks he awoke screaming from nightmares. As a reward, King Amrath appointed Hilfred to the prestigious post of personal bodyguard to the princess.

But she had never thanked him, nor forgiven him for not saving her mother. Her anger was always between them. Arista wanted to apologize, but it was too late. Too many years had passed, too many cruelties, followed by too many silences like the one that had just hung between them.

"What's going on?" Arista heard Thrace's voice and walked toward it.

"What's wrong, Thrace?" The princess found the farmer's daughter and the deacon in the main hallway. The girl was dressed in her thin chemise nightgown. They both looked concerned.

"Your Highness!" the girl called to her. "Do you know what is happening? Why was the bell ringing?"

"The contest is starting soon, if that's what you mean. I was on my way to watch. Are you feeling better? Would you like to come?" Arista found herself asking. She was aware of the irony, but being with Thrace was not the same as being escorted by Bernice and Hilfred.

"No, you don't understand. Something must be wrong. It's dark. No one would ring the bell at night."

"I didn't hear a bell," Arista said, pulling the cloak over her shoulders.

"The village bell," Thrace replied. "I heard it. It has stopped now."

"It's probably just part of the combat announcement."

"No." Thrace shook her head, and the deacon mimicked her. "That bell is only rung in emergencies, dire emergencies. Something is terribly wrong."

"I'm sure it's nothing. You forget. There is practically an army outside just itching for their chance to fight. Anyway, we certainly can't find out standing here." Arista took Thrace's hand and led them out to the courtyard.

Because it was the second night, the event had moved into

full extravagance. Outside, the high grassy yard of the manor's hill was set up like a pavilion at a tournament joust. The raised mound of the manor's motte offered a perfect view of the field below. Colorful awnings hung stretched above rows of chairs with small tables holding steins of mead, ale, and bowls of berries and cheese. The archbishop and Bishop Saldur sat together near the center, while several other clergy and servants stood watching the distant action unfolding on the hillside beyond the castle walls.

"Oh, Arista, my dear," Saldur called to her, "come to see history being made, have you? Good. Have a seat. That's Lord Rufus out there on the field. It seems he tires of waiting for his crown, but the vile beast is late in showing this evening and I think it is making His Lordship a tad irritated. Do you see how he paces his stallion? So like an emperor to be impatient."

"Who is to come after Rufus?" Arista asked, remaining on her feet, looking down at the field below.

"After?" Saldur looked puzzled. "Oh, I'm not sure, actually. Well, I hardly think it matters. Rufus will likely win tonight."

"Why is that?" Arista asked. "It isn't a matter of skill really, is it? It is a matter of bloodline. Is Lord Rufus suspected of bearing some known ties to the imperial family?"

"Well, yes, as a matter of fact he has claimed such for years now."

"Really?" Arista questioned. "I have never heard of him ever making such a boast."

"Well, the church doesn't like to promote unproven theories or random claims, but Rufus is indeed a favorite here. Tonight will prove his words, of course."

"Excuse me, Your Grace?" Tomas said with a bow. He and Thrace stood directly behind Arista, both still appearing as nervous as mice. "Do you happen to know why the village bell was rung?"

"Hmm? What's that? The bell? Oh that, I have no idea. Perhaps some quaint method the villagers use to call people to dinner."

"But, Your Grace—" Tomas was cut off.

"There," Saldur shouted, pointing into the sky as the Gilarabrywn appeared and swooped into the torchlight.

"Oh, here we go!" the archbishop shouted excitedly, clapping his hands. "Everyone pay attention to what you see here tonight, for surely many people will ask how it came to be."

The beast descended to the field and Lord Rufus trotted forward on his horse, which he had had the foresight to blind with a cloth bag to prevent it from witnessing the pending horror. With his sword held aloft, he shouted and spurred his mount forward.

"In the name of Novron, I—the true heir—smite thee." Rufus rose in the stirrups and thrust at the beast, which seemed startled by the bold confidence of the knight.

Lord Rufus struck the chest of the creature, but the blow glanced away uselessly. He struck again and again, but it was like striking stone with a stick. Lord Rufus looked shocked and confused. Then the Gilarabrywn slew Rufus and his horse with one casual swipe of a claw.

"Oh dear lord!" the archbishop cried, rising to his feet in shock. A moment later the shock turned to horror as the beast cast out its wings and, rising, bathed the hillside in a torrent of fire. Those in the yard staggered backward, spilling drinks and knocking over chairs. One of the pavilion legs toppled and the awning fell askew as people began to rush about.

With the hillside alight, the beast turned toward the castle and, rising higher, let forth another blast that exploded the wooden stockade walls into sheets of flame. The fire spread from dry log to dry log until the flames swept fully around, ringing the castle. It did not take long for those buildings close to the walls, those roofed with thatch, to catch, and soon the bulk of the lower castle and even the walls surrounding the manor house were burning. With the light of fire surrounding them, it was impossible to see where the Gilarabrywn had gone. Blind as to the whereabouts of the flying nightmare, and feeling the intensity of the heat growing all around them, the servants, guards, and clerics alike scattered in terror.

"We need to get to the cellar!" Tomas shouted, but amidst the screams and the roar of the flames devouring the wood, few heard him. Tomas took hold of Thrace and began to pull her back toward the manor. With her free hand Thrace grabbed Arista's arm, and Tomas pulled both back up the slope.

In shock, Arista put up no resistance as they dragged her from the yard. She had never experienced anything like this. She saw a man on fire running down the slope screaming, thrashing about as flames spiraled up his body. A moment later, he collapsed, still burning. There were others, living pyres racing blindly about the yard in ghastly brilliance, one by one collapsing on the grass. By instinct, Arista looked for the protection of Hilfred, but somewhere in her soup-like mind, she remembered she had ordered him to remain on guard in her room. He would be looking for her now.

Thrace held her arm in a vise grip as the three moved in a human chain. To her left she saw a soldier attempt to breach the wall. He caught on fire and joined the throng of living torches, screaming as his clothes and skin burned away. Somewhere not far off where the fire had spread to the forest, a tree trunk exploded with a tremendous crack. It rattled the building.

"We have to get down in the cellar," Tomas insisted. "Quickly! Our only hope is to get underground. We need—"

Arista felt her hair blowing in a sudden wind.

Thrump. Thrump.

Deacon Tomas began praying aloud as out of the smoke-clouded night sky, the Gilarabrywn descended upon them.

CHAPTER 12

SMOKE AND ASH

Crawling out of the well into the gray morning light, Hadrian entered an alien world. Dahlgren was gone. Only patches of ash and some smoldering timber marked the missing homes, but even more startling was the absence of trees. The forest that had hugged the village was gone. In its place was a desolate plain, scorched black. Limbless, leafless poles stood at random, tall dark spikes pointing at the sky. Fed by smoldering piles, smoke hung in the air like a dull gray fog, hiding the sky behind a hazy cloud from which ash fell silently like dirty snow, blanketing the land.

Pearl came out of the well. Not surprisingly, she said nothing as she wandered about the scorched world, stooping to turn over a charred bit of wood, then staring up at the sky as if surprised to find it still there now that the world had been cast upside down.

"How did this happen?" Russell Bothwick asked no one in particular, and no one answered.

"Thrace!" Theron yelled as he emerged from the well, his eyes focusing on the smoking ruins atop the hill. Soon everyone was running up the slope.

Like the village, the castle was a burned-out hull; the walls were gone, as were the smaller buildings. The great manor house was a charred pile. Bodies lay scattered, blackened by fire, torn and twisted. The corpses still smoked.

"Thrace!" Theron cried in desperation as he dug furiously into the pile of rubble that had been the manor house. All of the village men, along with Royce, Hadrian, and even Magnus, dug in the debris, more out of sympathy than hope.

Magnus directed them to the southeast corner, muttering something about the earth speaking with a hollow voice. They cleared away walls and a fallen staircase and heard a faint sound below. They dug down, revealing the remains of the old kitchen and the cellar beneath.

As if from the grave itself, they pulled forth Deacon Tomas, who looked battered but otherwise unharmed. Just as the villagers had, Tomas wiped his eyes, squinting in the morning light at the devastation around him.

"Deacon!" Theron shook the cleric. "Where is Thrace?"

Tomas looked at the farmer and tears welled in his eyes. "I couldn't save her, Theron," he said in a choked voice. "I tried, I tried so hard. You have to believe me, you must."

"What happened, you old fool?"

"I tried. I tried. I was leading them to this cellar, but it caught us. I prayed. I prayed so hard, and I swear it listened! Then I heard it laugh. It actually *laughed*." Tomas's eyes filled with tears. "It ignored me and took them."

"Took them?" Theron asked frantically. "What do you mean?"

"It spoke to me," Tomas said. "It spoke with a voice like death, like pain. My legs wouldn't hold me up anymore and I fell before it."

"What did it say?" Royce asked.

The deacon paused to wipe his face, leaving dark streaks of soot on his cheeks. "It didn't make sense, perhaps in my fear I lost my mind."

"What do you *think* it said?" Royce pressed.

"It spoke in the ancient speech of the church. I thought it said something about a weapon, a sword, something about trading it for the women. Said it would return tomorrow night for it. Then it flew away with Thrace and the princess. It doesn't make any sense at all, I'm probably mad now."

"The princess?" Hadrian asked.

"Yes, the princess Arista of Melengar. She was with us. I was trying to save them both—I was trying to—but—and now..." Tomas broke down crying again.

Royce exchanged looks with Hadrian and the two quickly moved away from the others to talk. Theron promptly followed.

"You two know something," he said accusingly. "You got in, didn't you? You took it. Royce got the sword after all. That's what it wants."

Royce nodded.

"You have to give it back," the farmer said.

"I don't think giving it back will save your daughter," Royce told him. "This thing, this Gilarabrywn, is a lot more cunning than we knew. It will—"

"Thrace hired you to bring me that sword," Theron growled. "That was your job. Remember? You were supposed to steal it and give it to me, so hand it over."

"Theron, listen—"

"Give it to me now!" the old farmer shouted as he towered menacingly over the thief.

Royce sighed and drew out the broken blade.

Theron took it with a puzzled look, turning the metal over in his hands. "Where's the rest?"

"This is all I could find."

"Then it will have to do," the old man said firmly.

"Theron, I don't think you can trust this creature. I think

even if you hand this over, it will still kill your daughter, the princess, and you."

"It's a risk I am willing to take!" he shouted at them. "You two don't have to be here. You got the sword—you did your job. You're done. You can leave anytime you want. Go on, get out!"

"Theron," Hadrian began, "we are not your enemy. Do you think either of us wants Thrace to die?"

Theron started to speak, then closed his mouth, swallowed, and took a breath. "No," he sighed, "you're right. I know that. It's just..." He looked into Hadrian's eyes with an expression of horrible pain. "She's all I've got left, and I won't stand for anything that can get her killed. I'll trade myself to the bloody monster if it will let her live."

"I know that, Theron," Hadrian said.

"I just don't think it will honor the trade," Royce said.

"We found another over here!" Dillon McDern shouted as he hauled the foppish scholar Tobis Rentinual out of the remains of the smokehouse. The skinny courtier, covered from head to foot in dirt, collapsed on the grass, coughing and sputtering.

"The soil was soft in the cellar..." Tobis managed, then sputtered and coughed. "We—dug into it with our—with our hands."

"How many?" Dillon asked.

"Five," Tobis replied, "a woodsman, a castle guard, I think, Sir Erlic, and two others. The guard—" Tobis entered into a coughing fit for a minute, then sat up, doubled over, and spat on the grass.

"Arvid, fetch water from the well!" Dillon ordered his son.

"The guard was badly burned," Tobis continued. "Two young men dragged him to the smokehouse, saying it had a cellar. Everything around us was on fire except the smoke-house, so the woodsman, Sir Erlic, and I all ran there too. The dirt floor was loose, so we started burrowing. Then something hit the shed and the whole thing came down on us. A beam caught my leg. I think it's broken."

The villagers excavated the collapsed shed. They pulled off a wall and dug into the wreckage, peeling back the fragments. They reached the bottom, where they found the others buried alive.

They dragged them out into the light. Sir Erlic and the woodsman looked near dead as they coughed and spat. The burned guard was worse. He was unconscious, but still alive. The last two pulled from the smokehouse ruins were Mauvin and Fanen Pickering, who, like Tobis, were unable to speak for a time but, other than numerous cuts and bruises, were all right.

"Is Hilfred alive?" Fanen asked after having a chance to breathe fresh air and drink a cup of water.

"Who's Hilfred?" Lena Bothwick asked, holding the cup of water Verna had brought. Fanen pointed to the burned guard across from him and Lena nodded. "He's not awake, but he's alive."

Search parties spread out and combed the rest of the area, finding many more bodies, mostly those of would-be contes-tants. They also discovered the remains of Archbishop Galien. The old man appeared to have died not from fire, but from being trampled to death. His servant, Carlton, lay inside the manor, apparently not content to die by his master's side. Arista's handmaid, Bernice, was also found inside the manor, crushed when the house collapsed. They found no one else alive.

The villagers created stretchers to carry Tobis and Hilfred

out of the smoky ruins to the well, where the women tended their wounds. The old common green was a charred patch of black. The great bell, having fallen, lay on its side in the ash.

"What happened?" Hadrian asked, sitting down next to Mauvin. The two brothers huddled where Pearl had once grazed pigs. Both sat hunched, sipping from cups of water, their faces stained with soot.

"We were outside the walls when the attack came," he said, his voice soft, not much louder than a strained whisper. He hooked his thumb at his brother. "I told him we were going home, but Fanen, the genius that he is, decided he wanted his shot at the beast, his chance at glory."

Fanen drooped his head lower.

"He tried to sneak out, thought he'd give me the slip. I caught him outside the gate and a little way down the hill. I told him it was suicide; he insisted; we got into a fight. It ended when we saw the hill catch on fire. We ran back. Before we reached the front gate, a couple of carriages and a bunch of horses went by at full gallop. I spotted Saldur's face peeking out from one of the windows. They didn't even slow down.

"We went looking for Arista and found Hilfred on the ground just out front of the burning manor house. His hair was gone, skin coming off in sheets, but he was still breathing, so we grabbed him and just ran for the smokehouse. It was the last building still standing that wasn't burning. The dirt floor was soft and loose, like it had recently been dug up, so we just started burrowing with our hands like moles, you know. That Tobis guy, Erlic, and Danthen followed us in. We only managed to dig a few feet when the whole thing came down on us."

"Did you find Arista?" Fanen asked. "Is she..."

"We don't know," Hadrian replied. "The deacon says it took her and Theron's daughter. She might still be alive."

The women of the village tended the wounds of those found at the castle while the men began gathering what supplies, tools, and food stores they could find into a pile at the well. They were a motley bunch, haggard and dirty, like a band of shipwrecked travelers left on a desert island. Few of them spoke, and when they did, it was always in whispered tones. From time to time, villagers would weep softly, kick a scorched board, or merely wander off a ways only to drop to their knees and shake.

When, at last, the men were bandaged and the supplies stacked, Tomas, who had cleaned himself up, stood and said a few words over the dead, and they all observed a moment of silence. Then Vince Griffin stood up and addressed them.

"I was the first to settle here," he said with a sad voice. "My house stood right there, the closest to this here well. I remember when most of you were considered newcomers, strangers even. I had great hopes for this place. I donated eight bushels of barley every year to the village church, though all I seen come of it was this here bell. I stayed here through the hard frost five years ago and I stayed here when people started to go missing. Like the rest a' you, I thought I could live with it. People die tragically everywhere, be it from the pox, the plague, starvation, the cold, or a blade. Sure, Dahlgren seemed cursed, and maybe it is, but it was still the best place I'd ever lived. Maybe the best place I ever will live, mostly because of you all and the fact that the nobles hardly ever bothered us, but all that's over now. There's nothing here no more, not even the trees that was here before we came, and I don't fancy spending another night in the well." He wiped his eyes clear. "I'm leaving Dahlgren. I s'pose many a' you will be too, and I just wanted to say that when you all came here, I saw you as strangers, but as I am leaving, I feel I'm gonna be saying goodbye to family, a family that has gone through a lot together. I...I just wanted you all to know that."

They all nodded in agreement and exchanged muttered conversations with the people nearest them. It was decided by all that Dahlgren was dead and that they would leave. There was talk about trying to stay together, but it was only talk. They would travel as a group, including Sir Erlic and the woodsman Danthen, south at least as far as Alburn, where some would turn west, hoping to find relatives, while others would continue south, hoping to find a new start.

"So much for the church's help," Dillon McDern said to Hadrian. "They were here two nights and look."

Dillon and Russell Bothwick walked over to where Theron sat against a blackened stump.

" 'Spect you'll be staying to find Thrace?" Dillon asked.

Theron nodded. The big man had not bothered to wash and he was coated in dirt and soot. He had the broken blade on his lap and stared at it.

"You think it'll be back tonight, do ya?" Russell asked.

"I think so. It wants this. Maybe if I give it back, it will give Thrace to me."

The two men nodded.

"You want us to stay behind and give you a hand?" Russell asked.

"A hand with what?" the old farmer asked. "Nothing you can do, either of ya. Go on, you both have families of your own. Get out while you can. Enough good people have died here."

The two men nodded again.

"Good luck to you, Theron," Dillon said.

"We'll wait awhile in Alburn to see if you show up," Russell told him. "Good luck."

Russell and Tad fashioned a sled from charred saplings and loaded what little they had on it. Lena mashed up a salve, which she applied to Hilfred's burns, and left it and a pile of bandages with Tomas, who took it on himself to stay with the soldier. And so it was that with only a few things to pack up and carry with them, the bulk of the villagers were on their way westward by early afternoon. No one wanted to be anywhere near Dahlgren after sunset.

⚓

"What are we doing here?" Royce asked Hadrian as the two sat on a partially burned tree trunk. They were just up the old village path from the well, near where the Caswells' two little wooden grave markers used to be. Like everything else, they were gone, nothing left to mark their passing. Hadrian and Royce could see Deacon Tomas sitting with Hilfred, who still lay unconscious.

"This job has cost us two horses and over a week's worth of provisions, and for what?" Royce went on, and with a sigh broke off a bit of charred bark and absently tossed it. "We should head out with the rest of them. The girl is likely dead already. I mean, why would it keep her alive? The Gilarabrywn holds all the cards. It can kill us at will, but we can't harm it. It has hostages, while all we have is half a sword that it doesn't really need but apparently would just like to have. If we had both parts of the sword, Magnus could put them back together and we could at least bargain from a position of some strength. We could even have the dwarf make us all swords, and maybe even spears with the right name on it. Then we could have a go at the bastard, but right now, we have nothing. We are no threat to it at all. Theron thinks he's going to bargain, but he doesn't have anything to bargain with. The Gilarabrywn set this up only to save itself the tedium of hunting for that sword."

"We don't know that."

"Sure we do. It won't keep those girls alive. It probably had them for lunch already, and when night comes, old Theron will be standing out there like a fool with exactly what it wants. He'll die and that will be that. On the other hand, his stupidity will buy time for the rest of us to get away. Considering his whole family is gone and his daughter is most likely already dead, it's probably for the best."

"He won't be standing there alone," Hadrian said.

Royce turned with a sick look on his face. "Tell me you're joking."

Hadrian shook his head.

"Why?"

"Because you're right; because everything you just said will happen if we leave."

"And you think if we stay, it will be different?"

"We've never quit a job before, Royce."

"What are you talking about? What job?"

"She paid us to get the sword for her."

"I got the sword. Her old man's got it right now."

"Only part of it, and the job won't be finished until he has both parts in his hands. That's what we were hired to do."

"Hadrian." Royce ran a hand over his face and shook his head. "For the love of Maribor, she paid us *ten silver*!"

"You accepted it."

"I hate it when you get like this." Royce stood suddenly, picking up a charred piece of scrap. "Damn it." He threw it into a pile of smoking wood that had once been the Bothwicks' home. "You're just going to get us killed, you know that, right?"

"You don't have to stay. This is my decision."

"And what are you going to do? Fight it when it comes? Are you going to stand there in the dark swinging swords that can't hurt it?"

"I don't know."

"You're insane," Royce told him. "The rumors are all true; Hadrian Blackwater is a damn loon!"

Hadrian stood to face his friend. "I'm not going to abandon Theron, Thrace, and Arista. And what about Hilfred? Do you think he can travel? You try dragging him through the woods and he'll be dead before nightfall, or do you want to try stuffing him in the well all night and think he'll be just fine in the morning? And what about Tobis? How far do you think he'll get on a broken leg? Or don't you give a damn about them? Has your heart gotten so black you can just walk away and let them all die?"

"They will all die anyway," Royce snapped at him. "That's just my point. We can't stop it from killing them. All we can do is decide whether to die with them or not, and I really don't see the benefit in sympathy suicide."

"We can do something," Hadrian asserted. "We're the ones who stole the treasure from the Crown Tower and put it back the very next night. The same two that broke into the invincible Drumindor, we put a human head in the Earl of Chadwick's lap while he slept in his tower, and busted Esrahaddon out of Gutaria, the most secure prison ever built. I mean, we can do *something*!"

"Like what?"

"Well..." Hadrian thought. "We can dig a pit, lure it there, and trap it."

"We'd have better luck asking Tomas to pray for Maribor to strike the Gilarabrywn dead. We really don't have the time or the manpower for excavating a pit."

"You have a better idea?"

"I'm sure I could come up with something better than luring it into a pit we can't dig."

"Like what?"

Royce began walking around the still smoldering stick forest, angrily kicking anything in his path. "I don't know, you're the one who thinks we can do something, but I know one thing: we can't do squat unless we can get the other half of that sword. So the first thing I would do is steal it tonight while it's gone."

"It would kill Thrace and Arista for certain if you did that," Hadrian pointed out.

"But then you could kill it. At least there would be the closure of revenge."

Hadrian shook his head. "Not good enough."

Royce smirked. "I could always steal the sword while you and Theron fool it with the blade Rufus was using." Royce allowed himself a morbid chuckle. "There's at least about a single chance in a million that might work."

Hadrian's brow furrowed in thought, and he sat down slowly.

"Oh no, I was joking," Royce said, backpedaling. "If it could tell the blade was missing last night, it can tell the difference between the real thing and a copy."

"But even if it doesn't work," Hadrian said, "it might give me time to get the girls away from it. Then *we* could dive in a hole—a small hole that we do have time to dig."

"And hope it doesn't dig us out? I've seen its claws; it won't be hard."

Hadrian ignored him and went on with his train of thought. "Then you could bring the other half of the sword, have Magnus forge it, and then I can kill it. See, it was a good thing you didn't kill him after all."

"You realize how stupid this is, right? That thing decimated this whole village and the castle last night, and you are going to take it on with an old farmer, two women, and a broken sword?"

Hadrian said nothing.

Royce sighed and sat down beside his friend, shaking his head. He reached into his robe and pulled his dagger out. He held it out in its sheath.

"Here," he said, "take Alverstone."

"Why?" Hadrian looked at him, puzzled.

"Well, I'm not saying Magnus is right, but, well, I've never found *anything* that this dagger can't cut, and if Magnus is right, if the father of the gods did forge this, I would think it could come in handy even against an invincible beast."

"So you're leaving?"

"No." Royce scowled and looked in the direction of the tower of Avempartha. "Apparently I have a job to finish."

Hadrian smiled at his friend, took the dagger, and weighed it in his hand. "I'll give it back to you tomorrow, then."

"Right," Royce replied.

⤝

"Did your partner leave?" Theron asked as Hadrian approached him, walking up the slope of the scorched hill that had once been the castle. The old farmer stood on the blackened hillside, holding the shattered sword and looking up at the sky.

"No—well, sort of. He's headed back inside Avempartha to steal the other half of the sword just in case the Gilarabrywn tries to double-cross us. There is even a chance it might leave Thrace and Arista in the tower while it comes here, and if it does, Royce can get them out."

Theron nodded thoughtfully.

"You two have been real good to me and my daughter. I still don't know why, and don't tell me it's the money." Theron sighed. "You know, I never gave her credit for much. I ignored her, pushed her away for so many years. She was only my daughter, not a son—an extra mouth to feed that would cost us money to marry off. How she ever found the two of you and got you to come all this way to help us is…well, I just don't think I'll ever understand that."

"Hadrian," Fanen called to him. "Come down here and see what we've got."

Hadrian followed Fanen down the hill to the north edge of the burn line, where he found Tobis, Mauvin, and Magnus working on a huge contraption.

"This is my catapult," Tobis declared, standing proudly next to a wagon on which a wooden machine sat. Tobis looked comical in his loud-colored court clothes, propped up on a crutch Magnus had fashioned for him, his broken leg strapped down between two stiff pieces of wood. "They dragged it out here when I was bumped from the roster. She's exquisite, isn't she? I named her Persephone after Novron's wife. Only fitting, I thought, since I studied ancient imperial history to devise it. Not easy to do either. I had to learn the ancient languages just to read the books."

"Did you just build this?"

"No, of course not, you silly man. I am a professor at Sheridan. That's in Ghent, by the way. You know, the same place as the seat of the Nyphron Church? Well, being brilliant, I bribed some church officials, who let slip the true nature of the competition. It would not be a ridiculous bashing match between sawdust-filled heads, but a challenge to defeat a legendary creature. This was a puzzle I could solve, one that I knew did not require muscle and a lack of teeth, but rather a staggering intellect such as mine."

Hadrian walked around the device. A massive center beam rose a good twelve feet, and the long thick arm was a foot or two longer than that. It had a sack bucket joined to a lower beam with torsion-producing cords. On either side of the wagon were two massive hand cranks connected to a series of gears.

"Well, I must say, I have seen catapults before and this doesn't look much like them."

"That's because I modified it for fighting the Gilarabrywn."

"Well, he tried," Magnus added. "It wouldn't have worked the way he had it set up, but it will now."

"In fact, we fired a few rocks already," Mauvin reported.

"I've had some experience with siege weapons before," Hadrian said. "And I know they can be useful against something big, like a field of soldiers, or something that doesn't move, like a wall, but they're useless against a solitary moving enemy. They just aren't that fast or accurate."

"Yes, well, that's why I devised this one to fire not only projectiles but nets as well," Tobis said proudly. "I'm very clever that way, you see. The nets are designed to launch like large balls that open in mid-flight and snare the beast as it is flying, dropping it to the ground, where it will lie helpless while I reload and take my time crushing it."

"And this works?" Hadrian asked, impressed.

"In theory," Tobis replied.

Hadrian shrugged. "What the heck, it couldn't hurt."

"Just need to get it in position," Mauvin said. "Care to help push?"

They all put their backs to the catapult, except, of course, for Tobis, who limped along spouting orders. They rolled it to the ditch that ringed the bottom of the motte and within range to fire on anything in the area near the old manor house.

"Might want to get something to hide it—rubble or burnt

wood, maybe, so that it looks like a pile of trash," Hadrian said. "Which shouldn't be hard to do. Magnus, I was wondering if you could do me a favor."

"What kind?" he asked as Hadrian led him back up the hill toward the ruins of the manor house. The grass was gone, and they walked on a surface of ash and roots that made Hadrian think of warm snow.

"Remember that sword you made for Lord Rufus? I found it, still with him and his horse on the hill. I want you to fix it."

"Fix it?" The dwarf looked offended. "It's not my fault the sword didn't work; I did a perfect replica. The records were likely at fault."

"That's fine, because I have the original, or part of it, at least. I need you to make an exact copy of what we have. Can you do it?"

"Of course I can, and I will, in return for your getting Royce to let me look at the Alverstone."

"Are you crazy? He wants you dead. I saved your neck from him once already. Doesn't that count?"

The dwarf stood firm, his arms crossed over the braids in his beard. "That's my price."

"I'll talk to him, but I can't guarantee it."

The dwarf pursed his lips, which made his beard and mustache bristle. "Very well. Where are these swords?"

Theron agreed to the plan as long as he got the piece back, and brought the broken blade to the manor's smithy, which now consisted of no more than the brick forge and the anvil. He would hold the blade during the exchange and hand it over immediately should the ruse be discovered.

"Hrumph!" The dwarf looked disgusted.

"What?" Hadrian asked.

"No wonder it didn't work. There are markings on both sides. There's this whole other inscription. See, this is the incantation, I bet." The dwarf showed Hadrian the blade, where a seemingly incomprehensible spiderweb of thin sweeping lines formed a long design. Then he flipped it over to reveal a significantly shorter design on the back. "And this side, I'm guessing, holds the name that Esrahaddon mentioned. It makes sense that all the incantations are the same; only the name is unique."

"Does that mean you can create a weapon that will work?"

"No, it's broken right along the middle of the name, but I can make an awfully good copy of this, at least."

The dwarf removed his tool belt, hidden beneath his clothes, and laid it on the anvil. He had a number of hammers of different sizes and shapes, and chisels all in separate loops. He unrolled a leather apron and tied it on. Then he took Rufus's sword and strapped it to the anvil.

"Carry those everywhere, do you?" Hadrian asked.

"You won't catch me leaving them on a horse's saddle," Magnus replied.

Hadrian and Theron began digging a pit on the side of the courtyard. They dug it on the site of the old smokehouse, making use of the already turned soil to ease their effort. Without a shovel, they used old boards that left their hands black. Within a couple of hours, they had a small hole big enough for the two of them to get down fully under the earth. It was not deep enough to avoid being dug up, but it might hide them from a blast of fire as long as it did not come straight down. If it did, they would be like a couple of clay pots fired in sand.

"Won't be long now," Hadrian told Theron as the two men sat covered in dirt and ash, looking up at the fading light. Magnus was using his smallest hammer, tapping away with a resounding *tink, tink*. He muttered something, then pulled a heavy cloth from a pouch on his belt and began rubbing the surface of the metal.

Hadrian looked out over the trees, feeling Alverstone inside his tunic. He wondered if Royce had made it to the tower. *Is he inside? Has he found Esrahaddon? Can the old wizard do anything to help them?* He thought of the princess and Thrace. *What has it done with them?* He bit his lip. Royce was probably right. *Why would it keep them alive?*

The sound of horses approached from the south. Theron and Hadrian exchanged surprised looks and stood up to see a troop of riders racing out of the trees. Eight horsemen crossed the desolate plain, knights in black armor with a standard of a broken crown flying before them. Leading them was Luis Guy in his red cassock.

"Look who is finally back." Hadrian looked over at Magnus. "You done yet?"

"Just polishing," the dwarf replied. He then noticed the riders for the first time. "This can't be good," he grumbled.

The riders trotted into the remains of the courtyard and pulled up at the sight of them. Guy surveyed the smoldering ruins of the old castle for a moment, then dismounted and walked toward the dwarf, pausing to pick up a burnt bit of timber, which he turned over twice in his hands before tossing it away. "It would seem Lord Rufus didn't do as well last night as we hoped. Did you forget to dot an *i*, Magnus?"

Magnus took a frightened step back. Theron stepped forward quickly, grabbed the original broken blade, and hid it under his shirt.

Guy noticed the act but ignored the farmer and faced the dwarf. "Care to explain yourself, Magnus, or shall I just kill you for lousy workmanship?"

"Wasn't my fault. There were markings on the other side that none of the pictures showed. I did what you asked; your research was to blame."

"And what are you up to now?"

"He's duplicating the blade so we can use it to trade with the Gilarabrywn," Hadrian explained.

"Trade?"

"Yes, the creature took the princess Arista and a village girl. It said if we return the blade we took from its lair, it will free the women."

"It *said*?"

"Yes," Hadrian confirmed. "It spoke to Deacon Tomas last night just before he watched it take the women."

Guy laughed coldly. "So the beast is talking now, is it? And abducting women too? How impressive. I suppose it also rides horses and I should expect it to be representing Dunmore at the next Wintertide joust in Aquesta."

"You can ask your own deacon if you don't believe me."

"Oh, I believe you," he said, walking up to face Hadrian. "At least the part about stealing a sword from the citadel. That is what you're referring to, isn't it? So, someone actually got into Avempartha and took the real sword? Clever, particularly when I know that only someone with elvish blood can enter that tower. You don't look very elf-like to me, Hadrian. And I know the Pickerings' heritage quite well. I also know Magnus here couldn't get in. That leaves only your partner in crime, Royce Melborn. He's rather small, isn't he? Slender, agile? Those qualities would certainly serve him well as a thief. He can see easily in the dark, hear better than any human, has uncanny balance, and is so light on his feet that he can move in almost total silence. Yes, it would be most unfair to all the other poor thieves out there using their normal, human abilities."

Guy looked around carefully. "Where is your partner?" he asked, but Hadrian remained silent. "That's one of the biggest problems we have; some of these crossbred elves can pass for human. They can be so hard to spot sometimes. They don't have the pointed ears, or the squinty eyes, because they take after their human parent, but the elven parent is always there. That's what makes them so dangerous. They look normal, but deep down they are inhumanly evil. You probably don't even see it. Do you? You are like those fools that try and tame a bear cub or a wolf, thinking that they will come to love you. You probably think that you can banish the wild beast that lurks inside. You can't, you know. The monster is always there, just looking for the chance to leap out at you."

The sentinel glanced at the anvil. "And I suppose one of you was planning on using the sword to kill the beast and claim the crown of emperor?"

"Actually, no," Hadrian replied. "Getting the women and running real fast was more the plan."

"And you expect me to believe that? Hadrian Blackwater, the consummate warrior who handles a blade like a Teshlor Knight of the Old Empire. You really expect me to believe that you're just passing through this remote village? That you just happen to be in possession of the only weapon that can kill the Gilarabrywn at the precise moment in time when the emperor will be chosen by the one who does so? No, of course not, you are just using what is arguably the most powerful sword in the world to make a trade with an insanely dangerous, but now talking, monster, for a peasant girl and the Princess of Melengar, whom you barely know."

"Well—when you put it that way, it does sound bad, but it's the truth."

"The church will be returning to continue the trials here," Luis Guy told them. "Until then, it is my job to make certain no one who is, shall we say, unworthy of the crown kills the Gilarabrywn. That most certainly includes a thieving elf-lover and his band of cutthroats." Guy walked over to Theron. "So I'll have that blade you're holding."

"Over my dead body," Theron growled.

"As you wish." Guy drew his sword and all seven seret dismounted and drew their blades as well.

"Now," Guy told Theron, "give me the blade or both of you will die."

"Don't you mean all four?" a voice behind Hadrian said, and he looked over to see Mauvin and Fanen coming up the slope, spreading out, each with his sword drawn. Mauvin held two, one of which he tossed to Theron, who caught it clumsily.

"Make that five," Magnus said, holding two of his larger hammers in his hands. The dwarf looked over at Hadrian and swallowed hard. "He's planning on killing me anyway, so why not?"

"There are still eight of us," Guy pointed out. "Not exactly an even fight."

"I was thinking the same thing," Mauvin said. "Sadly, there's no one else here we can ask to join your side."

Guy looked at Mauvin, then Hadrian, for a long moment as the men glared across the ash at each other. Then he nodded and lowered his blade. "Well, I can see I'll have to report your misconduct to the archbishop."

"Go ahead," Hadrian said. "His body is buried with the rest of them just down the hillside."

Guy gave him a cold look, then turned to walk away, but as he did, Hadrian noticed his shoulder dip unnaturally to his right and his foot pivot, toe out, as he stepped. It was a motion Hadrian had taught Theron to watch for, the announcement of an attack.

"Theron!" he shouted, but it was unnecessary. The farmer had already moved and raised his sword even before Guy spun. The sentinel thrust for his heart. Theron was there a second faster and knocked the blade away. Then, out of reflex, the farmer shifted his weight forward, took a step, and performed the combination move Hadrian had drilled into him: parry, pivot, and riposte. He thrust forward, extending, going for reach. The sentinel staggered. He twisted and narrowly avoided being run through the chest, taking the sword thrust in his shoulder. Guy cried out in agony.

Theron stood shocked at his own success.

"Pull it out!" Hadrian and Mauvin both yelled at him.

Theron withdrew the blade and Guy staggered back, gripping his bleeding shoulder.

"Kill them!" the sentinel shouted through clenched teeth.

The Seret Knights charged.

Four Knights of Nyphron attacked the Pickering brothers. One rushed Hadrian, another launched himself at Theron, and the last took Magnus. Hadrian knew Theron would not last long against a skilled seret. He drew both his short sword and the bastard and slew the first Knight of Nyphron the moment he came within range. Then he stepped in the path of the second. The knight realized too late he was walking into a vise of two attackers as both Hadrian and Theron cut him down.

Magnus held up his hammers as menacingly as he could, but the little dwarf was clearly no match for the knight, and he retreated behind his anvil. As the seret got nearer, he threw one hammer at him, which hit the seret in the chest. It rang off his breastplate, causing no real harm, but it staggered him slightly. Realizing that the dwarf was no threat, the seret turned to face Hadrian, who raced at him.

The seret swung down in an arc at Hadrian's head. Hadrian caught the blade with the short sword in his left hand, holding the knight's sword arm up as he drove his bastard sword into the man's unprotected armpit.

Mauvin and Fanen fought together against the four attackers. The elegant rapiers of the Pickerings flew—catching, blocking, slicing, slamming—every attack turned back, every thrust blocked, every swing answered. Yet the two brothers could only defend. They stood their ground against the onslaught of the armored knights, who struggled to find a weakness. Mauvin finally managed to find a moment to jump to the offense and slipped in a thrust. The tip of his blade stabbed into the throat of the seret, dropping him with a rapid jab, but no sooner had he done so than Fanen cried out.

Hadrian watched as a seret sliced Fanen across his sword arm, the blade continuing down to his hand. The younger Pickering's sword fell from his fingers. Defenseless, Fanen desperately stepped backward, retreating from his two opponents. He tripped on the wreckage and fell. They rushed him, going for the kill.

Hadrian was too many steps away.

Mauvin ignored his own defense to save his brother. He thrust out. In one move, he blocked both attacks on Fanen—but at a cost. Hadrian saw the seret standing before Mauvin thrust. The blade penetrated Mauvin's side. Instantly the elder Pickering buckled. He fell to his knees with his eyes still on his brother. He could only watch helplessly as the next blow came down. Two swords entered Fanen's body. Blood coated the blades.

Mauvin screamed, even as his own assailant began his killing blow, a cross slice aimed at Mauvin's neck. Mauvin, on his knees, ignored the stroke, much to the delight of the seret. What the knight did not see was Mauvin did not need to defend. Mauvin was done defending. He thrust his sword upward, slicing through the attacker's rib cage. He twisted the blade as he pulled it out, ripping apart the man's organs.

The two who had killed his brother turned on Mauvin. The elder Pickering raised his sword again but his side was slick with blood, his arm weak, eyes glassy. Tears streamed down his cheeks. He was no longer focusing. His stroke went wide. The closest knight knocked Mauvin's sword away and the two remaining seret stepped forward and raised their swords, but that was as far as they got. Hadrian had crossed the distance and Mauvin's would-be killers' heads came loose, their bodies dropping into the ash.

"Magnus, get Tomas up here fast," Hadrian shouted. "Tell him to bring the bandages."

"He's dead," Theron said as he bent over Fanen.

"I know he is!" Hadrian snapped. "And Mauvin will be too if we don't help him."

He ripped open Mauvin's tunic and pressed his hand to his side as the blood bubbled up between his fingers. Mauvin lay panting, sweating. His eyes rolled up in his head, revealing their whites.

"Damn you, Mauvin!" Hadrian shouted at him. "Get me a cloth. Theron, get me anything."

Theron grabbed one of the seret who had killed Fanen and tore off his sleeve.

"Get more!" Hadrian shouted. He wiped Mauvin's side, finding a small hole spewing bright red blood. At least it was not the dark blood, which usually meant death. He took the cloth and pressed it against the wound.

"Help me sit him up," Hadrian said as Theron returned with another strip of cloth. Mauvin was a limp rag now. His head slumped to one side.

Tomas came running up, his arms filled with long strips of cloth that Lena had given him. They lifted Mauvin, and Tomas tightly wrapped the bandages around his torso. The blood soaked through the cloth, but the rate of bleeding had slowed.

"Keep his head up," Hadrian ordered, and Tomas cradled him.

Hadrian looked over at where Fanen lay. He was on his back in the dirt, a dark pool of blood still growing around his body. Hadrian gripped his swords with blood-soaked hands and stood up.

"Where's Guy?" he shouted through clenched teeth.

"He's gone," Magnus answered. "During the fight, he grabbed a horse and ran."

Hadrian stared back down at Fanen and then at Mauvin. He took a breath and it shuddered in his chest.

Tomas bowed his head and said the Prayer of the Departed:

> *"Unto Maribor, I beseech thee*
> *Into the hands of god, I send thee*
> *Grant him peace, I beg thee*
> *Give him rest, I ask thee*
> *May the god of men watch over your journey."*

When he was done, he looked up at the stars and in a soft voice said, "It's dark."

CHAPTER 13

ARTISTIC VISION

Arista did not want to breathe. It caused her stomach to tighten and bile to rise in her throat. Above her stretched the star-filled sky, but below—the pile. The Gilarabrywn built its mound, like a nest, from collected trophies, gruesome souvenirs of attacks and kills. The top of a head with dark matted hair, a broken chair, a foot still in its shoe, a partially chewed torso, a blood-soaked dress, an arm, so pale it was blue, reaching up out of the heap as if waving.

The pile rested on what looked to be an open balcony on the side of a high stone tower, but there was no way off. Instead of a door leading inside, there was only an archway, an outline of a door. Such false hope teased Arista as she longed for it to be a real door.

She sat with her hands on her lap, not wanting to touch anything. There was something underneath her, long and thin like a tree branch. It was uncomfortable, but she did not dare move. She did not want to know what it really was. She tried not to look down. She forced herself to watch the stars and look out at the horizon. To the north, the princess could see the forest, divided by the silvery line of the river. To the south lay large expanses of water that faded into darkness. Something out of the corner of her eye would catch her attention and she would look down. She always regretted it.

Arista realized with a shiver that she had slept on the pile, but she had not fallen asleep. It had felt like drowning—terror so absolute that it had overwhelmed her. She could not recall the flight she must have taken, or most of the day, but she did remember seeing it. The beast had lain inches away, basking in the afternoon sun. She had stared at it for hours, not able to look at anything else—her own death sleeping before her had a way of demanding her complete attention. She sat, afraid to move or speak. She was expecting it to wake and kill her—to add her to the pile. Muscles tense, heart racing, she locked her eyes on the thick scaly skin that rippled with each breath, sliding over what looked like ribs. She felt as if she were treading water. She could feel the blood pounding in her head. She was exhausted from not moving. Then the drowning came over her once more and everything went mercifully black.

Now her eyes were open again, but the great beast was missing. She looked around. There was no sign of the monster.

"It's gone," Thrace told her. It was the first either of them had spoken since the attack. The girl was still dressed in her nightgown, the bruises forming a dark line across her face. She was on her hands and knees, moving through the pile, digging like a child in a sandbox.

"Where is it?" Arista asked.

"Flew away."

Somewhere nearby, somewhere below, she heard a roar. It was not the beast. The sound was constant, a rumbling hum.

"Where are we?" she asked.

"On top of Avempartha," Thrace answered without looking up from her macabre excavation. She dug down beneath a layer of broken stone and turned over an iron kettle, revealing a torn tapestry, which she began tugging.

"What is Avempartha?"

"It's a tower."

"Oh. What are you doing?"

"I thought there might be a weapon, something to fight with."

Arista blinked. "Did you say 'to fight with'?"

"Yes, maybe a dagger, or a piece of glass."

Arista would not have believed it possible if it had not happened to her, but at that moment, as she sat helplessly, trapped on a pile of dismembered bodies, waiting to be eaten, she laughed.

"A piece of glass? A piece of glass?" Arista howled, her voice becoming shrill. "You're going to use a dagger or a piece of glass to fight—*that thing*?"

Thrace nodded, shoving the antlered head of a buck aside.

Arista continued to stare openmouthed.

"What have we got to lose?" Thrace asked.

That was it. That summed up the situation perfectly. The one thing they had going for them was that it could not get worse. In all her days, even when Percy Braga had been building the pyre to burn her alive, even when the dwarf had closed the door on her and Royce as they dangled from a rope in a collapsing tower, it had not been worse than this. Few fates could compare to the inevitability of being eaten alive.

Arista fully shared Thrace's belief, but something in her did not want to accept it. She wanted to believe there was still a chance.

"You don't think it will keep its promise?" she asked.

"Promise?"

"What it told the deacon."

"You—you could understand it?" the girl asked, pausing for the first time to look at her.

Arista nodded. "It spoke the old imperial language."

"What did it say?"

"Something about trading us for a sword, but I might have gotten it wrong. I learned Old Speech as part of my religious studies at Sheridan and I was never very good at it, not to mention I was scared. I'm still scared."

Arista saw Thrace thinking and envied her.

"No," the girl said at last, "it won't let us live. It kills people. That's what it does. It killed my mother and brother, my sister-in-law, and my nephew. It killed my best friend, Jessie Caswell. It killed Daniel Hall. I never told anyone this before, but I thought I might marry him one day. I found him near the river trail one beautiful fall morning, mostly chewed, but his face was still fine. That's what bothered me the most. His face was perfect, not a scratch on it. He just looked like he was sleeping under the pines, only most of his body was gone. It will kill us."

Thrace shivered with the passing wind.

Arista slipped off her cloak. "Here," she said. "You need this more than I do."

Thrace looked at her with a puzzled smile.

"Just take it!" she snapped. Her emotions breached the surface, threatening to spill. "I want to do *something*, damn it!"

She held out the cloak with a wavering arm. Thrace crawled over and took it. She held it up, looking at it as if she were in the comfort of a dressing room. "It's very beautiful, so heavy."

Again Arista laughed, thinking how strange it was to fly from despair to laughter in a single breath. One of them was surely insane—maybe they both were. Arista wrapped it around the young girl as she clasped it on. "And here I was ready to kill Bernice—"

Arista thought of Hilfred and the maid left—no, ordered—to stay in the room. Had she killed them?

"Do you think anyone survived?"

The girl rolled aside a statue's head and what looked like a broken marble tabletop. "My father is alive," Thrace said simply, digging deeper.

Arista did not ask how she knew this, but believed her. At that moment, she would believe anything Thrace told her.

With a nice hole dug into the heart of the debris, Thrace had yet to find a weapon beyond a leg bone, which she set aside with grisly indifference, to use in case she found nothing better, Arista guessed. The princess watched the excavation with a mix of admiration and disbelief.

Thrace uncovered a beautiful mirror that was shattered, and struggled to free a jagged piece, when Arista saw a glint of gold and pointed, saying, "There's something under the mirror."

Thrace pushed the glass aside and, reaching down, grabbed hold and drew forth the hilt half of a broken sword. Elaborately decorated in silver and gold encrusted with fine sparkling gems, the pommel caught the starlight and sparkled.

Thrace took the sword by the grip and held it up. "It's light," she said.

"It's broken," Arista replied, "but I suppose it's better than a piece of glass."

Thrace stowed the hilt in the lining pocket of the cloak and went on digging. She came across the head of an axe and a fork, both of which she discarded. Then, pulling back a bit of cloth, she stopped suddenly.

Arista hated to look but once more felt compelled.

It was a woman's face—eyes closed, mouth open.

Thrace placed the cloth back over the hole she had made. She retreated to the far edge and sat down, squeezing her knees while resting her head. Arista could see her shaking and Thrace did not dig anymore after that. The two sat in silence.

Thrump. Thrump.

THEFT OF SWORDS

Arista heard the sound and her heart raced. Every muscle in her body tightened and she dared not look. A great gust of air struck from above as she closed her eyes. She heard it land and waited to die. Arista could hear it breathing and still she waited.

"*Soon,*" she heard it say.

Arista opened her eyes.

The beast rested on the pile, panting from the effort of its flight. It shook its head, spraying the platform with loose saliva from its lips, which failed to hide the forest of jagged teeth. Its eyes were larger than Arista's hand, with tall narrow pupils on a marbled orange and brown lens that reflected her own image.

"*Soon?*" She didn't know where she found the courage to speak.

The massive eye blinked and the pupil dilated as it focused on her. It would kill her now, but at least it would be over.

"*Thou know'st my speech?*" The voice was large and so deep she felt it vibrating her chest.

She both nodded and said, "*Yes.*"

Across from her, the princess could see Thrace with her head up off her knees, staring.

The beast looked at Arista. "*Thou art regal.*"

"*I am a princess.*"

"*The best bait,*" the Gilarabrywn said, but Arista was not sure she heard that right. It might also have said, "The greatest gift." The phrase was difficult to translate.

She asked, "*Wilt thou honor thy trade or kill us?*"

"*The bait stays alive until I catch the thief.*"

"*Thief?*"

"*The taker of the sword. It comes. I crossed the moon to deceive it that the way 'twas clear, and have returned flying low. The thief comes now.*"

"What's it saying?" Thrace asked.

"It said we are bait to catch a thief that stole a sword."

"Royce," Thrace said.

Arista stared at her. "What did you say?"

"I hired two men to steal a sword from this tower."

"You hired Royce Melborn and Hadrian Blackwater?" Arista asked, stunned.

"Yes."

"How did you—" She gave that thought up. "It knows Royce is coming," Arista told her. "It pretended to fly away, letting him see it leave."

The Gilarabrywn's ears perked up, suddenly tilting forward toward the false door. Abruptly, but quietly, it stood and, with a gentle flap of its wings, lifted off. Catching the thermals, the beast soared upward above the tower. Thrace and Arista heard movement somewhere below, footsteps on stone.

A figure appeared in a black cloak. It stepped forward, passing through the solid stone of the false door, like a man surfacing from below a still pond.

"It's a trap, Royce!" Arista and Thrace shouted together.

The figure did not move.

Arista heard the whispered sound of air rushing across leathery wings. Then a brilliant light abruptly burst forth from the figure. Without a sound or movement, it was as if a star appeared in place of the man, the light so bright it blinded everyone. Arista closed her eyes in pain and heard the Gilarabrywn screech overhead. She felt frantic puffs of air beat down on her as the beast flapped its wings, breaking its dive.

The light was short-lived. It faded abruptly though not entirely and soon they could all see the man in the shimmering robe before them.

"*YOU!*" The beast cursed at him, shaking the tower with its voice. It hovered above them, its great wings flapping.

"Escaped thy cage beast of Erivan, hunter of Nareion!" Esrahaddon shouted in Old Speech. *"I shall cage thee again!"*

The wizard raised his arms, but before he made another move, the Gilarabrywn screeched and fluttered back in horror. It beat its great wings and rose, but in that last second, it reached down with one talon, snatching Thrace off the tower. It dove over the side, vanishing from sight. Arista raced to the railing, looking down in horror. The beast and Thrace were gone.

"We can do nothing for her," the wizard said sadly. She turned to see Esrahaddon and Royce Melborn beside her, both looking over the edge into the dark roar of the river below. "Her fate lies with Hadrian and her father now."

Arista's hands squeezed the railing stiffly. She felt the drowning sensation again. Royce grabbed her by the wrist. "Are you all right, Your Highness? It's a long way down, you know."

"Let's get her downstairs," Esrahaddon said. "The door, Royce. The door."

"Oh right," the thief replied. *"Grant entry to Arista Essendon, Princess of Melengar."*

The archway became a real door that stood open. They all entered a small room. Off the pile, safe behind walls, Arista felt the impact at last and she was forced to sit before she fell.

She buried her face in her hands and wailed, "Oh god, dear Maribor. Poor Thrace!"

"She may yet be all right," the wizard told her. "Hadrian and her father are waiting with the broken sword."

She rocked as she cried but she did not cry only for Thrace. The tears were the bursting of a dam that could resist the flood no longer. In her mind flashed images of Hilfred and that last unspoken word; of Bernice and the cruel way she had treated her; and of Fanen and Mauvin, all of them lost. So much sorrow could not be put into words; instead, the emotions exploded out of her as she shouted, "The sword, what sword? What is all of this about a sword? I don't understand!"

"You explain," Royce said. "I need to find the other half."

"It's not there," Arista told him.

"What?"

"You said the sword was broken?" Arista asked.

"In two parts. I stole the blade half yesterday; now I need to get the hilt half. I'm pretty certain it is in that pile up there."

"No it isn't," Arista said, shocked that her brain was still working enough to connect the dots. "Not anymore."

◈

The wizard led the way down the long crystalline steps, pausing from time to time to peer down a corridor, or at a staircase. He would think for a moment, then shake his head and push on, or mutter, "Ah, yes!" and turn.

"Where are we?" she asked.

"Avempartha," the wizard replied.

"I got that much already. What *is* Avempartha? And don't say it's a tower."

"It is an elven construction, built several millennia ago. More recently it has been a trap that has held the Gilarabrywn, and more recently still, it has apparently been its nest. Does that help?"

"Not really."

Although perplexed, Arista did feel better. It surprised her how easy it was to forget. It felt wrong. She should be thinking about the ones lost. She should be grieving, but her mind fought against it. Like broken limbs that refused to support any more weight, her heart and mind were hungry for relief. She needed a rest, something else to think about, something that did not involve death and misery. The tower of Avempartha provided the remedy. It was astounding.

Esrahaddon led them up and down stairs, through great rooms, and across interior bridges that spanned between spire shafts. Not a torch or lantern burned, but she could see perfectly, the walls themselves giving off a soft blue light. Vaulted ceilings a hundred feet high spread out like the canopy of a forest, with intricately lined designs that suggested branches and leaves. Railings, appearing as curling tendrils of creeping vines, sculptured from solid stone in vivid detail, ran along walkways and down steps. Nothing was without adornment, every inch imbued with beauty and care. Arista walked with her mouth open, her eyes shifting from one wonder to the next—a giant statue of a magnificent swan taking flight, a bubbling fountain in the shape of a school of fish. She recalled the crude barbarity of King Roswort's castle and his disdain for the elves—beings he likened to rats in a woodpile. *Some woodpile.*

There was a music to this place. The muted humming of the falls created a low, comforting bass. The wind across the tips of the tower played as woodwinds in an orchestra—soft reassuring tones. The bubbling and trickling of fountains lent light, satisfying rhythms to the symphony. Into this harmony crashed the voice of Esrahaddon as he recounted his first visit to the tower centuries before and how he had trapped the beast inside.

"So since you trapped the Gilarabrywn nine hundred years ago," she said, "you plan to trap it here again?"

"No," Esrahaddon told her. "No hands, remember? I can't cast that powerful of a binding spell without fingers, girl; you should know that better than anyone."

"I heard you threaten to cage it again."

"The Gilarabrywn doesn't know Esra doesn't have hands, does it?" Royce put in.

"The beast remembered me," the wizard said, taking over. "It assumed I was just as powerful as before, which means aside from the sword, I am about the only thing the Gilarabrywn fears."

"You just wanted to scare it off?"

"That was the idea, yes."

"We were trying to get the sword and hoped we might also save the both of you in the process," Royce told her. "I obviously didn't expect it to grab Thrace, and there was absolutely no way I could have guessed she would have taken the sword with her. You're certain she took a sword hilt from the pile?"

"Yes, I was the one who spotted it, but I still don't understand. How does the sword help? The Gilarabrywn isn't an enchantment; it's a monster that the heir must kill and ..."

"You've been listening to the church. The Gilarabrywn *is* a magical creation. The sword is the countermeasure."

"A sword is? That doesn't make sense. A sword is metal, a physical element."

Esrahaddon smiled, looking a bit surprised. "So you paid attention to my lessons. Excellent. You're right, the sword is worthless. It is the word written on the blade that has the power to dispel the conjuration. If it is plunged into the body of the beast, it will unlock the elements holding it in existence and break the enchantment."

"If only you had been the one to take it, we'd have a way to fight the thing."

"Well, you did save me, at least," Arista reminded them. "Thank you."

"Don't thank us too soon. It's still out there," Royce told her.

"Okay, so Thrace hired Royce—I don't know how that transpired, but okay—still I don't understand why *you're* here, Esra," she admitted.

"To find the heir."

"There isn't an heir," she told them. "All the contestants failed and the rest are dead, I'm sure. That monster destroyed everything."

"I'm not talking about that foolishness. I'm speaking about the real Heir of Novron."

The wizard came to a T-intersection and turned left, heading for a staircase that lead down again.

"Wait a minute." Royce stopped them. "We didn't come this way."

"No *we* didn't, but I did."

Royce looked around him. "No, no, this is all wrong. Here I was letting you lead and you clearly don't have a clue where the exit is."

"I'm not leading you to the exit."

"What?" Royce asked.

"We're not leaving," the wizard replied. "I am going to the Valentryne Layartren and the two of you are coming with me."

"You might want to explain why," Royce told him, his voice chilling several degrees. "Otherwise you are jumping to a pretty big conclusion."

"I'll explain on the way."

"Explain now," Royce told him. "I have other appointments to consider."

"You can't help Hadrian," the wizard said. "The Gilarabrywn is already at the village by now. Hadrian is either dead or safe. Nothing you can do will change that. You can't help him, but you can help me. I spent the better part of two days trying to access the Valentryne Layartren, but without your hands, Royce, I can't reach it, and it would take days, perhaps weeks, for me to operate alone, but with Arista here, we can do it all tonight. Maribor has seen fit to deliver both of you to me at the precise moment I need you most."

"Valentryne Layartren," Royce muttered, "that's elvish for *artistic vision*, isn't it?"

"You know some elvish, good for you, Royce," Esrahaddon said. "You should pursue your roots more."

"Your roots?" Arista said, confused.

They both ignored her.

"You can't help the people back at the village, but you can help me do what I came here to do. What I brought you here to help me with."

"You need us to help you find the true Heir of the Empire?"

"You're normally quicker than this, Royce. I'm disappointed."

"I thought you were keeping it a secret."

"I was, but circumstances have forced me to reconsider. Now quit being so stubborn and come with me. You might look back on this moment one day and reflect on how you changed the course of the world by simply walking down these steps."

Royce continued to hesitate.

"Think," Esrahaddon said. "What can you do for Hadrian?"

Royce didn't answer.

"If you run down the steps, race through the tunnel, swim out to the woods, and kill yourself running to the village, what will that accomplish? Even if you miraculously manage to reach the town before Hadrian is killed, how will that help? You will be standing there exhausted and dripping wet. You don't have the sword. You can't harm it. You can't scare it. I doubt you can even distract it, and if you do, it will only be for a moment. If you go, it will only be to your own death, and for no reason at all. Hadrian's fate does not lie in your hands. You know I'm right, or you wouldn't still be listening to me. Now stop being stubborn."

Royce sighed.

"Thank the gods," the wizard said. "Let's get moving."

"Wait a minute." Arista stopped them. "Don't I get a say in this too?"

The wizard looked back at her. "Do you know the way out?"

"No," she replied.

"Then no, you don't get a say," the wizard told her. "Now, please, we've wasted enough time. Follow me."

"I remember you being nicer," Arista shouted at the wizard.

"And I remember both of you being faster."

They were off again, heading deeper into the center of the tower. As they did, Esrahaddon spoke again. "Most people believe this tower was built by the elves as a defensive fortress for the wars against Novron. As both of you most likely have guessed, that's not true. This tower predates Novron by many millennia. Others think it was built as a fortress against the sea goblins, the infamous Ba Ran Ghazel, only that's also not true, since the tower predates their appearance as well. The common mistake here is that this is a fortress at all—that's the result of human thinking. The fact is, the elves lived for eons before man or goblin, and perhaps even before dwarves entered the world. In those days they had no need for fortresses. They didn't even have a word for war, as the Horn of Gylindora controlled all of their internal strife. No, this wasn't some defensive bulwark guarding the only crossing point on the Nidwalden River, although that certainly became its use many eons later. Originally, this tower was designed as a center for the Art."

"He means magic," Arista clarified.

"I know what he means."

"Elven masters would travel here from the world over to study and practice advanced Art. Still, this wasn't just a school. The building itself is an enormous tool, like a giant furnace for a blacksmith, only in this case, the building works as a focusing element. The falls function as a source of power and the tower's numerous spires are like the antennae on a grasshopper or the whiskers of a cat. They reach out into the world, sensing, feeling, drawing into this place the very essence of existence. It is like a giant lever and fulcrum, allowing a single artist to magnify their power almost beyond reason."

"Artistic vision..." Royce said. "It's a device that will allow you to use magic to find the heir?"

"Sadly, not even Avempartha has that much power. I can't find something I've never seen, or something I don't know exists. What I can do, however, is find something I do know, something that I am very well acquainted with, and something I created for the specific purpose of finding later.

"Nine hundred years ago when Jerish and I decided to split up in order to hide Nevrik, I made amulets for them. These amulets served two purposes: one was to protect them from the Art, thus preventing anyone from locating them by divination; the other was to provide me with a means to track them with a signature only I know how to recognize.

"Of course, Jerish and I assumed it would only take a few years to assemble a group of loyalists to restore the emperor, but as we all now know, that didn't happen. I can only hope that Jerish was smart enough to impress upon the descendants of the heir to keep the necklaces safe and to hand them down from one generation to the next. That might be asking too much, since—well, who could imagine that I would live so long?"

They crossed another narrow bridge, which spanned a disturbingly deep gap. Overhead were several colorful banners with iconic images embroidered on them with large single elven letters. Arista noticed Royce staring at them, his mouth working as if he was trying to read. On the far side of the bridge, they reached a doorstep where a tall ornately decorated archway was drawn into the stone, but no door was present.

"Royce, if you wouldn't mind?"

Royce stepped forward and, laying his hands on the polished stone, pressed.

"What's he doing?" Arista asked the wizard.

Esrahaddon turned and looked at Royce.

The thief stood before them uncomfortably for a moment, then said, "Avempartha has a magical protection that prevents anyone who doesn't have elvish blood from entering. Every lock in the place works the same way. Originally, we thought no one else but I could enter—oh, and Esra, because he had been invited years ago—but it turns out that if an elf invites you, that's all that is needed. Esra found the exact elvish wording for me to memorize for the invite. That's how I got you in."

"Speaking of which..." Esrahaddon motioned toward the stone arch.

"Sorry," Royce said, and added in a clear voice, "Melentanaria, en venau rendin Esrahaddon, en Arista Essendon adona Melengar," which Arista understood as *Grant entry to the wizard Esrahaddon and Arista Essendon, Princess of Melengar.*

"That's Old Speech," Arista said.

"Yes." Esrahaddon nodded. "There are many similarities between Elvish and Old Imperial."

"Whoa!" Looking back at the archway, Arista suddenly saw an open door. "But I still don't understand. How is it you can grant us—oh." The princess stopped with her mouth still open. "But you don't look at all—"

"I'm a *mir.*"

"A what?"

"A mix," Esrahaddon explained, "some elven, some human blood."

"But you never—"

"It's not the kind of thing you brag about," the thief said. "And I'd appreciate it if you kept this to yourself."

"Oh—of course."

"Come along. Arista still needs to play her part," Esrahaddon said, entering.

Inside, they found a large chamber carved perfectly round. It was like entering the inside of a giant ball. Unlike the rest of the tower, and despite its size, the room was unadorned. It was merely a vast smooth chamber with no seam, crack, nor crevice. The only feature was a zigzagging stone staircase that rose from the floor to a platform that extended out from the steps and stood at the exact center of the sphere.

"Do you remember the Plesieantic Incantations I taught you, Arista?" the wizard asked as they climbed the stairs, his voice echoing loudly, ricocheting repeatedly off the walls.

"Um...the ah..."

"Do you or don't you?"

"I'm thinking."

"Think faster; this is no time for slow wits."

"Yes, I remember. Lord, but you've gotten testy."

"I'll apologize later. Now, when we get up there, you are going to stand in the middle of the platform on the mark laid out on the floor as the apex. You will begin and maintain the Plesieantic Phrase. Start with the Gathering Incantation; when you do, you will likely feel a bit more of a jolt than you would normally, because this place will amplify your power to gather resources. Don't be alarmed, don't stop the incantation, and whatever you do, don't scream."

Arista looked fearfully back at Royce.

"Once you feel the power moving through your body, begin the Torsonic Chant. As you do, you will need to form the crystal-matrix with your fingers, making certain you fold inward, not outward."

"So with my thumbs pointing out and the rest of my fingers pointing at me, right?"

"Yes," Esrahaddon said, irritated. "This is all basic formations, Arista."

"I know it, I know it—it's just been a while. I've been busy being Melengar's ambassador, not sitting in my tower practicing conjurations."

"So you've been frivolously wasting your time?"

"No," she said, exasperated.

"Now, when you've completed the matrix," the wizard went on, "just hold it. Remember the concentration techniques I taught you and focus on keeping the matrix even and steady. At that point, I'll tap into your power field and conduct my search. When I do, this room is likely to do some extraordinary things. Images and visions will become visible at various places in the room and you might even hear sounds. Again don't be alarmed. They aren't really here; they will merely be echoes of my mind as I search for the amulets."

"Does that mean *all* of us will be able to see who the real heir is?" Royce asked as they reached the top.

Esrahaddon nodded. "I would like to have kept it to myself, but fate has seen fit to force me a different way. When I find the magical pulse of the amulets, I'll focus on the owners and they will likely appear as the largest image in the room, as I'll be concentrating to determine not only who wears them, but where they are as well."

The platform was only faintly dust-covered and they could easily see the massive converging geometric lines marked on the floor like rays of the sun, all gathering to a single point in the exact center of the dais.

"Them?" Arista asked as she took her position at the central point.

"There were two necklaces: one I gave to Nevrik, which

will be the heir's amulet, and the other to Jerish, which will be the bodyguard's. If they still exist, we should see both. I would ask that you not tell anyone what you are about to see, for if you do, you could put the heir's life in immense danger and possibly imperil the future of mankind as we know it."

"Wizards and their drama." Royce rolled his eyes. "A simple *please keep your mouth shut* would do."

Esrahaddon raised an eyebrow at the thief, then turned to Arista and said, "Begin."

Arista hesitated. Sauly had to be wrong. All that talk about the heir having the power to enslave mankind was just to frighten her into being their spy. His warnings that Esrahaddon was a demon must be more lies. He was secretive, certainly, but not evil. He had saved her life that night. What had Sauly done? How many days before Braga's death had Saldur known...and done nothing? Too many.

"Arista?" Esrahaddon pressed.

She nodded, raised her hands, and began the weave.

CHAPTER 14

AS DARKNESS FALLS

The night wind blew gently across the hilltop. Hadrian and Theron stood alone on the ruins of the manor above what had been a village. A place of countless hopes that lay buried in ash and wreckage.

Theron felt the breeze on his skin and remembered the ill wind he had felt the night his family died. The night Thrace ran to him. He could still see her as she raced down the slope of Stony Hill, running to the safety of his arms. He had thought that was the worst day of his life. He had cursed his daughter for coming to him. He had blamed her for the death of his family. He had put on her all the woe and despair that he had been too weak to carry. She was his little girl, the one who always walked beside him wherever he went, and when he shooed her away, as he always did, he would catch her following at a distance, watching him, mimicking his actions and his words. Thrace was the one who laughed at his faces, cried when he was hurt; the one who sat at his bedside when he lay with fever. He never had a good word for his daughter. Never a pat or praise that he could remember. Not once did he ever say he was proud of her. Most of the time he had not acknowledged her at all. But he would gladly give his own life merely to see his little girl run to him again, just once more.

Theron stood shoulder to shoulder with Hadrian. He held the broken blade hidden beneath his clothes, ready to draw it out in an instant to appease the beast if needed. Hadrian held the false blade the dwarf had fashioned, and he, too, kept it hidden, explaining that if the Gilarabrywn knew in advance where its prize was, it might not bother with the trade. Magnus and Tobis waited down the hill out of sight behind a hunting blind of assembled wreckage while Tomas worked at making Hilfred and Mauvin as comfortable as possible at the bottom of the hill.

The moon had risen and climbed above the trees and still the beast had not come. The torches Hadrian had lit in a circle around the hilltop were burning out. Only a few remained, but it did not seem to matter, as the moon was bright, and with the canopy of leaves gone, they could see well enough to read a book.

"Maybe it's not coming," Tomas said to them, climbing up the hill. "Maybe it wasn't supposed to be tonight or maybe I was just hearing things. I've never been very good with the Old Speech."

"How's Mauvin?" Hadrian asked.

"The bleeding stopped. He's sleeping peacefully now. I covered him in a blanket and created a pillow for him from a spare shirt. He and the soldier Hilfred should—"

There came a cry from the tower that turned their heads. To his amazement, Theron saw a brilliant explosion of white light flare at the pinnacle of the tower. It was there one moment and then faded as suddenly as it had appeared.

"What in the name of Maribor was that?" Theron asked.

Hadrian shook his head. "I don't know, but if I had to guess, I'd say Royce had something to do with it."

There was another cry from the Gilarabrywn, this one louder.

"Whatever it was," Hadrian told him, "I think it's headed our way."

Behind them, they could faintly hear Tomas praying.

"Put in a good word for Thrace, Tomas," Theron told him.

"I'm putting a word in for all of us," the cleric replied.

"Hadrian," Theron said, "if by chance I don't survive this and you do, keep an eye on my Thrace for me, will you? And if she dies too, see to it we are buried on my farm."

"And if I should die and you live," Hadrian said, "make sure this dagger I have in my belt gets back to Royce before the dwarf steals it."

"Is that all?" the farmer asked. "Where do you want us to bury you?"

"I don't want to be buried," he said. "If I die, I think I would like my body to be sent down the river, over the falls. Who knows, I might make it all the way to the sea."

"Good luck," Theron told him. The sounds of night fell silent, save only for the breath of the wind.

This time, with no forest in the way, Theron could see it coming, its wide dark wings stretched out like the shadow of a soaring bird, its thin body curling, its tail snapping as it flew. It did not dive as it approached. It did not breathe fire or land. Instead, it circled in silent flight, arcing in a wide ellipse.

As it circled, they could see it was not alone. Within its claws, it held a woman. At first, Theron could not tell who it was. She appeared to be wearing a richly tailored robe but she had Thrace's sandy-colored hair. As it circled the second time, he knew it was his daughter. A wave of relief and heightened anxiety gripped him. *What has become of the other?*

After several circles, the beast lowered like a kite and softly touched the ground. It landed directly in front of them, not more than fifty feet away, on the site of the now collapsed manor house.

Thrace was alive.

A massive claw of scale-covered muscle and bone tipped with four foot-long black nails surrounded her like a cage.

"Daddy!" she cried, in tears.

Seeing her, Theron made a lunge forward. Instantly the Gilarabrywn's claw tightened and she cried out. Hadrian grabbed Theron and pulled him back.

"Wait!" he shouted. "It'll kill her if you get too close."

The beast glared at them with huge reptilian eyes. Then the Gilarabrywn spoke.

Neither Theron nor Hadrian understood a word.

"Tomas," Hadrian shouted over his shoulder. "What's it saying?"

"I'm not very good at—" Tomas began.

"I don't care how well you did in grammar at seminary, just translate."

"I think it said it chose to take the females because it would create the greatest incentive for cooperation."

The creature spoke again and Tomas did not wait for Hadrian to tell him to translate.

"It says: 'Where is the blade that was stolen?' "

Hadrian looked back at Tomas. "Ask it 'Where is the other female?' "

Tomas spoke and the beast replied.

"It says the other escaped."

"Ask it 'How do I know you will let us all live if I tell you where the blade is hidden?' "

Tomas spoke and the beast replied again.

"It says it will offer you a gesture of good faith, since it knows it has the upper hand and understands your concern."

It opened its claw and Thrace ran to her father. Theron's heart leapt as his little girl raced across the hill to his waiting arms. He hugged her tight and wiped her tears.

"Theron," Hadrian said, "get her out of here. Both of you get back to the well if you can." Theron and his daughter did not argue and the Gilarabrywn's great eyes watched carefully as Theron and Thrace began to sprint down the hill. Then it spoke again.

" 'Now, where is the blade?' " Tomas translated.

�<

Looking up at the towering beast and feeling the sweat dripping down his face, Hadrian drew the false blade out of his sleeve and held it up. The Gilarabrywn's eyes narrowed.

" 'Bring it to me.' " Tomas translated its words.

This was it. Hadrian felt the metal in his hands. "Please let this work," he whispered to himself, and tossed the blade. It landed in the ash before the beast. The Gilarabrywn looked down at it and Hadrian held his breath. The beast casually placed its foot upon the blade and gathered it into its long talons. Then it looked at Hadrian and spoke.

"The deal is complete," Tomas said. "But..."

"But?" Hadrian repeated nervously. "But what?"

Tomas's voice grew weak. "But it says, 'I cannot allow those who have seen even half my name to remain alive.' "

"Oh, you bastard," Hadrian cursed, pulling his great spadone sword from his back. "Run, Tomas!"

The Gilarabrywn rose, flapping its great wings, causing a storm of ash to swirl into a cloud. It snapped forward with its head like a snake. Hadrian dove aside and, spinning, drove his sword at the beast. Rather than feeling the blade tip penetrate, however, Hadrian felt his heart sink as the point of the spadone skipped off as if the Gilarabrywn were made of stone. The sudden shock broke his grip and the sword fell.

Not losing a beat, the Gilarabrywn swung its tail around in a sharp snap. The long bone blade on the tip hummed as it sliced the air two feet above the ground. Hadrian leapt over it and the tail glanced off the hillside, stabbing into a charred timber. A quick flick and the several-hundred-pound log flew into the night. Hadrian reached inside his tunic and drew Alverstone from its sheath. He crouched like a knife fighter in a ring, up on the balls of his feet, waiting for the next attack.

Once more, the Gilarabrywn's tail came at him. This time it stabbed like a scorpion. Hadrian dove aside, and the long point sunk into the earth.

He ran forward.

The Gilarabrywn snapped at Hadrian with its teeth. He was ready for that, expecting it, counting on it. He jumped aside at the last minute. It was so close one tooth sliced through his tunic and gashed his shoulder. It was worth it. He was inches from the beast's face. With all his strength, Hadrian stabbed Royce's tiny dagger into the monster's great eye.

The Gilarabrywn screeched an awful cry that deafened Hadrian. It reared back, stomping its feet. The tiny blade pierced and cut a slice. It shook its head, perhaps as much in disbelief as in pain, and glared at Hadrian with its one remaining eye. Then it spat out words so laced with venom that Tomas did not need to translate.

The beast spread its wings and drew itself up in the air. Hadrian knew what was coming next and cursed his own stupidity for having allowed the creature to move him so far from the pit. He could never make it there in time now.

The Gilarabrywn screeched and arched its back.

There was a loud *twack!* A wad of rope netting flew into the air like a ball. With small weights tied to the edges, which traveled faster than the center, the net flew open like a giant wind sock, enveloping the flapping beast even as it tried to take flight.

Its wings tangled in the net, the Gilarabrywn dropped to the hilltop, crashing down with a heavy thud, the impact throwing up bits of the manor house's stairway banister, which flew end over end before shattering in a cloud of ash.

"It worked!" Tobis shouted, as much in shock as in triumph, from the far side of the hill.

Hadrian saw his opportunity and, spinning around, charged the monster. As he did, he noticed Theron following him.

"I told you to take Thrace and run," Hadrian yelled.

"You looked like you needed help," Theron shouted back, "and I told Thrace to head for the well."

"What makes you think she will listen to you any more than you listen to me?"

Hadrian reached where the Gilarabrywn lay on its side thrashing about wildly, and dove at its head. He found its open eye and attacked, stabbing repeatedly. With a terrible scream, the beast raked back with its legs, ripping the net open, and rolled to its feet again.

Hadrian, so intent on blinding the beast, had stepped on the netting. When the monster rose, Hadrian's feet went out from under him. He fell flat on his back, the air knocked from his lungs.

Blind, the beast resorted to lashing out with its tail, sweeping it across the ground. Caught trying to stand up, Hadrian was struck by the blunt force of the tail.

❦

Hadrian rolled and tumbled like a rag doll, sliding across the ash until he stopped in a patch of dirt, where he lay unmoving.

Freeing itself fully of the net, the beast sniffed the air and began moving toward the one who had caused it pain.

"No!" Theron shouted, and charged. He ran for Hadrian, thinking he could drag him clear of the blind beast before it reached him, only the beast was too fast and reached Hadrian at the same time Theron did.

Theron picked up a rock and drew forth the broken blade he still carried. He aimed for the exposed creature's side and, using the rock as a hammer, drove the metal home like a nail.

This stopped the Gilarabrywn from killing Hadrian, but the beast did not cry out as it had when Hadrian had stabbed it. Instead, it turned and laughed. Theron struck the blade with the rock again, forcing the metal deep, but still the beast did not cry out. It spoke to him, but Theron could not understand the words. Then, having little trouble guessing where the farmer stood, the Gilarabrywn swiped at him with his claw.

Theron did not have the speed or agility that Hadrian had. Strong as he was for his age, his old body could not move clear of the blow in time, and the great nails of the beast stabbed into him like four swords.

⚬

"*Daddy!*" Thrace screamed, running to him. She scrambled up the slope, crying as she came.

From their blind, Tobis and the dwarf fired a rock at the Gilarabrywn and managed to hit its tail. The beast spun and charged furiously in their direction.

Falling to her hands and knees, Thrace crawled to Theron's side and found her father lying broken on the hill. His left arm lay twisted backward, his foot facing the wrong direction. His chest was soaked in dark blood and his breath hitched as his body convulsed.

"Thrace," he managed to say weakly.

"Daddy," she cried as she cradled him in her arms.

"Thrace," he said again, gripping her with his remaining hand and pulling her close. "I'm so—" His eyes closed tightly in pain. "I'm so—pr—proud of you."

"Oh god, Daddy. No. No. No!" she cried, shaking her head.

She held him, squeezing as hard as she could, trying by the force of her arms to keep him with her. She would not let him go. She could not; he was all there was. She sobbed and wailed, clutching his shirt, kissing his cheek and forehead, and as she held him, she felt her father pass away into the night.

Theron Wood died on the scorched ground in a pool of blood and dirt. As he did, the last tiny remnant of hope Thrace had held on to—the last foothold she had in the world—died with him.

There was a darkness of night, a darkness of senses, and a darkness of spirit. Thrace felt herself drowning in all three. Her father was dead. Her light, her hope, her last dream, they had all died with his last breath. Nothing remained upon the world that *it* had not taken from her.

It had killed her mother.

It had killed her brother, his wife, and her nephew.

It had killed Daniel Hall and Jessie Caswell.

It had burned her village.

It had killed her father.

Thrace raised her head and looked across the hill at *it*.

No one who had been attacked had ever lived. There were never any survivors.

She stood and began to walk forward slowly. She reached into the robe and pulled out the sword that had remained hidden there.

The beast found the catapult and shattered it. It turned and blindly began to search its way back down the hillside, sniffing. It did not notice the young girl.

The thick layer of ash that it had created quieted her steps.

"No, Thrace!" Tomas shouted at her. "Run away!"

The Gilarabrywn paused and sniffed at the sound of the shout, sensing danger but unable to determine its source. It tried to look in the direction of the voice.

"No, Thrace—don't!"

Thrace ignored the cleric. She had passed beyond hearing, beyond seeing, beyond thinking. She was no longer on the hill. She was no longer in Dahlgren, but rather in a tunnel, a narrow tunnel that led inescapably to only one destination...*it.*

It kills people. That's what it does.

The beast sniffed the air. She could tell it was trying to find her; it was searching for the smell of fear it created in its victims.

She had no fear. *It* had destroyed that too.

Now she was invisible.

Without hesitation, fear, question, or regret, Thrace quietly walked up to the towering monster. She gripped the elven sword in both hands and raised it above her head. Putting the full weight of her small body into it, she thrust the broken sword into the Gilarabrywn's body. She did not have to put so much effort into it; the blade slipped in easily.

The beast shrieked in mortal fear and confusion.

It turned, recoiling, but it was already too late. The sword penetrated all the way to the hilt. The essence that was the Gilarabrywn and the forces that bound it shattered. With the snapping of the bonds that held it fast, the world reclaimed the energy in a sudden violent outburst. The eruption of force threw Thrace and Tomas to the ground. The shock wave continued down the hill, radiating out in all directions, beyond the burnt desolation to the forest, launching flocks of birds into the night.

Dazed, Tomas staggered to his feet and approached the small slender figure of Thrace Wood at the center of a cleared depression, where the great Gilarabrywn had once been. He walked forward in awe and fell prostrate on his knees before the girl.

"Your Imperial Majesty," was all he said.

CHAPTER 15

THE HEIR OF NOVRON

The sun rose brightly over the Nidwalden River. The clouds had moved off and by midmorning the sky was clear and the air cooler than it had been. A light wind skimmed across the surface of the river, raising ripples, while the sun cast a brilliant gold face upon the water. A fish jumped above the surface and fell back with a plop. Overhead, birds sang morning songs and cicadas droned.

Royce and Arista stood on the bank of the river, wringing water out of their clothes. Esrahaddon waited.

"Nice robe," the princess said.

The wizard only smiled.

Arista shivered as she looked out across the river. The trees on the far bank looked different than the ones on their side, a different species, perhaps. Arista thought they appeared prouder, straighter, with fewer lower branches and longer trunks. While the trees were impressive, there was no evidence of civilization.

"How do we know they are over there?" Arista asked.

"The elves?" Esrahaddon questioned.

"I mean, no one has seen an elf" — she glanced at Royce — "a pure-blood elf — in centuries, right?"

"They are there. Thousands of them by now, I should think. Tribes of the old names, with bloodlines that can be traced to the dawn of time. The Miralyith, masters of the Art; Asendwayr, the hunters; Nilyndd, the crafters; Eiliwin, the architects; Umalyn, the spiritualists; Gwydry, the shipwrights; and Instarya, the warriors. They are all still there, a congress of nations."

"Do they have cities? Like we do?"

"Perhaps, but probably not like ours. There is a legend of a sacred place called Estramnadon. It is the holiest place in elven culture...at least that we humans know of. Estramnadon is said to be over there, deep in the forests. Some think it is their capital city and seat of their monarch; others speculate it is the sacred grove where the first tree—the tree planted by Muriel herself—still grows and is cared for by the Children of Ferrol. No one knows for certain. No human is likely ever to know, as the elves do not suffer the trespasses of others."

"Really?" The princess looked at the thief with a playful smirk. "Perhaps if I knew that before, I might have guessed Royce's heritage sooner."

Royce ignored the comment and turned to the wizard. "Can I assume you'll not be returning to the village?"

Esrahaddon shook his head. "I need to leave before Luis Guy and his pack of hounds track me down. Besides, I have an heir to talk to and plans to make."

"Then this is goodbye. I need to get back."

"Remember to keep silent about what you saw in the tower—both of you."

"Funny, I expected the heir and his guardian to be unknown farm boys from someplace—well—like this, I suppose. Someone I never heard of."

"Life has a way of surprising you, doesn't it?" Esrahaddon said.

Royce nodded and started to head off.

"Royce," Esrahaddon said softly, stopping him, "we know that what happened last night wasn't pleasant. You should prepare yourself for what you're going to find."

"You think Hadrian's dead," Royce said flatly.

"I would expect so. If he is, at least know that his death may have been the sacrifice that saved our world from destruction. And while that may not comfort you, I think we both know that it would have pleased Hadrian."

Royce thought a moment, nodded, then entered the trees and disappeared.

"He's definitely elvish," Arista said, shaking her head and sitting down opposite Esrahaddon. "I don't know why I didn't see it before. You've grown a beard, I see."

"You just noticed?"

"I noticed before, been kinda busy until now."

"I can't really shave, can I? It wasn't a problem while I was in Gutaria, but now—does it look all right?"

"You have some gray coming in."

"I ought to. I am nine hundred years old."

She watched the wizard staring across the river.

"You really should practice your art. You did well in there."

She rolled her eyes. "I can't do it, not the way you taught me. I can do most of the things Arcadius demonstrated, but it's a bit impossible to learn hand magic from a man without hands."

"You boiled water, and you made the prison guard sneeze. Remember?"

"Yes, I'm a veritable sorceress, aren't I?" she said sarcastically.

He sighed. "What about the rain? Have you worked on that incantation any more?"

"No, and I'm not going to. I am the Ambassador of Melengar now. I've put all that behind me. Given time, they may even forget I was tried for witchcraft."

"I see," the wizard said, disappointed.

The princess shivered in the morning chill and tried to run her fingers through her hair but caught them in tangles. Stains and wrinkles dotted her dress. "I'm a mess, aren't I?"

The wizard said nothing. He appeared to be thinking.

"So," she began, "what will you do when you find the heir?"

Esrahaddon only stared at her.

"Is it a secret?"

"Why don't you ask me what you really want to know, Arista?"

She sat trying to look naïve and offered a slight smile. "I don't understand."

"You aren't sitting here shivering in a wet dress making small talk with me for nothing. You have an agenda."

"An agenda?" she asked, not at all convincingly, even for her own tastes. "I don't know what you mean."

"You want to know if what the church told you about your father's death is true or not. You think I used you as a pawn. You are wondering if I tricked you into being an unwitting accomplice to your own father's death."

The act was over. She stared, stunned at the wizard's bluntness, barely breathing. She did not speak but slowly nodded her head.

"I suspected they might come after you because they are having trouble following me."

"Did you?" she asked, finding her voice. "Did you orchestrate my father's death?"

Esrahaddon let the silence hang between them a moment, then at last replied.

"Yes, Arista. I did."

At first, the princess did not say a word. It did not seem possible that she had heard him correctly. Slowly her head began to shake back and forth in disbelief.

"How..." she started. "How could you do that?"

"Nothing I nor anyone else says can explain that to you—not now, at least. Perhaps someday you'll understand."

Tears welled up in her eyes. She brushed them away and glared at the wizard.

"Before you judge me completely, as I know you will, remember one thing. Right now, the Church of Nyphron is trying to persuade you that I am a demon, the very Apostle of Uberlin. You are likely thinking they are right. Before you damn me forever and run into the embrace of the Patriarch, ask yourself these questions. Who approved your entrance into Sheridan University? Who talked your disapproving father into letting you attend? How did you learn about me? How was it that you found your way to a hidden prison that only a handful of people knew existed? Why were you taught to use a gemstone lock, and isn't it interesting that the very gem you used on your door was the same as the signet ring that unlocked the prison entrance? And how was it that a young girl, princess or not, was allowed to enter Gutaria Prison and leave unmolested not once, not twice, but repeatedly for months without her activities ever being questioned or reported back to her father the king?"

"What are you saying?"

"Arista," the wizard said, "sharks don't eat seafood because they like it, but because chickens don't swim. We all do the best we can with the tools we have, but at some point you have to ask yourself where the tools came from."

She stared at him. "You knew they would kill my father.

You counted on it. You even knew they would eventually kill me and Alric, and yet you pretended to be my friend, my teacher." Her face hardened. "School's over." She turned her back on him and walked away.

❦

When Royce reached the edge of the burnt forest, he spotted a series of colorful tents set up around the old village common. The tents displayed pennants of the Nyphron Church, and he could see several priests as well as imperial guards. Other figures moved slowly over the hill near the old castle grounds, but nowhere did he see anyone he knew.

He kept to the cover of the trees when he caught the sound of a snapping twig not too far off. Slipping around, he quickly spotted Magnus crouched in the underbrush.

The dwarf jumped in alarm and fell backward at his approach.

"Relax," Royce whispered, sitting down next to where the dwarf now lay, nervously watching the thief.

Glancing down the slope, Royce realized that the dwarf had found an excellent position to watch the camp. They were on a rise behind a series of burnt trees where some of the underbrush had survived. Below, they had a perfect view of each of the tent openings, the makeshift horse corral, and the latrine. Royce guessed there were about thirty of them.

"What are you still doing here?" Royce asked.

"I was breaking a sword for your partner. But I'm leaving now."

"What happened?"

"Huh? Oh, Theron and Fanen were killed."

Royce nodded, showing no outward sign of surprise or grief.

"Hadrian? Is he alive?"

The dwarf nodded and went on to explain the events that had transpired that evening.

"After it was dead, or dispelled, or whatever, Tomas and I checked on Hadrian. He was unconscious, but alive. We made him comfortable, covered him in a blanket, and put a lean-to over him, the Pickering kid, and that Melengarian soldier. Before dawn, Bishop Saldur and his crew returned, dragging two wagons with them. The way I figure it, either Guy reported what happened and he was coming back with help, or they heard it when the beastie died. They pulled in and, fast as rabbits, had these tents up and breakfast cooking. I spotted the sentinel in their ranks, so I hid up here. They moved Hadrian, Hilfred, and Mauvin into that white tent, and soon after, they put a guard on it."

"Is that all?"

"Well, they sent a detail out to bury the dead. Most they buried on the hill up there near the castle, including Fanen, but Tomas made some big stink and they took Theron down the road to that last farm near the river and they buried him there."

"Perhaps you forgot to mention how you found my dagger?"

"The Alverstone? I thought you had it."

"I do," Royce said.

Magnus reached for his boot and cursed.

"When you investigated my background, you must have stumbled across the fact that I survived my youth by picking pockets."

"I remember something about that," the dwarf growled.

Royce pulled Alverstone from its sheath as he glared at the dwarf.

"Look, I'm sorry about killing that damn king. It was just a job I was hired to do, okay? I wouldn't have taken the job if it hadn't required a uniquely challenging masonry effort. I'm not an assassin. I'm not even good enough to be considered a pathetic fighter. I'm an artisan. Truth be told, I specialize in weapons. That's my first love, but all dwarves can cut stone, so I was hired to do the tower work; then the job got changed, and after half a year's work, I was going to be stiffed if I didn't knife the old man. In hindsight, I can see I should have refused, but I didn't. I didn't know anything about him. Maybe he was a bad king; maybe he deserved to die; Braga certainly thought so and he was the king's brother-in-law. I try not to involve myself in human affairs, but I was caught up in this one. It's not something I wanted; it's not something I looked for; it just happened. And it's not like someone else wouldn't have done it if I hadn't."

"What makes you think I'm upset you killed Amrath? I'm not even mad that you trapped the tower. Closing the door on me was the mistake you made."

Magnus inched away.

"Killing you would be as easy as—no, easier than—slaughtering a fatted pig. The challenge would lie in causing the maximum amount of pain before inflicting the death."

Magnus's mouth opened, but no words came out.

"But you are a very lucky dwarf, because there's a man still alive in that tent who wouldn't like it—a man you covered in a blanket and put a lean-to over."

Down below he spotted Arista as she entered the camp. She talked to a guard, who pointed toward the white tent. She rushed to it.

Royce looked back at the dwarf and spoke clearly and evenly. "If you ever touch Alverstone again without my permission, I'll kill you."

Magnus looked at him bitterly; then his expression changed

and he raised an eyebrow. "Without your *permission*? So there's a chance you'll *let* me study it?"

Royce rolled his eyes. "I'm going to get Hadrian out of there. You are going to steal two of the archbishop's horses and walk them over to the white tent without being spotted."

"And then we can talk about the *permission* thing?"

Royce sighed, "Did I mention I hate dwarves?"

❦

"But, Your Grace—" Deacon Tomas protested as he stood in the large striped tent before Bishop Saldur and Luis Guy. The pudgy cleric made a poor showing of himself in his frock caked with dirt and ash, his face smudged, his fingers black.

"Look at you, Tomas," Bishop Saldur said. "You're so exhausted you look as if you'll fall down any minute. You've had a long two days, and you've been under tremendous stress for months now. It is only natural that you might see things in the dark. No one is blaming you. And we don't think you are lying. We know that right now you believe you saw this village girl destroy the Gilarabrywn, but I think if you just take a nap and rest, when you get up, you'll find that you were mistaken about a great many things."

"I don't need a nap!" Tomas shouted.

"Calm down, Deacon," Saldur snapped, rising abruptly to his feet. "Remember whose presence you are standing in."

The deacon cowed and Saldur sighed. His face softened to his grandfatherly visage and he put an arm around the man's shoulders, patting him gently. "Go to a tent and rest."

Tomas hesitated, turned, and left Saldur and Luis Guy alone.

The bishop threw himself down in the little cushioned

chair beside a bowl of red berries some industrious servant had managed to gather for him. He popped two in his mouth and chewed. They were bitter and he grimaced. Despite the early hour, Saldur was desperate for a glass of brandy, but none had survived the flight from the castle. Only the grace of Maribor could account for the survival of the camping gear and provisions, all of which they had lazily left in the wagons when they had first arrived at the manor. In the turmoil of their exodus, they had given little thought to provisions.

That he lived at all was a miracle. He could not recall how he had crossed the courtyard, or how he had reached the gate. He must have run down the hill, but had no recollection of it. His memory was like a dream, vague and fading. He did remember ordering the coachman to whip the horses. The fool wanted to wait for the archbishop. The old man could barely walk, and the moment the flames hit, his servants deserted him. He had had as much chance of survival as Rufus.

With Archbishop Galien's death, the command of the church's interest in Dahlgren fell to Saldur and Guy. The two inherited a disaster of mythic proportions. They were alone in the wilderness, faced with crucial decisions. How they handled them would decide the fate of future generations. Who actually held authority remained vague. Saldur was a bishop, an appointed leader, while Guy was only a constabulary officer whose jurisdiction extended mostly to apostate members of the church. Still, the sentinel actually spoke with the Patriarch. Saldur liked Guy, but appreciation for his effectiveness would not prevent him from sacrificing the sentinel if necessary. Saldur was certain that if Guy still had had his knights about him, the sentinel would have taken command and he would have had no choice but to accept it, but the seret were dead and Guy himself wounded. With Galien also dead, a door had opened, and Saldur planned to be the first one through.

Saldur looked at Guy. "How could you let this happen?"

The sentinel, who sat with his arm in a sling and his shoulder wrapped in bandages, stiffened. "I lost seven good men, and barely escaped with my life. I wouldn't call that *allowing* it to happen."

"And how exactly did a bunch of farmers defeat the infamous seret?"

"They weren't farmers. Two were Pickerings and there was Hadrian Blackwater."

"The Pickerings I can understand, but Blackwater? He's nothing but a rogue."

"No, there's more to him—him and his partner."

"Royce and Hadrian are excellent thieves. They proved that in Melengar and again in Chadwick. Poor Archibald still has fits over them."

"No," Guy said, "I think they're more than that. Blackwater knows Teshlor combat, and his friend Royce Melborn is an elf."

Saldur blinked. "An elf? Are you sure?"

"He passes as human, but I'm certain of it."

"And this is the second time we've found them with Esrahaddon," Saldur muttered in concern. "Is this Hadrian still here?"

"He is in the infirmary tent."

"Put a guard on him at once."

"I've had him under guard since he was dragged to the tent. What we need to concern ourselves with is the girl. She's going to prove herself to be an embarrassment if we don't do something," Guy said, and slipped his sword partway out of its sheath. "She is in grief over the loss of her father. It wouldn't be surprising if she threw herself over the falls in a fit of despair."

"And Tomas?" Saldur asked, reaching for another handful of berries. "It is clear he won't be quiet. Will you kill him too? What excuse will you give for that? And what about all the others in this camp that heard him going on all morning about her being the heir? Do we kill everyone? If we did, who would carry our bags back to Ervanon?" he added with a smile.

"I don't see the humor in this," Guy snapped, letting his sword slide back down in its sheath.

"Perhaps that's because you are not looking at it the right way," Saldur told him. Guy was a well-trained and vicious guard dog, but the man lacked imagination. "What if we didn't kill her? What if we actually made her the empress?"

"A peasant girl? Empress?" Guy scoffed. "Are you mad?"

"Despite his political clout, I don't think any of us, including the Patriarch, were particularly happy with the choice of Rufus. He was a fool, to be sure, but he was also a stubborn, powerful fool. We all suspected that he might have had to be killed within a year, which would have thrown the infant empire into turmoil. How much better would it be to have an empress that would do whatever she was told right from the very start?"

"But how could we possibly sell her to the nobles?"

"We don't," Saldur said, and a smile appeared on his wrinkled face. "We sell her to the people instead."

"How's that?"

"Degan Gaunt's Nationalist movement proved that the people themselves have strength. Earls, barons, even kings are afraid of the power which that commoner can gather. A word from him could launch a peasant uprising. Lords would have to kill their own people, their own source of revenue, just to keep order. This presents them with the undesirable choice of accepting either poverty or death. The landholders will do almost anything to avoid such an event. What if we tapped that? The peasants already revere the church. They follow its teachings as divine truth. How much more inspiring would it be to offer them a leader plucked from their own stock? A ruler who is one of them and able to truly understand the plight of the poor, the unwashed, the destitute. Not only is she a peasant queen, but she is also the Heir of Novron, and all the wonderful expectations that go with that. Indeed, in our greatest hour of need, Maribor has once again delivered unto his people a divine leader to show us the way out of darkness.

"We could send bards across the land repeating the epic tale of the pure, chaste girl who slew the elven demon that even Lord Rufus was powerless against. We'll call it *Rufus's Bane*. Yes, I like it—so much better than the unpronounceable *Gilarabrywn*."

"But can she be made to play her part?" Guy asked.

"You saw her. She's nearly comatose. Not only does she have no place to go, no friends or relatives, no money or possessions, she is also emotionally shattered. She'd slit her own wrists, I suspect, if she gets a knife. Still, the best part is that once we establish her as empress, once we have the support of the people so fervently on our side, no noble landholder would dare challenge us. We can do what we planned to do with Rufus. Only instead of a messy murder that would certainly invite suspicion and accusations, with the girl, we can simply marry her. The new husband will rule as emperor and we can lock her in a dark room somewhere, pulling her out for Wintertide showings."

Guy smiled at that.

"Do you think the Patriarch will agree?" Saldur asked him. "Perhaps we should send a rider back today."

"No, this is too important. I'll go myself. I'll leave as soon as I can saddle a horse. In the meantime—"

"In the meantime, we will announce that we are considering the possibility that this girl is the heir, but will not accept her unconditionally until a full investigation is conducted. That should buy us a month. If the Patriarch agrees, then we can send out rabble-rousers to incite the people with rumors that the church is being forced by the nobles and the monarchs to not reveal the girl as the true heir. The people will be denouncing our enemies and demanding that she take the throne before we even announce her."

"She will make the perfect figurehead," Guy said.

Saldur looked up, picturing the future. "An innocent girl linked with a mythic legend. Her beautiful name will be everywhere and she will be loved." The bishop paused and thought. "What is her name, anyway?"

"I think Tomas called her... Thrace."

"Seriously?" Saldur grimaced. "Well, no matter, we'll change it. After all, she's ours now."

∽

Royce looked around. There was not a single sentry left outside. Several still moved about on the hilltop, but they were far enough away to ignore. Satisfied, he ducked through the flap of the white tent. Inside, he found Tobis, Hadrian, Mauvin, and Hilfred on cots. Hadrian was naked to his waist, his head and chest wrapped in white bandages, but he was awake and sitting up. Mauvin, though still pale, was alert, his bandages bright white. Hilfred lay wrapped like a mummy and Royce could not be sure if he was awake or sleeping. Arista stood bent over his cot, checking on him.

"I was wondering when you would get here," Hadrian said.

Arista turned. "Yes, I thought you would have arrived much sooner."

"Sorry, you know how it is when you're having fun. You lose all track of time, but I did locate your weapons, again. You know how upset you get when you don't have your swords. Can you ride?"

"If I can walk, why not?" He raised an arm and Royce offered his shoulder, helping him to stand.

"What about me?" Mauvin asked, holding his side and sitting up on his cot. "You're not going to leave me, are you?"

"You have to take him," Arista declared. "He killed two of Guy's men."

"Can you ride?" Royce asked.

"If I had a horse under me, I could at least hang on."

"What about Thrace?" Hadrian asked.

"I don't think you need worry about her," Royce told him. "I was just by the bishop's tent. Tomas is demanding that they declare her empress."

"Empress?" Hadrian said, stunned.

"She killed the Gilarabrywn right in front of the deacon. I guess it made an impression."

"But what if they don't? We can't leave her."

"Don't worry about Thrace," Arista said. "I'll see she's taken care of. Now you all need to get out of here."

"Theron wanted at least one of his children to be successful," Hadrian muttered, "but empress?"

"You need to hurry," Arista said, helping Royce pull Mauvin to his feet. She gave all three of them a kiss and a gentle hug and then pushed them out like a mother sending her children to school.

Outside the tent, Magnus arrived with three saddled horses. The dwarf looked around nervously and whispered, "I could have sworn I saw guards watching this tent earlier."

"You did," Royce replied. "Three horses—you read my mind."

"I figured I needed one for myself," the dwarf replied, pointing at the shortened stirrups. He looked at Mauvin with a scowl. "Now it looks like I'll need to get another."

"Forget it," Royce whispered. "Ride with Mauvin. Take it slow and make sure he stays in the saddle."

Royce helped Hadrian up onto a gray mare, then started to chuckle to himself.

"What is it?" Hadrian asked.

"Mouse."

"What's that?"

Royce pointed to the horse Hadrian sat on. "Of all the animals he had to choose from, the dwarf stole Mouse."

Royce led them away from the camp, walking the horses across the scorched land, where the ash muffled their movement. He kept a close eye on the distant sentries. No outcry, no shouts, no one appeared to notice, and soon they slipped into the leafy forest. Once there, he turned back toward the river in order to throw off anyone who might look for their tracks. Once he had them safe in a shallow glen near the Nidwalden, Royce ordered them to stay put while he went back.

He crept up to the edge of the burned area. The camp was as it had been before. Satisfied they had made a clean escape, he walked back toward the river. He found himself on the trail that led to the Woods' farm and the shell of the old building. Inexplicably, the fire had never reached this far and it remained untouched. There was one change, however; in the center of the yard, where they had first seen the old farmer sharpening his scythe, there was a mound of earth. A stack of stones borrowed from the walls of the farmhouse circled the oblong mound. At its head, driven into the ground, was a broad plank, and burned into it were the words:

THERON WOOD FARMER

Royce could just make out the additional words scratched into the plank below that:

Father of the Empress

As Royce stood reading the words, he noticed it—a chill making the hair on his skin stand up. Someone was watching him. On the edge of his sight, a figure stood in the trees. Another stood to his left. He sensed more behind him. He turned his head, focused his eyes to see who they were—nothing. All he saw were trees. He glanced to his left and again nothing. He stood still, listening. Not a twig snapped, nor a leaf crinkled, but he could still feel it.

He moved away from the clearing into the brush and circled around. He moved as quietly as he could, but when he stopped, he was alone.

Royce stood, puzzled. He looked for tracks where he had seen the figures, but none existed, not even a bent blade of grass. At last, he gave up and returned to where he had left the others.

"All's well?" Hadrian asked, sitting atop Mouse with the sun on his bare shoulders and his chest wrapped in broad strips of white cloth.

"I suppose," he said, mounting up.

He led them southwest along the highlands near the falls, following a deer trail that cut through the deep forest. It was the same trail he had found in his hours searching for a tunnel to the tower. Hadrian and Mauvin appeared to be doing better than expected, though each of them winced in pain whenever his horse took a misstep.

Royce continued to look back over his shoulder but nothing was ever there.

By midafternoon they had cleared the trees and found the main road heading south to Alburn. Here they paused to check Mauvin's and Hadrian's bandages. Mauvin started to bleed again, but it was not bad and Magnus turned out to be almost as good a nurse as he was a sword smith, fashioning a new pad for his side. Royce searched through the saddlebags and found Hadrian a suitable shirt.

"We should be fine," Royce told them, going through their inventory. "With a little luck we should reach Medford in a week."

"In a hurry, are you?" Hadrian asked.

"You might say that."

"Thinking about Gwen?"

"I'm thinking it's time I told her a few things about myself."

Hadrian smiled and nodded.

"You think Thrace will be all right?"

"Tomas seems to be watching out for her pretty well."

"Do you think they'll really make her empress?"

"Not a chance." Royce shook his head and handed the shirt to him. "What do you plan on doing now?" Royce asked Magnus.

The dwarf shrugged. "You mean assuming you don't kill me?"

"I'm not going to kill you, but your old employer, the

church, might now that you've turned on them. They will be coming after you just the same as they'll be after Mauvin and Hadrian. And without the church's support, you won't last long on your own. Towns in Avryn aren't too friendly to your kind."

"Nowhere is."

"That's what I meant." Royce sighed. "I know of a very out-of-the-way place you might be able to hold up at. A place the church isn't likely to visit. They need a lot of stonework done and could use an experienced craftsman like you."

"How do they feel about dwarves?"

"I don't think you'll have a problem. They're the kind of people who tend to like everyone."

"I could do with getting back to stonecutting." Magnus nodded.

"Myron will drive him crazy with his quest to get the monastery exactly the way it was," Hadrian said. "They've gone through five builders so far."

"I know," Royce replied with a little grin.

Royce climbed back on top of Mouse as Magnus went ahead to check on Mauvin.

Hadrian shook out his shirt before slipping his arm in the sleeve. "Arista told me you two were with Esrahaddon in the tower last night. She said he needed help with something, but wouldn't tell me what it was."

"He was using the tower to look for the Heir of Novron," Royce replied.

"Did he find him?"

"I think so, but you know how Esra is. It's hard to be sure of anything when dealing with him." Hadrian nodded and winced as he pulled the shirt over his shoulders.

"Having troubles?"

"You try getting dressed with broken ribs sometime. It isn't so easy."

Royce continued to look at him.

"What is it? Am I that entertaining?" Hadrian asked.

"It's just that you've worn that silver medallion ever since I've known you, but you never told me where you got it."

"Hmm? This?" Hadrian said. "I've had this forever. My father left it to me."

GLOSSARY OF TERMS AND NAMES

ADDIE WOOD: Mother of Thrace, wife of Theron

ALBERT WINSLOW, VISCOUNT: Landless nobleman used by Riyria to arrange assignments from the gentry

ALBURN: Kingdom of Avryn ruled by King Armand and Queen Adeline

ALENDA LANAKLIN, LADY: Daughter of Marquis Victor Lanaklin and sister of Brother Myron of the Winds Abbey

ALLIE: Daughter of Wyatt Deminthal

ALRIC BRENDON ESSENDON, PRINCE: Member of ruling family of Melengar, son of Amrath, brother of Arista

ALVERSTONE: \al-ver-stone\ Royce's dagger

AMBROSE MOOR: Administrator of the Manzant Prison and Salt Works

AMRATH ESSENDON, KING: \am-wrath\ Ruler of Melengar, father of Alric and Arista

AMRIL, COUNTESS: \am-rill\ Noblewoman that Arista cursed with boils

ANTUN BULARD: Historian and author of *The History of Apeladorn*

APELADORN: \ah-pell-ah-dorn\ Four nations of man, consisting of Trent, Avryn, Delgos, and Calis

AQUESTA: \ah-quest-ah\ Capital city of the kingdom of Warric

ARCADIUS VINTARUS LATIMER: Professor of lore at Sheridan University

ARCHIBALD BALLENTYNE: Earl of Chadwick

ARISTA ESSENDON, PRINCESS: Member of ruling family of Melengar, daughter of Amrath, sister of Alric

ARMAND, KING: Ruler of Alburn, married to Adeline

ART, THE: Magic, generally feared by nobles and commoners due to superstition

ARVID MCDERN: Son of Dillon McDern of Dahlgren

AVEMPARTHA: Ancient elven tower

AVRYN: \ave-rin\ Central and most powerful of the four nations of Apeladorn, located between Trent and Delgos

BALLENTYNE: \bal-in-tine\ Ruling family of the earldom of Chadwick

BA RAN GHAZEL: Goblins of the sea

BELINDA PICKERING: Extremely attractive wife of Count Pickering, mother of Lenare, Mauvin, Fanen, and Denek

BELSTRADS: \bell-straads\ Family of knights from Chadwick, including Sir Breckton and Wesley

BERNICE: Handmaid of Princess Arista

BERNUM RIVER: Waterway that bisects the city of Colnora

BETHAMY, KING: Ruler reputed to have had his horse buried with him

BLACK DIAMOND, THE: International thieves' guild centered in Colnora

BLACKWATER: Last name of Hadrian and his father, Danbury

BLYTHIN CASTLE: Castle in Alburn

BOCANT: Family who built a lucrative industry from pork, second most wealthy merchants in Colnora

BOTHWICKS: Family of peasant farmers of Dahlgren

BRECKTON BELSTRAD, SIR: Son of Lord Belstrad, knight of Chadwick, considered by many to be the best knight of Avryn

BRODRIC ESSENDON: Founder of the Essendon dynasty

BUCKET MEN: Term for assassin used by the Black Diamond thieves' guild

BYRNIE: Long (usually sleeveless) tunic of chain mail formerly worn as defensive armor

CALIAN: \cal-lay-in\ Pertaining to the nation of Calis

CALIANS: Residents of the nation of Calis, darker in skin tone, with almond-shaped eyes

CALIS: \cal-lay\ Southern- and easternmost of the four nations of Apeladorn, considered exotic, in constant conflict with the Ba Ran Ghazel

CASWELL: Family of peasant farmers from Dahlgren

CENZARS: \sen-zhars\ Wizards of the ancient Novronian Empire

CHAMBERLAIN: Someone who manages the household of a king or nobleman

COLNORA: \call-nor-ah\ Largest and wealthiest city of Avryn, merchant-based, grew from a rest stop at a central cross-roads from various major trade routes

COSMOS DELUR: Colnora's richest resident

CRIMSON HAND: Thieves' guild operating out of Melengar

CROWN TOWER: Home of the Patriarch, center of the Nyph-ron Church

CUTTER: Assassin of the Black Diamond, best friend of Royce, boyfriend of Jade

DAGASTAN: Major and easternmost trade port of Calis

DAHLGREN: \dall-grin\ Remote village on the bank of the Nidwalden River

DANBURY BLACKWATER: Father of Hadrian

DANTHEN: Woodsman from Dahlgren

DAREF, LORD: Nobleman of Warric, associate of Albert Winslow

DARIUS SERET: Founder of the Seret Knights

DAVENS, SQUIRE: Boy who Arista had a youthful crush on

DEGAN GAUNT: Leader of the Nationalists

DELANO DEWITT, BARON: Nobleman who hires Hadrian to steal Count Pickering's sword

DELGOS: One of the four nations of Apeladorn. The only

republic in a world of monarchies, Delgos revolted against the Steward's Empire after Glenmorgan III was murdered and after surviving an attack by the Ba Ran Ghazel with no aid from the empire.

DELORKAN, DUKE: Calian nobleman

DELUR: Family of wealthy merchants

DENEK PICKERING: Youngest son of Count Pickering

DILLON MCDERN: Dahlgren's blacksmith

DIOYLION: \die-e-leon\ *The Accumulated Letters of Dioylion*, a very rare scroll

DIXON TAFT: Bartender and manager of The Rose and Thorn Tavern

DROME: God of the dwarves

DRONDIL FIELDS: Count Pickering's castle, once the fortress of Brodric Essendon, the original seat of power in Melengar

DRUMINDOR: Dwarven-built fortress located at the entrance to Terlando Bay in Tur Del Fur

DRUNDEL: Peasant family from Dahlgren consisting of Mae, Went, Davie, and Firth

DUSTER: Moniker used by Royce while a member of the Black Diamond

ECTON, SIR: Chief knight of Count Pickering and military general of Melengar

EDMUND HALL: Professor of geometry at Sheridan University, reputed to have found Percepliquis, declared a heretic by the Nyphron Church, imprisoned in the Crown Tower

ELAN: The world

ELDEN: Large man, friend of Wyatt Deminthal

ELLA: Cook at Drondil Fields

ELVEN: Pertaining to elves

ENDEN, SIR: Knight of Chadwick, considered the second best to Breckton

EREBUS: Father of the gods, also known as Kile

ERIVAN: \ear-ah-van\ Elven empire

ERLIC, SIR: Knight competing in Dahlgren contest

ERVANON: \err-vah-non\ City in northern Ghent, seat of the Nyphron Church, once the capital of the Steward's Empire as established by Glenmorgan I

ESRAHADDON: \ez-rah-hod-in\ Wizard, onetime member of the ancient order of the Cenzar, convicted of destroying the Novronian Empire and sentenced to imprisonment

ESSENDON: \ez-in-don\ Royal family of Melengar

ESSENDON CASTLE: Home of ruling monarchs of Melengar

ESTRAMNADON: \es-tram-nah-don\ Believed to be the capital or at least a very sacred place in the Erivan Empire

ESTRENDOR: \es-tren-door\ Northern wastes

ETCHER: Member of the Black Diamond thieves' guild

FALINA BROCKTON: Real name of Emerald, waitress at The Rose and Thorn Tavern

FANEN PICKERING: \fan-in\ Middle son of Count Pickering

FAULD, THE ORDER OF: \fall-ed\ Post-imperial order of knights dedicated to preserving the skill and discipline of the Teshlor Knights

FENITILIAN, BROTHER: Monk of Maribor, made warm shoes

FERROL: God of the elves

FINILESS: Noted author

FLETCHER: Maker of arrows

GALEANNON: \gale-e-an-on\ Kingdom of Avryn, ruled by Fredrick and Josephine

GALENTI: \ga-lehn'-tay\ Calian term

GALEWYR RIVER: \gale-wahar\ Marks the southern border of Melengar and the northern border of Warric and reaches the sea near the fishing village of Roe

GALIEN, ARCHBISHOP: \gal-e-in\ High-ranking member of the Nyphron Church

GALILIN: \gal-ah-lin\ Province of Melengar ruled by Count Pickering

GEMKEY: Gem that opens a gemlock

GEMLOCK: Dwarven invention that seals a container and can only be opened with a precious gem of the right type and cut

GENTRY SQUARE: Affluent district of Melengar

GHAZEL: \gehz-ell\ Ba Ran Ghazel, dwarven name for goblins, literally: Sea goblins

GHENT: Ecclesiastical holding of the Nyphron Church

GILARABRYWN: \gill-lar-ah-bren\ Elven beast of war

GINLIN, BROTHER: \gin-lin\ Monk of Maribor, winemaker, refuses to touch a knife

GLAMRENDOR: \glam-ren-door\ Capital of Dunmore

GLENMORGAN: 326 years after the fall of the Novronian Empire, this native of Ghent reunited the four nations of Apeladorn; founder of Sheridan University; creator of the great north-south road; builder of the Ervanon palace (of which only the Crown Tower remains)

GLENMORGAN II: Son of Glenmorgan. When his father died young, the new and inexperienced emperor relied on church officials to assist him in managing his empire. They in turn took the opportunity to manipulate the emperor into granting sweeping powers to the church and nobles loyal to the church. These leaders opposed defending Delgos against the invading Ba Ran Ghazel in Calis and the Dacca in Delgos, arguing the threat would increase dependency on the empire.

GLENMORGAN III: Grandson of Glenmorgan. Shortly after assuming the stewardship, he attempted to reassert control over the realm his grandfather had created by leading an army against the invading Ghazel that had reached southeastern Avryn. He defeated the Ghazel at the First

Battle of Vilan Hills and announced plans to ride to the aid of Tur Del Fur. Fearing his rise in power, in the sixth year of his reign, his nobles betrayed and imprisoned him in Blythin Castle. Jealous of his popularity and growing strength, and resentful of his policy of stripping the nobles and clergy of their power, the church charged him with heresy. He was found guilty and executed. This began the rapid collapse of what many called the Steward's Empire. The church later claimed the nobles had tricked them, and condemned many, most of whom reputedly ended their lives badly.

GLOUSTON: Province of northern Warric bordering on the Galewyr River, ruled by the marquis Lanaklin

GREAT SWORD: Long sword designed to be held with both hands

GRIGOLES: \gry-holes\ Author of *Grigoles Treatise on Imperial Common Law*

GUARDIAN OF THE HEIR: Teshlor Knight sworn to protect the Heir of Novron

GUTARIA: \goo-tar-ah\ Secret Nyphron prison designed to hold Esrahaddon

GWEN DeLANCY: Calian prostitute and proprietor of Medford House and The Rose and Thorn Tavern

HADRIAN BLACKWATER: Mercenary, one-half of Riyria

HALBERD: Two-handed pole used as a weapon

HEIR OF NOVRON: Direct descendant of demigod Novron, destined to rule all of Avryn

HELDABERRY: Wild-growing fruit often used to make wine

HESLON, BROTHER: Monk of Maribor, great cook

HILFRED: Bodyguard of Princess Arista

HIMBOLT, BARON: Nobleman of Melengar

HOUSE, THE: Nickname used for Medford House

HOYTE: Onetime First Officer of the Black Diamond

IMPERIALISTS: Political party that desires to unite all the kingdoms of men under a single leader who is the direct descendant of the demigod Novron

JADE: Assassin in the Black Diamond, girlfriend of Cutter, friend of Royce

JERISH GRELAD: Teshlor Knight and first Guardian of the Heir

JERL, LORD: Neighbor of the Pickerings known for his prizewinning hunting dogs

JULIAN TEMPEST: Chamberlain of Melengar

KILE: Master sword smith, named used by Erebus when in the form of a man

KRINDEL: Prelate of the Nyphron Church and historian

KRIS DAGGER: Weapon with a wavy blade, sometimes used in magic rituals

LANAKLIN: Ruling family of Glouston

LANIS ETHELRED: \eth-el-red\ King of Warric, Imperialist

LANKSTEER: Capital city of the Lordium kingdom of Trent

LENA BOTHWICK: Wife of Russell, farmer in Dahlgren

LENARE PICKERING: Daughter of Count Pickering and Belinda, sister of Mauvin, Fanen, and Denek

LINGARD: Capital city of Relison, kingdom of Trent

LONGWOOD: Forest in Melengar

LOTHOMAD, KING: Lothomad the Bald, ruler of Lordium, Trent, expanded territory dramatically following the collapse of the Steward's Reign, pushing south through Ghent into Melengar, where Brodric Essendon defeated him in the Battle of Drondil Fields in 2545

LOWER QUARTER: Impoverished section of the city of Medford

LUIS GUY: Sentinel of the Nyphron Church

MAGNUS: Dwarf

MANDALIN: \man-dah-lynn\ Capital of Calis

MANZANT: \man-zahnt\ Infamous prison and salt mine located in Manzar, Maranon

MARANON: \mar-ah-non\ Kingdom in Avryn, ruled by Vincent and Regina

MARES CATHEDRAL: Center of the Nyphron Church in Melengar, run by Bishop Saldur

MARIBOR: \mar-eh-bore\ God of men

MASON GRUMON: \grum-on\ Blacksmith in Medford

MAURICE SALDUR, BISHOP: Head of Nyphron Church in Melengar, friend of the Essendon ruling family

MAUVIN PICKERING: \maw-vin\ Eldest of Count Pickering's sons

McDERN: Peasant family living in Dahlgren

MEDFORD: Capital of Melengar

MEDFORD HOUSE: Brothel run by Gwen DeLancy and attached to The Rose and Thorn Tavern

MELENGAR: \mel-in-gar\ Kingdom in Avryn, ruled by the Essendon royal family

MELENGARIANS: Residents of Melengar

MELISSA: Head servant of Princess Arista, nickname Missy

MERCS: Mercenaries

MERLONS: Solid section between two crenels in a crenellated battlement

MERTON, MONSIGNOR: Eccentric priest from Ghent, known to talk aloud to Maribor

MILLIE: Hadrian's horse

MIR: Person with both elven and human blood

MONTEMORCEY: \mont-eh-more-ah-sea\ Excellent wine imported through the Vandom Spice Company

MOTTE: Man-made hill

MOUSE: Royce's horse

MURIEL: Goddess of nature, daughter of Erebus, mother of Uberlin

MYRON: Monk of Maribor, son of Victor, brother of Alenda

NAREION: \nare-e-on\ Last emperor of the Novronian Empire

NATIONALISTS: Political party led by Degan Gaunt that desires rule by the will of the people

NEVRIK: \nehv-rick\ Son of Nareion, the heir who went into hiding

NIDWALDEN RIVER: Marks the eastern border of Avryn and the start of the Erivan realm

NOVRON: Savior of mankind, son of the god Maribor, demigod who defeated the elven army in the Great Elven Wars, founder of the Novronian Empire, builder of Percepliquis

NOVRONIAN: \nov-ron-e-on\ Pertaining to Novron

NYPHRON CHURCH: The worshipers of Novron and Maribor, his father

NYPHRONS: \nef-rons\ Devout members of the church

PARTHALOREN FALLS: \path-ah-lore-e-on\ The great cataracts on the Nidwalden near Avempartha

PATRIARCH: Head of the Nyphron Church who lives in the Crown Tower of Ervanon

PAULDRON: A piece of armor covering the shoulder at the junction of the body piece and the arm piece

PERCEPLIQUIS: \per-sep-lah-kwiss\ The ancient capital of the Novronian Empire, named for the wife of Novron

PERCY BRAGA, ARCHDUKE: Lord Chancellor of Melengar, winner of the title of Grand Circuit Tournament Champion in Swords, the Silver Shield, and Golden Laurel; uncle to Alric and Arista, having married King Amrath's sister

PICKERING: Noble family of Melengar and rulers of Galilin. Count Pickering is known to be the best swordsman in Avryn and believed to use a magic sword.

PICKILERINON: Seadric, who shortened the family name to Pickering

PLESIEANTIC INCANTATION: \plass-e-an-tic\ A method used in the Art to draw power from nature

PRICE: First Officer of the Black Diamond thieves' guild

RATIBOR: Capital of the kingdom of Rhenydd

RENDON, BARON: Nobleman of Melengar

RENIAN, BROTHER: \rhen-e-ahn\ Childhood friend of Myron the monk

RHELACAN: \rell-ah-khan\ Great sword that Maribor tricked Drome into forging and Ferrol into enchanting, given to Novron to defeat the elves

RHENYDD: \ren-yaed\ Kingdom of Avryn, ruled by King Urith

RILAN VALLEY: Fertile land that separates Glouston and Chadwick

RIONILLION: \ri-on-ill-lon\ Name of the city that first stood on the site of Aquesta but was destroyed during the civil wars that occurred after the fall of the Novronian Empire

RIYRIA: \rye-ear-ah\ Elvish for *two*, a team or a bond

RONDEL: Common type of stiff-bladed dagger with a round handgrip

ROSE AND THORN, THE: Tavern in Medford run by Gwen DeLancy, used as a base by Riyria

ROSWORT, KING: Ruler of Dunmore

ROYCE MELBORN: Thief, one-half of Riyria

RUFUS, LORD: Ruthless northern warlord, respected by the south

RUSSELL BOTHWICK: Farmer in Dahlgren, husband of Lena

SALIFAN: \sal-eh-fan\ Fragrant wild plant used in incense

SAULY: Nickname of Maurice Saldur, used by those closest to him

SENON UPLAND: Highland plateau overlooking Chadwick

SENTINEL: Inquisitor generals of the Nyphron Church, charged with rooting out heresy and finding the lost Heir of Novron

SERET: \sir-ett\ Knights of Nyphron. The military arm of the church first formed by Lord Darius Seret, who was charged with finding the Heir of Novron.

SHERIDAN UNIVERSITY: Prestigious institution of learning, located in Ghent

SPADONE: Long two-handed sword with a tapering blade and an extended flange ahead of the hilt allowing for an extended variety of fighting maneuvers. Due to the length of the handgrip and the flange, which provides its own barbed hilt, the sword provides a number of additional hand placements, permitting the sword to be used similarly to a quarterstaff, as well as a powerful cleaving weapon. The spadone is the traditional weapon of a skilled knight.

SUMMERSRULE: Popular midsummer holiday celebrated with picnics, dances, feasts, and jousting tournaments

TABARD: A tunic worn over armor usually emblazoned with a coat of arms

TEK'CHIN: Single fighting discipline of the Teshlor Knights that was preserved by the Knights of the Fauld and handed down to the Pickerings

TENENT: Most common form of semi-standard international currency. Coins of gold, silver, and copper stamped with the likeness of the king of the realm where the coin was minted.

TERLANDO BAY: Harbor of Tur Del Fur

TESHLORS: Legendary knights of the Novronian Empire, greatest warriors ever to have lived

THERON WOOD: Father of Thrace Wood, farmer of Dahlgren

THRACE WOOD: Daughter of Theron and Addie

TILINER: Superior side sword used frequently by mercenaries in Avryn

TOBIS RENTINUAL: History professor at Sheridan University

TOLIN ESSENDON: Son of Brodric, who moved the capital to Medford and built Essendon Castle

TOMAS, DEACON: Priest of Dahlgren village

TORSONIC: Torque-producing, as in the cable used in crossbows

TRENT: Northern mountainous kingdoms

TRUMBUL, BARON: Mercenary

TUR: Small legendary village believed to have once been in Delgos, site of the first recorded visit of Kile, mythical source of great weapons

TUR DEL FUR: Coastal city in Delgos, on Terlando Bay, originally built by dwarves

UBERLIN: The god of the Dacca and the Ghazel, son of Erebus and his daughter, Muriel

URITH, KING: Ruler of Ratibor

VALIN, LORD: Elderly knight of Melengar known for his valor and courage but lacking strategic skills

VANDON: Port city of Delgos, home to the Vandom Spice Company, which began as a pirate haven until Delgos became a republic, when it became a legitimate business

VENLIN, PATRIARCH: Head of the Nyphron Church during the fall of the Novronian Empire

VERNES: Port city at the mouth of the Bernum River

VILLEIN: Person who is bound to the land and owned by the feudal lord

VINCE GRIFFIN: Dahlgren village founder

WARRIC: Kingdom of Avryn, ruled by Ethelred

WESBADEN: Major trade port city of Calis

WESTBANK: Newly formed province of Dunmore

WESTERLANDS: Unknown frontier to the west

WICEND: \why-send\ Farmer in Melengar who lends his name to the ford that crosses the Galewyr into Glouston

WINDS ABBEY: Monastery of the Monks of Maribor near Lake Windermere in western Melengar

WINTERTIDE: Chief holiday, held in midwinter, celebrated by feasts and jousts

WYATT DEMINTHAL: Onetime ship captain, father of Allie

WYLIN: \why-lynn\ Master-at-arms at Essendon Castle

extras

orbit

meet the author

Michael J. Sullivan

After finding a manual typewriter in the basement of a friend's house, MICHAEL J. SULLIVAN inserted a blank piece of paper and typed *It was a dark and stormy night, and a shot rang out.* He was just eight. Still, the desire to fill the blank page and see where the keys would take him next wouldn't let go. As an adult, Michael spent ten years developing his craft by reading and studying authors such as Stephen King, Ayn Rand, and John Steinbeck, to name just a few. He wrote ten novels, and after finding no traction in publishing, he quit, vowing never to write creatively again.

Michael discovered forever is a very long time and ended his writing hiatus ten years later. The itch returned when he decided to write books for his then thirteen-year-old daughter, who was struggling in school because of dyslexia. Intrigued by the idea of a series with an overarching story line, yet told through individual, self-contained episodes, he created the

Riyria Revelations. He wrote the series with no intention of publishing it. After presenting his book in manuscript form to his daughter, she declared that it had to be a "real book," in order for her to be able to read it.

So began his second adventure on the road to publication, which included drafting his wife to be his business manager, signing with a small independent press, and creating a publishing company. He sold more than sixty thousand books as a self-published author and leveraged this success to achieve mainstream publication through Orbit (the fantasy imprint of Hachette Book Group) as well as foreign translation rights including French, Spanish, Russian, German, Polish, and Czech.

Born in Detroit, Michigan, Michael presently lives in Fairfax, Virginia, with his wife and three children. He continues to fill the blank pages with three projects under development: a modern fantasy, which explores the relationship between good and evil; a literary fiction piece, profiling a man's descent into madness; and a medieval fantasy, which will be prequel to his best-selling Riyria Revelations series.

Find out more about the author at www.michaelsullivan -author.com and his blog www.riyria.blogspot.com.

interview

When did you know you wanted to be an author?

I was really young, no more than seven or eight, and a friend and I were playing hide-and-seek, and I found a typewriter in his basement. It was a huge black metal upright with small round keys. I completely forgot about the game and loaded a sheet of paper. I swear, the very first thing I wrote was: "It was a dark and stormy night, and a shot rang out." I thought I was a genius.

When my friend found me, he was clearly oblivious to the value of the discovery I had made. He wanted to go outside and do something fun. I thought about explaining to him that I couldn't imagine anything that could be more fun than what I was doing. I looked at the blank page and wondered what might come next: Was it a murder mystery? A horror story? I wanted to find out; I wanted to fill the page; I wanted to see where the little keys would take me.

We ended up going alley-picking until my mother called me for dinner. Alley-picking was the art of walking down the alley between the houses and seeing if there was anything cool being thrown away that we could take for ourselves. I had hoped that someone was throwing away a typewriter — no one was, and I went to bed that night thinking about that typewriter, thinking about that page and that first sentence.

What made you start writing? Were you a big reader? Did you ever add to that first sentence?

I'm a bit ashamed to admit that I hated reading in my youth. The first novel I tried was a book called *Big Red*, which was about a boy and his dog. I was on my way to my sister's farm and would have nothing to do for four hours. This was before DSs, DVDs, VCRs—before all the entertainment acronyms. It was also before Sirius, and I knew that twenty minutes after we left Detroit there would be nothing but static on the radio—hence the reason for the book. I finished it out of a sense of perseverance rather than enjoyment. When I was forty I wanted to be able to say, "Yes! I read a book once! It was excruciating, and took half a year, but by god, I did it!" Then whomever I was speaking to would look upon me with awe and know they were in the presence of a learned man. The reality was, the book was boring and put me to sleep.

Then I read Tolkien's *The Hobbit* and *The Lord of the Rings.* I loved them in a way I never dreamed it was possible to love a book. When I closed the last page of *The Return of the King*, I was miserable. My favorite pastime was over. As I mentioned before, this was before all those letters, before Xboxes and PS 2s and 3s, back when television had only three stations and cartoons were something shown only on Saturday morning. I went to the bookstore with my brother looking for another series like that one and was dismayed to come up empty.

There was nothing to read. I sat in my room, miserable. I made the mistake of telling my mother I was bored and she put me to work cleaning the front closet. I pulled out what looked like a plastic suitcase.

"What's this?" I asked.

"That? That's your sister's old typewriter. Been in there for years."

I never finished cleaning the closet.

Can you tell us about your background in writing? Where did you go to college? Do you have an MFA?

Usually this question comes from aspiring writers, and they always look disappointed when I tell them the answer: I never took a class in writing or English, beyond those required in high school. I never read a book on creative fiction. I never went to a seminar or a writers' conference. And I didn't attend my first writers' group until after I had published my first book. What I know about writing I taught myself.

My family didn't have the money to help me pay for college. My father, a crane operator at Great Lake Steel, died when I was nine, and after that my mother paid the bills with the money she made as a gift wrapper for Hudson's department store and my social security checks (that stopped coming when I turned eighteen). Still, I was pretty good at art and received a scholarship to the Center for Creative Studies in Detroit, but it ran out just after my first year. I did manage to land a job as an illustrator/keyliner, though. Then kids came along and my wife made more money, so I stayed home. I was twenty-three.

By this time we had moved to the remote northern corner of Vermont, literally over a thousand miles away from everyone we knew. I had lots of time on my hands, particularly when our daughter was taking naps and the idea of trying to write a publishable book rose to the top of my consciousness. I was teaching myself to write by reading books. I went to the local general store (yes, just like in *Green Acres*) and looked for the books with the golden seal indicating they were Nobel or Pulitzer Prize winners. These were not the books I would normally choose to read. At the time, I was into Stephen King, Isaac Asimov, and Frank Herbert, but I was trying to learn—so I figured I should learn from the best, right? I purposely forced myself to read widely, especially the stuff I did not like. They were the ones that always won the awards, the abysmally boring novels with paper-thin plots and elaborate prose.

I would pick a particular author, read several books by them, and then write a novel using what I had gleaned from reading their books. I didn't just write a short story—I wrote whole novels, then rinsed and repeated with the next author. I found something in each writer's style, or technique, that I could appreciate, and worked at teaching myself how to do what they did. In a way, I was like Silar from the television series *Heroes*, where I stole powers from other authors and added them to my toolbox. From Steinbeck I learned the transporting value of vivid setting descriptions. From Updike I found an appreciation for indirect prose that could more aptly describe something by not describing it. From Hemingway I discovered an economy for words. From King, his ability to get viscerally into the minds of his characters...and so on. In addition, I wrote in various genres: mystery, science fiction, horror, coming-of-age, literary fiction—anything and everything. I did this for ten years.

My writing improved with each novel. I finally wrote what I thought was something worthy of publishing and spent maybe a year and a half trying to get an agent before I finally gave up. Ten years and untold thousands of hours is a long time to work at something and achieve at least what I thought at the time to be nothing. Ten years, ten books, a ton of rejections, and not a single reader. It was time to give up this pipe dream.

So how did you "get back on the horse" as it were? What got you to start writing again?

It was years later; we had left Vermont and were living in North Carolina. The kids were old enough for day care and I went back into advertising. I had been a one-man band running an advertising department at a software company, and then I left that to create my own advertising agency, where I was the creative director. As to writing novels, I had vowed never to write another creative word.

Years passed, and my second daughter, Sarah, was struggling in school. She's dyslexic, which makes reading difficult. Not being good at something means it isn't any fun. So I got her books—good books—books I loved: *The Hobbit*, *Watership Down*, Chronicles of Narnia, Chronicles of Prydain, and that new book that I was hearing about—that thing about the kid who was a wizard or something... *Harry Potter*. It was sitting around on a table one afternoon. Beautiful, brand-new book—I'm a sucker for a pretty book. I cracked it and started reading and was transported. What I liked the most was how easy it was to read—it was just plain fun.

I started writing again, but this time for the sheer fun of it and with the hopes of making something for my daughter that would help her to like reading. I wasn't writing in anyone's style. I was done trying to make the great American novel. I just wanted to enjoy making something I would like to read. Still, the authors I had studied were there, lurking beneath the surface. When I wanted to paint a vivid setting, Steinbeck was whispering in my ear. When I hunted for a special turn of phrase, Updike lent me his hounds, King gave me a road map into the characters' heads, and when I wrote a run-on sentence, "Papa" scowled at me.

Why did you decide on a series instead of writing a single book and adding sequels after?

It may seem strange, but two of the biggest inspirations for the Riyria Revelations were the television shows *Babylon 5* and *Buffy the Vampire Slayer*. The thing about them that I found fascinating was the layered plots. *B5* in particular was amazing in that the entire five-year series was mapped out before the first episode was shot. I think this might be the first, and only, time that's ever happened. Yet it allowed for the unique opportunity for viewers to watch episodes and look for clues to the bigger questions that were hinted at from time to time and in small doses. In addition, Straczynski—the show's creator—layered his plots, something that was mimicked to a lesser degree in *Buffy*. This really impressed me, and I wondered if it could be done in a book series. So I actually mapped out the entire series before writing it. I was never making a series of books, but rather one long story in six episodes.

You use a lot of humor in your books; talk to us about that.

During the late sixties and early seventies a lot of the movies were pretty depressing. Many of them were tough dramas like *Chinatown* or were dreary accounts of the aftermath of the Vietnam War, such as *Coming Home*. For me, it was a terrible time to be a moviegoer. Then I saw *Butch Cassidy and the Sundance Kid*. I really liked the mix of drama and humor. Sometimes at the most tense spots a bit of humor is the perfect ingredient, and to me, far more realistic.

I also mentioned *Buffy the Vampire Slayer* and that's another great example. Joss Whedon is a master of mixing drama and humor. I don't presume to put myself into his league, but the hours of enjoyment I had in watching something I wouldn't normally be attracted to was definitely an influence on me.

Royce and Hadrian are a great pair; where did the inspiration for them come from?

It's funny, because many people assume I'm a big fan of Fafhrd and the Gray Mouser, but I've never read any of those stories. Any similarities are purely coincidental. I already mentioned *Butch Cassidy and the Sundance Kid*, and there was a television show called *I Spy* that I enjoyed while growing up, and I'm sure at a subconscious level there is a lot of that seeping into my characters, but their origins actually go way, way back—more than twenty years. It was when I was living in Vermont, and to help pass the cold, boring winters I started writing a chain story with two other friends. It basically started with two characters walking into a tavern and getting together a crack team to go on an adventure into an ancient dungeon. We would write a few pages and mail it on to the next to add to the tale. Yes, it was long ago...before there was e-mail.

My friends soon became bored, and not too happy that I would rewrite the parts they wrote, but I really loved the concept of two buddies, each with their own strengths, each very different, but having a relationship that really works for them. My daughter tells me it's classic bromance, but that's a term that came into vogue long after Royce and Hadrian came to life. I really like creating characters that I would like to hang out with. Being a writer means you get to create your own imaginary friends.

How did you decide on the writing style for the series?

The Riyria Revelations was born out of my trying something new. My last novel before this, even though it was written years previously, was a true literary fiction piece. Short on plot, long on character development, with sentences that were composed with great care and required a tremendous amount of contemplation and polishing.

As I already mentioned, I loved the *fun* of *Harry Potter*. This wasn't Steinbeck; it was simple, and light, and just a good enjoyable read. Riyria just flowed from my head to the keyboard. I wrote the first book in a month, the second a month later. Its style was designed to be light. I had a huge story to tell, one of complex themes, numerous characters, and dozens of twists where things are not always what they seem. This idea would be unmanageable in a heavy-handed style. I'm already asking a great deal of the reader—to keep track of everything that happens over the course of six separate novels as if they were one long book. To make the trip as comfortable as possible for my readers I attempted a style I had never tried before—invisibility.

The idea is to make the story pop off the page and make the writing disappear. Neither awkward prose nor eloquent phrases should distract the reader from immersion in the action and the world unfolding before them. I have needed on many occasions to rewrite passages that were too pretty, too sophisticated, for fear the reader would notice them and pause to reflect. I have other works that do this. For the Riyria Revelations I wanted to keep it simple. The result, I have discovered—much to my delight—is a book that reads like a movie in the reader's mind. As you can tell, a lot of my references have been from television and movies, and I think that also sets the tone and pace in these books. I'm not so much trying to create another Lord of the Rings so much as a good old-fashioned Errol Flynn movie or sixties Western.

This, then, is the "light-hand" approach that some have read about on my website. While I know that I am not the first to employ it, it remains something of a rarity in the fantasy realm. For me, this is a great disappointment, for while I enjoy a beautifully written novel—I love a great story.

Why did you choose to use such established fantasy tropes in your series?

For years now I have heard fans of the traditional "Tolkienesque" fantasy novels lament the repetitive themes and exhausted archetypes of the genre. They are tired of the same old hero-vanquishing-evil and want something new, something more real, more believable. Which to me sounds like someone saying they love chocolate, they just wished it wasn't so chocolaty and that it tasted more like vanilla. Many writers struggle to appease, whether that means turning an old theme on its head or going for the gritty and morbid. During the past few decades this trend has resulted in fantasy going dark: Evil often wins. Heroes don't exist.

This happened before.

The motion-picture industry turned out happy endings for decades, then in the sixties things began to change. Gritty, realistic films began to pop up, and antiheroes like The Man with No Name arrived in the Italian Western. The trend solidified in the seventies, with moviemakers like Scorsese, De Laurentiis, Coppola, and Kubrick, who often focused on complex and unpleasant themes. It was theorized that the public was tired of the old good-triumphs-over-evil stories because it was so out of sync with the realities of the

American experience during the age of Watergate, the Vietnam War, the Civil Rights movement, and the Sexual Revolution.

Then *Star Wars* debuted in 1977 and everything began to change again.

I remember seeing *Star Wars* the weekend it opened. I wasn't expecting anything, and I was debating between it and the cartoon movie *Wizards*. Only one early review for *Star Wars* was out, a small block article in the *Detroit News* that slammed it for being unoriginal and using just about every movie cliché that existed, but the review did add that it was surprisingly entertaining. It was the comment about movie clichés that tipped the scales for me. I never cared for the gritty realism of *Midnight Cowboy* and *Taxi Driver*. I liked the old films, the ones I saw on television that I was too young to have seen at a theater. When the movie ended and the credits were rolling, I had one thought—so that's a movie.

I saw the same scenario play out to some degree in the fantasy book world. This time it was a novel series by a new author who made the unforgivable mistake of writing a hero story using every clichéd trapping available. It was actually the tale of a young boy destined to defeat an evil dark lord and save the world from destruction. It even had an old mentor wizard guiding him as well as a motley crew of humorous sidekicks (not unlike *Star Wars*). According to the professed mentality of the consumer, the books should have been laughable. In serious times, people don't want trite tales of do-gooders with happy endings. They should have been panned as the worst kind of old-fashioned echo. Instead, there is a Harry Potter theme park in Florida now.

So I have to wonder—what's the deal?

An aspiring writer friend of mine was working on a book in which a talking cat plays an important role. He presented part of his story to a writers' workshop and the overwhelming response was that the talking cat was cliché—a tired device as old as *Alice in Wonderland*. He was depressed afterward, and over drinks he asked me if his story was even worth pursuing anymore, as it wouldn't work without the cat. I told him that the cat doesn't matter. All that matters is if the story is good and if it is well written.

You see, I don't think people so much hate to read the same type of story, they just hate to read bad stories. There are an infinite number of ways to combine old ideas to create new books. If the plot is good, if the reader cares for the characters, if the setting feels real, then it doesn't matter if it's about talking cats or boys destined to defeat an evil dark lord. And trying to write a completely original story is sort of like trying to compose music with all original notes. It's not necessary, and I'm not even certain it's possible.

Some people have told me that I should alter the names of things to make the world more unique, less generic, but I chose to use elves and dwarves, kings and queens, castles and churches, precisely because everyone knows what they are—I don't have to explain them. The less time I have to take explaining the basics of my world, the more time I have to tell a great story and the less work readers have to go through to imagine themselves in the world.

How did you get published?

Well, as I mentioned, I wasn't planning on publishing. I had put that aspect behind me. But I did want my books to be read…Heck, all authors do. Originally I gave it to a few friends and they, not surprisingly, expressed their enjoyment...but, hey, they are my friends so I wouldn't expect less.

I mentioned that my daughter is dyslexic. This means she has a few strange quirks. She is easily distracted by the color of the background on a computer screen, whether a door is left ajar or a light is on in another room. When I finished *The Crown Conspiracy* I presented her with a stack of double-spaced 8½" × 11" pages, and she looked at me as if I were crazy.

"I can't read it this way...you said you were writing me a book...I need binding; I need a smaller page size."

I just sighed.

For anyone who has read my blog, or read or listened to any of my other interviews, you know that my wife is the engine behind my writing. She is an extremely competent person who will break any door and rise over any challenge—even something as daunting as publishing. And she is a great businessperson. So when I finally resigned myself that I should give publishing one more chance, I laid my plan well. I wrote a terrible query letter and presented it to my wife, along with my inept plan of mailing it to one agent a month for the next twelve months.

"Seriously?" she told me with a raised eyebrow. "Send me a copy to rewrite and go back to your editing...I'll take care of this."

Yes! I thought. Now I just might have a chance.

Robin was the one who, after a hundred or so rejections, got Aspirations Media (a small independent press based in Minnesota) to publish my first book. They had planned on putting out the second book in April 2008, but in March they informed us they really didn't have the cash for the printing. We negotiated the rights back and published the next four ourselves under the Ridan Label, a publishing company Robin set up. When the original print run of *The Crown Conspiracy* sold out, that reverted to us as well. By October 2010 we had kept up the breakneck pace of releasing one book every six months and saw a nice following both from readers and book bloggers.

With the release of book five the sales went up exponentially. For the first time in my writing career I was actually contributing some money to the household. And I was even able to pay off some pretty high credit card debt we had built when my single-income wife had been laid off not once but three times over a two-year period—OUCH!

A few months earlier, we had several publishers in the Czech Republic asking for foreign rights. Knowing that there was no way she could handle this on her own, Robin went in search of an agent to broker this deal. And landed Teri Tobias (who had sold foreign rights for Dan Brown and Patrick Rothfuss). She had left her position as foreign rights director at Sanford J. Greenburger Associates to start her own agency.

The books were doing so well by the fall of 2010 that Robin got thinking there might be an opportunity to try New York again. Neither of us thought it would happen, or so fast, but to our amazement we received an offer from Orbit in just a couple of weeks. So Riyria has taken a strange path. It has been published through a traditional small press, self-published (primarily as e-books), and now through a big-six publisher.

introducing

If you enjoyed
THEFT OF SWORDS,
look out for

RISE OF EMPIRE

Volume Two of the Riyria Revelations
by Michael J. Sullivan

Amilia made the mistake of looking back into Edith Mon's eyes. She had never meant to—she had never planned on raising her stare from the floor—but Edith startled her and she looked up without thinking. The head maid would consider her action defiance, a sign of rebellion in the ranks of the scullery. Amilia had never looked into Edith's eyes before, and doing so now, she wondered if a soul lurked behind them. If so, it must be cowering or dead, rotting like a late-autumn apple; that would explain her smell. Edith had a sour scent, vaguely rancid, as if something had gone bad.

"This will be another tenent withheld from yer pay," the rotund woman said. "Yer digging quite a hole, ain't you?"

Edith was big and broad and missing any sign of a neck. Her huge anvil of a head sat squarely on her shoulders. By contrast, Amilia barely existed. Small and pear-shaped, with a plain face and long, lifeless hair, she was part of the crowd, one of the faces no one paused to consider — neither pretty nor grotesque enough to warrant a second glance. Unfortunately, her invisibility failed when it came to the palace's head maid, Edith Mon.

"I didn't break it." *Mistake number two*, Amilia thought.

A meaty hand slapped her across the face, ringing her ears and making her eyes water. "Go on," Edith enticed her with a sweet tone, and then whispered in her ear, "lie to me again."

Gripping the washbasin to steady herself, Amilia felt heat blossom on her cheek. Her gaze now followed Edith's hand, and when it rose again, Amilia flinched. With a snicker, Edith ran her plump fingers through Amilia's hair.

"No tangles," Edith observed. "I can see how ya spend yer time, instead of doing yer work. Ya hoping to catch the eye of the butcher? Maybe that saucy little man who delivers the wood? I saw ya talking to him. Know what they sees when they looks at ya? They sees an ugly scullery maid is what. A wretched filthy guttersnipe who smells of lye and grease. They would rather pay for a whore than get ya for nothing. You'd be better off spending more time on yer tasks. If ya did, I wouldn't have to beat ya so often."

Amilia felt Edith winding her hair, twisting and tightening it around her fist. "It's not like I enjoy hurting ya." She pulled until Amilia winced. "But ya have to learn." Edith continued pulling Amilia's hair, forcing her head back until only the ceiling was visible. "Yer slow, stupid, and ugly. That's why yer still in the scullery. I can't make ya a laundry maid, much less a parlor or chambermaid. You'd embarrass me, understand?"

Amilia remained quiet.

"I said, do ya understand?"

"Yes."

"Say yer sorry for chipping the plate."

"I'm sorry for chipping the plate."

"And yer sorry for lying about it?"

"Yes."

Edith roughly patted Amilia's burning cheek. "That's a good girl. I'll add the cost to yer tally. Now as for punishment…" She let go of Amilia's hair and tore the scrub brush from her hand, measuring its weight. She usually used a belt; the brush would hurt more. Edith would drag her to the laundry, where the big cook could not see. The head cook had taken a liking to Amilia, and while Edith had every right to discipline her girls, Ibis would not stand for it in his kitchen. Amilia waited for a fat hand to grab her wrist, but instead Edith stroked her head. "Such long hair," she said at length. "It's yer hair that's getting in the way, isn't it? It's making ya think too much of yerself. Well, I know just how to fix both problems. Yer gonna look real pretty when I—"

The kitchen fell silent. Cora, who had been incessantly plunging her butter churn, paused in mid-stroke. The cooks stopped chopping and even Nipper, who was stacking wood near the stoves, froze. Amilia followed their gaze to the stairs.

A noblewoman adorned in white velvet and satin glided down the steps and entered the steamy stench of the scullery. Piercing eyes and razor-thin lips stood out against a powdered face. The woman was tall and—unlike Amilia, who had a hunched posture—stood straight and proud. She moved immediately to the small table along the wall, where the baker was preparing bread.

"Clear this," she ordered with a wave of her hand, speaking to no one in particular. The baker immediately scooped his utensils and dough into his apron and hurried away. "Scrub it clean," the lady insisted.

Amilia felt the brush thrust back into her hand, and a push sent her stumbling forward. She did not look up and went right to work making large swirls of flour-soaked film. Nipper was beside her in an instant with a bucket, and Vella arrived with a towel. Together they cleared the mess while the woman watched with disdain.

"Two chairs," the lady barked, and Nipper ran off to fetch them.

Uncertain what to do next, Amilia stood in place watching the lady, holding the dripping brush at her side. When the noblewoman caught her staring, Amilia quickly looked down and movement caught her eye. A small gray mouse froze beneath the baker's table, trying to conceal itself in the shadows. Taking a chance, it snatched a morsel of bread and disappeared through a small crack.

"What a miserable creature," she heard the lady say. Amilia thought she was referring to the mouse until she added, "You're making a filthy puddle on the floor. Go away."

Before retreating to her washbasin, Amilia attempted a pathetic curtsy. A flurry of orders erupted from the woman, each announced with perfect diction. Vella, Cora, and even Edith went about setting the table as if for a royal banquet. Vella draped a white tablecloth, and Edith started setting out silverware only to be shooed away as the woman carefully placed each piece herself. Soon the table was elegantly set for two, complete with multiple goblets and linen napkins.

Amilia could not imagine who could be dining there. No one would set a table for the servants, and why would a noble come to the kitchen to eat?

"Here now, what's all this about?" Amilia heard the deep familiar voice of Ibis Thinly. The old sea cook was a large barrel-chested man with bright blue eyes and a thin beard that wreathed the line of his chin. He had spent the morning meeting with farmers, yet he still wore his ever-present apron. The grease-stained wrap was his uniform, his mark of office. He barged into the kitchen like a bear returning to his cave to find mischief afoot. When he spotted the lady, he stopped.

"I am Lady Constance," the noblewoman informed him. "In a moment I will be bringing Empress Modina here. If you are the cook, then prepare food." The lady paused a moment to study the table critically. She adjusted the position of a few items, then turned and left.

"Leif, get a knife on that roasted lamb," Ibis shouted. "Cora, fetch cheese. Vella, get bread. Nipper, straighten that woodpile!"

"The empress!" Cora exclaimed as she raced for the pantry.

"What's she doing coming here?" Leif asked. There was anger in his voice, as if an unwelcome, no-account relative was dropping by and he was the inconvenienced lord of the manor.

Amilia had heard of the empress but had never seen her—not even from a distance. Few had. She had been coronated in a private ceremony over half a year earlier on Wintertide, and her arrival in Aquesta had changed everything.

King Ethelred no longer wore his crown, and was addressed as "Regent" instead of "Your Majesty." He still ruled over the castle, only now it was referred to as the imperial palace. The other one, Regent Saldur, had made all the changes. Originally from Melengar, the former bishop had taken up residence and set builders working day and night on the great hall and throne room. Saldur had also declared new rules that all the servants had to follow.

The palace staff could no longer leave the grounds unless escorted by one of the new guards, and all outgoing letters were read and needed to be approved. The latter edict was hardly an issue, as few servants could write. The restriction on going outside the palace, however, was a hardship to almost everyone. Many with families in the city or surrounding farms chose to resign, because they could no longer return home each night. Those remaining at the castle never heard from them again. Regent Saldur had successfully isolated the palace from the outside world, but inside, rumors and gossip ran wild. Speculations flourished in out-of-the-way corridors that giving notice was as unhealthy as attempting to sneak away.

The fact that no one ever saw the empress ignited its own set of speculations. Everyone knew she was the heir of the original, legendary emperor, Novron, and therefore a child of the god Maribor. This had been proven when she had been the only one capable of slaying the beast that had slaughtered dozens of Elan's greatest knights. That she had previously been a farm girl from a small village confirmed that in the eyes of Maribor, all were equal. Rumors concluded that she had ascended to the state of a spiritual being, and only the regents and her personal secretary ever stood in her divine presence.

That must be who the noblewoman is, Amilia thought. The lady with the sour face and perfect speech was the imperial secretary to the empress.

They soon had an array of the best food they could muster in a short time laid out on the table. Knob, the baker, and Leif, the butcher, disputed the placement of dishes, each wanting his wares in the center. "Cora," Ibis said, "put your pretty cake of cheese in the middle." This brought a smile and blush to the dairymaid's face and scowls from Leif and Knob.

Being a scullion, Amilia had no more part to play and returned to her dishes. Edith was chatting excitedly in the corner near the stack of oak kegs with the tapster and the cup-bearer, and all the servants were straightening their outfits and running fingers through their hair. Nipper was still sweeping when the lady returned. Once more everyone stopped and watched as the lady led a thin young girl by the wrist.

"Sit down," Lady Constance ordered in her brisk tone.

Everyone peered past the two women, trying to catch the first glimpse of the god-queen. Two well-armored guards emerged and took up positions on either side of the table. But no one else appeared.

Where is the empress?

"Modina, I said sit down," Lady Constance repeated.

Shock rippled through Amilia.

Modina? This waif of a child is the empress?

The girl did not appear to hear Lady Constance and stood limp with a blank expression. She looked to be a teenager, delicate and deathly thin. Once she might have been pretty, but what remained was an appalling sight. The girl's face was white as bone, her skin thin and stretched, revealing the detailed outline of her skull beneath. Her ragged blonde hair fell across her face. She wore only a thin white smock, which added to the girl's ghostly appearance.

Lady Constance sighed and forced the girl into one of the chairs at the baker's table. Like a doll, the girl allowed herself to be moved. She said nothing and her eyes stared blankly.

"Place the napkin in your lap this way." Lady Constance carefully opened and laid the linen with deliberate movements. She waited, glaring at the empress, who sat, oblivious. "As empress, you will never serve yourself," Lady Constance went on. "You will wait as your servants fill your plate." She was looking around with irritation when her eyes found Amilia. "You—come here," she ordered. "Serve Her Eminence."

Amilia dropped the brush in the basin and, wiping her hands on her smock, rushed forward. She lacked experience with serving but said nothing. Instead, she focused on recalling the times she had watched Leif cutting meat. Taking up the tongs and a knife, she tried her best to imitate him. Leif always made it look effortless, but Amilia's fingers betrayed her and she fumbled miserably, managing to place only a few shredded bits of lamb on the girl's plate.

"Bread." Lady Constance snapped the word like a whip and Amilia sliced into the long twisted loaf, nearly cutting herself in the process.

"Now eat."

For a brief moment, Amilia thought this was another order for her and reached out in response. She caught herself and stood motionless, uncertain if she was free to return to her dishes.

"Eat, I said." The imperial secretary glared at the girl, who continued to stare blankly at the far wall.

"*Eat, damn you!*" Lady Constance bellowed, and everyone in the kitchen, including Edith Mon and Ibis Thinly, jumped. She pounded the baker's table with her fist, knocking over the stemware and bouncing the knives against the plates. "*Eat!*" Lady Constance repeated, and slapped the girl across the face. Her skin-wrapped skull rocked with the blow and came to rest on its own. The girl did not wince. She merely continued her stare, this time at a new wall.

In a fit of rage, the imperial secretary rose, knocking over her chair. She took one of the pieces of meat and tried to force it into the girl's mouth.

"What's going on?"

Lady Constance froze at the sound of the voice. An old white-haired man descended the steps into the scullery. His elegant purple robe and black cape looked out of place in the hot, messy kitchen. Amilia recognized Regent Saldur immediately.

"What in the world..." Saldur began as he approached the table. He looked at the girl, then at the kitchen staff, and finally at Lady Constance, who at some point had dropped the meat. "What were you thinking…bringing her down here?"

"I—I thought if—"

Saldur held up his hand, silencing her, then slowly squeezed it into a fist. He clenched his jaw and drew a deep breath through his sharp nose. Once more he focused on the girl. "Look at her. You were supposed to educate and train her. She's worse than ever!"

"I—I tried, but—"

"Shut up!" the regent snapped, still holding up his fist. No one in the kitchen moved. The only sounds were the faint crackle of the fire in the ovens and the bubbling of broth in a pot. "If this is the result of a professional, we may as well try an amateur. They couldn't possibly do worse." The regent pointed at Amilia. "You! Congratulations, you are now the imperial secretary to the empress." Turning his attention back to Lady Constance, he said, "And as for you—your services are no longer required. Guards, remove her."

Amilia saw Lady Constance falter. Her perfect posture evaporated as she cowered and stepped backward, nearly falling over the upended chair. "No! Please, no," she cried as a palace guard gripped her arm and pulled her toward the back door. Another guard took her other arm. She grew frantic, pleading and struggling as they dragged her out.

Amilia stood frozen in place, holding the meat tongs and carving knife, trying to remember how to breathe. Once the pleas of Lady Constance faded, Regent Saldur turned to her, his face flushed red, his teeth revealed behind taunt lips. "Don't fail me," he told her, and returned up the stairs, his cape whirling behind him.

Amilia looked back at the girl, who continued to stare at the wall.